THE LORE
OF IRELAND

THE LORE
OF IRELAND

*An Encyclopaedia of Myth,
Legend and Romance*

Dáithí Ó hÓgáin

THE BOYDELL PRESS

First published 2006
The Collins Press, West Link Park, Doughcloyne, Wilton, Cork
and
The Boydell Press, Woodbridge
Paperback edition 2023

ISBN: 978 1 84383 215 7 (Hardback)
ISBN: 978 1 83765 112 2 (Paperback)
Irish ISBN: 978 1 905172 16 0

Transferred to digital printing

The Boydell Press is an imprint of Boydell & Brewer Ltd.
PO Box 9, Woodbridge, Suffolk IP12 3DF, UK
and of Boydell & Brewer Inc.
Mt Hope Avenue, Rochester, NY 14620–2731, USA
website: www.boydellandbrewer.com

A catalogue record for this book is available from the British Library

This publication is printed on acid-free paper

Edited & typeset by Dominic Carroll, Ardfield, Co. Cork

Dedication

Ba mhaith liom an saothar seo a thoirbhirt dom chéile ionmhain Caitríona, dom chlann Aisling, Orla, Niamh, Ruán, agus Sadhbh, dom mhuintir agus dom chairde ar fad, agus do gach n-aon ler mian seanchas, scéalaíocht, agus éigse.

Contents

Preface

This book is intended as a reference work for all those with an interest in Irish folklore and traditional literature, be they the scholarly, the imaginative or the merely inquisitive. An attempt has been made to include all the important strands of tradition, and for this purpose specific headings have been selected. Within each entry, cross-references enable the reader to investigate related material and lore of a similar kind. It is not possible within the space limitations of a work like this to include every aspect of local lore or many refinements of literary genre, but it is intended that indications given in the references following each entry will enable the reader to pursue further paths of enquiry.

Dáithí Ó hÓgáin
in earrach na bliana 2006

Guide to References, use of Patronymics & Pronunciation

Cross-references

Words set in small capitals indicate a cross-reference to a separate entry (cross-references are used only when the matter in question is narratively functional or when required to illustrate the context, rather than when merely an incidental item in the discourse); for example:
According to the old historians, the son and successor of Eoghan was FIACHU MUILLEATHAN.

References

Words set in capitals within references indicate a general area of study, and are followed by references to other publications or manuscript collections; for example:
STORYTELLING IN IRELAND: Delargy (1969); Mac Cana (1980).

References to publications and manuscript collections (following each entry) usually correlate with the bibliography. Volume numbers within these references are set in italics; for example:
O'Grady, *i* (1892), 404–6
refers to O'Grady, Standish Hayes, *Silva Gadelica*, volume 1 (London, 1892), pages 404–6.

Titles of periodicals, journals and manuscripts are abbreviated and italicised; for example:
JCS refers to *Journal of Celtic Studies*
IFC refers to Irish Folklore Collection, Delargy Centre, University College, Dublin.

Where footnotes refer to articles published in periodicals, both the initials and surname of the author is used; for example:
J. O'Neill in *Ériu, 3,* 92–115.
Initials are also used to distinguish between authors with the same surname.

Where an author has more than one publication from the same year listed in the bibliography, an italicised abbreviation for each publication is used so as to distinguish between publications (with the abbreviation included with publication details in the bibliography); for example:
Hyde, *GF* (1899)
refers to Hyde, Douglas, *Giolla an Fhiugha* (London, 1899).

Patronymics

Patronymics were the usual way of distinguishing individuals in early Ireland – for example, Conall mac Suibhne indicated 'Conall son of Suibhne'. From the late Middle Ages onwards, however, group surnames came into vogue; thus Maolmhuire Mac Suibhne entails the surname Mac Suibhne (anglicised as MacSweeney or MacSwiney). The reader will note the difference in that lower-case *m* is used for 'mac' in patronymics, whereas upper-case *M* is used for 'Mac' in surnames. The same rule applies to the word 'ua', which originally meant grandson, but was later petrified as Ua (later standard Ó) in surnames. Entries, being arranged alphabetically, accord with this system; for example, Alasdair Mac Dhomhnaill is entered under *M* as Mac Dhomhnaill, Alasdair, whereas Tadhg mac Céin is entered under *T*.

Pronunciation of Irish-language Entries

For a guide to Irish-language pronunciation, fonts provided by the International Phonetics Association have been utilised (*see* the entries *ABAIR* and BADHBH, and the section entitled 'Pronunciation of Irish-language Entries', page 513).

List of Entries

abair The post-medieval Irish form of the imperative verb meaning 'speak' (pronounced *abər*'). It derives from the Old Irish *as-beir*, literally 'out-bring' in the sense of producing from the mouth a word, phrase or speech. It is the usual request when an oral performance is being sought; for example, *abair scéal* (tell a story!), *abair dán* (recite a poem!) or *abair amhrán* (sing a song!). Thus the telling or relaying of information or lore is basically understood as by means of the spoken word. Much of the lore in this book was in essence oral, although it should be stressed that the written medium has also played an important role in the preservation of lore, and a considerable amount of Irish traditional narrative was originally invented as literature. The word for 'write' in Irish is *scríobh*, an early borrowing from Latin, but it is significant that the traditional writers tended to see themselves as telling in much the same sense as if they were speaking.

Because written sources in the Irish language date back to the sixth century AD, the tradition of storytelling has existed in literary form, beside the oral tradition, for a long time. This has meant that in certain contexts the oral and literary streams are distinct from each other, whereas in other contexts there is a close interplay between them. In dealing with each item of lore presented in this book, an attempt has been made to clarify its nature vis-à-vis these two streams, as well as distinguishing the genre or genres of lore into which it fits.

STORYTELLING IN IRELAND: Delargy (1969); Mac Cana (1980).

Abán Leinster SAINT of the early sixth century AD. A biography of him was written towards the end of the eighth century in the monastery of Magh Arnaidhe (Moyarney, near New Ross, County Wexford); the monastery claimed him as its founder. Somewhat later recensions of this biography in Latin and Irish survive.

The Leinstermen (LAIGHIN) ascribed their conversion to Abán. His name is titular, meaning 'little abbot', and he was of the Dál gCormaic, one of the ancient Leinster septs; thus he was known as Abán mocu Cormaic, but his biography takes *mocu* in the sense of son rather than of descendant, and we read that he was the son of a local KING called Cormac, and that his mother Milla was sister to a bishop called Iubhar. In his youth, he expressed a desire for the monastic life rather than for kingship; as a result, he was chained and held in captivity by his parents. After the chains miraculously fell away, he was allowed to pursue the religious life.

When still a mere boy, Abán showed his miraculous power by restoring to life and wholeness a calf that had been devoured by a wolf. When he was twelve years old, he wished to accompany his uncle Iubhar on a journey to Rome, but Iubhar slipped away to the ship while Abán was sleeping. The youngster followed and, as the ship left port, he walked on the waves to join its crew. In Italy, he again showed his power by lighting a lamp with his breath, by restoring to life a queen who had just died, and by overcoming ravenous monsters. On his return to Ireland, he banished demons from the sea by confronting them while riding his staff on the water, and angels told him that God had given him power over the sea.

Abán was reputed to have also founded several churches outside of Leinster, particularly in Munster, where the biography claims he performed several miracles. Other lore centred on his manner of establishing and defending monasteries: on his orders the wolves acted as shepherds to protect his flocks, and ravaging armies found themselves transfixed until they abandoned their destructive intent. His feast day is 16 March.

O'Hanlon, *3* (1875), 394–5; Stokes (1905), 82, 98–9, 398; Plummer, *1* (1910) 3–33 & *1* (1922), 3–10; Kenney (1929), 318–19; IFC 189:81–3, 203:11–12, 406:13–15.

Ábhartach mac Ildathaigh One of the leaders of the mythical TUATHA DÉ DANANN and an adept at music. His name meant 'the deft fellow, son of the multi-coloured'. His dwelling was in the tumulus called Sídh Buí (Shivey, Desertcreat, County Tyrone).

First mentioned in texts of the twelfth

century, he is praised as a great warrior and is also represented as having strong magical powers and as using apples to seduce women. One medieval story told of how, by the power of his music, he won a beautiful lady of the Tuatha Dé called Doireann. Another story described how two young women were in love with Ábhartach. One of these was Miadhach, daughter of a Tuatha Dé king called Eachdhonn, and the other was the king's foster-daughter Morann. At the king's exhortation, Morann agreed to give up Ábhartach, which impressed Eachdhonn so much that he offered great wealth to Miadhach if she would leave Ábhartach to Morann. Miadhach refused, whereupon her father grew angry and magically turned her into a crane.

A long prose text from the late sixteenth century gives a humorous twist to the lore of Ábhartach. It describes how an ungainly man called the Giolla Deacair (Difficult Servant), once came to the FIANNA as they hunted at Cnoc Áine (Knockainey, County Limerick). This stranger had an ill-tempered and frightfully ugly HORSE, which the foolish CONÁN MAOL mounted. He could not get the horse to budge, and so fourteen others of the Fianna also mounted the horse. With the fifteen on the nag's back, the Giolla Deacair raced away at great speed, followed by the animal. They were chased by the Fianna leader, FIONN MAC CUMHAILL, and his men all the way to Dingle Bay, where they took to the water and disappeared. Fionn and some others travelled overseas to search for their comrades and, with the aid of two marvellous helpers whom they met, managed to locate the Giolla Deacair in a wondrous foreign clime. The culprit then revealed himself as Ábhartach mac Ildathaigh, the most powerful wizard in the world. He offered compensation to Fionn, but the latter forgave him all. Conán Maol, however, was vengeful, and demanded that fourteen of the finest women in that country should come with him to Ireland on the nag's back, with Ábhartach's own wife tied to its tail. This was agreed, but as soon as they reached Cnoc Áine all the strangers disappeared into thin air.

In this text, the name and general image of Ábhartach as an otherworld personage have been taken from the medieval literature. The author of the story, however, borrowed the designation 'Giolla Deacair' and the idea of a trickster using magical abilities from a slightly earlier humorous text (see CEITHEARNACH CAOILRIABHACH). The motif of the wondrous horse, which he elaborated greatly, seems to have had a different kind of source – oral stories concerning magical HORSES that come from a lake or the sea, and burlesque accounts of several people scrambling onto one horse. Ábhartach was used as a personal name in Ireland, and a large stone marking a burial site in Errigal, County Derry was called after some man who bore that name: Leacht Ábhartaigh (anglicised Slaghtaverty); this meant 'the monument of Ábhartach', and in time it was interpreted as referring to the famous wizard. Thus in late folklore it was claimed that Ábhartach was vulnerable only in one spot of his body. Becoming aware of this through the ritual of chewing his own 'thumb of knowledge', Fionn mac Cumhaill cast his spear at Ábhartach and slew him. Fionn, it was claimed, buried Ábhartach with his head downwards so as to ensure that the wizard would not return to life, and then raised the monument over him.

GENERAL: Stokes (1900), 85; J. Fraser in Ériu, 8, 44; L. Duncan in Ériu, 11, 188; Ní Shéaghdha (1967), 52; G. Murphy (1933), 28–30; Carney (1945), 95; C. McGrath in Éigse, 7, 88, 92.
DOIREANN: Bergin (1970), 113; McKenna (1939), 32; McKenna (1947), 123; Gwynn (1935), 117.
MIADHACH AND MORANN: Ní Shéaghdha (1945), 85–91; see also Christiansen (1931), 418–19; Mac Néill (1908), 21; G. Murphy (1953), 21.
GIOLLA DEACAIR: O'Grady, 1 (1892), 257–75; Ó Siochfhradha (1938). See Ó hÓgáin (1988), 228–32, 339.
LEACHT ÁBHARTAIGH: OSL Derry (1834), 30–1.

Adhamhnán (AD 627–704) Biographer of COLM CILLE and abbot of the community founded by that SAINT on the island of Iona off the west coast of Scotland. His father was of the same stock as Colm, and Adhamhnán himself was apparently born and reared in the region of County Donegal. His name (earlier written Adamnán) was a diminutive of Adam, but is anglicised as Eunan.

He went to Iona some time around the year 670, became abbot in 679, and wrote the biography of Colm Cille some years later, using traditions of the saint that had survived both orally and in writings during the few generations since his death. One of his sources was an old monk who had known Colm Cille himself. Among other works written by Adhamhnán was a description in Latin of the holy places of Palestine, based on what he heard from a Gallic bishop called Arculf who was shipwrecked and took refuge on Iona. In the year 697, a law drafted by him was enacted at a convention in Biorra (Birr, County Offaly). This law, entitled *Cáin Adamnáin*, was applicable to both Ireland and Scotland, and it specified that women, children and clerics should be protected from attack both in times of war and peace. It was claimed that he drafted the law to fulfil a promise he once made to his mother when she was upset at seeing a woman injuring another in battle.

Adhamhnán is featured in several medieval texts. He was especially associated with the high-king of TARA, FIONNACHTA, his somewhat older contemporary. We read that when Fionnachta was riding along a road once, the young Adhamhnán ran out of the way but tripped on a stone and broke the milk vessel that he had been carrying on his back. Realising that the youth was a clerical student, Fionnachta paid for the vessel and brought Adhamhnán with him to a banquet. Their friendship continued for a long time, until Fionnachta was tricked by St MOLING concerning the *BÓRAIMHE* tribute, whereupon Adhamhnán reproached the high-king bitterly for his foolishness. This is very dubious history, not least Adhamhnán's role in the tribute controversy. Along with the several more localised accounts of Adhamhnán making legal and political arrangements, it seems to be no more than an echo from the social importance of the *Cáin Adamnáin* tract.

Another role attributed to him, however, does have an historical origin. Two years after a fierce Saxon attack on Breagha (the plain of County Meath) in 684, he went to visit the king of Northumbria and secured the release of 60 captives who had been taken in the raid. The account given in the medieval literature is quite dramatised, claiming that when he arrived with his monks on the shore of the Saxons' territory, the current was so rapid that his boats could not land. By a miracle, Adhamhnán made a great wall of the sea and therefore landed safely on dry land. Gripped with dread of the saint, the Saxons submitted to him, surrendered their booty, and promised not to plunder Ireland again.

One story describes how Adhamhnán once shut himself into his cell on Iona for three days, and how the monks grew anxious for him and went to investigate. Through the keyhole they saw the child JESUS, surrounded by a beautiful light, sitting in Adhamhnán's lap.

An additional text attributed to the authorship of Adhamhnán, but actually composed as late as the tenth century, is his 'vision' entitled *Fís Adamnáin*. It purports to describe a vision that he had when at Birr for the convention, in the course of which his soul went from his body and visited heaven and hell. This belongs to a genre popular in the literature of early medieval Ireland (*see* FURSA *and* BRÉANAINN). The feast day of Adhamhnán is 23 September.

BIOGRAPHICAL: Anderson & Anderson (1961), 92–8; Stokes (1905), 196, 210–11, 244–5; Anderson & Anderson in *RC*, *13*, 98–117; R.I. Best in *AIM*, *2*, 10–20; O'Donovan (1860), 72–85; O'Grady, *1* (1892), 404–6; K. Meyer in *ZCP*, *5*, 495–6.

CÁIN: K. Meyer in *Anecdota Oxoniensia*, *12*.

FÍS: J. Vendryes in *RC*, *30*, 349–83; *see also* Boswell (1908); Dillon (1948), 132–9.

GENERAL: Kenney (1929), 245–6, 283–7, 429–33, 443–5, 799; O'Hanlon, *9* (1875), 476–533.

Ailbhe SAINT who reputedly died in AD 527, founder of a monastery at Imleach Iubhair (Emly, County Tipperary).

The literature regards Ailbhe as a contemporary of PATRICK, and claims that his mission was in progress in Munster before that of Patrick. There are indeed some indications that his image took on aspects of pre-Christian tradition. Imleach Iubhair meant 'the omphalos at a yew-tree', and might originally have been a pre-Christian sanctuary, while the name Ailbhe itself – meaning 'rock' – may have been given to him as a reflex from ancient lore. St Ailbhe was probably an historical character, and his fame as abbot of Emly was so well established that a metrical list of monastic rules (called *Riagol Ailbi Imlecha*) was being attributed to him from the eighth century onwards.

The biographical account of the saint, however, dates to the twelfth century, and is so late that it can contain but a few vestiges of the earlier tradition. It is full of conventional miracles that have obviously been borrowed from biographies of other Irish saints. The description of his birth and youth show that at least the meaning of his name had not been forgotten. We read that his parents lived in the territory of the Artraighe or Araidh Cliach (on the modern Limerick–Tipperary border), that his father's name was Olcnais or Ollchú (both names signifying a wolf), and that his mother Sanclit was a servant of the local king, Crónán. That king was very hostile to Olcnais, and he ordered that the baby be exposed to wild beasts. The little boy was therefore placed under a large rock in a lonely place, but a wolf bitch carried him away to her den and suckled him with her own pups. He was eventually found, and was reared by some Briton slaves.

When Ailbhe came of age, he went to the Continent and was educated there by a bishop called Hilarius. Returning to Ireland, he was spreading the Christian faith in Munster when Patrick reputedly arrived there. He recognised Patrick as his superior and was given Emly as his See. In this role, Ailbhe was said to have been the mentor of several other Munster saints, and of ÉINNE, for whom it was claimed he got possession of Inishmore off the Galway coast. According to one tradition, as he grew older Ailbhe wished to retire to some place where he could live in solitude, and chose the island of Thule near the Arctic Ocean. The king of Munster, Aonghus mac Nadfraoich – who did not wish to see so pious a saint leave his territory – placed guards at the seaports and so prevented him from doing so.

The association of a rock with his childhood is a reflection of his name, and the name given to his mother seems to be a corruption of the Latin word *sancta*. The name given to his father, however, was probably based on speculation by the medieval writers, who knew that an important place in central Leinster was anciently known as 'the plain of Ailbhe'. An epic story concerned a wild hound called Ailbhe after whom it was claimed the plain had been named (*see* CONALL CEARNACH concerning Mac Da Thó). This would have suggested a wolf name for the saint's father, as well as the Romulus motif of suckling by a wolf (*see* CORMAC MAC AIRT). From this it would appear that the saint's rescue by a wolf was imposed onto an earlier tradition that he was given directly to a group of Britons who were in bondage in the area, and that he had been looked after by them. The mention of Hilarius, if it refers to the fifth-century bishop of Arles of that name, is a curiosity, but the connection of this bishop with Ailbhe is hardly more than speculation by a medieval writer.

A possible scenario for the history of Ailbhe would be that his mother was a Briton slave in the territory of the Araidh Cliach – perhaps as early as the fifth century – and that her son got the Christian faith from her and from her compatriots. Having come to prominence among the peoples of that area, he would appear to have established Christianity at a cultic site known as Meadhon Mairtine (the 'centre' of a small tribe called Mairtine). With the growing power of the great EOGHANACHT sept, this site became known from the yew-symbolism of that sept as Imleach Iubhair. The association of Ailbhe with the mission to Inishmore came from a later monastic settlement under Eoghanacht influence on that island.

We read that Ailbhe died at Emly, and local tradition holds that he was buried in the grounds of the monastery there. It was believed down to recent times that he protected the crops, and water from his well was sprinkled on the fields to prevent the sparrows from eating the corn. A LEGEND in existence since the Middle Ages – and still current – claims that when he was a boy and in service with a farmer, he miraculously confined the birds in a roofless barn (*see* SAINTS). His feast day is 12 September.

O'Hanlon, *9* (1875), 278–97; Stokes (1905), 194, 206–7, 262–3, 399; Plummer, *1* (1910), 44–64; Kenney (1929), 313–15; Heist (1965), 118–31; L de Paor (1993), 227–43, 251–2; 'Fáinne Fionn' in *The Irish Rosary*, *16*; J. O'Neill in *Ériu*, *3*, 92–115; Stokes & Strachan (1903), 265, 379; J. Szöverffy in *Éigse*, *8*, 128–9; IFC 556:141–2.

Ailill Mythical name with an original meaning of 'brilliant one' or 'phantom', a designation of the ancestor-deity in some contexts. That the solar father-deity (*see* AODH RUADH RÓ-FHEASA *and* EOCHAIDH) could be thought of as appearing in ghostly human or animal form is evident from some early traditions (*see* CONAIRE, FIONN *and* MANANNÁN). In fanciful Munster and Ulster genealogies, names are cited of characters called Ailill Find (the epithet, later *fionn*, meaning 'bright'). In the genealogy of the LAIGHIN (Leinstermen), there is mention of a mythical Ailill Áine, the sobriquet here underlining the name Ailill and meaning 'lustrous'. The genealogists claimed that Ailill Áine was the grandson of UGHAINE, whose name meant 'sheep-conceived', and there are several indications that the name Ailill for the ancestral deity was especially associated with patronship of the sheep-herds. Due to the designation Ailill Áine, Ailill could be thought of as the consort of a lady called Áine, and so in the Munster EOGHANACHT lore the ancestor figure was regarded as partner of a GODDESS called ÁINE. This supposed Eoghanacht ancestor was known as AILILL ÓLOM, the sobriquet here being taken to mean 'ear-bare', an appropriate symbol for a sheep-deity. An earlier form was Aulom, the first element of which could have been from a Celtic *ovo* (sheep) – in that case, the meaning would have been 'definite sheep'. The fact that an historical leader of the CONNACHTA in the fifth century AD

was known as Ailill Molt (Ailill the Wether) shows that the SHEEP-cult associated with the deity under this name was well established by then. The probability is that such a cult was a survival from ancient Celtic culture, and was known to the various population groups in early Ireland.

Play upon Ailill as a patron of herds has given rise to some dramatic lore. In the ULSTER CYCLE, the husband of the celebrated MEADHBH of Connacht is called Ailill mac Máta, and his famous bull – called, significantly, the bright (*find*) horned one – is a source of envy for Meadhbh, thus causing the disastrous war. Otherwise in that cycle, a character called Ailill Find is the husband of Fiodhais, a lady who has a wonderful herd of cattle. Furthermore, as a pseudonym for the father-god as sun-deity, Ailill seems to have survived in the loosely structured sub-literary tradition, to surface in various forms under the name Aillén (little Ailill). For instance, in medieval story, one Aillén mac Midhna was a fiery destroyer of TARA until vanquished by FIONN MAC CUMHAILL, while another Aillén was a triple-headed monster that emerged from the cave of Cruachain (Rathcroghan, County Roscommon) and devastated Ireland until slain by AMHAIRGHIN MAC ÉIGIT SALAIGH. 'Ailill' came into use as a personal name at an early period, and in the later literature is usually written as 'Oilill'.

T.F. O'Rahilly (1946), 300; Olmsted (1994), 383–4, 479; O'Brien (1962), 502; Stokes (1900), 47–50; M. O'Daly (1975), 48.

Ailill Molt Semi-historical CONNACHTA leader and KING of the western province in the late fifth century AD. He was the son of NAITHÍ, and the medieval historians claimed that he extended his power over his relatives – the progeny of NIALL – thus becoming king of TARA for a while (according to the Annals, from AD 461–82). This reign of his at Tara may be a fabrication, and rather than a struggle for the kingship, the Battle of Ochae (Faughan Hill, County Meath) in which he was defeated and slain was probably the result of a raid by him on territory held by Niall's family.

His name AILILL had mythical origins, and this seems to have been what attracted the epithet Molt (Wether) to him, for Ailill was a mythical appellation of the deity as patron of sheep. Such a deity, called Moltinus, was known to the ancient Continental Celts. A late and fanciful tradition was that the epithet of the historical Ailill Molt derived from the circumstance that, before his birth, his mother Eithne took a desire for wether-mutton. All such available sheep were brought to a hill called Tulach na Molt (literally, 'Mound of the Wethers'), to be slaughtered for her there. This hill is also known as Mullach Rua (Mullaroe, Skreen, County Sligo).

T.F. O'Rahilly (1946), 300, 400–1; Mac Niocaill (1972), 16–21; F.J. Byrne (1973), 85, 231–2; H. Wagner in *ZCP*, *38*, 21; O'Donovan (1844), 22, 96–7; Dinneen, *3* (1908), 42–4.

Ailill Ólom Mythical KING of Munster and a dramatic figure in the cultic-lore of the leading sept in early Munster, the EOGHANACHT. He was a version of the father-deity in the guise of the brilliant phantom AILILL, and his sobriquet (originally, Aulom) with a meaning 'definite sheep' or 'ear-bare' reflected the role of the deity as patron of herds. The honouring of such a ram-deity would indicate that the Eoghanacht regarded themselves as a wealthy sheep-herding people.

Several details of Ailill Ólom are found in eighth- and ninth-century texts. We read that his dwelling was on the hill called Cláire (in the parish of Galbally, County Limerick), and that he lived for 90 years – 30 years for each of three periods. The first period was before his reign, the second was as king, and the third after he was deposed by LUGHAIDH MAC CON. He was sometimes claimed to have been father of EOGHAN MÓR rather than his son, as the synchronisers usually had it. Possibly Ólom was in origin a mere nickname for Eoghan, for he was regarded – like Eoghan – as the ancestor and archetypal king of the Eoghanacht sept whose prestige was celebrated by the lore. In this role, he was the mate of the land-GODDESS ÁINE, and a dramatic but somewhat hostile description in

one text has him raping her at her hill of Knockainey, County Limerick. She tore his ears off in the struggle, and thus the appellation Ólom was explained. An elaboration of this episode states that in anger at being maimed, he drove his spear through her, killing her. The medieval literature represents Ailill as having for his wife Sadhbh, daughter of CONN CÉADCHATHACH and sister of ART. This, of course, is a synchroniser's trick, in order to portray diplomacy between the great rival dynasties of the CONNACHTA at TARA and the Eoghanacht in Munster.

Ailill Ólom, with his seven sons and his army, was said to have defeated the ÉRAINN forces of Lughaidh mac Con at the Battle of Ceann Abhradh (the Ballyhoura hills on the present Limerick–Cork border). This was probably an echo of how the Eoghanacht first took the kingship of Munster. Some accounts state that Ailill acted treacherously towards Lughaidh, who was his foster-son, but all agree in having Lughaidh retire to Scotland and return from there at the head of a large army. At the Battle of Magh Mucramha (near Athenry, County Galway) the exile defeated the combined forces of Ailill and Art. Ailill's seven sons were slain, and he himself was deposed from the kingship of Munster. Lughaidh took the HIGH-KING-SHIP at Tara, but later handed it over to the renowned CORMAC MAC AIRT, and went south in order to restore his friendship with Ailill. It was said that Ailill had a barbed spear and that there was a prohibition (*GEIS*) on him against straightening it. It happened that he once put it under his tooth to straighten it, and the poison passed from it into the tooth. It corrupted his breath and blackened the tooth, causing great pain and anguish to him. When Lughaidh came, however, Ailill turned this ailment to advantage, for he infected his foe with it under pretence of kissing him.

A curious aspect of these accounts of Ailill is that their attitude is rather hostile to him. This can be explained by the hypothesis that elements of them derive from ancient rivals of the Eoghanacht in Munster, and that they have been further effected by propaganda of the Connachta and Uí NÉILL, who regarded the Eoghanacht as their principal competitors in the early medieval period.

M. O'Daly (1975), 4, 38–65, 74–93: Meyer (1910), 6–13; K. Meyer in *AIM, 3*, 27–9; W. Stokes in *Irische Texte, 3*, 304–7; Dillon (1946), 16–23; M. Dillon in *Ériu, 14*, 154–65; M. Ó Dúnlainge in *Irisleabhar na Gaedhilge, 18*, 75–81.

Áine Otherworld woman in Irish literature and folklore. The name originally meant 'lustre' or 'brightness'. In archaic times, this designation Áine was used as an epithet for male as well as female deities, and it occurs in place names in different parts of Ireland.

The medieval literature has several mentions of an otherworld lady called Áine. She was, for instance, claimed to have been a daughter of MANANNÁN, and one story told of how a warrior called Étar (later, Éadar) fell in love with her but died of a broken heart when she rejected him; he was reputedly buried at the place that since bears his name, Beann Éadair (Howth, County Dublin). The major emphasis, however, settled on a woman called Áine who was associated with Munster and particularly with the EOGHANACHT sept. Her residence was an otherworld palace at Cnoc Áine (the hill of Knockainey, County Limerick), which is situated in the centre of the pasture-lands of the rich Munster plain. She was therefore a version of the land-GODDESS, and as such became the patroness of sovereignty for the Eoghanacht of that area.

This Eoghanacht connection seems to have been based on the widespread cult of AILILL, and it is clearly expressed in an eighth-century text that has AILILL ÓLOM going at Samhain (the November feast) in the evening to attend his horses at Knockainey and lying down there to sleep. The hill was stripped of its grass during the night, and he was puzzled as to who did that. He travelled to Leinster to a seer-poet called Fearcheas mac Comáin, who advised that they go together to investigate on the following Samhain. When they did so, Ailill fell asleep on the hillside while listening to the cattle grazing, and the king of the *sídh* (otherworld dwelling), called Eoghabhal, appeared accompanied by his daughter Áine. She was playing music on a bronze instrument. Fearcheas slew Eoghabhal and Ailill raped Áine, for which treatment she cursed the assailants.

This text is hostile towards Ailill, and a later version of the story develops the narrative further by having Ailill slay Áine with his spear in anger at her pulling off his right ear. The origin of the tradition, however, was that Ailill was an Eoghanacht ancestor-figure and was the mate of Áine. She was thus ancestress of the Eoghanacht, which was a way of stressing the right of that sept to the kingship of Munster. Indeed, the name of the father invented for her, Eoghabhal (yew-fork), is a simple derivation from the sept's own name.

The medieval scholars considered it necessary to give an account of the 'prehistory' of Áine. They therefore claimed that in the time of the TUATHA DÉ DANANN, Eoghabhal and his family sought territory from Neachtan (i.e. NUADHU), and were advised to go and take the hill called Drom Collchoille. The tribes who were then in possession of the hill gave battle to Eoghabhal and his men, and the latter were being repulsed. Then Áine promised to gain the victory for Eoghabhal on condition that her name be on the hill forever afterwards. This was agreed, and she scattered the foe by the force of magic and put them to flight. The hill was accordingly known as Cnoc Áine, and it was divided into four parts – Uainidhe's portion to the north, that of Fear Fí to the south, Eoghabhal's portion to the west, and Áine's to the east. This, of course, is a mere rationalisation and dramatisation of Áine's connection with the hill. Her real history was that of a land-goddess, functioning as a compound symbol of agricultural prosperity and septal sovereignty.

The claim of Áine's patronage and ancestry was stressed again in a striking manner by the great Norman lords of the area at the end of the Middle Ages. These were the Geraldines who, in the four-teenth century, called their first Earl of

DESMOND, Maurice, 'the king of Áine'. Maurice's son, Gearóid Iarla FitzGerald, they referred to as the 'son of the cavalier of bright Áine'. This Geraldine propaganda is reflected in folklore that portrays Gearóid Iarla as her actual offspring. Maurice the first earl, we are told, one day saw her bathing in Lough Gur, a short distance from Knockainey. He took her cloak, an action that magically put her in his power, and then lay with her, by which act Gearóid Iarla was conceived. This story is the result of a fusion between the Eoghanacht myth of Ailill and a medieval Continental LEGEND concerning a swan-maiden. As a result of this fusion, Áine was supposed in folklore to be sometimes seen bathing in that lake in the form of a MERMAID.

Independent of the Geraldine lore, Áine survived in folk tradition as a latter-day figure of the land-goddess. She was given an aetiological role, and various large rocks at Knockainey hill were said to have been placed there by her. She is popularly called Áine Chliar, the sobriquet being explained as *cliar* (a wisp), but in reality it reflects the local pronunciation of Cliach, the genitive of the territory's ancient name Cliú. The extended name of Knockainey in Irish is in fact Cnoc Áine Cliach. In the nineteenth century, it was customary for local inhabitants to hold midsummer festivities (*see* TIME) on the hill. Bunches of straw (*cliara*) were lit and carried to the summit of the hill, and then scattered in the cultivated fields and among the cattle to bring prosperity. Áine was reputed to be sometimes seen on the hill on that night. She was said to be 'the best-hearted woman who ever lived', and a legend still current in the area tells of how she appeared in the form of a beggar woman to a local poor family. The family was kind to the old woman, and when she had left they found a new sheep in their field. All their affairs prospered while they kept the sheep, but when they sold it the initial poverty returned. This association with sheep could well be a distant echo of a sheep-cult connected with names such as AILILL ÓLOM and AILILL ÁINE.

The particular strength of the Áine tradition in east Limerick is due to the early appropriation of her by the Eoghanacht. That 'Áine' survived as a general designation for a goddess is clear, however, from the folklore associated with the name in widely scattered areas. At Dun Áine (Dunany, County Louth), the weekend immediately after the Lughnasadh festival (*see* TIME) was regarded as sacred to her, and people refrained from going to sea for its duration. In County Derry, the parish of Lios Áine (Lissan) has many associations with the same name, and it contains another hill called Cnoc Áine. Here she was also said to take an interest in local affairs. Once, when a cowherd was asleep, she awakened him and informed him that the cattle had strayed into an oat field. She touched his head, leaving five grey finger marks on his fair hair. She was supposed to have once been an ordinary woman, but was abducted into the hill, and a local family, Ó Corra (Corr), was reputedly descended from her. She was the family's BANSHEE, and her wailing was heard as a presage of the death of members of that family. Another hill called Cnoc Áine is in the parish of Teelin, County Donegal, and here Áine is said to have been an ordinary girl who, tired of harsh orders from her father, went into the hill long ago. She lives there in a beautiful palace and passes her time 'spinning the sunbeams and making gold cloth of the thread'.

LITERATURE: T.F. O'Rahilly (1946), 280–90; Gwynn (1913), 114–15: W. Stokes in *RC*, *15*, 330–1; W. Stokes in *Irische Texte*, *3*, 83; Stokes (1900), 104–5; R.I. Best in *Ériu*, *3*, 162–3; M. O'Daly (1975), 4, 38–9; M. Dillon in *Ériu*, *14*, 154–65; Best & O'Brien (1957), 546; O'Grady, *2* (1892), 575–6; Mac Cionnaith (1938), 205.

FOLKLORE: D. Fitzgerald in *RC*, *4*, 186–90, 195; IFC 1799:8, 117–19; M. MacNeill (1962), 30, 181, 307, 567, 591–2, 680; Ó Muirgheasa (1934), 403–4; P. Mac Seáin in *Béaloideas*, *31*, 72–3; Ó hEochaidh, MacNeill & Ó Catháin (1977), 36–41, 375.

Airghialla A collective name for septs inhabiting much of west and south Ulster, and a little of north Leinster. The name meant 'givers of hostages'. A variant spelling is Oirghialla, and that general region is still known by it (anglicised Oriel).

These septs – stretching respectively from the west of modern County Derry to the north of modern County Meath –

were known as the Uí Mhic Chairthinn, Uí Fhiachrach Arda, Fir Chraoibhe, Uí Chréamhthainn, Fir Lí, Uí Thuirtre, Fir Airthir, Uí Mhéith and Mughdhorna. They were originally ÉRAINN. With the northward expansion of the CONNACHTA in the fifth century AD (*see* ULSTER CYCLE), they felt themselves under pressure, but they survived through becoming allies and satellites of these powerful neighbours; hence their collective name, which indicates the arrangement of giving hostages by them to the Connachta – a custom apparently initiated by NIALL, who had the epithet Naoi-Ghiallach, meaning 'nine-hostaged'. It was later claimed that there was a hostage from each of the nine Airghialla septs and that, out of respect for them, these hostages were placed in chains of gold by the HIGH-KINGS at TARA.

The Airghialla even claimed direct relationship with the Connachta, and the legend of the three COLLA brothers stressed this. The conceit was obviously of some political value for it was borrowed by the mixed Érainn and Laighin sept called Uí MHAINE, who held on to their territory against the Connachta west of Lough Ree on the Shannon.

In the medieval period, branches of the Airghialla took on surnames such as Maguidhir (Maguire), Mac Mánais (McManus), Mac Mathúna (McMahon), Mac Gormáin (Gorman), Ó hAnrachtaigh (Hanratty), Mac Maicín (Mackin), Mac Cuarta (McCourt), Ó Conghaile (Connolly), Mac an Fhailghigh (MacNally), Ó hÉighnigh (Heaney, Hegney), Ó hAnluain (O'Hanlon), Mac Gnímh (Agnew), Mac an Bheatha (McVeagh) and Ó Cearbhaill (Carroll of Louth).

T.F. O'Rahilly (1946), 224–6, 232–34; O'Brien (1962), 139–55, 414–23, 435–7; K. Meyer in *ZCP*, 8, 317–24; Mac Niocaill (1972), 12–15, 39; F.J. Byrne (1973), 72–4, 318; O'Donovan (1847), 134–55; W. Stokes in *Irische Texte*, 3, 350–3; Ó Muraíle, 2 (2003), 2–101 & 3, 460–73.

Aithirne Fictional satirist in the ULSTER CYCLE. His name originally meant 'little glutton', and his character developed out of anti-POET sentiment. This was probably part of clerical antipathy to those poets of the sixth and seventh centuries who were slow to accept Christianity and who upheld their traditional rights to demand large rewards for their work. Aithirne is given the various sobriquets Áilgheasach (importunate), Amhnach (savage), and Díbheach (miserly), and was said to have been son of the poet FEIRCHEIRDNE. As a typified satirist, his name was sometimes reinterpreted as *Áithrinne* (meaning 'sharp-pointed').

Several texts tell of the adventures of Aithirne. The magical power of his verse was said to have been demonstrated even before his birth. His mother, when pregnant, went into a house where a feast was being prepared, and the baby leaped in her womb when it got the whiff of ale. The ale-man refused her a drink, however, and the unborn baby was heard to speak a stanza that caused the barrels to burst asunder. The ale spilled all over the house, and Aithirne's mother managed to drink three draughts of it from her palm. Another account has Aithirne, when a grown poet, satirising a river that yielded no fish to him. The river (the Mourne in Counties Tyrone and Donegal) rose up in a flood of anger and swept people, animals and property with it to the sea. The alarmed Aithirne then recited a verse of praise to 'clean away' the insult, and the river restored all and subsided.

He is portrayed as ferociously demanding and so greedy that he would never share his food with anybody else. We are told that he used to always eat his meals in private for fear anybody would observe him and wish to join him. One day, he went into a wood to cook a pig, but a stranger approached, much to his discomfiture. Aithirne demanded to know the stranger's name so that he could compose a satire on him, but the stranger gave a jumble of words that could not be rhymed. The stinginess of Aithirne is expressed metaphorically in an account that has him going to the otherworld dwelling of Brí Leith (near Ardagh, County Longford) to acquire there the three 'herons of refusal and inhospitality' for his own house. One of these would tell a visitor not to enter, another would tell him to depart, and the third would tell him to keep away from the house.

Aithirne's acquisitive nature is illustrated in a long text of the eleventh century entitled *Tallaind Étair* (the Battle of Howth). It describes how he went to Eochaidh mac Luchta, the one-eyed KING of Connacht, who was a most generous man. Eochaidh offered him any gift he desired, and Aithirne demanded his only eye. The king plucked the eye out and gave it into the palm of the poet. On taking his leave, Aithirne remarked that this was proper vengeance for a raid that Eochaidh had made on the Ulster court at Eamhain Mhacha. Continuing on his journey to Munster, Aithirne visited the king of that province and insisted on sleeping with the queen, even though she had given birth on the same night. The people of south Leinster assembled before him offering all kinds of gifts in order to avoid his satire, but he refused all in the hope that they would kill him and thus draw on themselves the wrath of his native Ulster. He was finally appeased with a precious brooch that a horse accidentally kicked up from a grave-mound. On reaching the court of the Leinster king, Meas Geaghra, he demanded to sleep with the queen. Fearing satire and resultant dishonour, Meas Geaghra acquiesced.

Aithirne remained a year there, and then took his leave, bringing with him thrice-50 wives of Leinster nobles. The Leinstermen (LAIGHIN) escorted him courteously out of their territory as far as the borderland at Tealchuma (just north of Dublin), and he left them there, without giving any thanks. As soon as he had passed from the hospitality of their territory, the furious Leinstermen felt justified in seeking revenge and gave chase, but they were intercepted by an Ulster force led by king CONCHOBHAR MAC NEASA, and a fierce battle ensued. The Ulstermen retreated as far as Éadar (Howth, County Dublin), where they ensconced themselves. For eight days they were besieged there, with no food or drink except clay and sea water. Aithirne had 700 cows in the fortress, but he refused a drop of milk

even to dying men. Meas Deadh, a pupil of CÚ CHULAINN, performed great feats in defending the fortress, but was slain just as Ulster reinforcements landed by sea. Enraged by this, Cú Chulainn led a sortie from the fort, and the Leinstermen were put to flight, but many warriors on both sides were slain. CONALL CEARNACH followed the Leinstermen and slew their king, Meas Geaghra, in single combat.

Aithirne was, however, once outwitted by his host. This was the poet AMHAIRGHIN MAC ÉIGIT SALAIGH, himself a former pupil of the infamous satirist. Having stayed a night, Aithirne was about to leave but was persuaded by Amhairghin's rhetoric to remain for the duration of autumn. Again he was persuaded to remain for the winter and the spring, until summer came and Amhairghin made a poetic speech allowing him to depart. The pupils of Amhairghin wished to hear some of Aithirne's poetry, so Amhairghin called for a bull, a calf and a sheep to be brought in and killed in his honour. Aithirne recited verses forbidding the killing of each, but finally was satisfied with a pig. Amhairghin had saved his house from satire by the high standard of his own poetry. Otherwise, we read in praise of a woman of Ulster, called Duanach, who she was so rich and munificent that even Aithirne once lauded her.

The death of Aithirne came about when he overstepped himself with a demand. We read that king Conchobhar sought a new woman after the death of DEIRDRE, and a suitable maiden was found – Luaine, daughter of a chieftain of the TUATHA DÉ DANANN. When he heard of this, Aithirne and his two sons demanded that she become their lover. She refused, and Aithirne with a satire caused three blisters of shame to rise on her face. She died as a result, and Aithirne fled with his sons to a dwelling that he had at the River Boyne. The druid CATHBHADH warned the enraged Ulstermen that Aithirne could send 'destructive monsters against you – satire and ridicule and reddening, barking and burning poison and bitter words'. Cú Chulainn, however, advised them to kill Aithirne, and the

10

satirist's dwelling was accordingly set ablaze by the Ulstermen. The bitter poet perished within.

The stories concerning Aithirne all belong to the period between the eighth and the eleventh century, and no accounts of him survived in post-medieval folklore.

NAME: C. Marstrander in *ZCP, 7*, 376–82.

ACCOUNTS AND STORIES: R. Thurneysen in *ZCP, 12*, 398–9: E.J. Gwynn in *ZCP, 17*, 152–6; E.J. Gwynn in *Ériu, 13*, 13–28, 57; W. Stokes in *RC, 8*, 47–64; W. Stokes in *RC, 24*, 270–87; M.E. Dobbs in *Études Celtiques, 5*, 154–61; R.I. Best in *Irish Texts, 1*, 32–3; K. Meyer in *Ériu, 7*, 1–9; Meyer (1912), 57; L. Breatnach in *Celtica, 13*, 1–31.

DUANACH: M. Dillon in *Ériu, 11*, 51.

GENERAL: P. Henry (1978), 55–65, 240.

Amhairghin Glúngheal

Mythical or fictional POET in early Irish literature. His name (earlier, Amorgein) probably meant 'song-conception', and would have originally been a kenning for the art of poetry itself. His epithet, Glúngheal, means 'bright-kneed', but its import is obscure; it may indicate that, belonging to the pre-Christian era, his knee was not darkened by being accustomed to a praying posture.

He is featured in the pseudo-history, where he appears as one of the sons of MÍL, who led the Gaelic people in their invasion of Ireland. The role assigned to him makes him the most important of the invaders, for he is the first of them to touch the soil of Ireland, and he becomes the counsellor of his brothers and the chief negotiator with the incumbent race, the TUATHA DÉ DANANN. A dramatic detail is included to the effect that his wife Scéine was drowned off the shore where they landed; that harbour is thus claimed to have been called after her – Inbhear Scéine (Kenmare Bay, County Kerry). That place name itself is of pseudo-learned derivation, being based on a corrupted reference in an early Latin geography. As Amhairghin first lands, he recites a great mystical rhetoric in which he exults in being a poet, claiming to be at one with the whole environment. He is wind, sea, bull, hawk, dewdrop, flower, boar, salmon, lake and hill, and he further claims to be the point of a warrior's weapon and 'a god who fashions inspiration in the head'. This composition is really an argument by the professional poets of medieval Ireland for social primacy, but there is also an echo of ancient ritual concerning the metamorphic power of seer-poets (*see* FIONN).

He and his brothers successfully effected the conquest of Ireland, and we read that Amhairghin arbitrated on their various claims, and then himself settled at Inbhear Mór (Arklow, County Wicklow), where he built a causeway. Contention broke out between the sons of Míl, however, and Amhairghin was slain by Éireamhóin in a battle at Bile Teineadh (Billywood, near Moynalty, County Meath).

C.-J. Guyonvarc'h in *Ogam, 12*, 448–9; Macalister (1956), 30–47, 106–7, 110–21, 156–9; M. Dillon in *Ériu, 11*, 50; L. Breatnach in *Ériu, 32*, 45–93; Dinneen, *2* (1908), 80–107 & *3*, 30–3.

'INBHEAR SCÉINE': T.F. O'Rahilly (1946), 198.

Amhairghin mac Éigit Salaigh

Mythical character, professional POET to king CONCHOBHAR MAC NEASA in the ULSTER CYCLE. He is sometimes given the epithet '*iarghiunnach*' (shaven behind), which is probably a reference to a tonsure employed by the DRUIDS.

This character was another development from the imagery associated with the name Amhairghin (*see preceding entry*). The earliest reference to him is in a recension from the end of the eighth century of the birth-story of CÚ CHULAINN. There he is presented as tutor to Cú Chulainn, the drama of that young hero being heightened by the acquisition in this way of mythic wisdom. This indeed seems to have been the context in which a character called Amhairghin was introduced into the Ulster Cycle, and we read that Amhairghin and his wife Fionnchaomh reared Cú Chulainn in their fortress of Dún Imbrith in Muirtheimhne (north County Louth). It is further stated that CONALL CEARNACH was the foster-brother of Cú Chulainn, the former being son of Amhairghin and Fionnchaomh. It thus appears that Amhairghin was introduced into the cycle as a tutor in the early part of the eighth century, and that he was soon put in the role of Conall's father in the rapidly developing lore. In this text, Amhairghin stakes his claim to be a suitable tutor for a child hero, and his words are the basis for his portrayal in the succeeding literature: 'I am praised for every quality, for my courage, for my wisdom, for my fortune, for my maturity, for my eloquence, for the nobility and bravery of my offspring. Whoever is a prince, I am a poet. I deserve the status of a KING. I slay each warrior. I give allegiance to nobody but Conchobhar.' The echoes here in phraseology from the poetry and portrayal of his namesake, AMHAIRGHIN GLÚNGHEAL, show that the other poet figures in the background. There are other passages in the literature that equally show the exalted status of Conchobhar's poet. A ninth-century text, for instance, refers to a three-headed monster that emerged from the cave of Cruachain (Rathcroghan, County Roscommon) and laid Ireland waste until 'Amhairghin, father of Conall Cearnach, slew it in single combat in the presence of all the Ulster men'. This monster is called 'ellén', which can be related to the fiery Aillén slain by the famous warrior-seer FIONN MAC CUMHAILL.

Another ninth-century text tells of Amhairghin's childhood, claiming that until he was seven years old, he was an ugly backward child. His father, Éigeat Salach (dirty artisan), was a blacksmith, and one day the poet AITHIRNE sent his servant to the forge to redden his axe. The child spoke a rhetoric to the servant, who raced back to Aithirne and told him what he had heard. Fearing that he would be upstaged, Aithirne went to kill the child. Éigeat, however, made a clay statue of his son, and Aithirne – in the dim light of the forge – struck that with his axe in mistake for the child. Hotly pursued, Aithirne then fled to his own fortress, where he was besieged by the enraged Ulstermen. Eventually, peace was arranged, according to which Aithirne agreed to take the boy Amhairghin as his pupil and to teach him the skills of poetry. Thus when Aithirne grew old, Amhairghin succeeded him as chief poet of the province. Another

medieval story tells of how – when Amhairghin was a qualified poet – Aithirne came to visit him and sought a pretext to satirise him, but Amhairghin was so good a host that he could find no pretext.

The general portrayal of Amhairghin is that of a faithful supporter of Conchobhar, who is nevertheless socially on a par with that king. Thus his wife Fionnchaomh is described as Conchobhar's sister, and Amhairghin acts as as mediator between Conchobhar and FEARGHUS MAC RÓICH in their disputes. Invariably he is a stout fighter. An interpolation in the epic text *Táin Bó Cuailnge* (*see* ULSTER CYCLE) tells of how he had a portentous vision at Tailtiu (Teltown, County Meath), and immediately afterwards went to confront CÚ ROÍ, who was advancing against Ulster. He and Cú Roí began pelting each other and the stones met in the air. They then agreed to a truce, according to which Amhairghin would allow no armies to pass and Cú Roí would retire from the campaign. But when Cú Roí resumed his march, Amhairghin began casting again. Conall Cearnach supplied him with stones and javelins, and the number of men he killed in this way was uncountable. Amhairghin is mentioned in several musters of Conchobhar's army, and he is represented as fighting side by side with CORMAC CONN LOINGEAS when the latter was slain by the Connachtmen in the house of Da Choga.

Van Hamel (1933), 6–8, 12, 30; M. Joynt in *Ériu*, 10, 133–4; M. O'Daly (1975), 48–9; Meyer (1912), 57; R.I. Best in *Irish Texts*, 1, 32–3; C. O'Rahilly (1976), 103–6, 111–18; W. Stokes in *Irische Texte*, 3, 390–5; Ó Cadhlaigh (1956), 465 ('*Aimhirghean*').

amphibians, reptiles and molluscs

Frogs were in some narrative tales portrayed as enchanted people or fairies in disguise, but this idea was not strong in ordinary folk belief. Little other lore was concerned with frogs, except that their croaking betokened rain, as also did their coming into the dwelling-house. Frogspawn was sometimes explained as being the remains of a falling star, but contrariwise the appearance of evil spirits could be compared to frogspawn. Lizards were regarded as dangerous and quite sinister, and a voracious appetite was ascribed to them (*see* ANIMAL TALES, type 285B). A belief that probably derives from speculation regarding the chameleon is that the lizard, if cut into pieces, could join itself together again. If a person were brave enough to lick a lizard, it was said that he would have power to cure burns by applying his tongue to them. Ireland was noted in antiquity for the fact that it had no snakes, but it was not until the Middle Ages that the explanation was given that the country lacked such creatures because they had been expelled by St PATRICK. With regard to the more homely molluscs, snails and slugs were often used in divination – for example, young people traced their track over a slate to decide whether a certain boy or girl would marry within the year.

GENERAL: S. Ó Súilleabháin (1942), 302–3; Ó Danachair (1978), 25; P.V. O'Sullivan (1991), 125; Ó hÓgáin (1995), 46.

SNAKES: D. Ó hÓgáin in *Béaloideas, 51*, 95–6 (citing early foreign writers such as Solinus, Isidorus and Bede); O'Meara (1982), 50–2.

Anglo-Irish The generic term Anglo-Irish can be used for people of English origin in Ireland or for their contribution to Irish culture. English settlers in Ireland were often referred to as *Gaill*, an inaccurate term that had earlier been applied to the NORSEMEN, but the more usual term for them was *Sasanaigh* (literally, 'Saxons'). Although the origins of the Anglo-Irish lay in the conquest and subjugation of Ireland, in time they came to play a full and important part in the life of the country.

NORMAN control of Ireland, followed by their English successors, left the native GAELIC people in a state of disarray and their culture deprived of its own social institutions. Since the Norman invasion, small but significant settlements of Anglo-Norman communities were in particular areas, most notably the Pale, as County Dublin and contiguous areas came to be known. By the sixteenth century, however, the native Irish culture had begun to reassert itself everywhere, so that even people of English descent in Dublin spoke Irish and could hardly converse in English at all. Thereafter, there were rapid and

huge changes. In the reign of Queen Mary, a 'plantation' (i.e. dispossession of the natives and their replacement by English settlers) was carried out in the Midland counties of Laois and Offaly. This was followed by the dispossession of the great Norman-Gaelic lords of Munster, and the plantation of that fertile province. The seventeenth century saw a succession of plantations – that of Ulster, that of most of the country east of the River Shannon by the Cromwellians, and finally a new plantation by the Williamites.

By the beginning of the eighteenth century, the native Irish were left with title to less than a sixth of the whole country. The native people in almost all areas were reduced to tenantry on the lands that they once held under their own septal system. The social proximity to their leaders, and with it the whole system of mutual obligations, came to an end, being replaced by a system of feudalism and exploitation. The majority of the landlords were strangers, the law was a severe instrument to guarantee the status quo, and the official culture and language was exclusively English. From the end of the seventeenth century, the Irish language was in sharp decline, and by the time of the Great Famine it was spoken by only about half of the people. Thereafter, with the death and emigration of a further quarter of the population, the decline was even greater. Everywhere, English was the language of law, of education, of economics and of advancement.

The new landlordism was a severe imposition on the people, but not all of the TYRANT landowners and judges were of English stock. Some, indeed, were descendants of the native chieftains who had changed sides in the vicissitudes of Irish history. It should also be said that many of the patriotic leaders who gave their lives resisting the cruel system were themselves descendants of English settlers. In the forefront of Irish revolutionary history are thoroughly English names such as Theobald Wolfe Tone, Jemmy Hope, Robert Emmet and John Mitchel. The list of great thinkers and reformers includes Thomas Davis, Isaac Butt and Charles

Stewart Parnell. The great names of modern Irish literature include Jonathan SWIFT, Maria Edgeworth, Lady Augusta Gregory, Douglas Hyde, John Millington Synge and William Butler Yeats.

Most of the Anglo-Irish were unilingual or bilingual, depending on the language situation in the country, just as the rest of the Irish people were. They made a significant contribution to the folk tradition of Ireland, not only in material culture such as house types, farming techniques and food varieties, but also in terms of customs and beliefs. Many international FOLK-TALES must have reached Ireland in recent centuries through the medium of English, as did shorter types of lore, especially concerning GHOSTS and superstitions. There was no formal drama in Gaelic Ireland, but in towns and cities it was customary for the English settlers to stage plays dealing with religious and political matters. The transference of traditional English folk dramas to Ireland resulted in the mummer traditions popular in the provinces of Ulster and Leinster since the seventeenth century (see SPORTS AND PAS-TIMES). In these mummer plays, characters from Irish history were introduced side by side with, and sometimes replacing, original English figures such as Jack Straw, Robin Hood and Prince George.

The English commonly spoken in Ireland is in essence a language learned through social necessity from the seventeenth to nineteenth centuries. Its intonations, pronunciations and many of its expressions are direct derivatives of Irish. In recent generations, a variant of 'standard' English has tended to be accorded prestige among the professional classes. There is no substantial connection to be noted with pre-seventeenth-century English, but researchers have accorded due attention to two notable exceptions: these concern the survival of a variant of Middle English from the twelfth century down to the nineteenth century in two specific areas – the baronies of Forth and Bargy in south Wexford, and the barony of Fingall in north Dublin. There was naturally some influence from Irish, but it was the strange character of the English words which caused English travellers in these areas to suppose that all the speech was Gaelic. The speech of Forth and Bargy was called Yola (literally, 'Old'). In the seventeenth and eighteenth centuries, a number of colourful Christmas carols were composed in English in that part of Wexford, and are still sung.

There are many Anglo-Irish surnames, some of which are confused with native Irish surnames, and others of which have been gaelicised. The most numerous (with Gaelic variants) include Smith (Mac Gabhann), King (Mac an Rí), Wood (Vúd), Mitchell (Mistéal), Walker (Vácúir), Hall (de Hál), Gray (de Grae), Stevenson or Stenson (Mac Stiofáin), Davis (Dáibhis), Jackson (Mac Siacais), Dickson (Mac Risteaird), Gibson (Mac Giolbaird), Clayton (Cléatan), Burrowes or Burgess (Brugha), Burtchaell (Buirséal), Studdart (Studart), Blood (Lúid), Gaule (Gál), Skinner or Shinnors (Sionúr) and Smithwick (Smíste).

ENGLISH LANGUAGE IN IRELAND: J.J. Hogan (1927); Bliss (1976) & (1979).

DRAMA: Fletcher (2000); Gailey (1969).

MIDDLE ENGLISH SURVIVALS: Bliss (1976), 20–9; Dolan & Ó Muirithe (1979).

CHRISTMAS CAROLS: Ó Muirithe (1982).

animal tales Of the 300 international plot types concerning animals listed in the Aarne/Thompson catalogue of folktales, versions of over a third have been collected from Irish oral lore, and it is clear that such narratives have been equally popular in different parts of the country down to recent times. Being folktales, these stories are told for entertainment purposes, and the animals in them have roles that make the narrative attractive and interesting but always fanciful. As such, they are easily distinguished from ordinary zoological lore and superstition (for which see the entries on various kinds of animals).

These folktales are almost all short and pithy, and the most frequent actor in them is the clever fox. For example, a story that has been collected in many different parts of the world, and which is listed in the catalogue as type 1, was and remains very popular in Ireland. It tells of a fox that sees a man bringing a load of fish in a horse-cart. The wily animal lies down on the road at a place where the cart will pass and pretends to be dead. The man notices him and, thinking of the value of the fur, throws him into the cart and travels on. As soon as the man's back is turned to him, the fox throws the fish one by one onto the road behind, and finally jumps quietly off the cart, gathers up the fish, and brings this great stock of food to his den.

Type 2 tells of a trick that the fox plays on the wolf in icy weather when it is difficult to get anything to eat. He advises the wolf to make a hole in a frozen lake, and states that if he puts his tail through the hole the fish will bite at it. He should then swish the tail quickly upwards, and so catch the fish. The wolf does as he is told, but soon his tail becomes stuck in the ice. Men come on the scene to kill the wolf, and the unfortunate animal can only escape by leaving his tail behind. This story is sometimes told abroad concerning a bear rather than a wolf, and in these cases it serves to explain why bears have short tails. There have been no bears in Ireland in historical times, but wolves survived until the eighteenth century; the latter animal was therefore the choice.

Other stories that have the fox outwitting the wolf include type 9B, which has both farming together, with the fox demanding the top of the corn and the bottom of the potatoes; and type 31, which has both trapped in a well, the fox climbing onto the other's back in order to escape. A story that was very popular in Ireland, as abroad, concerns how the two enter a cellar at night and begin to gorge themselves with food (type 41). The fox eases off at the eating after some time, and walks in and out through the narrow entrance, while the wolf jeers him for his apparently eccentric behaviour. The wolf eats so much that his body greatly expands, and therefore he cannot make his getaway when humans come. His more clever companion had kept a careful eye to his waistline and thus got cleanly away.

Other stories tell of the fox's attempts to catch animals to eat, such as studying the character of a cock in order to entrap him (type 61). When they meet, the clever beast praises the beautiful singing voice of the cock and gives a friendly hint on how to make the voice even more musical. Even the best of singers, he states, improve on their voice when their eyes are closed, and the foolish cock does accordingly, only to be jumped on and gobbled up. A very simple, but widespread, little story tells of how the fox rids himself of fleas (type 63). He does this by plucking a hair from his fur and holding it in his mouth while sitting in the river. Slowly but surely he submerges himself in the water, allowing just enough time for the fleas to travel upwards to avoid being drowned. He finally submerges his nose, leaving only the hair above, and then drops that into the water.

One story concerning the fox found in different parts of Ireland has not been widely collected abroad. This (a variant of type 67) tells of how he steals into a butcher's shop but is trapped by the butcher who bars the door. The resourceful animal begins to throw everything he can seize into the fire. Eventually, when the whole shop is in danger of becoming a conflagration, the butcher leaves the door to quench the flames, and the fox slips out and away. The clever fellow is not always so successful when he encounters domestic animals, however. Thus a cat and a fox debate the matter of agility (type 105). The fox boasts that he knows and can perform many tricks, and challenges the cat to match him in this. The cat knows but one trick, and therefore has to concede that his opponent is superior to him. Just then a savage dog comes on the scene, and the cat climbs up a tree with incredible speed, while the fox is unable to do so and is devoured. Climbing was the cat's one trick.

A very interesting story found throughout most of Europe since medieval times and popular throughout Ireland concerns the death of the king of the cats (type 113A). We are told that a man once met a huge cat that attacked him and that he with difficulty managed to slay. Before it died, the fierce animal told him that it was the king of the cats. On his return home, the man told his wife that the king of the cats was dead and, hearing this, the old domestic cat sleeping by the fireside jumped up and left the house. Some versions have a more macabre ending, with the domestic cat leaping at the man's throat and killing him as the bearer of bad tidings.

Several of these folktales deal with the relationships between animals and humans. Irish versions of a worldwide story (type 130) have an assorted group of animals joining forces to rout robbers from a house used as a hideout. Another story (type 155) must be a comparatively recent borrowing from abroad, for a serpent is a main actor in it although no such creatures are found in Ireland. A man sees the serpent trapped under a tree and releases it, whereupon the ungrateful creature announces its intention of devouring its rescuer. The man remonstrates, and they agree to call on a passing fox to adjudicate. The fox states that he must see the situation re-enacted in order to help him make up his mind and, once the tree is placed on top of the serpent again, he declares the most just solution would be to allow matters to remain as they were in the first instance.

The narratives can entail something of an aetiological sense. For instance, one story (which has been but sparsely collected abroad but which remains popular in Ireland) tells of an argument long ago between a cat and a dog regarding which of them should live inside the house (type 200D). To settle the question, they decided to have a race, and the one that reached the house first should have the privilege. The dog was winning the race, but he stopped to attack a poor beggar man whom he did not recognise, and so the cat reached the house first. A more widespread story (type 217) describes how a cat is destined to always behave according to its nature. A certain man has his cat so well trained that it holds a candle for him while he reads. However, a visitor (in Irish versions usually a poor travelling scholar) bets

that he can make the cat drop the candle, and accordingly releases a mouse from his pocket. The mouse races across the table, with the eyes of the cat rivetted on it. When a second mouse is released, the cat can no longer control its nature, but flings the candle aside and gives chase.

Stories about birds also feature. The fanciful idea that these once held a parliament to decide on the functions and habitats of each of them is found widely (type 220), as is the related story of how the wren became king of the birds (type 221). It was decided that whichever of them could fly the highest would be given that exalted office, and in the contest the eagle flew away above every other bird. The wren hid in the eagle's tail, however, and when the great bird tired and could get no higher the wily little fellow jumped out and went higher still.

According to another story (type 222), a dispute between the wren and the mouse caused a great battle between the bird and animal kingdoms. The winged creatures sided with the wren, and the quadrupeds sided with the mouse, and as the two armies faced each other, the fox offered to be umpire for them. He was to stand on a hill and indicate the trend of the battle by his tail. If the quadrupeds were winning, he would raise it, and if the birds were winning, he would lower it. The animals were soon overcoming their foes, and the fox accordingly raised his tail. The bee, however – who had not decided which side to take – threw in his lot with the birds and went and stung the fox's posterior. With a howl of pain, the fox lowered his tail to protect himself. Seeing this, the birds were encouraged and they routed the animals off the field. Ever since, the birds have jurisdiction both in the air and on the ground, whereas the quadrupeds are confined to the earth. This story is often told – in Ireland as overseas – as an introduction to another FOLKTALE (*see* WONDER TALES, *type 313*).

One rare international folktale (type 232C) is well evidenced in Ireland. We are told that a wren was once a farmer, and he had twelve sons that looked exactly like himself. A harsh winter came and he ran out of food and had to borrow some grain. When the following harvest came, the wren had a fine crop, but he made no effort to repay the debt. The creditor went to collect his due, but was confronted with the thirteen identical birds and did not know to whom he should address his demand. The old wren was very pleased to in this way avoid paying, and he and his sons continued nonchalantly to thresh the grain as the bewildered creditor looked on. At last, the creditor thought of a plan. He shouted out enthusiastically that the old wren was a far better worker than any of his sons, and at that one of the wrens jumped up and beat his breast with pride. It was the old wren, pleased that at last his paternal chiding of the sons had been justified, but the creditor then knew to whom he should address his demand.

Regarding fish, the only folktale that has become widespread in Ireland is an explanation of why the plaice has a crooked mouth (type 250A). We are told that it acquired this deformity because it once mocked a hungry SAINT who desired a fish, and a detail is often added to the effect that the salmon acquired its agile leap because it generously jumped into the breast of the holy man on the same occasion.

A variant of type 285B has been known in Ireland since medieval times. This international folktale tells of how a snake enters a person's stomach and is enticed out again by being made thirsty, and in the Irish adaptations a lizard is substituted for the snake. Two occurrences of the plot in medieval Irish literature (see MAC CONGLINNE and FURSA) turn the offending creature into a demon of gluttony.

As opposed to folklore, the rarity of animal tales in Irish literary tradition can be accounted for by the fact that they are of so fanciful a character as to be difficult to include in the literary narratives, the usual objective of which was to present material as historical data. It is also likely that many of the international animal tales did not become current in Ireland until recent centuries. For ordinary lore concerning different species of animals, see

folk custom and belief in the List of Genres, page 509.

GENERAL: Aarne & Thompson (1961), 21–87; S. Ó Súilleabháin & Christiansen (1967), 33–57; S. Ó Súilleabháin (1942), 558–9, 650–3 & (1973), 14–16.

Aodh An ancient designation for the sun-deity. The name (earlier, Aedh) was in Celtic *aedos*, and its original meaning was 'fire'. Since the sun-deity was synonymous with the divine ancestor, Aodh was an alternative name for the Irish father-deity, the DAGHDHA, who was sometimes called AODH RUADH RÓ-FHEASA.

Another variant of the character's name was Aodh Álainn (Fiery Lustrous One). Even a deviation shows by import that this was the true tradition – the medieval pseudo-historians, in their attempts to synchronise mythical names, claimed that the successor of the Daghdha as KING of Ireland was one Dealbh-aodh (literally, 'fire-shape'). Since the appellation Aodh referred to the father-deity, it was not unknown for tribes to take their names from it – for instance, tribes called Aedha and Aedhnai in Ireland, and the Aedui among the Continental Celts. In the present work, the name is spelt Aodh according to the modern orthography. From an early period, it was also popular as a personal name. It is inaccurately anglicised as 'Hugh'.

AODH: RIA Dictionary, s.v. 'áed'; G. Murphy (1953), lxviii; Olmsted (1994), 43, 170–1, 478; E. Hogan (1910), 13; Ó hÓgáin (2002), 11–13, 271. DEALBHAODH: RIA Dictionary, s.v. 'delbaéth'; Macalister (1941), 124–5; W. Stokes in *Irische Texte*, 3, 358–9; Ó hÓgáin (1999), 141.

Aodh Allán Son of FEARGHAL MAC MAOLDÚIN, and UÍ NÉILL high-king from AD 734–43.

One annalistic source gives a dramatic account of his conception and birth. We read that his mother was the daughter of Conghal, who preceded Aodh's father Fearghal as HIGH-KING. She was a nun, but was the secret lover of Fearghal. Once, when he was told that she had a tryst with her lover, Conghal came in a rage to discover them, but his daughter hid Fearghal under the bedclothes and sat on top of him. While in this position, a large cat came and ate chunks from his legs, but

Fearghal seized the cat and quietly choked it. Believing his daughter to be innocent, Conghal drowned the man who had informed him of her affair and sought her forgiveness for his suspicion. Nevertheless, she conceived and gave birth, and secretly handed her baby boy to two women with instructions to drown him. Instead of doing so, they kept him, and four years later the nun-mother unwittingly admired the child and confessed that she was guilty of murdering a child born to herself. She was overjoyed to learn that this was in fact her son, and the boy Aodh was quietly delivered to Fearghal to be reared.

This story seems to be apocryphal, for elsewhere the name of Aodh's mother is given as Bríghe, daughter of Orca mac Carrthain. One account states that when he grew up, Aodh was boisterous and crude, in contradistinction to his younger brother NIALL FRASACH, who was well-mannered and kindly. It happened once that they simultaneously visited their father at the royal fortress of Aileach (Greenan Hill, in northeast County Donegal). Fearghal had them put into separate quarters and, when he visited them in turn, was very pleased with the gentle comportment of Niall but disgusted by the uproar and filth of Aodh's company. He therefore foretold that Aodh would be energetic and hard-willed, whereas Niall would be pious and prudent.

This reputation of Aodh was not general, however, and some of the literature regards him as a cultured man who was accustomed to compose verse. There is no doubting that he was an able, if ambitious ruler, and he succeeded in exerting his control over the regional KINGS by a combination of war and diplomacy. His most powerful opponent was the Munster king CATHAL MAC FIONGHUINE, but the two met at Tír Dhá Ghlas (Terryglass, County Tipperary) in the year 737 and peace was arranged between them. Aodh fell six years later, fighting against his relative, Domhnall mac Murchadha, at Seireadh Magh (near Kells, County Meath).

O'Donovan, *1* (1848), 326–41 & (1860), 22–31; Macalister (1956), 390–3; Dinneen, *3* (1908), 146–9; K. Meyer in *ZCP*, *13*, 143–4; F.J. Byrne (1973), 114–18, 147–8, 208–10.

Aodh Eangach A prophesied KING in medieval Irish lore. The name AODH had the original meaning 'fire'. The epithet Eangach has not been satisfactorily explained. Interpretations of it vary from 'brilliant' and 'pennoned' to 'vociferous' and 'bird-voiced'.

The idea that a great leader called Aodh Eangach would come was part of the propaganda of the royal UÍ NÉILL sept in the latter centuries of their dynasty. It seems to have developed in or about the ninth century, and was supposed to have been a prophecy made by the earlier St BEARCHÁN. The image may actually have sprung from the figure of Aodh Finnliath, the Uí Néill HIGH-KING from AD 862–79 who gained several victories over the Norse raiders. Especially when the sept's power began to decline from the beginning of the eleventh century, poets were wont to flatter various Uí Néill leaders with the conceit that the lauded individual was the prophesied Aodh Eangach. A thirteenth-century poem claims that Bearchán had prophesied long before that 'a pillar would be erected by the side of TARA, and from it Aodh Eangach would emerge'. The imagery here suggests the fiery pillar of Exodus that led the Hebrews out of Egypt, and this is supported by one explanation of 'Aodh Eangach' as 'he who leaves a trail of fire'. Clearly both the name and the personality were left open to various interpretations, but the basic point is that he would lead from the royal centre Tara.

The prophecy attributed to Bearchán also states that the messianic figure would be a 'red-handed one' (*crobhdhearg*) – i.e. his hand would be red from fighting and battles. Such an image was generally expressed by the term *lámhdhearg*, and was known to the earlier literature in the general sense of great warriors. For alliterative reasons it was applied especially to the warriors of Leinster. Once it was attached to the Uí Néill prophecy, however, it became domiciled in that context, and in postmedieval times the red hand was the family crest of the O'Neills and thus of the province of Ulster, where they predominated. Bearchán was reputed to have foretold that

18

Aodh Eangach would defeat his rivals and win the battle at Liathdroim, which was a variant poetic name for Tara.

Belief in such a prophecy lingered for a long time, and much reference was made to it during the rebellion of the great Aodh Ó Néill, Earl of Tyrone, against ELIZABETH I at the end of the sixteenth century. Before the Battle of the Yellow Ford in 1598, a professional poet told the earl's assembled army that Bearchán had long ago prophesied a defeat of the English there. In this case the prediction was proved correct. An English report of the same time, in describing a push by the earl towards Dublin, makes much of his arrival at Tara 'where the old doating prophecy was that if O'Neill could come and shoe his horse he should be king of all Ireland'.

R. Thurneysen in ZCP, 12. 237–8; A.O. Anderson in ZCP, 18, 29–31; N.J. Williams (1980), 64, 280–1, 321; Breathnach & Ó Lochlainn, 1 (1948), 178–9; J.G. O'Keeffe in Irish Texts, 4, 41; Wood (1933), 173; J. Carney in Dillon (1968), 155–7; Ó hÓgáin (1985), 124–7, 136, 333.

Aodh Ruadh Ró-Fheasa

An alternative name for the ancestor-deity, the DAGHDHA, who was also known as EOCHAIDH. The name Aodh meant 'fire', representing the sun, and the epithet *ruadh* (modern, *rua*) meant 'ruddy' or in anthropomorphic terms 'red-haired'.

The full designation, Aodh Ruadh Ró-Fheasa, may have originally belonged to the ancestral lore of the LAIGHIN (Leinstermen). It can be translated as 'Aodh the all-knowing red one'. The soubriquet *Ró-fheasa* – meaning literally 'of great knowledge' – accords with the lore of the typical seer FIONN, who ritually obtained knowledge from an ancestor figure. In the Leinster genealogies, indeed, FIONN FILE is claimed to have been son of a personage with the curious name Find File mac Rosa Ruadh. This patronymic was no more than a learned inversion of the appellation Ruadh Ró-fheasa. As a personage, Aodh Ruadh survived in the developing lore of Fionn, becoming associated like him with the Boyne river, and being invested with the power to appear in the form of a salmon there. Echoing also his solar symbolism, a variant name for him was GOLL (one-eyed).

As the cult of Fionn developed into lore concerning FIONN MAC CUMHAILL and an otherworld rival, Fionn was portrayed as fighting against an otherworld figure alternately called Aodh and Goll.

The final curious twist to the history of this personage occurred sometime in the eleventh or twelfth century when, due to folk etymology, his name became confused with the place called Eas Ruadh, which means 'the red waterfall' (it is anglicised as Assaroe, the waterfall at Ballyshannon, County Donegal). Thus we read of a fictional king of Ireland called Aodh Ruadh who had been drowned at Assaroe, and of a wonderfully wise salmon that resided there called Goll Easa Ruaidh. The latter salmon surfaces in redactions of the story of FIONNTAN and in a very popular Irish FOLKTALE (see OLDEST CREATURE). *See also* DEARG and DONN as names for the male deity.

Meyer (1912), 98; W. Stokes in Irische Texte, 3, 356–7; T.F. O'Rahilly (1946), 318–20; O'Brien (1962), 21–3, 99, 118–19; Ó Muráile (2003), 2, 198–200.

Aodh Sláine

HIGH-KING of the Uí NÉILL, who reigned from AD 598–604. He was son of DIARMAID MAC CEARRBHEOIL. Sláine is the place name Slane in County Meath, and its association with him suggests that he lived there at some stage.

A striking birth-tale is told of Aodh Sláine in a tenth-century text. According to it, his father Diarmaid had two wives, Maireann and Mughain. The latter was jealous of Maireann and, knowing that her rival was bald, she determined to shame her at the festival of Tailtiu (Teltown, County Meath). She therefore bribed a woman satirist to knock from Maireann's head the royal diadem that hid her blemish. Immediately it fell, Maireann exclaimed: 'May God and Ciarán help me!' Through a miracle of St CIARÁN (of Clonmacnoise), beautiful golden hair grew on her head before anybody noticed that she was bald. Moreover, God caused Mughain to be barren for what she had done, and the king lost interest in her. In desperation, she sought the assistance of St Finnian of Magh Bhile (Moville, County Down), and he blessed water and gave it to her to drink. As a result, she became pregnant and gave birth to a lamb. Again he blessed water for her, and she bore a silver fish. On the third occasion he blessed Mughain herself, and as a result of this she gave birth to Aodh Sláine.

This story was composed as propaganda for Aodh's descendants, and it was obviously intended to offset an earlier tradition that belittled them. Aodh, in fact, slew his nephew Suibhne mac Colmáin (*see* DIARMAID MAC CEARRBHEOIL) and was in turn slain by Suibhne's son Conall at Loch Seamhdaidhe (Loughsewdy, east of Athlone, County Westmeath). The seventh-century biography of COLM CILLE has that SAINT warning the young Aodh Sláine against kin-slaying, stating that, if he becomes guilty of it, his seed will have the kingship for a short time only. This would have been well remembered, for most of the high-kings from the eighth to the tenth century were direct descendants of Conall mac Suibhne.

The descendants of Aodh Sláine only managed to hold the HIGH-KINGSHIP intermittently. Some of them became lords of north Breagha (in County Meath), and had their headquarters at Cnoghbha (Knowth). From their leader in the ninth century, Ceallach, they took the surname Ó Ceallaigh (Kellys of Meath).

O'Grady, *1* (1892), 74–5, 82–4 & 2, 469–72; W. Stokes in *Irische Texte*, *3*, 342–5, 417; Best & Bergin (1929), 133–6; Anderson & Anderson (1961), 236–7; Macalister (1956), 372–5; O'Donovan, *1* (1848–51), 226–7; K. Meyer in *AIM*, *3*, 47–8; F.J. Byrne (1973), 96–8, 281–2.

Aoibheall Otherworld lady and protectress of the Dál gCais sept (later known as O'Briens) in County Clare. The name meant 'sparkling' or 'bright', and reflects a common attribute of a GODDESS in ancient Irish culture.

Aoibheall was associated particularly with the rock called Craig Liath (Craglea, near Killaloe, County Clare) – where the Dál gCais had a fortress since the sixth century AD – and all indications are that she was originally the patroness of the general area of east Clare and north-west Tipperary. The twelfth-century tract on king BRIAN BÓRAMHA states that on the night before the Battle of Clontarf, Aoibheall appeared to him and foretold that he would be killed in that contest and that the first of his sons whom he would see on that day would succeed him as KING. The son was Donnchadh, and it is clear from the account that Aoibheall was acting in the capacity of goddess of sovereignty. Later adaptations of the theme have her appearing to either Donnchadh or his brother MURCHADH and giving details of what would befall various members of the royal family. One account aptly names her as *banfháidh Ó mBriain* (the prophetess of the O'Briens).

The post-medieval poets numbered Aoibheall as one of the principal otherworld women of Munster. The eighteenth-century Clareman Brian Merriman made her the chief actor in his celebrated Rabelaisian poem *Cúirt an Mheán Oíche*. In this, she presides over the midnight court of frustrated women who complain of male impotency. Little folklore concerning Aoibheall exists, but in County Cork she is made the sister of CLÍONA in a late oral LEGEND.

T.F. O'Rahilly in *Ériu*, *14*, 1–6; Todd (1867), 200–1; W.M Hennessy (1871), 1, 8–9; Mac Cionnaith (1938), 322–3; E. Mac Néill in *Irisleabhar na Gaedhilge*, *7*, 10; Ó Murchú (1982); T.J. Westropp in *Folk-Lore*, *21*, 186–7.

Aonghus *(earlier, Oengus)* Mythical chieftain among the TUATHA DÉ DANANN. He resided at Brugh na Bóinne (the tumulus of Newgrange in County Meath), and was thus often referred to as 'Aonghus an Bhrogha'. His father was the DAGHDHA, and his mother was BÓINN, the eponymous goddess of the Boyne river. The name Aonghus means 'true vigour', and must in origin have been a description of a divinity.

An alternative appellation for him was 'Mac ind Óc', which is a curious one, for *óc* (modern, *óg*) is ungrammatical as a genitive if the appellation meant 'the son of the youth'. It is therefore accepted that the original form was either *maccan óc* or *in mac óc*, both of these meaning 'the young boy'. 'Maccan' (later, Macán) corresponds to the Welsh mythical figure Mabon and to the British Celtic Maponos, who was identified in inscriptions with the classical Apollo. It appears from this that Aonghus was the youthful expression of some Celtic deity. To standardise the orthography, the alternative appellation of Aonghus is in this work cited as the Mac Óg.

A ninth-century text tells of the conception, birth and early life of Aonghus. According to it, the Daghdha, who was KING of Ireland, desired Bóinn, the wife of 'Ealcmhar' (a nickname for NUADHU) who resided at the Brugh. The Daghdha sent Ealcmhar away on a journey and then, by magic, made the night disappear and banished hunger and thirst from Ealcmhar so that the latter would not notice the passing of time. Nine months went by as one, and in the meantime the Daghdha lay with Bóinn and she bore him a son. When Ealcmhar returned, he remained ignorant of what had happened. The child was called the Mac Óg because his mother said that 'young is the son who was begotten at the beginning of a day and born between that and evening'.

The Daghdha brought him to the home of MIDHIR, where he was reared for nine years and became a champion hurler. One day he quarrelled with another player, however, and the opponent told him that Midhir was not his father. He demanded the truth of Midhir and learned who his real parents were. Accompanied by Midhir, he went to meet the Daghdha at Uisneach (Ushnagh, County Westmeath), seeking land as his heritage. The Daghdha told him to go to Brugh na Bóinne at Samhain (the November feast), to threaten Ealcmhar there, and to demand possession of the Brugh for a day and a night. He did this, but when the day and night were over he refused to relinquish the Brugh to Ealcmhar. They went to the Daghdha to seek his judgement, and the Daghdha ruled that 'it is in days and nights that the world is spent', thus tricking Ealcmhar out of his dwelling. As compensation, Ealcmhar was given a nearby home, and the Brugh became the property of Aonghus.

Other versions of how he came to possess the Brugh have him tricking the Daghdha himself rather than Ealcmhar, and these seem to represent the orthodox form of the story. A twelfth-century poem, which makes the Daghdha both the brother and lover of Ealcmhar's wife Bóinn, has Midhir directing Aonghus on how to trick his father out of the Brugh, with the same verbal ambiguity concerning day and night being used. Midhir, meaning 'arbitrator', would be an appropriate name for the one who passes judgement. The time trick was part of ordinary folklore, and it was employed in this mythic context in order to dramatise ideas that were intrinsic to the tradition of the Daghdha. These included the understanding that time was composed of darkness for the dead and light for the living (see DONN and FIONN), and the dead ancestors presiding over the affairs of the living (see KINGSHIP). The story quite artistically illustrates also that the blooming of youth denies the process of aging – at the youthful stage of life time passes slowly and vitality seems to be permanent. It was natural for the Irish to associate this feeling with a character from the divine realm, for one of the terms to describe the otherworld made it the timeless realm Tír na nÓg (the Land of the Young People). A much earlier idea seems to have been the ultimate basis of the story – namely, that the new sun ushers in a new era, and this appears to have been part of the ancient pre-Celtic cultus of the Newgrange tumulus, which became associated with the Daghdha (q.v.).

In the text on the second Battle of Moytirra (see MYTHOLOGICAL CYCLE), Aonghus is portrayed as a dutiful son to his father. When the Daghdha was in servitude to BREAS, the satirist CRIDHINBHÉAL was eating his food. Aonghus, called the Mac Óg, advised him on how to get rid of the satirist and also suggested what payment he should seek from Breas. This payment was one black heifer from among a great herd of the cattle of Ireland that Breas' FOMHÓIRE people had taken as tribute. Breas thought the Daghdha's choice a stupid one, but later the whole herd followed the heifer back into the possession of the Tuatha Dé Danann. The plot of the adviser and the ruse, occurring again in this case, must be a reflex from the old story that had Aonghus being advised to trick Nuadhu.

In line with the common triplication of deities in early Ireland, Aonghus was referred to in some sources as one of three sons of the Daghdha. His divine status is underlined by the prominent place among the Tuatha Dé that is accorded to him in several texts. Most dramatic of these is *Aislinge Oenguso* (The Vision of Aonghus). According to this, when Aonghus was asleep one night he saw a beautiful maiden approach, but before he could touch her she disappeared. Such visits by her to him continued for a year, and he fell sick for love of her. His physician decided to call his mother Bóinn, and she searched Ireland for a year but failed to find the maiden. Then his father, the Daghdha, was sent for. The Daghdha enlisted the help of Bodhbh, the Tuatha Dé king of Munster who resided in Sídh ar Feimhin (the cairn on Slievenamon, County Tipperary). Bodhbh discovered that the maiden was Caer Iobharmhéith, and that she was at Crotta Cliach (the Galtee Mountains, County Tipperary), and he brought Aonghus to meet her. They found her at Loch Béal Dragan (Lough Muskry on the Galtees), accompanied by thrice-50 maidens linked together by a silver chain. Caer herself wore a silver necklace and her chain was of burnished gold. Bodhbh then explained that she was from Sídh Uamhain, an otherworld residence in the province of Connacht.

When Aonghus returned to Brugh na Bóinne and told this to his father, the Daghdha went to Connacht and compelled Eathal Anbhuail, father of Caer, to reveal that his daughter went in the forms of a bird and of a girl on alternate years. At the following Samhain (November) she would be a bird at Loch Béal Dragan, and the Daghdha instructed Aonghus to go there and call her to him. He did so, and found her in the shape of a beautiful white swan, in the company of thrice-50 others. She went to him, and he too became a

swan, following which they embraced each other and flew three times around the lake. They then flew together to Brugh na Bóinne and put the dwellers of that place to sleep with their beautiful singing. Caer remained with Aonghus in the Brugh after that. The text confuses the narrative somewhat by having the Daghdha go to queen MEADHBH and her husband Ailill mac Máta to enlist their help against Eathal Anbhuail. These characters from the ULSTER CYCLE led an assault on Eathal's dwelling, and Ailill threatened to kill that king unless he gave information on his daughter. It is probable that the story was first written in the eighth century, and that the material from the Ulster Cycle was introduced (on the pattern of the NEARA narrative) in or about the tenth century.

Being the archetypal youth, several stories concerning love were told of Aonghus in medieval times. It was said that he loved a daughter of Ealcmhar, but that she went with Midhir instead, and Aonghus cast his food – 'the blood-red nuts of the wood' – onto the ground in anger. It was said also that he loved Dreibhriu, daughter of EOCHAIDH FEIDHLEACH, and that CLÍONA was drowned while going to visit Aonghus after she had fallen in love with him. In the origin-LEGEND of Loch nEachach (Lough Neagh in Ulster), Aonghus was described as assisting an eloping couple, EOCHAIDH MAC MAIREADHA and Eibhliu, wife of Eochaidh's father. Aonghus gave them the loan of his horse, which was so huge that it could carry them and all their chattels out of danger. When they stopped to rest, the horse urinated and thus gave rise to the great Lough Neagh. The exuberance of youth is suggested in a mention of how Aonghus also had a wonderful multi-coloured mantle, which appeared to be of one colour only in the eyes of a man about to die. Another text makes MANANNÁN the patron of Aonghus and the presenter to him of a wonderful dun cow, and further relates the story of EITHNE, a beautiful maiden loved by him.

In late medieval and post-medieval literature Aonghus is introduced into some stories of the FIANNA CYCLE as a *deus ex machina.* Most strikingly, he is made the patron and protector of the handsome young hero DIARMAID UA DUIBHNE. He intervenes to rescue the eloping Diarmaid and Gráinne when Fionn's men are close to capturing them and, after Diarmaid's death, he takes the corpse to his own residence at Brugh na Bóinne and lays it in burial under a great stone there. The reason why he became associated with Diarmaid was undoubtedly his fame in the context of youth and love. One medieval text claims that Aonghus forged four kisses of his into 'four birds which charmed the young people of Ireland'. On the basis of his connection with Diarmaid, later stories have him intervening to assist the Fianna in a cattle-raid and rescuing them from dire straits in 'the land of the giants'. Despite his glamorous imagery, however, Aonghus is not featured in late folklore stories.

NAME: de Vries (1961), 39; T.F. O'Rahilly (1946), 516–17; Carney (1964), 112.

BIRTH AND GAINING OF BRUGH: O. Bergin & R.I. Best in *Ériu*, *12*, 142–7; L. Duncan in *Ériu*, *11*, 188–92; V. Hull in *ZCP*, *19*, 53–8; L. Gwynn in *Ériu*, *7*, 210–38; Gwynn (1906), 18–21.

MAPONOS: A. Ross (1974), 463–6; Green (1992), 140; Olmsted (1994), 380–4.

HELPING THE DAGHDHA: Gray (1982), 30–1, 70–1.

THREE SONS OF THE DAGHDHA: Macalister (1941), 156–7, 190–1; Gwynn (1924), 92–3, 108–9.

VISION OF AONGHUS: Shaw (1934).

LOVE STORIES: Gwynn (1913), 40–3, 386–9; Stokes (1892), 56–7.

MANTLE: Vendryes (1953), 13–14. See Stokes (1905), *CTS*, 31.

DIARMAID: Ní Shéaghdha (1967), 22–3, 28–9, 38–9; G. Murphy (1933), 96–7.

HELPING THE FIANNA: Mac Néill (1908), 5–6; G. Murphy (1933), 392–9; Stokes (1900), 13–14.

KISSES: W. Stokes in *RC*, *16*, 68–9; O'Curry (1873), 478–9.

GENERAL: Gray (1982), 127–8; Stokes, *CTS* (1905), 31.

Aristotle The celebrated Greek philosopher of antiquity, concerning whom several anecdotes became popular in medieval Europe after the rediscovery of his writings.

The best known of these anecdotes was commonly represented in art and sculpture in medieval Europe, but was very rare in Ireland. Aristotle had been the tutor of the famous Macedonian conqueror, Alexander the Great, and it was said that Alexander brought a beautiful young woman from Greece and that Aristotle fell in love with her. She assured him that she would become his lover on one condition only: that he go on his hands and knees and allow her to ride on his back in the public street. While he was thus engaged, Alexander came on the scene and enquired of the great philosopher why he was humbling himself so. Aristotle was quick with an excuse, saying that he was doing this as a lesson for Alexander, for 'if a woman thus makes a fool of an old man like me, how necessary it is for a young man like you to beware of female wiles?'

Probably as a result of this story, Aristotle was often associated in medieval European lore with women – how he pitted his great wit against their charms and guile. One such story was borrowed from an equally apocryphal tradition concerning the famous ancient Latin poet, Virgil. It was said that a certain young lady invited Virgil to visit her in a high tower by means of a basket hung on ropes. Halfway up the ropes, she ordered him to be left there in the basket so that all could see and ridicule him. When told in Ireland, Aristotle rather than Virgil was the dupe in this story.

Most Irish stories of Aristotle have him contending with his own wife. For instance, it is told that he was accustomed to spending nights on the roof of his house, studying the stars with a telescope that he had placed on a table. His wife was displeased at being left alone at night and, unknown to him, placed a silver coin under each leg of the table, so that when he began his observations on the following night he was alarmed by what he saw. 'A great tragedy lies ahead,' he remarked, 'for either the heavenly bodies have begun to descend, or the earth has begun to rise!' His wife pointed out to him how he had been fooled, and his embarrassment was so great that he retired from the stargazing. This anecdote was derived from *The Seven Sages of Rome* – a popular medieval Latin text translated into several languages, including Irish. The dupe in that text was not Aristotle, however, and the inclusion of the great philosopher may have been an Irish development of the anecdote.

Irish storytellers describe Aristotle as continually tussling with his wife, who was jealous of his wisdom and who repeatedly asked him how he had gained it, but to no avail. Once, when seeing a sow in heat, Aristotle remarked to his wife that the soup from that sow's meat would be poisonous. His wife secretly killed the pig and gave its soup to Aristotle for his dinner. He had drunk the soup before he realised the trick she had played on him. 'Since I am about to die,' he said, 'I may as well tell you the secret of my wisdom! You will get it all if you undress and sit for a considerable while on a cold flagstone!' She did this, and caught a severe cold, with the result that she died along with him. Some storytellers said that he wrote many books on the wiles of women, but that after all this he observed a woman playing a new trick, and – realising that all his books were useless – ordered that they be burned. The idea that the philosopher's books were burned or buried on his orders was already current in the ancient classical world, probably as an explanation of the difficulty of obtaining good copies of his works. The notion that he was preoccupied with women was, however, a humorous development in later lore. A common saying in Irish placed special emphasis on this: 'Notwithstanding his great learning, there were three things which Aristotle failed to understand – the work of the bees, the coming and going of the tide, and the mind of women!'

The question of the sea tides was long associated with Aristotle. There was a tradition in ancient Greece and Rome, indeed, that he tried so hard to study the tide at close quarters that he was actually drowned in the sea. More historical is his connection with bees, for he did actually write a treatise on these insects. As a result of this, a LEGEND grew up in the Middle Ages – a legend still current in Irish folklore – that in order to observe the work of the bees closely, he constructed a glass cover around a beehive and then sat down to study the

bees in safety. The clever little insects, however, smeared the glass with honey so that he could not see them.

In medieval Europe, great intellectuals of the past were sometimes thought to have been magicians. In accord with this, the folklore of County Kerry claims that Aristotle tried to gain immortality through a secret ritual. He instructed his servant to decapitate him, place the head in a box and bury it in the ground for 24 hours. The head would then speak and the boy should exhume it, but the boy fell asleep and when he awoke it was too late and Aristotle could never again be restored to life.

Aristotle's wise maxims could, however, be given more dramatic and resounding echoes. An old system of popular education in Ireland was to assemble lists of advices, and from the seventeenth century onwards one such list was entitled 'Comhairle na Barrscolóige dá Mhac' (The Counsel of the Leading Scholar to his Son). Probably in the hedge-schools of the eighteenth century, a connection was made between this *barrscológ* and the celebrated philosopher. The brilliant scholar, it was said, was married to a sister of Aristotle, and the result of this union was three extremely clever sons. When they grew up these three boys went incognito to their uncle Aristotle and became his servants. In the course of their work they found occasion to ask him some questions, which he unsuspectingly answered, and then they abruptly left his service. Realising the trick played on him Aristotle sent murderers after them, but the three clever boys exchanged roles with three dupes, and thus the dupes were slain. When the three heads were brought to Aristotle, he examined them carefully and then remarked: 'These are not they – the three clever fellows would have had much more compact brains!'

Then Aristotle foretold that one of the three would one day receive *croch gheal* (the bright gallows) of Dublin city. This prophecy was later fulfilled in an unexpected way, for the three were engaged to build a treasure-house by the mayor of Dublin. They left a stone loose in the building, and by this means were enabled to come back secretly at night and steal from the treasury. Two of them were caught and executed, but the third continually evaded capture. Finally, in exasperation, the mayor offered his daughter, together with a pardon, to the extremely clever fellow if he would come forward and admit the theft. He did so, and thus got the girl in marriage – she was a blonde girl with the unusual name of Croch. This plot is in fact an international one (*see* ROMANTIC TALES, type 950). It was in a chap-book edition of *The Seven Sages of Rome* used by the hedge-schoolmasters, and would have been thus joined with the names of Aristotle and the *barrscológ*.

The Irish form of the philosopher's name is Arastotail, but in Hiberno-English his name is sometimes imaginatively rendered as Harry Stottle!

ARISTOTLE, VIRGIL IN EUROPEAN LORE: A.J. Morris in Wilgus & Sommer (1967), 151–9; Spargo (1934).

LADY AND ALEXANDER: Aarne & Thompson (1961), type 1501; IFC Almqvist Tapes.

BASKET: IFC 472:169–76.

ASTRONOMY: IFC 913:196, 1492:271–3.

SEVEN SAGES OF ROME: K. Campbell (1907); D. Greene in *Béaloideas*, 14, 219–36; Brunner (1933), 6–7.

WIFE: R. Flower in *Béaloideas*, 2 (1930), 97–8; Ó Duilearga (1948), 262–3, 430 & in *Béaloideas*, 29, 50–1; IFC 35:212–13, 394:34–5, 913:197–8, 915:105–6.

VIEWS ON WOMEN: T. Breathnach in *An Stoc 7–8* (1920), 6; IFC 472:176.

BEES: Ransome (1986), 80–1; C. Nic Dhonnchaidh in *An Claidheamh Soluis*, 28/10/1911, 3; Ua Murchadha (1939), 119; IFC 152:225, 306:485–6, 407:370, 828:517–18, 864:466–7, 1234:447.

BURIAL OF HEAD: IFC 6:152–60, 362–73.

NEPHEWS: S. Ó Súilleabháin & Christiansen (1967), 187–8, several of the listed versions; IFC 204:42–9, 55, 306:482–6, 913:194–8; chapbook edn., anon, *History of the Seven Wise Masters*.

GENERAL: S. Ó Flannagáin in *Béaloideas*, 3 (1932), 49–50; M.J. Murphy (1975), 108; IFC Index.

Art Mythical KING of Ireland, son of CONN CÉADCHATHACH. The name originally meant 'bear' – apparently a pseudonym for a warrior – and he had the sobriquet Aonfhear (earlier, Óenfer), which meant 'singular man' or 'champion'.

The literature, as was its wont, derives the sobriquet from a narrative episode.

When his brother Connla departed in a boat for the otherworld realm, the disconsolate father Conn gazed upon Art and remarked that this remaining son was now 'the lone one' (*oenfer*). He proved a dutiful son, for when Conn brought the polluted woman Bé Chuma to TARA and banished him for a year at her request, he accepted his father's wishes. He returned at the end of the year and found Conn unable to check the misfortune that had overtaken his reign. Bé Chuma challenged him to a game of *ficheall* (the early Irish form of chess). Art won the first game and demanded as his prize the warrior's wand that CÚ ROÍ once had. Bé Chuma searched the otherworld dwellings of Ireland and found it for him. Then she won a game and imposed as a condition on him that he seek out and find a beautiful lady called Dealbhchaomh.

Art went abroad and eventually came to a wonderful island of women, where he was cordially received. They gave him directions to where Dealbhchaomh was, a place that could only be reached by overcoming several great obstacles. These included treacherous oceans and forests, fierce hags, and a nigh-invulnerable warrior. Art overcame all the obstacles and slew both of Dealbhchaomh's warrior parents in single combat. He and Dealbhchaomh became lovers, and he brought her back to Ireland with him. When he reached Tara, Dealbhchaomh advised him to expel his stepmother Bé Chuma from the country. This he did, thereby relieving Conn and the realm of the woman who had brought them such misfortune.

This text is late, dating from around the thirteenth century, and most of the episodes in it are taken from an international FOLKTALE that was very popular in Ireland (*see* WONDER TALES, type 313) and in which a youth performs difficult tasks to gain a maiden and then elopes with her.

The theory of the medieval historians was that Conn was succeeded as king by his brother-in-law CONAIRE MAC MOGHA LÁMHA, and that Art in turn succeeded Conaire. In contradiction of the sagas, these historians also claimed that Art was the survivor of three sons of Conn – the other two, Connla and Crionna, having been slain by Conn's jealous brothers. Art's own reign is not much stressed in the literature. The historians claimed that his wife was called Meadhbh Leathdhearg, but this is merely an echo from the cult of the goddess of Tara kingship, MEADHBH. Another woman associated with him was the wife of a certain Gnáthal mac Conruith, who is represented in a text of around the ninth century as having been king of Tara. This text is a rather confused one, and the king who is really meant seems to be Conaire mac Mogha Lámha. We read that the woman loved Art, and tricked her husband out of the kingship for his sake. This, however, was over-imaginative and conflicted with the generally held tradition that Art was king by right and by justice. As with his father Conn, he was portrayed as an ideal king. Although – living before the Christian period – he was a pagan, two angels hovered over him in battle on account of the 'truth of his rule'. It was also claimed that he won several battles against the Leinstermen (LAIGHIN) and compelled them to yield the BÓRAIMHE tribute to him.

An eighth-century text states that he had no male heir, but the night before the Battle of Magh Mucramha (in east Galway) he slept with Achtan, the daughter of a druid, and in this way begot his famous son CORMAC. He was slain in the battle next day, and his foe LUGHAIDH MAC CON took the kingship of Tara. This situation is developed in a text from the tenth or eleventh century, according to which Art was out hunting one day when he had a vision of angels and was inspired to foretell the coming of Christianity to Ireland. He also foresaw the Battle of Magh Mucramha and how he would be defeated there.

J. Pokorny in ZCP, 17, 204–5; T. Ó Máille in ZCP, 17, 138–9; M. Dobbs in ZCP, 20, 171–3; R.I. Best in Ériu, 3, 149–73; W. Stokes in Irische Texte, 3, 334–7, 360–1; O'Donovan, 1 (1848), 106–9; Macalister (1956), 334–5; L. Gwynn in Ériu, 6, 136; M. O'Daly (1975), 52–5, 64–9, 152; Best & Bergin (1929), xxxv, 296–9.

GAME MOTIF: R. Power in Scottish Studies, 28, 69–89.

Badhbh *(earlier, Bodhbh)* A war-GODDESS and announcer of death, who usually appears in the form of a scald crow. Her name comes from Celtic *bodua*, with a meaning such as 'fighting lady'. She was frequently referred to, from her role in the context of battle (*cath*), as Cath-Bhadhbh or Badhbh Chatha. This was very old, for a slightly defaced Gaulish inscription refers to 'Cattubodva', and Greek and Roman writers describe the ancient Continental Celtic belief in the scald crow as a divine being hovering over battlefields. Ultimately, one may consider that this was a form taken by the mother-goddess who, in the context of bloodshed, was desirous of recovering her own progeny.

In medieval Irish sources, the Badhbh is described as one of three sisters, all daughters of Ealcmhar, a leader of the TUATHA DÉ DANANN (*see* NUADHU). The other two sisters of this trio are called Danainn and MACHA, and all three – on behalf of the Tuatha Dé – magically bring sleet and strong showers against the enemy in battles. The two others are also given the name MÓR-RÍOGHAIN, and there is a strong tendency in the literature to regard the Badhbh herself as being an actual synonym of the Mór-Ríoghain. All of this indicates that the Badhbh was in fact a representative of the triplicated mother-goddess DANU.

To medieval Irish writers, the image of the Badhbh was somewhat repulsive, and there was a tendency to view her as a personage who exulted in slaughter for its own sake. One medieval gloss describes her 'fruit-crop' as 'the heads of men that have been slain', and she has little of the function of protectress in these accounts. Her name Badhbh was clearly being used by the writers when they wished to stress the negative aspects of the Mór-Ríoghain (q.v.). She was the 'red vehement Badhbh' who was joyful when human women are sorrowful at the slaughter of their men-folk. Portrayals of perennial hostility to humans had their effect even on the relationship between the war-goddess and CÚ CHULAINN. Thus in the account of his death compiled at the end of the Middle Ages, the name Badhbh is given to one of the demonic children of Cailitín who plotted the hero's destruction. Taking the shape of a carrion crow (*feannóg*), this Badhbh tries to entice him into a magical ambush and, failing in this, goes to him disguised as one of his serving-ladies to summon him to what will be his doom. When he is dying, this Badhbh again assumes the form of a crow and alights shrieking on the pillar to which he has tied himself, thus showing that his life is at an end.

Horrible as she was, however, she still tends to favour one side in a battle and helps that side to achieve victory, and this is probably an echo of her original function as the warlike aspect of the land-goddess. A tenth-century description of an historical battle, in which FEARGHAL MAC MAOLDÚIN, HIGH-KING of the Uí NÉILL, was defeated by the Leinstermen (LAIGHIN) in AD 722, has dramatic mention of her in such a partisan context. She is called 'the red-mouthed and sharp-faced Badhbh', and is said to have raised an exultant shriek over the decapitated head of Fearghal. A description of another historical battle – this one between the men of Leinster and the men of Ossory in the year AD 870 – has equally sinister imagery: 'Great indeed was the din and tumult that occurred between them then, and the Badhbh raised her head between them, and there was massive killing between them.'

One particular type of portrayal of the war-goddess became conventional in the literature. An eighth-century text has the Mór-Ríoghain as a horrible woman who strikes terror into the hearts of men. The text further states that 'horrible are the huge entrails ... many are the spoils that she washes'. This recurs in several other accounts. By 'spoils' is meant weapons, even parts of bodies, but more usually the blood-soaked clothes of warriors is to be understood. The word used for the spoils is *fadhbh* (earlier, *fodhbh*), which is an obvious phonemic parallel to *badhbh* (earlier, *bodhbh*), and a stylistic connection was made between the two words within the overall context of war. Before his death, Cú Chulainn is described as meeting the Badhbh as a beautiful young woman at a ford 'lamenting and moaning, washing in cold water purple hacked wounded spoils'. The account of the death of the mythical warrior CORMAC CONN LOINGEAS contains the prophecy: 'The red-mouthed Badhbh will shriek around the house, for corpses she will be solicitous.' Before he died, this Cormac met the Badhbh by a riverside. She was a red woman, and when she lowered her hand the water became red with gore and blood. She was washing his spoils, thereby portending disaster for him.

This imagery was readily applied to battles fought in the late Middle Ages. A near-contemporaneous account of the Battle of Corcomroe Abbey in County Clare, fought in the year 1317, has Donnchadh Ó Briain meeting such a being on his way to oppose his kinsman Toirdhealbhach. She is described as a hideous hag and is washing mangled heads and limbs by the shore of a lake. He asks her who she is, and discovers that she is the protecting Badhbh of his opponents. She foretells the slaughter of Donnchadh and of his army, a prophecy that is fulfilled. The same hag is said to have taken Toirdhealbhach's part again the following year when he was contending with a NORMAN army under Richard de Clare. As he and his army crossed a river, de Clare saw 'a sharp and bare-mouthed Badhbh' washing armour and rich robes from which red blood poured into the water. She stated that de Clare and his followers would soon be slaughtered, and this prophecy was also fulfilled.

The war-goddess as such does not occur in later folklore, but her influence is to be noted in the popular tradition of the BAN-SHEE, whose crying is heard at night as a portent of death. In several counties in the southeast of Ireland, the banshee is in fact known by variants of the appellation *badhbh*; for instance, the *bodhbh* (pronounced bou in Counties Carlow, Wexford, south Wicklow and south Kildare; the *bodhbh chaointe* (lamenting badhbh, pronounced bo'hi:nt'ə) in County Kilkenny and adjacent parts of Laois and Tipperary; and the *badhb* (pronounced baib) in County Waterford. *See also* BODHBH DEARG.

DERIVATION OF NAMES: Olmsted (1994), 285, 411; W.M. Hennessy in *RC, 1*, 32–5; RIA Dictionary, s.v. '*badb*', '*fodb*'.

CARRION CROW AND CONTINENTAL CELTS: Ó hÓgáin (2002), 22, 41–3, 55, 242, 244 (drawing on Livy 7.26; Silius Italicus 3.340–3; Aelianus, *Natura Animali*, 10.22).

TRIPLICATED GODDESS: Gray (1982), 118, 128; Macalister (1941), 122, 154, 160; J. Frazer in *Ériu, 8*, 29–48; Ó Cuív (1945), 20, 26–7.

'FRUIT CROP': W.M. Hennessy in *RC, 1*, 36.

CÚ CHULAINN: C. O'Rahilly (1976), 7, 118, 121; Van Hamel (1933), 89–91, 95–6, 113.

CORMAC CONN LOINGEAS: W. Stokes in *RC, 21*, 156–9.

HISTORICAL BATTLES: W.M. Hennessy in *RC, 1*, 40; Ó Riain (1978), 8; O'Grady (1929), 1, 104–5, 140–1.

FOLKLORE: Lysaght (1996), 34–40.

GENERAL: W.M. Hennessy in *RC, 1*, 32–55; P.L. Henry in *Études Celtiques, 8*, 407–11.

Baile mac Buain

Baile mac Buain Fictional youth of Ulster in a love story written in or about the eleventh century. His name was fancifully derived from the place name Tráigh Bhaile ('the strand of the homestead', at Dundalk, County Louth), and he was given the epithet Binnbhéarlach, which means 'sweet-spoken'.

The story tells of how he arranged a love tryst with a Leinster princess called Aillinn. They were to meet at a house in Ros na Ríogh (Rosnaree on the River Boyne), and Baile set off southwards towards that place. On the way, he and his companions stopped to rest their horses, and were approached by an ugly fleet-footed stranger who told them that Aillinn had been killed by the warriors of Leinster as she came to meet Baile. On hearing this, the young man fell dead with disappointment. His followers buried him there, and thus the writer conveniently explains the place name Tráigh Bhaile. The malicious stranger then went south to Suí Laighean (Mount Leinster) and, entering the bower of Aillinn, told her that her lover was dead. She also died from a broken heart, and was buried in that place. A yew tree grew from the grave of Baile, with the likeness of his head in the upper branches, while an apple tree grew from the grave of Aillinn, with her likeness on its top. Seven years later the Ulster POETS made a writing tablet from the yew tree, while the Leinster poets made a writing-tablet from the apple tree. At the feast of TARA, CORMAC MAC AIRT – mythical high-king of Ireland – was much taken with the beauty of the stories read by these two sets of poets, and wished to see their tablets. When he held them, the two tablets leaped together and became entwined in each other like woodbine on a branch. They could not be parted, and they were kept in the treasury of Tara for a long time until the citadel was burnt in a raid.

Just as the character of Baile mac Buain was suggested by the place name Tráigh Bhaile, Aillinn's name is similarly derived from the large Leinster hill fort called Ailleann (Knockaulin, County Kildare). The story itself is a much ornamented version of an international narrative plot (*see* ROMANTIC TALES, type 970). The tragedy in the international plot is caused by feuding parents, but they have here been replaced by the malicious and spirit-like stranger, who seems to be an Irish development from medieval demon-lore.

O'Curry (1873), 472–5; K. Meyer in *RC, 13*, 220–5 & (1894), 84; V. Hull in *JCS, 1*, 94–7.

Balar

Balar *(also Balor, Bolur)* Mythical tyrant, who was sometimes given the sobriquet Bailcbhéimneach (strong-smiting). His name seems to have originally meant 'the flashing one', and would have been Boleros in ancient Celtic. Classical authors such as Ptolemy and Diodorus Siculus attest to a promontory in Cornwall being anciently known as Bolerion, and the inference is that a figure with such a name was associated with that place (probably Land's End). The Irish Balar is described in the early literature as grandson of an obscure personage called NÉT, and is said to have met his death at Carn Uí Néit (the cairn of the grandson of Nét). This is Mizen Head in County Cork. Such associations with promontories may be due to the prevalence of lightning storms at such places. In prehistoric forms of the Irish MYTHOLOGICAL CYCLE, therefore, Boleros would seem to have had a function connected with that of the Gaulish thunder-god Taranos.

With the recession of mythic rationale, the dramatic potential of Balar's destructive role increased. Probably because of his association with sky storms and with south-western promontories, his image was somewhat influenced by that of the sky deity, whose eye was the sun (*see* DAGHDHA). In one early source he is called Balar 'Birugderc' (piercing-eyed), showing that the flashing effect of lightning was thought of as emanating from his eye. So it was said that he had a fearsome eye that destroyed hosts 'by its poison'. His role in Irish tradition is confined to the myth of LUGH, to whom his daughter gave birth against his wishes and by whom he was eventually slain. In that context, he appears as a leader of the sea-pirate race called FOMHÓIRE, who oppress the divine race TUATHA DÉ DANANN to whom Lugh belonged by his father's line. In the medieval literature, Balar is associated with the north and is said to have been king of the Hebridean Islands off the coast of Scotland. The general imagery of the Fomhóire has, however, been much influenced by that of the Norse raiders who harassed Ireland in the ninth and tenth centuries (*see* NORSEMEN), and there is no reason to doubt the greater antiquity of his connection with the seas off the south-west coast.

The story of the second Battle of Moytirra (*see* MYTHOLOGICAL CYCLE) can be reduced to two basic levels of plot – the struggle between two supernatural races on the one hand, and the killing of a tyrant by his prophesied grandson on the other. That Balar was not originally involved in the former level is suggested by the fact that BREAS, rather than him, is the overall commander of the Fomhóire, and that Breas' role is much more central to the plot of the battle. The Balar-Lugh level, of course, presents a titanic clash to reciprocate the other level, but here the clash is more immediate and individualistic. Sensing this, the medieval writers did not hesitate to add some further touches. They borrowed from the biblical contest between David and Goliath, and had the weapon used by Lugh the same as that used by David, a slingshot, which we are told drove the eye back through Balar's head. Balar's own portrayal has also been tempered by the image of Goliath – he is of enormous size in our earliest text on the Moytirra battle, and when he falls dead 'thrice nine' of his own soldiers are crushed underneath him. Folk versions of the story are more true to the original format, having Lugh slaying Balar with a great javelin or spear.

Otherwise, Balar is described in the literature with rather spontaneous dramatic touches. We read that the eye was never opened except on a battlefield – it had a polished ring in its lid, and it required four men to lift this lid. A rather ingenious, though superfluous, explanation is given of how the eye became poisonous; when his father's druids had been brewing a magic concoction, Balar had come to observe the work and the fumes had settled on the eye, bringing with them their venomous power.

A variant description of Balar's death was current from at least the twelfth century. According to it, he survived the loss of his eye in the battle and was pursued by Lugh all the way to Mizen Head. When cornered and certain of his doom, he tried to exact vengeance by telling Lugh that he could gain all of his grandfather's power by performing a certain act. This was to place the severed head of Balar on top of his own. Having decapitated the tyrant, Lugh instead laid the head on a large rock, and it was immediately dashed to pieces. Variants of this episode have survived in later folklore recensions of the Lugh myth, though Mizen Head is no longer mentioned in them. In these tellings, Balar is said to have had his base on Tory Island off the Donegal coast, and is said to have oppressed Ireland with cruel taxes. This is derived from the medieval literature, which situated the stronghold of the Fomhóire on that rocky island and portrayed them as robbers and exactors of tribute. Various landmarks are pointed out on the island, such as the site of his fortress (Dún Bhalair), the nigh inaccessible peak on which he had a tower (Túr Bhalair) and where his daughter was kept, and a deep cleft where he used to keep prisoners. The withering effects of his evil eye were pointed out in phenomena as varied as the black tips of the rushes and the barren slopes of the mountains Muckish and Errigal on the mainland.

In folk versions of the Balar myth, his grandson Lugh was assisted by a friendly smith called Goibhleann (*see* GOIBHNIU). This Goibhleann had a marvellous cow (the GLAS GHOIBHNEANN), which Balar tried to steal from its owner. A variant account of these episodes was current in County Monaghan, according to which Balar drove the cow and its calf down into Leinster, but when they reached the coast near Dublin the cow tried to turn back, and Balar raised the lid from his eye to see what was troubling her. Immediately the cow and her calf were turned into rocks, which are now the two Rockabill islands off Skerries. His eye was reputed to have had a similar effect in County Mayo, the folk at Cong claiming that rocks in the locality were men who had been petrified by its glance. As might be expected, descriptions of how he employed his unique faculty are lavishly dramatised; for instance, the following account from Mayo: 'He had a single eye in his forehead, a venomous fiery eye. There were always seven coverings over this eye. One by one Balar removed the coverings. With the first covering the bracken began to wither, with the second the grass became copper-coloured, with the third the woods and timber began to heat, with the fourth smoke came from the trees, with the fifth everything around grew red, with the sixth it sparked. With the seventh they were all set on fire, and the whole countryside was ablaze!'

ORIGIN: T.F. O'Rahilly (1946), 58–60; Gray (1982), 133.

BATTLE OF MOYTIRRA: Gray (1982); Ó Cuív (1945).

HIS EYE IN LITERATURE: Gray (1982), 60–1.

SEVERED HEAD: Ó Cuív (1945), 6, 9; Mac Néill (1908), 35, 135.

FOLK VERSIONS OF THE MYTH: *see* LUGH.

LANDMARKS IN DONEGAL: OSL: Donegal (1835), 46–51, 81–97, 129–30, 229 & Westmeath (1837), 152; S. Ó Searcaigh in *An Claidheamh Soluis*, 17/9/1910, 3; IFC 56:392.

MONAGHAN LORE: H. Morris in *Béaloideas*, 7, 244–6. *See also* É. Ó Tuathail in *Béaloideas*, 3, 128–9.

MAYO ACCOUNTS OF THE EYE: OSL: Mayo (1838), 110–12; T. Ó Cillín in *Béaloideas*, 4, 88. *See also* M. MacNeill(1962), 598.

Banba A leading lady among the otherworld people, the TUATHA DÉ DANANN, according to the medieval writers of pseudo-history. Her name (originally Banbha) meant '[place of] women's death', and occurred as an ancient toponymic in south Wexford and in County Meath. In the latter instance the region of Banba included the royal centre of TARA, and thus the toponymic came to be used as an alternative name for the land-GODDESS there. When adopted into the framework of mythology, Banba was given a fundamental role.

In an eighth-century text, she was described as the leader of thrice-50 women and three men, the first group ever to settle in Ireland, which was thus known as 'the island of Banba of the women'. In later versions of this story, Banba's role was given to the lady CEASAIR, who was stated to have been her daughter. The pseudo-historians also claimed that Banba survived the biblical Deluge by standing on top of the prominence over the River Shannon near Portroe, County Tipperary called Tul Toinne (hill of the flood). That prominence reputedly remained above the waterline.

Banba's survival enabled the writers to claim that she was wife of Mac Cuill, one of the three Tuatha Dé KINGS of Tara at the time of the invasion of the country by the sons of MÍL. We read that after these invaders conquered the Tuatha Dé, they met Banba at Sliabh Mis (Slieve Mish, County Kerry). She sanctioned their rule in Ireland, but asked that her name be on the country henceforth. The same promise was exacted by two other Tuatha Dé queens, FÓDLA and ÉIRE; thus Ireland had three eponymous goddesses. The pseudo-historians were clearly bringing together various long-standing poetic terms for the country, making use of the ancient Celtic format of the triplicated goddess. Along with Éire (earlier, Ériu) and Fódla, Banba continued until modern times to be referred to rhetorically as a lady symbolising Ireland.

E. Hogan (1910), 95; Macalister (1939), 176–7, 184–5, 196–7 & (1941), 122, 152, 182 & (1956), 34; de Vries (1963), 135, 152; J. Carey in *Éigse*, 22, 38–9.

banshee *(in Irish,* bean sí*)* Female spirit that, in folk belief, is heard to cry when the death of a member of an Irish family is imminent. The designation means 'otherworld lady', and the banshee is invariably a solitary being. Her cry is described as plaintive and very much like that of a keening woman of this world. It is usually heard in the vicinity of the family dwelling and therefore near in location to the person who is about to die. However, some accounts have her cry being heard at the family home although that person be far away, even in a foreign country.

The banshee tradition is peculiar to the Gaelic world, and it must originally have sprung from the idea that a GODDESS cares for the fortunes of specific noble families. In the early story of FRAOCH, the impending death of that hero is announced by the cries of otherworld women, and in other texts we read of his own death being foretold to BRIAN BÓRAMHA by the goddess AOIBHEALL, and of the goddess MÓR lamenting over the grave of CATHAL MAC FIONGHUINE. That there is continuity between this and the later folklore of the banshee is strongly suggested by the folk insistence that the banshee laments only those who have Ó or Mac in their surname – i.e. families of noble Gaelic descent. This notion provides a clue as to how the folk belief developed from the original idea that goddesses protected the rulers and inhabitants of their particular areas. Firstly, it is clear that the folklore is not totally in accord with the literary tradition, which uses the term *bean sí* or *síbhean* equally for an otherworld lady, but with somewhat different connotations. Such a woman in the literature is not solely associated with death, but makes her appearance to inspire poets, and through them to encourage the chieftains to success and prosperity. When she appears in order to lament a dead leader, it is usually after the death has occurred, and according to the age-old convention of KINGSHIP, her sorrow is magnified by the fact that the dead hero was her mystical spouse. In folklore, on the other hand, the banshee is concerned only with death and with its announcement before it occurs. It is thus clear that the folk tradition has selected but one aspect of the original idea, and has placed it into the context of the general belief in omens presaging death. Such omens – for instance, the appearance of certain birds or the hearing of certain noises – are expressions of the folk attitude to the enigma of death. So the banshee of popular belief, though originally a patron goddess, has become an enigmatic being, a strange voice crying from the portals of the unknown.

It is difficult to date precisely when this change occurred, but it seems obvious that stress on otherworld women as protectresses of Gaelic families has to do with the confiscations of land in Ireland by the English government. There are certain indications that the new profile of the banshee developed in the south-eastern part of Ireland, probably during the seizure of land there by the English in the sixteenth and seventeenth centuries. This area preserves a very special designation for the being that is in fact a survival of the name BADHBH, and which occurs frequently in the old literature as that of a goddess of war. Its survival as the usual designation for the banshee in the southeast is probably an echo of the fighting that was a necessary corollary to the claim on the land in that period.

Belief in the banshee has survived with surprising strength all over Ireland, and in urban as well as rural parts. Although it is claimed that she presages the death only of those with Ó or Mac in their surnames, in practice many names of non-Gaelic origin are included in the selection. She is much more often heard than seen, although some people claim to have caught a glimpse of her, and in such accounts she is usually portrayed as old in appearance, combing her long white hair as she laments. A small number of narratives have become attached to her, and it is significant that these are particularly strong in Leinster. The most popular concerns how, after she has been heard to lament at night, a man finds her comb in the morning and takes it into his house. Next night a terrific wailing is heard outside his house, accompanied by knocks on the window. Realising that it is the banshee seeking her comb, the man puts it in the tongs and gives it out through the window. The comb is taken, and the tongs is twisted or broken, by which the man understands how that would have been the fate of his hand had he extended it.

Lysaght (1996) & in *Béaloideas, 59*, 67–82, 221–2; D. Ó hÓgáin in Owens (1987), 63–5, 119.

Barra *(earlier, Bairre)* Patron SAINT of Corcaigh (Cork city), which owes its origin to a monastery reputedly established by him at the end of the sixth century AD. His full name was Barrfhind or Findbhairre (later, Fionnbharra, meaning 'fair-haired'). It is anglicised as Barry or Finbar.

A fanciful biography of him was written in Latin in the late twelfth century, and there are later versions in both Latin and Irish. We read that a certain Amhairghin was chief smith to Tighearnach, a west Munster king. Against the king's commands, Amhairghin cohabited with a beautiful female slave, and when she became pregnant the king ordered that the couple be burned alive. The fire could not be lit due to a rain storm, however, and the unborn child spoke from its mother's womb, warning the king to abandon his intention. Amhairghin took the mother and child to his house at Achadh Durbchon (now Macroom, County Cork), and he was baptised there and given the name Loan. When he was seven years old, three clerics got permission to take him with them to study in Leinster. A doe gave her milk to feed him at Ros Coille (now Muckalee in north Kilkenny) and the clerics tonsured him there, giving him the new name Fionnbharra (fair crest).

We read that the saint's first foundation was at Achadh Bó (Aghaboe, County Laois), but that he soon left this to CAINNEACH and moved on to Cliu (an area in east Limerick), where he raised from the dead the recently deceased wife of a local king. He then established a school for clerics at the lake in west Cork that became known as Gúgán Barra. The founding of

many other churches, and the counselling of many other clerics, were attributed to him, until eventually he was guided by an angel to the marsh at the mouth of the River Lee called Corcaigh. There he was given a site for a hermitage, which in time grew into the celebrated monastery.

Barra is also described as going to Rome to obtain episcopal orders, and it is claimed that a flame from heaven came onto the hand of Pope GREGORY THE GREAT as he consecrated him. Later, when Barra asked St Eolang of Achadh Bolg (Aghabullogue in west Cork) to be his confessor, the latter placed Barra's hand in that of God Himself. God was taking Barra to heaven until beseeched by Eolang to allow him to remain on earth in order to continue with his good work. Nobody could ever after look on Barra's hand because of its radiance, but he used to cover it with a glove. We read that when Barra died, he was buried at Cork, and the sun stood still in the heavens and shone brilliantly for twelve days while his obsequies were being performed.

Some foundations in other parts of Ireland and even in Scotland were attributed to him. A possible explanation for this is that various monasteries were founded under the direct or indirect influence of Cork, but it is more likely that the name was derived from myth and applied to various saints, especially those who were seafarers. 'Barrfhind' is a term used to describe the sea waves in the early texts concerning the mythic MANANNÁN, and it is significant that some descriptions of St Barra resemble Manannán. He rides on horseback across the sea from Wales to Ireland, for instance, and effortlessly picks a salmon from that watery 'plain'. The memory of Barra survived strongly in the lore of the southwest of Ireland. One folk LEGEND claims that he banished a monster from the lake of Gúgán Barra, and that the monster fled up through the River Lee before departing through Cork Harbour. His feast day is 25 September.

BIOGRAPHICAL: Kenney (1929), 401–2; Plummer, *1* (1910), 65–74 & *1* (1922) 11–22; Stokes (1905), 196, 210–11, 402; O'Hanlon, *9* (1875), 547–85; L. Ó Buachalla in *JCHAS, 68,* 104–6; Ó Riain (1994).

SEA FEATS: Ó Riain (1994), 138–9; Stokes (1905), 40–1.
FOLKLORE: *Irish Independent*, 12/5/1932, 6; anon in *JCHAS*, 11
(second ser.), 76; IFC 327:289–96, 437:396, 452:275–8, 939:304–5,
1014:262–4.

Beag mac Dé A prophet, whose death is recorded at the year AD 553. Beag (earlier, Becc) means 'small', and the earlier form of his patronymic was Ded or Deadh, a septal designation common among the ÉRAINN. In the medieval literature, this element of his name was changed to 'Dé' (genitive of *dia*, i.e. 'god'), and was explained as referring to his having got the gift of prophecy from God. Due to this rather incongruous interpretation, he came to be regarded as a Christian SAINT, even though it is not certain that he was a Christian at all.

Several anecdotes are told of him in tenth-century literature, and these are clearly taken from oral tradition of the time. As with POETS, it was claimed that he showed his ability from childhood. After he was born, people were talking about him, and they remarked that he was very small. The baby spoke and said that he knew as much as any big child concerning the end of the world, and then gave a series of pessimistic prophecies. Another account has him as a grown man in the house of Mac Arda, king of the Ciarraighe Luachra (a sept in County Kerry) on the night that St BRÉANAINN was born. The king asked Beag what did he see, and Beag answered that he saw that a child had been born between them and the sea who would be king over Mac Arda forever. Similarly, Beag was said to have prophesied the beneficent rule of St CIARÁN of Clonmacnoise, and the success of the monastery of COLM CILLE at Ceanannas (Kells, County Meath).

He spent the most notable part of his career in the employ of the high-king DIARMAID MAC CEARRBHEOIL. We read that once, as he left the royal stronghold of TARA, he encountered three men, each of whom asked him a question. The questions related to how long would the fortress be occupied, what was the depth of the nearby river, and how thick was the bacon-fat that year. Beag answered all three questions together truthfully with the four words *pas go tóin amárach*. This phrase responds backwards to the questions – *pas* being a three-finger measure, *go tóin* meaning as far as one's posterior, and *amárach* being 'tomorrow'. We also read that Beag once spoke to nine people at once, and with a single discourse replied to all the different talk of the nine. Cryptic and accurate speech of this kind was an attribute of the most skilled poets according to Irish folk tradition.

The spontaneous knowledge of Beag was usually put to more practical uses. When Mughain, wife of the high-king Diarmaid, was pregnant, she and her husband went onto the green of Tara for fresh air, and they saw a troop of riders approach, led by Diarmaid's grandson and leading heir, Suibhne mac Colmáin Mhóir, king of the Dál Riada. Immediately Mughain cried out, and her husband suspected that she did this for love of Suibhne. Beag, however, explained that the cry was an indication that her unborn child would kill Suibhne. This was later proved correct, for the baby was AODH SLÁINE, who slew Suibhne and was in turn slain by Suibhne's son. On another occasion, Diarmaid was being praised by his poets, but Beag remarked that he saw 'the fierce hound which shall destroy the mansion'. Diarmaid asked what he meant, and Beag replied that the high-king's foster-child would bring about his death. The foster-child was Aodh Dubh, son of a minor northern king Suibhne, whom Diarmaid himself had slain. Beag prophesied in detail how Diarmaid would die, and in order to avoid this, the high-king had Aodh Dubh banished to Scotland.

Notwithstanding this precaution, Diarmaid was worried from that time onwards. One night he dreamed that two men came to him – one in clerical garb and the other a military man. They took his diadem from him and divided it among them. When he awoke and told of his dream, Beag explained it to mean that his reign was doomed, that his kingdom would be divided between the clergy and the laity, and that ill would come of that arrangement. On yet another occasion, Beag gave a long list of prophecies to the high-king concerning the future of Ireland, these being again of a very pessimistic nature. Diarmaid doubted the prophecies regarding his own death and questioned his DRUIDS on the matter, but they confirmed what Beag had said. Incensed at Diarmaid's distrust of him, Beag decided to leave Tara, but he had not gone far when he met Colm Cille. It had been foretold that Beag would give three false prophecies before his death, and so, when the two met, Colm asked when would Beag himself die. Beag replied that he had seven years of life remaining, and on being further pressed reduced it to seven months. Colm expressed doubts, and he then admitted that he had a mere seven hours to live. All these prophecies were false, for death was nearer still, and the saint then said that he had come to prepare Beag for it. He administered the last rites to him, and so the prophet died.

The genealogists devised fanciful genealogies. One source has him descended from Maine, son of NIALL, and another claims that he was of the DÁL GCAIS of Munster.

Flower (1926), 311–12; R.I. Best in *Ériu*, 4, 162; Stokes (1890), 23, 28, 100, 118, 350 & (1905), 132–3; Plummer, *1* (1910), 98 & *1* (1922), 45; O'Grady, *1* (1892), 74–5, 78–80 & *2*, 470; K. Meyer in *ZCP, 9*, 169–71; O'Donovan, *1* (1848), 150–1, 196–7, 438–9; W.M. Hennessy & McCarthy, *1* (1887), 52–3, 154–6; Ó Cadhlaigh (1950), 77–87.

Bearach *(earlier, Berach)* SAINT of the sixth century AD. Two biographies of later date survive, one in Irish and the other in Latin. His name, a common one, meant 'sharp-witted'.

We read that the coming of Bearach was prophesied by St PATRICK, and that he was born at Gort na Luachra (Gortnalougher, County Leitrim). He was fostered by a monk called Daigh mac Cairill at Magh Muirtheimhne (the plain of north Louth). Once, when a woman and boy refused to allow him to grind some wheat in a hurry, the boy fell into the mill and the woman died, but Bearach restored both to life. The boy's father, who was a nobleman, in gratitude gave him the site for a monastery

in that place, Raon Bhearaigh (near Inishkeen, County Monaghan). Bearach then went to the royal centre of TARA, but was refused a drink there. After he left, all the beer disappeared from the vats. The KING sent for him, and when he blessed the vats all was restored, whereupon he was given a site for another monastery. This was Díseart Bhearaigh (either Dysart, County Westmeath or Kilbarrack, County Dublin). Proceeding to the monastery of CAOIMHGHIN at Glendalough, he was given control of the refectory there and worked many miracles to provide food for the monks when it was lacking. He also banished many demons from the place by ringing his bell and singing psalms.

We read that, after seven years, he left Glendalough, with his books being drawn in a chariot by a stag. The stag lay down at Cill Bhearaigh (Kilbarry, in Termonbarry, County Roscommon), and it was there that he founded his most celebrated monastery. There also he performed many miracles, including the raising to life of warriors slain in battle. The site on which he built the monastery had earlier been given to a POET named Diarmaid, who refused to relinquish his claim to it. Bearach and Diarmaid searched Ireland for somebody willing to adjudicate between them, but nobody would do so for fear of the saint's curse and the poet's satire. In their search they finally visited the Scottish king Aodán mac Gabhráin. Finding two great mounds of snow at the entrance to the royal fortress, Bearach told Diarmaid to blow on these. Immediately he did so they blazed into fire. When Aodán was told what had happened he prostrated himself before Bearach, and he directed them to go to the kings of Teathbha and Breifne in Ulster. Bearach performed several miracles in the presence of these kings, and they ruled in his favour. Diarmaid attempted to satirise them for this, but Bearach placed his palm over the poet's mouth and declared that he would never compose again. He also foretold that Diarmaid would die in a year from that day. At the end of the year, the poet shut himself into a church, but he was slain by a strong spear-cast made by a hunter at a passing

stag. Diarmaid's son Cú Allaidh then undertook to curse Bearach's territory, but he was
slain by Concheanann, a companion of the
saint. Bearach was displeased at this act and
imposed penance on Concheanann.

Other miracles attributed to Bearach
included protecting the people against
famine and sickness, and he was reputed
to have changed a bog into a lake near
Kilbarry in order to swallow up an aggressive army that was raiding the septs under
his protection. His feast day is 15 February.
Kenney (1929), 402–3; Stokes (1905), 60, 74–5; Plummer, *1* (1910),
75–86 & *1* (1922), 23–43; O'Hanlon, *2* (1875), 534–52; D. Ó Corráin
& Maguire (1981), 31.

Bearchán SAINT of the sixth century AD,
founder of a monastery at Cluain Sosta
(Clonsast, County Offaly). His name was
a diminutive of the common one, Bearach
(*see the preceding*). He reputedly was of the
Dál Riada (a sept of County Antrim), and
had the nickname 'Fear Dá Leithe' (literally, 'man of two halves'), which is explained
by his having spent half of his career in
Scotland and the other half in Ireland. There
is no surviving biography of Bearchán, but
he must have had great prestige, as he was
represented as the foreteller of many major
happenings. The principal work attributed to him was a long verse text that
referred to events of the period from the
sixth to the twelfth century in Ireland and
Scotland. It is difficult to decide on a date
for the genesis of this text, but it is clear
that it was supplemented and rearranged
from time to time. Further prophetic verses
were attributed to him after the Middle Ages,
and during the Elizabethan Wars much use
was made of prophecies by which he was
claimed to have foretold Irish victories
over the English. He was reputed to have
been one of the four great saint-seers of
Ireland, the other three being COLM CILLE,
MOLING and BRÉANAINN.

No doubt on account of his fame as a
prophet, a curious anecdote concerning
him has been collected from the folklore
of west Cork. This anecdote – of obscure
derivation – describes how he had a vision
in which it was revealed to him that his
death would come when three kings came

uninvited to his house. Three such guests
did indeed come, and when he told them
of his vision, they promised to protect him.
Placing him under an overturned vat, they
stood guard around it, but soon a cowherd
arrived and lulled them to sleep with
music. When they awoke in the morning,
they found nothing left of Bearchán but his
bones beneath the vat.

There was some confusion between
himself and his namesake Bearchán of
Glasnevin (in Dublin), who was better
known as Mobhí. This Mobhí was of the
Luighne of Connacht, and was reputed to
have been delivered of his mother after her
death, as a result of which he had a flat
face. He was one of the mentors of Colm
Cille. His death was given as AD 545 and
his feast day is 12 October. The feast day
of St Bearchán of Clonsast is 4 December.
GENERAL: Stokes (1905), 76–7, 249, 256–7; O'Donovan (1864),
326–7; D. Ó Corráin & Maguire (1981), 31–2; A.O. Anderson in *ZCP*,
18, 1–56; Todd (1867), 204–5, 225, 307; O'Curry (1873), 412–18, 421,
432, 627–8, 670; Walsh & Ó Lochlainn, *1* (1948), 178–9;
FOLKLORE STORY: Hyde (1899), 210–11 & (1915), 63–5; A. Kelleher
& G. Schoepperle in *RC, 32*, 53–8.
MOBHÍ: Stokes (1905), 216–17, 222–5.

bees These valuable insects were more
generally kept in former than in recent times.
Although a tradition held that they were
introduced by a certain St Modhomhnóg of
Tiobar Fhachna (Tibberaghny, County
Kilkenny) in the seventh century is certainly
apocryphal, it does appear that the
Christian monasteries practiced bee-
keeping on a large scale. Bees were believed
to be blessed creatures, probably because of
the use of their wax to make church candles,
and one medieval LEGEND describes a
swarm of bees building a little container
around a lost communion wafer to protect
it. They were also thought to be possessed
of special wisdom, and to take an acute
interest in the affairs of their owners. If a
bee entered the house it was regarded as a
good omen, and the bees in their hive
would be told in advance of projects that
the family intended to undertake in the
belief that they might effect a beneficial
influence. When a member of the family
died, it was customary to place a black

piece of cloth on the hive so that the bees could join in the mourning. *See also* ARISTOTLE *and* GOBNAIT.

F. Kelly (1997), 108–14; Cross (1952), 45, 69; Plummer (1925), 217; E. J. Gwynn in *Ériu*, 2, 83; S. Ó Súilleabháin (1942), 42–3; IFC Index.

birds The heroic literature shows that in pre-Christian times birds were understood to be intermediaries between this world and the otherworld (*see, for example*, CONAIRE *and* CÚ CHULAINN). Deities could take on the form of birds, and in Christian lore this was adapted and transformed so that angels were portrayed as appearing in that form (*see, for example*, PATRICK).

There are several reports that the DRUIDS used the flight of birds as auguries, and they were believed to have been able to interpret the cry of the raven. A vestige of this survives in folklore, which claims that ravens and hooded crows are birds of ill omen, and that to hear them hovering over or squawking near the house betokens the death of some relative. Similar ideas are still current regarding other types of birds. For instance, if, for the first time in the year, a person hears the cuckoo's cry in his left ear, that is a portent that the person will die before the year is out; and it is still widely believed that to harm a swan brings death or some other misfortune to a person. If a farmer harms a swallow, it is claimed that he will soon notice blood in the milk given by his cows.

It is regarded as a very unlucky thing to see a pigeon enter the dwelling-house. On the other hand, if crows make their nest in trees near the house each year, and then fail to return one year, that is known as 'the curse of the crows' and also betokens bad luck. The magpie is generally considered an unlucky bird, and one old tradition states that it was brought to Ireland by the soldiers of CROMWELL. To see a single magpie betokens bad luck, but the effect of this can be removed if, on seeing it, a person immediately removes his hat. Some people claimed that the magpie got its black-and-white colouring because when the other birds went into mourning at the death of JESUS CHRIST, it did so only half-heartedly. The jackdaw is also an unlucky bird to see, and if one falls down the chimney that is taken as a portent of a death in the family. The singing of the thrush was much valued for its musical timbre and that of the blackbird for its clear notes, but the voice and appearance of the latter was often taken to be a sign that rain was coming. Contrariwise, to see and hear the lark in the morning was taken as a sign of good weather for the day. Another respected bird was the plover, which was considered a great delicacy, and was said to have been introduced to Ireland by BRIAN BÓRAMHA.

The eagle was reputed to be the most long-living bird, but was believed to be dangerous, and to seize and carry away in its talons lambs, other small animals and even children. The hawk was thought to have the best eyesight of all the birds, and 'the eye of a hawk on a mountain top' was proverbial for sharpness. Some more curious ideas were current until recently concerning the behaviour and nature of certain birds. When the corncrake sang, for instance, it was said that it lay on its back, thinking that it was holding up the sky with its uplifted legs. Even more striking was the opinion held of the barnacle goose, which was said to be hatched from barnacle shells and thus not to be properly a fish. This meant that the Lenten fast would not be broken by eating the barnacle goose, a situation that in medieval times was accepted in Ireland and elsewhere by ecclesiastical authorities.

The robin was said, in Ireland as abroad, to have got its red breast from its attempts to stanch the blood on the brow of Jesus Christ at the Crucifixion. It was also said to have assisted the Virgin Mary on the Flight into Egypt. Mary was cut by brambles, but the little bird followed on and covered the trail of blood with leaves so that the pursuers would not find it. The robin was thus held in high regard as a blessed bird, and it should never be killed, nor should its nest be interfered with. Because of the assistance it rendered to Jesus, the robin was regarded as a bird anxious to console the sick and dying, and some people claimed that it was wont to alight on the window sill of a house and sing to comfort a dying person within. In some Munster versions of folktales, the robin was described as a supporter and encourager of heroes in mortal combat, and these stories refer to the helpful bird as '*spideog mhuintir Shúilleabháin*' (the robin of the O'Sullivans). Its particular association with that family is puzzling, but it may have arisen from the pseudo-tradition that the family's ancestor Súildubhán mac Maolughra gave away his eye through his generosity (*see* AITHIRNE *and* EOCHAIDH). In that case, the appearance of a helpful robin to stanch the blood from Súildubhán's face would have been a natural improvisation.

The wren's reputation was less respected. Although this little fellow was reputed to be king of all the birds in widespread narrative lore (*see* ANIMAL TALES), it was regarded in Ireland as a treacherous bird. Various redactions of one LEGEND told of how it had betrayed Irish soldiers by beating its wings on the shields or drums of a sleeping hostile army, whether of the NORSEMEN or the Cromwellians. It was even said to have betrayed St Stephen, the first Christian martyr, by flapping its wings to attract his pursuers when he was hiding. This is the popular explanation given for the custom of 'hunting the wren' on St Stephen's Day, when it is still customary in many parts of the country for groups of people in disguise and playing music to go from house to house collecting money to 'bury the wren'. In former times, they really brought with them, on a pole, the body of an unfortunate wren. The custom – which was known also in Wales, England and France – seems to have been introduced into Ireland in the late Middle Ages (*see* MOLING). The ultimate origin of antipathy to the wren may, however, be much older – perhaps the wren was thought of as a symbol of the severe winter season, and its expulsion would therefore have been a ritual act. It has been plausibly suggested that antipathy towards the wren results from efforts by medieval ecclesiastics to abolish vestiges of druidic practices concerning the bird. A ninth-century glossary fancifully derives a term for the wren, *drean*, from

draoi-éan (druid-bird), and similar echoes could be interpreted from a medieval text that gives a detailed list of prognostications from the wren's movements.

A. Ross (1974), 302–77, 417–46; R.I. Best in *Ériu, 8*, 120–3; O'Meara (1982), 38–47, 77–80, 83–4; Wood-Martin, *2* (1902), 140–50; S. Ó Súilleabháin (1942), 289–93 & in *Béaloideas, 10*, 136–40; Ó Danachair (1978), 25; S. Ó hEochaidh in *Béaloideas, 37–8*, 246–316; L. Ó Dochartaigh in *Béaloideas, 45–7*, 164–98 & *50*, 90–125; Meyer (1912), 40; B. Ó Cuív in *Éigse, 18*, 43–66; Danaher (1972), 243–50; P.V. O'Sullivan (1991), 21–7, 30–50; Ó hÓgáin (1995), 78–82.

Bodhbh Dearg A KING of the otherworld people, the TUATHA DÉ DANANN. His name (from Celtic *Boduos*), had a meaning such as 'the fighting man', and he thus seems to be derived from the father-deity in his role as warlord. The epithet (meaning 'red') also indicates such an origin (*see* DEARG).

Such fearsome imagery connected with his name has been lost in Irish tradition. In the early text on the Vision of AONGHUS, Bodhbh is described as 'the king of the otherworld of Munster' (*ríg síde Mumhan*) and has his residence in Síd al Feimhin (the cairn on top of Slievenamon, County Tipperary). He is a friend of the Daghdha, and is famous for his knowledge throughout Ireland, which knowledge he uses to assist the love-sick Aonghus to find a beautiful maiden. He does not play a leading role in any story, however. Later medieval literature made both him and MIDHIR sons of the Daghdha, and one source refers to hostility against him by the sons of Midhir. There are various mentions of sons and daughters of his own. In a late medieval text, it is related that he was elected as king of all the Tuatha Dé Danann, much to the dissatisfaction of LIR, and a reconciliation between these two was only effected by Bodhbh Dearg offering his foster-daughter in marriage to Lir. Bodhbh is portrayed as a kindly uncle-figure, who greatly grieves at the fate that befalls the children of that marriage (*see* LIR).

NAME: Holder, *1* (1896), 461; Pokorny (1959), 114; Walde & Pokorny, *2* (1930), 126; Olmsted (1994), 411.
OCCURRENCES IN LITERATURE: Shaw (1934), 50–6; Stokes (1900), 139, 350; Ní Shéaghdha (1945), 197; E. O'Curry in *Atlantis, 3*, 385 & *4*, 114–41; Gwynn (1935), 152.

Bóinn Eponymous GODDESS of the River Boyne. The name (earlier, Bóind or Bóand) is derived from a primitive Irish form, *bóu-vinda*. This is one of the earliest cited Irish toponyms, occurring in Ptolemy's geography in the form Buvinda. Ptolemy's work dates from the second century AD, but may be based on sources somewhat earlier still. This – correctly Bouvinda – could be taken to mean 'illuminated cow', suggesting a goddess in bovine shape. The Celtic word *vind-* covered a semantic range from the colour white to illumination and wisdom. In this latter sense, it was personified as a great seer, known in old Irish as Find (*see* FIONN), and there is good reason to believe that the name of the river was closely connected with the cult of this personage. Thus Bóinn would originally have been the wisdom-giving cow associated with the archetypal seer. Her imagery is paralleled from another early Indo-European source, Sanskrit literature, which symbolised sacred rivers as milk flowing from a mystical cow. In early Irish literature, it is said that if a person drinks water from the River Boyne in June he will become a seer-poet.

The goddess in bovine form was anciently worshipped by the Continental Celts under names such as Damona and Stirona, and there is some evidence that the name Bouvinda was also used for her abroad in connection with springs. In that case, the Bouvinda cult would have existed in Celtic areas abroad before being brought to Ireland and connected to the particular Irish river. It seems, indeed, that Bouvinda was originally another name, or an epithetical name, for the great river-goddess of the Continental Celts called DANU – namely, Danu Bouvinda, or 'Danu the milk-giving and inspiring'. As might be expected, the cult underwent its own particular development in Ireland.

In the medieval literature, Bóinn is described as the wife of Neachtan, which was a pseudonym for NUADHU, and thus we can see that at some early stage of Irish tradition the cult of the seer Fionn had that of Nuadhu superimposed on it. The reason for this seems to have been the rich aquatic imagery associated with Nuadhu, and hence it was claimed that the source of the river was a well called the Sídh (otherworld dwelling) of Neachtan. The medieval PLACE-LORE states that only Neachtan himself and his cup-bearers could approach this well, and the eyes of anybody else who looked on its water would burst. One day, however, Bóinn boldly approached the well to examine it, and three gushes came from it, injuring her foot and hand, and blinding one of her eyes. She raced away from there, but the water rose after her and followed her all the way to the sea, thereby giving rise to the Boyne river.

This account, though not in itself ancient tradition, incorporates an archaic idea concerning the craft of seers and POETS – i.e. the light of inspiration that blinds. Perhaps with equal significance, it gives various poetic names to the Boyne, and goes on to declare that it is the same as the Banna at home and a variety of foreign rivers such as the Severn, the Tiber, the Euphrates, the Jordan and the Tigris. In other words, the Boyne has the mythic essence appropriate to rivers, an idea that must have grown out of the belief that the mother-goddess works through rivers and that she brings fertility into the world through union with the father-deity in the sky.

As great mother, Bóinn is portrayed as a partner of the father-deity, for a ninth-century story tells of the DAGHDHA becoming her lover. This he does by a trick, sending her husband away on business for nine months. This period appears to be only a day, and in the meantime he lies with Bóinn and she gives birth to AONGHUS of Newgrange, the archetypal youth. The imagery here seems to have been influenced by traditions concerning the divine youth called the Mac Óg (*see* AONGHUS) and an older personage (*see* NUADHU). We may presume that such imagery was borrowed from British Celtic lore concerning the deities Maponos and Nodons, but the original myth would appear to have been that Fionn, representing seer-craft, was born out of the union of the Daghdha and Bóinn.

The source of the River Boyne – in the

townland of Newberry, near Carbury, County Kildare – is still regarded as a sacred place. It is a holy well, dedicated to the Holy Trinity and frequented on Trinity Sunday. Perhaps as an echo of its ancient imagery, the water of the well is believed to hold a cure for failing eyesight. *See also* SIONAINN.

NAME AND ORIGIN: RIA Dictionary, s.v. '*boand*'; Holder (1896), *1*, 646–7; T.F. O'Rahilly (1946), 3; P.K. Ford in Larson (1974), 67–74; Ó hÓgáin (1988), 17–18, 325 & (1999), 110–13, 234; Olmsted (1994), 352–6.
OTHERWORLD SOURCE OF RIVER: Dillon (1969), 6.
IN LITERATURE: Knott (1936), 6; Gwynn (1913), 26–39, 286, 480–2; G. O'Nolan in *ZCP*, *8*, 516–19; Van Hamel (1956), 37–8; W. Stokes in *RC*, *15*, 315–16 & *CTS* (1905), 18–19; O. Bergin & R.I. Best in *Ériu*, *12*, 142–7.
TRINITY WELL: OSL: Kildare (1837), *1*, 93; IFC 946:113–14.

bóraimhe A tribute that the medieval historians claimed was due to the royal Uí NÉILL sept from the Leinstermen (LAIGHIN). The word (also spelt *bóramha*) meant 'cattle-computation', and the idea of this specific tribute was invented in or about the eighth century AD to explain and justify the record of warring by the Uí Néill against Leinster, which continued sporadically for several hundred years.

A text written in the eleventh century purports to give the history of this tribute. It describes how a Leinster king called Eochaidh mac Eachach married the daughter of TUATHAL TEACHTMHAR, and then married a second daughter while pretending that the first was dead. When they discovered the truth, the ladies died from shame, and Tuathal as revenge defeated Eochaidh in battle, slew him, and ravaged his province. To secure peace, the Leinstermen agreed to pay a massive tribute. It consisted of thrice-50 hundreds each of cows, pigs, wethers, mantles, silver-chains and copper cauldrons, as well as a special huge cauldron and 30 red-eared cows and calves with bronze halters and spancels and bosses of gold.

We read that Tuathal's successors continued to collect this *bóraimhe*, once in each reign, until the time of CAIRBRE LIFEACHAIR. When this king tried to collect it he was faced by a Leinster army headed by Breasal Béalach and supported by FIONN MAC CUMHAILL. Cairbre was defeated, and the tribute was not again levied until 30 royal maidens were slain

in TARA by the forces of the Leinster king Dúnlaing. The Leinstermen, however, continually rebelled against it, and were often successful, defeating even NIALL himself in twelve battles. Niall's son LAOGHAIRE next tried to impose the tribute, but he was captured on the first attempt and was slain on the second. Ailill Molt, son of NAITHÍ, also tried to take the *bóraimhe*, but the Leinstermen defeated him several times, as they did also his successors down to Aodh mac Ainmhireach, who suffered a momentous defeat and was slain by the Leinster king BRANDUBH.

A few of Aodh's successors managed to collect the tribute, but several others failed, until FIONNACHTA became high-king and took it twice. He tried to take it a third time, but the Leinster king Bran Múit enlisted the support of St MOLING. This SAINT went to confer with Fionnachta, and by a verbal trick secured final remission of the onerous tribute. He persuaded the high-king to give the Leinstermen respite *go Luan*, which Fionnachta understood to mean 'till Monday', but which Moling interpreted as 'till the Last Day' (*see* TIME).

K. Meyer in *Ériu*, *4*, 72; W. Stokes in *RC*, *13*, 32–124; O'Grady (1892), *2*, 495–7.

Bran mac Feabhail Fictional character in a text written in northern Ulster in the early eighth century AD. The writer was playing on the place name Srúibh Brain (Stroove Point, County Donegal, at the opening of Lough Foyle). This place name meant 'the headland of the raven', but since Bran (raven) was often used as a man's name, the author or his source invented a noble seaman called Bran. He further claimed that this seaman was son of a certain Feabhal, which name was deduced from Loch Feabhail (Lough Foyle). It was easy to imagine such a character as a great sea voyager embarking or landing at Srúibh Brain, which point faced the open sea.

The text is the earliest example of the genre of *imram* (later, *iomramh*, and meaning 'rowing'). It describes how an otherworld lady with a silver branch came to Bran at his palace, the location of which is not given. The branch emitted beautiful music, and she revealed that it was from an apple tree in the realm of Eamhain (for which otherworld realm, *see* MANANNÁN). She further disclosed that this was a faraway island, and she described its wonders and invited Bran and his men to row there. She then disappeared from sight, and Bran set out on the sea with thrice nine for a crew. When they were two days on their journey, they encountered Manannán, who described the sea as his estate and gave them instructions on how to reach the island of Eamhain before sundown. Coming to that island, Bran rowed around it and saw a crowd of people staring and laughing at his crew. One of his men went ashore, and immediately he began to stare and laugh like the rest. They next encountered the Island of Women, the inhabitants of which invited them ashore. They remained there in great delight and joy for what they thought was a year, though it was in fact many years.

Then one of the crew, called Neachtan, grew lonely for Ireland and decided to return home, and Bran agreed to accompany him. Bran's paramour advised him not to go, and if he did go not to set foot on the land. Reaching Ireland at Srúibh Brain, they spoke from the boat to the people, who said that they had heard old lore of 'Bran's rowing'. Neachtan jumped from the boat, but as soon as he touched the soil of Ireland he withered away as if he had been buried for hundreds of years. Bran told of their adventures and wrote his account in OGHAM. Then he departed, and no more was heard of him.

This is a curious text, much of it in verse, and it is based in part on pre-Christian ideas of the otherworld. The writer was a Christian, but he wrote his text as a poetic tour de force rather than a serious philosophical work. The MOTIF of a man who ages on his return from the timeless otherworld was an international one (*see* WONDER TALES, type 470).

ORIGINAL PLACE NAMES: E. Hogan (1910), 498, 617; R.I. Best in *Ériu*, 2, 22; A. Mac an Bhaird in *Ainm*, 5, 2.

GENERAL: Mac Mathúna (1985); Meyer & Nutt (1895–97); Van Hamel (1941), 1–19. *See also* Dillon (1948), 101–31; Oskamp (1970), 40–3.

For visits to pre-Christian Irish otherworld, *see* Cross (1952), motifs F370, F373.

Brandubh Leinster KING who died *c.*AD 605. His father's name was Eochu, and the name Brandubh itself means 'raven-black'. He was one of the characters who figure most prominently in stories of the kings.

A text from around the eleventh century states that Eochu was for a while exiled in Scotland. His wife Feidhilm gave birth to twin boys, and on the same night and in the same house, Ingheanach, wife of a king called Gabhrán, gave birth to twin girls. Feidhilm gave one of her sons in exchange for one of the baby girls, but she inserted a grain of gold into his shoulder so that he might be identified later. Eochu returned to Ireland with his family, and his son Brandubh became king of Leinster. The other boy grew up to be Aodán mac Gabhráin, a celebrated leader of the Dál Riada sept and king of Scotland. Aodán came to wage war on Leinster, but his real mother Feidhilm went to meet him and proved his identity to him through the grain of gold, as a result of which he made peace with Brandubh. This imaginative story has no basis in history, but derives from popular lore concerning confusion of new-born babies. Medieval romance also brought Brandubh into association with the adventures of MONGÁN, whose father was an ally of Aodán mac Gabhráin.

Brandubh was reputed to have delivered 'seven blows against Breagha', but by far his greatest victory over the royal Uí NÉILL of that area (in County Meath) was in the year 598 at the Battle of Dún Bolg (Dunboyke, near Hollywood, County Wicklow). Here the Uí Néill high-king Aodh mac Ainmhireach, who was attempting to collect the *BÓRAIMHE* tribute, was slain and his army scattered. By the eleventh century a whole series of narratives had become associated with this battle, with quite dramatic representations of the participants. We read that the high-king Aodh had a son called Cumascach, who went about the country demanding the privilege of sleeping with the wife of each local king. When he came into Leinster, Brandubh spread the rumour that he was gone abroad and disguised himself and his men as servants. As a feast

40

was being prepared for Cumascach, his satirist Glasdámh recognised by the great bounty that the cook was Brandubh in disguise, and accordingly put Cumascach on his guard. However, Brandubh had the doors of the house locked from the outside and set fire to it. Glasdámh begged to be allowed out, as he had been given food and was thus a true guest. Brandubh gave him permission to depart, but instead of himself doing so, Glasdámh allowed Cumascach to escape in his clothes. However, Cumascach was slain by one of Brandubh's men as he left the territory.

The high-king Aodh, to avenge the death of his son, brought his army south, and encamped at Dún Bolg. Brandubh sent Bishop Aodán of Glendalough to arrange a truce, but the high-king insulted him by insisting that the bishop touch his private parts. Aodán cursed him, saying that the king's own sexual organs would be taken by a she-wolf. Returning to Brandubh, Aodán advised him to bring his men into the enemy camp in baskets strapped to oxen, under the pretext of delivering food as tribute. He also recommended that a troop of unbroken horses be brought with rocks attached to their tails. Brandubh managed to make a truce with the Ulstermen in Aodh's force, and then challenged the high-king's champion to combat and slew him.

He sent a spy called Rón Cearr, disguised as a leper, into Aodh's camp in order to arrange the treacherous food delivery, but the high-king recognised 'a warrior's eyes in the leper's head' and continued his preparations for battle. Nevertheless, he was put off his guard when the Leinstermen arrived with a huge amount of food. The hidden soldiers sprang from the baskets and the wild horses were released, causing pandemonium in the camp. A wall of spears and shields was put around the high-king by his followers, and he retreated. Rón Cearr, however, attacked him, slew his bodyguard, and dragged him from his horse and beheaded him. He put the head of Aodh into his food satchel and brought it to Brandubh. Variant accounts have both Cumascach and Aodh slain by

Brandubh himself, thus further underlining the martial ability of the Leinster king.

The death of Brandubh is dramatised in the hagiographical literature, which has St MAODHÓG as his spiritual adviser and supporter. We read that a man called Saran 'the squinter' slew Brandubh, and when Maodhóg realised that the king had died without being shriven, he prayed and fasted for a long time, and by this means had the king restored to life. Brandubh, however, was unwilling to return to the sinful world and, having received the Last Rites, desired to go to heaven and therefore died again immediately. He was buried at Maodhóg's monastery at Fearna (Ferns, County Wexford). Saran repented of his deed and was forgiven, but as punishment his arm fell off.

K. Meyer in ZCP, 12, 134–7; R.I. Best in Loomis Studies (1927), 381–90; W. Stokes in RC, 13, 54–95 & 17, 160–1; A. Maniet in Éigse, 7, 98–110; Plummer, 2 (1910), 149 & 1 (1922), 185–6, 188, 215–17, 230–2 & 2 (1922), 383; Heist (1965), 238–44, 417; Dinneen, 2 (1908), 408–11 & 3 (1908), 114–15; F.J. Byrne (1973), 142–9; Dillon (1946), 41, 49, 106–11.

Bréanainn SAINT of the sixth century, the date of whose death is variously given as AD 571, 575 and 581. His name was rendered in Latin as Brendanus and thus in English as Brendan. He was a great founder of monasteries – the best known of these being at Clonfert and Annaghdown in County Galway, Inishadroum in County Clare, and Ardfert in County Kerry. Reputedly also a great traveller, he was said to have visited Scotland, Wales and Brittany, in which places his cult was strong in medieval times. Biographical accounts of him in Irish and Latin had their genesis in the eighth century, and his fame owed much to a fantastic text, *Navigatio Brendani*, which was written about a hundred years later.

Bréanainn belonged to the Ciarraighe Luachra, a sept that inhabited the area around Tralee Bay in County Kerry. Many place names in that area reflect his cult, most notably the towering Cnoc Bhréanainn (Mount Brandon) in the Dingle Peninsula. The Ciarraighe were a maritime people, and no doubt their sea travels helped to spread the cult of their saint and also to give him the image of a mariner par excellence. All of the surviving accounts of his life are conflations of the original biography and the *Navigatio*. From an analysis of these and some other material, the following emerges as a general outline: Bréanainn was born the son of one Findlugh of the Ciarraighe Luachra. Before she gave birth, Findlugh's wife dreamed that her bosom was full of pure gold and that her breasts shone like snow. A bishop called Earc explained to her the meaning of this, and the prophet BEAG MAC DÉ also foretold the wondrous birth. This event was accompanied by several marvellous happenings, including a fair drop (*braen-fhind*) that fell from heaven onto him, thus giving his name. The latter motif is transparently fanciful, for the name Bréanainn was apparently quite common in early Ireland, being a borrowing of the Welsh word for a KING, *brenhin*.

We further read that the child was fostered for five years by the nun, St ÍDE, and then was sent to be educated by Bishop Earc. Later he went to Connacht, and having studied there for some time returned to be consecrated by Earc. The love of God so increased in him, however, that he was given a vision of a secret island in the ocean to which he might withdraw from the world. This was Tír Tairngire (the Land of Promise). When he reached that island, he was told to return and teach the true way of living to the Irish people. This he did, and many more adventures are related of him. It was claimed that he cursed 50 rivers because fishermen on them were stingy with him, so that these rivers never after had fish, and that he blessed 50 more, with the opposite effect. He also turned a man into an otter because that man had stolen his cows.

On account of his short temper, Íde instructed him to leave Ireland and to go on missionary work to Britain. He rowed thither, and among the miracles performed by him there we read of such unrealistic wonders as the taming of savage lions and the banishing of sea-monsters. Notably, many of the miracles attributed to him are connected with water, such as

the changing of 50 seals into HORSES to ransom a prisoner from the high-king DIARMAID MAC CEARRBHEOIL. The horses proved unmanageable to the king's riders and raced to the River Boyne, where they assumed their original form. Bréanainn died at the home of his sister at Eanach Dúin (Annaghdown), and according to his instructions, his body was conveyed to his monastery at Cluain Fhearta (Clonfert) in a small chariot accompanied by one monk only.

Bréanainn's sea voyage to Tír Tairngire is a Christian adaptation of the Celtic otherworld situated in an overseas island (*see* MANANNÁN). Such a voyage to the otherworld was a striking and dramatic theme, and its occurrence in the legend of Bréanainn prompted a scholar in the early ninth century to compose the *Navigatio*. This scholar used some other material also from pre-existing Irish literature, particularly the account of the voyage of MAOL DÚIN. His text begins by having a monk called Barrfhind come to Bréanainn at Clonfert and tell of the marvellous Land of Promise. Following on this, Bréanainn, with fourteen of his monks, built a light wooden boat covered with ox hides and set sail westwards, entrusting their fate to God. After 40 days they reached land, where one of their company died, and then set sail again and reached the Island of Sheep. Later they began to cook their food on another island, which turned out to be in reality a great fish, and they encountered a flock of birds, one of which spoke and gave them directions for their journey. They next reached an island where they were welcomed by a community of monks who had a beautiful church, and continuing on their journey, they came to a marvellously smooth sea.

Having revisited these places, they headed for the open ocean. They encountered huge sea-beasts, and spent some time on various other islands, one of which had three choirs of anchorites and another being luscious with grapes. A gryphon attacked them at sea, but the bird that had already advised them appeared and slew the gryphon, and they then came upon MARVELS such as a crystal-clear sea and a pillar in the ocean that stretched to the sky and that contained a chalice for Bréanainn to celebrate Mass. They reached the Island of Smiths, the inhabitants of which threw burning lumps of clay at them as they sailed by. Bréanainn said that this was hell, and they also had to cope with a great fiery mountain from which demons came to take one of their number. Sailing south, they met with Judas seated on a lonely rock in the ocean enduring punishment for having betrayed JESUS CHRIST.

On a small island they met a hermit called Paul, who was very old and clothed only in his long white beard. Paul explained that he had been educated by St PATRICK, who had directed him to seek that lonely abode, and he had been fed for 30 years there by an otter that caught fish for him. For another 60 years he had been sustained by a marvellous well, and he now gave Bréanainn directions to the Land of Promise. Finally, they came to that island, which was surrounded by mist and lit up by a mighty light. They met a youth there, who explained that God had kept them journeying for seven years so that they would see 'His varied secrets in the great ocean'. Bréanainn and his surviving companions returned home to a warm welcome by his own community.

The text of the *Navigatio* was translated into several languages and had a strong influence on European culture. It was often taken literally, even in terms of actual navigation. At home in Ireland, due to the several dedications to him, the memory of Bréanainn survived in many places. His feast day, 16 May, is celebrated in west Kerry by the climbing of Mount Brandon. *See also* SAINTS.

BIOGRAPHICAL: Kenney (1929), 406–20; Plummer, *1* (1910), 98–151 & *1* (1922), xvi–xxii, 44–95; Stokes (1890), 99–115, 349–54 & (1905), 112–13, 404.

NAVIGATIO: Selmer (1959); O'Meara (1978); Oskamp (1970), 20–38. INFLUENCE OF *NAVIGATIO*: P.E. MacFhinn in *An Síoladóir, 3* (1921), 143–7.

FOLKLORE: Croker (1829), 75–80; M. MacNeill (1962), 682; OSL: Mayo (1838), 202–5; IFC 25:376–7, 124:138–40, 336:253–4, 492:67–119, 628:428, 945:*passim*, 947:*passim*.

Breas A mythical or fictional KING of the otherworld race, TUATHA DÉ DANANN. Breas (earlier, Bres) meant 'brave', and according to the text on the second Battle of Moytirra (*see* MYTHOLOGICAL CYCLE), it was a sobriquet, the character's real name being Eochu Bres.

That text gives a detailed account of Breas' life. We read that a maiden of the Tuatha Dé called Ériu (i.e. Éire, the name of the country) was by the seashore when a stunningly handsome young man came to land in a silver vessel. He wished to make love to her, and she consented. Before departing, he gave her a ring and told her to give it to nobody but the person whose finger it would fit. He also told her that he was Ealatha, king of the FOMHÓIRE, and that she would bear him a son. Thus was Breas conceived. He grew up, and when NUADHU was removed from the kingship because of his blemish, Breas was installed in his place on condition that if he became oppressive he would resign. He soon began to connive with the Fomhóire, however, in their levying of tribute on Ireland. He made virtual slaves of OGHMA and the DAGHDHA, and further outraged the Tuatha Dé by refusing to entertain them as a king should do for his subjects. Finally, a poet of the Tuatha Dé, CAIRBRE MAC ÉADAOINE, satirised him for his stinginess, and 'from that hour there was nothing but blight on Breas'.

The Tuatha Dé demanded his resignation, but agreed to his request to remain in office till the end of seven years. Intending to use this respite to assemble the Fomhóire, he went to his mother and enquired about his paternity. She gave him the ring that Ealatha had left with her, and it fitted his middle finger perfectly. He and she then set out for the domain of the Fomhóire, where they were welcomed, and their dogs and horses outran those of the Fomhóire in friendly racing contests. Breas' father Ealatha recognised him from the ring, but refused him assistance to regain Ireland since he had not ruled justly. He did, however, direct Breas to BALAR and to Inneach mac Dé Domhnann, two other Fomhóire kings. These assembled a mighty host and came with Breas to Ireland, but they were defeated by the Tuatha Dé in the great Battle of Moytirra. Captured after the battle and in order to be given quarter by LUGH, he offered to ensure that the cows would always be in milk and that there would be four harvests every year in Ireland. These conditions were refused by the Tuatha Dé, and then he offered agricultural advice to Lugh – namely that ploughing, sowing and reaping should all be done on a Tuesday. On account of this advice, Breas was released. The end of the text has him back with his father Ealatha in the latter's fortress in the realm of the Fomhóire.

It would be difficult to claim any great antiquity for the character of Breas, as distinct from the theme of the Fomhóire (q.v.). His name seems to be a mere echo from the divine personage EOCHAIDH, borrowed into the Fomhóire context by some early medieval writer and made to suit that context. His birth-story follows a pattern that had some popularity with early medieval storytellers. This pattern is found also in the birth-story of MONGÁN, whose father was said to be the sea-deity MANANNÁN. On the Continent, it was the birth-story of the founder of the Merovingian dynasty. Common to these stories is the paternity by a sea-spirit and, just as the element 'maris' or 'mer' was the reason why the plot was applied to the Merovingians, so also the element 'muir' (i.e. sea) – as popularly applied to the Fomhóire – attracted the plot to Breas.

Another MOTIF borrowed from folklore is that of a father recognising his son through a ring-token left with the child's mother. It is noticeable that the motif does not suit the narrative context in the case of Breas, for there is no need of a recognition scene, but the author was anxious to dramatise his text with whatever material he had to hand. A further borrowing from folklore is the nature of Breas' advice concerning agriculture, for a common superstition held that it was unlucky to begin a new undertaking on Monday (see TIME).

None of the other accounts given of Breas differ substantially from that in the Moytirra text, although there was some confusion regarding his ultimate fate. The first redaction of the pseudo-historical *Lebor Gabála* states that he was slain in the Battle of Moytirra. An alternate tradition is found in other redactions – i.e. that he met his death at the hands of Lugh at Carn Uí Néit (Mizen Head, County Cork). This is a reflection from the lore concerning Balar (q.v.), but in his case Breas was said to have died through treachery. Lugh magically made bog water appear as milk in his eyes, and he was poisoned from drinking it. In the post-medieval text on the Moytirra battle, he is said to have been beheaded by Lugh in single combat in the course of the fighting. Yet another account – given in the text on the 'first' Battle of Moytirra – states that Breas died after taking a drink while hunting on Sliabh Gamh (the Ox Mountains, County Sligo). No accounts of him survived in post-medieval folklore.

Gray (1982), 26–39, 50–1, 66–71, 133–4; Macalister (1941), 118–19, 148–9, 176–7, 228–9; Gwynn (1913), 216–23; J. Frazer in *Ériu*, 8, 58–9; Ó Cuív (1945), 49–50, 73.

FOLKLORE MATERIALS: Kurth (1893), 137, 150–6, 501; Aarne & Thompson (1961), type 873; S. Ó Súilleabháin (1942), 356.

Breasal Bó-Dhíobhadh

Fictional HIGH-KING of Ireland in prehistory. He is described as having been son of the mythical Rudhraighe (*see* ULSTER CYCLE). The name Breasal was common in early Ireland, and it meant 'brave in combat'.

We read that he ruled for eleven years, and that during his reign a great pestilence came on the cattle of Ireland, so that one bull and one heifer alone survived. His epithet *bó-dhíobhadh* means 'lacking in cattle', and on account of its alliteration seems to have been originally associated with a king called Breasal Beoil or Breasal Béalach, who had a prominent place in the early Leinster genealogies. The loss of cattle was not an unusual occurrence in early Irish warfare, and one story in fact told of how this Leinster Breasal resisted payment of the cattle-tribute called *BÓRAIMHE* to the high-king CAIRBRE LIFEACHAIR. The name is found in association with the seeking and taking of cattle in another medieval text also, for we read of one Breasal, son of the sixth-century high-king DIARMAID MAC CEARRBHEOIL, forcibly taking a cow from a nun. The attribution of a name such as Breasal Bó-Dhíobhadh to a fanciful high-king of Ulster stock probably arose from the fame of the great cattle-raid in the ULSTER CYCLE, and the meaning of the epithet was in turn reinterpreted by the writers of pseudo-history.

A fanciful medieval story describes Breasal Bó-Dhíobhadh as calling the men of Ireland to build a great tower for him. His sister came also, and she undertook by magic to make the sun stand still in the heavens to give them light enough to complete the building. Breasal, however, went aside from the crowd and incestuously lay with his sister, as a result of which her magical power was spoiled and the sun moved on. It became dark, and work on the tower was discontinued. By this contrived fiction was explained the name of the tumulus Dubhadh ('darkening' – i.e. Dowth, County Meath).

O'Brien (1962), 120, 271; O'Donovan, *1* (1848), 84–7; M. Dillon in *Ériu, 11,* 43–4; Meyer (1914), 2, 15; Gwynn (1924), 270–2 & (1935), 152; Macalister (1956), 294–5; Dinneen, *2* (1908), 180–1; T.F. O'Rahilly (1946), 268; F.J. Byrne (1973), 137–9, 320; J. Carey in *PHCC, 10,* 27, 32–3.

Brian Bóramha *(AD 926–1014)*

Leader of the DÁL GCAIS sept of County Clare and HIGH-KING of Ireland from AD 1002 until his death. The name Brian had apparently come into general use in his time, being an adaptation of the earlier Brión, probably under the influence of the Breton name Brien. His epithet is pronounced 'Bórú' in modern Irish, it being a variant of the word *BÓRAIMHE.* This meant a cattle-tribute, but it came to be applied to Brian in a roundabout way. In a contemporary poem, he is referred to as 'Brian from Bóramha', by which place was meant Béal Bóramha, on the right bank of the River Shannon just north of Killaloe, County Clare. The place name means 'the port of the cattle-tribute', and it is apparent that he was either born or reared at the large ring fort there. Since Brian himself became in time a great collector of tribute, the term

bóraimhe was soon regarded as applying directly to his own activities.

Brian was the son of the Dál gCais chieftain Cinnéide, and he and his elder brother Mathghamhain waged a persistent war against rival septs, and particularly against the Norse settlers, until Mathghamhain was installed king of Munster in the year 968. Eight years later, Mathghamhain was slain by the rival sept of Ó Donnabháin of Bruree, County Limerick, and Brian became the leader of the Dál gCais. He went from strength to strength, until he compelled the reigning Uí NÉILL high-king, Maoilsheachlainn mac Domhnaill, to abdicate in his favour in the year 1002. Brian had his headquarters at Ceann Cora (the head of the weir, called in English Kincora). This was situated on the high ground of the present town of Killaloe. His power was unchallenged until a crisis that developed in 1014 and which led to the great Battle of Cluain Tairbh (Clontarf, County Dublin), in which he won a decisive victory over the NORSEMEN and their Leinster allies. He was himself slain, however, in the course of the battle.

After the death of Brian, there was over a century of contention between various powerful families for the HIGH-KINGSHIP, and it was during this time that his descendants had a text compiled to assert their leading claim. These descendants were called Uí Bhriain (O'Briens), and their text was entitled *Cogadh Gaedheal re Galloibh* (The War of the Irish with the Foreigners). It described in heroic terms the career of the great Brian.

The text states that, at an early stage, Mathghamhain was daunted by the power of the Norse in Munster and came to terms with them. Brian, however, continued a guerrilla campaign with a small band of men, and eventually persuaded his brother to resume the fight. Their victorious campaign against the Norse is described, culminating in a total victory at Sulchóid (Solohead, County Tipperary) in 968, after which they took Limerick itself. Having described the subsequent events, and how Brian avenged the death of his brother, the text goes on to portray his reign as high-king as a period of unparalleled peace and prosperity in Ireland. We read that during the reign, a lone woman travelled from Tory (Island) in the north of Ireland to Glandore (County Cork) in the south 'carrying a gold ring on a horserod, and she was neither robbed nor molested'. The text further claims that Brian appointed learned men as educators and funded the purchase of books from abroad, and had bridges, causeways and roads constructed. He is also described as a great patron of religion, a reflection of the historical fact that Brian made a celebrated visit to Armagh soon after he gained the high-kingship, proclaiming that bishopric supreme in the Irish church and assigning to himself the title 'Emperor of the Irish'.

Brian's victory at Clontarf on Good Friday of the year 1014 is one of the great historical moments in the memory of the Irish. Although the Norse settlements around major seaports were not unduly affected by the Irish victory, it signalled an end to their raiding and expansion. Therefore the Battle of Clontarf was traditionally taken to mark the final overthrow of Viking power in Ireland, and conventional accounts of it were based entirely on the *Cogadh* text. There we are told that on the night before the battle, the otherworld lady AOIBHEALL appeared to Brian and told him that he would be killed next day. This proved true. As the tide of battle turned against the Norsemen, a fleeing Danish warrior called Brodir saw Brian praying in his tent and thought at first that he was a priest. Discovering who he in fact was, Brodir attacked him, and the elderly Brian defended himself stoutly. With a sword stroke he severed Brodir's left leg at the knee and right leg at the foot, but the dying Dane smashed Brian's head to pieces with his axe. This may be inaccurate, and a varying account is given by a Norse writer in the *Brennu-Njals Saga*. This Norse saga was written in the thirteenth century, but the account of the Battle of Clontarf given in it is believed to be based on a lost twelfth-century text. That account tells of Brodir deliberately seeking out the king's tent during the battle, bursting through the bodyguards, and slaying Brian before being himself captured and put to death. The fact that the Norse author was himself a Christian and very favourable to Brian adds some weight to his testimony.

All the later Irish literary accounts make use of the material in the *Cogadh* text, and it is not surprising that most of the stories concerning Brian in folklore are in one way or another derived from that source also. In these stories, the courage and decisiveness of Brian is extolled, and one story common in Munster lore gives a scenario that is obviously derived from the capture of Limerick. We are told that he went secretly to examine the structure of a great Norse fortress, and decided that it could only be taken if the gates were opened to him. Riding by a hut, he saw a woman lamenting there, and was told by her that she was married to a Dane and that, since no food was available, her husband had ordered her to cook their baby for a meal. Brian took pity on her and gave food to her, and in the conversation he discovered what the password to the fortress was. On the following night Brian and a band of men gained access to the fortress by using this pass, and they fell upon the sleeping Vikings and slew them.

A more widespread story tells of how the Norsemen were so oppressive that they quartered a soldier in every house in Ireland – a detail sprung from the *Cogadh* text – but Brian sent word around secretly that every household was to kill their unwelcome guest on a certain night. At the appointed time this plan was put into operation, each household lighting a sheaf of straw as a signal to their neighbours that the deed was done and encouraging them to do likewise. Hearing of what had befallen their kinsmen in Ireland, the Norsemen abroad gathered a great force and invaded Ireland, thus leading to the Battle of Clontarf. This is a curious tradition, and it must be an echo of the slaughter of the Danes in England at St Brice's feast by King Ethelred in the year 1002. This episode was described in various Saxon and Norman chronicles, and probably entered Irish lore from some such source, becoming connected with Brian because he was considered by tradition the great archetypal opponent of the Norse.

The *Cogadh* text itself is hardly more accurate in the reason it cites for the great battle. After the death of his wife – the daughter of a Connacht king – in 1009, Brian had married Gormlaith, sister of the Leinster king Maolmhórdha. When Maolmhórdha was visiting Kincora, he asked his sister to repair a button on a fine silk tunic that had been presented to him by Brian, but she flung the tunic into the fire and reproached him for being Brian's vassal. This caused Maolmhórdha to ponder on all his past quarrels with Brian, and in this strained frame of mind went to observe a game of chess between Brian's son MURCHADH and a relative. Maolmhórdha's prompting caused Murchadh to lose the game, and the latter taunted the Leinster king with having earlier been an adviser to the Norsemen when they lost against Brian. In high dudgeon, Maolmhórdha said that he would go to advise them again, and began to foment the renewed Norse activity that led to the battle. A Galway folk LEGEND has Brian rather undecided as to whether he should wage total war on the Norsemen, but he is advised by a SAINT to go to a certain well on Ard-Oileán (high island) off the coast. He does this, and notices the water of the well turn red, which he takes as a sign that he will triumph. This attractive little legend is in fact based on the name of that well, Tobar Bó Rua (well of the red cow) being misunderstood as 'Tobar Bóramha', which would be pronounced similarly.

Late literary tradition makes much of Brian's reputed poet and adviser, the miniature Muircheartach mac Liag. There probably was a poet known as Mac Liag, but the verses on Brian and his court attributed to him are of much later date than the tenth-eleventh century. A story in one late text has Mac Liag returning to Kincora after a poetic trip around Munster. He tells Brian of how he has been very well received and loaded with presents by CIAN MAC MAOLMHUAIDHE and how another chieftain, Domhnall mac Dubhdhábhoireann, has given him but a belt and a piece of flint. Much to Brian's surprise, the poet values Domhnall's generosity the more, and Mac Liag explains that this was because Domhnall was the poorer of the two. Late folklore describes how Brian's affairs at Kincora were looked after for him in his absence by a dwarf counsellor, who is probably an echo of the Mac Liag personage.

There is much folk speculation at Killaloe and its surroundings concerning the layout of Brian's headquarters – the roads, bridges, courtyards, stables, fields, wine cellars and such. A fanciful legend, in contradiction of history, tells of how a daughter of Brian was betrothed to a young king of Leinster. The latter came to collect his bride, but the girl's mother was displeased with the arrangement and sent soldiers to attack and slay the Leinsterman at the hill of Thountinna, overlooking the east bank of the Shannon. When he discovered what had been done, Brian was very sad, and ordered that the slain king be entombed under a heap of rocks on the hilltop from where he could always have a view of his native Leinster. The queen in that story is an echo of Gormlaith, Brian's formidable queen. She had an eventful life, having been married three times – to the Norse king of Dublin, to the high-king Maoilsheachlainn and to Brian. The traditional historians thus alluded to her ambitious use of matrimony as 'three leaps' to kingship.

Folklore contains some stray traditions about Brian that are nevertheless significant when taken in their broad context. A Cork account, for instance, claims that when a cow lies down in a field she sighs for the good life in the time of Brian, a notion that directly parallels northern lore of CORMAC MAC AIRT. A Kildare source claims that plover were first introduced into Ireland by Brian because of the wariness of these birds, and that the great king trained them to give the alarm if any enemy approached his camp. A Limerick tradition was that Brian had placed a massive chain across the River Shannon from Cratloe to

Carrig so that the Vikings could not bring a fleet into the country at that point.

The descendants of Brian, who were dominant in Munster for many generations, bore the surname Ó Briain (anglicised O'Brien). Some offshoots of the O'Brien family took further surnames, such as Mac Mathúna (MacMahon of Munster), Ó Consaidín (Considine), Mac Giolla Iasachta (MacLysaght) and Mac Briain (MacBrien).

NAME: K. Meyer in *Ériu*, *4*, 68–73.

COGADH: Todd (1867).

BRENNU-NJÁLS SAGA: Magnusson & Pálsson (1960), 341–52.

LATER TEXTS: R.I. Best in *Ériu*, *1*, 74–112; E. Mac Néill in *Irisleabhar na Gaedhilge*, *7*, 8–11, 41–4, 55–7; Goedheer (1938).

ETHELRED: Garmonsway (1972), 133–5; Ashdown (1930), 46–7, 97.

FOLKLORE: Chatterton, *2* (1839), 108; *JKAS*, *3*, 185; Westropp (1914), 26–32 & in *Folk-Lore*, *24*, 365–9, 505; Gregory (1926), 35; *Irisleabhar na Gaedhilge*, *5*, 111; *Béaloideas*, *8*, 109; Ó hÓgáin (1985), 69–77, 328–9; IFC 41:332–5, 237:271–2, 323:251–2, S376:218–19, S538: 71–2; S631:224–6.

MAC LIAG: C. Ó Lochlainn in *Éigse*, *4*, 34–43; R.I. Best in *Ériu*, *1*, 94–102.

GORMLAITH: W.A. Trindade in *Études Celtiques*, *23*, 150–1.

GENERAL: Ó Ceallaigh (1908); Westropp (1914); Dinneen, *3* (1908), 223–77; Macalister (1956), 402–5; Kierse (1983).

Bricriu *(later, Bricne)* Mythical character in the ULSTER CYCLE, a troublemaker who is described as 'poisonous' and 'evil-tongued'. He is stated to have been son of a certain Carbad (literally, 'chariot'), which indicates that his characterisation was somewhat improvised.

A little lake in the west of County Down is called Loch Bricreann (Loughbrickland) – this means 'the lake of Bricriu', from which one can gather that Bricriu was the name of some ancient landholder in that area. The name, based on the adjective *breac* (speckled), meant 'little spotted fellow'. Some fanciful early writer decided to portray this character as a satirist, which image was suggested by the use of *breac* in early Irish sources to describe a type of satiric poetry – mixed praise and vituperation (*see* POETS). Although little verse is attributed to him, it seems that Bricriu, like the other satirist AITHIRNE, was envisaged as a poet. This would account for why his speech was always taken seriously and why his provocation never brought retaliation

on him. He was portrayed as a courtier of CONCHOBHAR MAC NEASA, mythical KING in the Ulster Cycle, towards whom, as towards others, he combined friendship with malice. We are told that he could not refrain from encouraging strife, for 'if he made a secret of anything which was in his mind a purple boil would grow on his forehead as large as a man's fist, and he used to say to Conchobhar, "It will burst from the boil tonight, o Conchobhar!"'

He was particularly effective at causing dissension at drinking feasts, when the warriors were drunk and thus open to flattery and prone to competition. In the text on the dispute between the poets FEIRCHEIRDNE and NÉIDHE MAC ADHNA, the blame for the dispute is placed on Bricriu. He encouraged the young Néidhe to sit in the chair of the chief poet by falsely stating that Feircheirdne was dead, and then went to Feircheirdne to inform him of Néidhe's ambition. Similarly, at the feast given by Mac Da Thó (*see* CONALL CEARNACH), Bricriu did his best to promote strife between the warriors of Ulster and of Connacht, who were ominously seated together. He proposed that the pig be divided by combat, adding 'you have all flattened each other's noses before!'.

The principal story concerning his mischief-making is *Fled Bricrend* (the Feast of Bricriu), which was composed around the eighth century and survives in an eleventh-century inflation. It describes how he had a special mansion built for a great feast to which he invited Conchobhar and the Ulster nobles. They were reluctant to go, knowing that he would incite them against each other, but Bricriu threatened a worse fate if they refused. He said that he would cause them all to kill each other, would set son against father, and would even set the two breasts of every Ulsterwoman beating against each other until they were destroyed. The Ulstermen therefore agreed to go to the feast. Bricriu, meanwhile, spoke privately to three great warriors – LAOGHAIRE BUACH, CONALL CEARNACH and CÚ CHULAINN – and promised each separately that he would give him the champion's portion of the food and drink at the feast. Accordingly, when the guests arrived, these three warriors began to argue and came to blows. They were separated at the request of Seancha, Conchobhar's peace maker, who directed that the champion's portion be divided among them until it be decided which of them was the greatest. Bricriu had in the meantime sought to make matters worse by talking to the wives of the three warriors and saying to each of these that they should be first to enter the mansion. Hungry for precedence, the women raced each other and arrived outside the mansion with a great tumult. The doors were closed, but Cú Chulainn by his strength lifted a side of the mansion so that his wife Eimhear could enter.

Next day, Conchobhar advised them to go to CÚ ROÍ, and that he would decide between them. On the way, they met a giant, who overcame both Laoghaire and Conall but was overcome by Cú Chulainn. They returned to the Ulster court at Eamhain Mhacha, but once there, the other two claimed that tricks had been played on them. They then set out for the court of queen MEADHBH in Connacht, where they faced an ordeal with three savage CATS from the cave of Cruachain, and again Cú Chulainn alone triumphed. He further proved best at armed combat and horse racing. Meadhbh privately gave a present to each of the three – a goblet of bronze to Laoghaire, a goblet of white gold to Conall, and a goblet of red gold to Cú Chulainn. On their return to Ulster, however, the other two claimed that Cú Chulainn had bribed Meadhbh, so they were again sent to Cú Roí in Munster. There a phantom overcame Laoghaire and Conall when they were put on night-watch at Cú Roí's fortress, but Cú Chulainn again prevailed. Cú Roí, who apparently was himself the phantom, awarded the honours to Cú Chulainn, but the verdict was once more disputed on their return home, and Cú Chulainn decided to forego his claim in the interests of peace.

Soon after, a monstrously ugly churl dressed in a grey cloak arrived at Eamhain Mhacha. The churl said that he had searched many foreign parts for a warrior the match of himself, but had so far failed. The test he proposed was that a warrior be allowed to decapitate him and that he be allowed to decapitate that warrior on the following night. Muinreamhar (Fat Neck) was the first to accept the challenge. He cut the churl's head off, and the churl picked it up and went out. Next night, however, Muinreamhar absented himself, thus avoiding his side of the bargain. Similarly, Laoghaire and Conall decapitated the churl, but did not come to fulfil the second condition. Only Cú Chulainn was willing to lay his own neck on the block. The churl raised his axe but brought down its back rather than its blade. He then told Cú Chulainn to arise, for the champion's portion was undoubtedly due to him only. The churl was Cú Roí, who had come in disguise to ensure that his judgement was upheld.

Curiously, Bricriu does not figure at all in the second part of this story, and it has been suggested that two separate narratives were combined. It is more likely, however, that the inventor of the story took a rather liberal attitude to his material, starting from a typically mischievous situation engineered by Bricriu and going on to adapt the beheading game from floating medieval lore. It is significant that the order of events contradicts that in *Táin Bó Cuailnge* (*see* ULSTER CYCLE), where Meadhbh sees Cú Chulainn for the first time during the campaign, and Bricriu is killed at the end of the campaign.

Within his loose terms of reference, the writer of *Fled Bricrend* did nevertheless achieve some unity of plot, and the way in which Bricriu's mischief actually works to the benefit of Cú Chulainn is not discordant with tradition. In the accounts of the birth of Cú Chulainn (q.v.), he is one of the Ulstermen who first discover the otherworld house in which that hero's mother resides, and thus could be regarded as in some sense a patron of the hero. In the *Táin* and other stories, he stings Cú Chulainn into greater efforts in battle when such are required. Cú Chulainn accordingly improves his performance, though he resents such comments. In one eleventh-century text, the hero is trying to slip into a feast when Bricriu announces his entry and calls for him to be attacked and killed. Cú Chulainn angrily threatens, 'I will give you a strong blow, o stupid Bricriu of the bitter words, which will quickly afflict you if you do not control your bad tongue!' In a later medieval text – the quest for the sons of Daol Dearmaid – incitement by Bricriu at another of his feasts is the cause of great trouble for Cú Chulainn (q.v.), culminating in a very difficult task that he must perform overseas.

Bricriu's more usual custom is to provoke trouble by suggestions and remarks made at the most sensitive times. 'I give my word,' he is quoted as saying, 'that a whisper is more valuable to me than a roar to another person!' Thus in an account of why FEARGHUS MAC RÓICH left Ulster, it was Bricriu who destroyed the truce between Conchobhar and Fearghus by reminding the latter of how he had been wronged. Then he advised Fearghus to go to the court of Meadhbh, and himself went to Connacht to fuel Meadhbh's ambitions. However, he could not refrain from sarcastically foretelling failure for Meadhbh's son MAINE when that prince went to Ulster to court the maiden Feirbh. While at Meadhbh's court, he schemed to bring about Fearghus' raid on the king of the Gamhanra, as told in the story of the lady FLIODHAIS. Fearghus, however, was so stung by one of Bricriu's insults at Cruachain that he once flung a chess piece at him and fractured his skull, as a result of which the satirist spent a long time convalescing. When the two bulls were fighting fiercely at the end of the *Táin*, Bricriu came with the rest of Meadhbh's forces to watch them. In their violent struggle, the bulls trampled on Bricriu and killed him. *See also* CONGHAL CLÁIRINGNEACH.

BOIL: W. Stokes in *Ériu*, *4*, 32–3.

BRICRIU AND FEIRCHEIRDNE: W. Stokes in *RC*, *26*, 12–13.

FLED BRICREND: Henderson (1899); S. Thompson (1955–58), motif P632.2.

BRICRIU AND CÚ CHULAINN: C. O'Rahilly (1976), 61; J.C. Watson (1941), 13–14, 39–40; W. Stokes in *RC*, *14*, 424–71; E. Windisch in *Irische Texte*, *2 (2)*, 173–4.

WHISPER: J.C. Watson (1941), 12–13, 39.

BRICRIU AND FEARGHUS: D. MacKinnon in *Celtic Review*, *1–4*, passim; Windisch in *Irische Texte*, *2 (2)*, 211, 214; K. Meyer in *RC*, *10*, 227; C. O'Rahilly (1976), 124.

MAINE: Windisch in *Irische Texte*, *3*, 445–556.

DEATH: C. O'Rahilly (1976), 124.

GENERAL: Ó Cadhlaigh (1956), 467; M.A. O'Brien in Dillon (1968), 67–78.

Brighid Mythical lady of the TUATHA DÉ DANANN, originally a Celtic GODDESS. Her name (earlier, Brigit) meant literally 'the exalted one'.

Similar designations for places and tribes in Britain and on the Continent seem to have referred to highlands and highlanders. There is evidence that this caused the mother-goddess to be worshipped by Celtic inhabitants of such areas under the pseudonym Briginti or Briganti. The most notable instance is that of the tribe called Brigantes, who controlled the whole area of central Britain dominated by the Pennine Hills. This tribe had the eponymous Briganti as their principal goddess, and offshoots of them settled in south-eastern Ireland in or about the first century AD (*see* LAIGHIN). It was probably through such settlements that the cult of this goddess came to Ireland, Brigit being the Irish adaptation of the name. Interestingly, the goddess is also called Brigh in Irish sources, and this corresponds with a Continental variant of her name, Briga.

Briginti may indeed have been the Gaulish and British goddess whom Caesar equated with the Roman patroness of arts and crafts, Minerva. In line with this, a ninth-century Irish glossary describes Brighid as a POETESS and daughter of the DAGHDHA. She was 'a goddess whom poets adored because her protection was very great and very famous'. She had, the glossarian states, two sisters, both also called Brighid – a factor that exemplifies the Celtic tendencies to triplicate deities.

There are several indications that Brighid had agricultural fertility as her function besides the inspiring of poetry. The medieval compendium of Irish myth and pseudo-history, the *Lebor Gabála*, in listing Brighid among the Tuatha Dé Danann (q.v.), again refers to her as 'Brighid the poetess, daughter of the Daghdha', and states that she had two oxen. One of these was called Fea and the other Feimhean, and from them were named Magh Fea (the plain of the Barrow in County Carlow) and Magh Feimhin (the plain in south-east County Tipperary). Along with these oxen was 'Triath, king of the swine, from whom is named Treithirne'. Treithirne was the name of a plain in west County Tipperary, and the mythical boar in question was more usually called the Torc Triath. It is further stated in the *Lebor Gabála* that these three animals used to cry out after rapine had been committed in Ireland, and all of this suggests that Brighid was a sort of guardian-goddess of domestic animals. This suggestion is strengthened by the cult of St BRIGHID, who is in folk culture the patroness of farm animals and whose feast day is the first day of spring. It was once known as *Oímelg*, meaning 'lactation', a word that the scribes sometimes confused with *imbolg* (parturition). This was a direct reference to the birth of young animals in the spring. It is highly likely that the festival was originally connected with the goddess, much of whose imagery was subsumed in that of the SAINT.

The medieval writers, in trying to normalise the connections between various characters of the Tuatha Dé, made Brighid (in the form of 'Brigh') the wife of BREAS and gave her a son called Ruadhán. In the statement that she was mother of the 'three gods of Danu', these writers seem, however, to have been reflecting early tradition. DANU, the mother of the gods, was otherwise claimed as the mother of these three, and the statement thus echoes the original role of Brighid as an aspect of the mother-goddess. This type of portrayal is repeated in an account that claims that Brigh was the first to lament the dead with weeping and shrieking. She did this when her son Ruadhán was slain in a treacherous attempt on the life of GOIBHNIU. It may even be that the term *brigit* came into common usage as an epithet for 'exalted' goddesses, for the ninth-century glossarian writes that 'among all the Irish a goddess used to be called Brigit'.

The fact that many hills in Ireland were called Brigh or Brí is probably due to the same simple way of describing them as being high, as was the case with places called Briga in Celtic areas abroad. The cult of the actual goddess, however, seems to be reflected in the name Brighid given to some Irish rivers, just as some rivers were anciently called by names such as Briga and Briginti in Britain and on the Continent.

CELTIC GODDESS: Holder, *1* (1896), 533–43; Binchy (1970), 12–14; Mac Cana (1970), 34–5; A. Ross (1974), 452–6, 514; Green (1995), 36, 196–7; Olmsted (1994), 358–60.

IN IRELAND: Meyer (1912), 15; Macalister (1941), 132–3, 158–9, 196–7; Gray (1982), 56–7, 119; W. Stokes in *RC, 16*, 150–3; E. Hogan (1910), 127–8.

Brighid (c.*AD 439*–c.*524*) Leinster SAINT who founded a celebrated convent at Cill Dara (Kildare). Her name in early form was Brigit. In modern Irish orthography it is spelt Bríd, and in anglicised form appears as Bridget and Bride.

The earliest surviving reference to her dates from around the year 600. It occurs in an origin story of the Fotharta sept, and in it she is stated to have been of that sept, is called 'truly pious Brig-eoit', and is described as 'another Mary'. All sources agree that she was of the Fotharta, and to this day a favourite designation for her is 'the Mary of the Irish'. The early development of her cult was closely connected with the rise to power in Leinster of a new sept, the Uí Dhúnlainge. The sept's leader, Faolán mac Colmáin, seized the KINGSHIP of the province around the year 633. He was married to a woman of the Fotharta, and his brother was bishop of Kildare. It was therefore of great benefit to this new king to stress the importance of Brighid. At the request of the Kildare Church, a Latin biography of the saint, *Vita Brigitae*, was compiled in or about the year 650 by a cleric called Toimtenach, who used the pen name Cogitosus. A striking feature of this work is the lack of real information on the historical Brighid, who had lived in the previous century. It can be inferred from this that very little personal memories survived of the holy woman of the Fotharta who had founded the convent.

Cogitosus' text is basically a compendium of miracles, and the most valuable part of it is the description of Kildare as an ecclesiastical centre.

Cill Dara means 'the church of the oak-tree', and the presence of such a tree (*see* DRUIDS) at the site suggests that it might have been regarded as a sacred place in pre-Christian times. The feast day of the saint, 1 February, is the beginning of spring and was anciently known as Oímelg (literally, 'lactation'). Cogitosus stated that it was the date of the saint's death, but it is safe to assume that this was a mere rationalisation of the cultic date. In Irish Christian tradition, St Brighid has always been regarded as the special patroness of farm animals and crops, and these are precisely the functions that one would expect of a pre-Christian divinity of spring. It is significant that the saint shares her name with the Celtic goddess BRIGHID, who in Ireland was honoured for her 'protecting care'. It is therefore probable that a pagan sanctuary at Kildare was Christianised by a holy woman of the Fotharta. This would have meant that the cult of that sanctuary became attached to her, including the GODDESS-name Brighid, which may have been a title borne by the chief druidess there.

The synthesis of paganism and Christianity under the name of Brighid was easily achieved, and Cogitosus' own text betrays this in the nature of some of the miracles. Like a protecting goddess, the saint is portrayed as having the power to multiply such things as butter, bacon and milk, to bestow SHEEP and CATTLE, and to control the WEATHER. Celtic goddesses were frequently associated with fire, light and thermal waters, and it is noteworthy that such images are also instanced by Cogitosus. The Christian ethos of the text should not, however, be underestimated, for the basic theme running through it is Brighid's great charity due to her faith in God, and her sympathy for all His creatures. Moreover, the style in several places echoes phrases from the Bible and other early Christian literature. For instance, St Brighid changes water into ale, gives sight to a blind man, and renders fierce animals tame.

Some of the LEGENDS are localised variants of widespread MOTIFS, such as the account of a maiden who has a silver brooch given into her charge by a cunning and lustful man, who secretly steals it and casts it into the sea. He then demands either the brooch or that she become his sexual slave, but she sought the advice of the saint. As they were speaking, a man came with a fish for Brighid, and on opening the fish the brooch was discovered inside. The motif of a ring or coin miraculously recovered from a fish's stomach occurs in several early Christian sources (including Matthew's Gospel 17:27), but the overall plot here is an Irish development. Variants of it are found in the story of FRAOCH and in the British biography of St Kentigern.

Another legend given by Cogitosus is of a pattern familiar in Irish hagiography: a miraculous trick played by the saint on an overbearing king. In Brighid's case, we read that the king (presumably a Leinster monarch of an earlier dynasty than the Uí Dhúnlainge) had a pet fox that performed many kinds of tricks, and an unfortunate man killed it, thinking it to be wild. The man was seized and sentenced to death, and the angry king told him that this would be his fate unless he could produce a fox of equal intelligence and skill. A wild fox came to Brighid, sheltering under her cloak, and she produced it at the royal court, where it equalled the skill of the dead fox in every regard. The man was accordingly released, and soon after, the fox escaped from the court and returned to its wild state.

A direct borrowing of a motif from apocryphal lore of the child JESUS in Continental literature is instanced by Brighid hanging her clothes on a sunbeam. Cogitosus states that she was dazzled by light and mistook it for a tree, and that the clothes stood there.

The theme of light and fire is especially stressed in ninth-century biographies of Brighid in Irish and Latin texts that are based on sources somewhat older than themselves. Here we are told that the house in which she slept seemed to onlookers to be on fire, a detail coinciding with a twelfth-century claim that a perpetual fire had been kept burning in the convent of Kildare. Although these motifs are borrowed from Continental sources, their application to Brighid is probably a reflection of older native tradition of the goddess. Cogitosus had stated that Brighid's father was called Dubhthach and her mother Broicseach, and that she had spent her youth at agricultural labour for them, such as churning butter, tending the harvest, and shepherding the flocks. The ninth-century biographies show the same awareness of her agricultural functions, but they differ from Cogitosus in stating that Brighid's mother Broicseach was the slave of Dubhthach and that he sold her to a druid. The druid therefore had care of Brighid as a child, but later he sent her back to her father.

Such a lowly background for the saint could well reflect the original tradition, and an acquaintance with druidry would have been important to a person who undertook the task of Christianising a pagan sanctuary. These biographies also reflect imagery in keeping with druidic practice, such as the mystical production of milk and the feeding of the child Brighid on the milk of a special white red-eared cow (*see* CORC DUIBHNE). Much of this is, however, rationalised in the context of Christian morality – Brighid being described as continually giving butter and even cows to the poor and the needy. In one touching scene, she does the servile work in place of her poor mother who has an eye disease, and she works so eagerly and well that the druid decides to set Broicseach free and himself accepts baptism.

Additional healings of the sick and injured are included in these biographies, but the most striking departure from Cogitosus is the bringing of Brighid into contact with saints of other paruchiae, such as Mel and BRÉANAINN, and especially with PATRICK himself. The latter case reflects the success of the Kildare Church in gaining recognition as the principal see of Leinster from the Church of Armagh. We read that she met Patrick at Tailtiu

(Teltown, County Meath) and solved for him a problem affecting his retinue. A woman claimed that Patrick's assistant Bron was the father of her child, but Brighid caused the tongue of the woman to swell when she repeated the lie. Those present wished to burn the woman for her perjury, but Brighid did not allow them to do that and instead told the woman to do penance. A variant telling has the child itself speaking in Latin to Brighid and telling who the real father was. This story makes Patrick somewhat dependent on Brighid, and the circumstance is repeated when Brighid persuades a pagan man to accept baptism from Bron. Patrick's preeminence, however, is accepted when he instructs Brighid to bring a priest about with her always as her charioteer, so that converts can be baptised by the priest without delay.

The later medieval biographies increase her itinerary to cover areas of the country far from Leinster, and in this they doubtlessly reflect the spreading influence of her cult. They also add some material to the original portrayals, some of it cultural elements surfacing in the literature for the first time. For instance, an account in Irish from around the eighth century gives the druid's name as Maithghean, and states that he knew from the noise of a chariot in which Broicseach was being conveyed that she had a marvellous child in her womb. The account also gives the striking detail that Brighid was born as her mother brought milk into the druid's house at sunrise – the mother had one foot outside the threshold and the other foot 'neither without nor within'. The mystery and paradox involved here, and the redolence of ancient beliefs concerning sacred kingship and sacred POETS, seem to be more vestiges of druidic lore.

Narratives of Brighid were developed through medieval times by further additions from Continental hagiography. A ninth-century text has a man coming to woo the young, and as yet unprofessed, Brighid. Her stepbrothers try to compel her to accept the marriage, but she knocks out one of her eyes so as not to be attractive to the suitor. When the family allow her to remain a virgin, she miraculously restores sight to herself. The story is repeated in later sources, and it survived in the recent folklore of north Leinster and south Ulster. The name of the suitor, Dubhthach mac Lughair, is borrowed from the early Patrician texts, and it is obvious that the story cannot be older than the eighth century. Its plot was, in fact, taken from the lore of the Continental saint Lucy, and was suggested by the symbolism of light associated with both of these holy virgins.

It is apparent that the cult of Lucy influenced that of Brighid in other ways in medieval times. Lucy's feast day, 13 December, coincided with the winter solstice in the old calendar and was thus seen to usher in the lengthening of daylight. In Irish, the saying that refers to Brighid's feast day, 1 February, is that 'from Brighid's feast day onwards the day gets longer and the night shorter', although in fact that change occurs from the winter solstice – the presumption must therefore be that this saying was in origin a rather inaccurate borrowing from the Lucy lore. It could well be, also, that some of the paraphernalia associated with the feast of Brighid in Irish folk life – such as processions of young girls with the leader dressed up as the saint – shows the influence of the Lucy cult, which was very popular in western European countries in the Middle Ages.

A very curious little folk legend, which was known throughout Ireland, illustrates the close connection made between Brighid, 'the Mary of the Irish', and the Virgin Mary. A quite anachronistic tradition, it seems to have been invented for the purpose that it itself expressly states – namely, to explain why Brighid's feast day comes immediately before that of Mary, on 2 February – a date shared with Candlemas. We are told that when Mary and the child JESUS were fleeing into Egypt, they found the road blocked by a party of soldiers, and Mary did not know what to do. Just then Brighid came on the scene and offered to deflect the attention of the soldiers from the fugitives. She did this by donning a garish headdress with lighted candles attached to her hair, and the soldiers were so intrigued by this that they did not notice Mary and Jesus slip by. In thanks for this assistance, Mary told Brighid that henceforth the feast of the Irish saint would come one day before her own.

The best known of all the folk legends of Brighid purports to explain how she obtained the land for her convent at Kildare. We are told that the local chieftain refused to give her any more ground than the amount her cloak would cover. At that, she took off her cloak and laid it on the ground, and it began to miraculously spread. It spread so much and encompassed such a wide area that the dumbfounded chieftain begged her to stop it before he had lost all his territory. She did so, and the area covered by the cloak, we are told, became the site for her foundation. Some variants of the legend have an aetiological dimension, explaining that the ground was levelled by the cloak and thus includes the great flat plain known as the Curragh of Kildare. This folk legend dates to the late Middle Ages and is, in fact, an Irish version of a well-known FOLKTALE. This (see HUMOROUS TALES, type 2400) has a trickster gaining as much land as an ox hide can enclose by cutting the hide into thin strips and encircling a large area with these strips. A noted literary version of this motif was told by Virgil (*Aeneidos* 1. 367–8) concerning Dido, foundress of Carthage, and it may well be that the Irish version concerning Brighid was devised by a medieval clergyman who knew that. In his or in other hands, the rather unethical act of the international folktale was transformed and given the moral force of a miracle.

It is clear that the Fotharta sept, branches of which were scattered throughout Leinster, played a large part in the dissemination of the Brighid lore in early times, and apart from Kildare, her cult is strongly localised at Fothairt (Faughart, County Louth) – a place deriving its name from the sept. The traditional belief is that the saint was born there. It was, however, undoubtedly ecclesiastical sources that in the Middle Ages caused the spread of the lore of St Brighid throughout Ireland and even to Wales and Scotland. This is still evidenced by the widespread occurrence of her name in toponymics, but – at least in the post-medieval era – lore of her has depended less on local dedications than on the high profile of her feast day in the traditional calendar (*see* TIME). Until recent generations, this day, 1 February, was marked by a great variety of folk custom and belief, particularly in association with agricultural matters. It is probable that aspects of these traditions stretch back to the pre-Christian lore of the Celtic goddess Brighid, and it is even possible that they derive from pre-Celtic lore predating that goddess herself.

Foremost among the customs was that of the *Cros Bhríde* (Brighid's Cross), a small cross woven from rushes or straw and placed under the rafters of the dwelling-house so as to ensure health and good fortune for the ensuing year. Sometimes such a cross was put in the cow byre to protect the livestock. The most common kind of cross throughout the country was lozenge-shaped, with the rushes or straw wound around sticks, and with up to five such cross-lozenges formed into the shape of a larger cross. Also common were crosses with unaligned arms and ones with interwoven patterns. A cross within a circle was a variant found only in Munster, and in Ulster a simple three-legged type was sometimes used for cow byres.

Equally prevalent was the custom of leaving a piece of cloth outdoors from sunset to sunrise on the eve of the feast in the belief that the saint would touch it overnight and thus confer on it protective and curative properties. This was known as the *brat Bhríde* (Brighid's mantle) and was kept in the home for the following year. It was believed to be efficacious in healing sick animals, and if placed on the head of a calf or foal would ensure that the young animal's mother would suckle it. In County Galway, a belt decorated with little crosses was woven from hay or straw ropes, and both people and CATTLE were passed through it in order to secure the protection of the saint. A more general practice was to include the residue from the making of Brighid's Crosses in new spancels for the cows, so as to protect them during the ensuing year.

In most of the country, it was customary on the eve of the feast day for groups of people, particularly young girls, to go in disguise from house to house, singing and dancing, and to collect either eggs or money from the householders. The leader of the group was usually a girl dressed as the saint and carrying a home-made doll, called a *brídeog* (little Bríd) or in English a 'biddy'.

For late folklore connecting Brighid with a mythical Leinster king, *see* LABHRAIDH.

EARLIEST REFERENCE: O'Brien (1962), 80–1; Ó hAodha (1978), 42.

FAOLÁN: F.J. Byrne (1973), 131–56.

COGITOSUS: F. Ó Briain in *ZCP*, *36*, 112–37.

COGITOSUS' TEXT: Bollandus & Henschenius (1863), 1 February, 135–41; S. Connolly in *JRSAI*, *117*, 5–27.

BROOCH AND FISH: Aarne & Thompson (1961), types 736A, 930D (*see* WONDER TALES). See also Brewer (1901), 142–4; Plummer, *1* (1910), clxxxv; D. Ó hÓgáin in *Béaloideas*, *60–1*, 64.

CLOAK ON SUNBEAM: *See* R. Wildhaber in Carlen & Steinegger, *2* (1974), 228–37; Plummer, *1* (1910), cxxxix; Aarne & Thompson (1961), type 759B.

OTHER BIOGRAPHIES: Ó hAodha (1978); Bollandus & Henschenius (1863), 118–34, 141–55; P. Grosjean in *Irish Texts*, *1*, 2–21; Stokes (1890), 34–53, 318–36; Heist (1965), 1–37.

OTHER EARLY MATERIAL: Stokes & Strachan, *2* (1903), 327–49; R. Thurneysen in *Irische Texte*, *3*, 71; Meyer, *HB* (1912).

DATING AND FEAST DAY: D. McCarthy in *Peritia*, *14*, 255–80.

POSSIBLE ANTIQUITY OF LORE: Ó Catháin (1995).

FOLK CUSTOMS AND BELIEFS: Danaher (1972), 13–37; S.C. Ó Súilleabháin (1977) & in Gailey & Ó hÓgáin (1982), 242–53; Ó Duinn (2002).

FOLKLORE STORIES: Ó hÓgáin (1985), 16–26, 323–4; M. Ó Briain in *Béaloideas*, *53*, 52–7; IFC, much material. See also types 782, 2400 in Aarne & Thompson (1961) & in S. Ó Súilleabháin & Christiansen (1968).

GENERAL: Kenney (1929), 356–64, 801; E.G. Bowen in *Studia Celtica*, *8–9*, 33–47; O'Hanlon, *2* (1875), 1–224.

Butler, Margaret *Countess of Ormond* (c. *1466*–c. *1539*) Wife of Piaras Rua Butler, eighth Earl of Ormond, and a celebrated woman of her time. She was daughter of Gerald FitzGerald, the great Earl of Kildare known popularly as Gearóid Mór. Her marriage to Piaras in 1485 was an attempt to form a bond between the two great rival NORMAN families, the Geraldines and Butlers, but this did not have the desired result, and Margaret witnessed the destruction of her nearest relatives by the English authorities, aided by her husband.

Before he became Earl of Ormond, Piaras Rua had to contend with a cousin for the position, but he was staunchly supported by the Kildare Geraldines. For some years, he led a very difficult life and, according to near-contemporary accounts, 'was forced to hover and lurk in woods and forests'. He was accompanied by Margaret in these miserable circumstances, and we read that in the wilderness once, when she was heavily pregnant, she begged her husband to bring her some wine to drink. This spurred her husband on to greater efforts, and he slew his rival and gained the earldom. It is clear that Margaret had a reputation for a great appetite in her own time. Writing in 1571 Edmund Campion describes her as 'a rare woman, and able for wisdom to rule a realm, had not her stomach overruled herself'.

Richard Stanihurst, who wrote six years later, was quite hostile to her because of the manner in which she sided with her husband in his scheming against her Kildare kindred. Nevertheless he admitted that there was some ambiguity in her nature. 'She was a sure friend, a bitter enemy, hardly disliking where she fancied, not easily fancying where she disliked', he writes, and goes on to describe her as 'man-like, tall of stature, very rich and bountiful'. Several writers refer to her as religiously devout and charitable, and one source credits her with being 'the very best woman of her time for hospitality and munificence'.

It is likely that the faction of the Butlers who had been defeated by Piaras would have resented her even more than they did her husband, for it was through her that Piaras got the assistance to defeat them. Secondly, the Geraldine family themselves would have felt quite hostile to her on account of her connivance with the ungrateful plotting of Piaras against them. As a result, her portrayal in folklore is that of a powerful but greedy and vindictive woman. LEGENDS concerning her were

current until recent times in County Kilkenny, where she was known as *Máiréad Ní Ghearóid* (Margaret daughter of Gerald) and also as 'the great Countess'. A nineteenth-century source relates that 'she emulated, if not excelled, her lord in feats of arms', and goes on to describe her as 'having always a numerous train of armed followers, well-trained and accoutred, at her command, by whose aid she levied blackmail on her less powerful neighbours'.

Folklore in general tends to focus on more immediate and personal details, and so the folk legends tell of tricks and ruses by which the countess tried to inveigle possessions from various individuals. We are told that when she resided in Granny Castle, in the south of County Kilkenny, she often visited the head of the Mandeville family, who had a fine estate at Ballydine, near Carrick-on-Suir. While there, she noticed a contrivance by which a bell rang in the mansion every time a salmon was caught in a net placed by Mandeville's servants in the River Suir. Overcome with envy, she exclaimed aloud that Ballydine would yet be hers, but Mandeville indignantly rebuffed her. Not to be outdone, the countess bestowed 'the praise of the envious' on Mandeville's sixteen fine sons, as a result of which all of the boys soon died. This story combines two old but different elements – the MOTIF of a bell attached to a salmon net (*see* CANO MAC GARTNÁIN *and* COMHDHÁN), and the folk belief that an 'evil tongue' can be physically destructive. It is probably on account of the association of this belief with Margaret that she was sometimes referred to as *an Chuntaois mhallaithe* (the cursed Countess).

Another legend has her visiting the head of the Walsh family, called *an tOidhre Breathnach*, who lived at Inchacarran Castle. He was a very generous host, and on one occasion asked the countess to name any dish in the world and he would have it prepared for her. She said that she desired more than anything else a plateful of special morsels of meat, and she specified that the type of morsel she had in mind can only be found in a tiny part of the thigh of an ox. Walsh realised how he had been fooled, but he had given his word, and had no choice in honour but to order the slaughter of as much of his CATTLE as was necessary for the purpose. Thus seven whole herds were sacrificed in order to appease the craving appetite of the Countess of Ormond.

We are further told that she wished to take his lands from Walsh and, with this in mind, again chose an unguarded moment while being merrily entertained in his house. She begged as a small request of him that she could have the use of as much fertile ground as one bottle of flax seed might be sown in. He instantly granted the request, but soon realised that he had again been tricked and that she intended to spread the seed far and wide. On this occasion, he was prepared, however, so when she came with her servant and the bottle of seed, he directed her to start the sowing in the thick brush of Coolanass, where the seed would soon be used up to no avail.

Another tradition claims that she kidnapped the son of the Walsh chieftain, and that this episode gave rise to extreme hostility between them. So great did their hatred grow that the countess and Walsh hanged messengers sent from each to the other. The tree on which Margaret hanged her unfortunate victim was long known as *Sceach na Cuntaoise* (the Countess' Bush), a large whitethorn in the parish of Tullahought. In north Kilkenny, the countess was said to have hanged people from a jutting stone in front of her stone 'seat' on the top of Ballyragget Castle. Though the tradition must preserve some grain of truth, such a reputation for cruelty was hardly deserved. That reputation seems rather to have been a relic of the violent tenor of her time and the anomalous situation in which she lived.

The fact that she was a Geraldine living among Butlers is echoed in a legend of her sept (*see* DESMOND) that in Kilkenny was attached specifically to her. We are told that when she was in the great castle at Carrick-on-Suir once, she looked through the window and saw Butler of Kilcash driving in his carriage. By use of magic, she

caused his horses to sink into the pavement, but he in return caused a pair of horns to grow on her head so that she was stuck in the window, much to the amusement of the spectators, until they released each other. *See also* SEVEN BISHOPS.

Campion (1633), 161; Bryan (1933), 92–5, 214–15; O'Grady (1929), 167; Lord Dunboyne in *Old Kilkenny Review, 18,* 45; Carrigan, *3* (1905), 53; FitzGerald (1951), 129–30; CR: Pádraig Ó Néill MSS; OSL: Kilkenny 2 (1839), 199; IFC 2143:487–507.

Butler, Margaret *Lady Iveagh (1673–1744)* Noblewoman celebrated in folklore for her saintliness and generosity. She was daughter of William Burke, seventh Earl of Clanrickard, and her sister was the wife of Patrick SARSFIELD. Margaret married firstly in 1689 Brian Mac Aonghusa, fifth Viscount Iveagh (in County Down). After his death, she married in 1696 Colonel Thomas Butler of Kilcash Castle, County Tipperary, by whom she had three sons and five daughters. Residing at Kilcash, she was predeceased by her husband and several of her children.

She was noted for her charm and virtue, and in an oration delivered at her funeral in Kilcash, the parish priest Father Richard Hogan remarked on how she was lamented by vast crowds of people who had benefited from her kindness. He drew attention to the fact that her residence was open to all ranks of society and a refuge for those who had fallen into poverty. She was, he said, a great patron of the clergy, and had devoutly attended several Masses each day. Added to the affection in which she was held, this oration contributed to her enduring saintly image in popular memory. Folk tradition claims that she used to feed the BIRDS every morning and that these creatures would descend onto her shoulders and palms. She was also said to have been expert in cures, studying many books of medicine and using herbs to heal a large number of people. She was lauded in poetry during her lifetime and in subsequent generations.

P. Power in *JWAS, 1,* 189–91; P.J. Griffith in *JWAS, 15,* 27–9; Hardiman, *2* (1831), 417; O'Daly (1850), 198–201; Maher (1954), 30–1, 43–5; Ó hÓgáin (1981), 51–2, 82–3; Flood & Flood (1999), 59–69, 85–99; P. Ó Milléadha in *Béaloideas, 6,* 185.

Butler, Theobald *(+1206)* Ancestor of the Butler family, earls of Ormond. His real name was Theobald Walter, and he was brother of the archbishop of Canterbury and a favourite courtier of King John II. Coming to Ireland with that king, he was granted large tracts of land in north Tipperary and south Wicklow. Equally important, he was given the lucrative control of the wine patent for Ireland, from which derives the family name de Bouteillier ('bottle-bearer', gaelicised as de Buitléir). His descendants held this patent, which entitled them to a payment on all imported wine, until 1811, when they sold it to the Crown for a huge sum.

The very powerful earls of Ormond felt it appropriate to give a heroic profile to their ancestor. Thus in a genealogical text written in the sixteenth century, we are told that Theobald first landed in Ireland at 'an tInbhear Mór' (the bay of Arklow), and when he came ashore, drew his sword, put its point into the earth beneath him, and announced: 'I pledge my word that I will not return this sword to its sheath or its protective scabbard until I attain to the farthest part of Ireland, unless my demise come!' The text goes on to state that he made good his words, never stopping until he reached Inis Umhaill (Innishowle, west Mayo). Then he returned to Arklow, put up his sword, and declared that the surrounding coastal area was so fine that he wished to live his life there and be buried there.

This account is highly fanciful, changing the status of Theobald to that of a great conqueror and attributing to him several different episodes in the history of the family. Quite skilfully, the author converts the wine patent into a much more resounding commission, namely 'the first patent from the English king to make conquest in Ireland'. King John did indeed confer Arklow on him, but he was not buried there, although his direct successors were. The writer of the text was borrowing imagery from the lore of AMHAIRGHIN GLÚNGHEAL, reputedly the first of the Gaelic people to set foot on the soil of Ireland in prehistoric times, and also the reputed builder of the causeway at Arklow. The Butlers did acquire land by conquest in County Mayo, but not until Theobald was long dead, and the district in question was suggested to the author by the fact that it officially became Ormond property in the sixteenth century. In the meantime the Butlers had come to control most of Counties Tipperary and Kilkenny, where their fine castles can still be seen.

Curtis (1923), 100–2, 170, 430; Carrigan, *3* (1905), 51–2; O'Grady (1929), 162–77; Lord Dunboyne in *Old Kilkenny Review, 18,* 37–52.

Cailleach Bhéarra *(Hag of Beara)* Mythical old woman in Irish literature and folklore, associated with the Beara Peninsula in west Cork. The peninsula's designation comes from *bérre*, with a meaning such as 'the short place', indicating that grass does not grow copiously there. The early sources state that the hag's own name was Boí, and they also refer to her as the *sentainne* (old woman) of Beara.

In origin, she was undoubtedly a GODDESS, or a special manifestation of the land-goddess. The southwest of Ireland was anciently associated with the otherworld, especially that of the dead (*see* BALAR *and* DONN), and the idea of a HAG of great age domiciled there seems to have been a combination of such sombre imagery with the negative or ugly aspect of the land-goddess. Her name Boí was a variant of the word for a cow (*bó*), and ancient Irish lore seems to have contained the notion that an old cow-goddess lived on an island off the western coast (*see* CORC DUIBHNE). At the tip of the Beara Peninsula is an island called Inis Boí (later, Oileán Baoi), which was regarded as the residence of this celebrated hag. The Corca Laíghdhe, a leading sept of west Munster whose territory encompassed the Beara Peninsula, claimed this Boí as their ancestress; and a neighbouring sept, the Corca Dhuibhne, claimed that she had been the foster-mother of their ancestor, Corc Duibhne.

She is featured in a poem written around the year AD 900, which portrays her as a miserable old yellow-skinned woman lamenting her youth. She says that in the past she has been beautiful and has drunk mead and wine with kings, an image that shows she represented the goddess of sovereignty (*see* KINGSHIP). All of this has been reset by the poem in a moral context, however, and she speaks as one who, after a pleasurable life in youth, is taking the veil of a nun in her old age. The word *cailleach* (from the Latin word for a veil, 'pallium') originally signified a nun, but had come to mean an old woman. The new word, with its image of a covered head, was considered suitable to the portrayal of the goddess in her elderly form, and this in turn suggested to the author that Boí had become a nun. That CUMAINE FADA is claimed to have been the SAINT who invested her suggests that the poem is of Munster derivation.

The Hag of Beara is not traditionally portrayed as a nun, but rather as a wise and somewhat sinister old woman. In early stories, however, she could also have the aspect of youth. One such – now lost but current in the tenth century – told of a love affair she had with the warrior FOTHADH CANAINNE. Another medieval description centres on her more prominent image. We read that 'she had fifty foster-children in Beara' and that 'she passed into seven periods of youth, so that every husband used to pass to death from her of old age, and her grandchildren and great-grandchildren were peoples and races'. It is this portrayal of her as an old woman surviving from the distant generations of the past that is found in folklore. In fact, it was commonly said of a person of very advanced years that he or she was 'as old as the Cailleach Bhéarra!'

The medieval literature claims that St Cumaine Fada had blessed the veil and placed it on her head, after which age and infirmity came upon her. From this has sprung a widespread folk LEGEND that tells of a monk who visited her and enquired concerning her age. She said that she had killed a bullock each year and had thrown a bone from it onto the loft of her house. The monk sent his servant up to the loft to count the bones, but the task took so long that the monk lost patience. He then asked her to relate to him the greatest

wonder she had ever seen, which she did (*see* MARVELS). Aetiological lore of the older type concerning her was, as one might expect, strongest in west Munster. As an echo of her origin as a goddess, she is triplicated by the claim that she had two sister hags, who lived respectively on the Kerry peninsulas of Dingle and Iveragh. One folk legend tells of how she fell on hard times, and the Dingle hag decided to render her some assistance by presenting her with an extra island. The Dingle hag put a straw rope around the island and began to drag it south, but it split in two and the straw broke at the Iveragh Peninsula, and so the islands of Scariff and Deenish remain in that place. Another legend tells of the extremely sharp eyesight the hag of Beara had. It happened that the Iveragh hag was one day working in her house at Bolus, when she heard a shout outside. It was the Hag of Beara warning her that her cow had gone into the corn field outside the house. The hag of Beara had seen this happening at a distance of almost 20 miles across the sea.

Another legend has her being asked how she has lived for so long. Her answer is that the top of her head had never seen the air, the sole of her foot had never touched the ground, she had never eaten except when she was hungry, and she had never stayed in bed after awakening. In this context, she personifies ideas of healthy living, and a Connacht variant adds to these some principles of hygiene. The Hag of Beara, we are told, never carried mud on her feet from one place to another, and never threw out dirty water until she had first brought in clean water. The lore of west Galway tells of how, when at sea one night with her sons they complained of the severe cold. She told them to scoop water into the boat and fill it, and then to scoop the water out again, and in this way they kept themselves warm with the exercise until morning.

We are also told that she had a great bull called the Tarbh Conraidh, and every cow who heard his bellow calved within a year. The bull once swam after a cow across a creek, and the hag jumped after him, struck him with her rod, and turned him into a rock in the sea. This simple account is obviously of late derivation, but the general tradition that connects her with the landscape in different parts of the country is older. Standing stones are often said to have been people and animals transformed by her, and she is said to have described how various aspects of the landscape came about, such as lakes drying up and mountains taking their place. All of this must reflect the spread of her fame from Munster in medieval times, when she had not yet lost the imagery of a land-goddess.

In fact, lore surviving from land-goddess cults in various places was preserved by the application of her name to them. This is especially clear in the folklore of Scotland, where the Cailleach has undergone radical transformation, being represented as a female spirit of the wilderness and protectress of WILD ANIMALS. In the folklore of Connacht, north Leinster and south Ulster, the Hag of Beara was closely associated with corn and harvesting. There was widespread allusion to a hag (*cailleach*) as spirit of the harvest, which was said to race from the scythes in the form of a small animal, especially that of a hare (*see* HAGS). The strong likelihood is that – at some time since the Middle Ages and in the northern half of the country – the imagery of this harvest hag got confused with lore of the Cailleach Bhéarra, thereby causing the latter to become a kind of embodiment of the harvest-spirit. It is curious to note that neither lore of the harvest-animal nor of the Cailleach Bhéarra as a great reaper was known in Munster.

A man who could work as fast as a racing hare would, of course, be a phenomenally fast reaper, and so the idea could develop of a contest between a reaper and the Hag of Beara. Thus we are told that the Cailleach Bhéarra once had a huge corn field and that she issued a challenge to all and sundry to engage in a reaping contest with her. Every man who took up the challenge was defeated by her in the reaping race, and had his legs cut from under him by a stroke of her sickle or scythe. Eventually, a wily man discovered that she had a black beetle hidden in the handle of her implement, and realising that this was a magical device to give her great speed, he killed the beetle and thus defeated the hag in the contest. She then revealed to him her great age and told him some details from her life, which vary from version to version but usually contain some accounts of her love affairs when young.

A common tradition tells of how she used to sow in late winter and harvest the green corn before the autumn gales came. This corn was known as *coirce na bhFaoillí* (the oats of February), and it was contrasted in a proverb with the mixed oats and straw of a crop sown in March, and the wisps and bags of chaff that resulted from April sowing. We are also told that the hag revealed to people a better method of threshing than that which had hitherto been current. She did this with a verse, recommending that the flail should be made with a holly stick as handle and a hazel stick as striker, and that the sheaves should be threshed one at a time on a clean floor. Such items of lore were obviously mnemonic devices for farmers that became attributed to the Hag of Beara so as to underline conventional wisdom. In folklore, she is often known by an alternative form of her name, Cailleach Bhéarrach.

LITERATURE: G. Murphy (1962), 74–83, 206–8 & in *Proceedings of the Royal Irish Academy*, 55:C, 83–5; Meyer (1892), 6–7, 208–10 & in *Otia Merseiana*, *1*, 119–28; V. Hull in *ZCP*, *19*, 174–6; Mac Cana (1980), 48, 58; M.C. Dobbs in *RC*, *49*, 440; F.J. Byrne (1973), 166–8, 211; Jackson (1990), 3, 48.

FOLKLORE: Meyer (1892), 131–4; S. Ó Súilleabháin (1942), 493; Ó Duilearga (1948), 255–7, 428–9; M. MacNeill (1962), 160–1, 573; S.P. Moore in *Éigse*, *8*, 78; Ó Crualaoich (2003) & in *Béaloideas*, *56*, 153–78; IFC Index.

Caillín SAINT of the fifth or sixth century, who founded a monastery at Fiodhnacha (Fenagh, near Ballinamore, County Leitrim). The name means 'little cowl', and he was of the Conmhaicne sept of west Connacht.

A long account of him in Irish survives, devoted to his founding of the monastery and citing many poems concerning him. This, the 'Book of Fenagh', was compiled in the year 1516, but incorporates the contents of an earlier text that was probably written in the twelfth century. The account given of Caillín is a quite fanciful one, with much added by the later author. We read that Caillín was fostered and educated by the longevous FIONNTAN and sent by him to Rome to be educated as a Christian. Twelve years after the arrival of St PATRICK, he returned to Ireland as a bishop and was given much honour and authority by Patrick and the other early saints. When founding his monastery at Fenagh, he was at first opposed by the local king Feargna and his druids. Through the saint's prayers, Feargna was swallowed up by the ground and the druids were turned into stones. Feargna's son, called Aodh Dubh, was an extremely ugly fellow, but he was helpful to the saint and was therefore rendered handsome and had the kingdom conferred on him by Caillín.

We read that God sent an angel to Caillín to give him great knowledge, and this allowed the saint to be portrayed as a notable sage and harbinger of social and political events. The fourteenth and fifteenth-century chieftains of the northwest of the country and their POETS found this portrayal suitable as background to events of the time, and so the Book of Fenagh has much material – couched in prophetic terms – relating to the triumphs and ambitions of the strong septs bearing the surnames Ó Dónaill, Ó Néill and Ó Ruairc. The latter sept (rulers of the Cavan–Leitrim area) had Caillín as their special patron. The saint, whose feast day was 13 November, was portrayed fancifully in another late medieval text, where he is claimed to have been a stepbrother of the seventh-century poet SEANCHÁN.

The folk memory of Caillín in Leitrim is derived from the Book of Fenagh; and in the area especially associated with the Conmhaicne sept, Connemara in west Galway, he is said to have built a church at Bannon and to have had a bell with a tremendously loud sound.

Kenney (1929), 400–1; W.M. Hennessy & Kelly (1875); Macalister (1939); Mac Giollarnáth (1941), 11–13, 259; IFC 62:264, 75:158–9, 158:64–6, 559:200–1, 655:187–99.

Cainneach *(c.AD 521–c.599)* SAINT who founded the monastery of Achadh Bó (Aghaboe, County Laois). His name (which meant 'pleasant person') is anglicised as Canice, Kenneth and Kenny.

Cainneach was for a while a member of the community of COLM CILLE on the island of Iona. Three Latin texts on his life survive, and these are based on an original biography compiled perhaps as early as the eighth century. We read that he was born in Gleann Ghaimhin (Glengiven, County Derry), and that his father Laidheach was an accomplished POET. In his youth, Cainneach was employed as a cowherd, but he soon opted for ecclesiastical education. He went to Wales, where he was ordained a priest by St Cadoc, and on his return home to Glengiven, he converted to Christianity the chieftain of his own sept, the Corca Dhálann. We read also that while with Colm Cille in Scotland, Cainneach founded several churches in that country. Returning to Ireland, he clashed with the king of Meath, called Colmán Beag, who had carried off a nun from her convent and held her captive on an island. The king, seeing Cainneach approach in a fiery chariot, was terrified and repented of his action. Soon after, Colmán died, and Cainneach prayed over his grave and had his soul released from torment into heaven.

Cainneach became a close friend of the king of OSRAIGHE (south County Laois and County Kilkenny), and when that king was besieged by enemies and his fortress set on fire, the saint miraculously passed through the flames and brought him to safety. On another occasion, Cainneach miraculously preserved the boy DALUA from a cruel death at the hands of a group of Leinstermen. The literature describes Cainneach as in appearance a low-sized, bald-headed man. He was celebrated for his beautiful handwriting in copying sacred texts, and also for his eloquence in speech, and it was said that he had been taught these special skills by JESUS Himself, who came to him once when he was in solitude at Inis Locha Cré (Holy Island, near Roscrea, County Tipperary).

Although it is not mentioned in the

surviving literature, it is apparent that he founded a church at Kilkenny, thus giving that place its name (Cill Chainnigh). The folklore of the Aghaboe area claims that after his death, the people of Laois and the people of Kilkenny argued over which of them should have his body for burial. They fell to blows, ignoring his coffin, and when they looked again there were two coffins, thus allowing both parties to be pacified. This story is in fact a borrowing from the lore concerning the burial of the national saint, PATRICK. The feast day of Cainneach is 11 October.

Kenney (1929), 394–5; Anderson & Anderson (1961), 220–1, 352–7, 500–1; Heist (1962), 182–98; Plummer, 1 (1910), 152–69 & 2, 18; IFC 946:124–31, 134, 217–19.

Cairbre Catcheann Fictional character who, it was claimed, had led a revolt of the *aitheach-thuatha* (subject-peoples) against the nobility in ancient Ireland. For the name Cairbre, *see* CORMAC MAC AIRT. His epithet means 'cat-headed', and he was said to have been of the Luighne sept, who lived near TARA.

The story of him was an invention by the pseudo-historians as part of the propaganda of the royal Uí NÉILL dynasty, who fancifully applied the term *aitheach-thuatha* to the septs collectively known as ÉRAINN. We read of how Cairbre, with two other leaders called Monach and Buan, spent three years preparing a feast for the nobles at Magh Cró (in east County Mayo). When the guests were drunk, Cairbre and his men slew them all. The plan was not, however, a complete success, for a great FAMINE came on Ireland on account of the unjust KINGSHIP of the usurpers. Accordingly, when Cairbre died, messages were sent to the three young heirs to the kingship, who had been in their mother's wombs when the revolt had occurred and who had since been refugees in Scotland. These three – Fearadhach Fionn, Corp Ólom and Tiobraide Tíreach – were invited to return to Ireland, and the subject-peoples offered them their loyalty forever. Fearadhach became king of Tara.

Another tradition had a character called Cairbre Catutchenn as an ancient king of the Érainn of Munster. In this case, the epithet meant 'hard-headed', and it is obvious that the pseudo-historians shortened it to mean 'cat-head', which image was seen by them as suitable to a usurper. *See also* MORANN.

O'Brien (1962), 121; Ó Raithbheartaigh (1932), 60, 107–14, 122–6, 210; T.F. O'Rahilly in Ryan (1940), 101–10.

Cairbre Lifeachair Fictional high-KING of Ireland, son of the celebrated CORMAC MAC AIRT.

His name (earlier, Coirpre Lifechar) was based on a vestige of myth concerning the TARA kingship. This, of Leinster provenance, had the element *corb* in names of archetypal KINGS at that centre, and from it also the name of Cormac mac Airt himself may have come. One emanation of this name is Cairbre Cluitheachair, also associated with the ancient Leinster control of Tara (*see* LAIGHIN). His sobriquet meant 'lover of games', and it is apparent that Cairbre Lifeachair was an analogous name. The sobriquet in this case meant 'lover of the Liffey', this latter (*Life*) being the designation of the plain of Kildare. The river that ran through this plain, originally called the Ruirtheach, was referred to as *Abha na Life* (the river of the Liffey), hence the tendency to call the river by the name of the plain.

His Leinster connections were kept alive by his name (identical with the region of Cairbre in County Kildare) and by his sobriquet, and we find it variously stated that his mother was a daughter of the great Leinster king CATHAOIR MÓR and that he was fostered by the Leinstermen. The character of this Cairbre as delineated by the medieval pseudo-historians, however, was as a son of the high-king Cormac mac Airt, whom the CONNACHTA propagandists claimed as their own. Accordingly, Cairbre Lifeachair in tradition was a staunch scion of the Connachta who had taken Tara from the Leinstermen. He is several times mentioned as a prince at the court of his father, not only in stories of the celebrated Cormac, but also in stories of the great Leinster hero FIONN MAC CUMHAILL.

The annalistic record claims that he was

killed in battle against the Fotharta – branches of which sept inhabited various parts of Leinster – in a battle at Gabhra (Gowra, County Meath) in the year AD 284. This, of course, is pseudo-history, but it may be based on some garbled old tradition known to the medieval storytellers. This battle was reinterpreted, in or around the eleventh century, as having been fought by Cairbre against the FIANNA troop of Fionn, and this latter idea became the accepted one. We read that, seated on a white horse in that battle, Cairbre cast his spear at the great Fianna warrior OSCAR, mortally wounding him, but that he was himself slain by the dying Oscar.
GENERAL: Macalister (1956), 338–41; W. Stokes in *Irische Texte*, *3*, 336–7 & in *RC, 13*, 50; K. Meyer in *ZCP, 11*, 110; M. Dillon in *Ériu*, *11*, 44; T.F. O'Rahilly (1946), 139–40, 268–9; O'Donovan, *1* (1848), 158; Ó Muraíle, *2* (2003), 204.
BATTLE AGAINST FIANNA: *see* FIANNA CYCLE.

Cairbre mac Éadaoine *(earlier, Corpre mac Étaine)* Mythical POET of the TUATHA DÉ DANANN, his mother being a poetess called Éadaoin.

He was reputed to have composed the first satire in Ireland. It so happened that when he visited BREAS, then king over the Tuatha Dé, he met with the inhospitality typical of that king. He had to spend the night in a dark and bare little hut with nothing to eat but stale cakes. Next morning, he made a quatrain deriding the stinginess of his host and declared that 'the prosperity of Breas is no more!' As a result, the good fortune of that king began to fade. Before the second Battle of Moytirra (*see* MYTHOLOGICAL CYCLE), Cairbre again assumed the role of the archetypal poet by promising to use his magical power as a weapon, satirising the foe so that 'through the spell of my poem they will not be able to contend with warriors'.

There are a few other incidental references to Cairbre. We are told, for instance, that he composed a praise-poem on the great shield of MANANNÁN, and as a result was given the shield, but he passed it on to the DAGHDHA. The medieval tradition was that he died of sunstroke, and that his mother died from sorrow for him.

Gray (1982), 34–5, 52–3, 119–20; Meyer (1912), 25, 98; Arbois de Jubainville (1903), 96; Mac Néill (1908), 35; Macalister (1941), 226–7; V. Hull in *ZCP, 18*, 63–9.

Cano mac Gartnáin Ruler of a petty kingdom in the Isle of Skye in the seventh century AD. He was grandson of the celebrated Aodán mac Gabhráin (+608), KING of the Dál Riada sept, whose kingdom straddled the Sea of Moyle with substantial territories in Antrim and western Scotland.

After he was ejected from Skye in 668, Cano with his brothers and supporters spent two years in Ireland before he regained his territory. He was slain in the year 688, but was later made the hero of a literary romance entitled *Scéla Cano Meic Gartnáin*. The essence of the romance was composed in the ninth century, but the full surviving text dates from over a century later. The events described in it are unhistorical for Cano, son of Gartnán, died a generation or two later than most of the characters who are made to figure in the action. Among these characters are Aodán mac Gabhráin and Aodán's son, Gartnait or Gartnán – grandfather and father respectively of Cano. Curiously, in the romance Gartnán is wrongly described as Aodán's nephew.

The story has Gartnán and his 'uncle' Aodán contending fiercely for the kingdom of Scotland. We read that Gartnán lived in Inis Moccu Chéin (an island near Skye) in a fine palace surrounded by wealth and prosperity. He had 50 fishing nets attached to ropes with a bell at the end of each rope so that whenever a fish was caught a bell would ring. A son was born to him, and the child was called Cano and put into fosterage. Gartnán had a vat full of gold and silver concealed in the sand at low tide, and had the four men who hid it killed, so that only he, his wife and his son knew of it. Sometime later his foe Aodán mac Gabhráin sacked and ravaged the island and slew Gartnán himself. Cano escaped to Ireland with some followers. The joint kings of Ireland, DIARMAID MAC AODHA SLÁINE and his brother Bláthmhac, welcomed them.

Meanwhile, Aodán searched for the hidden vat of treasure and found it, reputedly

63

with the help of the devil. With this treasure, he sent servants to bribe the joint kings of Ireland to murder Cano, but the daughter of Diarmaid overheard the plotting and warned the intended victim. Cano went with twelve swordsmen and broke in on the discussions between Aodán's men and the two joint kings. Diarmaid and Bláthmhac gave assurances that they would not betray him, and advised him to follow the bribers and take the treasure from them. This he did, but he allowed these men to go free in return for promises of loyalty.

Cano went hunting with his followers and was amazed when, for the first time, he failed to shoot swans and ducks. Arriving in the province of Connacht, however, he met and fell in love with Créidh, daughter of king GUAIRE and wife of the warrior Marcán. She put all to sleep with a magic spell at a feast, but Cano refused to lie with her or to elope with her. Nevertheless before he departed he left a stone as a token with Créidh, promising to return for her when he secured the kingship of Scotland. This was a stone received by his mother from two otherworld women who came to her when she was in child-bed, and its preservation was linked to the preservation of Cano's own life. On leaving Connacht, he went south to Dún mBaíthe (Dunboy, west Cork), where he was received with great hospitality by a chieftain of the Corca Laíghdhe sept called Iollann mac Scanláin. Soon messengers arrived from Scotland to announce that the kingship had been awarded to him, and he departed for his native land, loaded with presents from Iollann. As he left the shore, a dark red wave splashed into his boat, and he interpreted this as a presage of death for Iollann. A year later, Iollann was indeed slain by two Munster rivals, and Cano brought an army of Saxons, Britons and Scots to avenge him. He established the son of Iollann as over-king of the Corca Laíghdhe sept.

Cano tried on several occasions to meet Créidh, but was always prevented from doing so by armed bands under the control of Colcu, son of Marcán. On one occasion, as he crossed the sea to meet her,

he was intercepted by three ships under the command of Colcu and he was cut down. When Créidh saw the pallor of death on his face, she dashed her head against a rock, and Cano's life-stone was shattered underneath her. Cano died in Scotland nine days later.

The writer of this text used a variety of elements in his plot. He seems to have been under the influence of the story concerning the above-mentioned Diarmaid mac Aodha Sláine and his wife Beagfhola; but he also forged some of the narrative from the three-cornered plot popular in early medieval times – i.e. the old husband opposed by the lover of his young wife (see DEIRDRE and DIARMAID UA DUIBHNE). Several folklore elements are also utilised, such as the idea of hidden TREASURE, the MOTIF of an external soul (see WONDER TALES, type 302), and the bloody wave as a presage of death.

THE CHARACTERS: Binchy (1963), xvii–xxvii.

THE STORY: Binchy (1963), 1–19. *See also* Carney (1955), 189–242; S. Ó Coileáin in *Ériu, 32*, 115–36.

Caoilte *(earlier, Caílte)* A great athlete and faithful comrade of FIONN MAC CUMHAILL in the FIANNA CYCLE. His full name is Caoilte mac Rónáin, and he figures prominently in stories of Fionn in both literature and folklore.

In a Leinster genealogy from the sixth or seventh century, the characters Fionn, Tulcha and Caoilte are referred to as three descendants of Baoiscne. Tulcha was represented in medieval lore as a brother of Fionn, and Caoilte as Fionn's nephew, but this early reference groups the three together as if they constituted a unit. It may be that such a unit echoed the triplication of FIONN. The name was a descriptive based on the adjective *caol* (earlier, *cáel*, meaning 'slender'), and therefore meant the 'athletic fellow'. In medieval times, however, it was regarded as a compound of *caol*, with another adjective *te* ('warm' or 'energetic'), reflecting accurately his fame as a runner.

Already in texts from the eighth to ninth century, he is said to have had special athletic skills, and texts of comparable date describe him as Caoilte *cos-luath* (fleet-footed). He was so celebrated for such accomplishments that a twelfth-century Welsh author borrowed him under the guise of *Sgilti ysgawndroet* (Sgilti light-foot). The Welsh text utilises a common folklore plot concerning a number of characters with extraordinary abilities (*see* WONDER TALES, type 513), and there are many indications that this plot had already influenced the lore of Caoilte in Ireland in the tenth or early eleventh century. Thus we find an old friend and helper of Fionn, Fiacail Fí, being described as so fast a runner that he wears balls of lead around his neck to check his speed. This MOTIF parallels one in the folklore plot that has a fast runner tying one leg under his belt to slacken his speed. Nowhere else is Fiacail claimed to have been a great runner, so it is reasonable to assume that in the case of Fiacail Fí the motif has been borrowed from the folklore plot through the medium of Caoilte.

It may well be that it was a text concerning MONGÁN, written at the end of the eighth century, which cast Caoilte in the definite image of a stupendous runner. Here he comes from the realm of the dead in the southwest of Ireland in order to settle a dispute between Mongán and his POET in east Ulster concerning the site of a warrior's burial. This portrayal of him running across the whole sweep of Ireland is repeated in later sources, such as the twelfth-century text *Agallamh na Seanórach*, which has him speeding from Tonn Chlíona (Glandore Bay, County Cork) to Tráigh Rudhraighe (Dundrum Bay) in a single day. The title of this text means 'The Colloquy of the Old Men', and it focuses strongly on Caoilte who, along with OISÍN, is described in it as a survivor of the ancient Fianna troop who lives on to meet St PATRICK and to relay much of the ancient lore to that SAINT. The occurrence of Caoilte in such a role is probably due to the eighth-century text cited above that has him as one coming from the past to convey antiquarian lore.

The colloquy gives other insights into the development of the character Caoilte.

His speed is compared to that of the wind, and it has him running two tense races. In one case, an ugly HAG comes to the Fianna at Cruachain (Rathcroghan, County Roscommon) and demands that they race against her. When the contest begins, Caoilte runs ahead of her, and then turns around and cuts her head off with a sword. In another case, the challenger is a beautiful young lady from the otherworld dwelling at Beann Éadair (Howth, County Dublin) who is defeated in a long race by Caoilte. The motif of racing against a woman comes from the folklore plot (type 513 referred to above), but the contrasting images of Caoilte's two competitors here – ugly hag and beautiful maiden – are those of the GODDESS of sovereignty. This suggests a connection between Caoilte and Fionn's struggle with CORMAC MAC AIRT, of which the character Gráinne is also an echo (*see* DIARMAID UA DUIBHNE).

The connection is seemingly confirmed by a story written towards the end of the tenth century that tells of how Fionn wooed Gráinne at TARA, but she demanded as a gift from him the male and female of each WILD ANIMAL in Ireland to be brought in one drove to her. Caoilte undertook this seemingly impossible task, and succeeded in bringing that great 'straggling drove' (*corr-imirce*) to Tara. Other recensions of this story, though written somewhat later, preserve echoes of the original struggle between Fionn and Cormac. We read that Fionn attempted to seize power at Tara, but his plan was thwarted by Cormac and he was taken prisoner. In order to secure his release, Caoilte engaged in a campaign of attrition against the high-king, and so swift was he that he could not be captured. Eventually, he went in disguise to Cormac and demanded to know what ransom the king would accept for Fionn's release. The ransom was the male and female of every creature in the land, and Caoilte accordingly succeeded in bringing it to Tara and thus had Fionn set free. This story is in fact drawn from two different sources – folklore concerning a man who can herd rabbits by blowing his magic pipe (*see*

WONDER TALES, type 570), and the account of Noah's Ark in the Bible. It was a good and dramatic story, and soon became very popular in folklore, where Caoilte was said to have brought a herd of hares to Tara and to have placed them there in a house with nine open doors. By his speed and continuous racing around that house, he kept all the hares within until morning.

Other suitable motifs were joined by the folk to the image of Caoilte the mighty runner. A late folk story from County Galway illustrates this well by its deft selection of materials from various Fianna stories and from ordinary lore. We are told that the king of Ireland wished to have a fistful of sand brought to him every morning from each of the four shores of Ireland, for he would know by smelling them whether the foot of a foe had landed during the night. Three men offered to do this for him each day. The first man said that he would have the sands collected as quickly as a leaf falls from a tree, but this did not satisfy the king. The second man said that he would do so as fast as a cat slinking between two houses, but again the king was not satisfied. The third man was Caoilte, and he said that he would do it as fast as a woman changes her mind. The king was impressed and asked him to go and collect the sands. 'I have just returned with them!' said Caoilte, having performed the task in the blink of an eye.

GENERAL: Meyer (1895), 45–8 & (1910), xxiii & in *RC*, 5, 198, 200 & in *ZCP*, 1, 458–61; Stokes (1900), 1–3, 103, 115, 136, 182, 189, 205; Mac Néill (1908), 6, 19–21; G. Murphy (1933), 124–40; Ní Shéaghda (1945), 67–83; N. Ross (1939), 40–59; Ó hÓgáin (1988), 177–85, 296–8, 337, 344, 357 & in Almqvist, Ó Catháin & Ó Héalaí (1987), 241–2; IFC 1010:85–6, etc.

SGILTI: J.G. Evans (1907), 232.

Caoimhghin SAINT who died *c*.AD 618. Founder of the monastic settlement at Gleann Dá Loch (Glendalough, County Wicklow), his name (earlier, Coemgen) is anglicised as Kevin.

The surviving biographies of him, in Latin and Irish, date from several centuries after his time, being compiled principally to add to the prestige of the famous monastery of Glendalough. We read that his coming was foretold by both St PATRICK and the epic hero FIONN MAC CUMHAILL. His father's name is given as Caomhlugh, of the Dál Messin Corb sept of Leinster, and his mother was reputedly called Caomhall. Both names, containing the adjective *caomh* (gentle) seem to have been invented by the biographers. The texts state that he was born without any pain to his mother, and such an easy pregnancy may have been the reason why the child was given the name Coemgen (literally, 'gentle conception'), although the texts themselves explain the name as 'beauteous birth'. We read that twelve angels with golden lamps attended his baptism by St Crónán, and that the fort in which he was reared was never subject to frost or snow. A mysterious white cow used to come to give its milk for the child's sustenance.

When Caoimhghin grew up, he was told by an angel to study for the priesthood and, when he received holy orders, the same angel instructed him to go to the lonely place called Gleann Dá Loch (literally, 'the valley of the two lakes'). There he wore only the skins of WILD ANIMALS and would lie by night on bare stones doing penance. He banished a great monster from the lesser of the two lakes into the larger one, and as a result sickness of men and of beasts was healed by a visit to the lesser lake. The monster in the other lake takes the illnesses and is thereby left too weak to inflict harm on anybody. When, however, the monster turns on its side, the water rises as high as the peaks of the surrounding mountains, and a person who sees that is destined to die within a week.

Caoimhghin performed great self-mortification. For seven years, he ate only nettles and sorrel and was accustomed to stand up to his waist in the water while reciting the vespers. His psalter once fell into the lake, but an otter came and saved it from being wetted. The saint went to live all alone in a cave, and was on the point of death from fasting and penance when he was discovered. It happened that the cow of a certain farmer of the locality had a marvellous milk yield. The herdsman grew curious and, following the cow, found that she got her marvellous milk through licking the feet of the saint. When the farmer heard of this, he arranged that the saint be brought in a litter to his house, and the dense trees of the wood bent of their own accord to allow the litter to be carried through them. The rescuers looked after the saint, and helped him to build a church and the residence that were the basis of the great monastery. In the valley, he was at peace with all nature, and we read that, when he prayed, the little BIRDS would often perch on his hands and shoulders. One fanciful little anecdote told of how, while fasting during Lent, a blackbird landed on one of his outstretched palms and made its nest there. Noticing this, the saint kept his hand in the same position until the blackbird's young were hatched.

Soon he was joined by others seeking the monastic life. It was claimed that in order to gain recognition for the foundation, he travelled to Rome and was granted the boon that seven pilgrimages to Glendalough were equal in spiritual value to one pilgrimage to that great city. Among the miracles attributed to him were the restoring to life of recently deceased people, the provision of food for his community of monks when such was not available, and making a wolf substitute itself for a doe in providing milk for a foster-child of his. The helpful otter used to bring a salmon from the lake for the monks every day, but one member of the community decided to kill that otter in order to make a glove from its skin. Understanding this, the animal disappeared, and the angry Caoimhghin ordered the monk to leave the community. It was also said that during a time of scarcity, the saint sought food for his monks from some women who were carrying cheese in their baskets. The women pretended that the baskets contained nothing but thread, whereupon Caoimhghin turned the cheese into stones.

Most of the LEGENDS related of him in the medieval literature survived in local folklore, though often altered and embellished. One striking instance is that concerning a maiden who fell in love with

him, and who, according to the literature, was driven away with nettles by the celibate saint and afterwards became a nun. Later folk versions of this legend have Caoimhghin causing the persistent lady to fall from a precipice into the larger lake at Glendalough. A folk legend which is post-medieval and has no counterpart in the literature purports to tell of how he gained the site for his monastery. A chieftain of the local noble family Ó Tuathail, we are told, ridiculed the saint's entreaties for a site. Observing a goose with a broken wing, Ó Tuathail mockingly promised as much land as that goose would encircle in its flight, whereupon the injured bird rose into the air and encircled all of the valley. It is hardly necessary to point out that this legend is apocryphal, and it is also anachronistic, for the family of Ó Tuathail (anglicised O'Toole) did not settle in the area until the twelfth century.

Another popular tradition has it that no larks ever sing at Glendalough, the saint having so ordained because he was aggrieved at larks who caused the builders of his cathedral to rise too early in the morning and thus feel tired and listless at their work.

Glendalough was one of the greatest centres of monasticism and of learning in early medieval Ireland, and the remains of the foundation are particularly striking in their beautiful surroundings. Caoimhghin's feast day is 3 June.

Kenney (1929), 403–4; Plummer, 1 (1912), 234–57 & 1 (1922), 125–67; Heist (1965), 361–5; Ó Nuanáin (1936); Lover (1834), 1–16; Prevost (1846), 170–1; IFC 143:1771, 485:269–70, 946:128–34, 1140:275–7, S917:245–7, 327, 337, 370, 413–14, S918:139–40, 207.

Cathal mac Fionghuine (+AD 742)

KING of Munster, whose reign began in the year AD 721. The name Cathal was a very common one in early Ireland, meaning 'battle-strong'.

This king was of the EOGHANACHT, the royal Munster sept, and belonged to the branch that inhabited the area of Gleanndamhain (north-east Cork). His father Fionghuine had been king of the province for a short period, as had his uncle and his cousin. After acceding to the kingship, Cathal undertook a campaign against the Uí NÉILL high-king FEARGHAL MAC MAOLDÚIN. For a while he was allied to the Leinster king Murchadh mac Brain, but he was not involved in the decisive Battle of Allen in 722 when Fearghal was defeated and slain by the Leinstermen. The account of that battle has the severed head of Fearghal being brought to the court of Cathal at Gleanndamhain and being accorded high respect there.

In the following years, Cathal was in continuous conflict with both the Uí Néill and the Leinstermen, barely escaping with his life from the latter at the Battle of Bealach Éile (near Borrisoleigh, County Tipperary) in 735. Two years after this, he had a conference with the new high-king AODH ALLÁN at Tír Dhá Ghlas (Terryglass, County Tipperary), at which the two magnates appear to have reached some sort of agreement, and Cathal was involved in no other serious conflict. He was buried at the famous monastery that had been founded by St AILBHE at Emly, County Tipperary. In a text concerning a lady called Mór, he was confused with his great-grandfather Cathal mac Aodha, and as a result the goddess MÓR MUMHAN was claimed to have uttered a verse of lamentation over his grave.

Medieval Munster writers represented Cathal as having been in effect the king of all Ireland. They claimed that he was a great patron of POETS and an extraordinarily generous host. This was the main reason why he was featured in the goliardic text concerning MAC CONGLINNE and a vision of abundant food. There we read that Cathal had a demon of gluttony within him as a result of dainties he ate and which had been tampered with by the magician of the high-king Fearghal.

F.J. Byrne (1973), 205–11; Mac Airt (1951), 104–9; O'Donovan, 1 (1848), 314–19, 328–9, 334–5; Ó Riain (1978); Best & O'Brien (1957), 627–8; Ó Donnchadha (1940), 147.

Cathaoir Mór *(earlier, Catháir Már)* Quasi-historical ancient Leinster KING, whose character derives from a title given by the LAIGHIN (Leinstermen) to their early kings. That title would have been in its Celtic form *Catuveros* (battle-man) until the fourth century AD, when the power of the Leinstermen was at its highest. Its early Irish form, *Cathaír*, developed from this, the title being considered the name borne by a famous progenitor, and the epithet *Már* (great) was accordingly added. Thus the early medieval writers regarded Cathaoir Mór as the ancestor of the foremost septs of the Leinstermen, and claimed that he had ruled at TARA.

There was no small amount of confusion concerning his floruit. The Annals and sagas regarded his reign as having belonged to the second century AD, but this contradicts the more reliable genealogical sources, whose evidence would place him 200 years later. His ambit at least is historical, for it is clear that the Leinstermen held Tara for some time before the rise of the CONNACHTA in the fourth to fifth century. He is referred to in literature dating from the late sixth or early seventh century as a kindly, generous and noble leader. The genealogists claimed that he ruled Tara for 30 years, and that he had the same number of sons, but only ten of these were given prominence. A fictional document, styled 'The Testimony of Cathaoir Mór', seems to have been in existence by the eighth century. It describes the grants of wealth and privilege bequeathed by Cathaoir to the various Leinster septs. Listed are his sons from whom the leading septs traced their descent, and the major royal sites of the Leinstermen are enumerated, significantly including Tara. A medieval prose commentary on the testimony states that 'Cathaoir Mór was for three years in the KINGSHIP of Ireland', and that he was defeated and slain at the Battle of Magh Ágha (near Teltown, County Meath) by CONN CÉADCHATHACH.

The title *Cathaoir* may have still distinguished the last Leinster king of Tara, although the battle between such a character and Conn was an invention and did not become well established in tradition. One late version portrays Conn as a child and has his people already in possession of the citadel. We read that Conn was playing hurling at Cruachain (Rathcroghan,

County Roscommon) when a DRUID told him that Tara was being sacked by Cathaoir. The youngster gathered together a band of soldiers and set out to defeat the Leinstermen. No full account of these matters survives from the Leinster viewpoint, but there is an echo of such in the mentions of how Cathaoir fell in the Battle of Magh Ágha at the hands of the Luighne. This sept, mercenaries to the Connachta, were portrayed as bitter enemies of the Leinstermen in the early accounts of the hero FIONN MAC CUMHAILL.

The medieval PLACE-LORE has several mentions of Cathaoir. One story describes him celebrating the feast of Tara, and when the assembled host was inebriated a warrior called Garman stole the queen's golden coronet. He was pursued from Tara by Cathaoir's men and, after a long chase, was seized at the mouth of the River Slaney and drowned there – hence, we are quite speculatively told, that place was known as Loch Garman (Wexford). The inventor of this story conveniently ignored the fact that an Old Irish genitive 'Garman' would have required 'Garmu' in the nominative form.

Another story tells of how Cathaoir dreamed that a beautiful lady appeared to him. She was pregnant for a long time and then gave birth to a son. Cathaoir next dreamed that he saw nearby a fragrant tree that gave all kinds of fruit and from which the most pleasant music came. On awakening, Cathaoir's druid, Brí mac Baircheadha, interpreted the dream for him. The lady was the Sláine (River Slaney), her son was the harbour of Loch Garman, and the great tree was Cathaoir himself. Its music was his 'noble eloquence when appeasing a multitude', and the wind that shook down its fruit was his great generosity. This account owes much to biblical themes such as the tree of Jesse, which symbolised genealogy, and the tree seen by the Babylonian king Nebuchadnezzar in a dream, which personified that king himself. These themes were combined by the medieval writers with the native Irish kingship metaphor of a strong protective tree for a good ruler.

Yet another story has Loch Garman being named from the death there of Cathaoir's swine-herd, while Cathaoir himself and his ten sons were said to have been buried at Tulach Eoghain (near Morett, County Laois). Though these references are quite contrived, they illustrate how, in the medieval mind, Cathaoir was regarded as synonymous with the ancient culture of Leinster.

T.F. O'Rahilly (1946), 268, 549; O'Brien (1962), 121, 535; Meyer (1914), 14–16; Dillon (1962), 148–78; Macalister (1956), 330–1; W. Stokes in Irische Texte, 3, 370–1; Gwynn (1913), 168–83, 508–10 & (1924), 172–5, 282–7, 450–1; D. Murphy (1896), 57–8; Ó Caithnia (1984), 97–8.

Cathbhadh Mythical warrior-DRUID in the ULSTER CYCLE. His name (from Celtic *Catubatuos*) would have originally meant 'battle slayer'.

According to one version of the birth of king CONCHOBHAR MAC NEASA, Cathbhadh slew the twelve tutors of the girl Neas. She then went armed in search of the killer, whose identity was unknown to her, and was surprised by Cathbhadh while bathing. He forced her to become his wife and brought her with him to his home in the district of Ros (in south County Armagh), where Conchobhar was born. Other accounts do not mention his warrior prowess, but instead concentrate on his magical and prophetic powers. He is said to have taught his magical skills to the noble youths in Conchobhar's warrior academy at Eamhain Mhacha, and to have thus given instruction to CÚ CHULAINN. He announced what was the most auspicious day to first take arms, which knowledge was quickly put to effect by Cú Chulainn. He also specified to Conchobhar's son, CORMAC CONN LOINGEAS, the magical injunctions (*see GEIS*) by which that prince should abide in his life. Cathbhadh's status was high in the royal court. For instance, there was a prohibition on the Ulster men to speak before the KING spoke at an assembly, but the king himself was prohibited from speaking until Cathbhadh had his say.

His function of adviser to Conchobhar is evidenced in the story of DEIRDRE, for when that lady was born, he foretold that she would bring disaster to the Ulstermen.

He is referred to as the maternal grandfather of the three sons of Uisliu, including Deirdre's lover Naoise, but he was tricked into supporting Conchobhar in the king's treachery against them. When they were fighting invincibly against Conchobhar's men, who attacked them in violation of guarantees, the king asked Cathbhadh to restrain them, saying that he feared they would destroy Ulster. He gave a solemn promise that if they were restrained, he would not harm them. Cathbhadh accordingly used his magic to bring a great surge of sea under their feet on the plain, and so they were seized and done to death on Conchobhar's orders. One account states that Cathbhadh cursed Conchobhar after that treachery, declaring that none of his progeny would rule at Eamhain Mhacha; but the Ulster Cycle in general has him remaining loyal to Conchobhar.

His advice is always mentioned as being far-sighted and wise. For instance, when the cattle-raid of Cooley was over and the king thirsted for revenge against Connacht, he was advised against further warring by the druid. Cathbhadh also tried to restrain Cú Chulainn from going to his death when a trap had been set for him by hostile magicians.

C.-J. Guyonvarc'h in *Ogam*, *12*, 197, 449–50; K. Meyer in *RC*, *6*, 173–182; W. Stokes in *Ériu*, *4*, 22–3; C. O'Rahilly (1976), 19–20, 105; J.C. Watson (1941), 4–16; Hull (1949), 43–6; W. Stokes in *Irische Texte*, *2*, 122, 143, 146–52; E. Hogan (1892), 2–13; Ó Cadhlaigh (1956), 467.

cats A rather ambiguous attitude was taken to these animals. On the one hand, they were much valued for their service in keeping mice and rats at bay, but on the other hand were suspected of having a deep and sinister side to their nature.

The old literature has some fierce cats as opponents of heroes (*see* CÚ CHULAINN, FIONN MAC CUMHAILL *and* SEANCHÁN), yet domestic cats are portrayed as gentle companions of SAINTS, as in one text that has a little pet cat supplying fish for three hungry monks on an island. A tradition dating back to medieval times, in fact, claims that mice were created by the devil to plague humans, but that St MARTIN created the cat to control these pests. In a

humorous vein, it was said that the cat had long ago bought three gifts for itself – these were equal light by night and day, the forgetfulness of the housewife, and the ability to keep its feet from getting wet.

The sinister view of cats seems to spring from their ability to see in the dark and from their nocturnal lifestyle. A fanciful notion claims that the domestic cat dreams three times each night of killing its owner, but is deterred from this by fear of the household DOG. Other lore seems to derive from an ancient fear that a cat might take the soul of a deceased person – it was, for instance, considered unlucky to allow a cat to remain in a wake-house or to cross the path of a funeral. The dramatic image of an all-black cat evoked superstitious feeling – to meet with such a cat is usually regarded as a sign of bad luck, but some people consider it the opposite. *See also* ANIMAL TALES (types 105, 113A, 200, 217), and for lore of wild cats *see* WILD ANIMALS.

F. Kelly (1997), 121–4; Cross (1952), 44, 52, 55, 60, 64, 73, 82; Flower (1926), 522; Wood-Martin, *2* (1902), 122–6; S. Ó Súilleabháin (1942), 43–4; Ó Duilearga (1949), 371, 449; Ó Danachair (1978), 25; Ó Catháin (1982), 45–53; P.V. O'Sullivan (1991), 19–20, 107–12; Ó hÓgáin (1995), 68–70; E.R. Ó Néill in *Béaloideas*, *59*, 167–88, 255–8.

cattle A great deal of lore was concerned with the creatures with whom humans were in regular daily contact and on whom people's livelihood largely depended. Of these, the cow was one of the most valuable and valued.

The medieval historians fancifully stated that the first cattle ever in Ireland were four oxen introduced by PARTHALÁN. This was, of course, invention, for cattle have been domesticated in Ireland since the fourth millennium BC. Both archaeology and pseudo-history agree, however, that these animals have been of paramount social importance in Ireland for a very long time, and this is reflected in the medieval literature concerning wars and raiding (*see* BÓRAIMHE, DONN CUAILNGE *and* ULSTER CYCLE). The necessity of milk for sustenance and nourishment caused a quasi-mystical power to be often associated with it (*see* BRIGHID, CORC DUIBHNE, FLIODHAIS

70

and GLAS GHOIBHNEANN), and this was further stressed by perennial ideas that make cows stand at a kind of functional juncture between this life and the otherworld realms. The image of a divine white cow seems to have been early established in Irish myth (*see* BÓINN), and it spilled over into LEGENDS of SAINTS. Especially notable is the fact that the literature repeatedly refers to white red-eared cows as being particularly valuable and obtainable from otherworld sources. It has been plausibly suggested that this type of dual colouring derives its imagery from a breed that still survives in Britain, having been introduced there during the Roman occupation. FAIRY cows are sometimes in later folklore claimed to have these colours, and it is believed that the fairies are more likely to take a white cow from a farmer's herd than any other colour. By extension of this, a white cow is said to be very unlucky on a farm. The type of cow most sought after by the old farmers was a *droimfhionn*, which signifies a dark-coloured animal with a streak of white on its back. These were believed to be great milkers, as also were cows with crooked horns.

An Irish proverb claims that 'the cow is one of the pleasant trees of Paradise', and another states that she is leather and meat, milk and butter. Since cows were of central importance to the livelihoods of farmers, and since they were prone to illness, interference with them by otherworld beings was much feared. The fairies were believed to take a special interest in livestock, and so to placate them the first measure of milk taken from a cow would be thrown into the air for them. Notwithstanding this, it was thought that the fairies would not hesitate to take away a fine cow if they were in need of one in their realm. Cracks in a cow's hide were interpreted as resulting from fairy darts being shot at her, these darts being a preliminary to abduction. In order to prevent this, various methods were employed that were believed to be effective against the fairies, such as tying a red ribbon to the cow's tail, rubbing dung to her udder, or causing her to inhale some puffs of smoke.

Although on big farms the cow byre was a separate building, down to the nineteenth century, the cow byre of the small farmer was often under the same roof as the dwelling-house. It was a sort of extension of the main kitchen, with a drain carrying the waste material away from the house. This arrangement allowed the cattle to contribute to house-heating in the winter, and increased the sense of close proximity felt towards the cows. Since St BRIGHID was the special patron of cattle, crosses dedicated to that saint were hung in the cow byre and were believed to give very good protection; while on St John's Eve (*see* TIME), the cows might be driven through bonfires, or have their udders singed with a blessed candle at Easter.

The same methods of protection were believed to be effective against the other chief source of danger to cattle: envious and avaricious neighbours. Certain people, who were reputed to have the evil eye (*see* HUMAN LIFE), were much feared by farmers, and would at all costs be kept away from a herd. Similarly, if a neighbour used a whitethorn stick to drive one's cattle, the worst was suspected of him. Some neighbours were also suspected of attempting to take milk by magical means, especially on May Eve (*see* TIME). On the positive side, it was considered lucky to keep a GOAT or a virgin cow with the herd, and in some places the cows were made to swim in a river or even the sea to bring them good fortune.

Regarding the actual milking itself, there was a belief that music caused a cow to increase her yield, and so milkers would often sing or whistle as they worked. It was customary in many places at the beginning of summer to bring the herd to new pasture until the end of autumn. The summer pasture would be unused land on a hillside or mountainside, and was known as *buaile* – hence the frequency of this element (anglicised booley) in Irish place names. Temporary dwellings were erected on the chosen locations, and often the young people who tended the cattle would live in these for weeks on end. The practice of transhumance was current in other countries also, but in Ireland – which has little sunny WEATHER apart from these

71

months – it had a special aesthetic attraction. It afforded the young people the opportunity of prolonged absence from the authority of their elders, and they availed of it to congregate, dance and make merry. From the word *buaile* comes the Hiberno-English term 'hooley', which refers to an enjoyable get-together accompanied by singing and dancing.

Some lore also was attached to the keeping of bulls. In olden times, these dangerous animals were often allowed to roam quite freely, and people needed to be on their guard against them and to be ready to avoid or outwit them. If cornered by a bull, one should keep one's nerve and attempt to bluff it by, for instance, making a feint towards it while shouting wildly. It was said that a bull would never attack a lunatic or a naked person. According to one curious tradition, a bull should never be placed in a field where there was an echo, because on hearing his bellowing repeated, he would think that another bull was present. He would thus be constantly restive, and in time would pine away and die.

A practice very common in medieval times, but which has died out in recent centuries, was to bleed cattle for food. A vein in the animal's shoulder was opened and the blood caught in a vessel – when congealed, this was heated into edible balls, which provided much-needed nutrition in times of scarcity.

Lucas (1989); F. Kelly (1997), 27–66; Cross (1952), 44, 51–82, *passim*; Macalister (1939), 272 & (1940), 8, 58; Wood-Martin, *2* (1902), 126–31; S. Ó Súilleabháin (1942), 31–5 & (1967), 21–5; Ó Duilearga (1948), 371, 449; M. MacNeill (1962), 674–5; Ó Danachair (1978), 25; Danaher (1984), 14; M.J. Murphy in *Ulster Folklife, 3*, 71; Ó Catháin (1980), 75–80; P.V. O'Sullivan (1991), 9–11, 112–24.

Céadach Fictional character, a handsome young hero and lover in the FIANNA CYCLE. The name was not unusual, being derived from *céad* (hundred) and therefore denoting a man of some wealth.

The late medieval literature has several mentions of a warrior called Céadach, variously claimed to have been a son of the Scandinavian KING, the Saracen king and the king of Thule. There does not seem to have been any specific narrative of him in existence at that time, and the mentions were simply a way of stressing how the fame of the Fianna troop was so great that foreign princes came to join it. It is virtually certain that a romance story concerning Céadach was composed in the sixteenth or seventeenth century, although no manuscript of that text survives. Versions of the story have been collected from folklore all over Ireland and western Scotland in the last two centuries, which suggests that manuscripts of it were once quite common.

The story tells of how Céadach was the son of a foreign king and that he joined the Fianna and became a close confidant of the troop's leader, FIONN MAC CUMHAILL. He and another young man, usually called Lon Dubh, were in love with the same girl. She chose Céadach, and Lon Dubh sought as recompense the right to strike one undefended blow on his rival. Soon afterwards, Fionn was embarking on an overseas adventure, and he took the two young warriors with him. Céadach showed great valour on the expedition, but on their return home, Lon Dubh struck the promised blow, and in the ensuing struggle both young men were killed. Fionn had arranged with Céadach's sweetheart that he would raise a black sail if her lover were dead, but he raised a white sail instead. When she saw the dead body, she was disconsolate, but noticing two birds magically revive a third, she copied their actions and brought Céadach to life again.

The composer of this story clearly had a good imagination, and it is difficult to trace any possible sources used by him, apart from some version of the medieval romance of Tristan and Isolde, which is clearly echoed by the sails MOTIF.

Bruford (1969), 123–33, 258–9; Ó hÓgáin (1988), 257–8, 341.

Ceallach Cleric of the mid-sixth century, bishop of Cill Alaidh (Killala, County Mayo). His name, which meant 'champion', was a common one in early Ireland.

Memory of the career of this bishop Ceallach seems to have survived orally until medieval times in his native area of Uí Fhiachrach Muaidhe (in east Mayo).

He was the son of the Connacht king EOGHAN BÉAL, who died in the year 543 and was succeeded by his brother Ailill Ionbhanna. It is apparent that this Ailill contended with Ceallach for the KINGSHIP and deprived him of it, but there is no direct evidence regarding this. A biography of Ceallach written in the twelfth century purports to give details of these events, but it creates a great distortion by substituting for Ailill the celebrated Connacht king GUAIRE, who in fact lived a century later.

The text of this story, which is entitled *Caithréim Cellaig*, describes how before he died, Eoghan Béal instructed his followers to install Ceallach as king in his place, as his other son Muireadhach was too young. Ceallach was a monk at the monastery of St CIARÁN at Clonmacnoise, and the men of Uí Fhiachrach Muaidhe persuaded him to leave that monastery and to become king of Connacht. Ciarán was displeased at this, and cursed Ceallach for abandoning his vocation. The king of the southern Uí Fhiachrach – here called Guaire – plotted to depose Ceallach and eventually drove him in flight from his territory. Ceallach returned to Ciarán's monastery and resumed the clerical life there, sending what remained of his followers to join his young brother Muireadhach.

The fame of Ceallach's holiness spread, and he was appointed bishop of Killala. He was extremely popular, a great host and patron of the arts. We read that once, when he approached near to a fortress of Guaire, he did not go to meet the king. Guaire sent an invitation to him, and Ceallach promised to come as soon as his Sunday observances were completed. Guaire's messenger, however, misrepresented his reply as a refusal and, as a result, Guaire grew angry and ordered the bishop to leave his territory. Ceallach went to an island on Loch Claon (a pseudonym for Lough Conn, County Mayo) and spent Lent there, accompanied by four young clerics. Meanwhile, Guaire became aware that the youth Muireadhach was frequently visiting Ceallach there and grew frightened that Ceallach would advise his young brother to make a bid for the kingship.

Guaire's own advisers fed his fear, and on their instructions, he bribed Ceallach's four clerical companions to murder him. This they did by driving their spear points into him and rending him with their swords. His body was left to the carrion crows and wild beasts, but all who consumed his flesh and blood died as a result.

When Muireadhach came to the island and found his brother missing, he set out in search of him. A fierce wolf came from the woods and slew nine of Muireadhach's men, whereupon Muireadhach attacked and slew the wolf. Thus he got the nickname Cú Choingeilt (consuming hound) from his companions. Finding Ceallach's body, he realised what had happened and swore vengeance. He cursed a graveyard where burial was refused to the body for fear of Guaire, and it was struck by lightning and destroyed. Two wild stags came drawing a hearse, and when the corpse was put into the hearse, they brought it to a cemetery in the Eisreacha (an area near Killala, County Mayo). After the burial, the stags used to plough for the local people by day and come to lick the grave of holy Ceallach in the evening.

Cú Choingeilt collected a force of men and made several alliances, including that of the high-king at Tara. On his return to Connacht, he met a swine-herd guarding pigs that belonged to the four murderers of Ceallach. The swine-herd welcomed him, and brought him disguised as a servant to the fortress of the four. Noticing that all were becoming drunk, he sent the swine-herd to call his men. They came and seized the four murderers – the ex-clerics Maol Chróin, Maol Dalua, Maol Seanaigh and Maol Deoraidh. Cú Choingeilt had the four taken out next morning, and had them impaled, dismembered and gibbetted. Following this savage revenge, conflict broke out between Cú Choingeilt and Guaire, the latter being forced to sue for terms. Guaire gave his daughter Geilghéis in marriage to Cú Choingeilt, but he also plotted treachery. Using the unwitting St Ciarán as a mediator, he invited his young rival to his fortress, promising to cede the kingship of Connacht to him. When he got Cú Choingeilt in his power, however, he wasted no time in having him slain. As remarked above, the attribution of these crimes to Guaire is quite unhistorical and due to a mistake of the writer of *Caithréim Cellaig*. The feast day of Ceallach is 1 May.

O'Hanlon, *5* (1875), 1–15; Kenney (1929), 456–7; Mulchrone (1933); T. Ó Concheanainn in *Éigse*, *11*, 35–8.

Cealtchar *(earlier, Celtchair)* Fictional warrior in the ULSTER CYCLE. The character may have been suggested by the place name Ráith Chealtchair (literally, 'concealed fort'), an early designation for Downpatrick in County Down.

Once, Cealtchar was understood as the name of a person who had owned the dwelling, and that person was naturally claimed to have been the ancestor of the Rosraighe sept of that area. His image was also developed according to the semantic range of the name. This, *celtchair* or *celtair*, was often taken to indicate 'a concealed thing', and by extension was a poetic term for a spear. Thus it was claimed that the character Cealtchar had been a great spearman who resided at Dún Leathghlaise (Downpatrick). He was described as son of an otherwise unknown personage called Uitheachar or Uithidir. Huge and ugly in appearance, he had a large nose, large ears and rough grey hair. Rugged also in manners, he fought alongside CONCHOBHAR MAC NEASA in all that king's major engagements and is mentioned as present in several dramatic scenes of the Ulster Cycle.

Usually a background figure, one text from the eleventh century focuses attention on him. We read that his wife Brígh Bhreathach once went to the house of a very rich man of Ulster called Blái Briugha. There was an injunction (GEIS) on this Blái that he must sleep with a woman who came alone to his house, and so he slept with Brígh. Cealtchar heard of this, and he drove his spear through Blái as the latter was playing chess with Conchobhar. The spear stuck in the wall behind Blái, and a drop of blood from it fell on the chessboard near the enraged king. Fleeing Conchobhar's anger, Cealtchar went to the territory of the DÉISE (Decies, in south-east Munster),

but a settlement was reached and he was allowed to return home. Conchobhar imposed on him as compensation for Blái's death that he must relieve the Ulstermen of the three worst misfortunes that should befall them.

Soon after, a Munster warrior called Conganchneas came to ravage Ulster as vengeance for the death of his brother CÚ ROÍ. This Conganchneas (horny-skin) got his name from the fact that javelins and swords did not wound him but merely glanced off his skin. Cealtchar was sent by Conchobhar to rid the province of him. Encountering Conganchneas, Cealtchar beguiled him by offering his daughter Niamh to him as well as a massive dinner every evening. Niamh soon inveigled from Conganchneas the secret of how he might be killed. 'Red-hot iron-spits must be driven into my soles and through my shins,' he said. She told her father, and when Conganchneas was asleep, Cealtchar drove the irons into him and then beheaded him. Cealtchar had the fallen warrior buried at the place of his demise and a cairn erected over him.

The second misfortune Cealtchar had to tackle was a vicious hound called the Luchdhonn (brown mouse), which every night devastated some dwelling in Ulster. It used to return to a cave in a certain valley and sleep there during the day. One morning, it found Cealtchar at the cave waiting for it. He thrust a hardened alder stick into the hound's mouth, and when its teeth locked on the stick, he shoved his hand down its throat and tore its heart out. Exactly a year after that, three whelps were found at the cairn of Conganchneas. One of these became the hound of Mac Da Thó (*see* CONALL CEARNACH), a second was the hound of Culann the smith killed by CÚ CHULAINN, and the third was raised by Cealtchar. He called it Daolchú (chafer-hound) because it was jet black. This hound was ferocious to everyone except Cealtchar himself, and when he was away from home one day, it escaped and began to devastate the province. This was therefore the third misfortune from which Cealtchar had to deliver Ulster. He went to the valley where the hound was, and called it. It came and licked his feet, but he speared it through the heart. When he withdrew the spear and raised it, a drop of the hound's blood ran along it and fell on Cealtchar himself. It went right through him and killed him.

The source for this story is clearly the tradition regarding the death of Cú Roí (q.v.). Conganchneas is described as brother to that hero, and the narrative employs a FOLKTALE plot (*see* WONDER TALES, type 302) already used in the context of Cú Roí. From that folktale, we have the MOTIF of the secret betrayed by a GIANT's wife, and that of the external soul of the giant – here complicated by the extension of his personality onto hounds. These animals were no doubt suggested by the name of Cú Roí, and the influence of the slaying of a great hound by Cú Chulainn is also clear. The name Conganchneas is borrowed from the text of *Táin Bó Cuailnge* (*see* FEAR DIADH), while the venomous drop of blood from a slain opponent is probably taken from accounts of the death of the tyrant BALAR.

Cealtchar had a celebrated spear (*lúin*). We are told that when it was expected to be used, it had to be bathed in a cauldron of blood, for otherwise its shaft would burst into flame and it would go through its bearer. It was discovered by Cealtchar on the field of the great second Battle of Moytirra (*see* MYTHOLOGICAL CYCLE), and after his death passed into the possession of DUBHTHACH DAOL ULADH. Dubhthach was himself slain by it, as was CÚSCRAIDH MEANN MACHA later. It is clear that the character of Cealtchar owed much of its development and appeal to this fantastic spear. The weapon's name, *lúin Chealtchair*, with all its connotations of secrecy and danger, was suggestive of sinister drama. An offshoot of the association of Cealtchar with spears is a reference to a great javelin-cast made at him by CEAT MAC MÁGHACH. This javelin entered his thigh and passed through his testicles, so that from that day forward he had no progeny. A fanciful genealogical tradition, on the other hand, had it that Cealtchar had several sons and was the ancestor of the Uaithne and Araidh septs in Munster and the Luighne sept in Connacht.

RÁITH CHEALTCHAIR: E. Hogan (1910), 569.
GENERAL: C. O'Rahilly (1976), 107, 113, 301; Meyer (1906), 24–31, 43–5; Thurneysen (1935), 12–13; Ó Cadhlaigh (1956), 467.
SPEAR: Knott (1936), 37–8; J.C. Watson (1941), 33, 58; E. Hogan (1892), 78.
GENEALOGY: O'Brien (1962), 278–80, 541.

Ceasair *(earlier, Cessair)* Fictional lady, leader of the imagined first ever settlement in Ireland. Her travels covered much of the country, showing that her portrayal is influenced by imagery of the land-goddess. It is significant that one tradition has her as daughter of BANBA, an obvious version of such a GODDESS, and that she was substituted for her mother in a dramatic narrative.

In developing that narrative, the medieval pseudo-historians claimed that Ceasair was a granddaughter of the biblical Noah and that she came to Ireland to escape the Deluge. 'She thought it probable that a place where people had never come before, and where no evil or sin had been committed, and which was free from the world's reptiles and monsters, that place would be free from the flood.' She arrived 40 days before the Deluge, but two of her three ships were wrecked and only one came ashore at Corca Dhuibhne (the Dingle Peninsula, County Kerry). The total crew of that ship was 50 women and three men. Ceasair's father Bith, son of Noah, was one of these, as well as Ladru the pilot and the celebrated FIONNTAN. The name Ladru meant 'robber', indicating some lost story concerning him, whereas the name Bith may have had mythical origins, as it meant 'world'. The three men divided the women among them at Cumar na dTrí nUisce ('the juncture of the three waters' – i.e. where the Rivers Suir, Nore and Barrow meet). Ceasair was part of Fionntan's share. The other two men soon died and were buried at Ard Ladrann and Sliabh Beatha respectively. Left alone with all the women, Fionntan felt inadequate and fled from them. Ceasair died from a broken heart on account of his absence, and was buried at a place called Cúil Ceasra. The other women did not long survive her, and Fionntan alone remained.

A variant account states that Noah had refused entry into his Ark to these three men because he considered them robbers, and that Ceasair had offered to bring them to safety if they accepted her leadership. She consulted an idol that directed them to travel to Ireland. Ceasair was also given an agricultural role, it being claimed that she brought into Ireland the first SHEEP ever to be in the country. The medieval historians had a further tradition that, whereas Ceasair and her group were the first settlers in Ireland, three fishermen from Spain had earlier discovered the country, having been blown hither by a gale. They returned to Spain to collect their wives, but the Deluge overtook them and drowned them at Tuagh Inbhir (the estuary of the River Bann) before they could land.

Fictional though these accounts are, there may be some native myth lying behind them. There were several traditions of mythical drownings in early Ireland that purported to explain the origin of great breakers off the coast. The breaker at Tuagh Inbhir, for instance, was explained as having resulted from the drowning there of a maiden called Tuagh. She had been kidnapped by the wizard Fear Fí, who had enchanted her and left her on the beach there while he sought a boat, but she was overcome by the wave. A similar story attached to the drowning of CLÍONA by a breaker at Glandore, County Cork; and the designation Tuile Ladrann (flood of Ladru) for a breaker off north Mayo suggests that the above-mentioned Ladru was associated with some lore of a drowning at that place. Lore of inundations was known to the Celts outside of Ireland also, and this story type may have concerned the attempt of a robber to seize a water-goddess and the reaction of the waters to the attempt.

The MOTIF of a single male surrounded by many women, and fleeing from them, may also have been based on indigenous Celtic tradition. A thirteenth-century story describes how a mariner called Ruadh mac Ríghdhoinn was accosted at sea by nine otherworld women. He became their lover,

but when one of them became pregnant by him, he fled from them to the mouth of the nearest river. The women pursued him and cast his newborn baby onto the rocks, where it perished. The women then cried out that this was 'a great tragedy' ('*Ollbhine!*'), from which statement the toponymic Ailbhine (Delvin river, County Meath) is fancifully derived. That such otherworld water-women or river-goddesses may lie behind the Ceasair story is suggested by the way in which the women are there divided into three groups at the meeting of the three rivers.

The name Ceasair would have meant 'shower of hail' or the like, but whatever mythological significance it originally had has been subsumed by a simple place name. Some medieval antiquarian in the vicinity of County Galway noticed that Ard Ladrann (Ardamine near Gorey, County Wexford) and Sliabh Beatha (Slieve Beagh near Fivemiletown, County Tyrone) underlined the roles of the characters Ladru and Bith. That antiquarian then sought to focus attention on his own area by using the local place name Cúil Ceasra ('showery hinterland' – i.e. Coolcasragh near Tuam, County Galway). This he interpreted as 'the slope of Ceasair', and claimed that Ceasair had died there.

GENERAL: Macalister (1939), 166–252; Arbois de Jubainville (1903), 36–42; Rees & Rees (1961), 113–15; J. Carey in *Éigse*, 22, 37–48.

CELTIC INUNDATIONS: Duval (1971), 189, 193, 307; Ó hÓgáin (2002), 18–19, 241–2 (sources: Strabo 7.2.1; pseudo-Aristotle, *Ethica Eudemia* 3.1.25; Stobaeus, *Florilegium*, 3.7.390); Irish version in Gwynn (1924), 226.

CELTIC RIVER-GODDESSES: T.F. O'Rahilly (1946), 3–6; Green (1995), 89–116; Ó hÓgáin (1999), 63–8, 108–13 (Continental sources: Strabo 4.4.6; Pomponius Mela, *De Chorographia*, 3.48). *See* BÓINN, DANU *and* SIONAINN.

SEA STORIES: Gwynn (1913), 210–14 & (1924), 58–62; Best & O'Brien (1957), 749; Van Hamel (1933), 39–41; J. Carey in *Éigse*, 22, 41–6.

Ceat mac Mághach
Mythical Connacht champion who figures in several stories of the ULSTER CYCLE.

The name (earlier, Cet) seems identical with the Gaulish name Cettos, both indicating endurance, which was probably an attribute of some antique Celtic deity. Both it and the patronymic (nominative Mághu) may have belonged to the native population of the western province before the CONNACHTA sept took over. In view of Ceat's leading profile as a Connacht warrior, it is significant that the part he plays in the cattle-raid of Cooley is minimal, and this further suggests that his origins do not lie in the ambit of Ulster lore. The strong likelihood is that he was a figure of such celebrity in the early folklore of the western province as to be naturally included in an Ulster–Connacht conflict once that conflict became a context in which writers situated their stories. In these stories, Ceat always plays the role of a hostile outsider, the greatest single warrior with whom the Ulstermen must contend.

According to one source, the mother of CONALL CEARNACH was a sister of Ceat, and when Ceat came to visit and saw the baby, he knew that it would be a great slaughterer of Connachtmen. So he put his foot on the baby's neck, intending to kill it, but was prevented by the mother. Conall's neck was twisted ever after. In his continual attacks and combats, Ceat later left his mark on several other leading Ulster warriors. He cut off the arm of Lámh Ghábhaidh, knocked an eye out of the head of Eoghan mac Durthachta, cut the heel off Sál Cholgan, made the same warrior's son Meann dumb, wounded Muinreamhar mac Gheirginn so that his neck was continually swollen, wounded CÚSCRAIDH in the throat so that he spoke ever after with a stammer, and rendered CEALTCHAR infertile with a cast of his javelin. He had thus a victory to boast of over the various great warriors of Ulster who were present at Mac Da Thó's feast, when he demanded the right as leading warrior to carve the PIG. When Conall Cearnach entered, however, Ceat relinquished that privilege to him.

The literature represents Ceat as having been for a time at the court of the high-king EOCHAIDH FEIDHLEACH and as having shared with Conall Cearnach the leadership of Eochaidh's army (see FINN EAMHNA). When the conflict between

Ulster and Connacht gathered momentum, however, his main function was raiding and plundering the northern province. He is described as 'a slaughterous hound' and 'a perpetually foraying enemy against the Ulstermen for as long as he lived'. In one of his daring raids, he took the brain-ball of Meas Geaghra that was held as a trophy in Eamhain Mhacha; and it was with this that he delivered his most devastating blow of all. Waiting his opportunity, he shot it from a sling at king CONCHOBHAR MAC NEASA, and it was as a result of this deadly shot that Conchobhar eventually died.

Ceat followed up this triumph by slaying Conchobhar's son and successor, CORMAC CONN LOINGEAS, and soon after made another deadly raid into Ulster. When he departed with the heads of thrice-nine men, Conall Cearnach was sent after him. Snow had fallen, and Conall followed his track as far as Breifne (in County Leitrim), where he saw his chariot-horses outside a house. Reluctant to engage so fierce a warrior, Conall contented himself with placing as a token a wisp from one of the horse's manes on the front of Ceat's chariot. He then headed eastwards towards Ulster, but when Ceat found the wisp, he recognised Conall's work and went to seek him out. They met at Áth Cheit ('Ford of Ceat', on the River Shannon) and fought so furiously that both fell. Conall rose again, badly wounded, but Ceat was dead.

Notwithstanding the indications that his origins lay in the oral lore of western septs in ancient times, the character of Ceat figures only in Ulster Cycle literature and is not known to the folklore of recent centuries.

T.F. O'Rahilly in *Ériu, 13, 166–7*; W. Stokes in *Irische Texte, 3,* 392–5, 404–7; Thurneysen (1935); M.E. Dobbs in *RC, 43,* 284–7, 304–31; Meyer (1906), 2–21, 36–41, 45; Dinneen, *2* (1908), 200–9; Ó Cadhlaigh (1956), 468.

Ceithearn mac Fionntain Fictional character in medieval Irish literature. The word *ceithearn* had the collective meaning of 'a troop of soldiers' and was also used to denote a single soldier or 'kern'.

This character seems to have been developed due to a fanciful etymology of the toponymic Dún Ceithirn (the fortress of the troop), a large stone-fort in the parish of Dunbo in north County Derry. When it came to be understood to mean the fortress of a man called Ceithearn, this character underwent rapid development. Because one Fionntan mac Néill Niamhghlonnaigh was remembered as a local king in the same area of northern Ulster – having his fortress at Dún Dá Bheann (Mountsandel) – it was thought appropriate to make Ceithearn a son of this ruler.

Ceithearn appears in the ULSTER CYCLE in its embryonic form as early as the seventh century, where he is said to have been slain with a rowan-spear by FEARGHUS MAC RÓICH, and a ninth-century elaboration claims that Fer Deodae (i.e. FEAR DIADH) did the killing on Fearghus' behalf. In revenge, Ceithearn's son Solcheann slew Fiacc, son of Fearghus. A different account is given in the developed eleventh-century telling of the great cattle-raid of Cooley, where Ceithearn is described as one of twelve leading champions of Ulster. In that text, he comes alone to attack the army of queen MEADHBH, taking the place of the hero CÚ CHULAINN who is worn out by wounds and fatigue. He himself suffers a grievous wound, but resumes the fight and is slaughtered in the midst of the foe. His father Fionntan then comes to avenge him.

The name given to his father corresponded to that of the celebrated old seer FIONNTAN, and his own name Ceithearn qualified him as a warrior. Ceithearn mac Fionntain, accordingly, paralleled in his person the dual aspects of seer and warrior as found in the famous FIONN MAC CUMHAILL. The introduction of Ceithearn into this context gives him the distinction of being one of the very few characters who appear in two different cycles of Irish story. By the twelfth century, he was mentioned in the FIANNA CYCLE, for we read that after the young Fionn got the gift of wisdom from tasting the salmon of the Boyne, he went to Ceithearn to receive instruction from him in the craft of poetry. Here Ceithearn is described as a sage, and

his role is no doubt due to the associations of his patronymic.

NOMENCLATURE: Vendryes et al., Lexique, C, 58–9, 86–7; E. Hogan (1910), 379; J.C. Watson (1941), 1–2, 124; Ó Cadhlaigh (1956), 468, 475.

GENERAL: E. Windisch in Irische Texte, 2.1, 174; P.L. Henry in Mac Mathúna & Ó Corráin (1977), 56–62; C. O'Rahilly (1976), 96–101; K. Meyer in RC, 5, 202.

Ceithearnach Caoilriabhach

(Narrow-striped Kern) Designation of the principal character in a humorous text composed around the year 1514.

We read that the chieftain Aodh Dubh Ó Dónaill was feasting with his retainers in his dwelling at Béal Átha Seanaigh (Ballyshannon, County Donegal) when a stranger appeared among them. His costume had narrow stripes on it, his boots let in the water, his mantle was old and tatty with a naked sword protruding from it behind, and in one hand he carried three javelins of charred hazel. Aodh Dubh asked who he was and received the answer: 'My use and wont is to be in Islay one day, another in Cantyre, a day in Man, a day in Rathlin, and yet another on Slievecarn – for I am a ranting rambling roving fellow!' He had passed by the doorman unnoticed, and he boasted that he could not be prevented from leaving whenever he wished. Furthermore, he insulted the musicians of Aodh Dubh, saying that their playing sounded worse than the devils wielding sledgehammers in hell. He then himself took a harp and played, and so sweet and enchanting was the music that it would heal the sick and the wounded. Aodh Dubh recognised that the strains were of the otherworld.

The stranger then continued with his saucy answers. 'One day I am sweet, another I am bitter!' he declared, and refused a fine suit of clothes proffered to him. Aodh Dubh had twenty foot-soldiers within and twenty horsemen without to ensure that he could not depart, but the stranger passed out between them while they struck each other thinking that they were striking him. He gave a herb to the gatekeeper, telling him that if rubbed to the palates of the men killed in the tussle it would revive them. He instructed the gatekeeper to demand land and twenty cows from Aodh Dubh as payment for this service.

Just at that very time, Seán Mac Gearailt (i.e. John Fitzgerald), son of the Earl of Desmond, was holding an assembly in his dwelling at Cnoc Áine (Knockainey, County Limerick), and the kern dressed in striped clothes approached, announcing that he had come from Ó Dónaill in the north. He was given a drink and fell asleep until the following morning. When he arose, Seán asked him to play music and show his learning, but the stranger failed dismally at both tasks. Being ridiculed, he took the book and harp and performed magnificently. Seán remarked that he was a man of truly sweet art, and received the reply: 'I am sweet one day, and sour another day!' In the afternoon, Seán took him walking around the hill, and the stranger described how he had seen long ago there great hunts by FIONN MAC CUMHAILL and his men. Engrossed in this account, Seán turned to look at him, but found that the visitor had disappeared in the twinkling of an eye.

In Leinster (probably in County Wicklow), the head of the bardic Mac Eochaidh family was laid up with a broken leg for a long time, and all the best twelve physicians of his province had failed to cure him. To him, the narrow-striped kern next appeared, claiming to be a medical student and saying that if Mac Eochaidh abandoned his stinginess and churlishness he would be healed. The poet promised this, and his visitor then applied a herb to his leg. Immediately, Mac Eochaidh leaped up and began to run so swiftly that his twelve physicians could neither restrain nor catch him. Then the kern warned the poet to remain generous, or else he would come to him and break the two legs so badly that they could never again be healed. In a flush of gratitude, Mac Eochaidh offered the kern 300 each of horses, cattle, sheep and pigs, as well as his daughter in marriage. A great feast was prepared for the kern, but he raced away from them faster than a hare.

He ran so swiftly that he reached Sligo in an instant. The chieftain of that area, Ó Conchúir, was preparing to go on a campaign against Munster on account of a dispute between two hags over the ownership of a basket. One of the hags, from Munster, had taken the basket from the Connacht one, and Ó Conchúir was determined to avenge this insult to his province. The kern enlisted in his force, and the Connachtmen took great prey in Munster – including two cows and a hornless bull from the southern hag as compensation for her Connacht rival. The kern took his bow and arrow, and alternately repelled the Munster pursuers and drove the prey, ensuring that the raiders crossed the River Shannon safely. On their return home, Ó Conchúir drank a draught without offering one to the kern, and the latter took his leave of him. The chieftain tried to persuade him to stay and offered him his choice of reward, but in an instant the kern had disappeared.

He next visited Tadhg Ó Ceallaigh (chieftain of Uí Mhaine in the east of County Galway), and offered to perform tricks for the company at the residence of that chieftain. His first trick was to lay three rushes on his palm and to blow away the middle one only, which he did by holding the other two with his fingertips. One of Tadhg's men protested that he could also do this, but when he tried his fingers got magically caught in the palm. The kern, having won the bet, cured him with a herb, and then said that he had another trick – he could wag one ear while the other stood still. He did this by wagging one ear with his hand. When the same retainer of Tadhg tried to do it with his own ear, it came clean away from his head, and he again had to be cured by the kern.

Then the kern took a thread of silk from his bag and threw one end of it into the air, and it stuck in a cloud. He further took from his luggage a hare, a beagle, a servant-boy and a pretty girl, who all climbed up the thread into that cloud. Commotion was heard from the cloud above, and the kern remarked that harm was being done. He pulled in the thread, and it transpired that the beagle had killed the hare and the boy had gone 'between the two legs of the lady'. The kern cut the boy's head off with a sword stroke, but Tadhg protested at this, and he resuscitated the boy, putting the head on backwards. Again Tadhg protested, and he turned the head around to its proper position, but then he immediately disappeared.

The kern next appeared at the house (in County Carlow) of Mac Murchú Caomhánach, styled 'KING of Leinster'. There he announced himself as the *giolla deacair* (difficult servant). He criticised the harpists of that chieftain, and they seized their swords to kill him. All of their blows fell on their own heads, however, and on seeing this slaughter the nobles ordered that the kern be seized and hanged. He was accordingly taken to the gallows and dispatched, but on the executioners' return to the house, they found him waiting for them there alive. They realised to their consternation that they had hanged the closest confidant of Mac Murchú Caomhánach, but the kern restored him to life, together with the harpists who had been killed in the earlier melée. The chieftain turned to check if all were alive, and when he looked back again the kern had gone. He went to Cill Scíre (Kilskeer, County Tyrone) to the house of Seán Ó Dónalláin, where he was given a meal of thick milk and wild apples. He departed unexpectedly from there also, and no tidings of him were ever found after.

Some later manuscripts state that the kern was MANANNÁN in disguise 'because he used to be thus visiting everybody as a trickster', but this is merely a rationalisation of the story based on such appearances of Manannán in other accounts. The author seems to have been an Ulsterman, for he has Mac Eochaidh praise the people of that province and say that the kern came from there. It is clear that he made a compilation of trickster material based on lore of travelling POETS and gleemen. The Ceithearnach Caoilriabhach has the attributes of such men, including the characteristic saucy and antithetical answers. It is very likely that the author himself was one of them. Some of the noblemen are clearly identified by the author himself – Aodh Dubh Ó Dónaill, Seán Mac Gearailt, Tadhg Ó Ceallaigh and Seán Ó Dónalláin. The others can be identified as Féilim Ó Conchúir, Maolmhuire Mac Eochaidh and Art Buí Mac Murchú Caomhánach. These, being contemporaries of the author, were probably among his hosts when he went on tour.

The specific imagery of the kern would have been suggested to the author by card-playing, which was extremely popular in sixteenth-century Ireland. The knave in a suit of cards was represented as both a trickster and a soldier (i.e. a kern), and was portrayed with striped trousers. It therefore appears that the noblemen who occur in the text enjoyed playing at cards, and that the author was teasing them on this account.

The text was very popular in manuscripts, and it passed into popular lore. In recent generations, good oral versions of it have only been collected in Scotland, but some of the episodes have been collected in connection with other characters from the folklore of Ulster.

O'Grady, *1* (1898), xii–xiii, 276–89; Ua Muirgheasa (1912); Bruford (1969), 153–4, 253; IFC 169:387–8; OSL: Donegal (1835), 121–2.

Céitinn, Seathrún *(c.1570–c.1650)*

Priest, POET, theologian and historian, his name in anglicised form is Geoffrey Keating. Born in Tubbrid, near Cahir, County Tipperary, he was educated at Bordeaux and Salamanca. He was ordained a priest and became a doctor of theology, and in the year 1610 returned to Ireland. Appointed curate in his native parish, he wrote many poems and two long theological treatises in Irish. His fame as a preacher spread, and he was appointed parish priest of Outeragh and then of Tullaghorton (both County Tipperary).

In 1613 his name appeared among a list of priests being watched by government spies on suspicion of 'seducing' the people into rebellious feelings. His preaching was definitely forthright. It was said that he delivered a sermon on adultery that was understood by a certain influential lady of his locality to be directed against her, and that she complained him on this account to Donough O'Brien, Earl of Thomond, who was then holder of the office of president of Munster under the English regime. His standing with the authorities was further lessened, according to tradition, when he protested against the treatment of some tenants by a local landlord, and he was proclaimed an OUTLAW in 1622. Taking himself to the Glen of Aherlow, folklore claims that he hid away there for a while in a cave, and that he travelled about in disguise while collecting manuscript materials for his research. The death of the Earl of Thomond in 1624 left him free to engage in this research without hindrance.

He travelled much of Ireland seeking out manuscripts, and in or about 1633 completed his most celebrated work, a history of Ireland entitled *Foras Feasa ar Éirinn*. It circulated widely in manuscript form and in the succeeding centuries was a basic source of information for POETS, scholars and antiquarians. The term *béaloideas* (literally, 'oral education') was used by him several times in his writings to designate 'oral tradition'. It is now the usual term in Irish for folklore, and it was apparently coined by Céitinn himself.

Céitinn was parish priest of Cappoquin, County Waterford in 1634, but references to him after that date are uncertain. His name appears in a 1644 dedication over the doorway of a church in Tubbrid. The name of a deceased parish priest is also mentioned in the inscription, but it is not clear whether the reference to Céitinn himself indicates that he was dead or alive at the time. One report has it that he died at a castle belonging to the Butler family at Reahill, near to his birthplace. Another tradition, however, has it that he was murdered by a Cromwellian soldier in St Nicholas' Church in Clonmel in 1650. A Kerry folk account is in general accord with this, claiming that he was saying Mass in a lonely place when his congregation noticed soldiers approaching. When they told this to the priest, he instructed everybody to stay where they were, for if they ran they might be shot. He continued with the Mass then, but when the soldiers came they could see neither priest nor congregation there. Three days later, however, Seathrún Céitinn was caught and decapitated.

This LEGEND is of a type usually told of fugitive priests in seventeenth- and eighteenth-century Ireland, according to which the priest is saying Mass at a rock in the wilderness for fear of arrest. A group of soldiers come to the spot but cannot see him. However, it is often said that one of the soldiers, who was baptised a Roman Catholic, has the power to see the priest, who is accordingly arrested and put to death.

BIOGRAPHY: T. O'Sullevane in Clanricarde (1722), cxxvi–cxxix; W P. Burke in *JWAS*, *1*, 173–82; Mac Giolla Eáin (1900), 3–7; B. Ó Cuív in *Éigse*, *9*, 263–9; Cunningham (2000), 14–47.

HISTORY BOOK: Comyn, *1* (1902), & Dinneen, *2–4* (1908–14).

TERM *BÉALOIDEAS*: D. Ó hÓgáin in *Béaloideas*, *70*, 83–98.

FOLKLORE: R. Flower in *Béaloideas*, *2*, 204; Ó hÓgáin (1985), 206–8.

MASS ROCKS: F.P. Carey in *Vexilla Regis* (1957), 99–116.

Cian mac Maolmhuaidhe (c.*AD* 960–1015) Son of the EOGHANACHT king

of Munster. The name Cian was a common one, meaning 'enduring' or 'resilient'. His father Maolmhuaidh was slain in battle against BRIAN BÓRAMHA in the year 978, but he himself made peace with Brian and married his daughter Sadhbh. He fought on Brian's side at the Battle of Clontarf, but was afterwards slain in the struggle for the KINGSHIP of Munster that followed on Brian's death.

He is the subject of a romance composed in the fourteenth century entitled *Leigheas Coise Chéin* (The Healing of Cian's Leg). According to this, the stewards of Brian Bóramha went to collect rent in west Munster, and when they came to the house of Ó Cronagáin of Coireall (an unidentified place), that man was not at home. The wife of Ó Cronagáin, however, refused the rent to them. Hearing this, Brian in anger despoiled Ó Cronagáin's land, but he encountered the culprit's wife, and she insisted that their overlord was Cian and that he had never sought rent from them. Impressed by her speech, Brian returned her greyhound and sheep to her, and promised to make restitution to her husband for the damage that had been done to him if he reported to the royal fortress of Ceann Cora (Kincora, County Clare).

Soon after, Ó Cronagáin set out for Brian's court, and on the way caught a greyhound that was half white and half green. Brian welcomed him, and Ó Cronagáin asked for a set of beagles that the high-king had received as a gift from the king of France. This was granted to him and, foregoing the promised compensation, he went off towards home on the following day. At Sliabh Luachra (east of Killarney), his hounds coursed a hare, and the hare jumped into his bosom and became a beautiful young woman. She brought Ó Cronagáin to an otherworld dwelling and, at his request, slept with him that night. In the morning, she went with him to his home at Coireall, and when they arrived there, they found that his wife had gone away.

For three years, the otherworld lady stayed with Ó Cronagáin, and at the end of that time persuaded him to entertain Brian Bóramha there. Cian also was invited, and when he saw the woman fell completely in love with her. She rejected his advances, whereupon Cian knocked her down, but she was immediately changed into a mare and raced from the house. Cian tried to restrain her, but she kicked him, breaking his leg. Next day, Cian was brought to his own home, but his physicians failed to heal the leg. On the exact same day at the end of a year, he was alone in bed while his household was at Mass. A stranger came to him, announcing that he was his nephew and that he had heard Mass at Réamas na Ríogh (Rheims, France) that very day. He further said that he had once had a sweetheart in an otherworld dwelling at Cnoc Rafann (Knockgraffon, south Tipperary). He had slighted her, and she had laid a condition (*GEIS*) on him to leave Ireland. In France, he had procured a foreign princess as wife for the French king and had himself married a daughter of the German emperor. She bore him three sons, but she was taken from him by a warrior who overcame him and left him bound for a year. After his release, he had accidentally wounded himself with his own spear. A young princess of Orkney had healed him with a special poultice, and he now applied that same poultice to Cian's leg and cured it immediately.

The nephew called himself Macaomh an Fhágáin (the Vagrant Youth). Cian wished to know more of his adventures, and the Macaomh explained as follows: he had had affairs with other women besides his wife, and by the Orkney princess he had a son who called himself Macaomh an Uaignis (the Solitary Youth). He had met with this son on the search for his wife, and eventually they found her. His other three sons had refused to accept the pre-eminence of the Solitary Youth, and thus the Vagrant had to depart without delay in order to settle matters between them. Thus ended the account given to Cian by his adventurous visitor.

This story is found in a mere two manuscripts. It is a loose and ill-constructed text, but better manuscripts of it must have existed, and the story became popular in folklore, especially in Gaelic Scotland. Oral versions give an explanation for the disappearance of Ó Cronagáin's otherworld wife, which seems to have been a vital part of the narrative in the lost manuscripts. She had, we are told, threatened to leave him if he ever reminded her of how she had been a hare at the mercy of his dogs. This MOTIF is reminiscent of the folk LEGEND of the Quin family of INCHIQUIN, County Clare, from which it was probably borrowed. The influence of literary stories of CÚ ROÍ is evident from the motif of binding a vanquished rival in love, from the designation 'man of the grey cloak' for one of the Vagrant's associates, and also from his speedy travel abroad. However, the specific reference to mystical travel between Rheims and Ireland seems to be derived from the lore of bilocation of SAINTS.

Todd (1867), cxl, cxcii–cxciv, 212–15; O'Grady, *1* (1898), 296–305; Bruford (1969), 134–6, 144, 262.

Ciarán the older SAINT of the fifth and early sixth centuries, founder of the monastery of Saighir (Seirkieran, near Birr, County Offaly). He was reputed to have been 'the first-born of the saints of Ireland'.

His name implies that he was dark haired, and is anglicised as Kieran.

It is apparent that a biography of him was composed by a monk of the Seirkieran community in or about the eighth century, but the surviving accounts have added much to that original. Though they differ considerably among themselves, the general outline is clear. His father Lughna was from the territory of the OSRAIGHE (south Laois and Kilkenny), and he settled in Corca Laíghdhe (later, Corca Laoi, west Cork) and married a woman called Liadhain there. Before the saint's birth, she had a vision of a star coming from heaven and entering her mouth. Ciarán was fostered in Cléire (Clear Island) and, having spent 30 years there, set out for Rome.

In Italy, he met St PATRICK, who gave him a bell and told him to return to Ireland and to found a monastery at the place where the bell would ring of its own accord. He returned, and when the bell rang at Saighir, he commenced the building of his monastery there. He was helped in his task by a wild boar, a wolf, a badger and a fox, which animals became his first monks. An anecdote tells of how the fox once stole the saint's shoes to eat them in his den, but Ciarán sent the badger to bring him forcibly and ordered him to do penance for the misdeed. Soon a large number of men and women arrived to become his monks and nuns. A series of miracle stories are related of him, including raising people from the dead, providing food where none previously existed, and healing the sick and afflicted.

When Patrick reputedly arrived in Munster, Ciarán went to join him on his missionary work. One anecdote tells of how a man was seized by the king of Munster because he had stolen Patrick's horse, and of how Ciarán ransomed the man for his weight in gold. After the king had received the gold, however, it melted away and vanished. A similar story tells of CATTLE paid by Ciarán to ransom his namesake CIARÁN of Clonmacnoise from a local king – these cattle also melted away and vanished when their purpose was fulfilled. The idea that Ciarán preceded the

mission of Patrick must be old, for in some striking instances he is made to parallel John the Baptist, the precursor of JESUS. We read of him as a pioneer of monasticism in the wilderness, wearing nothing but skins of WILD ANIMALS and refusing ordinary food, all of which sounds like residue from an ancient portrayal. Another striking MOTIF is his reputed custom of keeping a fire perpetually lighting in his monastery – this has all the marks of a borrowing from Irish pre-Christian ritual (*see* entry on St BRIGHID).

His association with Cape Clear on the south-west coast seems to be historically accurate. The surviving literary accounts have him spending his youth there, and they make the association again in a different context, stating that he used to go to pray with his foster-mother on a lonely rock off the southern coast of Munster. He would return miraculously to Seirkieran on the same day. Ciarán is still remembered in the folklore of Clear Island, as well as at Seirkieran, and his feast day is 5 March.

Kenney (1929), 316–18; Plummer, *1* (1910), 217–33 & *1* (1922), 103–24; O'Grady, *1* (1892), 1–16; Heist (1965), 346–52; P. Grosjean in *Analecta Bollandiana, 59,* 217–71; O'Hanlon, *3* (1875), 115–48; IFC 40:96–8, 88:198–201.

Ciarán the younger SAINT who died *c*.AD 550, and who founded the great monastery of Cluain Mhac Nóis (Clonmacnoise, County Offaly). This monastery, in the seventh and eighth centuries, claimed ecclesiastical precedence over most of Connacht and Munster as well as a large part of Leinster. The name, as in the case of his older namesake CIARÁN of Saighir, is anglicised as Kieran.

His biography was written at Clonmacnoise in or about the ninth century, and versions of it survive in both Latin and Irish. We read that he was son of a carpenter called Beoán of the Dál nAraidhe sept (in Counties Antrim and Down) and of Darerca, a woman of the Ciarraighe sept (in County Kerry), and that even before his birth there were signs of his future greatness. His coming was, it was claimed, prophesied by the three major saints of Ireland, PATRICK, BRIGHID and COLM CILLE. When Darerca was pregnant with him, the high-king's DRUID announced that the chariot in which she travelled resounded as it did under one destined for KINGSHIP.

His youth is also much dramatised. The first miracle performed by him was the restoration to life of a dead horse belonging to the son of the high-king and, to give him the profile of a young hero par excellence, he was described as slaying a savage hound that attacked him, as CÚ CHULAINN had done. He was sent by his parents to herd cattle, and while engaged at this work a fox befriended him and carried about his psalter for him. The fox, however, began to eat the book and while doing so was set upon by hounds. He had no choice but to race for safety into Ciarán's cowl, and thus both book and fox were saved.

One day, Ciarán insisted on joining his mother in dyeing cloth, and did his task so well that the cloth turned all it touched into its own colour. Having performed several other miracles, he went to the monastery of St Finnian at Cluain Ioraird (Clonard, County Meath). His mother refused him permission to take a cow from the herd with him, but he blessed a brown cow and it followed him. This was the celebrated *odhar Chiaráin* (dun one of Ciarán) that used to give enough milk for all the monastery's needs. While studying at Clonard, a stag used to come and hold his book on its antlers while he read. Once, when a girl fell in love with him, Ciarán persuaded her to become a nun by saying that if she offered her maidenhood to God she would be united with himself in a true sense. Ciarán became very famous as a sympathetic saint, ransoming slaves and befriending the poor with special fervour. He also had a marked agricultural function, and several of his miracles are concerned with reaping and milling, ensuring copious harvests and plenty of food.

We read that he decided to found his monastery at Clonmacnoise on account of the beauty of the place. He was assisted in the building by DIARMAID MAC CEARRBHEOIL, and as a reward promised Diarmaid that he would be high-king of Ireland. When this came to pass, the two maintained their friendship, and Ciarán became the confessor of the high-king. This situation allowed for lore to develop of Ciarán playing a leading part on a very public stage. We read that once, when Diarmaid held the assembly of Tailtiu (Teltown, County Meath), a woman accused her husband of being unfaithful to her. The husband denied this, but his wife insisted that he swear on the matter 'under Ciarán's hand'. He accordingly swore with the saint's hand laid upon his neck, but he was swearing falsely, and as a result a tumour came upon him and his head fell off. All wondered at this, and Ciarán took him to the monastery of Clonmacnoise, where the headless man remained for seven years, being reconciled to his wife before his death. The saint was also said to have miraculously come to the rescue of Maireann, one of Diarmaid's wives, who was being shamed by a rival wife at the fair of Tailtiu (*see* AODH SLÁINE). Maireann had no hair, but when her diadem was knocked off at the instigation of the rival, Ciarán caused beautiful tresses to grow on her head. On yet another occasion, Ciarán was asked by the high-king's assembly at Uisneach (Ushnagh, County Westmeath) for assistance in a period of drought, and he consented and caused a downpour of much-needed rain on the land.

To distinguish him from his older namesake, this saint was often referred to as *Ciarán Chluana* (i.e. of Clonmacnoise), whereas the other saint was known as *sean-Chiarán Saighre* (old Ciarán of Saighir). One story connects the two to each other. We read that Crichid, the farmer of Clonmacnoise, went to Saighir and impiously quenched the perpetual fire that burned there. On his way home, Crichid was devoured by wolves, whereupon Ciarán of Clonmacnoise went forth, obtained fire from heaven in place of the quenched fire, and restored Crichid to life. While the two saints feasted together at Saighir, Ciarán of Clonmacnoise prayed that the monastery be wealthy, whereas the older Ciarán prayed that wisdom be always in Clonmacnoise. When he felt his death approaching, Ciarán of Clonmacnoise had the monks bring him out into the sunlight. He looked at the sky and said 'hard is that road, but necessary'. We read that he was 33 years of age at the time of his death. This latter detail is obviously based on the life of JESUS who, like Ciarán, was 'the son of a carpenter'. Another tradition had it that Ciarán died young because the saints of Ireland grew jealous of him and prayed for his death.

Several relics of him survived until medieval times. The hide of his dun cow was kept at Clonmacnoise, and it was believed that the soul of a person who was placed on it when dying would gain heaven. The stone that had always served as a pillow for him was also preserved, as was a robe allegedly given by him to St SEANÁN, who sent it floating down the River Shannon to the latter's monastery. We further read that, at his death, he presented his bell to CAOIMHGHIN – this bell was called the *bobán* and was long preserved at the monastery of Glendalough.

Several of the stories passed from the written texts into popular lore, and some other details were added. In the folklore of west Offaly, for instance, a sudden gust of wind was known as 'Ciarán's wind', and this was explained by a LEGEND. Ciarán and St Manchán, we are told, decided to arrange the boundary between their paruchiae by rising early one morning and walking towards each other. The dividing line would then be drawn from where they would meet. Manchán accordingly left his monastery (at Lea Monaghan, County Offaly) with the first light of day and began to walk towards Clonmacnoise. Ciarán was a heavy sleeper, and was only woken by the voice of Manchán insisting that the boundary must be at Clonmacnoise itself. Ciarán, however, prevailed on his rival to allow him as far as he would throw his cap. He uttered a prayer, and a sudden squall blew the cap far away into the air. The two saints ran after it, and it came down at Bloomhill, which henceforth was the boundary between them.

In the folklore of County Meath, a humorous account was given of how Ciarán was said to have had a difference of opinion with COLM CILLE. The two saints had churches at Castlekieran and Kells respectively, and we are told that Ciarán took a cross from Kells and Colm went to Castlekieran in high dudgeon and took it back. Ciarán followed on and caught up with him as he crossed the River Blackwater, whereupon the two holy men struggled with each other in the water and the cross fell and was broken.

Several legends of the saint were current in the folklore of the Clonmacnoise area. It was said that a local chieftain once refused him food though he was starving, and Ciarán threatened that the chieftain would die of thirst. This happened so, for each time the chieftain put a goblet to his mouth the drink disappeared through it. It was also said that Ciarán was once mocked by a local man who said that he was 'no more a saint than the robin on yonder bush'. No sooner had he said these words than Ciarán changed into a robin and flew to a hawthorn bush that grew nearby. The man fell on his knees and begged pardon, and the saint returned to his usual shape. The feast day of Ciarán of Clonmacnoise is 9 September.

Kenney (1929), 376–82; Bieler (1979), 146–7; Stokes (1905), 202–5 & (1890), 117–34; Plummer (1910), *1*, 200–16; Heist (1965), 78–81; Macalister (1921); O'Grady, *1* (1892), 72–4, 82–3, 416; O'Hanlon, *9* (1875), 199–237; OSL: Meath (1836), 18–22; IFC 157:505–6, 179:141–3, 946:157–60, 256, 947:222–4, 1103:421–4, 1910:148–9.

Clíona *(earlier, Clidna, Clíodhna)* Supernatural lady in literary and oral tradition. Her name probably meant 'the territorial one', and represented a function of the patron GODDESS. Showing her otherworld nature, she was sometimes given the epithet Ceannfhionn (fair haired).

A medieval story tells of how she fell in love with AONGHUS and went from her dwelling in Magh Meall (the Pleasant Plain) in a bronze boat to meet him. She was accompanied by a man called Iuchna, who acted treacherously towards her. He played magic music so that she fell asleep, and a great flood came and drowned her at Cuan Dor (the bay of Glandore, County

Cork). An alternative account – which expressly makes her one of the TUATHA DÉ DANANN – states that she eloped from Tír Tairngire (the Land of Promise) with a handsome young warrior called Ciabhán. They landed at Trá Théite (the strand at Glandore), and Ciabhán left her in his boat while he went to hunt. The wave then came and drowned her. These accounts seem to have arisen from an actual designation of the tide at that place as the Wave (*Tonn*) of Clíona. This was one of the great waves of Ireland, according to the ancient topographical system, and her association with it was an expression of the idea that the deities resided in, and that goddesses were patronesses of, water (*see* CEASAIR).

In post-medieval tradition, Clíona was regarded as one of the principal otherworld women of the province of Munster. She was said to reside in a palace under Carraig Chlíona, a conspicuous large rock surrounded by smaller ones in a lonely part of the parish of Kilshannig, south of Mallow in County Cork. To the POETS she was an inspirer of their art, but she also had the reputation of being a seducer, as evidenced by a poem composed as a colloquy in west Munster in the eighteenth century and which became very popular in the folklore of that area. In this text, she comes to the celebrated poet Cearbhall Ó DÁLAIGH, inflicts a terrible thirst on him, and then promises to relieve him of it if he will lie with her. Cearbhall realises that to go with her means death, and so refuses to comply.

A folk LEGEND told in County Cork concerned Clíona and her reputed sister AOIBHEALL, who were claimed to have been daughters of a DRUID who lived in the fort of Castlecor, near Kanturk. Both the ladies were in love with a young chieftain of the Ó Caoimh (O'Keeffe) family, but Aoibheall was his favourite and he was engaged to be married to her. Clíona enlisted the help of an old nurse skilled in magic, and so caused Aoibheall to pine to the point of death. She then told Aoibheall that she would have her cured if she renounced her love for Ó Caoimh, but Aoibheall refused and Clíona struck her

with a magic wand, turning her into a white CAT. The unsuspecting chieftain later married Clíona, and they lived happily for a long time until the old nurse took ill and on her deathbed was struck by remorse. She sent for the chieftain and told him what had happened. The wand was by that time lost and the beautiful white cat could not be restored to its former shape, but Ó Caoimh in his fury ordered Clíona from his dwelling. She went to live at Carraig Chlíona and remains there ever since. She had given birth to a son of Ó Caoimh, and was thus regarded as the otherworld ancestress of that sept.

With the same general theme, another curious legend of her was told throughout Munster in recent centuries. According to this, a young man called Seán mac Séamais Mac Gearailt (John fitz-James Fitzgerald) was betrothed to a lady and a great dance was held to celebrate the engagement. Seán, who was a very handsome fellow, was dancing magnificently when he suddenly dropped dead, and it was believed that he had been 'carried away' by the FAIRIES and specifically by Clíona. A young girl, Caitlin Óg Chéitinn, daughter of a 'wise woman' (i.e. a folk-healer), went to Carraig Chlíona and demanded that he be returned. She spoke in verse outside the rock and Clíona answered in the same metre from within. A long contest in poetry ensued, with Clíona insisting on holding on to the handsome young man, but when Caitlin Óg demanded a massive dowry for Seán, she released him back into the world.

This legend is connected with an actual event that occurred in August 1737, when John Fitzgerald, the young Knight of Glin, suddenly fell ill at a ball in Youghal to celebrate his engagement to Isabel Butler. He died next day in Cork and was buried there. This John had seven years earlier formally renounced the Catholic religion and had conformed to the official Protestant Church. He was a Gaelic poet and was a close friend of several of the leading Munster poets of his time. His change of faith was motivated by a desire to avoid confiscation of his property, and was generally believed to have been contrived. As such it would have been the subject of humorous repartee between himself and other versifiers, and it is apparent that some such versifier alluded to the change as if it were an abduction of him by the fairies. This was a type of poetry often remembered in oral tradition, and his tragic death would in time be confused with it, thus giving rise to the legend.

According to local lore in north Cork, Clíona was many times seen leading the fairies in a nocturnal dance at her conspicuous rock, and it was also claimed that she sometimes gambolled about in the form of a large white rabbit. The stone circle of Carraig Chlíona was regarded as an eerie place, and nobody would venture there at night for fear of being abducted by her and her fairy host.

WAVE LEGEND: Stokes (1392), 12–13 & (1900), 108–9 & in *RC, 15,* 437–8; Gwynn (1913), 206–15.

CLÍONA AND POET: Ó hÓgáin (1982), 215–23.

CLÍONA AND AOIBHEALL: Kennedy (1870), 133–5; J.G. White in *JCHAS, 17,* pt. 2, 45–50, 74–82; IFC 42:130–3, 98:268–86.

SEÁN MAC SÉAMAIS: B. Ó Cuív in *Béaloideas, 22,* 102–11; P. Breathnach in *Celtica, 24,* 55–7; IFC Catalogue (numerous versions).

JOHN FITZGERALD: Gaughan (1978), 66–9, 148–50; Ó Foghludha (1937), 5–10 & (1946), 14, 84–6; RIA MS 12 F 6:21–5.

Cnú Dearóil

Cnú Dearóil Fictional otherworld minstrel in the FIANNA CYCLE. The word *cnú* (nut) was used in the figurative sense of 'favourite' and thus his name meant 'little nut'.

The character seems to have been derived from Crom Dearóil (little hunchback), a stock name in the early literature – a Crom Dearóil, for instance, occurs as a student of the druid CATHBHADH in the ULSTER CYCLE, and another of the name is described as the steward of St Móibhí at Glasnevin in Dublin.

Cnú Dearóil is not found in the literature until the twelfth century, and was probably added to the retinue due to Fionn being considered a *ríghfhéinnidh* (Fianna KING), according to the medieval convention of kings having gifted dwarf attendants. We read that he belonged to the otherworld community residing within Sídh Ban Feimhin (Slievenamon, County Tipperary), but that he was banished by the other musicians of that community due to jealousy of his splendid playing. FIONN MAC CUMHAILL was hunting that day between Aherlow and Slievenamon when he heard music and, looking around, saw the little man playing the harp. He was only four times as tall as Fionn's fist, and his harp was but three fists high. The Fianna troop was delighted with his music, and he remained with them, teaching their own musicians. He was also a wonderful singer. The Fianna went to the otherworld residence of DONN (off the south-west coast) to find a wife for him – Bláthnaid, who was a mere fist higher than him. Fionn had great affection for the tiny couple, and in bad WEATHER used to shelter them under his cloak.

CROM DEARÓIL: J.C. Watson (1941), 16–37; Meyer (1911), 80.

DWARF CONVENTION: Harward (1958).

CNU DEARÓIL: Stokes (1900), 18–20, 145, 165, 168; Ní Shéaghdha, *1* (1942), 50–8 & *2,* 51, 112–13 & (1945), 16, 24.

Cobhthach Caol

Cobhthach Caol Fictional KING of Ireland, whose reign was put down to the fourth century BC. Sometimes his name has the appendix Breagha – i.e. pertaining to the area around TARA.

Son of UGHAINE, he was said to have reigned for 50 years, but he figures narratively only in the Leinster myth of LABHRAIDH. He treacherously killed his brother Laoghaire Lorc, Labhraidh's grandfather, and seized the kingship. He also killed Ailill, Labhraidh's father, but was in turn slain by Labhraidh in the conflagration at Dinn Ríg. The name Cobhthach meant 'victorious', while Caol (earlier, Coel) meant 'meagre' or 'thin'. The sobriquet is explained by reference to the great envy he bore towards his brother Laoghaire, which caused him to waste away. The fact that Cobhthach occurs in the genealogies among the fictional ancestors of the CONNACHTA would explain why the Leinstermen (*see* LAIGHIN) selected him as the hostile tyrant in the Labhraidh myth.

Macalister (1956), 268–79; T.F. O'Rahilly (1946), 102–16.

Cod

Cod A fictional warrior in a romantic tale entitled *Eachtra Chlainne Ríogh na* hIorbhuaidhe (The Adventure of the Children of the King of Norway), which was composed by an anonymous Irish author in the seventeenth century. From one character in the tale being called the Macaomh Mór, it would appear that its author knew either the story of CONALL GULBAN or that of IOLLANN AIRMDHEARG.

The tale was poorly constructed but had many attractive episodes. According to it, Cod is the eldest son of the Norwegian king. While hunting with his two brothers, they meet the lady Féithlinn, who is enchanted and wishes to be released from the magic. She compels them by magical injunction (*see* GEIS) to search the world until they find her again and thus release her. On their quest, they have many adventures in strange lands, during which they learn that Féithlinn has been given the form of a CAT. In a treacherous attack orchestrated by the Macaomh Mór, two of the brothers are slain, and Cod alone survives. He encounters Féithlinn when she is in the form of a swan, and she places a mantle on his brothers to preserve them intact. Cod goes in search of a balsam to revive them, and is directed by a mysterious lady called Bé Thoinne to the Forest of Wonders, where he has further adventures – contending with opponents such as a headless corpse, a wizard harpist, and a fierce ox with golden horns. Meanwhile, Féithlinn finds the balsam and again meets Cod, who disenchants her by becoming her lover. He then departs on other adventures, and Féithlinn uses the balsam to restore his brothers to life. The two brothers go to war with the king of the world, and are taken prisoner by that king's daughter and placed in a city that is surrounded by a river of fire. Cod comes to assist them, and a friend whom he has gained through his adventures shows him a special stone that will quench the flames of the fiery river. Cod captures the city and himself becomes king of the world.

Although the tale was long and rambling, it was frequently read out from manuscripts and – in much reduced form – became popular with some of the older folk storytellers. There was a popular saying, '*ní scéal go scéal Choid*', meaning 'every story is less than the story of Cod', which must reflect the difficulty storytellers encountered in memorising its details rather than any particular quality of the narrative itself. These oral variants were often influenced by the plot of an international WONDER TALE (type 302), which entailed a similar quest for a lady.

Hyde, *GF* (1899), xi–xvi, 50–199; Bruford (1969), 79–84, 255–6, 278.

Colla Three mythical brothers of the name Colla Uais, Colla Meann and Colla Fochra. According to the pseudo-historians, they were the ancestors of the AIRGHIALLA septs in south Ulster. The earlier form of the name Colla was Conlae, which seems to be derived from a Celtic *Condollos*, meaning 'directing great one'.

The leading figure of the three was Colla Uais, whose name reflects the most powerful of the Airghialla septs, the Uí Mhac Uais. The Uí Mhac Uais were the furthest south of the Airghialla, on the immediate border of the Connachta (in the north of modern County Meath). These brothers were reputed to have made significant conquests in that area of Ulster in the fourth century AD. It is clear, however, that the actual conquests referred to were the work of NIALL and his sons a century later, and that the Airghialla septs were trying to expropriate some Connachta traditions. It may be that the basic lore they picked up involved a triplication of the mythical ancestor of the Connachta, CONN CÉADCHATHACH. Some early sources, in fact, have it that the Collas slew Eochu Muighmheadhon, father of Niall, in the Battle of Dubhchumar (where the Boyne and Blackwater meet at Navan), and that Colla Uais ruled for four years between Eochu and Niall.

The altered tradition of the three Collas as Airghialla ancestors is evident from the eighth century onwards. This claimed that they were nephews of the high-king Fiachu Sraibhthine, who was himself son of CAIRBRE LIFEACHAIR. Fiachu had a wonderful son called Muireadhach Tíreach, who was his champion in battle. Once, when Muireadhach was away in

Munster leading his father's army, the three Collas made an attempt to seize the throne. Fiachu's DRUID told him that he had a choice: victory and no more kings among his descendants, or to be slain and his descendants to be kings. Fiachu decided on the latter, and he thus was defeated and slain by the Collas in the Battle of Dubhchumar. Alarmed at the approach of Muireadhach's army, however, the Collas fled to Scotland, where they spent three years. Finally, they returned to TARA all alone and were received and forgiven by Muireadhach for having slain his father. They remained loyal to the high-king, and after some time, he advised them to go north and make 'sword-land' of Ulster. Enlisting allies from the province of Connacht, the Collas advanced north and won six great battles against the ULAIDH (Ulstermen). The seventh battle lasted a whole day and night, until blood reached the girdles of the warriors. The Ulstermen were completely routed, and the Collas pursued them all the way east to Gleann Righe (the Newry Valley). Thereafter the conquering brothers carved out their kingdom in south Ulster.

This story of the conquests by the three Collas enabled the Airghialla to underline the part they had played as allies in the northward expansion of the Connachta, thereby guaranteeing their territories against a possible takeover from Tara.

NAME AND CONNACHTA CONNECTION: T.F. O'Rahilly (1946), 225–31, 500.

EARLY TRADITION: K. Meyer in ZCP, 13, 378; Mac Carthy (1892), 93.

STORIES: M.A. O'Brien in Ulster Journal of Archaeology (ser. 3), 2, 170–7; K. Meyer in ZCP, 8, 317–20; G. Mac Eoin in ZCP, 8, 36, 63–82; Gwynn (1913), 200–5, 512; O'Grady, 2 (1892), 461–2, 505–7; Dinneen, 2 (1908), 356–65; T.F. O'Rahilly (1946), 224–32; F.J. Byrne (1973), 72–4.

Colm Cille SAINT and missionary, born at Gartan (County Donegal) around AD 521 of the royal UÍ NÉILL sept, his father Feidhlimidh being a grandson of CONALL GULBAN. His mother Eithne was from Leinster. In the year 546 he founded a monastery at a place that became known as his 'oakwood', Doire Cholm Cille (i.e. Derry). His later foundations included one at Dairmhaigh (Durrow, in north County Offaly). In 563 he left Ireland with twelve companions and settled on Oileán Í (Iona, an island off the south-west coast of Scotland). From there, he began a mission to the PICTS and to the Irish settlers of Scotland. He died on Iona in the year 597. He was originally called Criomhthann, 'Colm Cille' being a nickname meaning 'dove of the church'. The word *colm* is derived from the Latin Columba, a form often used as the saint's name.

It is apparent that a short biography of him was written by Cuimíne Ailbhe, seventh abbot of Iona, in the middle of the seventh century, but the earliest full work on him was the celebrated *Vita Columbae*, written in three sections or 'books' in or about the year 685 by the ninth abbot, ADHAMHNÁN, who, like Cuimíne, was a relative of Colm. The first section gives accounts of Colm's feats of clairvoyance and of his prophecies relating to immediate events and to people whom he knew and met. The second section describes miracles performed by him – such as producing food, healing illnesses, controlling the WEATHER at sea – and the deaths of several tyrants who were hostile to the Iona community. The third section seems to be a reproduction of the work of Cuimíne Ailbhe and is more directly biographical.

We read in that third section of how, before the birth of Colm, an angel appeared to his mother to announce that he would be a great saint; and further that when the baby was born, light radiated from the room where he slept. He was educated by a bishop called Finnian, who observed an angel continually accompanying him. Reference is made to how, after he became a monk, he was 'excommunicated by a certain synod for some trivial and quite pardonable offences', and how the charges against him were proved to be incorrect. In this controversy, BRÉANAINN took his part, announcing that he had seen a bright pillar precede him as a sign that he was ordained by God to lead souls to heaven.

Accounts are given of various visions, in which Colm saw angels and demons, as well as the souls of the blessed departing to their reward. The most dramatic account concerns how, when on Iona, he realised that a monk had fallen from the round tower of his monastery at Durrow, and sent an angel to rescue him. Before the monk reached the ground, the angel caught him, with the result that he suffered no injury. During his visions, Colm was surrounded by light, and on these occasions he 'saw openly manifested many secrets hidden since the beginning of the world'.

He foresaw his own death and announced this to his monks on Iona. As the final hour approached, weary with age, he went to sit in the monastery's granary, and a white horse that used to carry the milk pails galloped up to him. The horse laid its head upon the saint's breast and began to whinny, to shed tears, and to foam at the mouth in sadness. A monk tried to drive the horse away, but he was restrained by Colm, who said: 'Let him be, for he loves me!' Returning indoors, he appointed his colleague Baíthéne as his successor, and died before the altar in the monastery chapel, blessing his community. It was night time, and a great light in the shape of a pillar was seen in the heavens over a wide area as his soul departed. For the three days of his obsequies, a great tempest blew, but it subsided immediately when he was buried.

In the second section of *Vita Columbae* is related the most engrossing of all the stories concerning the saint. This concerns the renowned monster of Lough Ness in Scotland. We read that when Colm came to the bank of the River Ness, he met there a group of people preparing to bury a man who had been seized and bitten by a water monster (*aquatilis bestia*) as he swam there. The body had been recovered by some boatmen using hooks. Colm told one of his men, called Lugne moccu Min, to swim across and collect a boat from the other bank, but as Lugne was in midstream, the monster roared and rushed on him with open maw. Colm made the Sign of the Cross in the air with his hand and commanded the monster to retreat, whereupon it fled terrified back into the water.

This is the earliest recorded instance of the common Irish MOTIF that has water-monsters being banished by saints, a motif that sprang from the influence of the Apocalypse of John on the folk imagination. In the Apocalypse, a dramatic description is given of a great dragon being confined to a lake of fire at the end of the world. Much play is made of that scene in an acrostic hymn entitled 'Altus Prosator', which seems to have originated in the monastery of Iona. In the hymn, reference is made to the 'great horrible frightening dragon' of the Apocalypse (*draco magnus deterrimus terribilis*) that dwells in the depths of land and sea. Although it seems to have been written a generation or two after his time, the 'Altus' was traditionally regarded as Colm's own composition. It may have been so regarded because it echoed his actual treatment of topics, and one can envisage Colm declaring that by holiness the dragon of evil could be consigned to such a realm. The image became so intimately connected with him, that his role in the lore known to Adhamhnán had been transformed from that of relayer into that of actor.

It is probable that several hymns were composed by Colm, and down through the centuries a vast number of poems have been fancifully attributed to him. These vary in subject from prayer and celebration of the beauties of nature to occasional stanzas and prophecies of all kinds. He thus came to be regarded as the saint with a special partiality to those who made verse, and it was claimed that he had himself been trained in the schools of the POETS. The nucleus of this tradition may have existed in his own lifetime, for Adhamhnán refers to poems composed in Irish in praise of the saint, and claims that one of these protected its composer from enemy attack.

The text of a long verse eulogy on Colm survives. It is called the *Amhra* [Marvel] *of Colm Cille,* dates to around the year AD 600, and is attributed to the chief-poet of Ireland at the time, DALLÁN FORGAILL. The text is in extremely obscure language, of a type known as *bélra na filed* (rhetoric of the poets), and various glosses were written on it by medieval scribes. According to these glosses, Dallán Forgaill began the eulogy in gratitude for the saint's intervention on behalf of the poets when they were in difficulty. Adhamhnán recounted how Colm was present at a convention in Drom Ceat (Daisy Hill, near Limavady, County Derry) at which the high-king Aodh mac Ainmhireach made an agreement with the king of the Dál Riada of Antrim and western Scotland, Aodán mac Gabhráin. The glossarians claimed that one of the issues discussed at that convention was the situation of the poets, who had been guilty of extortionate behaviour and had become a major problem to the nobles, and that Colm had saved them from banishment by suggesting that their numbers and privileges be reduced. When Dallán began to compose his eulogy in thanks for this, the saint directed him to postpone composition of it until after his death. By the time that Colm died, Dallán had lost his eyesight, but it was miraculously restored to facilitate him in carrying out his task.

The medieval biographies in both Latin and Irish are based on Adhamhnán's text, but they add some striking traditions. One of these concerns how he came to be called Colm Cille: when he was a child, the other children noticed how often he visited the church to recite the psalms, and they used to enquire 'Has the little dove come to the church today?' Another such tradition concerns how his teacher, the monk Cruithneachán, taught him the alphabet: for each letter the child learned, Cruithneachán gave him a bite of sweet-tasting bread, and so he soon knew all the letters.

A very dramatic innovation was introduced into lore of him in or about the twelfth century. This has no historical foundation, but has become one of the best-known stories of Colm. According to it, he got a loan of a book of the Gospels from St Finnian of Maigh Bhile (Moville, County Down) and secretly copied it. Finnian, on realising what had been done, demanded the return of the book and the copy as well. Colm objected, saying that the copy was his, and the matter was referred to the high-king DIARMAID MAC CEARRBHEOIL for judgement. Diarmaid ruled 'to every cow her calf and to every book its copy'. Colm angrily retorted that it was a bad judgement and would be avenged. Another quarrel added to the tension, for Colm gave sanctuary to a prince who had killed a man in violation of the high-king's protection. Ignoring Colm's sanctuary, Diarmaid put the prince to death. Nurturing these two grievances against the high-king – who was of the southern branch of the Uí Néill – Colm encouraged the northern Uí Néill to make war on him. As a result, Diarmaid was defeated by the northerners with great bloodshed at the Battle of Cúl Dreimhne (Cooldrevny, at the foot of Benbulben, County Sligo).

We read that Colm later repented of having caused so much slaughter, and vowed that as penance he would never again set foot on the soil of Ireland, never again set eye on the Irish people, and never again partake of the country's food or drink. So he departed in sorrow for Iona. Years later, when he attended the convention of Drom Ceat, he avoided breaking his vow by having a sod of Scottish clay under his feet, having his eyes shrouded in cloth, and using only food and drink brought from Scotland.

The Battle of Cúl Dreimhne was fought in the year 561, and in it Diarmaid mac Cearrbheoil was indeed heavily defeated by an alliance of the northern Uí Néill and the Connachtmen. Colm's sympathies would naturally have been with his own close relatives in that battle, but apart from this there are several indications that he was generally on good terms with the high-king. None of the early sources make reference to the copying of a book as the cause of Colm's exile, and indeed Adhamhnán mentions two return visits Colm made from Iona to Ireland. It appears that some medieval scholar invented the idea of 'the battle of the book' on foot of the rather quaint way in which Adhamhnán dated the departure of Colm to Iona. 'Two years had passed after the battle of Cúle Drebene', he wrote, 'as it has been told to us, when the blessed man first sailed away from Ireland.' It is not possible to say if the 'trivial and very pardonable offences' mentioned by Adhamhnán were at all related to manuscript copying or to partiality towards the northern Uí Néill, but the very reference to accusations would have helped to develop the LEGEND. The plot of how Colm circumvented his vow was borrowed from popular storytelling of medieval times (see HUMOROUS TALES, type 1590).

All of this lore is featured again in the celebrated biography *Beatha Colaim Chille* compiled by Mánas Ó DÓNAILL in the year 1532. This makes use of not only many of the earlier texts but also of oral tradition concerning the saint that was current in the Donegal area at the time. For instance, in Ó Dónaill's work we read that before Colm was born, an angel directed that a particular flagstone floating on a lake be brought to his mother, and that she gave birth on that stone. His mother's bleeding stained the earth, and therefore the red clay of that place, Gartan, has many curative and protective properties. Such properties are still said to attach to that clay.

Concerning Colm's public life, the most dramatic of the many legends in Donegal folklore concerns how he converted the inhabitants of Tory Island to Christianity. We are told that the ruler of the island was at first hostile to the saint, but agreed to give him as much land as his cloak would cover. When Colm spread his cloak, it covered the whole island, whereupon the ruler grew angry and set a savage hound on him. Colm made the Sign of the Cross and the hound fell down dead, and following this the ruler submitted. Colm left as a blessing that the clay of the island would always be effective in banishing rats, wherever it was brought. The cloak-spreading motif is an obvious derivation from the lore of St BRIGHID; whereas the idea of the efficacious clay of Tory – not mentioned by Mánas Ó Dónaill – seems to have been supplied by some partisan of Tory who was acquainted with Adhamhnán's text. There it is stated

that Colm blessed Iona, so that 'the poison of vipers shall in no way have power to harm either men or CATTLE within the boundaries of this island'.

There was indeed a Columban monastery on Tory Island in early medieval times, and a kindred legend based on a monastic foundation concerns Glencolmcille in the south of County Donegal. There it is said that the saint banished a horde of demons from the glen and ordained that ever after the area was to be a sanctuary for the weak and for all those in need.

Probably on account of the legend of 'the battle of the book', Colm was popularly regarded as a short-tempered saint. It was said that, though very charitable, he was impatient and quite haughty with beggars who came to seek alms outside of the time of day set aside by him for this purpose. He was cured of his high-handedness, however, when JESUS appeared one day disguised as a beggar seeking alms. On being impatiently handed a lump of dough, the beggar man threw it into the fire and immediately ears of corn sprouted from the fireplace. Recognising who his visitor was, Colm begged forgiveness, and ever after gave generously to the poor at any hour of day or night. The motifs here are borrowed from the lore of St MARTIN.

There was a persistent tradition that, after his death on Iona, the body of Colm was miraculously transferred home to Ireland. Norse raiders of Iona in the year 825 sought out the shrine in which his body had been placed in order to plunder it, and the tradition grew up afterwards that these raiders – finding no treasures there – cast the coffin out to sea and that it floated over to Ireland. When the coffin was discovered by monks on the northeastern coast, and found to contain the saint's body, these monks brought the body to Downpatrick and interred it there alongside PATRICK and BRIGHID. The belief that these three great saints of Ireland are buried together is unhistorical, but it proved very attractive to the popular mind. One folk account has it that when Colm's coffin came ashore, a cow licked it and her milk yield increased greatly as a result. The local people went to investigate what had caused the cow to give so much milk, and they discovered the coffin and the body of the saint inside. When they brought the corpse to Downpatrick, the graves of Patrick and Brighid moved apart so as to allow room for Colm to be buried between them.

The powerful sept Ó Dónaill of Donegal claimed the special protection of Colm Cille, and down to Elizabethan times always brought into battle a special relic, which was believed to guarantee them victory. This relic was a copy of the Psalms and was known as the *Cathach* [battler] of Colm Cille. The manuscript, which dates from the sixth century, was said to have been written by the hand of the saint himself. It still survives, as does a casket of later date in which it was carried.

An anthology of prophetic poems traditionally ascribed to the saint was published in the year 1856 and several times subsequently. This anthology has had a great influence on popular lore in Ireland, as these 'prophecies of Colm Cille' are taken to refer to many developments in recent generations and even in the contemporary world. The feast day of Colm is 9 June.

AMHRA: W. Stokes in *RC*, *20*, 30–55, 132–83, 248–9, 400–37 & *21*, 133–6. *See also* P. Henry (1978), 191–212.

ADHAMHNÁN'S TEXT: Anderson & Anderson (1961).

ALTUS PROSATOR: Bernard & Atkinson, *1* (1898), 62–89. *See* Kenney (1929), 264–5; Richter (1999), 202–4.

MEDIEVAL BIOGRAPHIES: Stokes (1890), 20–33, 299–317; Heist (1965), 112–13, 366–78, 420; C. Plummer in *AIM*, *3*, 1–4.

Ó DÓNAILL TEXT: O'Kelleher & Schoepperle (1918).

FOLKLORE: Ó hÓgáin (1985), 26–35, 51–2, 324–5; S. Ó hEochaidh in *Irisleabhar Muighe Nuadhat*, 1963, 33–50; J. Szövérffy in *Éigse*, *8*, 108–132; IFC Index.

CATHACH: Kenney (1929), 629–30.

'PROPHECIES': O'Kearney (1856).

GENERAL: Kenney (1929), 263–5, 422–42, 802–3; F. Kelly in *Ériu*, *24*, 1–34 & *26*, 66–98; Dinneen, *3*(1908), 48–113; Ó Searcaigh (1967); O'Hanlon, *6*(1875), 255–593; Szövérffy (1988).

Comhdhán A celebrated jester of Munster who reputedly lived in the early seventh century AD. His name was originally Comhghan, a common enough one in early Ireland, deriving ultimately from a Celtic *Comagagnas*, with a meaning such as 'fellow leader'. The name was misinterpreted, however, as a variant of *comhchan*, with a meaning such as 'reciter', which was one of the terms used to indicate a minor POET.

He was said to have been a stepbrother of the saint CUMAINE FADA. That is probably untrue, but this jester may have been an historical character, known also as Moccu Cerda (son of the Ceard-people), which suggests that he belonged to the Ceardraighe sept of south-west Munster. It is apparent that attempts to make sense of these confused designations, Moccu Cerda and Comhghan, brought about the two nicknames by which he came to be known in later medieval literature. One of these nicknames was Comhdhán (equal arts), and the other Mac Dá Chearda (son of two skills). These nicknames were of similar import, and they were explained by his possessing wisdom and madness in equal measure. He was the archetypal wise fool, and one source refers to him as 'the chief poet of Ireland and the leading fool of Ireland'.

The medieval literature exhibits his legend in developed form, associating him with the south-eastern end of Munster. He is described as son of Maolochtraigh, king of the DÉISE sept, and of Mughain, mother of Cumaine. He and Cumaine are credited with having jointly composed a learned poem on the place-lore of Magh Feimhin (the plain of south Tipperary), and various anecdotes concerning them are related in a text from the twelfth century or thereabouts. According to this text, Comhdhán was the chief fool of Ireland, yet when he was in his senses, he would deliver judgements the wisdom of which nobody could contradict. When the foolishness predominated, he could walk dry-shod on water and could sleep underwater, and the aquatic creatures were friendly towards him, nestling in his palms. Likewise, he slept on dry land when there was inclement WEATHER and the BIRDS would come and shelter him. How he became a fool is explained by an affair he had with the wife of his father's DRUID. The druid sang an incantation on a wisp and cast it in his face,

93

confusing his senses. He became a perpetual wanderer, but Cumaine loved him and delighted in his conversation. Cumaine used to ask him all types of questions concerning morality, and received in return the most profound answers.

It happened that a Munsterman called Mac Teléne, who was a fermenter of strife, was once at the court of king GUAIRE of Connacht. He boasted that Munster excelled Connacht, citing Cumaine for sportsmanship, bishop Moronóc for foolishness, and Comhdhán for poetry. Guaire thought such attributes rather incongruous for these three characters, and he detained Mac Teléne until the boast could be investigated. A year later, the three characters came to the Connacht court, and Guaire hid an egg under the cover of Cumaine's chair, but the SAINT sat on it without breaking it, thus proving his agility. He also showed superb ability at chess. Moronóc took 50 hurley sticks from a group of youths and closed the door on the sticks so that it knocked the curved heads off them all. He then lay in the king's bed with his boots full of mud, and tied his laces to the bed so that when he arose, he knocked both Guaire and Cumaine to the floor. Meanwhile, Comhdhán recited an extempore stanza that proved his ability at poetry, so Guaire had to admit the truth of Mac Teléne's assertion and accordingly had to release the boaster.

Several of the details from these anecdotes are retold in a long text written a few centuries later. This text gives a humorous biography of Comhdhán, and is entitled *Imtheachta na nÓinmhididhe* (The Adventures of the Fools). It describes how, after the death of his wife Mughain, the Déise king Maolochtraigh remarried, and the new queen fell in love with Comhdhán. This love was not returned, and so his stepmother grew to hate Comhdhán and to plot his destruction. Once, when he won a horse race, the king's druid was praising him, but the queen told the druid that Comhdhán was courting his wife. The druid grew jealous, and as Comhdhán was washing his horse in a river, he struck him with a magic wand, as a result of which Comhdhán was sick for a year. His hair fell out and he became a complete idiot. A young man called Odhrán pitied him, and he developed a special affection for Odhrán and gave him all his possessions. One day, Comhdhán followed the women to the forest to collect fruit, and he remained there overnight. He was attacked by wolves, and next day went towards his father's house, stopping at an oratory on the way.

Meanwhile, his half-brother Cumaine had come to seek tidings of him. By promises of all kinds of food, he was prevailed on to follow Cumaine to his hermitage. Comhdhán did not wish it to be known that he was following on, and he covered his head with a lump of moss, foolishly thinking that this concealed him. Soon after, Cumaine and Comhdhán came upon a group of men erecting a wall from felled trees, and the men explained that they were building a barricade between them and the property of a monastery. On the saint's advice, they desisted, however, and they brought Comhdhán and Cumaine with them to their master, Fínghein, king of Munster, who royally received the two guests. When Fínghein's queen joked that Comhdhán should marry her as yet unborn daughter, however, the fool took the remark seriously and fled from that place. He ran all the way until he came to the court of king Guaire in Connacht. On being told that a 'huge red-haired churl' was outside trying to fell a tree, Guaire went to welcome him. Comhdhán recited enigmatic poems, which Guaire understood to refer to his condition and his recent adventures. Guaire instructed the local children to put their hands around the tree, and this ruse succeeded in preventing Comhdhán from trying to cut it with his axe. The king then brought the fool into his fortress.

Soon after, Guaire's horses were stolen and Comhdhán followed the robbers, being under the impression that they were preparing the horses for racing with the king's consent. He met with the robbers, who found it feasible to go along with his delusion, but on his amicable return to Guaire, the king was furious with him for befriending them, and plotted treachery against him. He sent him to collect heron's eggs in a lonely place, and then sent cut-throats after to kill him. Comhdhán unwittingly led the pursuers to where the horse thieves were, and the latter took this to be a warning from him and fled. Guaire and his party came upon Comhdhán sitting alone in the robbers' hut and, angry at their chiding, the fool left them and returned to Munster. He next visited the court of the Leinster king Conaing, and there met again with St Cumaine, after which he returned to Connacht.

The exasperated Guaire sent messengers to collect the high-king's jester CONALL CLOGACH, in the hope that the latter might be able to teach some sense to Comhdhán. Conall, however, was an equally great fool, and in order to entice him to come with them, Guaire's men had to pretend that there was much better food in Connacht than at the Ulster fortress of the high-king DOMHNALL MAC AODHA. They left lumps of rich food along their track all the way to Guaire's court, and Conall followed along at a distance. When the two fools met, they kissed each other, eyed each other, and engaged in conversation about each other's physical appearance. They were given massive cauldrons of meat and porridge from which to eat. Noticing a fly alight on Conall's nose, Comhdhán plastered him with roasting porridge in an attempt to kill it. Conall thanked Comhdhán for defending him, and the latter was very pleased with his new reputation for heroism. Then Guaire decided to have a bath and requested their assistance. They went to a wood to get timber for the fire, and Guaire arranged to have a golden ring mounted on a stick in their path. When they saw this, they made little of it, saying that they had come to seek timber rather than gold. Conall found a suitable piece of timber, and the disappointed Comhdhán begged him to exchange it for the ring. Returning to the palace, Conall cast the ring aside with indifference.

One of Guaire's retainers suggested that the fools should make a circuit of Connacht, and so they set out next day and reached Ros Comáin (Roscommon). They were well received there, but complained of the quality of the butter and Conall flung it onto the fire. It blazed up, and in an attempt to quench it, Comhdhán threw flax onto the fire, and Conall threw straw after it. The house caught fire and soon the whole town was in a state of conflagration. The fools fled, and as it was a dark night, they thought that the saint of that place had deprived them of their sight for what they had done. Reassured by the sunrise next day, they stopped at a house on their way, but being badly received there, walked withershins around the house and cursed it. Eventually, they met with Cumaine, who treated them very well, and then they set out on a circuit to many different parts of the country. They soon began to bicker and to insult each other, however. When they came to the dwelling of the Munster king Fínghein, Conall stole some meat from the steward and Comhdhán disapproved of this. They then decided to part company, Conall returning to Ulster and Comhdhán going to visit Cumaine. The latter gave a hermitage to Comhdhán at a place called Inis Glinne, in Gleann Uisean (Killeshin, County Laois), and Comhdhán made a fish weir for himself there. He arranged a bell on the weir in such a way that it rang whenever a fish was caught. He spent the rest of his life in prayer and devotion and died in the arms of his saintly stepbrother.

The author of this text was well read in the medieval literature, and was quite selective in his treatment of the materials. He altered the story of the druid's wife so as to avoid accusing Comhdhán of adultery, introducing the well-known MOTIF of a lustful and treacherous stepmother – probably on the pattern of the story of the Leinster hero MAOL FHOTHARTAIGH, whose name resembles that of Maolochtraigh (*see also* ROMANTIC TALES, type 870C). The companionship of the two fools may have been suggested by a similar setting in the story of SUIBHNE; while the bell announcing the catching of a fish is borrowed from the story of CANO MAC GARTNÁIN, probably due to fancifully etymologising Inis Glinne (holm of the valley) as 'holm of the fishing-frame [*glinne*]'. The emphasis on tricks associated with food may have been suggested by the story of MAC CONGLINNE, in which Comhdhán had a mention. The author also had a good sense of humour, and did not hesitate to borrow from oral lore current in his time. Such adaptations by him included popular tales concerning fools frightened, dealings with robbers, and fatal results from swatting an insect (*see* HUMOROUS TALES, types, 1321, 1527 *and* 1586A). He also seems to have known the ANIMAL TALE, type 130, which concerns robbers and the burning of a house; and the text recounts concerning Conall Clogach other far-flung humorous tales.

Comhdhán occurs also in the love story of LIADHAIN, in which he brings a secret message in verse to that lady from her lover Cuirithir. Despite his entertaining character, however, he is not featured in the later folklore, under either name Comhdhán or Mac Dá Chearda.

ORIGIN OF NAME: McManus (1997), 73, 107, 208.

GENERAL: Meyer (1892), 6–7 & (1902), 12–17 & (1912), 5; Stokes (1905), 168; J.G. O'Keeffe in *Ériu*, 5, 18–44; Gwynn (1913), 200–5, 512; Calder (1917), 372; Ó Cadhlaigh (1939), 113–56, 217–22; G. Mac Eoin in *ZCP*, 36, 74–82; Jackson (1990), 3, 42, 47–8; S Ó Coileáin in *Ériu*, 25, 103–13.

Comhghall *(c.AD 515–602)* SAINT who founded the monastery of Beannchair (Bangor, County Down). The name Comhghall was a common one in early Ireland, with a meaning such as 'suitably strong' – it is anglicised as Congall. This saint was of the sept called Dál nAraidhe (in south Antrim and north Down).

A friend of COLM CILLE, Comhghall spent some time with that saint on the mission to Scotland. He was also the teacher of the renowned missionary Columbanus (*c.*543–615), who carried the message of Christianity to many parts of continental Europe and founded the famous monastery of Bobbio in Italy. Although the prestige of Comhghall himself was great, the two versions of his biography that survive seem to date from as late as the twelfth century. These texts are in Latin, but they make use of much earlier material that was probably in Irish.

We read that the priest who baptised him was blind, but got his sight from a well which miraculously sprang up to give water – a detail borrowed from the lore of PATRICK. When Comhghall grew up, he had to substitute for his father in a local war because the father was too old to fight, but he was allowed to go home when snow fell on the army camp and miraculously left him untouched. On opting for the religious life, he went to the monastery of Cluain Eidhneach (Clonenagh, County Laois), the abbot of which was St Fionntan, and then visited CIARÁN at Clonmacnoise. Returning to Ulster, he took holy orders and established the monastery of Bangor. Several miracles of healing and even of raising the dead are attributed to him, and we read that, due to his holiness, his cell was brilliantly illuminated when he retired there. Once, when grain was scarce, a rich man refused to give of his copious store to the monks, and Comhghall told him that mice would eat all his corn. This accordingly happened, and other anecdotes tell of how the saint overcame various tyrants and robbers.

Comhghall crossed over to the community of Colm Cille on the island of Iona, and we read that together with Colm and CAINNEACH, he set out to convert the king of the PICTS, Brude. Coming to Brude's fortress, Comhghall caused the gate to open, Colm opened the doors, and Cainneach caused the king's hand to wither when it brandished a sword against them. On accepting the faith, Brude's hand was restored to him. We further read that after Comhghall returned to Bangor, a foreign monk visited that monastery to contend with him in austerities. Comhghall brought the visitor to a river at midnight, with an invitation to join him in singing the psalms there. As they stood in the river, the water alternated between great heat and great cold, and the stranger had to admit defeat. On another occasion, Comhghall restored to health Caointighearn – wife of the Dál nAraidhe king, FIACHNA MAC BAODÁIN – after she had been given poison by one of her handmaids. The handmaid repented, and was forgiven and saved from punishment by the saint.

Several churches in both Ireland and Scotland were dedicated to Comhghall, and his feast day is 10 May.

Kenney (1929), 395–7; Anderson & Anderson (1961), 314–19, 490–3, 500–1; Stokes (1905), 410; Plummer, 2 (1910), 3–21; Heist (1962), 332–4, 420; K. Meyer in *Irisleabhar na Gaedhlige*, 4, 229 & in *AIM, 3*, 9–10; O'Hanlon, 5 (1875), 152–84.

Conaire Mythical KING of TARA, his name is a compound of *cú* ('hound', figuratively 'warrior') and *aire* (protector), and meant 'warrior-lord'. He is sometimes given the epithet Mór (great), or Caomh (handsome).

The principal text concerning Conaire is *Togail Bruidne Da Derga* (The Destruction of Da Dearga's Hostel). This was compiled in the eleventh century from two distinct texts of earlier date. The story was already in writing in the eighth century, containing material that seems to be an echo of how the Leinstermen displaced the ÉRAINN, who were previously dominant there. Conaire, who represents such a group, is a somewhat enigmatic figure, but it is clear that the MOTIFS associated with him derive from a cult of sacral kingship. We read that his father, a king called Eterscéle, had no issue until he married a young girl, Meas Buachalla, who had been abandoned by her parents. The girl had been impregnated by an otherworld man who came to her in a BIRD-skin. This spectre had told her that she would give birth to a son, 'and that boy may not kill birds, and Conaire shall be his name'.

The young Conaire was sent into fosterage in Magh Life (the Curragh of Kildare), and when he grew to early manhood, Eterscéle died. Conaire was summoned to attend a 'bull-feast' at Tara, which involved a seer sleeping on a bull hide in expectation of a vision that would reveal who should be the new king. He set out in his chariot, and on his way saw some huge birds and pursued them as far as the sea near Áth Cliath (Dublin). There the birds took off their skins, taking human form, and one of them told him that he was forbidden to cast at birds. He further instructed Conaire to go naked to Tara, where he would be installed as king. Meanwhile, the seer at the bull-feast had a vision of 'a naked man coming along the road to Tara at dawn, bearing a stone in his sling'. Conaire came thus, and his fosters ers met him on the road and clothed him with royal garments. The motto he adopted as king was 'to enquire of wise men so that I myself may be wise'.

Conaire's reign ushered in a period of great happiness and good fortune in Ireland. His three foster-brothers, however, began to reave and plunder. Conaire, out of love for them, refused to put them to death, but instead banished them to Scotland. Meanwhile, he unwittingly broke several prohibitions (*see* GEIS) that the bird-men had imposed on him when they told him that he was to be king. Finally, when benighted on the road called Slíghe Chualann (going south from Dublin), he decided to visit the hostel (*bruidhean*) of his friend Da Dearga. This hostel is described as being built astride the Dothair (known in English as the Dodder river), the water flowing through the middle of the hall. Its location is unclear – one theory situates it near the source of the Dodder at Bohernabreena in the Dublin mountains, but a more likely situation would be at the bridge over that river at Donnybrook, in the south of the present Dublin city.

As he travelled towards the hostel, Conaire perceived three red men riding along in front of him, and remembered that one of his prohibitions was against following three such men into Da Dearga's house. Failing to dissuade the three strangers from preceding him, he resigned himself to his fate. He entered the hostel, and the three red men sat down with him. A horrid-visaged woman came to the door and foretold that 'neither skin nor flesh of you will escape from the house you have entered, except what the birds will take in their claws'. His three foster-brothers had in the meantime landed at Trácht Mhuirbhthean (Merrion Strand, Dublin) with an army of marauding Britons, and were marching towards the hostel. They made a surprise attack, but Conaire killed hundreds of the foe before he could reach his weapons, and hundreds more when he grabbed the weapons. The raiders set fire to the hostel three times, but each time the conflagration was quenched by the defenders. Then DRUIDS who were with the raiders put a magic thirst on Conaire, and since all the liquid in the hostel had been expended in quenching the flames, he grew weak and was slain by two of the foe. His severed head spoke a verse in praise of his champion, Mac Cécht, who had fought tremendously by his side.

Other fragmentary sources shed light on aspects of this story. We read, for instance, that the foster-brothers of Conaire were also known as 'the three red-heads of the Leinstermen', and it is obvious that the three mysterious strangers who rode ahead of him to the hostel were originally the same trio as these. It is also striking that the name of his host, Da Dearga – also called simply Dearg – signifies redness, and the original story must have had that character in the role of foe rather than of friend. DEARG, indeed, was a common personification of death in early Irish literature. In the basic stratum, therefore, Dearg as Death would have been one of the aspects of the fated life of the sacred king. It would appear that memories of Leinster aggression were superimposed on, and confused with, such rituals of kingship.

A different account of Conaire's accession to the kingship states that his mother, Meas Buachalla, was of otherworld origin and was herding for king Eterscéle when she was made pregnant by him. She kept the child's paternity secret until Eterscéle died, and then told Conaire to go to Tara, for he was the son of the dead king. She collected an otherworld army for him, and when they reached Tara, Conaire had to undergo a series of ritual tests to prove his claim. The tests included mounting a chariot to which were yoked two stallions of one colour that had never before been harnessed. If he were not the true king, the HORSES would rear up against him, but they stood still when he approached. The royal cloak also fitted him, and the flagstones magically moved to let him pass. The chariot-horses then coursed tamely around the citadel, and the upright ritual stone – the Lia Fáil – at the head of the course there cried out against the axle of his chariot as it always did for the true king. This account also refers to variant traditions concerning Conaire's birth, including the ideas that Meas Buachalla was the daughter of her lover Eterscéle, and that she had sojourned for a while in the otherworld dwelling called Sídh Breagha Léith, near Tara. It is clear that the sacral kingship was the central and basic subject of the Conaire legend, and that this was underlined by the use of a variety of motifs relating to the otherworld.

Several of the non-dominant septs regarded Conaire as their ancestor, thus giving them a claim on the kingship and indirectly preserving the memory that the Érainn once controlled Tara. The dominant Uí NÉILL dynasty also used his name for their own benefit, and one tradition had it that Conaire took compensation from the Leinstermen for the death of his father at their hands. He is thus, rather anachronistically, claimed to have originated the BÓRAIMHE, a tribute imposed by the Uí Néill on Leinster. The medieval literature also exhibits a duplication of this mythical king by the annalists (see CONAIRE MAC MOGHA LÁMHA). There are no late literary accounts of Conaire, and he was unknown in the folklore of recent centuries.

GENERAL: Knott (1936); L. Gwynn in *Ériu*, 6, 130–41; Macalister (1956), 300–1; Gwynn (1913), 116–19; O'Brien (1962), 120; Dinneen, 2 (1908), 230–3; T.F. O'Rahilly (1946), 82, 117–30, 202; F.J. Byrne (1973), 59–63, 323; Dillon (1948), 25–31; Ó Muraíle, 2 (2003), 194. LOCATION OF HOSTEL: O'Curry, 3 (1873), 136; Joyce, 2 (1903), 172–3.

Conaire mac Mogha Lámha

Fictional KING of Ireland, son-in-law and successor of CONN CÉADCHATHACH.

This character is clearly a double of the great CONAIRE, and was invented by the historians in order to facilitate chronology.

Like his prototype, the epithet *caomh* (handsome) is added to his name, and the medieval writers themselves were sometimes confused as to which Conaire they had in mind. This Conaire mac Mogha Lámha was one of the three joint kings of Munster, and was favoured by Conn after EOGHAN MÓR took the whole province of Munster to himself. Conaire married Sárait, daughter of Conn, and Conn designated him his heir.

We read that he reigned at Tara for eight years, and was slain by one Neimheadh mac Sraibhghind (*see* NEIMHEADH), who then married the bereaved queen. However, the three sons of Conaire went to their uncle ART for assistance. These three were each called Cairbre, and they travelled to Munster and gave battle to Neimheadh, who had as ally Lughaidh mac Con. This was claimed to have been the Battle of Ceann Abhradh (the Ballyhoura hills on the Limerick–Cork border), other and differing accounts of which exist (*see* LUGHAIDH MAC CON). At any rate, Neimheadh was defeated, and he fled to the protection of his new wife at Ard Neimhidh (Great Island, Cork Harbour), but one of the three brothers slew him in her arms. Sárait remarked that the deed was a great disgrace (*aisc*) – hence the slayer became known as Cairbre Músc, the epithet being explained as a derivative of *mó a aisc* (greatest was his disgrace). A variant tradition had it that the disgrace of Cairbre Músc resulted from his lying with his own sister (*see* CORC DUIBHNE).

T.F. O'Rahilly (1946), 201–3; Macalister (1956), 334–5; L. Gwynn in *Ériu, 4,* 144–53; Jackson (1938), 1–14, 31–4, 74–5; W. Stokes in *Irische Texte, 3,* 312–17; Dinneen, *2* (1908), 276–81.

Conall Cearnach Mythical warrior in the ULSTER CYCLE. The name Conall derives from a Celtic *Cunovalos* or *Cunovalios*, meaning 'strong like a wolf', and in origin this character seems to have been the eponymous ancestor of the Conaille sept that inhabited parts of Counties Armagh, Down and Louth. His sobriquet meant 'triumphant', an appropriate one for such a hero.

Conall Cearnach was probably adopted into the nascent Ulster Cycle in the seventh or early eighth century, perhaps following the rise to prominence of the Conailli at this time. He was soon given a major role. The literature makes him son of the poet AMHAIRGHIN MAC ÉIGIT SALAIGH, his mother being identified as Fionnchaomh, daughter of the druid CATHBHADH and sister of king CONCHOBHAR MAC NEASA. Fionnchaomh was for a long time childless, but on a DRUID's advice went and washed at a certain fountain. She took a drink of water there, and a chafer (beetle) was in the drink. As a result, she gave birth to a baby boy. The chafer was stuck in the baby's hand, and she had to cut it out. This story parallels the birth-narrative of Conchobhar and is obviously borrowed from that source.

Another account deviates from the genealogy ordinarily given to Fionnchaomh, and claims that she was of the Connacht people and sister to the warrior CEAT MAC MÁGHACH. According to this, Ceat heard it foretold that Fionnchaomh would give birth to a child who would 'never be a night without a Connachtman's head hanging on his belt'. Ceat therefore placed the baby under his heel to crush its neck, but before the marrow of the neck was destroyed, Fionnchaomh intervened and had the baby returned to her. As a result of this, Conall ever after had a slanted neck. This account gives a false etymology for his name, stating that Fionnchaomh condemned Ceat's act as 'wolfish treachery' (*con-fheall*). Several artificial attempts were also made to explain the sobriquet Cearnach, such as relating it to the protuberance (*cern*) cut from his hand to release the chafer, or a protuberance from the side of his head after a blow was struck on him in battle. One imaginative interpretation was that the epithet derived from the Latin root 'cern', meaning 'perceive', and it was said that Conall could see as well by night as by day, so sharp was his eye.

Conall Cearnach was much used as a character in the filling-out of the Ulster Cycle in the early medieval period, and in this regard his occurrence in the early heroic text *Táin Bó Fraích* is of special significance. The original of this text seems to have been written towards the end of the eighth century. It features, with Conall, the hero FRAOCH, and these two characters may have been suggested to the author by their rather incidental appearances in early versions of *Táin Bó Cuailnge* (*see* ULSTER CYCLE). That author tells of how Fraoch, when setting out to search for his wife, his sons and his stolen cattle, met Conall at Beanna Bairche (the Mourne Mountains, County Down). They went together to the Alps, where they found the cattle being guarded at a fortress by a savage serpent. Conall, 'the finest hero of the Ulstermen', attacked the fortress and destroyed it. The serpent went harmlessly into his belt, and having released it again he and Fraoch brought the kidnapped people and cattle back to Ireland. The most plausible explanation of the serpent's strange behaviour is that the episode was suggested to the author by a similar episode in the seventh-century biography of St Samson of Dol in Brittany. That the author of *Táin Bó Fraích* was a cleric is indicated by the occurrence of the Lombards as hostile people. The Lombard kingdom was overthrown by the Franks, with papal backing, in the year AD 775, and this was probably the event that prompted their inclusion.

The literature represents Conall Cearnach as having been for a while in the employ of the high-king EOCHAIDH FEIDHLEACH, for whom he and Ceat were army commanders during the rebellion of Eochaidh's three sons, the FINN EAMHNA. This may be an echo of an alternate tradition to the more general one that he was among the leading warriors in the Ulster court of Conchobhar. A certain instability in the role initially assigned to him in the literature is evidenced by the fact that he is erroneously mentioned among Meadhbh's soldiers in *Táin Bó Cuailnge*, while later in the same text he is one of Conchobhar's foremost fighters. One unsupported source has Féibh, daughter of Conchobhar, as his wife, and he is therefore made father of Fiacha mac Fir Féibhe, one of the Ulster exiles in Connacht (*see* CORMAC CONN LOINGEAS).

A text written about the year 800 made Conall Cearnach the foremost warrior of Ulster. This was *Scéla Mucce Meic Dathó*

(The Story of the Pig of Mac Da Thó). It told of how Mac Da Thó, a Leinster king, had a great hound called Ailbhe that was sought after by both Conchobhar and queen MEADHBH of Connacht. The hound's owner cleverly promised it to both sides, and when both Ulstermen and Connachtmen arrived to collect the animal, he invited them to a feast in his huge house. A massive PIG was cooked for the feast, and the two companies sat ominously opposite each other. The satirist BRICRIU, as was his wont, started mischief by suggesting that the only way to divide the pig was by feats of arms. A boasting contest began, and Ceat mac Mághach went to the pig, knife in hand, and challenged any Ulsterman to equal his feats. He described how he had humiliated in battle their leading champions, and it seemed that the apportioning of the pig must be left to him.

Then Conall Cearnach entered the house, exchanged greetings with Ceat, and told him to leave the pig. Ceat questioned his accomplishments and Conall answered: 'I swear as my people swear that, ever since I took a javelin in my hand, I was slaying a Connachtman every day, and destroying them by fire every night, and I have never slept without a Connachtman's head under my knee!' Hearing this, Ceat backed down, but he remarked that if another Connacht warrior, by name Anluan, were present, that warrior would have been able to contend with Conall. 'But he is,' said Conall, drawing Anluan's head from his belt and flinging it at Ceat's chest so that a spurt of blood came through his lips. Conall then apportioned the pig. He allowed but a fourth part of it to the Connachtmen, however, and fierce fighting broke out between the two sides. Mac Da Thó released the hound to see which side it would take, and it chose the Ulstermen. The Connachtmen were routed, and the hound pursued the chariot of Meadhbh and her husband as far as the Plain of Ailbhe in central Leinster. It was slain there by the charioteer Fear Logha.

This type of contest at a feast was a very ancient aspect of Irish culture. Writing of the Continental Celts, Greek and Latin authors mentioned how leading warriors among these were honoured with the finest pieces of meat, and how disputes and challenges to duels were common at their feasts. The Celts allowed the thigh bone of the cooked animal to the bravest warrior, 'and if any one challenged this the two arose and fought a duel to the death'. These classical writers also described how the heads of slain enemies were brought about by the Celts as trophies.

The cult of heads is reflected also in a text of the tenth or eleventh century. This tells how Conall's two brothers were slain by the men of Leinster in the battle at Howth, which was brought about by the satirist AITHIRNE. The Leinster king, called Meas Geaghra, later had his hand cut off by a servant during a quarrel. Conall, thirsting to avenge his brothers, caught up with Meas Geaghra at the ford of Casán Claonta (Clane, County Kildare). Meas Geaghra protested that it was ignoble to fight a one-handed man, so Conall tied one of his own hands to his side. The river was reddened by the fierce combat that ensued between the two, but Conall proved superior. Meas Geaghra, before being slain, suggested that Conall place his head on top of his own. Having decapitated him, however, Conall placed it on a rock, and a drop came from it and cut through the rock to the ground. When he then placed the head over his own, it straightened his neck so that the twist that had caused him to be called *Conall Claon* was removed.

Conall left that place in his own chariot, putting his charioteer into that of Meas Geaghra. On his way, he met the dead king's wife, Buan, showed her the head, and took her into his chariot. The head reddened and whitened alternately, and Buan explained that her dead husband was smarting from having once declared in an argument with Aithime that no Ulsterman would take her. She then began to lament her husband, and herself fell dead from the trauma. Conall told his servant to cut the brains from Meas Geaghra's head and to mix them with lime into a ball. This was

done, the head itself being left with the body of Buan, and Conall took the brainball with him and deposited it in Eamhain Mhacha, the Ulster capital. It was later snatched away by Ceat mac Mághach and used as a projectile to inflict a mortal wound on Conchobhar mac Neasa (q.v.). This adventure of Conall again shows signs of being a literary compilation, its purpose being to explain the origin of the brainball that killed Conchobhar. The episode of the destructive drop from Meas Geaghra's head parallels a MOTIF in the account of the death of Cealtchar, both based in all probability on a similar motif in the mythological lore of LUGH and BALAR. It is also apparent that the situating of Meas Geaghra's death at Casán Claonta (literally, 'the twisted pathway') was due to a play on Conall's reputed nickname, Claon (earlier, *claen*), referring to the twist in his neck.

Conall Cearnach was accorded a special role in the youth-biography of CÚ CHULAINN, who was given as a child into the care of Conall's mother Fionnchaomh. Thus the two heroes were reared together, Conall being somewhat older in years. On the day that Cú Chulainn took arms, Conall was guarding a frontier post, and the younger hero asked him to leave the duty to himself. Conall refused, and Cú Chulainn insisted on going further south to find combat. Conall followed on in his chariot to give protection, but the youngster flung a stone and broke the harness of the chariot, which caused Conall to return to his post in a fit of pique. Later on, Conall was bested by Cú Chulainn in the tests for the leading warrior that resulted from the feast of Bricriu (q.v.), but no real hostility between the two is ever portrayed.

When Cú Chulainn was treacherously slain, Conall wreaked vengeance on those responsible. This is described in the text *Deargruathar Chonaill Chearnaigh*, the earliest version of which dates from the eleventh century. According to this, Cú Chulainn and Conall had arranged that if one of them were killed the other would avenge him. After the slaying of Cú Chulainn, therefore, his wife Eimhear sent for his foster-brother, who was then at Inbhear Mór (Arklow, County Wicklow). Conall set out, and on his way his charioteer, in anticipation of the *deargruathar* (crimson-raid), was overcome by fear and died. Conall released one horse from his chariot and continued on horseback. He met the great steed of Cú Chulainn, the Grey of Macha, which led him to where its master lay dead. Astride his own fierce mount, called the Dearg Drúchtach, Conall tracked the retreating killers of his friend, and met with Lughaidh mac Con Roí at a ford. He agreed to allow Lughaidh to return to his native Munster on condition that he face him in single combat later. Conall next met and slew MAINE, son of Meadhbh, and put the head of the dead man on a withe. Continuing his offensive, he slew among others the family of Cailitín, who had by magic brought about the death of Cú Chulainn, and then headed south to keep his appointment with Lughaidh. The latter had lost one hand at the killing of Cú Chulainn, and to equalise the combat Conall tied his own hand to his side. Having cut Lughaidh's head off, Conall left it on a stone and it split the stone. He then went to Ulster and presented the heads of the dead enemies to Eimhear. It is clear that the description of the combat with Lughaidh is based on the somewhat earlier description of that with Meas Geaghra.

It is noticeable that the story-writers were anxious to give cohesion to the major stories of the Ulster Cycle, and Conall Cearnach was seen as a suitable personage to employ in that context. So, after the death of Cormac Conn Loingeas, we read that the Ulster nobles appointed Conall as administrator of the kingdom and then offered the throne to him. He, however, declined this since he considered himself too old to lead them into battle, and instead he recommended that his pupil CÚSCRAIDH MEANN MACHA be made king, and he gave a series of wise counsels to Cúscraidh on how to govern. When Cúscraidh was duly installed, he divided his territory among the nobles, allotting the land between Drogheda and Iveagh to Conall. We are further told that the area was as a result known as Caoille Chonaill (Conall's Division), but this designation is merely a reflection of the fact that it was the ancient territory of the Conailli, the people who had Conall Cearnach as ancestor-hero.

The versatility of Conall is clearly shown in the story of one of his greatest feats, the slaying of the ferocious Ceat mac Mághach (q.v.). Indeed, the ongoing contest between these two 'slaughter hounds' (*árchoin*) is a background theme running through most of the Ulster Cycle. After one of Ceat's most devastating raids on Ulster, Conall followed him through the snow to Breifne (an area in Cavan–Leitrim) and slew him in single combat at a ford on the River Shannon. Conall himself was nearly dead after the furious contest. A hostile warrior, Béalchú of Breifne, found him lying on the ground and took him to his house with the intention of allowing him to recover and then slaying him in combat. As Conall's condition improved, however, Béalchú grew fearful and plotted treachery. He accordingly told his three sons that he would leave the doors of his house open and directed them to go at night and kill Conall in his bed. Suspecting this, Conall forced Béalchú to lie in the bed. Béalchú first closed the doors, but when he had fallen asleep, Conall reopened them and thus Béalchú was mistakenly slain by his own sons. Conall then attacked the sons and slew them. This account, found in an eleventh-century text, is an adaptation of the plot of a folk story that has a giant being outwitted in that way by a smart man (*see* HUMOROUS TALES, type 1119). The plot was considered appropriate to Conall's dexterity.

All of this presupposes a long martial career continuing for Conall after the main events of the Ulster Cycle were over, but a variant account has him repairing to the court of queen Meadhbh in Cruachain after the deaths of Conchobhar and Cú Chulainn. 'Great sorrow and misery and leprosy befell him, so that there was no strength in his feet to go about.' Meadhbh and her husband Ailill mac Máta had him fed for a long time, even though he ate mighty meals. He used to entertain the men of Connacht rather riskily every day by describing how he had slain their sons and brothers and fathers. Finally, when Meadhbh became jealous of her husband's affair with another woman, she prevailed on Conall to kill him. Conall was in turn slain by the enraged Connachtmen. His head was kept in the western province, but the Ulstermen had a prophecy that if they drank milk out of the skull they would become strong again.

Conall Cearnach was so celebrated a character in medieval culture that the various septs who – like the Conaille – were designated as CRUITHNIGH by the genealogists (*see* PICTS), claimed descent from him. He remained well known to the literati, and some of the texts in which he played leading roles continued to circulate in manuscript down to recent centuries. His name was thus known to those oral storytellers influenced by written sources. In Ulster folklore, it was said that he joined the Roman army and was present at the Crucifixion of JESUS. On his return to Ireland, when asked why he was so dejected, he remarked that anybody who had seen what he saw could never again be merry. This LEGEND is a simple development of the tradition that Conchobhar mac Neasa was informed of the Crucifixion. Local onomastic lore at Ballyconnell, County Cavan insisted that Conall had been slain there by some of Meadhbh's soldiers who followed him from Connacht, and the same claim was made on behalf of Rathconnell, County Westmeath, but both these are late identifications of the hero with other individuals called Conall referred to in place names.

NAME AND ORIGIN: Pokorny (1959), 1112; McCone (1996), 130; Meyer (1912), 25; F.J. Byrne (1973), 89–90, 118, 323; W. Stokes in *Irische Texte, 3*, 390–5; T.F. O'Rahilly (1946), 230; Olmsted (1994), 335–6. FRAOCH: Meid (1974), 13–16, 44; Carney (1955), 26–7, 57–60. EOCHAIDH FEIDHLEACH: M.E. Dobbs in *RC, 43*, 284–7, 304–27. *TÁIN BÓ CUAILNGE*: C. O'Rahilly (1976), 5, 105, 120, 122. FIACHA: W. Stokes in *Irische Texte, 3*, 406–7. CONTEST OVER HEADS: Thurneysen (1935); Jackson (1964), 35–7; N.K. Chadwick in *Scottish Gaelic Studies, 4*, 120–6. CONTINENTAL CELTIC FEASTS: M. Tierney in J. Raftery (1964), 31–2 (sources in Athenaeus 4.40 – 154); Diodorus Siculus 5.28).

MEAS GEAGHRA: W. Stokes in *RC, 8*, 47–64. CÚ CHULAINN: C. O'Rahilly (1976), 17, 21; Best & O'Brien (1956), 451–3; Van Hamel (1933), 115–33. CÚSCRAIDH: R.I. Best in *Ériu, 8*, 170–90. DEATHS OF CEAT AND BÉALCHÚ: Meyer (1906), 36–42, 45. DEATH OF CONALL: K. Meyer in *ZCP, 1*, 102–11. GENEALOGIES: T.F. O'Rahilly (1946), 349–50; O'Brien (1962), 555. FOLKLORE: S. Ó Súilleabháin in *Béaloideas, 21*, 25–6, S. MacManus (1951), 159–61; OSL: Cavan (1836), 96 & Westmeath, *1* (1837), 215–17; IFC 89:152, 1126:2–3, 283, 1141:117–51, S964:173, S966:135, 354, S967:329.

Conall Clogach

Foolish man who figures in Irish literature, reputed to have been a stepbrother of the sixth-century high-king DOMHNALL MAC AODHA.

In the celebrated biography written by ADHAMHNÁN, St COLM CILLE is said to have blessed the boy Domhnall at the Convention of Drom Ceat (Daisy Hill, near Limavady, County Derry) in the year AD 575, and to have foretold that he would excel his brothers. This was developed by medieval writers with the suggestion that Domhnall's mother was pleased, but the legal queen of Aodh mac Ainmhireach was angry that her own son had been superseded by this. She bitterly referred to the SAINT as 'a crane-like cleric' and, on hearing this, Colm Cille remarked that she and her maidservant – who assisted her in plotting against him – might themselves be cranes until doomsday. They accordingly were turned into two cranes and remained in a nearby river ever after.

One of Domhnall's stepbrothers, called Conall, had a distinguished career and died in 604, but this did not deter the writers from giving a bizarre account of him. We read that Conall incited the rabble to throw stones at Colm Cille and his monks at Drom Ceat, and that in retaliation the saint cursed him and deprived him of the KINGSHIP. Colm assembled his monks and had them ring their bells against the transgressor, on account of which he came to be known as Conall *Clogach* (i.e. of the bells). He was deprived of his reason by the saint's curse, and thus became the royal jester at his brother's court at Dún Chinn Craoibhe (somewhere to the south of Ballyshannon, County Donegal).

One late medieval text gives details of his folly, stating that he used to spend each day guarding the frontier against Tír Chonaill (i.e. the Donegal area), and would strike three blows with his cudgel on the ground there to keep the boundary from moving overnight when he returned to his brother's royal fortress. As he went home one night, he met with the high-king's men, who had just hanged the mother of a gang of robbers and were burying her in a bog-hole. Noticing that Conall had seen them, they secretly replaced the body with that of a dead GOAT. The foolish Conall later pointed out to the robbers where he thought their mother was, but they found the goat there instead. 'Had your mother a beard and horns?' he asked. Later, his royal brother Domhnall played a trick on him by having some Connacht visitors pretend to be messengers with tidings that Conall Clogach had been eaten by wolves at his frontier post. Conall wept at the news of his own death, but one warrior seized him and declared that he had rescued the fool and brought him safely there. This text goes on to tell of how Conall Clogach went to Connacht and met the Munster fool COMHDHÁN there, and of their numerous escapades together. This account incorporates several plots from folklore (*see* HUMOROUS TALES, types 1600 and 1313, and other types referred to under Comhdhán).

Anderson & Anderson (1961), 230–1; B. Ó Cuív in *Éigse, 11*, 183–7, 290; W. Stokes in *RC, 20*, 426–8; K. Meyer in *ZCP, 10*, 48–9; O'Kelleher & Schoepperle (1918), 346–51, 376–7; Dinneen, *3* (1908), 88–91; Ó Cadhlaigh (1939), 136–56.

Conall Corc *(also called simply Corc)* Legendary KING of Munster in the fifth century AD. Apparently an early ruler of the EOGHANACHT sept, little can be deduced regarding his actual history from the LEGENDS told of him in literature of the eighth and succeeding centuries.

He is described as son of a certain Lughaidh (viz. 'Corc mac Luighdheach') and fourth in line of descent from AILILL ÓLOM. His mother was called Boilce, a female satirist of the Britons, who put a binding request on Lughaidh to lie with her. In this way, Conall was conceived, and he was fostered by a sorceress called Feidhilm, who was nicknamed Láir Dhearg (Red Mare) – hence he was also known as 'Corc mac Láire'. A group of sorceresses once gathered at Feidhilm's house, and she concealed the boy under the hearth. One of the visitors remarked: 'I destroy only what is under the cauldron,' and immediately the fire darted at the child and burned his ear. Thus he got the nickname Corc, which meant 'red'. Next day, a diviner examined the boy's palm and told him that if he freed captives whenever he could, his name would be famous.

The boy was later adopted by his cousin, the Munster king Criomhthann mac Fiodhaigh. When he grew up, Criomhthann sent Conall to Leinster to collect tribute, and while there, he ransomed three captives – one of whom, Gruibne, went to Scotland. However. Criomhthann's wife tried to seduce him and then, in spite, lyingly told her husband that Conall had asked her to lie with him. This is an early Irish example of a far-flung storytelling MOTIF (*see* ROMANTIC TALES, type 870C). Criomhthann sent Conall to the king of the PICTS in Scotland with a coded message in OGHAM on his shield. Arriving in that country, Conall was caught in a snowdrift and was rescued by Gruibne, who was herding swine there. Gruibne understood that the message on his shield was a signal to the Pictish king Fearadhach to kill the bearer, so he changed it to mean that Fearadhach's daughter should be given to Conall. Fearadhach hesitated, but Conall and his daughter came together and she became pregnant by him. She gave birth to a son, and after some wrangling, Fearadhach accepted Conall as his son-in-law. This part of the narrative is also based on an international plot (*see* ROMANTIC TALES, type 930).

Conall had two more sons by his Pictish wife, and on Criomhthann's death, he returned to Munster, bringing his wife and children with him. As they arrived, snow fell and they lost their way in the storm. On the very same day, a swine-herd had seen a vision of a yew tree on top of the great rock of Caiseal (Cashel, County Tipperary) and angels descending to an oratory in front of it. The swine-herd told this to his master Aodh, king of the Múscraighe sept, and Aodh's DRUID explained that this meant that the kingship of Munster would be centred there and that the first person to light a fire under the yew tree would be king of the province. Aodh wished to go at once, but the druid advised him to wait till morning. Thus it happened that Conall arrived at the rock before him and, quite unaware of the prophecy, lit a fire there. When Aodh arrived and submitted to him, Conall understood all, and within a week had established himself as king of Munster. The place was accordingly known as Caiseal Coirc (the castellum of Corc).

This legend of Corc, with its early folk-lore material, was obviously put together at the behest of the Eoghanacht sept, of whom Conall Corc was one of the most famous ancestors. The place name Caiseal is a borrowing from Latin, and it seems that all the tradition of that place had Christian sources – as in this legend. For that reason, the lore in this form cannot be much older than the texts. The stress on pagan elements is so marked, however, and the lore so clearly illustrates the transition of the Eoghanacht from paganism to Christianity, that its origin probably belonged to the sixth or seventh century.

Conall Corc is little referred to in the later tradition, but a seventeenth-century source gives a slightly varying account of how he got his name. According to this, his mother was called Bolgbháin, and the hero's father was legally married to another woman. Two idiots deliberately injured the child Conall. He was hidden from them under the cauldron, but they lifted the cauldron and burned his ears.

K. Meyer in *AIM*, *3*, 57–63; V. Hull in *Proceedings of the Modern Language Association*, *56*, 937–50 & *62*, 892–906 & in *ZCP*, *18*, 420–1 & *27*, 64–74; M. Dillon in *Ériu*, *16*, 61–73; W. Stokes in *Irische Texte*, *3*, 311–12; Dinneen, *2*(1908), 368–87; Dillon (1946), 34–7; F.J. Byrne (1973), 183–9; M. Schlauch in *JCS*, *1*, 152–66; D. Sproule in *Ériu*, *36*, 11–28.

Conall Gulban Son of the celebrated king NIALL. In the mid-fifth century AD, Conall carved out a kingdom for himself in west Ulster.

In the push northwards from TARA, he was accompanied by his brothers Eoghan, Cairbre and Éanna. Conall's new territory came to be known from him as Tír Chonaill (most of County Donegal), and his descendants were called Cinéal gConaill. Similarly, Eoghan's name was given to Inis Eoghain (the northern Donegal peninsula) and Tír Eoghain (Tyrone), and his descendants were called Cinéal nEoghain (the northern branch of the Uí NÉILL).

Conall got his epithet from the conspicuous mountain Beann Ghulban (Benbulben) in the south of his territory. His fame was promoted in succeeding centuries by his descendants, the Cinéal gConaill, whose leading family from medieval times onwards took the surname Ó Domhnaill (later, Ó Dónaill). Later genealogists claimed that Conall had been the favourite son of his father Niall, but in reality Niall was succeeded as KING of Tara by LAOGHAIRE, who was probably the eldest son. In the province of Connacht, Niall's brothers Fiachra and Brión had formed their own kingdoms, their descendants being known as Uí Fhiachrach and Uí Bhriúin. Fiachra was an outstanding warrior, as also was his son NAITHÍ.

The medieval Cinéal gConaill writers weaved old memories of politicking between all these powerful relatives into a comprehensive narrative that heroised Conall. According to this, when Conall was a boy, his uncle Fiachra was so impressed by the lustre in his face that he took him as a foster-son from Niall. The boy was sent by Fiachra to be educated by Muireadhach Meann, king of the Calraighe sept (in County Sligo). Part of his training was to run each day from a pillar-stone towards Beann Ghulban, and the place where he halted to draw his breath was marked by Muireadhach. Next day, he would have to run further, until eventually he could reach the peak without pausing at all. When people remarked that 'Conall runs bravely on Gulba', the DRUID of Muireadhach called him 'Conall of Gulba' – hence his full name. Once, when Conall's uncle Brión visited Muireadhach's dwelling, a leading soldier among the visitors boasted that he could do the same feat, but he dropped dead in the effort.

Soon a war broke out between the provinces of Ulster and Connacht, and the Ulstermen burned the fortress of Muireadhach and slew that king. Conall went to Tara for assistance, and his brothers joined him. Their father Niall counselled that compensation should be accepted from the Ulstermen, but Fiachra urged Conall against this. In a fierce battle at Áth Cró ('the ford of blood' – i.e. Ballyshannon, County Donegal), Conall and his brothers, assisted by Fiachra and Naithí, defeated the Ulstermen. Conall himself beheaded the Ulster king Cana. Laoghaire then returned to Tara, taking Cana's wife with him, and Fiachra and Naithí returned to their fortress at Cruachain (Rathcroghan, County Roscommon). Conall, supported by Eoghan, Cairbre and Éanna, continued his campaign against the Ulstermen. Finally, in a battle at Cruachan Droma Lighean (near Lifford, County Donegal), the other three were facing defeat, but the wounded Conall rose from his sick-bed, slew the enemy leader and inspired his army to rout the foe. The four brothers then divided their conquered territories between them, Conall's portion being from Loch Súilighe (Lough Swilly) to Drobhaois (River Drowes).

Following this, war broke out in Connacht between Fiachra and Brión, and Naithí came to Conall seeking help for Fiachra. Conall gathered his forces, defeated Brión and cut a trail of destruction southwards, defeating even the Munster king Lughaidh Meann. However, Brión captured Fiachra and sent him to Niall at Tara as a prisoner. Conall again defeated the reassembled forces of Brión at Damhchluain (near Tuam, County Galway), after which Brión was slain. The combined armies of Conall and Naithí subdued all Connacht,

after which Naithí was installed as king of the province. The two leaders then went to Tara; they were reconciled to Niall and Fiachra was released.

A later medieval text retells much of this, and further increases Conall's status by claiming that he was chosen as high-king as successor to Niall, but that Laoghaire coaxed the kingship from him. A long list of battles gained by Conall in many parts of the country is given, and we read that 'the valour of Niall of noble deeds was in no son of his except in Conall'. This text describes the hero as meeting his death at Dún Chonaing (near Fenagh, County Leitrim), while chasing a group of raiders of the Masraighe sept (of County Leitrim), who had stolen horses from Tara. Conall was slain while unarmed and accompanied by but a few of his men, and he was buried at Dún Bhaile (now Fenagh).

The Cinéal gConaill had long been interested in gaining ecclesiastical prestige for themselves. Thus we read in a seventh-century biography of PATRICK that Conall was the most receptive of all Niall's sons to the message of the great saint. He welcomed Patrick, accepted baptism, and gave him land for a church at Domhnach Phádraig (Donaghpatrick, County Meath). There may well be some truth in this, but it is much developed in the ninth-century biography of the saint, which has Patrick telling Conall that 'your brothers' seed will submit to your seed forever'. A later medieval source claims that, on that occasion, Patrick drew the sign of a red cross on Conall's shield, thus giving to the hero's Ó Dónaill descendants their family crest.

The fame of Conall Gulban was so great that when, in the sixteenth century, an anonymous Donegal writer decided to compose a romantic story, he made this celebrated ancestral figure the hero of it. This text, entitled *Eachtra Chonaill Gulban*, departs almost completely from the genuine tradition, situating most of its action overseas in the general manner of post-medieval romances. It opens by describing how Conall was trained by Muireadhach Meann by making him run up Beann Ghulban, and then we read of how – quite anachronistically – the German emperor sought help from Niall after Italy was overrun by the Turks. Niall is here described as having three sons – Laoghaire, Eoghan and Conall – and the first two insist on joining their father on the expedition. Only Conall is willing to remain at home and protect Ireland. After Niall's fleet has departed from Beann Éadair (Howth, County Dublin), Conall decides to visit the beautiful Eithne, daughter of the Leinster king. She is strongly guarded at Nás (Naas, County Kildare), but Conall vaults into her apartment and departs carrying her on his shoulder. She complains that he is carrying her away in flight, and so he waits for her guard and slays an entire company of them. On reaching Beann Éadair, he falls asleep with his head on her lap, and a stranger called the Macaomh Mór (Large Warrior) arrives in search of the Leinster king's daughter. Eithne pretends that she is not her, but the Macaomh is so enamoured of the lady who addresses him that he takes Eithne anyway, and departs with her over the sea.

When Conall awakes, he finds out from a local shepherd what has happened. The shepherd also tells him that a ship is always at Beann Éadair when an Irishman needs it, and so Conall finds a ship and sets sail in search of his loved one. He lands in Scandinavia, where he defeats a whole team of young hurlers and then goes to *Teach na nAmhas* (the House of Mercenaries), where he is attacked. Seizing one man by the ankles, he uses him as a club to ward off the rest. When Conall falls asleep, the Scandinavian king sends a hundred warriors to attack him, but Conall dreams of fierce lions and awakes and slays them all. The king's daughter Doireann falls in love with him and sends her druid Dúnadhach to cure him of his wounds. The druid then places him in the princess' bed, but Conall puts a sword between them and she grows angry. She engages a great warrior called Amhas Órarmach (Golden-armed Mercenary) to kill him, but in a fierce and protracted combat, Conall overcomes and binds the Amhas. He then puts the king's whole army to flight and

binds the king himself, but Dúnadhach intervenes and makes peace between them.

A great feast is held, and a strange warrior called Ridire an Ghaiscigh (the Knight of the Feat) arrives, seizes the king, and throws him to the floor. Conall fights the newcomer, defeats him, and then demands to know if he was ever in a more difficult position than now. The Ridire tells of how he met the Macaomh with Eithne, and how he had fought for Eithne but had been overcome by the Macaomh and thrown over a sea cliff. He had landed in a griffin's nest and eventually managed to kill the griffin. Next, he had fallen in with man-eating giants but had again escaped, and had then proceeded to Scandinavia. Hearing from him that Eithne had won a promise from the Macaomh not to be made his wife for a year, Conall enthusiastically sets out again on his quest, accompanied by Dúnadhach, the Amhas, and the Ridire. In Crete, Conall defeats in single combat the prince IOLLANN AIRMDHEARG, and enlists him also as a supporter.

They arrive in Syria, and coming to the Macaomh's fortress at a place called Pampilana, they kill hordes of the foe. Then Conall fights the Macaomh, and after four days of combat defeats him but spares his life on promise of tribute. In order to compensate the Macaomh for the loss of Eithne, Conall and his men go to Caledonia to win a fine princess for him. They encounter great opposition there, finding that 500 men they kill each day come alive again overnight. Conall lies among the dead, and thus discovers that a HAG comes with a bottle of balsam to revive them. He slays the hag, and some days later strangles three poisonous hounds with his bare hands. In a general battle, the army of the Caledonian king is defeated, and the princess is won for the Macaomh. News arrives, however, that Eithne has been kidnapped by the Greek king to be his son's wife. In a great battle, Conall and his followers defeat the Greeks and sack Athens.

Learning that the Turks have won many battles against the German emperor and have advanced into Europe, Conall and his helpers set out to the rescue with a mere hundred knights. Slipping into the Turkish camp, Conall slays the enemy emperor, but he and his five companions have to retreat in the face of great odds. In the darkness and confusion, Conall's brother Laoghaire unwittingly fights the Amhas, and similarly with Eoghan and the Macaomh. Conall, however, recognises in each case an Irish groan from his brothers, and calls off their opponents. Next day, Conall and his men join the army of the German emperor, and in a massive battle, the Turks are completely overthrown. Conall returns to Ireland with his father and brothers, and his later career is summarised in keeping with the earlier sources.

The author of this text obviously cared little for historical or geographical accuracy, and included any dramatic material at his disposal. As well as using a version of the earlier biography of Conall, he borrowed some plots from current folklore (*see* ROMANTIC TALES, type 953 *and* HUMOROUS TALES, type 1137). The motif of a hag magically reviving slain warriors is found also in the thirteenth-century Norman-French romance *Perceval*, and this may have drawn on the same lost Irish source from which the author of *Eachtra Chonaill Gulban* got it. This romance of Conall Gulban, with its colourful imagery, became very popular in manuscripts, and from being read out it was picked up by oral storytellers in the eighteenth and nineteenth centuries. Several versions have been collected from folklore – all shortened and tending to omit the details that are not necessary to the basic plot. That plot, as preserved by the oral tellers, centres on the abduction of Eithne, Conall's adventures in Scandinavia, his defeat of the Macaomh, and his final routing of the Turks.

BIOGRAPHIES: P. Breathnach in *Irisleabhar Muighe Nuadhat* (1932), 43–52 & (1933), 34–41; G. Lehmacher in *ZCP*, 14, 212–69; W.M. Hennessy & Kelly (1875), 138–55, 312–31.
PATRICK: Bieler (1979), 132–3 & (1971), 149–50; Mulchrone (1939), 46; Stokes (1887), 70–3, 148–51, 464–7, 478–81; Burke (1884), 747; O'Kelleher & Schoepperle (1918), 12–13.
ROMANCE AND ORAL VERSIONS: IFC 1121 (edn. by Roibeard Ó Scannláin). Discussions and lists of versions in Bruford (1969), 15–17, 72–9, 253–4, 279 & in *Béaloideas*, 31, 1–50.

Conán Maol Mischievous character in the FIANNA CYCLE, brother of the great warrior GOLL MAC MORNA. The name Conán is a diminutive of *cú* (literally, 'hound' but figuratively 'warrior'), and the epithet means 'bald'.

His mischief-making is probably a survival from the early hostile portrayal of Goll and thus of the whole Morna clan. There is an early reference to a certain Maol mac Morna, and such a character may have been envisaged as having a druidic tonsure, an image also found in relation to the Fianna leader, FIONN MAC CUMHAILL. It is of interest that Conán Maol shares his first name with another character who was hostile to Fionn, namely Conán son of the Liath Luachra. We read that this latter character waged a long campaign against the Fianna, killing many of them. His father's designation (the Grey of Logher) shows him to have belonged to west Munster, hostile territory for Fionn (q.v.), and it was in that area that he eventually crept up on and captured Fionn himself. He told Fionn that he wished to enlist in the Fianna, and the latter had no choice but to agree. However, Fionn never forgave him, and eventually encompassed his death by sending him to woo the daughter of a man who had vowed to kill any such wooer.

Accounts of Conán Maol mac Morna begin in the twelfth-century literature, and it is noticeable that the author of the most developed Fianna text of that period, *Agallamh na Seanórach*, confuses the son of Liath Luachra with Goll's brother. It may therefore be that Conán Maol was in origin a composite figure drawn from a certain Maol mac Morna and this other Conán. Already in the twelfth-century sources, he has a comprehensive personality as an impulsive and quite malicious man. A very sinister side to his character is illustrated by one episode in which, during the great war between Fionn and Goll, he and two of his supporters seize three young women who are under Fionn's protection. When they are brought to Goll's camp, that warrior wishes to return them as a means of making peace with

Fionn, but Conán Maol insists on killing them. This is probably an echo of the cruel nature of Fionn's archetypal foe who originally gave rise to the more noble Goll (q.v.). It represents an extreme in the portrayal of Conán, whose mischief is usually of a less-sinister type.

We read that 'he never sought justice from anyone, and he gave his curse to those who did justice to him', and he was notorious for jibes and incitement. A fifteenth-century lay goes so far as to call him 'the destructive man of the Fianntroop' (*fear millte na Féinne*). This word for destruction has a special meaning in the term for a magically destructive eye, *súil mhillte*, so it is not surprising that folklore attributes to Conán the power of killing his enemies by looking at them through his fingers. He had requested that power, we are told, from an otherworld lady in an allegorical house that Fionn and some of the Fianna once visited, and the lady had granted it to him. However, on Fionn's advice, she did not let him know that his request had been granted, for, if he knew it, he might kill the Fianna themselves if a fit of pique came on him.

Conán Maol was portrayed as a troublesome buffoon in the post-medieval literature of the Fianna Cycle (q.v.), and his actions afford comic relief in some texts. A favourite situation is to have him tussling with hideous HAGS, resisting their amorous advances or fighting viciously with them. According to one such text, when many of the Fianna were released after being stuck to the floor in a magical dwelling, there was not enough liquid to release Conán, so he had to be forcibly torn free, leaving the skin of his back behind him. Folk narrative added some details in its retellings of the popular text, claiming that the other Fianna warriors attached a sheepskin to his back in place of his own skin, and that he was sheared each year and thus provided socks for all the Fianna! He is further ridiculed in a verse text composed in south Ulster in the late eighteenth century. According to this, he is invited to an otherworld dwelling by a little man called Cab an Dosáin (Tufty

Mouth). During the night there, he tries to go to the bed of a beautiful young woman, but imagines that he is being sucked into a bog and that savage CATS are attacking him. His shouts awaken the other dwellers, and they find him sitting on a candlestick, with a kitten licking his mouth. When all had again retired, he succeeded in reaching the woman's bed, but she made him reverse sexual roles, and then he imagined that he was going to give birth and called for a midwife. Fionn, however, managed to have Conán freed from his weird surroundings 'because he had some magic himself'. This story is a combination of a somewhat earlier text on the character called MAC NA MÍCHOMHAIRLE and of an international narrative plot (*see* HUMOROUS TALES, type 1739). *See also* FEARDHOMHAIN.

GENERAL: Stokes (1880), clxxii & (1900), 52, 113, 186, 203–5; Ní Shéaghdha (1967), 24; Mac Néill (1908), 57; G. Murphy (1933), 258; Ó hÓgáin (1988), 165–6, 272–3, 295–6, 336, 342, 344, 357. CONÁN SON OF THE LIATH LUACHRA: Stokes (1900), 101–2; Mac Néill (1908), 1–3; Gwynn (1924), 362–6; L-C. Stern in *RC*, *13*, 7–10; Ní Shéaghdha (1967), 56–64.

Conchobhar mac Neasa

Mythical KING in the ULSTER CYCLE. The name Conchobhar is a compound of *cú* (i.e. hound; figuratively, warrior) and *cobhar* (desirous). Its original meaning would then appear to have been 'one who is desirous of warriors', a typical designation for the king in heroic society.

As holder of the office of sacral kingship, the figure of Conchobhar must have been of importance in the LEGENDS of the ancient ULAIDH people, from whom the province of Ulster got its name. Echoing lore of him that circulated in antiquity, we have several embellished accounts of Conchobhar from early in the literature, and by medieval times, the corpus of the Ulster Cycle functioned as a kind of general biography of him.

It is curious that he is designated from the name of his mother Neas (earlier, Nes). This could be considered a vestige of some matriarchal system, but it more likely derives from the convention of personifying sovereignty as a woman (*see* GODDESSES). In accordance with this, descriptions of his birth were invented that in underlying his royal status gave pride of place to his mother. Neas, it is claimed, was daughter of a fictional earlier king of the province called Eochu Sálbhuidhe. She had twelve foster-fathers, who were all slain by the DRUID-warrior CATHBHADH as they drank together one night. The identity of their killer was not known, and Neas was so enraged that she took to reaving the countryside in blind fury. One day, while unarmed and bathing in a lake, she was seized by Cathbhadh who made her swear to become his wife. One account states that Conchobhar was their offspring; but another has a high-king of Ireland, Fachtna Fáthach, as his father. Yet another source states that Neas was fertilised by a drink of water she had brought to Cathbhadh and some drops of which she herself consumed. The water was from the Conchubhar, which was the name of a stream (apparently in the vicinity of Lough Ross, County Armagh); thus, it is said, the child got its name. This explanation is based on the false identification of two different words, the stream's name being a compound of *con* (cumulative) and *cubhar* (foam). An additional MOTIF used in order to connect him with this river seems to have been borrowed from lore of FIONN MAC CUMHAILL. According to it, Conchobhar was born holding a worm in each hand, and immediately fell into the river, from which Cathbhadh rescued him.

The tradition that gained currency was that Fachtna Fáthach was the real father and that Cathbhadh acted as guardian to the child; this allowed for a story to develop that rationalised Conchobhar's accession to the throne of Ulster. The reigning king, FEARGHUS MAC RÓICH, wished to have Neas as wife, and she agreed on condition that he allow her son to hold the kingship for one year. The province prospered during that year, and Neas advised Conchobhar to win the support of the nobles by favouritism and bribery. This stratagem worked so well that, at the end of the year, the nobles decided to retain Conchobhar as king. He then ordered that Fearghus be banished,

and a civil war followed between the two. Peace was eventually made between them, the basic conditions of it being that Conchobhar should remain king and that Fearghus should become seneschal of the province. The king of TARA, EOCHAIDH FEIDHLEACH, who had supported Fearghus in the war, now gave his daughter in marriage to Conchobhar. That daughter was MEADHBH, but she soon left her bridegroom through vanity and returned to her father at Tara.

Conchobhar is portrayed as a good and able administrator of his kingdom. During his reign in Ulster, the crops grew lusciously, cattle were easily fattened, and the rivers and lakes gave plenty of fish. Peace and prosperity radiated from his court at Eamhain Mhacha (Navan Fort, County Armagh), where he had fine buildings erected. As an ideal and wise king, he is imagined as having been in step with the logic of the cosmos. His household, for instance, consisted of 'the number of men which is the number of days in the year'. He held a great assembly each year at Samhain (November), the feast with greatest emphasis in the old Irish calendar (*see* TIME), and all the Ulstermen were dutybound to attend this assembly; any man who failed to do so lost his reason and died. Conchobhar was also a model of systematic planning, establishing depots and armouries, and instituting an academy at Eamhain Mhacha where boys were trained in feats of arms. Regarding his duties as king, he spent each morning in solving the administrative problems of the province, and then divided the day into three parts. The first part he spent observing the boys perform athletic feats, the second part playing chessboard games, and the final part feasting with music and entertainment.

Echoes of more primitive features survive through the model patterns, however – features that accord with the fertility symbolism of the Ulster kingship evidenced by the character of Fearghus mac Róich (q.v.). Thus we read that Conchobhar slept with the bride of each of his subjects on the first night after a wedding, and slept on one night also with the wife of any householder whom he visited on his royal circuit. His sister Deichtine was the mother of the great CÚ CHULAINN, but one tradition had it that Conchobhar was in fact the father of that hero through an incestuous union with Deichtine. He certainly was quite amorous, for we read that after Meadhbh, he married three of her sisters – Clothra, Eithne and Mughain.

As a warrior, Conchobhar is represented as brave and resourceful, as in *Táin Bó Cuailnge* (*see* ULSTER CYCLE) when he shows his valour after he and his men are released from the magical debility previously imposed on them by the lady MACHA. When the *Táin* campaign was over, he languished in Eamhain Mhacha impatiently planning vengeance on Meadhbh and the rest of Ireland for the damage they had inflicted on his province. Gathering his forces by land and sea, he made such preparations for terrible war that three great sea waves shook portentously (*see* ENVIRONMENT). The various kings who had opposed him now offered huge compensation in gold, but Conchobhar refused and moved his army south to Ros na Ríogh (Rosnaree on the River Boyne). He was confronted there by the forces of Cairbre Nia Fear, king of Tara. During the fighting, Conchobhar's shield, the Óchaoin, shrieked out and was answered by all the other shields of the Ulstermen. When Cú Chulainn slew Cairbre, the enemy took flight, and he entered Tara in triumph. Cairbre had been married to Conchobhar's sister Feidhlim, and the victor now gave the prestigious kingship of Tara to the son of that couple, called Earc. This story first appears in a twelfth-century manuscript and is obviously a late sequel to the *Táin* narrative, but it is interesting to note that there is no attempt – even at that late stage – to have Conchobhar installed at Tara as high-king of all Ireland.

The unsavoury manner in which he ousted Fearghus from the Ulster throne was not seen to reflect overmuch on Conchobhar's character. It was based on a vestige of ancient ritual that had Fearghus as a divine patron entrusting that kingship to the reigning sovereign – the story itself being no more than a rationalisation of this vestige. The early medieval writer, who thus rationalised the material, found it necessary to dramatise it in personal terms, and for this purpose he attributed a shrewd opportunism to Conchobhar. This trait of opportunism was not perpetuated by other writers, but one notable exception was a story that developed early in the ninth century – the tragedy of DEIRDRE. This story in fact goes further than its precedent, allotting to Conchobhar a cynically cruel and treacherous role, but in general the older type of portrayal held firm and Conchobhar was envisaged in a remarkably consistent light through the centuries.

True to the original meaning of his name, he is invariably described as a figure of authority surrounded by his great martial champions and, significantly, his death occurs when for once the sacred person of the king is exposed unprotected to the foe. This, his death-tale, is found in several versions and seems to have originated in the eleventh century. According to it, the Leinster king Meas Geaghra was slain by CONALL CEARNACH, and his brain, mixed with lime, was preserved as a trophy in Eamhain Mhacha. CEAT MAC MÁGHACH, the Connacht warrior who continuously ravaged Ulster, stole the trophy away. Mindful of a prophecy that Meas Geaghra would avenge himself after death, Ceat kept the brain-ball by him as a missile, with which he intended to do maximum harm to the Ulstermen when the opportunity should arise. Eventually, during a skirmish between the two provinces, he got his chance. He persuaded a group of Connacht women to beg Conchobhar to go apart from the Ulster army and show his kingly person to them, and then lost no time in shooting the brain-ball from a sling at his quarry. The missile lodged in Conchobhar's head and, thus seriously wounded, the king was rescued and taken away by the Ulster warriors. On examining the wound, the surgeon Fínghein decided that Conchobhar's life would be endangered if the ball were removed, but that he would live if he avoided all exertion.

111

For seven years, Conchobhar remained seated, but then one day he noticed the earth trembling and the sun darkening and, on enquiring of the druid Cathbhadh what was the meaning of this, was told that a good man called JESUS CHRIST had been crucified in the east. Outraged by this news, Conchobhar rose up in great anger, and the ball fell from his forehead. The blood that sprang from his head baptised him before he died, and so he was the first Irishman to become a Christian. Variants of this story have as bearer of the sad tidings to Conchobhar, not Cathbhadh but a Leinster POET called Bachrach, or even a Roman tribute-collector called Altus. One version of the story has the king rising from his throne and racing furiously to a nearby wood, where he slashes at the trees, in his delirium imagining them to be the crucifiers of Christ.

This story became popular in the folklore of Ulster, but the idea of baptism by blood was too enigmatic, and that detail dropped out and was replaced by a whole new extension to the account. Only his body had died, it was said, and God had preserved his soul and deposited it in the hollow of his skull. Much later, when St PATRICK was preaching the faith in Ireland, he heard a voice speaking to him from a clump of rushes. This was the voice of Conchobhar's soul, and Patrick soon discovered the skull in the rushes. The voice explained how the brain-ball had been lodged there, and Patrick said that in order to reach heaven, the body must be revived and baptised. Conchobhar's soul then cried out pathetically that it feared to endure death a second time, whereupon Patrick was so overcome with pity that tears flowed from his eyes down onto the skull and Conchobhar was thus baptised. His soul ascended to heaven in the form of a dove. This legend is derived from a medieval Latin tradition that claimed St GREGORY the Great had baptised the dead emperor Trajan, Patrick and Conchobhar being seen as good substitutes for these two worthies in the Irish context.

Conchobhar does not figure prominently in recent folk tradition, apart from this latter legend and occurrences in oral versions of stories like that of Deirdre and Macha, as well, of course, as the fragmentary oral survivals of the Cú Chulainn stories.

NAME: C. Watkins in *Ériu, 19*, 114–16.
BIRTH AND ACCESSION: K. Meyer in *RC, 6*, 173–82; W. Stokes in *Ériu, 4*, 18–38; V.E. Hull in *Irish Texts, 4*, 4–12.
REIGN AND WISDOM: W. Stokes in *Ériu, 4*; Van Hamel (1933), 20–1, 64–5; M. Dillon in *Ériu, 11*, 44–8, 51. *See also* references under ULSTER CYCLE.
ROS NA RÍOGH: E. Hogan (1892).
DEATH: Meyer (1906), 2–21; Dinneen, *2* (1908), 198–205; J. Szovérrfy in *ZCP, 25*, 183–210; Bruford (1969), 99; Ó hÓgáin (1985), 11–2.
GENERAL: Ó Cadhlaigh (1956), 38–44, 135–61, 371–82, 427–9, 469.
See WILD ANIMALS.

Conghal Cláiringneach Fictional KING of Ireland, situated in prehistory. The name means 'warrior-valour' and the sobriquet 'flat-nailed'. There apparently were several stories in medieval literature concerning him, but no good early account survives. There is, however, a long text dating from around the fifteenth century that retells episodes known to the literature for several centuries anterior to it. These episodes have synchronised Conghal with the ULSTER CYCLE.

The text, which was written in east Ulster, tells of how Lughaidh Luaighne, king of Ireland, divided the province of Ulster into two parts, placing Conghal Cláiringneach over one part and FEARGHUS MAC LÉIDE over the other. The nobles demanded that their province be united under one king, and the poet Fachtna Fionn brought the two rulers to TARA to request this of Lughaidh Luaighne. In Tara, Lughaidh's daughter Fionnabhair fell in love with Fearghus and prevailed upon her father to give the Ulster kingdom to him. Tracts of land in each province were offered in compensation to Conghal, but he rejected this and left Tara in anger. He went to the king of Meath, Cairbre Crom, who encouraged him to avenge the insult, and several banished princes joined him there.

As he returned to Ulster, Conghal met Criomhthann Caomh, son of Lughaidh Luaighne, at the Boyne and killed him. When Lughaidh was given news of this, he was in great sorrow. He gave Fionnabhair in marriage to Fearghus mac Léide, who then undertook to go home to Ulster and banish Conghal. Fearghus held a great feast at the Ulster capital, Eamhain Mhacha, at which his namesake, Fearghus mac Rosa, was present. Contention arose between the followers of the two, and when Mac Rosa suspected that a military tribute due to him from Mac Léide would not be honoured, he withdrew his forces from Eamhain and joined Conghal's army.

Conghal sent the POETS Fachtna Fionn and Bricne (i.e. BRICRIU) to Eamhain to ask his friends and kinsmen to join him, but Bricne began to make threats against these and they refused to come over. On the advice of his tutor, Conghal turned away from fighting his fellow Ulstermen, but he allowed Fearghus mac Rosa to attack and destroy the fortress of Niall Niamhghlonnach at Dún Dá Bheann (Mount Sandel, near Coleraine) in revenge for the insults he had received at the feast. In retaliation, Niall attacked the army of Conghal and Mac Rosa at Aonach Inbhir Thuaighe (at the mouth of the River Bann). In a fierce battle, Niall was slain and his forces scattered.

The poet Fachtna Fionn then advised Conghal to go overseas with his followers, and they did accordingly. After several adventures in Scotland and elsewhere, they returned to Ulster and were rejoined by Fearghus mac Rosa, and headed for the hostel of Boirche (in south-east County Down), where Fearghus mac Léide was then sojourning. Mac Léide and his men came out to face the foe but were routed, and Conghal then decided to advance on Tara. He sent Fachtna to challenge Lughaidh Luaighne, who asked for a night's respite in order to gather his forces. He was given that, but in the battle next day, he came face to face with a rampant Conghal and was beheaded. His Luaighne sept was decimated, and Conghal then took the kingship of Ireland. Fearghus mac Léide came to Tara to surrender, and Conghal did not banish him but gave the throne of Ulster to a warrior called Ros Ruadh.

The portion of the text that describes Conghal's adventures abroad is obviously a late medieval invention, and indeed may have been composed by the writer of the text himself. It tells of how Conghal was betrothed to Taise Thaoibhgheal, daughter of king Donn of the otherworld, who is here said to have lived on Rathlin Island. The king of Uardha (cold country), called Nabgodon, desired Taise. When Conghal and his men were feasting with DONN at the latter's hostel, this Nabgodon attacked them with a great force, and in a vicious struggle Conghal beheaded Nabgodon and all the attackers were slain. Conghal and his men were a long time recuperating from their wounds, and emissaries were meanwhile sent to Fearghus mac Léide, who bestowed a tract of land on Taise and even offered the Ulster kingship to Conghal. The latter, however, decided to go to Scandinavia, and he and his men were royally entertained by the king of that country, called Amhlaoibh. Bricne mischievously went to the king's beautiful daughter Beiuda and told her that Conghal was in love with her. She said that he must bring her three wonderful birds, a certain great chariot-yoke, and a certain great helmet. These things were on a faraway sea-fortress controlled by the amazon Muirn with a great force, but after many fighting feats, Conghal and his men procured them. On his return to Scandinavia, he refused to marry Beiuda, since she had sent him into such danger. Then he went to Scotland and took several islands, and received the homage of the kings of the Britons and Saxons before deciding to return to Ireland.

The death of Conghal was made to follow logically on his great campaign for the kingship. It was said that he went to Munster to take hostages on account of the help that Lughaidh Luaighne had received from that province. The Munstermen refused the hostages, and in the ensuing battle were defeated, and Lughaidh's son Cairbre was wounded and remained lame ever after. This Cairbre had two sons, Duach (alternately, Duí) and Déadhadh. These contended with each other, and Duach had his brother blinded. He was therefore known as Duach Dallta Déadhaidh (Duach who blinded Déadhadh). Conghal died at the hands of Duach, who then assumed his grandfather's throne, but no details of that episode survive.

It is obvious that some of the characters and the events in this text are based on rather confused memories of tradition. The influence of lore concerning such figures as FEARGHUS MAC LÉIDE, FEARGHUS MAC RÓICH, RUADH RÓ-FHEASA, BRICRIU and LUGHAIDH MAC CON is discernable, as are struggles between the Ulaidh and the kingship of Tara (here represented by the 'Luaighne' – i.e. the Luighne sept of the ÉRAINN).

Macalister (1956), 296–7; MacSweeney (1904); Dinneen, 2 (1908), 180–3.

Conlae Fictional son of CÚ CHULAINN in the ULSTER CYCLE, tragically slain by his father in single combat. The name was not unusual, being of ancient derivation (see COLLA), and seems to have been selected by an early medieval writer for this character because it could be interpreted as 'warrior-like'. Later interpretations are evidenced by the forms Conlaed (warrior-essence) and Conlaoch (warrior-hero).

The story of Conlae first appears in a text of the late ninth century, *Aided Óenfir Aífe* (the Death of Aoife's Only Son), and is a version of an international HERO-TALE plot (see ROMANTIC TALES, type 873). We read that when Cú Chulainn was learning arms in Scotland, he overcame in combat the female warrior Aoife, and she consented to lie with him. He gave her a ring and requested of her that if she gave birth to a baby boy, to send the child to Ireland as soon as he could wear that ring. Cú Chulainn further said that the boy should be instructed to tell his name to no single warrior. Seven years later, the Ulstermen were assembled on the shore of Trácht Éise (at the Newry estuary) when they saw a youth coming over the waves in a boat. The youth refused to tell his name to various warriors who went one by one to meet him, and he overcame them all.

Eimhear, the wife of Cú Chulainn, suspected the youth's identity, and she tried to restrain her husband from going to face him; but Cú Chulainn ignored her entreaties and demanded his name of the youth. The latter begged that two men be sent against him so that he might tell it, but to no avail, and a terrible combat commenced between the two. They went fighting into the water, and Cú Chulainn shot his javelin, the *ga bolga*, at his opponent through the water. The youth's entrails were torn out and he died. Seeing the ring on the youth's finger, Cú Chulainn took the body in his arms and laid it before the Ulstermen. 'Here is my son for you, men of Ulster!' he said.

It is clear that the starting point for this narrative was the older account of the wooing of Eimhear by Cú Chulainn (q.v.), which described how that hero learned arms in Scotland and fought Aoife. The spirit of the international hero tale was not properly integrated into the context, as the author – mindful of the short life of Cú Chulainn – had to make Conlae an accomplished fighting warrior at the tender age of seven. Two other versions, which do not long postdate that text, exhibit a desire to make the story more logical. One of these, a verse redaction, makes Conlae nine years old when he comes to Ireland. The other, in prose, mentions no age, but changes the background to his conception in order to render it less complicated. Thus whereas both Aoife and another lady, Uathach daughter of Scáthach, were lovers of Cú Chulainn in Scotland according to the story of the wooing of Eimhear, here Aoife herself is made Scáthach's daughter.

The manuscript copyists of the Middle Ages intruded an account of Conlae's conception into their text of the wooing of Eimhear, thus gaining respect and acceptance for the new narrative. In later literary tradition, the two stories were usually paired together, and inflated versions of both were written in the sixteenth century and re-copied in several manuscripts for the following two hundred years. So it is not surprising to find that in folklore the story of 'Conlaoch', son of Cú Chulainn, is invariably told as a sequel to the latter's sojourn in Scotland. Several versions of this combination have been collected from the recent oral lore of Counties Donegal and Galway, and in them Aoife is always fused with the daughter of Scáthach. Not surprisingly, the story of Conlaoch was popular also in the west of Scotland, where a special lay concerning his tragic biography was composed and passed on orally.

NAME: T.F. O'Rahilly (1946), 230–1, 500; Olmsted (1994), 398.

OLDEST VERSION: Van Hamel (1933), 9–15; T.P. Cross in JCS, 1, 176–82.

OTHER RECENSIONS: Gwynn (1924), 132–5; J.G. O'Keeffe in Ériu, 1, 123–7.

LATER VERSION: Ua Ceallaigh (1935), 25–38.

FOLKLORE: Ó Súilleabháin (1942), 598; Bruford (1969), 94, 256–7; J.F. Campbell (1872), 9–15.

Conn Céadchathach *(earlier, Cond Cétchathach)* Mythical KING of Ireland. His name meant 'wise leader', and the sobriquet 'of the hundred battles'. The imagery in these names is that of a great conquering leader. *Conn* is the Irish version of an old Celtic word for sense or intelligence, and its ancient Celtic source, *Condos,* was also in use in Gaul as a personal name.

It was natural that a sept emerging to power and predominance in late prehistoric Ireland should regard such an ideal name as being that of their ancestor, hence that sept called themselves CONNACHTA. By the time Irish saga-lore was committed to literature, the political and military interests of the Connachta had caused many traditions of him to develop. Much of this can be instanced from the surviving medieval texts.

The earliest stratum of tradition concerning him is echoed in a text that dates from around the ninth century, but which undoubtedly reflects much earlier material. This tells of how a certain Fínghein mac Luchta was visited each November feast (*see* TIME) by an otherworld lady called Rothniamh. She used to relay to him information concerning all the affairs of Ireland. One year when she came, she told him that many wonders were to occur on that night. A son would be born to a king called Feidhlimidh, and that son would unite the five provinces and be the progenitor of 53 kings of Ireland. On the

same night, a stream would break from the earth that would be the River Boyne. Also, an ancient tree called Mughain that had been sown by FIONNTAN MAC BÓCHNA would be uncovered, and Fionntan himself would awake from a long slumber and would relay ancient lore. Furthermore, lost TREASURES would be discovered by the TUATHA DÉ DANANN in their otherworld dwellings; the five great roads of Ireland would be discovered; and among other wonders, great lakes and rivers would appear and nine bright birds would sing beautiful music over the rampart of TARA.

Later, when Conn became king of Ireland, he was told by his DRUID that Fínghein was the only man in the country who did not give fealty to him. He sought out Fínghein, who then served him for 50 years until falling in battle. Conn himself, it was claimed, reigned for no less than 53 years, and his floruit was put down to the second century AD. It was claimed that he immediately succeeded the great Leinster king CATHAOIR MÓR as ruler of Tara, and some sources state that he in fact defeated and slew Cathaoir in a battle at Magh Ágha (the plain around Teltown, County Meath). We read that no reign ever was better than that of Conn. There was no robbery, no sickness, no bad WEATHER, and the trees were well foliated, the crops were copious, and the rivers were full of fish. No sharp weapons were carried, one ploughing in spring yielded three crops, and the cuckoo's cry was heard on the cows' horns. 'A hundred clusters grew on each stem, a hundred nuts in each cluster.'

It is clear from this text that when the Connachta took over the Boyne Valley, they expropriated the cultic-lore of that area and connected it to their mythical ancestor. Their anxiety to make Conn the culture-hero of the Boyne Valley was, as the text shows, matched by their anxiety to make him the perfect king of Tara. The Connachta were successful in their ambitious policies, but they did have to contend with long and sustained opposition from other septs. Memories of this are embodied in the tradition of a great conflict between Conn and the Munster hero EOGHAN MÓR (also known as Mugh Nuadhat). Eoghan, it was said, made himself king of the southern province by ousting the three incumbents. One of these three, called Aonghus, sought help from Conn and received six battalions. He was, however, defeated and slain by Eoghan, who thereby came into direct conflict with Conn. Eoghan defeated the high-king in ten successive battles, forcing him to divide Ireland in halves between them. Conn had the northern half and Eoghan took the southern half. Hence the names 'Leath Choinn' and 'Leath Mhogha' for the two halves of the country (*see* CONNACHTA *and* EOGHANACHT).

A developed and inflated telling of the conflict between Conn and Eoghan is given in the late-thirteenth-century text, *Cath Maighe Léna* (The Battle of Moylena). Here Eoghan's father is described as displacing two rivals for the Munster kingship and as gaining that office for Eoghan. The two displaced men were called Macnia mac Luighdheach and CONAIRE MAC MOGHA LÁMHA, and they went to Conn for help. They were well received at Tara, and Conn gave them his daughters in marriage, as well as a third daughter to Iomchadh Airmdhearg, a prince who had been banished from Ulster. Relations between Conn and Eoghan deteriorated as a result, and Conn gathered his forces and advanced into Munster. After several skirmishes, he encountered the Munster forces at Carn Buidhe (near Kenmare, County Kerry). A fierce battle ensued, with Eoghan on the losing side. He escaped in a boat and departed the country for Spain.

Sometime later, Eoghan returned to Carn Buidhe with a strong Spanish force and demanded of Conn that Ireland be divided in two halves between them. Left with no choice, Conn agreed, and the division lasted for a long time. When Eoghan went on a circuit of his territories later, he noticed that many ships belonging to Conn were in Dublin Bay, and he demanded that the bay should also be divided equally. Conn refused, and a new war began between them. Eoghan brought his forces to Moylena (just north of Tullamore, County Offaly), and Conn made an unexpected attack on him there. In a prolonged struggle, Eoghan's armies were wiped out and he himself slain. Conn was then the unchallenged king of Ireland, and he re-established Macnia and Conaire as joint kings of Munster.

Another tradition told of a special clash with the Leinstermen, whose king Eochaidh mac Earca once refused to pay the BÓRAIMHE tribute. At Maistiu (Mullaghmast, County Kildare) Conn was routed by the Leinster forces. As he fled, he was overtaken by two Leinster warriors and wounded by them. He slew the two, but Tara was taken and remained in the possession of Eochaidh for seven years. However, Conn's fortunes revived and he regained the royal citadel and compelled Eochaidh to once more yield the tribute. Such traditions of Conn's struggles against provincial kings echo the emerging power of his sept, the Connachta, although in the form in which they have come down to us, the stories anachronistically portray Conn like a medieval king claiming sovereignty over the whole country.

Accounts vary concerning the length of his reign, ranging from twenty to 53 years, but there is general agreement that he was succeeded – according to his own wishes – by his son-in-law Conaire mac Mogha Lámha, who was in turn succeeded by Conn's son ART. Since Conn was, through pseudo-historical and historical kings, claimed by the Connachta and their UÍ NÉILL descendants as their great progenitor, it was important for them to emphasise his role as ideal king and founder of a dynasty. One early text is entitled *Buile Chuind Chétchathaigh* (The Vision of Conn of the Hundred Battles), and it gives a long list of kings who succeeded him. Another text, put together in the eleventh century, turns this into the form of a story. One day, we read, Conn went for a walk on the rampart of Tara, accompanied by his druids and his POET Cessarn. He trod on a stone, which screamed under his foot. Cessarn explained that the number of cries the stone made signified the number of his descendants who would rule Ireland. Then a great mist descended and they found themselves in a beautiful plain. Entering a magnificent house, they found there a girl with a crown of gold and a golden cup, and a phantom sitting on the throne. The phantom was LUGH, and the girl was the sovereignty of Ireland. She gave a giant ox-rib and hog-rib to Conn, as well as a cup of red ale (*see* KINGSHIP), and the phantom named the future kings. Cessarn wrote them down in OGHAM script on staves of yew, and then the vision disappeared.

Such vision stories had some vogue in the medieval literature concerning Conn. We read that he was on the hill of Uisneach (Ushnagh, County Westmeath) one day, accompanied by his son Connla, when a beautiful lady from the otherworld approached. Only Connla saw the lady, and she called on him to go to Magh Meall (the Pleasant Plain). Conn's druid sang a spell against her so that she departed, but as she did so she threw an apple to Connla. For a whole month, Connla would partake of no food but that apple. Then, when they were at the seashore one day, the otherworld lady returned. She had a boat of glass, and Connla entered that vessel and went away with her.

Conn's other son Art also features in a late medieval narrative involving the otherworld. According to this, when his beloved queen Eithne died, Conn was very depressed and went alone one day to Beann Éadair (Howth, County Dublin). There he met a young woman of the Tuatha Dé Danann, called Bé Chuma, who had been expelled by her own people for an indiscretion she had committed with a son of MANANNÁN. She went with Conn to Tara and lived with him for a year. She demanded that he banish Art, and he did so, but as a result there was neither corn nor milk for the whole year in Ireland. The druids were consulted, and they blamed the misfortune on the presence of the woman and further revealed that deliverance could only come through the sacrifice of the son of a sinless couple. Conn undertook to seek out such a youth. He went to Beann Éadair, where he found a boat that brought him to a beautiful island called Tír na nIongnadh (the Land of Wonders). He found there a prince called Séaghdha Saorlabhraidh (Fortunate Noble-speaker),

whose parents had never come together except at his conception. Conn told Séaghdha that if he bathed in the waters of Ireland, the country would be delivered from its misfortunes, and Séaghdha agreed to go with him.

On reaching Tara, preparations were made to slay the boy, but Conn and his men relented. Realising the situation, the boy called on them to slay him, but just then a strange woman approached with a cow and told them to kill the cow instead. This they did, and two birds emerged from the carcass. One bird had twelve legs and the other but one leg. They fought, and the one-legged bird conquered the other. The woman then explained that Séaghdha was as the one-legged bird, with justice on his side, while the druids were as the other. She was the boy's mother, and she declared that the druids should be hanged and advised Conn to put his concubine Bé Chuma from him. Conn could not get himself to do this, and Bé Chuma remained at Tara for some time until Art defeated her at chess, outdid her in questing, and banished her from the country. The theme of the innocent boy who is to be sacrificed on the advice of druids is borrowed from a Welsh source – Nennius' account of the boy Ambrosius in *Historia Brittonum* – but it has been reshaped here in a rather awkward attempt to insert Christian symbolism into Celtic otherworld lore.

The death of Conn, as befitted a great hero, could only come about through treachery. He had, we are told, a brother called Eochaidh 'Yellow Mouth' who continually upset his reign. This Eochaidh went into Ulster, and Conn sent five envoys after him to ensure he was well behaved. The envoys met Eochaidh on Sliabh Breagha (the hill-range north-west of Slane, County Meath) and slew him there. The Ulstermen were displeased at this, but peace was made between them and Conn. However, an Ulster king called Tiobraide set out for Tara with a group of his men. They were all disguised as women. Conn was standing on an eminence, preparing for the Festival of Tara, and he considered that they were a group of visiting Ulsterwomen.

Seizing the opportunity, they fell upon him and slew him. One account states that the otherworld lady Rothniamh reappeared just before this episode to foretell disaster, and that on the death of the great high-king, war broke out again between the provinces, rivers overflowed, great trees fell, the salmon in the Boyne river screamed, and the four great waves of Ireland lamented him (see ENVIRONMENT).

It is significant that Conn was born at Samhain (the November vigil) and died also at Samhain, for this was reputedly the date of the Festival of Tara (q.v.), the major cultic centre of kingship. The antiquity of this lore of Conn is evidenced by the occurrence of the episode of Eochaidh 'Yellow Mouth' in a saga that has been dated to the seventh or eighth century. There Eochaidh is described as Conn's uncle who was his rival for the kingship and who, after doing much harm to Conn, sought and was granted protection in Ulster. Eochaidh was slain by Conn's son Asal, accompanied by five other men, and Conn had to give heavy compensation to the Ulster king FEARGHUS MAC LÉIDE as a result. The compensation included a noblewoman of his own sept and a parcel of land known as Níth, just north of the Boyne. The episode is briefly mentioned in a poem of even earlier date, perhaps as early as the sixth century – in that text, Conn is described as *cétchorach* (i.e. of the hundred treaties), which was either an alternative or an older form of his epithet.

NAME: T.F. O'Rahilly (1946), 281–3, 514–15.

BIRTH: Vendryes (1953), 1–25; Gwynn (1913), 238–9.

MAGH ÁGHA: Dillon (1962), 168–9; Macalister (1956), 332–3.

WONDERFUL REIGN: Vendryes (1953), 25–6.

CONN AND EOGHAN: V. Hull in ZCP, 19, 59–61; O'Curry (1855); Jackson (1938).

VISION: Thurneysen (1912), 48–52; K. Meyer in ZCP, 12, 232–8 & 13, 370–82.

CONNLA: J. Pokorny in ZCP, 17, 193–205.

BÉ CHUMA: R.I. Best in Ériu, 3, 149–73. Ambrosius story in Van Hamel (1932), 52–61.

DEATH: O. Bergin in ZCP, 8, 274–7; M. Dobbs in ZCP, 20, 161–72; D.A. Binchy in Ériu, 16, 33–48; Breatnach (1996), 90–107.

GENERAL: Macalister (1956), 332–5; Dinneen, 2 (1908), 260–7; Gwynn (1935), 156; O'Brien (1962), 563; T.F. O'Rahilly (1946), 184–92; Dillon (1946), 11–14; Ó Caithnia (1984), 94–8.

Connachta The sept that seized control of the Boyne Valley in the fourth century AD. They had apparently been settled for a while before that in an area west of the River Shannon, and are best regarded as being of FÉINE origin. They became known as Connachta, meaning 'descendants of Conn', and tradition concerning that mythical king CONN CÉADCHATHACH had its origin in their tribal lore.

By the time that Irish traditions were first being committed to writing in the late sixth century AD, the Connachta had control over almost all the north Midlands, and their political and military interests were at a zenith. Having put many other septs under tribute to them, they were claiming to be HIGH-KINGS of Ireland. In the south, the EOGHANACHT – who seem to have also had a Féine origin – exercised comparable power over Munster from their royal seat at Cashel. The early medieval literature therefore portrays the respective mythical ancestors of these septs – Conn and EOGHAN MÓR – as two ancient magnates who divided Ireland between them. The dividing line is claimed to have run from Áth Cliath Meadhraighe (Maaree, south-east of Galway) to Áth Cliath Duibhlinne (Dublin). It consists of a number of low mounds across the centre of the country that could be imagined as a series, known as Eisgir Riada (the Driving Ridge).

The truth seems to be that the Connachta seized TARA from the LAIGHIN (Leinstermen) in or about the fourth century AD, and within a few generations had struck north-wards, destroyed the great centre of the ULAIDH at Eamhain Mhacha, and taken much land in western Ulster as well. They also added greatly to their lands in the region west of the Shannon, in the province then known as Ól nÉacmacht. Their great king in this period was NIALL, who had many sons, and they all followed his policy of expansion. So great was the explosion of their power in that period that the sons of these sons took pride in a new designation, Uí NÉILL (Grandsons of Niall).

The western branch of the sept kept the old appellation, Connachta, and this soon replaced Ól nÉacmacht as the provincial name (rendered in English as 'Connacht' or 'Connaught'). That province, according to the literature, was ruled by brothers of Niall called Fiachra, Brión and Ailill – from whom the branches of the sept there came to be known as Uí Fhiachrach (in west and south Connacht), Uí Bhriúin (in north-east and central Connacht), and Uí Ailealla (in Tirerill, County Sligo). The son of Fiachra, NAITHÍ, and his son again – called AILILL MOLT – seem to have made claims on the Tara kingship, but this western branch of the Connachta soon contented themselves with their power base west of the Shannon. In Modern Irish, an inhabitant of the western province is called 'Connachtach' (plural, Connachtaigh).

Apart from the aforementioned, other leading mythical or legendary figures of traditional Connachta lore were UGHAINE, TUATHAL TEACHTMHAR, CORMAC MAC AIRT and CAIRBRE LIFEACHAIR. There are individual entries in this work also for later celebrated descendants of the Connachta, including ADHAMHNÁN, AODH ALLÁN, AODH SLÁINE, COLM CILLE, DIARMAID MAC AODHA SLÁINE, DIARMAID MAC CEARRBHEOIL, DOMHNALL MAC AODHA, FEARGHAL MAC MAOLDÚIN, FIONNACHTA, MUIRCHEARTACH MAC EARCA, NIALL FRASACH, NIALL GLÚNDUBH, Ó DÓNAILL (Aodh Balldearg and Mánas) and Ó NÉILL (Eoghan Rua). See also AODH EANGACH. For the descendants of the western Connachta, there are entries on GUAIRE, RAGHALLACH, Ó CONCHÚIR (Cathal Crobhdhearg) and Ó RAGHALLAIGH (Giolla Íosa).

For surnames of the many families descended from Niall, see UÍ NÉILL. Surnames taken in medieval times by the three western septs of the Connachta include the following:
Uí Fhiachrach – Ó Dubhdha (O'Dowd); Ó Maolruaidh (Mulroy); Mac Firbhisigh (MacFirbis, Forbes); Ó Mocháin (Maughan); Ó Leannáin (Lennon); Ó Flaithile (Flatley); Ó hEidhin (Hynes); Ó Cléirigh (Clery); Ó Seachnasaigh (Shaughnessy); Mac Giolla Cheallaigh (Gillkelly); Mag Fhionáin (Gannon); Ó

Gáibhtheacháin, modern Ó Gacháin (Gaughan); Ó Learghusa (Larrissey).
Uí Bhriúin – Ó Conchúir (O'Connor of Connacht); Ó Flaitheartaigh (O'Flaherty of Galway); Mac Diarmada (McDermott); Ó Máille (O'Malley); Mac Donnchaidh (McDonagh); Ó Ruairc (O'Rourke) and offshoot Ó Raghallaigh (O'Reilly of Cavan).
Uí Ailealla – Ó Murghaile (Morley).
GENERAL: T.F. O'Rahilly (1946), 173–5, 222–6; Jackson (1938), 39, 97; O'Brien (1962), 133–6, 172; K. Meyer in ZCP, 8, 291–302; F.J. Byrne (1973), passim; Ó Muraíle, 1 (2003), 278–687 & 3, 376–460.

Corc Duibhne Fictional ancestor of the ÉRAINN sept called Corca Dhuibhne in west Munster. His name was a fanciful personification of the septal designation – corca in fact meant 'a race of people', and Duibhne (little dark lady) was a pseudonym of the land-GODDESS. This pseudonym appears in the earlier form Dovinia on several west Munster OGHAM stones.

The legend of the character Corc Duibhne first appears in a text of the tenth or eleventh century. We read that his parents were Cairbre Músc and the sister of that warrior, Duibhind. These were the children of CONAIRE MAC MOGHA LÁMHA, king of Munster, and twin boys were born of their incest. The first of the twins to emerge had a ruddy colour, and thus was called Corc (literally, 'red'). The men of Munster wished the child to be burned and so avoid the shame on their province, but a DRUID offered to take Corc out of Ireland. He brought the baby to an island off the west coast called Inis Boí, after his wife Boí, who was better known as the CAILLEACH BHÉARRA. There Corc was reared by the druid and Boí, being bathed in the sea each morning on the back of the white red-eared cow that his fosterers owned. Eventually, the boy through magic changed the cow into a rock in the sea, and the druid brought him back to the mainland. The young Corc joined with the DÉISE sept who, according to the story, were soon after banished from TARA by CORMAC MAC AIRT. They went to east Munster and settled there, and Corc Duibhne chose as his habitation the peninsulas in the west of that province.

There is no mention of the character Corc Duibhne in the earlier, eighth-century account of the expulsion of the Déise from Tara, and it is clear that this story was invented by the Corca Dhuibhne in the interval. The principal source used by them was the legend of CONALL CORC, reputed founder of the royal Munster dynasty, the EOGHANACHT.

GENERAL: V. Hull in ZCP, 27, 28–37; F.J. Byrne (1973), 166–7. DOVINIA: Macalister, 1 (1945), 152–3, 167–8, 170–1 nos. 156, 175, 178; McManus (1997), 108, 115, 201.

Cormac Conn Loingeas Mythical or fictional warrior, son of Ulster king CONCHOBHAR MAC NEASA.

Cormac's mother was Clothra, daughter of EOCHAIDH FEIDHLEACH and sister of MEADHBH. The scattered fragments of biography devoted to him in the medieval literature bring him into the ambit of his famous aunt. We are told that he was one of the guarantors for DEIRDRE, and when his father treacherously reneged on that agreement, he joined with FEARGHUS MAC RÓICH in rebellion. Together they went to Cruachain and joined the forces of Meadhbh there. This group of Ulster defectors to Connacht was called the *dubhloingeas* (meaning 'numerous exile band'), and thus was explained Cormac's sobriquets Conn Loingeas (head of exile bands). He was in Meadhbh's great muster for the cattle-raid of Cooley (see ULSTER CYCLE), but, like Fearghus, could not disguise his sympathy for his fellow Ulstermen and his reluctance to oppose them. He praised CÚ CHULAINN to his Connacht listeners, grew violently angry when Meadhbh denigrated Conchobhar's military skills, restrained an enraged Fearghus from slaughtering myriads of Ulstermen in the last great battle, and vehemently urged on the brown Ulster bull in its combat with its Connacht rival. All of this is literary fiction, postdating the Deirdre story that was seen as a rationalisation of Cormac's sobriquets.

The original import of his name, however, would have had the element 'Conn' going with the first word rather than with the third. Thus 'Cormac Conn' (Cormac the Leader) would have been the character's proper designation, both of these elements having mythic dimensions in early Irish tradition and being interchangeable in that context as names for a hero (see CORMAC MAC AIRT *and* CONN CÉADCHATHACH). A significant part of the biographies of these heroes was a period of displacement or exile (*loingeas*). It is therefore obvious that the designation Cormac Conn Loingeas had roots far anterior to the story of Deirdre and even to the idea that some Ulstermen defected to the court of Meadhbh.

An indication of what those roots were is provided by the only full story concerning the character, the text *Togail Bruidne Da Choca*, which was fashioned in or about the ninth century and tells of how he died. According to this, after the death of his father Conchobhar, the Ulstermen sent AMHAIRGHIN MAC ÉIGIT SALAIGH and other emissaries to Cruachain offering Cormac the KINGSHIP of his native province. Cormac set out for Ulster with 300 men, but on the way broke several prohibitions (see GEIS) that the druid CATHBHADH had put on him at his birth. These prohibitions forbade hunting at particular places, repairing his chariot with a yoke of ash, and swimming in a particular lake. Another broken prohibition involved listening to the music of the harpist CRAIFTINE, who came to play for him. Craftine did this out of malice because Cormac was the lover of his wife Sceanbh. Reaching the River Shannon at Athlone, Cormac saw a woman there before him. She was the Badhbh and she was washing a bloody garment. When she raised her hand, all the water rose up with it, and so Cormac crossed over without wetting his feet. Such a crossing was, however, also one of the things prohibited to him by Cathbhadh.

Soon after, Cormac and his men encountered and routed a Connacht army that was returning from raiding Ulster. One of his men, Loiniach, was angered by this change in alignments and returned to inform the Connacht court, while – weakened from the fighting – Cormac's force decided to rest at the hostel of Da Coga (near Drumraney, County Westmeath) –

again in violation of a prohibition on him. Amhairghin tried to dissuade them from doing so, saying that Da Coga was a subject of Meadhbh, but he was overruled, and when reinforcements from Ulster arrived, all settled down at the hostel for the night. Amhairghin had a dream of doom, and they were soon surrounded and attacked by a large force of Meadhbh's soldiers. The hostel was set on fire by the attackers, and in a ferocious conflict almost all of Cormac's men were slain. He himself fell in hand-to-hand fighting with a certain Corb Gaillne and the formidable CEAT MAC MÁGHACH. Only three survived: Amhairghin, DUBHTHACH DAOL ULADH and Fiacha mac Fir Féibhe, and they were met by a desolate Fearghus mac Róich, who had rushed from Cruachain in an attempt to prevent the slaughter.

This story parallels the death of CONAIRE at the hostel of Da Dearga, and is obviously derived from that source. The reason seems to have been an old tradition that a character called Cormac Conn Loingeas was also slain in a besieged hostel, such a tradition being detritus from a ritual of deposing a king. Sources outside of the Ulster Cycle give the name of Cormac Conn Loingeas as that of a TARA king. In reality it seems to have been a mere designation that reflected imagery found also in association with such as Conn, Cormac and Conaire. Such a mythic figure of kingship would be the source from which was formed the character of Cormac son of Conchobhar mac Neasa.

A late medieval reference gives to Cormac the pseudonym *Nia an Chairn* (Champion of the Cairn), and claims that he protected his province from intruders at *Fionncharn na Foraire* (the White Cairn of the Lookout) in the Fews Mountains (in County Armagh). This was a fanciful interpretation of the ancient designation of that cairn, which commemorated the burial there of some forgotten hero, the burial being considered a territorial marker.

K. Meyer in *AIM, 5*, 18; J. O'Neill in *Ériu, 2*, 176–7; Hull (1949), 47–8; C. O'Rahilly (1976), 1, 52; W. Stokes in *Irische Texte, 3*, 402–5 & in *RC, 21*, 149–65, 312–27, 388–402; T.F. O'Rahilly (1946), 130–40, 284, 485–6.

Cormac mac Airt Mythical HIGH-KING of Ireland. The most celebrated of all kings in Irish tradition, the medieval historians put down his reign to the period AD 227–66. He was sometimes given the epithet Ulfhada (earlier, Ulfhota), which meant 'long-bearded'.

It may be that there was a spectacular local king of TARA called Cormac in the third century, but he could not have been ruler of all Ireland at that time. The name is an abbreviation of *Corbmac*, which, with the components reversed, would be the same as *Mac-corb*. The noun *mac* (literally, 'son') was sometimes in Old Irish sources used in warriors' names, and the element *corb* seems to have signified 'destroyer' or the like. It occurs in ancient septal designations of sections of the LAIGHIN, and a certain Cú Chorb (meaning 'hound/warrior of destruction') was regarded as the ancestor of all the kings of these Leinstermen. Cú Chorb was reputed to have had four sons – Nia Corb, Cormac Lusc, Cairbre (earlier, Coirpre) Cluitheachair and Meas Corb. The latter was claimed as their progenitor by the Uí Gharrchon, the sept to which the earliest definitely historical kings of Leinster – in the fifth century AD – belonged. This sept, like others of the Cú Chorb line, fell into relative obscurity in succeeding centuries. The strong likelihood, therefore, is that the appellation Corb was associated with a section of the Leinstermen who had controlled Tara in the third or fourth century.

'Cormac Lusc' is the most suggestive of the names, but another striking echo of the nomenclature is a certain Cairbre Nia Fear. The first element in this character's name is a diminutive of *Corb* – the word Nia meant 'champion', and *fear* (literally, 'man') was sometimes used as a synonym for *mac* (son). This character was cited by the synchronisers of history as having been king of Tara, but not a high-king of Ireland – a position that would suit the political reality of late-prehistoric Ireland.

It therefore appears that a figure known as Cormac was the fanciful ancestor of, or the actual leader of, a Leinster group that for a while controlled Tara, and that he therefore came to be seen as an archetype of the sacral kingship associated with that place (q.v.). When the ascendant CONNACHTA sept gained control of Tara, they expropriated the cult of kingship and adopted Cormac into their own genealogy. They made him out to have been a son of ART, and therefore grandson of their own eponymous ancestor CONN – hence his usual appellations 'Cormac mac Airt' and 'Cormac ua Coinn'. In their own propaganda interests, they portrayed him as the man to whom Tara owed all its splendour and as an ideal king whose power brought good fortune and prosperity to the whole country. That legendary royal names could be borrowed from the genealogy of one dynasty into that of another is evidenced also by the way in which the Leinstermen – impressed by the prestige attaching to the mythical Ulster king CONCHOBHAR MAC NEASA – claimed that one of their great ancient kings had been called Conchubhar Abhradhrua. In turn, the Ulstermen borrowed the name Cormac from the Connachta, hence their character CORMAC CONN LOINGEAS. Perhaps this latter borrowing accounts also for the rather inconsequential epithet that describes Cormac as long-bearded, for *Ulfhota* may be a deliberate corruption of *Uladhta* (of the Ulstermen) and thus an attempt in the Connachta interest to negative the Ulster borrowing.

The Connachta propaganda developed from the fifth to the seventh century, and from it derives the image of Cormac found in all the medieval literature. In his reign, we read, the rivers of Ireland were overflowing with fish, forests were difficult to travel due to the amount of fruit on the trees, and the plains were difficult to travel because of all the honey. Peace reigned supreme, crops grew copiously, and cows had a massive milk yield. An echo of the taking of Tara survived in a tradition that 'Cormac grandson of Conn' was defeated by the Leinstermen and banished to Caladh Truim (Galtrim, County Meath). We read that the Leinstermen were led by Meadhbh Leathdhearg, demonstrably the GODDESS of sovereignty (*see* MEADHBH),

and that she herself held the kingship for fourteen months and lay with Criomhthann Cas, son of the celebrated Leinster king CATHAOIR MÓR, before Cormac managed to regain power. Other sources state that Meadhbh had been the wife of Art, and that she would not allow Cormac – Art's son by another woman – to come to Tara.

These are stray echoes from earlier Connachta propaganda concerning Cormac, but it is clear that the Connachta and UÍ NÉILL historians soon decided that it was better to delete all claims of the Leinstermen to the Tara kingship. Accordingly, an epic biography of Cormac mac Airt was composed, the surviving text of which dates from the eighth century. It can be synopsised as follows:

On the night before the Battle of Magh Mucramha (in east Galway), Art slept with the daughter of the DRUID Olc Aiche. Her name was Achtan, and before he left, Art gave her as tokens his sword and a golden ring. He was slain in the battle next day, and his foe LUGHAIDH MAC CON took the kingship. Achtan gave birth to her baby, Cormac, and the druid signalled five protective circles about him – against wounding, drowning, fire, sorcery and wolves. Then one day, when Achtan was asleep on a green, a wolf-bitch came and took the child away. This wolf suckled him until he was discovered by a trapper called Luighne Fear Trí and returned to his mother. Fearing the hostility of Lughaidh mac Con, Achtan took the child to the north of Ireland to seek the protection of Art's foster-father Fiachna Casán. While crossing a mountain at night time, the wolves of Ireland gathered to take back Cormac, but a herd of wild horses protected the mother and son. They reached the dwelling of Fiachna, and Cormac grew up there. On reaching the age of 30, his druid grandfather told Cormac that a certain day was auspicious for an attempt at gaining the kingship. Taking the sword and ring of his father Art, he set out for Tara all alone. As he approached the citadel, he met with a woman who was crying because the king had declared her

SHEEP forfeit for grazing in the queen's field of woad. 'One shearing for another would have been more just!' said Cormac. When word of this was brought to Lughaidh, the usurper recognised the truth of the judgement. He suspected that this was a son of Art and realised that his own false reign was at an end. Therefore, when Cormac came, Lughaidh received him and handed over the kingship to him.

The elements of Connachta tradition that went to invent this biography are clear. Lughaidh's moral acceptance of Connachta supremacy is an obvious case in point. Less obvious, though also significant, is the role played by the character Fiachna (or Fiachra) Casán, otherwise associated with the Airghialla septs of the north Midlands who paid tribute to the Connachta (see COLLA). This Fiachna was also featured as a helper of Cormac's fancied ancestor TUATHAL TEACHTMHAR. Furthermore, there is the helpful role played by a character called Luighne. Although this character in the text belongs to the Leyney area of County Sligo – which area took its name from the Luighne sept – another branch of that sept was in the vicinity of Tara. The Luighne near Tara were permanently loyal to the Connachta. Both the Airghialla and Luighne appear to have been of ÉRAINN stock, and their occurrence in this biography reflects their role as supporters of Connachta hegemony.

Versions of Cormac's birth-story some centuries later also echo Connachta propaganda of early centuries. According to these, Cormac's mother was called Éadaoin and her father Olc Aiche was a smith. The helper was called Lughna Fear Trí, and the pregnant Éadaoin went in a chariot to seek him out. When journeying through the region of Corann (in County Sligo), she gave birth to her baby in her chariot. This is based on a false etymology for the name, viz. *carb-mhac* (chariot-son). Éadaoin told her handmaid to make a bed of leaves for them on the roadside and to watch over them as they slept, but the handmaid herself fell asleep also and a wolf-bitch came and brought the baby away to one of the caves at Céis Chorainn (Keshcorran, County Sligo). When Lughna heard of this, he offered a rich reward to anybody who would recover the child. Later one Grec (ancestor of the Grecraighe sept) found the little Cormac playing with the wolf cubs at the mouth of the cave. Grec informed Lughna of this, and thus he was discovered by Lughna. Cormac grew up to be an extremely handsome, strong and kindly boy. One day, he and Lughna's sons were playing and he struck one of them. The other boys teased him with having no father, whereupon Cormac went to Lughna and demanded to know the truth. Having told him that he was the son of Art, Lughna and his allies – a sept called the Fir Chúil – went with the boy to Tara. The woman who owned the sheep there was called Beannaidh, and when Cormac gave the proper judgement on their shearing, rather than their confiscation, the usurper Lughaidh mac Con was removed from the kingship by 'the men of Ireland'.

Another source has it that Cormac's mother was called Éachtach, and we read that when she became pregnant, she had a vision of her head being taken from her body and a large tree growing from her neck. Art explained this to mean that she would give birth to a great king who would rule all Ireland. There were differing accounts also of the confrontation between Cormac and Lughaidh mac Con at Tara. For instance, one source has it that when Cormac corrected the judgement of Lughaidh, the usurper realised who he was. He charged at the boy, who raced from him three times around Tara before jumping the rampart and making his getaway. Lughaidh remained for another year in the kingship – during which time no grass or foliage or corn grew – and then was driven out of Tara by the men of Ireland and Cormac was installed in his place. One curious description dramatises the ritual contrast between 'true' and 'false' kingship – when Lughaidh gives the wrong verdict on the sheep, one side of his palace collapses, but it stays and falls no further when Cormac gives the correct verdict. Thus Cormac is made the founder of true kingship, and this is underlined by the claim that he restored Tara 'as it had never been before' and built the great 'Fortress of the Kings' and other edifices there.

Some ideas used in the development of the myth are quite clear. Cormac is portrayed as the SOLOMON of the Irish, several accounts referring to his wise decisions and counsels; like Romulus, he is suckled by a wolf-bitch; and like JESUS, he had a threatened youth and began his public life at the age of 30. The founding of the Connachta–Uí Néill dynasty, therefore, was patterned in this story along the lines of three other great foundations – i.e. those of the Jerusalem Temple, of the city of Rome, and of the Christian faith. These ideas cannot have been earlier than the Christianised Ireland of the sixth to seventh century, but some more ancient ideas can also be traced. Since Lughaidh mac Con belonged to the ÉRAINN people, his contest with Cormac could well reflect the taking of Tara by the Leinstermen from the Érainn in or about the third century (see CONAIRE). Because of the appellation 'mac Con' (literally, 'son of hound/wolf') the image of suckling by such an animal was very probably first associated with him in particular, and in the perspective of the Leinstermen his reign could be symbolised as a wolf herding sheep – thus introducing the idea of sheep into the embryonic myth. The wolf-imagery would naturally have transferred to Cormac due to the classical account of Romulus.

In the medieval literature, elaborate descriptions are given of the splendour of Cormac's great banqueting hall at Tara, called the Teach Miodhchuarta, and of his methods of administration. Neither was the dramatic potential of his personal life ignored. A tenth-century text tells of a beautiful girl called Eithne, daughter of the Leinster king CATHAOIR MÓR, who was in fosterage with the exceptionally generous hospitaller Buichead. The brothers of Eithne so played upon Buichead's generosity that he became impoverished, his seven herds of cattle reduced to a mere seven cows and one bull. He left Leinster and went to live at Ceanannas (Kells, County Meath), bringing only his small herd, his wife and his foster-child. Eithne worked hard for her foster-parents, and one day, Cormac met her as he rode through the countryside on his horse. He admired the diligence with which she worked, and on learning who she was proposed marriage to her. Buichead, however, hesitated with his permission, saying that he could not give her as he was not her father, whereupon Cormac had her carried off at night and she conceived by him. Later, the marriage was arranged, and Cormac gave a massive bride-price to Buichead – all the animals that he could see from the rampart of Ceanannas for a whole week. Thus Buichead returned to the Leinstermen with an even bigger herd than before.

Other texts tell of how Cormac fell in love with a beautiful woman called Cearnait, daughter of the king of the PICTS, whom an Ulster raiding party had brought as a captive from Scotland. Cormac asked for her, and she became his mistress, but Eithne through jealousy made her a slave whose work was to grind a large amount of grain with a quernstone every day. Cormac contrived to meet with her again, and she became pregnant by him. He pitied her when he saw how hard she had to work, and so sent abroad for a tradesman to construct a mill – the first ever in Ireland. Thus Cearnait was freed from her gruelling labour.

Another story concerning Cormac's family life occurs in a fourteenth-century text that seems to be based on earlier materials. According to this, he was alone in Tara on a May morning (see TIME) when he saw a young beautifully dressed stranger approach. The stranger had a branch with three golden apples on it, which, when he shook it, gave forth exquisite music capable of healing all illnesses. Cormac asked for the branch, and the stranger gave it to him in return for the right to make three requests. The stranger then departed, but returned exactly a year later and asked for Cormac's daughter Ailbhe to go with him. The king reluctantly agreed. Exactly a year later, he returned again and in similar manner took Cormac's son,

CAIRBRE LIFEACHAIR, with him. Finally, on the third May Day, he took Eithne herself. Cormac was disconsolate, and he followed the stranger. He came to an unknown land, where he saw several strange sights. There the stranger revealed that he was MANANNÁN and that his country was Tír Tairngire (the Land of Promise). Manannán had brought him there to show to him the nature of true wisdom (see POETS). Cormac had his family returned to him, and was given a present of a beautiful goblet, which broke into three pieces when a lie was spoken in its presence and became whole again when the truth was told. He was entertained with a banquet, at which he fell asleep, and next morning awoke on the green of Tara with all his family and the goblet. One late medieval tradition claimed that Cormac brought three fine goblets from overseas to Ireland, but that they were buried after his death and were not found again until the reign of the high-king Aodh Oirdnidhe in the ninth century.

The famous high-king had another treasure, a wondrous sword that shone in the darkness like a candle and was so sharp that it could cut a hair on water. It had belonged to a young man called Socht, but one of Cormac's administrators, Duibhdhriu, took it from Socht while he was drunk and had his own name inscribed on the inside of the hilt. Afterwards Duibhdhriu claimed the sword as his, offering the inscription as proof. Socht replied that the sword was found driven through his grandfather and that this proved that Duibhdhriu was the murderer. Hearing this, Cormac ordered Duibhdhriu to pay *wergild* for Socht's grandfather. Duibhdhriu confessed the trick he had played, and was given an additional fine by Cormac for that. Cormac then revealed that the sword had once belonged to CÚ CHULAINN, and that it had been used by the Ulstermen to slay his own grandfather Conn (q.v.). The judge Fíothal agreed with Cormac that he should have the sword as *wergild*; and it, with the branch and the goblet, constituted the three special treasures of Cormac. This story is in fact a variant of a folk plot that

was quite popular in medieval Europe (*see* ROMANTIC TALES, type 978).

A striking aspect of the Cormac lore is how he was on several occasions forced to go into exile (*loingeas*) from Tara. This theme must have originated in the context of the struggles of the Connachta to gain and hold that sacral centre of kingship from contending peoples such as the ÉRAINN, the LAIGHIN and the ULAIDH. It had special emphasis in the myth of the eponymous ancestor of the Connachta, Conn (q.v.), and its antiquity in the lore of both Conn and Cormac is evidenced by the appellation Cormac Conn Loingeas (q.v.), which was borrowed as the name of an exile prince into the ULSTER CYCLE. In the specific case of Cormac mac Airt, at least three exiles are described by the medieval literature. The Ulstermen (Ulaidh) are given the chief role as his enemies, and one source rationalises this by having them depose him for a year on two separate occasions. This must ultimately reflect the fourth-to-fifth-century conflicts as the Connachta attempted to extend their sway north of the River Boyne. A text entitled *Cath Crinna* was composed, probably in the ninth century, describing such a conflict, and an expanded version of it dates from the later Middle Ages. According to this text, Cormac brought the Ulstermen to a feast in the north of Breagha (the plain of Meath), but hostilities were scarcely disguised and the servant of the Ulster king scorched Cormac's hair with a candle. To avenge the insult and re-establish his power, Cormac went to his maternal cousin, TADHG MAC CÉIN, and sought his help, promising him as much land of Breagha as his chariot would encircle after the battle until sunset. Tadhg also told Cormac how to come unawares upon the great warrior LUGHAIDH LÁGHA, who had been the slayer of Art. Acting upon Tadhg's instructions, Cormac came upon Lughaidh Lágha as he was taking a bath, and stood over him with naked sword, demanding *wergild* for his father. Lughaidh promised the head of Fearghus 'Black-tooth', king of Ulster. The battle against the Ulstermen was fought at

Crionna (on the River Boyne near Mellifont), and Cormac stayed apart, accompanied by a servant dressed exactly like himself. Lughaidh Lágha brought a head to the servant, thinking it that of the Ulster king and that the servant was Cormac. He made the same mistake with a second head, and when he came the third time with the real head of the Ulster king, he slew the servant in a fit of pique. Tadhg fought magnificently, and when the battle was won demanded fulfilment of the promise of land. Swooning from the effects of the fighting, he set off in his chariot, intending to encompass Tara itself on his route, but the charioteer – a partisan of Cormac – headed away from Tara every time he swooned. Finally, the unfortunate Tadhg found himself at the River Liffey and knew that he had been tricked.

Returning to Tara, Tadhg sought medical attention for his wounds. Cormac arranged that both he and Lughaidh Lágha should be treated by physicians whom he bribed to insert beetles into their wounds. When Lughaidh was near to death, Cormac came and asked him how his father Art had comported himself when slain. Lughaidh was livid at the question and answered bitterly: 'He bleated like a he-goat, he bellowed like a bull, he screeched like a woman!' His anger was indeed so great that his wounds burst open, the beetles fell out, and he was healed. Tadhg got a message to the Munster king AILILL ÓLOM, who sent good physicians to him. They feigned to pierce his stomach with a red-hot iron and, through his terror, he thrust the beetles and other vermin from himself and was also healed. In order to avoid war with him, Cormac gave the fee of the land that his chariot had encircled. The attribution of treachery to Cormac is atypical, and this story was obviously written in the interests of Munster – to which province Ailill Ólom, Lughaidh Lágha and Tadhg mac Céin belonged.

The second push against Cormac occurred when Eochaidh Gunnat succeeded Fearghus as Ulster king. One night, Cormac saw in a dream this Eochaidh coming and taking the captives' pillar from Tara and placing it in Cruachain (Rathcroghan, County Roscommon). He also saw his wife Eithne lying with Eochaidh for a year and then returning to himself. His druids explained this to mean that the Ulstermen would drive him from Tara and that Eochaidh would take and hold his kingship for a year. This proved true, for the kings of the other provinces joined with Eochaidh and defeated Cormac's army. They slew his stepbrother and close ally, Nia son of Lughna, and drove Cormac's own mother Éachtach out of her dwelling. The disconsolate Cormac fled west to Cruachain, where he gathered his supporters about him. Returning to Tara, he defeated the Ulster army – Lughna's other son Lughaidh slaying Eochaidh Gunnat – and thus Cormac regained his power.

Towards the end of the ninth century, a genealogical text was compiled that claimed that Cormac was expelled for a time from Tara by Fiachu Araidhe, ancestor of the Dál nAraidhe sept of north-east Ulster. He had to go to Rafainn (Knockgraffon in south Tipperary) and submit to the Munster king FIACHU MUILLEATHAN in order to get his support. With the help of a strong southern force, therefore, Cormac gave battle to Fiachu Araidhe and defeated him at the Battle of Fothairt (Faughart, County Louth). Cormac then regained Tara, and it is clear that this text was written in the Munster interest. A notable aspect of it is the role of counsellor in the battle assigned to the druid MOGH RUITH, who resided at Dairbhre (Valentia Island, off the Kerry coast). For his services, we read that this druid was awarded territory in Magh Féine (near Fermoy, County Cork).

The same selection of Munster characters is found in the text *Forbhais Droma Damhghaire* (The Siege of Drom Damhghaire – now Knocklong, County Limerick). In its present form, this text dates from as late as the fourteenth century, but the basis of it must be several hundred years older. Again, it is a Munster story, and this time the southerners teach a lesson to Cormac rather than lend him assistance. It describes how the high-king once ran short of beef to feed his numerous household. One of his administrators reminded him that he collected only one tribute from Munster, even though that province was divided into two parts. When this was demanded, the Munster king Fiachu Muilleathan refused to pay double tribute, and so Cormac brought his army south and besieged Fiachu at Drom Damhghaire. Fiachu was in a desperate position, but the druid Mogh Ruith came from Dairbhre and magically supplied the besieged Munstermen with water. Cormac's own druid Ciothruadh advised him to have his men cut down trees and set fire to them. If the wind blew south towards the besieged army, they should attack, and if it blew north they should go home. Mogh Ruith advised the Munstermen to do likewise, and then blew a magic breath that became a black cloud and floated towards Cormac's men. The cloud fell among them as a sinister shower of blood. Mogh Ruith also caused the Munster fire to explode into a conflagration, and the smoke from it blew north. The men of Munster then charged after it, sweeping Cormac's army before them, and to stave off utter ruin, Cormac had to pay compensation and give hostages to Fiachu at the fortress of Rafainn.

Another Munster tradition described how this Fiachu Muilleathan was treacherously slain at the instigation of Cormac. The genesis of such texts concerning Cormac's dealings with the Munstermen obviously belongs to a period after his epic biography was well established – i.e. in or about the seventh century. Another interesting development in this period was the association of Cormac with the hero FIONN MAC CUMHAILL, who came to be portrayed as the leader of troops serving the high-king as a semi-independent army (see FIANNA CYCLE). This arose from a conflation of the Connachta–Uí Néill lore of Cormac and the Leinster lore of Fionn. As a vestige of the ancient hostility between the Connachta and the Leinstermen, it continued to evidence within it a certain

amount of tension between the two characters (see FIONN and CAOILTE). The writers developed the idea that Cormac's daughter, Ailbhe, had been Fionn's wife, and the celebrated Gráinne of Fianna romance (see DIARMAID UA DUIBHNE) was another reputed daughter of the high-king. Moreover, the eventual overthrow of the Fianna in battle was attributed to Cormac's son, Cairbre Lifeachair (q.v.).

The way in which Cormac's reign was used to punctuate the pseudo-history is well exemplified in a story invented in or about the ninth century, claiming that the DÉISE had once lived near Tara but had been forced from there and had settled instead in south-east Munster. It was said that the Déise leader, Aonghus Gaíbhuaibhtheach, had in the course of a tussle blinded Cormac in one eye, thus causing a war and leading to Cormac eventually banishing him and his people from Tara. Since a blemish disqualified one from holding the kingship (q.v.), Cormac had to abdicate, and his son Cairbre Lifeachair became high-king in his place. Cormac left Tara for the last time and went to live at the palace of Cleiteach (near Slane, County Meath).

This story provided a rationale for accounts of Cormac's final days. A text of the late ninth or early tenth century quotes a long list of advices given by him to his son Cairbre concerning how a king should rule. This is one of several Old Irish texts that are based on the type of Latin gnomic writings known as *speculum principis*. Not long after this, an account developed of how the great high-king died, imputing Christian sanctity to him. It was claimed that his goodness, and his insistence that not things themselves but the creator of things should be adored, meant that he was in effect a Christian even though he lived before the coming of St PATRICK to Ireland. One medieval text describes how two otherworld women came to Tara and were mutilating the people there until Cormac placed his kingdom under the protection of the true Christian God. The otherworld women then announced that the power of paganism had been broken. We further read of

127

how Cormac ordered that, after his death, he not be buried in Brugh na Bóinne (Newgrange, on the River Boyne) because the pagan kings had been buried there. Instead, he wished to be buried at Ros na Ríogh (Rosnaree), a short distance down the river on the opposite bank, with his face eastwards towards the rising sun.

He went to a feast at the home of a noble called Spealán, and a piece of bread given to him at the feast contained a fish bone. As he was eating, a dispute broke out between two kerns. Cormac was startled by the commotion, and the fish bone caught in his neck and he choked from it. Accounts differ as to the reason the fish bone was in the bread, the original explanation being that it was inadvertently kneaded into it, but later versions suggest that the druids were responsible as they disapproved of his Christian leanings. After his death, these druids determined that he be buried in Brugh na Bóinne despite his orders, but a flood rose on the river as they attempted to cross it. His bier was swept down to Ros na Ríogh, and on the following morning, the body was found lying there. So he was interred at that place in accordance with his wishes.

His fame lived on in the folklore of the northern half of the country. A quatrain cited in the old literature concerning the reign of Conn has in recent centuries been exclusively referred to as the reign of Cormac. This has been collected from the folklore of Irish-speakers in Irish throughout Ulster, Connacht and north Leinster, and it states that 'in the time of Cormac mac Airt/life was pleasant and enjoyable/there were nine clusters on each branch/and nine branches on each stem'. It was also said that when a cow lies down on the grass, the great sigh she heaves is for the happy days of his reign long ago.

In the same broad region, versions of the story of his threatened youth, and of his coming to Tara as a youth to claim the kingship from Lughaidh mac Con (q.v.), continued to be told by word of mouth. In County Sligo, it is claimed that, as a baby, his mother gave birth to him near the well at Cloonagh, near the mountain of Céis Chorainn, and that a stone there bears the mark of his head. Immediately after his birth, the wolf-bitch snatched him away a kilometre southwards to one of the several caves that form a huge geological terrace on the western side of the mountain. This cave is called Uamhaigh Chormaic, and it is claimed that he was suckled by the wolf there until he was seven years of age. His mother's father, said to have been the local chieftain Ó Dóláin Doinn, then rescued him after roasting beef nearby and drawing the wolves away from the cave by the scent. This localisation of the story in the region of Corann, where the caves of Keshcorran dominate the landscape, dates from the twelfth century at least, and seems to have resulted from the fact that these caves contained the dens of wolves.

Folklore over a wide northern area claimed that Cormac was posthumously baptised by Patrick when the SAINT one day came across a clump of rushes from which a voice spoke. The voice explained that it was Cormac's soul, which had been confined there because it could not enter heaven. Patrick shed tears of sympathy, which baptised his soul, and it rose to heaven in the form of a white dove. This LEGEND was borrowed from the lore of CONCHOBHAR MAC NEASA, but in recent centuries, the Cormac versions have become more numerous than those concerning Conchobhar.

A late recension of the story of Cormac's quest to the land of Manannán was current in manuscripts of recent centuries, and it gave rise to a new narrative in Donegal folklore. This told of how Cormac had to go to a strange country to recover 'the sword of light' and how he succeeded in this task with the help of a shaggy-looking but very fleet pony. It was told as a loose version of an international FOLKTALE that was quite popular in Ireland (see WONDER TALES, types 313 and 550). The common imagery of wisdom shared by Cormac with Solomon led to Cormac's name being sometimes substituted in late folklore for that worthy (see SOLOMON and ROMANTIC TALES, type 920).

128

CORB AS SEPTAL NAME: O'Brien (1962), 9, 23–8, 94–5, 565; Smyth (1982), 15–20, 186.

ULFHADA: W. Stokes in *Irische Texte*, 3, 336–7; T.F. O'Rahilly (1946), 486.

SALUTORY REIGN: O'Grady, 1 (1892), 89–90.

MEADHBH AND LEINSTERMEN: M. Power in *ZCP*, 11, 42–3, 52–3; Ní Shéaghdha (1945), 174.

BIOGRAPHIES: Ó Cathasaigh (1977), 107–33; V.E. Hull in *Ériu*, 16, 79–85; M. O'Daly (1975), 15, 52–3, 56–9, 64–73; O'Grady, 1 (1892), 253–6; M. Dobbs in *ZCP*, 20, 171–82; Dinneen, 2 (1908), 298–301.

ADMINISTRATION: O'Grady, 1 (1892), 90; Stokes in *Irische Texte*, 3, 198–9; Gwynn (1903), 20–37.

EITHNE: Stokes in *RC*, 25, 18–39, 225–7; Greene (1955), 27–44; P. Mac Cana in *Études Celtiques*, 8, 86–7.

CEARNAIT: K. Meyer in *Hibernica Minora*, 2, 75–6; Gwynn (1903), 20–3.

GOBLET STORIES: Stokes in *Irische Texte*, 3, 193–8; E.J. Gwynn in *Ériu*, 2, 186–8.

SWORD: Stokes in *Irische Texte*, 3, 199–202. *See* D. Strömbäck in Brown & Foote (1963), 178–90.

EXILES AND BATTLES: R. Thurneysen in *ZCP*, 20, 222–3.

CRIONNA: O'Grady (1892), 2, 491–3 & 1, 319–26; O'Brien (1962), 403–5.

EOCHU GUNNAT: J. Carney in *Éigse*, 2, 187–97.

FIACHU ARAIDHE: Meyer in *ZCP*, 8, 313–14.

DROM DAMHGHAIRE: M-L. Sjoestedt-Jonval in *RC 43*, 1–123 & 44, 157–86.

ADVICES: Meyer (1909).

SALTER OF TARA: W. Stokes in *Irische Texte*, 3, 199; O'Donovan, 1 (1848), 116–17.

RELIGION AND DEATH: Best & Bergin (1929), 127; R.M. Smith in *Irish Texts*, 4, 16–18; Meyer in *Irisleabhar na Gaedhilge*, 4, 69–70; Hull in *Ériu*, 16, 85; Power in *ZCP*, 11, 43; Ní Shéaghdha (1945), 175–6; O'Donovan, 1 (1848), 114–17.

FOLK QUATRAIN: Laoide (1905), 111 & (1913), 61; G. Nic Gréagóir in *An Claidheamh Soluis*, 20/6/1908, 6; É. Ó Tuathail in *Béaloideas*, 3, 123, 131; IFC (several versions).

COW: IFC 706:535.

FOLK BIOGRAPHIES: Ó Tuathail (1933), 123–4 & (1934), 13. For other versions and discussion, *see* the entry on LUGHAIDH MAC CON.

KESHCORRAN: OSL: Sligo (1836), 150, 160–3.

BAPTISM: Ó Tuathail (1934), 13–14; S. Ó Súilleabháin in *Béaloideas*, 21, 178; IFC Index.

'SWORD OF LIGHT': IFC 56:321–44, 104:263–81.

GENERAL: O'Donovan, 1 (1848), 110–21; Dinneen, 2 (1908), 282–353; Ó Cathasaigh (1977); Ó Cadhlaigh (1927).

Cormac mac Cuileannáin *(AD 831–908)* Scholar and bishop of Cashel.

He became KING of Munster in 902. Among other learned works – both sacred and secular – Cormac is accepted as the author of the influential Irish glossary, *Sanas Cormaic*, compiled towards the end of the ninth century. This is perhaps the earliest dictionary in any European vernacular language. Cormac belonged to a lesser branch of the EOGHANACHT sept, and he may have agreed to serve as king of the province in order to avoid dissension among the more powerful branches.

Though a holy and devout man, by the year 905, he was embroiled in politicking and then in warfare with other kings. The Annals have it that in this he was unduly influenced by the ambitious abbot of Scattery Island, Flaithbheartach, who was to succeed him in the kingship. Advancing into Leinster as far as Magh Léana (Moylena, north of Tullamore, County Offaly) in 907, Cormac won a great victory over the UÍ NÉILL high-king, Flann Sionna. He then raided Connacht, but his success was short-lived. In the following year, at Bealach Mughna (Ballaghmoon, County Kildare), he faced Flann again, but this time the high-king had with him the combined forces of the king of Leinster and the king of Connacht. Cormac was heavily outnumbered, and in addition was deserted in the battle by many of his own supporters. As the fighting went against him, he retreated, but his horse jumped into a ditch and he was unseated. His followers put him back on the horse, but his mount slipped on the bloodied road and fell backwards. Cormac's back and neck were broken, and he was beheaded by the foe. When the head of Cormac was brought to him, Flann kissed it out of respect, instead of placing it under his thigh as was the custom by a victor with the vanquished.

It was said that Cormac had a premonition of the result of the fatal battle, and that he considered it a bad omen when Flaithbheartach's horse fell into a deep trench, unseating its rider, as the troops were being reviewed. Cormac is described as, before the battle, distributing a basinful of apples among his people from his own hand, as a token of his affection for them. Cormac loved music, and one text varies the apple-motif by having him present an apple to each of three entertainers as a way of engaging them to play music for him on the following night. The entertainers were among the slain, and the Leinster king, Cearbhall mac Muireagáin, sent one of his retainers to the battlefield to see if the contract would be honoured. The retainer saw the heads of the entertainers return to their bodies and play sad music for the slain king until dawn. The author of this story was clearly indebted to the earlier tradition of the entertainer Donn Bó (*see* FEARGHAL MAC MAOLDÚIN). Cormac was buried with respect by his opponents at Díseart Dhiarmada (Castledermot, County Kildare), and it was believed that he worked several miracles after his death. He was traditionally regarded as a very pious man, generous to the poor and a great patron of learning. *See also* NIALL GLÚNDUBH.

O'Donovan (1848–51), 554–69 & (1860), 200–25; Stokes (1862), v–xiii; Meyer (1912); Kenney (1929), 11–12, 15; J.G. O'Keeffe in *Irish Texts*, *3*, 8–10; Dinneen (1908–14), *3*, 194–214; F.J. Byrne (1973), 324.

cosmology There are no direct sources for ancient pre-Christian cosmology in Ireland, and clues as to basic formats must be sought through interpretation of later literary material. For instance, we can deduce that the DAGHDHA was a male deity with solar connotations, and DANU (otherwise called the MÓR-RÍOGHAIN) was his female consort representing the land and the waters. Indications are that the union of these two was thought to give rise to social prosperity, and that seercraft was portrayed by the druidic class as a kind of divine child resulting from that union (*see* FIONN). An elaborate system of doctrine attached also to the role of KING as a mediator between the solar deity and human society. On a more general level, the relationship between the worlds of the dead and of the living seems to have been expressed by the division of TIME into dark and bright periods.

Vestiges of mythology indicate that other cosmological ideas were influential also. Dramatic narratives concerned tussles between divinities who represented natural forces in particular contexts, and such symbolism attracted the Indo-European myth of a great primordial battle between two sets of deities (*see* TUATHA DÉ DANANN *and* FOMHÓIRE). Otherwise, aspects of nature and of the landscape could be interpreted to have divine origins, with stress on the image of the world as a four-posted house (*see* ENVIRONMENT), on the conceit that rivers were conduits of otherworld energy (*see* BÓINN *and* SIONAINN), and on the notion that aspects of the landscape had sprung from or had been fashioned according to the bodies of deities (*see* DANU, DONN CUAILNGE, *etc.*).

Christian cosmology could pick upon and develop aspects of this lore that did not involve theological difficulty. For instance, the image of the Celtic father-deity could be switched to the Christian God, who was described as the master-builder of the world (*see* GOBÁN SAOR), and JESUS could be described as the true sun that would never be extinguished. Just as the people once faced with respect the rising sun in the east, in Christian times they also faced east in reverence for the Holy Land where Jesus had lived. The bounty of the Daghdha could be described as a praiseworthy trait, but incomplete by comparison with the Christian God, who was all-bountiful and morally perfect (*see* PATRICK). Finally, the 'Land of Promise' mentioned in the Christian Bible could become an Irish *Tír Tairngire*, which was almost synonymous with the otherworld island where the dead went according to pre-Christian Irish tradition (*see* DONN *and* ENVIRONMENT). On land also, sacred locations could keep their force – ritual springs became holy wells where SAINTS baptised their converts, and great trees – earlier considered as junctions with the sky-deity – became symbols of holiness that gave protection to the hermitages of the saints.

Among the ordinary people, the issues were less philosophical than imagistic and dramatic. Thus in folklore, heaven was thought of as somewhere above the sky, where God reigned in happiness with the angels and saints. On the other hand, the devil of Christianity resided in hell, which was thought of as a terrible place somewhere away under the ground. In actual

Irish folklore, however, the devil appears more in the guise of a malicious trickster than as a powerful and repulsive monster. The location of the Christian purgatory was more a matter for conjecture – it might be a place hidden away in some unfathomable region, but it might also be a state of existence in some lonely or damp part of the ordinary ENVIRONMENT. The ancient Celts believed that the soul was immortal, and in early Irish belief the dead could live on, not only in the realm of the setting sun but also in the tumuli that dot the landscape. Something of such older native ideas survived side by side with Christian belief. For instance, the dead might enter a hill where a tumulus was situated, a door being heard to slam in the hillside after them; or departed people might be encountered by visitors to a FAIRY fort. With regard to the departure of the soul to the afterlife, it was often thought that a long journey through a mysterious realm lay ahead of that soul, and so food and clothes would be placed with the corpse in the coffin. In some places, it was even thought that the dead person lingered for a month in the cemetery, and food was left on the grave each day for him or her. At Samhain (Halloween – see TIME), all the dead were believed to return for a brief visit to the graveyard in which they were buried.

In a more theological Christian sense, God the Father, in heaven, is referred to by appellatives such as *Dia na glóire* (God of glory), *Rí an Domhnaigh* (the King of Sunday), and more affectionately simply as *an Fear thuas* (the Man above). In ordinary speech in the IRISH LANGUAGE, it is usual when referring to God to add the remark 'praise be to Him forever', and there were several sayings of reassurance such as 'God is strong, and He has a good Mother'. He was thought of as the champion of the poor and oppressed, and a simple little story illustrating His justice was common. According to it, a rich man sneeringly asks a poor man what God is doing just now. 'He is making a wheel,' says the poor man, 'and that wheel of God will keep turning!' That every single human should have hope, however, is illustrated

by the traditional saying: 'God never closed one door but He opened another.'

There was much speculation as to how and when an end would come to the world. Since the Resurrection of Jesus was on a Sunday, it was thought in medieval Europe that the final dissolution would occur also on that day of the week, and so the General Judgement would be on a Monday (*see* SAINTS). A variety of cataclysms were thought of as preceding the Last Day, but the old belief was that Ireland would be covered by the sea seven years before that time (*see* PATRICK). A general idea, in Ireland as throughout Europe, was that the end of the world would come when all the seats vacated in heaven by the fallen angels would be filled by the human race.

In recent generations, many humorous anecdotes centre on the situation at the gates of heaven, which is said to be guarded by St Peter with a great bunch of keys. Tongue-in-cheek accounts are given of various famous personalities – from the political and social world – arriving at these gates and conversing with Peter. Quite incongruously, the personalities are more usually living rather than deceased individuals, and the opportunity is taken to give comical or satirical portrayals of them.

CELTIC LORE: MacCulloch (1911), 165–232, 333–90; Ó hÓgáin (1999), 39–68.

CHANGE TO CHRISTIANITY: Ó hÓgáin (1999), 184–216.

GENERAL JUDGEMENT ON MONDAY: D. Ó hÓgáin in *Béaloideas*, 51, 110–14.

RELIGIOUS FOLKLORE: Ó Súilleabháin (1942), 20–1, 215–50, 516–19, 548.

Craiftine *(earlier, Craibhtine)* Celebrated harpist in medieval Irish fiction. His name seems to be derived from *Crobhtine*, with a meaning such as 'lithe-handed fellow'.

In Leinster tradition, he was claimed to have been the faithful harpist of the mythical king LABHRAIDH, accompanying that KING on his adventures abroad and later helping him to seize a fortress by playing music that magically put the defenders to sleep. Indeed, the magical beauty of his music was instrumental in causing the hitherto-dumb Labhraidh to speak. Later, however, his music had a disastrous effect, for he made a new harp from the timber of a tree to which Labhraidh had whispered his secret. When the harp was played publicly, it proclaimed the secret that Labhraidh had the ears of a horse.

In Ulster tradition, Craiftine was mentioned as a harpist who held a grudge against CORMAC CONN LOINGEAS, because the latter was the lover of his wife Sceanbh. Knowing that Cormac was under magical prohibition (GEIS) not to listen to his music, he played the harp for Cormac in an effort to hasten that warrior's demise.

LABHRAIDH: W. Stokes in *ZCP, 3,* 4–6 & in *RC, 20,* 429–33; Dillon (1946), 4–10; B. Ó Cuív in *Éigse, 11,* 174; Dinneen, *2* (1908), 160–75. CORMAC: W. Stokes in *RC, 21,* 152–7.

Cridhinbhéal *(earlier, Cridenbél)* Fictional satirist, one of the otherworld people, TUATHA DÉ DANANN. The meaning of the name – alternately given as Crichinbhél, Crithinbhél and Crichinphél – is unclear, but the most likely interpretation is *cridhe ina bhéal* (heart in mouth) in the sense that POETS were believed to speak directly from their emotions without thinking.

When king BREAS oppressed the Tuatha Dé, the DAGHDHA was made to construct an earthwork around the KING's fortress. Cridhinbhéal, described as 'an idle blind man', asked the Daghdha for the three best bits of his food each night. The requests of satirists were not normally refused, so the Daghdha complied and as a result was miserable and hungry. He was, however, advised by his son, the Mac Óg (i.e. AONGHUS), to put three gold coins into the food for Cridhinbhéal. He did this, and the gold stuck in the satirist's stomach and killed him. When the Daghdha was accused of murder by Breas, he protested that he had but given gold to Cridhinbhéal. The satirist's stomach was cut open, and when the gold was found there, the Daghdha was released.

It is not expressly stated in the text, but what the Daghdha was implying was that Cridhinbhéal had consumed the coins out of greed. In folklore, behaviour of this type was often humorously ascribed to misers (*see* HUMOROUS TALES, type 1305C).

Otherwise, Cridhinbhéal is described as among the Tuatha Dé host in battles. His name was a puzzle to the medieval writers, and they made various attempts to explain it. One such – based on the 'heart in mouth', interpretation – speculated that he could not keep a secret. Alternately, it was said that he was so ugly that his mouth was in his breast. Another explanation given was 'mouth of sparks' (*crithir-bhéal*) from the fierceness of his poems; and yet another – even more fanciful still – claimed that he was the first lampooner ever to quench a torch with the power of his words.

Gray (1982), 28–31, 120; W. Stokes in *Irische Texte, 3,* 384–5, 422; Macalister (1938), 154–5, 184–5.

Criomhthann Nia Náir Fictional KING of Ireland situated in prehistory. The name Criomhthann, meaning 'fox', was a common one in early Ireland. His sobriquets were originally Nia Nár and meant simply 'noble warrior' (*see* NÉT).

He was said to have been begotten by LUGHAIDH RIABHDHEARG on Lughaidh's own mother Clothra. One medieval text tells of how he went on an adventure to Éadar (Howth, County Dublin) with an otherworld lady called Nár, thus deriving his appellation Nia Náir (warrior of Nár). He spent a month and a fortnight in the otherworld place there and brought many TREASURES from it, but died soon after. The treasures included a golden chariot, a great chessboard, and a mysterious 'mantle of Criomhthann'. A variant account fancies that Nár refers to the shame (*náir*) that he felt on account of his incestuous birth – it states that his reign lasted for sixteen years in all, and that he died after falling from his horse.

Macalister (1956), 302–5; Dinneen, *2* (1908), 234–5; W. Stokes in *Irische Texte, 3,* 332.

Crom Archetypal pagan in folk tradition, represented as an opponent of PATRICK in that saint's mission.

In an eleventh-century text, he is called Crom Cruach and described as an idol of the pagan Irish. The personage intended is synonymous with an idol called Cenn

Cruaich, which is referred to in a biography of Patrick from the ninth century. Cenn Cruaich has twelve sub-GODS, and his statue in Magh Sléacht (the plain of Tullyhaw, County Cavan) is demolished by the SAINT and sinks into the ground. Crom Dubh, like Cenn Cruaich, originally derives from the image of the Antichrist in Christian thought. In folklore, he is usually called Crom Dubh. The name has been taken to mean 'black stoop', but it may have actually signified 'dark croucher', an image of the devil.

A late medieval LEGEND evidences a change in the characterisation of Crom Dubh, portraying him as a great sinner who after his death was being carried away by demons, but Patrick intervened and saved him. The saint's reason for doing this was that Crom had each year given a bullock to the poor for their sustenance. It is obvious that the Antichrist image of Crom had been forgotten and that he was now seen as a mere mortal.

Another and connected development was the substitution of Crom for DÁIRE in the legend of how the latter gave a cauldron as a gift to Patrick. Thus in folk versions of that legend, it is always Crom Dubh who presents Patrick with either a cauldron or a bullock, and the saint shows that his thanks written on a piece of paper outweighs the gift on a scales. Convinced by this, Crom is converted. Other and more ancient imagery is reflected in the assigning of the encounter between Crom and the saint to the festival of Lughnasa (see TIME). This festival has long been celebrated on the Sunday nearest to 1 August, which was therefore known in most of the country as 'Crom Dubh's Sunday'. Since Lughnasa is a harvest festival anciently dedicated to LUGH, it is likely that the myth once represented Lugh's contest with BALAR, and that Patrick and Crom have taken the place of these.

Gwynn (1924), 18–23; Mulchrone (1939), 55–6; M. MacNeill (1962), 26–32, 452–74, 598–600, 681; Ó hÓgáin (1985), 6–8, 323.

Cromwell, Oliver *(1599–1658)*

English parliamentary leader and lord protector of the British Commonwealth. The merciless nature of his nine-month campaign in Ireland in the year 1649 left a deep imprint on Irish feeling, and 'the curse of Cromwell' (*scrios Chromail*) is regarded as an imprecation of the worst kind.

With his large and seasoned army, Cromwell cut a pathway of slaughter through the country, but folklore strikingly concentrates on some personal accounts of him that have little or nothing to do with his actual campaign. In fact, the corpus of oral narrative concerning him in Ireland clearly reflects propaganda against him by the Royalists in England in his own time. No doubt the Irish, from their own experience of him, felt that they had little reason to doubt what his English enemies said about him.

The Royalist party in England claimed that a tapestry of the devil hung in the room where he was born. This is developed in Irish folklore into the claim that when Cromwell drilled his soldiers in a field, he had a picture of the devil hanging on the gate at the entrance, and every time he himself passed through the gate, the devil bowed to him. Royalist cartoons of his own time in England usually represented Cromwell in the company of the devil, and an echo of this in Irish folklore is the story of how a friar once encountered Cromwell, who was mounted on a fine horse. The terrified friar saluted the 'two gentlemen', and when Cromwell queried who the other gentleman was, he found that the devil could be seen riding behind him.

It was noticed in England that Cromwell's death on 3 September 1658 came exactly seven years to the day after his last great victory, at the Battle of Worcester in 1651. The story thus grew up that he had sold his soul to the devil before that battle in return for seven years of success. This idea too became very popular in Ireland, where it was believed that Cromwell had got his great military power from that infernal source. The correspondence was even closer than this, for a great storm was raging in the south of England as Cromwell lay dying, and the Royalists interpreted this as the devil coming for the soul of his agent. Memory of this storm and of its supposed significance survived in Irish folklore, and accounts collected in this century describe how, at the time of his death, a hellish vessel was seen on the sea, being dragged along by black dogs while its sinister captain announced that he was coming for Cromwell. A satiric poem written in England at the time of Cromwell's death and published in broadsheet described the deceased tyrant being brought over the River Styx to Hades, and one Kerry folk account echoes actual lines from that poem.

In a play performed in Cork city in the year 1685, Cromwell was represented 'with a gilded nose tweaked by Beelzebub as he carried him off'. The emphasis on his large nose was derived from contemporary propaganda in England, which nicknamed him 'Copper Nose', 'Ruby Nose and 'Nose Almighty'. Irish folklore preserves this detail also, it being claimed that Cromwell had a nose of either copper or brass.

Some aspects of his image in Irish lore seem, however, to be independent developments. An example is a story that claims that he once came to Ireland in disguise in order to discover what kind of people the Irish were and how he could overcome them. He arrived at a house where a man was being waked, and after a while offered money to the widow if she would cut a slice from the corpse. She indignantly refused, but relented when he increased his offer. He further bribed a man at the wake to trip up a drunken friend and knock him into the fire. Very satisfied when he noticed this weakness of character, Cromwell remarked 'Ireland is mine', and said that the Irish would sell and roast one another for money. This story is no doubt a rationalisation of an unfortunate tendency in the Irish experience, but it may echo some vestiges of the propaganda against the Irish that was current in England in Cromwell's own time. This propaganda painted the Irish as barbaric and cannibalistic monsters, and to its influence was largely due the ruthlessness of Cromwell's actions in Ireland.

One particular story was widely told in both the provinces of Munster and Connacht. This purports to tell of dealings that Cromwell had with a prophet called Maoilsheachlainn Mac Amhlaoibh, chieftain of Duhallow, County Cork (the surname is anglicised as MacAuliffe). There really was a chieftain of that name living at the time, and he did compose some verses of prophecy concerning the general state of Ireland, but accounts of his involvement with Cromwell must have been a special narrative growth unconnected with the historical Maoilsheachlainn. We are told that his mother was taken away into a FAIRY fort, where she became the lover of an otherworld man, and that when she was pregnant, she was left back into the ordinary world. Her husband, the chieftain, was unaware that he was not the father of the child she was bearing, and so that child grew up and in time succeeded the old chieftain. This was Maoilsheachlainn, and because of his otherworld origin, he had the power of prophecy.

One night, Maoilsheachlainn dreamed of a cobbler in England who would rise to great power and would one day control all Ireland. This cobbler's name was Cromwell. Maoilsheachlainn lost no time in setting out for England, and after a long search located that cobbler. The latter turned out to be a genial fellow who was amused at what he regarded as the mad fantasies of the Irishman, so he agreed to sign a covenant in his blood that he would never evict Maoilsheachlainn from his property. Time passed, and when Cromwell rose to power and was ravaging Ireland, he came to Duhallow to seize land there. However, when shown his signature on the covenant, he honoured his word and did not evict Maoilsheachlainn.

Being quite curious as to his future, Cromwell queried the prophet on it, and was given apparently reassuring answers. Some tellings claim that Maoilsheachlainn prophesied that he would never again be in danger if he survived that day. Cromwell, however, went to a forge to have his horse shod and, being impatient, stuck a gun barrel into the furnace to convert it into a shoe, and was shot by a bullet that had been left in the discarded gun. Other versions state that the prophecy was that Cromwell would live as long as he liked, but that he cut his own throat in a fit of anger as he shaved. Yet others have it predicted that his power would last in Ireland as long as he was in the country, and he accordingly left instructions for his body to be buried here. The soil of Ireland, however, rejected his corpse and cast it out into the sea between the two countries, the resultant tussle between English and Irish waters causing that sea to be rough ever since.

The story of Cromwell's dealings with this prophet is basically borrowed from the biography of Merlin, whose reputed prophecies were taken very seriously in the political life of seventeenth-century England. Merlin, according to the account of him given by Geoffrey of Monmouth, was the son of a demon-spirit and gave ambiguous prophecies to the tyrant ruler Vortigern. Some conceit that placed Cromwell in the role of Vortigern must have been current in Royalist circles, and when this was borrowed to Ireland, an Irish prophet associated with that period would have been substituted. Maoilsheachlainn was the one chosen for this role, for that name is pronounced in Munster as 'mlokhlin', and Merlin not dissimilarly.

GENERAL: S. Ó Súilleabháin in Dégh, Glassie & Oinas (1976), 473–83; Ó hÓgáin (1985), 281–6, 345–6 & in *Sinsear*, 2, 73–83.

ROYALIST PAMPHLETS: R. Laache in *Edda*, 2, 175–227 (compare especially verse on p. 218 to IFC 667:206–8).

MAC AMHLAOIBH: C. O'Rahilly (1925), 20; Ó Donnchadha (1940), 214.

Cruithnigh *(earlier, Cruithin)* This was an old designation for certain groups of people who inhabited parts of Ireland. It is an Irish adaptation of the British Celtic term *Priteni*, with a meaning such as 'shapers' in the sense of decorating their bodies with designs. It is apparent that this name was used for earlier Celtic settlers in Britain by new arrivals from the Continent, such as the Belgae in the final centuries BC. The Romans used the term, in the Latin form *Britannii*, for all the inhabitants of Britain – hence the name of the island. The older Celtic form survived to give the island's designation *Prydein* in Welsh.

The groups in Ireland called Cruithin included Tuath Chruachna (at Croghan, County Roscommon), the Loíghis (who have left their name on County Laois), the Conaille of Muirtheimhne (in north Louth and south Armagh), and the Dál nAraidhe, who occupied parts of Counties Antrim and Down. Some famous personages of story belonged to such Cruithin – such as the mythical CONALL CEARNACH of the Conaille and the historical MONGÁN of the Dál nAraidhe. Although the genealogists' claim that the Cruithin in general were descended from Ír, son of the fictional MÍL, was a polite fabrication, it is more reasonably suggested that there were Cruithin elements scattered throughout much of the country, with some even in Munster. Furthermore, a few tribes not specifically classed as Cruithin by the genealogists but settled in the east of the country at an early period may have originally been designated by the same name. Such include the Fotharta (in parts of Louth, Offaly, Carlow and south Wexford), who were the most significant of the tribes paying tribute to the LAIGHIN. They may also include the coastal Cualainn of east Wicklow and adjacent areas, and the Manaigh, who spread from south Leinster northwards to leave their name on County Fermanagh (*Fear Manach*). The tradition of the Manaigh themselves was that they left Leinster and travelled northwards after Éanna, son of the LAIGHIN king, was killed by their leader Eochaidh Gunnat. The Partraighe in County Mayo could well have had a similar origin.

The origins of these various groups in Ireland is obscure, but they were probably immigrants into Ireland in the early centuries AD, some perhaps being refugees from the Roman legions. Their settlement in the country may have been facilitated by their willingness to serve as mercenaries and as marchers to strong Irish tribes. They must have lost their original dialects before long, for by the beginning of the literary records, in the sixth century AD, there is no indication that their speech differed from the rest of the country.

Little or nothing survived concerning the early history of the Cruithin, and so a story was fabricated on the matter.

135

According to this, they landed at Inbhear Sláine (the mouth of the River Slaney at Wexford) and were welcomed by a Leinster KING called Criomhthann Sciathbhéal. This king was troubled by a group of Britons called Tuath Fiodhgha, who had poison-tipped weapons and thus were slaying many of his men. A DRUID of the Cruithin, called Drostan, advised that the milk of six-score hornless white cows be poured onto the battlefield. This was done, and all of Criomhthann's wounded men lay in the milk and were immediately healed. The Tuath Fiodhgha were defeated, and the power of the Cruithin grew greatly. Cathluan was the name of their king, and he took over Scotland for them. The Gaelic king ÉIREAMHÓIN, however, drove them out of Ireland. They had no women, and one of their leaders, called Cruithne, came to Ireland to seek wives from Éireamhóin. They were given the widows of the men who had been drowned in the initial attempts by the sons of Míl to land in Ireland. There was a condition attached to this arrangement, however – namely that the Cruithin would have women as their leaders henceforth.

This curious account contrasts with the understanding of the medieval historians that the Cruithin were of the same stock as the earlier settlers called ÉRAINN. The use of the term Cruithin to designate the indigenous inhabitants of Scotland is of interest, as these inhabitants were a mixture of an ancient people speaking a distinct language and of early Celtic settlers in Scotland. The early Celts in Britain were, as we have seen, termed *Priteni*. When the Romans used a corruption of this term, *Britannii*, to describe the Celts of Britain in general, the Latin term *Picti* (painted ones) was used to refer to the mixed indigenous and Celtic peoples in the north and east of Scotland. From this comes the English term 'Picts'.

Although the chronology involved in the Irish account of the origin of these Cruithin of Scotland is unrealistic, the account must in part be based on early tradition, such as the idea that the Picts practised a matrilineal system of inheritance,

which was suggested by the number of women rulers mentioned in the regnal lists of these people. The boast that the Irish had imposed that system on them in return for Irish wives was already current in the early eighth century, for it is mentioned by the Anglo-Saxon historian, Bede. It probably reflects politicking on the part of the Gaelic settlers (*Scoti*) from the fifth century AD onwards, from whom Scotland takes its name. There is no indication that Irish Cruithin were involved in any of this, but because of the same old designation shared by them with the Picts, the Irish writers considered them to be the same people. All that was known of Pictish language and culture in early medieval Ireland pertained only to Scotland, and it may be that none of the Cruithin of Ireland were actually PICTS at all. There was no post-medieval tradition concerning the Cruithin or Cruithnigh.

Some of the above septs remained quite powerful until medieval times, and the genealogists consider that the following were among the surnames taken by them at that time:

Tuath Chruachna – Ó Rodaí (Ruddy); Ó Tormaigh (Tormey); Mac an Bhaird (Ward of Connacht); Ó Móráin (Moran/Morahan of Connacht).

Loíghis – Ó Mórdha (Moore).

Conaille – Ó Cronghaile (Cronley); Ó Conghalaigh (Connolly of Ulster); Ó Caoinneacháin (Kinahan of Ulster).

Dál nAraidhe – Ó Mainnín (Mannion); Mac Giolla Riabhaigh (MacIlrea); Mac Aonghusa (McGuinness); Mac Artáin (McCartan); Ó Muireadhaigh (Murray); Ó Loingsigh (Lynch of Ulster); Ó Ceallaigh (Kelly of east Ulster).

Fotharta – Ó Nualláin (Nolan); Ó Lorcáin (Larkin of Leinster); Ó Dorchaí (Darcy).

GENERAL: T.F. O'Rahilly (1946), 341–84; Wainwright (1955).

CRUITHIN GROUPS IN IRELAND: O'Brien (1962), 41, 80–98, 153–5, 195, 375, 433–4; Ó Muraíle, *2* (2003), 102–5, 258–61, 350–9, 472–93 & *3*, 472–83, 496–501, 548–55, 634–49; T.F. O'Rahilly (1946), 34–5; K. Meyer in *ZCP, 8,* 313.

MEDIEVAL STORY: T.F. O'Rahilly (1946), 342–6; Macalister (1956), 175–85; J. Fraser in *Loomis Studies* (1927), 407–12; G. Mac Eoin in *Studia Hibernica, 4,* 138–54.

IRISH REFERENCES TO PICTS AS 'CRUITHIN': T.F. O'Rahilly (1946), 340–2; RIA Dictionary, s.v. '*Cruithen*', '*Cruithnech*'.

Cú Chulainn Mythical champion who predominates in the ULSTER CYCLE. His name is traditionally interpreted to mean 'the hound of Culann'. *Cú* (i.e. hound) was a common designation for a warrior in early Irish literature, and whatever the original import of the second part of his name, it is clear that he had his source in a cult of martial prowess.

The literature tells that prior to his first great exploit, he was called Sétanta (pronounced Séadánta), which name is similar in appearance to that of a small Celtic tribe in western Britain, the Setantii. It is unclear whether the two designations are actually connected, but if the eponym Setantii was borrowed from British Celtic into Irish, it could have given a form such as Setainte, with a fanciful singular such as Setanta. The Setantii tribe are reported by Ptolemy (a geographer of the second century AD) as inhabiting an area in modern Lancashire, and there is a strong possibility that a group of them settled across the sea in the area of County Louth. It has been suggested that they had an eponymous GOD called Sentonotios, which name would mean 'wayfarer'. Support for this comes from a medieval Irish text, in which the name is given as Sédana and explained as referring to *sét* (route), and from the fact that the chariot was a vehicle especially associated with this hero. The name Cú Chulainn signified 'the warrior of the smith', but the smithcraft in this instance seems to have special reference to vehicles, for the word *cul* signified a chariot.

The literature describes Cú Chulainn as a native of Muirtheimhne (in present-day County Louth), and the indications therefore are that his cult originally belonged to a group of Setantii that had settled in that area, bringing the war chariot with them. Such a migration would perhaps have occurred as early as the first or second century AD, when the tribes of that part of Britain were being savaged by the Roman legions. Other nomenclature connected with Cú Chulainn seems to reflect displacement or movement of Celtic tribes from the same period. His javelin, for instance, is called the *ga bolga*, reminiscent

of the Belgae, a prominent Celtic people of western Europe, strong groups of whom had settled in Britain. The name given to the father-in-law of Cú Chulainn, Forgall Manach, preserves that of the Manapii – these may be connected to the Belgic Menapii, whose name was reported from south Leinster and branches of which spread to Ulster.

The ULSTER CYCLE was already in existence as a narrative framework before Cú Chulainn was introduced into it as a superhero. This adaptation seems to have been made to the Cycle in the late seventh century, Cú Chulainn being inserted in place of a young warrior called Fiacc as the leading fighter for the Ulster forces. The warrior imagery of Cú Chulainn of Muirtheimhne was so impressive as to cause him to be substituted for this Fiacc of Ulster. In the Cycle's central epic, *Táin Bó Cuailnge*, he single-handedly defends the province of Ulster against the great army of queen MEADHBH of Connacht. The sheer drama of his portrayal in that text highlights the fact that much distinctive lore attached to him, and this must have been drawn from the tradition of Muirtheimhne, which was on the southern border of the Ulstermen. We read of his body becoming transformed by the *riastradh*, which is a kind of battle-frenzy. He shakes from head to foot and revolves within his skin, his features turn red, one eye becomes monstrously large while the other becomes tiny, his mouth grows huge and emits sparks, his heart booms in his chest, his hair becomes spiked and glowing, and the 'warrior light' comes from his brow. This description is obviously an echo of ancient ideas concerning the inspiration of a warrior.

At the height of the battle campaign, Cú Chulainn risks his life to 'show himself to the women and the POETS', and this motif would appear to be a survival in narrative of some ancient warriors' ritual. Relevant also is the fact that his character covers a wider range than feats of arms alone, and that there is a mystical significance in some of his actions. In order to delay the enemy army, for instance, he twists an oak sapling into a hoop and writes a message on it while using but one arm, one leg and one eye. This was apparently a ritual of war employed by magical poets, and parallels the pose adopted by LUGH during battle. In fact, Lugh is introduced into the *Táin* as the otherworld patron of Cú Chulainn, who comes to relieve him when he is fatigued from fighting, thereby allowing him to sleep for three whole days.

An early eighth-century text tells the story of the conception and birth of Cú Chulainn, giving him a close blood relationship to the Ulster king CONCHOBHAR MAC NEASA. We read that a flock of BIRDS landed on the plain of Eamhain Mhacha, where the royal court was, and devoured the grass there. Some of the Ulster warriors pursued the birds in their chariots, with Conchobhar's sister Deichtine acting as his driver. Night overtook them at Brugh na Bóinne (Newgrange, County Meath), and a great snow fell. The Ulstermen were given shelter by a couple who lived in a solitary house there. The man told them that his wife was in birth-pangs, and Deichtine went to her assistance. A baby boy was born, and at the very same time a mare dropped two foals at the door of the house. The Ulstermen brought the foals to the baby, and Deichtine nursed him. When morning came, they found themselves alone at the Brugh, except for the baby and the foals. They returned to Eamhain Mhacha, but the baby grew ill and died. When the heartbroken Deichtine took a drink, a tiny creature slipped into her mouth. She dreamed that night that Lugh came to her and said that he was the father of the baby and that it would be born again through her. She became pregnant, and it was suspected that her brother the king was responsible, so Conchobhar gave her in marriage to one of his warriors called Sualdamh. She miscarried and grew pregnant again – this time by her husband – and gave birth to a son, whom she called Sétanta.

The patronage of Lugh for Cú Chulainn, as shown in these texts, indicates that there was some connection between the two personages. They should not be identified with each other, however, for the intensive, and seemingly basic, warrior focus of Cú Chulainn is quite different from the polytechnic imagery of Lugh. The most likely explanation for the connection would be that the image of Cú Chulainn was influenced by the Lugh cult in the Louth–Meath area.

The text on Sétanta's birth further states that the child was given to a smith called Culann, who was to be his tutor. When at play, Sétanta killed Culann's hound, and then said to the smith: 'I will be your hound' – hence his acquired name 'Cú Chulainn'. This episode is a secondary invention, for – as we have seen – the name originally signified 'chariot warrior' or the like. The writers were clearly feeling it necessary to give some description of the hero's youth, but were unsure as to how the existing material should be handled and developed. The text, for instance, betrays some confusion as to who Sétanta's real father was, and the reader suspects that Sualdamh and Lugh were variously considered in that role. It is noteworthy also that in the accounts of his birth and youth, the roles of paternity and fosterage played by these figures have been duplicated by the inclusion of characters who are central to the Ulster Cycle – characters such as Conchobhar mac Neasa and Fearghus mac Róich. This confusion suggests that at the time of Cú Chulainn's first occurrences in the literature, his lore had only recently been Ulsterised.

One account, from the ninth century, has his mother called Deichtire rather than Deichtine. She is here also the sister of Conchobhar, but her husband is apparently of the otherworld. She and her maidens were the 50 birds who allured the Ulstermen to the strange house, where BRICRIU met her and her husband. Mischievous as usual, Bricriu returned to Conchobhar and spoke of the lady's great beauty, without mentioning who she was, and when the king heard of the lady, he desired that she be brought to him. On her way thither, however, she revealed that she was in travail, and so she was excused from sleeping with the king. The night passed thus, and when the Ulstermen awoke next morning, they found the baby Sétanta in Conchobhar's lap. This version, with its extra attempts at dramatisation, confuses the tradition still further, and it is significant that general indecision also relates to the question of the hero's rearing. One version of the birth-story states that he was given by Conchobhar to another sister, Fionnchaomh, and was reared by her and her husband, the seer AMHAIRGHIN MAC ÉIGIT SALAIGH, in their dwelling on the plain of Muirtheimhne. This also states that the seneschal FEARGHUS MAC RÓICH wished to be the child's tutor, and elsewhere Fearghus is indeed given this function.

Accounts of the birth of Cú Chulainn were becoming quite fanciful by the twelfth century, when some writers were claiming that he was born in the otherworld residence called Sídh Troim (east of Slane, County Meath), and that the Connacht warrior CEAT MAC MÁGHACH passed by that place soon after. Ceat had with him his own foster-parents and their newly born son Laegh, and he asked Laegh's mother to allow the other child to drink from her also; thus, we read, Cú Chulainn and his charioteer Laegh were suckled at the same breast. The medieval genealogists, for their part, invented a pedigree for Cú Chulainn that brought his line backwards to Cearmaid, son of the DAGHDHA, and thence through TIGHEARNMHAS to ÉIREAMHÓIN, son of MÍL.

The compiler of the developed version of *Táin Bó Cuailnge* attempted to reconcile the differing strands by having Fearghus relate a youth biography of the hero. According to this, the boy Sétanta persuaded his mother (who is here said to have lived with her husband in the plain of Muirtheimhne) to allow him to go to Eamhain Mhacha and play with the youths there. He set off, continually casting his javelin ahead of him and catching it before it touched the ground, until he reached his destination. Seeing the youths hurling there, he joined the game without their permission. The enraged boys flung all their sticks, their playing balls and their

shields at him, but he rained off all the blows and the battle-frenzy came upon him with the usual bodily transformation. He laid low 50 of the youths, and the rest fled before him. Conchobhar and Fearghus had their chess game upset by the rout, and Conchobhar seized the boy. On learning that he was Sétanta, the king made peace between him and the other boys, and those who had been injured were restored to health by their guardians.

Sétanta, however, refused to sleep in Eamhain Mhacha until his head and feet were propped up with stones so that they were equidistant from the floor. He insisted on not being disturbed in his sleep thus, and broke the forehead of a man who tried to awaken him. Once, when the boy was sleeping, the Ulstermen were defeated by their enemies in a great battle. Awakening, Sétanta went to the battlefield with his hurley, rescued Conchobhar and his son CORMAC CONN LOINGEAS, and brought them home safely. When Eamhain Mhacha was attacked on another occasion, and the Ulstermen laid low with the curse of debilitation that was on them (*see* MACHA), the boy repelled the marauders with stones and with his hurley. We are told that when he rescued Conchobhar and Cormac, Sétanta was egged on by the war-goddess BADHBH, who spoke to him from among the corpses on the battlefield. This GODDESS is repeatedly associated with him, appearing in various forms when he is locked in battle. She again underlines the intensive imagery of war in his portrayal.

Regarding the idea that the boy Sétanta killed a hound, another passage inserted into the *Táin* rationalises this through use of a monster-slaying motif. The account is put into the mouth of the warrior Conall Cearnach, supplementing what has been said by Fearghus. Since Sétanta excelled all his fellows at games and athletic feats, the account goes, the king was intensely proud of him. Once, when Conchobhar was invited to a feast, he asked the boy to accompany him and his nobles, but Sétanta was busy playing games and said he would follow on. The feast was being hosted by the smith Culann, who kept a monstrous hound to guard his fortress by night. Conchobhar forgot that the boy was coming, and the hound was released. Soon Sétanta came, playing his tricks with his hurley and ball, and the hound attacked him. The boy seized the ferocious beast by the throat and back, and dashed its head against a pillar-stone. Conchobhar's men rushed out of the fortress, and to their amazement and relief found the boy safe and the hound dead. Culann, however, felt the loss of his great hound, and Sétanta offered to guard his property for him until another DOG could be found. Thus he came to be known as Cú Chulainn. Some medieval sources in fact give him a secondary or alternative designation – namely, Cú na Ceirde (the Hound of the Craftsman/Smith).

This inserted passage in the *Táin* has another warrior, Fiacha mac Fir Féibhe, tell of how Cú Chulainn gained official recognition as a warrior when he was a mere seven years old. The druid CATHBHADH prophesied that whoever took up arms on a certain day would forever be remembered in story and, overhearing this, the boy went to Conchobhar seeking weapons. He broke the first fifteen sets of spear and shield, and then was given the king's own set. When Cathbhadh said that his life would be short, Cú Chulainn answered that he would be content with this if he achieved fame. Similarly, when Cathbhadh prophesied that the name of whoever mounted his first chariot on that day would live forever in Ireland, Cú Chulainn broke twelve chariots and was given the chariot of Conchobhar. He set out and slew the three sons of Nechtan Scéine, who had killed as many Ulstermen as were then living. He also captured live a fine stag and twenty swans, roped them to the chariot, and returned thus to Eamhain Mhacha with the heads of the three conquered warriors. In his frenzy, he threatened to slaughter all, but Conchobhar ordered the women of Eamhain to go out naked to him. Seeing the women thus, Cú Chulainn covered his face, and the Ulster warriors seized him and plunged him consecutively into three vats of cold water. The first vat burst asunder, the second boiled up with huge bubbles, and the third was lukewarm. Then he went and sat on the king's knee, which henceforth was his public seat.

It is clear from this that various ideas from antiquity, particularly those associated with initiation rites of warriors, are embedded in the tradition of Cú Chulainn. The *Táin* portrays him as the complete warrior, excelling in all the tricks of the trade, and parts of the text look like echoes from lore that functioned as a kind of training manual. His accomplishments include athletic skills, deft use of a sling, controlled and accurate wielding of a sword, methods of throwing a javelin and warding it off with a shield, and howling to upset a foe. The descriptions given of his skills greatly exaggerate human potential – he could, for instance, cut the sod from under his opponent or shave him with sword strokes, leap onto the opponent's shield and leap over a flying javelin, but this may be as much the result of oral preservation of the tradition as of deliberate dramatic inflation. The names given to many of his martial tricks are quite obscure and seem equally to be the debris of ancient skills. Of special interest is his mode of fighting with his great Carbad Searrdha (Scythed Chariot), which had cutting instruments attached to its axle on either side. Latin writers describe how the Continental Celts used similar devices, and this constitutes yet another distinctive parallel between Cú Chulainn and Celtic culture outside of Ireland.

Another text is worthy of study with regard to the development of the biography of the new hero. This is *Tochmarc Emire* (The Wooing of Eimhear), the original of which was written in the late eighth century but which underwent much reworking and expansion during the following 200 years. It tells of how Cú Chulainn outdid all the Ulster warriors at walking on ropes and 'the apple-feat and the feats of the javelin and the sword-edge', and how the Ulstermen grew jealous of their women's admiration of him and decided that a wife must be found for him. Conchobhar had all Ireland searched for a suitable girl, but nowhere could such be found. Then Cú Chulainn himself went to woo one Eimhear (earlier, Emer), daughter of Forgall Manach in the Lughlocht of Lugh (south of the River Boyne in County Meath). They spoke in riddles to each other, and she set conditions on her love. She said that he must first slay hundreds of men, do 'the feat of the salmon leap', deliver a sword stroke that slew several but spared men selectively, and go sleepless from November till August. Cú Chulainn promised to perform the feats and left her.

When Eimhear's father heard of their encounter, he went in disguise to Eamhain Mhacha and advised that Cú Chulainn should go to Scotland to study the warrior's art with a female tutor called Scáthach. He thereby hoped to have the young hero killed. Cú Chulainn set out for Scotland and learned tricks there from a warrior called Domhnall – how to walk over fire and to perform on the point of a spear. Going to meet Scáthach, he came to a bouncing bridge that knocked off it all but the most accomplished warriors. His battle-frenzy came upon him and he crossed the obstacle by performing the salmon leap. He then became the lover of Scáthach's daughter Uathach, and forced Scáthach herself to give him further martial training. War broke out between Scáthach and another warrioress called Aoife, and Cú Chulainn overcame Aoife in single combat and she lay with him. He learned many tricks from her, relating to such things as juggling, leaping, running, casting, fighting and chariot-driving.

Returning to Ireland, he found Eimhear's home so well guarded that he could not take it for a whole year. Then he charged the defenders with the scythe-wheeled chariot and slew 309 of them. Giving the salmon leap over the rampart, he thrice over slew nine men, sparing one man in the middle of them each time. Having thus performed all the tasks required of him by Eimhear, he took her away to Eamhain Mhacha. The mischievous Bricriu stated that Eimhear must sleep the first night with king Conchobhar as was the usual custom. To allay the hero's rage at this and deflect his attention, Conchobhar ordered him to gather a herd of swine and deer and birds and to bring them to Eamhain. The nobles saw to it that further trouble was avoided by having Fearghus and Cathbhadh sleep in the same bed with Conchobhar and Eimhear, and thus assure that the honour of Cú Chulainn was not compromised. The episode of the stupendous herding in that account was probably borrowed from the Fianna lore of CAOILTE.

A story composed soon after the Wooing of Eimhear also survives in a somewhat later recension than its original. This is *Serglige Con Cúlainn* (The Wasting-sickness of Cú Chulainn), and it tells of how the hero fell in love with an otherworld lady called Fann (earlier, Fand). On the feast of Samhain (November) some wonderful birds settled on a lake in the plain of Muirtheimhne, and each of the women longed to have a pair of them. Cú Chulainn got the birds for them with his sling, but there were none left for his wife (identified in the text variously as Eimhear and Eithne Inghubha), and he promised to find some for her. He failed to catch two magic birds soon after, however, and then fell asleep. Two women came and beat him, and as a result, he was sick in Eamhain Mhacha for a whole year. At the next feast of Samhain, a man appeared beside his bed and told him that an otherworld lady called Fann awaited him. He returned to where he was a year before and was told by a lady called Lí Ban there that if he fought for her husband for the duration of one day in the otherworld he would have the love of Fann. He did this, and spent a month with Fann in the otherworld. When he bade her farewell, they arranged a tryst at Iubhar Cinn Tráchta (Newry, County Down). His wife, however, came to that place to attack Fann, and the latter returned to the otherworld, leaving Cú Chulainn to her.

Other adventures related of the hero in the medieval literature include the awarding of the champion's portion to him after the feast of BRICRIU, his contest with CÚ ROÍ for the lady Bláthnaid, and the tragic single combat he fought against his own son CONLAE. There is rich personal colouring in the various accounts, and much of this can be related to the heroic milieu. For instance, he is described as having three faults, being 'too handsome, too brave and too young'. He has two marvellous chariot-horses the Liath Mhacha (Grey of Macha) and the Dubh Shaingleann (Black of Saingliu). These are presumably the same as the two foals mentioned in the birth-story, but they had to be recovered by him as described in a recension of the text on the feast of Bricriu. There we are told that the Grey came out of a lake (*see* HORSES) and was mounted by Cú Chulainn and ridden rough throughout Ireland before he brought it tame to Eamhain at nightfall. The Black was acquired in similar circumstances.

He had great weapons, too, especially the *ga bolga*, which is described as a barbed javelin that hacked at its victim causing multiple wounds. He also had a great spear called Duaibhseach (literally, 'grim'), a massive shield and helmet around which demons of the air shrieked, and a visor he got as a present from the deity MANANNÁN. One account claims that his shield, in contrast to the silver ones of the other Ulster warriors, had a dark engraving and bore the name Dubhán. Much extravaganza is employed in describing his appearance. His hair was of three different colours, and he had four colourful dimples in each cheek, seven pupils in each eye, seven fingers on each hand and seven toes on each foot. He had some distinctly magical powers, such as when he wrote a message in OGHAM script compelling the enemy to cease their advance in the *Táin*. Also in that text, when mocked by the women on account of his youth, he 'took a handful of grass and chanted a spell over it, and they all thought that he had a beard'. The more practical side of his adventures is also stressed – his charioteer Laegh accompanies him on most of his great exploits, performing the service of chiding him into greater efforts when such are required.

As champion of the Ulster Cycle, Cú Chulainn is described in many accounts as saving king Conchobhar and his men when they are in dire straits. Thus in the ninth-century text *Mesca Ulad* (The Intoxication of the Ulstermen), he and another warrior called Fionntan argued over which of them should host the king and his company at an ale feast. It was decided that the night should be divided into two halves, with Fionntan having the first. But the disgruntled Cú Chulainn, when his turn came, brought the company on a drunken tour all over Ireland, ending up in the fortress of Cú Roí at Teamhair Luachra (in County Kerry). Here Meadhbh and her husband Ailill were already visiting, and the Ulstermen received a feigned welcome and were then locked into an iron-walled house. The house was made red hot, but Cú Chulainn broke a way out with his sword. He broke down the door of a second house in which they were confined, and then led the Ulstermen in an all-out attack on their tormentors. The fortress was destroyed and Cú Chulainn later entertained Conchobhar and the other warriors in his own fortress of Dún Déalgan (Dundalk, County Louth). The motif of entrapment in a red-hot iron house is an obvious borrowing from an earlier Leinster story concerning LABHRAIDH.

An account of the death of Cú Chulainn was already in circulation by the tenth century. Cú Chulainn, we read, had killed a warrior called Cailitín during the war with Meadhbh, and Cailitín's wife gave birth posthumously to sextuplets – three sons and three daughters. Meadhbh sent these children abroad to study sorcery, and on their return incited them against Cú Chulainn. Then she herself invaded Cuailnge (the area of Cooley, County Louth), thereby drawing Conchobhar and his Ulster warriors into battle again. Conchobhar, having got a report that treachery was planned against Cú Chulainn, called him to Eamhain and ordered him to remain there until the war was over. The hero was kept there in the company of Eimhear and the women and DRUIDS of Ulster. The children of Cailitín came, however, and by magic made it appear that Eamhain was being attacked. For three days this continued, with Cú

Chulainn being restrained by his guardians. Then Conchobhar sent word that the hero be brought to the Valley of the Deaf, where he could no longer hear the din of battle. He was followed there by the children of Cailitín, and one of them put herself into the shape of Niamh, a young lady for whom Cú Chulainn had a particular affection. She went to where he was and told him that he was needed in the battle. He set forth, and on his way met the three daughters of Cailitín, who were roasting the meat of a dog. They invited him to eat with them. There was a prohibitive GEIS on him against refusing an invitation to a meal, but equally he was prohibited from eating dog-meat on account of his name. He tried to extricate himself by taking the meat in his hand and hiding it, but much of his strength left him nevertheless.

When he joined the battle, the sons of Cailitín had prepared three special javelins, and three sons of men whom Cú Chulainn had slain were ready to throw these javelins. The first cast killed the charioteer Laegh, the second lodged in the side of the great Grey, and that horse raced into the lake from which it had come. The third javelin struck Cú Chulainn. It was flung by Lughaidh, son of Cú Roí, and it caused the hero's intestines to fall out. He staggered to the nearby lake to take a drink, and a raven that was drinking his blood tripped over the intestines. Amused at this, the hero gave a last great laugh. He tied himself to an upright stone so that he would face his enemies standing, and then died. For three days, the foe did not dare approach him, until one of Cailitín's daughters put herself in the shape of a crow and landed on the stone. Realising that he was dead, the warriors approached, but they could not remove the sword from his hand. Lughaidh cut the veins of the hand, and the sword fell, severing Lughaidh's own hand as it did so. The medieval writers employed much fancy in claiming to identify the burial place of the great warrior. Some sources say that he was interred in the otherworld residence of Sídh Troim, whereas others state that his head and his hand were brought to Tara and buried there.

The fame of so great a warrior caused one eleventh-century writer to make a connection between him and St PATRICK. This writer described how, when the saint was trying to convince the high-king LAOGHAIRE of the truth of Christianity, Cú Chulainn appeared as a phantom driving his great chariot and told Laoghaire to believe in the new religion. He described some of his own great feats in arms and outlined the values he had held in life. These were to protect his people, and to be 'a boy among boys, a man among men, triumphant at a ford, strong in face of satire, stronger still in face of praise'. As a result, we are told that Laoghaire was converted to Christianity and Cú Chulainn was released from hell into heaven. It is clear from this that the lore of Cú Chulainn was being made more adaptable to the mentality of medieval culture, and that the writers were growing more fanciful. One text, for instance, has Cú Chulainn meeting on the Boyne river an otherworld man called Seanbheag (old dwarf), who is a splendid harpist and who travels in a small boat of bronze. Seanbheag presents the hero with clothes that protect their wearer against burning and drowning, as well as a shield and spear that guarantee victory in combat. Another medieval account tells of how Eimhear eloped with a NORSE prince called Tuir Gleasta, but Cú Chulainn followed them to Norway, slew his rival and recovered his wife.

A twelfth-century text evidences an effort to set Cú Chulainn in the context of medieval romance without losing the flavour of the indigenous lore. This tells of a feast held in Cooley by Conall mac Gleo Ghlais, who invited Conchobhar and the nobles of Ulster. The king, however, neglected to bring Cú Chulainn with him, and the hero set off in a huff to find adventures for himself. He told his charioteer Laegh that there was a *geis* on him to kill a man on every journey he made from Eamhain Mhacha. At the seashore, he met a huge warrior, Goll mac Carbada from north Germany, who was coming to put

Ireland under tribute. In a fierce contest, Cú Chulainn, encouraged by Laegh, beheaded the intruder with his short-sword, called the 'Cruaidín Cadadcheann'. Returning then to Eamhain, he found the court empty of its nobles, who had all gone to the feast, and in a pique decided to burn the place. He was restrained, however, by the verse of Suanan Sailcheann, the king's poet.

He then set out for Cooley and on the way met a ferocious character called Garbh who lived in Gleann Ríghe (the Newry Valley, County Down) and who refused to allow any warrior to pass through his territory. This Garbh had just killed 50 of Conchobhar's men as they travelled to the feast. Cú Chulainn slew Garbh with his short-sword, and also slew an horrific hound that Conall mac Gleo Ghlais had released at night to protect his fortress. Refused entry to the feast, Cú Chulainn tore a great standing stone from the ground and slew thrice 50 of the servants with it. Bricriu urged the warriors to combine and kill Cú Chulainn, but Fearghus mac Róich and Conall Cearnach took his part. The tumult continued until Conchobhar's diplomat, Seancha mac Ailealla, waved his 'branch of peace'. Then Cú Chulainn told of his adventures and was reconciled to the others. He intended to leave Ulster for a year on account of the insult he had received, but Conchobhar offered him whatever compensation he sought. Cú Chulainn was satisfied to leave the amount to be decided by the judges and poets, and even then took only a third of what he was awarded.

In the story of the feast of Bricriu, Cú Chulainn got public recognition as the champion of Ulster, but he had to undergo many ordeals to prove his pre-eminence. The situation in that text would naturally have appealed to later writers, and so – in the thirteenth century – another story was composed that made use of it, again having the hero undertake adventures as a result of Bricriu's machinations. This story told of how Bricriu held another feast and, when all were assembled, said that no warrior should partake until he had first performed a great martial deed. Cú Chulainn

accordingly set out for Connacht, and took away from there a girl who loved him. She was called Fionnchaomh and was the daughter of a local king called Eochaidh Ronn. When Cú Chulainn spent the night at Meadhbh's court, Eochaidh came in most aggressive mood, but Cú Chulainn drove a spear through the neck of his horse and seized him with his hands. Meadhbh made peace between them, but Eochaidh enjoined Cú Chulainn to discover what caused the exile of three sons of a warrior called Daol Dearmaid.

The hero returned to Eamhain Mhacha, but could not rest there on account of what had been enjoined on him. He felt as if the clothes on his body and all surrounding him were ablaze, so he set out to find the answer. At Dundalk, he saw a boat, and in his anger slew all its crew except a prince who was on board. This prince told him that the boat was a magical one and would itself direct him on his quest. It accordingly brought him to a strange island where, in answer to his question about the sons of Daol Dearmaid, he was directed to another island where their sister Achtland lived. She slipped away from her husband with Cú Chulainn, and brought him to the land in which the sons of Daol Dearmaid were. There Cú Chulainn fought a tremendous duel with a fierce warrior called Eochaidh Glas. The answer to the question is not clarified in the text, but apparently this Eochaidh Glas was holding the three young men in subjection. Cú Chulainn, using astounding acrobatic skills in the duel, slew his opponent with the *ga bolga*. He then returned to Eamhain Mhacha in Ulster and told of his adventures.

This story, although using the traditional background, is strongly influenced by a new genre being adopted from other languages into Irish storytelling at the time. This genre – the *'romain d'aventure'* – featured quests that led to curious adventures in strange and faraway countries. Although the theme of great heroes making conquests abroad was found in the Ulster Cycle and other Irish heroic literature from an earlier date, plots dependent on fantastic places and loosely strung episodes were a novelty. That genre was of a quite different character to the indigenous lore of Cú Chulainn, and it had comparatively little vogue in his case. However, in the seventeenth century, a group of anonymous writers from the Armagh–Louth area composed half a dozen prose texts that were inspired by the story of the quest for Daol's sons. The earliest and best of these was the Pursuit of Gruadh Ghriansholais, a beautiful lady who came to Ireland fleeing from a hideous GIANT and seeking the help of Cú Chulainn. She was daughter of the king of Antioch. Protection was given, but the giant snatched her from Cú Chulainn, and the hero set out overseas to recover her. After many ferocious encounters with giants and formidable warriors, he rescued the lady and reunited three love-crossed couples before returning in triumph to Ireland.

The author of this text took great liberties with pre-existing material of the Ulster Cycle – for example turning Conchobhar's physician Fínghein Fáithliaigh into a FAIRY who comes in a cloud to cure the hero's wounds. Much play is also made of Cú Chulainn's great war-chariot, the Carbad Searrdha, which is claimed to have exuded poison in battle. Similar motifs occur in the other texts of this group, with Cú Chulainn and comrades like CONALL CEARNACH, FEAR DIADH and Ailill Fionn (see FLIODHAIS) contending with giants and dragons, overcoming sorcery, rescuing ladies, and always returning in bloodstained victory.

Some garbled versions of these late prose texts have been collected from the folklore of the north of Ireland, arising no doubt from readings of manuscripts. Popular also, particularly in Connacht, was a lay concerning Cú Chulainn, which had been composed in the sixteenth or seventeenth century after the pattern of many such lays in the FIANNA CYCLE. This has a Scandinavian champion called Garbh mac Stairn coming to Ireland to demand tribute. At TARA – rather inappropriately for the Ulster Cycle – he met Conchobhar mac Neasa and the Ulster warriors, and all agreed to render the tribute except Cú

Chulainn. Bricriu chided Garbh with this, and as a result those two warriors fought a combat non-stop for seven days and nights. On the eighth morning, Garbh was beheaded by Cú Chulainn with a mighty sword stroke. No original manuscript of this lay has been found, but such must have been in the background.

The fact that so dramatic a character as Cú Chulainn has not been accorded a higher profile in folklore mirrors the fortunes of the Ulster Cycle generally, for that cycle seems to have been almost exclusively a learned tradition for the past 500 years or more. General folk biographies of him have indeed been collected from the oral lore of Connacht and Ulster, as well as from western Scotland, but these derive most if not all of their material from literary accounts compiled in modernised language from the fourteenth to the seventeenth century – accounts that continued to be copied by scribes down to recent generations. Accordingly, some details from his birth-story have been current in Donegal folklore, while in Galway a confusion of the sources has led to him being identified with one of the children born to MACHA after her race against the horses of Conchobhar. His slaying of Culann's hound is general, as is an abbreviation of his training with the female warriors and the tragic story of how he slew his son Conlae. Some of his feats in the *Táin*, as well as episodes from his death-story, were well known in the lore of County Louth, due no doubt to their local associations.

In the texts of the *Táin* epic, we find a quaint little anecdote that has Cú Chulainn, in a fit of martial anger, slay two chroniclers, called Roán and Roae. As a result of this, we read, the account of the *Táin* was lost for a long time. This gave rise to a burlesque narrative that was known over most of the Gaelic world. In it, a humorous plot from the common stock of folklore has been adapted to this context (see HUMOROUS TALES, type 1376A). According to this narrative, Cú Chulainn agrees to tell a smith about an adventure of his, provided that no woman is listening. He describes how he had come upon a giant who had stolen a cow and was roasting it. Cú Chulainn tried to interfere, but all his martial efforts were in vain and he ended up by being flung by the giant into the cow's horn! The smith's wife was listening to this account of the hero's humiliation, and she shouted out that he should properly be called, not Cú na gCleas (the hound of the skills), but Cú na hAdhairce (the hound of the horn). When Cú Chulainn heard this, he was humiliated and angry, and killed the eavesdropper in a fit of pique, thus leaving the remainder of the engrossing story untold. This narrative, with its deflation of heroism and its joking at the learned respect given to the Ulster Cycle, exhibits the typical playful humour often found in oral narrative.

The distancing of Cú Chulainn from the ordinary stock of oral tales did not generally result in ridicule, however, for the learned respect for him that persisted among literary men guaranteed his status. To antiquarian speculation of recent centuries is due the practice of explaining place names in different parts of Ireland by reference to the literary stories of Cú Chulainn.

ORIGINS: Jackson (1964); Sjoestedt (1982), 75–98; de Vries (1963), 72–86; C.-J. Guyonvarc'h in *Ogam*, *13*, 592–8 & *19*, 266; Rivet & Smith (1979), 456–7; Olmsted (1994), 348–52.
RITUALISTIC DESCRIPTIONS: C. O'Rahilly (1970), 61–3 & (1976), 14–15, 24–5, 68–72; Van Hamel (1933), 102–4; R.I. Best in *Ériu*, *5*, 72; W. Sayers in *Ériu*, *32*, 163–7.
BIRTH: Van Hamel (1933), 1–8; E. Windisch in *Irische Texte*, *1*, 134–45; K. Hollo in *Ériu*, *49*, 13–17.
INVENTED GENEALOGY: O'Brien (1962), 285.
'CÚ NA CEIRDE': Gwynn (1913), 256–9; C. O'Rahilly (1976), 13; Meyer (1906), 44; W. Stokes in *Irische Texte*, *3*, 398–9; Dillon (1953), 13.
BOYHOOD DEEDS: C. O'Rahilly (1976), 13–26.
EIMHEAR: Van Hamel (1933), 16–46, 60–68.
SCÁTHACH AND AOIFE: Van Hamel (1933), 47–60.
WASTING SICKNESS: Dillon (1953).
HORSES: Van Hamel, 4, 92, 107–17; Henderson (1899), 38–40; Best & O'Brien (1956), 448–53.
WEAPONS: C. O'Rahilly (1970), 58–62 & (1976), 64–8; E. Hogan (1892), 102; R.I. Best in *Ériu*, *5*, 72; M. Dillon in *Ériu*, *11*, 54–5. See Ó Cadhlaigh (1956), 121–3, 381.
PERSONAL DESCRIPTIONS: *see* Ó Cadhlaigh (1956), 103–5.
INTOXICATION OF ULSTERMEN: J.C. Watson (1941).
DEATH AND BURIAL: Best & O'Brien (1956), 442–53; Van Hamel 69–118; K. Hollo in *Ériu*, *49*, 17–18.
PATRICK: Best & Bergin (1929), xxxiv–xxxv, 278–87; K. Meyer in *AIM*, *3*, 48–56.
SEANBHEAG AND EIMHEAR: K. Meyer in *RC*, *6*, 182–5.
GOLL MAC CARBADA AND GARBH: W. Stokes in *RC*, *14*, 396–449.
DAOL DIARMAID: E. Windisch in *Irische Texte*, *2 (1)*, 164–217.
LATE ROMANCES: T.F. O'Rahilly (1924); Ní Chléirigh (1941) & (1942); Ni Mhuirgheasa & Ó Ceithearnaigh (1952).
GARBH MAC STAIRN: Christiansen (1931), 86–9; Áine Bhreathnach in *An Stoc* 6/1919, 2; IFC 793:406–10, 1012:421–3, 1236:60–6.
LATE VERSIONS OF MEDIEVAL STORIES: Ua Ceallaigh (1935); W. Stokes in *RC*, *29*, 109–52, 312–14; C. O'Rahilly (1961), xlvii–lix.
CHRONICLERS SLAIN: C. O'Rahilly (1976), 32; R. Thurneysen in *ZCP*, *8*, 543; J.F. Nagy in *ZCP*, *49–50*, 603–4.
FOLKLORE: Ó Súilleabháin (1942), 597–9; Bruford (1969), 93–9, 104–5, 237–8; Hyde (1901), 330–8; C. Maguire in *New Ireland Review*, *25*, 181–9; Quiggin (1906), 236–41; Mac Giollarnáth (1936), 37–46; L. Mac Coisdhealbha in *Béaloideas*, *9*, 55–8; OSL: Louth (1836), 94–7, 103–4, 155; IFC Catalogue.

Cú Roí Mythical KING of Munster who figures prominently in the ULSTER CYCLE. Cú (hound) was a frequent appellation for a warrior in ancient Ireland, but the meaning of the second part of the character's name is unclear. It was sometimes written *Ruí*, and an earlier form would have been *Raui*, apparently the genitive of a Celtic word meaning 'roarer' or the like.

The lack of clarity in the name has led to several different suggestions as to its origin, one theory going so far as to claim that Cú Roí was an echo of an historical character. This was Carausius, an officer in the Roman navy who belonged to the Celtic tribe of Menapii in modern Belgium. In the year AD 286, Carausius seized the reins of government in Britain and proclaimed himself emperor. He held out against the might of Rome for seven years, until killed by treachery. Obviously, the career of such a great leader would make a deep impression on the surviving Celtic peoples, but even if he did influence Irish mythical narrative, it is clear that several indigenous mythical elements are involved in the portrayal of Cú Roí.

In medieval Irish literature, Cú Roí was usually said to be 'son of Dáire'. This DÁIRE was claimed as ancestor by the ÉRAINN, which was the designation given to septs other than the predominant CONNACHTA and EOGHANACHT. Among the leading septs of the Érainn were several Ulster groups, and in the south the Corca Laíghdhe (in present-day County Cork). The Corca Laíghdhe claimed descent from Lughaidh, son of Dáire. This is significant, for a mythical character who figured prominently in early Munster tradition was LUGHAIDH MAC CON. The Ulster Cycle has a son of Cú Roí, called Lughaidh mac Con Roí, as slayer of CÚ CHULAINN, and there is little doubt but that originally all of these three Lughaidhs were one and the same character. The title 'son of Dáire' would have been a ritual one, either for a divine figure or for a tribal leader, and its occurrence here is due to the fancy of genealogists who were acquainted with the close association between the characters Cú Roí and Dáire and wanted to rationalise it.

A seventh-century Latin text represents Dáire as the possessor and bestower of a cauldron, which sets him in the role and function of the Celtic GOD of plenty. This imagery is paralleled in a ninth-century poem, which states that Cú Roí had a cauldron into which 30 oxen would fit, as well as a huge vat and a dish wrought from silver and gold. Another reference in the poem gives an indication of the source from which the composers of the Ulster Cycle borrowed Cú Roí. He is described as 'the high-king of the mounds of TARA'. This gets indirect support by the text on the Intoxication of the Ulstermen (see CÚ CHULAINN), where Cú Roí is said to reside at a place called Teamhair Luachra in Munster. There does not appear to have been such a place, and it is likely that the whole story told in this text was originally concerned with the real Teamhair (TARA, County Meath). A petrified toponymic, Temhair Érann, survived in the ancient literature, and its original meaning must have referred to Tara having been in the possession of the Érainn people before the LAIGHIN (Leinstermen) and CONNACHTA in turn gained control of it.

This situation is also reflected in the tradition of another Érainn king, CONAIRE, who is cast in the role of ritual king to whom many fateful prohibitions (see GEIS)

attach. Among the conditions are that Conaire should not stay away from Tara for nine nights in succession, that he should not stay in a house from which firelight could be seen after sunset, and that a single woman or man should not enter his house after sunset. These seem to echo ancient ideas concerning a cosmic function of the king as guarantor of the life-giving energy of the sun. One very old text states that the king was prohibited from being in bed in Tara at sunrise and from travelling over the plain of Cuileann (in County Louth) after sunset. An idea that corresponds to all of this occurs regarding Cú Roí, though much ornamented and enhanced by a style-conscious medieval writer: 'Cú Roí never reddened his sword in Ireland from when he took arms until he died, and the food of Ireland did not pass his lips since when he had reached the age of seven for as long as he lived, because Ireland could not contain his pride or his fame or his supremacy or his valour or his strength or his courage ... In whatever part of the world Cú Roí should happen to be, he chanted over his fortress every night, so that it revolved as quickly as a millstone, and the entrance was never to be found after sunset.'

Other references to him are in a similarly striking vein. He wages campaigns in foreign parts, conquers countries in the eastern and southern world, and is even called by the title 'king of the world'. Such references accord with the theory that Cú Roí was Carausius, who was a great admiral, but the general drift of the ideas suggests a more ancient origin. Cú Roí 'traverses the briny stream', he 'holds helm on the southern sea', and his appearance is that of a 'blazing lion'. Notwithstanding their medieval flavour, these references all have solar symbolism, and it is not accidental that Conaire is haunted by the colour red and is consumed in a great fire, while the figure of Dáire was often associated with fire, with redness, and even with one-eyed figures (see GOLL MAC MORNA). This suggests that the lore of Cú Roí derives from the rituals of KINGSHIP, but that it has confused the complementary roles of the sun-deity as patron, and the sacred king as mediator who guarantees good fortune.

The Ulster Cycle, in which he occurs, preserves no direct accounts of Cú Roí's ritual role, but instead associates him with the west Munster area. This is to be expected, for the Érainn people were strongest in that area in the early literary period. His fortress is designated as Cathair Chon Roí (Caherconree on the Slemish mountain, west of Tralee), and it is from this base that he operates in the general corpus of the Cycle. In the text on the feast of BRICRIU, for instance, the three leading Ulster warriors go to Caherconree to have him decide which of them is the greatest. Cú Roí is not present when they arrive, but the huge phantom who tests them on their night watch is apparently him in disguise. He finally settles the matter between them by going to the Ulster court at Eamhain Mhacha in the shape of a massive and very ugly churl wearing a great dark-grey cloak. He proposes to each of the three warriors that they decapitate him and that he will do the same to them in return. Of the three, only Cú Chulainn is willing to fulfil his side of the bargain, and so Cú Roí names him as the champion. In the story of the Intoxication of the Ulstermen, however, Cú Roí is represented as a foe of Ulster and as foe even of Cú Chulainn. He is a close ally of MEADHBH and her husband Ailill mac Máta, and the fosterer of their son. Again, in *Táin Bó Cuailnge*, his forces (the Clann Deadhadh) are among Meadhbh's combined armies, although their part is a minor one. Cú Roí himself is a reluctant participant in that campaign. His only spectacular act during it is to engage in a great stone-throwing contest with the Ulster warrior Muinreamhar. Like CONALL CEARNACH, his role in tradition depended on other lore of the Ulster Cycle besides the *Táin*.

The best-known story of Cú Roí concerned his death, of which there were several medieval renderings. The story seems to have developed, or at least to have been put into the context of the Ulster Cycle, in the late ninth century. The earliest surviving version tells of how Cú Roí, disguised in a grey cloak, assisted the Ulstermen in a raid on a sept called Fir Fálgha. In the raid, several treasures were taken, including 'the three cows of Iuchna', a fine cauldron, and Bláthnaid, daughter of the Fir Fálgha king. When he was refused a share of the spoils, the enraged Cú Roí took these three best treasures – cattle, cauldron and woman – for himself. Cú Chulainn tried to prevent him, but was overcome by Cú Roí and had his hair shorn and he was daubed with cow dung. The great Cú Chulainn had to hide himself with shame for a year until his hair grew again. Bláthnaid, however, loved Cú Chulainn, and she schemed with him to come to Caherconree and destroy Cú Roí.

The earlier recension of the story states that she betrayed to Cú Chulainn the fact that Cú Roí's soul resided in a salmon in a certain pool, and that when Cú Chulainn killed that salmon with his rival's sword, Cú Roí's strength drained away. The somewhat later recensions have Bláthnaid asking Cú Roí to have a fine dwelling built for her. She arranged that when all his warriors were thus engaged collecting and erecting stones, she would give the signal to Cú Chulainn that her captor was undefended. This she did by letting some milk from the cows flow downstream to where Cú Chulainn was waiting with his forces. She secretly tied Cú Roí's hair to the bedpost after bathing him and, thus discommoded, he was slain by Cú Chulainn and most of his men slaughtered. Bláthnaid paid for her treachery, however, for Cú Roí's poet FEIRCHEIRDNE watched her closely until he found her standing on a cliff at Ceann Beara (probably on the Antrim coast). He threw himself at her, and both he and she were dashed against the rocks below. An obscure praise-poem on Cú Roí is also attributed to Feircheirdne, but it contains no references to further narratives.

The 'Fir Fálgha' were in reality the mid-Leinster sept known as the Uí Fháilghe, and this story has incorporated an independent LEGEND that told of a herd of cows owned by an ancient king of that people, called Iuchna Eachbhéal. According to

148

that legend, the cows loved Iuchna so much that they broke their horns in lamentation at his death. One speculative genealogical text has the same Iuchna as maternal uncle of Cú Roí, and this may have suggested the idea that Cú Roí would attempt to take the celebrated cows. The pre-existing theme of the cauldron of Cú Roí provided another valuable item for the story, while his reputation as a great warrior betrayed would attract the MOTIF of a treacherous wife. It is obvious that two sources have been used in connection with this latter motif – one being the biblical account of Samson and Delilah, and the other a plot from the common stock of folklore (see WONDER TALES, type 302). Cú Roí's appearance to the Ulstermen in disguise, and wearing a grey cloak, was borrowed from the story of Bricriu's feast.

The death-tale of Cú Roí seems to have been very popular in medieval lore, and it gave rise to the rather unconventional idea that Cú Chulainn had killed the famous salmon of the Boyne (see FIONN MAC CUMHAILL) and took away the wife of Ealcmhar (see NUADHU) there. It was equally popular with manuscript writers from the eleventh to the thirteenth century. These writers did not understand who the Fir Fálgha of the story were, with the result that they situated the great raid by Cú Roí and the Ulstermen at Cantyre in Scotland, or alternately on the Isle of Man. This latter was the place mentioned in the retelling by the historian Seathrún CÉITINN in the seventeenth century. A few tellings of the story have been collected from folklore, deriving directly from Céitinn's work, but otherwise no accounts of Cú Roí survived in later oral tradition.

ORIGINS: T.F. O'Rahilly (1946), 5–6, 77–80, 321–2; J. Rhys in *JRSAI*, 21, 651–7; R. Thurneysen in *ZCP*, 9, 232–3.
POEMS ON HIM: W. Stokes in *Ériu*, 2, 1–14; K. Meyer in *ZCP*, 3, 37–46; J. Rhys in *JRSAI*, 21, 652–3.
BRICRIU'S FEAST: Henderson (1899).
INTOXICATION OF ULSTERMEN: J.C. Watson (1941).
DEATH: R.I. Best in *Ériu*, 2, 18–35; Meyer in *RC*, 6, 187–8; R. Thurneysen in *ZCP*, 9, 189–234; J. Baudis in *Ériu*, 7, 200–9.
SALMON AND EALCMHAR: Meyer in *ZCP*, 8, 120; V. Hull in *ZCP*, 29, 305–14.
FOLKLORE: Bruford (1969), 95–7, 251.

Cumaine Fada *(c.AD591–662)* A learned Munster SAINT, and abbot of the monastery founded by BRÉANAINN at Clonfert. He was the author of a hymn in honour of the Apostles and of an influential penitential treatise. A praise-poem on him also survives, reputedly composed at his death. His appellation Cumaine was a common nickname, meaning 'stooped fellow' – the modern form of it is Cuimín. It would not appear to have been his original name, but was probably acquired, like his epithet (earlier written *Fota*), which means 'long' or 'tall'.

Several accounts of him are given in the medieval literature. According to a short and fanciful biography in Irish from the ninth or tenth century, he was son of Fiachna, king of the western section of the royal EOGHANACHT sept of Munster. We read that Fiachna, when intoxicated, begot the child on his own daughter and then ordered that it be thrown to the wild beasts. However, the baby was put in a milk pail and left on the arm of a cross outside the convent of Cill Íde (Killeedy, County Limerick), and the abbess discovered him there and fostered him, giving him the name Cumaine (Little Pail). When Cumaine learned of his origin, he went away to be educated by St BARRA at Cork, and spent twelve years studying there. An inspired fellow student told him that he would die in Corcach, so Cumaine hastily left that place. He went to visit his father's royal court – situated in the text at Cashel – and gave wise counsel to the king, who did not realise who the young cleric was. Everybody remarked on how closely the two resembled each other, and Cumaine spoke a verse to his father suggesting their relationship. When Fiachna understood, he promised Cumaine authority over all the monasteries in his territory, and in return Cumaine promised heaven to his father. This story of the incestuous birth and reconciliation to his father seems to be an early version of an international plot (see ROMANTIC TALES, type 933).

We read that Cumaine spent the rest of his life preaching throughout Ireland, and eventually came to a monastery at Corcach

Bheag in the territory of the Uí Fidhgheinte (a sept in east Limerick). He had been avoiding a place called Corcach all his life, and realised too late what name this location bore. The text is damaged at this point, but the account must have ended with his death. Variant later recensions of his biography have Cumaine's mother as queen of the DÉISE sept (in County Waterford), and have him as a baby being saved from the River Suir by the fisherman of St DÉAGLÁN and being reared by St ÍDE. As he grew up, he left her convent and wandered about idly until one day he took shelter in the hollow of a tree. A continuous dripping of rain filled that hollow, and meanwhile he noticed a man nearby building a house patiently with lathe upon lathe. Realising that learning could only be acquired in similar manner through patience, he returned to Íde's convent and resumed his studies. His connection with both Déaglán and Íde is anachronistic, both of these saints having been long dead before his birth. Also fanciful was the account of how he blessed an elderly and barren couple, thus causing them to give birth to St Molaga of Tulach Mhín (near Fermoy, County Cork).

A long tradition of verse and story makes Cumaine the half-brother of a famous Munster jester, COMHDHÁN, and both are involved in the early medieval story of LIADHAIN. One source states that Cumaine was 'the vessel of wisdom in his time', and his feast day was 12 November.

Kenney (1929), 241, 266, 420–1; G Mac Eoin in *Béaloideas, 39–41*, 192–205 & in *Ériu, 28*, 17–31; Stokes (1905), 242–3; F.J. Byrne in *Ériu, 31*, 111–22; Bernard & Atkinson (1898), *1*, 16–21 & *2*, 108; Stokes (1905), 242–3; O'Donovan (1864), 304–5; Meyer (1902), 16–23 & (1912), 43; J.G. O'Keeffe in *Irish Texts, 3*, 12–16; Ó Cadhlaigh (1939), 188–9; S Ó Coileáin in *Ériu, 25*, 92–113.

Cúscraidh Meann Macha

A fictional Ulster warrior and KING, son of CONCHOBHAR MAC NEASA. The name Cúscraidh (variant, Cumhscraidh) was found in the toponymic Inis Cúscraidh or Inis Cumhscraidh (Iniscourcey, near Downpatrick, County Down). Whoever this may originally have referred to, the developers of the ULSTER CYCLE imagined

him to have been a great warrior. The second part of the name must have been added later, for Meann Macha (conspicuous part of the plain) was the area around Tullycorbet in County Monaghan. The similar-sounding name Coscrach (the triumphant) occurred among the ancestors of the royal line of the AIRGHIALLA in that area, and this would explain why Meann Macha was applied as a sobriquet to the old fictional hero.

The medieval writers, however, selected for their purpose another meaning of the word *meann* – namely, stammerer. We read that Cúscraidh met and contended with the fierce Connacht fighter CEAT MAC MÁGHACH in a lonely place. Ceat wounded him in the neck with a javelin, and his vocal cords were thus damaged. Another source states that Ceat wounded him in the mouth, cutting away the tip of his tongue, and that the women of Ulster used to woo him afterwards by themselves affecting a stammer.

He is stated to have had a magnificent spear, with ferrules of silver that of their own accord whirled around bands of gold on the spear when conflict was imminent. Cúscraidh was the pupil of CONALL CEARNACH, and after the death of Conchobhar, Conall tried hard to secure the kingship for him. He refused that office, however, in order to avoid civil war among the Ulstermen. After the death of his brother CORMAC CONN LOINGEAS, he accepted the kingship and was given a series of wise counsels by Conall concerning how a king should behave. He ruled well, but after three years a dispute broke out again with Connacht over a patch of territory, and this led to war. The two armies met in a fierce battle at Airteach (Frenchpark, County Roscommon), and the Connachtmen were defeated, but Cúscraidh himself was slain by a warrior called Mac Éacht wielding a famous spear that once belonged to CEALTCHAR.

Once the character Cúscraidh Meann Macha became known to the literati, it was fancifully claimed that a sub-tribe of the ÉRAINN people in Munster, called Meannraighe, were descended from him.

NAME: E. Hogan (1910), 537, 676; MacLysaght (1973), 60.
COSCRACH: O'Brien (1962), 183, 420; Ó Muraíle, *2* (2003), 14.
GENERAL: Thurneysen (1935), 13–14; W. Stokes in *Irische Texte*, *3*, 404–5 & in *RC*, *21*, 150–1; R.I. Best in *Ériu*, *8*, 170–90; C. O'Rahilly (1976), 110, 302 & (1970), 120, 346; Ó Cadhlaigh (1956), 471.
MEANNRAIGHE: E. Hogan (1910), 537; O'Brien (1962), 279; Pender (1947), 214.

Daghdha A leading mythic character in Irish literature, one of the TUATHA DÉ DANANN, who was demonstrably the principal deity in ancient times. He is usually referred to with the definite article – namely, *an Daghdha* (the Daghdha).

The name (earlier, Dagdae) derives from a Celtic *dago-Dewios*. The second element in that Celtic designation (literally, 'sky') was cognate with other Indo-European terms for the male sky-deity (for example, Indic *Dyâus*, Latin *Deus*, Greek *Zeus*). The first element in the designation meant 'good', and thus the real meaning of his name was 'good GOD', though good not specifically in the moral sense but rather in the sense of technical precision. This explanation is given in the important text on the second Battle of Moytirra (*see* MYTHOLOGICAL CYCLE), when the Tuatha Dé were making their military preparations.

From the surviving portrayals, he can be identified with the father-god whom Caesar claimed was regarded by the Gauls as their ancestral deity. Medieval texts in fact state that the Daghdha had the alternative name EOCHAIDH Ollathair, the sobriquet here meaning 'father of many'. He was also known by appellations indicating blazing brightness, such as Aedh Álainn (Fiery Lustrous One) and AODH RUADH RÓ-FHEASA. This suggests his identification with the sun rather than the sky, and it seems that an earlier indigenous sun-cult influenced the image of the sky-deity among the western Celts. References to the Daghdha under such names portray him as an ancestral figure distinguished by great wisdom (*see also* FIONN).

The Daghdha was said to have had as his residence Brugh na Bóinne (the tumulus at Newgrange on the bank of the River Boyne in County Meath). This was in fact a great Stone Age passage tomb – dating to the third millennium BC – through the long passage of which the sun shines at the winter solstice. It is obvious that the archaic people who built the site placed great emphasis on social renewal by the sun. When Celtic culture reached the area, it was therefore natural that the Celtic sun-god be domiciled there. A frequent theme in the old literature is that Brugh na Bóinne was the residence of the Daghdha. In that role, he is described as the father of the youth-deity AONGHUS, having caused the sun to stop for nine months so that the youth could be conceived and born discretely. When Aonghus grew up, however, he tricked the Daghdha out of possession by a verbal trick – he borrowed the residence for a night and a day and then claimed that all eternity was encompassed by counting TIME in this way. The verbal trick played on the father-deity appears to have been a medieval dramatisation of early lore. According to this lore of the DRUIDS, time was composed of darkness for the dead and light for the living (*see* DONN *and* FIONN), and the father-deity relinquished his control over the affairs of the living to the presiding king (*see* KINGSHIP). There was probably an amalgam of such Celtic ideas with an earlier and indigenous rite of the Newgrange tumulus concerning how generations displace each other just as the new sun displaces the old.

Some basic attributes of the Daghdha are described in the account of the second Battle of Moytirra. These attributes are hugeness, generosity and a voracious appetite. He possessed a mighty cauldron from which 'no company ever went away unsatisfied', and the narrative again and again stresses the massive and momentous nature of his imagery. He is represented as willingly building a fortress for king BREAS, and then being forced to build a great rampart around that fortress. During this work, he was deprived of food due to the demands of the satirist CRIDHINBHÉAL and his life was miserable. However, through the advice of his son, the Mac Óg (i.e. AONGHUS) he outwitted both Cridhinbhéal and Breas, and chose as payment for his work a single black heifer from Breas' herd. This heifer he later used to entice back all the cattle the FOMHÓIRE oppressors had taken from the Tuatha Dé, for when she called her calf it attracted them.

The images of progenitor and gourmand also surface in the Moytirra text. Before the battle, we are told, he went to a tryst with the MÓR-RÍOGHAIN, goddess of land and of war, on the bank of the River Unshin in Connacht. She had one foot on either side of the river when the Daghdha mated with her there. Then he went to a parley at the Fomhóire camp, and they – knowing that he loved porridge – filled a great cauldron with it for him and added vast quantities of milk and meat. They poured all this mixture into a hole in the ground and forced him to eat it. He took his ladle, which was big enough for a man and a woman to lie together in it, and ate the whole meal, scraping up even the gravel in the process. His belly was greatly distended as a result, and he fell asleep. On awakening, he left the camp, dragging his mighty club after him. The club was so massive that eight men would be required to carry it. He had it mounted on wheels, and as he dragged it along, the wheels made a track as deep as a dyke between provinces. He soon met a beautiful young woman of the Fomhóire and sought intercourse with her, but his huge belly made this impossible. The woman mocked him and flung him to the ground, and after he had disgorged himself, he mated with her. She then promised magical assistance to the Tuatha Dé in the forthcoming battle, as the Mór-Ríoghain had also promised. When the battle was joined, the Daghdha wrought havoc on the foe with his mighty club.

These passages are full of crude humour, but in them the writer is burlesquing what were in reality ancient mythical ideas of copiousness and fertility in association with the deity. At the end of the text, a more exalted capability is attributed to the Daghdha when he expertly plays the three kinds of magical music on a harp. In the text on the first Battle of Moytirra, he is claimed to have been a god of druidry, and is described as using the great club with deadly effect in the fight. His magical power is stressed in direct association with the club in a passage in an eighth-century text. Here we are told that the club had a rough end and a smooth one. When he put the rough end on the heads of nine men together, it slew them immediately, and when he put the smooth end on them, they were revived. The emphasis on his club and cauldron recall the Gaulish deity Sucellos (literally, 'good striker') who was portrayed on monuments as having a mallet and a jar. Sucellos was often represented in the company of the river GODDESS Nantosuelta, so it is reasonable to assume that the Gaulish 'Sucellos' was a pseudonym for *dago-Dewios* and thus identical with the Daghdha.

Traits of the Daghdha mentioned in the literature include cunning, sternness and strength. Although often thought of as a ponderous personage, adjectives (such as *dian* and *deis*) indicating swiftness are also coupled with the name of the Daghdha; like other deities (for example, DIAN CÉACHT), this would suggest that he was able to make himself available without delay to his devotees. His great cauldron, which is claimed to have been brought into Ireland from abroad by the Tuatha Dé Danann, may in origin have been connected with his solar imagery (*see* CÚ ROÍ *and* DÁIRE). Interestingly, he is also referred to as *Daghdha donn* – the epithet here can be taken to mean 'swarthy', but it also echoes the father-deity's guise as DONN.

Although an ancestral and therefore original figure, the medieval writers were very keen to attribute a genealogy to the Daghdha. In pseudo-history he is claimed to have been, like Breas, a son of Ealatha, which would give him Fomhóire paternity. This might well be a reflection of his association with fecundity, which would coincide with the agricultural imagery of the Fomhóire. In the account of the second Battle of Moytirra, he is said to have had two brothers, NUADHU and OGHMA, but this is no more than a late instance of the tendency to triplicate deities. Elsewhere there is no scarcity of references to his immediate family. One medieval account, obviously echoing earlier lore, makes him the husband of the Mór-Ríoghain, and he is also stated to have been lover or husband of the eponymous river-goddess BÓINN. By the latter he was father of Aonghus (q.v.), for whom he gained possession of Brugh na Bóinne (the Newgrange tumulus in County Meath). That landmark, we are told, was built by the Daghdha himself, and another great edifice attributed to his labours was the Grianán of Aileach (in County Donegal, a few miles from Derry city).

As ruler over the Tuatha Dé, it is said that the Daghdha determined the residences of the various leaders of that divine people. When he himself lost Brugh na Bóinne to Aonghus, he had to resort to several other residences of his own. These included the tumuli at Leithead Lachtmhaighe (Leadmore, near Kilrush, County Clare) and at Cnoc Báine (Ballygawley, near Clogher, County Tyrone); but, most strikingly, the cairn on top of the mountain called Ó Chualann (the Sugerloaf, in north County Wicklow), from which he could look northwards towards the great Brugh.

Several Tuatha Dé worthies were said to have been children of the Daghdha, including Aodh Caomh, Cearmaid and BRIGHID, and one source even goes so far as to make DIAN CÉACHT his son. An account of a daughter called Ainge states that the Daghdha made a tub for her that would drip while the sea was in flood and become stable when the sea subsided. His hugeness is emphasised in one text by the casual, though serious, remark that his countenance was 'broader than half a plain'. Another text has him clearing twelve plains in one night, and cutting the path of twelve rivers in another night, and describes him as controlling the WEATHER and the crops for the Tuatha Dé. This aetiological and environmental sense in the lore of the Daghdha underlines his divinity. The story of how his son Cearmaid was slain by Lugh, after he sought to seduce the latter's wife, reflects some ancient lore of sexual jealousy connected

with the Daghdha, for similar themes occur in accounts of two other sons of his. These were Aodh Caomh – who was slain by the jealous husband after he had seduced the wife of Corrchend – and Conán, who was killed while trying to win a maiden called Cealg from her father.

The literary writers did not hesitate to invent new stories of the Daghdha. A tenth-century source has him using his club to expel a sea-monster and making the sea itself recede, thereby causing to surface the plain of Muirtheimhne (in north County Louth). Continuing fascination with the great club is evidenced by a text from about the twelfth century that purports to tell its origin. In this, after Cearmaid was slain by Lugh, the Daghdha put the dead body of his son on his back and set out for the eastern world in search of a resuscitating cure. He met three men carrying TREASURES along the road, and one of these treasures was the club. He inveigled it from them to examine it, and then touched the three with its killing end. He touched Cearmaid with the revivifying end, and his son was restored to life and health. He finally revived the three strangers, and they allowed him to keep the club on permanent loan.

The Daghdha's own death was claimed by the pseudo-historians to have taken place as the result of a wound inflicted by a woman. This was Ceithlinn, wife of BALAR, with whom – according to some versions of the second Battle of Moytirra – he engaged in single combat. She stabbed him with a javelin, and though he survived the wound, it continued to trouble him. He succeeded Lugh as king and ruled over the Tuatha Dé for 80 years, but eventually the wound took its toll and he died from it. This reworking of the tradition, with its strained chronology, is due to the pseudo-historians. A text of around the ninth century, with its timelessness, is nearer to the mythic perspective. Here the Daghdha is represented as still living when the Tuatha Dé were overcome by their successors, the sons of Míl. As part of the struggle, the Tuatha Dé destroyed the corn and milk of the newcomers, but when the sons of Míl made peace with the Daghdha, he returned these products to them.

Later mentions of the Daghdha make him the father of other Tuatha Dé personages such as BODHBH DEARG and MIDHIR, but his image did not undergo much further development.

DERIVATION OF NAME: Mallory & Adams (1997), 230–1.

OTHER NAMES: Gray (1982), 44–5; T.F. O'Rahilly (1946), 466–7; Meyer (1912), 98; W. Stokes in *Irische Texte*, 3, 354–7; Macalister (1941), 120–1.

NEWGRANGE: *See* AONGHUS. Also Ó hÓgáin (1999), 23, 60–4, 107–10.

CAULDRON & CLUB: Gray (1982), 24–5; J.C. Watson (1941), 27–9.

MOYTIRRA: Gray (1982), 24–5; J.C. Watson (1941), 28–31, 42–51; 54–5, 70–1; J. Frazer in *Ériu*, 8, 16–17, 30–3, 38–9, 44–5.

SUCELLOS: Thévenot (1968), 133–42; Sjoestadt (1982), 52–7.

TRAITS: L. Gwynn in *Ériu*, 7, 219–16; E. Gwynn (1906), 18–21.

MÓR-RÍOGHAIN: Gray (1982), 44–5; Gwynn (1906), 18–19 & (1924), 196–201.

BÓINN: Gwynn (1906), 10–11, 18–21.

EDIFICES: Gwynn (1906), 18–19 & (1924), 92–121.

HIS OTHER RESIDENCES: V. Hull in *ZCP*, 19, 55.

HIS CHILDREN: Macalister (1941), 120–1, 158–9; Gwynn (1924), 92–121, 292–3, 350–3, 362–7; O. Bergin in *Loomis Studies* (1927), 400–2. For Cearmaid *see also* LUGH.

ENVIRONMENT: Stokes (1892), 8–9; Gwynn (1924), 108–9; Bergin & Best in *Ériu*, 12, 142–51.

MUIRTHEIMHNE: Van Hamel (1933), 35–6; Gwynn (1924), 294, 454.

ACQUISITION OF CLUB: O. Bergin in *Loomis Studies* (1927), 402–6.

DEATH: Ó Cuív (1945), 7, 48; Macalister (1941), 184–5.

WAR WITH SONS OF MÍL: V. Hull in *ZCP*, 19, 55–7.

GENERAL: Gray (1982), 121; Olmsted (1994), 43–7.

Dáire Name of a mythical personage in early Irish lore. Literally it meant 'the fruitful one', and there are several indications that it was an alternative designation for the DAGHDHA. Dáire was honoured by the ancient Érainn people, a group of which – in the area of present County Armagh – owed their collective name, Dáirine, to him.

The Daghdha was regarded as a great ancestor, and Dáire fulfils the same function through his frequent occurrences in the early portions of genealogies. In these, he is given various identities – such as Dáire Doimhtheach, Dáire Barrach, Dáire mac Sídhe Bhoilg and Dáire mac Deadhadh – in order to render the different pedigrees credible. In a seventh-century biography of St PATRICK, he parallels the Daghdha more immediately by being the possessor of a fine bronze cauldron, brought to Ireland from abroad. The cauldron MOTIF occurs again in the context of the mythical CÚ ROÍ, who is represented as son of Dáire. Like Cú Roí also, a character called Dáire Sírchréachtach was fancifully claimed to have made many conquests abroad, and it is thus apparent that the images of Cú Roí and Dáire were synonymous at some stage of tradition. Elsewhere we find the name Dáire being given to the owner of the great bull, the DONN CUAILNGE, and appellations of characters such as Dáire Donn and Dáire Dearg indicate that the name was originally on a functional par with others, such as DONN and DEARG.

It is noticeable that Dáire mac Deadhadh appeared in early Munster lore as a KING to whom it was prophesied that he would die if his daughter gave birth to a son. This seems to have been a borrowing from the tradition of FIONN MAC CUMHAILL (*see* NÓINE). Again, in the FIANNA tradition, the name Dáire occurs in alignment with GOLL to designate a figure hostile to Fionn, and this can be explained by the early influence of Balar's prophesied grandson LUGH on Fionn's image.

T.F. O'Rahilly (1946), 7, 48–9, 210, 275–6, 454–5, 551; Olmsted (1994), 44–5; O'Donovan (1849), 4–5; C. O'Rahilly (1962), 1, 39; K. Meyer in *RC*, 5, 197; G. Murphy (1933), 66–73; O'Brien, 189, 288; Ó hÓgáin (1988), 14–15, 357.

Dál gCais Sept of County Clare. The designation means 'tribe of Cas', referring to an ancestor of theirs called Cas, who lived early in the fifth century AD.

In origin, the sept derived from the DÉISE of south-east Munster, a branch of whom settled in the area that became known as Déis Bheag (the east of County Limerick). The northernmost of these 'little Déise' had as their centre the hill fort of Carn Fhearadhaigh (Cahernorry). In time, they moved further north, to a place near the banks of the River Shannon, where a fortress was erected by Cairtheann, grandson of Cas. With the advent of Christianity, a church was erected there and became known as Saingeal (literally, 'chancel', now Singland, east of Limerick city). This church was dedicated to St PATRICK, and the Dál gCais were later to claim that, during his mission, Patrick himself had visited Cairtheann there and had left his blessing on the sept. Singland became an important sacred site in the lore of the Dál gCais, and in later times the tradition grew up that the last great battle in Ireland would be fought there.

The sons of Cairtheann lost no time in subduing some territory to the north of the river, in present-day County Clare. One of them, Aonghus, settled in the flat countryside between the Rivers Fergus and Shannon. His descendants were dominant within the sept for several generations, inaugurating their chieftain, or 'KING', under a great tree that grew on a mound on the plain of Magh Adhair, about 6 kilometres west of Tulla. To the east, in the hilly country at the bend of the Shannon, was the settlement of Aonghus' brother Eochaidh 'Red-Spot'. Towards the end of the sixth century, a grandson of this Eochaidh – called Aodh Caomh – built a fortress on the lower slope of Craig Liath (the Hill of Crag), overlooking the southern tip of Lough Derg. This hill had been associated with the land-GODDESS of pre-Christian belief, known in that area as AOIBHEALL, and the goddess lived on in Dál gCais lore as a FAIRY lady, the patroness and protectress of the sept.

In terms of Christianity, too, the sept were determined. It was either Aodh Caomh or his son Cathal who welcomed St DALUA to the area in the early seventh century, and the sept soon had a special SAINT of their own: FLANNÁN, son of Toirdhealbhach, grandson of Aodh Caomh. The saint's father Toirdhealbhach, through his other son Mathghamhain, was the progenitor of the line that became dominant in the whole sept. Later Dál gCais historians would claim that – to foreshadow their future triumph – Toirdhealbhach cut down an ancient yew tree, symbol of the royal EOGHANACHT sept, at Emly, County Tipperary.

The rise to such power was to be slow and difficult, however, particularly because of the activities of the NORSEMEN in the Limerick area. When Toirdhealbhach's descendant Lorcán became chieftain of the sept in AD 934, he constructed a strong new fortress of stone called *Ceann Cora*, meaning 'head of the weir' (in English, 'Kincora'). It was situated on the low hill where the Catholic church now stands in the town of Killaloe. Lorcán's son Cinnéide continued the war against the Norsemen, as did his son again, Mathghamhain, who in 964 wrested the kingship of Munster from the royal EOGHANACHT sept. Upon the assassination of Mathghamhain in 976, his brother, the famous BRIAN BÓRAMHA, became leader.

Descendants of the Dál gCais were very numerous. The genealogists list many surnames, including the following:
Mac Bruaidí (Brody); Mac Con Mara (MacNamara); Mac Eochaidh (Keogh of north Munster); Mac Fhlannchaidh (Clancy); Mac Raith, later Mac Craith (McGrath of north Munster); Ó hAichir (Hehir); Ó hÁinle (Hanly); Ó hArtagáin (Hartigan); Ó Beoláin (Boland of Munster); Ó Cearnaigh (Kearney of Munster); Ó Céilleachair (Kelleher); Ó Cinnéide (Kennedy); Ó Coinn (Quin of Munster); Ó Coirc (Quirke); Ó Con Duibh (Conway of north Munster); Ó Conaing (Gunning); Ó Deadha (O'Dea); Ó Floinn (Flynn of north Munster); Ó Fionnmhacáin (Finucane); Ó Gráda (O'Grady); Ó hEachiarainn (Ahearne, Ahern, Heron); Ó hIcí (Hickey); Ó hIfearnáin (Heffernan); Ó hÓgáin (Hogan); Ó hUrthaile (Hurley); Ó Loingsigh (Lynch of Clare); Ó Lonargáin (Lonergan); Ó Maoldhomhnaigh (Moloney, Downey); Ó Meadhra (O'Meara); Ó Riagáin (Regan); Ó Seancháin (Shanahan); Ó Seasnáin (Sexton); Ó Síocháin and Ó Séacháin (Sheehan, Sheahan); Ó Slatraigh (Slattery).

For the most famous Dál gCais surname, Ó Briain (O'Brien), and its offshoots, *see* BRIAN BÓRAMHA.

GENERAL: Todd (1867), cvi–cxxxiv, 247; Heist (1965), 290; O'Brien (1962), 235–45, 427; Ó Donnchadha (1940), 293–325; F.J. Byrne (1973), 180–1, 325; Ó Muraíle, *2* (2003), 598–645 & *3*, 680–95.

SINGLAND PROPHECY: D. Ó hÓgáin in *Béaloideas, 42–4*, 251–3; Ó Foghludha (1938), 47.

Dallán Forgaill POET who lived at the end of the sixth century AD, composer of a celebrated hymn in honour of St COLM CILLE entitled the *Amhra* (literally, 'marvel'). 'Dallán Forgaill' meant 'the blind man of eloquence', and was really a nickname.

According to the medieval literature, Dallán was the chief-poet of Ireland and was indebted to Colm Cille for this position. It was claimed that the SAINT had successfully pleaded the case of the poets at the Convention of Drom Ceat (in County Derry) in the year 575. Dallán had been banned from composing and the poets in general were in danger of being banished from the country until Colm reconciled them to the UÍ NÉILL high-king Aodh mac Ainmhireach and to the nobles. As part of the solution, Colm insisted that Dallán, on account of his surpassing knowledge and skill, be made the chief-poet (*ard-ollamh*). Dallán began soon after to compose the *Amhra* for Colm, but the latter, out of humility, forbade him to go beyond the prologue. Colm did, however, give him permission to compose the full eulogy once the saint himself had died, and told him that his sight would be restored for the purpose. Dallán asked how he would know if and when Colm had died, and the saint told him that a man on a speckled HORSE would bring the news, and that the first words that man would speak to him should be used to begin the poem. Dallán did accordingly after the saint's death in AD 597, and so the *Amhra* began with the words '*ní disceoil d'uibh Néill*' (it is no paltry news for the descendants of Niall). Colm was the great saint of this royal sept.

The medieval writers knew little about Dallán himself, but the general tradition was that he belonged to the Masraighe sept of the ULAIDH and that he was a native of Maighin (Moynehall, just south of Cavan town). His real name is given as Eochaidh son of Colla, and some writers identified him with EOCHAIDH ÉIGEAS. This seems to be a confusion due to a shared name, however, and one medieval quatrain mentions as three leading and distinct poets SEANCHÁN, Eochaidh Éigeas and Dallán

Forgaill. There are some indications that Eochaidh Éigeas was the eldest of these three, and that Dallán inherited his position as leading poet, while Seanchán was definitely the youngest. Early sources refer to Dallán as *mac Forgaill* (son of Forgall) or even as *ua Forgaill* (indicating a grandson). Neither of these appellations intend Forgall as the name of a progenitor, but rather that the poet Dallán was the 'essence' of wise declaration.

In two early stories, a poet called Forgall is described as being present at the palace of MONGÁN at Moylinny, County Antrim. It is possible that this is a genuine tradition, for the cycle of stories concerning Mongán apparently derives from eulogies composed for him by poets. Forgall is here described as proud and rapacious, a factor that leads to suspicion that the lore of the Drom Ceat convention is in the background. The strong likelihood is that by this Forgall was meant Dallán himself, albeit portrayed in a manner not necessarily true to character. Mongán died a reasonably young man in the year 624, and the dating would thus accord with the idea that he and Dallán were acquaintances.

The medieval literature claims that Seanchán succeeded Dallán as chief-poet, and there is no compelling reason to doubt this. However, an account grew up of the circumstances that is definitely romance rather than history. We read that he was inveigled by Aodh Fionn, king of Breifne (the Cavan area), to go and seek a fine shield from a rival, Aodh mac Duach, king of Airghialla (the general area of south Ulster). Dallán accordingly went and recited a poem in praise of the Airghialla king, and then demanded the shield as payment. The king offered gold and silver and herds of cattle, but refused to part with his shield, and then Dallán threatened to satirise him. Aodh mac Duach protested that such extortion had been forbidden by Colm Cille and the other saints at Drom Ceat, but Dallán recited a demeaning poem and then departed. Because he had abused his art, he lived but three days thereafter. On his deathbed, he proclaimed that Seanchán was the most worthy to succeed him, and that poet came and recited an eulogy over his corpse, describing him as the greatest poet of Ireland and comparing his intellect to 'a great flooding of the sea-tide'.

His association with Colm Cille, and the pious nature of his celebrated poem in praise of that saint, caused Dallán himself to be regarded by ecclesiastical historians as an especially holy person. Already by the eighth century he was being described as a saint and had a feast day, 19 January, allotted to him. Furthermore, due to the fame of the *Amhra* for Colm Cille, a tendency grew for similar associations to be made between him and other saints. Thus in or about the ninth century, a short *Amhra* for SEANÁN was attributed to him, undoubtedly at the instigation of that saint's community in Scattery Island on the Shannon. In later medieval times, Dallán was claimed to have composed a praise-poem for St CONALL CAOL of Inishkeel, County Donegal, and this type of pious portrayal of him continued in stark contradiction to the secular lore. We read that he was once visiting the monastery of Conall Caol when sea pirates attacked and beheaded him. They flung his head into the sea, but it was swept ashore, and when one of Conall's monks placed it on his body, it stuck thereto as before, so that he was buried whole at Inishkeel. This story, though unhistorical, is the only account of Dallán to have survived in folklore. The real place of Dallán's burial is unknown, but he can hardly have lived long into the seventh century.

W. Stokes in *RC, 20*, 31–55, 132–83, 248–89, 400–37 & *RC, 21*, 133–6 & in *ZCP, 3*, 220–5 & (1905), 54–5, 414; O'Donovan (1864), 30–1; Connelan (1860), 258–62; J. Travis in *Speculum, 19*, 89–103; Meyer, *1* (1895), 45–56; Joynt (1941), 1–9; O'Kelleher & Schoepperle (1918), 486; O'Hanlon, *1* (1875), 496–503; S. Ó Coileáin in *Ériu, 28*, 33–7; Ó Searcaigh (1967), 23–5, 42–3; IFC 948:45.

Dalua

Dalua SAINT of the late sixth century. His name meant 'the beloved Lua', and is synonymous with that of another and different saint, MOLUA.

According to a text that may go back to the eighth century, St CAINNEACH once came upon a gruesome sight in south Leinster – a group of men were sacrificing a boy by flinging him into the air so that he would fall on the points of their spears. By the saint's prayer, the boy was not injured by his fall, but was so terrified by the ordeal that his eyes were crooked to the end of his days. This boy was Lua, and the local king Cormac mac Diarmada gave him to Cainneach. He seems to have been educated in that saint's monastery at Aghaboe (in County Laois), and in time became noted for sanctity.

Coming as a vagrant holy man to the territory of the DÁL GCAIS – which sept at the time held territory straddling the River Shannon in east Clare and north Limerick – Lua was welcomed to the area. The sept's chieftain – either Aodh Caomh or his son Cathal – encouraged Lua to erect a hermit's cell, which he did on a little island in the river. This island was later called Inis Lua or Friar's Island, and the little foundation there became famous as a place of pilgrimage in succeeding generations. Either the place of embarkation on the western side of the river – about a kilometre upstream from the island – took its name from that cell, or else Dalua founded another cell at that place. At any rate, the location on the bank of the river has long been known as Cill Dalua (the modern picturesque town of Killaloe).

The island itself was submerged in the hydro-electric scheme of 1930, and the remains of the little cell were brought to the town of Killaloe and reconstructed there in the grounds of the Catholic church. The feast day of Dalua is 11 May. *See also* FLANNÁN.

Kenney (1929), 395, 404, Heist (1965), 193; Kierse (1983), 20–2.

Damer, Joseph

Damer, Joseph *(1630–1720)* An English entrepreneur who moved to Ireland in 1662 and bought up large estates from Cromwellian settlers in County Tipperary. He filled these lands with SHEEP, and set up a very successful business in the export of wool. He also set up a banking business in Dublin and became so rich that the English government itself was heavily in debt to him.

Damer had the reputation of being a

miser. Dean SWIFT, who disliked him, wrote that 'he walked the streets and wore a threadbare cloak, he dined and supped at charge of other folk'. He never married, and at his death left his great wealth to two nephews – the property at Roscrea to his namesake Joseph, and his own house and surrounding estate at Shronell to John. The total will amounted to nearly half a million pounds, a stupendous sum for the time, and it is doubtlessly from this that the common Irish proverb 'as rich as Damer' derives. Amazement and speculation gave rise to much folklore concerning how he first became rich. Joseph Damer had begun his career as a civil servant in Cromwell's administration, and so it was said that he had stumbled onto the TREASURES of one of the monasteries confiscated in Ireland. The treasure had been hidden by the monks in barrels covered with tallow, and it was fancied that Damer had been a chandler who bought these 'tallow-barrels' and found to his surprise and delight what they contained.

After his death, the mantle of archetypal magnate fell on his nephew John, who married in 1726. It was, however, an unsuccessful alliance. Folklore claims that his wife eloped with an army officer, and this Damer also was childless. Around the year 1740 he commenced the building of a huge mansion at Shronell. This mansion, of which only a portion of the wall now remains, was said to have had a window for every day of the year. Folk accounts of John have a large element of farce. It is said that he went about in rags, while he had his servants magnificently accoutred for the sake of pomp, and that he used even to come in disguise to the servants and beg money from them. There was reputedly a secret room in his mansion, with its doors heavily padlocked, and in this room he had stored an incredible treasure of golden sovereigns. He loved to spend long periods alone in this vault, gazing at the glittering sovereigns and delightedly letting them run through his fingers.

A story grew up about him, which is in reality a variant of one of Aesop's fables (*see* HUMOROUS TALES, type 1305A).

According to this, a travelling tailor came to him one day and offered to make a proper suit of clothes for him. He immediately asked how much would that cost, and the tailor said that all he required as payment was one look at Damer's gold. The magnate thought the tailor was a foolish fellow and that this was a good bargain, so he agreed. When the fine suit was finished, he brought the tailor to his secret room and showed him the gold. The tailor looked at it for a little while and Damer, growing curious, enquired what could he gain from this. 'It does me the same good to be looking at it,' said the tailor, 'as it does yourself, sir!'

When John died in 1768, the enormous wealth passed to his nephew, again called Joseph, and the son of this Joseph was an inveterate spendthrift who frittered away his vast inheritance on gambling, drinking and expensive clothes. The theme of futility was thus complete, and folklore continually added to its accounts of the gold of 'great Damer' – who was, in reality, a composite character drawn from the various eccentric members of that family. Many kinds of MOTIFS involving acquisitiveness became attached to the name in Munster tradition. A popular international FOLKTALE told of a trickster who made a contract for as many sovereigns as would fill his hat, and so it was said that Damer struck such a bargain with the devil in return for his soul. The shrewd Damer tricked the evil one by putting a hole in his hat and placing it over a hole in the floor of his mansion. There was a huge room underneath, into which the sovereigns continued to shower, and in exasperation the devil withdrew from the deal, forfeiting the huge amount of sovereigns to Damer. Another story had it that Damer was originally a poor rat-catcher and that he was employed by a rich lady to clear her house of the pests. He stole a huge amount of gold sovereigns from her by secreting them in the bellies of the dead rats as he disposed of them.

The final loss of Damer's great wealth was also the subject of speculation. It was said that jackdaws found their way into his vault and, coin by coin, took away all the bright metal objects in their beaks. Some tree cutters in the area were reported to have become wealthy later through the unexpected windfall from the birds' nests. There is some evidence that the charge of callous greed laid against Damer was not justified in the cases of any of the bearers of the name. However, the vast wealth contrasted strongly with the general living conditions of the time, and was in itself a very dramatic phenomenon. It was therefore ideal material for folklore, which has a strong tendency to personalise memories and to put ideas into physical form.

A.M. Fraser in *Dublin Historical Record*, 3, 41–53; J.M. Hone in *Studies*, 39, 419–26; D.J. O'Sullivan in *Journal of the Irish Folk Song Society*, 25, 37–9; Danaher (1964), 112; S. Ó Duilearga in *Béaloideas*, 29, 27, 138; D. Ó hÓgáin in Nolan & MacGrath (1985), 139–47, 446–8.
FOLKLORE PLOTS: Aarne & Thompson (1961), types 1130 (hole in hat), 1305–1305A; S. Thompson (1955–1958), motifs B756, M210–211, N527, Q272.

Danu Mother-GODDESS referred to in the MYTHOLOGICAL CYCLE and in some ancient toponymics. The name occurs only in the form *Danann* (earlier, *Danand*), a refashioned nominative. This form was more properly the genitive, as in the significant description of the otherworld beings as TUATHA DÉ DANANN (literally, 'peoples of the goddess Danu'). 'Danand' or 'Danann' is described in the medieval literature as a *bandé* (goddess), and sometimes as a mythical *bandruí* (DRUIDESS).

This goddess must have been worshipped from antiquity by the Celts, for several river names in Europe – most notably the Danube – are based on a Celtic word *Dánuv*. This would appear to have been the name of an Indo-European river-goddess with a form such as Dehanu – which survived in the figure of Dánu, a river-goddess in Sanskrit literature, and also perhaps in the mythical Greek princesses called Danaides, one of whom discovered a river that never dried up. In medieval Welsh literature, a lady called Dôn is described as the mother of a family of mythical wizards, a factor that strongly suggests her identity with the Irish goddess.

The name Danu was identified by medieval Irish writers with 'Anu'. This latter (alternately, 'Ana'), seems to have been a pet name for 'mother', and when applied to Danu was fancifully connected with an Old Irish word *anai*, which meant 'wealth'. Thus Anu is described as the goddess to whom the province of Munster owed its special prosperity. Two mountain tops near Killarney, County Kerry were called Dá Chích nAnann (literally, 'the Two Paps of Anu'), and a ninth-century glossary states of Anu that 'good was the food which she gave'. The status of mother-goddess is strongly suggested by the glossary, which declares that Anu was 'the mother of the Irish gods' – a near-enough equivalent to the Welsh Dôn.

It is clear that the Irish goddess was associated with the land rather than with rivers, but this change of function could have taken place in antiquity – the fructifying waters giving rise to fertility of the soil. Another early text calls Ireland *iath nAnann* (the land of Anu). This usage, like the toponymic Dá Chích nAnann, would have rendered the final element similar, and later identical, in sound with 'nDanann', and it may indeed have been such usages that allowed Danu to be referred to with ease as Anu. As a land-goddess, she was identified by the writers with the MÓR-RÍOGHAIN, which seems to have originally been an epithetical title for her. It is likely, indeed, that Danu was originally the proper name that lies behind several designations, such as ÁINE, BADHBH, BRIGHID and other titular names of Irish goddesses.

Little narrative concerning Danu is found in the literature. She is claimed to have been the mother of the three brothers who killed the father of LUGH. Their father was Tuireall, and Danu's association with them is due to the designation of Tuatha Dé Danann as Trí Dé Danann, which left the impression that she had three sons. Tuireall was claimed to have been an alternative name for Dealbhaoth, described as Danu's own father, but this piece of incestuous scandal is nothing more than a product of the imagination of some medieval writer. Even more obviously fictional is a medieval account that has her (under the name Donand) being slain by a warrior of the FOMHÓIRE called Dé Domhnand.

Danu was in fact given varying paternities, causing some writers to imagine various mythical ladies bearing the name. Ultimately, as mother-goddess, Danu was not in need of parentage.

INDO-EUROPEAN SOURCE: Mallory & Adams (1997), 174, 232, 487; Rees & Rees (1973), 50–3, 364; Holder, 1 (1891), 1224–38; M. Müller in RC, 1, 135–6.

DANU/ANU IN IRELAND: G. Murphy (1953), 208–10; Meyer (1912), 3; W. Stokes in Irische Texte, 3, 288–9; E.J. Gwynn in Ériu, 13, 40, 63; Macalister (1941), 122–3, 128–3, 156–7, 160–1, 188–9, 192–3, 208–9, 226–7; Gray (1982), 122–3; M.C. Dobbs in RC, 49, 442; Olmsted (1994), 367, 479; Ó hÓgáin (1999), 64–8.

de Courcy, John (c. 1150–1219) A NORMAN leader who was a fierce fighter and who conquered much of the north of Ireland in 1177. He was chief governor of Ireland between 1185 and 1195, but lost the favour of King John I and was dispossessed by Norman rivals, the de Lacys, in 1205. He was imprisoned for a while in England, but was released and seems to have died at sea.

During his reign in Ulster, de Courcy was a generous patron of the Benedictine monks. He founded a large establishment for them near his headquarters in Downpatrick, and encouraged them to develop prophecies in his favour. One of the great traditions cultivated by the Benedictines in France was the chivalric one concerning Ogier the Dane. This Ogier, or Othgerius, was reputedly one of the chief knights of the Christian Frankish emperor Charlemagne in the ninth century. It was said that he had quarrelled with Charlemagne and had been imprisoned, but was released to lead a successful campaign against Saracen invaders of the Frankish empire. It is apparent that this legendary MOTIF was applied to de Courcy in the time of his misfortune.

A written Latin version of this de Courcy legend was in existence in or about 1565, when it was translated into English in the Book of Howth, on behalf of the St Lawrence family, lords of Howth, who were descended from de Courcy's sister. According to it, when de Courcy was imprisoned in the Tower of London, the English and French kings agreed to settle a dispute over a castle by a single combat between their champions. Unable to find a suitable champion, King John sent emissaries to de Courcy, who was lying miserable and unkempt in a dungeon. After much persuasion, de Courcy agreed, but demanded that his great sword be brought from Downpatrick to him. Upon seeing his ferocious appearance, the French champion fled the field, and de Courcy then asked that a large piece of timber be placed in the ground, with a coat of mail and a helmet on it. He gave a terrible look at the kings, and then – with one stroke – cleaved the mail and helmet through to the timber. The marvelling kings enquired why he had looked at them so, and he replied that if he had missed, 'by St Patrick of Down' he would have slain both kings in a fit of anger. The account claims, unhistorically, that King John then restored to him his territories in Ireland, but that de Courcy was drowned on his way hither.

This story was relayed again and again in written sources from the sixteenth to the nineteenth century, and versions of the plot came to be told of various Irish heroes in the presence of foreign authorities – see, for example, Ó SÚILLEABHÁIN (Dónall Cam).

HISTORY: Curtis (1923), 86–112; Scott & Martin (1978), 175–81, 235, 333–4, 353.

LEGEND OF OGIER: Bédier, 2 (1926), 298–334.

LEGEND OF DE COURCY: Brewer & Bullen (1871), 112–17.

OTHER VERSIONS: D. Ó hÓgáin in Studia Hibernica, 31, 175–89.

Déaglán SAINT who founded the monastery of Ard Mhór (Ardmore, County Waterford). He was claimed to have been one of the missionaries who predated PATRICK in the south of Ireland, but it is difficult to confirm this, and his floruit is likely to have been in the late fifth and early sixth century AD. His name (earlier, Déclán) seems to have meant 'beloved deacon'. It is anglicised as Declan.

His biography, surviving in Latin and Irish, dates from the twelfth century but incorporates some older material. We read that his father was called Earc mac Tréin and was of the Leinstermen, and that his mother Déithín gave birth to him without pain. At his birth, his head struck against a stone, and this caused the stone to have a cavity. Rain from this *carraig Dhéagláin* (Déclan's rock) used afterwards to heal all types of sickness. Until he was seven, he was fostered by his maternal uncle Dobhrán, who lived in the DÉISE territory (County Waterford), and then was educated by a bishop Colmán and a holy hermit called Diomna. When he came of age, seven men who had seen a ball of fire in the sky at his birth came to him and became his followers. They set out to Rome with him, and met St AILBHE, who was sojourning there. Déaglán, it is claimed, was appointed bishop by the Pope, and while in Italy also met Patrick, who had not yet undertaken his mission to Ireland. We read that while Déaglán was saying Mass one day, a little black bell came from heaven to him. He entrusted this bell for safekeeping to one Rúnán, son of the king of Rome, who wished to accompany him on his return to Ireland.

They set out on the homeward journey, but could not find a ship to bring them over Muir nIocht (the English Channel). Then an empty ship miraculously appeared and took them from the mainland to the south of Britain, and after spending some time there, they embarked for Ireland. Rúnán, however, left the little black bell on a rock on the shore and did not remember it until they were well out to sea. Discovering this, Déaglán prayed to God and that rock began to float on the sea. The saint directed that the boat follow the floating rock, and in this way they landed at Inis Aird na gCaorach (High Sheep Island), whereupon the king of the Déise gave this island to him. Déaglán struck the water with his crozier, and immediately the sea drained and the island was joined to the mainland. This was the site on which he began to build his great monastery of Ardmore.

The biography attributes several other miracles to Déaglán. He banished a PLAGUE from the people of Caiseal (Cashel, County Tipperary) and restored to life seven noble hostages who had died from that plague while in the custody of Aonghus, king of Munster, there. As a result of this, tribute from the Munster kings was ever after due to his monastery. It is also claimed that he welcomed and assisted Patrick when that great saint reputedly arrived in Munster, for they had formed a mutual bond of friendship when they met on a highway in Italy.

A series of more personal LEGENDS are also cited in the biography. Once, a certain wealthy man named Dearcán invited him to dinner and served up the meat of a dog under pretence that it was mutton. Déaglán, however, noticed the dog's claw in the meat and upbraided his host, whereupon Dearcán repented and was converted. On another occasion, Déaglán was on a journey and his horse went lame. He harnessed a stag to the chariot in its place, and when the journey was finished, released the stag back into the wilderness. We also read of how the palace of the Déise king Cionaodh took fire and how Déaglán cast his crozier into the conflagration, thereby quenching it immediately. Furthermore, when an enemy fleet approached with the intent of plundering and destroying Ardmore, he sent the holiest member of his community, Ultán, to confront them. Ultán raised his left hand against the ships, and they all sank immediately. The sailors were turned into stone, and they are the rocks in the sea off Ardmore. The latter story has been borrowed into this context, for elsewhere Ultán is described as banishing a massive invasion fleet at the request of the high-king DIARMAID MAC CEARRBHEOIL. We read that he was busy caring for the children of women who had died in a great plague, and only his left hand was free when the messengers from Diarmaid arrived. He therefore raised that hand, remarking that if his right hand were free he would have raised it and, as a result, 'no foreigner would ever invade Ireland'.

161

Much of such fanciful material in the literary lives survived also in the folklore of County Waterford. A boulder that lies on the shore at Ardmore is identified as the rock that floated over the sea carrying his bell. It rests on two other rocks, thus leaving a little passage underneath through which people crawl on all fours to relieve themselves of ailments. The legend of the dog meat is a derivative of a FOLKTALE plot concerning the divining power of a wise man (see WONDER TALES, type 655). In oral lore of Déaglán, however, it is much developed by having the saint make the Sign of the Cross over his plate, and the dog jumps up, restored to life, and races barking from the house. This oral form results from the addition to the literary account of a story of a holy man who miraculously brings a dead animal back to life after eating its meat (see RELIGIOUS TALES, type 750B). An early tradition had it that Déaglán first brought rye into Ireland, the full of his shoe of it, as St FÍONÁN CAM first brought wheat. The feast day of Déaglán is 24 July.

GENERAL: Kenney (1929), 310–13; Plummer, 2 (1910), 32–59; Power (1914), xvi–xxvi, 1–73, 150–77; Stokes (1905), 112–13; O'Hanlon, 7 (1875), 307–54; OSL: Waterford (1841), 159–66; Hyde (1915), 87–94; IFC 22:70, 413, 84:8–10, 87:86, 251:329–31, 259:54–68, 492:331, 614:162–5, 947:307.

ULTÁN AND DIARMAID: Stokes (1905), 198–201.

EATEN ANIMAL RESTORED: Plummer, 1 (1910), cxliii.

Dearg (earlier, Derg) Name of a mythic personage in ancient Irish lore. Literally, it means 'red', and Dearg had rather sinister associations with slaughter and death.

In the surviving sources, he does not have a uniform identity, and it is apparent that the name and personality had by the literary period become a dramatic device to build tension in texts. The character Da Dearga, in whose hostel CONAIRE was slain, is a case in point. Da Dearga is also directly referred to as 'Derg' in the medieval text of this story, and indeed the element da was a shortening of dia, meaning 'GOD'. His divinity is further suggested by the occurrence of three horsemen called Derg who presage death for Conaire and who ride 'the HORSES of Donn', as it is by the parallelism between 'the house of Derg'

and 'the house of Donn' in the text itself. The conclusion must be that Dearg is in some way equivalent with the better-known death-god DONN. Perhaps Dearg was an appellation for Donn in the context of violent death, or given the history of the Conaire myth, it might well be that it was the name by which Donn was generally known to the early Leinstermen.

In the tradition of the Leinster hero FIONN MAC CUMHAILL, Dearg appears as a hostile otherworld figure, and this seems to have originated in a fanciful dialectic between Donn and the original FIONN. 'Dearg', like 'Donn', occurs in several texts as an epithet with the name DÁIRE, who in turn also appears to have been a double of the DAGHDHA. This whole complex of ancestral figures would have been borrowed some centuries before Irish literature began into the context of Fionn (q.v.).

One offshoot of this is a very curious story, found in an eighth-century text, which describes how Fionn mac Cumhaill had a servant called Dearg Corra. A paramour of Fionn made advances to this servant, who rejected her, and she in revenge claimed that he had tried to rape her. Believing the false charge, Fionn banished the servant from his presence, but later, while hunting, came across him again in the forest. Dearg Corra was eating a meal along with a blackbird, a trout and a stag. His identity was hidden by 'a cloak of concealment', but he was recognised through the magical knowledge of Fionn. The plot of this story has been borrowed from an extraneous source (see ROMANTIC TALES, type 870C), but the imagery onto which it has been superimposed is quite distinctive.

That imagery corresponds to Celtic engravings in several parts of western Europe that have a human figure accompanied by a stag and other animals. One of the engravings preserves the name Cernunnos, which meant 'the horned [or peaked] one', an interpretation which can also be put on the name Dearg Corra (the red peaked one). This suggests that surviving vestiges of ancient Celtic belief became attached to the divine appellation Dearg. Imagery of sacred deer, of course, proved attractive to the developing lore of Fionn mac Cumhaill, which had deer-hunting as one of its favourite themes. The connection of Dearg with wild deer continued within that context, and medieval storytelling had his daughter coming in the shape of a doe to Fionn (*see* OISÍN).

GENERAL: T.F. O'Rahilly (1946), 125–9, 276; Knott (1936); K. Meyer in *RC*, 25, 346–9; Ó hÓgáin (1988), 15, 46–9, 324, 328.

CERNUNNOS: Olmsted (1994), 335–7.

Deirdre *(earlier, Deirdriu)* Fictional lady of great beauty in the ULSTER CYCLE. The name seems to have originally been a diminutive of *der* (girl); but a fanciful interpretation (substituting '*dér*') would give a meaning such as 'the tearful one' or 'the sorrowful one'.

Probably a popular name for girls, it was thought appropriate to be used for the leading lady in a tragic story of Ulster. The composer of the story took it to be derived from *dér*, and for his purpose extracted a meaning such as 'she who brought sorrow'. This story of Deirdre was a version of the three-cornered plot concerning competition between an old man and a young man for the hand of a lady. It is apparent that the plot circulated in the folklore of antiquity and became popular among the Celts of northern Britain and of Ireland. Other versions of it included the romance of Tristan and Isolt, and the elopement of DIARMAID UA DUIBHNE with Gráinne.

The first surviving text of the Deirdre story dates from the ninth century and is entitled *Loinges Mac n-Uislenn* (The Exile of the Sons of Uisliu). It tells of how king CONCHOBHAR MAC NEASA and the Ulstermen were drinking at the house of the storyteller Feidhlimidh when an unborn baby cried out in the womb of Feidhlimidh's wife. The lady gave birth to a girl. The druid CATHBHADH foretold that the child would cause great slaughter, and the warriors called for her to be put to death. Conchobhar, however, said that he would take the child, who was called Deirdre, and had her fostered in a place apart in the care of the nurse Leabharcham. She grew up to be the most beautiful woman in Ireland. One day, as she watched her foster-father flaying a calf

in the snow, a raven came and drank the blood, and she remarked that the man of her desires must have hair dark like the raven, cheeks red like blood, and body as white as the snow. Leabharcham told her that there was such a man, and his name was Naoise (earlier, Naíse), one of the three sons of Uisliu. Deirdre soon after contrived to meet Naoise. 'A fine heifer is passing by,' said Naoise. 'The heifers are always fine,' she answered, 'where there are no bulls.' 'You have the bull of the province, the king of Ulster,' said he. 'Between the two of you, I would choose a young bull like you!' answered Deirdre. Remembering Cathbhadh's prophecy, Naoise rejected her; but she seized him by the ears and threatened him with shame and derision if he refused to take her away (*see* GEIS).

Naoise then collected his two brothers, Aindle and Ardán, and took her away with him. Unable to avoid Conchobhar's vengeance in Ireland, they crossed to Scotland, but Deirdre's beauty soon attracted the jealousy of the king of that country to Naoise, and they had to repair to a lonely island in the sea. The Ulstermen pitied their plight and prevailed upon Conchobhar to allow them to return. Three celebrated warriors – FEARGHUS MAC RÓICH, DUBHTHACH DAOL ULADH and CORMAC CONN LOINGEAS – went to Scotland and escorted them home on Conchobhar's surety. On their arrival at the royal court of Eamhain Mhacha, however, the king had the three sons of Uisliu treacherously slain by his mercenaries. Fearghus and his fellow guarantors were livid at this, and they ravaged the province in vengeance and departed to the hostile court of queen MEADHBH in Connacht. Conchobhar forced the grieving Deirdre to live with him for a year. At the end of the year, he asked her whom of all men she hated most, and she answered Eoghan mac Durthacht, for it was Eoghan who had killed Naoise. 'Well, you will live with Eoghan!' said the king. Next day, she was made to travel in a chariot, with Conchobhar and Eoghan on either side of her. The king mockingly remarked that her eye was like that of a sheep between two rams. Deirdre, unable to bear any more, hurled herself from the chariot and dashed her head to pieces against a rock.

This story did not long predate its first occurrence in literature. It was introduced into the Ulster Cycle as an explanation for the desertion of Fearghus mac Róich (q.v.), a happening that had previously been explained in other ways. Also, the portrayal of Conchobhar is conspicuously more ruthless than in other stories. Elsewhere, he is ambitious but not cruel, and the age-ing vindictiveness shown by him here is a direct result of the role of the old suitor in the borrowed three-cornered plot.

An expanded version of the romance was written in the fourteenth century, and became quite popular in manuscripts; and again, the seventeenth-century historian CÉITINN gave a short retelling in his influ-ential work. There is also an eighteenth-century redaction, written in Ulster, which gives more detailed descriptions of some of the episodes; while in Scotland a lay was composed that tells the story in a more con-versational form. It is therefore not surprising that the romance of Deirdre has survived strongly in folk tradition, many tellings hav-ing been recorded in both Ireland and Scotland in recent generations. These oral versions have been current for a long time, for they include the beginning of the story (not found in the fourteenth-century text) and the MOTIF of the unborn-child's cry (missing in all but the earliest text). They also have two important innovations. Conchobhar has a house built with a leaden roof for Naoise and his brothers, and when they are inside the house, the doors are locked on them and the house set on fire. The intention is to leave them to a horrid death, but in most versions they break out and die fighting. This motif is borrowed from the firing of an iron house in the medieval literary tale called *Mesca Ulad* (*see* CÚ CHULAINN). Secondly, when Deirdre dies, she is buried in the same graveyard as Naoise, and a tree grows out of each grave. Branches of the two trees intertwine. This is an adaptation of an international motif that has been current in Ireland for many centuries (*see* ROMANTIC TALES, type 970).

NAME: RIA Dictionary, s.v. *'der'*, *'dér'*.
EARLIEST TEXT: Hull (1946).
OTHER VERSIONS: Mac Giolla Léith (1993); D. McKinnon in *Celtic Review*, 1, 12–17, 104–31; Ua Ceallaigh (1927), 65–88.
CÉITINN'S VERSION: Dinneen, 2 (1908), 190–7.
LATE ULSTER REDACTION: B. Ó Buachalla in *ZCP*, 29, 114–54.
SCOTTISH LAY: J.F. Campbell (1872), 12–29.
FOLKLORE: Bruford (1969), 99–105, 264–5; S. Ó Súilleabháin (1942), 599 & (1974), 23–9.

Déise An amalgam of ÉRAINN septs in south-east Munster. The designation meant 'vassals', and was probably applied to them by the strong EOGHANACHT sept, who claimed to be over-KINGS of the whole province of Munster. Déise is sometimes anglicised in the form 'Decies'.

The vassalage seems to have been more nominal than real, however, for the Déise were quite powerful in their own right. In the course of the fifth and sixth centuries, they sent out settlements to the northwest, taking over part of present-day County Limerick, which became known as Déis Bheag (Little Decies). A branch of this Déis Bheag spread across the River Shannon into east Clare, where they gave rise to the strong medieval sept known as DÁL GCAIS. The Déise could make little progress to the north, where they were faced with the Eoghanacht, but they fought several successful engagements with their neighbours to the north-east, the OSRAIGHE and LAIGHIN. More signifi-cantly, they crossed the sea to Wales in the sixth century, establishing settlements in the territory of the Demetae (now Dyfed). The tradition was that one of their chief-tains called Eochaidh Allmhuir had led this migration and that he was the ances-tor of the later Welsh kings of Dyfed.

The fact that so successful a people were known by a name indicating vas-salage caused some difficulty for the his-torians and chronologists. Early medieval writers claimed that they had once occu-pied territory near TARA, but had been banished from there by the high-king CORMAC MAC AIRT. This was based on the fact that a similar name, Déis, was borne by a people who resided there (Deece, County Meath). The main actor in that account, and the reputed leader of the Déise, was one Aonghus (earlier, Óengus) Gaíbhuaibhtheach. This Aonghus had a terrible spear, from which his epithet derives and to which three heavy chains were attached. The story tells of how a son of king Cormac, called Ceallach, abducted a girl from Aonghus' territory, and Aonghus – chided by a woman from whom he once sought food – determined to avenge the act. He went to Cormac's palace at Tara and ran Ceallach through with his spear. As he withdrew it, a link from one of its huge chains struck Cormac and blinded him in one eye. As a result, seven great battles were fought between the armies of Aonghus and Cormac, with the result that Aonghus and his Déise were banished from their territory and had to retire to Munster.

This shadowy leader – also called Aonghus Gaífhuileach (spear-bloody) – can be identified with one Óengus Bolg, a GOD-figure of ÉRAINN myth. A further fanciful and anachronistic tradition has it that the Déise refugees were given their land by the Eoghanacht king Aonghus mac Nadfraoich, who actually lived in the fifth century AD. Historical reality was hardly less dramatic. Having successfully withstood the pressure of their Gaelic neighbours and then the NORSEMEN of Waterford for several generations, the Déise chiefs were finally overthrown in their County Waterford strongholds by the NORMAN invaders in the twelfth century. See CORC DUIBHNE and DÁL gCAIS.

The principal families descended from the Déise of Waterford are, since medieval times, known by the surnames Ó Faoláin (Whelan or Phelan) and Ó Bric (Brick). See DÁL gCAIS for that sept.

SOURCES: K. Meyer in *Ériu, 3,* 135–42 & (1912), 75; V. Hull in *ZCP, 27,* 14–63, 362–3, 374–5; Pender (1947), 209–17; O'Brien (1962), 156–8, 394–402; Ó Muraíle, *2* (2003), 102–5 & *3,* 472–5.

GENERAL: T.F. O'Rahilly (1946), 63–5; F.J. Byrne (1973), 180–4; T. Ó Cathasaigh in *Éigse, 20,* 1–33.

Desmond, Earl of Desmond is the anglicised form of Deasmhumhain (literally, 'south Munster'), and was the general term for most of Counties Limerick, Kerry and Cork, along with parts of Counties Tipperary and Waterford. The two principal leaders with this title who are remembered in folk LEGENDS are Gerald FitzGerald (1338–98), the third earl, and Gerald FitzGerald (1532–83), the fifteenth earl. Leaders in their respective epochs of the Munster branch of the powerful FITZGERALDS, they were both known in Irish as Gearóid Iarla (Gerald the Earl).

The earlier Gearóid Iarla succeeded to the earldom in 1358, and served two periods as chief justiciar for Ireland. He was a leading example of the gaelicisation of the NORMAN lords, and was a noted composer of love poetry in the IRISH LANGUAGE. The Annals state that 'Ireland was full of the fame of his wisdom'. Lough Gur in County Limerick, where he had a castle, was at the centre of the earldom of Desmond, and nearby is Knockainey (in Irish, the '*Cnoc*', or hill, of ÁINE). This Áine was in Gaelic tradition the GODDESS of Munster sovereignty, and as such was described in an early text as the mate of AILILL ÓLOM, mythical KING of the royal EOGHANACHT sept. The Geraldines, as the new Norman overlords of Munster, were not slow to expropriate such symbolism to themselves. Thus we find the professional POET Gofraidh Fionn Ó Dálaigh, who was in the employ of the Geraldines in the fourteenth century, referring to Gerald's father, Maurice, the first earl, as 'Áine's king', and to Gerald himself as 'the son of Áine's knight'. It is striking to find this idea embedded in a story that was current in the recent folklore of the Knockainey area. According to this, Maurice was walking one day by the shore of Lough Gur when he saw the beautiful otherworld lady Áine bathing. He seized her cloak, which act magically put her into his power, and then lay with her. In this way, Gearóid Iarla was conceived, and when he was born, Áine appeared at the castle of the earl to present the child to him. This story is in reality a conflation of two distinct traditions – the Gaelic one whereby the Munster king lies with Áine (*see* AILILL ÓLOM), and a Continental legend that tells of how certain great families had a swan-maiden ancestress. The conflation must reflect actual policy of the Geraldines themselves, who wished to place their Norman heritage within a Gaelic framework.

Another Continental legend that became applied to Gearóid Iarla was that concerning a 'swan-knight' – a legend quite popular in French, German and English literature of the late Middle Ages. This tells of a knight who appears in a boat accompanied by a swan, marries a lady, but goes away with the swan again when she breaks a taboo by asking about his identity. In the folklore of Gearóid Iarla, it takes the form of a taboo that Áine puts on Maurice not to show surprise at anything his son does. When Gearóid grows up, he shows his magical agility by leaping into a bottle and out of it again, and the father shows astonishment. At that, Gearóid leaves the castle, enters the water of the nearby Camogue river, and swims away in the form of a goose. An old saying in Irish refers to how island geese never return to the same habitat, and since an island on Lough Gur was known as Gearóid's Island, the proverb was claimed to refer to this episode. The story, however, contradicts the mass of the folklore concerning Gearóid Iarla, which accords with history in having him succeed to the earldom and gain fame in that position. It must have been attracted to him because of its similarity to the Áine story, not earlier than the sixteenth century, for it was at that time that the most celebrated MOTIF concerning Gearóid gained currency. This was that he had not really died, but had disappeared from this world in a mysterious manner.

This motif is closely connected with the political fortunes of the great Desmond family in the generations after the death of Gearóid, their most famous and popular earl. During the fifteenth century, the rulers of England grew increasingly nervous of the growing power of the Desmond earls, who ruled Munster like kings. The Geraldines, however, were astute, and despite continued provocation and even judicial assassination, they managed to maintain their position. Tension mounted in the early decades of the sixteenth century, with

anti-Geraldine rumours being circulated in England to the effect that they were plotting to invade that country and seize power there. The other major branch of the Geraldine family, that of Kildare, was much to the fore at this time, but was decimated by the English after a failed rebellion in 1534. In Munster, the year 1558 saw the succession to the Desmond earldom of Gerald FitzGerald as fifteenth earl, the first of the name in his line since the celebrated Gearóid Iarla. He was, however, deprived by the English of his vast family estates and himself kept in captivity in London for long periods. He was allowed to return home to Lough Gur in 1573, but immediately began to take a defiant pro-Irish stance, and within a few years had joined his cousin James FitzMaurice FitzGerald in rebellion. Hopes ran high, and messianic prophecies were circulated to bolster the Geraldine campaign.

Remnants of these prophecies in later folklore show that the new Gearóid Iarla was being portrayed as embodying the great Geraldine spirit of his ancestral namesake. From their contacts with the Gherardini in Florence (see FITZGERALDS), they would have heard the lore of the messianic emperor Frederick II, who had died in 1250 but who was claimed to be alive and waiting to return, and there are several indications that imagery of that emperor became entwined in the minds of the Geraldine supporters with the hoped-for return of their fortunes through the agency of a Gearóid Iarla. Thus popular fancy began to claim that the Gearóid Iarla of olden times had not died at all, but had disappeared mysteriously from one of his castles and was waiting to return at the hour of the family's greatest need. In line with the image of Frederick also, Gearóid was said to have been a great scholar who dabbled in magic, and so one particular legend grew up to explain how he had disappeared. It was said that in his castle at Lough Gur, he had a secret room in which he used to perform magic spells. His wife grew curious and asked to be allowed to witness a performance. He warned her not to utter a sound while the magic was in progress, no matter what she saw. Then he began to assume different shapes, one of them so frightful that she screamed. The taboo was broken, and the whole castle sank to the bottom of the lake, bringing with it Gearóid and all his household. He therefore was said to dwell beneath the water, enchanted until the opportune time for him to return and restore all as before.

The central messianic legend was of greater import. Versions of this are found throughout Europe concerning different great figures of history, but in Gearóid's case it seems to have been a direct borrowing from Frederick. It is said that a man was passing by Lough Gur one night when he saw a light in the side of a hill there. He went to investigate and found the entrance to a cavern, in which he saw an army of knights and horses all asleep. There was a beautiful sword on the floor, and as the man began to draw it from its scabbard, the army began to awaken. Finally, its leader, Gearóid Iarla, asked in a loud voice had the time come yet, but the man took fright and ran away. The army fell to slumbering again, and the entrance to the cavern could not be found later.

The second Earl Gerald of Desmond, in history, was not a very competent military man, and by 1583 his cause was completely lost and he himself treacherously slain. The sequel to this disastrous rebellion was the devastation of Munster by the Elizabethan armies, so that an annalist felt obliged to state that 'the lowing of a cow or the voice of a ploughman could scarcely be heard from Dunquin to Cashel'. The great affection for the Geraldine family, however, lived on, as did the hope that one of them would free the country. There are repeated references to this mystical belief in literature and social documents from the seventeenth to the nineteenth century, and the legends of Gearóid's enchantment and of his sleeping army are still told. An alternative telling claims that the enchanted earl rides around Lough Gur on midsummer night once every seven years. He is mounted on a fine white stallion shod with silver shoes, and when these shoes wear down, he will return.

Variants of this corpus of messianic lore have been told for several centuries concerning the earls of KILDARE, the O'Neills and O'Donnells in Ulster, and a chieftain called Dónall Ó DONNCHÚ at the Lakes of Killarney. It is clear that in these cases, the corpus has been borrowed from the lore of the Desmond earl.

Munster folklore has also assimilated other legends of magic and the otherworld to the celebrated name, Gearóid Iarla. Two such legends of Continental origin concern his magical practices. According to one, he, with the poet Black David FitzGerald (+1581) and (anachronistically) Dónall Ó Donnchú, learned magic from the devil at a secret school. The devil demanded as payment that one of them should stay with him, but they each told him to 'take the man behind me' and he ended up with nothing but the shadow of Dónall. The other legend tells of how Gearóid was riding from his residence at Castleisland, County Kerry one day, and as he passed through the town, a magician looked through a window and put a spell on him. As a result, the earl and his horse were sinking into the ground, but Gearóid quickly used his own magic to put a pair of horns growing on the head of his assailant. The latter could not withdraw his head through the window because of the horns, and Gearóid would not remove the horns until the other spell was also withdrawn. Several stories tell of Gearóid's appearances, such as visiting a blacksmith late at night to have his horse shod (see DONN), or meeting a benighted horse dealer and inviting him into his castle under Lough Gur to discuss a sale with him. The spirit of Gearóid Iarla is also reputed to protect the ENVIRONMENT at Lough Gur, and one story tells of how he caused the horse of a local TYRANT landlord to bolt, with serious or even fatal injury to its rider, after the latter had planned to drain the lake or forbid access to it by local people.

G. Mac Niocaill in *Studia Hibernica*, 3, 7–59; L. Mac Cionnaith (1938), 201–6; D. Fitzgerald in *RC*, 4, 186–99; Ó Siochfhradha (1932), 42–4, 53–4; Ó hÓgáin (1985), 78–86, 141–57, 329–30, 335–7 & in *Béaloideas*, 42–44, 213–308 & in Bonanno (2000), 17–24.

Dian Céacht *(earlier, Dían Cécht)* Mythical physician in early Irish literature. The original meaning of the name seems to have been 'swift traveller', and it may in fact have been a pseudonym for a GOD of healing.

Dian Céacht is mentioned very early in the literature. Reference in seventh- and eighth-century texts have him as a physician and an arbitrator on matters concerning leeches. An incantation against ailments refers to 'the salve which Dian Céacht left with his family, so that anything on which it is laid is healed'. A ninth-century glossary directly calls him 'the healing sage of Ireland', and a later writer repeats this description and calls him a 'god of health'. Caesar refers to such a god among the Gauls, but does not give his name and calls him 'Apollo'. It is likely that Dian Céacht, the one who travels swiftly when required to heal his devotees, is the Irish version of this deity. In a tenth-century text, Dian Céacht is indeed described as 'going roads of great healing'.

The medieval writers in general made him the physician of the TUATHA DÉ DANANN, an adept at magical cures, and in that role he occurs in several texts. In the MYTHOLOGICAL CYCLE, he and his three brothers are mentioned as physicians in the first Battle of Moytirra. In the second battle, however, two sons and a daughter are the trio who feature with him. They make a well into which the wounded of the Tuatha Dé are cast to be healed while Dian Céacht and his family sing incantations by it. Before the same battle, he makes a promise that typifies his image: 'Any man who is wounded, unless his head be cut off, or the membrane of his brain or his spinal cord be severed, will be fully healed by me.'

It was appropriate, then, that it was he who healed the blemish of the Tuatha Dé king NUADHU. That king having lost his hand in the first Battle of Moytirra, Dian Céacht put a silver arm on him that had 'the vigour of every hand in it'. The great physician's son Miach, however, interfered and himself set about healing the king. In nine days, skin grew on the hand, it

became manageable, and it became so deft as to catch wisps of burnt bulrushes. Dian Céacht was displeased at being upstaged by his son and struck him three times on the head with a sword, but Miach cured himself of each wound. Then Dian Céacht struck him a fourth blow, which cut his brain and killed him. Three hundred and sixty-five herbs grew out of Miach's grave, one for each of his joints and sinews. The young man's sister Airmeith collected the herbs, and Dian Céacht mixed them so that nobody would ever again know their full healing qualities. This is based on an ancient idea that the spirit of a person resides in a tree or plant that grows from his grave, and also on the common folk belief that there is a herb appropriate for each and every illness.

We also read that Dian Céacht put every type of herb that grew in Ireland into a well between Moytirra and Lough Arrow. This well was known as Tiopra Sláine, and was reputed to have been his great healing well. Some medieval sources invent further details of relatives and associates, but very few adventures are related of him. We are told that he cured Tuirill *(see LUGH)* by making an emetic draught for him, and that he destroyed serpent-like creatures that infested the heart of a son of the MÓR-RÍOGHAIN. Much of this lore can be viewed as debris of the ancient mystique and rituals associated with the art of healing.

In a more heroic vein, Dian Céacht is described as slaying a great serpent that threatened to devastate the countryside surrounding the River Barrow in south Leinster. This is clearly an echo of the medieval imagery that equated plagues with dragons and the like *(see SAINTS)*. It is also stated that he restored the eye MIDHIR had lost in an accident, and a late variation on this particular theme is given some humorous colouring. According to this, Miach, the son of Dian Céacht, replaced the eye of Nuadhu's door-keeper with that of a CAT. Skilled though this operation was, it left the door-keeper at a disadvantage, for the eye remained open at night watching mice and birds, whereas by day it slept while its bearer should be at work. The same late text burlesques the MOTIF of the replacement of Nuadhu's arm by stating that Miach performed the operation in a bizarre manner. First he removed a beetle that had nested in the king's other arm, and then he replaced the lost limb with that of the king's swine-herd. This is an echo from a folk plot (*see* WONDER TALES, type 660).

NAME: T.F. O'Rahilly (1946), 472–3.

EARLY REFERENCES: D. Binchy in *Ériu*, *20*, 1–3, 22–3; Stokes & Strachan, *2* (1903), 249; Meyer (1912), 36; W. Stokes in *Irische Texte*, *3*, 356–9.

MEDIEVAL LITERATURE: J. Frazer in *Ériu*, *8*, 34–5, 44–5; Gray (1982), 24–5, 32–3, 40–3, 50–1, 54–7, 122–3; Gwynn (1906), 62–3 & (1924), 182–5; Macalister (1941), 112–15, 122–3, 216–17, 228–9; O'Duffy (1888), 1–3.

LOSS OF HERBAL KNOWLEDGE: S. Thompson (1955–58), motif E631.3; MacCulloch (1905), 108–16; S. Ó Súilleabháin (1942), 284; IFC 85:352–5.

GENERAL: Ó hÓgáin (1999), 78, 87, 229–30.

Diarmaid mac Aodha Sláine

HIGH-KING of the UÍ NÉILL, son of AODH SLÁINE, who reigned jointly with his brother Bláthmhac from AD 642 to his death in 664. Both he and Bláthmhac died of the PLAGUE called the *Buidhe Chonaill* (literally, 'Yellow of Conall').

Diarmaid was said to have been reared by a woman called Sineach Cró, and a saga entitled *Cath Chairn Chonaill* was compiled in the tenth century concerning her influence on him. We read that the men of Connacht were taking her cattle and that she chided Diarmaid with doing nothing to stop this. She said that he had the nickname Ruanaidh (scarlet) because he was a coward, and smarting under this, Diarmaid invaded the western province. Eventually, the Connacht king GUAIRE opposed him at Carn Chonaill (Ballyconnell, near Gort, County Galway). Guaire was defeated, and had to submit to the high-king, but so generous was he that Diarmaid knelt before him in respect, and the two kings were reconciled.

From the same period comes another story of Diarmaid, which tells of how he left the citadel of TARA one day with his foster son Criomhthann and travelled to Áth Troim (Trim, County Meath). A beautiful woman approached them in a chariot there, and she agreed to return to Tara with Diarmaid and be his wife. He gave her as token a little brooch, and hence she became known as Beagfhola (earlier, Becfola, meaning 'little wealth'). However, she tried to seduce Criomhthann, and he agreed to a tryst with her. She set out for the appointed place on a Sunday morning, accompanied by a handmaid, but wolves attacked them at Dubhthor (the northern boundary of Meath) and killed the handmaid. Beagfhola fled into a tree to avoid them. From the tree, she saw a fire in the forest and, going there, met a handsome young man magnificently accoutred. He paid no heed to her, but she followed him into his boat on a nearby lake.

They crossed over to an island, where she shared his meal and got into his bed, but still he paid her no attention. Three warriors exactly like him came in the morning, and he joined them. The group fought four other warriors who arrived on the scene, until all were bloody. The young man then returned to her and revealed that his name was Flann, grandson of Feadhach. His three companions were his brothers, and the other group were relatives. The island had belonged to Feadhach, and the two groups were fighting for it. It was a marvellous island, with sufficient food always available for its inhabitants. Beagfhola wished to remain with him, but he told her to return to Diarmaid, and said that if he gained possession of the island, he would come for her. She found her handmaid alive and well – for the wolves had merely been calves from the island – and they returned to Tara. There she found Diarmaid rising from his bed as if no time had passed since she left him.

Exactly a year later, she and Diarmaid saw a wounded man passing the door of their dwelling. The man was Flann, and Beagfhola went away with him. Soon after, four clerical students arrived and announced that St Molaise of Damh-Inis (Devenish on Lough Erne) had sent them, for a farmer on the island had that morning seen two groups of four warriors fighting there. All had fallen but for one wounded man. The saint had buried the other seven, and Diarmaid directed that the gold and silver of their accoutrements be used to ornament Molaise's shrine, satchel and crozier. Beagfhola was never seen again.

This story provides a unique blend of pre-Christian and Christian tradition, with Devenish being portrayed as an island sanctuary for both world views. It is clear that the author, who initially presented Beagfhola as an immoral being, could not resist portraying the otherworld of pre-Christian belief in an attractive light. Diarmaid also figures in the medieval literature concerning CANO MAC GARTNÁIN and SEANCHÁN, and concerning several of the saints, including FÉICHÍN and MOCHUDA.

A great-grandson of Diarmaid, called Fógartach, was high-king of the Uí Néill from AD 722–24. From him descended the lords of south Breagha (in south-east County Meath) whose centre was Loch Gabhair (Lagore). They later took the surname Mac Fhógartaigh (Gogarty).

Macalister (1956), 378–81; W. Stokes in *ZCP*, *3*, 203–19 & in *Irische Texte*, *3*, 344–7; Meyer (1912), 98; Binchy (1963), 5; O'Grady, *1* (1898), 85–7; M. Bhreathnach in *Ériu*, *35*, 59–91.

Diarmaid mac Cearrbheoil

HIGH-KING of the Uí Néill, who reigned in the years AD 544–65. His father was Fearghus 'Cearrbheoil', this epithet (earlier, Cerrbeoil), meaning 'crooked mouthed', and Diarmaid's patronymic therefore comes from his father's nickname. In later texts, his name is written as Diarmaid mac Cearbhaill.

After the death of Muircheartach mac Earca, the two claimants to the throne were Diarmaid and his distant cousin Tuathal Maolgharbh. The latter won the contest, and he forced Diarmaid to go into hiding. One text describes an incident that reputedly occurred during this period. Being at Snámh Dá Éan (now Farnagh, County Westmeath), Diarmaid saw the smoke of a fire in the distance and, going to investigate, found St CIARÁN the Younger building the foundations of his monastery at Clonmacnoise. One of Diarmaid's DRUIDS

remarked that it was an inopportune time for undertaking a building, but Diarmaid disregarded this and assisted the SAINT in driving a stake into the ground. Ciarán prophesied to him that, as a result of this, he would be high-king on the next day.

Hearing this, one of Diarmaid's followers, Maol Mór, volunteered to go and assassinate Tuathal Maolgharbh. His plan was to bring a pup's heart on the point of his spear and to tell Tuathal that this was the heart of Diarmaid, and then to stab the unsuspecting high-king with the same spear. Diarmaid agreed to the plan, and lent his own horse to Maol for the venture. This was a black horse, and it was very fleet-footed. Maol accordingly went and slew Tuathal, but he failed in his effort to escape and was himself slain. Diarmaid then advanced on TARA and, encountering no opposition, assumed the office of high-king for himself. This tradition is a curious one, and it is difficult to determine what basis it had. The account of the assassination may preserve some historical data, for we read that an expression grew up from it – namely, *éacht Mhaoil Mhóir* (the feat of Maol Mór), to denote a pyrrhic victory.

The account goes on to say that in appreciation of his prophecy, Diarmaid offered to Ciarán all of the plain around Clonmacnoise. That place had been until then occupied by one Flann Fionn, an enemy of the king. Diarmaid attacked the house of Flann and set fire to it. Flann was wounded and jumped into a bath tub to escape the heat, but notwithstanding this, he perished in his own house. Ciarán grew angry at the manner in which the land was acquired for him, and he declared that Diarmaid himself would suffer a similar triple death by wounding, drowning and burning.

Diarmaid, as was customary, began his reign by celebrating the feast of Tara. The nobles of Ireland demanded that the arrangements regarding precedence at this feast should strictly accord with ancient ordinances, and Diarmaid brought the various wise men of Ireland to detail what these ordinances had been. None could do this satisfactorily, however, until the antediluvian seer FIONNTAN came on the scene and gave a full description of the ancient history and lore of Ireland. This account, by selecting Diarmaid's installation as the occasion for Fionntan's mythical announcements, shows how important his reign was regarded by the medieval writers. One reason for this was the fact that Diarmaid stood chronologically between two worlds, the ancient pagan one and the new Christian one. Diarmaid himself may have still been a pagan. He seems to have been at least a half-pagan, for he is represented as having druids in the forefront of his retinue and as mixing their counsels with those of Christian saints.

There is much ambiguity. We read that when his son Breasal forcibly took a cow from a nun to provide a feast for his father, she complained to Diarmaid and he brought Breasal to a river and drowned him there. Then he regretted having done this, and went to COLM CILLE to implore the assistance of that saint. Colm brought him to the ascetic Beagán who, when he saw Diarmaid, spoke crossly to him. 'Into the ground with you, o kin-slayer!' he said, and the high-king sank to his knees in the earth. Nevertheless, Colm prevailed upon Beagán to help, and the ascetic raised his hand and began to pray. He brought 50 men called Breasal from hell, and eventually brought the desired Breasal and restored him to life.

In the seventh-century biography of Colm Cille, Diarmaid is referred to as 'ruler of all Ireland', ordained by God's will, yet his relations with Colm himself were – if tradition is to be credited – far from good. Medieval writers state that the saint gave his protection to Curnán, a Connacht prince who had killed a man in a hurling match at Tara, and that, notwithstanding this, Curnán was put to death by the high-king. A further development in the saga of their relations was the LEGEND of how Colm secretly copied a book and how Diarmaid adjudged that the copy must be surrendered to the owner of the original. These disagreements were cited as the incidents that brought about the Battle of Cúil Dreimhne (Cooldrevny, between Drumcliff and Sligo) in the year 561, a battle that Diarmaid and his southern Uí Néill forces lost to a combined army of Connachtmen and northern Uí Néill. The actual role of the saint in this battle was probably no more than as a supporter of his northern kindred, and the theme of bitter personal hostility between himself and Diarmaid seems to have originated from an attempt to synchronise their respective careers.

Individuals gifted with prophecy, whether saints or druids, were given significant roles in the lore of Diarmaid. This emphasised the ritual nature of the kingship he embodies, but its special focus was on the question of his death. One account gives the leading part to the celebrated prophet BEAG MAC DÉ, who was among the high-king's retinue. Beag, we are told, had suggested that Diarmaid's foster-child Aodh Dubh, a prince of the Dál nAraidhe sept of east Ulster, would cause his death. Aodh would give him a poisoned drink while Diarmaid would be wearing a shirt woven from a single seed of flax and a cloak of wool from a single sheep; moreover, his ale would be brewed from a single grain, his bacon would be a pig that was never farrowed, and the ridge-pole of the house would fall on his head. Hearing this, Diarmaid was alarmed and had Aodh Dubh banished from Ireland. To test Beag's prophecy, he consulted his druids on the matter, and to his dismay found that their prognostications were similar. There was obviously much duplication in the tradition of prophecies concerning Diarmaid's death – these being variously attributed to Ciarán, Beag and the druids.

To further complicate the matter, another saint, RUADHÁN of Lorrha, was portrayed as a portender of doom for the king. We read that Diarmaid's reign was generally a good one, and that he was wise and kindly. However, one of his administrators, called Aodh Baclámh, was an evil fellow who swaggered about the countryside collecting the taxes. His custom was to carry the high-king's spear crosswise in his arms, and to demand that the entrance to each nobleman's fortress be made wide enough to allow him to thus pass through it. A Connacht noble, Aodh Guaire by name, was enraged at his fortress being knocked down to suit this whim, so he slew Aodh Baclámh and then fled to Ruadhán for sanctuary. For fear of Diarmaid, Ruadhán sent him to Britain, but soon he had to leave there because of Diarmaid's threats. Aodh Guaire returned to Ruadhán, and the saint hid him in an underground chamber called Poll Ruadháin in one of his monasteries (Pollrone, County Kilkenny). Diarmaid went there, demanding to know where the fugitive was, and – unwilling to tell a lie – the saint said he did not know 'unless he be under where you are standing'. The high-king departed in frustration, but knowing that Ruadhán would not lie, he soon realised where Aodh Guaire was. He therefore returned and seized the fugitive in violation of the saint's sanctuary.

Aodh Guaire was brought to Tara to be put to death, but Ruadhán followed on, accompanied by St BRÉANAINN, and demanded that the prisoner be released. Diarmaid refused, insisting that as king he had the necessary legal authority. The saints chanted curses and rang their bells against him, and then fasted against him, and one night he dreamed that a great tree was cut down by foreigners. Realising that the foreigners signified clerics, he called Ruadhán and began to upbraid him. They exchanged maledictions, Diarmaid insisting that Ruadhán's monasteries would be deserted and that his body would be blemished. Ruadhán laid his curse on Tara, and then pointed out the ridge-pole that would fall on the high-king. Finally, Diarmaid agreed to release Aodh Guaire, and they were reconciled.

The multiple prophecies must, however, be fulfilled; and so it happened that when the high-king was on his royal circuit, he was approached by a strange warrior who invited him to visit the fortress called Ráth Bheag (near Donegore, County Antrim). The warrior had a beautiful daughter, and he invited Diarmaid to sleep with her. She gave him a shirt and cloak, and her father gave him bacon and ale – all of the unusual types that had been foretold. Then he noticed that the house had new rafters, and was told by his host that they were made from a ridge-pole found floating on the sea. Realising that his doom was at hand, Diarmaid tried to rush from the house, but his former foster-child, Aodh Dubh, was at the door and ran him through with a spear. The house was set on fire, and he climbed into a vat of ale to avoid the flames. The beam of the house fell on his head, and he thus died a triple death from wounding, fire and drowning.

That Diarmaid was slain by Aodh Dubh is an historical fact. ADHAMHNÁN, in his biography of Colm Cille written in the seventh century, describes how this Aodh Dubh later sought to be ordained a priest in Scotland but was cursed by Colm for killing Diarmaid. The curse was that he would be 'pierced with a spear' on the prow of a ship and would fall into the water and 'die by drowning', which indeed was the way in which he died. There is little reason to doubt the statements that Colm rejected Aodh Dubh and that Aodh Dubh was killed in a sea fight, but the connection between the two events must be considered a narrative accretion. A saint's curse would be thought of as having a markedly unusual effect, causing the idea of a multiple death to be borrowed from folklore (see ROMANTIC TALES, type 934A). This reputedly cursed death of Aodh Dubh then influenced the memory of the death of Diarmaid at the hands of Aodh Dubh. Diarmaid himself was, after all, himself a murderer as well as a victim of murder, for his collusion in the death of Flann Fionn was notorious enough. The MOTIF of a multiple death therefore spread into all this lore – from the death of Aodh Dubh backwards in time to that of Diarmaid, and from that backwards again to the death of Flann Fionn.

The kernel of Diarmaid's saga seems to be the opposition between druidic and Christian advices – in other words, the struggle of the two religions for influence over him – and his actual violent death would have been a suitable event to which a striking moral could be attached. The claim that a saint had warned him of it beforehand would illustrate the ultimate powerlessness of an earthly king and also demonstrate the divine accuracy of Christian prophecy. That there were remnants in existence of sacrificial imagery in connection with the deaths of kings is evidenced by the myth of Conaire, and three-fold enigmatic circumstances would highlight such drama. The basic idea that Diarmaid was unable to compete with the Christian religion and with its saints is echoed also by an episode in his saga that has St Ruadhán outsmart him regarding horses. We read that after he had released Aodh Guaire, Ruadhán sent 30 dark-grey sea HORSES to him as a gift. Not realising the unusual origin of these fine steeds, Diarmaid put them racing, but they would accept neither bridle nor whip and returned to the sea.

SOURCES: Anderson & Anderson (1961), 71–5, 84–9, 278–83; Macalister (1956), 384–7; O'Grady, *1* (1982), 66–84; K. Meyer in *ZCP*, *7*, 305–7; Best & Lawlor (1931), 102–7; P. Walsh in *Irisleabhar Muighe Nuadhat* 1926, 3–11.

THEME OF THREE-FOLD DEATH: K. Jackson in Ryan (1940), 535–50.

GENERAL: Ó Cadhlaigh (1950); Mac Cana (1970), 29–31; F.J. Byrne (1973), 87–105. For a mistaken identification of this Diarmaid, *see* MAOLODHRÁN.

Diarmaid ua Duibhne

Handsome young hero in the FIANNA CYCLE. The name Diarmaid was derived from *dí-fhor-maid*, meaning 'unenvious', and was common in early Ireland. The second part of his name signifies 'descendant of Duibhne', which connects him with the Corca Dhuibhne sept of west Kerry.

In the medieval literature, he is also referred to as Diarmaid Donn, Diarmaid mac Duinn Uí Dhuibhne and Diarmaid mac Duinn meic Donnchadha. All of these appellations connect him with the Kerry area – containing echoes not only of Corca Dhuibhne but also of the deity Donn, and the branch of the western EOGHANACHT known as the Uí Dhonnchadha. The indications are, therefore, that the original appearance of the character in lore of FIONN MAC CUMHAILL was connected with

that part of the country. In some stories from the eighth century onwards, Fionn is opposed to the western Eoghanacht and abducted women from them; and it would have been natural to have a character with such appellations portrayed as an opponent of his in these matters. Simultaneously, in the Midlands, Fionn was being portrayed as an opponent of the high-king CORMAC MAC AIRT, as part of the conflicting claims of CONNACHTA and LAIGHIN septs on the Boyne Valley and the cult-centre of TARA. Sovereignty was envisaged alternately as a beautiful lady and as a miserable HAG; thus, the contest between Cormac and Fionn could be viewed as a struggle concerning a beautiful lady called Gráinne, a name that in fact meant 'ugly one'.

There are several references that show that an account of how Diarmaid eloped with Fionn's woman Gráinne was part of the repertoire of storytellers from the ninth century onwards. This indicates that a fusion had taken place between Fionn's hostility towards Cormac and his hostility towards the western Eoghanacht. The narrative structure used to rationalise this fusion was quite a popular one in early medieval Irish storytelling – i.e. the three-cornered plot of old man, young man and young woman, such as is found in the case of DEIRDRE. Although it was well known, we have no full version of this romance of Diarmaid and Gráinne from medieval times, the earliest surviving recension dating from the fifteenth century. This recension contains some late accretions, but it no doubt preserves faithfully the original structure. It can be summarised as follows:

After the death of his wife Maighnis, Fionn was a widower for a year, and having been told that Cormac had a beautiful daughter called Gráinne, he sent a message to the high-king concerning her. Gráinne consented to marry Fionn, and a great betrothal feast was held at Tara. At the feast, however, Gráinne saw the young warrior Diarmaid among Fionn's company and fell in love with him. She gave a sleeping draught to all those present at the feast except Diarmaid, and then tried to persuade him to carry her away. He was reluctant to do so, out of loyalty to Fionn, but she threatened him with magical destruction (*see* GEIS) if he refused. They departed from Tara and went west, crossing the River Shannon, and encamped in a wood called Doire Dá Bhaoth. Next day Fionn set out in pursuit, and his trackers found their trail. OISÍN sent Fionn's great hound Bran to warn the fugitives and also got a man with a massive voice to shout a warning, but Diarmaid ignored both messages, and instead gave three kisses to Gráinne in the full sight of the enraged Fionn. The spiritual AONGHUS, who had been the fosterer of Diarmaid, came to support the elopers, and he took Gráinne away from that place under a cloak of concealment, while the athletic Diarmaid vaulted over Fionn's men and escaped.

The fugitives next went to the southwest. Diarmaid caught a fish in the River Laune and they spent the night there. A young warrior called Muadhán came to them and became their servant. Going further west over the Caragh and Beigh rivers, they met with three mercenaries from the Channel Islands who had come to Ireland at Fionn's request with 1,000 men and three poisonous hounds to hunt Diarmaid. Not recognising Diarmaid, they took up his challenge to athletic contests of riding a barrel downhill, jumping onto a pointed spear, and walking on a sword edge, and in this way lost many of their men. Finally, they realised who Diarmaid was and set their hounds on him, but Diarmaid, with the help of Muadhán, slew both hounds and then slew the mercenaries. Soon after, Muadhán left them, and Diarmaid and Gráinne travelled northwards again. As they crossed a stream, a spurt of water struck Gráinne's leg and she remarked that it was bolder than Diarmaid. It was then that they became lovers, for hitherto Diarmaid had left a fish bone between them as they slept as a proof to the pursuing Fionn that they had not been unfaithful to him.

Coming to a forest, they got permission from an ogre called the Searbhán to settle there, providing they did not interfere with the fruit on his tree. However, Gráinne became pregnant and craved for some of these berries, and Diarmaid had to slay the ogre in an horrific combat. Fionn with his trackers reached that place and surrounded the tree, in the branches of which the lovers had taken refuge. Again, Aonghus came to their assistance, and they escaped in similar manner as before. Aonghus then went to Fionn and to the high-king Cormac and agreed terms with them regarding Diarmaid. The fugitive couple were allowed to return to Diarmaid's native territory of west Kerry, and he and Gráinne got further land from Fionn and Cormac in Leinster and Connacht. They lived happily for a long time and had several children. However, Fionn still secretly planned revenge against Diarmaid.

While residing in north Connacht, the couple were awakened one night by hounds baying and the sounds of a boar-hunt. Fionn had organised this hunt because it had been prophesied of Diarmaid, when he was a child, that he would meet his death through hunting the great boar of Beann Ghulban (Benbulben, County Sligo). Suspecting treachery, Gráinne tried to restrain her husband from going to face the boar, but next day, when Diarmaid heard that the Fianna warriors were being slaughtered by the boar, he went to face it. When the fierce beast charged him, Diarmaid leapt onto its back, and after a tremendous struggle was thrown off and his stomach ripped open. Then, with the stump of his sword, he stabbed the boar through the navel, killing it. Diarmaid was in the pangs of death, and Fionn refused twice to bring him a drink of water, even though water from Fionn's palms contained a cure. On the third occasion, Oisín threatened his father that he would kill him if he did not comply with Diarmaid's request. Fionn therefore brought the drink, but before he reached him Diarmaid was dead. Aonghus then came and brought the body of Diarmaid to his otherworld dwelling on the River Boyne.

Most manuscripts of this text end with Gráinne inciting the warrior sons of Diarmaid to take vengeance on Fionn, but one manuscript has Gráinne eventually marrying Fionn and bringing about a reconciliation between him and these sons. An extra narrative is added to the story in a fourteenth-century lay. According to this, Diarmaid and Gráinne had a daughter called Éachtach (Proficient). When a messenger quickly brought the news of Diarmaid's death to this Éachtach, she assembled her three brothers and they undertook a campaign of reaving against Fionn. After three full days of destruction, they were surrounded by Fionn and his battalions. Éachtach engaged Fionn himself in single combat, in which his shield was destroyed, and Daolghus – who went to Fionn's assistance – was cut in halves by her golden sword. Fionn was badly wounded and would have been slain but for the intervention of his supporter Lodharn, who slew the maiden. According to this recension, Diarmaid's sons were also slain in the fighting.

There are several points of similarity between the portrayal of Diarmaid and that of Adonis in classical myth. As with Adonis, the literature often refers to the beauty of Diarmaid's person and to the lustre of his countenance, and his death fighting a fierce boar is a direct parallel. This can best be explained by postulating that the early medieval composer of the Diarmaid and Gráinne story had read the account of Adonis given in Ovid's *Metamorphoses*. This would also explain why Diarmaid is associated with Benbulben, a place so far away from his native territory, for Ovid describes how the boar that killed Adonis had a savage and crooked snout. An Irish word for such a snout is *gulba*, and thus it is likely that Diarmaid's boar had some such designation that suggested Beann Ghulban as the locale of the fight. Regarding the involvement of Aonghus, this was already part of the story in the eleventh century, and may have been so from the beginning. It seems that it was occasioned by the special concern of Aonghus for young lovers, and that it was patterned on the assistance rendered to the beleaguered Cú Chulainn by Lugh.

This story of Diarmaid and Gráinne has been current in the folklore of both Ireland and Scotland for several centuries, and the main events of it are situated in various localities by the oral tradition. Indeed, the dolmens – ancient burial portals, common in the Irish landscape, consisting of a flat stone raised on top of two others – have long been known as 'beds of Diarmaid and Gráinne'. The folk fancy is that the lovers slept on top of these during their flight from Fionn, and it is believed that if a childless woman sleeps on one of them, she – like Gráinne – will conceive.

These folk versions have contained two special motifs since the end of the Middle Ages. One concerns the manner of Diarmaid's death. Instead of dying in combat with the boar, he is said to have slain it without sustaining any mortal injury to himself. The wily Fionn, however, realised that the boar had one poisonous bristle and therefore asked Diarmaid to measure the beast from snout to tail. To do so, Diarmaid stood on its back, but he slipped and the bristle pierced him, with fatal results. The other motif in oral versions is Diarmaid's celebrated love-spot. This was situated on his forehead or neck, and any woman who saw it would fall helplessly in love with him. Marks on the body, made from various concoctions, were part of love-magic in ancient and medieval tradition, and it must have come into this narrative from such a source. Diarmaid's love-spot (*ball seirce*) became his great distinguishing mark in folklore, and he was known as 'Diarmaid of the women'.

In post-medieval oral versions of a visit made by Fionn to an allegorical house, Diarmaid is said to have got his love-spot as a gift from an otherworld lady representing youth there. It seems clear that the character of Diarmaid owes its origins to the story of his elopement with Gráinne, but in the subsequent literature, he figured prominently in many stories. For accounts of other adventures involving him, *see* FIANNA CYCLE.

NAMES: Stokes (1900), 7, 43, 86, 100; O'Rahilly (1927), 267; Ní Shéaghdha (1967), 130.

ELOPEMENT: early references: Meyer (1910), xxiv; Mac Cana (1980), 46, 57, 86; Ní Shéaghdha (1967), x–xiv, 130–6. Fifteenth-century text: Ní Shéaghdha (1967). Version in Scottish lay: N. Ross

(1939), 70–6. Oral versions: Ní Shéaghdha (1967), xviii–xxix; Bruford (1969), 106–9, 265–6.

ÉACHTACH: Mac Neill (1908), 45–7.

LOVE-SPOT: Bruford, 108, 265; Meyer & Nutt, *1* (1895), 69; de híde (1933), 125; IFC 1170:277; Ó hÓgáin (1985), 269–70 & in *Comhar, 7* (1979), 16–18.

GENERAL: Ó hÓgáin (1988), 166–77, 336–7, 358–9 & in Almqvist, Ó Catháin & Ó Héalaí (1987), 216–18, 227–31.

dogs These animals have been domesticated in Ireland since the fifth millennium BC. Their importance is clear from the various roles given to them in the medieval literature. In stories of FIONN MAC CUMHAILL and the FIANNA, for instance, some dogs or hounds are faithful friends, whereas others are fierce fighters in the armies of the foe. The hounds said to have hunted and fought for Fionn were undoubtedly examples of the huge and handsome breed known as Irish wolfhounds, which were in high demand abroad and were exported in great numbers in medieval times.

A story, mentioned in ninth-century stories, claims that there were no lapdogs in early Ireland because the Britons had forbidden the export of them to this country. While visiting a friend in Britain, however, Cairbre Músc, son of Conaire, deliberately smeared his dagger with fat, thereby causing a beautiful lapdog to gnaw at the dagger and damage it. He demanded the dog itself in compensation, and it was given to him. It was a bitch, and it produced three pups. To settle a quarrel in Ireland, Cairbre gave a pup each to CORMAC MAC AIRT and AILILL MOLT, and kept one himself.

Dogs were appreciated not just as good workers on the farm but also as protectors of the house from both physical and spiritual marauders. It was generally held that a dog would know if a GHOST were present, and would show this by making its coat stand on end and baying. The dog was considered to have almost human intelligence and, in some ways, even more. A faithful dog, for instance, would know of its master's impending death and would make that clear by its behaviour, refusing to be parted from the master. This sixth sense extended also to the WEATHER, and various signs were taken from the behaviour of dogs in that regard. As 'man's best friend', it was considered natural and proper to talk to a dog, but one should never ask a question of it, for it was feared that the dog might answer in a human voice, thereby causing ill luck and perhaps even death to the questioner.

It was said in Ulster that when St COLM CILLE once saw a spaniel defeat an Irish hound in a fight, he prophesied that the Spaniards would one day control Ireland. *See also* ANIMAL TALES (types 178A, 200) *and* ROMANTIC TALES (type 934B).

HISTORY: F. Kelly (1997), 114–21; Graham (1885); E. Hogan (1897); Gardner (1931).

LAPDOG STORY: Stokes (1862), xlviii–l, 29–30.

GENERAL: Cross (1952), 44, 53–5, 59–61, 65–6, 72–5, 77–80, 82; S. Ó Súilleabháin (1942), 44–6; Danaher (1966), 93–100; P.V. O'Sullivan (1991), 14–15, 97–102.

Domhnall mac Aodha HIGH-KING

of the UÍ NÉILL, who reigned from AD 628–42. He was son of another high-king, Aodh mac Ainmhireach (for whom *see* COLM CILLE *and* BRANDUBH).

In his biography of Colm Cille, ADHAMHNÁN describes how that SAINT blessed the boy Domhnall, and foretold that he would outlive all his brothers, be a famous king, and die peacefully in his bed – all of which proved to be true.

Domhnall was a shrewd and able king. Initially, he had as ally the Ulster king Conghal Caoch, but when the two quarrelled and clashed, Conghal had to flee to Scotland. He enlisted the support there of Domhnall Breac, king of the Dál Riada sept that controlled western Scotland and some territory in County Antrim. The result of this was a great battle fought at Magh Rátha (Moira, County Down) in the year 637. In this battle, the high-king gained a complete victory over the forces of Domhnall Breac and Conghal Caoch. A text that dramatised these events was composed early in the tenth century, being based on surviving tradition at that time. According to it, Conghal Caoch was the foster-son of the high-king Domhnall, and his epithet *caoch* (one-eyed) was due to his having been stung in the eye by a BEE in Domhnall's orchard. The Ulstermen demanded the eye of Domhnall's son as compensation, but the high-king decreed only that the swarm be destroyed so that the guilty bee should perish.

The text goes on to describe how, when Domhnall held the feast of TARA, Conghal sat on his left-hand side. A dozen eggs were brought to the high-king, and Conghal ate one of them secretly. When Domhnall began to divide the eggs, he noticed that one was missing and accused Conghal of stealing it. Conghal refused to remain at the feast, despite Domhnall's attempt to resolve the quarrel by offering him a golden egg. He went to Scotland to the Dál Riada king, and returning with a strong force began to ravage the territory of the high-king's mother. The saints of Ireland attempted to effect a reconciliation between himself and the high-king, but Conghal was determined to become ruler of Ireland. The armies met at Magh Rátha. Domhnall the high-king entrusted command of his forces to a warrior called Dúnchadh, while he himself played chess in his tent, with his dwarf acting as a look-out. The battle lasted for three days. Dúnchadh killed Conghal's horse, but gave him his own in place of it. Similarly, he destroyed Conghal's shield and sword, but replaced them with his own. Hearing that the high-king was at his tent praying, Conghal thought of going to make terms with him, but in the continuing fighting slew the royal jester CONALL CLOGACH. Then the high-king himself went into the fighting, calling on the name of God, and his forces overwhelmed the foe. Conghal was slain, as well as the Dál Riada king, but one strong man of the Scots escaped by swimming. The loyal Dúnchadh was also slain, and the high-king lamented him in verse. Domhnall also honoured the head of his slain opponent Conghal, reciting a poem of praise for him.

A more intricate narrative is given in a text from the eleventh century entitled *Fled Dún na nGéd* (The Feast of Dún na nGé, a fortress near Dowth, County Meath). According to this, the high-king

Domhnall dreamed that his pet whelp went raging from him and gathered the Irish and Scottish packs, as well as those of the Saxons and Britons, against him. These hounds were only defeated by Domhnall and his men after seven battles. Alarmed by the dream, Domhnall leaped naked from his bed, but he was restrained by his wife who assured him that his forces were so strong that he had nothing to fear. Domhnall went to his hermit brother Maol Cobha to have the dream interpreted, and Maol explained that the whelp was his fosterling, and that the fosterling would rebel and get the support of foreigners and only be defeated after seven battles. Domhnall had two princes in fosterage, Conghal Caoch and RAGHALLACH of Connacht, and Maol recommended that these two be dismissed, but the high-king refused to do so out of honour and affection for them.

Domhnall prepared for the feast of Tara, sending out his stewards to collect as many goose eggs as possible. These stewards forcibly took eggs from the maidservant of a saint who used to stand all day to his armpits in the River Boyne and each evening eat an egg together with some cress from the river. When the saint discovered what they had done, he laid a curse on the feast the high-king was preparing. Just before the feast was held, a hideously ugly couple arrived, bringing a tubful of goose eggs. Domhnall welcomed them and gave them food, but they could not be satisfied, and departed saying that they were from hell and had come to be first at the feast and thus ensure that trouble would ensue.

When the kings of all the provinces had assembled, Domhnall welcomed them, but before they sat to eat, Conghal took a bite from one of the eggs. Domhnall was told of the saint's curse, and he then realised that Conghal – who had been the first to partake of the eggs – would be the one to oppose him. The twelve leading saints of Ireland were brought to bless the feast and have the curse removed from it, and they did so, but the effect on Conghal could not be undone. At the feast, Conghal was not put sitting in his customary place beside the high-king and, furthermore, was served the egg of a hen rather than of a duck. Urged on by his outraged Ulstermen, Conghal was seized with rage and began to recite his grievances against Domhnall. Among the things he mentioned was the fact that he had gained the HIGH-KINGSHIP for Domhnall by slaying his predecessor SUIBHNE MEANN. He had run Suibhne through with his spear as that high-king was playing chess, and the dying Suibhne had flung a chessman at him and completely destroyed his eye, which had earlier been stung by the bee. Then Conghal stormed out of the feast, despite all Domhnall's efforts to pacify him.

He gathered his forces in Ulster, and then crossed to Scotland to seek support from the king of that country, Eochaidh. The latter had promised never to oppose Domhnall mac Aodha, but he allowed his four sons go with Conghal. Eochaidh's chief-DRUID, Dubh Diadh, and the other druids cautioned against the undertaking, but Conghal pushed ahead and went to seek the support of the king of the Britons. While he was at that court, a strange warrior arrived who demanded the marrowbone given to the greatest warrior at a feast. He won this through combat, and then proved that he was Conán Rod, the long-lost son of the British king and queen. He wore a ring on his finger given him by his mother when he had left twenty years before to learn feats of arms, he had a grain of gold under his shoulder that the queen had long ago inserted there, and he gave conclusive proof of his identity by removing a stone that no liar could move and by riding two horses that no liar could ride. He also joined the force of Conghal.

Fortified by warriors of the Scots, Britons and Saxons, Conghal crossed to Ireland, but in the massive slaughter at Magh Rátha was defeated and slain. Conán Rod was slain by Ceallach, son of Maol Cobha, and of all the foreigners only one man escaped alive. This was the druid Dubh Diadh, who by magic flew through the air and reached Scotland with a dead warrior attached to each leg, for Conghal

had tied his men together for the battle.

This text claims that it was in that battle that the Dál n-Araidhe king SUIBHNE GEILT went mad, and several echoes from the Suibhne story are found in it. Other sources known to the writer obviously included an account of the sojourn of LUGHAIDH MAC CON in Scotland and his triumph in the Battle of Magh Mucramha; the story of the birth of the Leinster king BRANDUBH (MOTIF of gold grain in shoulder); the story of CONLAE, unrecognised son of Cú Chulainn; and the tradition of the Connacht king GUAIRE, who also had a hermit brother who was a prophet. Domhnall's brother Maol Cobha was not in actual fact a hermit, but had been high-king until defeated and slain by Suibhne Meann. His survival as a hermit in this instance is therefore an anachronism.

Anderson & Anderson (1961), 47–50, 230–1, 316–17, 474–7; C. Marstrander in *Ériu*, *5*, 226–47; O'Donovan (1842); R. Lehmann (1964); Macalister (1956), 376–7.

donkeys Although much associated with the country in modern tourist brochures, the donkey was a late introduction into Ireland and did not become common until the eighteenth century. Because of the international folk LEGEND claiming that it got the cross on its back as a reward for carrying JESUS CHRIST, it was said to be a blessed animal that should always be treated with kindness. It was widely believed that a child suffering from chincough (whooping cough) could be cured by being made to pass under a donkey's belly.

Swinfen (1975), 13–22; S. Ó Súilleabháin (1942), 36–7; P.V. O'Sullivan (1991), 91–7.

Donn Mythical figure in Irish literature and folklore. The name simply represents the adjective *donn*, meaning 'brown'. This was sometimes written *dond*, which is incorrect, for the word derives from a Celtic *dhuosnos*.

In ancient times, the adjective usually signified 'dark', and the character Donn is perennially associated with the shadowy realm of the dead. He is, however, also represented as an ancestor of those who die, and his name therefore seems to have been originally an epithet of the deity known as the DAGHDHA. Donn is referred to in several early texts. Particularly striking is a reference in the death-tale of CONAIRE, who is slain by three red-haired men, 'sons of Donn, king of the dead at the red tower of the dead'. These three are further quoted as saying, 'we ride the HORSES of Donn – although we are alive, we are dead!'

In treating of this shady personification of death, the writers of pseudo-history rationalised him into one of the leaders of the fanciful ancient migration to Ireland of the Gaelic people. These writers described how one Donn, son of MÍL, was drowned at Inbhear Scéine (Kenmare Bay, County Kerry). In this, they were echoing an earlier belief that in that area the deity inhabited the island known as Teach Duinn (literally, 'Donn's House', now called Bull Rock). One ninth-century source attributes a very significant statement to this personage: 'To me, to my house, you shall all come after your deaths.' That rocky island in fact has a dolmen-like shape, with the sea passing beneath it, and it could easily be likened to the pre-Celtic burial dolmens on land. Also, when viewed from the mainland, the setting sun shines through the archway underneath it, and this may also have helped its assimilation to Donn, a figure of the father-GOD Daghdha in his role as underworld deity during the dark hours (see TIME).

Sources from the eighth to the tenth century refer to Teach Duinn as the place 'where the dead assemble', and describe deceased people as travelling to and from it. Repeated references in the literature show that Teach Duinn was regarded as the western extremity of Ireland, and it is tempting to connect the locating of Donn there with some accounts given by the second-century Greek writer Plutarch. Referring to a deity who lives in a sleepy state on an island off the land to the west of Britain, Plutarch calls him by the name of a Greek god of the dead, Cronus; and again, the same writer describes how fishermen in that land were wont to hear strange boats travelling at night to a distant destination where the names of those who disembarked were called out.

The word *donn* could be viewed as the opposite of *find*, which meant 'illumination' or 'brightness', and that the Celtic otherworld included a dialectic between these two colours is clear from the early lore of the personage FIONN. Such a dialectic was, indeed, the background to the conflict in the ULSTER CYCLE between the two great bulls called the Finnbheannach and the DONN CUAILNGE. Its genesis must be quite old, but originally the figure represented by Donn was not in any way dependent on Find, and Donn survived in tradition as a great personage in his own right. Medieval literature tends to associate his name with each and every otherworld place, but since the name had come to be used in a generalised sense to mean 'otherworld lord', it is clear that most of these allusions are not to him specifically. Folk tradition testifies that two locations in addition to Bull Rock preserved definite vestiges of his cult. These were Cnoc Fírinne (Knockfierna, a very conspicuous hill in the middle of County Limerick) and the 'Dumhcha' or great sand dunes at Dunbeg on the west coast of County Clare.

At Knockfierna he was known as Donn Fírinne, and the entrance to his palace was believed to be through a cavity near the summit of the hill. Folklore told of people being brought into the hill to be with Donn when they died, and this was not seen to conflict with Christian belief since it was rationalised by the opinion that such people were not really dead but had been kidnapped by him. He was said to often leave his residence at night riding a white horse, and such folk accounts of him have been influenced by LEGENDS of other spiritual beings. For instance, he once took a man with him on a terrifying ride throughout Ireland (see GHOSTS), and was said to take away accomplished hurlers to join his team in hurling matches against rival otherworld communities (see FAIRIES). Like the fairies, he resented people interfering with his hill by ploughing on its slopes, but, being quite genial, preferred to appear and warn people to stop rather than to take immediate action against them.

One type of narrative illustrates how a cluster of MOTIFS got attached to him. We are told that he visited a blacksmith one night and asked for his horse to be shod. He wrenched off one of the horse's legs and gave it to the blacksmith to have the shoe put on it. The terrified smith complied, and then Donn replaced the leg on the horse perfectly, saying that he was to lead his cavalry that night in a battle against a rival host. The unorthodox method of shoeing the horse is borrowed from a far-flung folklore plot (*see* RELIGIOUS TALES, type 753), but the general situation described is of special interest. That situation corresponds to a legend found in a medieval NORSE text concerning the Norse god Odin, who similarly appeared to a blacksmith to have his steed Sleipnir shod before a great battle far away. It seems likely, therefore, that this account of Donn is indebted to a residue of lore from the Norse settlements of medieval Limerick.

Other items of lore concerning Donn can also be related to Odin. Like the Norse deity, he sometimes rode his horse through the sky, and was regarded as a great personification of the WEATHER. Thunder and lightning meant that he was travelling wildly in the sky, and if clouds were over the hill of Knockfierna, that was taken to mean that he was gathering them together and would soon release them in the form of rain. The portrayal of Donn as a phantom rider led to a connection being made between him and another ghostly figure of Limerick lore, Gearóid Iarla FitzGerald, the Earl of DESMOND, and as a result of this, the image of a wizard was borrowed from that earl to Donn. Thus one folk narrative has a man being brought into a fine palace in Knockfierna and finding there Donn as an old man clothed in white and instructing a large number of young students in 'the mysteries of the creation since the stars began to shine'.

In County Clare, he was known as Donn na Duimhche (Donn of the Dune), being also often encountered as a night horseman, and one legend develops the motif of his fairy army. We are told that a hostile fairy host was driving away all the CATTLE from a local farmer when Donn and his army intercepted them and, in a bitter otherworld battle, rescued the herd. This Clare tradition of Donn stretches back for a considerable time. It was well known to the POET Aindrias Mac Cruitín, who around the year 1740 alluded to Donn na Duimhche in one of his works. Complaining of his miserable circumstances and of the niggardly treatment he had received from the gentry of the area, the poet begged Donn to open his door to him and receive him into his palace 'under the waves'. The maritime aspect of this lore of Donn in west Clare is a close parallel of the tradition of Bull Rock (Teach Duinn). The medieval pseudo-historians described several people as being drowned at the sand dunes (*dumhcha*) at Teach Duinn, and the literature also referred to this great personage of the south-west Kerry coast as Donn Dumhach or Donn Dumhaighe (i.e. of the dunes). The shore off Doonbeg, County Clare was very dangerous for boats, and it was therefore easy to make the mistake of identifying the Kerry dunes with the larger ones on the Clare coast. The identification was probably first made by some scholar in post-medieval times and, as a result, the lore of Donn became associated with the latter area.

In his poem, Aindrias Mac Cruitín made an offer to Donn to 'groom the steeds of your phantom cavalry'. It is apparent from this that the poet knew of the fairy-horseman image, this having been borrowed into the Clare lore from that of Donn Fírinne at some time previous to the eighteenth century. The origin of this earlier Donn Fírinne of Limerick is more complicated. His epithet is a corruption of Frigrinn, which was an ancient name for the locality, the hill being originally called Cnoc Frigrinne. The likelihood is that this tradition grew out of some rhetoric or text that situated Donn at various hill-cairns regarded as otherworld dwellings. As a result of the corruption to *Fírinne* (literally, 'truth'), and of Donn's associations with the elements, the people of County Limerick claimed that the hill was so called because its aspect enabled 'truthful predictions to be made about the WEATHER'. The connection with Odin and the variety of the fairy legends attached to Donn Fírinne would suggest that his lore was well established in Limerick by the late Middle Ages.

GENERAL: Pokorny, 1 (1959), 271; K. Müller-Lisowski in Béaloideas, 18, 142–99; T.F. O'Rahilly (1946), 481–4 & in Hermathena, 23, 203–4 & in The Irish Monthly, 53, 257–63; Ó Luaighnigh (1935), 7–9; Bruen & Ó hÓgáin (1996), 142–3, 229–31; Ó hÓgáin (1985), 152–4, 234–6, 337.

BULL ROCK: M. Mac Cárthaigh in Dinnseanchas, 2, 51.

PLUTARCH REFERENCES: Moralia: 419, 941; Brown (1943), 339–41.

ODIN MATERIAL: Jónsson (1957), 390–2; C-M. Edsman (1949), 117–19.

Donn Cuailnge Mythical bull, the chief object of the great CATTLE-raid (*Táin Bó Cuailnge*) in the ULSTER CYCLE.

When the compilers of the *Táin* narrative in the sixth or seventh century decided that cattle-raiding would be the basis of their account of an epic war, they naturally sought material with bovine imagery that could be dramatised. The ancient GOD of the dead was DONN, and since death was a major theme in the context, the compilers were inclined to give a leading role to a great bull called Donn. Cuailnge (Cooley, County Louth) seems to have been an area in which herds were concealed during real cattle-raids (*see* ULSTER CYCLE), and thus the bull was said to belong to that area. The mythical background to this Donn Cuailnge is clear from the fact that he is contrasted with another great bull called the Finnbheannach (earlier written 'Findbennach'). The name of this latter bull is interpreted as 'the white horned one', but the first element in it suggests that it is an emanation from the ancient divine personage Find (*see* FIONN).

There are several indications that metamorphosis was an attribute of deities in ancient Irish tradition, and a ninth-century text underlines the mythic significance of these two bulls in accordance with this. They are described as the final manifestations of two opposing beings after a whole series of transformations. Originally, we are told, they belonged to the otherworld community, being two PIG-keepers

there called Friuch and Rucht. These two quarrelled and cast spells over each other's pigs, with the result that they were dismissed by their employers. Then they turned themselves into BIRDS of prey and continued their contest, and later took on respectively the forms of FISH, stags, warriors, phantoms and dragons, fighting each other all the while. Eventually, they became maggots. One of them went into a spring in Cooley and was consumed by a cow belonging to Dáire mac Fiachna. The other was consumed from a Connacht spring by a cow of queen MEADHBH and her husband. These two cows bore bull-calves, the former the Donn Cuailnge and the latter the Finnbheannach.

The plot of this story is borrowed from folklore (*see* WONDER TALES, type 325), but the basic idea can be accepted as reflecting divine transformations of Donn and Find that have been carried over into the new context of the *Táin* epic. The name of the Donn Cuailnge is taken to reflect a brown colour (*donn*), but the bull is also called the Dubh Cuailnge (black of Cooley). This colour variety in fact reflects the imagery of the deity Donn, who was also sometimes called Dubh. The designation of the bull's owner further reflects ancient lore of the deity, for the name DÁIRE was often used in association with Donn.

The same text on the pig-keepers' transformations describes the Donn Cuailnge as being fierce, strong, and so huge that 30 boys could ride on its back. In the *Táin*, we are told that it could bull 50 heifers in a single day, that the heifers that did not calve on the following day would burst, and that no demons would dare come into the canton where the great animal was. Its role is further dramatised in related texts. For instance, the MÓR-RÍOGHAIN once took a cow from Connacht to be bulled by the Donn Cuailnge, and the calf that resulted grew into a fine young bull that was slain in combat by the Finnbheannach. On seeing this, queen Meadhbh swore that she would not rest until she saw that calf's sire being confronted by the Finnbheannach.

The great cattle-raid began when Meadhbh was refused a loan of the Donn Cuailnge by its owner. Later, when Meadhbh's army was in a position to capture the bull, the Mór-Ríoghain appeared to it in the form of a bird, and warned it to go with its heifers to a safe place. Eventually, Meadhbh succeeded in taking the bull, and she retained it on her retreat to Connacht after defeat at the hands of Cú CHULAINN and the Ulstermen. On reaching Meadhbh's court at Cruachain, the final inevitable clash occurred when the Donn Cuailnge and the Finnbheannach encountered each other. The most dramatic account states that they fought all day and all night, travelling throughout Ireland and terrifying everybody who heard their rending and bellowing in the darkness. When morning came, the Donn Cuailnge was seen passing by Meadhbh's court with the carcass of its rival on its horns. It then headed towards home, dropping parts of the dead bull at various places and thus giving rise to several place names. Reaching Cooley, it slaughtered many people in its rage, then put its back against a mound, and the heart burst in its breast.

Roider (1979); E. Windisch in *Irische Texte, 2 (2)*, 239–56; K. Meyer in *RC, 10*, 212–28; C. O'Rahilly (1976), 30, 46–8, 124 & (1970), 35–6, 48–9, 133–6 & (1961), 44–5, 58–9, 157–62; M.E. Dobbs in *ZCP, 14*, 395–420.

Donnelly, Dan *(1788–1820)* Famous boxer from Dublin who graced the ring between the years 1814–19. In Irish, his name was Dónall Ó Donnghaile. He was a carpenter by trade, and only got the reputation of a fighter after he reacted to teasing by ruffians. He was persuaded to become a professional boxer by a sports enthusiast from County Kildare, Captain William Kelly, who became his trainer.

Folklore stresses the great power of his punches, as in an account of how he was discovered by Kelly. Hearing of his boxing skill, Kelly had gone to Dublin to seek him out, and noticed a strange youth lay low a tavern-full of men with a single blow to each. Upon enquiring, he was told that the youth was indeed Donnelly. Another account has Dan meet his trainer in a different way. He

was doing some journeywork as a carpenter, and when passing by Kelly's estate noticed the owner being badly beaten in a sparring bout by a rough-looking fellow. Dan shouted out to Kelly that attack was the best form of defence, and Kelly changed his tactics and laid low his opponent. He then invited Dan to dinner on condition that he try some sparring himself, but Dan easily knocked down every man put against him.

A narrative collected in County Galway asserts that a short while before his birth, the great boxer's mother ran a race against a horse and won it. This was, of course, a great portent for the unborn child. The story itself is based on the medieval Irish myth of MACHA, which circulated in Irish manuscripts, but it was suggested by the actions of Dan's mother who, after he defeated an acclaimed English boxer called George Cooper at the Curragh in 1815, is reported to have led a victory parade through Dublin with her bosom exposed and shouting: 'There's the breast that suckled him!'

Dan's first bout in the ring was against the boxing champion of Dublin. He won after sixteen rounds of slugging, but a folklore account telescopes this by claiming that 'Donnelly punched him, and he did not punch him a second time, for the other man could take no more!' The most dramatic aspect of Dan Donnelly in the folk mind was – as a song states – 'the fist that overthrew his rivals o'er and o'er!' In fact, Dan competed in only three professional bouts. The first two of these took place on the Curragh of Kildare at a place since known as 'Donnelly's Hollow', but the third victory was gained in England. This factor shot him into a traditional role of the great Irish sportsman who defeats an English adversary on the latter's own soil.

It was claimed that King George IV was so impressed with the Irish boxer's prowess that he knighted him. There is scant historical evidence for this claim, but folklore uses the opportunity to attach another undercurrent of ideology to the supposed conferring of honour. A Kildare account portrays the conversation between monarch and pugilist as man-to-man drama. 'So you

182

are the best man in Ireland,' said the king. 'I am not, my liege,' answered Donnelly. 'I'm the worst man in Ireland, but I'm the best man in England today!'

Myler (1976); G.A. Little (1943), 112–16; de híde, *AR* (1933), 78–82; Ms Greene in *JKAS, 3,* 259.

druids/druidesses Members of the learned caste or priestly profession in Celtic and early Irish culture. The word 'druid' is probably derived from a Celtic *dru-wid*, which would have meant 'very knowledgeable'.

The Greek and Latin writers attest to the importance of the druids among the Celtic Gauls. They were at the centre of society, making decisions on matters of tradition, custom, and law, and also on general questions concerning nature and human life. Continental and Irish sources alike make it clear that the druids in their teaching placed great emphasis on the five elements – sky, earth, sea, sun and moon – holding these to preside over human affairs. According to the classical writers, the Continental druids also taught the doctrine of transmigration of souls, and practised divination of the future from auguries, and several echoes of such beliefs and practices can be found also in Irish tradition (*see* FIONN).

In writing of the Continental Celts, Julius Caesar refers to the druidic belief that the Celts were all descended from one ancestral father and adds: 'For this reason they count periods of TIME not by the number of days but by the number of nights; and in reckoning birthdays and the new moon and new year their unit of reckoning is the night followed by the day.' This system of counting of nights before days was known to other early European people also, and terminology reflecting it survives still in Irish and other Celtic languages (in Irish, for instance, *oíche* means both night and eve). It is clear that Caesar saw a connection between the darkness of night and the lord of the dead ancestors, but the functional link between this and the computing of time raises a question. The sun, which brings the light of day, is, of course, the basic determiner of time, but for the Celts, time seems to have been computed by the sun's absence.

We can explain this by the proposition that knowledge of time, as other abstract knowledge, came from the realm inhabited by the ancestors, the realm into which the sun descends in the west each night. It is apparent that Irish lore of the great ancestor (*see* DAGHDHA) reflects the ancient druidic genealogical system, and that the MOTIF of alternation between figures representing darkness and light (*see* DONN *and* FIONN) is derived from the druidic computation of time. The teaching was that, just as the night represented the dead and the day the living, so the dark half of the year – which began at Samhain (November) – belonged especially to the dead, and the bright half – which began at Bealtaine (May) – highlighted the living community. In this context also can be mentioned the ancient Celtic custom of seeking knowledge from the dead ancestors by resorting to the burial mounds in darkness. The druids, it seems, claimed that they could thus bring light out of darkness (*see* POETS), and for them, Samhain was a very important time. As late as AD 1084 there is mention of a man who resorted to the prehistoric tumulus of Brugh na Bóinne (Newgrange, County Meath) every November to discover the future.

We read that the terminology used to describe a practitioner of mystical knowledge among the Continental Celts involved three terms, *druis, vatis* and *bardos*. These same words were used in early Irish literature in the form of *druí* (later, *draoi*), *fáith* (later, *fáidh*) and *bard*. In medieval Ireland, the terms were used respectively in the senses of 'magician', 'prophet' and 'versifier'. Whatever the nature of original druidic grades, these specific senses give a good insight into the general functions of the profession. The druid was believed to have mystical powers, to be a seer, and to utter sacred rhetoric. Irish tradition tends to use the word *bard* in the context of minor poets, and the more prestigious term for a poet is *file*. This word derives from a root meaning 'to see', and there are indications that it was used (in an original form *velet-*) in connection with the druids of the Continental Celts also. In Ireland, the *file* was a leading figure in the social order and his verse was reputed to have magical power. It is in fact clear that vestiges of druidism survived in the imagery of Irish poets after the introduction of Christianity made more overt expressions of the older beliefs unfeasible.

Some early Irish sources describe rituals whereby the druids gained knowledge. We read of how, to decide on who should be KING, they organised a bull-feast (*tarbh-fheis*) that consisted of killing a white bull, drinking its soup, and sleeping on its hide. The required information would be revealed through a dream in that situation. Similarly, their custom of lying on their 'wattles of knowledge' is described, and it is evident that the source of such inspiration was believed to be the spirits of dead ancestors (*see* FIONN). There can be little doubt but that much of the paraphernalia of the supernatural as found in early Irish literature emanated from teachings of the druids. These matters would include the idea of the otherworld realm – whether on western islands or in burial mounds – at least some aspects of the cult of kingship, and devices such as magical cloaks of concealment and magical fogs and winds.

In his account of the druids of Gaul, Julius Caesar describes the island of Britain as a kind of headquarters of the profession in his time, and he says that Gaulish druids resorted there to improve their education. Certain parallels to this are found in early Irish sources, which use the term Alba for the whole island of Britain. For instance, the druid-poetess Feidhilm, from whom queen MEADHBH of Connacht seeks a prophecy, is described as having come from Alba where she had learned *filidh-eacht* (seer-craft). There are several mentions of druidesses in Continental sources also. The word used by the Gauls for a centre of druidic ritual was *nemeton*. This appears in Irish in the form *neimheadh*, which had the meaning 'sacred place', and is in fact given as the name of a fictional druid-like figure.

These places seem to have often been close to trees – hence the Irish term *fiodhneimheadh*, where *fiodh* means a tree – and there are many indications that the cult of trees was very strong among druids. A somewhat fanciful derivation of the word 'druid' – first cited by Pliny and still held by some scholars – is 'oak scientist' (Gaulish *dru*, Irish *dair*, meaning oak). The favourite tree of the Irish druids, however, was clearly the rowan, and it was on wattles of this tree that the Irish practitioners slept in order to have prophetic visions. The hazel tree was also important, as evidenced by the druid's name Mac Cuill (son of hazel) and also by the lore concerning nine hazel trees at the source of the River Boyne, the nuts of which had a nucleus of wisdom (*see* BÓINN). Both Continental and Irish sources also stress the druidic custom of drawing auguries from the flight of BIRDS, especially of the raven.

The narratives concerning druids in Irish literature all come from Christian sources, and in them these pagan priests are portrayed in a generally negative light. Aspects of their original status, however, come through in some texts. A good example is the druid CATHBHADH, who is portrayed as on a par with the king of Ulster, and in some contexts even has precedence over him; thus we read that nobody could speak before this druid in the assembly of the Ulstermen, and an incident is related to illustrate this. When trying to rouse the warriors from their debilitation, Sualdamh, father of CÚ CHULAINN, shouts a warning to them concerning the rampant armies of Meadhbh. He does not wait for Cathbhadh to speak first, and so, when he mounts a horse, it rears under him and his shield turns against him and severs the head from his shoulders.

Not surprisingly, the druids were portrayed as opponents of the SAINTS in medieval hagiography. Already in a seventh-century biography of PATRICK, a verse is attributed to two druids who sadly prophesy the end of their own power and the coming of new ways. These two are called Lochru and Lucet Mael, and we read of a great contention at TARA between

Patrick and the latter. This is druidism through a hostile perspective, and Lucet is patterned on biblical figures such as the Babylonian wizards of Nebuchadnezzar and Simon Magus, the magician who opposed St Peter. However, certain of his attributes may be authentic, such as his name Lucet, which is meant to indicate a devotee of Lugh, and his epithet Mael (later, Maol), which means bald and may refer to a druidic tonsure. The skills attributed to Lucet are probably a reflex of lore then current concerning druids: he causes snow to fall and brings a thick fog over the land. Other skills attributed to druids in the medieval literature are the creation of illusions (especially in battle), interpretation of dreams, curing of illnesses, discovery of thieves, giving of shrewd military advice, and cursing of people and places hostile to them. A principal means of performing all these functions was through chanting spells or uttering rhetorics. This custom lies at the basis of the culture of the Irish poets (q.v.), and there is continuity between the ancient lore of druids and the traditional images of the latter.

Whereas the tradition could survive under the guise of versification, it was handled with varying degrees of tolerance. When the context being described was explicitly belonging to old pre-Christian times, druids and their craft could figure in the literature because of their antiquarian and dramatic value. This is so in cases of druids associated with the TUATHA DÉ DANANN and with pseudo-historical kings such as CORMAC MAC AIRT and EOGHAN MÓR. In other contexts, prophecies supposedly made by druids and pagan seers could be used as an argument in favour of Christianity, as is evident from prophecies concerning Patrick and several other saints that were attributed to the celebrated FIONN MAC CUMHAILL. Finally, there are traditions that reflect the historical situation of the Christian mission confronted with druidism. A realistic echo of this is found in the accounts of the sixth-century high-king DIARMAID MAC CEARRBHEOIL, who is represented as having both druids and saints as advisers at his court. His leading

prophet, in fact, is an interesting example of how the mystical imagery from the two cultures could influence each other. This is BEAG MAC DÉ whom the writers converted retrospectively into a saint.

Although the druid survived as a dramatic personage in ordinary narratives of ancient heroes (see CONALL GULBAN), the tendencies in the hagiographical literature were different. There the general picture is of druids as malicious wizards. See also FEIRCHEIRDNE and MOGH RUITH.

Chadwick (1966); Piggott (1968); P. Henry (1978), 40–8; le Roux & Guyonvarc'h (1968); Plummer, *1* (1910), clviii–clxiii; Bieler (1979), 74–7, 92–7; Ó hÓgáin (1999), 54–127; E. Mullally in *Éigse*, *31*, 89–101; W. Stokes in *RC*, *17*, 416–17.

Dubhthach Daol Uladh Fictional warrior in the ULSTER CYCLE. The name Dubhthach was a common one, meaning 'black-haired', and does not seem to have had any mythical content.

This Dubhthach figures as one of the warriors who constituted the exile band of FEARGHUS MAC RÓICH in Connacht. His sobriquets (earlier, Dóel Ulad) mean 'chafer of the Ulstermen', and he is described as particularly ruthless, killing several women on his first foray when Fearghus rebelled against king CONCHOBHAR MAC NEASA. In retaliation, all of his family were put to death, and he in turn continually wreaked vengeance for this on the Ulstermen. Sometimes he worked in company, but he was equally effective when raiding alone. His portrayal is sinister, having rough, jet-black hair, a bloody eye, and the head of a ravenous wolf on each shoulder of his armour. For a while, he was the possessor of the great spear of CEALTCHAR, and he was accustomed to bathe its point in a vat of dark blood.

Dubhthach was obviously a character invented to heighten the drama in the texts. One medieval source states that 'as everybody deems it a horror to see the insect called the chafer, so the Ulstermen deemed it a horror to see Dubhthach'. We are told that he also had the nickname Daolteangach (chafer-tongued) because his speech was poisonous and bitter, as a result of which the tongue had grown black in his head. When his wife was among the women who admired the beauty of CÚ CHULAINN during the cattle-raid of Cooley, Dubhthach was overcome by jealousy and suggested that the young hero be attacked unawares and killed. Hearing this, Fearghus reprimanded him severely for his cruelty in killing women and youths. Despite his hatred for his native province, Dubhthach remained loyal to CORMAC CONN LOINGEAS and fought alongside him in Cormac's last stand. He was one of the few survivors on that occasion, but was eventually slain by his frightful spear when it was in the hands of a certain Feidhlimidh.

J.C. Watson (1941), 32–3, 37, 40–2; W. Stokes in *Irische Texte, 3*, 398–9; Hull (1949), 47–8; C. O'Rahilly (1976), 7–8, 72–4, 107; Knott (1936), 37–8; W.M. Hennessy (1889), xiv–xvi, 37–9; Ó Cadhlaigh (1956), 472; D. McKinnon in *Celtic Review, 2*, 112–21, 202–5.

duellists Single combat was a high point of many of the old heroic stories, such as those of the FIANNA CYCLE and ULSTER CYCLE. There is evidence, also, that it was a social reality, though not perhaps as much in Ireland as in feudal Europe, where divine justice was claimed to be revealed by such contests.

What appears to have been a combination of English feudal practice and native Irish heroism is illustrated by an account of a duel fought in the year 1583 in the courtyard of Dublin Castle before the assembled legal authorities. The combatants were two rival members of the Ó Conchúir Failghe sept of the Midlands, and they fought with swords. After a fierce contest, Tadhg Ó Conchúir slew Cathal Ó Conchúir, and the presiding judge – the English chief secretary for Ireland – remarked that he would like to see 'the same end of all the O'Connors in Ireland'.

From the seventeenth century onwards, heroism in combat came to be expressed by the native Irish population in terms of faction-fighting. These contests usually took place at fairs and places of assembly, and involved a large crowd of wattle-wielding fighters on each side. The wattles were ash plants of about 3 feet in length, and with a hard knob on the striking end, often reinforced with lead. A variety of moves were employed in the fighting, with the wattle being used for defence as well as attack. The origins of the factions are difficult to trace, but they seem to have been a tangle of local loyalties and family feuds, all expressed in a crude type of heroism. On the afternoon of a market day, when most of the business transactions were finished, a few leading figures belonging to rival factions would begin to taunt each other. Sometimes, a man would chant a verse to insult the opposing faction, and would trail his coat around in a circle challenging any one of them to tread on it. The result of this was inevitably a clash in which increasing numbers of followers would become involved. Terrible injuries, and sometimes even deaths, would occur, and the outcome of one such faction-fight would give cause for another on the next assembly day. Membership of the various factions was more or less stable, and nicknames were applied to them and boastfully proclaimed. In Munster, the principal division was between the *Seana-Veastaí* (Old Vests) and the *Carabhataí* (Cravats), but various more localised nicknames were also used. Factions had their own ritual challenges, their own mocking-songs on their opponents, and even their own war cries; favourite among the latter was '*Fág an Bealach!*', meaning 'Clear the Way!'

Just as pointless a phenomenon – among the ANGLO-IRISH gentry – was the practice of duelling with pistols. Although this was technically illegal, most of the leading personages in the legal profession, including even chief justices, fought such duels. Various extra-legal regulations governing duels were drafted; for instance, at the Clonmel assizes of the year 1777, a series of detailed rules was laid down specifying how duels should be conducted. These rules soon spread throughout the country and were referred to as 'the 36 commandments'. It was claimed that no gentleman could take his proper station in life until he had 'smelt powder', and at assizes and elections, members of the governing class were frequently seen to fight each other with pistols. It is reported that one gentleman, in quieting his child who was crying because it had been bullied by others, assured the child as follows: 'I'll give you a case of nice little pistols tomorrow. Come now, don't cry, and we'll shoot them all in the morning!' The same writer remarks that the first two questions always asked when a young man was wooing a rich lady were, 'What family is he of?' and 'Did he ever blaze?'

There was a lingering tradition of duels fought with swords, sometimes on horseback. One migratory LEGEND is told of different characters in various parts of Ireland telling of how in such a sword contest, neither man could gain the advantage over the other. Finally, the hero noticed that his opponent was wearing a coat of mail inside his shirt, and was dismayed until his servant shouted out: 'How would you kill a PIG at home?' Taking the hint, the hero drove his sword through the unfortunate opponent's throat. Pistols, however, were the favourite weapon, and the duellists were referred to as 'fire-eaters'. The usual fashion in other countries was for a pair of pistols to be chosen, and one of these given to each combatant. In Ireland, however, each combatant would bring his own pair of pistols and stand with one in each hand, ready to blaze away.

The actual pistols owned by celebrated duellists were sometimes given nicknames – all of which suggested sudden death – such as Bás gan Sagart (Death without a Priest), Súth an Deataigh (Soot of Smoke), or Crochaire an Chorda (Hangman with the Cord). Some families were said to have their own hereditary sets of pistols, handed down from one generation of fire-eaters to the next. In addition, sets of pistols would be kept at inns for the convenience of guests, ready to be used if they were needed. In such a case, if the gentlemen in their cups decided on a duel for the next morning, before retiring to sleep they would leave the order: 'Pistols for two, and breakfast for one!'

One much-lauded duellist was Richard Butler-Lowe (1742–1821) of Rosegreen, County Tipperary. Known as Risteard Riabhach (Speckled Dick), he was for a while high-sheriff of County Tipperary,

and was a relative of Sir John Butler, Earl of Ormond, for whom he substituted once in a duel in the Parade of Kilkenny. It was said that he had enchanted pistols that had come down to him in the family from the celebrated sixteenth-century Earl Black THOMAS BUTLER. Once, when a relative was being arraigned in Clonmel for shooting a bully, Risteard Riabhach objected to an adjournment for the gathering of more evidence. He stood up in the body of the court, levelled his pistols at the judge, and demanded that a decision be made there and then. His relative was acquitted. On another occasion, it was said, he led several leading duellists into a court at Abington, County Limerick, and forced the judge to acquit a defendant also accused of a shooting.

An even more famous fire-eater was Clareman, Seán Buí Mac Conmara (c.1780–1836), who acted as a second for Daniel O'CONNELL in the latter's famous duel in 1815. He was known in Irish as Seán an Mhaighriasc because he was reared in Moyriesk near Ennis, and in English as 'Fireball' McNamara. He was said to have fought no less than 45 successful contests and, like many expert marksmen, could shoot an apple off the head of a person at quite a distance. He reputedly had an estate at the Burren, County Clare, and one of the legends concerning him tells of how, having lost all his property at card-playing, he went to Dublin to try his fortune there. He had one good suit of clothes left, and he put it on and went to a great ball, at which he saw a man insulting a noble young lady. With drawn sword, Fireball challenged the man, who impudently trod on Fireball's shoes as a sign that he was accepting. In the ensuing fight, Fireball ran him through, and then left in a hurry lest he be apprehended. The young lady, however, had fallen in love with the dashing stranger, and she enquired after him all over Ireland. Eventually, she arrived at Burren Head and found him hunting there. They married, and lived happily together, she using her money to restock his estate with cattle.

Sometime later, she read in the newspaper that her elderly father was challenged to a duel in England by an expert gunman, who was a cousin of the man slain in Dublin by Fireball and was thirsting for revenge. Fireball travelled to England in a hurry, and arrived on the field as the opponent was complaining that the 'cowardly old beggar' had not come yet. 'Well,' said Fireball, 'why not excuse the poor old man?' The duellist reacted angrily. 'One would think,' he snapped, 'that you were going to take his place!' 'On the spot!' said Fireball. He had been forbidden by law to give a challenge, but could accept one, so they squared up to each other. The challenger had the first shot, but it missed. Fireball advised him to withdraw, but this request was ignored, and Fireball shot at him with devastating accuracy. Fearing that he would be arrested, he left the field immediately, and soon met his wife's parents coming dolefully to their downfall, or so they thought. 'The most generous lord to the poor in all England is going to his death today,' moaned the old lady, 'and all because of a disobedient daughter in Ireland!' 'Not so,' said Fireball, 'the business is already completed!' But they would not believe him, and so he returned to Ireland. When they arrived on the field, however, they saw for themselves what had happened, and they surmised that the stranger they had met was none other than their errant son-in-law. So they sent messengers to search Ireland until they discovered that Fireball and his wife lived at Burren Head, and every year after, the kindly old English lord sent nine barrels of gold to the young couple. Later, we are told, MacNamara's son was sent to school in Dublin and fought a duel there. Fireball's wife reacted to this news with the proverbial saying: 'What would the son of the CAT do but kill a mouse?'

Many of the duellists were 'squireens' – Irishmen or Anglo-Irishmen of the landlord class who swaggered idly about the country. A particularly obnoxious fire-eater in eighteenth-century Dublin was one Bryan Maguire, an ex-soldier who was accustomed to stroll up and down the streets kicking dirt onto passers-by or otherwise angering them. When a man complained,

he would immediately pull out a brace of pistols and offer the complainant his choice. When Maguire wished to call a servant, he disdained to ring the bell with his finger, but instead rang it with a pistol shot from some distance.

DUELLING IN EARLY IRELAND: Joyce (1903), 152–4; Kelly (1991), 211–13; O'Grady, *1* (1892), 377; Danaher (1964), 31–2.

FACTION-FIGHTERS: O'Donnell (1975); Danaher (1962), 148–52.

FIRE-EATERS: Danaher (1964), 32–6; Barrington, *2* (1830), 1–58; Barry (1981); J.E. Walsh (1979), 21–32; J. Kelly (1995).

BUTLER: Ó hÓgáin (1981), 59, 89–91; J.F. Lynch in *JCHAS, 2* (second series), 446.

MAC CONMARA: Ó hÓgáin (1985), 293–7, 346; IFC Index.

MAGUIRE: J.E. Walsh (1979), 29–30.

Dwyer, Michael *(1772–1825; in Irish, Micheál Ó Duibhir)* Leader in the RISING OF 1798 in County Wicklow. He held out against the English authorities in the fastnesses of his native county for five years after the rebellion had failed, and eventually secured acceptable terms of surrender. Having been imprisoned in Dublin for two years, he agreed to go to Australia and spent the remainder of his life there.

As a guerrilla leader, Dwyer was daring, resourceful and effective, and he became a great popular hero. Many stories were told of his agility and cleverness in evading capture. He often used disguise, and he could mislead and confuse the soldiers in a variety of ways. Once, it is said, he put a troop to flight by placing hats on haystacks, thereby giving the impression that he was accompanied by a large body of men. When all else failed, he could use his great running and swimming ability to make his getaway. A whole new road that allowed for the rapid deployment of troops was constructed by the authorities in a futile attempt to capture him. Known as the Military Road, it runs southwards right across the Wicklow Mountains. No doubt many of the accounts of his breathtaking escapes were current in his own time, spreading among the community as soon as they were effected. Much of the folklore concerning him has an air of desperate humour. For instance, we are told that soldiers once surrounded the house in which he was staying in the Glen of Imaal, and Michael had no choice but to slip into the piggery, where he hid behind a big and rather fierce sow. The soldiers came to look in the sty, and the sow stood on her hind legs and began to attack them. Michael prodded her into the fray, and the confused redcoat soldiers decided that nobody could stay there with such an ill-tempered animal, and departed.

Michael was an expert climber, and used the mountain slopes to fatigue his enemies and to speed his own progress. Not only the terrain but wild nature itself was in sympathy with the popular hero, as is clear from an account of what befell him when he once spent the night sheltering in a cave on Lugnaquilla Mountain. When he woke up, it was a beautiful sunny morning, and he began to light his pipe and relax. A robin flew into the cave and began to upset his blanket. He attempted to grab the BIRD, but it flew away. The bird soon returned with an aggressive air, as if it were going to attack him, and Michael thought this strange. He went to the cave entrance and, when he looked out, saw that the hillside was red with soldiers. He drew out his strong sea whistle and blew a blast on it. When the soldiers heard this, they thought he was giving a signal to a large body of men to attack them, and they fled. Michael himself wasted no time in running down the opposite side of the mountain, thankful to the little bird for its timely warning.

Cullen (1938); Dickson (1944); O'Donnell (2000); P. Ó Tuathail in *Béaloideas*, 5, 174–8; IFC Index.

Éadaoin *(earlier, Étain)* Mythical lady of the TUATHA DÉ DANANN. One source mentions a POETESS of the Tuatha Dé with this name (*see* CAIRBRE MAC ÉADAOINE), while another introduces her as an otherworld helper of the Munster king EOGHAN MÓR in his travails. Her name was based on *ét* (later, *éad*), meaning 'envy', and thus designated 'she who evokes envy'. Her original significance can therefore be seen as that of the GODDESS of sovereignty who leads to rivalry between aspirants to KINGSHIP.

She is featured in a very colourful story written in the ninth century. According to this, after AONGHUS had got possession of Brugh na Bóinne (the Newgrange tumulus in County Meath), his foster-father MIDHIR went to visit him there. Midhir attempted to separate two fighting youths, and had one of his eyes knocked out by a holly prick in the struggle. DIAN CÉACHT came and healed him, but he nevertheless demanded compensation from Aonghus. What he sought was the most beautiful maiden in Ireland, Éadaoin Eachraidhe, daughter of Ailill, king of Ulster. Aonghus went to Ailill, who demanded that twelve plains be cleared for him and twelve rivers be created. All of this was done by Aonghus' father, the DAGHDHA, and after Aonghus gave Éadaoin's weight in gold and silver, he was allowed to bring her home with him. He gave her to Midhir, who tarried for a year thereafter in the Brugh. At the end of the year, Midhir and Éadaoin went to Midhir's own dwelling at Brí Léith (now Slieve Golry near Ardagh, County Longford).

Éadaoin was not long there, however, when Midhir's first wife Fuamnach, with a stroke of a magic wand, turned her into a pool of water. The water turned into a worm, and the worm into a beautiful fly that followed Midhir wherever he went. Midhir knew that it was Éadaoin, and he loved only her. However, Fuamnach caused a magic wind to blow the fly away from Brí Léith and out onto the seashore, where the transformed Éadaoin lived for seven years in misery. Then she managed to reach Brugh na Bóinne, where Aonghus protected her and kept her in a beautiful sun bower. Fuamnach contrived to go to the Brugh when Aonghus was absent, and again she blew the fly away. It alighted on a house in Ulster and fell into the drink of the wife of a warrior called Étar. The woman conceived, and in this way Éadaoin was born a second time.

When EOCHAIDH AIREAMH became king of Ireland, his subjects refused him tribute until he got a queen. He sought out the most beautiful woman in the country, and found that she was Éadaoin, daughter of Étar. He took her to TARA and married her. The king's brother Ailill

Anghubha fell sick from love of her, and in order to save his life, she arranged a tryst with him on a hill near the court. However, the man who came in the shape of Ailill was none other than Midhir, who had kept Éadaoin under observation since her second birth. She refused to go with him, and returned to Eochaidh. Ailill Anghubha, whose lovesickness had been magically caused by Midhir, regained his health. Sometime later, Midhir arrived at Tara and invited the king to play chess. Eochaidh won several games and exacted great prizes from him. These included horses, pigs, cattle and sheep, as well as magical tasks such as the clearing of stones from a large plain, the placing of rushes over another plain, the construction of a forest over yet another, and the building of a causeway over a bog. Finally, Midhir won a game and demanded as prize a kiss from Éadaoin. This was arranged for a month hence, but at the appointed time Eochaidh had his court at Tara surrounded with warriors inside and outside. Notwithstanding this, Midhir suddenly appeared among them, and taking Éadaoin in his arms, took her out through the skylight. In the form of swans, they flew together to Sídh ar Feimhean (the cairn on Slievenamon, County Tipperary).

In a vain search for them, Eochaidh and his men began to dig up the cairn on Slievenamon, and realising that the lovers were not there turned their attention to Midhir's own dwelling at Brí Léith. Midhir immediately appeared to them and offered to let Eochaidh have the lady back. Accordingly, 50 women arrived at Tara, all looking exactly like Éadaoin. She was the best woman in Ireland at serving drink, so Eochaidh asked the women to do that. He chose one lady, and the others departed. But he had chosen wrongly, for the lady was his own daughter, with whom Éadaoin had been pregnant when she left him. Before he realised his mistake, he lay with his daughter, and of that was born a baby girl. This child was cast out on Eochaidh's orders, but she grew up to be a fine maiden, and became the wife of Eterscéle and thus the mother of the great CONAIRE.

This story of Éadaoin has the background of kingship myth, but the plot uses a variety of MOTIFS borrowed from folklore (*see* WONDER TALES, types 313, 325). These motifs include the transformations of Éadaoin, the magical flight of the lovers, and the attempt by Eochaidh to select her from among the identical women. The motif of incest at the end of the story was borrowed from medieval hero-lore and employed to make unique the ancestry of a famous character. The description of the road building corresponds closely to an extensive timber road from the second century BC that has been discovered at Corlea, County Longford. It may be that memory of that actual road became embedded in the early lore of Midhir and Éadaoin, and thus surfaces in the story.

Another early medieval text refers to Éadaoin as the otherworld wife of Eochaidh Feidhleach rather than of Eochaidh Aireamh, but that text has none of the great adventures of the above account.

GENERAL: O. Bergin & R.I. Best in *Ériu*, *12*, 137–96; Knott (1936), 1–3. For folklore motifs *see* Christiansen (1959), 148–50.

THE ROAD: D. Ó hÓgáin in B. Raftery (1997), 359–66.

Éibhear Son of the fictional MÍL of Spain, and one of the imagined leaders of the Gaelic people in their settlement of Ireland. His name (earlier, Éber) was forged by the pseudo-historians who noticed that Iberus, the name of the River Ebro in Spain, resembled Eberus, a Hiberno-Latin form of Hibernus (Irishman). The epithet Fionn (fair-haired) was sometimes added.

After their victory over the TUATHA DÉ DANANN, we read that Éibhear ruled the south of Ireland for a year, while his brother ÉIREAMHÓIN ruled the northern half. A border dispute, however, led to a battle between them in which Éibhear was defeated and slain. The medieval genealogists fancifully claimed that the leading sept of Munster, the EOGHANACHT, was ultimately descended from Éibhear.

Macalister (1956), 10–175 (*passim*); T.F. O'Rahilly (1946), 195–9; O'Brien (1962), 186–94.

Éinne *(earlier, Enda)* SAINT who died *c.*AD 530; the founder of a monastery on

Inishmore, the largest of the Aran Islands, County Galway.

The surviving biography, in Latin, is a late conflation of several earlier accounts. We read that his father was called Conall Dearg and that his mother, Aoibhfhinn, was a granddaughter of the king of Arda (Ards, County Down). He had several sisters, one of whom, Fanchea, was celebrated as a saint in her own right. Initially he pursued a warrior's life, but Fanchea persistently tried to direct him towards the Church and eventually succeeded in this. He is described as going to Britain and to the Continent for his education, and, on returning to Ireland, as founding several churches near the River Boyne. With the support of St AILBHE, he got permission from the Munster king to set up a monastery on Inishmore, and he and his monks set out for that island but could find no boat to bring them there from the mainland. They stood on a large rock on the shore, and this rock miraculously floated on the water and conveyed them over. We read that, in all, he had ten monasteries built on Inishmore, assigning half of the island to himself, but contention arose concerning this division. An angel appeared to him with two gifts – a copy of the Gospels and a priest's chasuble – and on account of this heavenly intervention, the dissenting monks accepted his decision.

Several dramatic miracles are attributed to him. Once, his monks complained that a dangerous rock was troublesome to them at sea, and Éinne brought an angel to split the rock with a sword of lightning. The result was a chasm through the rock allowing safe passage to the port. Éinne was celebrated for the strictness of his rule, and one tradition has it that to ensure that each of the monks had a clear conscience, he used to order them one by one to go on the sea in a little timber boat. If there was any sin on the monk's soul, the saltwater would penetrate the body of the boat. Only one man of the community continually passed this test – he was called Gigniat, and had entered the monastery as a boy. Many of the famous saints of Ireland were said to have visited Éinne on Inishmore, and to have been instructed by him. A late literary tradition has COLM CILLE visiting him, but we read that the two saints quarrelled, and Colm left the island with their friendship rather strained after Éinne refused him permission to build a church there.

The literary sources are embellished by local folklore concerning Éinne and his community. It is said, for instance, that the inhabitants of Inishmore at first resented his coming to them, but that he miraculously drove the horses of the island's chieftain, Corbán, across the sea to the other islands. This convinced Corbán that he should submit to the saint. The contention between his monks concerning the division of the island is also remembered in folklore, as is his quarrel with Colm Cille. In the latter case, a version of a common Irish folk LEGEND of saints is told, according to which Éinne agreed to divide the island with Colm, and they made an arrangement concerning the division. Éinne was to go to the eastern end of the island and Colm to the western end, and having both said Mass at sunrise, they would start to walk towards each other. The point at which they met would be the boundary between them. However, Colm cheated by starting to walk without saying Mass, and as a penance was ordered to leave Inishmore and not to build a church within earshot of Éinne's bell, which had a very wide range. The feast day of Éinne is 21 March.

Kenney (1929), 373–4; Plummer, 2 (1910), 60–75; O'Kelleher & Schoepperle (1918), 158–61; O'Hanlon, 1 (1875), 1–11 & 3, 911–21; IFC 77:26–9, 157:522–3, 158:121–8, 238:617–22, 303:112, 413:12–13, 461:72–85, 669:135–7.

Éire The name of the country, anglicised Ireland. Its earlier form was Ériu, from a Celtic *Iveriu*, meaning 'land', and a further derivative ÉRAINN was used to refer to the bulk of the population of Ireland.

The land-GODDESS of the country had this (Ériu > Éire) as one of her names, and from it the English and other forms – such as Irlanda – are derived. The dative of Éire is Éirinn, and its genitive is Éireann. The goddess Éire is represented in medieval pseudo-history as one of the three queens of Ireland of the TUATHA DÉ DANANN at the time of the invasions by the sons of MÍL. She resided at Uisneach (Ushnagh, County Westmeath), regarded as the ritual centre of Ireland. To further underline her function as land-goddess, she is described as wife of the KING called Mac Gréine (Son of the Sun). The name of this fictional king echoes the solar cult of kingship, and the marriage of male sun with female earth was an archaic and basic convention in Irish ritual (*see* DAGHDHA). According to the medieval writers of pseudo-history, after the sons of Míl conquered the Tuatha Dé, they met Éire at Uisneach. She sanctioned their rule in Ireland, but asked that her name be on the island henceforth, and she was assured by AMHAIRGHIN GLÚINGHEAL that Éire would be its principal name. *See also* BANBA *and* FÓDLA.

T.F. O'Rahilly in *Ériu*, 14, 7–28; Macalister (1941), 122, 152, 182 & (1956), 34–6, 76–8.

Éireamhóin Son of the fictional MÍL of Spain, and imagined leader of the Gaelic people in their settlement of Ireland. The name (earlier, Éremon) was invented by the pseudo-historians on the basis of Ériu (later, Éire), the name of the country.

After the Tuatha Dé Danann delayed them by tricks and magic, we read that Éireamhóin led his people into Ireland through the Boyne estuary. Having defeated the Tuatha Dé at the battle of Tailtiu (Teltown, County Meath), he and his brother Éibhear divided the kingdom of Ireland between them, he reigning in the northern half and Éibhear in the south. It was said that the two brothers cast lots concerning their men of art, and that Éireamhóin won the poets for the north, while Éibhear won the harpists for the south. Within a year, the brothers had a dispute concerning border territories, and in a battle between them at Brí Damh (near Geashill, County Offaly), Éibhear was defeated and slain. Éireamhóin was then unchallenged king of Ireland, and he dug two royal forts: Ráth Oind in Cualu (north Wicklow), and Ráth

Bheathaigh (Rathbeagh, in north Kilkenny). He fought several other battles, in one of which his opponent was another brother of his, the poet Amhairghin Glúngheal. Having reigned for seventeen years, Éireamhóin died at Airgeadros (Silverwood, by the River Nore), and was buried at Ráth Bheathaigh nearby.

The medieval genealogists, in their attempts to derive all the Irish septs from the sons of Míl, contrived to claim Éireamhóin – through UGHAINE – as the common ancestor of the LAIGHIN, ÉRAINN and CONNACHTA.

Macalister (1956), 10–175 (*passim*); T.F. O'Rahilly (1946), 195–9; O'Brien (1962), 129–30.

Eithne Mythical or fictional lady of the TUATHA DÉ DANANN. Her name was based on the word *ét* (later, *éad*), for 'envy', and meant 'the little one of envy'. It therefore signified 'she who causes envy' among rival aspirants, and in this she reflected the function of the GODDESS of KINGSHIP. A variant of the name, with the same meaning, was Eithliu (*see also* ÉADAOIN).

A survival of the role of territorial goddess is found in the river name Eithne (rendered in English, 'Inny', with one in Counties Cavan, Westmeath and Longford, and another in County Kerry). One source, indeed, claims that Eithne was a variant name for the river-goddess BÓINN. The ritual significance of the name has long been lost in narrative tradition, however. An echo is found in the mother of LUGH called Eithne or Eithliu in medieval literature, for Lugh was sometimes regarded as a symbol of kingship. Other reputed bearers of the name had similar associations, such as the mothers of kings LUGHAIDH LÁGHA and CONAIRE, and the wives of kings CONN, CORMAC MAC AIRT and CONCHOBHAR MAC NEASA. Unconnected with the office of sovereignty, however, was Eithne Inghubha, reputedly the wife of CÚ CHULAINN.)

An imaginative story of another Eithne is told in a text from about the fourteenth century. This lady is described as of the TUATHA DÉ DANANN, being daughter to the steward of AONGHUS. Along with

Curcóg, daughter of MANANNÁN, Eithne was reared in the fosterage of Aonghus at Brugh na Bóinne (the Newgrange tumulus in County Meath). When she grew up, she was a beautiful girl, but was insulted by a remark passed by a visitor to the Brugh, and as a result would touch neither food nor drink. After seven days, Aonghus offered her the milk of a dun cow, one of two marvellous cows he and Manannán had brought from India. Eithne herself milked the cow and drank its milk, which tasted like honey and wine. When Manannán in his dwelling at Eamhain Abhlach heard the news, he summoned the maiden to him, for he knew the remedy for every ailment. When Eithne arrived, she would only partake of the milk of the other marvellous cow from India, the speckled animal Manannán had. Then Manannán understood that when she was insulted in Brugh na Bóinne, her 'guardian demon' had left her and had been replaced by a guardian angel. She was thus no longer one of the Tuatha Dé, but had become a Christian and would accept nourishment only from the righteous land of India.

For many ages, she lived on the milk of the two cows, until St PATRICK came to Ireland. After bathing in the River Boyne one day, the *féth fiadha* (invisibility of the Tuatha Dé – *see* DRUIDS) left her, and she met a cleric and went with him to his hermitage near the Brugh. Patrick himself soon arrived there, as did Aonghus and his people in search of her. The latter demanded her back, but Patrick refused and tried unsuccessfully to convert Aonghus, who departed with a cry of anguish. Eithne was baptised, died a fortnight later, and was buried with Christian honour.

RIVER NAMES: E. Hogan (1910), 403–4.

MOTHERS, WIVES OF KINGS: T.F. O'Rahilly (1946), 163–4, 553.

STORY: L. Duncan in *Ériu, 11*, 184–225.

Elizabeth I *(1533–1603)* Queen of England from 1558 until her death. Because of her oppressive policies regarding Ireland, and the devastation caused by her armies, Elizabeth is remembered with hostility in the popular tradition of the country.

The major charge laid against her in fanciful lore is that of promiscuity. A poem from the mid-seventeenth century refers to her as 'monstrous Elizabeth who did not marry but who refrained from no man', and adds that she was treacherous and made a wasteland of Ireland. A folk LEGEND collected in County Leitrim in the following century accords well with this. It tells of how Brian 'na Múrtha' Ó Ruairc, chieftain of the O'Rourkes of Breffny, was invited to London by her in order to pledge his fealty. When she saw that he was a handsome man, she arranged that he be accommodated in a sumptuous apartment in her palace. He was visited in his bedroom on several nights by an unknown lady, and he noticed by the moonlight on one occasion that his visitor was wearing a fine ring. Next day, he saw the same ring on the queen's finger and hinted genially that he recognised her. On the following night, an assassin was sent to dispatch him. This story is apocryphal, for in reality Brian had been in rebellion against Elizabeth and had travelled from his homeland to Scotland to seek assistance. However, the Scottish king James VI (later, James I of England) handed him over to the English and he was kept in the Tower of London until he was hanged in 1591. Brian was a very brave man, and some contemporary sources suggest that he had some correspondence with the queen when he was imprisoned in London. On one occasion, he refused to bow to her Privy Council, and when asked did he bow to the images of SAINTS replied that there was a great deal of difference between the saints and them. Respect for Brian's courage seems to have been confused in Ireland with rumours of Elizabeth's amours, thus giving rise to the legend.

Later folklore accounts claim that Elizabeth slept with a different man each night, and in the morning had each of her lovers sent to the block. The MOTIF of an anonymous nocturnal lover is found in the reverse form under the influence of an international FOLKTALE that tells of how a princess tries to identify a rogue. Thus we are told that Elizabeth used to have a man brought to her boudoir each night and, since she could not see him properly in the dark, would quietly cut a piece of his coat or a lock of his hair so as to identify him on the morrow and have him executed. An Irishman outwitted her, however, by cutting the hair of all her soldiers while they slept. Next day, she failed to pick out the man, but uttered a verse warning whoever had fooled her not to try it again.

The context that has people visiting her to advance their interests in Ireland puts Elizabeth in a somewhat better light. There were indeed some celebrated visits by Irish leaders to her court, such as that in 1562 of the proud Ulster chief Seán Ó Néill, who spoke only Irish and kept his kerns by him as bodyguard, and the visit in 1593 of the dramatic Gráinne Mhaol Ní MHÁILLE, whose wits were well equal to those of Elizabeth herself. Folklore has Elizabeth behaving with wisdom and humanity on such occasions. A legend from Cork tells of how she conferred one side of the River Bandon on a man called Fitzgerald in return for services rendered to her cause in Ireland. He remarked, however, that things were better in pairs, so she told him to take the two sides. An account from Wicklow claims that one of her officers brought the head of the chieftain Feidhlim Ó Tuathail to her in expectation of a grant of that chieftain's land. Elizabeth, however, conferred no more on the opportunist than a smile and the shawl she was wearing on her neck.

We are told that Elizabeth was very superstitious, and kept a playing-card – the ace of hearts – under the seat of her throne, believing that as long as it was there she would not die. One story claims that she had a servant-girl from Ireland, whom she relied on greatly. As she grew old, she became quite demented, and one day called the servant-girl to her as she lay prostrate in her bed of gold. In their conversation, the girl referred to all the Irish people whom the queen had caused to be killed, and remarked that death was now near and all her gold could not keep her alive. After her death, it is claimed that a terrible stench came from her coffin, this obviously being a hostile perspective on the fact that her corpse had been kept for five weeks before her royal funeral in London.

C. O'Rahilly (1952), 21; de híde (1933), 144; Walker (1786), appendix, 81–2; D. O'Sullivan, *2* (1958), 121–2; Hardiman, *2* (1831), 286–305; Gregory (1926), 37–8; Ó hÓgáin (1985), 162–3; IFC 259:457, 648, 924:403–5, 1007:784, 1114:175–6, S507:142.

environment People in Ireland, as everywhere else, have speculated on the nature of the physical world around them, giving rise to a rich imaginative lore.

The sky and its phenomena are an obvious subject of such lore. The DRUIDS are said to have been keen students of the heavenly bodies, and the early literature has several mentions of oaths being taken by reference to sun, moon and stars. The sun figured most prominently in ancient tradition, and the lore of EOCHAIDH shows how it could be personified. There are other indications, such as in descriptions of the mythical BRIGHID, CONAIRE, and in seasonal lore generally (*see* TIME) of how the sun was understood to be the source of energy, both agricultural and mystical. In folk speech, the sun and moon are sometimes referred to as if they have influence on human affairs, and in Irish 'by the strength of the sun and moon' was a common exclamation. What appear to be echoes of ancient beliefs are the idea that if a woman slept in the sunlight she was more likely to become pregnant, and that the waxing of the moon was a propitious time to undertake new work, whereas its waning was the opposite. The light of the full moon was said to make FAIRIES more active in their affairs, and it was also supposed to cause insanity in some people.

Fanciful explanations were offered, especially to children, of the obvious aspects of these bodies. The sun was said to be inhabited by a fox, and food melting due to its heat was referred to as being eaten by him, while the 'man in the moon' was said to have once been a boy who was transported there due to his laziness at sweeping with a brush or drawing water with a bucket. Thunder and lightning were similarly claimed to be the angels drilling and flashing their swords, and December snow was picturesquely explained as the geese being plucked in heaven for the Christmas feast. The young ones were also told that a crock of gold was hidden at the foot of the rainbow. On a more serious note, the latter phenomenon was said to be a token of God's promise to mankind that the world would never again be destroyed by flood, but it was not altogether auspicious, for its appearance over a house was taken to portend the death of some member of that family. Various stories told of how persons were born under a certain star and, as a result, had either good or bad fortune in their lives, while a meteor was taken to be a soul passing from purgatory to heaven. A sunburst through clouds, causing clear rays to descend to the earth, was interpreted as the track made by the souls of good people passing to heaven immediately after death.

Landscape and sea had many traditions attached to them. Lonely places and regions far out on the ocean were regarded as special haunts of fairies and kindred beings. In early Irish myth, the otherworld was thought of as an overseas realm (see MANANNÁN) or an island where the sun sets (see DONN), and the survival of such a mythical idea in folk belief is instanced by the fancy that there was a mystical island where people remain perpetually young called Tír na hÓige or Tír na nÓg. Usually it was thought of as situated off the west coast, and the imprint made on the sea by the sunrays was pointed out as the image of this island. It was imagined that towns, farms and crowds of people could be seen there. The otherworld island was often called uí Bhreasaíl, but was known locally also by other names, such as Ladra, off the north-west coast, Beag-Árainn, off the Galway coast, and Cill Stuithín, off the coast of Clare. The early literature describes four great waves of Ireland that cried out on the death of a true KING: these were the Wave of Tóim in Dingle Bay, the Wave of CLÍONA in Glandore Bay on the south-west coast, the Wave of Rughraidhe in Dundrum Bay and the Wave of Tuaidhe at Ballintoy on the north-east coast. Because of its danger and unpredictability, folklore tends to personalise the ocean. It

was believed that 'the sea takes its own share', by which was meant that a person who saved another from drowning was himself in danger of meeting with such a tragic end.

It was fancifully said that various lakes came about when a woman forgot to replace the lid on a copious well, or when some supernatural person or animal urinated in that place. Almost all Irish rivers have feminine names, and the early literature associates several of them with variants of the land-goddess (see GODDESS, BÓINN and EITHNE). A common folk LEGEND tells of how a voice is heard at a river every seven years declaring 'now is the time, where is the person?' by which is meant that it is destined that individuals will be drowned there periodically. Lakes were also much feared and speculated upon. Some of them were said to be so deep as to have no bottom, and traditions abounded of ancient cities having sunk beneath them. Boatmen could often at night see lights and hear the muffled sounds of bells coming from these underwater cities.

The veneration accorded to holy wells, each of them dedicated to a particular SAINT, seems to have had its origin in pre-Christian religion, but it became thoroughly Christianised due to the importance of wells for baptism by early missionaries. Thus we are often told in both literature and folklore of a saint causing a well to miraculously spring up by striking the ground with his crozier. On the feast day of the particular patron saint, people gathered at the local holy well to pray, and this 'pattern' (Irish patrún, from the actual word 'patron') was a great occasion for, in addition to prayer, communal celebration such as music, dancing and even drinking. Many cures were associated with these wells, and it was usually said that a supplicant saw a mystical FISH in the water as a sign that a cure was to be obtained. Various local traditions told of a holy well being desecrated by some individual, and it becoming dry as a result but reappearing at a new location nearby. A special tree grew beside most of these wells, and pilgrims attached a piece of cloth to it or inserted a coin into it as a token of their veneration.

There are several references in both literary and folklore sources to special stones in the landscape that spoke at certain times and gave oracles. Such stones were consulted to discover guilty parties in theft and dishonest land claims, and not only might they speak out clearly but they could also cause misfortune to one who swore falsely upon them. Such beliefs may have originated in the standing stones that marked burial sites of great ancestors, the ancestral voices being considered to still communicate to this world through them. More fanciful ideas existed also to the effect that certain great boulders in the landscape could move about at certain times, and even descend to river banks to drink. Some people even claimed that stones softened with the rising moon, and that drops of perspiration could be seen on them.

Lonely parts of the countryside, especially at night, were reputed to be places of contact with the otherworld, and some quite disturbing traditions were associated with them. Most striking was the belief in the *féar gortach* (hungry grass), said to be a patch of grass – mostly on mountainsides – on which a person might unwittingly walk with the result that he or she became afflicted by a great hunger. This could cause death, and to avoid such an eventuality many wayfarers brought some bread with them in their pockets, for eating the bread could obviate the effect of the magical hunger. In lonely places, also, a *ceo draíochta* (magic fog) was believed to sometimes descend around a person, causing him or her to stray interminably until light of day brought release from the ordeal. This belief can be compared with accounts in the medieval literature of how heroes found themselves surrounded by a fog as an introduction to an otherworld adventure.

Of the flora, most attention was focused on trees. The early literature describes several great trees of ancient Ireland, and these seem to have been landmarks for assemblies. Most celebrated of them was the Bile Tartain at Ardbraccan, County Meath, said to have been an ash of gigantic size.

Others were the yew of Mughain near Ballaghmoon in County Kildare, the yew of Ros at Old Leighlin in County Carlow, an ash called 'Dáithí's Branch' at Farbill in County Westmeath and another ash called 'the Branch of Uisneach' at Ushnagh in the same county. The sites of many of the great trees were taken over by monastic communities, and there are several mentions of such in the biographies of the saints. In early and medieval Ireland, a great tree growing at the inauguration centre of a sept was regarded as a symbol of that sept's nobility and endurance, and it was considered a disastrous defeat if a rival group cut down the tribal tree (see especially Eoghanacht). The belief long survived that a very old and notable tree, termed a bile, was in some way sacred, and accounts in both literature and folklore tell of misfortune befalling people who interfered with such a bile or cut it down.

Concerning magical properties, the early literature associates the hazel with seers (*see* BÓINN *and* DRUIDS), but in ordinary folklore pride of place is very much accorded to the rowan. This, called in Irish *caorthann* and also known as 'mountain ash', was believed to be especially efficacious. A piece of rowan was put in the milk pail and around the churn to prevent magical milk stealing (*see* TIME: Bealtaine), and was kept in the house in the belief that it prevented fire.

Cross (1952), 20–32, 46–7; Wood-Martin, *2* (1902), 46–115, 152–9, 206–61; S. Ó Súilleabháin (1942), 251–88; E. Ettlinger in *Ogam, 14*, 485–91; Danaher (1964), 67–78, 114–19; A.T. Lucas in *JCHAS, 68*, 16–54; Ó Danachair (1978), 24–5; Ó hÓgáin (1995), 29–49 & in Lysaght, Ó Catháin & Ó hÓgáin (1999), 247–60; B. O'Reilly in *Béaloideas, 59*, 83–7, 222–3.

Eochaidh *(earlier, Eochu)* A name of mythical origin that occurs as that of several characters in medieval literature. It is a derivative of *ech* (later, *each*), which means 'HORSE', and the name is often associated with equine imagery. The suggestion is that a deity could be envisaged as a great horseman, but in some contexts could indicate stallion-like reproductive ability (*see* FEARGHUS MAC RÓICH).

The most striking instance of the name

being attached to a divinity is that of the DAGHDHA, who had the alternative designation of Eochaidh Ollathair (i.e. Eochaidh the Father of Many). As appears from the rituals of KINGSHIP, this father-deity as the divine patron was represented by the sun. We may presume that the divine male principal was given a title such as 'Eochaidh Daghdha' (with a meaning such as 'horseman the good god'), and was imagined as the presiding horseman of the heavens whose eye was the all-seeing sun. With the sun as eye, he was also referred to as AODH RUADH RÓ-FHEASA. There are some indications that the sacrifice of a horse was an archaic ritual connected with the inauguration of kings in Ireland, and if so, such a ritual would have had both social and mythic connotations.

In accordance with this understanding of the ultimate male ancestor, there was a tendency to give the particular name Eochaidh to antique characters in the genealogies of several septs. In the EOGHANACHT pedigrees, a character called Echdae was mentioned as husband of the goddess ÁINE – his name would have meant either 'horse-like' or 'horse-god'. Furthermore, a persistent theme in the mythology of Celtic GODDESSES was the race in which these ladies showed their speed, sometimes in contention with horses (*see* MACHA *and* MEADHBH). Designations of deities were frequently used as names for mythical or, in some cases, historical kings.

One significant tradition is instanced by a story concerning a certain fictional king, Eochaidh mac Luchta. We read that he was a very generous man and had but one eye. When AITHIRNE visited his court, Eochaidh offered that importunate poet the choice of his wealth as a gift. Aithirne demanded 'the only eye in your head to be given to me in my fist', and Eochaidh complied. He knocked the eye out with his own finger and presented it to the poet. He then asked his servant to direct him to water so that he might wash his face. The servant remarked that the socket (*dearc*) was red (*dearg*) from the blood, and Eochaidh said that the water should ever after be called Deargdhearc (hence, Lough Derg on the River Shannon). God

was so impressed with the magnanimity of Eochaidh that He miraculously gave him two eyes as reward. A variant of this story has FEIRCHEIRDNE as the importunate poet, rather than Aithirne.

It is apparent that this motif is very old, it being an exemplary one to demonstrate how generous the true king should be to poets. A similar story is found in ancient Sanskrit literature, and one could argue that the motif was an Indo-European one underlining the duty of a king to be as supportive of his subjects as the presiding deity is. In this sense, the deity in the heavens could be thought of as one-eyed due to his generosity. Elsewhere there is mention of a character called Eochaidh Aonshúile (i.e. of the One Eye), and there can be little doubt that Eochaidh mac Luchta was a character invented from the debris of the cult of the deity.

The later medieval literature gives a further twist to the story, attempting to historicise it more convincingly. Here we read that a local ruler in Munster, Eochaidh mac Maolughra, plucked out his eye to satisfy the extortionate demand of a Scottish DRUID called Labhán. St RUADHÁN, who witnessed this, prayed to God that the druid's two eyes should pass into the head of the king, and so it happened. Thus the king acquired the nickname 'Súil Labháin', and from him was derived the Eoghanacht family surnamed Ó Súilleabháin. This version was quite anachronistic with regard to its characters, connecting the sixth-century Ruadhán with Súildubhán mac Maolughra who flourished in the tenth century. The name Súildubhán in fact meant 'dark-eyed', and a false etymology – *súil amháin* (one eye) – led to the invention of a character named Labhán. It may be, indeed, that Eochaidh was not the real name of the historical Súildubhán, but that it was attached to him because of this lore.

EOCHAIDH AS FATHER-GOD: T.F. O'Rahilly (1946), 34, 290–4, 467–9, 552–3; Olmsted (1994), 43–5, 169–71; O'Brien (1962), 613–17; Dillon & Chadwick (1973), 126.

GIVING OF EYE: W. Stokes in *RC, 8,* 48–9 & *15,* 461–3; Gwynn (1913), 338–47; T.F. O'Rahilly (1946), 59, 175–9; Jackson (1938), 182; M. Dillon (1969), 4; Plummer, *1* (1922), 329; Ó Donnchadha (1940), 147–8; Dinneen, *3* (1908), 58–9.

Eochaidh Aireamh Fictional KING of Ireland situated in prehistory. His sobriquet means 'ploughman'.

He is described as brother and successor of EOCHAIDH FEIDHLEACH, and his reign as lasting fifteen years. In the original lore, he was probably in fact a double of Eochaidh Feidhleach, and since the names of both suggest agriculture, they may be remnants of a divine patron of that skill. In the ninth-century text on the wooing of ÉADAOIN, Eochaidh Aireamh appears as a king of TARA and human husband of that metamorphosed lady of the otherworld. Various sources place his death at Freamhain (Frewin, County Westmeath), where he was burned by one Siugmhall. Elsewhere, this character Siugmhall appears as an otherworld being or deity who resided in Sídh Neanta (a fort near the north of Lough Ree on the River Shannon). His name may originally have meant 'powerful thunderbolt', and the tradition that he killed Eochaidh Aireamh could be a remnant of myth. A secondary account, in the Éadaoin story, develops the lore by making Siugmhall the grandson of MIDHIR, Eochaidh's rival for the lady. According to this, Eochaidh had a fortress in Frewin, and the burden of his sustenance fell on the sept called Fir Chúil who belonged to that district. Mórmhaol was king of the Fir Chúil, and his brother was Siugmhall. These two gathered their forces and attacked Eochaidh's fortress. They burned it and slew the king himself.

Macalister (1956), 298–9; O. Bergin & R.I. Best in *Ériu*, *12*, 137–96; Gwynn (1935), 161; Dinneen, *2* (1908), 228–9; T.F. O'Rahilly (1946), 52–3.

Eochaidh Éigeas POET of the sixth century AD, who is mentioned as having been present at the Convention of Drom Ceat (Daisy Hill, near Limavady, County Derry) in the year 575. His epithet means 'poet' or 'sage'. He was son of Aonghus of the leading ULAIDH sept called Dál bhFiatach, and first cousin of the Ulster KING Muireadhach Muindearg, who reigned in the early sixth century. The genealogies state that Eochaidh guested with the AIRGHIALLA noble Daimhín, and

was buried in Domhnach Cuilinn (probably at Slieve Gullion, County Armagh).

Some medieval writers incorrectly identified him with DALLÁN FORGAILL, whose real name is also given as Eochaidh. It seems likely that he was somewhat older than Dallán, and was the leading poet in Ulster before the latter came to prominence. His prestige must have been considerable, for he was described in the medieval literature as the chief-poet of Ireland and is given the title Rígh-Éigeas (King-poet). Little detail is given concerning him, except that in one story he is claimed to have been employed as court poet by the king of Dál nAraidhe (in south Antrim and north Down), FIACHNA MAC BAODÁIN. In that capacity, we read, he was upstaged by Fiachna's brilliant young son MONGÁN.

Although they knew next to nothing of him or of his life, the writers of pseudo-history were so impressed by the fame of his name that they projected it backwards in their chronology onto a fictional king of ancient Ireland, OLLAMH FÓDLA (literally, 'high-poet of Ireland') whose real name, they claimed, was Eochaidh Éigeas. The leading poetic family of Leinster, surnamed Mac Eochadha (anglicised Keogh and Kehoe), were not descendants of Eochaidh Éigeas, but they fancifully claimed that their ancestor Eochaidh was named after him because of his poetic skill.

O'Brien (1962), 278, 322, 407; W. Stokes in *RC*, *20*, 42; Joynt (1941), 1; Dinneen, *3* (1908), 80–1, 94–5; E. Knott in *Ériu*, *8*, 155–60; Mac Airt (1944), 256; Mac Cionnaith (1938), 399.

Eochaidh Feidhleach Fictional KING of Ireland, who was claimed to have been contemporaneous with Julius Caesar. The sobriquet *feidhleach* probably meant 'one who yokes', and a medieval text supposes that it was during his reign that the ox-yoke was first used in Ireland. An alternative explanation, 'righteous', is given for Eochaidh's sobriquet, but this seems to be incorrect, as he is said to have had a brother called EOCHAIDH AIREAMH – the epithet here meaning 'ploughman'. This brother is probably a double of Eochaidh Feidhleach himself, and suggests that the name was in origin the appellation of the deity EOCHAIDH in the context of agricultural patronage.

The actual character of Eochaidh Feidhleach is not, however, regarded as in any way supernatural. He figures in the ULSTER CYCLE, where he is described as king of Ireland and the first descendant of COBHTHACH CAOL to gain that primary office. We are told that he took the kingship by defeating and slaying the Ulsterman Fachtna Fáthach at the battle of Leitir Ruibhe (in the area of Corran, County Sligo). Fachtna was the father of CONCHOBHAR MAC NEASA, who consequently schemed against Eochaidh. The latter, for his part, supported FEARGHUS MAC RÓICH against Conchobhar and made several attempts to have the province of Ulster submit to him. He reigned for twelve years, and we read that during that time, there was a golden age in Ireland. Peace, generosity, courtesy towards women, and love of the arts prevailed. Cows gave milk copiously, trees gave much fruit, and the waters were full of fish. 'No noise was heard from woods of howling wind or showers of rain, but the great plains were covered with dew until the middle of each bright fine day.' This was so because in the third year of Eochaidh's reign, JESUS CHRIST was born in the Holy Land.

Eochaidh, however, had some bitter disappointments. Two of his sons were killed in the victorious battle of Leitir Ruibhe. Then three other sons, called the FINN EAMHNA, rebelled against him. It was said that he had an argument with his queen Cloithfhionn over a chess game, and she as a result left TARA and went to live at the Ulster court in Eamhain Mhacha. She took her three sons, the Finn, with her, and at her instigation they declared war on their father. They ignored all his entreaties and were defeated and slain in the battle of Comar (near Navan, County Meath). Eochaidh was disconsolate, and his heart burst in his breast with sorrow. He was buried with his three rebellious sons, as he had directed, in a great mound at Croghan. Eochaidh was said to have had several other children, including Conall Anghlonnach, who later became a leading warrior in

Ulster, and the celebrated MEADHBH.

He gave the kingdom of Connacht to one Tinne mac Connrach after Tinne and his men built a fossa around the *rath* of Croghan in one night. When Tinne later slew Meadhbh's suitor, Fiodhach mac Féig, Eochaidh turned against Tinne, deposed him, and gave the Connacht throne to Meadhbh. On account of the episode concerning the three Finn, it was said that Eochaidh recommended that any future king have somebody other than a son to succeed him, for in that way sons would not be rivals of their fathers. According to the pseudo-historians, his brother Eochaidh Aireamh became king after his death.

W. Stokes in *Irische Texte, 3*, 330–1; M.E. Dobbs in *RC, 39*, 1–32 & *40*, 404–23 & *43*, 277–342; K. Meyer in *AIM, 5*, 17–22; J. O'Neill in *Ériu, 2*, 173–81; Macalister (1956), 298–9; Gwynn (1935), 161–2; Dinneen, *2* (1908), 182–7; Knott (1936), 1–2.

Eochaidh mac Maireadha Fictional
character in a medieval story which may preserve echoes of ancient myth.

The story claims that Mairidh was a king of Munster, and that he had two sons, Eochaidh and Ríbh. Eochaidh fell in love with his father's wife, a young woman called Eibhliu, who had been fostered by AONGHUS of Newgrange. Eochaidh carried Eibhliu away, accompanied by many of his retainers. On their way, a stranger killed their horses but Aonghus appeared and gave them a marvellous steed that carried all their baggage. Aonghus warned them not to allow the steed to rest and urinate, else it would cause their death. On reaching Ulster, however, the horse did urinate, causing a spring to rise. Eochaidh built a house by the spring and settled there, but one day a woman forgot to replace the cover on the well and it flooded the area, drowning Eochaidh and most of his family. Thus was formed Loch nEachach (the Lake of Eochaidh – i.e. Lough Neagh).

One version duplicates the plot by having another otherworld lord MIDHIR first killing their horses and then offering them a marvellous steed. This animal urinated and thereby gave rise to Lough Ree on the Shannon. We read that later, when their horses were killed again, Aonghus presented them with the second steed. All of the versions are somewhat disjointed, being retellings of an original account. It is likely that the original account described how Eibhliu (*see* GODDESS) was abducted by Eochaidh. Midhir – perhaps the original name of Mairidh – tried to prevent the abduction by killing the horses, and Aonghus came to the rescue with the wondrous steed. This steed later gave rise to Lough Neagh by urinating there. This, the largest lake in Ireland, in fact got its name from the sept Uí Eachach, who inhabited the area and whose name signifies 'descendants of Eochaidh'. It is quite likely that the sept was so called from the cult of the deity EOCHAIDH, and that the story is an elaboration of the equine imagery of that deity.

GENERAL: Gwynn (1913), 450–9, 560–1 & (1924), 62–9, 388–91; W. Stokes in *RC, 16*, 151–3; O'Grady, *1* (1892), 233–6; T.F. O'Rahilly (1946), 291, 499; K. Meyer in *ZCP, 8*, 307–8.

UÍ EACHACH SEPT: O'Brien (1962), 467.

Eoghan Béal

KING of Connacht, who died in AD 543. His epithet (earlier, Bél) means 'mouth' and is explained as meaning that he was 'the spokesman for all the people around him'.

A brief account of his career is given in the twelfth-century text on his son CEALLACH. This states that he raided all the other provinces of Ireland and was consistently successful on his campaigns. Eventually, he clashed with the sons of MUIRCHEARTACH MAC EARCA, who brought a great force from Ulster to plunder Connacht. As they were returning north with massive booty, Eoghan attacked them at Sligo. The Ulstermen were put to flight, but Eoghan himself was mortally wounded. Before he died, he told his people to install Ceallach as king in his place. He also instructed them to bury him in the plain of Uí Fhiachrach (now north Mayo and west Sligo) with his javelin in his hand. He was to be standing upright and facing north, and this would ensure that the Ulstermen would not triumph over Connacht. This was done, and the Uí NÉILL of the north were continually defeated by the Connachtmen until

they came with a great force, took the body of Eoghan from its grave, and reburied him at Loch Gile (Lough Gill, County Sligo) with his face downwards. This burial MOTIF is apparently a borrowing from the lore of LAOGHAIRE.

Mulchrone (1933), x, 1–3; K. Meyer in *Archiv für celtische Lexikographie, 3*, 303–4.

Eoghan Mór

Mythical ancestor of the dominant sept in early medieval Munster, the EOGHANACHT. 'Eoghan' came from a Celtic *Iwo-genos*, meaning 'yew-conception' or 'conceived by the yew tree'. The name bears evidence for the Celtic cult of trees, the sept identifying themselves by the symbol of that particular tree. The epithet *mór* signified 'great', especially in the sense of a family ancestor. Eoghan Mór was sometimes claimed to have been the father of AILILL ÓLOM, sometimes the son of that personage, and the medieval genealogists tried to rationalise this confusion by claiming that one Eoghan was the grandfather of another. It is likely that Ólom, or Ailill Ólom, was in origin a mere nickname for Eoghan, as the ancestor and archetypal king of the sept.

The genealogists claimed that the father of the first Eoghan was called Mugh Néit (servant of NÉT). This Nét was associated with the ÉRAINN people of Munster, and given that that area belonged to the Érainn people, this would suggest a subservience of the Eoghanacht to these people at an early stage – possibly a tactical one before the power of the Eoghanacht themselves was established over most of Munster. Eoghan himself was referred to as Mugh Nuadhat (servant of Nuadhu). NUADHU was a divinity and ancestor figure held in high regard by the LAIGHIN (Leinstermen), and this designation of Eoghan seems to be the result of Leinster influence on the Eoghanacht in the sixth century AD. The Leinstermen had previous to that time been engaged in a long struggle against the growing dominance of the CONNACHTA, and their anti-Connachta propaganda would have had appeal to the rulers of Munster. The whole lore of Eoghan, indeed, involves a bitter struggle against the mythical ancestor of the Connachta, the celebrated CONN CÉADCHATHACH. The tradition that he and Conn divided Ireland in two equal halves between them must be early, probably dating to the sixth century when their respective septs were dominant in large areas of the country.

The literature, as was its wont, gives a fabricated explanation of the designation Mugh Nuadhat. According to this, Eoghan was the foster-son of the Leinster king Dáire Barrach, who once undertook to fortify Dún Aillinne (Knockaulin, County Kildare), and engaged a famous builder, Nuadhu, for the work. A servant was digging the trench and was unable to remove a huge stone he came across. Eoghan was among a group of onlooking youths. The other youths refused to help, but Eoghan went into the trench and lifted the stone on his own. With one throw, he placed it in the southern angle of the fortress, where it remained ever after. 'You have a noble servant today, o Nuadhu,' remarked a DRUID, and thus Eoghan became known as 'Mugh Nuadhat'.

A series of epithets was connected to his name, such as Eoghan Taidhleach (bright), Eoghan Fial (generous) and Eoghan Fithiceach. This latter was interpreted in several ways: it was claimed that he invented wooden spades (*fidhflheaca*) so that his men could dig out the site of a fortress; and alternately that he had three forts, each called Fighfhec (woven and bent), because they were made of trees thus interlocking. The real explanation seems to be that *fithec* was a corruption of fiodhach (tree-natured), referring to the sept's yew connection, but it was taken to mean a tunnel that Eoghan constructed for storing provisions.

Already by the ninth century the Munster genealogists were promoting the fancy that Eoghan had come to Ireland from abroad, landing with his followers at Inbhear Colptha (the estuary of the Boyne). He was informed by his prophets that a great FAMINE was coming in Ireland, and they advised that he store up a large amount of food. This he did, storing the provisions away in souterrains connected with his three fortresses, and when the famine came, he shared this food with the men of Ireland in return for the KINGSHIP of the country. This is obviously contrived by some early medieval scholar to bolster the prestige of the Eoghanacht. The coming of Eoghan to Ireland is somewhat confused, for the surviving text at some points suggests that it was his sons who came rather than himself. It clearly echoes the *Lebor Gabála* account of the sons of MÍL, while the famine MOTIF is borrowed directly from the Old Testament account of Joseph in Egypt.

The Spanish connection is developed in another text, entitled *Tochmarc Momera*, in which Eoghan is portrayed as going from Ireland to Spain following on advice given to him by three strange prophets. They told him that he would marry the daughter of the king of that country, that there would be four children of the marriage, and that the descendants of these children would rule Ireland between them. (A Spanish druid made similar prophecies to the king of that country, who is curiously given the name ÉIBHEAR.) Eoghan arrived in Spain, accompanied by his foster-brothers, and married the princess, who was called Momera. The Spanish druid then told Momera to catch a salmon that came every seventh year to the River Éibhear (the Ebro) and to make a shining cloak of its scales for Eoghan. She did so, and thus Eoghan gained the epithet Taidhleach. Having spent nine years in Spain, he returned to Ireland, bringing his wife and the druid with him, as well as a strong Spanish force. The druid foretold that he would divide Ireland with another, and this prophecy was fulfilled when he and Conn came to their agreement.

A text entitled *Cath Maighe Léna*, which dates to the late thirteenth century, gives a full account of the deeds of Eoghan, incorporating details from several earlier sources. The text seems to have been compiled in the Beara Peninsula in west Cork as an attempt to underline the Eoghanacht ancestry of the Ó Súilleabháin sept that had settled there some generations before. It situates some of the action in Beara and, anachronistically, suggests that the peninsula took its name from Eoghan's fictional Spanish wife.

Here again in this text, his nickname is explained with the claim that he helped the servant of a Munster fort builder called Nuadhu Dearg. We read that Munster was at that time divided into three parts, one portion being ruled by Eoghan's father, who is called – apparently as a reflection of Eoghan's nickname – Mogh Néid. Eoghan's mother, Síoda, had a dream of seven emaciated black cows that gored and killed seven fine white cows, and a druid explained this as a presage of seven bounteous years followed by seven years of famine. Eoghan and his father had cellars constructed in which they stored a great quantity of grain in the good years. With the onset of famine, the other Munster lords came to them in desperation seeking food, and Mogh Néid promised to assist them on condition that the whole kingdom of Munster be given to his son. This was agreed, but the other two regional kings, CONAIRE MAC MOGHA LÁMHA and Macnia mac Luighdheach, went to Conn Céadchathach for help. Conn gave them his daughters in marriage, and he divided Munster on their behalf.

The armies of Conn and Eoghan met at Carn Buidhe (near Kenmare, County Kerry), and Eoghan was defeated. An otherworld lady called Éadaoin who resided in that area came to his assistance, making rocks appear as soldiers in the eyes of the foe, and under cover of this she spirited away Eoghan and what remained of his army. She placed them in seven ships in Kenmare Harbour, and that night the unyielding Eoghan made three sorties ashore against the forces of Conn. They spent nine more nights having their wounds healed by Éadaoin, and then Eoghan sailed with his followers to Spain. Arriving there, he was given a bright (*taidhleach*) cloak by Béara, the daughter of the Spanish king. She had made that cloak from the skin of a wondrous salmon she had caught. Eoghan married this princess, and all went well for nine years, until he grew lonesome for home. The Spanish king gave him a fleet and an army, and thus he set out for Ireland, bringing his wife with him.

When he reached Carn Buidhe, both Conaire and Macnia submitted to him, and many other nobles of Ireland came into alliance with him, including the Ulster and Leinster kings. Conn had no choice but to compromise, and accordingly Ireland was divided into two equal portions between himself and Eoghan. The dividing line was from Áth Cliath Meadhraighe (Maaree, south-east of Galway) to Áth Cliath Duibhlinne (Dublin), and this arrangement lasted for a long time. When Eoghan demanded that Dublin Bay be divided equally between them, however, hostilities resumed. Conn made a surprise attack on Eoghan's forces at Magh Léana (Moylena, just north of Tullamore, County Offaly), and in a prolonged and vicious contest, Eoghan's army was routed. Eoghan stood alone, fighting fiercely against the foe. He and Conn wounded each other, and then several warriors transfixed the dying Eoghan with their spears.

NAME: McCone (1996), 131; Meyer (1912), 44.

ACCOUNTS: K. Meyer in *ZCP, 8*, 312–13; V. Hull in *ZCP, 19*, 59–61; Jackson (1938); O'Curry (1855); W. Stokes in *Irische Texte, 3*, 298–309; T.F. O'Rahilly (1946), 184–92; F.J. Byrne (1973), 199–201.

Eoghanacht The strongest sept in the southern half of Ireland from about the fifth century AD until the Middle Ages. The designation means 'Eoghan-people', referring to the mythical EOGHAN MÓR. Indications are that the Eoghanacht originated in one of the early groups known as FÉINE.

The name Eoghan contains a Celtic *iwo*, the word for a yew tree, and the fact that the sept used that tree as their symbol is shown by the names of other mythical characters of theirs, such as Eoghabhal (yew-fork). A variant of the septal name, indeed, was Fir Í (from a Celtic *veri iwi*, meaning 'men of the yew'). The image of the yew tree as the sept's talisman is clear from the account of how one of their legendary figures, Conall Corc, established Caiseal (Cashel, County Tipperary) as their headquarters after a yew tree appeared on top of the great rock there. The Eoghanacht had several other strongholds in that area of south County Tipperary, such as Cnoc Rafann (Knockgraffon), Áth Cró (near Cahir) and Áth Asail (Athassel).

It seems that the Eoghanacht came to envisage their spiritual ancestor not only as being synonymous with the yew tree, but as actually residing in it. That species of tree is particularly noted for its longevity, for its great height, and for the pliability and strength of its timber, thereby rendering it a suitable symbol for a dynasty. It may be that its special connection with a great ancestor developed from a custom of planting a tree over the burial mound of a leader – after each shedding of its leaves, the tree restored itself and this could be taken when appropriate as reflecting the tribe's fortunes.

With the expansion of their power, three major branches of the Eoghanacht developed – that at Cashel, another in east Limerick centring on Knockainey, and another at Loch Léin (the Killarney lake). All three groups had traditions of great yew trees, but the east Limerick one is the most dramatic. Knockainey (Cnoc Áine) was the mystical seat of the sept's tutelary GODDESS, whom they called ÁINE, and she is described as daughter of the otherworld man Eoghabhal. Furthermore, she was said to have a brother called Fear Fí or Fear Í, a personification of the variant name for the sept, Fir Í. An eighth-century text claims that this character was a musician who lived in a yew tree at the waterfall on the River Maigue at Cathair Easa (Caherass, County Limerick). Another tradition claims that the yew itself could not be seen at that place, only its reflection in the water.

According to the old historians, the son and successor of Eoghan was FIACHU MUILLEATHAN. Fiachu himself was probably a historical person, in which case the supposed relationship between him and Eoghan would reflect how the sept claimed a mythical ancestor as the 'father' of their first-known ruler. Their genealogy claims that Fiachu's son and successor was Ailill

Flainn Bhig, whose son again was called Lughaidh and was the father of CONALL CORC. Spreading minor branches of theirs to some faraway parts of Munster in the sixth century, the Eoghanacht were soon powerful enough to send settlers further afield. One such settlement went to the Aran island off the coast of modern County Galway – becoming known as the Eoghanacht Árann – while another constituted the major part of the Irish settlements in Cornwall at that time. The main participants in this latter adventure were the Uí Liatháin, a small sept from east County Cork who claimed to have been of the same ancient stock as the Eoghanacht lords.

The main rivals of the Eoghanacht from the eighth century onwards were the sept called DÁL GCAIS in modern County Clare. Later writers, indeed, claimed that a Dál gCais king of that time, Toirdhealbhach, cut down a great yew tree that grew in the Eoghanacht territory at Imleach (Emly, County Tipperary). This was fanciful, but in the late tenth century, the Dál gCais leaders, Mathghamhain and BRIAN BÓRAMHA, did indeed take the kingship of Munster from the Eoghanacht. After the death of Brian, the fortunes of the Eoghanacht revived somewhat, but they finally lost the plain of Cashel to the NORMANS in the late twelfth century. The leading branches of the sept then migrated westwards from County Tipperary. Pre-eminent among these was the family surnamed Mac Cárthaigh (anglicised MacCarthy), which occupied most of modern County Cork and was descended from the Eoghanacht king of Cashel, Cárthach (+1045). Their chief rivals were the family surnamed Ó Súilleabháin (anglicised O'Sullivan), who were descended from a tenth-century Eoghanacht chieftain called Súildubhán (*see* EOCHAIDH). Contention between these two families led to the massacre in 1214 of many of the leading O'Sullivans by the MacCarthys at a feast at Raheen, near Cork, after which the O'Sullivans settled in south Kerry and the extreme west of County Cork.

Surnames taken in medieval times by descendants of Eoghanacht septs include the following:

Mac Cárthaigh (MacCarthy); Ó Súilleabháin (O'Sullivan); Ó Donnabháin (O'Donovan); Ó Coill (Quill); Ó Coileáin (Collins); Ó hAichir (Hehir); Ó Míocháin (Meehan); Ó Donnchú (O'Donoghue); Ó Mathúna (O'Mahony); Ó Muircheartaigh (Moriarty); Ó Gairbhia (Garvey, Garvin of Munster); Ó Caoimh (O'Keeffe); Mac Amhlaoibh (McAuliffe); Ó Ceallacháin (O'Callaghan); Ó Ríordáin (O'Riordan).

SOURCES: O'Brien (1962), 190–234, 388–90; K. Meyer in *ZCP, 8*, 312–15; Ó Muraíle, *2* (2003), 542–99 & *3*, 648–81; M. O'Daly (1975), 38–41, 58–61, 76–81; M. Dillon in *Ériu, 14*, 154–65 & *Celtica, 10*, 9–14; Todd (1848), 220; Gwynn (1924), 58, O'Grady, *2* (1892), 575; Stokes (1862), xliii & (1900), 140 & in *RC, 13*, 438; Heist (1965), 290.

GENERAL: T.F. O'Rahilly (1946), 184–92, 288; Mac Niocaill (1972), 5–9; 33–5, *passim*; F.J. Byrne (1973), 165–201.

Érainn *(also, Érna)* General name, derived from a Celtic designation *Iverni*, which was applied to several septs in early Ireland. It had an original meaning such as 'land-dwellers' (*see* ÉIRE).

It is apparent that the septs known as Érainn were descended from the earliest Celticised groups in Ireland. We have no clear idea of the identities of these groups, but all indications are that the Celts of Britain used the general term *Iverni* for them and for the indigenous non-Celtic peoples alike. The Iverni in reality must have been a fusion of pre-Celts and Celtic incomers, but from the third century BC, the Celticised elements were dominant among them. In Ireland itself, the various groups were known by different names, most prominent being the Vinducati, Soborgii, Darinii and Uluti towards the north, the Ceuleni and Aucii on the east coast, the Lugunii in the north Midlands, the Gamarnates in the west, and the Autinii and Veldobri in the south.

The Iverni, by gaining possession of the major hill forts and burial sites of the country, expropriated the prestige of these places and perpetuated their cults in Celtic guise. One of the most important of the ritual hill-top sites was TARA, where the Iverni seem to have remained in possession until the second century AD or thereabouts. The literature preserves some memories of this situation (*see* CONAIRE

and LUGHAIDH MAC CON), and the Érainn were regarded by the genealogists as distinct from other somewhat later arrivals, such as the CONNACHTA, EOGHANACHT, LAIGHIN and CRUITHNIGH (*see* PICTS). Tradition held that the Érainn were *aitheach-thuatha* (vassal-tribes), which probably reflects the fact that from the third and fourth centuries AD, many of their tribes were becoming tributary to the Laighin, Connachta and Eoghanacht.

Irish was the common language of dominant and tributary septs alike, as is clear from the provenance of OGHAM inscriptions, most of which belonged to Érainn territories. The change from Celtic word-forms to those known as Old Irish was taking place at the same time as the Iverni were in decline, and thus their generic name was changing to Érainn. The names of the leading septs at the time were also changing: the Darinii, Uluti, Lugunii, Ceuleni, Gamarnates and Autinii becoming respectively Dairine, Ulaidh, Luighne, Cualainn, Gamhanraidh and Uaithne.

The literature relates the term Érainn particularly to non-Eoghanacht septs in the south, of whom the most influential in early medieval times were two amalgams of tribes along the banks of the Rivers Nore and Suir, which became known as the OSRAIGHE and the DÉISE. Of the Érainn tribes in Munster, the Uaithne and Iobhdhaigh south of the Shannon maintained their independence for some centuries, while the Ciarraighe, Músgraighe and Corca Laíghdhe in west Munster did so until the Middle Ages. In central Munster, however, only a remnant of the Fir Mhaighe Féine survived Eoghanacht pressure. Most of the non-Connachta septs west of the River Shannon were Érainn – including the Gamhanraidh, Calraighe, Meadhraighe and another branch of the Ciarraighe (in the province of Connacht), and the Corca Baiscinn and Corca Mruadh (in County Clare). The Conmhaicne were a widely scattered people with an Érainn genealogy – groups of them were in central Connacht, in west Galway, and in Longford east of the Shannon. Earlier, the ULAIDH in the northeast had been especially powerful, while the Dál Riada made the first Irish settlements in Scotland in the fifth century AD. An amalgam of Érainn septs in the west and south of Ulster survived by calling themselves AIRGHIALLA and becoming tributaries of the Connachta and their Uí Néill descendants.

The Érainn of Tara were long remembered – that is, the old rulers of that area before the Laighin took it from them. When the Laighin were themselves displaced from Tara by the Connachta, Érainn groups such as the Luighne (or Luaighne), Gaileanga and Ciannachta held on in the area. As clients of the Connachta, the Luighne and Gaileanga set up secondary settlements west of the Shannon (in modern Counties Sligo and Mayo), and the Ciannachta set up one of their own to the north in the Roe Valley (County Derry). In the general southeast of the country, Érainn groups were much reduced by the Laighin, and some completely assimilated, such as the Cualainn (in east Wicklow) and the Lámhraighe (scattered on the western borders of the Laighin). The Beanntraighe were another scattered sept, one group of them being in County Wexford and another in west Cork.

Some major figures in early Irish mythology were long established in Érainn lore. These include appellations of ancestral GODS such as the DAGHDHA, DÁIRE and DONN; while LUGH is represented by the Érainn lore of LUGHAIDH MAC CON and their septal name Luighne. Another name that they had for the ancestor-deity was Ailill Érann (Phantom of the Érainn), whom they also called by the name Bolg (lightning) – hence the designation FIR BOLG for less prominent Érainn groups in northern and western parts of the country. At some stage, they identified this Bolg with AONGHUS, calling their ancestor Aonghus Bolg. The cult of Danu as mother-GODDESS must also have been known to them from an early period, as well as some of the goddess-river names.

In time, the adoption of a novel term to refer to an Irish person weakened the force of most of the older designations.

This was the Welsh word *Gwyddel* (i.e. an Irishman) that was, in or about the sixth century AD, borrowed into Irish in the form *Goídel* and soon became '*Gaedheal*' (plural, *Gaedhil*). Though this was at first used particularly for themselves by the septs of FÉINE derivation who were predominant in the pre-medieval centuries, the medieval genealogists insisted that all the early inhabitants of Ireland were of common stock, and accordingly claimed that all were properly *Gaedhil* (*see* GAEL). The term Érainn thus became obsolete, both in its original meaning and in its narrowed sense.

Its original meaning, however, had something of a rebirth in post-medieval speech with the use of the word *Éireannach* (plural, *Éireannaigh*) to describe an inhabitant of Ireland. It retains this general meaning in contemporary speech, with the term Gael being used of a person who belongs to, or identifies with, the IRISH LANGUAGE and the native culture.

For large Érainn groups and their descendants, *see* the entries under AIRGHIALLA, DÉISE, OSRAIGHE and ULAIDH. For the Uí MHAINE of Connacht, *see* MAINE Mór. Surnames taken in medieval times by descendants of other Érainn groups include the following: Ó hIarlaithe (O'Herlihy); Ó hIfearnáin (Heffernan); Ó Laochdha (Leahy); Ó Cathaláin (Culhane or Cahalan); Ó Daghnáin (Dinan); Ó Dubhagáin (Duggan); Ó Riagáin (O'Regan of Cork); Ó Buachalla (Buckley); Ó Cochláin (Coughlan); Ó hIonghardail, modern Ó hUrdail (Harrington); Ó Duinnín (Dinneen of north Cork); Ó Conchúir (O'Connor of Kerry); Ó hAodha (Hayes); Ó Murchú (Murphy of Cork); Ó Sé (O'Shea); Ó Fáilbhe (Falvey); Ó Coirc (Quirke); Ó Floinn (Flynn of Cork); Ó hEidirsceoil (O'Driscoll); Ó Béice (Beeky, Begg, of Cork); Ó Cobhthaigh (Coffey); Ó Laoghaire (O'Leary); Ó Conaill (O'Connell); Ó Curnáin (Courtney); Ó Ciabháin (Keevane); Ó hAonghusa (Hennessy of Cork); Ó Nuáin (Noone); Ó Finn (Finn); Ó Baiscinn (Baskin); Ó Leannáin (Linnane); Ó Maolchorcra (Mullarky); Mac Bruaidí (Brody); Ó

Conchúir (O'Connor of Clare); Ó Lochlainn (O'Loughlin); Mac Fhlannchú (Clancy); Ó Cathail (Cahill of Munster); Ó Flaitheartaigh (O'Flaherty of Clare); Ó Mainnín (Mannion of Clare); Ó Fearghail (Farrell of Longford); Ó Sioradáin (Sheridan); Ó Ciardhubháin (Kirwan); Ó Ceanndubháin (Canavan); Ó Ciaragáin (Kerrigan); Mac Raghnaill (Reynolds); Ó Giollagáin (Gilligan); Mac Sheanlaoich (Shanley, Gantly); Ó Maoilmhiaigh (Mulvey); Ó Maoilchiaráin (Mulkerrin); Mac Fhionnbhairr (Gaynor); Ó hEadhra (O'Hara); Ó Gadhra (O'Gara); Ó Cearbhaill (Carroll of Tipperary); Ó Meachair (Meagher, Maher); Ó Dulchaointigh (Delahunty); Mac Corcráin (Corcoran); Mac Conchúir (MacNaugher or O'Connor of Derry).

GENERAL: T.F. O'Rahilly in *Ériu*, *14*, 7–28 & (1946), 48–54, 61, 75–91, 391–4; E. MacNeill (1919), 61–97; L Ó Buachalla in *JCHAS*, *49*, 25–9; Ó Raithbheartaigh (1932), 53–92, 101–31; O'Brien (1962), 155, 168–71, 186–93, 246–9, 254–68, 287–321, 367–87, 391–3, 424–9, 431, 439; K. Meyer in *ZCP*, *8*, 305–9; Ó Muraíle, *2* (2003), 104–41, 418–74, 492–501, 644–83 & *3*, 476–81, 696–715.

fairies *(in Irish, sí)* The otherworld community that, according to Irish folklore, inhabits the landscape side by side with, but usually invisible to, the human race.

The word *sí* (earlier, *sídh*) originally meant a mound, and the early Irish literature has several references to otherworld dwellers in the tumuli and cairns that dot the countryside. One ultimate source of the Irish tradition of fairies, therefore, was the idea of the community of the dead living on in their burial chambers, and it is noticeable that lore of the dead (*see* GHOSTS) still tends to become confused with that of the fairies in living oral narrative. In a more basic sense, there are some indications that the concept of the living dead was one of the fountainheads of the ancient Celtic pantheon of mythic beings (*see especially* DONN). These mythic beings were, however, also understood to be a kind of spiritual community whose nature was on a different plane to that of the human race. As such, they were called by the literati the TUATHA DÉ DANANN, and were described as living in a timeless realm from which they could appear to people at will and provide glittering visions of their existence. The evidence indicates that at some stage in antiquity, Irish versions of widespread and varied beliefs about otherworld communities were assimilated to lore of the living dead, and that from this evolved the *sí* people of general Irish tradition.

The Tuatha Dé were portrayed as patrons and bestowers of things involving social prestige, such as arts and skills, and even KINGSHIP itself. That the fairies of folklore are indebted to them is obvious from the special intensity with which this MOTIF is found in Irish folk LEGENDS. Many such legendary accounts tell of how celebrated POETS and musicians got their skills as gifts from the fairies. The occasions and methods of communication with the fairies in such cases is also enlightening. Usually, the person who is to receive the gift falls asleep at some location not ordinarily frequented by humans and therefore regarded as otherworldly. It may be a 'fairy *rath*' (an ancient tumulus or relic of an earthenwork fort), a riverside (water being anciently associated with Celtic deities), or a cairn on a hill top. The fact that the sleep parallels shamanic rites, and that the locations are the same as those involved in ancient seer-craft (*see* FIONN), makes it clear that this aspect of fairy legend is a survival from native rituals. It has been strengthened, however, by poetic and metaphoric conventions. For instance, it was customary to describe brilliant harpists and other musicians as coaxing wondrous and otherworldly sounds from their instruments, and to compare their music to that played in the otherworld.

The fairies are said to live in the air and in the sea as well as on land, and thus all folklore concerning communal otherworld beings can be classified under this general heading. Among the aspects of fairy lore to which a pre-medieval origin can be attributed are the numerous traditions concerning otherworld animals – especially CATTLE and HORSES – that come from *raths* or lakes or the sea, and mingle with animals of this world. Similarly, the fairies sometimes take animals away into their world, a form of economic thieving that may owe its origin to ancient animal sacrifice. The fairy dwellings, when a human gains access to them, are beautiful places, decorated with precious metals and with sumptuous food and drink and melodious music, and can therefore be seen to preserve the standard traits of the realm inhabited by the Tuatha Dé.

The medieval literature concerning the seer hero FIONN MAC CUMHAILL has many references to visits to Tuatha Dé strongholds that, like the dwellings of the fairies in the late folklore, are often situated within cairns and *raths*. As in folklore, Fionn is given gifts in these residences – for example, a marvellous knife or goblet. Gift items of a similar nature are also brought from the otherworld in texts that situate it in a marvellous land overseas (*see* BRAN MAC FEABHAIL *and* CORMAC MAC AIRT), and it is therefore clear that we are dealing with one continuous tradition that derives ultimately from the divine realm of mythology. We read in one twelfth-century text that every otherworld dwelling in Ireland was open at Samhain (the November feast – *see* TIME), an idea that is reflected in folk beliefs that the fairies are especially to be encountered at May and November, as groups of them are wont to change their residence from one *rath* to another at these two basic junctures of the Irish year.

It is likely also that the folk belief that great battles are sometimes fought between different fairy communities is a reflection of ancient lore – for instance, the mythic battle described in the literature between the Tuatha Dé and the Fomhóire (*see* MYTHOLOGICAL CYCLE). In line with this battle imagery, folk belief holds that the most dangerous type of encounter is with the *slua sí* (trooping fairies), a kind of battalion of shock troops who are sometimes abroad at night and who lay low anybody who gets in their way. There was a strong folk assumption that one should never refer to the fairies by their name (whether *sí*, or the diminutive and somewhat disparaging *sióga*, or the English word 'fairies'), and so

several circumlocutions were used – for example, *na daoine maithe* (the good people) or *na daoine uaisle* (the noble people). This is also redolent of early belief, and there can be little doubt that similar caution was employed in connection with mythical and quasi-mythical beings in ancient Ireland.

The survival of early Irish myth in folklore is amply illustrated by the portrayal of several individual personages as functionaries in the landscape – for example ÁINE, CLÍONA, DONN *and* FINNBHEARA, and it is noticeable that these are usually assimilated to the fairies in the living lore. There is an interesting duality in the folk attitude to these personages and to the fairies themselves. On the one hand, they are exalted beings who can be good patrons, but on the other hand are understood to be on a parallel with humans and even in competition with us, engaged in their own agricultural pursuits and wishing to keep their own sections of the landscape as their special property. This tendency to regard the otherworld community as a parallel to the human one is evidenced at all stages of Irish literature. For instance, otherworld women could become the lovers or even wives of mortal men, an idea that is at least as ancient as the theme of the GODDESS of sovereignty, symbolising KINGSHIP, who is mate to the reigning king. Such alliances occur again and again in the literature – for example, *see* the entries concerning AONGHUS, ART, BRAN MAC FEABHAIL, CONAIRE, CORMAC MAC AIRT, CRIOMHTHANN NIA NÁIR, CÚ CHULAINN, DIARMAID MAC AODHA SLÁINE, ÉADAOIN, FIONN MAC CUMHAILL, LAOGHAIRE MAC CRIOMHTHAINN, MUIRCHEARTACH MAC EARCA, NIALL and OISÍN.

Ancient Ulster kingship personified as a goddess gave rise to the story of MACHA as an otherworld lady. In her case, a floating folklore motif was employed that had a man marrying a wife from the otherworld, and she leaving him when he broke a taboo. The Macha tradition had some influence on later folklore (*see* INCHIQUIN *and* DONNELLY). Independently of the Macha tradition, however, the folklore motif gave rise to a different oral legend in coastal areas of western Ireland, concerning a man who married a MERMAID.

All of this raises the much-debated issue of Celtic influence on the Romantic literature of medieval Europe, especially in so far as fairy lore is concerned. It seems likely, for instance, that the French legend of Mélusine was based on a Celtic, or even Irish, source; and whatever the reality behind the problem of the 'Breton lays' in medieval French, portrayal of the fairy realm in Arthurian and related literature derives largely from Celtic sources. Continental romance in turn had a marked influence on Irish literature of the late Middle Ages, but little of that influence is mirrored in the folk tradition. The medieval Irish attitude to the otherworld did, however, undergo a profound change due to one external influence: that of Christianity. The monks who committed the ancient lore to writing had, from the beginning, been somewhat uncomfortable theologically when describing the otherworld of pre-Christian belief. At times, these writers regarded it as a simple realm of story, while at other times they felt compelled to reduce its characters to the plane of ancient history, and only when its mythical and spiritual nature became too awkward to handle did they fully reject it. Theologians on the Continent were less tolerant, and when confronted with the age-old popular idea that spiritual communities live on beside the human community, they used biblical references to condemn it. One such polemic gained widespread currency – that the fairies were remnants of the fallen angels who had been driven out of heaven by God after the revolt of Lucifer.

This idea spread to Ireland and was adopted into the lore of the Irish *sí*, probably towards the end of the Middle Ages. It is referred to in a text of the early fifteenth century that identifies the fairies with the Tuatha Dé Danann. Describing them as dwellers in mounds and under water, the writer comments: 'Some say that they were demons of a different grade who came with the exiled band of Lucifer from heaven. They assume airy bodies for the purpose of destroying and tempting the descendants of Adam.' Irish folklore softened this portrayal, claiming that, as the fairies fell from heaven, God relented somewhat and said that 'where they are, may they stay there'. Thus the fairies came to inhabit air, land and water. In order to fill the seats left in heaven by their expulsion, God created the human race with the distinctive trait of having red blood in their bodies, whereas that of the fairies is white. Any whitish-coloured liquid seen on the ground in the early morning might accordingly be explained as blood spilt when two hostile groups of fairies clashed and fought a battle during the night.

Having lost their places in heaven, the fairies were believed to be anxious to regain them, and to underline the situation, a special Irish folk legend was developed and became very popular. We are told that a priest, while travelling at night, was met by a group of fairies who asked him would they ever gain salvation, and when he answered in the negative, they began to wail pitifully. A variant of this has the fairies asking a man to put the question to the priest as he consecrates the Host at Mass. The priest again gives the negative answer, and warns the man that when he goes to tell this to the fairies, they will be very angry and he must dig a hole in the ground, enter it, and place a shovel and spade in the form of a cross over himself as protection. The notion that fairies are in contention with humans for places in heaven was further developed as a rationale for why the fairies sometimes abducted people. Thus we are told that they wished to assimilate and intermarry with humans so that their race would gain more red blood, the qualifying trait for the lost seats.

Belief in abduction by otherworld beings must be quite ancient in Ireland. The medieval literature has several instances of young men and young women being enticed away by the Tuatha Dé (*see, for example*, CORMAC MAC AIRT *and* CÚ CHULAINN) and, apart from the context of courtship, such abduction would be a natural explanation for sudden death or unexplained deterioration in health. There was much fairy-lore concerning the taking away of women who had just given birth, the fear of abduction in the case of such a woman reflecting the perceived vulnerability of her health. A favourite narrative explanation was that a young mother of the fairy community had died and that the fairies were seeking a wet nurse for their orphaned child. Human children were also in danger of abduction, and this belief had a social dimension, for the threat of fairies was frequently used as a means of warning children to stay safely near their home. Some narrative explanations for the abduction of young children were quite involved. Boys were said to be especially vulnerable, not only because they were reputedly more able workers but also because of the traditional idea that the male gives more of its properties to offspring and thus would give more human blood to the fairy race.

Regarding the abduction of children, a legend that spread throughout western Europe became very popular in Ireland. This has parents leaving their child, who is pining and causing them great worry, in the care of a babysitter, usually a tailor. Much to the astonishment of the babysitter, the child begins to act like an intelligent adult. He stands up in the cradle and begins to speak of events long ago, perhaps also asking for a drink of liquor or even playing fine music on a set of pipes. Realising what he is, the tailor reddens his pin or some other metal implement in the fire and approaches the child while wielding it. At that, the child jumps from the cradle and races screaming out through the door. The babysitter warns the departing changeling to send the stolen child back, and soon after, the real child, for which the strange creature had been substituted, is returned. A popular formulation of the legend has the babysitter applying a special test to the changeling – he heats a drink for it in an eggshell and, on seeing this, the child laughs and says it has never seen such a silly thing in its long life, thereby betraying its real nature.

Another migratory legend, also found throughout Ireland, describes an attempted abduction of a young woman by three strange old women who come on each of three nights to help her at her spinning. Growing suspicious, the young woman on the third night goes to the door and shouts out that the top of the nearby hill is on fire. Duped by this, the three old women race from the house and up the hill to save their otherworld residence from the supposed flames. This legend was inspired by two international FOLKTALES, one of which tells of how an impish little man tries to inveigle her child from a young woman by helping her at spinning, and the other telling of how three old women help a girl to spin an impossible amount in one night and thus become the bride of a prince. Particularly developed recensions of the legend state that the three fairy women lived on Slievenamon, County Tipperary. The name of that eminence, Sliabh na mBan, means literally 'the mountain of the women', and it has a cairn on its top long associated with the otherworld. It may well be that this Irish folk legend originated in that area.

The *slua sí* can sometimes be understood as a fairy cavalcade abroad at night seeking to take some human away with them for no apparent reason. This appears to be an indigenous Irish theme, in which they are synonymous with the otherworld of the dead, and there are even accounts given of 'fairy funerals' seen at the time of the death of some local person. A legend told in several parts of the country describes how a recently deceased young woman appears to her sleeping husband and asks him to be in a certain place on the following night, when she will be riding with the fairy host. When the cavalcade comes by, he must watch for the grey horse on which she will be mounted, and if he grabs her without delay, she will be returned to him. He goes to the place as directed and sees the cavalcade passing. Among them, he recognises several people of his acquaintance who have died. When he rushes to grab his wife, however, the grey horse shies and bolts, and the cavalcade immediately disappears, leaving him alone. The motif upon which this legend was constructed – that of a man trying and failing to recover his wife from the otherworld – can be traced back in Irish tradition to the tenth century at least, as it occurs in the story of Éadaoin. Ultimately, it seems to derive from ancient European lore such as found in the Greek story of Orpheus.

Common in different parts of Ireland also was a north-west European legend that tells of how a midwife was once called out to tend to a fairy woman who was giving birth. When the child was born, she was given some ointment to rub on its eyes so as to strengthen its eyesight, and by accident rubbed her own eye with the ointment. She was then brought back to her own house safe and well. Sometime later, however, she was at a market and recognised one of the men there who had been in the fairy dwelling. She spoke to him, and he realised that she could see him because of the ointment she had rubbed to her eye. Angered at being thus visible to her, he put his finger in her eye and blinded it. The idea that the fairies are resentful of human intrusion into their world is common. For instance, if a house is deliberately or inadvertently built over a pathway used by them, great tumult will be heard and items will get flung about. One of the fairies may appear and explain that the dwellers in that house will have no peace until the situation is corrected, either by demolishing the house completely or by removing whatever part of it is blocking the path.

The fairies can, however, be quite benevolent to people in some ways. They might confer gifts or skills on people, and they might even come to the rescue of an individual who badly needed help. Several individuals, especially those with SPECIAL POWERS of healing, were said to be 'in the fairies' and to travel the countryside with them at night, gaining all types of information in the process. Another Continental legend was adopted to illustrate this notion of quick magical travel, and versions of it were common throughout the country. It concerns a man who meets the fairy host one night, and they invite him to come with them. They give him a special cap and tell him to mount a ragwort weed as if it were a horse. When he does so, he finds himself brought into the air and, travelling thus with the fairy host, comes to a wine cellar in a foreign country. There he drinks his fill, but when morning comes finds himself alone and is arrested for breaking into the cellar. He is sentenced to be hanged, and is placed on the gallows with a rope around his neck. He manages, however, to draw the fairy cap from his pocket, and when he puts it on his head, he is raised into the air. Soon he finds himself back home, standing beside the ragwort in the very place that he met the fairies.

The Irish fairies were not imagined as being very different in form or appearance to the human race, except that they might be somewhat paler in hue and might be dressed in clothing of silk and satin. The idea that they were smaller in size than humans was not general in Ireland. Similarly, a wide range of activities parallelling those of the human community were attributed to them. They were believed to be ruled by kings and queens, inside their dwellings were many chambers and great assembly halls, and they often held great feasts. It was usually said, however, that a human visitor who partook of their food could not return to the ordinary world. This idea is far-flung and very old, occurring, for instance, in ancient Middle Eastern literature.

The fairies engaged in farming, went incognito to the humans' markets to buy and sell stock, and could appear at will to seek the loan of some implement from a farmer or his wife. They often rewarded those who assisted them in some way. In SPORT and entertainment, too, their tastes resembled those of humans. Their music, often heard at night, was exceedingly beautiful, and they were much given to hunting and to playing hurling. A story told in many parts of the country concerns a great hurler who was taken away at night to play for a team of fairies in a match against another such team in a field beside a *rath*.

The hurler scored, following which the vision of the match suddenly disappeared and he found himself at home in bed. This motif is current since medieval times. A twelfth-century text claims that in the time of St PATRICK, one Aodh, son of the Leinster king Eochaidh Leathdhearg, was a great hurler. While playing magnificently at Sí Liamhna (the *rath* near the king's residence at Castlelyons, County Dublin), this young man was taken away hand in hand by the two daughters of the otherworld lord BODHBH DEARG. He spent three years in the otherworld, at Brugh na Bóinne (Newgrange, County Meath), before escaping during another hurling match there and returning to his family.

The hostile aspect of the fairies included their supposed propensity to shoot tiny darts at fine cattle or fine horses and thus cause them to pine away and belong to them. A ribbon or other piece of cloth of red colour was believed to be an effective protection against them, and various religious amulets were used for that purpose also. Another means of protection arose from the fact that the fairies themselves were very fastidious and disliked anything dirty. Therefore, it was thought wise to keep the foot-water in the house, and in some places it was customary to sprinkle a drop of urine on children before they left the house, so as to keep fairy abducters at bay.

Fairy dwellings may be of many types, all relatively remote from human concourse and all with a certain aura of mystery. The oldest attributions must have been to tumuli and cairns, but in late medieval times, the no-longer understood earthenwork forts (popularly called '*raths*', '*lisses*' and 'moats') were added. Further variety of location was provided by stone circles, hills and even invisible caverns in mountainsides, not to mention fanciful underwater palaces. If any person damaged a place believed to be a fairy dwelling, misfortune or even death would befall him – a belief that was instrumental in preserving many archaeological sites in the countryside. A solitary bush or tree was often regarded as belonging especially to the fairies, and if it were cut down, they would similarly exact vengeance.

Although such beliefs in a parallel otherworld community may never have been unanimously held in Ireland, they were widely held at all stages of history, so strongly indeed that stories and superstitions have become intertwined in each other with many kinds of permutations. Rather spontaneous beliefs, too, could spring up. For instance, strange lights seen at night were believed to be the fairies trying to send a benighted traveller astray, and a heavy mist was believed to be caused by them with a similar intent. It was thought necessary to be diplomatic towards the fairies in ordinary human nourishment – for instance, the first drops of milk from a cow or of newly distilled whiskey should be thrown into the air for them. The belief that a whirlwind is caused by fairies as they pass by is of a kind likely to be quite ancient, but it must have been reinforced by the similarity in sound of its title *sí gaoithe* (originally, *sidhe gaoithe* and literally meaning 'thrust of wind') with the word *sí* (originally, *sídh*) for the fairies themselves.

INDICES & DISCUSSIONS: Cross (1952), 243–73; S. Ó Súilleabháin (1942), 450–79 & (1967), 826; Ó Danachair (1978), 32; Wood-Martin, *2* (1902), 1–25; Wentz (1911); Briggs (1977) & (1978); B. Almqvist in *Béaloideas*, *59*, 271–2.

POETS & MUSICIANS: Ó hÓgáin (1982), 168–202; R. uí Ógáin in *Béaloideas*, *60–1*, 197–214; Ralls-MacLeod (2000), 25–51; B. Hilliers in *PHCC*, *14*, 58–75.

DWELLINGS AT NOVEMBER: K. Meyer in *RC*, *5*, 202; S. Ó Súilleabháin (1967), 83.

ORIGIN OF FAIRIES: R. Th Christiansen in *Béaloideas*, *39–41*, 95–111.

TUATHA DÉ AS FALLEN ANGELS: Ó Raithbheartaigh (1932), 197–201.

QUERY RE. SALVATION: Ó Catháin (1985), 79; Almqvist in *Béaloideas*, *59*, 271.

CHANGELING: Mac Philib (1980) & in *Béaloideas*, *59*, 121–31.

SPINNING WOMEN: S. Ó Súilleabháin & Christiansen (1967), types 500–1; Áine O'Neill in *Béaloideas*, *59*, 189–96, 258–63; J. Dunne in Maher (1954), 68–9.

ABDUCTED WIFE: Ó Duilearga (1948), 291–3, 435; Cross (1952), motifs F322.2–5; Hunt (1912), 155–8.

MIDWIFE: Christiansen in *Lochlann*, *6*, 104–17; Mac Cárthaigh (1988) & in *Béaloideas*, *59*, 133–43.

FAIRY CAP: Christiansen (1958), type 6050; Briggs (1976), 148–50, 409–12; Ó Duilearga & Ó hÓgáin (1981), 257–60; Almqvist in *Béaloideas*, *59*, 272.

FAIRY FOOD: Almqvist in *Béaloideas, 59*, 272; Ó hÓgáin in *Béaloideas, 68*, 90.
HURLING: Stokes (1900), 116; S. Ó Súilleabháin (1942), 460–1.
ANTHOLOGIES: Ó Duilearga (1948), 291–323, 434–40; D. MacManus (1959); Ó hEochaidh, Ní Néill & Ó Catháin (1977).

famine There were many famines in Irish history, culminating in the Great Famine of 1845–49, during which almost two million people died from hunger and disease, and another two million emigrated; this halved the population of Ireland. The specific word for 'famine' is *gorta*, but the Great Famine was often referred to simply as *an drochshaol* (the bad time).

Many oral accounts of the misery of the Great Famine survived in oral tradition into the twentieth century. Accounts abounded of corpses by the roadside, of families closing the doors of their cabins to die together or carrying each other's corpses to the graveyard, of mass graves and of outbreaks of disease such as typhus and cholera. The failure of the potato crop due to blight was the immediate cause of the hunger, and this blight spread from western Europe. Having seen its effect, the people regarded the blight as a deadly pestilence, and so folk tradition held that a great murky fog was seen to descend on the fields, and that the blight came from this fog. Soon after, the people noticed horrid black spots on the potato leaves, and this developed into a great stench from the fields as the crop rotted away. Many attempts were made to explain why such a terrible catastrophe should befall the people. There had been flourishing potato crops in the years leading up to the Famine, and some considered that the wasteful and self-assured attitude of the people had tempted fate. 'Wilful waste,' they said, 'made woeful want!' Bad agricultural methods were also blamed, as well as the frightfully unjust division of land and resources under the landlord system. There had also been premonitions, according to lore. In the months preceding the Famine, the seasons had shown great volatility – ominous mists, and storms of rain and wind alternating with periods of terrible quiet and silence. In accordance with ancient

PLAGUE-lore, a horrid dragon-like animal had even been seen in the sky, crazy to descend and wreak havoc on the land.

A belief that long predated the Great Famine concerned the *fear gortach* (hungry grass). This was a patch of grass a person might unknowingly step on, and the result would be extreme hunger and growing fatigue unless relieved by some food. It seems to have originated in medieval Ireland when, due to the frequent confluence of famine and plague, grass growing from the grave of a victim was thought to be infectious.

S. Ó Súilleabháin (1942), 397, 534–6; R.J. McHugh in Dudley Edwards & Williams (1956), 391–436; Porter (1995).

Fear Diadh Mythical or fictional warrior in the ULSTER CYCLE. Several variants of his name are found in the medieval literature – including Fer Déa (man of a goddess), Fer Deodae (divine man) and Fer Dedh (man of fire). One variant, Fer Deadh, preserves what is apparently the original meaning.

An earlier form of Fer Deadh would have been Fer Dedad, or in the plural Fir Dedad, which looks like a tribal name. In fact, the many ÉRAINN groups were often called Clann Dedad, which is equivalent in meaning to Fir Dedad. It is apparent that a group of Érainn left their name on a ford (*áth*) on the River Níth, north of the Boyne, which ford was accordingly known as Áth Fher Dedad. Etymology, be it true or false, was regarded by the medieval writers as crucial to the acceptance and development of lore. The memory of Fir Dedad would have been quite obscure in that area, and so their designation could easily be reshaped into an imagined heroic personage of old. Moreover, the obscure name was given a new form and interpretation: Fer Diad (literally, 'man of smoke'). To the antiquarians of early medieval Ireland, it presented no problem to interpret the place name as being 'the ford of Fear Diadh' – i.e. Áth Fhir Diadh (later anglicised as Ardee, County Louth).

The proximity of this to the area of the cult of CÚ CHULAINN meant that a connection could be made between the two warriors. The first surviving mention of the warrior Fear Diadh is in a text from the ninth century. He (Fer Deodae) is there described as son of FEARGHUS MAC RÓICH and slayer of CEITHEARN MAC FIONNTAIN, and it is clear from this that he had already by that time become associated with the Ulster Cycle. As that cycle developed and its characters became synchronised, Cú Chulainn and Fear Diadh were represented as having as youths been trained in arms together. Thus in a tenth-century text we are told that they were educated by the female warrior Scáthach in Scotland.

One of the other students of Scáthach was one Lóch Mór, who is represented in the epic story *Táin Bó Cuailnge* (*see* ULSTER CYCLE) as a former companion who was slain in single combat by Cú Chulainn. There are several indications that it was on the pattern of this episode that a combat between Fear Diadh and Cú Chulainn was introduced into the text of the *Táin* in the eleventh century. Loch is described as having a horny skin (*conganchnes*), which meant that he could not be killed by ordinary means, and Cú Chulainn had to use his deadly javelin, the *ga bolga*, to slay him. Both details are repeated in the account of Fear Diadh's clash with the great hero. Again, the *Táin* describes how another young comrade of Cú Chulainn, called Fear Baoth, is weaned away from his friendship by queen MEADHBH, who offers her daughter Fionnabhair to him if he will fight Cú Chulainn. This is repeated also in the case of Fear Diadh. Furthermore, the *Táin* account shows signs of forced rearrangement in order to make Fear Diadh fit into the context. He had been, for some reason, described as the son of Damhán, and the writer who invented the combat of Fear Diadh with Cú Chulainn used phonemic similarity to add a wider dimension to this patronymic. Thus he described Fear Diadh as coming from Iorras Domhnann (Erris, County Mayo). The Domhnainn sept (*see* LAIGHIN) in that area were reputed to be one of the fiercest fighting groups in Meadhbh's army, and it was considered appropriate to identify Fear Diadh as one of them, even though such a

western origin contradicted the ambit he shared with Cú Chulainn.

The inserted episode in the *Táin* has Fear Diadh at first refusing to fight Cú Chulainn on account of their friendship. Meadhbh plied him with drink and offered her daughter to him, but he continued to refuse until she lyingly suggested that Cú Chulainn had boasted of superiority over him. So he went to face his former comrade in single combat, a combat that is made to accord with tradition by situating it at Áth Fhir Diadh. The confrontation at the ford of the two erstwhile friends is described with great drama. In the first recension of the *Táin*, Fear Diadh insults his opponent by calling him a squint-eyed fellow, and the two then fight fiercely, using all their tricks learned from Scáthach. Cú Chulainn, however, has his charioteer Laegh pass the *ga bolga* downstream to him and, catching it between his toes, casts it into the anus of Fear Diadh. The latter lowers his shield, and Cú Chulainn pierces him through the heart. Badly wounded himself from the combat, Cú Chulainn then laments his fallen friend. This account is amplified in the later recensions to include a preliminary conversation between the warriors in which each beseeches the other to withdraw from the ford and in which they dolorously recall their past friendship. They are described as fighting for four days before Fear Diadh is slain. Each evening after the first two days' fighting, they embrace each other and exchange food, drink and healing herbs. On the third evening, however, they break off all contact, and after a fierce conflict, Cú Chulainn slays him with the *ga bolga*. Fear Diadh dies in the arms of his friend turned foe.

This is the only major episode in the whole tradition that features Fear Diadh. He is mentioned incidentally in other texts, and figures as a comrade in arms in some post-medieval romances concerning Cú Chulainn (q.v.).

Van Hamel (1933), 49; P.L. Henry in Mac Mathúna & Ó Corráin (1997), 56–9; C. O'Rahilly (1976), 78–95, 275 & (1970), 71–100 & (1961), 83–110; R.I. Best in *ZCP*, *10*, 274–308; M. Nettlau in *RC*, *10*, 330–46 & *11*, 23–32, 318–43. For an alternative understanding of the name, *see* E.P. Hamp in *Ériu*, *33*, 178.

Feardhomhain Mythical or fictional young warrior in the FIANNA CYCLE. The name seems to have been a common one, meaning 'minor' or 'young man'.

The medieval literature mentions him several times as one of the followers of FIONN MAC CUMHAILL. It varies as to his identity, but generally regards him as a Leinster scion. Texts from the eleventh to the thirteenth century give varying recensions of a story concerning his tragic death. According to this story, he had a sister called Finnine and she was either ill-treated or killed by her husband, Conán mac an Léith Luachra, as a result of which Feardhomhain engaged Conán in combat, and both were slain in the fierce duel. There is a suggestion that Fionn was in some way responsible for the tragedy. Another medieval source mentions how Feardhomhain slew a monster in Loch Lurgan (a lake west of the Bog of Allen in County Offaly), and there can be little doubt but that a substantial literary account of Feardhomhain once existed, though it is now lost.

An oral story, very popular in the folk-lore of County Donegal, seems to be based on that lost text. A folk identification of Loch Fhinne (Lough Finn) in that county with Finnine was the probable reason for the survival of the story in this form. We are told that Fionn wished to bring about the death of Feardhomhain and, knowing him to be a brave youth, advised him to avoid a fierce PIG that inhabited a certain glen. Feardhomhain, as expected by Fionn, went to the glen with his three dogs. Each dog was killed in turn by the pig, and then Feardhomhain and the fierce beast fell fighting each other. The young hero's sister, called Finngheal, went to assist him, but she was drowned in Lough Finn in her haste.

There are elements in this story concerning Feardhomhain that seem to have been unknown to the medieval writers, and the likelihood therefore is that the lost literary romance was written – like other works of its kind – in the sixteenth or seventeenth century. Its author would have read the mentions of Feardhomhain in the earlier texts, from which he took the character of Feardhomhain's sister and the theme of Fionn's treachery. He portrayed the water-monster slain by Feardhomhain as a fierce pig, for he knew of the situation of a brave youth acting on ambiguous advice concerning such an animal from the story of DIARMAID UA DUIBHNE, and perhaps even from the biography of Fionn himself.

P.L. Henry in Ériu, 18, 158–9; Stokes (1900), 78–9, 101–2, 113, 123–4, 355; M.E. Dobbs in Ériu, 14, 166–9; Mac Néill (1908) 12–13, 25; M. Dillon in Ériu, 11, 44; Gwynn (1924), 362–7; Plummer, 2(1910), 250; G. Murphy (1953), 3–6, 181; Ó Catháin (1985), 69–70, 85–6; Ó hÓgáin (1988), 255–7, 341, 358.

Fearghal mac Maoldúin High-KING of the UÍ NÉILL from AD 710–22. He died in that year in battle against Leinster – a battle that is the subject of the text *Cath Almaine*, composed in the tenth century and rewritten sometime later.

The original author derived the character and general milieu from the historical Annals, and dramatised these in his narrative. According to the text, Fearghal and the Munster king CATHAL MAC FIONGHUINE were old adversaries, but peace was arranged between them. Fearghal planned to invade Leinster to collect the BÓRAIMHE tribute, and he gathered a large army for this purpose. One of his recruits was a youth called Donn Bó, a widow's son, whose mother allowed him to go only on his safety being pledged. The invasion force went astray in the winter weather, and Fearghal's men took from a leper his only cow and burned his house. The leper cursed them for this. At their camp, Fearghal called on Donn Bó to entertain the company, for he was the best in Ireland at storytelling and poetry and music. Donn Bó refused, however, and the jester told stories instead. At Almhain (Allen, County Kildare), the Leinster army opposed them in a fierce battle, and both Fearghal and Donn Bó were slain.

That night, the Leinstermen held a triumphant feast, and when one of them went out to the battlefield, he heard the voices of the dead singing for Fearghal, and their musicians playing. The voice of Donn Bó was the sweetest of all, and so the Leinsterman brought that head into the feast. It was placed on a pillar and, when asked to sing for the men of Leinster, turned to the wall so as to be in darkness, and then sang. All the company wept, so sad was its voice. When brought back to the battle-field, the head asked to be replaced on its body, and when this was done, Donn Bó revived and so returned safe to his mother as pledged. Cathal mac Fionghuine, how-ever, was angry at the slaying of Fearghal, with whom he had made peace. To placate him, his erstwhile Leinster allies brought the head of the high-king to a feast at Gleann Damhain (Glanworth, County Cork), where Cathal was then residing. Cathal had the head washed and combed and dressed in satin, and then prepared a great feast. The head blushed in the pres-ence of the Munstermen and thanked God for the reverence shown to it, after which the feast was distributed among the poor. Cathal then brought the head back to the Uí Néill, Fearghal's royal sept.

The most striking aspect of this story is the MOTIF of the speaking heads of the dead. This was an ancient feature of war-rior-lore (*see* CONALL CEARNACH *and* FIONN MAC CUMHAILL) to which the author of this narrative gave an aura of mystery and of pathos. Fearghal was the father of two other celebrated high-kings, AODH ALLÁN and NIALL FRASACH.

Ó Riain (1978); O'Donovan (1860), 20–49; Macalister (1956), 384–9.

Fearghus mac Léide (*earlier, Fergus mac Léte*) Mythical KING of Ulster. He seems to have originally been a double of the better-known mythical king of the province, FEARGHUS MAC RÓICH, and as such would be another version in saga of the patron deity of ancient Ulster kingship. His patronymic Léide probably in origin meant 'the grey one', an appellation of the father-deity (*see* MACHA *and* MIDHIR).

The major account of him dates from the late seventh or early eighth century. According to this, he gave his protection to Eochaidh 'Yellow Mouth', who had been exiled by CONN CÉADCHATHACH. When Eochaidh was slain by Conn's men,

Fearghus demanded compensation. This was agreed, and it included the handing over of a parcel of land called Níth to Conn, as well as the handing over of the mother of one of the assassins. She was Dorn, a noblewoman of Conn's people, and she was treated by Fearghus as a menial servant. Soon after this, Fearghus went on a trip to the sea coast with his charioteer, and fell asleep there. Sprites (*luchorpáin – see* LEPRECHAUN) came to him and took away his sword. Then they carried him to the sea, and when his feet touched the water, he awoke and seized three of the sprites. He demanded that they grant him three wishes: the power of swimming under seas, pools and lakes. His desire was granted to him, with the stated exception of going under Loch Rudhraighe in his own territory (i.e. Dundrum Bay, County Down).

Time passed, and one day, Fearghus decided to swim under Loch Rudhraighe. While in the lake, he encountered a dread-ful monster (*muirdris*) that alternately inflated and contracted itself like a bel-lows. At the sight of it, his mouth was turned to the back of his head, and he fled to the land. He fell asleep there, and the charioteer went to the wise men of Ulster at the court of Eamhain Mhacha. Realising that a man with a blemish should not be king (*see* KINGSHIP), but wishing to retain Fearghus in that office, the wise men decided to conceal the blemish. They arranged that only nobles would attend him in his palace, and this stratagem suc-ceeded for seven full years. Fearghus remained unaware of his condition, but one day, the enslaved Dorn was washing his head. Judging that she was working too slowly, Fearghus struck her with a whip, whereupon she was overcome by anger and taunted him with the blemish. He cut her in two with his sword, and then went straight to Loch Rudhraighe to contend with the monster. For a day and a night they fought in the water, and even-tually Fearghus emerged showing the head of the slain monster to the Ulstermen. Overcome by his efforts, however, he fell down dead, and for a whole month the bay remained red from the struggle that had taken place there.

Some early myth obviously lies behind this account. We are told that the sprites put into his ears herbs that enabled him to be a prodigious swimmer, and a variant description has one of them giving him a cloak that, when wound around his head, gave him that ability. It is noteworthy that his supposed double, Fearghus mac Róich, is portrayed as a great swimmer who is also killed while in water, and this suggests that some aquatic symbolism attached to the ritual of ancient Ulster kingship. Some further support for this is given by the classification of Tonn Rudhraighe (the tide in Dundrum Bay) among the great waves of Ireland that cried out upon the death of a king. It is likely that such aquatic symbolism combined with memories of a fourth-to-fifth-century conflict between the Ulstermen and the CONNACHTA sept at Tara (see ULSTER CYCLE), and that the result was the legend of how Conn gave to Fearghus the land and woman as compensation. This much is indeed described in a poem predating the text that has been summarised here. The poem mentions Dron's taunt to Fearghus and states that the latter was killed in Loch Rudhraighe. The monster is not mentioned, and both it and the sprites must be an addition to the legend. They are apparently derived from the influential writings of the early-seventh-century scholar Isidorus of Seville, who describes such fantastic sea-dwelling creatures.

Around the thirteenth century, some writer developed the story of Fearghus' death into a burlesque narrative, laying greatest stress on the sprites. According to this, on the very night that Fearghus hosted a great banquet at Eamhain Mhacha, the king of the land of the leprechauns hosted a feast for his own people. This king, called Iubhdán, boasted of the greatness of his warriors, but his POET Eisirt burst out laughing, saying that one of Fearghus' warriors could overcome all of Iubhdán's battalions. Eisirt was allowed to depart in order to prove his assertions, and he travelled to Ulster, where he was received with much amusement. He was

so small that he could stand on the palm of Fearghus' dwarf poet Aodh. After three days and three nights, Eisirt, accompanied by Aodh, returned to his own country. Iubhdán and his court were terrified when they saw the 'giant' Aodh, and Iubhdán decided to go himself to see Ulster. He set out, with his queen Bébó, and arrived secretly at Eamhain Mhacha by night. Attempting to eat porridge there, he fell into the cauldron, and was rescued next morning by the amused courtiers. Fearghus ordered that he be put with the rabble of the household, but relented when Iubhdán promised to remain with him. He was accordingly given excellent quarters, and he and his queen became celebrities in Eamhain Mhacha. Eventually, the leprechaun people came with seven battalions to take him back. They bargained for his release, using both threats and offers of ransom. The only ransom Fearghus would accept was Iubhdán's shoes, and so the leprechaun king was released.

The reason Fearghus desired the shoes was that previously, while swimming in Loch Rudhraighe, he had encountered a monster (sinach) and had barely escaped with his life. The monster's breath had twisted his mouth towards the back of his head. The blemish was kept a secret from him until he and his queen one day quarrelled over precedence in the use of the bath-stone. He struck her, breaking one of her teeth, and she in anger told him of his blemish. He therefore chose Iubhdán's shoes, for he believed they could protect him when he went to encounter the monster again. Accordingly, he confronted it a second time, and in a ferocious fight slew it with his great sword (called the caladhbholg). But the monster's vicious tooth tore his heart, and so he expired, mourned by his poet Aodh and the rest of the Ulster people.

It has been suggested that a manuscript version of this story was read in English to Jonathan Swift, and that he got from it the idea of contrasting a land of giants with a land of pygmies, which is the basis of his famous work Gulliver's Travels. At the other end of the timescale, it is believed that the sword of Fearghus derives from ancient Celtic myth. The medieval literature lists Fearghus mac Léide among the several heroes who for a time had possession of the *caladhbholg*, and for his part, Fearghus mac Róich was also the wielder of a great sword. Another mythical Ulster king, who seems ultimately to be identical with both of these, was known as Fearghus Foga (literally, 'Fearghus of the Spear'). He was said to have been the inventor of the spear, and it emerges from this that a typical weapon of great warriors was associated with the personification of Ulster kingship. It has been argued that such a great weapon, called *bolgos* (meaning 'lightning') was an attribute of the ancient Celtic war-deity, and it is significant that in Irish the compound *caladhbholg* (i.e. hard-spear) was used to designate a fearsome weapon of war. The word *bolg* was easily confused with the ordinary word for a bag (see FIR BOLG), and since *colg* means a sword, it was natural that *caladhcholg* should be substituted for the earlier form, so the typical weapon became a sword. In Welsh sources, it is also a sword, though the original *bolgos* survived there in its aspirated form, viz. *caledvwlch* – hence Arthur's great 'Caliburnus' or 'Excalibur' in later romantic literature.

Apart from the saga of his death, Fearghus mac Léide is given an occasional background role in the developed Ulster Cycle in the Middle Ages. As if to echo their ultimate identity, he is there stated to have been 'the close colleague of Fearghus mac Róich'. He is given a major role in the post-medieval romance of *Conghal Cláiringneach*, where it is said that the province of Ulster was divided between himself and Conghal, but that relations broke down between them, and Fearghus was defeated in battle by Conghal and deprived of his realm.

EARLY TEXTS ON HIS DEATH: D.A. Binchy in *Ériu*, *16*, 33–48.

ISIDORUS INFLUENCE: Carney (1955), 125.

BURLESQUE TEXT: O'Grady, *1* (1892), 238–52.

POSSIBLE INFLUENCE ON SWIFT: Mercier (1962), 27–31, 187–8.

NAME OF SWORD: T.F. O'Rahilly (1946), 43–74.

FEARGUS FOGA: T.F. O'Rahilly (1946), 68, 226–8.

GENERAL: Binchy in Dillon (1968), 40–52.

Fearghus mac Róich Mythical KING and seneschal in the ULSTER CYCLE. The name Fearghus (earlier, Fergus) meant 'virility'; and the original form of his patronymic, *ró-ech*, meant 'great stallion'.

He is represented as possessing great sexual energy, having large genitals and requiring seven women to satisfy him. Several other figures in the regnal lists of the ancient ULAIDH (Ulstermen) were also called Fearghus, and since these lists were fabricated from myth, it is apparent that the name had some ritual significance. He was sometimes referred to as Fearghus mac Rosa Ruaidh, which designation must be of secondary origin. According to this tradition, his mother had the unlikely name, for a woman, of Róch, and his father was Ros Ruadh son of Rudhraighe (for whom *see* ULSTER CYCLE). There can be little doubt, however, that this Ros Ruadh originated in an attempt by genealogists to connect the Ulaidh with the prestigious cult of the Boyne Valley (*see* FIONN *and* AODH RUADH RÓ-FHEASA). Otherwise, the character of Fearghus mac Róich springs from genuine ancient Ulster tradition. We are told in the literature that he was king of the province at first and that he later became seneschal. This is a strange arrangement biographically, and suggests that he was anciently regarded as an original king of Ulster who was the patron of successors to that office. In all probability, *fergus* had once been a cultic attribute of kingship, entailing equine imagery (*see* EOCHAIDH), and had in time become a cult name for the monarchs of the Ulaidh. When the fortunes of the Ulaidh waned in the fourth and fifth centuries AD, this attribute and its mythic personification would have been understood as in some way abandoning them.

There is evidence that Fearghus mac Róich was a leading figure in the saga *Táin Bó Cuailnge* (*see* ULSTER CYCLE) from its inception. An obscure verse text dating from the early seventh century AD has him deserting his own people because of his attachment to queen MEADHBH, and further states that, having been proclaimed by the Ulster king CONCHOBHAR MAC NEASA, he and his associates went south to TARA. A somewhat later text, *Fochond Loingse Fergusa meic Róig*, describing the cause of his exile, has him resenting the lavish way in which Conchobhar entertains strangers compared to the lack of respect shown for himself, and has him dallying with Meadhbh unknown to her husband when he reaches her court. The MOTIF that Fearghus had left Ulster and joined the foe was obviously open to several rationalisations. In the biography of Conchobhar, we are told that he was tricked out of the throne. He was king of Ulster until falling in love with Neas, the mother of Conchobhar, and she agreed to become his wife on condition that he relinquish the kingship to her son for a year. When the year was ended, the nobles of the province were so pleased with Conchobhar that they decided to keep him permanently in the office, and Fearghus was displaced. Yet another account has Fearghus being banished by the ambitious Conchobhar and going to Tara where king EOCHAIDH FEIDHLEACH gave him his daughter in marriage. From there, he commenced a war against Conchobhar, and when peace was eventually restored between them, Fearghus was allowed to return to Ulster and was made seneschal. This, despite the confused rationalising, preserves an echo of an original role as patron of the monarchy.

The notion that Fearghus became seneschal neutralised the theme of desertion, but it did not obliterate it, and so a new explanation was felt necessary. This was done by having him desert the province a second time, and a plot was adopted from floating lore external to the Ulster Cycle, one which also had a woman as the cause of conflict between two men. Thus the tragic story concerning DEIRDRE came into existence. Memory of Fearghus' cult was weakening, and here he was confined to a secondary role in the action, being not the lover of Deirdre but her guarantor. We are told that he deserted Conchobhar after that king had treacherously violated his sureties for the beautiful young woman and her lover. Fearghus

declared war on Conchobhar, burned the royal fortress of Eamhain Mhacha, ravaged the province, and departed with many Ulster warriors to the hostile court of Meadhbh in Connacht. Later he fell in love with FLIODHAIS, wife of the king of the Gamhanraidh, an ÉRAINN sept (who lived in the Erris area of Mayo). She abandoned her husband, who was slain and his fortress plundered by Fearghus. Fliodhais then became Fearghus' wife, and she brought her great herd of CATTLE to him.

The literature also states that in retaliation for his desertion, Conchobhar had all of Fearghus' kin who remained in Ulster slaughtered. Fearghus thirsted for revenge, and was thus in the forefront when Meadhbh launched her great attack on Ulster in *Táin Bó Cuailnge*. His loyalties were, however, divided as he had not lost his affection for Ulster, and since he had once been the tutor in arms of CÚ CHULAINN, he resorted to several ruses to protect his native province and in particular his beloved pupil. He was the owner of a great sword (*see* FEARGHUS MAC LÉIDE) that was stolen from him by Ailill mac Máta when the latter had discovered him dallying with his wife Meadhbh (q.v.). Ailill restored this sword to him before the final great battle in the *Táin*, and with it he sheared the heads off three hills so as to quench his martial vigour and not wreak havoc on his fellow Ulstermen.

When the great campaign was over, Fearghus grew homesick and returned to Ulster against Meadhbh's wishes. He settled in the southeast of the province and remained there until his wife Fliodhais died. Then, in yet another departure, he went back to Meadhbh's court at Cruachain (Rathcroghan, County Roscommon). He went swimming once in a lake called Loch Finn, near Cruachain, and so great a swimmer was he that all the gravel and stones from the bottom of the lake came to the surface. Meadhbh dived in after him and entwined herself about him, and he swam thus around the lake. Her husband Ailill, growing jealous, remarked to his brother, the blind POET Lughaidh, that 'the stag and the doe are acting splendidly in the lake',

218

and encouraged the oracular Lughaidh to cast a javelin at them. This Lughaidh did, with unerring aim, and the javelin struck Fearghus in the breast. The great man managed to swim ashore before he died, and was buried in that place. The motif of death in water is apparently part of the ancient lore concerning him (*see* FEARGHUS MAC LÉIDE), but otherwise this story is a creation of the tenth or eleventh century.

Although the sexual prowess of Fearghus and his association with women like Neas, Meadhbh and Fliodhais must represent old tradition, most of the narratives concerning him found in the literature were invented as linkages in the complex of lore that centred on *Táin Bó Cuailnge*. This function is brought out clearly in the idea (which first appears in twelfth-century sources) that he was responsible for the preservation of the *Táin* epic itself. According to this, the story of the great cattle-raid had been lost and the poets of Ireland failed to recover more than a few fragments of it. The chief-poet SEANCHÁN began a great quest for the story, and success was finally achieved by going to the grave of Fearghus beside Loch Finn and addressing an incantation to the dead warrior. Fearghus arose from the grave, surrounded by a mist, and revealed the story from beginning to end before returning to the clay. This no doubt originated with pre-medieval play by scholars upon the image of Fearghus, with use being made of the ancient custom of seeking inspiration at the burial sites of the noble and wise dead (*see* DRUIDS). Other uses were found for his striking personality: pondering on the great dramatic theme of him deserting his beloved Ulster, and aware of the special connection between the ULAIDH and the ÉRAINN, the genealogists associated him with some Érainn tribes in faraway places. Thus, though mythical, Fearghus mac Róich was cited as the ultimate ancestor of the Ciarraighe (in Counties Kerry and Galway), the Araidh (in Counties Tipperary and Limerick), and the Corca Mruadh (in County Clare).

Fearghus mac Róich does not figure prominently in the later literature. He is described in one eleventh-century text as travelling to Spain to avenge a Munster chieftain who was beheaded by marauders, and he is given background roles in the post-medieval romance of CONGHAL CLÁIRINGNEACH and in some rambling literary tales of the seventeenth century (for sources *see* CÚ CHULAINN). Little memory of him survives in folklore, apart from some examples of the story of Fliodhais collected in County Mayo. When he was driving away the cattle herd of Fliodhais from the Erris Peninsula, it is said, a GIANT slew him with holly darts shot from a bow. This giant, called 'the Fool of Barr Uisce', pretended to be a simpleton, whereas in reality he was a very clever fellow. This is obviously a distorted echo from the manuscript descriptions of how Fearghus was killed by the blind poet Lughaidh. The hero's grave was pointed out at Tammy, north-east of Bangor-Erris, but this was but one of several onomastic identifications no doubt inspired by the tradition of how the poets sought out his grave. The most striking onomastic detail echoes his basic image of virility, for the upright stone at TARA was known to local Irish-speakers in the nineteenth century as *bod Fhearghusa* (the phallus of Fearghus).

ORIGINS AND SEXUALITY: T.F. O'Rahilly (1946), 480–1; F.J. Byrne (1973), 51–2; W. Stokes in *Ériu*, 4, 26; M.E. Dobbs in *Ériu*, 8, 136.

SEVENTH-CENTURY TEXT: J. Carney in *Ériu*, 22, 73–80; P.L. Henry in Mac Mathúna & Ó Corráin (1997), 56–64.

FOCHOND TEXT: V. Hull in *ZCP*, 18, 293–8; D. McKinnon in *Celtic Review*, 1, 208–27.

OTHER ACCOUNTS: *see* CONCHOBHAR MAC NEASA, DEIRDRE, FLIODHAIS *and* CÚ CHULAINN.

DALLYING WITH MEADHBH AND LOSS OF SWORD: C. O'Rahilly (1976), 76 & (1970), 68; D. McKinnon in *Celtic Review*, 1, 228–9.

MEDIEVAL ACCOUNT OF DEATH: Meyer (1906), 32–5.

SPANISH SOJOURN: Gwynn (1924), 346–51.

PHALLIC STONE: F.J. Byrne (1973), 51.

GENERAL ACCOUNTS: Ó Cadhlaigh (1956), 38–42, 228–33, 267–83, 439–46, 473–4.

Féichín SAINT who died in AD 665, founder of a monastery at Fobhar (Fore, County Westmeath) and at several other places. His name was a common one in early Ireland, and meant literally 'little raven'.

Concerning his life, one Latin text and

two Irish ones survive. One of the Irish texts may be a translation from the original, but lost, Latin biography compiled in or about the ninth century in one of the monasteries founded by the saint. We read that his coming had been prophesied by COLM CILLE, and that his father Caolcharna was of the royal UÍ NÉILL of TARA, and his mother Lasair was of the royal EOGHANACHT sept of Munster. As a baby, he used to be put sleeping between his parents, but when morning came, they would find him on the bare floor with his arms outstretched in the form of a cross. A flock of angels hovered over his head, and as he grew up, he performed many miracles. Having been educated at the monastery of St Náithí at Achadh Chonaire (Achonry, County Sligo), he was instructed by an angel to go and found a monastery at Iomaidh (Omey Island, off the Galway coast).

He reputedly had several dealings with the joint HIGH-KINGS, the brothers DIARMAID MAC AODHA SLÁINE and Bláthmhac. We read that he sought recognition for their claims from their predecessor as high-king, DOMHNALL MAC AODHA. Domhnall at first refused Féichín's request, but the saint fasted against him and brought snowdrifts to his kingdom and a fiery sword between himself and his queen. Domhnall then relented, but the royal DRUID – who continued to oppose the saint – was swallowed up by the ground. Notwithstanding this account of his friendship towards them, Diarmaid and Bláthmhac are sometimes represented as in conflict with Féichín. Once, when Bláthmhac seized hostages from him, he caused that king's fortress to burst into flames and thereby gained his submission. On another occasion, Diarmaid had seized a friend of Féichín called Aodán. Féichín went to the royal fortress, miraculously entered through the closed gates, and caused a man who opposed him there to drop dead. On restoring the man to life, he was allowed to take Aodán with him. This Aodán, who became one of Féichín's monks, was the strongest man of his time, with a huge stomach, and the saint was sore pressed to limit his appetite.

Having been instructed by an angel to go to Fore, Féichín set up his famous monastery there. We read that he never sought the help of kings or nobles for fear of slipping into arrogance. He was, however, assisted by the generous Connacht king GUAIRE in time of FAMINE. The queen of the high-king Diarmaid also assisted him in looking after a leper, whom Féichín carried on his back to her fortress. This leper was JESUS CHRIST Himself in disguise, and He left a crozier as a gift for the saint. When on an urgent journey once to secure the release of a hostage, one of Féichín's chariot-horses dropped dead, and a water-horse from a nearby river pool came and took its place. The hostage was being held by the king of Leinster, Ailill mac Dúnlaing, at Dún Náis (Naas, County Kildare), and when Ailill refused to release him, an earthquake shook that place and the chains fell off all the hostages there. Ailill died, but was restored to life by Féichín in return for the release of the hostages and an end to the tribute paid by the saint to him for the site of Fore. Féichín returned the strange animal to its pool, instructing it to never again appear to man (see HORSES). The biography claims that when Féichín died, a multi-coloured column was seen ascending from Fore to heaven, and for the following seven days, the devil and his minions found it impossible to visit Ireland.

One medieval source gives a speculative anecdote by way of explaining the saint's name. We read that when he was a child, his mother noticed him one day gnawing a bone and remarked 'yonder is my little raven!' As well as Féichín, the saint was sometimes referred to by a hypocoristic form of his name, Mo-éca. His memory survives in the folklore of the Fore area, the monastery there being reputed to have 'seven wonders' associated with it. These are the situation of the edifice over a bog, the image of an anchorite in a stone, water in a well that will not boil, a mill without a mill-stream, a stream that flows uphill, a tree the timber of which will not burn, and a massive stone lintel raised by an angel over the church entrance in response to Féichín's prayers. His feast day is 20 January.

Kenney (1929), 458–9; Stokes (1905), 48–9, 421 & in *RC, 12*, 318–53; Plummer, *2* (1910), 76–86; O'Hanlon, *1* (1875), 356–82; OSL: Westmeath (1837), 1–28, 80–5 & Louth (1835–36), 41–3, 47–8; IFC 62:264, 75:64–6, 58–9, 656:83–115, 946:201–2, 1133:50–5, 69–70, 1160:551–3.

Feidhlimidh mac Criomhthainn

(AD 771–847) Leader of the Cashel branch of the EOGHANACHT and KING of Munster from 820 until his death. The name Feidhlimidh was a very popular one in early Ireland, meaning 'guardian'. This Munster king was also celebrated as an ecclesiastic.

He became a lay member of the ascetic community of monks called *céilí Dé* (companions of God), and also reputedly held the office of bishop of Cashel. A renowned warrior, he gained several victories in battle over Munster rivals, over the royal Uí NÉILL, and over the men of Connacht and of Leinster. As well as his military triumphs, he forced many monasteries to submit to his ecclesiastical authority. In the year 838 he met the Uí NÉILL high-king Niall Caille at Cluain Conaire (Cloncurry, County Kildare), and they arranged a pact of non-aggression between them. However, they clashed three years later at Carman near the very same place. Feidhlimidh was defeated in the battle, and in his flight left his crozier behind him in the brambles.

Feidhlimidh had quite a reputation for composing extempore verse, and the medieval literature cites anecdotes concerning repartee between him and various characters. One such has him arguing in verse with a young cleric by the Samhaoir (River Morning Star, County Limerick), and another has a cleric of the Uí Chormaic sept (of County Clare), as he sang to the harp, poetically seeking Feidhlimidh's help against those who had laid waste his monastery. Yet another has the king expounding in verse a crude witticism concerning a senior of Clonmacnoise, after he had ravaged that Leinster monastery. We read that Feidhlimidh had previously been refused hospitality by the senior while travelling outside his own territory disguised as a pauper and accompanied by his wife,

servant and dog. Now he triumphantly ordered in verse how the foul reception accorded to him on that occasion be avenged. The wife, servant and dog of the senior should be joined with the senior himself, by the nose of each being put into the anus of another.

A longer text, written in the eleventh century, describes Feidhlimidh going on his royal circuit to west Munster. It was snowing heavily and, since there was nowhere else to go, he decided to visit the house of the satirist Gulaidhe at Áth Lóiche (Dunloe, County Kerry). This Gulaidhe had often benefited from the king's bounty, but he was himself a bitter and stingy old fellow. He had a young daughter who was just as sharp in her speech as himself, and on hearing the king's arrival trumpeted outside, he sent this girl to greet the visitors. She spoke to Feidhlimidh in rich rhetoric, protesting that everything was miserable and scanty about the house. So daunted was the king by her speech that he offered her a large tract of land, and she then took him by the hand and led him into the house. For three days, he was entertained there with fine food.

A longer version of this story, in modernised form, is found in manuscripts from the seventeenth century onwards. In it the satirist is called Gul, and his daughter is called Sadhbh and is allotted a much-developed series of stylised and slick replies. She routs the three leading poets of Feidhlimidh with her clever remarks when she comes upon them relieving themselves. 'The poets were bulled together,' she says, and they state that she should tie the newly born calves, but she retorts that the cows should first be allowed to lick their calves! When, having been well entertained, Feidhlimidh is leaving the house, he promises her a gift the next time he meets her. She slips out through a back-door and meets him outside, and he is therefore constrained to give her his suit and his horse. Feidhlimidh sends a scholar called Donnúir to seduce the girl, and after Donnúir succeeds, he goes to Feidhlimidh's palace at Cashel seeking payment. At table, Donnúir insists on dividing the goose, which he rhetorically does and allots the major portion to himself.

Most of the jokes and anecdotes found in these texts seem to have been borrowed from folklore, and some are still to be found in oral tradition quite independent of Feidhlimidh (*see* POETS). The account of the smart girl outwitting the king has the appearance of a distorted version of a popular folklore plot (*see* ROMANTIC TALES, type 875) and the expanded version of that story has taken into its ambit another such plot (*see* HUMOROUS TALES, type 1533). This expanded version has, in its turn, had an influence on the folklore concerning poets, particularly in Munster, where manuscripts of it were quite popular.

In the Munster literature, Feidhlimidh appears as 'a brave, saintly, and well-spoken king' who travelled around with a bishop at each shoulder and surrounded by clerics and wise advisers. In other words, he was seen as a sort of Irish Charlemagne, a role that possibly he himself tried to emulate. Like the Frankish emperor, he was even regarded by some as a saint, and – doubtlessly under Munster influence – 28 August was allotted to him as a feast day. The infamy of his deeds was, however, remembered elsewhere, and the Annals report that his death resulted from the destruction by him of the famous monastery of Clonmacnoise in the year 846. When he returned home to Munster after this escapade, he dreamed one night that he was visited by the patron saint of the monastery, CIARÁN, who prodded him in the stomach with his crozier. As a result of this, Feidhlimidh was overtaken by a 'flux of the belly', from which affliction he died in the following year.

BIOGRAPHICAL: Mac Airt (1951), 114–15, 124–31; D. Murphy (1896), 131–40; O'Donovan, *1* (1848), 434–73; Hughes (1966), 182–212; F.J. Byrne (1973), 211–29.

ANECDOTES AND POETRY: K. Meyer in *ZCP, 3,* 34 & *5,* 500 & *10,* 44–5; Ó Donnachadha (1940), 95–103.

CLEVER GIRL: Meyer (1894), 65–9; Ó Gallchobhair (1915), 93–114; C. Ó Cadhlaigh in *An Lóchrann,* 12/1911 & 2/1913; Breatnach (1996), 44–9. *See also* MIS.

Féine The standard Irish name for the Féni, originally Vénii, an ancient Celtic population group of people who were situated in the south of Ireland and also in the north Midlands. The old Celtic name meant 'hunters' or 'warriors'.

A group bearing the name Vénii may have arrived from the area later known as Brittany, where tribes called Veneti and Venelli are attested from the first century BC. All of this is obscure, and such new groups would need to embed themselves well among the indigenous population in order to attain to lasting strength. It can, at any rate, be accepted that by the second century AD, people called Vénii had come to dominate much of east Munster. It may be that, at some stage, a section of them broke off from the rest and began to move northwards. Alternately, a quite distinct group of Vénii may have become ensconced in the north Midlands, perhaps by sailing in from an earlier settlement in Wales (called Venedotis) through the Boyne estuary. It has sometimes been suggested that this northern settlement was no more than a merger of indigenous peoples in that area, but if so, it is difficult to explain why these were specifically called Vénii.

The northern group claimed descent from an ancestor called Owogenos (literally, 'SHEEP-conceived'), a type of ram-GOD appropriate to a people whose chief economic concern was animal husbandry. They used the title *Condos* (wise head) for their leaders, and their power grew to such an extent that in or about the fourth century AD, they took over the kingship of TARA in County Meath. The group called Vénii in Munster called their ancestor Iwogenos (son of yew) – there may have been a ritual reason for this, as the cult of the yew tree was known in Ireland, as evidenced from its common occurrence in a personal name of that ancient time, Iwocatus (yew-battler). With the development in Ireland from common Celtic into Old Irish, by the fifth century the designation Vénii had become Féni, and later still Féine, while Owogenos had become UGHAINE, Iwogenos had become EOGHAN, and *Condos* was personalised into a character called CONN. The later claim by their descendants that Ireland was divided equally between the two Féine groups seems to echo an early identification of them with each other. This was expressed through a myth of rivalry between two great leaders called Conn and Eoghan, mythical ancestors of the CONNACHTA and the EOGHANACHT respectively.

The Celtic word for hunter-warriors became *fianna* (*see* FIANNA CYCLE) in ordinary Irish speech from the sixth or seventh century AD, but the form Féine shows that its vowel did not mutate in the tribal name. In medieval Ireland, the designation Féine gradually lost its original meaning and came to be used in the general sense of 'nobility' or 'genuine antiquity'. The tribal name survived, however, in the toponymic Magh Féine, the plain around Fermoy in east County Cork, and in Áth Féine, a ford on the River Gaine near Multyfarnham, County Westmeath.

A. Mac an Bhaird in *Ainm*, *5*, 9; D. O'Brien in *Ériu*, *11*, 182–3; L. Ó Buachalla in *JCHAS*, *49*, 25–9; E. Hogan (1910), 520; F.J. Byrne (1973), 8–9, 328; Ó hÓgáin (2002), 193–6, 204–5.

Feircheirdne *(earlier, Ferchertne)* A mythical POET, who occurs in a number of different contexts in the early literature. His name is a personification, meaning 'man of precise craft', the craft referred to being poetry. To the writers, such a name was suggestive of a poet par excellence, and could thus serve as an archetype of the profession in whatever context.

One of the seventh-century biographers of St PATRICK refers to onomastic information preserved by an ancient poet of that name and calls him 'one of the nine DRUID-prophets' who belonged to Breagha (the County Meath area). This formulaic description suggests that Feircheirdne was known only through verse attributed to him and, given the name, such verse might have been composed by any expert of the poetic craft. This interpretation is borne out by the way in which Feircheirdne is accorded differing situations in the scheme of things. The earliest context in which he is set is the myth of the Leinster king LABHRAIDH, whose poet he is claimed to have been. He is there credited with the composition of the very archaic poem on the destruction by Labhraidh of the fortress of Dinn Ríg. In the developed story concerning this event, it is said that he, together with the harpist CRAIFTINE, accompanied Labhraidh when that KING was banished from Ireland. His statements are represented as invariably containing the truth, and he is absolutely loyal to the Leinster culture-hero Labhraidh.

Feircheirdne is again the name of an archetypal poet in an eighth-century text that assigns his most dramatic role to him. This text is entitled *Immacallam in Dá Thuarad* (The Colloquy of the Two Sages), and in it he is represented as an elderly poet of the Ulstermen. When the chief-poet of the province, Adhna, died, his official robe was conferred on Feircheirdne. Adhna, however, had a young beardless son called NÉIDHE who was studying poetry in Scotland, and he got tidings of what was happening by interpreting the sound of a sea wave. He immediately went to the Ulster capital Eamhain Mhacha to claim the robe for himself. Feircheirdne was absent when he arrived, and the mischievous BRICRIU persuaded the youngster to don the robe. Néidhe fixed grass on his face and sang a charm over it to make it appear as a beard, and sat in the chief-poet's chair. Feircheirdne was indignant when he returned and discovered this, and a vehement contest in words ensued between him and Néidhe. They contended in rhetorics, riddles and metaphors in the obscure poetic speech. Eventually, Néidhe yielded precedence to the older man, who then made a series of prophecies about evil times to come in Ireland. Néidhe surrendered the prestigious robe to Feircheirdne, and was about to throw himself at his superior's feet when Feircheirdne graciously stayed him and bestowed lavish blessings on him. A later gloss on the text states that the earth was swallowing the young poet for his discourtesy until Feircheirdne prevented this by proclaiming 'Stay!' Finally, Néidhe hailed Feircheirdne as *comrar dána* (a casket of poetry), and accepted him as a second father.

That text was part of the ULSTER

CYCLE, but it was quite unique there and not really synchronised with the cycle's other stories. Feircheirdne is mentioned en passant in some of the other texts, but the cycle generally has other characters – such as AITHIRNE and AMHAIRGHIN MAC ÉIGIT SALAIGH – as the chief-poets of the Ulster king. Though Feircheirdne is claimed as Aithirne's father, he really duplicates him. For example, the story of how an importunate poet demands to be given the one eye of a generous king was properly told of Aithirne, but a late medieval text substitutes Feircheirdne for him. Another text of the same period borrows a description of Aithirne and relates it of Feircheirdne, viz. 'the lakes and rivers drain before him when he satirises, and they rise up when he praises them'. The name Feircheirdne is also given to the poet of the warrior CÚ ROÍ in that cycle. Here he avenges the death of Cú Roí by jumping to his death from a cliff top, bringing with him Bláthnaid, the false wife of the warrior. A long poem on Cú Roí, which praises his qualities and laments his tragic death, is attributed to this Feircheirdne.

Bieler (1979), 84–5; Meyer, 2 (1914), 7–9 & in AIM, 3, 43–4 & in ZCP, 3, 40–6; Stokes, CTS (1905) & in Irische Texte, 3, 364–5, 380–1: J.C. Watson (1941), 24–5; C. O'Rahilly (1961), 141.

Feiritéar, Piaras (c. 1610–53) Nobleman and poet from the Dingle Peninsula, County Kerry. He fought for several years against the Cromwellian army. When returning home from peace negotiations, he was seized in violation of a promise of safe conduct, and was hanged in Killarney.

Folklore concerning Piaras is very popular in the Dingle Peninsula, most of the anecdotes centring on some verse or other said to have been composed by him or by somebody whom he encountered. His nobility is stressed by traditions that associate him with fine horsemanship. He was said to have had seven fine stallions, all of different colour and all possessed of great speed, stamina, agility and courage. Apart from the delight which he took in HORSE racing, it is said that he also loved gambling and that he was an expert at cards. The poetry composed by him and that survives in manuscript treats especially of love, and this aspect of his personality emerges as a basic theme in his folk portrayal. It is said that he once courted a rich lady and was preparing to marry her. While visiting her father's mansion, however, a blind but wise man who was sitting in the corner of the parlour spoke a quatrain to the effect that 'the white mare has foaled'. The import of this was unclear, but Piaras understood it to be that the lady was of easy virtue, and he took the warning and cancelled the wedding. It was alleged that when he was captured later, this lady spared no effort to have him hanged.

The historical Piaras was in fact the leader of a group of several hundred men, and with this little army managed to hold out longer against the Cromwellian forces than any other leader in the country. All of this is much personalised in the folk LEGENDS, which visualise him as outwitting and tricking the enemy with a mere handful of soldiers of his own. His castle was situated on a cliff overlooking the sea near Sybil Head, and it is said that a large body of English soldiers once came to attack it. The sea had made a cleft beside the castle, and Piaras told his men to increase the size of this cleft and to build a false bridge over it. When the enemy came in sight of him and his working party, he quietly gave a signal to his men and they raced towards the castle as a feint. The soldiers rushed after them directly, crowding onto the false bridge, which gave away under their weight, and large numbers of them dropped into the sea far below and were drowned.

There is even a tendency to envisage Piaras as a solitary fugitive, and we are told that a favourite hideout of his was a cave in a nigh inaccessible part of the Great Blasket Island. We are told that several groups of soldiers were sent into west Kerry to apprehend him, and that he was captured once. The soldiers, however, were hungry and tired after their long search, and decided to stop at a local house for a meal. Piaras gave a hint to the woman of the house to quietly pour water into the barrels of the soldiers' guns, which had been left aside as they ate. Then he himself jumped up and ran away. The soldiers tried to shoot him, but their guns would not fire. They followed him on foot as far as his cave, which could only be entered through a narrow gorge. Unknown to them, there was a hole in that entrance, and as they came in, he flung them one by one through the hole and into the perilous sea below. He used this hideout for a long time, but it was a lonely life there, and he is said to have once composed a quatrain complaining to God that he had no company there but the darkness of the cave and the noise of the waves.

Piaras, who in one of his poems described the English policy towards the Irish as 'the games played by the brave little CAT with the mouse', was taken treacherously by the enemy forces at Castlemaine. One folk legend states that the arresting officer noticed a seagull at some distance from them and promised Piaras his freedom if he could compose a stanza and twenty, every one ending with the word *siar* (west), before the gull rose from the ground. Piaras began to compose with absolute fluency, but the gull rose when he had sixteen stanzas made. He was brought to Killarney, where he was put to death on Cnocán na gCaorach (Fair Hill). Folklore states that a priest and a bishop were hanged along with him. The bishop handed a little stone to him, saying that while he held that in his mouth he could not be hanged. So it was, the rope failing to choke Piaras twice. On the third occasion, however, he spat the stone from his mouth, saying that none of his descendants would be called remnants of the gallows, and so he was hanged. The MOTIF of the miraculous stone was part of general folk belief, but there is no evidence that Piaras was in the company of two clergymen when executed. The folk account may have developed from a well-known reference in a seventeenth-century poem by Sean Ó Conaill, a cleric of Kerry. This reference is to 'the wise and generous man, Piaras Feiritéar of fine traits, Conchubhar, Tadhg, and Bishop Baothlach, who were

hanged on the gallows of Cnocán na gCaorach'. The two priests referred to – Conchubhar Mac Cárthaigh and Tadhg Ó Muircheartaigh – were hanged at the same place a year after Piaras, whereas Bishop Baothlach Mac Aogáin was hanged three years before. The folk accounts of Piaras' death seem therefore to have sprung from a misinterpretation of these lines.

Ua Duinnín (1903); Jackson, *SB* (1938), 37–40; C. O'Rahilly (1952), 78, 156–7; Ó hÓgáin (1985), 174–8, 219, 338; IFC Index.

Fiachna mac Baodáin *(earlier, Fiachnae mac Baetáin)* KING of the sept called Dál nAraidhe (in south Antrim and north Down), who died in battle against his cousin and namesake Fiachna mac Deamháin of the Dál bhFiatach (in County Down) in the year AD 626.

He was also known as Fiachna Lurgan, and was a celebrated warrior. A lost saga described an attack that he made on the Saxons of Dún Guaire (i.e. Bamborough in England), and elsewhere the medieval literature describes him as having been king in Ireland and Scotland. He may even have claimed the HIGH-KINGSHIP of Ireland for a while. One annalistic account borrows from the youth biography of the epic hero CÚ CHULAINN in order to underline the greatness of Fiachna. His mother was of the rival Dál bhFiatach sept, and we read that on seeing a wolf attack sheep, she wished that she would conceive a son who would thus treat her husband's people. When the young Fiachna was born, his father disliked him because he resembled his mother too much, and so she brought him to a place apart to be reared. One day, however, the child seized some meat from his fellows and went to his father's court with the meat on a spit. Baodán set a fierce hound on him, but the young Fiachna stabbed the animal through the heart with the spit. At the same time, he grabbed in his other hand a hawk that had swooped for the meat, and on seeing this, his mother was so shocked that she could never conceive again.

We further read that Fiachna was given the epithet *find* (fair-haired) in order to distinguish him from his rival namesake,

Fiachna mac Deamháin, who was accordingly given the epithet *dubh* (black-haired). These two fought many battles, and Fiachna Find was always the victor because St COMHGHALL, who was of his sept, supported him with prayers. However, Fiachna Dubh went to Comhghall and insisted that the SAINT pray for him also, as Comhghall had been fostered by the Dál bhFiatach. Both men were preparing for another battle, and the perplexed saint offered Fiachna Find the choice of victory and loss of heaven or defeat and eternal happiness. Fiachna Find chose the latter, and so was defeated and slain.

Fiachna mac Baodáin figures prominently in the stories that grew up around the name of his more famous son MONGÁN.

F.J. Byrne (1973), 111–12; O'Grady, *1* (1892), 390–3.

Fiachu Fear Mara Fictional character situated in prehistory. The medieval writers claimed that a KING of Ireland called Aonghus Tuirmheach lay with his own daughter in drunkenness, and as a result the girl gave birth to Fiachu. The child was put by Aonghus into a little boat, dressed in the purple robe of a king's son, with a golden fringe on it. He was put out to sea at a fortress called Dún Aighneach (apparently on the Donegal coast), but was discovered on a nearby beach by fishermen, who took him ashore and reared him. Hence he was known as Fear Mara (son of the sea). The name Fiachu (later, Fiacha) was a common one, being a petform of *fiach* (raven).

Fiachu was said to have been father of Eterscéle and thus grandfather of CONAIRE. The account of his birth must have been prompted by the suggestion of incest in Eterscéle's fathering of Conaire, but the plot used is an international one, probably based in this instance on the pseudo-account of the birth of Pope GREGORY THE GREAT (*see* ROMANTIC TALES, type 933).

W. Stokes in *Irische Texte, 3*, 312–13; Macalister (1956), 284–7, 472–3; Dinneen, *2* (1908), 176–9; T.F. O'Rahilly (1946), 81–2.

Fiachu Muilleathan Mythical KING of Munster, regarded as contemporaneous with CORMAC MAC AIRT. Fiachu (later

form, Fiachaidh) was one of the most famous ancestors claimed by the powerful EOGHANACHT sept.

The best-known story of him occurs in texts from the eighth century onwards. According to this, he was the son of Eoghan, son of AILILL ÓLOM, and he was born posthumously. We read that before the Battle of Magh Mucramha in which he perished, Eoghan met a DRUID at Druim Díl (Drumdeel, near Clonmel, County Tipperary). The latter had a daughter called Moncha, and realising that Eoghan would be slain, this druid told her to sleep with the warrior so that the future kings of Munster might descend from himself. After the death of Eoghan, and when her time came to give birth, Moncha was with her father by the River Suir at Rafae (Knockgraffon, County Tipperary). The druid told her that if the child were born on that day he would be the chief jester of Ireland, but if she delayed the birth until the following day, he would be the most powerful king in the country. She therefore went into the river and sat on a stone to delay the baby's coming. Next day, the baby was born, but Moncha died from her efforts. Due to the forced delaying of the birth, the head of the baby Fiachu was widened out against the stone, and he was thus given the sobriquet Muinleathan or Muilleathan (broad-crowned). He was also known as Fear Dá Liach (man of two sorrows), on account of the deaths of his father and mother.

The posthumous birth of Fiachu parallels that of Cormac mac Airt, but in the case of Fiachu it fulfilled a specific political purpose, for the druid Díl was said to have been of the Creacraighe, a sept of the OSRAIGHE. It is likely that the borrowing from the Cormac context was done in or around the seventh century by the Creacraighe themselves, for they used the story to claim special privilege from the Eoghanacht. One variant, which discredits this Creacraighe claim, states that the druid reared two girls who were very alike in appearance. One of them was his own daughter, the other was the daughter of Eoghan. He pretended that Eoghan's daughter was his, and in this way sent her to her own father and claimed that her baby was his own descendant.

Other accounts of Fiachu are closely intertwined with the lore of Cormac (q.v.), but they are obviously Munster inventions. He helps Cormac at the Battle of Crionna, and then triumphs over him in the Battle of Drom Damhghaire when the high-king invades Munster. An account of Fiachu's death is found in a late source. According to this, a son of TADHG MAC CÉIN, called Conla, was a fosterling of Cormac, and he fell sick from leprosy at TARA. Cormac told him that the only possible cure would be for him to bathe himself in the blood of a king. Conla therefore went south to the court of Fiachu, who was his relative, at Rafae. He was warmly received there. One day, he and Fiachu went swimming in the Suir at Áth Aiseal (Athassel), and when the opportunity arose, he drove his spear through Fiachu in the water. The dying Fiachu showed his nobility by ordering his retainers not to put Conla to death.

M. O'Daly (1975), 14, 50–1, 64–5; W. Stokes in *Irische Texte, 3*, 306–9; Dinneen, *2* (1908), 272–5, 322–5; F.J. Byrne (1973), 67.

Fianna [Cycle] A large corpus of stories relating to the band of warriors led by the mythical FIONN MAC CUMHAILL. The stories, the first of which appear in eighth-century texts, have been very popular in both literature and folklore for over 1,000 years.

The word – in earlier form *fianna* (singular, *fian*) – was used for young hunter-warriors (*see* FÉINE). Such groups of young men were a social reality in many early societies, as it was part of a warrior's training to live for a period in the wilderness in order to learn how to hunt and fight. Originally, it had no connection with the name 'Fionn', but when the Leinstermen (LAIGHIN) used Fionn as a symbol of their efforts in the fifth to sixth century to regain the Boyne Valley from their UÍ NÉILL foes, it is apparent that a Leinster version of the hunter-warrior cult got especially connected with Fionn. Thus in narrative, Fionn came to be regarded as a great *féinnidh*, or leader of a troop of *fianna*.

The early medieval stories of Fionn show the influence of the life of such young men. As well as being a seer and warrior, we find him described as a great hunter, and much of the terminology associated with that occupation is connected with him (*see* DEARG, OISÍN *and* OSCAR). Very much in accord with the mentality one would expect to find in such youth-cults, Fionn and his comrades are represented in the early literature as great feuders and womanisers. One early text, in fact, claims that the youthful Fionn had 'a woman in waiting for him in every region near him', and that these women were 'good to support the *fianna*'. The socially disruptive actions of Fionn and his companions in the earlier literature is intelligible when seen in that context of youthful fancy, and the early sources are in fact at pains to stress that *fianna* were distinct from the bands called *díbheargaigh*, who were groups of tribeless and desperate men. Yet an aura of youthful rebellion survived within the lore of Fionn and his comrades, and in time became one of the most fertile themes in the whole corpus of stories concerning them.

By medieval times, the only *fianna* who were really important in the narrative lore were the celebrated band of Fionn. A further development – which portrayed an unsteady reconciliation between the Leinster Fionn and the great high-kings of Uí Néill lore, CONN CÉADCHATHACH and his grandson CORMAC MAC AIRT – led to the band becoming known as 'the Fianna of Ireland'. They were portrayed as a kind of volunteer army led by Fionn that served the high-king and that was basically divided between the influences of two great families – that of Fionn (called the *clanna Baoiscne*) and of GOLL MAC MORNA (called the *clanna Morna*). The theme of this rather enigmatic force gave medieval writers many opportunities to employ their fancy. Some descriptions echo what would have been the real material life of early *fianna* groups. We read of how Fionn and his men hunted deer and wild PIGS to provide food for themselves, and how they cooked the meat on spits or at sites called *fulachta fian* – ancient cooking pits, the remains of which survive in many parts of Ireland. These pits consist of a wooden trough connected to a stream, and the method of cooking was to place the meat there in water, which was brought to the boil with heated stones. The erection of hunting booths with brace and ridge-pole is also described, as is the covering of the floor with heather, rushes and foliage to lie on. Several texts mention a type of hummed refrain, called the *dord fiann*, made so as to call to their comrades for assistance when in danger. It was produced by drawing the lips together, and sometimes was accompanied by the clashing of spear shafts.

A more military perspective gradually came to the fore in the writers' musings on Fionn and his Fianna. An eleventh-century text claims that the high-king Cormac appointed thrice-50 chiefs of the Fianna, with Fionn as the chief-of-staff. When a volunteer was accepted into the Fianna, his family undertook not to avenge him if he died in that service, and likewise they were not held responsible for his acts while he was in that force. To be accepted was no easy matter, for the applicant must be a POET and also a supreme athlete. One test was for the applicant to stand in a hole in the ground and ward off a spear-cast from each of nine warriors; another was to race through the forest pursued by many warriors without upsetting his hair or cracking a twig under his foot; yet another was at high speed to jump over a branch as high as his forehead and bend under another as low as his knee, and he must also be able to draw a thorn from his foot without slackening speed.

Various numerical fancies were used to describe the organisation of the Fianna, which force was sometimes said to consist of three great battalions and other times of seven. More consistent was the relative importance accorded to the personnel. A twelfth-century account states that the five leading warriors were Fionn, LUGHAIDH LÁGHA, OSCAR, Goll and CAOILTE. The pre-eminence of a half-dozen or so heroes was a recurrent feature of the Fianna lore, Lughaidh Lágha often being replaced by

his son MAC LUGHACH. The storied OISÍN and the swashbuckling young warrior DIARMAID UA DUIBHNE also figured among the elite group, while Goll's brother CONÁN MAOL was the anti-hero of the tradition. A theme – probably suggested by the imagery of Caoilte as a great runner – was borrowed from folklore and became very popular in the literature from the eleventh century onwards. This involved some marvellous helpers who come to assist Fionn in performing difficult tasks. Thus we read in twelfth-century texts of three Norwegian princes who enter the service of Fionn, having in their possession a marvellous hound that coughs up gold and ale as desired; and also of helpers from several foreign countries who drain a troublesome lake for Fionn. We read further of a member of the Fianna called Leargan, who was so swift a runner that he could herd the deer as others did the cows.

Sources from the following centuries add much to the fanciful traits of individual members of the Fianna. We read of how Fionn was assisted by a group of strangers with a variety of great skills, and thus succeeded in rescuing children who had been kidnapped by a GIANT. Some of the descriptions are quite humorous. Thus a man called Daolghus was the tallest member of the Fianna, and Mac Méin was the smallest, a sharp-tongued female messenger called Deardubha was the worst person in the Fianna, and Fionn's fire-attendant was the slowest worker. Some sources stress that Fionn's favourite retainer was the brilliant dwarf musician CNÚ DEARÓIL. A fifteenth-century writer with a taste for the exotic presents the Fianna as a type of incongruous society – including in it a deaf warrior who hears everything, a warrior with a wooden leg who can outrun all, a blind man who never made an inaccurate spear-cast, a woman of Fionn who was dead by night and alive by day, and a warrior who on alternate years was a woman and a man.

Some medieval sources postulate that long before Fionn was born, there had been great contests for power between his father Cumhall and Goll mac Morna. This was developed backwards from the account of the birth of Fionn (q.v.), which had his father defeated and slain by Goll at the Battle of Cnucha (Castleknock, County Dublin). Notwithstanding this, all sources agree that the golden age of the Fianna began with Fionn's accession to the leadership. A text written in the tenth century lists ten great battles fought by the Fianna under his command, and later sources attribute many more to him. Actual accounts of only a small number of these battles survive, however, and it is unlikely that there were many more such accounts. Already in the eighth or ninth century, a story was being told of a fierce battle fought against Fothadh Airgtheach, brother of FOTHADH CANAINNE, at Ollarbha (Larne, County Antrim), and the later literature claims that only 600 of the Fianna warriors survived it. In the tenth or eleventh century, another account of a battle in the northeast of the country was gaining currency. According to this, Fionn had left two Connacht princes – students of his called Art and Eoghan – to guard the shore at Tráigh Rudhraighe (Dundrum Bay, County Down). These princes were accompanied by 400 warriors and the same number of servants, and as night fell, they saw a huge fleet of Norse ships approach. The NORSEMEN – led by kings called Conus and Conmhaol – came ashore and were immediately attacked by the Connacht princes and their small force. Meanwhile, Fionn was sleeping in his camp, and he had a vision of two grey seals drinking from his breast. His poet, Fearghus Fíonbhéil, explained that this indicated that the Connacht princes were in danger, and Fionn rushed to that place. He found all the Norsemen slain and the two brave princes themselves mortally wounded.

The name of this strand, Tráigh Rudhraighe, was pseudo-etymologised as having the element *ruadh* (red), and this allowed for a standard convention concerning a great slaughter to be attached to it. This convention had places before a great battle being named with the element *fionn* (white), and afterwards with *dearg* (crimson) – *see* FEARGHUS MAC LÉIDE. So

a writer from west Munster, who knew this story of Tráigh Rudhraighe, decided to compose another story on the same pattern but situated on the 'white strand' best known to him – i.e. Fionntráigh (Ventry, County Kerry). From several mentions of this story in twelfth-century texts, we know that it was already in existence by then, but the earliest full recension to survive is from the fifteenth century.

That recension tells of how a 'king of the world', called Dáire Donn, sailed to Ireland with a massive fleet, and guided by a renegade member of the Fianna, anchored off Ventry. Fionn had sentries posted on all the major shores of Ireland, and the sentry at Ventry was one Conn Crithir. This Conn immediately attacked the invaders, and was assisted by three mysterious women who loved him and engaged their magic in his favour. Soon after, a strong man of the Fianna called Taistealach arrived and overcame the champion wrestler of Dáire. Conn sent Taistealach to alert the Fianna, and on his way told a group of the otherworld people, TUATHA DÉ DANANN, who hastened to the place to hold off the invaders until Fionn could muster his forces. The first great leader of the Fianna to enter the fray was Oscar, who slew whole companies of the foe and routed the French king; the king raced demented from the field. A great warrior called Dolar Durba came ashore, performing wonderful tricks with a hurley and ball, and he was attacked by a young Ulster prince who came to assist the Fianna. All day and all night long, they fought, and in the morning were both found dead on the shore. The incessant fighting led to a great depletion in the ranks of the Fianna, and eventually Fionn decided on one great battle against the invaders. The fighting was atrocious, but gradually the Fianna gained the upper hand. The Norse king was slain by an Ulster warrior of the Rudhraighe clan, Conmhaol son of Dáire was slain by Goll mac Morna, and Fionn beheaded Dáire himself in a tremendous tussle. When only one of the invaders remained alive, he took to the sea but was followed by a young student of Fionn called Caol. Both sank to the bottom of the ocean in deadly combat, and the story ends with Caol's young wife lamenting him in verse.

There are echoes in that text from the epic called *Táin Bó Cuailnge* in the ULSTER CYCLE, and also from the story of the king SUIBHNE who went mad, and it is obvious that the writer or writers of the text did not scruple about borrowing material from any source to hand. A similar attitude prevailed in the composition of most late medieval and post-medieval stories of the Fianna. Few of the texts are of significant artistic value, but their combined effect and the manner in which the themes were continually developed makes them more than worthy of notice. Furthermore, their neat combinations of adventure and melodrama led to their easy absorption into popular culture, and versions of many of these literary tales have circulated widely in the Gaelic folklore of both Ireland and Scotland. They can be divided formally into two classes: richly ornamented prose narratives to be read aloud, and lays or versified texts that were recited in a chanting voice. In themes and in imagery, both classes are similar to each other, but whereas a lay tends to concentrate on one dramatic episode, the prose texts have more scope and can pile episodes on each other.

The starting point for this new development in the tradition was the long twelfth-century compendium called *Agallamh na Seanórach* (The Colloquy of the Old Men), in which the Fianna survivors, Caoilte and Oisín, tell many stories to St PATRICK. This text contains many stories of hunts, conflicts and adventures, with some of them retold in verse. Most of these narratives were the invention of the text's writer, even though they contain many earlier MOTIFS and themes. Two other recensions of the *Agallamh na Seanórach* – adding new matter – were written in succeeding centuries. The combined effect of all three recensions was to cause a standardisation of the lore, and it is noticeable that the same types of setting are found in all the subsequent literary tales of the Fianna, whether in prose or

verse. A favourite theme was the simmering rivalry between the Baoiscne and Morna clans, which is sometimes described as breaking out at feasts when the warriors become drunk and boastful.

This is best exemplified in a prose story written in the fifteenth or sixteenth century. It describes how Fionn held a feast at his headquarters of Almhu (the Hill of Allen, County Kildare), during which Goll showed extraordinary generosity towards the poets who entertained them. Noticing that Goll was bestowing wealth from his Scandinavian tribute, Fionn grew jealous and claimed that the exacting of such tribute should be his own prerogative. Goll explained how, long ago, he had been driven from Ireland by Fionn's father Cumhall, and how he had conquered Scandinavia and thus earned the tribute. He further recalled that, at a later stage, he had rescued Fionn from captivity in Scandinavia. Tempers became frayed, and when Fionn was reminded of how Goll had slain his father, a fierce conflict broke out between the two clans. Fionn lost 1,200 men and women in the fighting, and Goll lost eleven men and 50 women. The poet Fearghus Fíonbhéil, however, got them to desist, and it was agreed that the question of compensation for injuries should be decided by the judges of the high-king Cormac. The celebrated judge FÍOTHAL made a ruling that was accepted by all, according to which the Baoiscne clan were exempted from payment because of their great losses in the fight, and the Morna clan were exempted because it was they who had been first attacked.

Several lays tell of how an otherworld visitor – usually either AONGHUS or MANANNÁN – comes in disguise to the Fianna to cause some problem or other for them or to teach them a lesson. This theme was a rather spontaneous one, and was an innovation in the lore. Older origins can be postulated for the many stories that tell of the Fianna being trapped in a sinister otherworld dwelling, for this situation seems to be a development in narrative from visits to the world of the dead made by Fionn's prototype, the seer

FIONN. An eleventh-century story tells of how Fionn and a few companions were forced to fight all night long in a sinister dwelling, and later writers revelled in such fancies. Thus we read of how three savage witches trapped a group of the Fianna in the hill of Céis Chorainn (Keshcorran, County Sligo), but they were released by the great Goll, who slew the three witches. Another story tells of how the Fianna were hunting in the Galway area when they were invited to lodge in his dwelling by one Eochaidh Beag Dearg, a hostile lord of the Tuatha Dé Danann. The cantankerous Conán Maol insisted that himself and fourteen others only should go to the dwelling. When they reached there, these fifteen found themselves surrounded by hundreds of hostile warriors. Fionn learned of their danger through chewing his thumb of knowledge, and accompanied by his son Aodh Beag, quietly went to the place and joined them. Two huge assassins entered, but they were in turn overcome by Conán in cumbersome combats, and Conán also slew a horrendous HAG. When morning came, the seventeen Fianna warriors took the field, but they were hopelessly outnumbered, and all seemed lost when the seven battalions of the Fianna arrived and slaughtered the whole army of Eochaidh Beag Dearg.

These stories of entrapment are each entitled *Bruidhean*, a word that meant a hostel, and which came to have sinister connotations (*see* CONAIRE). The most dramatic such Fianna story is called *Bruidhean Chaorthainn*, and tells of how a Scandinavian king called Colgán invaded Ireland but was defeated and slain by the Fianna in a great battle. Míodhach, son of Colgán, surrendered to Fionn and was well treated, being given land at the Shannon estuary, but he secretly plotted revenge. After several years, he connived with 'the king of the world', called Sinsear, and it was arranged that a massive invasion force would come to Ireland when Míodhach had trapped the Fianna leaders in his mansion. This mansion was built by three magicians, and Fionn and his companions were invited to a feast there. While there,

they found themselves stuck to the ground, and when Fionn chewed his thumb, he realised the treachery that had been arranged. Unable to escape, he told his companions to strike up their special hum, the *dord Fiann*. Oisín, who had not come to the feast, grew suspicious, and sent two Fianna warriors to investigate. Realising what was afoot, these two – one of whom was Fionn's son Fiachna – fought bravely against the foe but were vastly outnumbered and slain. Just as Fiachna fell, the great warrior Diarmaid ua Duibhne arrived on the scene. Diarmaid beheaded Míodhach, and then stood guard over the mansion to protect the Fianna captives. However, the troublesome Conán Maol, who was within, was ravenously hungry, so Diarmaid had to go and forcibly take sumptuous food and drink from the very hands of the king of the world, who was feasting in another mansion nearby. He next slew the three magicians, and rubbed their blood to the captive Fianna warriors, which enabled them to rise from the floor. There was not enough blood left to free Conán, so he had to be pulled from the floor, leaving behind him a slice of skin from his poll to his buttocks. All the Fianna then assembled, and in a frightful battle the invaders were completely overthrown, Oscar beheading the king of the world himself.

Many lays tell of a great single warrior coming to Ireland and challenging the warriors of the Fianna to single combat. The basic structure of these lays has Fionn and his men being shamed by the rampant stranger, but the latter is eventually overcome by one of the Fianna. Goll is the champion in some cases, but more usually it is the mighty Oscar. An unusual and original twist is given to this motif of the strange visitor in a prose text from the sixteenth century, which concerns tricks played on the Fianna by the wizard ÁBHARTACH MAC ILDATHAIGH. This strange character, calling himself the Giolla Deacair (Difficult Servant), comes to the Fianna as they hunt at Cnoc Áine (Knockainey, County Limerick), and magically brings fifteen of the Fianna overseas.

231

Fionn can only retrieve them by enlisting the assistance of two marvellous helpers.

A quite original little story was written around the year 1600. This tells of how a stranger came from overseas to the Fianna at Binn Éadair (Howth, County Dublin) and demanded that they set a man to race against him, the wager being the mastery of Ireland. His name was Caol an Iarainn (Slender Fellow of the Iron), and the perplexed Fionn set out for Tara to find the great runner Caoilte. As he passed through a forest, he met a huge ugly man with a grey cloak, who moved extremely slowly but claimed that he alone could defeat Caol. After some persuasion, Fionn agreed to let this stranger race for the Fianna. The course was to be from Binn Éadair to Sliabh Luachra (in south Kerry) and back, and when they set out, Caol surged ahead. The grey-cloaked churl behaved very strangely, stopping for huge feeds and at some stages even retracing his steps to collect pieces of his torn garment. However, as the end of the race approached, he moved like the wind, and easily defeated Caol. The piqued Caol drew his sword, but the churl threw a handful of meal and berries at him, which knocked his head off. The churl then replaced his head on the shoulders, but back to front, and thus Caol had to return to his own country. Then the wind and the sun lit up the face of the churl, and Fionn realised that it was none other than Manannán in disguise, who had come to assist them in their dire straits.

Some writer in or about the eleventh century noticed that the annalistic record had the fictional high-king CAIRBRE LIFEACHAIR, son of Cormac, being slain by the Fotharta, a sub-sept of Leinster, at the Battle of Gabhra (Gowra, County Meath). Since the reign of this Cairbre was understood to coincide with the latter part of Fionn's career, the writer considered this a good opportunity to describe how the Fianna finally met their end. He accordingly invented the idea that that battle was a great clash between them and Cairbre, and that in it the high-king was slain by the great Oscar. The idea developed rapidly, and a fourteenth-century redaction

of it has a dispute over hunting rights as the cause of the battle. We must presume that the general setting was after the death of Fionn (q.v.), but this redaction states quite anachronistically that the great leader had gone on a pilgrimage to Rome when the dispute began. At any rate, Cairbre is described as mustering a mighty force from both Ireland and abroad, and the Fianna as fighting bravely in the battle, though utterly outnumbered. Oscar, as usual, is in the leading role. Cairbre casts a deadly spear at him, but mortally wounded as he is, he manages to slay the high-king and then flings himself against the crack regiment of the foe before being himself destroyed. We read that 'until both sea-sand and stars are counted, one-third of a third of those whom Oscar, son of Oisín, slew may not be reckoned'. The day is won by the Fianna, but they themselves have been decimated, and of all their leaders, only Caoilte and Oisín survive. An earlier, though now lost, version of this story must have been the basis in the twelfth century for the composition of *Agallamh na Seanórach*, which tells of how these two old heroes live on after the battle to meet St Patrick.

The writing of new Fianna prose stories continued into the eighteenth century, with use being made of miscellaneous motifs from the earlier tradition. One text from that period, written in County Clare, has an ugly little fellow introducing himself to the Fianna as Maol Ó Manannáin and challenging them to a race. Diarmaid accepts the challenge, but the little man outruns him through much of Ireland. He then brings the Fianna to a feast at his magical dwelling. There they encounter magical pigs and other wonders, including a monstrously naughty boy and a beautiful young lady. The dwelling disappears at daylight, leaving the Fianna lying naked on the plain of Tara. Their host, we read, was in reality DONN, who had come from his otherworld residence in the sandhills of west Clare to tease them. A novel-length prose text, written in County Limerick around 1770, introduces Dearg, a son of Fionn and his wife Ailbhe. At the age of seven, Dearg was already a great fighter and runner, and so eager was he that Fionn had him confined while the Fianna hunted a ferocious boar. Dearg, however, escaped, and tackled the boar at Cnoc Áine (Knockainey, County Limerick). Leaping onto its back, he stabbed it continually all the way to where the three rivers meet at Waterford, and killed it there.

Variants of many of the Fianna stories, and motifs from them, are still found in the folklore of Irish-speaking areas. The chanting of Fianna lays, however, no longer survives in Ireland, though versions of several of these lays can still be heard in the western islands of Scotland. The Fianna tradition had a strong influence on world literature and culture in an indirect way, through the highly inaccurate reproductions of Scottish lays by James Macpherson in the late eighteenth century. The works of Macpherson were translated into many languages, and were well known to writers, philosophers, artists and composers of music in Europe and America. For further material, *see* the full list of entries on the Fianna Cycle in the List of Genres, page 509.

WORDS *FIAN*, *FIANNA* AND EARLY TRADITION: Meyer (1910), v–xvi; R. Sharpe in *Ériu*, *30*, 75–92; K. McCone in *Ériu*, *35*, 1–30; Nagy (1985), 41–79, 240–55; Ó hÓgáin (1988), 33–43, 103–4; Pettersson (1999), 23–35.

FEUDING AND WOMANISING: Meyer (1912), 87–8; Ó hÓgáin (1988), 43–50. *See* FIONN MAC CUMHAILL.

LIFE IN WILDERNESS: D. de hÍde in *Lia Fáil*, *1*, 104–6; Meyer (1912), 46; Stokes (1900), 21–2, 25, 43–4, 74, 183; Dinneen (1908), 328; R. Thurneysen in *ZCP*, *13*, 262; Joynt (1936), 20–1; G. Murphy (1933), 178, 204–6; Mac Piarais (1908), 17; Ní Shéaghdha & Ní Mhuirgheasa (1941), 82–3; Ó hÓgáin (1988), 74–7.

ACCEPTANCE TO MEMBERSHIP: O'Grady (1892), 92–3; Ó hÓgáin (1988), 104–5.

ORGANISATION AND LEADING MEMBERS: Stokes (1900), 21, 67–8, 93, 160–3; Ní Shéaghdha (1945), 184–5; Joynt (1936), 8, 11, 38; Dinneen (1908), 326–32; Ó hÓgáin (1988), 139–41.

MARVELLOUS HELPERS: Best & O'Brien (1965), xvi, 1001–3 & in *ZCP*, *3*, 433–4; Stokes (1900), 6, 106, 108, 123–4, 149–52, 154, 168–73, 182, 211; D. de hÍde in *Lia Fáil*, *1*, 107; Ní Shéaghdha, *2* (1942), 16–27; Christiansen (1931), 78–83; Macalister (1941), 134–6; Joynt (1936), 21–34; Ó hÓgáin (1988), 183–91.

FANTASTIC RETAINERS: Stokes (1900), 328–9; Joynt (1936), 8, 14; Ní Shéaghdha (1967), 20; Ó hÓgáin (1988), 141–3.

GREAT BATTLES: Stokes (1900), 21–5, 31–2, 88–90; E. Mac Neill

(1908), 37; G. Murphy (1933), 86, 124; C. O'Rahilly (1962); Christiansen (1931), 84–5; Ó hÓgáin (1988), 143–50, 289, 335.

COLLOQUY OF THE OLD MEN: Stokes (1900); D. de hÍde in *Lia Fáil*, *1*, 79–107; Ní Shéaghdha *1–2* (1942) & *3* (1945).

MORNA vs. BAOISCNE CLANS: *see* Ó hÓgáin (1988), 159–66, 336 & GOLL MAC MORNA.

ENTRAPMENT: Ní Shéaghdha, *2* (1942), 47–53; E. Mac Neill (1908), 91–2; K. Meyer in *ZCP*, *5*, 22; Ó Siochfhradha (1941), 149–50; G. Murphy (1933), 60–4; Ó hÓgáin (1988), 202–7, 288–89, 338.

KESHCORRAN: Ní Shéaghdha & Ní Mhuirgheasa (1941), 3–15; Ó hÓgáin (1988), 204–5.

EOCHAIDH BEAG DEARG: Ní Shéaghdha & Ní Mhuirgheasa (1941), 40–91; Ó hÓgáin (1988), 207–12, 288.

QUICKEN MANSION: Mac Piarais (1908); Ó hÓgáin (1988), 212–16, 288.

SINGLE COMBATS: Stokes (1900), 4, 126–9. 163–7; G. Murphy (1933), 222–32, 248–78, 298–328, 362–8; Ó Siochfhradha (1941), 28–31; Ó Gallchobhair et al. (1915), 17–46; E. Mac Neill (1908), 61–73; Ó hÓgáin (1988), 217–28, 339.

'DIFFICULT SERVANT': *see* ÁBHARTACH MAC ILDATHAIGH.

'GREY-CLOAKED CHURL': Mac Piarais (1906); Ó hÓgáin (1988), 258–61.

DONN STORY: T. Ó Caomhánaigh in *Lia Fáil*, *3*, 91–113.

DEARG STORY: RIA 24 B 14:151–271; Bruford (1966), 50–1, 259.

END OF THE FIANNA: E. Windisch in *Irische Texte*, *1*, 158; Stokes (1900), 1, 31, 222; E. Mac Neill (1908), 37, 48, 81; G. Murphy (1933), 32–57, 108; N. Ross (1939), 148–51; Ó Siochfhradha (1941), 200–12; Ó hÓgáin (1988), 149–50.

GENERAL DISCUSSIONS: S. Ó Súilleabháin (1942), 588–97; Ó Cadhlaigh (1947); MacKillop (1986), 69–266; Alqmvist, Ó Cathain & Ó Héalaí (1987), 1–264; Ó hÓgáin (1988), *passim*.

Finn Eamhna

Finn Eamhna The triplet sons of EOCHAIDH FEIDHLEACH, their individual names being given as Breas, Nár and Lothar. These characters are a confused echo in medieval literature from the ancient triplication of the mythic FIONN.

Within the ULSTER CYCLE, they were given a new role as residents of the Ulster court at Eamhain Mhacha, and were made sons of the TARA king Eochaidh Feidhleach. Because the word *eamhain* could mean twins, they came to be regarded as triplets, born together to Eochaidh's queen Cloithfhionn. When she became estranged from her husband, we are told, she took them with her to Eamhain Mhacha, where she and the Ulster king CONCHOBHAR MAC NEASA continually urged them to oppose their father. Eventually, they gathered their forces to mount an offensive against Eochaidh, and went south to Cruachain (Rathcroghan, County Roscommon), where their sister Clothra then reigned as queen of Connacht. She, however, refused to join them and tried to dissuade them from the undertaking, going so far as to make sexual offers to them, but all to no purpose. Her two DRUIDS also tried to dissuade them, prophesying disaster, but they were killed by the angry triplets.

When they arrived at Tara, Eochaidh sent his own druid Glúincheann to offer them two-thirds of his kingdom, but they refused. Eochaidh then fasted against them, and next morning fierce battle was joined at Comar (near Navan, County Meath). During the battle, Lothar flung a stone at his father, and 'no stronger shot was made ever since'. It struck Eochaidh in the chest, laying him unconscious. Then three great warriors – who were commanders of Eochaidh's army but who had until then been restrained by Eochaidh – took the field. These were CONALL CEARNACH, CEAT MAC MÁGHACH and Raon mac Róicheadail, and they routed the army of the Finn. They followed the three Finn themselves to Connacht and slew them there. Eochaidh was disconsolate when he saw the heads of his three sons. He directed that the heads be buried with their bodies, and with himself, at Cruachain. He then died from sorrow, and his instructions were carried out.

The treble imagery of the Finn was extended imaginatively by claiming that all three together were fathers of the hero LUGHAIDH RIABHDHERG, having begotten him on their sister Clothra on the night before the Battle of Comar.

W. Stokes in *Irische Texte*, 3, 332–3; T.F. O'Rahilly (1946), 486; M.E. Dobbs in *RC*, 43, 277–342; K. Meyer in *AIM*, 5, 17–18; J. O'Neill in *Ériu*, 2, 174–5.

Finnbheara

Finnbheara Leader of the FAIRIES of the province of Connacht, according to folklore. He was said to preside over an otherworld community in Cnoc Meadha (Knockmaa, some miles to the southwest of Tuam, County Galway).

The name is a corruption of Findbharr (later, Fionnbharr), a designation with mythical origins (*see* BARRA). The origin of Finnbheara was probably an epithetical *findbharr* (literally, 'fair top') to describe the summit of Knockmaa or a cairn on it, and this term would easily have been reinterpreted as the name of an otherworld being resident there. There is mention of the TUATHA DÉ DANANN chieftain Findbharr of Cnoc Meadha in the twelfth-century FIANNA text *Agallamh na Seanóach*, and he occurs again in the fifteenth-century *Feis Tighe Chonáin*, where he is an otherworld rival of FIONN MAC CUMHAILL for the hand of a lady. The Finnbheara of folklore is represented broadly in the same vein, several oral LEGENDS telling of how he enticed beautiful young women away into his preternatural realm. It is therefore probable that this Fianna text had a strong influence on the development of the character in folklore.

Several other narratives were attached to Finnbheara. As a fairy chieftain, he was said to lead his host in contention with rival otherworld groups. In this, he acts as the counterpart of DONN according to ancient convention of alternating brightness and darkness. Lore of Donn as a fairy leader was current since the Middle Ages in Clare and Limerick, and the portrayal of Finnbheara has been coloured by the fairy imagery of that personage. Thus a popular legend told of how – like Donn – Finnbheara came one night to a blacksmith to have his HORSE shod before a great battle. In Finnbheara's case, some details are added, for his horse was three-legged, and next day the blacksmith was rewarded by having cash blown to him on the wind. Finnbheara and his followers engaged each year in a hurling match against the fairies of other provinces, and when they won, the crops of Connacht bloomed.

Accounts were current also of how he invited humans into his palace in Knockmaa for feasts. These feasts were variously considered as ruses to entice people away into the fairy realm, or as entertainment offered in good faith by Finnbheara. Like Donn, he is often portrayed as the benefactor of local inhabitants. He once appeared for the purpose of healing a sick woman, and on another occasion assisted the popular local landlord Hacket when the latter could find no suitable jockey for his horse in a race. Finnbheara himself appeared and took the mount, winning easily before vanishing again.

Stokes (1900), 140–2; Joynt (1936), 49–56; L. Duncan in *Ériu, 11*, 193–4; T.F. O'Rahilly (1926), 58; Neilson, *2*(1845), 56–9; Wilde (1888), 42–5, 259–63; Ó Fotharta (1892), 33–5; Hyde (1910), 86–91; Wentz (1911), 42, 122; S. Ó Súilleabháin (1942), 452–3, 495–6; M. MacNeill (1962), 593.

Fíonán Cam SAINT of the early seventh century, founder of a monastery at Cionn Eitigh (Kinnitty, County Offaly). His name is based on *fíon* (wine), and probably meant worthy, while the epithet *cam* meant squint-eyed.

He was of the Corca Dhuibhne sept of Kerry, and his mother's name is given as Becnat. We read in a medieval text that she was bathing after sunset in Loch Léin (the greater lake of Killarney) and that a golden salmon impregnated her there, and thus Fíonán was conceived. One old tradition claimed that he had been the first person to bring wheat to Ireland, having conveyed it hither from Leatha (Latium, Italy) in his shoe. There are several recensions of his biography, the fullest being a late version in Irish. Altering the earlier tradition somewhat, this claims that his mother conceived by dreaming that a golden FISH entered her mouth, and during her pregnancy no rain or snow fell on her. The young Fíonán soon showed great knowledge and miraculous powers, impressing St BRÉANAINN, who directed him to leave Kerry and go north and build a church where he would meet a herd of wild boars. He therefore set out, and in this manner made Kinnitty the site of his foundation. The rest of the biography describes miracles performed by Fíonán, particularly by way of healing sick and injured people and animals, and several of these are borrowed from the accounts of other saints.

A special tradition has Fíonán Cam banishing a plague from Uíbh Ráthach (the south-western part of County Kerry). He became somewhat confused with his namesake, St Fíonán Lobhar (i.e. the Leper), who also lived in the Killarney area. His feast day is 7 April, but it was celebrated in Kerry on 16 March.

Kenney (1929), 421–2; Stokes (1905), 112–15, 423; Plummer, *2*(1910), 87–95; Heist (1965), 153–60; R.A.S. Macalister in *ZCP, 2*, 545–65; C. O'Rahilly (1952), 81, 162; O'Hanlon, *4* (1875), 57–72.

Fionn Name of a mythical seer whose image stands behind much of the learned lore of early Ireland. The earlier form of the name – usual in the manuscripts – was Find, but in the present work the name is spelt according to modern orthography.

The origins of this personage must be sought in remote antiquity. A present-stem *weid* was behind words in several Indo-European languages to indicate knowledge in the sense of something seen and thus understood – for instance, Latin *vid-*, Germanic *wit-*, and Indic *véda*. Another construction, *wind-*, was either a variant present-stem based on the same root, or a word of different origin that could be confused with it. In Celtic, this became *vind-*, with a range of meaning from brightness to wisdom. Among the Continental Celts, 'Vindos' was a personal name, meaning 'the bright one' or 'the fair-haired', and a compound of it, 'Vindobona', occurred as a toponymic (modern Vienna). The first element here can be taken as a personal name, since *bona* (meaning a cluster of houses) tended to be connected with such – thus Vindobona would have meant 'settlement dedicated to Vindos'. A Celtic deity called Vindonnus is indeed attested on the Continent, and it is reasonable to assume that this was a lengthened form of Vindos, a personification of wisdom with bright countenance. This antique Fionn appears in the character Finnéigeas (*Findéces*) described as a mystical tutor of FIONN MAC CUMHAILL. The name Finnéigeas (Fionn the seer) was identical in meaning with the 'avatar' name FIONN FILE, and thus the rhetorical designation of Fionn would anciently have meant 'the bright seer'. This would represent a play upon the druidic claim to communicate with the world of the dead ancestors, to bring light out of darkness (*see* DONN, DRUIDS *and* POETS).

235

The first echo of the character's name in Ireland is provided by Ptolemy's geography, which dates from the second century AD. This is the second part of the compound 'buvinda', a transliteration of archaic Irish *bóu-vinda* for the river now known as the Boyne. The name of this river was redolent of the nourishing and sustaining streams of milk and wisdom, and underlined social and mystical well-being (*see* BÓINN). Moreover, it flowed through the rich and luscious Boyne Valley, the most coveted part of Ireland, which had a prestige and serenity all of its own due to the large number of ancient monuments left there by earlier peoples. The Celtic culture was spreading rapidly throughout Ireland in the late centuries BC, mingling with earlier cultures. It was therefore natural for speakers of Celtic to rationalise these ancient monuments – especially mounds and burial chambers – by locating their own deities in them. In the development of this culture of the spiritual environment, the seers would have played the leading role, and so a figure who personalised the cult of the seers was of primary importance. In this way, the character Vindos would have been intimately associated with the artefacts and the surroundings of the area, and especially with the river that flowed through the valley.

The seers would have stressed their own social importance by portraying the waters of that river not only as the life-giving force to the surrounding countryside, but also as the source of their mystical stream of wisdom. Imagery such as this bears witness to ancient strata of lore, promulgated by a learned caste, that survived to be reflected in the early literature. Among the varied allusions, one can decipher a conceit whereby the wonder-child, reflecting the druidic interest, was born from the female river that had been fructified by the male sun. In this context, sense can be made of early Irish kennings for poetry and wisdom such as 'the splendour of sunrise', 'the dews of a goddess', and 'the navel-string of the infant'. There were many layers of meaning to be extracted from such imagery, including the typical seer as a reflection on the waters of life of the ancestral sun shining overhead. Not only was the function of the mother-deity fulfilled by Bóinn, but the father-deity himself lingered behind the ancestral solar designation AODH RUADH RÓ-FHEASA. Both such parents may, indeed, in origin have been alter egos of DANU and the DAGHDHA respectively; and the whole complex may thus reflect an Indo-European inheritance.

It is curious that Fionn does not figure among the divine race called the TUATHA DÉ DANANN by the medieval writers, but the reason for this must be that, as a typical and representative seer, he was usually imagined as a human person. His name does, nevertheless, appear in the mythical parts of genealogies, and the literature has mention of three characters whose designation reflects a divine triplication of him (*see* FINN EAMHNA). Lacking any narrative records from so early a period, the lore concerning this archetypal seer must be investigated through what survives concerning his emanations – characters such as MORANN, Fionn mac Cumhaill and others. A study of these suggests that certain ideas were basic to the image of Fionn and were expressed in a number of standard ways. Firstly, knowledge was believed to be got from the dead ancestors, an idea that gave immediate relevance to grave-mounds, cairns and such places. When ritually understood, this meant a great individual seer seeking out a wise predecessor, and there are several indications that this was expressed in a narrative concerning a wise youth called Fionn communicating with his ancestor, of whose sun-imagery his own was a reflection; thus the conceit of an old patron Finnéigeas giving knowledge and lustre to a young Fionn. It is likely that a direct survival of the designation for the old namesake is found in FIONNTAN, the antediluvian seer of medieval literature. His name (earlier, Fintan) can best be explained as deriving from a Celtic *Vindosenos* (literally, 'old Find'), and there are parallels to this in fossilised names that survive in medieval Welsh literature, viz. 'Gwyn hen' and 'Henwen'.

The youth of Fionn could be strikingly expressed in imagery of a divine child who symbolised wisdom. True knowledge was understood in early times as being inspirational rather than gradually acquired, and such a child was symbolic of fullness in the beginning. Lore seems to have been current concerning the baby Fionn emerging from mystical waters already physically mature in striking ways, such as having grown hair that was bright in colour in accord with his name, and speaking ritually. He was already fully possessed of wisdom, the word for which (*fios*) has the same probable root as his own name, and the babyish habit of thumb-sucking was for him a means of promoting his wisdom. The various images of Fionn – baby, young man and old ancestor – made sense in the mystical understanding of seers of their craft, which penetrated into future, present and past (*see* POETS). The mystical sense of wisdom involved the ability to experience different aspects of reality, and there are therefore several indications that metamorphosis was a basic element in early Irish seer rituals. This should be seen as a form of shamanism. Residues of it in narrative, deriving directly from lore concerning Fionn, are found in accounts of how such characters as Fionntan and MONGÁN went about in the forms of different animals, and thereby acquired extra knowledge.

A study also suggests that the cult of Fionn was influenced in the pre-literary period by the adoption of a new deity in the Boyne Valley, namely NUADHU, to whom a salmon-cult attached. Accordingly, the wisdom-giving waters of the Boyne were said to contain a special salmon sacred to Nuadhu. This caused some disruption in the earlier imagery, leaving the option to identify the salmon with the divine child Fionn or with the wisdom-giving ancestor. The latter option was the one chosen, the salmon and its possessor being set in the role of the old Fionn – Nuadhu being referred to as Nuadhu Fionnéigeas, and the salmon being called Aodh Ruadh Ró-Fheasa. In time, this elder-versus-youth pattern was dramatically developed

along the same lines as the Daghdha-versus-AONGHUS tradition, making the young Fionn not just seek knowledge from his ancestor, but actually outmanoeuvre him (*see* FIONN MAC CUMHAILL).

ORIGIN AND ANTIQUE LORE: Pokorny (1959), 1125–6; Holder, *3* (1896), 328–50; Mallory & Adams (1997), 337; Thevenot (1968), 110–12; K.H. Schmidt in *ZCP, 26*, 295–6; G. Murphy (1953), lxxviii–lxxxiii; Gwynn (1913), 34; Ó hÓgáin (1988), 3–26, 323–6 & (1999), 118–27; O'Brien (1962), 129–30, 642–3.

SOLAR AND WATER IMAGERY: Stokes, *CTS* (1905), 16–21, 28–9; P.K. Ford in Larson (1974), 67–74; Ó hÓgáin in Stewart (1998), 13–22.

Fionn File

Mythical ancient Leinster POET and KING, whose personality was derived from the druidic patron of knowledge FIONN. The full name of Fionn File in Celtic would have been Vindos Velitos, with a meaning such as 'the bright seer'.

The Leinstermen (LAIGHIN) lost the Boyne Valley in or about the third century AD (*see* CATHAOIR MÓR *and* TARA), and for a long time hankered after that rich area. Since he was symbolical of the Boyne culture, the obscure figure of Find (i.e. Fionn) came to be regarded by these Leinstermen as a symbol of kingship. Thus Fionn File, alluded to as son of one Ros Ruadh (i.e. AODH RUADH RÓ-FHEASA), and one of three brothers, was claimed by the Leinstermen to have been a great ancient king of theirs. One of the mounds at Tara, Dumha Find, was indeed claimed to have been his burial site.

Fionn File was regarded as a great poet, and some early compositions were attributed to him – none of them, however, earlier than the sixth century AD in date. As befits their attribution to such a personage, these poems treat of the mythical history of Leinster. Later still, in tales of medieval date from the ULSTER CYCLE, Fionn occurs as the standard Leinster king. For instance, in one account of the war caused between the Ulstermen and the Leinstermen by ATHAIRNE – when the two armies filled Magh nEalta (the plain of Dublin) – Fionn File cast a shot at the youthful Ulster warrior Meas Deadh, causing him to fall into a well and drown there. Another fiction was that Fionn himself was slain by CONALL CEARNACH when that

Ulster hero wreaked vengeance on Leinster for the death of Cú CHULAINN. The genealogies claim that one of the brothers of Fionn File was a certain Cairbre Nia Fear, king of Tara. One fanciful story had Fionn File, on a visit to Tara, being offended by the mean food offered to him by his niece Bé Ghealchneas (Maiden of Bright Skin), the daughter of Cairbre. Fionn satirised her stinginess, with the result that she fell dead.

More significantly, the name of Cairbre Nia Fear can be considered a vestige of lore from the Leinster control of Tara (*see* CORMAC MAC AIRT), and the format of the genealogies suggests that chief among the Leinster septs that held Tara in that period were the Uí Gharrchon. After the loss of the Boyne Valley, this was also the sept that ruled Leinster to the end of the fifth century AD, and at that time, Ailleann (Knockaulin, County Kildare) was in the heart of their territory. This was one of the largest hill-top forts in Ireland, and since the Leinster kings were now being inaugurated at that site, the mythical Fionn File was claimed to have had his residence there. In the early sixth century, the Uí Gharrchon were uprooted from Knockaulin also and driven east into the Wicklow mountains, and this may account for the 'freezing' of the lore concerning Fionn File. Henceforth the front line against the dominant Uí NÉILL was held for the Leinstermen by a sept to the west of them, the Uí Fhailghe, and through this latter sept another emanation from the ancient Fionn flourished and underwent intense development in narrative. This was the celebrated FIONN MAC CUMHAILL.

Nothing else of import attaches to the tradition of Fionn File, except that the genealogists fancifully named as his third brother a character from the Ulster Cycle, the Connacht king Ailill mac Máta (for whom, *see* MEADHBH).

Meyer, *HB* (1912) & (1914), 9–14; E. Hogan (1892), 22, 58; Ó Cadhlaigh (1956), 475; T.F. O'Rahilly (1946), 179; Gwynn (1903), 46–8, 81 & (1906), 80 & (1913), 56–8, 108, 158; W. Stokes in *RC*, *15*, 318–19 & in *Folk-Lore, 3*, 472; Ó hÓgáin (1988), 28–9; O'Brien (1962), 1, 5, 8, 15, 18–24, 99, 643; Ó Muraíle, *2* (2003), 192, 200–2.

Fionn mac Cumhaill The most celebrated hero in Irish literature and folklore. Stories concerning him are continuous in the literature for well over 1,000 years. In the earliest texts, his name occurs in the Old Irish form *Find*, in Middle Irish it is written *Finn*, and in Modern Irish *Fionn*. This latter form, which has been current for many centuries, is the one used here.

Fionn mac Cumhaill is always portrayed as a great warrior-seer. He can be viewed as an emanation of the archaic seer FIONN (i.e. *Find*) or, indeed, as a continuation in tradition of that personage. This Fionn was archetypal in the cult of wisdom in the Boyne Valley, and the LAIGHIN (i.e. Leinstermen) adopted lore of him into their own tradition when they gained control of that prime area in the third or fourth century. A leading Leinster sept, the Uí Gharrchon, associated the archetypal seer with their great centre at Ailleann (Knockaulin, County Kildare), calling him FIONN FILE. Another sept, the Uí Fhailghe, inhabited a large territory in the west of the province (encompassing parts of present-day Counties Kildare, Offaly and Laois). This Uí Fhailghe sept also had the lore of Fionn from the Boyne Valley, and centred it on a hill in the heart of their territory called Almhu (the Hill of Allen, County Kildare), which apparently was a sacred site. They called the personage Fionn son of Cumhall.

The Leinstermen were driven from the Boyne Valley by the ascendant Uí NÉILL sept in the fifth century, and by the beginning of the sixth century the Uí Gharrchon had been routed. The Uí Fhailghe then assumed the leadership of Leinster, and for some years engaged in a determined but futile struggle against the Uí Néill. All the indications are that in this struggle they used the imagery of the seer Fionn as a symbol of their efforts to regain possession of the Boyne Valley and that, as part of this, Fionn was portrayed as having been a great war leader. The cult of war was particularly stressed in the case of young trainee warriors known as FIANNA, and thus Fionn was fancifully said to have been the leader of a mythical Fianna band long ago. This context explains how Fionn mac Cumhaill is at one with the ancient seer of the Boyne Valley, and also with the fighting and hunting life of young men whose base is said to have been in the Uí Fhailghe territory. This composite character of the warrior-seer, originating in the early sixth century, underwent rapid narrative development in the following generations, and reflecting the abiding hostility of the Leinstermen to the Uí Néill, provided an increasingly dramatic corpus of stories.

Already in the seventh century, the Leinster genealogists were at work finding a place for Fionn in their tracts. They described him as a descendant of NUADHU, and invented martial-sounding names for his immediate ancestors. His father Cumhall was said to have been son of Tréanmhór (literally, 'strong and big'), son of Sualt (wholesome), son of Ealtan (having troops), son of Baoiscne (stalwart). Various attempts have been made to explain the name of his father, Cumhall, but none seem satisfactory. It may well have been associated with the ancient Fionn of the Boyne Valley before the Leinstermen borrowed the lore, and there are indications that its original form was 'Umhall'. This may have been a variant name for the divine ancestor, with a meaning such as 'the bronze one', which calls to mind the bronze cauldron of the solar father-deity (*see* DÁIRE), and the fact that metals in the earth were thought to have a special connection with the sun. All of this underlines the mystical origin of the lore (*see* FIONN FILE *and* NOÍNE). Echoes of shamanic practices can be clearly recognised in the early literature concerning Fionn mac Cumhaill – for instance, in the accounts that he had a special hood that, according as he turned it on his head, allowed him to assume animal form such as a hound or a deer.

A number of stories concerning this Fionn are found in texts dating from the eighth century. Some of these are of Leinster provenance, and the others – from east Munster – show by the nomenclature employed in them that they are adaptations from Leinster. These attest to the fact that

lore of the young hunter-fighters had given rise to an identifiable band of invented warriors as companions of Fionn. Principal among these are CAOILTE and OISÍN, both of which may originally have been nicknames for Fionn himself.

The dual function of Fionn as fighter and seer are brought out in a story that tells of how he had a woman of the Luaighne sept as lover, but she lay with a warrior of his band called Cairbre. Fionn's jester Lomhna saw them and, when he let Fionn know, Cairbre killed him. When Fionn found the decapitated body, he put his thumb into his mouth and uttered a rhetoric proclaiming that this was Lomhna. He set out in pursuit of Cairbre, and found him in an empty house cooking FISH, with Lomhna's head on a spike by the fire. The head was complaining that it had been given nothing to eat, and was threatening Cairbre with the destruction Fionn would bring on him. At that, Fionn attacked Cairbre and slew him. Apart from the Fianna context of fighting over a woman, this account stresses three important aspects of Fionn's power of wisdom. Firstly, he places his thumb in his mouth in order to gain knowledge, a trait inherited from the image of the ancient Fionn as a child-seer. Secondly, he puts the knowledge gained by him into an obscure rhetoric, which was the standard custom of inspired POETS. Thirdly, the head of a dead man speaks in his presence. This seems to have been a combination in the Fionn context of two different early factors – one being the idea that Find gained information from the dead ancestors, and the other the general custom of fêting the heads of dead warriors (*see* CONALL CEARNACH *and* FEARGHAL MAC MAOLDÚIN).

The same themes recur in other texts of the period – for instance, in a Munster adaptation of the lore that describes how his Fianna abducted women from Dún Iascaigh (Cahir, County Tipperary), and how Fionn kept one of the women for himself. She desired one of his servants, called Dearg Corra, but he rejected her. Nevertheless, he was banished by a jealous Fionn at her instigation. Sometime later,

Fionn met with a strange and mystical figure in the forest, and to discover who it was, put his thumb in his mouth. He was illumined by his wisdom and sang a rhetoric stating that it was Dearg Corra. This strange servant (*see* DEARG) had the attributes of a deer-deity, and thus seems to reflect some hunting lore current among Fianna bands. The general plot employed in this story is the international one known to scholars as 'Potiphar's Wife' (*see* ROMANTIC TALES, type 870C), the occurrence of which shows how the narratives concerning Fionn were being developed at the time. Deer lore also lies behind the name of Oisín (q.v.), who was regarded as Fionn's son and in relation to whom another well-known plot was borrowed (*see* ROMANTIC TALES, type 873). The story describes how Fionn, having searched for a whole year throughout Ireland for Oisín, found the son cooking a PIG in a lonely place. Fionn struck him and Oisín seized his weapons, but then they recognised each other, argued in verse, and were reconciled. The language of this text concerning Oisín seems to belong to the eighth century, but it may be slightly later than that. Nevertheless, the fact that Fionn is portrayed in it as an elderly man with a grown-up son again shows how comprehensive the narratives had become by that time.

An eighth-century text that seems to be a composite between Leinster and Munster lore brings Fionn into contact with another famous *fianna* leader of early myth, FOTHADH CANAINNE. We read that Fionn carried off a woman called Badhamair from Dún Iascaigh, but a Leinster warrior called Cuirreach Life decapitated Badhamair. Fionn beheaded Cuirreach in revenge, but this led to conflict with the half-brother of that man, who was Fothadh. After some time, they made peace with each other, and Fionn invited Fothadh to an ale feast. Fothadh, however, said that he would not drink ale 'unless it be in the company of white faces', and accordingly Fionn went to Dá Chích Anann (the hills called the Two Paps, near Killarney) and slew the husband of Fothadh's sister with a spear-cast there. He

brought the head of this man to the feast, but the episode caused the hostility between Fionn and Fothadh to be renewed with great ferocity. An account from around the same time goes further and puts Fionn into the context of mythical Munster history by having him track down and slay one Fearcheas, the man who had killed LUGHAIDH MAC CON.

This type of lore is quite crude and savage, no doubt reflecting the life of young warriors of the time, but the greater stress remained on the aspect of Fionn as a poet-seer. In the eighth century also, a story was invented to rationalise the strange power he had of putting his thumb in his mouth to gain knowledge. According to this, when he and his men were on the banks of the River Suir cooking a pig, an otherworld being called Cúldubh came from Sídh ar Feimhean (the cairn on top of Slievenamon, a mountain in east Tipperary) and snatched the pig from them. Fionn followed him, and as he entered the cairn, threw his spear at Cúldubh and killed him. A lady who had been distributing drink inside the cairn tried to close the door, but Fionn inserted his thumb between the door and the post to keep it open. The thumb was hurt, and Fionn put it into his mouth. Since it had been inside the otherworld dwelling, the thumb had got the power of wisdom, and so, as soon as it was in his mouth, he began to sing a rhetoric concerning Cúldubh. This method of killing an otherworld foe with a spear-cast as the foe enters his dwelling recurs in several stories of Fionn, and in some of these the episode is said to have happened at Samhain (the November feast – *see* TIME). Samhain was the festival of the dead, and this complex is probably an echo of the ancient cult of Find who got knowledge from the ancestors. The actual killing of the otherworld foe can be traced to the influence of the LUGH myth on the cult before Find was transformed into Fionn mac Cumhaill. That cult had Lugh defeating his tyrant grandfather, and it is reasonable to assume that when it was superimposed onto the existing lore of the seer-hero, it transformed his contest with the wise predecessor into one of physical combat.

When put to creative use in the early Middle Ages, vestiges of Fionn's contact with the ancestors led to dramatic accounts of visits by him to otherworld dwellings. Perhaps the most striking early example of this was a story, current in the ninth century but now lost, which described an adventure of Fionn in Dearc Fhearna. This was the great prehistoric cavern at Dunmore, County Kilkenny, which was described as one of the 'three dark places of Ireland'. Such otherworld dwellings visited by him could be either bright and inspiring or dark and threatening, a variability that can be assumed to be debris from the alternation between darkness and light in ancient druidic lore (see DONN *and* FIONN).

An aesthetically pleasing development was the attribution to him, in place of rhetorics, of mystical nature poetry that can be taken to reflect the inspiration of the seer at one with his ENVIRONMENT. A more planned development of his image seems to be echoed by eighth-century engravings on a stone cross at Drumhallagh in north Donegal, which show a figure with thumb in mouth sitting over an engraving of a bishop with a crozier in his hand. This suggests that the Church was using the image of Fionn, as a great ancient prophet, to its own advantage by claiming that he had foretold the coming of St PATRICK 'the Adze-Head'. A later medieval text is probably echoing this when it claims that Fionn once sat on the rock of Cashel, County Tipperary, put his thumb into his mouth, and foretold the coming of that great saint. Fionn was by then well on his way to portrayals that reflected wide human interests and no small amount of curiosity. For instance, the claim began to be made that he had a 'tooth of knowledge' with which he chewed his thumb – this was a natural transference of the source of his wisdom due to the idea of chewing.

A series of texts written from the tenth to the twelfth century, when taken together, amount to a kind of biography of Fionn mac Cumhaill, preserving many ancient elements and adding new adventures and situations to the lore. There are some minor contradictions between these texts, but one can draw from them an outline of his life and actions that became generally accepted. The material from all the texts, taken together, will be arranged here in as logical a pattern as the sources permit.

Fionn, we read, was of the Uí Thairsigh, a sub-sept to the Uí Fhailghe, who inhabited a place called Glaise Bolgain. This place is unidentified, but there are indications that it was in the vicinity of Almhu (the Hill of Allen), and we can assume that this hill was a cult centre in the Uí Fhailghe territory and that special responsibility for it rested with the Uí Thairsigh. His mother was Muirne, daughter of a DRUID called Tadhg mac Nuadhat, who lived in a white mansion on Almhu. A warrior called Cumhall sought Muirne as wife, but this was refused by her father, and then Cumhall abducted her. Tadhg went to the high-king CONN CÉADCHATHACH for assistance and, as a result, the abductor had to fight a battle against Conn's forces at Cnucha (Castleknock, County Dublin). Nine hours before the battle, Fionn was begotten, and Cumhall was defeated and slain at Cnucha. The aggrieved Tadhg threatened to kill his daughter before she gave birth, but she and the child were protected by Cumhall's sister Bodhmhall, who lived with her husband Fiacail Fí at Teamhair Mhairge (a peak of the Slievemargy hills between Counties Laois and Kilkenny). The basic themes of the Fionn literature are here set out. Fionn, as the Uí Fhailghe, is in basic hostility to the royal CONNACHTA sept of Conn; and his grandfather Tadhg mac Nuadhat is a tyrant developed partly from NUADHU and partly from BALAR. Imagery from the latter figure is clear from accounts of how, when Fionn grew up, he demanded combat or possession of Almhu from Tadhg, and the latter abandoned the place to him. Almhu is through the whole tradition described as Fionn's special fortress, but these medieval accounts of how he obtained it were not in the mainstream of the lore.

There are indications that as a reflex of

ancient lore concerning Find and the River Boyne, an early narrative described the baby Fionn as a great swimmer. Special connections with water and sea are found in the related birth-stories of the other wonder-children, MONGÁN, MORANN, and NOÍNE, and – as we shall see – various narratives tell of great feats performed by Fionn in water. These feats are connected with his name in such a way as to suggest that involvement with water was an important and basic theme in his tradition. Similar to Morann, a birth-story of the Ulster king CONCHOBHAR MAC NEASA has the child falling into water immediately after birth. We read that Conchobhar was born with a worm in each hand, and this is paralleled in folklore accounts of Fionn's birth, according to which he was thrown into the sea on the orders of his grandfather, but emerged holding an eel in his hands. It seems plausible to suggest that this episode concerning Conchobhar was taken from an existing story of Fionn. One late medieval text, in fact, seems to echo such a story by having the child Fionn strangle a dangerous stoat.

The caul on the head of the child Morann is also relevant, for when Morann is thrown into the sea, the monstrous caul is reduced to a collar about his neck. The Fianna lore had a marked tendency towards diffusion of MOTIFS and their recurrence in different contexts, and it could well be that the basis for all of these portrayals was a narrative image of the child Find emerging from the Boyne river with the spirit of wisdom in his head. Frequent terms for Fionn's wisdom in the early literature were *imbas* (a compound of *fios*, and meaning 'full knowledge') and the enigmatic *teinm laeda* (which probably meant 'chant of fire'). The paradoxical image of fire in water would well suit his mystical knowledge, and that this should be in the head of the child-seer accords well with the portrayal of inspiration in early Irish rhetoric (*see* POETS). It is clear that right through the tradition, Fionn's shining hair reflects both his name and his wisdom.

The fullest medieval account of Fionn's youth is entitled *Macgnímartha Find*. It describes how Cumhall, a warrior of the Uí Thairsigh, was outnumbered by the forces of Conn at Cnucha, and was slain by a great fighter called GOLL MAC MORNA This Goll was also an emanation from the image of Balar, and when the child Fionn was born, Muime had to take herself and it into hiding from him. She gave the child into the safekeeping of Bodhmhall, described as a nurse of young *fianna*. He was reared for six years on Sliabh Bladhma (Slieve Bloom, County Laois), and we read that his first hunt was when he brought down a duck on a lake with a dart. He went travelling for a while with a group of poets, and a disease struck him so that he became mangy and was thus called 'Demne the Bald'. This is probably an echo of some kind of poetic or druidic tonsure. The name Demne is unclear, but it may be a corruption of *daimhne* (little stag), and may thus reflect the Fianna context of hunting. At any rate, it functions narratively to stress an event by which he is claimed to have got his real name. We read that he went on several occasions to the plain of the Liffey (i.e. the Curragh of Kildare) and overcame all the youths there at hurling. On the final occasion, they were swimming and tried to drown him, but he drenched nine of them in the water. After his departure, the local chieftain was told by the boys that the stranger was fair-haired (*fionn*), and he remarked that this was the proper name for Demne.

The heroic youth had by this time grown so agile that he could outrun deer, and thus did the hunting for his two female guardians. They, however, advised him to leave the area for fear of his father's enemies, the family of Morna, and he went to west Munster. No chieftain would keep him in his service there for fear of the sons of Morna, and so he went east and met a smith at Cuilleann (Cullen, County Tipperary). He became the lover of the daughter of this man, and the latter made two great javelins for him with which he killed a ferocious wild pig. Then he went to Connacht in search of his father's brother Criomhall, and on the way met and slew one of the warriors who had wounded Cumhall at the Battle of Cnucha.

242

Criomhall was lying low in a forest with the remnants of Cumhall's band, and after a brief visit to him, Fionn went towards the Boyne Valley to learn the craft of poetry. Now follows the best known of all the adventures of Fionn.

Rather illogically, in view of the events the text has already described, the hero is again called Demne and stated to be a mere seven years old when he meets on the banks of the Boyne with a seer called Finnéigeas (whose name means simply 'Fionn the Seer', and who thus can be seen as a variant of Fionn's older double). This Finnéigeas had been for seven years seeking to catch the salmon of knowledge in that river. He had just then caught it, and entrusted it to the visitor for cooking, warning him not to eat it. As he cooked it, however, Fionn burned his thumb and put it to his mouth, thus getting the gift of wisdom. When he heard this, Finnéigeas said that the lad should be called not Demne but Fionn. This is clearly a folk narrative that the author has inserted into his text, but it has been changed somewhat to suit the Leinster genealogical lore. The name Nuadhu Finnéigeas is found elsewhere in the literature, and it can be accepted that this is the same character as the 'Finnéigeas' of the story.

This account of how Fionn gained wisdom is very popular in folklore of both Ireland and Scotland. The folk versions portray the opponent as a one-eyed figure who intends to kill the boy Fionn, but when the latter gets the knowledge, he realises this and kills the cyclopean figure. This is in agreement with the dramatic theme of the tyrant grandfather that had long before permeated the lore from the LUGH context. The author of this text seems to have omitted it because he thought it inappropriate to the image of Nuadhu, who in the genealogies was a respected ancestor of the Leinstermen. The account itself is another rationalisation of the motif of Fionn's thumb of knowledge, and it can hardly be older in origin than the ninth or tenth century. It uses motifs from an international narrative plot (*see* WONDER TALES, type 673), but its closest

correspondent is a medieval Icelandic account of Sigurd the dragon slayer, who accidentally burns his thumb while cooking the heart of a dragon and, realising that his companion intends to kill him, takes pre-emptive action. The relationship between the stories concerning Fionn and Sigurd is extremely complicated, but it is likely that the images of both heroes were perceived to be similar and that their lore influenced each other due to NORSE–Irish contacts in or about the tenth century. The imagery of the Boyne salmon was long associated with Fionn due to the influence of Nuadhu (q.v.), but the international wonder-tale plot was probably attached to him from Sigurd, while Sigurd got his thumb and the slaying of his opponent from Fionn.

After this episode, the medieval text states – again rather incongruously – that Fionn went to study poetry with a warrior called CEITHEARN MAC FIONTAIN (another echo of Fionn's older double). He accompanied Ceithearn when the latter went to woo a beautiful otherworld maiden at Sídh Éile (the Hill of Croghan, County Offaly) at November, but the venture was abandoned when one of their men was slain by an otherworld agency. The author was here dealing with some tradition that he did not clearly understand, but he repeats the theme in the event which follows. This has Fionn meeting with the warrior Fiacail, who gave him a javelin and told him to go to the Paps of Anu (in County Kerry) and sit down between these two mountain peaks in the following November. He cast his javelin at an otherworld man who entered the dwelling there, and then went to Sídh Éile and seized a woman to hold as hostage for the return of the javelin. Having recovered it, he was told by Fiacail that the otherworld warrior he had slain had been the killer of Ceithearn's man.

Fionn then went with Fiacail to join a Fianna band at Inbhear Colptha (the Boyne estuary), and while there was placed on sentry duty at their camp for the night. He heard a shriek from the north, and going to Sliabh Slángha (Donard Mountain,

County Down) saw three horned other-world women who fled into the dwelling there. He snatched the brooch of one of them, and she begged him to return it, but the text breaks off here. It is obvious that the author has been telling different versions of one basic story – i.e. of how Fionn slew with a spear-cast an otherworld warrior who came to do some harm to mortals. This, as suggested above, seems to have had its ultimate roots in the motif of the one-eyed destructive Balar who was slain by Lugh. When adopted into the Fionn context, that motif had become split into two basic recensions – the foe as a one-eyed fearsome warrior and the foe as a fiery otherworld foe. That this division occurred in the Fionn lore around the sixth or seventh century is suggested by the development of the character who in medieval times became known as GOLL MAC MORNA.

A well-written twelfth-century text gives the most dramatic version of the motif, showing clearly how the archetypal foe had been split into two personages and synchronised into the developing tradition of Fionn. This tells of how Fionn, at the age of ten, went to the court of the high-king CONN CÉADCHATHACH at Tara for the November feast. The KING was desolate, for every year on that night the citadel was burned down by an otherworld being called Aillén, who came playing magical music to lull everybody to sleep. Fionn offered to stand guard, and was given a spear by one Fiacha (apparently a variant of the previous Fiacail). When he heard the magical harp music, he stayed awake by pressing the spear point to his forehead, and then jumped up to face the fiery being. Aillén released a blaze from his mouth, but Fionn quenched it with his cloak and put the burner to flight. Fionn followed him to Sliabh Fuaid (Fews Mountain, County Armagh) and as Aillén entered the hill-top cairn there, Fionn cast his spear at him and slew him. Fionn then returned to Tara with the head of Aillén, and so grateful was the high-king to him that he installed him as head of all the Fianna of Ireland. The slayer of Fionn's father, Goll mac Morna, accepted this with

good grace, and the three battalions of the high-king's soldiers put their hands in the hand of Fionn as a token of their loyalty. Thus Fionn became the leader of the Fianna, an elevated position in which he could even be referred to as *righfhéinnidh* (Fianna king).

The synchronisation and pseudo-historicising had thus proceeded quite far. Fionn mac Cumhaill, the archetypal hero of the Leinstermen in their struggle against the expanding sept of Conn, had now become the commander of Conn's own army. The dramatic potential of the old hostilities was remembered, however, and so – right through the tradition of Fionn – a poorly concealed friction continued between Fionn and Conn's heirs, as did open rivalry between Fionn and Goll. Indeed, it became conventional to regard the Fianna as comprised of two different groups – one the Baoiscne clan of Fionn and the other the Morna clan of Goll – and several stories are based on periodic breaches between these two.

Friction with Conn's grandson, the celebrated high-king CORMAC MAC AIRT, became endemic to the career of Fionn, who was regarded as a sort of alternative king, and so echoes from imagery of the GODDESS of sovereignty came into play. Since the goddess could be alternately beautiful and hideous, this competition between Cormac and Fionn gave rise to the idea that Cormac had a beautiful daughter called Gráinne (literally, 'the ugly one'). We read in tenth-century texts that Fionn wooed and married Gráinne, but she hated him and loved instead a young man called Diarmaid, with whom she eloped. As a result of this dispute, Fionn was banished for a while by Cormac. The story survives in full only in a later recension, but its origins seem to have lain in a confusion between Fianna lore of abduction and the goddess imagery (*see* DIARMAID UA DUIBHNE). One of the tenth-century texts goes on to relate how Fionn wooed a second daughter of Cormac, called Ailbhe. In the courtship, Fionn used his gift of enigmatic speech and engaged in a riddle contest with the maiden – a theme related to a common ROMANTIC TALE (type 875). This marriage was a happy one, and we read that as a result of his union with Ailbhe, some marvellous things happened to Fionn – including the appearance of a white-and-purple spot on his breast, and his hair taking on a colour of gold (another echo from the imagery of his name).

An extremely rich lore grew up concerning the adult life of Fionn, some of it contradictory, and it will be dealt with presently. Accounts purporting to tell of how he met with his death were already current in the ninth century. The Luaighne or Luighne sept of Tara (*see* ÉRAINN), anciently mercenaries of the Connachta, were always portrayed as special enemies of his, and they play a large part in stories of his demise. We read that it was prophesied to him that if he drank from a horn, he would die, and so he always drank from goblets. However, he once took a drink from a spring at a place called Adharca Iuchbha (literally, 'the horns of Iuchbha'), and when he put his thumb into his mouth and chewed, he realised his death was near. Then he proceeded to the Boyne river, to an area controlled by the Luaighne. His foes gathered about him there and, in a fierce struggle, slew him. They brought his head with them, and when they began to cook fish, the head spoke and asked for a morsel. This was the learned tradition.

An alternative account, based on folklore, was already current in the eleventh century, and was still common until recent times in oral tradition. According to this, he had once been challenged by an otherworld lady to leap backwards and forwards across the Boyne river, or from one cliff to another in Luachair Deaghadh (south-east Kerry). The woman enjoined on him to do this jump once every year, and when he grew old and attempted it, he fell and was killed. It is interesting to note that the two locations mentioned in the context of Fionn's death were regarded as enemy territory for him in the early literature. The Boyne area was so regarded because of the control of it by the Connachta and their Luighne subordinates. In the case of the Luachair area of Kerry, this belonged to the western branch of the Eoghanacht sept, rivals of the eastern Eoghanacht of Cashel who had borrowed the Fionn imagery from Leinster.

The delineation and development of Fionn's character continued apace through the Middle Ages. Apart from wisdom, bravery and good looks, the quality most attributed to him was generosity, and some quite creative images were used to illustrate this. We read that if the leaves were gold and the waves silver, Fionn would have given them all away; and so hospitable was he that a troublesome man, whom everybody would avoid, would be invited by Fionn to stay in his house as long as he lived. There were varying accounts of his family. We have mentioned his marriages to Gráinne and Ailbhe, but other sources have him marrying Smirnat (daughter of FOTHADH CANAINNE), Luchar (sister of the same Fothadh), Bearrach Bhreac (foster-sister of GOLL MAC MORNA), Maighnis (sister of the same Goll), Scoithfhionn, Daolach, a Scottish princess called Áine, and otherworld women called Scáthach, Sadhbh and Blái Dheirg. His children are not consistently ascribed to definite wives, but they included the sons Raighne, Iollann, Caoince, Faolán, Aodh Beag, Fearghus, Faobhar, Dáire Dearg and the famous Oisín, while the daughters mentioned are named Grian, Aoi, Samhaoir, Caon and the Lughaidh who became the mother of MAC LUGHACH.

Various other members of his Baoiscne clan are mentioned, and we are left in no doubt that they were a hardy and efficient fighting force. A lay from the thirteenth century describes how at a feast in TARA once, the high-king Cormac insulted Fionn and told him that he would make him pass under the fork of the cauldron. An argument broke out, and the Morna clan sided with Cormac. Fionn and his clan left, and sixteen of them decided to make a foray against Tara as revenge for the insult. They accordingly drove away 1,000 head of cattle, but the mustered forces of Cormac soon caught up with them. The mere sixteen men turned about, made a vicious charge at Cormac's army, and took the king's son CAIRBRE LIFEACHAIR as a hostage. Fionn's son Faolán would accept no ransom except that Cormac himself pass under the fork of the cauldron. Cormac had no choice but to comply, so as to spare the high-king embarrassment, Fionn himself graciously did so also.

The greatest compendium of medieval lore concerning Fionn is entitled *Agallamh na Seanórach* (The Colloquy of the Old Men). Written in the twelfth century and added to in two later versions, it relays scores of stories about the hero and his Fianna troop, placing them in the mouths of Oisín and Caoilte when they were claimed to have lived on and met St Patrick (*see* FIANNA CYCLE). Among these stories, the relations of Fionn with the otherworld continued to evoke most interest. Accounts of his visits to such places usually have the otherworld as a bright and shining place inside some hill-top cairn or other. A common format is to have him and his men hunting through the countryside and, on chasing a fast deer or pig, finding themselves in a strange place, where they are entertained to a great feast. One story has him, with five companions, spending a whole year in the cairn on Slievenamon, and engaging in many otherworld battles in support of their hosts there.

Visits of Fionn and his men to supernatural dwellings prompted some medieval writer to compose an allegory based on the situation. The earliest surviving text of this allegory is a rather confused one dating from around the fifteenth century, and there is no doubt but that it was composed several centuries earlier. It gained great popularity, enough to influence a Norse story of Thor in the thirteenth century, and it is still current in the folklore of the Irish language. It tells of how Fionn and five of his men were benighted while hunting, and came to a strange house. They found there an old man, a beautiful young woman and a ram. A meal was served up to them but, before they could eat, the ram butted the table, knocking all the food on the floor. One by

one, Fionn and each of his men tried to tie the ram to the wall, but failed. Finally, the old man did so without any bother. They ate and then went to bed. During the night, Fionn tried to go to the room of the young woman, but she rejected him, saying that 'you had me once, and you will not have me again'. Puzzled by this strange household, Fionn sought explanations from the old man before they left next morning. He was told that the ram was the world, the old man was age, which subdues all, and the beautiful lady was youth. The oral versions state that, on their departure, the lady gave a special distinctive gift to each of the warriors.

There is a sinister side to the otherworld also. The hostility of Dearg to Fionn, as instanced above in the story of Dearg Corra, recurs in accounts concerning the daughter of that personage. A poem from about the fifteenth century tells how, when Fionn was once drinking with his comrades and their wives in his dwelling on the Hill of Allen, a strange woman arrived and challenged the ladies present to put on her cloak. She explained that only if a woman were chaste would it cover her completely. Most of the ladies present failed the test miserably, and none quite succeeded. At that, the stranger revealed that she was the daughter of Dearg, and had once been the mistress of Fionn. She had come to create unrest among the Fianna. Fionn cursed her and ordered her to leave immediately. There was an old tradition concerning Fionn and this otherworld lover, who was in reality hostile to him. She probably was also the unnamed otherworld lady whom – according to late medieval sources – the hero met one day by the shore of a magical lake near Sliabh gCuillinn (Slieve Gullion, County Armagh). She sadly proclaimed that her bracelet had fallen into the lake, and inveigled Fionn into diving for it. When in the water, he was transformed into an old man, and was hardly recognisable to his comrades when they found him. They then besieged the hill-top cairn where Cuilleann, father of the malicious lady, dwelt. Cuilleann was forced to give a rejuvenating drink to Fionn, but the hair of the hero remained grey.

A story told in texts from the eleventh century describes how a Munster prince presented him with a fine black racehorse, and Fionn set out on a long gallop with this HORSE, accompanied by Caoilte and Oisín on their mounts, until he reached a hillock called Bairneach (south of Killarney). They found a strange house in a glen there and entered, but were set upon within by monstrous people, and had to stay fighting all through the night. With the coming of morn, their attackers and the house faded from view. The idea of Fionn and his men being trapped in sinister otherworld palaces became very popular with the post-medieval writers, who composed several texts on this theme (see FIANNA CYCLE). Its culmination was in the popular folk account of how the Fianna escaped from hell (see OISÍN).

The most colourful text concerning a visit to the otherworld has Fionn going into the mysterious fortress of a certain Conán at Ceann Sléibhe (possibly the headland of that name in west Kerry). Entitled *Feis Tighe Chonáin*, it was written in the fourteenth or fifteenth century by a quite imaginative author, and in it Fionn tells several of his own adventures to his otherworld host. Having conceived a desire for Conán's daughter Findearbh, he was eventually allowed to sleep with her, and a marriage was arranged for a month hence. However, when Fionn and his company arrived for the wedding, they were fiercely attacked by a large contingent led by Findearbh's otherworld wooer Fionnbharr. Conán and his people fought bravely to defend their guests, but the slaughter was massive, and the text mentions no more of the wedding.

Fionn is invariably portrayed as a great hunter of deer and wild pigs, and we read that he used to sit on hill tops to direct the chase. This led to lore concerning his hounds, many of which are mentioned but the most famous being Bran and Sceolaing. Several texts in the medieval literature tell a story of how he acquired this great set of hounds. We read that the king of the Dál nAraidhe (in Counties Antrim and Down) desired Fionn's aunt Uirne as

wife and, when the warrior LUGHAIDH LÁGHA guaranteed that she would be well treated, Fionn agreed to the marriage. However, Uirne was magically turned into a hound by the king's first wife and, as a result, Lughaidh Lágha went and slew the king. Uirne regained her own shape and became the wife of Lughaidh. She bore him triplets, but at the same lying-in brought forth two pups also. These were therefore the cousins of Fionn, and they became his great hunting DOGS. It is clear that some author had been reflecting rather fancifully on the hound-lore associated with LUGHAIDH MAC CON. The image of Bran was particularly developed. It was a massive hound, with its head as high as Fionn's own shoulder. It had two white sides, a purplish haunch, four bluish feet, and a fierce eye in its shapely head. It and Fionn used to make great noise together at feasts, and whenever the Fianna were hungry, Bran would go into the forest and bring their meal to them. Fionn loved the hound with exceptional intensity, and a late medieval writer saw the potential here for pathos. We read that Bran was yelping impatiently once when the quarry was being risen, and Fionn angrily struck it on the head with the leash. The offended Bran stared at its master with tear-filled eyes, then wrenched itself free, and raced to a lake where it drowned itself. Every time afterwards that Fionn heard the baying of a hunting hound, his heart was near to breaking.

Many battles were said to have been fought and won by Fionn, but the number of them actually described is less. These, as well as his military strategies and his household retainers, are discussed in the entry FIANNA CYCLE. A very fertile idea that grew up in the medieval lore – probably due to the imagery of the great runner CAOILTE – was that of helpers who assist him in the achievement of difficult tasks. Thus we read in the twelfth-century colloquy of how a lake burst forth on Sliabh Bladhma (Slieve Bloom, County Laois) and was spreading out to cover all Leinster. Fionn, however, managed to avert that catastrophe through the help of magicians and female warriors from India, Germany, England and France, who sucked up all the water. Such motifs were obviously borrowed from general folklore plots concerning marvellous helpers with incredible abilities (*see* WONDER TALES, type 513), and they became a frequent aspect of stories concerning the Fianna (q.v.).

In a text from the fifteenth century or thereabouts, we read of how Fionn was hunting one day when he was approached by eleven strange youths, who said that they were searching for a worthy master. They explained that they each had a great ability, these abilities being respectively answering questions, kindling fires, serving at table, dividing wealth, listening, strength, tracking, running, shooting, climbing and stealing. Fionn took them into his employ, and brought them with him to Dublin. The king of that place asked Fionn to protect his wife who was about to give birth, for she had already borne seven babies and they had all been taken away by a GIANT at night. Fionn undertook this task, and told his helpers to use their special skills to serve a meal for the household and to stand guard. However, the giant came and put his hand through the roof. The strong helper tore the limb away from its body, but the giant put in the other hand and took the baby away. Fionn, with his tracker and other helpers, followed on by land and sea. They came to an island, the lord of which challenged them to race against his daughter for her hand. If she won the race, they would lose their heads, but Fionn's fast runner defeated her and thereby won the beautiful princess for Fionn. Resuming their quest for the stolen baby, they came to a great cliff in the sea. The climber scaled this cliff and saw the giant sleeping there with all of the children of the king and queen of Dublin, as well as two fine pups. He told this to Fionn, who instructed him to bring the thief on his back to the cliff top, and in this way the children were recovered by Fionn. The giant, however, followed on, but was beheaded by Fionn, and all returned happily to Dublin. The pups became the two great hounds of Fionn, namely Bran and Sceolaing.

This story, versions of which have been very popular in folklore, has a complicated history. A narrative was current in medieval times in either Ireland or Wales concerning how a baby was stolen by a giant hand coming through the roof, and this narrative had attached to itself the well-known Celtic motif of animals who are congenital with humans. The independent Irish story of how Bran and Sceolaing were born also became attached to this, and so Fionn was brought into the story. He in turn caused the plot to be much lengthened by the inclusion of folk plots concerning extraordinary helpers (WONDER TALES, types 513 and 653, both of which are embedded in this developed story).

The dramatic scenario of Fionn opposing a giant proved very productive in later Irish folklore. Such accounts usually have Fionn triumphing through wile, and several folklore plots were borrowed to illustrate this. The most frequent account – collected all over Ireland and also in Scotland and the Isle of Man – can hardly be more than a few centuries old. It describes how a giant visits Fionn's house intending to engage him in combat, but the clever Fionn jumps into the cradle and pretends to be the baby. As he waits for the 'father' to come home, the giant plays with the 'baby', who wastes no time in biting off the visitor's finger. When told by Fionn's wife that the Fianna children are born with sharp teeth, the giant imagines that Fionn himself must be an horrific fighter and flees in dread. This is a Gaelic ecotype (*see* FOLKTALE) of an international narrative plot (*see* HUMOROUS TALES, type 1149).

A more recent stratum of lore, particularly strong in the English language, has Fionn himself portrayed as a giant. Elements of this grew from the tendency towards hyperbole in Gaelic narrative, and also from the custom of associating various landmarks with Fionn. The medieval literature already has mention of *Suí Finn* as the name of a mountain top, the notion being that he sat there to observe the hunt. Variants of this place name occur all over Ireland for hill tops and mountain ledges, and folk fancy increases the size of Fionn to suit the elevations. Similarly, certain great flagstones are claimed to have been his griddle, and even level hill tops his table. Some great boulders are said to have been stones thrown by Fionn in contest with giants. Quite comical are claims that he tore up great sods from the ground and threw them overseas at a giant in England. Thus, in such a contest, the island known as Ireland's Eye off the Dublin coast was a sod torn from the ground by him in County Wicklow, thereby causing the larger lake to spring up at Glendalough; and this is more than matched by another claim that the Isle of Man is a sod flung by him from the site of Lough Neagh.

It is clear that, having held the stage in many centuries of storytelling, Fionn has come to represent many aspects of the human psyche – positive and negative, traditional and innovatory, serious and humorous.

EARLY SOURCES: O'Brien (1962), 22–3, 45, 99; Meyer (1903) & (1906), 30–1 & (1910), xvi–xxii, 1–3, 18–27 & in ZCP, 8, 105, 117–18; V.E. Hull in ZCP, 30, 17–20; M. O'Daly (1975), 82–8; Ó Muraíle, 2 (2003), 196–8.

SHAMANICHOOD: Meyer (1910), 50; M. Dillon in Ériu, 11, 49.

LOMHNA: Stokes (1862), 34–5; Meyer (1912), 87–8; Dillon in Ériu, 11, 48–9, 58–61.

DEARG CORRA: Meyer in RC, 25, 344–8; E.J. Gwynn in Ériu, 11, 152–3.

CUIRREACH: Meyer in RC, 14, 242–3; Hull in Speculum, 16, 323–4.

CÚLDUBH: Meyer in RC, 14, 245–6 & 25, 344–6; Hull in Speculum, 16, 329–33; Ó hÓgáin (1988), 52–5.

WISDOM POETRY AND PROPHECIES: F. Henry (1940), 109–10; Stokes (1900), 52, 148; J.G. O'Keeffe in Irish Texts, 4, 39–44; Ó hÓgáin (1988), 37–8, 70–2, 329.

YOUTHFUL ADVENTURES: Gwynn (1906), 72–6 & (1910), 72–7; Meyer (1885), 72–6 & (1910), xxii–xxxi, 46–51 & in RC, 5, 195–204 & in ZCP, 1, 458–65; W.M. Hennessy in RC, 2, 86–93; R. Thurneysen in ZCP, 13, 251–82; Hull in ZCP, 18, 422–4; Hull & J.R. Reinard in Speculum, 11, 42–58; Stokes (1900), 47–50 & in RC, 7, 289–307; L-C. Stern in ZCP, 13, 12–22; Christiansen (1931), 20–5; G. Murphy (1953), 103–4; Bruford (1969), 132–3; Ó hÓgáin (1988), 81–102, 275–9, 342.

FIONN AS RÍGHFHÉINNIDH: Stokes (1900), 50, 146 & in Irische Texte, 3, 199 & in RC, 7, 292; Meyer (1910), 44; Gwynn (1913), 130, 250; Stern in ZCP, 1, 472; O'Grady, 1 (1892), 92–3; Best, Bergin & O'Brien (1967), 1275–87; Ó hÓgáin (1988), 102–5.

GRÁINNE: see DIARMAID UA DUIBHNE.

AILBHE: R. Thurneysen in ZCP, 13, 254–6; Ó hÓgáin (1988), 106–7.

DEATH OF FIONN: Meyer (1910), xxi, xxv–xxvi, 92–8 & in ZCP, 1, 462–5; Gwynn (1906), 12; Best, Bergin & O'Brien (1954), 131;

O'Donovan, 1 (1848–51), 120; Stokes (1887), 536 & (1900), 50 & in RC, 17, 21 & in RC, 23, 310; Meyer (1885), 73–5; J.G. O'Keeffe in Irish Texts 4, 41; Ó hÓgáin (1988), 108–13, 279–81.

GENEROSITY OF FIONN: Stokes (1900), 4, 116, 211; N. Ross (1939), 190–2; Ó hÓgáin (1988), 118–20, 335.

FIONN'S RELATIVES AND FAMILY: Hull in ZCP, 18, 422–4; Meyer (1885), 74 & (1910), xxix; Stokes (1900), 29, 60–2, 78–81, 86–8, 102, 178–80; E. Mac Neill (1908), 25; G. Murphy (1933), 20–9, 104, 108; Ní Shéaghdha (1967), 1, 96; Ó hÓgáin (1988), 105–8, 151–9.

CORMAC–FIONN WAR: E. Mac Neill (1908), 4–6; G. Murphy (1933), 344–60.

AGALLAMH: Stokes (1900); Ní Shéaghdha (1942) & (1945); D. de híde in Lia Fáil, 1, 79–107.

ALLEGORICAL STORY: Joynt (1936), 14–20; R. Power in Béaloideas, 53, 217–94; Ó hÓgáin (1988), 234–40, 339–40.

HOSTILE LADIES: T.P. Cross in Modern Philology, 16, 158–62; Stokes (1900), 68–9, 135–6, 208; Joynt (1936), 34–40, 44; Ó Siochfhradha (1941), 74–9, 81–5.

OTHERWORLD HOUSE AS TRAP: Stokes in RC, 7, 290–305 & 13, 3–12; E. Mac Neill (1908), 28–30; Ní Shéaghdha, 1 (1942), 169–81.

FEIS TIGHE CHONÁIN: Joynt (1936), 1–57.

FIONN'S HOUNDS: G. Murphy (1933), 198–202 & (1953), 103–4, 123; Stokes (1900), 5–9, 62–3, 97; Ó hÓgáin (1988), 123–32, 190, 333–4, 359.

MARVELLOUS HELPERS: Stokes (1900), 123; Ó hÓgáin (1988), 183–91. See FIANNA CYCLE.

FIONN AND GIANTS: Joynt (1936), 21–34; Stokes (1900), 3, 58–9, 62–3; D. de híde in Lia Fáil, 1, 98; G. Murphy (1953), xvi; S. Ó Súilleabháin & Christiansen (1967), 218–19; E. Evans in Ulster Folklife, 21, 85–9; Ó hÓgáin (1988), 188–90, 303–10, 345–6.

FOLKLORE: Ó hÓgáin (1988), 275–310, 342–6.

DISCUSSIONS: Christiansen (1931); Ó Cadhlaigh (1947); G. Murphy (1953); Nagy (1985); MacKillop (1986); Ó hÓgáin (1988); Pettersson (1999).

Fionnachta HIGH-KING of the Uí NÉILL from AD 674–95. The basic form of his name seems to have been Fíonsneachta (meaning 'snow-wine' in the sense of possessing wine as plentiful as snow), and it was often accompanied by the epithet Fleadhach (bountiful).

His father was called Dúnchadh and, though a brother of the high-kings Bláthmhac and DIARMAID MAC AODHA SLÁINE, was not prominent in political life. Fanciful lore therefore grew up to explain how Fionnachta became high-king. It was said that he was a poor man, and that he and his wife had but one ox and one cow between them. The king of Fir Rois (a sept inhabiting parts of Counties Monaghan, Armagh and Louth) was benighted in a storm and took shelter at the hut of Fionnachta.

The latter killed the ox and cow in order to feed the king and his company, and out of gratitude that king later presented him with a large herd of cattle, pigs and sheep, and many other riches besides. This account may be based on a folklore plot (*see* RELIGIOUS TALES, type 750B).

One day, as Fionnachta was on his way to a banquet, he met the young St ADHAMHNÁN, who was travelling as a poor scholar. Adhamhnán ran out of the horse's way, and let fall a pitcher of milk that he was carrying on his back. The pitcher was smashed and, seeing this, Fionnachta offered to pay for its cost and brought Adhamhnán and his five fellow students with him to the banquet. The tutor of Adhamhnán then prophesied that Fionnachta would one day be high-king and that Adhamhnán would be his adviser until insulted by him. The prophecy was verified, though in a less than honourable manner, when Fionnachta fought a battle against his own cousin Ceannfhaolaidh to gain the throne.

After Fionnachta remitted the *BÓRAIMHE* tribute to St MOLING on behalf of the Leinstermen, Adhamhnán quarrelled with his decision because he regarded it as an insult to the supremacy of their UÍ NÉILL sept, and thus the second part of the prophecy was fulfilled. Under pressure from Adhamhnán, Fionnachta changed his mind and vainly tried to capture Moling, who cursed him as a result. We read that this curse led to Fionnachta being treacherously slain by close relatives who were rivals for the kingship. He and his son Breasal were in a tent at Greallach Dolaidh (Girley, near Kells, County Meath) when they were attacked and beheaded.

O'Donovan (1860), 70–85, 94–7; W. Stokes in *RC*, *13*, 98–117; Macalister (1956), 382–3; O'Grady, *1* (1892), 402–6; Dinneen, *3* (1908), 138–41.

Fionnchú SAINT who died *c.*AD 664, founder of a monastery at Brí Gobhann (Brigown, now Mitchelstown, County Cork). The name (earlier, Findchú) meant 'fair-haired hero'. It was sometimes written as Findchua and is anglicised as Fanahan.

He was noted for his self-mortification in order to save souls from hell, and an apparently early source places emphasis on this. We read that when a corpse was brought to his church, he used to spend the night in the mortuary with it, suspending himself from the wall by an iron sickle in each armpit. By this sacrificial practice, he prevented the devil from approaching and taking the soul of the dead person.

The tradition of Fionnchú developed greatly through the Middle Ages, and a biography in Irish from the eleventh or twelfth century adds MOTIFS that make him more of a romantic hero than a conventional saint. According to this biography, he was son of an Ulsterman called Findlugh, who was banished after plotting against the high-king of Ireland. Findlugh had made pregnant a girl called Iodhnait, and this girl was looked after by the Munster king. Once, when she sought a drink of ale from some brewers and was refused, the child in her womb spoke a rhetoric and caused the vats to burst. When the child was born, he was baptised by St AILBHE, and when he reached seven years of age was noticed by the visiting Ulster saint COMHGHALL, who took the boy to his celebrated monastery of Bangor (in County Down). When Fionnchú was guarding the monastery's meadow one day, the king of Ulster placed his horses there and refused to move them, but Fionnchú turned the horses into stones and caused the angry king to sink to his knees into the ground. He restored both king and horses when Comhghall begged him to do so. He became a close friend and confidant of Comhghall and, when the latter died, succeeded him as abbot.

Having spent seven years in the abbacy of Bangor, Fionnchú returned to the south and was given a site for a new monastery by the king of Munster. Seven smiths came to assist him in the building, and hence the place was known as Brí Gobhann, which meant 'the hillock of the smiths'. They made seven iron sickles for him, and he hung himself on these for seven years so as to ensure a place in heaven for himself. From his monastery of Brigown, this biography claims, he sallied forth on several occasions to assist those in need of military support. He helped Seachnasach, king of TARA, to repel foreign marauders; helped a king of Leinster called Nuadhu against the Uí Chinsealaigh sept that was challenging him; helped the Munstermen to rout an invading Ulster army and defeat an attempted invasion by the royal Uí NÉILL sept of Tara; and helped the Connachtmen against another foreign set of raiders. On each occasion, he first offered peace to the aggressors, and only when the offer was rejected did he play his role of *cathaighe conghalach* (valiant warrior). In that role, he led the fighting men into battle, brandishing his crozier, emitting fire from his mouth, and causing the foe to shrink and to lose their vigour. The text rather fancifully derives his name from his great martial competence, stating that he fought like a hound (*cú*) in a battle on behalf of his mother's sept, the Ciarraighe. Finally, he went to Rome to repent of the battles he had fought, dying there within a year.

The artificial character of this biography is obvious. For instance, the bursting of the ale vats is borrowed from the lore concerning the satirist AITHIRNE, while the episode of the Ulster king grazing his horses on a sacred site is based on a story of St PATRICK. A Leinster king called 'old Nuadhu Éigeas' is anachronistically borrowed from the mythology of that province (*see* NUADHU). Nevertheless, the account is rich in adventure, and variants of it survived in the folklore of the Mitchelstown district. Fionnchú's feast day is 25 November.

Kenney (1929), 457–8; Stokes (1905), 246 & (1890), 84–98; O'Donovan (1864), 316–19; IFC 128:133, 407:332–3, 556:142–9, 155–6, 947:148–51.

Fionntan Mythical seer in Irish literary tradition. He is described as son of Bóchna or Bóchra, who does not appear as a character. The patronymic really meant 'sea', and originally must have reflected an aspect of myth concerning water as a source of wisdom for seers. The name Fionntan (earlier, Fintan) is probably derived from a Celtic compound *Vindo-senos*, which would have

meant 'old Find'. This suggests that Fionntan was a variant in ancient lore of the great mythical seer Find (*see* FIONN).

Fionntan was portrayed as a seer who had lived for hundreds of years and who thus had detailed knowledge of past events. The writers of pseudo-history interpreted Bóchna as the name of his mother, and claimed that his father's name had been Labhraidh. Fionntan, they said, had come to Ireland with the lady CEASAIR and her group of settlers 40 days before the Deluge described in the Bible. There were 50 women and three men in the group, and Fionntan took Ceasair as wife. When the two other men died, all the women came to him, but he fled from them. A poem put into his mouth tells of how the flood came and he alone survived it. He was hidden in the earth at Tul Tuinne (Tounthinna, the hill over the River Shannon near Portroe, County Tipperary), and remained there until the inundation had passed away.

One text, accepting the pseudo-historical setting for him, nevertheless embodies some genuine mythic elements. This has him in conversation with a hawk from Acaill (Achill, County Mayo) and gives him the opportunity to tell his story in detail. He was fifteen years of age when the Deluge came, and lived for five-and-a-half thousand years thereafter. During that period, he had gone through transformations – first as a one-eyed salmon, then as an eagle, and then a falcon, before re-assuming his own shape. In their conversation, the hawk tells that it too is very old, and has witnessed all the major events of the country's history, such as the various reputed settlements, the Battles of Moytirra (*see* MYTHOLOGICAL CYCLE), the deeds of CÚ CHULAINN, the reigns of CONN CÉADCHATHACH and many other KINGS, until the coming of Christianity. Here we note the relaying of such heroic lore within the setting of the international storytelling MOTIF of the OLDEST CREATURE.

This text also introduces a new motif into the lore of Fionntan, claiming that he had once met a strange man who offered him a branch of fruit, and that when he ate this fruit, he was rejuvenated. Another text tells that at the time of the Crucifixion of JESUS, a stranger called Trefuilngid came from abroad and persuaded Fionntan to become a Christian. The stranger relayed to him a vast quantity of knowledge concerning the history and geography of the country. As a result of these encounters, Fionntan was replete with the ancient lore of Ireland.

It is clear that these texts have confused the original notion, which was that Fionntan himself had through his longevity and wanderings in various shapes acquired all the information. He could thus boast concerning Ireland that 'I am knowledgeable in its feasts and in its cattle-raids, in its destructions and its courtships, in all that has been done'. This statement is, in fact, a synopsis of what the POETS and learned men of early Ireland should know, and it underlines Fionntan's role as a mythical projection of such sages. One text has him dramatically fulfilling that role by coming to the historical high-king DIARMAID MAC CEARRBHEOIL and answering all the questions put to him by the king and his assembly at TARA. The basic myth involved is how the great seer gained much of his wisdom through transforming himself into the forms of various animals (see FIONN).

The format of the Fionntan story that survives, however, has him recast fully in the terms of reference of medieval culture as a Christian witness to Ireland's pagan past. The account of his meeting with the high-king has him describing the proper procedures for the ruling of Ireland, and then states that he went to Dún Tulcha (at Kenmare Bay, County Kerry). Worn out by age, he prepared for death and received the sacraments from a bishop called Earc. The text states that the place of his burial was unknown, but that some people considered that he had been carried away to some secret place to await the final Resurrection.

Macalister (1939), 166–229; K. Meyer in *AIM 1*, 24–39; R.I. Best in *Ériu*, 4, 121–37; Gwynn (1903), 2–5 & (1913), 236–9 & (1924), 256–7; Vendryes (1953), 4–6, 36–7; D. Hyde in *The Celtic Review*, 10, 138–40; W.M. Hennessy & Kelly (1875), 6–11, 98–9, 248–75; Mac Cionnaith (1938), 202–4.

Fíothal Fictional judge at the court of the celebrated high-king CORMAC MAC AIRT. The name (also written Fítheal) meant literally 'calf', and there are some indications that the character originated in the same context of FIANNA hunting-lore as OISÍN and OSCAR.

A fourteenth-century poem states that Fíothal was one of two brothers of FIONN MAC CUMHAILL, and claims that this was an old tradition. The other brother of Fionn named in the poem is Féinnidh (Fianna-leader), and it is therefore likely that this tradition was an echo of an ancient triplication of Fionn, the hero with a strong residue of ritual and myth. Fionn was in one text given the name 'Demne', which probably meant 'little stag', and in meaning this would approximate to the name Fíothal. It therefore seems that Fíothal was adopted into the context of Cormac from Fianna lore when these two hostile sagas were being synchronised with each other in or about the eighth century. This situation may be reflected in one text in which a young man called Socht, son of Fíothal, is claimed to have been a hostage at the court of Cormac at the same time as Fíothal himself was a judge there. In the later medieval literature, Fíothal is represented as an arbitrator in disputes between the FIANNA generally, as well as between Fionn and Cormac. Several collections of wise maxims were assembled and claimed to have been instructions given by him.

The seventeenth-century historian Seathrún CÉITINN relates a relevant story that he apparently had from some written source. This describes how Fíothal, when dying, gave four advices to his son Flaithrí, viz. not to rear a king's son, not to tell a dangerous secret to his wife, not to promote the son of a slave, and not to entrust his wealth to the keeping of his sister. After Fíothal died, Flaithrí decided to test the advices. He therefore promoted the son of one of his servants, and that young man grew extremely rich; and Flaithrí also entrusted a portion of his own treasures to his sister. He then took the son of Cormac as a pupil, and soon after left the boy with a swine-herd in the forest, with instructions to hide him away until summoned. Returning home, he affected great dejection and, on being pressed by his wife concerning this, at length told her that he had killed his royal pupil, and bound her to secrecy in the matter. Immediately, however, she informed the authorities, and Flaithrí was seized. The young man whom he had promoted was one of his strongest accusers, wishing for an opportunity to gain Flaithrí's property at a low price. Flaithrí called on his sister to go bail for him, but she denied that he had ever entrusted money to her. Realising the dire straits he was in, he called for a private conversation with Cormac, and told the KING where the prince was. He was therefore allowed to send word to the swineherd, and the prince was released. Flaithrí then explained that he had been testing the advices of Fíothal and had found them to be good.

This story is based on a common folklore plot, but its details represent a rather rare variety (*see* ROMANTIC TALES, types 910 *and* 911). Miscellaneous mentions of advices against telling a secret to one's wife and promoting a slave in ninth and tenth-century texts suggest that the plot was known in Ireland by that time, and at some stage in the interval it got attached to Fíothal. There was probably a tendency to consider the name of this judge as synonymous with his profession, and one source even situates him at the fifth-century court of the high-king LAOGHAIRE.

Mac Neill (1908), 18; G. Murphy (1933), 104–5, 110–11, 132–7 & (1953), 108, 371; Ní Shéaghda & Ní Mhuirgheasa (1941), 38–9; W. Stokes in *Irische Texte, 3*, 199–202; R.M. Smith in *RC, 45*, 1–92 & 47, 30–8; Dinneen, 2 (1908), 338–43; Á. Ní Chróinín in *Éigse, 3*, 67–8; Binchy (1978), 1654.

Fir Bolg A people who, according to the medieval historians, occupied Ireland in ancient times. The designation meant *Bolg*-men, and seems to have in reality meant 'those who swell' with battle-fury. It was similar to the Celtic population name found in Britain and north-western Europe under the form Belgae. Another instance of the word occurs in 'Bolgios', the name or title of a famous Continental Celtic leader; while the name of the javelin of CÚ CHULAINN was *ga bolga*, probably a reflex from the famous battle-fury of that mythical hero. It is apparent that a group of early Celtic settlers in Ireland were called Bolgae or such, although they probably had no connection with the actual Belgae. The genealogists of early medieval times often designated septs by prefacing *fir* (men) to their name; hence these ancient inhabitants came to be known as Fir Bolg.

What the narrative literature tells of this population group is, however, mere conjecture and fantasy. They were claimed to have been descendants of Semeon, grandson of NEIMHEADH, who left Ireland and went to Greece. His progeny increased till they were numbered in thousands, but they were enslaved by the Greeks, being made to carry loads of clay onto bare rocks in order to turn the barren landscape into a fruitful plain. It was claimed that they carried this clay in bags (*boilg*) – hence the fanciful derivation of their name as 'bag-men'. An alternative notion was that the Greek king gave them to inhabit a territory full of venomous reptiles, and that as protection against these creatures, they carried about with them bags of Irish clay. Eventually, they left Greece and set sail for Ireland.

When they arrived, their five leaders divided the country among them from the vantage point of Uisneach (Ushnagh, County Westmeath), which was regarded as the exact centre of the country. Thus the writers of pseudo-history explained the origin of the division of Ireland into five provinces; the word *cúige* (fifth) is still used for a province, even though since medieval times there have been only four. The idea of the Fir Bolg was used not only for aetiological explanation, but also for the synchronising of data. Thus we are told that, properly speaking, the descendants of Semeon who came into Ireland were in three sections. These were the Fir Bolg proper, the Gaileoin, and the Fir Domhnann. As in the case of the first section, fanciful etymologies were used to explain the designations of the other two. The Gaileoin, we are told, were named from 'the javelins of

253

wounding' (*gai leoin*) with which they dug the clay in Greece; while the Fir Domhnann were named from the deepness (*domhaine*) of the clay when it was heaped onto the rocks. In reality, Gaileoin was an alternative name for the LAIGHIN (Leinstermen), and the Fir Domhnann were a group settled in various parts of Ireland whose name is cognate with the Celtic Dumnonii of Britain and western Europe. Whatever the relationships between these various Celtic groups in antiquity, the medieval historians imagined them as having been one extended tribe.

The Fir Bolg, it was claimed, were in possession of Ireland for 37 years, until the coming of the TUATHA DÉ DANANN, who conquered them at the first Battle of Moytirra (*see* MYTHOLOGICAL CYCLE). Some medieval historians claimed that after this battle, the Fir Bolg settled in islands off the coasts of Ireland and Scotland. Much later, presumably, the Fir Bolg were claimed to have been driven from these islands by the CRUITHNIGH, and they returned to Ireland. They entered the service of the TARA king Cairbre Nia Fear, and gave him sureties; but they later rebelled against him because of the heavy taxes he imposed on them. Their leader was Aonghus, son of Umhor, and he brought them to Meadhbh in Connacht, who gave them lands in the islands and outlying areas. The enraged Cairbre, however, enlisted four warriors to destroy them: CÚ CHULAINN, CEAT MAC MÁGHACH, CONALL CEARNACH and Ros mac Deadha. The pseudo-historians continued in this fanciful vein, claiming that Cairbre's men eventually overthrew the Fir Bolg in all their new strongholds.

The pseudo-historians claimed that the greatest of these strongholds was the massive cliff fortress on Inishmore, the largest of the Aran Islands, County Galway. Seizing on a pre-existent name or inventing a new name for the edifice, they claimed that this had been constructed by Aonghus and his Fir Bolg. Archaeology indicates that this fortress, Dún Aonghusa, was constructed in the final centuries BC, and the medieval writers, like modern theorists, recognised

the likelihood that the builders were some group of people who had retreated to the islands and who felt themselves beleaguered there.

The pseudo-historians, of course, were satisfied to let fancy explain ancient edifices, and also the fate of ancient peoples. More realistically, other medieval writers described the eventual assimilation of the Fir Bolg to the ÉRAINN, which was the designation of the general body of non-dominant septs in early medieval Ireland.

BELGAE, BOLGIOS, *GA BOLGA*: Ó hÓgáin (2002), 10, 51, 2, 102–4, 147–60, 197.

GENERAL: Macalister (1940), 144–9 & (1941), 1–111; A.G. Van Hamel in *ZCP*, *10*, 160–3, 186–90; Ó Raithbheartaigh (1932), 53–92, 101–31; J. Carey in *CMCS*, *16*, 77–83; Ó Muraíle, *1* (2003), 206–47.

fish The salmon was the favourite fish of many generations of Irish people, and accordingly this fish has more lore attached to it than any other of its species. The famous 'salmon of knowledge', eaten by FIONN MAC CUMHAILL, was used as a symbol by the ancient seer-POETS, not only due to mystical ideas but also to the fine taste and nutrition of this fish. Because of its superb jumping ability, the salmon was regarded as the epitome of good physical and mental condition, and so *sláinte an bhradáin* (the health of the salmon) was a standard term used in wishing a person well. It was so closely identified with human beings, indeed, that each person was said to have an internal 'salmon of life' in their body (*see* HUMAN LIFE), and drowned people were sometimes said to appear after death in the form of large black salmon on a river.

Little narrative lore was current about other types of fish, apart from the tendency to explain marks on some of them as having been left by JESUS CHRIST while He was a fisherman on earth, and the widespread claim that the plaice got its crooked mouth from mocking St PATRICK or some other of the SAINTS (*see* ANIMAL TALES, type 250A). An interesting belief was that many holy wells had a little trout in them (*see* ENVIRONMENT). This trout, usually white in colour, was believed to be sacred, and for a sick devotee at the well to see it was a token that a cure was imminent.

The eel, on account of its unusual appearance and mode of travel overland, was an object of much speculation. Its tenacity gave rise to the idea that dead eels might sometimes come to life again, and that HORSE-hair left in water for a long time turned into an eel. There were some sinister echoes in the lore, such as a tradition that large eels could sometimes be seen going into graves to eat corpses. In inland parts of Munster, a story of how a captured seal was called back to the sea by its comrade has come to be told of an eel from a lake (*see* WILD ANIMALS). On stories concerning fish, *see also* OLDEST CREATURE *and* WONDER TALES (type 736A).

Cross (1952), 46, 51, 54, 56–9, 61–2, 68, 73–7, 79, 82; O'Meara (1982), 37–8, 65; Wood-Martin, 2 (1902), 109–13; S. Ó Súilleabháin (1942), 297–300; Ó Danachair (1978), 25; D. Fitzgerald in RC, 4, 186; IFC Index.

FitzGerald Surname of the leading NORMAN-Gaelic family in Ireland. The eponymous ancestor was Gerald of Windsor, who married Nesta, son of the king of north Wales, Rhys ap Tewdwr. The son of this union, Maurice FitzGerald, came to Ireland with the Norman conqueror Richard de Clare (Strongbow) in 1169, and got widespread lands in Ireland.

From Maurice's son Gerald, lord of Offaly, were descended the Earls of KILDARE; and from another son, Thomas, were descended the Earls of DESMOND. Both earldoms were founded in the early fourteenth century. The surname was gaelicised as Mac Gearailt, and collectively the family was known as 'Gearaltaigh' in Irish and 'Geraldines' in English. For two centuries, the two great Geraldine earldoms were predominant in Ireland, occupying a kind of middle ground between English and native Irish interests, but they were both decimated by the English authorities in the sixteenth century.

Their prestige was high throughout Europe, and a leading family of Florentine magnates, the Gherardini, claimed relationship with them and kept in close contact with them. The supposed connection with the Gherardini seems to have arisen from the activities in Florence of a Munster cleric, Father Maurice FitzGerald, who made the acquaintance of the nobles of that city as he travelled through Florence in 1413. The result was frequent correspondence between the Gherardini and both Geraldine earldoms. The Renaissance poet Ludovico Ariosto referred approvingly to 'il Conte de Childera' and 'il Conte di Desmonda' in his famous poem *Orlando Furioso*; and the genealogists invented an ancestry for the Italian and Irish families. This traced their origin to a companion of the ancient Greek hero Aeneas of Troy, on whom Aeneas conferred the region of Etruria, or Tuscany, where the city of Florence later stood. This unnamed warrior was thus claimed to have been the ancestor of both the Gherardini and the Geraldines, the latter reputedly descended from a Florentine knight called Rollo who joined the Norman invasion of England. As a result of this fabrication, the Geraldines were often referred to in Irish tradition as 'the Grecian family'.

There were many famous members of the Geraldine family in Irish history, but the most significant old stories are discussed here under the headings DESMOND and KILDARE.

Meehan (1878); FitzGerald (1951); A. Fitzgibbon in JRSAI, 14, 246–64; Kildare (1858) & (1872); Bryan (1933); Ó hÓgáin in Bonanno (2000), 17–24.

Flann mac Lónáin A chief-POET of Ireland, whose death is put down to AD 918 or 920. Son of one Lónán, his name Flann was a common one, meaning 'blood-red'. He was known as Flann Aidhne, which indicates that he was a native of Aidhne, an area in south Galway and north Clare.

Little is known concerning him. Possibly due to his skill in storytelling, a source from near to his own time relates an adventure concerning himself and a dramatic character from ancient lore. We read that Flann and his subordinate poets were once in an empty house, very hungry, when an ugly GIANT came to them with a cudgel in one hand and a bullock in the other. In return for the promise of a milking cow, he killed and divided the bullock among them and then departed. A year later, he returned with five other giants to demand the cow that had been promised. Mac Lónáin demanded to know his name, and he said that he was Fiodhbhadhach (forest-man). Flann recited a poem describing the situation, and the stranger then said that this recitation was the 'cow' that he had come for. He revealed that he was none other than AONGHUS, the 'Mac Óg'.

One source gives to Flann the reputation of surliness and greed. We read that after his death, his harpist offended another poet, Mac Liag, by praising his great knowledge to the detriment of the latter. Flann, the harpist said, could name all the places to be seen from Sliabh nEachtga (Slieve Aughty, south Galway). Mac Liag said that he would have the harpist hanged by the morning, but Flann appeared at dawn and proved by a poem that he knew all the lore in question. This story is obviously of a type with the discovery of the *Táin* epic by SEANCHÁN and the proof of the antiquarian knowledge of MONGÁN. Another late medieval source develops this notion by stating that Flann was murdered and was buried in Tulach Mochaimhe (near Terryglass, north Tipperary), but he arose on the day after to recite a poem on himself and the other five people interred with him.

O.J. Bergin in *AIM*, 1, 45–50; Gwynn (1913), 532–3; J.G. O'Keeffe in *Irish Texts*, 1, 22–4; C. Ó Lochlainn in *Éigse*, 4, 42–5.

Flannán SAINT who died in AD 778, abbot of the monastery of Cill Dalua (Killaloe, County Clare). The name is a diminutive of Flann ('blood-red'), which was a common name in early Ireland.

Flannán was son of Toirdhealbhach, a king of the sept called DÁL GCAIS in that area. This Toirdhealbhach was the son of Aodh Caomh, who had patronised St DALUA. A brother of Flannán, called Mathghamhain, was the progenitor of the sept's major line that culminated in the famous BRIAN BÓRAMHA. It is thus not surprising that the memory of Flannán – as their own special Churchman – was regarded with great respect by the Dál gCais, and that he was heroised by the compilers of his biography.

The surviving biographical text, in Latin, dates from the twelfth century and is very fanciful. Perhaps realistically, it states that he was educated by a monk called Blathmet and then by Dalua, founder of the Killaloe monastery, and while still young decided to become a monk. Accounts of his miraculous power are soon to the fore, however. When sent once to work at a mill, he remained at his task overnight, and his fingers emitted light after he had breathed on them. Dalua was so impressed by the young man that he resigned from the abbacy and persuaded Flannán to succeed him. Flannán then went to Rome to be consecrated by the Pope, and on his journey crossed the sea on a rock that miraculously floated for him. On his return, he delivered so effective a sermon to his congregation that his father Toirdhealbhach, who was listening, decided to give up his throne and become a monk. The king thus quietly departed for the monastery of Lismore (in County Waterford), where he was accepted by St Colmán, who was the abbot there.

Several of Flannán's adventures concern how he overcame robbers and brought them to repentance. For instance, the meat of oxen they steal cannot be cooked and turns rotten before the robbers' eyes. We further read that, on one occasion, he turned into stone a group of jesters who threatened to satirise him. During his episcopate, the crops grew copiously and the sea was full of fish, the trees full of fruit, and the poor were generously cared for. This is a borrowing of the conventional description of the kingship of a good ruler. A new monastery, founded for the Dál gCais by Flannán, is now the site of the Church of Ireland cathedral in the town of Killaloe. His relics were kept there, and were much venerated. His feast day is 18 December.

Kenney (1929), 404–5; Malone (1902).

Fliodhais Fictional lady (earlier, Flidais), famous for her CATTLE. Her name (originally meaning 'wet one') referred to liquid, and in particular to milk. She is sometimes given the epithet *foltchaoin*, which means 'soft-haired'.

Some accounts have her as one of the TUATHA DÉ DANANN, among whom she is said to have had four daughters, but her husband is not named. In what appears to be the original tradition, she is described as wife of a fictional Munster king Adhamair (earlier, Amadair) and, through this husband, mother of another king, NIADH SEAGHAMAIN, who was fancifully claimed to have been a milker of deer. Thus she was said to have had a herd of deer as well as of cattle, and both wild and domesticated animals were known as her 'cattle' (*buar Fliodhais*). The fact that her name is not declined would lead to suspicion that she was an invention of the writers. The apparent explanation is that the genitive of a noun *flidas* was connected to the name of Niadh Seaghamhain, and that this in time was taken to be the name of his mother. In this way, a fictional lady called Fliodhais coincided with the image of the mother-goddess as patron of milking animals (*see* the associations of the MÓR-RÍOGHAIN and of BRIGHID with cattle, and of OISÍN's mother Blái Dheirg with deer).

Fliodhais, having grown out of Munster genealogical lore, was soon given a different context. Doubtlessly because of her role as patron of cattle, she was brought into association with the Ulster worthy, FEARGHUS MAC RÓICH – who had equine connections – and became his consort. We are told that she alone could satisfy his sexual appetite, whereas when she was absent he required no less than seven women. One of the tales of the ULSTER CYCLE told of how Fearghus wooed and won her. Here she is described as wife of Ailill Fionn (earlier, Ailill Find), king of the Gamhanra sept (in present-day County Mayo). When at the court of queen MEADHBH, the satiric poet BRICRIU arranged for Fearghus and her to meet. They fell in love with each other, and accordingly began to plot against Ailill Fionn. The latter, suspecting treachery, made captives of Fearghus and his men when they came to feast at the fortress of Fliodhais. She, however, plied her husband with drink, knowing that he would release

Fearghus through his noble nature when his senses were befuddled. Once free, Fearghus joined Meadhbh's forces in an attack on his rival. Ailill Fionn fought bravely against vastly superior odds. When all his men had fallen, he asked a smith called Ceartan to allow him to escape in that smith's boat, but Ceartan refused, whereupon Ailill Fionn beheaded him with a slingshot as he sailed away. Fighting alone against his foes, Ailill was slain; and Fliodhais, together with her herd of wonderful cattle, became the possession of Fearghus. Fliodhais remained the wife of Fearghus until she died in his company long after in Ulster.

This story, which portrays both Fearghus and Fliodhais in an atypically treacherous light, was composed as early as the tenth century, and it remained popular in manuscripts for a long time. Because of its association with the area, versions of the story have been popular in the folklore of north-west Connacht in recent centuries. These versions, however, have altered the name of Ailill Fionn to Dónall Dualbhuí, and that of Fliodhais is sometimes altered to Muinchinn. Dónall, whose sobriquet means 'yellow-tressed', was in fact stated to have been father of Ailill Fionn in the manuscripts, some of which have him slain in single combat by Fearghus. The most prized beast among the herd of Fliodhais was a wonderful white cow called the Maol (hornless one), and one milking of this 'Maol Fliodhaise' would be full nourishment for 300 men and their families. It was said that during the combat between Fearghus and Dónall, the Maol rested on the hill of Mullach Rua (Mullaroe, Skreen, County Sligo), from which circumstance that hill was sometimes known as Tulach na Maoile.

The easier memorability of his name accounts for why Dónall was substituted for Ailill Fionn in the oral lore. He is described as a great warrior who ruled the Erris Peninsula, and the folklore claims that Fliodhais or 'Muinchinn' colluded with Fearghus when the latter came from Ulster to visit the area. Ceartan is described as a

GIANT, and Dónall drowned him by holing his boat with a slingshot. Regarding the contest between Dónall and Fearghus, we are told that Muinchinn secretly exchanged the swords of the two champions in their scabbards, leaving Fearghus with the magical weapon of Dónall. Thus Fearghus slew the cheated Dónall, and took his wife and all his property. On crossing a river, however, Fearghus thought to himself that he could not trust a woman who had betrayed her husband, so he drowned her there. That river, which flows out of Carrowmore Lake, is thus called the Munchin after her. It is also claimed that as Fearghus with two other warriors were driving the cattle away from Erris, a giant killed the three of them with holly darts shot from a bow. It is further claimed that Dónall was buried near his fortress, which is pointed out as Dún Dónaill (Dundonnell in the valley of Glen Castle, Erris, County Mayo).

LITERATURE: Macalister (1941), 122–3, 132–3 & (1956), 282–3; O'Brien (1962), 362; Thurneysen (1921), 319–20; Gwynn (1924), 70–5; E. Windisch in *Irische Texte, 2 (2)*, 206–23 & *3*, 294–5; D. MacKinnon in *Celtic Review, 1–4, passim*; M. Dobbs in *Ériu, 8*, 133–52; O'Donovan (1844), 96–7; Dinneen, *2* (1908), 176–9; Ó Donnchadha (1940), 45–6.
FOLKLORE: OSL: Mayo, *1* (1838), 13–14, 157–8, 170, 397; O'Donovan (1844), 97; L. Mac Coisdhealbha in *Béaloideas, 13*, 206–8; Bruford (1969), 97, 265.

Fódla A leading lady among the otherworld people, the TUATHA DÉ DANANN, according to the medieval writers of pseudo-history. Her name (earlier written *Fótla*) meant 'swarded one', and she was a personification of Ireland.

Making use of the earlier convention of a triplicated land-GODDESS, the medieval writers claimed that she, ÉIRE and BANBA were three queens of the Tuatha Dé, married to three mythical KINGS. The husband of Fódla was Mac Céacht. After the defeat of him and his brother kings by the sons of MÍL, we read that Fódla met the conquerors at Sliabh Eibhlinne (Slieve Felim, east County Limerick). She sanctioned the newcomers' control of Ireland on condition that they allow the country to be called by her name forthwith.

Macalister (1941), 122, 152, 182 & (1956), 34, 38, 76.

folktale A term used to designate an oral story with a well-balanced plot, which is told for entertainment purposes and generally needs little belief from either tellers or listeners to bolster it.

Stories of this kind are found in many different countries and languages. The plots of many of them have maintained a more-or-less uniform structure over wide areas of the world, and the stories are thus referred to as 'international FOLKTALES'. Scholars have identified about 3,000 of these international plot 'types', and versions of over a third of the types have been collected from Irish folklore. The best known of them are synopsised in this book under the headings ANIMAL TALES, HUMOROUS TALES, RELIGIOUS TALES, ROMANTIC TALES and WONDER TALES. As will be clear from these entries, some types have been known in Ireland for a considerable time and have been embedded in our literature, whereas others have been adopted more recently.

Much scholarly debate has taken place concerning the origins and means of transmission of international folktales, and some of the most difficult problems arise from variability in the plot structures. There is no doubt that in living folk tradition, storytellers have a certain degree of independence in their selection and embellishment of plots. For this reason, international types may appear with special adaptations in some areas, and such are referred to by scholars as 'ecotypes'. Furthermore, two or more of such types can be combined by storytellers to make composite narratives, and some particular combinations can occur frequently over wide areas. In general, however, it is quite impressive to note how individual types maintain a more-or-less standard international form. It is clear that though the composers are anonymous to us, the plot of each international type was originally composed in a logical pattern, with MOTIFS interlinking in such a way as to provide an interesting and lasting narrative.

Each type is made up of a particular selection and arrangement of motifs, and it is the suitability of these selections and arrangements that guarantees the popularity and spread of the types. Storytellers do sometimes make new arrangements of such motifs and add to them, thus creating new plots. However, idiosyncratic plots that lack balance and cohesion seldom achieve any permanence in oral tradition.

INTERNATIONAL TYPES: Aarne & Thompson (1961).

IRISH VERSIONS AND ECOTYPES: S. Ó Súilleabháin & Christiansen (1967); S. Ó Súilleabháin (1942), 557–88; Christiansen (1959).

NON-STANDARD TYPES IN IRELAND: S. Ó Súilleabháin (1942), 611–51.

Fomhóire Destructive supernatural race in the MYTHOLOGICAL CYCLE. Their designation (earlier, Fomoiri) meant 'underworld phantoms', but from a confusion of the archaic word *mor* or *mór* (phantom) with *muir* (sea) they came to be regarded as sea pirates.

Based on original theories as to the symbolism of light and darkness (*see* DRUIDS), the Fomhóire were the opponents of the divine TUATHA DÉ DANANN in the Irish version of the Indo-European myth of a great struggle between a divine race and a destructive one. The surviving text that describes this – the so-called 'second' Battle of Moytirra (*see* MYTHOLOGICAL CYCLE) – has the Fomhóire living in regions to the north of Ireland such as Scandinavia and the Hebrides. This is obviously a reflex from the Viking raids on medieval Ireland, and prior to this portrayal, the Fomhóire were apparently regarded as underwater spirits, and ultimately as spirits residing in the nether regions of the earth. Such an origin is echoed in the Moytirra text, in which some of them are associated with the soil and with agricultural skill. This text, based on an eighth-century account but with a good deal of material added by the eleventh-century redactor, gives the earliest detailed account of the Fomhóire. The LUGH myth had long been confused with the tradition of the Moytirra battle, and so Lugh's mother Eithliu (variously EITHNE) and her tyrant father BALAR had to be portrayed as Fomhóire in the context of that battle. The surviving text has the Tuatha Dé arranging the marriage between Lugh's parents, Cian and Eithne, as an attempt at rapprochement with the

Fomhóire, but the authentic plot had Cian gaining access to the maiden against her father's wishes and, as a result, Lugh being born.

The idea of love and marriage between the two races strengthened the idea that the Fomhóire were not necessarily sinister, as is clear from the description of the birth of BREAS in the same text. His father Ealatha is of the Fomhóire and is extraordinarily handsome. Breas was installed as their KING by the Tuatha Dé – partly as a diplomatic gesture to the Fomhóire – and he was given a Tuatha Dé wife (*see* BRIGHID). When he connived with the Fomhóire in imposing tribute on Ireland and refused to entertain his subjects with the generosity of a king, the Tuatha Dé demanded that he resign. He went to the territories of the Fomhóire and arranged with two of their leaders, Balar and Inneach, to invade Ireland. They gathered a mighty force from the whole region between Scandinavia and Ireland, but in the Battle of Moytirra were defeated by the Tuatha Dé, with Balar being slain by Lugh. The POET of the Fomhóire, Loch Leathghlas, was given quarter by Lugh, as also was Breas. The price Breas paid for his life was agricultural advice, thus echoing the underground origins of his race.

The other source for descriptions of the Fomhóire is the medieval pseudo-historical compilation, *Lebor Gabála Érenn*. Here they are given a generally repulsive portrayal. In the time of PARTHALÁN, we are told, they were led by one Cichol Gricenchos, and they had 'single arms and single legs'. Parthalán and his people fought for a whole week with them and nobody was slain 'because it was a magic battle'. These are echoes of the great mythic contest described as the Battle of Moytirra, but the pseudo-historians – aware of the chronological difficulty of having the Fomhóire already in Ireland when the various pioneering groups arrived – stressed that they were not settlers but mere sea-raiders.

Accordingly, when the people of NEIMHEADH had settled in Ireland, they were oppressed by these Fomhóire, who had a fortress on Tor-Inis (Tory Island off the Donegal coast). This location was apparently chosen due to an early redaction of the Tuatha Dé-versus-Fomhóire clash that had the Fomhóire leaders residing in a great tower (Old Irish, *tor* – *see* MYTHOLOGICAL CYCLE). We read that at the time of Neimheadh, the Fomhóire were led by two kings, Conand and Morc, who had a great fleet and who demanded an exorbitant tribute – namely, two-thirds of the progeny and wheat and milk that Neimheadh's people had. The latter attacked the Fomhóire fortress on Tor-Inis and slew Conand, but Morc arrived with a huge fleet and, after an horrific contest, the survivors of Neimheadh's people withdrew and left Ireland.

In post-medieval literature, the designation *fomhóire* was applied in general to any strange grotesque beings required in narrative plots. In later Irish, they are often collectively called Fomhóraigh. The singular form of this – *fomhórach* – came to be used as a common noun to describe a huge and ugly enemy, so that a *fomhórach* was in the late literature the usual counterpart of the *fathach* or GIANT of folklore.

Gray (1982); Macalister (1939), 270–1 & (1940), 10–15, 122–5, 134–43; RIA Dictionary, s.v. 'fomóir', 'fomórda'.

Fothadh Canainne

Mythical warrior in early Irish literature. He is described as leader of a band of warriors (*fianna*) in Connacht.

It has been suggested that 'Fothadh' was the name of an ancestor-deity, and is cognate with the designation Votadini for a Celtic people in Britain. In Irish genealogies, Fothadh is an ancestor of the Uaithne sept of north-east Limerick and the adjoining part of Tipperary (*see* ÉRAINN), but he also has been intruded into Leinster genealogies, and it seems that he was originally connected with several septs, probably of the south Connacht area. Typical of a Celtic deity, he was often triplicated, giving rise to the characters Fothadh Canainne, Fothadh Cairptheach and Fothadh Airgtheach. These are described as three brothers who were the sons of a warrior called Mac Nia and his wife Fuinche,

but that is learned invention. A clue to their real identity is afforded by the according to them of nicknames such as 'Óendé', 'Clóendé' and 'Tróendé', all of which contain the word *dia*, which signifies a GOD. The trio were included in the lists of KINGS of Ireland drawn up by the medieval pseudo-historians, it being claimed that they ruled together for a year until Fothadh Airgtheach slew Fothadh Cairptheach and was himself slain by CAOILTE in a great battle at Magh Linne (Moylinny, County Antrim).

The sobriquet Canainne is a genitive, and an attested earlier form of it was Canann. It may be that this was a corruption of 'Danann' (*see* DANU), which would mean that Fothadh was anciently considered a consort of the land-goddess. Some references add weight to this, for Fothadh Canainne is mentioned as having been the mate of the CAILLEACH BHÉARRA, who was very much of a kind with Danu. In literary narrative, he is described as a great warrior and leader of a fierce band of fighters. In this context, he is connected with the most famous of all *fianna* leaders, FIONN MAC CUMHAILL. We read in a ninth-century text that he was half-brother to Cuirreach Life, who was slain in a feud with Fionn. This brought Fothadh and Fionn into conflict with each other, but a truce was arranged and Fionn invited his opponent to an ale feast. Fothadh stated that he was under an injunction (GEIS) not to attend a banquet except in the company of 'white faces', meaning heads of the dead, whereupon Fionn went and slew the husband of Téite, sister of Fothadh Canainne. This caused undying hostility between Fothadh and Fionn, and a huge number of warriors were killed in their feud. There may be an echo of Fothadh's original role as an ancestor-deity in this strange custom attributed to him of drinking with the dead.

His own death came about, according to the early literature, as the result of a love affair with the wife of a Munster *fianna* leader called Ailill Flann Beag. She eloped with him, which act led to a great battle at a place called Feic (apparently near Millstreet, County Cork) in which Fothadh was defeated and beheaded. After his death, the head recited to the woman a poem describing the battle.

The later literature has a character named Fathadh Canann as a member of Fionn's troop. One genealogical source preserves the tradition that he was a king, and states with great fancy that 'he obtained the government of the whole world from the rising to the setting sun, and he took hostages of the streams, the birds, and the languages'.

T.F. O'Rahilly (1946), 6, 10–11, 34; O'Brien (1962), 99, 264, 656; Macalister (1956), 340–3; M. Dillon in *Celtica, 5,* 73; M.C. Dobbs in *RC, 47,* 302 & *48,* 211; W. Stokes in *Irische Texte, 3,* 376–9; Meyer (1910), xv, 4–17 & in *ZCP, 7,* 299; V. Hull in *ZCP, 20,* 400–4; O'Donovan (1849), 4–7; G. Murphy (1953), 363–4.

fowl, domestic Whereas geese and ducks were widely kept on farms, most lore centres on hens and cocks.

It was popularly believed that hens had been brought to Ireland by the NORSEMEN, and that they frantically prepared every night to fly back to Scandinavia on the morrow. However, when they fell asleep, they forgot their plans and rambled about the farmyard the next day as before. They continue to harbour hostile feelings towards the Irish people, and their scraping on the floor of the kitchen is a vain attempt to set the house on fire.

Much folk custom centred on their eggs. These were marked with a cross for good luck when the hen began to hatch, and at Easter, baskets of fresh eggs were given as presents. Contrariwise, malicious individuals were reputed to put rotten eggs in the haystacks of neighbours in order to send bad luck to them. A crowing hen was believed to be unlucky in a farmyard, and was not left alive for long. However, when the cock crew he was claimed to be saying *'Mac na hÓighe slán!'* (the Son of the Virgin is safe!) in memory of how he once bore testimony to the Resurrection of JESUS CHRIST.

The crowing of a cock was believed to be efficacious against spirits, particularly that of a *coileach Mhárta* (March cock). This was described as a cock, all black in colour, which had been hatched out in March (*Márta*) and, in some cases, specifically on a Tuesday (*Máirt*). A story, found in several coastal areas, tells of how a sea captain once saw such a cock at a farmhouse near the shore. A thunderbolt was headed for the house, but the cock crew and thereby deflected disaster. Realising the worth of the animal, the captain offered a substantial amount of money for it to the housewife, who foolishly accepted the bargain. As soon as the captain had taken the cock away, fire broke out and consumed the house. This is a migratory legend, and versions of it are also found in neighbouring countries. *See also* ANIMAL TALES (type 61).

GENERAL: F. Kelly (1997), 102–8; O'Meara (1982), 76–7; S. Ó Súilleabháin (1942), 39–42; S. Ó hEochaidh in *Béaloideas, 37–8,* 210–46; P.V. O'Sullivan (1991), 50–4; Ó hÓgáin (1997), 67–8.

MARCH COCK: Ó Duilearga (1948), 305, 436; B. Almqvist in *Béaloideas, 59,* 274.

Fraoch Mythical Connacht hero in the ULSTER CYCLE. The name Fraoch (Old Irish, Fraech), derived from Celtic *Vroecos*, meaning 'heather' in the sense of 'bristling with warrior fury'.

An OGHAM-inscription on the roof of a cave at the ancient ritual site of Cruachu (Rathcroghan, County Roscommon) is dedicated to Vraicci maqi Medvvi (Vraecos son of Meduva). This was written in the late sixth or early seventh century AD, and the Vraecos in question is likely to have been a noble of the CONNACHTA – hence his title indicating that he belonged to the people of MEADHBH. It may have been a reader of the inscription in the late seventh century who invented a story imagining that the man interred in the cave was not really dead but had been brought to the otherworld there to recover from wounds. This storyteller was encouraged by the occurrence of two suitable place names in the vicinity – Dubhlinn Froích (the heathery dark pool) and Carn Froích (the heathery cairn). The first he fancifully interpreted as a pool where a man named Froech or Fraech was drowned, and the second as the cairn where the same man was finally buried after his death.

This story was developed and expanded in the eighth century by the writer of the prose text *Táin Bó Fraích*, who claimed that the father of Fraoch had been one Idath (later given as Fiodhach), and that his mother was an otherworld lady called Bé Find, sister of BÓINN. Fraoch was a supremely handsome youth, and his mother brought twelve red-eared white cows to him from the otherworld. Fionnabhair, daughter of queen MEADHBH and KING Ailill mac Mata, fell in love with him on hearing his repute. Hearing this, he went to the Connacht capital of Cruachain (Rathcroghan, County Roscommon), and was warmly welcomed there. Time passed by, and eventually he got an opportunity to meet Fionnabhair as she washed her hands by a river. She refused to elope with him, but gave him as token a thumb-ring she had received as a present from her father.

Fraoch then went and spoke to Ailill, who demanded all his wealth – including the twelve wonderful cows – as bridal price for the girl. Fraoch refused, and fearing that he would take Fionnabhair away without permission, Ailill planned treachery against him. He invited the young man to go swimming in the River Dubhlinn, and when Fraoch was in the water, Ailill looked in his wallet and saw the thumb-ring there. He flung it into the river, and a salmon consumed it, but Fraoch killed the salmon and hid it under the bank. Ailill then asked him to bring berries from a rowan tree that grew on the far side of the river, knowing that a water-monster dwelt there. In midstream, the monster attacked Fraoch, who called for his sword. Fionnabhair dived in and brought the sword to him despite the opposition of her father, who even threw a javelin in her direction. Fraoch slew the monster, and on his return – badly injured from the water – his mother and a group of other-world women came wailing there and took him into an otherworld dwelling that, like the royal court, was also at Cruachain. There he was quickly healed of his wounds, and Ailill visited the dwelling and invited him to a feast at the royal court. Fraoch sent a servant to find the salmon

he had hidden, and when Ailill demanded the ring of his daughter, it was presented on a dish with the cooked salmon. Ailill then consented to the marriage, and Fraoch for his part agreed to bring his herd of cows to Cruachain.

This account has obviously been adjusted to suit the context of Meadhbh's court as described in the Ulster Cycle. The original narrative must have told of how the hero was drowned or slain by the monster in the pool. Such a death of Fraoch is indeed described in the Cycle's main text, *Táin Bó Cuailnge* – there he goes to oppose CÚ CHULAINN in the water, the two warriors wrestle, and Fraoch is drowned. That is, however, a dislocation of the tradition of Fraoch's death, making it fit in with the tragic deaths of several other young warriors in single combat with the great Cú Chulainn. The MOTIF of the ring in the fish's belly is a borrowing from early lore (*see* WONDER TALES, type 736A), and was no doubt included by the author for extra dramatic effect.

Another story follows in *Táin Bó Fraích* as if tacked onto the first. It describes how, on his return home to collect his herd, Fraoch found that the cattle had been stolen, together with his wife (rather inappropriately in view of the preceding account) and his three sons. He set out in search of them, and was joined by CONALL CEARNACH in the quest. Arriving at the Alpine mountains, they found a great fortress there, where the captives were being held. They persuaded a female servant of Irish descent to leave the door of the fortress open for them at night, and thus took the fortress, and Fraoch rescued his family and cattle. Returning home, he joined Meadhbh and Ailill on the cattle-raid of Cooley (*see* ULSTER CYCLE). The story, in fact, is little more than an eighth-century improvisation to fill out the details of the preparations for that great cattle-raid and, like the account of Fraoch's death at the hands of Cú Chulainn, is very much a secondary development due to the borrowing of Fraoch into the Ulster Cycle.

There were different versions of the Fraoch narratives, for an eleventh-century verse text does not bring Fraoch and Conall so far overseas on their quest, but they go rather to an otherworld dwelling of DONN in Scotland. Again, around the thirteenth century, a new prose version was compiled. This unites themes from the earlier literature by having Bóinn put injunctions (see GEIS) on Fraoch against having a woman in his household, fighting Cú Chulainn, swimming between November and May, and pledging his arms. This text may well preserve some material from the original story prior to Ulster Cycle influence. Fraoch's lover here is not Fionnabhair, but Treabhlann, a granddaughter of the otherworld king AONGHUS, and the girl's guardian is one Cairbre mac Rosa Ruaidh, who forbids her to go with Fraoch. Treabhlann is tricked by the otherworld lord MIDHIR into believing that Fraoch is dead, and as a result dies from grief.

A fourteenth-century poem retells the first story, and this may also in some ways reflect the original plot, even though it accepts the Ulster Cycle context. According to it, Meadhbh herself loved Fraoch, and when he preferred her daughter, she planned treachery by sending him to bring her some rowan branches guarded by the water-monster. When he was attacked by the creature, Fionnabhair threw a knife to him and he slew it with the knife, but so badly wounded was he that he himself expired. Fionnabhair, it is implied, died from grief, and some place names are derived from the adventure. This poem passed into oral tradition in Scotland and remained popular there for many centuries.

OGHAM INSCRIPTION: Macalister (1945), 16–17; Olmsted (1994), 212–16 & in *Emania*, *10*, 11–16.

TÁIN BÓ FRAÍCH: Meid (1974).

COMBAT WITH CÚ CHULAINN: C. O'Rahilly (1976), 26–7.

RING IN SALMON: Carney (1955), 37–47.

OTHER VERSIONS: J. Carney in *Celtica*, *2*, 154–94; K. Meyer in *ZCP*, *3*, 166–75; D. Meek in *CMCS*, *7*, 1–37 & *8*, 65–85; N. Ross (1939), 198–207, 249–53; Gwynn (1913), 356–65.

LATE FOLKLORE: J.F. Campbell (1872), 29–33.

Fursa Missionary SAINT who died in or about the year 648. 'Fursa' may origi-nally have been his nickname, perhaps a hypocoristic form of *fursanta* (illuminat-ing). The medieval biographies of him state that he was the son of a Munster prince called Fionntan, and that his mother was daughter of Aodh Fionn, king of Breifne (in County Cavan).

According to these biographies, when Fursa came of age, he decided to be a monk, and went to a monastery that had been founded by BRÉANAINN on an island on Loch nOirbsean (Lough Corrib, County Galway). On the advice of Bréanainn, he settled at Ráth Mat, which became known as Cill Fhursa (near Headford). This set-tlement grew into a monastery, and some-time later, Fursa decided to go on a visit to his father, who had now become a local king in Munster. While sojourning in his native place, a sudden illness seized Fursa, and in the course of this illness, he had a great vision. Three angels brought him to a hill top, and when he looked down, he saw the world with four fires dangling above it. One of the angels explained that these fires were falsehood, covetousness, discord and cruelty. Gradually the fires grew together into one great conflagration, and a group of devils then assailed Fursa with false accusations. He was protected by the angels, who divided the flames before him to let him pass through. As he did so, the devils thrust towards him a man whom he had known in life and some of whose clothes Fursa had received when he died. For thus receiving the clothes of one who had died in sin, Fursa was burned on his shoulder and face, and these scars remained on him after he awoke and recovered from his illness.

Following on the vision, Fursa redou-bled his efforts at praying and preaching, and exactly a year from that day, an angel appeared to him and instructed him to con-tinue his work in Ireland for twelve years. When that period was concluded, he crossed the sea to England and began to preach there. He was well received by king Sigbert of East Anglia, and from there proceeded to the Continent, where he was supported by the Frankish king Clovis II. He had several years of missionary success, and after his death was buried at Peronne.

The celebrated vision of Fursa seems to derive from an experience that the saint himself had and which the Annals put down to the year 626, but the earliest account of it is given by the English historian Bede in 731. Bede was told of the vision by an old monk who had heard it from a man who had it from Fursa's own mouth. It was a cold day when Fursa had recounted it to that man, but the saint had nevertheless sweated profusely from the recollection of it. The vision became widely known in medieval Latin literature, and it was very likely the source that suggested to Dante the plot of his *Divina Comedia*. No doubt due to Fursa's image as a visionary, a text in Irish from around the ninth century attributes a series of pessimistic prophecies to him concerning social life of the future.

A medieval glossarian tells a fanciful anecdote concerning Fursa and his friend, St Maighniu. When Fursa once visited Maighniu at the latter's monastery (at Kilmainham, Dublin), out of affection for each other, they decided to exchange their ailments. Fursa thus transferred his headaches and piles to Maighniu, whereas the latter gave to Fursa a reptile that was in him. This reptile had a violent appetite, and in order to abate it, Fursa had to eat three portions of bacon each morning. Later, when he was abroad, a bishop censured him for his voraciousness, whereupon the saint caused the reptile to enter the bishop's throat. The bishop then understood, and Fursa recalled the reptile to himself. This anecdote is in fact an adaptation of an international folklore plot (*see* ANIMAL TALES, type 285B).

In disagreement with his Munster pedigree, one tradition claimed that Fursa was of the Conaille sept of Muirtheimhne (in County Louth), but this appears to have been a secondary development. His feast day is 16 January.

Kenney (1929), 500–3; W.M. Hennessy & McCarthy, *1* (1887–91), 108–9; Plummer, *1* (1896), 163–8; Heist (1965), 37–55; Bollandus & Henschenius (1863), 2 January, 401–8; Stokes (1905), 44–7, 190, 424 & in *RC*, *25*, 385–404; K. Meyer in *ZCP*, *9*, 168; O'Hanlon, *1* (1875), 222–86; IFC 132:139.

DANTE: *see* Boswell (1908).

Gael Generic word for Irish person of Celtic cultural background, for a speaker of the IRISH LANGUAGE, or for one who holds it or its tradition in affection.

In medieval Irish, the word was written *Gaedheal*, and its earlier form was *Goídel*. It is apparently a borrowing from around the sixth century AD of a Welsh term for an inhabitant of Ireland, viz. *Gwyddel* (meaning 'wild man', probably in the original sense of 'woodland dweller'). The dominant FÉINE septs of that time used the name (plural, *Goídil*) proudly for themselves, but the medieval genealogists and historians assured that it had the widest application. Thus the pseudo-historical tract called *Lebor Gabála* derives all the people of Ireland from the fictional Míl, whose ancestor was the equally fictional Gaedheal Glas.

The early Welsh referred to the Irish language as *Gwyddeleg*, and from this comes the term *Goídelc*. This became the ordinary name used by the Irish themselves for their language, and in medieval times it developed into *Gaeidhilg*. In modern Irish, it is written *Gaeilge*, but also has dialectal forms such as *Gaeilig*, *Gaeilinn* and *Gaeluinn*. From the same source, in Scotland, the Gaelic language is *Gàidhlig*, and on the Isle of Man it is *Gaelg*. Another derived term, *Gaeltacht*, basically refers to communities having native Irish culture, but now essentially means an Irish-speaking district. From the adjective of Gael – *Gaelach* – comes the English term Gaelic for any of the three languages Irish, Scottish Gaelic or Manx. Linguists use the term *Goidelic* to distinguish the common stock of these three languages as distinct from 'Britonic', the stock of the other surviving Celtic languages Welsh, Breton and Cornish.

T.F. O'Rahilly (1935), 5–6; E.P. Hamp in *PHCC*, *12*, 43–50; RIA Dictionary, s.v. '*Góidel*', '*Goídelc*'.

Garlach Coileánach Name of a fictional clever boy in Munster folklore who gives very witty answers. His mother has died and his father has remarried. The designation means 'puppish child', and is said to have been given to him because he was as badly treated as a DOG by his stepmother. It is possible, however, that the name originally referred to a clever child with the surname Ó Coileáin (anglice, Collins). Several anecdotes told in other parts of Ireland concerning unnamed stepchildren or orphans tend to be told exclusively of the Garlach Coileánach in Munster.

His stepmother, for instance, sent him to search for some straying calves with the order to search 'likely and unlikely places'. He climbed onto the roof of the house and, when the woman complained that he was wasting time, explained that he was beginning by searching the unlikely places. Some anecdotes have him informing his father through hints that he was suffering ill-treatment. For instance, he remarked when going to bed that he regretted his feet had not been washed nor had his forehead been kissed; and also that his mother, who was drowned, would return to the house if she could. He also is represented as telling his woes to a hole in the wall within the father's hearing. According to another widespread anecdote, his father killed a bullock to provide meat for the family, but the stepmother gave only the liver to the Garlach. After eating, the Garlach went outside and reported that it was a foggy clear night, with the wind from the south and frost gathering. 'That is strange weather,' said the father, to which the Garlach replied: 'No stranger than that there is nothing but liver in a bullock!' These stories usually have the father guaranteeing that the ill-treatment will end.

Alternately, it is said that the stepmother had a son of her own, who gave the Garlach many chores to do, such as gathering in the geese each evening for fear of the fox. When the stepmother died, the Garlach remarked to the other boy that he may no longer raise his finger by way of giving orders, and that henceforth he should collect the geese himself. Other smart comments attributed to the Garlach are riddles borrowed from an international FOLKTALE (*see* ROMANTIC TALES, type 921).

Ó Siochfhradha (1932), 296; Ó Murchadha (1939), 32–5; Ó Duilearga (1948), 157–8, 423; S. Ó Súilleabháin & Christiansen (1967), 177–80.

geis A term often used in Irish literature to imply a magical demand or injunction placed on a celebrated personage. The word itself has been variously explained. One theory relates it to *guidhe*, meaning request or prayer, while another theory is that in origin it meant 'happening' or 'destined occurrence'. It frequently occurs in its plural form *gessa* (later, *geasa*).

The idea seems to have been central to the ancient Irish ritual of KINGSHIP, the king being a sacred person whose function it was to maintain equilibrium in the society and in the ENVIRONMENT. The decisions made by such a person would be of great import, and his life and function were therefore considered to be hedged about by uncertainty. He must avoid any act that might tempt fate. By medieval times, the writers had become quite speculative in their accounts of such things; one long poem from the eleventh century describes seven purported *geasa* on the king of TARA, and five each on the provincial kings.

After allowing for imaginative additions and for over-neat enumeration, the actual things mentioned can be reduced to two types, which we may term 'mythical' and 'historical'. To the 'mythical' type belong such things as where a king should be at sunrise or sunset, or the way in which he should position himself at certain places – these could well be the residue of sun-myths and of sacred rituals (*see* KINGS) that lingered on as superstitions for a long time. They were probably always viewed selectively, only being referred to in order to bolster political or personal preferences. To the 'historical' type of *geasa*, on the other hand, belong prohibitions of a very specific and unique type. These may reflect some disaster that happened to either king or people on an earlier occasion, and there would naturally be a superstitious dread of a similar event happening again. Or they may reflect prophecies that had been made for some king or other. Examples of 'historical' *geasa* are many and varied – for instance, that on the Leinster king to 'ride on a dirty black-heeled HORSE across the plain of Maistiu', that on the Munster king 'to hold a border-meeting at Gabhrán', that on the Connacht king 'to go to an assembly of women at Seaghais', and that on the Ulster king 'to attend the horse-fair of Ráth Line in the company of the youths of Dál nAraidhe'. The importance of what was destined for a ruler, of course, would include not only his personal fate but also the fate of his followers.

The concept of *geis* probably originated from an idea that the GODDESS of sovereignty imposed certain conditions on her kingly spouse. From this, it would have spread to the contexts of great heroes also, and it is instanced in the cases of CÚ CHULAINN and FIONN MAC CUMHAILL, among others. It is indeed likely that the concept functioned as a necessary part of the social order in early Irish society, strategically designed *geasa* being a guarantee of the security as well as a check on the behaviour of both kings and warriors. In all events, the result of acting contrary to *geis* is the social destruction and the personal death of the individual. The meaning was indeed capable of being broadened into the notion that a special destiny was allotted to each individual person in life. The ending of an individual's life, being ultimately unavoidable, could be rationalised in this way, and it is noticeable that the occurrence of *geasa* in Irish literature is perennially linked to the breaking of them and therefore to death.

Probably as a reflex from the image of female sovereignty, the imposition of *geis* was represented in love stories as being a special privilege of women (*see*, for instance, DEIRDRE, and Gráinne in the entry on DIARMAID UA DUIBHNE). In the later romances and in folklore, such conditions became known as 'heavy *geasa* of magic', and they were much employed as a device to set a plot in motion. A hero may lose to a HAG at chess or cards, and as her prize, she imposes *geasa* on him to perform some seemingly impossible task.

RIA Dictionary s.v. '*geis*'; O'Donovan (1847), 2–25; M. Dillon in *PRIA*, *54 C1*, 1–25; Reinhard (1933); D. Greene in Bekker Nielsen (1979), 9–19; E.P. Hamp in *Ériu*, *32*, 161–2; A.M. Draak in Bleeker & Widengren (1969), 641–2; Bruford (1969), 284; P. O'Leary in *Celtica*, *20*, 85–107; T. Sjöblom in A. Ó Corráin (ed.) (2001), 83–100.

ghosts The native attitude to the dead in Ireland was that they formed a sort of otherworld community, and this tradition has survived into recent folklore in the context of the FAIRIES. A good deal of lore, in fact, has an interchangeable situation between fairy dwellings and the graveyards where the dead are buried. As is clear from the fairy lore, members of the otherworld community were imagined to live lives that were broadly parallel to those led by the human community, and they sometimes entered the human world for quite natural reasons, such as trading or seeking assistance. There was also a strong and ancient tradition that had the dead highly respected as preservers of ancient learning, and under certain conditions, they bestowed special types of knowledge on the world of the living (*see* FIONN, SEANCHÁN, POETS *and* FAIRIES).

Although there are accounts in the medieval literature of warriors after their own death indirectly exacting vengeance on enemies (*see* CONCHOBHAR MAC NEASA *and* MAOLODHRÁN), there seems to have been no generalised lore in early Ireland that had dead people gratuitously returning to cause terror or destruction. The hostility that the early literature sometimes describes as existing between the inhabitants of tumuli or cairns on one side and human heroes on the other is basically of the same type as competition between leading personalities in the ordinary world.

In early medieval times, the Church made 2 November the feast of All Souls, and since this came two nights after the ancient Celtic festival of Samhain (*see* TIME), much of the imagery concerning the community of the dead was switched to the new date. In a broader sense, the Christian religion gave rise to certain distinctive types of lore of its own concerning the dead. These can be divided into two categories: one concerns well-intentioned dead people, such as those who try to assist relatives when in either physical or spiritual need, or those who are in purgatory and who return to seek assistance for themselves in their plight; the other category concerns dead people who, through having led a bad life, have become evil spirits and maliciously return to do harm to the living. Finally, Irish folklore has many examples of ghosts of a type borrowed from the folklore of other countries in the post-medieval period.

There are some accounts in the medieval literature of SAINTS returning to protect their monasteries and monastic communities; for instance, SEANÁN and CIARÁN of Clonmacnoise who stabbed the wrongdoers with their staffs. The hagiographical texts also give several examples of how the saints could effect the release of souls from purgatory through the power of prayer. This, of course, would have been a point much stressed by clergymen down through the ages, but it is far more common for revenants in folklore to seek, not prayer, but the settlement of some debt they have left unpaid. A migratory LEGEND found in many parts of Ireland, as well as abroad, tells of how a man was once inadvertently locked into a church and, finding no way out, decided to bed down there till morning. At midnight, a priest came out onto the altar and indicated that he required somebody to be a server at his Mass. The man willingly undertook the task, and after Mass was over was thanked earnestly by the priest, who explained that he had been coming from purgatory every night for a long time. He had left one Mass unsaid in life and could not celebrate it until he got somebody to assist him, but now was free to enter heaven. A related story tells of a dead priest who inadvertently left behind a piece of paper on which a dumb man had written his confession, returning in an attempt to retrieve the paper and burn it.

It was said that revenants from purgatory looked pale and wan, and had thin legs. They could not speak until spoken to by a human, and the proper form of address to use with them was 'In God's name, what is troubling you?' Such a soul might return to seek assistance to his own house or to that of a friend, but stories also tell of souls encountered in quite unexpected places. Purgatory was usually understood as a great fiery flagstone or a cold and miserable lake, but some souls could endure their suffering in lonely parts of the earthly landscape – such as in the bark of a tree, beneath a leaf, or between foam and a river. One story tells of a horseman who heard a loud laugh from one such location and enquired who was there. A voice explained that it was a suffering soul that had just heard the news that a baby had been born – a baby who would grow up to be a priest and who would read a Mass that would gain the soul's release from purgatory. On hearing this, the horseman was struck by the magnitude of his own sins, and jumped from his horse, begging forgiveness from God. All his sins were wiped away between the saddle and the ground. Variants of this have a suffering soul offering to share its Mass with another and thus halve their respective terms, and God is so touched by this charity that He forgives both immediately.

A particularly poignant tradition concerns the souls of unbaptised children who anxiously seek baptism, without which they cannot enter heaven. It was customary to bury such babies on the perimeter of a graveyard, in a special little graveyard, or even in a boundary fence between two townlands. Being unbaptised, their souls were said to inhabit limbo, which in Irish folklore was said to be situated at Sruth Orthuláin (probably the River Jordan). A story that was quite popular around the country describes how a priest notices twelve lights in the sky one night, and realises that these are the souls of the children born to a poor woman who was held in low regard. All of them had different fathers, and all had died young. The priest understood that they had appeared to him this night in order to let him know that their mother was very ill and needed a priest. He therefore went and prepared the woman for death, and as he left her hovel noticed that one of the lights was dimmer than the rest. Realising that that light represented the only one of the children who had died without baptism, he recited the prayers of that sacrament, and immediately the light shone as strongly as the rest, before they all disappeared.

A story that can hardly be more than a few centuries old was current in several parts of the country. This tells of how a man meets with a pipe-smoking stranger one day, and they fall into conversation. The stranger offers him a puff of the pipe, and the man gratefully accepts it. On handing back the pipe, he prays God's blessing on the stranger. The latter, very pleased, explains that he is a soul from purgatory, and that he has now been released, for all that he required was that somebody should pray for his soul. This folk legend is told to explain the custom of saying a little prayer for the souls in purgatory whenever one enjoys the comfort of smoking a pipe. An old saying in Irish claims that 'every ghost knows his own business', and some accounts tell of specific people who returned to give necessary financial advice to their relatives or dependents. They may also return to protect the helpless – for instance, a dead mother warning the stepmother against ill-treating her children. Several versions have been collected of a story that has a ghost saving a living person from some evil spirits that are abroad. A man who is benighted on his journey is told by the ghost to leave the road for a little while, and soon he notices some hostile beings passing by. Such hostile beings can be in human or animal shape, but they are always regarded as evil spirits who intend to cause physical harm to people. They are either demons or damned souls, and more usually they appear as individuals who haunt some part of the countryside at night. A horseman or cart-man travelling by night, for instance, might suddenly notice a huge weight behind him, and on looking discover that a spirit is there. Such stories may tell of how the man gets respite from the spirit when he promises to return to the same place on the following night. He brings a priest with him, and the priest makes a circle with blessed water around the man and then banishes the spirit. The spirit in this type of story is invariably that of a dead woman, and a common formula for the conversation has the priest first asking the spirit what made a devil of her.

'I committed murder,' she answers, but the priest says that this was not the reason. 'I murdered children,' she says, but the priest again states that this was not what made her a devil. Then she admits that she killed children for money, and the priest agrees that the sin of professional infanticide has demonised her. She is banished in a flash of fire.

A late medieval text describes a conversation between St COLM CILLE and the devil, in which the evil one states in a semi-quatrain that the clergy deserve no respect because they preach for their own benefit. Challenging the saint to cap the verse, he says 'what is the semi-quatrain for this?' Colm answers in the same metre to the effect that the clergy's charity benefits those in need of it, and thus wins the debate. This is obviously a projection onto the spiritual realm of a practice common among poets of challenging each other. A similar stave anecdote was popular among the Irish-speakers of Munster, and it appears to have been invented by some scholar acquainted with the Greek story of Oedipus and the sphinx. According to it, a certain lonely place was haunted by an evil spirit wont to confront late-night travellers, recite two lines about a candle and candlestick, and challenge them to 'put a semi-quatrain to that'. All failed the test and were killed by the spirit until, one night, a drunken poet was passing by. Three times he capped the verse of the spirit, which disappeared in a sheet of flame and was never again seen there.

Evil spirits were said to often appear in the form of animals, particularly a black PIG or a black DOG, which nocturnal apparitions were identified with the devil himself. This type of lore was adopted from England in the sixteenth or seventeenth century, and has now become general throughout the country. Although it is never expressly stated in Irish folklore, the idea is that such sinister animals could physically attack a sinner and take him away to hell. Their real function is to warn people against staying out too late at night drinking, card-playing or otherwise misbehaving. Spirits were usually said to be encountered at intermediary places, such as a bridge, a crossroads, or a boundary fence. If confronted by some such apparition, the conventional advice was to recite a prayer and to make haste towards a stream or river, for it was believed that aggressive spirits could not cross running water. Other counsels were that one should not go out at night without some salt in one's pocket, some holy water, a hazel stick, or a black-hafted knife, all of which were believed to give good protection against spirits. Regarding the knife, one was advised to 'plunge and not withdraw', the effect of this being that the spirit decomposed into an unpleasant substance resembling slime or jelly.

Ghosts or spirits associated with buried or hidden troves are of different and quite old derivation (*see* TREASURE). More obvious is the tradition of the 'wild hunt' or 'dead hunt' – phantom horsemen and hounds heard, and sometimes seen, racing furiously across the sky. This tradition came into Ireland, probably in the medieval period, from other western European countries (*see* DESMOND, DONN *and* MARVELS). Miscellaneous accounts of hauntings, such as the idea that phantom armies can be heard at the sites of famous battles, are folk fancies that arise naturally from contemplation of events of the past. Definitely recent is lore concerning the 'white lady' seen at night in the grounds of various castles and large houses. She is usually interpreted as being the ghost of a young woman who was once a resident of the particular building, and who pined away or committed suicide after being disappointed in love.

Other apparitions may be more formidable, such as the reappearance at their former residences of notorious landlords or magistrates, often in the form of ferocious animals, though unable to do further harm to mortals. The headless coach or 'silent coach' (*cóiste bodhar*) was also associated with big houses and power abuse in former times. Because of a resemblance between such supposed coaches and actual horse-drawn hearses, however, they were also interpreted as vehicles coming from

the realm of the dead to bring people with them from this life. Thus a nocturnal ghostly carriage either seen or heard was taken to be a sign that somebody in the locality would soon die. If the vehicle touched a person or spattered blood on him, that was an indication that he would be taken away soon after, and accordingly people were advised that on hearing the approach of such a vehicle, they should lie face downwards on the ground and turn their coat inside out so as to be unrecognisable. In a similar way to ghostly coaches on land, ghostly ships or boats at sea were often taken as presages of death by shipwreck or drowning in the immediate area. A simpler presager of death was a cloud-formation in the sky that had the appearance of a funeral cortege.

A curious story was told in connection with the popular love song entitled 'Cailín Deas Crúite na mBó' ('The Pretty Milkmaid'), which was sung to a beautiful and plaintive air. According to the story, a priest was going on a sick call one night when he heard singing from behind a fence. He stood entranced by the air, and wondered who was singing it. So he went on tiptoes to the fence and looked into the field, only to discover that the beautiful notes were coming from the mouth of a massive black dog. Then the priest realised that the devil was using the song to delay him from tending to the person who was dying. How such a story got attached to the song is difficult to determine, but it may have originated in an admonition to priests not to pay too much attention to love songs.

A very distinctive body of lore centres on one particular spirit, which is called the *púca*. This spirit appears in the form of a horse or a calf, and is wont to run in under the legs of a benighted person and carry him on nightmare rides. A legend was commonly told of a particular man who was thus terrorised by headlong gallops on cliff tops for two successive nights. However, he got advice from a knowledgeable friend, and on the third night was prepared for the *púca*. He had steel spurs attached to his boots, and when the spirit hoisted him onto its back, he lacerated it mercilessly with the spurs. The *púca* begged to be let go, and the man complied on condition that the troublesome being would never again bother him. This story was told of several places, most notably of the aptly named Poll an Phúca (Poulaphouca, County Wicklow). The name of this spirit is cognate with the English 'puck', and the being itself seems to have originated as a type of troublesome demon in Continental lore of the early Middle Ages. The snail was nicknamed in Irish 'the *púca*'s spit', apparently because its horns resembled the demonic image of the spirit-animal. The *púca* was said to either spit or defecate on wild fruit at the beginning of November, thus rendering it unsafe to eat such fruit from then onwards.

The element of mystery attached in a greater or less degree to all ghostly manifestations, and the folk desire was to have the mystery solved. So, if a ghostly stranger made a brief but unexplained appearance in an area, this was regarded as a prelude to some misfortune, and any such event would be explained retrospectively by reference to it. One quite unnerving, though not very prominent, type of apparition was called in Irish *taise* and in English a 'fetch'. This is the image of a living person seen in a place where the person is not present. Such a puzzling phenomenon was taken to presage some accident or drowning. Most frightening of all was for a person to meet one's own fetch, a circumstance which betokened certain death.

There was a strong tendency to give preternatural interpretations for extraordinary phenomena, such as strange lights seen at night on land or sea, unidentified animals seen at dusk, or strange noises heard that sounded like footsteps or voices or tappings. By way of scepticism, however, there were many humorous accounts of people being over-nervous and prone to mistake ordinary things at night for some spirit or other.

MacCulloch (1911), 333–47; Cross (1952), 214–24; S. Ó Súilleabháin (1942), 479–92, 507–16 & in *Béaloideas, 21,* 32–105, 210–29, 286–9, 298–300 & (1967), 86–9; Danaher (1964), 108–13; P. Byrne (n.d.); Dunne (1977); Ó hÓgáin (1982), 369–73; Westwood (1987), 176–80;

A. O'Connor in *Sinsear, 1,* 33–41 & in *Béaloideas, 59,* 55–66; P. Lysaght in *Sinsear, 1,* 43–59 & in *Arv, 47,* 193–207; B. Almqvist in *Béaloideas, 59,* 270; Breatnach (1993).

giants Fanciful beings, with human traits, in folklore. They are rarely encountered in Irish literature. The Irish word for a giant is *fathach*, a post-medieval form of the word *aitheach*, which meant a rent-payer and which – through class distinction – was used in the context of an ignoble or uncouth fellow. This alone suggests that giant-lore in Ireland is not of ancient derivation.

Lack of understanding of the cultural landscape led people to think in terms of ancient individual rather than communal work. Therefore, neolithic burial sites such as court cairns were popularly understood to have been giants' graves, while dolmens may be referred to as beds of giants. Often, too, boulders in the landscape are imagined to have been flung into their present position long ago by giants using them as projectiles in fights. Otherwise, giants belong for the most part to fantastic or comic lore (*see* WONDER TALES, ROMANTIC TALES *and* HUMOROUS TALES). They are very popular in stories told to children. In such stories, a giant is thought of as a being living in the wilderness who is hostile to humans. Being so large, he may find it difficult to see his human opponent but identifies the opponent by his scent. A favourite saying of giants is 'Foo fa fum, I smell the blood of an Irishman!' This statement, with its strange phrase and its reference to nationality, underlines the alien and dangerous nature of the giant. In other countries, of course, giants refer to the relevant nationality in similar terms, and it is clear that such giant lore is international. It first occurs in Irish tradition in the medieval FIANNA CYCLE, and may not have reached Ireland before then.

S. Ó Súilleabháin (1942), 448–9; Christiansen (1959), 33–80.

Glas Ghoibhneann Famous cow in Irish folklore, which was said to have been a marvellous milker. Her name means literally 'the grey of Goibhniu', but is often corrupted into various forms, such as Glas Ghoibhleann and Glas Ghoibhneach.

GOIBHNIU was a mythical smith, probably in origin a Celtic GOD of smithcraft, but a special cow is not connected with him in the literature. In folk recensions of the myth of LUGH and BALAR in Ulster, however, she occurs as a cow owned by this same Goibhniu; and in the lore of southwest Munster, she is the cow owned by Goibhniu's folk counterpart Goibhleann. Some antiquity is furthermore suggested by the strength of the Glas Ghoibhneann LEGEND, which is told throughout Ireland and in western Scotland. This tells of how she filled with milk every pail put under her by her unnamed owner, but a jealous woman claimed that she had a vessel which the Glas could not fill, and accordingly that woman brought a sieve and began to milk the great cow. The Glas yielded a continuous stream of milk, enough to fill a lake, but it all ran through the sieve. Eventually, she became exhausted by the effort and died.

Variant accounts of the Glas state that she was a FAIRY cow that came in from the sea to a poor family, and that she yielded a great supply of milk for them and produced several calves. One day, however, a member of the family struck her with a spancel, and then she mysteriously disappeared, never to return. This is related to ordinary fairy lore, but it contains echoes also of ancient tradition of a cow-GODDESS (*see* BÓINN). It is likely that such a great cow was connected with the smith Goibhniu in early Irish lore, and that this particular story of her nigh-inexhaustible milk and her death was a narrative invented at some stage on the basis of ancient myth. Variants of the plot concerning such a great milker are found also in Wales and England, suggesting its origins go back to early medieval times at least.

Ó Duilearga (1948), 257–9, 429; S. Ó Súilleabháin (1942), 497; Cross (1952), 58, 173; Westwood (1987), 254, 314–16.

goats Probably because it seeks shelter immediately it senses the approach of rain, the goat is said to be able to foretell the weather and particularly to see the wind. It is also thought good to keep a goat in the field with CATTLE, as it will eat all noxious weeds. An extension of this idea is that the presence of a 'puck goat' (i.e. billy goat) among the herd will prevent cows from aborting and will cause them to increase their milk yield.

The most dramatic tradition associated with this animal was the custom in a few places of exhibiting a decorated billy goat at markets called 'puck fairs'. The best known of such fairs is held at Killorglin, County Kerry in August, but another survived into the late nineteenth century at Mullinavat, County Kilkenny. Similar displays of 'king' animals included a decorated ram at a SHEEP fair in Greencastle, County Down, and a white stallion at a HORSE fair in Cappawhite, County Limerick. The custom probably originated with the fairs held by the NORMANS in late medieval Ireland, the animal being enthroned as a proclamation that the market was in progress.

The popular explanation usually given for the origin of the Killorglin fair is that English soldiers were plundering the area long ago, but a puck goat collected all the farm animals and led them up a mountain to safety. Another explanation, however, is that when the Killorglin fair was first set up, no animals were brought there except for a solitary puck goat led by an old man. The townspeople were so grateful that they made the goat the symbolic king of the fair, and the spectacle of its enthronement attracted many sellers and buyers of animals. The puck goat, decked out with ribbons and a crown, is placed on a high stage for the three-day duration of the fair, which has become a major tourist attraction.

F. Kelly (1997), 77–9; Cross (1952), 43, 72; S. Ó Súilleabháin (1942), 37; M. MacNeill (1962), 289–302, 674–80; P.V. O'Sullivan (1991), 78–80; Ó hÓgáin (1995), 66–7.

Gobán Saor Famous craftsman of Irish legendary lore, concerning whom a number of anecdotes were told throughout the country.

The name seems to be a hypocoristic form of GOIBHNIU, the ancient GOD of smithcraft, while the sobriquet Saor means 'artificer'. There are indications that Goibhniu, and his Welsh counterparts Gofannon and Gwydion, were regarded as expert craftsmen generally, and Gobán could thus have functioned as an alternative form of the deity's name from an early period. One ninth-century religious poem refers to God, the constructor of the firmament, as 'Gobán', making it clear that such an appellation was appropriate to a master builder. An account from a century or so later claims that Gobán Saor was the son of a certain Tuirbhe who, by throwing a hatchet against it, stopped the tide from coming any further than Tráigh Thuirbhe (Turvey Strand, near Lusk, County Dublin). We read that Tuirbhe was one of the followers of LUGH, which puts him into the same cultural ambit as Goibhniu (*see* TUATHA DÉ DANANN). His story occurs in the PLACE-LORE, a quite unreliable source, but the allusion may echo the designation 'Gobán Saor' for Goibhniu.

'Gobán' also came into use as a personal name, and the fact that it was borne by several monks caused the medieval writers to confuse the imagery of the great craftsman Goibhniu with the monastic context. Thus we read in a biography of ABÁN that a distinguished wright called Gobán lived in the same neighbourhood as that SAINT. This wright charged high prices to the monks for his services and was blinded through their reproaches, but Abán caused his sight to be restored to him while he constructed a monastery. In the biography of MAODHÓG, we are told that Gobán was a member of that saint's community and that after his hand had been blessed by Maodhóg, he built a church with wondrous carvings in it. The accounts of MOLING tell of a 'famous artificer', called Gobán Saor, who built an oratory of timber for the saint. Gobán's wife insisted that he demand as payment for this the fill of the oratory of rye grain. Moling promised this, provided that Gobán could invert the oratory so that it could be filled. The saint thus thought to outwit the wright, but so skilful was Gobán that he succeeded in inverting it without the least damage. The Uí Dheagha sept (of County Kilkenny) contributed all their corn to its filling and the triumphant Gobán took away his grain,

only to find it turned into a heap of maggots on the morrow. It is noticeable that all of these three hagiographical accounts associate Gobán with south Leinster locations, and it therefore seems that lore of this particular avatar of Goibhniu originated in that area.

If so, it soon began to spread. Folklore shows that it has lost the actual identity of the master craftsman by applying the definite article to his name and calling him *an* Gobán Saor. What seems to be an echo of his original identity with Goibhniu is the folk belief that the Gobán was 'the only true smith who ever lived', but he is mainly featured in folklore as a great builder and carpenter. Several old monasteries, and particularly round towers, in different parts of the country are said to have been erected by him, and one common folk legend shows that the old tension between a pagan deity and Christian saints, though transformed, has not quite disappeared. The Gobán Saor, we are told, was once building a monastery, but when it was almost completed, the monks tried to lower his wages. He refused to renegotiate the arrangement, but they waited until he was on top of the building and then removed all ladders and scaffolding. They said that they would not allow him to descend unless he agreed to their proposal. The clever Gobán, however, began to throw down stone after stone of the building, saying that this was as easy a way as any to descend safely to the ground, whereupon the monks relented and paid him the full wages. That this legend is a development of the hagiographical accounts is obvious, but it adds the creative ingredient of quick wit attributed to the Gobán.

In the biography of Moling, Gobán's wife is called Ruaidhseach, and she is there portrayed as a shrewd and calculating woman. The best known of all the legends concerning him can be seen to be a further development on this theme. Told in folklore throughout Ireland and Gaelic Scotland, it relates how the Gobán and his son were once engaged in building a great castle for a king in foreign parts. They worked for seven years on the castle, and when it was nearing completion, the wily king planned to put them to death lest they might build an equally fine residence for somebody else. The Gobán, suspecting the king's intentions, said that he could not build the final turret without a tool he had inadvertently left behind him at home. This tool, he said, was called 'crooked and straight'. The king, unwilling to allow the Gobán or his son to depart, sent his own son to Ireland for it. But the name of the supposed tool was in fact a coded message, and when the Gobán's wife heard it, she knew that her menfolk were in danger. She told the foreign prince that it was in a deep trunk, and when he bent into the trunk to fetch it, she caught his two legs and threw him in. She locked the prince in the trunk, and then sent a message to the foreign king that if he wished to see his son again, he had better allow her husband and son home. The king had no choice but to comply. The central MOTIF of this legend – the outwitting of the selfish magnate by a builder who seeks an imaginary tool – was told in connection with various great buildings in western Europe.

When the clever wife became a major theme in stories of the Gobán Saor, the tradition came under the influence of a FOLKTALE that described a clever peasant girl (see ROMANTIC TALES, type 875). The plot of this folktale was not, however, applied to the Gobán's own wife, whose reputation was sufficiently established, but to his daughter-in-law. We are told that when his wife was due to give birth, the Gobán was away on business, and she was accompanied by another pregnant woman. The Gobán's wife gave birth to a baby girl, while the other woman had a boy. Knowing that the Gobán desired a son very much, they exchanged the babies. Time passed, and as the boy grew up, the Gobán – to his disappointment – noticed that his 'son' had inherited little of his own skill and intelligence. Eventually, the Gobán decided that the boy must marry a clever girl who would be able to look after his affairs for him, and so he sent him to the market with a sheep and instructions to

bring back 'the skin and its worth'. The boy was nonplussed, but at the market met a girl who advised him to sell the sheep to a butcher and then ask for the discarded hide. He did this, and when he returned home, the Gobán sent an invitation to that girl to come visit them. She must come neither dressed nor undressed, neither on the road nor off the road, neither by day nor by night. She cleverly fulfilled these conditions, and the Gobán arranged that she marry his boy.

The daughter-in-law proved to be as resourceful as the Gobán hoped. One day, he and his 'son' were on a long journey, and he asked the young man to shorten the road for him. The son did not know how to do this, and similarly failed when asked the same question on a second journey. Before they set out on a third journey, however, he consulted his wife, and she said that he should tell a story to the old man as they travelled. He did so, and this 'shortening of the road' pleased the Gobán very much. The master tradesman himself was full of quick wit, and some storytellers state that he came to understand the trick that had been played on him, and realised that the girl was in reality his daughter.

The origin of various tricks of the trade concerning building and carpentry were attributed in folklore to the Gobán Saor. For instance, on seeing his son trying unsuccessfully to build a straight wall, he invented the plumb line for the purpose, and he similarly invented a rule-cord for cutting straight pieces of timber. On one occasion, he came upon some poor men building a house that they could not complete because the three pieces of timber they had for joists were too short. The Gobán showed them how to make a cross-joist with these timbers, which held the roof just as well as beams of the proper length would. It was also said that he invented the method of placing 'a stone in and a stone out and a stone across' to ensure a solid structure in buildings. So deft and accurate was he that he could drive nails into the top of a high building without any climbing. He would throw a nail into the air, throw the hammer after it so that it would strike the nail into the proper place, and then catch the hammer again before it reached the ground.

Many of the medieval craftsmen had their own trademarks, which they left on buildings as testimony to their skill. At Holy Cross Abbey in County Tipperary, several examples of such trademarks left by artisans can be seen. They belong to the fifteenth-century reconstruction phase of the abbey, and one of the most striking and enigmatic of these is a carving in stone of a cat with two tails. The identity of the craftsman or craftsmen who used this symbol is not known, but in popular tradition became attributed to the Gobán Saor. A legend tells of how he once came to Holy Cross Abbey when a team of workmen were busy there. He joined in the work, but was not invited to dinner with the rest. He asked the foreman what should he be doing while the others ate, and was jeeringly told that he could make a cat with two tails if he wished. He did just that, and when the builders returned they found that carving there, but the Gobán had departed. This association with the Tipperary area led to another striking connection: some miles to the east of Holy Cross is a large bog, in the centre of which is a small 'island' of good grassy land. This, called Derrynaflan, was the site of an early monastic settlement, and a grave marked by stones there is claimed to be where the Gobán Saor is buried.

T.F. O'Rahilly (1946), 526; Stokes & Strachan, 2 (1903), 294; Gwynn (1924), 226–7; Stokes in RC, 16, 76–7 & (1907), 26–41; Plummer, 1 (1910), clxiii–clxiv & 1 (1922), 10, 188, 233, 238; Petrie (1845), 380–7; Wilde (1890), 224; Ó Duilearga (1948), 263–6, 430–1; Gregory (1926), 27–32; Kennedy (1866), 67–9; S. Ó Súilleabháin (1942), 496–7.

Gobnait SAINT traditionally associated with some places in Munster. Although she is considered to have lived in the sixth century, there is no early biography of her. Opinions vary – some regarding her as an historical person and others considering her a feminine version of the divine smith GOIBHNIU. One early popular etymology for her name was 'sharp-mouthed'.

Her cult was known since the eighth century at least, she being described as of the Múscraighe, a prominent ÉRAINN people of Munster. Her hermitage, it was said, was at Boirneach, the place later known as Baile Bhuirne (Ballyvourney, west Cork). There are also, however, parish dedications to her in Counties Kerry, Limerick and Waterford. According to Kerry lore, Gobnait was instructed by an angel to build her church wherever she saw white deer. She saw those beautiful animals in three places – Ballyvourney in County Cork, and Dunquin and Killorglin in County Kerry – and thus founded convents in these localities.

Devotion to her is strongest by far at Ballyvourney, where – according to some medieval sources – St Abán established a hermitage for her. One folk LEGEND has it that Gobnait's sister, who lived with her, contracted a fever. At the same time, the report spread that Abán had died, and loud lamentation for him spread throughout the countryside. Fearing that her sister would be disturbed in her illness, Gobnait prayed that she would not hear the tumult. The prayer was answered, and ever since no noise can be heard by a person who stands on a stone at that spot in Ballyvourney. It is further said that a PLAGUE was once approaching Ballyvourney, sweeping all before it, but Gobnait halted it and put it into a field which is since called *Goirtín na Pláighe* (the Enclosure of the Plague). No verdure or plant ever grew in that field afterwards. Another legend is told of how a band of raiders once attacked Ballyvourney. The report of the burning and looting reached Gobnait, who was tending to her beehive. She prayed to God that the people might be protected from their enemies, and immediately all the BEES rose up out of their hive and headed in a great swarm towards the raiders. They fell upon these marauders, stinging them furiously and putting them to flight. The bees then returned quietly to their hive, where the saint was waiting for them. The feast day of St Gobnait is 11 February.

O'Donovan (1864), 46; O'Hanlon, 2 (1875), 462–70; Stokes (1905), 72; Plummer, 1 (1922), 8, 15; Best & Lawlor (1931), 16, 248; Heist (1965), 264; Jestice (2000), 157–8; IFC 47:95, 947:100, IFC Index; Ciarán (n.d.), 5–7.

goddesses The literature has many accounts of otherworld ladies that can be taken to echo ancient myth. Its accounts are quite diffuse both in the names given to these ladies and to the themes concerning them, but certain underlying presumptions are clear.

Regarding the names, most of these were originally descriptions of aspects of particular localities and thus attributes of the otherworld women associated with these localities. Examples of this are ÁINE, AOIBHEALL, CLÍONA and Grian (literally, 'sun', the name of a goddess of east Limerick in ancient times). A few instances suggest a more basic system of appellations, such as BRIGHID (exalted one) or MÓR-RÍOGHAIN (phantom-queen), while the name DANU is attested from many parts of Europe and is patently of primitive Celtic or even of Indo-European derivation. The confusion is best explained by postulating that Danu was the original name for a river-goddess, and that her function was often transferred to that of earth-goddess. Accordingly, local variations of her cult, abroad and in Ireland, would have given rise to a variety of other names that could equally be applied to a patroness of agriculture and of productivity. Other aspects of these otherworld ladies, such as the tendency towards triplication and their ability to appear in different shapes, were associated with Celtic deities from antiquity.

The agricultural imagery is especially pronounced in the cases of Danu, Brighid and MACHA, but it occurs to some degree or other in the contexts of the others. The idea of fertility and of food production means that a goddess could be regarded as synonymous with the soil, but other aspects of the physical ENVIRONMENT were corollaries. Practically all Irish rivers have feminine names, the most famous such designation being BÓINN and SIONAINN. Identification with mountain tops is best instanced by the peaks called Dá Chích nDanann (the two paps of Danu), County Kerry. Being guarantor of food, the goddess would be inherently involved with social life, and this would be expressed ritually. As an echo of this, Irish literature at all stages stresses the symbolic unity of a KING with an otherworld lady. Such ladies are a metaphor for the land, sometimes very directly so, as when the three leaders of the fanciful Gaelic invasion (*see* MÍL) gain the kingship of Ireland by an agreement with three ladies of the TUATHA DÉ DANANN. The names of the three ladies – ÉIRE, BANBA and FÓDLA – are very relevant, for each is a name for the country. The latter two are used repeatedly by POETS to refer to Ireland, whereas the first is the term used for the country both in literature and in ordinary speech. Its earlier form was Ériu, from a Celtic *Iveriu*, meaning 'land', and a further derivative ÉRAINN was used to refer to the bulk of the population of Ireland.

In the literature of the MYTHOLOGICAL CYCLE, Éire is given a pivotal position as a woman of the Tuatha Dé beloved by the Fomhóire leader and thereby the mother of Breas, who is an adept at agriculture. Her importance is further underlined in a medieval text (*see* KINGSHIP) that describes a vision of her as 'the sovereignty of Ireland' giving a drink to each successive king of the country. The drink image is embedded in the name of a goddess of sovereignty associated in ancient times with TARA but who in the literature was transferred to the role of queen of Connacht – this was MEADHBH, whose name meant 'she who intoxicates'. Éire the otherworld lady represents Ireland in bad times and in good. Thus she can appear either as an ugly HAG or as a beautiful maiden. In the LEGEND of the great king NIALL, ancestor of the royal Uí NÉILL sept, she is transformed by his kiss from the ugly form into the beautiful one. This symbolises the reign of the proper king when misfortune is banished from Ireland and the whole country prospers. Through medieval times, the poets used the conceit that their patron kings and chieftains were spouses of the country or of a particular territory. This theme maintained its popularity as a poetic convention down to the nineteenth century, with Ireland (called Éire, Banba or Fódla) appearing in visions to poets and telling them that she has been deprived of her spouse and has been defiled and degraded by the English overlords.

Since the goddess represented the land, the forces of nature, and life in general, the king as her mate imposed social order on these things. This myth, of course, involved mutual obligations, and Irish literature shows that kingship was surrounded by many kinds of magical conditions (*see* GEIS) The medieval writers tended to make indiscriminate use of debris from early ritual, but – despite some dislocation – the idea of mutual obligation shows clearly in the account of the Ulster goddess MACHA and of the conditions she imposed on her husband, and of the dire consequences to the Ulster kingdom when she was abused. On the other hand, Macha is portrayed as being sexually attractive and as a warrioress. The sexual attraction is stressed in particular in the story of the otherworld lady ÉADAOIN, wife of the king of Ireland. It is also found in the story of Eibhliu, who was abducted by EOCHAIDH MAC MAIREADHA and from whom Sliabh Eibhlinne (Slieve Felim on the Limerick–Tipperary border) was reputedly named. The various ladies in medieval literature called EITHNE, though not all explicitly stated to be of the otherworld, should be included also in this context. The war function of the goddess is most clearly expressed in the accounts of the MÓR-RÍOGHAIN, and this is obviously an extension of the role of the land-goddess into that of protector of her territory.

The writers of the medieval PLACE-LORE made some quite spontaneous narratives out of the theme of goddesses at war. We read, for instance, of the royal lady Tailtiu of the FIR BOLG who, after the defeat of her people by the Tuatha Dé, was forced to clear forest-covered plains and died from exhaustion as a result. Further otherworld ladies described as having been held in captivity were Tea and Carman, both of them – like Tailtiu – patronesses of great assemblies in early Ireland. It may be that such subjection was a mythic theme, reflecting control of the powers of nature, but it is more likely to have been a mere extension of the

war-lore. The uncertain fortunes of war are instanced also in the case of the great god called the DAGHDHA, who was himself for a time subjected to servile captivity. The important point is that, whether triumphant like Macha or defeated like Tailtiu, the goddess is very powerful in terms of the landscape. Her aspect as patroness of animals is most clearly expressed in the traditions of BRIGHID and FLIODHAIS. Through an extension of agricultural symbolism into the realm of artistic production, Brighid functioned as a patroness of poets – a process also evidenced, in a more general context, by the role of the Tuatha Dé Danann.

Since the general welfare of the environment was, according to ritual, dependent on the relations between the reigning king and the earth-goddess, this is a recurrent theme in the biographical accounts of kings. The medieval literature has otherworld women coming to kings and becoming their wives or paramours, while even human queens have their portrayal influenced by ancient myths of goddesses. In folklore, too, the goddess lore has survived. Several otherworld ladies – such as Áine, Aoibheall or Clíona – have become fairy queens, while the imagery of a prodigious worker is still current in legends of the famous hag called the CAILLEACH BHÉARRA. Like the GODS, the goddesses of Irish tradition were often euhemerised and presented as fanciful historical characters.

Mallory & Adams (1997), 174, 231–3, 487; T.F. O'Rahilly in *Ériu*, 14, 1–28; Mac Cana (1970), 84–95; Sjoestedt (1982), 37–51; Ross (1967), 265–301.

gods The god-figures appear mostly in ancestral roles in pre-Christian Irish tradition, as patrons and protectors of the community. From archaeological data, we may assume that the ancestors were considered in that role by the ancient pre-Celtic communities of Ireland, and the alignment of some megalithic passage tombs and stone circles indicate that the sun was thought to represent the fructifying or paternal force. Such ideas were perpetuated and strengthened by the spread of Celtic culture in Iron Age Ireland. The Celtic view is encapsulated by the teaching of the Continental DRUIDS that the Gauls were 'all descended from a common father'.

The name of this father was Devos, the Celtic version of the Indo-European sky-god Deiwós. In Ireland, he became known as *dago-Deiwios* (good sky), which developed into the name of the DAGHDHA, the great father-figure of the early Irish. The Daghdha had several different names, some of which seem to have been specific to particular septs. The early Irish formula of oath-taking was 'I swear by him by whom my tribe [*tuath*] swear', thus alluding in the most important social context to the father-deity. It was usual to consider the father-deity as being synonymous with, or represented by, the sun. The Irish form of the Indo-European word for the sun, *séhaul-*, was *súil* (eye), showing that the sun was imagined as the eye of the all-seeing father-god in the sky. As is clear from lore of the Daghdha and his alter egos AODH RUADH, DÁIRE, DEARG, DONN and EOCHAIDH, this god was the patron of bountiful harvests, of wisdom, of the otherworld, and of KINGSHIP. Originally, we may assume that he was thought to be the husband of the maternal earth-GOD-DESS (*see* DANU), and to preside over the divine community, the TUATHA DÉ DANANN. The exact nature of the god-concept among the Celts and early Irish is, however, difficult to define. Symbolical patrons of various activities were often considered as gods (*see* DIAN CEÁCHT, FIONN, GOIBHNIU, LUGH, MANANNÁN, NUADHA *and* OGHMA). Although these may have ultimately been emanations from the father-deity, they were regarded as distinct individuals within Celtdom long before their cults reached Ireland, and so are never confused in Irish tradition with the Daghdha. For some processes involved in the replacement of the Daghdha and related figures by God the Father of the Christian faith, *see* PATRICK.

A large number of characters who occur in medieval Irish literature have vestiges of divine attributes, but not many personages are overtly divine. Analysis of what constitutes divinity in such cases is complicated

by the nature of the literature itself, since practically all the texts were written by Christians and much of them by clerics. Given this, the general lack of attempts at demonising the mythical characters is much to the writers' credit, but there is no guarantee that the lore is being set by them in its proper context. Consequently, it is difficult to decide whether the rather amorphous character of much of the mythological material is due to such a quality being inherent in Celtic tradition, or to deliberate debunking by the writers, or indeed to imperfect knowledge of the lore on the part of the writers. In reality, it is probably a mixture of all three causes.

The medieval writers, already faced with some confusion, adopted an approach towards the material that suited Christian beliefs and which also helped to put some coherent structure onto the lore of such personages; i.e. they portrayed them as characters of ancient times. That the writers were not altogether successful in their purpose is obvious from the remaining contradictions, but the pseudo-historical scheme did help to dramatise the lore. It allowed for the ancient gods to be portrayed primarily as great martial heroes, and this guaranteed that their imagery long outlived their relevance in Irish storytelling.

ORIGINS: Mallory & Adams (1997), 230–1, 556.

GENERAL: Mac Cana (1970), 11–73; Dillon & Chadwick (1973), 173–201; Sjoestedt (1982), 11–36, 52–61; Gray (1982), 117–32; Olmsted (1994), 43–7; Ó hÓgáin (1999), 59–64, 187–201.

Goibhniu Mythical smith of the TUATHA DÉ DANANN. The name is a simple derivative of *gobha* (modern, *gabha*) – the word for a smith – and his Welsh counterpart was the similarly mythical craftsman Gofannon.

There is no doubt that Goibhniu originally represented a deity. The 'science of Goibhniu', by which is meant smithcraft, is referred to in some early Irish charms that appeal to him for his protection. Generally, however, he is listed among the leading artisans of the Tuatha Dé, for whom he fashions spears to be used in the second Battle of Moytirra. During the preparations for that battle (*see* MYTHOLOGICAL CYCLE), Ruadhán, son of BREAS, went to spy on the Tuatha Dé, and noticing that Goibhniu was manufacturing such wonderful spears, attempted to kill him. He wounded Goibhniu with a newly made spear, but the smith managed to turn it back against Ruadhán, and drove it through his body.

An aura of wonder surrounded Goibhniu and his craft. We read that so marvellous was his skill that no spear made by him would miss its target and nobody who was pierced by it could survive. One tradition of special significance is that he held a great ale feast (*fled Goibnenn*) for the Tuatha Dé, and all who partook of this feast were preserved from age and decay. Such a role for Goibhniu has the mark of antiquity, for in Greek myth also a smith, Hephaistos, served drink to the GODS. The importance of Goibhniu is underlined by the fact that his character has survived in tradition. From an early variant of his name, Goibhninn, in folklore he is called Goibhneann or Goibhleann, and is reputed to have been the owner of a marvellous cow – *see* GLAS GHOIBHNEANN – whose milk yield was nigh inexhaustible.

He was said to have had a forge or smelting furnace in different parts of the country, but lore of this was particularly strong in the Beara Peninsula, County Cork. This again is significant, for there was a distinct tendency to situate deities in the south-west corner of Ireland (*see* BALAR, DONN *and* CAILLEACH BHÉARRA). He is said to have had his forge on the tiny island called Aolbhach (Crow Island), at the tip of the Reen promontory in Beara. A GIANT who lived in Beara once demanded that Goibhleann make a perfect razor for him. This Goibhleann did, using the blood of rats in the tempering of the steel, and so keen was the razor that with one dash it shaved off both beard and epidermis from the giant, without in any way causing pain. On this island, too, it is said, Goibhleann kept his marvellous cow, and when she desired to taste the grass of the mainland, she jumped back and forth over the 60-foot chasm without any bother. It was also said that Goibhleann buried his TREASURE on the island, killing his servant so that the GHOST would ever after protect it.

Oral versions of the LUGH myth survived in the north and west of Ireland, and in these Goibhleann figures as the smith who befriends the hero and forges a great spear for him. This is doubtlessly an echo from manuscript versions of the second Battle of Moytirra, but it is interesting to note that – as usual in folklore – he is in these versions also accompanied by his cow. Lore of him had a permanence and vibrancy of its own, and it is probable that one of the most celebrated characters in Irish folklore, the GOBÁN SAOR, was in origin an emanation from Goibhniu.

LITERATURE: Arbois de Jubainville (1903), 174–5; Stokes & Strachan, *1* (1903), 248; T.F. O'Rahilly (1946), 525–7; L. Duncan in *Ériu 11*, 188; Stokes (1900), 177, 189, 327; D.A. Binchy in *Ériu, 20*, 2; Gray (1982), 42–3, 50–1, 56–7, 125.

FOLKLORE: Curtin (1894), 1–34; OSL: Cavan & Leitrim (1836), 16–17; T. O'Sullivan in *Béaloideas, 6*, 168; IFC 51:9–17. *See also* LUGH.

Goll mac Morna

Leading rival of the hero FIONN MAC CUMHAILL in the FIANNA CYCLE of stories. Goll himself was a heroic character and a great warrior, and the leader of the Morna clan.

The origins of Goll mac Morna lie in the early lore concerning Fionn who, under the influence of the LUGH myth, was portrayed as being opposed by a fiery one-eyed foe. Designations given to this foe were Aodh (fire) and Goll (one-eyed), and it is significant that the medieval literature gives Aodh as the real name of Goll mac Morna, the latter resulting – we are told – from his loss of an eye at the Battle of Cnucha, in which he slew Fionn's father. In the synchronisation of the traditions about Fionn taking place in the tenth to twelfth century, this archetypal foe called Goll was made into the leader of those troops serving CORMAC MAC AIRT, who were hostile to the Leinster interest. The Luaighne sept, who had played this part in the earlier texts, thus had their function largely taken over by the Morna clan, who were reputed to be of Connacht origin.

The character called Goll had by this time become detached in narrative from the fiery otherworld foe of Fionn. We read, therefore, that when leadership of the Fianna was given to Fionn after he had slain the mysterious burner of TARA, Goll nobly accepted this and pledged his loyalty to the son of the man he had slain. The magnanimity of Goll continues in the succeeding literature, and he is described as exposing himself to many great dangers to protect Fionn and the Fianna. However, dramatic clashes between his clan and Fionn's Baoiscne clan are mentioned in several texts, and it was such a clash that brought about his tragic death. Various reasons are given for this final quarrel. One is that he had a dispute with Fionn over a PIG, and another is that the champion's portion was denied to him at a feast by a relative of Fionn called Caireall (for such a prerogative of champions, *see* CONALL CEARNACH). Yet another tradition had it that Fionn's daughter was married to Goll, and that Fionn, in some unexplained way, caused her death.

Whatever the cause, the result was that Goll and his clan went on a trail of destruction against Fionn's people. The Baoiscne clan counter-attacked, and the sore-pressed Goll crossed into Connacht and determined to hold the fords of the River Shannon. Hearing Goll snoring on the other side of the river one night, Fionn crossed quietly and stood over his foe with drawn sword. He generously allowed Goll to reach for his weapons, and at that very moment a large force of Goll's men came on the scene. Goll repaid the debt of generosity to Fionn by allowing him to depart, and actually escorted him back across the river. The war continued to go against him, and eventually Goll had to stand alone against his foes on a promontory on the west coast. A long poem describes a conversation he had with his wife – the only remaining one of his supporters – on that occasion. In it is described his great martial career, including conquests abroad as well as many victories at home. He pleaded with his wife to leave him for her own safety, but she refused, saying that no other man would be so kind to her. Eventually, worn out by hunger and fatigue, he was beheaded by one of Fionn's

men who swam onto the promontory.

It is clear that there was a strong effort by some Connacht writers in the late Middle Ages to make Goll the real hero of the Fianna Cycle, and they almost succeeded. The incendiary imagery of Fionn's ancient foe had not entirely left him, however. One poem states that, during his final war, his clan burned to death a large number of women, hounds and youths in Fionn's fortress of Almhu (the Hill of Allen, County Kildare). Other sources have this reflect somewhat less on Goll by attributing the savage act to his brother Garadh. We read that this Garadh, being rather advanced in years, was one day left by Fionn in charge of the women of the Fianna while the other warriors went to hunt. The women teased and mocked Garadh concerning his age, however, and, in a fit of rage, he locked them into the palace and burned them all. Since this would be an obvious cause of great conflict, there is a tendency in folklore to make it the grounds for the final split between Fionn and Goll. The destructive element also survived in accounts of another brother of Goll, the mischievous CONÁN MAOL.

GOLL: Ó Raithbheartaigh (1932), 94–8; K. Meyer in *RC*, 2, 90–2 & 5, 198; Stokes (1900), 56–62, 73–80, 132, 144–5, 183–7, 204–6, 219–20; Mac Neill (1908), 7–14, 17, 22–4, 60–1, 86–92; Best & O'Brien (1965), 978–88; N. Ross (1939), 60–8; Ó hÓgáin (1988), 159–66, 294–5, 359.

GARADH: Stokes (1900), 38–41; E.J. Gwynn in *Ériu, 1*, 13–37; Brewer & Bullen (1871), 7–8; Ó hÓgáin (1988), 154, 165, 359.

Gregory the Great Pope who reigned from AD 590 until his death in 604. Known in Irish tradition as *Gréagóir Pápa* and – on account of his association with the Gregorian chant – as *Pápa an Bhéil Óir* (the Pope of the Golden Mouth).

The writings of Gregory were held in high regard in the early Irish Church, and so, in Irish hagiography, he is the typical Pope. Several fanciful accounts of Irish SAINTS connect them with him. We read of St BARRA being ordained a bishop in Rome by Pope Gregory, when a flame comes on the Pope's hand from heaven, showing him that God had specially chosen Barra. Again, when Gregory died, St Colmán

Eala in his monastery (at Lynally, County Offaly) has a vision of myriads of angels descending to Rome to take the soul of the saintly Pope to heaven. One of the best-known LEGENDS of Gregory had, indeed, reached Ireland by the Middle Ages. This has the Pope celebrating Mass in Rome when a woman – who has baked the bread – doubts the presence of JESUS CHRIST in the Eucharist. A piece of the host turns into flesh, and only through the prayers of Gregory can the appearance of bread be restored to it.

This story is told in a biography of Gregory in Irish, which also details the tradition of how, when chosen for the papacy, Gregory went into hiding through humility and only consented to the office when he was discovered and brought back to Rome. The international account has, after Gregory's death, his body being buried in a golden casket in Rome, but the Irish version claims that he ordered the casket to be placed in the River Tiber. From there, we read, the casket floated out into the sea, and was finally deposited on Trácht Ghréagóra (Gregory's Strand) on Inishmore, the largest of the Aran Islands off the Galway coast. This curious tradition probably derives from a confusion of the Pope with another holy man called Gregory of Ard Mháil, who had a foundation there. Probably through this man, the Pope was even given an Irish ancestry, it being claimed that he was of the family of Deagha (see ÉRAINN), and he was specifically attached to the Corca Dhuibhne sept of west Kerry. This was due to a misunderstanding of the place name Caisleán Ghriaire in that area.

The tradition of Gregory lives on still on the Aran Islands, where – probably as an echo of the true situation – he is given an alternative name Ceannannach (white-haired). There is a church dedicated to this holy man on Inishmaan (the middle Aran Island), and it is claimed that he was beheaded by a TYRANT at Cleggan on the mainland. As is clear from the medieval literature, the confusion of names brought into focus much of the imagery of the famous Pope. In folklore, for instance, his 'golden mouth' gave rise to a weird story that describes how a man called Gréagóir, in penance for his verbal sins, cut off his mouth, but a golden mouth grew in its place. He left instructions that after his death, his corpse was to be put in a coffin and deposited into the sea between Inishmore and Inishmaan. That place is thus known as Gregory's Sound, but the coffin continually came to land and was eventually buried at Port Daibhche on Inishmore.

Widely instanced in Irish tradition is the plot of a medieval European FOLKTALE (see ROMANTIC TALES, type 933), that tells of the son of an incestuous union who, unaware of his origin, becomes Pope of Rome. The earlier European pattern of this plot did not give a name to the character, and most Irish versions follow this. However, the later European tendency to name Pope Gregory as the boy is evidenced in versions from County Cork. In these it is said that, on discovering the circumstances of his birth and in a pious attempt to rid himself of the stain, Gregory went to fast in a hut on an island and that his mouth became golden there from licking his lips with thirst.

For indirect influence of an early legend of Gregory the Great on Irish literary tradition, see PATRICK.

LITERATURE: Stokes (1905), 96–7, 425; Kenny (1929), 177, 219, 264–5, 451, 702, 720, 789, 805; Plummer, 1 (1922), lxiii–lxiv, 14–17 & 2, 220, 225, 264–5, 361 & (1925), 259–60; O'Kelleher & Schoepperle (1918), 24, 82, 206–15, 258, 487; K. Meyer in ZCP, 3, 36 & in ZCP, 12, 367–74; J. Vendryes in RC, 42, 119–53 & 43, 223–51; P. Grosjean in RC, 46, 223–51 & 49, 182–8; Ó Riain (1994), 244.

FOLKLORE: OSL: Galway, 3 (1839), 187–8, 287, 408–9; O'Hanlon, 3 (1875), 332–4; M. Nic Dhonnchaidh in An Stoc, 8/10/1928, 8; Munch-Pederson (1994), 178–9, 318; IFC 77:254–5, 612:224–8, 842:11–18, IFC Index.

Guaire KING of Connacht from AD 655 until his death in 666. Celebrated for his generosity, he was often referred to as Guaire Aidhne, since he belonged to the southern branch of the CONNACHTA sept known as Uí Fhiachrach, who inhabited the territory of Aidhne in east Galway. His royal fortress was Durlas, just east of the town of Kinvara.

It was said that in his youth he was stingy

and inhospitable, and when St COLM CILLE visited the province of Connacht, he was told about him. Colm went to him and explained that man comes into the world without possessions and leaves it in a similar manner. Furthermore, the world's wealth comes from God, and He is not grateful to those who ignore the poor. Guaire paid attention to the sermon and changed his ways, so that he became the most generous man in Ireland; hence he was known as Guaire *an oinigh* (i.e. of the hospitality).

This major trait of Guaire is stressed in another story that describes his military manoeuverings. Incensed at his cattle-raiding, the UÍ NÉILL high-king DIARMAID MAC AODHA SLÁINE launched an offensive against Connacht, and Guaire sent the cleric CUMAINE FADA to arrange a day's respite before battle. Cumaine met with the high-KING on a raft in the middle of the River Shannon. Diarmaid agreed, believing God to be on his side, and in the Battle of Carn Chonaill (Ballyconnell, near Gort, County Galway) inflicted a crushing defeat on Guaire. The latter fled from the battle with his servant, and reached a small convent where a lone nun dwelt. She looked after him, and Guaire caught a salmon in a nearby stream and cooked it. He lamented that this night he had to be satisfied with a salmon for a meal, whereas on other nights he had two bullocks for his retinue.

Finally, Guaire decided to go and surrender to Diarmaid. In token of submission, he took Diarmaid's sword between his teeth, and the high-king decided to test his generosity by sending a leper to beg from him during the ceremony. Guaire immediately threw his darts to the leper, and threw his shield to another man with a similar ailment, and a golden brooch to yet another. One of Diarmaid's men took the brooch from the leper, and on hearing this, Guaire gave him his belt of gold. This again was taken from the leper, and Guaire – who was still prostrate with the sword between his teeth – wept bitter tears because he had nothing else to give. He began to take off his shirt, but Diarmaid intervened and told him to arise. The high-king said that Guaire need

not suffer humiliation before him, since he was already subject to a better king – the God of heaven and earth. Then Diarmaid prostrated himself before Guaire, and brought him with him to the assembly of Tailtiu (Teltown, County Meath).

Guaire brought a large bag of money with him to Tailtiu in order to distribute it among the poor there. Diarmaid had ordered that nobody should beg from him at Tailtiu, but after three days, Guaire complained that he would die if none of the poor were to seek his assistance. On hearing this, Diarmaid revoked his order regarding begging, adding a bag of his own to that of Guaire. Then Guaire began to give with both of his hands to all and sundry, so that from the giving his arms grew longer than before. Other accounts state that his right arm was longer by half than his left, because that was the one he most used in giving to the poor.

An in-tale in this text explains that Guaire was destined to lose the battle against Diarmaid because of an earlier event. According to this, he had dealt ungenerously with St Caimín of Inis Cealtra (Holy Island in Lough Derg on the River Shannon) and, as a result, the SAINT had fasted for three days against him, praying that he might be weak against his foes. Guaire went with Cumaine Fada to be reconciled to Caimín, and peace was made between them, but Caimín said that he could not offset the coming defeat, as 'my throw has been cast and I cannot stop it now'. On that occasion, Cumaine and Caimín asked Guaire what was his chief desire, and Guaire replied figuratively that he wished that Caimín's chapel be filled with gold and silver, so that he could use the treasures as alms. Caimín then said that he wished that every kind of disease come on himself for love of God, and Cumaine Fada desired that the chapel be full of books that would help scholars to teach the Christian faith. The three wishes were granted, Guaire in time becoming so wealthy that he could be continually giving alms.

Guaire had a brother called Marbhán, who was a saint, a prophet and a POET, and who continually gave good advice to him. This Marbhán seems to have been a fictional character derived from the lore concerning Cumaine Fada (*see* SEANCHÁN). He is described as choosing to live the life of a swine-herd, so that the solitude of such a life would help him achieve greater holiness. Guaire asked him once why he preferred to live in the wilderness, and received a long answer that extolled the beauties of wild nature. Impressed by this, Guaire stated that he would give up all his kingdom if he could but live like that. The fame of Guaire's generosity caused him to be brought into association with the extortions of poets, and a writer in or about the eleventh century combined various elements of traditional lore in order to make him host to the ravenous company of the chief-poet SEANCHÁN. For a long time, Guaire acceded to the increasingly difficult demands of the poets, and was in danger of total impoverishment when Marbhán intervened to fend off Seanchán and his coterie. Further adventures concerning Guaire are found in the story of CANO MAC GARTNAIN and in the biography of St MAODHÓG.

Several separate anecdotes were told of him. We read that one Aonna, successor to CIARÁN of Clonmacnoise, was the confessor of Guaire. It happened once that a widow's son was arrested while trespassing in the royal garden. The widow was ordered to pay heavy compensation or, failing that, the young man was to be executed. She went to Aonna for help, and he gave her a quatrain of poetry to recite in the presence of Guaire. The quatrain was a reminder of death and hellfire, and when Guaire heard it from the widow, he immediately released her son. Sometime later, a fine horse belonging to Aonna was killed by a farmer, and Aonna demanded high compensation. The farmer went to Guaire for help, and Guaire gave him a quatrain to say. The quatrain accused Aonna of unjustly seeking compensation, and when Aonna heard it, he felt compelled to accept no more than a single cow.

Another anecdote told of how St Colmán mac Duach, the bishop of Guaire's

territory, spent Lent in the wilderness of Boirinn (the Burren area of north Clare). He was accompanied by a single clerk, and they fasted for a long time. After Mass on Easter Sunday, they sat to table, but there was no food. At the same time, Guaire was in his dwelling sitting down to a huge meal, and he wished that some holy man in need should have such food. Immediately, his great bowl rose into the air, carried by angelic hands, and went to Colmán in the wilderness. Guaire followed on and, after they had eaten, brought Colmán and the clerk with him to his dwelling at Durlas, where he presented them with three-score milking cows. Variants of this story in the later medieval literature add the detail that Guaire and his men followed the departing vessels on horseback, and that Colmán miraculously stuck their horses to the ground outside his hermitage until he had eaten his meal. They also state that the road between Durlas and Boirinn was since known as Bóthar na Mias (the Road of the Dishes). The anecdote remains popular in the folklore of east Galway to the present day.

Even after his death, Guaire's generosity was manifest. As he was being brought to the monastery of Clonmacnoise for burial, a beggar approached the corpse. Though dead, Guaire stretched out his hand and threw a fistful of sand at the poor man. Immediately it touched him it became gold, and this was the final act of charity done by Guaire.

COM CILLE: O'Kelleher & Schoepperle (1918), 138–41.

CEALLACH STORY: Mulchrone (1933).

KING DIARMAID: W. Stokes in *ZCP, 3*, 203–19.

RIGHT HAND LONGER: Dinneen, *3* (1908), 64–5; O'Grady, *1* (1898), 400.

CAIMÍN: Stokes (1890), 303–4; Kenney (1929), 386. Cf. O'Kelleher & Schoepperle, 60–3, 136–7.

MARBHÁN: K. Meyer in *ZCP, 3*, 455–7; Joynt (1941), 13–40.

AONNA: K. Meyer in *ACL, 3*, 1–2.

COLMÁN: J.G. O'Keeffe in *Ériu, 1*, 43–7; Kenney (1929), 456; Dinneen, *3* (1908), 64–7 (where Mac Duach is corrupted to 'Mochua').

COLMÁN AND GUAIRE IN FOLKLORE: Thoms (1834), 42; P. Kennedy in *Dublin University Magazine, 41*, 503; IFC 381:104–6, S36: 222–3, S48:66–7, S96:298–302.

DEATH: K. Meyer in *ZCP, 3*, 218.

GENERAL: O'Grady, *1* (1892), 396–401 & *2*, 497–8; Ó Cadhlaigh (1939).

For mistaken references to Guaire in a story, *see* CEALLACH.

hags Supernatural beings in the form of old women, who are described as inhabiting lonely parts of the Irish landscape. They derive ultimately from the land-GODDESSES, and represent these goddesses in their ugly guise. According to ancient tradition, the goddess takes on such guise in times of misery, whereas in good times she is a beautiful young girl.

Although the hag is thus an old native symbol, the Irish word for her is *cailleach*, based on the word *caille* (veil) – a borrowing from the Latin *pallium*. This supports the contention that the image of the hag as a permanently ugly being is not indigenous to Ireland. Even in late folklore, indeed, a hag still functions as a sort of protectress of the landscape and is not necessarily dangerous to humans. The most typical example is the CAILLEACH BHÉARRA, and lore of her is common throughout the Gaelic world, but less-famous hags are often mentioned in local lore. These, like the Cailleach Bhéarra, tend to have special connections with the landscape. Stones are said to have been dropped from her apron by a hag who was building a house long ago, for example, or a natural platform can be claimed as her residence. Similarly, many place names take forms indicating that they were the site of a hag's dwelling, bed or climbing-steps.

The great age of particular hags was often the subject of comment, as they were believed to have lived through many generations (*see* CAILLEACH BHÉARRA *and* MARVELS). They were also thought of as having tremendously keen eyesight, and their ability to thus discern climate variations such as thickening fog or signals of approaching storms meant that they could foretell the weather and sometimes even effect change in it. In the centre of Ireland, harvesters had a humorous tradition that the hare was in the corn and retreated before the reapers. Eventually, she took refuge in the final sheaf left uncut. The cutting of this last sheaf was therefore alluded to 'as driving out the hare', and – probably due to its resemblance to a hooded old woman – this sheaf was known as the *cailleach*. The farmer who was last of all in his area to cut the final sheaf in his fields, it was said, would have to support the hag for the winter. This was a way of ensuring good and prompt husbandry, and could also give an explanation as to why some farmers did not prosper. When cut properly and in good time, a farmer brought home his final sheaf and hung it in the house or shed for good luck. On the other hand, hostile neighbours could bring bad luck to a farmer by stealing his final sheaf and damaging or burying it.

A lay composed in the thirteenth century has the FIANNA warriors reaping a corn field at Breagha (County Meath) in order to expel a little deer from it; and this indicates that the folk fancy of a harvest animal was already current in the Midlands at that time. The word for a hare in Irish, *giorria* (*giorr-fhia*) meant 'small deer', and the identity of the deer in the lay with a hare is thus obvious even though the lay's writer tried to disguise it. The association of the hag with a hare strengthened this folklore of the harvest, for in European tradition a malicious old woman was believed to be able to take a hare's form (*see* WILD ANIMALS).

In narrative plots such as found in WONDER TALES and in the FIANNA CYCLE, the hag is a definitely hostile being. A favourite device with oral tellers of such stories is to begin an adventure by having the hero play cards or otherwise contend with a hag, resulting in the right of either side to impose tasks on the other. These tasks are in folklore called *geasa* or *deasa*, a slight semantic change to an old word indicating injunctions (*see* GEIS). The hero is allotted a nigh-impossible and extremely dangerous task by the hag, the performance of which requires him to depart for distant parts. In turn, the hero imposes restrictions on the hag until he returns from his adventure. He may, for instance, demand that she stand with one foot on the spire of a church and the other foot on the ground while eating nothing but grains of wheat blown by the wind and which she must catch in the eye of a needle. On his successful return, having completed the task, he finds the hag dead from her exertions. A less frequent MOTIF in HERO TALES concerns a hag who appears on a battlefield at night with a balsam to revive dead warriors – which activity can only be prevented by the hero finding the hag herself and killing her (*see* CONALL GULBAN).

HAG-LORE: S. Ó Súilleabháin (1942), 447–8; Christiansen (1959), 17–18; Bruford (1969), 9, 196–7.

HARVEST HARE: Evans & Thomson (1974), 127–41; E.E. Evans (1957), 162–3; Mac Néill (1908), 55–7.

hero tales Many genres of storytelling in Ireland can be listed under this term. In general, a hero tale (*scéal gaisce*) as understood in Gaelic Ireland was a narrative describing adventures of some real or imagined warrior of old acting in a pre-medieval or medieval setting. It could also be designated 'epic lore', with the proviso that these Irish stories are usually prose narratives rather than having the verse structure commonly associated with the word 'epic'. Thus literary historians and folklorists, when speaking of Irish hero tales, have in mind the types of lore discussed in this book under the headings MYTHOLOGICAL CYCLE, FIANNA CYCLE, ULSTER CYCLE and KINGS/KINGSHIP.

Also to be counted as 'hero tales' in this context are the medieval translations and adaptations into Irish of similar stories from other languages. These include some accounts of heroes from Greek and Latin epic (such as Herakles, Ulysses and Aeneas) and some accounts of heroes from English, French and Italian romance (such as Arthur, Galahad, Charlemagne, Bevis of Hampton, Guy of Warwick and Orlando). Since fuller and better versions of these stories are found in their original languages, these Irish versions of stories from other literatures are not discussed here.

Other stories involving heroic figures, such as WONDER TALES and varieties of historical LEGEND, are not usually encompassed within this specific term 'hero tales'.

LISTS AND DISCUSSIONS: G. Murphy (1961) & (1971); Bruford (1969); Mac Cana (1980).

high-king/high-kingship The title *ard-rí* (high-king) was originally an honorific one that could be used for any powerful ruler. As a specific political concept, the title came to the fore in the eighth century AD, when the Uí NÉILL kings were strong enough to claim a sort of overlordship over most of Ireland. This was in fact a continuation of the earlier social system by which a powerful regional king (often called *ró-rí* or *ruire*, meaning 'over-king') extended his power over several local kings and, while allowing for their autonomy, grouped them into a sort of confederation owing allegiance to him.

Historical Uí Néill kings, from the time of NIALL in the fifth century AD to the late eighth century, are referred to individually in this book as 'high-king of the Uí Néill'. This is done to avoid complication, even though in their time such a ruler would have been more appropriately referred to as a *ruire* presiding over the various branches of the populous and powerful Uí Néill sept in a broad area of the northern half of Ireland.

The medieval historians extended the concept of high-king backwards to cover early periods, claiming that the king who ruled at TARA had been general monarch of Ireland from time immemorial, and presenting a picture of Ireland as a sort of federal state, with the high-king reigning over a number of provincial kings. In this way, mythical kings of Tara, such as CONAIRE or CORMAC MAC AIRT, are in story claimed to have been high-kings of Ireland. Since this book is primarily concerned with storytelling, the traditional practice of referring to mythical and prehistoric kings of Tara as high-kings is retained, even though this does not accord with the actual reality of the past.

The title *ard-rí* continued in use for the most powerful Irish king down to the NORMAN conquest in the later twelfth century. This virtual high-kingship was a coveted position sometimes held by an Uí Néill leader, at other times by a leader of a rival sept – most notably BRIAN BÓRAMHA.

F.J. Byrne (1973), 40–7, 210.

horses Because of their social, economic and military importance, horses are the animals on which most emphasis is placed in Irish literature and folklore.

Archaeology shows that horses had been part of Irish life since the third millennium BC, but we lack direct evidence for the cultic importance of the animal until Ireland was Celticised. The medieval pseudo-historians were reflecting the status of the horse in their culture when they ascribed its introduction to the god LUGH. The harvest festival, called 'Lughnasa' after this deity, continued to be celebrated at many places in Ireland on the first Sunday in August down to the twentieth century, and remnants of it still remain. Horses continued to play a conspicuous part in the celebration of this festival. They were raced, usually in spontaneously organised contests on land but sometimes also in swimming races in lakes and rivers.

Lugh was a Celtic deity of Continental origin, and the Celts were indeed noted in Europe for their fine horsemanship, and their GODDESS of horses Epona was adopted as patroness by the Roman cavalry. Such a leading goddess could also be called Rigantona (revered queen), and in this form she survived as the MÓR-RÍOGHAIN in Irish tradition. A nickname for the Mór-Ríoghain was MACHA, who was especially associated with horses in Ulster myth. Since Epomaros (great in horses) was a designation among the Continental Celts for a GOD, it is clear that the deities were visualised after the manner of Celtic nobles as horse-lords. This primary importance of horses is reflected also by the fact that the DAGHDHA, the father-deity, was sometimes referred to as EOCHAIDH (which signified 'horseman'), and such equine mythology is apparent in the imagery of EOCHAIDH MAC MAIREADHA. Several mythical KINGS of early Ireland were given this name Eochaidh, and there was a tendency also to give the name to antique characters in the genealogies of several septs. In the pedigrees of the ancient kings of Munster, a character called Echdae was mentioned as husband of the goddess ÁINE. His name would have meant either 'horse-like' or 'horse-god'.

A significant echo is found in the name of the mythical Ulster king FEARGHUS MAC RÓICH, which name means literally 'male vigour son of great stallion'. This reflects an ancient conceit concerning kingship, the king being required to have 'male vigour', while his divine patron bore the nickname 'great stallion'. There are some very striking accounts in medieval Irish literature of the use of horses in early kingly rituals, such as in the myth of CONAIRE, who had to undergo a series of ritual tests to prove his claim to the TARA kingship. The tests included mounting a chariot to which were yoked two stallions of one colour that had never before been harnessed. If he were not the true king, the horses would rear up against him; but Conaire being the true king, they stood still when he approached. They then coursed tamely around the citadel, and the upright ritual stone at the head of the course there cried out against the axle of his chariot as it always did for the true king. Especially striking is the tradition that Conaire was under otherworld taboos not to enter his fortress at Tara after sunset and not to leave it before sunrise. When he eventually broke this prohibition, he found himself following three red horsemen to the place where he was slaughtered. The import of all of this is that the sun belongs to the father-deity, and that every earthly king must eventually relinquish his throne, being brought to it by horses and led away from it similarly. It may even be that the horse was seen as a type of psychopomp, bringing the dead king to the otherworld, and thereby mirroring the ritual role of a horse in his earlier inauguration.

The image of the father-deity in the context of the dead gave rise to the mythical character called DONN, and 'the horses of Donn' were alluded to as bringing dead heroes to the otherworld. This association of horses with the otherworld continued in the fertile imagination of the folk until recent times. At Knockfierna, County Limerick, Donn is represented as king of the FAIRY army, who leads his cavalry to battle against other fairy armies, ensuring that the fertile fields and crops of Munster are protected from spiritual foes. Also, in his role of protector and overseer of his territory, he often rides about alone at night on a fine white horse (*see* DONN FÍRINNE).

In the medieval literature, both heroes and SAINTS have their faithful horses, and folklore stresses the very close contact between horse and man by some curious traditions. We are told that horses once had speech, and for that reason one should always speak to a horse as if it were a Christian. Equine nature is said to be very closely akin to human, and one quite candid story told how Noah had forgotten to bring a stallion into the ark with him and that one of his sons had to perform its function. As a result, horses have a human ancestor, and they share several ribs with humans. Yet it is also said that the equine species have a certain animosity towards the human one, and that horses would kill people except for a fortunate quirk of their eyesight, for, to the convex eye of a horse, humans look several times bigger and stronger than they are, and we are told that this saves us from being savaged.

A common tendency in human thought is to express the social importance of things by attributing a spiritual significance to them. Accordingly, much lore represents horses as being very close to the otherworld. They can, for instance, see GHOSTS that remain unseen to the human eye, and many accounts tell of a horse stopping at a particular place and not moving despite the efforts of its rider or driver. If one looks forward between the two ears of the horse, it is claimed that the spirit or shade that has caused it to halt can be seen. Perhaps the origin of such ideas is in the very keen sense of smell that horses have and which causes them to notice many more things than humans do. Because of its crucial value for agriculture and transport, the owner of a horse tended to be himself quite nervous for its welfare, and thus beliefs abounded concerning many unexpected dangers that might lie in the animal's way. Often, when the owner would come to the stable in the morning, he would find the horse in a lather of sweat, and this was explained as the result of it being stolen overnight by some neighbour who rode with the fairies. These otherworld beings were themselves thought to be a danger to horses, as they might wish to abduct a fine one. From this arose the custom of tying a red ribbon or a piece of hazel to the horse, or of spitting on it, for all these things repelled the fairies. Moreover, it was said that the horse itself sneezed in order to keep these beings out of reach. One of the greatest dangers to the animal's welfare was believed to be the evil eye of some begrudging person, and to prevent this the Sign of the Cross was frequently made over the horse.

One type of horse was well able to defend itself, if tradition be credited. This was the 'true mare' (*fíorláir*), defined as the seventh filly foal born to its dam without any colt being born in the interval. No evil force could interfere with such a mare, and whoever was riding it was secure from all harm. If a racehorse, the true mare could never be bested. It was further believed that where the true mare fell to the ground at its birth, a shamrock grew. This shamrock had four leaves and was known as the *seamair Mhuire* (Mary's clover). It was considered to have curative and protective powers, and was a favourite talisman. Most horses have some luck attached to them, according to folklore. People liked to allow a horse to trample a little on seeds when sown, as this would cause them to sprout well, and the horse's halter was believed to bring good luck and should always be retained when the animal was sold. The horseshoe, of course, was believed to bring good luck, but this probably relates to its container shape rather than to its specific association with this animal.

Not all horses, however, were considered lucky. A foal born at Whitsuntide was held to have a vicious nature, and a white horse was generally considered an unlucky thing to see. A horse with four white feet was difficult to sell, as animals with this colouring were popularly believed to be of intractable disposition. There was much speculation, and there were many different maxims, concerning the best colour for a horse, but a white mark on the forehead was usually considered a good sign. A detailed system of evaluating good traits in a horse has been popular in Ireland for several centuries. According to this, the perfect horse should have 'three traits of a bull – bold walk, strong neck and hard forehead; three traits of a hare – bright eye, lively ear and swift run; three traits of a woman – broad breast, slender waist and short back'. The close relationship of equine and human is underlined by other parallels in beliefs concerning both, such as the idea that a foal born with a caul will be a great racehorse, and the rule that a mare in foal should never be put under a hearse or brought near to a corpse (*see* HUMAN LIFE). The basic reason for such parallelism is no doubt that for many people their very livelihood depended on having a horse, and the horse was often a human's sole companion on long journeys.

This close relationship between man and beast led to the notion that the ideal rider was one who appeared to be part of the same being as his mount. Expert horsemen, of course, were held in high regard, and their trade could be quite a lucrative one, especially for those who could handle wild or vicious stallions. Some individuals had this skill, which seems to have been due to a combination of courage and manipulation of the horse's keen sense of smell. Various substances with odour either pleasant or odious to the animal could be used to calm it, halt it firmly on the road, or drive it wild. One of the favourite items used to calm a horse was the substance found in a foal's mouth after its birth, but it was usually complemented by a variety of medical oils. The explanation given to the folk, however, was that a savage horse could be tamed by whispering into its ear a special secret word. The most celebrated of these horse-whisperers was James Sullivan, from Newmarket, County Cork, who flourished in the early nineteenth century. He met with astounding success, rendering tame and ridable even killer horses. In the year 1804 he performed his greatest feat when he so quietened a notorious stallion on the Curragh of Kildare that the animal actually took part in a race and won on the occasion. Lore of his native area claims that having

tamed a horse, he could with a word make it lie on its back with its four hooves in the air, so that a glass filled with drink could be balanced on each hoof.

An old saying in Irish is *capall le ceansacht*, meaning that a horse should be handled with gentleness. It was thought that horses had a special understanding of people, and that 'one should treat a horse like a Christian'. In fact, speaking to horses could have a natural soothing effect quite apart from any quasi-magical one. If a team of plough-horses was moving too fast, the ploughman would sing calmly to the horses, causing them to slow down as they listened to the song, as if they were 'timing the verse'. Sometimes, an extra man would walk beside the plough-team, whistling a tune to the horses; and some people were wont to sing a lullaby to soothe an uneasy or frightened horse.

A popular migratory LEGEND told of a strange horse that came from a lake and was captured by a local farmer. This water-horse became a valuable worker or racer for its owner, and the man profited much by it. One day, however, he struck the horse, with the result that it raced away again into the water. Some versions tell that the man was soon after drowned in the lake, and that stray pieces of his body were seen floating on the water as if he had been eaten by the horse. This legend, found also in parts of Britain and in Scandinavia, was already known in Ireland in medieval times. The account of how the hero CÚ CHULAINN got his two great chariot-horses is a variant of it, and other variants are found in the literature concerning the saints BRÉANAINN, FÉICHÍN, MAODHÓG and RUADHÁN. A colourful example from the folklore of County Clare claims that the celebrated fifteenth-century chieftain, Síoda Mac Conmara of Kilkishen, caught a water-horse and rode it for several years, but that it finally ran away with him and drowned him in a local lake. Other traditions of water-horses, describing them as progenitors of a notable line of local racehorses or workhorses, must have resulted from poetic conceits, such as statements that the exploits of a certain horse were seemed supernatural or were comparable to those of supernatural animals. The statements would be so resounding in tradition that they would in time be taken in a literal sense, that the particular horse itself was of supernatural origin.

Even when such ideas were considered silly, extraordinarily able horses could still be imagined to have otherworld connections. The celebrated little grey mare called Irish Lass belongs to the clear light of history – she raced on the Curragh of County Kildare in the mid-eighteenth century. She was popularly known as the Paidrín Mare, the *paidrín* being a rosary-beads that was hung around her neck before a particular race to help her to victory. The race, a match, took place on the Curragh of Kildare in the year 1749, and it was between Irish Lass and a noted racehorse of the time called Othello, a jet-black stallion with a ferocious temper. Later lore claimed that the stallion had sinister magical powers, and that it was heard to speak to its jockey during the race. The jockey riding Irish Lass was nicknamed Biorán (pin) because he was so light, and he was advised by a priest to take the lead from the start and to hold on to it, for Othello's magic would be too strong if the stallion got its head in front. Biorán obeyed these instructions, and won the race.

It was said that when the Paidrín Mare died, she was opened and it was found that there were a pair of wings attached to her heart that had helped greatly to increase her speed. This Pegasus-type image was associated with some other great racers also. One account from Kerry folklore of a great local racehorse claims that its owner raised it on goats' milk. Having won many races, the owner could not bear the thought of any horse defeating it as it grew older. 'He had a picture taken of himself mounted on the horse, and then put a bullet through it. The doctors opened the horse when it was dead, and they found wings on its heart. They considered that it was the goats' milk which caused that.' An account from County Mayo refers to an even more incredible trait that, it is claimed, was possessed by less than 'one horse in a million'.

This was the ability to draw breath through the anus as well as the mouth – 'any horse so distinctively endowed is supposed to be possessed of well-nigh supernatural staying power'.

GENERAL: F. Kelly (1988), 336 & (1997), 555–9; D. Ó hÓgáin in *Béaloideas*, 45–7, 199–243 & (1985), 279–80; B. Ó Cuív in *Celtica*, 2, 30–63 & 17, 113–22; Cox (1897); Danaher (1966), 100–6.

WATER-HORSES: Ellis (1851), 187–97; T.J. Westropp in *Folk-Lore*, 24, 376–7; D. Ó hÓgáin in *Béaloideas*, 45–7, 238–9; B. Almqvist in *Béaloideas*, 59, 107–20, 237–9.

human life The most immediate of all experiences, life itself, is naturally the subject of speculation. The worldwide tendency to regard three points of human living as being particularly important is well represented by Irish tradition. These points are birth, coming of age and death. In Irish literary biographies, whether of KINGS, heroes or SAINTS, special descriptions are given of these three crucial stages. In the folk custom and belief of Ireland, coming of age is generally replaced by marriage as the intermediate stage in the life of a person, and indeed there was a feeling that marriage was the only true introduction to adulthood.

The birth of children was a matter of great social importance and, as usual in such cases, was expressed in mystical terms. For example, it was said that sterility could be overcome if the childless couple slept on top of a dolmen, a type of Stone Age burial monument popularly regarded as the type of bed used by the great lovers DIARMAID UA DUIBHNE and Gráinne. The importance of fertility was underlined by fear of circumstances which might hinder it. It was believed, for instance, that conception would be prevented if an enemy tied a knot in a handkerchief at the time of marriage, and no child would be born to the couple until the malicious knot was untied. Pregnancy brought its own dangers. It was commonly believed that a woman with child should avoid meeting a hare, for if that animal crossed her path, the child would be born with a cleft palate, known as a *bearna mhíl*, or 'hare-lip'. The woman could prevent this if, when she saw a hare, she tore the hem of her skirt, thus transferring the blemish from the child to it. A pregnant woman should never enter a graveyard, for if she stepped over a grave, the child would be born with a clubbed foot, or *cam reilige* (cemetery twist).

When it came to birth itself, forms of the custom known to scholars as 'couvade' were practised in Ireland as in other parts of the world. This involved an attempt by the father to take some of the birth pangs away from his wife. Accordingly, he would often give his waistcoat or some other item of his clothing to his wife to wear in the belief that this would transfer the pains, or he might engage in strenuous work in the belief that this would relieve her of some of the physical exertion. The time of birth could be regarded as indicative of the future life of the child. Thus a child born at midnight was likely to have some special talents, such as extraordinary intelligence or even the ability to see otherworld beings.

Since marriage was the point when one adopted full social responsibility, many superstitions centred on the actual wedding itself. Some days of the week, especially Monday and Friday, were and still are considered unlucky as wedding days (*see* TIME). The colour green was believed to be an unlucky colour for a bride to wear, and it was also considered an ill omen for a glass or cup to be broken on the wedding day or if rain fell before the ceremony. There were certain practices that were reputed to bring good luck to the couple – throwing something after them as they left the church, for instance, or throwing coins into the air over their heads. It was customary in some places in the nineteenth century for all the men, with their wives behind them, to race on horseback from the church to the house of the newly-weds. This was known as 'the race for the bottle', the prize being a bottle of whiskey placed on a wall near the house. Socially, of course, marriage arrangements depended to a greater or less extent on class. Those who were in possession of land or in business tended to make matches for their offspring with economic prospects in view, while love matches were more common among the landless and the poor.

Folklore does not, in its concentration on the major points of life, exclude everyday matters. The human body being the general organ of life, much ordinary lore was current concerning it and its functions. Individual parts of the body were believed to display traits of the person. The eyes, for instance, were considered to be the mirror of the soul and thus by their expression revealed a person's mentality. Much hair on the body betokened strength, a split in the front teeth was a sign of a good singing voice, while a large forehead indicated intelligence. Much attention was focused on abnormalities, whether real or imagined. Lunacy was considered to result from water on the brain, which caused softness, and people with this affliction were believed to be extraordinarily agile at running or jumping. A simpleton was referred to as *duine le Dia* (meaning one specially selected by God), and was believed to have a paradoxical kind of intelligence that could show in unexpected ways. On the other hand, certain people were believed to have an evil eye, usually through their envious disposition but sometimes as an in-born trait for which they were not personally responsible. Those reputed to have such an eye were the cause of great anxiety, and they were often imagined to be staring peculiarly at a child or a farm animal, it being thought that as a result of this the health of child or animal would wither away.

Health was a major concern, particularly in the context of people's well-being, but also in the case of valuable domestic animals. As a result, many different kinds of cures were attempted, some natural and others more imaginative. A few very ancient ideas survived, such as that the essence of a healthy person could help to cure illness in another – hence breathing on a wounded part of the patient or applying saliva to it. Outdated theories of the anatomy were sometimes employed – such as curing headaches by bandaging the head into a rounded shape, or stopping nosebleeds by tying a string tightly around the little finger, thought of as the extremity of the body. More magical types of formulae were also used, such as drawing circles with red ink around ringworm to stop it from expanding, or drinking a concoction of dandelion to cure jaundice. There were many charm-prayers – called *orthaí* – that were believed to cure specific illnesses when recited devoutly.

Speculation concerning the observable physical traits of persons is inevitable, but neither was the question of the soul ignored. It was believed to be immortal, a point of teaching that the DRUIDS are reported to have had long before the coming of Christianity. The common folk idea that dead people could reappear in the form of an animal such as a BIRD or a hare may well be a survival of quite ancient and pre-Christian belief in reincarnation, but it is difficult to be sure of this. Little attempt was made generally to envisage the soul in concrete form, apart from a rather vague idea that it was akin to a little creature within the person. A migratory LEGEND, common enough in Munster, describes how a butterfly was seen to emerge from the mouth of a sleeping man, and when it returned to its source, the man awoke and related that he had dreamt of the very things over which the onlooker had observed the butterfly to hover. Another fancy, referred to in the medieval literature and still found in folklore, is that each person has a *bradán na beatha* (salmon of life) within the body, and that over-exertion could cause this little fish to be ejected, resulting in death if it were not immediately replaced.

Birds were also associated with the duration of life, but in an external role – for instance, the sudden appearance or unusual behaviour of ravens and crows could betoken death. A strange and sinister bird, described as large but of an unspecified kind, was believed to lay its wings over the bed of a sleeping person, thereby causing a nightmare. Sleep – an experience described as 'brother' to death – attracted much fanciful lore, it being thought to give a kind of access to the otherworld. Many people regarded dreams as being of great import, thinking that messages from dead relatives could be received through them, and that something that happened in a dream was a premonition of the future. The soul had precedence over the body in sleep as in death. It was said, for instance, that a sleepwalker could walk on water with as little difficulty as on land, but if awoken, he or she would drown. A common belief was that a certain duration of life had been allotted to each person, as if his or her death in particular circumstances could not be avoided. A curious idea, found in the early literature and surviving still in folklore, is that a certain sod is destined to be the spot on which a particular person will die. A prophet or wise companion of the person, or even an otherworld voice, may reveal to him how his destiny is connected with the sod, and the fulfilment of this in an unexpected way was the theme of many a dramatic narrative.

When the final illness approached, relatives of a sick person were usually more tense and inclined to take special note of things that otherwise would go unnoticed. Special attention might be paid to a bird perching on the window sill, a DOG howling at night, a picture that might chance to fall, or some strange sound heard outside, for any of these things could be taken as portents of death. As the old or ill person died, doors and windows would be opened to ease the passage of the soul; and after death, the curtains were drawn, the clock stopped, the mirrors turned to the wall, and any pet animals in the house put out. These customs may have originated in an idea that the soul could pass into some other object after death, but if so, no memory of such a rationale survives. There was definitely some amount of fear of the dead, and several customs illustrate this clearly. For example, round-about ways were taken by the funeral procession to the graveyard, and in some places, the coffin was carried around the graveyard a few times before burial. The obvious reason for this was to put astray the GHOST of the departed lest it should return to interfere in the affairs of those still alive. This did not contradict a sincere affection for the dead person, but the social role was considered to properly end at death.

The most important way of showing concern both for and at the dead was the custom of waking. Wakes of people who had died naturally after a long life were great social occasions, for as well as the lamenting of the dead person by keening women, there were several less desolate practices. At such a wake, stories were told, songs were sung, music and games were played, and there might even be dancing. The corpse was often given its own hand of cards in a card-game, and the smoking-pipe was extended to it as to all the living adults present. In these and other ways, efforts were made to show that the dead person was held in honour and affection, and that friendly memories remained.

There is no doubt but that ideas which, when taken philosophically, are incompatible with Christian teaching on the afterlife did survive (*see* COSMOLOGY). The people themselves seldom noticed such contradictions, but the clergy did, and for centuries strenuous ecclesiastical efforts were made to abolish the customs associated with wakes. Keening of the dead was considered a denial of the promise of heaven, and the robust nature of many of the wake games was considered disrespectful to the deceased. Nevertheless, most people, though very devout in their religious beliefs and practices, would feel hurt and aggrieved if they thought that they would not be 'waked properly' when they died. Until recently, the wake was the great backdrop against which the value of an individual to the community could be measured.

GENERAL: S. Ó Súilleabháin (1942), 177–250 & (1967), 39–55; Wood-Martin, *1* (1902), 285–340 & *2*, 26–45; Ó Danachair (1978), 22–4, 26–7; Ó hÓgáin (1995), 9–28, 71–8, 86–90.

THE SOUL VISUALISED: B. Almqvist in *Sinsear*, *1*, 1–22 & in *Béaloideas*, *59*, 269; RIA Dictionary, s.v. '*bratan*'; Dinneen (1927), s.v. '*bradán*'.

EVIL EYE: J. Borsje & F. Kelly in *Celtica*, *24*, 1–39.

CURES: S. Ó Súilleabháin (1942), 304–15, 432–4; Logan (1972).

DEATH: S. Ó Súilleabháin (1961); Ó Madagáin (ed.) (1978).

SOD OF DEATH: M. Carney in *Arv*, *13*, 173–9; Stokes, *CTS* (1905), 31; O'Grady, *1* (1892), 393; B. O'Reilly in *Béaloideas*, *59*, 88–90, 223–4.

humorous tales A great variety of stories of this nature are found in Ireland, with the best known of them corresponding with type-numbers listed in the Aarne/Thompson catalogue of international FOLKTALES. There the different genres of these entertaining stories are grouped together under headings such as 'Tales of the Stupid Ogre', 'Jokes and Anecdotes', 'Formula Tales' and 'Unclassified Tales'. Examples of Irish versions of the different kinds of humorous tales will, however, be discussed together here. These stories are usually short, but there is a strong tendency in Ireland to string a number of them together and thus to create somewhat longer units.

The outwitting of a GIANT, devil or HAG was a very popular theme in Irish storytelling, and narratives based on this usually involved a combined usage of ruses from different tale types. For instance, the smart hero fools the giant as to his strength by pretending to squeeze a stone with his hand whereas it is in fact a piece of cheese (type 1060), by pretending to cast a stone a long distance when in fact it is a bird that he throws (type 1062), and in an eating contest with the giant slips food into a concealed bag (type 1088). A very popular story, which is often the culmination of such contests, describes how a giant with murderous intent is tricked into killing his own offspring (type 1119). The hero, while sleeping in the giant's house, exchanges places with the giant's children in bed, who are thus slain in the darkness. This folktale has been known in Ireland for a long time, as its plot occurs in a medieval text that tells of how the warrior CONALL CEARNACH turned the tables on a murderous host.

A very widespread account, frequently a mere episode in longer narratives, describes how a man escapes from a ferocious one-eyed giant by blinding him with a hot iron (type 1137). Its earliest occurrence in Irish storytelling would seem to date from medieval times in the context of FIONN MAC CUMHAILL gaining wisdom from eating a special salmon (*see* WONDER TALES, type 673). In that case, it would have been borrowed from the Polyphemus story of Greek literature as a development of an indigenous Irish tradition that had the hero slaying a fiery one-eyed foe. Of less antiquity was the borrowing and reshaping of type 1149 to the context of Fionn. According to this, a giant visits Ireland to fight against Fionn, but the hero pretends to be a baby in the cradle, and Fionn's wife tells the visitor that this is their child. The giant plays with the 'baby', which bites off his finger, and the giant flees, thinking that if the baby is so fierce then Fionn himself must be a quite horrific warrior.

Type 1186 originated on the Continent in the Middle Ages, but appears not to have been introduced into Ireland until recent centuries. It is a satiric story against social TYRANTS, and the butt of it in Ireland is a bailiff who meets the devil while engaged in his work. They journey together and hear a woman curse a pig by saying 'may the devil take you!' The bailiff tells the devil to take the pig, but the evil one says that the woman did not wish it with her whole heart. Similarly, when another woman curses a child, the devil does not take it for the same reason. When a third woman sees the bailiff approach, however, she curses him 'to the devil', and the evil one seizes his companion. The bailiff protests in vain that the woman did not mean it with her whole heart.

Stories concerning the defeat of misers have been very popular in Irish tradition. These are grouped together under type 1305. One of Aesop's Fables describes how a miser is desolate when his gold is stolen from him, but is advised to comfort himself by imagining that he still has it, as he did not intend to spend it anyhow. In or about the eighteenth century, this gave rise to a special Irish ecotype (see FOLKTALE) concerning the magnate DAMER. A similar story is common in folklore – this tells of how, when he nears his end, a miser wishes to take all his gold with him on his departure from this life. He therefore orders that it be melted down so that he can drink it as liquid, but a trickster gives melted butter to him instead, and he dies deceived. That a variant of this was known for many centuries is suggested by an account in a medieval text that has the greedy satirist CRIDHINBHÉAL dying after

he has eaten pieces of gold.

Stupid persons are the butts of many of these folktales. Some such stories, still popular in folklore, were used in or about the fifteenth century by the author of a long text on the fools COMHDHÁN and CONALL CLOGACH. The stories include fools thinking that they themselves are dead (type 1313), fools taking fright without good reason (type 1321), robbers being put to flight from their den by an unwitting fool (type 1527), and a fool swatting a fly on a person's head, with fatal or near-fatal consequences (type 1586A). Type 1600 is told of Conall Clogach in the text, and scores of versions concerning other fools have been collected from recent folklore. These tell of a stupid fellow who sees the body of a murdered landlord's agent being buried in an unmarked grave and, on being questioned by the police, points out the place. The fool's relatives, who have been involved in the murder, have anticipated this and have substituted the body of a puck (i.e. billy goat) for the agent. On the grave being opened, the fool enquires 'Had the agent horns?' and the exasperated police give up their investigation.

One of the most popular of all stories in Irish folklore tells of how a boy is apprenticed to a master thief and soon shows his skills at that profession (type 1525). He steals a fine horse by disguising himself as an old woman selling liquor and making the grooms drunk. Then he steals sheep by leaving a good shoe on the road and its match further on, so that the shepherd leaves his herd to collect the shoes. Finally, he steals the sheet from under a rich couple in bed by creating diversions that cause them to briefly leave the bed. He asks his master to teach him the trick of escaping from the gallows, and when the old thief gives a demonstration, the clever youngster kicks a box away from underneath him and leaves him to hang. He then marries the old thief's wife and acquires all his loot.

Type 1533, which has a clever man carving a goose or deer to his own advantage, occurs in a seventeenth-century text (see FEIDHLIMIDH MAC CRIOMHTHAINN). In later folklore, it is usually told of some POET who composes a quatrain to describe his method of carving. Several varieties of type 1535 have been collected from Irish folklore. The most common pattern tells of how a poor man triumphs over his rich and selfish brother. The latter kills the poor brother's cow, but the poor man has some money concealed in the hide to fool him. Thinking to benefit in the same way, the rich fellow kills all his own cattle, but gains nothing. The enraged rich man puts his brother into a sack with the intention of flinging him over a cliff, but the poor man tells a dishonest cattle dealer that he is going to heaven and gets him to exchange places. The dealer trades his herd of cattle for this 'privilege', and later the poor man tells his brother that he found the cattle in the sea. The brother jumps over the cliff in search of more cattle and is drowned.

Known to Irish literature since the thirteenth or fourteenth century is type 1590, which describes how, while on another's property, a rogue swears that he owns the land he is standing on, having secretly put some of his own soil into his boots. Versions of this, excluding the moral dishonesty, occur in texts concerning COLM CILLE and MONGÁN. A very popular story in Irish folklore concerns an honest but unexpected gain (type 1645). It tells of a man who dreams of a TREASURE hidden near a certain bridge, and on going there is disappointed to find nothing. However, he meets a stranger who tells him that he has dreamt that it is near the man's own house, and on his return home, he finds the treasure. Another man gets rich in an even more unexpected way (type 1653). This man has an extremely foolish wife, and in desperation decides to leave her. As he departs his house, she begs to be allowed to follow him, and he tells her to 'pull the door after her' and come. She obeys him literally, pulling the door from its hinges and carrying it on her back. When night time comes, they climb a tree and use the door to sleep on. It so happens that a band of robbers gather under that tree to divide their loot, and the foolish

woman is so frightened that she cannot remain still above them. Eventually, the door slips and bangs all the robbers on the head, knocking them out, so that all their treasure falls to the man, giving him reason to be grateful to his wife.

Type 1739 is an hilarious tale, found widely abroad but not as common as might be expected in Ireland. It tells of how a cow's urine is substituted for that of a sick man, with the result that the doctor tells the man he is going to give birth to a calf. The man falls asleep and dreams that he has so given birth, and on seeing a calf when he awakes, believes that this is his offspring. In later folklore, the story has been collected only from south Connacht and Munster, but it was known to the Ulster author of an eighteenth-century story concerning CONÁN MAOL. Bizarre surroundings and happenings are the full subject matter of type 1930, which has a rogue describe a strange land to which he claims he has been. Prevalent among the strange sights described are landscapes made up of delicious foods and animals that behave uncharacteristically, such MARVELS being often described in the form of 'lying songs'. It is obvious that a version of such a humorous narrative was known to the medieval author who described the comic vision of MAC CONGLINNE.

A series of formulaic tales and catch-tales were told for and by children. Especially popular in this category were accounts of how a pancake rolled out through the door of a house and was pursued by several different animals until eaten by the fox (type 2025); of how a pig refused to go over a stile and of the roundabout way in which its owner had to engage the help of several animals and objects to compel it to do so (type 2030); and narratives that tease the listeners into asking questions that are saucily answered (types 2200 and 2204). Finally, the international type 2400 tells of how a rogue is offered as much land as he can cover with an ox hide, and he encloses a large area by cutting the hide into thin strips. The story is told in Ireland only in the context of the saints BRIGHID and COLM CILLE, and in it the trick-MOTIF has been changed into a mantle that miraculously spreads. This Irish ecotype originated in the late Middle Ages in the context of St Brighid (q.v.).

Aarne & Thompson (1961), 346–539; S. Ó Súilleabháin & Christiansen (1967), 196–343; S. Ó Súilleabháin (1942), 579–88, 640–9 & (1973), 22–4.

Íde SAINT who died c.AD 570, and who was the foundress of a convent at the place that became known as Cill Íde (Killeedy, County Limerick). The earlier form of her name was Íte, and she was also known as Mo-Íde – hence the form Míde for her name.

Next to BRIGHID, she is the most famous woman saint of Ireland; and some MOTIFS similar to those of Brighid got attached to her cult. For instance, the chamber in which she slept seemed to outsiders to be ablaze. Three recensions of her life exist in Latin, and it is thought that these may incorporate some material from a very early biography. It seems certain that she was a native of the DÉISE area (County Waterford), and it is claimed that she was daughter of one Ceannfhaolaidh, a man of noble lineage. We read that a young nobleman wished to marry her, and her father strongly opposed her desire to devote her life to JESUS CHRIST until an angel appeared to him in a vision and rebuked him. She founded a church in the Déise territory, but following the angel's directions, she went to Uí Chonaill Gabhra (west Limerick) and settled there at Cluain Chreadhail, which accordingly became known as Cill Íde. It is claimed that her first name was Deirdre, and that she became known as Íte because of her thirst (íota) for holiness. Several miracles are related of her, including healing ailments and having souls released from purgatory. She is represented as a particularly compassionate saint – one of her achievements, for instance, was to obtain pardon from a local king for a murderer on condition that he repent.

Íde was reputed to have been a great counsellor and educator. Among her pupils, it was claimed, was the celebrated BRÉANAINN, and she was referred to as 'the foster-mother of the saints of Ireland'. It is likely that her convent did in fact devote itself to the teaching of young boys, and

her care and kindness for them caused her to be imagined as a nurse suitable for the Christ-child Himself. Accordingly, a tenth-century source relates a touching story of her. We read that, for a long time, she endured without complaint a huge beetle that gnawed away at her side. When her nuns saw this beetle follow her from her cell, they killed it, but Íde was displeased, saying that the beetle was her fosterling. JESUS was so touched by this that He came as an infant to her, and Íde was so happy with this visit that she composed a beautiful poem beginning 'little Jesus is nursed by me in my little hermitage, though a cleric have much wealth all is false but little Jesus'.

Several LEGENDS of Íde are still current in the folklore of west Limerick. Some are borrowed from the lore of Brighid – for example, the miraculously spreading cloak and the man who had horse's ears but was made normal by the saint. As was natural in the rural community of west Limerick, she was popularly valued as a patroness of agriculture, and it is locally claimed that she was the owner of the famous cow called the GLAS GHOIBHNEANN. It was also said that she took pity on a poor farmer whose seed was being destroyed by sparrows, and banished all these birds into a nearby pond until his crop had been harvested. According to another legend, she provided a good catch for some penurious fishermen on the River Shannon. An unflattering tradition concerning the village of Tournafulla has it that some illnatured fellows there set dogs at her DONKEY as she passed through one day. The donkey took fright and, while jumping across two rivers which meet there, landed on a rock and left its hoofmarks on it. Another legend has it that a whitethorn tree at Killeedy grew from a thorn she plucked from the donkey's hoof – all the thorns on that tree were turned downwards and were therefore innocuous. Íde's feast day is 15 January.

Kenney (1929), 389–90; Stokes (1905), 42–5, 182–3; G. Murphy (1962), 26–9, 183–4; Plummer, 2 (1910), 116–30; O'Hanlon, 1 (1875), 200–17; N. Breathnach in *Irish Press*, 17/1/1978, 8; IFC 629:409–14, 947:385–8, S493–S497:passim.

Inchiquin Chieftain who, according to a folk LEGEND of County Clare and surrounding areas, married an otherworld lady and was deserted by her on his breaking of a prohibition.

The legend has been connected with various leaders of the Ó Coinn family of north-east Clare – most notably Conchúr Ó Coinn, who was chieftain of the sept from 1461–66. He was said to have first encountered the beautiful lady as he walked by Lake Inchiquin in his territory. She was bathing in the lake, and he seized her cloak. She thus was compelled to follow him to his residence, and she became his partner. She laid one condition upon him, however – that he was never to bring a guest to his house while she was there. Sometime later, he greatly enjoyed the horse races organised at Coad by the neighbouring chieftain, Tadhg Ó Briain, and then brought Ó Briain home with him for drinks. Sadly disappointed at how her prohibition had been broken, the otherworld lady recovered her cloak unknown to Conchúr and returned to the lake.

The story has obviously been influenced by the plot, found along the west coast of Ireland, of a man who married a MERMAID (*see* FAIRIES), but some distinct features of it (such as the horse racing and the bringing home of a stranger) point to the literary Ulster story of MACHA as its source. The Ó Coinn family of Clare (anglice, Quin) were an early offshoot of the DÁL GCAIS sept, and in the late twelfth century were much reduced by their strong rivals and far-out relations, the Ó Briain family (anglice, O'Brien). Of the latter family, Toirdhealbhach Ó Briain, HIGH-KING of Ireland, helped a relative of his, Conchúr Ó Briain, to set up a kingdom in central Ulster from 1078–84. The symbolism of Ulster kingship would thus have been relevant to the O'Brien lore, attracting the story of Macha, whose desertion of the ancient Ulstermen led to their downfall. Another fanciful connection was that the mythical Ulster king of the sagas was called CONCHOBHAR (later version, Conchúr), and this was the name of the short-lived O'Brien king in Ulster. The legend of Macha was thus well known to the O'Brien as an exemplar concerning kingship.

When the O'Briens coveted the territories of their neighbours in Clare, the legend would have served a similar purpose, especially as the family name of their local rivals was identical with that of their national rivals. The leading family of the north was the royal one of the Uí NÉILL, and these were pitted against the O'Briens on the national scale. From time immemorial, they were the leaders of the northern half, called Leath Choinn, and they included among their ranks the family name Ó Coinn, which was unconnected but identical with that of the Clare family. Thus the struggle of the O'Briens of south Clare against the Quins of north Clare echoed in imagery the struggle of the O'Briens of the south of Ireland against the O'Neills of the north of Ireland. In that context, the imminent fall from power of the Quins of Inchiquin could be portrayed in O'Brien propaganda as the desertion of the Quins by an otherworld lady. This would suggest the twelfth century as the time when the borrowing of the Macha plot took place. The plot is indeed echoed in a text with O'Brien influence written in the fourteenth century – *see* CIAN MAC MAOLMHUAIDHE. Its traditional connection with the fifteenth-century Conchúr Ó Coinn may result from the fact that his first name again reflected the situation in the mythical story.

T.J. Westropp in *Folk-Lore*, *24*, 378–81; Ó Duilearga (1948), 439; B. Almqvist in *Béaloideas*, *67*, 13–69; IFC Index.

O'BRIEN KINGDOM IN ULSTER: J. Hogan in Ryan (1940), 431–7.

insects As in other cultures, Irish lore concerning insects varied, some of them being regarded lucky and others unlucky because of quite superficial ideas concerning them.

The spider was considered the most blessed of insects, having once used its web to hide the fugitive JESUS CHRIST; it was therefore never killed, and was regarded as a harbinger of good luck in the house. The spider's web was commonly used to stanch the blood from wounds. Contrariwise, the cockroach or black chafer was detested as the betrayer of Christ by giving information to his pursuers. It was said to have been the only insect to enter Christ's tomb, and its antipathy to Christians – according to popular fancy – is still shown by the habit of raising its tail to curse its beholder. The accusation of betraying Christ is similarly levelled against the earwig, or 'clock', and the dung beetle in some areas.

The cricket was given both positive and negative significance – people believed that it was lucky to hear one in the house, but it was also said to betoken rain. If crickets left a house, this was taken to be an omen of an impending death in the family. People noticed the intricate work patterns of ants, and for these little insects to be unusually busy was taken as a sign of impending rain. It was sometimes thought by superstitious people that flies were demons in disguise, a notion strengthened by the frequent pronunciation of *deamhan* (demon) as *leamhan* (moth). A particularly curious idea was that fleas were lucky in a house, as it was thought they sucked poison out of the blood. To find a ladybird, or 'god-cow', in the garden was taken as a sign that the household was blessed, and this little insect should never be killed. *See also* SAINTS regarding Colmán Mac Duach.

Cross (1952), 24, 69; O'Meara (1982), 80–1; S. Ó Súilleabháin (1942), 300–2; Ó Danachair (1978), 25; P.V. O'Sullivan (1991), 124–6; Ó hÓgáin (1995), 80–2.

Iollann Airmdhearg Fictional hero in a romance tale written by an anonymous author in the late sixteenth or early seventeenth century. Iollann was a popular old Irish name, perhaps with an original meaning '[competent with] many swords'. The impressive name of this particular hero (literally, 'Iollann of the Red Weapons') was borrowed from that of a warrior in another romantic tale, that concerning CONALL GULBAN. Other details, such as the name of the Macaomh Mór and the MOTIF of attacking a king at a feast, were also borrowed from that tale. For most of the narrative, however, the author of the *Eachtra* (Adventure) of Iollann Airmdhearg used an international plot – *see* WONDER TALES (type 301).

We read of how a strange warrior forcibly knocks out the tooth of the Greek king, and also takes a precious goblet from him. The king's three sons – one of whom is Iollann Airmdhearg – set out to recover these items. They meet a noble lady, who tells them that the robber was the Macaomh Mór of Tír Fó Thoinn (Land Under Wave), and gives them a basket through which they can descend to that place. Iollann overcomes all the warriors in the underground world, and falls in love with a beautiful maiden called Éachtach there. His brothers act treacherously, however, by refusing to lower the basket after they themselves have ascended, bringing with them Éachtach as well as the king's tooth and goblet. Iollann has the Macaomh's wonderful steed, and with it gains many further triumphs and finds a magical basket that conveys him home. He takes employment with a fuller in Athens and shows great skill at his work. When his father the king falls sick with depression, Iollann in disguise heals him with the beautiful singing of birds in his magical basket. Iollann also slays a dragon that threatens to devastate Greece. Finally, when one of his brothers was marrying the reluctant Éachtach, Iollann comes in disguise to the wedding, binds by magic everybody there except his father and Éachtach, and then explains all. His two brothers are executed, and he himself marries Éachtach.

There were many manuscript copies of these adventures of Iollann Airmdhearg, and from being read out, the tale became very popular with traditional storytellers. Condensed versions of it were told over much of Ireland.

Bruford (1969), 84–8, 128, 259–60, 279; IFC 581 (edn. by Meadhbh Ní Chléirigh).

Irish language Known in Irish itself as *Gaeilge* (*see* GAEL), the Irish language is descended from the western (*Goidelic*) branch of ancient Celtic, a language spoken in much of central and western Europe until the triumph of the Roman Empire.

Celtic seems to have first reached Ireland in or about the fifth century BC, and to have gradually displaced the language or languages spoken by earlier inhabitants of the island. Primitive Irish must have remained comprehensible to speakers of other Celtic dialects for many centuries, and the OGHAM inscriptions show that the integral Celtic word forms had still not been forgotten in the fourth century AD. When Irish was first committed to writing two centuries later, however, many internal and final syllables had become syncopated, giving rise to a new morphology that clearly distinguished Irish from its Celtic sources. Because of continuing changes in the language, researchers classify three broad periods: Old Irish (seventh to ninth century), Middle Irish (tenth to thirteenth century) and Modern Irish (fourteenth century onwards).

The initial form of Modern Irish is often referred to as Classical Irish; this was promulgated by the literati as a standard literary system from the fourteenth to the early seventeenth century, after which political and social changes brought about the downfall of the native social order. A certain amount of regional variation in the spoken language must have always existed, but it is apparent that the marked differences in Irish dialects are of post-medieval provenance. The dialects can be generally divided into a northern one (Ulster Irish), a central one (now called 'Connacht Irish', but once belonging to most of Leinster as well), and a southern one (Munster Irish). It should be said that two other languages – Scottish Gaelic and Manx Gaelic – originated in Old Irish, but in the post-medieval period, these diverged significantly from the language spoken in Ireland.

In early times, a tendency had developed to soften some intervocalic consonants, and this gave rise to the aspiration of such consonants. It also gave rise to the feature – common to all surviving Celtic languages – of aspiration of initial consonants, usually with a grammatical sense. In Celtic, weakening of final syllables in preceding words could leave the phenomenon called 'eclipsis' on initial consonants and vowels – this also preserved grammatical significance in Irish. It should be noted that, in Irish generally, each consonant is pronounced as either palatal or non-palatal. This sound contrast (often referred to as 'slender' and 'broad') resulted from gradual phonemic changes in the Old Irish period. Standard orthography indicates the palatal quality of a consonant by placing the letter *i* before it, or either *i* or *e* after it. The letters *a, o, u* next to a consonant, or *e* before one, indicate that it is non-palatal, but an initial *r* in a word is almost always non-palatal. An acute accent over a vowel indicates lengthening, and long vowels determine the quality of consonants in the same manner as short ones do.

Stress is the most distinctive feature of differentiation between spoken dialects of Irish. Originally, strong stress was placed on the initial syllable of a word, and this was a major contributory factor to the historical changes in the language – from the syncopation of syllables in primitive Irish to the restructuring of verbal forms in Middle Irish, and the muting of some aspirated consonants within secondary syllables in the post-medieval period. It is clear that initial stress within a word was the norm in all parts of the country, and this did not generally affect secondary syllables, whether short or long. Such remained the situation until the medieval period, but thereafter it survived fully only in the central dialect. In the north, probably under Scottish influence, the strong initial stress tends to cause the shortening of long syllables elsewhere in the word. The opposite occurred in the south, where a secondary long syllable often attracts the stress onto itself and away from the initial. This southern development is thought to have been accelerated by the influence of Anglo-French spoken by the NORMAN settlers.

The vocabulary of the Irish language has, through the centuries, been influenced by several other languages, such as ecclesiastical Latin, and spoken Welsh, Norse, French, Scottish and English. The Irish language can therefore be said to reflect the general historical experience of the country in both linguistic and cultural terms. *Gaeilge* is the standard form of the language's name, but it is also referred to as *Gaeilig* in the north of the country, and *Gaelainn* or *Gaeluinn* in the south.

Ó Cuív (1969); Thurneysen (1961); McCone (1996); T.F. O'Rahilly (1932); de Bhaldraithe (1959); RIA Dictionary, *Gramadach na Gaeilge* (1968); Ó Dónaill (1977).

James II *(1633–1701)* King of England from 1685 until his deposition three years later by his daughter Mary and her husband WILLIAM OF ORANGE. He fled to France and, in 1689 – with the support of the French king Louis XIV – landed in Ireland. He raised a large but ill-equipped army, and was defeated by William in the Battle of the Boyne in 1690.

Although he had shown courage while fighting on land and at sea earlier in his career, his performance at the Boyne was a disaster, fleeing needlessly and leaving his army leaderless. He raced to Dublin, and from there to Wexford and Kinsale (County Cork), where he had first landed a year before. He sailed for France, publicly putting the blame for his defeat on the Irish who risked all for him and were left at home suffering the consequences of their naivety. His disdain for the Irish people was reciprocated, and he was remembered for the cowardice and cynicism he had shown. The traditional saying in Irish was that 'James had one English shoe and one Irish shoe when he lost Ireland', and he is always remembered by the nickname Séamas *an chaca* (literally, 'James of the dung'). At the Boyne, he had been completely outmanoeuvred by William, and was little more than a spectator while he remained there. His Irish followers claimed that he was preoccupied, not with fighting, but with a bout of diarrhoea, and hence the nickname.

Early in the battle, William had been wounded by a haphazard cannonball, but not seriously. Several of the Jacobites believed that he had been killed, and such a rumour spread to Dublin and even to Paris. There were other accounts also. One claimed that James' son, the Duke of Berwick, attacked and slew a small group of enemy officers, believing William himself to be among them and not willing to miss 'a splendid

opportunity for putting an end to this war'. Another account, perhaps more reliable, had it that a gunner in the Jacobite army had William well within his sights and range for a moment, but James forbade him to shoot and William was thus spared. This latter story survives in folklore, which has James beseeching the gunner not to 'make a widow of my daughter'.

A contemporary report says that after the battle, James entered Dublin 'in a manner stunned'. His chief-of-staff was the huge and courageous Richard Talbot, Duke of Tyrconnell, and an apocryphal story soon spread of how the wife of this Talbot asked James in Dublin what he would like to eat. The king replied that after such a breakfast, he had little stomach for a dinner. The idea of this encounter with Lady Tyrconnell later gave rise to a LEGEND that is still well known. According to this, she had been the first woman whom he met as he hurried into Dublin on his sweat-drenched horse. She sought news of the battle from him, and was told that the Irish had run away. The lady quickly retorted that his majesty had won the race. That James really was very nervous in his flight is clear from the report of a man who gave him a change of horses at Enniscorthy and noticed that he was riding with his pistols at full cock.

It is said, however, that James left one small benefit in Ireland, for it was believed that his blood could cure the skin disease scrofula – commonly known as 'king's evil'. Folk anecdotes were current that told of how he spilled a drop of his blood either accidentally or deliberately, and thereby healed people suffering from the ailment. The ability to cure this was the test of a true king, and the strong likelihood is that in the context of James, the MOTIF first became popular when he was held in high regard before the debacle at the Boyne. That, even more than his deposition, was the great turning point of his career. As one Irish folklore account states: 'The people liked James well enough before he ran, they didn't like him after that!' The folk memory contrasts the ineptitude of James with the dashing brilliance of one of his cavalry officers, Patrick SARSFIELD. According to one account, after the defeat, Sarsfield remarked to him in France: 'James, King and Prince, if you owned the whole world you would lose it!'

Bagwell, *3* (1916), 260–308: Ellis (1976), 62–5, 122–30, 144–9; Gregory (1926), 47–8, 55; de híde (1933), 146; T. Ó Concheanainn in *Éigse*, *14*, 225, 236; Bell (1956), 19; M.R. Toynbee in *Folk-lore*, *61*, 1–14; OSL: Wicklow (1839), 251–2; IFC 195:262, 794:489–92, 924: 489–95.

Jesus Christ *(in Irish, Íosa Críost)* In addition to the canonical texts of the New Testament, many accounts of Jesus and of His companions were current throughout Europe in apocryphal works in Latin and Greek. These works were very popular in medieval Irish Christianity, and many of them were translated into Irish. The Church in Ireland, indeed, was more tolerant of the apocryphal literature than it was in other countries and, as a result, the Irish sources are very important to a study of this whole phenomenon of unapproved accounts of Christ. Particularly important in early Irish devotional literature were versions of the works known as the 'Gospel according to the Hebrews', the 'Book of James' and the 'Gospel of Thomas', which gave fanciful descriptions of Jesus' youth, and 'the Gospel of Nicodemus' which told of Jesus' Passion, death and harrowing of hell.

It was, of course, considered in Ireland that Jesus had been born in mid-winter, with all the attendant harshness of climate at that time of year. Thus we read of several MARVELS that occurred at his birth, such as grapes ripening, palm trees flowering, wheat sprouting, lights appearing in temples, and babies speaking in their mothers' wombs. The sun shone in Bethlehem at midnight, and all those who were sick or afflicted were healed immediately in that hour. More obviously derived from Continental apocrypha are accounts of a great fragrance that filled the cave in which the Christ-child was born, and how He conversed with the three wise men who came with beautiful presents for Him. He soon showed His great wisdom and miraculous power. As a little boy, He shaped some clay into the form of BIRDS, and

when an over-pious man upbraided Him for doing this on the Sabbath, He clapped His hands and the clay images became alive and flew away to heaven. When sent to school, He showed that He knew more than the master, and other boys who tormented Him were miraculously struck down but were revived by Himself. The cross on which Christ was crucified, we read, was made from four different timbers – cedar, cypress, pine and beech.

The Gospel of Nicodemus, written in Greek in the fourth century AD, describes how, after the Crucifixion, the traitor Judas was going to hang himself, fearful of the prophecy that the dead Christ would rise again. Judas' wife, who was roasting a cock at the time, tried to reassure him by stating that this would no more happen than the dead cock would crow, whereupon the cock flapped its wings and crowed three times. Versions of this in medieval Irish literature have the woman as Judas' mother or sister rather than his wife, and have Judas himself boasting that the cock will not crow. The motif became very popular in post-medieval Irish iconography, the cock and cooking pot being on many tombstones and at the foot of little wooden crosses carried by penitents.

Not surprisingly, oral versions of this LEGEND were current throughout Ireland. According to these, the soldiers who had crucified Jesus were cooking a cock when one of them remarked that it was rumoured that the executed man would come back to life again. Another soldier denied this by reference to the cock, whereupon the dead bird arose from the cauldron, flapped its wings and cried out *'Mac na hÓighe slán!'* (the Son of the Virgin is safe). Ever since, it is claimed, cocks say this when they crow. These Irish folk versions have assimilated the situation to the canonical account of the cock crowing to signal Peter's denial of Christ, an account upon which the original apocryphal story was itself probably based.

Folklore tends to reflect philosophical ideas in its own physical way. Thus the Christian theory of history, which has the birth of Jesus ushering in a new era, gives rise in European folklore generally to the notion that the physical and cultural ENVIRONMENT was reshaped in many ways during the life of the Saviour. This is very much the case in Ireland also. We are told that Christ was once a fugitive and that the spider covered Him with its web so that his enemies could not see Him. This insect is thus regarded as blessed. The chafer beetle, however, is cursed, because it betrayed Christ. Some men were at work sowing corn when Christ passed by, and He told them that if questioned by His pursuers, they should not lie. The corn grew up overnight, and therefore when the search party arrived next day, the sowers told them that the fugitive had passed by when they were sowing. The soldiers were about to abandon their pursuit, but a chafer treacherously cried out '*inné!*' (yesterday!). It is also said that a PIG rooted clay over Christ to conceal Him, but a hen scraped it away and that, as a result, hens lay eggs painfully while sows bear their young with ease. The elder tree once refused to shelter Christ, but the ivy did so, hence the elder is the last tree to bear leaves while the ivy is evergreen. In a similar vein, the DONKEY got the cross on its back because it carried Christ on His triumphant entry to Jerusalem, and the robin (*see* BIRDS) got its red breast when it tried to remove a thorn or wipe the blood from the brow of the dying Saviour.

In human terms also, it is regarded as the time of beginnings. For instance, the Virgin Mary once remarked to her little son Jesus that He was her 'seven loves', and the child replied that she had left a sad inheritance to mothers, for ever after they would love their children so much as to cause heartbreak to themselves. A legend that has been international since medieval times tells of how, when Mary was pregnant, she asked her husband Joseph to fetch some fruit from a nearby tree. Joseph replied peevishly that she should ask the father of her child to do that for her, whereupon the tree bent down of its own accord so that she could get the fruit. Ever since, pregnant women long for fruit while old men get jealous of their young wives.

There is an element of humour in such lore, which does not, however, preclude piety. Another international story current in Ireland tells of how Jesus and Mary once met a blind man, and Mary privately asked Jesus to give him his sight. Jesus remarked that that might not be a good idea, because the man's wife was misbehaving with another man. Mary then asked that the wife be given an excuse also. So, when the cure was effected and the man saw what was happening, his wife remarked: 'If I was not fooling you, these people would not have taken pity on you and would not have given your sight to you!' Ever since, we are told, women have an excuse on the tip of their tongues.

An international story that was very popular in Ireland told of how Christ pointed out a mistake made by His leading apostle, St Peter (*see* RELIGIOUS TALES, type 774K). Less popular in oral tradition, though quite influential in the literature, was a story of how Christ miraculously caused a coin to be retrieved from the belly of a FISH (*see* WONDER TALES, type 736A). This motif, popular throughout the Christian world, occurs in fact in the Gospel of Matthew (17:26).

One of the best-known religious legends in Irish folklore has an even older source. This tells of how the child Jesus and His mother once sought lodgings at a house where a kind man was married to a high-handed woman. The wife curtly refused to allow them in, but the man told them that they could sleep in an outhouse. During the night, the man was severely smitten with a pain in his side, and his wife in desperation went to Jesus and Mary for help. Jesus told His mother to place her palm on the afflicted part and to recite the following prayer: 'A gentle man had a rude wife who put Jesus Christ sleeping in the straw. Mary's palm to the wound, in the name of the Father and the Son and the Holy Ghost!' The man was healed immediately, and so this prayer – which is in Irish and is called *Ortha an Ghreama* (the charm prayer for the stitch) – was commonly recited to heal such an ailment. Similar stories were current in

Hungary and Italy, and there can be little doubt but that these are survivals of a tradition once common in Europe. The ultimate source, in fact, seems to be a pre-Christian Egyptian story of how a rich woman refused shelter to the goddess Isis. When the woman's young son was stung by a serpent, Isis took pity on him and healed him with an incantation.

Popular piety in traditional Ireland was of such an immediate nature that there were folk prayers for almost all situations and to counteract many common ailments. The greatest devotion, however, centred on the suffering and Crucifixion of Jesus and on the sorrow of the Virgin Mary. Many variants of a heart-rending song described a conversation between the dying Christ and His mother as she stood at the foot of the cross.

APOCRYPHA IN IRELAND: E. Hogan (1895), 38–85; Carney (1964); B. Ó Cuív in *Éigse*, 15, 93–102; Atkinson (1887); G. Mac Niocaill in *Éigse*, 8, 76–7; Ó Maonaigh (1944); Ní Chróinín (1952); McNamara (1975), 37–125.

FOLKLORE: S. Ó Súilleabháin (1942), 548–51 & (1952), 3–31, 304–7; A. O'Connor in *Sinsear*, 2, 34–42; P. Ó Héalaí in *Léachtaí Cholm Cille*, 14, 151–72 & in *An Sagart*, 1–2 (1979).

PRAYERS: Ó Siochfhradha (1932), 360–404; Ó Laoghaire (1975).

ORIGIN OF STITCH LEGEND: T. Domotor in *Arv*, 28, 21–35.

VIRGIN MARY: Ó Domhnaill (1940); Partridge (1983); O'Dwyer (1988); Jestice (2000), 347–9.

Kildare, Earl of

Kildare, Earl of Leader of one of the two major branches of the NORMAN-Gaelic FITZGERALD family. The personage who stands immediately behind this designation in the folklore of Leinster and south Ulster was probably Gerald FitzGerald (1525–86), the eleventh Earl of Kildare. Known like several leaders of his family as Gearóid Iarla (Gerald the Earl), his stature was no doubt increased by the far greater fame of his predecessors, his grandfather and father, Gearóid Mór and Gearóid Óg respectively.

After the overthrow of his father and relatives in 1537, and while still a boy, he was protected by the native Irish chieftains and then spirited away to the friends and associates of his family in Florence. He was pardoned by Queen Mary in 1553 and was allowed to return to his native country. His return was greeted with great delight and expectation in Ireland, where the people – according to a contemporary English report – were 'so affectionate to this house that they would sooner a Geraldine come among them than God'. Although he disappointed such hopes, it is clear that suitable LEGENDS became attached to him at the time. These legends were borrowed from the lore of the other great Geraldine family, the Earls of DESMOND. So we are told that the Earl of Kildare once engaged in magical practices in a secret room in Kilkea Castle, but that when one spell went wrong, he became enchanted and since sleeps in a hidden cavern somewhere in County Kildare. Every seven years, he rides around the flat plain of the Curragh on a horse with silver shoes, and when these shoes are worn out, he will return to free Ireland. Since the eighteenth century at least, the MOTIF of the sleeping army of the Earl of Kildare is also found in connection with a location further north – the *rath* of Hacklim near Ardee, County Louth. The reason for this migration seems to have been the incidental occurrence of the name Gearóid in several local toponymics in that area.

Curtis (1936), 168; O'Donovan (1848–51), 1530–1; W. Fitzgerald in *JKAS*, 3, 13; D. Mac Íomhair in *CLAJ*, 14, 68–81: D. Ó hÓgain in *Béaloideas*, 42–4, 219–20, 230, 245, 255–6, 283–97.

kings/kingship

kings/kingship The king (in Irish, *rí*) was the most important personage in early and medieval society, and many beliefs and rituals attaching to his office seem to echo a role of 'priest-king' in more archaic times.

The echoes include the idea of truth (*fír*), which was the quality of a good king, and falsehood (*gó*), which attended a bad one. This has parallels in the ancient Sanskrit literature of India, and may be taken as an Indo-European system of valuation. One early Irish text states the position with a mystical flavour: 'Truth in a ruler is as bright as the foam cast up by a mighty wave of the sea, as the sheen of a swan's covering in the sun, as the colour of snow on a mountain. A ruler's truth is an effort which overpowers armies. It brings milk into the world, it brings corn and mast.' A general illustration of the belief is found in the references to the sacred prohibitions (*see* GEIS) that attended the office of kingship. These prohibitions show that the king, as mediator between supernatural powers and his community, was a power-point, and that social equilibrium depended on his observing the often difficult demands placed on him by the supernatural powers that bestow prosperity.

The clearest expression of these ideas was in the context of the ritual kingship of TARA. The myth of king CONAIRE states that two steeds of one colour, never before harnessed, were placed under a chariot and could only be controlled by the man who was destined to be king. A special mantle fitted only the true king, whose selection had further to be ratified by a vision of seers. When the chariot was driven by that man, two flagstones at Tara would open before it to allow it through, and the upright stone called the Lia Fáil screeched against its axle. The strange prohibitions on Conaire are also illustrative of the sacred nature of kingship. Especially relevant is the way in which he must accord with the movements of the sun – he must not be in bed at sunrise, must not cross a particular plain after sunset, and must not go to sea on the Monday after the Bealtaine feast (*see* TIME). This seems to be based on the idea that the sun-god was the father-deity of the tribe and therefore the patron of kingship (*see* GODS). The sacred prohibitions actually fulfilled a social purpose, for they tempered the authority conferred on the king with reminders that he was himself subject to rules and could lose office if general welfare did not result from his rule. It was held that if he suffered a blemish, the king must resign, and presumably in archaic culture a king would be removed from office or even sacrificed if his reign did not bring prosperity.

Sovereignty was posited as a gift proffered by the GODDESS, a gift of herself to the king who was thus her mystical spouse, who ritually incorporated the ancestor-deity. She symbolically offers him a drink, as in the medieval account of her appearance in the company of the god LUGH,

who gave a long list of future Tara kings to CONN CÉADCHATHACH. She is in fact the land-goddess, and the theme of her marriage to the proper ruler of a territory is a perennial one in Irish tradition. Under differing names, she may be the tutelary spirit of a particular area or of the whole country, the latter theme surviving as a patriotic convention in poetry down to recent times. It is likely that the whole complex of imagery and lore pertaining to kingship in Ireland should be regarded as residue of ancient rituals that accompanied the installation of kings, rituals that would have lauded their authority while reminding them of their responsibilities. That these responsibilities were broad-based is suggested by the frequent allusions in the literature to the good king as one who shows fierceness towards the strong and gentility towards the weak, a principle which in real life may have been honoured as much in its breach as in its observance.

The lore concerning great individual kings – whether mythical, fictional or historical – is discussed in this book under the headings of the individual names of these personages. Most notable among them are AILILL ÓLOM, BRIAN BÓRAMHA, CATHAL MAC FIONGHUINE, Ó CONCHÚIR [CATHAL CROBHDHEARG], CONCHOBHAR MAC NEASA, CORMAC MAC AIRT, CONAIRE, DIARMAID MAC CEARRBHEOIL, EOCHAIDH FEIDHLEACH, FEIDHLIMIDH MAC CRIOMHTHAINN, LABHRAIDH, LAOGHAIRE, NIALL, NUADHU and TUATHAL TEACHTMHAR. However, in the narratives derived from, or influenced by, international FOLKTALES, the figure of king is rather based on the European feudal model (*see* ROMANTIC TALES *and* WONDER TALES).

GENERAL: Dillon (1969); Binchy (1970); F.J. Byrne (1973), 7–69; J. Baudis in *Ériu*, 7, 101–7; R. Thurneysen in *ZCP*, 20, 213–27; C. Watkins in *Ériu*, 30, 181–98; M. Geriets in *Celtica*, 20, 29–52; de Vries (1961), 49–50; McCone (1990), 109–10; Enright (1996), 260–82; Koch & Carey (1997), 32–3.

LISTS OF KINGS: Macalister (1956), 137–565; O'Brien (1962), 117–28, 360–1; F.J. Byrne (1973), 275–301.

Labhraidh Mythical KING and ancestor of the Leinster people (LAIGHIN). His name is accompanied by the sobriquet Loingseach (exiled one), and alternately

Moen (later, Maon, meaning 'dumb') or Lorc (fierce). His legendary lore seems to contain the oldest tradition that the Leinstermen had concerning themselves, and may even contain a memory of how some section of them first came to Ireland.

An invasion by Labhraidh at the head of his Leinstermen is referred to in a few poetic fragments that may date from as early as the sixth century AD. One such fragment states that he destroyed by burning a fortress at Dinn Ríg (at Burgage, south of Leighlinbridge, County Carlow), and that he slew his foe COBHTHACH CAOL there. A full account is given in a ninth-century text, and here his conquest is for political reasons represented as a return to his rightful inheritance. Laoghaire Lorc, we are told, was king of Ireland, and he had a brother called Cobhthach, who wasted away from jealousy of him. Laoghaire went to visit the ailing Cobhthach, who feigned death. When Laoghaire reclined over him in mourning, the imposter stabbed him through the heart and killed him. Cobhthach then caused Ailill Áine, son of Laoghaire and king of Leinster, to be poisoned, and he himself usurped the kingdom. Ailill had a young son who never spoke and was therefore called Moen. One day on the playing field, Moen was struck on the shin by a hurley stick, and cried out: 'I am hurt!' 'The Dumb speaks,' *(labhraidh Moen)* said the other hurlers, and so that phrase became his name. When the usurper Cobhthach soon after asked his men of art who was the most generous nobleman in Ireland, in anticipation of praise for himself, they answered that Labhraidh Moen was. Overcome with jealousy, Cobhthach banished the youngster from the country, along with the poet FEIRCHEIRDNE and the harpist CRAIFTINE, who had praised him.

The banished trio betook themselves to Munster, to a people called the Fir Morca, whose king Scoriath gave them refuge. This king had a daughter called Moriath, who was closely guarded by her mother but who nevertheless fell in love with Labhraidh. One night while a feast was in progress, Craiftine played magic music on his harp so that the mother slept, and then Labhraidh went to the girl. When the mother awoke, she heard her daughter heave the sigh of a married woman and realised what had happened. Labhraidh admitted his role, and was accepted by Scoriath and gained a promise of help from that king to gain his inheritance. They went on a hosting together to the strong fortress of Cobhthach at Dinn Ríg and, having failed to capture it, resorted to a trick. Craiftine played sleep-music on the rampart while the besiegers covered their ears, and with the defenders overcome by sleep, Dinn Ríg was taken by storm. Labhraidh then sent a cordial invitation to Cobhthach to visit him, and for this purpose commenced the building at Dinn Ríg of a great banqueting hall. It was all of iron and took a year to complete. None of the builders spoke a word of their work, and we read that from this a proverb grew up to the effect that 'every Leinsterman has his own secret'. When all was ready, Cobhthach came with a great entourage, but he refused to enter the hall unless Labhraidh's mother and jester should go before him. On Labhraidh's instructions, the door was fastened with a great chain and thrice-50 bellows were blown until the building was red hot. Labhraidh then realised that his own mother was within, but she exhorted him to gain his vengeance at all costs, and Cobhthach, with all his followers, was destroyed.

This account is clearly inflated and was, to some extent, a distortion of the original tradition. The designation Fir Morca (i.e men of Morca) for the allies of Labhraidh, and the locating of that sept in Munster, are curious features, for the text itself states that Labhraidh was banished from Ireland. In fact, an appendage to the text states that the hero was called Labhraidh 'Loingseach' after he left the country, established a kingdom near Muir nIocht (the English Channel), and 'brought back two thousand two hundred foreigners with broad lances [*co laighnibh*] in their hands, from which they are called Laighin'. It may therefore be that Fir

Morca is a corruption of an earlier 'Armorica', and that this designation is an echo of Leinster origins, be these in Armorica (i.e. Brittany) or somewhere on the island of Britain. It is at any rate clear that there was ancient lore of how Leinstermen destroyed a fortress through a conflagration, for that is reflected also in the early saga of CONAIRE.

A later medieval tract gives a version of the story which is further expanded. This states that the young Moen was made by Cobhthach to eat a piece of the hearts of his father and grandfather and to drink a goblet of their blood. This, we are told, was why he became dumb. When banished, he went to Armenia and became a famous champion of the king of that land. He could not refrain from speaking out in praise of the beautiful music played by Craiftine, and thus his handicap was overcome. Returning to Ireland with a fleet of 300 ships, he landed at the Boyne estuary, marched to Dinn Ríg, and slew Cobhthach there. One man at Dinn Ríg asked another the question 'Does the exile speak?' and got the answer '*labhraidh*' (he speaks). There were therefore varying descriptions of how the hero first spoke, and this shows that the acquisition of his name reflects some basic idea that had become confused with the passing of time. There may have been a residual memory of differences between the dialect of the Leinstermen and the speech of earlier Celtic groups in Ireland. Alternately, or perhaps in addition to that, the king's eponymous speaking could refer to enunciation in formal or rhetorical language. The further epithet *lorc* connected with his name has the general meaning of fierce or voracious, but it is also taken to be synonymous with *moen*, or dumb. Thus the general imagery connected with Labhraidh concerns an abnormality or blemish of some kind.

This imagery invited personal drama, and a less-learned type of FOLKTALE was attached to Labhraidh in or about the tenth century. This (*see* RELIGIOUS TALES, type 782) was told of king Midas in Greek myth and had wide circulation in medieval Europe, but Labhraidh seems to owe the plot to the Welsh versions concerning king March ap Meirchion. It suited the context of Labhraidh, not only because of the notion of blemish, but also because of the stress placed in that context on magical music and on unexpected speech. So Labhraidh was said to have had horse's ears and, to preserve the secret, had every barber who cut his hair put to death. When a widow's son was appointed to the task, the alarmed mother beseeched Labhraidh to spare him and promised that he would not reveal whatever he discovered. This was agreed, but the young man grew sick and pined for three years with the burden of the secret. A DRUID advised him to go to a crossroads, to turn to his right, and to tell the secret to the first tree he met. He did this, and soon recovered his health. The tree in question was a willow, and Craiftine afterwards used the timber of that very tree to make a new harp. When the harp was played, the sound came from it as the words 'Labhraidh Lorc has the two ears of a horse'. Hearing this, Labhraidh was stricken with remorse for having put his barbers to death, and uncovered his ears for all to see his blemish.

The stories of how Labhraidh triumphed over Cobhthach and that concerning his ears were retold in the seventeenth century by Seathrún CÉITINN in his very influential history. Only the story of the horse's ears, however, survived in oral tradition. Versions of it have been collected from the folklore of many parts of Ireland. In many areas, it has undergone a further development, which brings the great mythical Leinster king into contact with the principal holy woman of that province, St BRIGHID. The literary biographies of Brighid described how she, by a miracle, gave eyes to a certain flat-faced man, and this episode provided the opportunity for a new twist to the story of Labhraidh's ears. So we are told – quite anachronistically – that Labhraidh was so depressed by his blemish that he went to seek consolation from the SAINT. He sorrowfully laid his head in her lap, and she blessed him. 'I see no blemish,' she said. He stood up and felt his head, and to his great delight found that he had ordinary human ears. Based on the literary account of the flat-faced man, and because of the mutual associations of Brighid and the horse-eared Labhraidh with Leinster, some imaginative person – probably an eighteenth-century clergyman – devised the new narrative.

ORIGINS OF LEINSTERMEN: O'Brien (1962), 1–9, 334–5; T.F. O'Rahilly (1946), 101–20; F.J. Byrne (1973), 130–6; Smyth (1982), 7–12.

DINN RÍG: W. Stokes in ZCP, 3, 1–14 & in RC, 20, 429–33; Dillon (1946), 4–9; O'Brien (1962), 17–19; H. Wagner in Ériu, 28, 1–16; Ó Muraíle, 2 (2003), 190–2.

CÉITINN'S TELLING: Dinneen, 2 (1908), 160–75.

HORSE'S EARS: B. Ó Cúiv in Éigse, 11, 167–87; M.Ó. Briain in Béaloideas, 53, 11–74. See also Gwynn (1913), 334–7.

BRIGHID AND LABHRAIDH: P. Ó Milleadha in Béaloideas, 6, 75; H.M. Roe in Béaloideas, 11, 189; M.Ó. Briain in Béaloideas, 53, 52–7. See Ó hÓgáin (1985), 24–5, 324.

Laighin Name for the confederation of peoples who inhabited the broad south-eastern part of Ireland. The word is from a Celtic *lagini* (lance-men), perhaps a re-interpretation of a different Celtic word *leiquni* (casters).

These peoples may have been composed mostly of the population indigenous to that area since antiquity, but it is clear that new groups were crossing from Celtic Britain, and perhaps some from Brittany, since the late Bronze Age into the early Iron Age, and intermingling with them. Principal among such groups were offshoots of the Brigantes, a powerful people in central Britain, from whom the cult of the goddess BRIGHID among the Laighin seems to have come. The Laighin soon gained control of the great hill fort later known as Ailleann (in modern County Kildare), and established it as their cultic centre. Another group who coalesced with them were called Gaileoin (from *gaiso-lingi*, meaning 'javelin-jumpers'), and together they extended their power over most of the south-eastern quarter of Ireland, reaching as far as the River Shannon in the west and Wexford in the south. Showing their origin more clearly, some other groups among the

Laighin have identical names with powerful tribes in Britain – such as the Bairrche (Celtic, *Barreki*) and Domhnainn (Celtic, *Dumnonii*). Intermittently throughout the territories of the Laighin, and particularly on the verges, were tribes referred to as *imeall-thuatha* (marginal peoples) – these may have been in some cases earlier ÉRAINN tribes who managed to preserve their identity, and in other cases later arrivals from Britain who were known as Cruithnigh (*see* PICTS).

The Laighin continued to expand their power, and some of them, or their clients, even spread across the River Shannon and settled in the far west. Most significant, however, was their taking of the prestigious ritual centre of TARA from the ÉRAINN in or about the second century AD. They expropriated the cult of the site and of the surrounding Boyne Valley (*see* BÓINN *and* FIONN FILE). A century or two later, however, they lost territory there to the emergent CONNACHTA, and henceforth their power was confined to southwards of the Boyne river. That area was known as their *cúige* ('fifth' part of Ireland), and took their name. In the fifth century, they extended their power eastwards across the Irish Sea, settling in a Welsh peninsula from which they were soon evicted but which retained their name in the form Lleyn.

The Laighin remained one of the strongest of the Irish provinces until the NORMAN invasion in the twelfth century. With the gradual extinction of the province of Midhe (Meath) to their north in Anglo-Norman times, the province of Laighin was understood to include that whole area as well as their traditional lands. So, in Modern Irish, the provincial name Laighin involves the twelve counties of Wexford, Carlow, Kilkenny, Laois, Wicklow, Dublin, Kildare, Offaly, Longford, Westmeath, Meath and Louth. The word *cúige* (fifth), is still used for a province (even though there are only four), and thus this province is more usually referred to as Cúige Laighean (Laighean being the genitive of the plural word Laighin). In English, the province is called Leinster. A duplicated ending is used in Modern Irish to indicate a Leinster person, 'Laighneach' (plural, Laighnigh).

Many worthies of Laighin extraction have entries in this book – including the mythico-fictional BRIGHID, CATHAOIR MÓR, FIANNA CYCLE, FIONN FILE, FIONN MAC CUMHAILL, LABHRAIDH and MANANNÁN; and the historical BRANDUBH, St BRIGHID, CAOIMHGHIN and MAOLODHRÁN.

Of the many surnames taken in medieval times by septs of Leinster origin, the most numerous nowadays include: Ó Broin (Byrne); Ó Tuathail (O'Toole); Ó Dubhlaoich (Dooley); Ó Murchú (Murphy of Wexford); Ó Riain (Ryan of Leinster); Ó hAodha (Hughes); Caomhánach (Kavanagh); Ó Cinsealaigh (Kinsella); Ó Treasaigh (Treacy); Ó Cuilinn (Cullen); Mac Giolla Cholmóg (Fitzdermot); Ó Cainnigh (Kenny); Ó Duibhir (Dwyer); Ó Donnagáin (Donegan); Ó Dubhluachra (Duloughry); Ó Fearghail (Farrell, Farrelly, of east Leinster); Ó Ceallaigh (Kelly of Wicklow); Ó Riagáin (Reagan); Ó Duinn (Dunne); Ó Conchúir Failghe (O'Connor of Faly); Ó Díomasaigh (Dempsey); Ó hAonghusa (Hennessy); Ó Duibh (Duff). *See also* OSRAIGHE.

GENERAL: O'Brien (1962), 1–79, 99–100, 334–57, 430–4; T.F. O'Rahilly (1946), 556; F.J. Byrne (1973), 130–64, 288–90; Ó hÓgáin (2002), 286; Ó Muraíle, *2* (2003), 180–307 & *3*, 522–76.

Laoghaire Son of the celebrated NIALL, and thus usually known as Laoghaire mac Néill. The earlier form of his name was Loíguire – it seems to have been in common usage, and it meant 'calf-guardian' or 'young official'. After Niall's death, his cousin Nath Í – leader of the western branch of the CONNACHTA – was to the fore for a while, but Laoghaire soon took over and reigned as KING at TARA until slain in battle with the Leinstermen in or about AD 461.

There is uncertainty concerning the length of his reign – traditional accounts claim it lasted 35 years, but it may have been much less. The question depends on the floruit of his father Niall, which is unsettled. All sources agree that the national saint PATRICK began his mission in the fourth or fifth year of Laoghaire's reign. The saint's seventh-century biographer

Muirchú gives a dramatic account of the meeting of the two. Laoghaire, he says, was a 'great king' and a 'fierce pagan' who had heard prophecies from his DRUIDS that such a missioner would come, and the expected event materialised when Laoghaire was in Tara performing his royal function of lighting a fire at Easter. Nobody was allowed to kindle a fire before the king on that night, but Patrick had lit his Paschal fire at Slane, and Laoghaire thus set out with his soldiers and druids to arrest him. Astounded by the saint's miraculous power, however, Laoghaire submitted and was converted to Christianity.

The other seventh-century biographer of Patrick, Tíreachán, gives a more accurate historical account, stating clearly that Laoghaire did not accept the Christian faith. He has the king declaring that his father Niall would not allow this, but had ordered that Laoghaire be buried on the ridges of Tara, facing south against the Leinster royal graves at Maistiu (Mullaghmast, County Kildare) 'because such is the fierceness of our hatred'. Tíreachán also mentions how two daughters of Laoghaire wished to follow Patrick, but the druids who reared them in Connacht tried to prevent them from doing so. The maidens came to the SAINT at a well near Cruachu (Rathcroghan, County Roscommon), and were instructed and baptised by him there. They then demanded to see the face of JESUS CHRIST, and died soon afterwards.

The subsequent texts repeat the claim that Laoghaire submitted to Patrick and adopted the new faith; and one eleventh-century source – stressing his supposed conversion – states that the mythic hero CÚ CHULAINN appeared to him while he disputed with the saint and exhorted him to become a Christian. The medieval literature also gives a dramatic account of his death. We read that he was captured by the Leinstermen in an attempt to collect the *BÓRAIMHE* tribute, and in order to be released swore by the elements not to seek that tribute again. However, sometime later he tried to re-impose the *bóraimhe*. It had been prophesied to him that he would die between Ireland and Scotland, and for this reason he always avoided travelling on the sea. There were, however, two hills in Leinster – one called Éire (Ireland) and the other called Alba (Scotland) – and as he moved south on a campaign against the Leinstermen, he was slain at Greallach Dá Phil (near Mullacash, County Kildare), between these two hills.

Such ambiguous prophecies were quite popular as a narrative device to heighten the drama in accounts of the deaths of kings. The MOTIF of being buried facing the foe was also a favourite narrative device, but it may encapsulate a burial custom in the cult of warriors, regarding the protection of territorial boundaries. In the case of his father Niall (q.v.), we read that the dead body of the warrior king was held aloft by his followers when going into battle.

GENERAL: Carney (1973), 8–13; Bieler (1979), 74–7, 84–99, 106–9, 127–45; Mulchrone (1939), 26–37; Stokes (1887), 562–7 & in *RC*, *13*, 52–3; Macalister (1956), 352–5, 530–1; Best & Bergin (1929), 278–87; G. Mac Eoin in *Studia Hibernica*, *8*, 21–48; C.G. Buttimer in *PHCC*, *1*, 63–78.

BOUNDARY BURIALS: Ó hÓgáin (1999), 49–50, 200.

Laoghaire Buach

Laoghaire Buach Fictional warrior in the ULSTER CYCLE. The name seems to have gained currency due to the historical fifth-century king LAOGHAIRE. The sobriquet (earlier, Buadhach) means 'victorious', and the name of the father of this fictional character is given as Connadh Buidhe.

Laoghaire is, in several texts, enumerated among the leading warriors at the court of king CONCHOBHAR MAC NEASA. In particular, he is featured as contending with CÚ CHULAINN and CONALL CEARNACH for precedence at the feast of BRICRIU. The only other noteworthy account concerns his death, which is described in an eleventh-century text. According to this, Mughain, wife of Conchobhar, cohabited with one of the king's poets, Aodh. When Aodh was sentenced to death by the angry Conchobhar, he asked that the mode of execution be drowning. At each lake to which he was taken, however, Aodh sang a spell that caused it to dry up (*see* POETS). There was a lake called Loch Laí in front of Laoghaire's house, and the poet's spell could not affect this, so he was brought there to be drowned. Incensed that a poet should be thus killed in his lake, Laoghaire rushed out of the house with sword in hand. He struck the crown of his head against the door lintel and his brains were spattered all over his cloak. Nevertheless, the dying Laoghaire slew 30 of the executioners before he himself expired, and the poet went free.

Henderson (1899); Ó Cadhlaigh (1956), 476; Meyer (1906), 22–3; M. Dillon in *Ériu*, *11*, 47–8, 51.

legend

legend In this book, the term 'legend' is used to denote a narrative that is told as if it were to be believed. The actual belief accorded may be fanciful rather than total, emotional rather than literal, but it can be argued that in any sense, the element of belief is much stronger than is expected of the genre known as FOLKTALE. Also, legends tend to be told of real persons or places, and even though there may be fantastic elements in them, they postulate real-life situations.

Many of the stories told in traditional Irish literature can, on this assumption, be considered as legends, and especially those stories concerning historical characters. The origin of a literary legend is not always clear, and analysis of the individual legend may be necessary so as to form an opinion on the matter. It may, for instance, be adapted from an earlier literary source, it may derive from pre-existing oral lore, or it may be simply fiction invented by the author. The same circumstances may hold true for an oral legend, but the survival of a legend in oral tradition demands a certain amount of communal interest in it and acceptance of it.

Both literary and oral legends are often of an historical nature, and contain echoes of historical events or of the cultural terms of reference of such events. There is a marked tendency in these legends to focus on individual characters, who are portrayed as larger than life. As will be clear to the reader, this book contains numerous literary and oral legends of historical characters, and an attempt is made in each case to determine the origin and development of each of these many narratives.

The MOTIFS in some legends are so user-friendly that they are borrowed by story-tellers from one context to another, especially if there is a clear resemblance between the two contexts. The resultant narratives are termed by scholars 'migratory legends'. A migratory legend of one personage can come to be told concerning a similar personage, and this holds true for many personality types. Examples, and cross-references to other examples, can be found in many entries in this book – for example, KINGS, OUTLAWS, POETS, SAINTS and TYRANTS. Legends usually have more than one MOTIF, but it should be remarked that a single motif may be attractive enough in itself to cause it to migrate – the storytellers in such a case may incidentally but logically reconstruct the pattern of a legend in a new environment.

Particularly prone to migration are legends dealing with the supernatural, many of which have come into Ireland from Britain or Continental Europe. The subjects of these legends are many and varied, and they can be treated as special types much after the manner of folktales. In this book, rather than having type numbers assigned to them, they are synopsised according to the phenomena with which they are associated. They include events that fulfil destiny (see ENVIRONMENT and HUMAN LIFE); individuals with magical powers, such as the Earl of DESMOND; creatures with preternatural powers, such as HORSES or CATTLE emerging from water, or an all-black March cock (see FOWL); the appearance of a man's soul in the form of a butterfly or salmon (see INSECTS and FISH); and the card-playing activities of the devil (see SPORTS AND PASTIMES). Several migratory legends are concerned with FAIRIES and GHOSTS, and some attach to fictional sea-people (see MERMAIDS/MERMAN) and to public catastrophes such as FAMINES.

There are a variety of narratives dealing with supposed events in contemporary settings. These also tend to be migratory and, indeed, the plots of many of them are told throughout much of the world. Since they most usually circulate among dense population groups, folklorists apply the term 'urban legends' to them – they are discussed in this book under the heading MODERN LEGENDS.

IRISH VERSIONS OF MIGRATORY LEGENDS, WITH SUGGESTED TYPE NUMBERS: B. Almqvist et al. in *Béaloideas, 59*, 1–325.

leprechaun Diminutive otherworld man in Irish folklore who is said to be the guardian of hidden TREASURE, envisaged as a crock of gold. He is invariably a solitary being, although he is sometimes reputed to be the shoemaker of the FAIRIES. The designation leprechaun (in Irish, *luprachán*) was in fact used for the being only in the north-Leinster area. In Ulster, the word was *luchramán*, in east Leinster, *loimreachán* and in south Leinster, *lúracán*, in Connacht, *lúracán* also, and in Munster, the series *luchragán, lurgadán* and *clúracán*. All of these designations are suggestive of his traits – echoing terms such as *luch* (mouse), *lúth* (agility), *lurga* (ankle) and *lom* (sparse). He was believed to be small, speedy, large-footed and rarely seen, and it is thus obvious that the basic designation was modified in accordance with folk imagination. The original term, attested in the early literature, was *luchorpán*, meaning literally 'little body'.

In the eighth-century text on FEARGHUS MAC LÉIDE, we read of a community of such diminutive beings, and they are represented as possessors of magical skill. When Fearghus seizes three of them, they bestow great swimming prowess on him as a condition for their release. Subsequent literary sources also make them bestowers of magical objects, such as a mantle or pair of silver-bronze shoes that enable a person to travel in water without drowning. These are adaptations of international MOTIFS concerning objects that provide for magical travel or magical finance. It is therefore obvious that the designation *luchorpán* was invented in Ireland when lore of dwarf communities was adopted from abroad by Irish writers, and that the solitary leprechaun of folklore is a post-medieval development from the literature.

Few stories concerning the leprechaun are general in Irish lore. The most popular describes how a man catches him and holds him firmly in his hand, demanding to know where his crock of gold is. If the man keeps his eyes firmly on the leprechaun, the little fellow must tell. However, he manages to deflect the captor's attention from him by warning that a ferocious beast is approaching, and when the man looks again, the leprechaun is gone. Another story tells of how he was captured by a man with the same demand, and that he showed the man a tree under which his treasure was buried. The man tied a ribbon or garter around the tree to identify it, and went to fetch a spade to dig up the treasure, but when he returned, he found that the leprechaun had disappeared and that every tree in the area was similarly marked.

Other more spontaneous accounts claim that the leprechaun is sometimes glimpsed as he flits through woody surroundings, or else as he sits on a toadstool smoking his pipe, but such descriptions are intended only for children. In Ulster lore, he has to an extent become assimilated to the brownie lore, which seems to have arrived from Scotland in the seventeenth century. These accounts have him, or a brownie, coming secretly at night to do farm work and housework for people to whom he is well disposed, but he leaves in a huff when a suit of clothes is left as a present for him. In Munster, the leprechaun is sometimes said to present people with a *sparán na scillinge* (purse of the shilling), which never becomes empty. However, those in receipt of this marvellous gift invariably misuse it, with the result that its contents change to dust. This is an old international motif.

GENERAL: Carney (1955), 103–10; D.A. Binchy in *Ériu* 16, 36–8, 41–2; D. Ó Giolláin in *Béaloideas*, *50*, 126–50 & *52*, 75–150 & *59*, 161–6, 254–5. MAGICAL OBJECTS: *See* Thompson (1955–58), motifs D1455, D1470, D1520.

Liadhain POETESS of the seventh century who reputedly belonged to the Corca Dhuibhne sept of west Munster. Her name seems to have meant 'the pale one'. A tragic love story concerning her is told in a text of prose and verse put together in the tenth century. Her name in modern form would be Liain.

According to this, Liadhain went on a circuit to Connacht and met there a poet called Cuirithir mac Dobharchon, who proposed marriage to her. She refused to abandon her circuit, but told him to come south for her to her home in Munster. When Cuirithir did this and arrived outside her house, he met there the wise fool COMHDHÁN, and asked him to go inside and tell Liadhain 'by your wit' that her lover was outside. Comhdhán entered and recited verses, stating that 'the son of the beast that stays at night under pools' was waiting for her. By this she understood that Mac Dobharchon (literally, 'son of the otter') was outside, and went with him. She was, however, 'under the spiritual direction' of St CUMAINE FADA – which probably meant that she had become a nun – and the SAINT forbade the two lovers to cohabit. After pleading, Cumaine agreed to let them spend one night together, but placed a clerical student between them in bed. Having been sent away by Cumaine, Cuirithir became a monk and went on pilgrimage to the territory of the DÉISE (in County Waterford). Hearing soon after that Liadhain was coming from the west to visit him, he went away across the sea in a coracle. Liadhain came to the flagstone on which he was wont to pray, and stayed on it sorrowfully until she died and was buried underneath. This story seems to have been suggested by an international narrative plot concerning lovers (*see* ROMANTIC TALES, type 970).

Meyer (1902); G. Murphy (1962), 82–5, 208–11.

Lir Fictional character, who is mentioned as a chieftain of the TUATHA DÉ DANANN in literary sources from the twelfth century onwards. He is referred to as 'Lir of Sídh Fionnachaidh', that place being the otherworld cairn on Deadman's Hill, County Armagh. This is probably due to learned speculation that connected the place name with descriptions of the sea as 'the white field [*fionnachadh*] of MANANNÁN'. Since Manannán was 'the son of the sea' (*mac Lir*), it would be natural for scholars to imagine his personalised father as associated with a place name like Fionnachadh.

In a text from the fourteenth century, 'Lir mac Luighdheach' is stated to have taken up residence in Sídh Fionnachaidh. It is not clear who the supposed father Lughaidh was, and this father may be an invention by the writer of the text. Further speculation is evident from another text of the same period in which Lir from Sídh Fionnachaidh is mentioned as a champion of the Tuatha Dé Danann who was slain by the human hero OISÍN of the Fianna. The only full narrative concerning him is in a text written in the late fifteenth century entitled *Oidheadh Chlainne Lir* (The Tragic Fate of the Children of Lir), and was probably written in the Erris area of west Mayo. It tells of how, after their defeat by the Gaelic people, the Tuatha Dé chose BODHBH DEARG as their new KING. Lir of Sídh Fionnachaidh was offended by this choice, but Bodhbh offered him one of his foster-daughters in marriage and so effected a reconciliation. This maiden was Aobh, and she bore him two sets of twins. The first set was a boy called Aodh and a girl called Fionnghuala. The second set was the boys Fiachra and Conn, in the bearing of whom she died. Lir was despondent, but Bodhbh gave him as second wife: Aoife, the sister of Aobh. Aoife at first loved her four stepchildren, but she grew jealous of Lir's affection for them and began to plot their destruction. Accordingly, she took them with her one day, ostensibly on a visit to Bodhbh, but in reality with the intent of killing them. She could not get herself to ply the sword on them, however, and instead struck them with a magic wand and turned them into swans at Loch Dairbhreach (Lake Derravaragh, County Westmeath). Fionnghuala besought Aoife to fix a term for their transformation, and Aoife said that it would last until a noblewoman from the south would marry a nobleman from the north.

When Bodhbh discovered what had been done, he changed Aoife into a demon, in which form she must wander through the air forever. For 300 years, however, the four swans remained on Loch Dairbhreach, conversing with the Tuatha Dé who came to see them by day and singing beautiful music for these visitors by night. Then they flew away to Sruth na Maoile (the Sea of Moyle between Ireland and Scotland), where they spent a further 300 years in cold and misery. After that, they spent 300 years off Iorras Domhnann (Erris, County Mayo), where they endured even greater misery. At the end of that time, they flew home to their father's dwelling of Sídh Fionnachaidh, but found the place empty and deserted. Returning to the west, they alighted on Inis Gluaire (Inishglory, an island in the bay of Erris). They met there the Christian missionary St Mochaomhóg, who treated them with great kindness, and they attended his religious services. Not long after, the Connacht king Lairgnéan married Deoch, the daughter of the king of Munster. Deoch desired the four wonderful swans as a wedding present, and Lairgnéan came to seize them, but their period of enchantment was now at an end, and they turned into three withered old men and an old woman. The SAINT baptised them, and they died happily and were buried together.

This story is based on the plot of a medieval LEGEND concerning swan-children, which seems to have originated in the twelfth century in the Netherlands or north-east France. This told of how a certain lord married a fairy lady, who could assume swan shape. She bore him six sons and one daughter, each of whom had a golden chain around the neck. By use of these chains, the children could transform themselves into swans, but their malicious grandmother had the chains taken from the boys and, as a result, they could not resume human form. Their sister, however, kept her chain and was therefore able to regain the boys' chains and disenchant them.

The area of Erris was extensively settled by the NORMAN family surnamed Fleming in the thirteenth century. The ultimate origin of this family was in Flanders, and they may have brought the plot of the story with them to the area. The author of *Oidheadh Chlainne Lir*, or his source, would have considered the Tuatha Dé Danann as an appropriate community among whom magic would have been prevalent. He would also have considered the name Lir to be appropriate in the context of the aquatic environment of swans. Furthermore, the author knew the text of *Buile Suibhne*, and noticed how in that text SUIBHNE underwent a swan-like transformation and sprouted feathers. He therefore allowed the Suibhne narrative to influence his version of the swan-children plot, and borrowed additional material from it, such as the roles of the husband and wife and of the saint at the end of the story.

It is a curious fact that the text *Oidheadh Chlainne Lir* had little influence on the Irish oral tradition, but the story is well known in recent generations from the many schoolbook retellings.

EARLY REFERENCES TO LIR: Stokes (1900), 46, 50–1, 140, 142; Ní Shéaghdha, *1* (1942), 36, 183–4, 195–201 & *2* (1942), 58 & (1945), 219; L. Duncan in *Ériu*, *11*, 188.

OIDHEADH CHLAINNE LIR: O'Curry in *Atlantis*, *4*, 113–57; Ua Ceallaigh (1927), 42–64.

MEDIEVAL LEGEND OF SWAN-CHILDREN: Baring-Gould (1872), 574–91; Gautier (1897), 77–81; French & Hale (1964), 859–73; Cramer (1971), 68–123; Lecouteux (1982), 110–19.

SUIBHNE CONNECTIONS: Carney (1955), 153–8.

Lugh Mythical hero, originally a Celtic deity. His name is often accompanied by the sobriquet Lámhfhada (long-armed), the idea being not of a physically long limb but that his weapons had long range. He was adept at the use of the javelin and the sling. Lugh was also known as the Samhildánach, meaning 'the one who possesses all the arts'.

Writing of the Gauls, Julius Caesar stated that they most worshipped a GOD whom he equated with the Roman Mercurius: 'They declare him the inventor of all arts, the guide for every road and journey, and they deem him to have the greatest influence for all money-making and commerce'. All the evidence points to Lugh (in Celtic, Lugus) as the deity in question. Sanctuaries with dedications to this personage have been discovered throughout Gaulish territories, and the Celtic place name Lugudunon (fortress of Lugus) survives in many forms – for example, Lyon,

Laon, Lauzun, Laudun, Loudon and Leiden. Many scholars have argued that his name connects him with light and is cognate with the Latin word *lux*; but it seems more likely that the proper derivation is from a Celtic word *lugio*, meaning an oath. Lugus would thus have originally been a patron of sworn contracts, a function that accords well with the description given by Caesar of the acclaimed Gaulish god. He was also the focus of a harvest cult, for there was a great festival at Lyon at this time of year, which the Romans forcibly changed into a celebration of the emperor Augustus (hence the name August for that month). The celebration of such a festival has long been current in Ireland, being called in Irish 'Lughnasadh' (*see* TIME), and thus providing a direct link between the mythology of the Continental Celts and the insular tradition of Ireland.

Medieval Welsh literature has some echoes from the deity Lugus, such as the character Lleu, who was given the sobriquet Llawgyffes (accurate arm), but clear and definitive lore concerning him is extant only in Irish sources. His cult appears to have been introduced into Ireland directly from Gaul or via Britain around the time of Christ, and perhaps by refugees from the devastation caused by the Roman armies. The cult soon replaced earlier harvest lore, and became the nexus of one of the four cardinal points of the Irish year. A glossary compiled in the ninth century, which embodies much ancient lore, explains Lughnasadh as 'an assembly held by him [i.e. Lugh] at the beginning of harvest each year', and another early source identifies this assembly as the great fair of Tailtiu (Teltown, County Meath). The origins of various communal activities relating to festive celebrations were also attributed to him – such as ball games, horse racing, and *ficheall* (the Irish form of chess).

Irish tradition at all stages represents Lugh as slaying his maternal grandfather, who was a TYRANT. This must derive, together with the harvest lore, from the cult of Lugus among the Continental Celts, as it conforms to a myth pattern prevalent among the ancient peoples of the Mediterranean. The pattern was known in Greek myth (Perseus), in Latin redactions of Persian myth (Cyros), and in ancient Babylonian culture (the Sargon inscription). Since the Greeks knew the plot, it is feasible to assume that the Celts of southern Gaul borrowed it from the long-established Greek colony at Marseilles, and applied it to their own harvest-god Lugus, who – under the designation Esus (lord) – was reputed to engage in great atmospheric contests with the thunder-god Taranos. The occurrence of Lugus' name in toponymics stretching northwards through Gaul and into Britain is evidence for the spread of his cult northwards. In Ireland – and perhaps also in Britain – the Taranos figure was better known by the designation Boleros (*see* BALAR).

The fullest description of Lugh is found in an eleventh-century Irish text, *Cath Maige Tuired*. The text incorporates material written down several centuries earlier, and describes the events surrounding what became known as the second Battle of Moytirra (*see* MYTHOLOGICAL CYCLE). It tells of the relations between the divine race, TUATHA DÉ DANANN, and the destructive race known as FOMHÓIRE. In an attempt to establish peace between the two races, we are told, one of the Fomhóire leaders called Balar gave his daughter Eithne to a young man of the Tuatha Dé called Cian, 'and she bore him the child of accomplishment, that is, Lugh'. Time passed by, and when the Tuatha Dé king NUADHU lost an arm in battle, he was deposed by his people on account of the blemish. They gave the throne to a Fomhóire prince called BREAS, but the reign of Breas became a period of great oppression. Smarting under this, the Tuatha Dé restored Nuadhu, who had been fitted with a silver arm. The Fomhóire then gathered a massive force in the northern zones of the world and, under the leadership of Balar, prepared to invade Ireland.

The Tuatha Dé were at TARA, planning the defence, when their door-keeper saw a handsome young warrior approaching.

The newcomer announced himself as Lugh, and was told by the door-keeper that he could not enter the citadel without having an art. Lugh said that he was a builder, but the door-keeper replied that they already had a builder and did not require another. Lugh said that he was a smith, but got a similar reply. Likewise when he said he was a champion, harpist, warrior, POET, historian, magician, physician, cup-bearer and brazier. Then Lugh said: 'Ask the king if he has one man who is skilled in all these arts, and if he has I will not enter Tara.' The door-keeper told the king that a stranger had arrived who was 'the man of every single art', and Nuadhu commanded that he be allowed to enter, 'because a man like that has never yet come into this fortress'. When he entered, Lugh performed a prodigious feat by throwing a great flagstone over the wall of the building, and then he played magical music on the harp.

Nuadhu decided to give him command of the Tuatha Dé in their hour of need, and Lugh inspected their forces, determining which particular skill each of the leaders possessed. When battle was joined with the Fomhóire on the plain of Moytirra (in County Sligo), Lugh slipped away from his bodyguard and circled around the warriors, 'on one foot and with one eye closed', while he chanted a spell. This was a magical device used by poets to weaken the foe. Horrific slaughter ensued, and Lugh came face to face with his Fomhóire grandfather. This fearsome warrior, Balar, had a destructive eye that was never opened except on a field of battle. Lugh cast a sling-stone at him, which drove the eye through his head, and it was gazing on his own host. He fell on top of the Fomhóire army, so that thrice nine of them died under his side.' The Fomhóire were routed, but Lugh spared the life of Breas in return for advice on ploughing, sowing and reaping the harvest.

In this narrative, the combat between Lugh and Balar has been inserted into the context of a struggle between two supernatural races (*see* MYTHOLOGICAL CYCLE). The combination of the two plots caused some difficulties, and the text of *Cath Maige Tuired* – even after several centuries of development – still betrays some disparate elements. The MOTIF that Lugh is predestined to slay Balar is not brought out clearly; the time of the battle is given as Samhain (the November feast) rather than Lughnasadh (August); and we are not told if Lugh continued to lead the Tuatha Dé. Despite the glorious role assigned to him, he was clearly an interloper, but in time was made to fit more comfortably into the Tuatha Dé company. References from about the tenth century state that after the death of Nuadhu, he was installed as their king by the Tuatha Dé at the hill of Tailtiu, and that he reigned as king of Ireland for 40 years. An eleventh-century text describes him as lord of the otherworld, living in a house of gold and silver and attended by the goddess of sovereignty (*see* KINGSHIP). He is called *an Scál* (the Phantom), is seated on a throne, and 'never was there seen in Tara one as wonderful as he'. In a poem written a century later, Lugh is said to have been reared on the otherworld island Eamhain Abhlach (*see* MANANNÁN).

One medieval writer, perhaps echoing some earlier tradition, states that Lugh had as wives two sisters called Buí and Nás. Buí was buried at Cnoghbha (Knowth, County Meath) and Nás at the place claimed to be called after her (Naas, County Kildare). The latter is pseudo-lore, for the word (and place name) *nás* actually meant a fair or assembly, but all of this may be an echo of early importance of Lughnasadh celebrations at these places. The same writer states significantly that it was in memory of these two wives that Lugh instituted the fair of Tailtiu, which, as suggested above, seems to have been the earliest great centre of his cult. Already by the eighth century, Lugh was being regarded as the otherworld father of CÚ CHULAINN, and it is clear that a broad mosaic of folklore concerning him was circulating in early medieval Ireland. One source applies the epithet *leathshuanach* (side-mantled) to him and explains it by claiming that 'a red colour used to be on

him from sunset till morning', while another states that he had a beautiful shirt of red-gold texture. These references suggest that some medieval writers were playing on the similarity of the name Lugh with the Latin *lux*.

With better warranty, the ancient tribal name Luighne (earlier, Luguni) was a derivative of his name, indicating devotion of that tribe to his cult, and a compound of his name, Lughaidh, was applied to various legendary leaders of the Luighne and other ÉRAINN peoples (*see* the following entries). Lughaidh became a common personal name and, in addition, several toponymics derive from 'Lugh' or were interpreted as such. The hero himself was sometimes referred to through his patronymic as Lugh mac Céin, but was more often called Lugh mac Eithleann – from Eithliu, an early form of his mother's name EITHNE. A poem from the fourteenth century refers to his coming to Tara and ascribes marvellous acrobatic skills to him on that occasion. These included prodigious jumping and swimming, as well as 'leaping on a bubble without bursting it'. He exemplified the process by which art and skill were extended into the realm of mystery and magic, and therefore was a prototype for several picaresque characters, such as the GOBÁN SAOR, Cearbhall Ó DÁLAIGH and perhaps even the CEITHEARNACH CAOILRIABHACH.

The attempts of medieval writers to synchronise the multiple vestiges of earlier mythology led to great confusion in names and characters. For instance, there was an enigmatic reference in the *Cath Maige Tuired* text to how Lugh procured weapons for the battle from the *trí dé Danann* (three gods of DANU). Some literary sources state that the father of this trio was called Tuirill, but others have Breas as their father. Yet other sources confuse Breas with Balar, with the result that Lugh is represented as gaining a singular victory over both in the Battle of Moytirra. A surveyor of the literature in the tenth century could speculate that three brothers, whose father had been killed by Lugh, would seek vengeance by killing Lugh's own father Cian. According to the story thus invented, Cian went in the shape of a lapdog to Brugh na Bóinne (the tumulus of Newgrange in County Meath) and was killed there by the sons of Tuirill (later, Tuireann), who were called Brian, Iuchair and Iucharba. The story soon became popular with writers. One version states that the three brothers were slain in revenge by Lugh on the Isle of Man, but others state that Lugh was satisfied with compensation. The *wergild* he demanded was seven precious things that were extremely difficult to obtain, including a mighty javelin. An expanded version of the story was written in the fourteenth century, according to which Lugh deliberately made the compensation difficult out of a spirit of malice. When the three brothers, having fulfilled the conditions, returned sick and weary from their exertions, their father beseeched Lugh to lend his mantle to them. This mantle had the magical property of healing all illness, but Lugh refused the request and let them die.

Despite its attractive plot – apparently suggested by the episode of Jason's fleece in Greek literature – and despite its frequent inclusion in manuscript compilations, this literary fabrication concerning the sons of Tuirill enjoyed no great popularity in oral storytelling. Another story from the medieval literature describes the death of Lugh as taking place at Uisneach (the Hill of Ushnagh, County Westmeath, also the venue of great assemblies in ancient times). He had, we are told, slain a certain Cearmaid 'through jealousy concerning his wife' and, in retaliation, the three sons of Cearmaid attacked Lugh at Uisneach. One of them thrust a spear into his foot, and Lugh retreated into a lake and was drowned there. This account has no warranty other than to fancifully explain the place name Loch Lughbhorta, and it was obviously suggested by the story of the sons of Tuirill.

Folklore attests that the presentation of Lugh depended on one great story from start to finish – i.e. his triumph over Balar. Several versions of this have been collected from the oral tradition in recent times in Irish-speaking areas in the west and northwest. The occurrence of the story in the folklore of these areas undoubtedly owes something to manuscripts. There are many references to the epic in literature, and even some literary retellings, and more of such written records must have existed but have been lost. Sligo and Mayo readers of the literature would note that the battle was fought at Moytirra in their own area and would thus be inclined to memorise the story. In Donegal, the place name Dún Lúiche (Dunlewy, at the foot of Mount Errigal) was popularly associated with Lugh because of its phonemic similarity to his name, and this appears to be the main reason for the story thriving in the folklore of that region. That these oral tellings have an integrity of their own, however, is illustrated by the fact that they give clearest expression to the basic motif – i.e. that Lugh is the prophesied youth who will slay his tyrant grandfather. They differ from each other in the order and arrangement of the plot, but their underlying pattern is as follows:

Balar was a one-eyed tyrant who lived on Tory Island off the Donegal coast. He had one daughter called Eithne, of whom it was foretold that if she gave birth to a son, that child would kill its grandfather. Balar therefore kept the girl locked away in a tower so that no man could gain access to her. However, a young man called Cian had intercourse with her, and as a result was seized and put to death by the tyrant. When she gave birth, the enraged Balar ordered that she and the child be set adrift in a boat. This was done, but they survived through the kindness of a smith called Goibhleann (*see* GOIBHNIU). When the child Lugh was growing to manhood, Goibhleann made a great spear for him. It happened that Balar coveted a marvellous cow, called the GLAS GHOIBHNEANN, which belonged to the smith. He took the cow and brought it with him to Tory, but Goibhleann succeeded in having himself accepted into Balar's service and contrived to gain possession of the cow's halter. The cow broke out of its byre on the island and swam after the halter all the way back to the mainland. Balar vowed to destroy Ireland in revenge for this, and on his campaign of devastation came to the forge of Goibhleann. His one eye was full of poison, and it destroyed all on which it gazed. Finding himself confronted by Lugh, Balar removed the covering from his eye, but Lugh threw the spear and blinded him. Before being decapitated, Balar said that if his severed head were put on top of Lugh's own, then all the power of Balar would pass to Lugh. Suspecting treachery, Lugh placed the head on a large rock, and a drop of poison fell from it and dashed the rock to pieces.

The theme of Goibhleann and his marvellous cow was introduced into these oral versions because of the occurrence of that character, under his earlier form Goibhniu, in the literary accounts of the Moytirra battle. A retelling of the Moytirra story from around the fifteenth century has Goibhniu busy in his forge during the battle. When Balar begins to uncover the eye, Goibhniu uses his tongs to fling to Lugh the heavy sling-stone with which he will slay the tyrant. The episode of the poisonous drop, not referred to in the earliest sources, occurs in the literature from late medieval times onwards – it being claimed that Balar was chased by Lugh all the way from Moytirra to Carn Uí Néid (Mizen Head, County Cork), where the beheading took place. Literary sources can thus be seen to lie behind definite aspects of the recent oral tradition concerning Lugh. The retention in them of a purer form of the plot of the tyrant-grandfather myth shows, nevertheless, that these folklore versions reflect a time when the cult of Lugh was still vibrant in the oral stream.

ORIGIN: H. Wagner in *ZCP*, *31*, 22–5; Holder, *2* (1896), 308–46; Thévenot (1968), 72–96; T.F. O'Rahilly (1946), 58–61, 310–17; Powell (1958), 120–7; M. MacNeill (1962), 1–11.

LUGUS/ESUS, TARANIS: Green (1992), 93–4, 205–7.

LLEU IN WALES: Gruffydd (1928), 60–4.

NINTH-CENTURY GLOSSARY: K. Meyer in *AIM*, *4*, 66–7.

TAILTIU AND SPORTS: Macalister (1941), 116–19, 128–9, 134–5; M. MacNeill (1962), 320–1.

MIDDLE-EASTERN MYTH: Rank (1914), 12–44; P. Saintyves in Couchoud (ed.) (1928), 229–72; Gruffydd (1928), 350–75; Krappe (1927), 1–43; Tovar (1961), 44–5.

BATTLE OF MOYTIRRA: Gray (1982); Macalister (1941), 118–21.

MEDIEVAL IRISH LORE: Van Hamel (1933), 41; Macalister (1941), 120–1; Knott (1957), 55; Gray (1982), 62; Gwynn (1913), 48–53, 122–3; Bergin (1970), 76–9.

LUGH AND CÚ CHULAINN: Van Hamel (1933), 5, 30; C. O'Rahilly (1976), 64–5, 70.

NAME DERIVATIVES: M. MacNeill (1962), 9; T.F. O'Rahilly (1946), 120; Bhreathnach (1971), 127–9.

TUIRILL: Macalister (1941), 128–31, 134–7; R. Thurneysen in *ZCP*, *12*, 239–50; O'Duffy (1888).

CEARMAID: Macalister (1941), 130–1; Gwynn (1924), 278–9; O. Bergin in *Loomis Studies* (1927), 399–406.

FOLKLORE: O'Donovan (1848–51), 18–21; Larminie (1893), 1–9, 241–5; Curtin (1894), 283–311; Gruffydd (1928), 65–76; Ó Searcaigh (1908), 3–7, 61; Laoide (1913), 63–5; Andrews (1913), 73–6; S. Ó Súilleabháin & Christiansen (1967), type 934C; D. O'Sullivan (1974), 17–22, 167; *Bentleys Miscellany*, *2*, 527–32; *An Gaodhal*, *12*, 78–81; E. Ó Tuathail in *Béaloideas*, *3*, 128–9; OSL: Donegal (1835), 46–51, 81–97, 129–30 & Mayo, *2* (1838), 41–2, 110–12; IFC, numerous versions.

GENERAL: Gray (1982), 126–7; M. MacNeill (1962), 3–11; Macalister (1941), 116–37; T.F. O'Rahilly (1946), 308–17.

Lughaidh Lágha

Lughaidh Lágha Fictional warrior of Munster, brother of AILILL ÓLOM. His sobriquet (earlier, Lágae) was fancifully explained to refer to a great 'hand-spear' which he had.

Lughaidh Lágha was a faithful supporter of LUGHAIDH MAC CON when Ailill acted treacherously towards the latter. He accompanied this namesake of his in exile to Scotland, and fought tremendously at his side on their triumphant return. He it was who slew the high-king ART in the Battle of Magh Mucramha (in east Galway). When Lughaidh mac Con later abdicated as high-king in favour of CORMAC MAC AIRT, Lughaidh Lágha refused to return to Munster with his friend, but instead determined to serve the son of the man he had slain.

The medieval literature thus envisaged him as a great warrior at the court of Cormac – in fact, one of the five greatest warriors that Ireland had ever seen, the others being LUGH, CÚ CHULAINN, CONALL CEARNACH and FIONN MAC CUMHAILL. He figures prominently in some late medieval stories concerning the latter, being described as the protector and husband of Fionn's aunt Uirne, and the opponent of GOLL MAC MORNA in a brawl that broke out at a great banquet held by Cormac. After this brawl, he returned to his own area of Eatharlach (Aherlow, County Tipperary), a point that echoes an alternative earlier tradition that he did not remain at Cormac's court but settled at Eatharlach. This is the situation described in the ninth-century text *Cath Crinna*, which has Cormac mac Airt enlisting his support for a battle against the Ulstermen. Again, Lughaidh Lágha fought magnificently in that battle, and before returning to Munster managed to survive a treacherous effort by Cormac to gain revenge for his father's death.

Though dramatised as a separate character by the medieval writers, it is clear that Lughaidh Lágha was originally an emanation from the Munsterised LUGHAIDH MAC CON.

T.F. O'Rahilly (1946), 61, 202; M. O'Daly (1975), 11–12, 40–1, 52–61: Stokes (1900), 163; G. Murphy (1953); 103–4; Ó Siochfhradha (1941), 146–50; O'Grady, *1* (1892), 320–5 & *2*, 478, 490–3. *See also* MAC LUGHACH.

Lughaidh Lámhdhearg Fictional KING of Ireland situated in prehistory. The medieval writers tell little of this king, except that he ruled for seven years. His sobriquet means 'red-handed', indicating his prowess in battle, and was no doubt added to the name Lughaidh for alliterative effect.

In accordance with the notion that ancient Ireland was divided into two halves (*see* CONN CÉADCHATHACH), we are told that a certain Conaing Beag-Eaglach ruled in the north and Eochaidh Uaircheas in the south. Lughaidh Lámhdhearg slew the latter in battle and reigned in the south until he fell at the hands of Conaing. The idea of a southern king called Lughaidh was probably suggested by the tradition of the Munster hero, LUGHAIDH MAC CON. The attractive alliteration of the name Lughaidh Lámhdhearg gave rise also to other incidental characters in the medieval literature with that name. A seventeenth-century source gives a curious explanation for the epithet of this fictional king, stating that he was so called 'because he had a spot or mark on his hand'. This is a reflection of lore concerning heroes with a distinctive mark on their bodies – *see* Ó CONCHÚIR, CATHAL CROBHDHEARG and Ó DÓNAILL (Aodh Balldearg).

GENERAL: Macalister (1956), 256–7; Best & O'Brien (1957), 480; Gwynn (1913), 200–5, 512; Dinneen, *2* (1908), 144–5.
OTHER WARRIORS WITH THE NAME: Ó Cadhlaigh (1956), 150, 228.

Lughaidh mac Con Mythical leader of the ÉRAINN people of Munster. The name Lughaidh was an affectionate form of that of the deity LUGH, and was probably a title given by the Luighne, an ÉRAINN sept, to their KINGS. Since a branch of the Luighne were at TARA from an early date, the original kingship in question was probably the kingship of that prestigious place. His patronymic 'mac Con' literally meant 'son of hound', but its true meaning would have been the figurative 'son of warrior'. A kindred character, Lughaidh mac Con Roí, occurs in the early literature, and the strong likelihood is that Lughaidh mac Con was – from time immemorial – associated with the celebrated CÚ ROÍ.

Writing in the seventh century, the biographer of St PATRICK, Tíreachán, relates how the SAINT revived a man who was long dead, having been slain by 'the warrior-band of Mac Con'. It is obvious from this that Tíreachán knew of a tradition concerning a great warlord of that name, and describes the episode as having taken place in Díchuil (an area in County Mayo), far from Munster. Cú Roí was originally associated with the north Midlands, and it is thus apparent that the character Mac Con – like Cú Roí – was transposed to Munster because of the prominent role played by Érainn septs in that southern province in the early literary period.

A character called Lughaidh Laíghdhe, who occurs in the medieval literature, was an emanation from him. This Lughaidh Laíghdhe, like Cú Roí, was said to have been son of DÁIRE, and he is represented as one of five brothers, all called Lughaidh by their father because he had heard a prophecy that a man of that name would be king of Ireland. One day when hunting, the seven young men met an ugly HAG, who asked them to lie with her. Lughaidh Laíghdhe alone consented, and she became a beautiful young woman. She explained to him that she was sovereignty, and that the kingship of Ireland would be his. This is a borrowing of the MOTIF of the dual aspects of sovereignty in the Uí Néill lore of NIALL, but it echoes an Érainn tradition about an ancient Tara king of theirs known as Lughaidh. The second part of this character's name (earlier, Loígde) was the designation of an Érainn sept of southwest Munster, the Corca Laíghdhe.

The mythical Érainn king was, however, most fully developed in the guise of Lughaidh mac Con. Already by the eighth century, dramatised and synchronised accounts of his adventures were in circulation, which reflect the conditions not so much of prehistoric Tara as of early medieval Munster. These accounts state that he was fostered by AILILL ÓLOM, mythical king of the dominant Munster sept, the EOGHANACHT. This Ailill had seven sons, the leading son having the old septal name of Eoghan. When on a journey once, Eoghan and Lughaidh mac Con came upon an otherworld musician called Fear Fí at Eas Máighe (Caherass on the River Maigue, County Limerick), they argued over which of them had first discovered the musician, and Ailill ruled in favour of Eoghan. The incensed Lughaidh complained of this, and when chided by Eoghan with being a vassal, he challenged his foster-brother to battle.

When the armies were assembled at Ceann Abhradh (the Ballyhoura hills on the Cork–Limerick border), Ailill tried to trick Lughaidh by inviting him to a parley. Lughaidh attended, against the wishes of his people, but he brought 700 of his men with him. This troop determined not to flee, and accordingly the men were fettered to each other. Ailill and Eoghan, however, slyly informed their ally Cairbre Músc that Lughaidh was making terms with them, and the enraged Cairbre gathered his own men and attacked the unsuspecting Lughaidh. The army of Lughaidh was completely overthrown, and he took

to flight with the remainder. His jester Da Deara had the exact same appearance as himself, and in order to save his chief, Da Deara put on Lughaidh's diadem. The jester was thus slain, but the fleeing Lughaidh was recognised by the kingly white calves of his legs, and Cairbre Músc cast at him and lamed him. Lughaidh nevertheless managed to get away, and he went to Scotland as a refugee.

That this lore of Lughaidh mac Con was not very old in the eighth century is indicated by the fact that there were variant explanations of the Battle of Ceann Abhradh. One was that Lughaidh mac Con and Ailill Ólom had only joined in the battle in support of opposite sides. The three sons of CONAIRE MAC MOGHA LÁMHA were giving battle to the killer of their father, Neimheadh mac Sraibhghind, and the principal of these three sons was Cairbre Músc. One version of the Ceann Abhradh story dispenses with the need for this other scenario by having Eoghan, rather than Cairbre Músc, wound Lughaidh. Yet another account has a warrior called Gnáthal (see ART) doing the wounding.

At any rate, after his flight to Scotland, Lughaidh and his followers were welcomed by the Scottish king – who did not know who they were – and they were seven years in that country, during which they won several battles for their benefactor. They did not reveal their identity, fearing that the king was an ally of the Irish high-king Art, who was a brother-in-law of Ailill Ólom. One day, when Lughaidh and the Scottish king were playing chess, an Irish POET arrived and gave news of events in Ireland. On hearing how his people in Munster were oppressed by Eoghan, Lughaidh knocked down a row of the king's chess pieces in anger. The king then realised who he was and decided to test him. He had dead mice placed as a meal before Lughaidh's followers, expecting that Lughaidh himself would not eat, but Lughaidh did eat and ordered his men to do likewise. 'They obey you!' said the king. 'I obey them too!' said Lughaidh. Then the king asked was he in fact Lughaidh. He replied truthfully and, much to his surprise, the Scottish king offered to help him with a host of Scots and Britons. Their ships stretched all the way from the Scottish to the Irish coast. Arriving in Ireland, Lughaidh swept all before him, and faced the combined forces of Art and Ailill Ólom at Magh Mucramha (the plain south west of Athenry, County Galway). Lughaidh tied his men together so that they would not flee, and hid half of the army in trenches. He won a great victory, with Art and the seven sons of Ailill being slain. He then advanced on Tara and took over the HIGH-KINGSHIP, which he held for many years.

The immediate source of these accounts was propaganda of the dominant CONNACHTA dynasties, and thus they show little of the point of view of the Érainn. So we read that, because he was a usurper, the reign of Lughaidh was a period of unfruitfulness and misery in the land. A son was posthumously born to Art, and when he – CORMAC MAC AIRT – came to Tara and proved a judgement of Lughaidh wrong, Lughaidh had to resign the kingship. He returned to Munster, and when he arrived at the dwelling of Ailill Ólom, his foster-mother Sadhbh warned him against the vengeance of her husband. Nevertheless, he went to see Ailill, who embraced him and put his cheek to his. With this pretence, Ailill touched him with his poisonous tooth, and within three days half of Lughaidh's face had melted away. Ailill then sent one of his retainers, the Leinster seer Fearcheas mac Comáin, after Lughaidh. Fearcheas chanted a spell over his spear and cast it at Lughaidh at a waterfall on the Bandon river, and thus Lughaidh was slain.

The strange appellation 'mac Con' gave rise to attempts to interpret it. One medieval text claims that when he was a baby in Ailill's fosterage, he crept to a bitch and was suckled by it, and hence he was called 'son of a hound' by way of a nickname. In folklore, memory of him survived in the context of the myth of Cormac mac Airt (q.v.), which became a traditional oral story in the north and west of Ireland. Coincidentally, therefore, memory of his lore reverted to its original area, while he was forgotten in Munster. Some oral tellings of the Cormac myth add a new motif to the image of Lughaidh. According to these, he could never sleep, and when the young Cormac came to Tara, Lughaidh told him that his reign had been miserable on that account. Cormac explained that the reason for this was that Lughaidh's father had been an otter that had once surprised his mother when she had gone to bathe in the Boyne river. On Cormac's advice, Lughaidh went and lay on a raft in the Boyne, and his otter-father came and took him underneath. This is a borrowing from a migratory LEGEND concerning a man who could not sleep because his father was a water-spirit (see MERMAIDS/MERMAN), while the water-spirit was assimilated to the otter because of a folk belief that otters (see WILD ANIMALS) keep their eyes open at night. The migratory legend got attached to Lughaidh because the 'hound' in his name (cú) was taken to refer to an otter (cú dobhráin, literally 'water-hound'), and because the misery of his reign could through it be rationalised into a personal ailment.

GENERAL: Bieler (1979), 154–5; Meyer (1910), 28 & (1912), 75; T.F. O'Rahilly (1946), 77–9, 201–2; W. Stokes in Irische Texte, 3, 322–3; M. O'Daly (1975), 9–11, 38–65, 74–93; R. Thurneysen in ZCP, 20, 222; M. Dillon in Ériu 11, 49 & 14, 154–65 & in PMLA, 60, 340–5; L. Gwynn in Ériu, 6, 136–7; M. Ó Dúnlainge in Irisleabhar na Gaedhilge 17–18, passim.

LUGHAIDH LAÍGHDHE: Stokes in Irische Texte, 3, 316–23.

DISCUSSIONS: Dillon (1946), 16–23; M.E. Dobbs in Journal of the Royal Society of Antiquaries of Ireland, 60, 165–87.

FOLKLORE: A.H. Krappe in Modern Language Review, 24, 200–4; O'Sullivan (1966), 21–37; Ó Tuathail (1934), 13; IFC 168:1–44, 169:822–31, 186:42–50, 289:376–93.

Lughaidh Riabhdhearg Fictional KING of Ireland whose reign was situated in prehistory. An earlier form of his sobriquet was Reo-derg, meaning 'red-stripe', and it probably referred to a battle wound.

He occurs in several texts as a foster son of CÚ CHULAINN, and obviously was one of the many characters invented to people the ULSTER CYCLE by the early medieval writers. The likelihood is that he was suggested by the character Lughaidh mac Con Roí, who was an echo in that cycle of the celebrated mythic hero of Munster, LUGHAIDH MAC CON. The character Lughaidh mac Con Roí was sometimes called *mac trí chon* (son of three hounds) because of a divine triplication of his father CÚ ROÍ. This suggested the idea that Lughaidh 'Reo-derg' had triple paternity, and so he was said to be *mac na dTrí Finn Eamhna* (son of the three FINN EAMHNA). This latter trio were seen by some writer as a tolerable alternative to the 'three hounds' in the context. The image of the red stripe provided the opportunity to rationalise the new character's triple paternity. Accordingly, it was said that the three Finn, in a fit of drunkenness, lay with their sister Clothra, and as a result Lughaidh was born. The child had red stripes that divided his body into three parts. His head resembled Nár, one of the three Finn; his breast resembled Breas, another of them; and from his belt downwards he was like the third of the Finn, Lothar. Thus he had the sobriquet Riabh nDerg (of the red stripes), which was later altered to the compound epithet Riabhdhearg. Some sources state that he had three stripes on his body, but others – computing for the three parts – give the number as two.

As a further development of his lore, it was claimed that he was reared by a certain Rumhal, king of Leinster, who was a brother to the 'Three Red-Heads' of that province (for whom, *see* CONAIRE). It was also claimed that these 'Red-Heads' slew Lughaidh Riabhdhearg – an idea speculatively derived from the image of three red stripes on his body, and probably also from the contrast between white (*fionn*) as the colour of his three fathers and red as the colour of three slayers. This slaying motif seems to have given rise to the notion that Lughaidh Riabhdhearg was a king of Ireland. The three Red-Heads of Leinster were the slayers of king Conaire, and thus Lughaidh was made the successor of Conaire, who was slain by the same trio. The claim that he had been a king was known to a medieval interpolator of the text on the 'Wasting Sickness of Cú Chulainn', who describes how Cú Chulainn gave Lughaidh a series of advices

on how to rule, and how Lughaidh went to TARA for the royal election.

His death at the hands of the Three Red-Heads reads awkwardly in the Annals, for nowhere else are Conaire and Cú Chulainn regarded as contemporaries, and so a new narrative was invented in the twelfth century based on imagery from the Wasting Sickness text. There the otherworld lady Fann and her sister came in the form of swans to woo Cú Chulainn. The new story therefore has Dearbhfhorgaill, daughter of the king of Norway, come with her handmaiden, both in the form of swans also to woo Cú Chulainn. In this case, however, that great warrior casts a stone at her. It lodges in her womb, and when Cú Chulainn sees her return to human shape, he sucks it out. He rejects her love and instead bestows her on Lughaidh. The couple, we are told, were happy and had children. Then, during a winter snow, the menfolk made pillars of the snow and, when they departed, the women went onto the pillars to compete concerning which of them could send their urine furthest through the snow. Dearbhfhorgaill was a reluctant competitor, but won the game. Thereupon, the other women were seized with jealousy, saying that if the men knew this, they would desire only her. So these women knocked her eyes out and cut off her nose, ears and hair. When Lughaidh returned to his house, accompanied by Cú Chulainn, he found his wife at the point of death. Lughaidh himself died from the shock, or according to some accounts threw himself on his sword. The furious Cú Chulainn overturned the house on top of the thrice-50 guilty women, killing them all.

The medieval literature variously gives twenty years, 25 years, and 26 years for Lughaidh's supposed reign. The motif of incest involved in his own birth was repeated in the tradition that he begat the future king CRIOMHTHANN NIA NÁIR on his own mother Clothra.

T.F. O'Rahilly (1946), 486–7; W. Stokes in *Irische Texte*, 3, 333, 375; Macalister (1956), 303–5; Dillon (1953), 3, 8–11; Van Hamel (1933), 62; C. Marstrander in *Ériu*, 5, 201–18; Gwynn (1924), 278–9; Dinneen, 2 (1908), 232–3; Ó Cadhlaigh (1956), 477.

Mac Conglinne The principal character in a medieval satiric story entitled *Aislinge meic Conglinne* (The Vision of Mac Conglinne).

From mentions of him among short lists of early-seventh-century comedians, it would appear that Mac Conglinne was an historical person. It was claimed that he studied at Armagh, became a skilled POET, and went on a scholarly circuit of Ireland, from which it may be adduced that he abandoned clerical studies to become a vagrant entertainer. He was an Ulsterman – being variously described as a native of Fahan (in County Donegal) and of the area around the River Bann. He was known by the nickname Anéra (non-refusal), and we read that he was refused nothing on account of his ability to praise and satirise. His own name is unknown, and he was usually referred to as Mac Conglinne from his patronymic (nominative, 'Cú Ghlinne', which meant 'warrior of the valley'). In the late tenth or early eleventh century, an anonymous author composed the story of his 'vision'. The original text is lost, but there are two surviving recensions. One of these seems to have been deliberately abbreviated, whereas the other is an expansive tour de force of humour and wit.

We read that the eighth-century Munster king CATHAL MAC FIONGHUINE fell in love with Líogach, sister of his rival, the Uí Néill high-king FEARGHAL MAC MAOLDÚIN. Cathal had never seen the lady, but their mutual love grew through reports of each other. Líogach used to send apples and sweets to Cathal, but at the behest of her brother, a scholar put spells on these dainties and, as a result, when Cathal ate them parasites formed in his stomach and one of these grew into a *lon craois* (demon of voracity). Cathal thereby had a voracious appetite, and for a year and a half impoverished the men of Munster as they tried to satisfy him.

At that time, the scholar Mac Conglinne was studying at Ros Comáin (Roscommon), and he decided to go on his poetic circuit to the Munster KING, since he had heard that there was plenty of good food wherever Cathal was. He arrived at the monastery of Corcaigh (Cork), the abbot of which was Mainchín (literally, 'little monk'), but got no welcome there. The guest house – a mere hut – was open to wind, rain and snow, the bedclothes were full of fleas and lice, and the bath water was putrid. There was nobody to attend to him, so he took out his book and began to sing the psalms. Hearing his voice, the abbot sent niggardly rations to him, but Mac Conglinne recited satiric quatrains on the monastery, and the servant reported these to Mainchín. The abbot, fearful that the quatrains would become known, ordered that the visitor be viciously flogged and drenched in the River Lee. This was done, and Mac Conglinne was flung naked and bleeding into the hut and locked therein till morning. On the next day, he was brought before the assembly of monks, and Mainchín ordered that, since he had insulted the Church, he should be crucified.

Mac Conglinne was taken to the green of Cork to be executed, but he asked for one boon before dying. This was to be allowed to eat some food from his satchel, as viaticum for the journey ahead of him. The request was granted, and he took a tenth of the little food that he had and offered it as tithes to the poor. As a group of paupers gathered around him, he told them of the savage way in which he had been treated, and further delayed his execution by drinking water from a well using the point of his brooch as a vessel. Finally, he was forced to cut his own passion tree, carry it on his back, and set it in the ground. All the while he reviled the monks, calling them curs and robbers until, stung in conscience by his remarks, they entreated Mainchín to give him a day's respite. After much persuasion. Mainchín agreed to this, and Mac Conglinne was left overnight tied naked to a pillar-stone.

During the night, an angel came to him and recited a vision, and Mac Conglinne put this vision into poetic form. When the monks came next day to crucify him, he recited the poem, which traced the descent of Mainchín back to Adam through a rich genealogy of food names. On hearing this, the abbot was speechless with surprise and rage, and Mac Conglinne continued to recite. His vision was of a journey through a sumptuous sea of milk and honey to a magnificent dwelling that consisted entirely of delicious food and drink. Now it so happened that Mainchín had dreamt that only through such a vision could Cathal mac Fionghuine be cured of his affliction, and so he ordered Mac Conglinne to go at once to the king. The scholar demanded that Mainchín's cloak be given to him if he succeeded, and the abbot reluctantly agreed to this.

Mac Conglinne then went to where Cathal was due to be that night, at the fortress of a noble called Piochán at Dún Cobha (somewhere in west Cork). Arriving there, he entertained the company with juggling and buffoonery. He offered to protect Piochán from the king's gluttony, and was promised as reward a golden ring, a British steed and a sheep from every herd between there and Cork. When Cathal arrived, he inveigled thirteen apples, one after another, from the king, this being the first time that Cathal gave food away since the demon entered him. In anger, Cathal finally flung all the apples to him, and then Mac Conglinne sought a boon and was promised it. He claimed that he had been cursed by the monks of Cork, and desired the king to sleep in his company one night in order to have the curse removed. Cathal was infuriated when he heard this, and had no choice but to fulfil his royal promise.

Having prevailed on Cathal to fast with him, Mac Conglinne had the king tied to the wall of the fortress and had delicious food of all kinds prepared. He began to cook most succulent meat and to eat it, as Cathal desperately tried to break his bonds and get to it. Mac Conglinne then began to recite a much inflated version of his food vision, which made the king delirious with desire and rage. The demon came as far as his mouth, ravenous for the food, and Mac Conglinne began to put pieces in front of it. Finally, the demon could restrain itself no longer, but sprang forth and seized a piece of meat in its claws and raced to the hearth with it. Mac Conglinne covered his own mouth and that of the king with his hands, and ordered that all leave the house. The doors were locked and the house set on fire, but the demon escaped onto a nearby rooftop. Mac Conglinne then addressed it, and it admitted that it could not have been overcome but by one as holy as himself. It was then banished into the air by Mac Conglinne. Cathal was so grateful to the scholar for his cure that he ordered a mighty reward to be given to him. This encompassed the things already promised, with the addition of a cow from every yard in Munster and a cloak from every church.

This story combines two plots from ordinary folk narrative – a reptile enticed from its victim's stomach (see ANIMAL TALES, type 285B), and a liar who tells of a land of wondrous food (see HUMOROUS TALES, type 1930). The original text seems to have been written as a satire on the monastery of Cork in particular, whereas, in its expanded form, it is directed at monastic life in general. It may have been meant for public recitation by medieval gleemen, being very stylised and rich in descriptions. The style was, however, so complicated that no variant of the text passed into oral tradition.

HISTORICAL PERSON: Meyer (1892), xxxix–xliii, 6–8, 114; Stokes (1905), 208; Jackson (1990), xxxix–xli.

THE STORY: Meyer (1892); Jackson (1990); B. Ó Buachalla in *Galvia*, 7, 43–9.

Mac Dhomhnaill, Alasdair

(c.1610–47) Leading officer in the war of the 1640s. Born on the island of Colonsay, off the west coast of Scotland, his clan (anglicised in Ireland as MacDonnell and in Scotland as MacDonald) were chiefs of Antrim as well as of western Scotland. His father was a famous warrior called Colla Ciotach (Colla the left-handed), and Alasdair himself was thus usually known as Alasdair Mac Colla. By the English he was called 'young Kolkitto'.

Lore concerning Alasdair's youth was very popular in western Scotland and in Antrim. It was said that, on the night of his birth, every sword rattled in its scabbard and every gunlock snapped. As a boy, he encountered a savage bull and slew it, and his father marvelled at his strength and determined to test it against his own. He therefore left his house one night, telling young Alasdair to protect it from possible attack by robbers. After some time, he returned, pretending to be a robber, and began to break the door in. The boy thrust a fork through the door and knocked an eye out of the head of the 'intruder'. It was also said that when Alasdair was sent ploughing, he lost his patience and struck one of the horses with his fist. The horse fell dead immediately.

The point of such extravagant stories is to underline that Alasdair was destined to be a great warrior, and this at least is in accord with history. While his father was being held hostage to guarantee his good behaviour, he joined the English army and was stationed at Coleraine, but on the outbreak of the 1641 rebellion in Ulster, he promptly deserted and became one of the leaders of the Irish forces. It was said in Scotland that a plot had been hatched in the English army to murder him, and that with this intent he was invited to a feast at Dunluce Castle in County Antrim. A letter was dispatched to his commanding officer to this effect, but the messenger, having been told that this officer was a tall dark man, mistook Alasdair for him. Alasdair pretended not to read the letter, but went to the feast and refused to surrender his sword, saying that it was 'in the bravest hand in Ireland'. His commanding officer asked jeeringly what was the next bravest hand, and Alasdair changed the sword into his left hand and said 'This one!' Since he was the only armed man present, he walked unimpeded from the castle and joined the Irish. These narratives of his youth and early life show the clear influence of ordinary FOLKTALES.

Alasdair was a very successful military leader in both Ireland and Scotland, and is believed to have originated as a military tactic the 'Highland charge', which consisted of the firing of one volley followed immediately by a headlong charge at the foe. He and James Graham, the Marquis of Montrose, won seven successive battles in Scotland, but in 1645 divided their forces and both were defeated. Alasdair fled to Ireland, where he joined the Irish forces of the Confederation of Kilkenny. Having achieved some naval successes against the forces of CROMWELL, the command of a company of Highlanders and Ulstermen in the Munster section of the Irish forces was assigned to him. This army, under the command of General Theobald Taaffe, was opposed by the Cromwellian forces under the notorious Murchadh Ó Briain, Earl of Inchiquin, whose incendiary tactics gave rise to a proverb in Irish to describe a frightened person as one who had 'seen Murchadh and his troop'. The two armies clashed at Knockanuss, near Mallow, County Cork, in November of 1647. Alasdair with his men charged the left flank of the enemy and swept all before them, but Taaffe's other lines gave way, and Alasdair was surrounded and captured. There are different traditions concerning his fate. One states that he was slain as he rode to a hill top to reconnoitre, another that he surrendered but was murdered in violation of safe conduct by an officer astounded to discover who his prisoner was.

Local Cork tradition has it that he was returning to the battlefield, having pursued his opponents a considerable distance, when he was made a prisoner. He was led off under a guard of five horsemen and, in crossing a stream, leaned forward to allow his horse to drink. In doing so, an opening in his armour was revealed, and one of the guards stabbed him through the back. The place where this happened is pointed out as the 'Chieftain's Ford', but the tradition is an apocryphal one (see a similar MOTIF in connection with Dónall Cam Ó Súilleabháin) and results from a confusion of Alasdair with that place name. Another Cork tradition states that after the battle, his wife came on the battlefield and, finding so many other women lamenting there that she could not be heard, remarked: 'If I cannot lament him, I will dance for him!' A well-known slow air entitled 'Caoineadh Alasdram' is said to have been composed as a lament for Alasdair, and a variant title for that air is 'Gol na mBan san Ár' (The crying of the women at the massacre). Alasdair was buried in a cemetery at Clonmeen, near Kanturk, County Cork, and his great sword was preserved at Loughan Castle in County Tipperary. This was said to have had a ball of ten-pounds weight running along the back from the hilt to the point in an indented groove, so that when swung it struck home with terrible force.

GENERAL: Laoide (1914); A. Matheson in *Transactions of the Gaelic Society of Glasgow, 5* (1958), 9–93; Mac Gill Fhinnein (1966), 69–73; Lorne (1898), 207–44; Hill (1873), 61–114; J. Buckley in *JCHAS, 5*, 128–32; Stevenson (1980); Ó hÓgáin (1985), 171–4, 338. FOLKTALE INFLUENCES: *See* Aarne & Thompson (1961), types 650A, 910K, 1559B.

Mac Fhlannchaidh, Baothlach

(in English, Boethius McClancy, +1598) Chieftain who belonged to a long line of Gaelic nobles and scholars, but who went into the service of ELIZABETH I and became high sheriff of County Clare. He was known in folk tradition as Bathlam.

When two ships of the Spanish Armada were wrecked in September 1588 near Spanish Point on the Clare coast, Baothlach wasted no time in hanging the survivors on a gallows near to his castle at Knockfinn. This callous act shocked combatants on all sides, and was long remembered. There was a tradition that the widows of the hanged men met every seventh year on the altar steps of a church in Spain to place a curse on Baothlach. He was reputed to have buried a large sum of money, and to have slain all those who knew of it. After his death, when his GHOST was conjured up, he explained that the TREASURE was buried in a river three jumps from the bank. His legs were thin from suffering in the afterlife, and when asked about this explained that it resulted from three things: the milk of five sheep he had stolen, the sweat of his hard-driven workers, and his disregard for the poor.

Frost (1893), 96–8, 271–2; Kilfeather (1967), 93–5; Holmer (1965), 219–21, 269–71; Ó Duilearga & Ó hÓgáin (1981), 272; Ó Duilearga in *Béaloideas, 17*, 175.

Mac Giolla Ghunna, Cathal Buí

(c.1680–1756) Ulster POET celebrated in folklore for a wild and rakish life. He was a native of County Fermanagh, and spent much of his life wandering around Leitrim, Cavan and Armagh. He was of sallow complexion, hence the epithet *buí* (yellow).

His reputation in folklore derives largely from the themes of drinking and womanising that he connects with himself in his poems, many of which are of a penitential nature. One of the songs, in a more humorous vein, became very popular with Ulster and Connacht folk singers. This tells of how he once saw the dead body of a yellow bittern in wintertime, and took it that the bird had died from thirst. This, he claimed, gave a licence to himself to continue drinking, as he resembled that bird in both colour and mentality. Several humorous anecdotes were told of his rakish habits. We are told that when a certain priest heard a report that Cathal was visiting his parish, he spoke from the altar threatening seven curses on anybody who would give lodgings to such a notorious fellow. That very night, a poor woman came to the priest's door and begged shelter for the night. The priest allowed her to sleep in the kitchen, but when he arose next morning found that she had departed, leaving only a note. The note was in the form of a quatrain, revealing that the 'old woman' had been Cathal in disguise and declaring that the priest's seven curses had now fallen on that clergyman himself. The priest looked frantically around his house and found that seven things were missing – his walking cane, riding whip, horse, dog, overcoat, hat and his servant-girl!

A very touching story was told concerning his death, and it seems to have developed as a kind of gloss on a striking line in one of his repentance poems. In this line, he states that 'through the intercession of the Mother I will get pardon and release from my pain'. According to the folk LEGEND, which became widely known, he lay dying in a miserable shack, and a local priest refused to go to attend him because of his wild life. A kindly neighbour eventually persuaded the priest to go and, as he approached, he noticed a strong light shining from the shack. Cathal had written his confession on the wall with a piece of charcoal, and as the priest tended to the dying poet, he noticed that a very modest and demure woman was waiting on him. After the poet had died, this woman disappeared, and the priest enquired in the neighbourhood as to who she might have been. He was told, however, that no woman would approach near to Cathal because of his reputation, from which the priest concluded that the strange lady had been the Virgin Mary who had come to succour the poor poet in his desolation.

Ó Buachalla (1975); IFC 1608:417–19, S929:218–19.

Mac Lughach Fictional grandson of FIONN MAC CUMHAILL, according to medieval literature. The designation means 'son of Lughaidh', and his own name is given as Gaoine.

One text states that he was the son of a warrior called Lughaidh Laghdha (a scribal misspelling for LUGHAIDH LÁGHA), hence his designation Mac Lughach. Some storyteller of the eleventh century, however, decided to make Lughaidh the name of his mother, and to connect popular MOTIFS concerning incest-births to him. We accordingly read that Lughaidh was a daughter of Fionn, and that she was in fosterage with the otherworld people, the TUATHA DÉ DANANN. Her brother, called Dáire Dearg, visited her in the otherworld dwelling and she became pregnant by him. In this way, Mac Lughach was born, and when he saw him, Fionn was pleased and remarked that he thought the child whole-some (*gaine*). While still a child, Mac Lughach killed a weasel, and when he was twelve years old was given for rearing to a great tutoress of young warriors called MONGFHIONN. However, he was so rough with his fellow students that they com-plained him to his grandfather, and Fionn then gave him a series of advices, telling him to be gentle towards women servants, POETS and the common people. In various literary texts, Mac Lughach figures as one of the Fianna warriors who were closest to Fionn in the latter's great adventures.

G. Murphy (1933), 66–78 & (1953), 206; Stokes (1900), 16–18; Ó hÓgáin (1988), 156–8, 360.

Mac Na Míchomhairle *(literally, 'the Son of Ill Counsel')* Hero of a comical text written in the late seventeenth cen-tury, probably in County Fermanagh.

The anonymous author calls himself Mac na Míchomhairle, and tells of his adventures in the first person. While walk-ing about one day, he sees a strange house and enters it. Within, he meets a *gruagach* (otherworld wizard) accompanied by a beautiful daughter. The wizard invites him to stay the night and states that if he takes part in a battle between otherworld armies next morning in Íle (Islay, off the Scottish coast), he may marry the beautiful maiden. She acts seductively towards Mac na Míchomhairle, and when they retire to sleep, he tries three times to travel the short distance to her bed. Each time, however, he goes astray and mistakes ordinary household items and domestic animals for savage regions and fierce beasts. He is dis-covered by the wizard and the maiden as he flounders about, much to his embar-rassment. Finally, he falls asleep, but awak-ens on the side of a old mound, with no house in sight.

The text is a prime example of the flow-ering of fanciful prose literature in the south Ulster area from the seventeenth to the nineteenth century. It is probably indebted to a celebrated adventure of FIONN MAC CUMHAILL in an allegorical house. For a related story, *see* CONÁN MAOL.

Ó Ceithearnaigh (1955); S. Watson (1979).

Mac Rustaing A celebrated gleeman of the early seventh century AD. He was known by his patronymic (son of Rustang), but his own name is given as Criotán.

He is listed as studying at the monastery of Armagh, being one of the fellow students of MAC CONGLINNE; and if tradition is to be credited, he followed the same path as that colleague to become an entertainer. The medieval literature states that he was a native of Ros Each

(Russagh, County Westmeath) and that he had the same mother as a saint called Caomhán 'the pock-marked', whose obit is given as AD 615 and whose feast day was on 14 September. It is probable that several anecdotes were in existence in the Middle Ages concerning the hilarity of Mac Rustaing. He was buried at Ros Each, and it was said that any woman who looked upon his grave would break wind or burst out laughing.

Some humorous text concerning Mac Rustaing seems to have been current in medieval Scotland and, as a result, he occurs in Scottish Gaelic literature and folklore, being called by variants of the name, such as Mac Ruslaing, Mac Ruslaich and Mac Rùsgail. As such, he is portrayed as a typical trickster in HUMOR-OUS TALES: in female disguise he seduces women, as a farm-hand he outwits stingy employers, and as a herd-boy he overcomes GIANTS by a variety of ruses.

Stokes (1905), 194, 206–8, Meyer (1892), xli, 7; W.J. Watson in *Scottish Gaelic Studies, 1,* 148, 210–11; Ó Duilearga (1948), 441; D.S. Thomson (1983), 191; Jackson (1990), 3, 48.

Mac Suibhne, Maolmhuire

(+1630) Chieftain of the MacSwiney sept of north Donegal from 1596 until his death. He was a brave warrior and an astute politician and survivor, changing sides repeatedly in the wars of the time and living to an old age.

Because of his cynicism, the dark-haired Maolmhuire (anglicised Myles) gained a quite sinister reputation in folklore. For his supposed loyalty to the English government, the staff of knighthood was conferred on him in 1599, and thus he was known to the folk as *Maolmhuire an Bhata Bhuí* (Myles of the Yellow Stick). This staff was said to have secreted within it a demon in the form of a black beetle, and it was claimed that Maolmhuire greased it with butter every day to feed its formidable occupant.

He quarrelled with members of the Ó Baoill (Boyle) family, and a story was commonly told in Donegal concerning an adventure involving himself and a certain Feidhlimidh Cam Ó Baoill. According to

this, Maolmhuire sent his servant to ask Feidhlimidh for the loan of a hound, but the latter claimed that he had no such animal. Knowing this to be untrue, Maolmhuire hatched a plot to gain revenge. He invited Feidhlimidh to a feast at his own dwelling in Doe, near Dungloe, and when the dupe had entered, he had the iron doors locked. When Maolmhuire pointed out a thin loaf being hardened by the fireside, likening it to a hungry thief of the Boyles, Feidhlimidh realised what was happening. He flung the loaf into Maolmhuire's face, kicked open the doors, and ran out to where his servant was waiting with two HORSES. Closely pursued by Maolmhuire and his horsemen, they raced all the way to Derry, where they managed to board a ship and make their getaway. This was said to have been the longest and hardest chase ever in County Donegal – the distance being 50 miles and including nine strands. In such a manner was Maolmhuire deprived of his quarry for the first time ever in his life. Folklore claims that he believed himself destined to die when thus overcome, so he lost all desire to live and soon expired.

P. Walsh (1960), 180–205; Ó Donaill (1952), 97–9; Ó Muirgheasa (1924), 26–9, 70–2; IFC Index.

Macha

Otherworld woman in the ULSTER CYCLE. Her real identity was the mother-goddess as patroness of KINGSHIP. Several sources describe her as a GODDESS of war, grouping her with other such mythical ladies.

The word *macha* meant a marked portion of land, and was the name by which the plain surrounding the sacred site of the ULAIDH, Eamhain, had come to be known. Hence the tumulus was called Eamhain Mhacha, and this in time led to the conjecture that the toponymic meant 'the tumulus of Macha'. The king of the Ulaidh was also referred to as the 'king of Macha', and all of this gave rise to a tendency to imagine that a personage called Macha had been associated with the site. The designation originally used by the Ulaidh for their cult-goddess was the usual MÓR-RÍOGHAIN, but the alternative name

Macha gave a special Ulster aura to this personage. Some sources in the medieval literature confirm that the Mór-Ríoghain and Macha were one.

That literature gives two separate accounts of Macha. According to one of these, three worthies – called Díthorba, Aodh and Ciombaoth – made an arrangement that they would alternate as kings of Ireland, each of them ruling for seven years at a time. When they had served three terms each, Aodh died and his daughter Macha 'the Red-haired' demanded his share for herself. She was refused, but through force of arms won her term. When Díthorba died, she in turn refused the kingdom to his five sons. She routed them in battle and herself married the other king, Ciombaoth. After the wedding, she went to Connacht disguised as a leper and encountered the sons of Díthorba as they were cooking a PIG. They shared their food with her, and one by one went into a wood to lie with her. She overcame each one, tied them up, and brought them back to Ulster, where she set them to building a fine fort for her. This account fancifully derives the name of the fort: Eamhain, as the *Eo-muin* of Macha. To mark out its perimeter, she used the clasp (*eo*) that she wore about her neck (*muin*). We read that she sat on the hill and planned the perimeter of the mound with the pin from her mantle. 'Her pin stretched further eastwards in front of her than behind her to the west – thus the mound is uneven'.

The other story of Macha is more significant, and in its earliest version, she is actually called the Mór-Ríoghain. According to it, an Ulster farmer called Crunnchu (later, Crunn), who was a widower, was visited in his house one day by a beautiful young woman. She looked after the household cares for him, entered his bed, and brought him good fortune in all his dealings. Her presence in his house was unknown to the Ulstermen, and she warned him not to mention her to any of them. She became pregnant by him, and when her time to give birth had almost come, he went to attend the assembly of the Ulstermen. At the assembly, the pair of chariot-horses belonging to king CONCHOBHAR MAC NEASA won all the races, and all present were loud in their praise of these horses. Crunnchu, however, boasted that he had a woman at home who could outrun them. Conchobhar had him arrested, and messengers were sent to bring the woman. She protested that she was pregnant, but when told that her husband would be killed if she did not race, she consented. She outran the horses, but collapsed at the finish and gave birth to twins. Before she died, she put a curse on the Ulstermen that in the time of their greatest need every man of them would be struck down with the pains she had suffered. In this way is explained the strange debility that struck the Ulster warriors at the crisis of the cattle-raid of Cooley (*see* ULSTER CYCLE). This debility was called the *ces noidhen* (difficulty of child bearing), but in time was altered to *ces noindhen* (difficulty of nine), which was taken to mean that the debility lasted for nine half-days.

The original explanation of the child-bearing theme in this context seems to have been that the otherworld lady could drain away the strength of warriors and leave them as weak as a woman in childbed. The twins (*emon*) are an incidental addition to the narrative, no doubt based on a misinterpretation of the name of the tumulus. Otherwise, however, this account is very significant, for it brings into focus the equine imagery in the Ulster cultus of kingship. This imagery derived from the sun-lore of EOCHAIDH and was reflected in the tradition of FEARGHUS MAC RÓICH. Illustrating the patron of kingship, it would naturally spread into the context of the father-god's partner, the divine patroness of the land. The race of the goddess would thus have been considered a suitably mystical way to refer to the course of a king's reign (*see also* MEADHBH), and such horse rituals are reported for the actual ceremonials of kingship. A further echo of the equine symbolism is provided by the Liath Mhacha (Grey of Macha) as the name of a famous horse in the Ulster Cycle. Liath was a designation often used for the ancestor-deity, and this horse –

which in the developed Cycle has become the charger of CÚ CHULAINN – may originally have been none other than a form of the father-deity.

Stories of otherworld ladies who leave their husbands after the breaking of a prohibition were found widely in folklore, and no doubt the theme of Macha leaving her husband was deliberately borrowed from floating lore. It was considered suitable to the Macha personage, for the lady of the folklore plot belonged to the otherworld, just as the Irish goddess did. We may speculate that the actual situation prevailing in the folklore plot was also suitable, for that entailed a supernatural condition similar to the types of *GEIS* that surrounded a ritual king. The folklore plot would accordingly have been borrowed in the context of a belief in the importance of placating the goddess and maintaining her protective function. King Conchobhar was referred to as the 'king of Macha', but the ritual myth was that he had taken the kingship from Fearghus mac Róich, and this allowed for some tension regarding her relationship to the reigning king. This ritual format was suitable to provide an explanation for the tragic destruction of the Ulster kingdom by the CONNACHTA in the fifth century AD. The curse placed by Macha on the Ulstermen would thus be a rationalisation of how the sovereignty passed out of their hands at that time.

The story of the building of Eamhain Mhacha was retold by the historian CÉITINN in the seventeenth century, but Macha is not named as a character in the late folklore. The MOTIF of her racing was, however, attractive enough to create echoes in some oral narratives. In County Galway, it is said that a race against a horse was run by the mother of CÚ CHULAINN before his birth; while County Clare lore has a derived LEGEND concerning a chieftain of INCHIQUIN. Some local scholar in the eighteenth century or thereabouts in mid-Ulster, on reading that Ciombaoth was the husband of Macha, caused the plot of her desertion of her husband to be told of the Mac Cionaoith (McKenna) family in that area. According to this, an otherworld

lady married a McKenna and had three children for him. He prospered as a farmer, but when he showed interest in another woman, she left him and brought all the farm animals with her into the waters of Tully Lough.

NAME: Gwynn (1924), 124–31; W. Stokes in *RC, 16*, 45; Mac Neill & Macalister (1916), 74; Macalister (1941), 122; Gray (1982), 128.
MACHA 'THE RED-HAIRED': K. Meyer in *ACL, 3*, 325–6; Best, Bergin & O'Brien (1954), 79–85.
MACHA AND HORSES: R. Thurneysen in *ZCP, 12*, 251–4: V. Hull in *Celtica, 8*, 1–42; Best & O'Brien (1956), 467–8.
'KING OF MACHA': E. Hogan (1892), 32; C. O'Rahilly (1976), 117–18.
CÉITINN'S TELLING: Dinneen, *2* (1908), 152–7.
OTHERWORLD WIVES: Cross (1952), motif F302.2; Briggs (1978), 145–50.
LATE FOLKLORE: Bruford (1969), 94; Ellis (1851), 106–42; B. Almqvist in *Béaloideas, 67*, 33–7.
GENERAL: Thurneysen (1921), 359–63; P. Henry (1978), 28–39; Ó hÓgáin (1999), 174–8.

Maine *(plural: Mainí)* Seven fictional sons of Connacht queen MEADHBH and her husband Ailill mac Máta were each known as Maine.

The name Maine was common enough in early Ireland (*see* UÍ MHAINE), but the idea of it being shared by seven brothers is obviously a literary fabrication. We are told that Meadhbh once asked a DRUID which of her children would kill her enemy, the Ulster king CONCHOBHAR MAC NEASA. The druid answered that the child was not yet born unless those born be renamed, and then explained that Conchobhar would fall by one called Maine. She therefore gave that name to all the seven sons whom she had borne to Ailill, and these became better known by the name Maine than by their own proper names, which, we are told, were Feidhlim, Cairbre. Eochaidh, Fearghus, Sin, Ceat and Dáire. Her plan did not have the desired result, however, for the prophecy referred to a different Conchobhar, who was a son of Arthur from Britain. This Conchobhar was killed by one of the seven, called Maine Andaí, whose proper name was Eochaidh. The ambiguous prophecy, as we have it, is somewhat confused. Its original form may have been that Conchobhar would be killed on one of the seven days of the week (genitive form, *sechtmaine*), which Meadhbh misunderstood to be a killing by one of seven men called Maine (*secht Maine*).

A dramatic story was invented concerning the personage of Maine Mórghor (properly, Sín). This told of how he went to court Fearbh, daughter of an Ulsterman called Gearg, accompanied by a troop of thrice-50 men. The mischievous BRICRIU remarked that they would spend but one day in Ulster. They were well received by Gearg, but as they were being entertained, a great wind blew and this was interpreted by the druid of Maine Mórghor as a bad portent. Meanwhile, an otherworld lady appeared to Conchobhar mac Neasa and told him that Maine was in his province. Conchobhar set out with a band of FOMHÓIRE mercenaries and attacked the dwelling of Gearg, who defended his visitors well but was slain. The otherworld lady also appeared to Meadhbh and told her that her son was being attacked. The fighting continued in Gearg's dwelling, and Maine Mórghor was slain. All of Conchobhar's men also died, except for himself and his servant Brod. He got reinforcements just in time before Meadhbh arrived, and her force was routed. Meadhbh herself was hurried away by her bodyguards, and Conchobhar plundered the dwelling of Gearg, taking away all its treasures.

Stories in which the Mainí figure generally have them as extensions of the interests of their mother. One account, for instance, tells of a rich hostelier called Reaghamhain who lived in Corca Moruadh (north County Clare). This Reaghamhain had a great herd of cattle and seven daughters who were in love with the Mainí. As Meadhbh was preparing for the cattle-raid of Cooley (*see* ULSTER CYCLE), she found the burden of feeding her great army quite heavy, and decided to send her sons to seek cattle from Reaghamhain. The Mainí met the girls, who eloped with them, bringing a large number of cattle, sheep and pigs. Reaghamhain and his men followed, and caught up with them as they forded a river. The Mainí sent the girls on with the cattle to their mother's court at Cruachain,

while they themselves held the ford by erecting a fence of briars and blackthorns. Meadhbh and Ailill came with a strong force to relieve them, and Reaghamhain agreed to give his daughters to the Mainí in return for his herd. The girls, however, were allowed to take seven-times twenty cows with them to help feed Meadhbh's army.

Another story of a cattle-raid was probably suggested by the preceding. According to this, Ailill and Meadhbh sent a message to Eochaidh Beag mac Cairbre, king of Cliu (an area in east Limerick), asking him to visit them. Before Eochaidh Beag set out, a woman came to him in a vision and warned him not to go without a retinue. When he awoke next morning, he found 50 fine steeds and riders' clothes for his men outside his dwelling. He was royally received at Cruachain, and agreed to Ailill's request for provision of a large number of cattle. On his way home, however, he and most of his men were killed by marauders. The otherworld lady apparently blamed Ailill for this, and sought vengeance against him. Soon after, he had a vision in which she and a warrior instructed him to seek cattle from Dartaid, daughter of Eochaidh Beag, who loved Ailill's son Órlámh. Accordingly, Órlámh set out with a troop and was welcomed by Dartaid, who agreed to go with him and to bring all her cows. The strange warrior and lady appeared also to a Munster champion called Corb Cliach and told him that Connachtmen were taking cattle from his territory. Corb attacked Órlámh's troop, and in the ensuing fight Dartaid and most of the troop were slain. Órlámh, who survived with a mere nine men, was probably understood to be one of the Mainí, although his is not one of their proper names in other sources. In *Táin Bó Cuailnge* (*see* ULSTER CYCLE), where he is killed by CÚ CHULAINN, he is described as son of both Ailill and Meadhbh.

Other mentions of the Mainí include the encounter of Cú Chulainn with Maine Athramhail (also known as Maine Andaí, and properly Feidhlim), whom he spares, in *Táin Bó Cuailnge* and the slaying by Conall Cearnach of Maine Mo-Eipirt (properly Eochaidh) after the latter had wounded the dying Cú Chulainn. We are told that Maine Andaí was slain by CEITHEARN MAC FLONNTAIN, and that Maine Máthramhail (properly Cairbre) fell in combat with Furbaidhe in an attempt to avenge his mother's death (see MEADHBH). Furbaidhe also fell in that fight.

K. Meyer in *AIM*, *5*, 21–2; J. O'Neill in *Ériu* 2. 184–5; Knott (1936), 12; E. Windisch in *Irische Texte*, *2 (2)*, 185–205, 224–38; W. Stokes in *Irische Texte*, *3*, 382–3; C. O'Rahilly (1976), 27–8, 48–9, 304; K. Meyer in *ZCP*, *9*, 175.

Manannán Otherworld lord and mythical mariner. The earlier form of the name was Manandán, and the patronymic *mac Lir* (son of the sea) is usually added.

His name appears in Welsh in the form Manawydan, which is based on the toponymic *Manaw*, the Welsh term for the Isle of Man. The toponymic seems to derive from an ancient population name such as *Manavii*, referring to dwellers near water. As frequently among ancient Celtic peoples, this may have encapsulated for that group a special name of their ancestor-deity – 'water-controller' or the like. With the passage of time and the influence of Christianity, the tribal deity would have survived only as a memory of some obscure personage who inhabited the island. Such a lingering memory could easily become fused with the well-known Celtic notion of an otherworld island off the western coast where the GOD of the dead dwelt (see DONN), and it was from such a fusion that the Welsh imagined a sea-dwelling wonder-worker or deity.

The Old Irish name of the island, *Manu*, was derived from the Welsh (i.e. later British) form *Manaw*, and therefore does not predate the third century AD. This suggests a late development for the character Manannán, whose name is based on *Manann*, the Irish genitive of *Manu*. It meant simply 'he of Manu', whereas the Welsh term Manawydan comes from the nominative form. The Irish and Welsh versions therefore seem to be two separate developments from the same basic lore. It would appear that it was the Irish who first gave the title *mac Lir* to him, and that this was in turn borrowed by the Welsh as

map Llyr. Whereas in surviving Welsh tradition, Manawydan was a master craftsman and trickster, it is noteworthy that the Irish preserved in fuller form the original lore of the personage, describing Manannán as the lord of a watery domain, the sea being his 'plain'. He was believed to control the WEATHER, and stories told of how he came periodically to intervene in the affairs of the men and women of this world.

His residence being in Manu, Irish storytellers made much of the ancient lore concerning the otherworldly nature of that place, and from this came a new legendary name for the Isle of Man. This was Eumania (later, Eamhain) meaning a tumulus or sacred place, a name suitable to lore of an otherworld lord who continues to take an interest in the world of the living. Probably from influence of the famous sacred site of KINGSHIP of the neighbouring Ulaidh people (see ULSTER CYCLE), an early Irish text describes the actual island as if it were a temple. The text claims that there was a unique tree on the island, and that 'four legs of white silver' were under the island, holding it up. With regard to the great tree, it was imagined that wonderful apples grew on it. This must have been in origin a separate tradition – similar to that of the Hesperides in Greek lore – and may have been part of the original ancestor-cult of the Manavii tribe. So Manannán was said to reside in Eamhain *Abhlach* (of the Apples), where all of life came to its full fruition.

The fertile lore concerning the otherworld ensured that the character Manannán underwent rapid dramatic development, and his mysterious realm came to be thought of in terms of a faraway otherworld, not distinctly identified with the Isle of Man but termed Magh Meall (the Pleasant Plain), or – under the influence of Christianity – Tír Tairngire (the Land of Promise). According with the earlier tradition, however, the ocean was poetically claimed to belong to him, it being to him 'solid earth' and 'a flowery plain', and its fish being his calves and lambs. He was described as driving his chariot over the waters, the waves were his HORSES, and he was accordingly 'the rider of the maned sea'. He had one particular horse called Enbharr (literally, 'water-foam'), and one kenning for the waves was 'the locks of Manannán's wife'. Sometimes, he himself was identified with the waves, and one text has him travelling in the following manner: 'For the space of nine waves he would be submerged in the sea, but he would rise on the crest of the tenth without wetting chest or breast.' The most humanising account is in a ninth-century glossary. Here he is described as 'a celebrated merchant who was in the Isle of Man', and furthermore as a great mariner who 'knew by studying the heavens when there would be fine weather and when there would be bad weather'.

A text from the eighth century has him coming from the Isle of Man to beget the hero-prince MONGÁN, and another from the same period has his wife Fann coming to seek the love of CÚ CHULAINN. In both these cases, he is presented as a spiritual being who appears and disappears at various places as he wills. A twelfth-century account has him visiting CORMAC MAC AIRT and bringing members of that king's family away to the happy otherworld. He is described as finely clad and carrying on his shoulder a branch with three golden apples. The apples touching each other made delightful music that would soothe to sleep all those who were sick or wounded. The parallel is obvious here between this 'Region of Apples' and its cognate, the Avalon of Arthurian Romance, which was derived from Celtic sources.

Manannán was not numbered among the divine community, TUATHA DÉ DANANN, in the earlier literature, but by the tenth or eleventh century, he was being treated as one of them. We read in a late medieval text that, after their defeat by the Gaelic people, he came from his overseas domain to the Tuatha Dé and advised them to take up residence in the mounds, hillocks and lonely places of Ireland. He appointed a special *sídh* (cairn-dwelling) to each of the Tuatha Dé nobles, and presented three great gifts to them. The first

of these gifts was the *féth fiadha* (literally, 'art of semblance'), understood as a cloak of concealment through which they could make themselves invisible. The second gift was the feast of GOIBHNIU, the celebration of which warded off age and death from their kings; and the third was 'the pigs of Manannán', which swine would come alive again after being hunted and killed. Then he made a circuit of the Tuatha Dé dwellings. A great feast was prepared for him by Ealcmhar (i.e. NUADHU) at Brugh na Bóinne (the Newgrange tumulus in County Meath), and the Brugh was freshly strewn with rushes before him as a welcome, but he disliked Ealcmhar and later acted against him. The same text also states that Manannán brought the divine youth AONGHUS on a trip to India, where they got two wonderful cows – a speckled one that Manannán kept afterwards on his domain in Eamhain Abhlach, and a dun cow which Aonghus kept at Brugh na Bóinne. The text also relates the story of the maiden EITHNE, who lives alternately in Eamhain Abhlach and Brugh na Bóinne, and for whom the milk of these two cows is full nourishment.

The attribution of wonderful weapons and accoutrements to Manannán seems to have been commonplace. References are made to a great shield, as well as a valuable knife and shirt, that had once been his property but came into the possession of the hero FIONN MAC CUMHAILL. In the post-medieval stories of Fionn, indeed, Manannán is treated as a *deus ex machina*. A fifteenth-century lay has him coming disguised as a warrior with a sword through his head, and inciting strife among the Fianna due to his hatred for them, but elsewhere he is friendly. In one late prose text, for instance, he helps them on a foreign adventure by carrying them in his wonderful boat. His image in the late literature is generally that of a friendly trickster, such as in two colourful texts that have him disguised as the CEITHEARNACH CAOILRIABHACH and a grey-cloaked churl (*see* FIANNA CYCLE).

Of special interest is a ballad from the Isle of Man, dating from around the end of the fifteenth century. Here we are told that rent in the form of rushes was paid to him by the inhabitants of the island. This – taken along with the medieval Irish reference to the strewing of rushes for him at Brugh na Bóinne – suggests that these wild plants, with their aquatic associations, were considered sacred to him. It also reveals that there was a permanence in the folklore concerning Manannán through the centuries. The same Manx ballad claims that Manannán was the first owner of the Isle, which is described as Ellan Sheeant (otherworld island), and he was able to conceal it from passing ships by use of a magic mist. This is undoubtedly connected with his power of *féth fiadha*, but the specific ability to remove territories from the human domain was also attributed to him. The sea, which was closely bound to him in metaphor, had a painfully obvious tendency to conceal islands and to flood the mainland. Thus a play on the territorial name Umhall (the Owles, County Mayo) caused a medieval writer to imagine that Manannán had once, by his magic, surrounded that whole area with a cliff of brass (*umha*).

The association of inundations with Manannán has a long tradition attaching to it. For instance, some sources claim that Oirbsiu was an alternative name for Manannán, and that this Oirbsiu died and was buried in Connacht, and that a lake burst forth over his grave. This was given as the origin-LEGEND of Lough Corrib, which according to that legend was originally known as Loch nOirbsen. Oirbsiu was described as the ancestor of the Conmhaicne, a sept of Leinster origin that had settled in that western area, and in all probability the name Loch nOirbsen was given to this lake by the Conmhaicne themselves. It would appear, indeed, that the tradition of Manannán was spread initially by the Leinstermen (LAIGHIN), and their adherents.

No doubt due to the reading of literary references, the tendency to associate waters with Manannán continued down through the centuries, and in the late folklore, several lakes were said to have got their names

from daughters of his. These included Lough Sheelin in County Cavan; Lakes Ennell, Owel and Derravaragh in County Westmeath; as well as Loughmonoge and Lake Glina in County Mayo. In line with this also is a folk legend from west Galway that describes another daughter as going boating in the Bay of Kilkieran. A storm arose, and she was in danger of being drowned until Manannán came to her assistance. He, through his magic, caused an island to appear there and she was thus enabled to reach land. The island is called Mana. A folk legend from north Donegal puts him in the role of an exasperated parent. Three sons of his resided at the mouth of Strathbreaga Bay, and they persisted in bickering with each other. The enraged Manannán refused to restrain the tide for them at that bay, and it burst in and drowned the three near Malin.

Other aspects of his literary portrayal also had their echoes in late folklore. In County Mayo it was said that he was a famous magician and resided at the castle of Mannin in the parish of Bekan, while west Galway lore claimed that he was a learned wizard to whom young men were sent to be educated. Furthermore, accounts have been collected from the folklore of the north-western parts of the country that repeat the notions that the sea waves are his horses and that storms are caused by his anger.

NAMES: Bromwich (1961), 428, 441–3; Rivet & Smith (1979), 410–11; J. Vendryes in *Études Celtiques*, 6, 247–51; H. Wagner in *ZCP*, 33, 4–5 & 38, 24; Ó hÓgáin (1999), 150–2, 240.

MANAWYDAN FAB LLYR: I. Williams (1930), 49–65.

ISLAND AS OTHERWORLD: RIA Dictionary, s.v. 'emon', 'emuin', 'emne'; Meyer (1912), 78; W. Stokes in *Irische Texte*, 3, 193; Bieler (1979), 106; Mac Mathúna (1985), 33–43; Ó hÓgáin (1999), 151–2, 241.

SEA-IMAGERY: Meyer (1900), 79–80 & (1912), 78; Gwynn (1913), 274–5; Dillon (1953), 26–9; Mac Mathúna (1985), 38-43.

GOLDEN APPLES: Mac Mathúna (1985), 33–8; Stokes in *Irische Texte*, 3, 193; O'Fihelly (1911), 7.

FRIENDSHIP WITH AONGHUS: L. Duncan in *Ériu*, 11, 184–225.

WEAPONS AND ACCOUTREMENTS: Mac Néill (1904), 21–2, 35.

SWORD THROUGH HEAD: G. Murphy (1933), 240–6.

HELPING THE FIANNA: Ní Mhuirgheasa (1954), 146–8.

MANX BALLAD: R.L. Thomson in *Études Celtiques*, 9, 521–31.

UMHALL: Gwynn (1924), 274–5.

OIRBSIU: W. Stokes in *RC*, 16, 276–7 & in *Irische Texte*, 3, 356–7;

Macalister (1941), 128–9; Wagner in *Ériu, 28*, 12.

FOLKLORE: OSL: Meath (1836), 91 & Westmeath, *2* (1837), 302 & Mayo, *2* (1838), 395, 398; IFC 57:124, 202:105, 1395:538, S1119: 363–4; S. Ó Duilearga in *Béaloideas, 6*, 298; Wagner in *ZCP, 38*, 15; MacCulloch (1911), 87.

GENERAL: J. Vendryes in *Études Celtiques, 6,* 239–54; G. Lemacher in *Ar Aghaidh, 10* (1945), 3.

Maodhóg SAINT who died *c.*AD 626; founder of monasteries at Fearna (Ferns, County Wexford), Drom Leathan (Drumlane, County Cavan) and Ross Inbhir (Rossinver, County Leitrim). His real name was Aodh (earlier, Aed) or its diminutive Aodán, and Maodhóg (earlier, Mo-Aedoc) is a hypocoristic form. It is sometimes anglicised as Mogue.

The several medieval accounts of his life are based on a biography compiled in Irish in or about the ninth century, but not now surviving. Probably reliable is the tradition that Maodhóg's father Sétna was of the Uí Mhac Uais, an AIRGHIALLA sept, and that his mother was called Eithne and was of the Uí Amhalghaidh, a northern sept of the LAIGHIN. Other details are less credible – for instance, that before his conception, a star was seen to enter the mouth of his mother. We further read that when the child was growing up, he was given by his father as a hostage to the high-KING Ainmhire at TARA. He so impressed Ainmhire that he was allowed to return to his parents, but he would accept his freedom only on condition that the other hostages were released also. Maodhóg was educated by ecclesiastics, and he soon showed his ability to work miracles. He once took pity on starving wolves, allowed them to take sheep from his father's fold, and then miraculously replaced the sheep. He was accompanied and protected by angels, and even succeeded in restoring to life a boy who had been drowned in Lough Erne. He and St Molaise were youthful friends, and when they were praying once at the foot of two trees, the trees fell away from each other. By this they understood that God willed them to part, and Molaise went north to build a monastery at Damh-inis (the island of Devenish on Lough Erne), while Maodhóg went south to the territory of the Uí Chinsealaigh sept (south-east Leinster).

We read that from there, Maodhóg went to Wales to study under St David and was given holy orders by him. In that country, he performed several other miracles, avoiding an assassination attempt by the servant of a jealous monk, cutting a new road through a forest by driving his ox-cart through it, and restoring the features of a flat-faced man. On his return to Ireland, he founded the monastery of Ferns in the Uí Chinsealaigh territory, and episodes are relayed that stress the importance of the saint in the political affairs of the area. When the Uí Chinsealaigh people took refuge from an invading army at his monastic site, he prevented that army from taking the sept's cattle by drawing a line with his crozier around the herd. A sole soldier who crossed that line was immediately struck dead. On another occasion, the Uí Chinsealaigh themselves were on a plundering expedition, and their king gave alms to Maodhóg. The king was overcome by sickness, and dreamed that he had been saved from hell by the alms he had given.

The king of all Leinster, BRANDUBH, was also indebted to Maodhóg when he clashed with the Uí NÉILL high-king Aodh mac Ainmhireach. It so happened that the high-king's son Cumascach came on a visit to Brandubh and insisted on sleeping with Brandubh's wife. The Leinstermen were so inflamed at this that they slew Cumascach, and the high-king came with a great army seeking vengeance. Maodhóg prayed earnestly for the success of Brandubh in the ensuing battle, with the result that the Leinstermen triumphed and the high-king was slain. Brandubh was later assassinated by a man named Saran. He was revived by Maodhóg, but he expressed a preference for the afterlife, and was allowed to return there when he had received the last rites from the saint.

Some of the LEGENDS refer to ordinary ecclesiastical matters. We read that Maodhóg was once bringing a team of oxen to a community of nuns, but he gave one of the oxen to a leper on the way. The nuns were angry because they could not plough with only one animal, but an ox came from the sea to do the work for them. Maodhóg went to Britain to visit the dying St David, but wished to return quickly to Ireland for an urgent appointment. On David's instructions, he went to the seashore and there found a wild animal (probably a sea-HORSE) that he mounted and which brought him across the sea to Ferns. This MOTIF of miraculous travel occurs in several contexts in the accounts of Maodhóg, such as in a claim that he was directed by an angel to go to see the ailing king of Connacht, who is anachronistically identified as GUAIRE. When Maodhóg approached Lough Derg, that lake dried up before him so that his chariot crossed it like a plain. He crossed a swamp in similar fashion and, when he arrived, healed the king of the sickness. On another occasion, Maodhóg was teaching a student when a golden ladder descended by his side. He went up the ladder and disappeared. When he returned, he told the student that St COLM CILLE had died and that he had gone to pay his respects to Colm in heaven.

When Maodhóg himself died, some of his miraculous power reputedly remained at Ferns, people being continually cured of ailments by his relics. Nobody could ever after him sleep in his bed without being overcome by weakness, and even his successor as abbot of Ferns, St MOLING, failed in this test. Fragments of Maodhóg's biography survived in the oral traditions of the two areas with which he was associated. In Cavan, it was said that the saint was born on a little island on Templeport Lough and was in danger of death. So as to ensure baptism, the baby was put sitting on a stone, and the stone floated across to the shore of the lake where a priest was waiting. The feast day of Maodhóg is 31 January.

Kenney (1929), 448–9; Stokes (1905), 54–5; Plummer, *2* (1910), 141–63, 295–311 & *1* (1922), 183–290; Heist (1965), 234–47; O'Hanlon, *1* (1875), 521–80; OSL: Cavan & Leitrim (1836), 19–20; IFC 54:89, 655:187–99, 948:220–1, 229–32, 972:517–18.

Maol Dúin Fictional character in a voyage text written in the late eighth century AD. It is a prose text, and there is a slightly later versified retelling, but in both versions the earlier form of his name, Máel Dúin, is used. The name meant 'warrior of the fortress', by which was probably meant the fortress called Dún Aonghusa on the Aran Islands, County Galway.

He is described as posthumous son of a warrior of Árainn (the Aran Islands) called Ailill Ochair Agha. His mother was a nun, and when he was born, she gave him to a queen to be reared along with three princes. As he grew up, he excelled his fellows in all things, and one of the three grew jealous of him and teased him with not knowing his parentage. Surprised by this, he went to the queen and insisted that she tell him the truth concerning his background. She told him who his father was, and he sometime later discovered that his father had been killed by marauders. Intent on vengeance, he discovered that the marauders were overseas, and a DRUID from Corca Moruadh (Corcomroe, County Clare) told him the day on which to begin building a boat and instructed him to take seventeen men on the enterprise. However, his three foster-brothers swam on board also. Reaching two small islands by night, they heard men feasting there, and one of them was boasting that he had slain Ailill. As Maol Dúin and his followers prepared to attack, a storm arose and carried their boat out to sea. When morning came, they found themselves far from land, and Maol Dúin reproached his foster-brothers for violating the druid's counsel and thereby bringing them into these perils.

Thus began their voyage into the unknown. They came across many islands, which surpassed each other in fantasy born of the author's imagination and interspersed with details from Irish myth and from medieval bestiaries. In the latter context, Maol Dúin and his companions had encounters with massive ants and birds, demon horses, and a monstrous CAT that guarded TREASURE. They came to an island of women, who became their lovers in an ageless realm, but eventually his men prevailed on Maol Dúin to set out for home. As they left, his own lover threw a ball of thread from the land to Maol Dúin and when he seized it, drew the boat back to the shore. This happened three times and, finally, when one of the crew caught the thread, Maol Dúin's POET Diúran cut off the man's hand and thus they escaped.

There are some elements in the text that derive from native Irish lore of the otherworld, such as an island of apple trees with beautiful golden apples (*see* MANANNÁN), and wondrous PIGS that disappear underground at night. On one island, they came to a lake that restored youth to those who bathed in it, and also restored health to the sick and injured. They also came to an island surrounded by a revolving wall of fire, which wall had one open doorway. Each time this doorway passed them, they caught a glimpse of all within – handsome people with beautiful clothes drinking ale from goblets of gold, with wondrous music being played for them.

The narrative has some interesting twists that show the originality of its author. On one occasion, for instance, Maol Dúin and his men beheld a silver pillar rising from the sea with a great silver net attached to it. Their boat went through a mesh of this net, and the poet Diúran took a piece of it with him, vowing to lay it on the altar at Armagh. This connection with the great cathedral of Armagh was inserted by the author as a pseudo-authentication of his story. The passage with most general relevance to literature concerns how they came to an island where an old Irish monk had settled. He explained that he was the sole survivor of fifteen disciples of St Bréanainn of Biorra (Birr, County Offaly). This account was one of the sources used by another early medieval writer, who described a celebrated voyage by the namesake of this saint, BRÉANAINN of Clonfert. The old monk whom Maol Dúin met was covered completely by his overgrown hair, and a parallel passage in the text describes another elderly Irish pilgrim clothed by his own hair. He had come there floating on a sod that miraculously grew to become an island.

The account of the birth and youth of Maol Dúin is an oblique instance of a plot that was very popular in Irish storytelling (*see* ROMANTIC TALES, type 873), while the theme of the fantastic voyage is borrowed from the earlier story of BRAN MAC FEABHAIL.

Van Hamel (1941), 20–77; Oskamp (1970); Dillon (1948), 124–31.

Maol Fhothartaigh *(earlier, Máel Fothartaig)* Leinster hero of the seventh century AD. He was the son of the king of the LAIGHIN, Rónán mac Colmáin, whose headquarters was at Nás (Naas, County Kildare) and who died around the year 624. His name indicates that he was dedicated as a 'devotee' (*maol*) to a SAINT of the Fotharta sept (perhaps St BRIGHID) at his birth.

At sometime in the eighth or ninth century, a story came to be told concerning both of these men. It was probably invented by a genealogist who knew the Greek myth of Phaedra and Hippolytus, which it resembles. The composer did not scruple to alter chronology, and he made Maol Fhothartaigh and his father contemporaneous with the king of Dál nAraidhe, Eochaidh Iarlaithe, who in fact died in the year 665. The fullest surviving text of the story dates from the tenth century, and in it Rónán is claimed to have been son of a certain Aodh rather than of Colmán.

We read that Rónán was married to a Munster lady called Eithne, and Maol Fhothartaigh was their son. The boy was much loved by the Leinster people, and was the darling of the girls and women. His mother died, and sometime later Maol Fhothartaigh encouraged his father to remarry. Rónán suggested the daughter of Eochaidh Iarlaithe, but was advised against it by Maol Fhothartaigh, who said that she was a skittish girl. Nevertheless, Rónán went to her father's court at Dún Sobhairce (Dunseverick, County Antrim) and brought her home as his wife. The new queen (who is not named) lusted after Maol Fhothartaigh and sent her maid to solicit him. In order to entice him, the maid herself slept with the hero, but he refused to go to the queen and instead departed for Scotland, accompanied by 50 warriors, so as to avoid her. After some time, the men of Leinster insisted that Rónán invite his son back from Scotland. So Maol Fhothartaigh returned, and again the queen forced her maid to solicit him. He sought advice from his friend Conghal, who promised him to set things right in exchange for the two great hunting hounds of Maol Fhothartaigh. Conghal sent a message to the queen that Maol Fhothartaigh would meet her, but when she came to the appointed place, Conghal himself was there instead. He reprimanded her severely and beat her with a horsewhip, but she vowed vengeance on him. 'I will bring a gush of blood to your mouth!' she said.

That night, Rónán was praising his son, who had not yet returned home from herding cattle in the wilderness, but the dishevelled queen said that Maol Fhothartaigh had tried to force his attentions on her. Rónán angrily accused her of lying, but she retorted that she would prove that it was true. Soon Maol Fhothartaigh entered and began to dry his legs by the fire. He recited a semi-quatrain about the cold weather, and she answered it, saying that it was cold for a man without his lover. Rónán took this to be an invitation by Maol Fhothartaigh and a rejection by her of the invitation, so in a rage he told one of his warriors called Aodán to drive a spear into his son. The spear transfixed Maol Fhothartaigh to the seat. As Conghal rose in surprise, his heart was pierced by a second thrust from Aodán, who further slew Maol Fhothartaigh's jester Mac Glas. Too late, Rónán realised his mistake.

In revenge, Conghal's brother went to Dún Sobhairce, lured the queen's father Eochaidh from his palace, and slew him and his wife and son. He then brought their heads to Leinster and flung them at the queen, who in desolation fell on her own knife. The two sons of Maol Fhothartaigh pursued Aodán and slaughtered him, and the men of Leinster rose against Rónán. The king, frantic with sorrow for having slain Maol Fhothartaigh and perplexed by the rebellion of his subjects, died of a broken heart.

For references to other occurrences in Irish literature of this plot of the lustful and treacherous stepmother, *see* ROMANTIC TALES, type 870C.

Greene (1955), 1–15; Dillon (1946), 42–8.

Maolodhrán Leinster hero of the seventh century AD, concerning whom some anecdotes are found in the literature of the ninth to tenth century. He belonged to the sept called Dál Meisin Corb that inhabited the area of south-west Wicklow. His name (earlier, Máel Odhráin) indicates that he was dedicated at his birth as a devotee (*maol*) to a Leinster SAINT called Odhrán.

The Annals record that in the year 650 Maolodhrán slew Dúnchadh and Conall, two sons of the UÍ NÉILL high-king Bláthmhac, at a mill. Bláthmhac shared the HIGH-KINGSHIP with his brother DIARMAID MAC AODHA SLÁINE, and they were grandsons of the famous DIARMAID MAC CEARRBHEOIL. The Maolodhrán stories substitute this latter high-king for Bláthmhac and, for dramatic effect, increase the number of slain sons to three – rather uninventively calling the third son by the name Maolodhar. We read that the three once went plundering in Leinster and came across Maolodhrán. They attacked and wounded him. The servant of Maolodhrán came to the rescue with the hero's HORSE, but was slain, and then Maolodhrán called his horse and mounted it. The three attackers fled before him and took refuge in a mill pond. Maolodhrán told an old woman who was working at the mill to turn the wheel, which she did, and the three were crushed to death. The high-king Diarmaid demanded that the Leinstermen hand Maolodhrán over to him on account of this, but his demand was rejected. He brought his army to Loch Gobhar (Lagore, County Meath) seeking vengeance, and encamped on an island in that lake. Maolodhrán managed to sneak in to the island at night and met the king as the latter went to relieve himself. Although he had been Maolodhrán's fosterer, Diarmaid did not recognise him in the dark, and asked him for some grass. Maolodhrán gave him a fistful of nettles and thistles, and when the king stung himself with these, he realised that his companion was no friend. Maolodhrán threatened to behead him, but spared him when Diarmaid agreed to forego vengeance for his sons. After that, Maolodhrán became Diarmaid's champion.

Another set of anecdotes tells of Maolodhrán's relations with his neighbouring sept of Uí Mháil (Imaal, south Wicklow). It is claimed that he slew large numbers of these in local warfare, but nevertheless had as wife the daughter of the Uí Mháil king, Aitheachda. Once, when this wife visited her own people, she was persuaded to betray Maolodhrán to them, and accordingly pointed out the bothy to which she and her husband retired by dropping pieces of phosphorescent timber behind her as she went with him. Soon the bothy was surrounded by men of the Uí Mháil and, realising this, Maolodhrán called out to them to allow their sister to escape. He himself then left the bothy wearing his wife's cowl, and in the darkness, they slew their own sister in mistake for him. Maolodhrán counterattacked so fiercely that he forced the Uí Mháil to make peace with him.

Aitheachda, however, plotted treachery, and he got the opportunity when Maolodhrán was visiting his house and taking a bath there. One of Aitheachda's men blinded the hero with embers used for heating the water, and then Aitheachda himself delivered the death blow with Maolodhrán's own lance. This was a devastating weapon that could kill 30 men with a single thrust. It used to be left on the roadside, resting on a fork, and if anybody passed without leaving something for it, it would spring at that passer-by and kill him. Following his death, Maolodhrán was buried in Gleann Dá Loch (Glendalough, County Wicklow), and then Aitheachda took the wife whom he then had, and also took the spear. Exactly a year later, Aitheachda was looking at this spear on a bridge, and the woman remarked that 'if ever a man was avenged after death, it is most likely that Maolodhrán will be!' At that, the dead hero appeared, grabbed the lance, and slew Aitheachda with it.

These were obviously popular LEGENDS that circulated among Maolodhrán's sept in early medieval times, and in them he has the typical image of an accomplished and resourceful folk hero who can only be slain through treachery. The lore of the special lance seems to have been derived from some ritual concerning war. It is called the *carr* (spear) of Bealach Duirghein (apparently Ballynabarny Gap), and we read that 'as long as it was covered and pointing south' the Leinstermen would not conquer their enemies to the north. Ballynabarny was in Maolodhrán's territory, and thus the great spear would have become associated with him. It is surprising that these legends did not survive into later tradition, but the explanation for this must be that the setting was too local and the influence of the Dál Meisin Corb too slight in the life of medieval Leinster.

O'Brien (1962), 36; Meyer (1894), 70–81; Greene (1975), 45–56; P. Walsh in *The Irish Book Lover*, 28, 74–80; Gwynn (1906), 64–5; W. Stokes in *RC*, 15, 305–6; G. Mac Eoin in *Ériu*, 15, 60–4; C.G. Buttimer in *Ériu* 19, 128–32.

Martin *(AD 316–97)* SAINT known variously in Irish as Mártan and Máirtín, his name being preceded by the title *Naomh*, which is usually reserved for native Irish saints. The cult of St Martin of Tours seems to have come to Ireland with the introduction of Christianity, and he was much venerated in the early Irish Church.

The influence of his biography, written by his contemporary and friend Sulpicius Severus, is evident in several early texts in Hiberno-Latin and Irish. In medieval Irish literature, Martin is claimed to have been the maternal uncle of St PATRICK, and his grave at Tours is said to have been discovered by COLM CILLE. He is also referred to, quite anachronistically, as a friend of St SEANÁN. As if to underline the importance placed on St Martin by the early missionaries to Ireland, the literature makes much of a copy of the gospels written by that saint, and variously claims that it was presented by him to Patrick, Colm Cille and Seanán.

Martin's feast day, 11 November, was the final festival before the full onset of winter, and it was customary at this time in different parts of western Europe to slaughter a bullock or FOWL for a great meal. An Irish text from about the eleventh century claims that this was begun by Patrick. We read that he was given the monastic tonsure by Martin, in thanks for which he made it his custom to present a PIG to monks and nuns on the eve of that saint's feast. The practice of killing a duck or hen on St Martin's Eve continued in most parts of Ireland until the beginning of the twentieth century. The Sign of the Cross was made with the blood of the slaughtered fowl on the door and in different parts of the kitchen while a prayer was addressed to the saint. This was believed to ensure good fortune during the ensuing winter.

There was a general belief in Ireland that no wheels should be turned on St Martin's Day, and it was especially important that no milling should be done. The explanation given for this was the unhistorical one that the saint had been a miller and that he had been accidentally crushed to death by his mill wheel. This lore probably developed from the fact that the grinding of corn was due to begin at that time of year, but was delayed out of reverence for Martinmas and in order to obtain the saint's blessing on the work. The saint was sometimes said to appear and take an animal away from people who failed to honour him at his feast, and in the south-east of the country was said to be seen riding a white HORSE on the sea as a warning to fishermen to refrain from work at Martinmas.

In the original biography of Martin by Sulpicius, the story was told of how Martin divided his cloak with a beggar and how JESUS later appeared to him in a dream wearing that garment. This story became known in Ireland as elsewhere, with the beggar being portrayed as Christ in disguise testing the charity of the saint. More popular in origin and spread was an account of Martin throwing a fistful of dough into the fireplace in the house of a stingy man, thereby causing a green tree to grow in the fire. This was borrowed from a folk LEGEND concerning JESUS CHRIST

himself. Another apocryphal source lay behind a story that Martin caused the first mice and cats to come into the world (*see* WILD ANIMALS).

Kenney (1929), 158–60, 810; Stokes (1887), xv, 8–9, 510, 560–1, 608 & (1890), 2, 7, 27, 62, 74; O'Kelleher & Schoepperle (1918), 96–7, 114–15, 258–61; S. Ó Súilleabháin in Richmond (1957), 252–61; Danaher (1972), 230–2; IFC Index.

marvels In medieval Ireland, there was a great interest in supposed wonderful happenings and strange traits relating to places. Most of this lore seems to have derived from ecclesiastical and learned sources.

As in other parts of Europe, didactic stories were frequently used by clergy, and such are found in several texts written in Irish and Latin. For instance, an admonition to properly observe the Easter ceremonies is marvellously dramatised in one medieval story in Irish from Dublin. It describes how a young married abbot of Droimneach (Drimnagh) left these ceremonies and fell asleep on a hill in the area. When he awoke, he found that he had become a woman. Totally confused, he allowed himself to be wooed and married by the steward of the church of Croimghlinn (Crumlin, nearby). Within seven years, he gave birth to seven children, and then again fell asleep on the same hill. He awoke to find that he was a man once more, and when he returned to his house, his wife told him that he had been absent less than one hour. Arrangements were made for the children to be reared between the steward and himself.

Also opposed to the marriage of clergy, though not localised, is an account of how the coffin of a priest's wife was too heavy to be carried. A wise man recommended that two other wives of priests be brought to shoulder it. They did so without difficulty, and the wise man remarked that two devils could easily carry one. This marvel was in later folklore adapted to the tradition of the wonderful HAG, the CAILLEACH BHÉARRA. We are told that, when asked by a priest what was the greatest wonder she had ever seen in her long life, that hag described how she had once witnessed a coffin of a dead land agent, which was so heavy that it could only be carried by other such agents. Finally, coffin and bearers were sucked into the earth, the import being that they were all damned. Variants have her telling the priest how she saw the spirit of a priest's paramour who had led an evil life being followed through the air or on the sea by demonic hounds.

The devil and his minions often appear in these didactic stories as insatiable foes of the spiritual welfare of humans. One account with a clear moral purpose tells of how a monk at the monastery of Armagh saw a devil there writing for a whole year in two books. In the smaller of the books, the devil wrote the sins of the people who confessed, whereas in the large book were a list of unconfessed sins. When all the community confessed their sins, the devil left in high dudgeon.

Several marvellous stories were told of the great Midland monastery of Clonmacnoise (founded by St CIARÁN on the River Shannon). We read that a bishop of that monastery, called Caoinchomhrac, was wont to retire with his monks to Inis Aondaimh (Devenish Island, in Lough Ree on the Shannon) in order to pray there. One day they were cooking a little PIG that had been given to them by hunters, when they saw a stranger come from the lake towards them. The stranger said that the dead pig was a monk who had been transformed, along with other young members of his community, for disobedience. The stranger was the monk's father, and on hearing his account, Caoinchomhrac had the pig buried honourably. At the stranger's invitation, Caoinchomhrac then dived into the lake and accompanied him to the underwater monastery. He repeated his visits often to that place. One Easter Thursday he noticed that his own monks had cooked pork for their meal and, angered at this breach of Lenten abstinence, left them and was never seen again. It was not known whether he had gone to the underwater monastery or had been brought to heaven by angels.

A blind man at Clonmacnoise, it was claimed, used to dive into the river and to emerge with an eel in each hand and foot. Also at Clonmacnoise, a grave was discovered with the body of a huge bearded man 15 feet long. It was said that in the year AD 748 ships were seen over the monastery in that place. This may have been no more than an unusual cloud formation, but the story was lavishly developed. We read that when the monks were chanting the psalms in the monastery one Sunday, they saw a ship in the air over them. The crew of the ship threw down an anchor, which got stuck in the church floor, and a man came swimming through the air from the ship to release it. He begged the monks to assist him, as he was being drowned, and they did so. The anchor was drawn up again, and the ship sailed away in the air. A variant telling has it that three ships appeared over Tailtiu (Teltown, County Meath) in 763, when the Uí NÉILL high-king Domhnall mac Murchadha was at an assembly there; and again this incident was set more elaborately in the reign of the tenth-century high-king Conghalach. We read that this king was holding an assembly at Tailtiu, when a man came from a strange sky-ship to redeem a dart that had been shot from the ship at a salmon in the air. This type of marvel must relate to the notion in medieval Europe that there were different levels of life, and that one of these was in the air between the earth and the skies.

A stranger marvel still was related of Ros Deala (Rossadalla, near Kilbeggan, County Westmeath), where it was reported that at the feast of St George in the year 1054, a fiery round tower was seen in the air for nine hours. A multitude of black BIRDS were in it, under the wing of a huge bird, and they flew to the earth and took many hounds with them in their claws, before dropping the dead bodies of the hounds. The huge bird tore an oak tree from its roots, and they finally flew back into the tower, after which the vision disappeared.

There seems to have been some local pride and prestige involved in the recounting of marvels. There was, for example, a mill at Cill Chéise (Kilkeasy, County Kilkenny) that would not grind any stolen grain; and at Loch na hOnchon (Loughnahanagan, County Wicklow), a shower of rain would fall when a particular rock there was struck with a stick. At the edge of the plain of Corann, County Sligo, there was a clear-water well that would fill and ebb according to the sea tide far away. A great wonder was told of a large stone cross that stood on the plain of Slane, County Meath – this was taken into the air and broken into pieces, which descended over a wide area of that plain. Of greater social use was a cross at the medieval Church of the Trinity in Dublin in the Middle Ages from which, it was said, a voice would be heard to support the truth in court cases.

The twelfth-century NORMAN writer, Giraldus Cambrensis, took a great interest in such marvels. He regarded Ireland as an extremely quaint place and was quick to collect and relay the strangest stories about its topography, climate and inhabitants. Some of the stories he heard from native Irish tradition, but others were fictional and uncomplimentary to the Irish. He claimed, for instance, that some of the inhabitants were half-human half-animal, which was probably a misinterpretation by him of LEGENDS such as that of SUIBHNE the lunatic. From Giraldus and from other unknown writers, Ireland got the reputation abroad of having many wonders. Several such details are found in a Norse work, *Kongs Skuggsjo*, written around the year 1250. It was claimed in that work that a wild man had been discovered in a forest in Ireland; this creature could not speak, and was very hairy, with a long mane hanging down his back to the ground.

Giraldus also refers to an island in a lake (probably Lough Ree on the Shannon) that no female, human or animal could enter without dying, and an island off the west coast (probably Inishglory, County Mayo) where exposed human corpses do not putrefy. With other writers, he mentions wells in different parts of Ireland with strange effects on humans, such as the hair of bathers turning grey or regaining its natural colour. Various medieval sources mention a well on Slieve Bloom, at the source of the River Barrow, which, if one looks on it, causes a deluge of rain to fall.

The rain can be stopped by sprinkling the well with holy water or milk of a cow of one colour. With a more historical perspective, Giraldus relates as a fact that two years before the Anglo-Norman invasion of 1169, and as a portent of what was to come, a massive FISH had been found in the bay of Carlingford (in County Louth). He claimed that this fish – probably a beached whale – had three golden teeth in its mouth that weighed about 50 ounces. *See also* FÉICHÍN *and* PLACE-LORE.

GENERAL: K. Meyer in *AIM*, 1, 76–9 & 3, 7–9 & in *Ériu*, 4, 1–16; W.M. Hennessy & McCarthy (1887–91), 1, 212–13; O'Donovan, 1 (1848–51), 346–7; O'Grady, 1 (1892), 87–9; Todd (1848), 192–219; A.G. Little (1908), xv–xvii; O'Meara (1982).

MARVELS SEEN BY CAILLEACH BHÉARRA: de híde (1933), 145–9; G. Ó Crualaoich in *Béaloideas*, 56, 166–9; P. Lysaght in Lysaght, Ó Catháin & Ó hÓgáin (1999), 136; S. Ó Súilleabháin & Christiansen (1967), 343.

Meadhbh Mythical queen of Connacht and a leading character in the ULSTER CYCLE. The name (earlier, Medb) originally meant 'one who intoxicates', and was used to denote the GODDESS of sovereignty. Early Irish sources symbolised the gaining of KINGSHIP as drinking ale proffered by an otherworld lady. Her cult, as a symbol of sovereignty, was very old; and her name in its original form, Meduva, was known also among the Continental Celts of antiquity. One medieval Irish text seems to echo this, describing Meadhbh as racing against HORSES. The combination of her representing ritual ale and horses must reflect some kingship symbolism, for the meaning 'horse-mead' is found in a Gaulish royal title, *Epomeduos*, as well as in the title of the Hindu inauguration ritual, *asvamedha*.

A character called Meadhbh Leathdhearg was associated with TARA, and a fortress there was called Ráth Mheadhbha after her. Her epithet means 'half-red' and probably referred to the bloody contests for the Tara kingship. She is represented as having had several husbands, a typical role for a personification of sovereignty, and one medieval text gives an apposite description of her role: 'Great indeed was the strength and power of that Meadhbh over the men of Ireland, for it was she who would not allow a king in Tara unless he had her as wife.' The text further describes her as 'a shrewd and wise woman, being fierce and merciless'. That description would be appropriate also to her namesake, Meadhbh of Cruachain (i.e. Rathcroghan, County Roscommon). This queen of the province of Connacht was also said to have had several husbands, and the literature invariably portrays her as a great manipulator of men and an adept at power and intrigue. Moreover, she is said to have been reared at Tara, and there is little doubt but that Meadhbh of Tara and Meadhbh of Cruachain were one and the same personage.

Symbolising the Tara kingship, the power struggle between the CONNACHTA sept that ruled there, and the ULAIDH of the north brought her cult into contact with that of the mythical Ulster king FEARGHUS MAC RÓICH. This power struggle of the fourth and fifth century is reflected in *Táin Bó Cuailnge*, a prose epic describing a cattle-raid and inter-provincial war that was first assembled around the year AD 600, when the name of the Connachta sept had become synonymous with the western province (*see* ULSTER CYCLE). Thus tradition came to situate Meadhbh's power centre at Cruachain. Regarding her husbands, one recension of the *Táin* has her boasting: 'I never was without one man in the shadow of another,' and she attempts to gain the great bull of Cooley (*see* DONN CUAILNGE) by offering its owner 'the friendship of my thighs'. One early account states that Fearghus deserted his native province out of lust for her.

It is clear that the dramatic potential of portraying her as a sex object was recognised from an early date, and that she quickly developed from a symbol of sovereignty into an attractive and cunning woman. We are told that her husbands – in consecutive order – were CONCHOBHAR MAC NEASA, Tinne mac Connrach, Eochaidh Dála and Ailill mac Máta. She left Conchobhar after a short time of marriage 'due to pride of mind', and returned to Tara. Later, we are told, Conchobhar

visited Tara and violated her while she bathed in the River Boyne. Then one Fiodhach mac Féig came to woo her, but he was intercepted and slain by Tinne mac Connrach, king of Connacht. Meadhbh's father, the high-king EOCHAIDH FEIDHLEACH, banished Tinne to the wilderness and installed Meadhbh as queen of Connacht in Cruachain. Eventually, she took Tinne as husband, but he was killed by Conchobhar in a battle at the River Boyne. Meadhbh was rescued from that battle and taken back to Connacht by Eochaidh Dála, whom she then allowed to be king of the province on condition that he marry her.

We read that Ailill mac Máta was a mere child when he was first brought to Meadhbh's court. His name would appear to have been attracted to the context of Meadhbh due to the famous cattle-raid in the *Táin*, for AILILL was the name of a great mythical patron of herds. The more general tradition claims him to have been of the ÉRAINN people, and his father's name is given as Máta mac Sraibhghinn. However, in one tract he is described as son of the LAIGHIN worthy, Ros Ruadh, and of a lady of the western province called Máta Muirisc. We read that because he displayed neither envy nor fear, and hoping to form a bond between Leinster and Connacht against the Ulstermen, the Connachtmen sought him as king. He grew up to be a fine champion, and Meadhbh deserted Eochaidh Dála for him. He is therefore the husband who figures in the *Táin* epic, and his forces are claimed therein to have been expert fighters of the Gaileoin, a branch of the Laighin. It is apparent that the compilers of the lore in or about the eighth century had noticed the name of one Ailill listed in Leinster genealogies as son of the mythical Ros Ruadh (*see* AODH RUADH RÓ-FHEASA), and – perhaps aware of some Laighin help once given to the Connachta against the Ulaidh – identified this Leinster Ailill with Meadhbh's husband.

In the surviving recensions of the *Táin* epic, the whole series of events is portrayed as caused by the pride and scheming of

Meadhbh, and this is the result of the increased dramatisation of her personality. She seeks the bull of Cooley in order to have her wealth equal that of her husband, she schemes to enlist the support of Fearghus and other powerful allies in her attack on Ulster, and she unremittingly plots to destroy the young CÚ CHULAINN who stands in the way of her ambitions. Moreover, she insists on herself being the leader of her assembled armies and belittles Ailill, whom she sees as having less determination than herself. One account shows him as a frustrated husband as he views her relationship with Fearghus. One day, we are told, he noticed the shaking of a hazel branch near the royal court, and on going to investigate found Fearghus and Meadhbh engaged in sexual intercourse. He took the sword from Fearghus' scabbard and put a timber one in its place, vowing not to return the weapon until the final great battle of the cattle-raid. When this latter conflict was over, Ailill took his revenge on Fearghus by having him slain by a javelin-cast when Fearghus was cavorting in a lake with Meadhbh.

The jealous way in which Meadhbh guarded her power is demonstrated by a reaction ascribed to her in the *Táin*. When she reviewed her troops and noticed the impressive troops of the Gaileoin sept, she feared that their prestige would so grow on the campaign as to outshine her own Connacht contingent and perhaps threaten her power. She therefore decided to have them slaughtered and was only dissuaded by the indignant objections of Fearghus. She then decided to have the Gaileoin warriors divided and dispersed among her forces.

Meadhbh's confrontations with Cú Chulainn, of course, were in the nature of high drama. In the initial stages of the cattle-raid, she affected to be dismissive of his ability, but was soon brought to view him more seriously. She slyly invited him to come unarmed to parley with her, and when, on his charioteer's advice, he did not fall for the trick, she prevailed upon his friend FEAR DIADH to oppose him in single combat. This she did by making Fear Diadh drunk with ale, promising him her daughter Fionnabhair as wife, and taunting him with cowardice. Cú Chulainn, who frustrated all her schemes, increased her hatred for him by humiliating her whenever they came face to face. At one stage during the campaign, he shot a pet BIRD from her shoulder, and later came upon her when she was alone and menstruating. She begged him to spare her, and he did so, 'not being a killer of women'. Eventually, Meadhbh had her revenge. She had the children of Cailitín trained in magic and sent them to kill Cú Chulainn, which by an ingenious manipulation of circumstances they succeeded in doing.

The portrayal of Meadhbh in the *Táin* whetted the appetite of medieval audiences, and accordingly more narratives were composed. We are told that she would only take a husband on three conditions – that he be without stinginess, without fear, and without jealousy. There is obviously some echo here also of her original function as goddess of sovereignty, but this echo again was dramatised. On account of her lax moral standards, her husbands could not allow themselves the luxury of jealousy, and so, until his patience finally snaps, Ailill is portrayed as extraordinarily tolerant of her affair with Fearghus. The condition of tolerance, however, did not apply to herself. When CONALL CEARNACH was exhausted from his horrific campaigns against her men, that great Ulster warrior made peace with her and went to recuperate to her court at Cruachain. He spent a year there, and meanwhile Meadhbh had noticed that her husband Ailill was keeping company with one of her ladies-in-waiting. She was overcome by jealousy, and prevailed upon Conall to slay Ailill, which he did by a quiet javelin-cast. Meadhbh, however, treacherously announced to the Connachtmen that Conall was the culprit and so encompassed his death also.

Her own death is described in an eleventh-century text. There we read that she killed her sister Clothra, who had preceded her as queen at Cruachain. Clothra had resided on an island in Lough Ree (on the River Shannon), but had been slain by Meadhbh there. A baby boy was delivered by putting swords through her side after her death, and he was called Furbaidhe (literally, 'the cut one'). Meadhbh herself went to live on that island and used to bathe every morning at a spring there. Once, when a great assembly was being held on the shores of the lake, the youth Furbaidhe saw a beautiful woman on the island going to bathe. He enquired who she was, and was told that she was his mother's sister. He had been eating cheese, and on hearing this put a hard lump of cheese in his sling and shot it with such accuracy and force that it struck her on the forehead and killed her. This, like many of the accounts of Meadhbh in the medieval literature, was a rather spontaneous composition with no tradition behind it. Furbaidhe in other accounts, indeed, was son of another sister of Meadhbh, called Eithne. In all cases, his father is claimed to have been Conchobhar mac Neasa, but the more usual format had him being cut from his mother Eithne after she drowned in a stream. The writers were obviously dealing with a jumble of names and were arranging them in narrative order by use of whatever MOTIFS suggested themselves. Meadhbh's husband, Ailill, for instance, was rather awkwardly claimed to have been a grandson of another of her sisters, Éile.

Meadhbh appears in a background role in several stories of the Ulster Cycle, such as the Feast of BRICRIU, the Intoxication of the Ulstermen (see CÚ CHULAINN), and the Adventure of NEARA. Though symbolising basic traits of the ancient goddess of sovereignty and of the war-goddess, her character as a power-hungry virago was very much the creation of the medieval literati. Apart from some onomastic recollections, she does not figure at all in the later folklore.

NAME AND SOVEREIGNTY: T. Ó Máille in ZCP, 17, 129–46; T.F. O'Rahilly in Ériu, 14, 14–21; E. Hogan (1910), 574; Gwynn (1924), 366; J. Puhvel in Puhvel (1970), 164–9; P. Henry (1978), 17–25; Dumézil (1973), 70–83.

SEXUALITY: C. O'Rahilly (1976), 32–3 & (1970), 3; K. Meyer in ZCP, 8, 305 & in AIM, 5, 17–22; T. Ó Máille in ZCP, 17, 130–9; J. O'Neill in Ériu, 2, 176–85; D. MacKinnon in Celtic Review, 1, 226–9.

AILILL MAC MÁTA: Meyer in AIM, 5, 18–21; O'Neill in Ériu, 2, 182–5; O'Brien (1962), 22–3.

MEADHBH'S PART IN TÁIN: C. O'Rahilly (1976) & (1970), passim.

GAILEOIN CONTINGENT: C. O'Rahilly (1976), 5–6.

ENCOUNTERS WITH CÚ CHULAINN: C. O'Rahilly (1976), 29, 31, 72, 123 & (1970), 35, 133–4.

SLAYING OF AILILL: K. Meyer in ZCP, 1, 102–11.

HER DEATH: V. Hull in Speculum, 13, 52–61; D. Wong in Études Celtiques, 32, 233–41.

GENERAL: Ó hÓgáin (1999), 133–4, 178–9.

mermaids/merman A mermaid is called appropriately in Irish either *maighdean mhara* (maiden of the sea) or *murúch* (earlier form, *murdhúchu*, meaning 'sea-singer' or 'siren'). The male counterpart – much more rarely mentioned – is called *murúch fir* or simply *fear mara* (man of the sea). References to such fictional beings in Irish literature are borrowed from Latin and other sources, and folklore of them seems also to be borrowed from abroad. When naturalised in Irish tradition, mermaids and mermen function as FAIRIES of sea, lake and river.

A mermaid called Lí Ban (literally, 'beauty of women') is featured in a fantastic story composed in the twelfth or thirteenth century. She is described as daughter of EOCHAIDH MAC MAIREADHA, who with most of his family was drowned when Lough Neagh burst forth in Ulster. She survived the inundation, being confined in her bower, which – though the lake rose all around it – the water did not enter. She expressed the wish to be turned into a salmon, and this happened accordingly. Her lapdog became an otter, and for a full 300 years, she roamed the seas. It so happened that a monk of the monastery of Beannchar (Bangor, County Down), called Beoán, was sailing by, and heard Lí Ban singing in the water and met her. She told him of her life, and promised to meet him a year hence at Inbhear Ollarbha (Larne, County Antrim). When that time came, she was caught in the fishing net of a monk called Fearghus, and many people came to marvel at her. A dispute arose between Fearghus and Beoán over which of them should have charge of her, and the monks fasted so as to gain inspiration from God concerning the matter. An angel told one of them that two stags would come from the grave of her sister Airiu, and that the stags should be yoked to her chariot and would bring her to the correct place. This was done, and Lí Ban was brought to a church, where the clerics gave her the choice of dying immediately and gaining heaven, or of tarrying for a further 300 years. She chose the former, and was baptised by St COMHGHALL of Bangor and christened Muirghein (sea-birth) or Muirgheilt (sea-prodigy).

This fanciful story makes use of the common MOTIF in medieval Irish literature of a personage marvellously living on from the remote pagan past so as to encounter the Christian missionaries. In this case, it was probably borrowed from the lore of PATRICK, for the additional motif of the stags settling a dispute derives from a LEGEND of the death of that SAINT.

The otherworld was long considered to be underwater in Irish tradition (see DONN, DRUIDS *and* MYTHOLOGICAL CYCLE), and this could give rise to lore of mermaid or merman type. A romance illustrating this was written in or about the fourteenth century. It tells of a young prince called Laoghaire, son of a fictional king of Connacht called Criomhthann Cas. We read that Criomhthan held an assembly by the shore of Éanloch (Lough Nen, County Roscommon; near Athlone). A finely dressed stranger approached through the mist, saying that his name was Fiachna and that he was of the *sídh* (otherworld beings). His wife had been taken from him by a *sídh* lord called Eochaidh, whom he had subsequently slain, but the woman had been taken by Eochaidh's nephew Goll, who lived in a fortress at Magh Meall (the Pleasant Plain). Fiachna had thus come to recruit warriors to assist him in battle against this Goll. Laoghaire agreed to go with him and was accompanied by 50 other young men. They dived into the lake after Fiachna and soon arrived in the otherworld. With their help, Fiachna defeated his foes and regained his wife. Fiachna's daughter married Laoghaire, and 50 other maidens of the otherworld

became the wives of his companions. At the end of a year, Laoghaire expressed the desire to visit his homeland, and Fiachna warned him to bring horses for his company to ride, and not to dismount. On their return, they met the assembled Connachtmen. King Criomhthann begged his son to stay, but to no avail, and Laoghaire returned to the otherworld and was not seen again.

This account is indebted to the theme of a one-eyed foe called Goll (see GOLL MAC MORNA), while the warning against touching natural land when returning from the otherworld was an international motif found in other Irish stories (see WONDER TALES, type 470).

Several plots of migratory LEGENDS entered Ireland during the Middle Ages, and some of these were in the context of imagined water-dwellers. It is apparent that, in one case, an Irish motif (see MACHA) came to be rationalised by mermaid imagery. According to this story – common along the western seaboard of Ireland – a man once saw a beautiful maiden on a rock by the shore. She had laid aside her cloak, and when he seized this she was in his power. She therefore went home with him and married him. They had several children, and all the time the husband kept the cloak hidden from her. Then one day, she discovered the cloak and returned to the sea. Certain families (such as the O'Sheas in Kerry, the Conneelys in Galway, the O'Dowds in Mayo, the O'Haras in Sligo and the Gallaghers in Donegal) are said to be descendants of this mermaid, and as proof of their origin these families are teasingly said to have webbed feet! This legend – some versions of which describe the lady as a seal maiden rather than a mermaid – spread to Scotland and to Iceland, probably in the late Middle Ages.

A very distinctive folk legend relates to a young nobleman surnamed Moore from Moorestown in the Dingle Peninsula of County Kerry who, it is said, could never sleep. He is always referred to as *Bodach Pharóiste Mhúraigh* (the Churl of Moore's Parish), and no first name is given for him.

According to the legend, he entertained a travelling scholar in his mansion, and as they sat up late at night discussing affairs, he confided his secret to the scholar. The latter said that he had once read that the offspring of spirits could not sleep and, on hearing this, Moore went to his mother and demanded to know how he had been conceived. She admitted that her husband had not been his father, but that she had gone swimming in the sea one day and that she had fainted in the water. She said that as a result of this, she had become pregnant, and Moore then realised that his real father had been a sea-spirit. Next day, he mounted his horse and rode into the sea, and was never seen again.

A variant of this story is found in the folklore of coastal areas of Connacht and west Ulster concerning LUGHAIDH MAC CON, the opponent of CORMAC MAC AIRT, and some commentators regard it as a survival in oral tradition of some early Irish myth. It is, however, more likely that it was a family legend which the Moores, an Anglo-NORMAN family, brought with them to Ireland after the Norman invasion. Another version of it is told in a thirteenth-century French lay of a character called Tydorel. This also contains the insomnia motif, which was probably added in medieval France to the basic plot of the legend – i.e. that a sea-being can be the father of a mortal man. This basic plot was attached to Merovech, the founder of the pre-medieval Merovingian dynasty, and from that source was adopted into Irish literature and appears in the birth-stories of Mongán and Breas. All of these have associations with the sea, and a fanciful etymology would equally allow the Moore family (de Múr) to claim affinity to the sea (mer in French and muir in Irish). That family has been settled in Kerry since the fourteenth century, and the legend could easily have been borrowed in the interval by sailors of the west coast and put in the new context of Lughaidh mac Con.

The lore of south-west Kerry presents in very colourful form another migratory legend concerning the people of the sea. This concerns a character called Cluasach

Ó Fáilbhe, claimed to have been a native of the Ballinskelligs area. He is said to have been a great sailor, and to have travelled with a sea captain called the Ceannaí Fionn (Fair-haired Merchant). Together they set out to discover where the end of the sea is. Having encountered many wonders on the voyage, they reached a great wall of brass, and considered that their quest was over. They examined the wall, but when they tried to draw anchor again, found that it was stuck at the bottom of the sea. Cluasach dived down to release it, but found himself in a fine city where a beautiful maiden invited him to stay with her. He agreed, but said that he first wished to return home to put his affairs in order. He therefore set sail again, but was followed by a great wave in which the beautiful lady swam. He threw a knife at the wave, knocking an eye from her head. However, a strange horseman came riding on the sea, stating that he was the lady's brother and warning the sailor to keep to his bargain. After a short visit home, Cluasach went to the seashore, was engulfed by a wave, and was seen no more. Before he departed, he said that he would send a burned sod to a local strand – Tráigh Phraisce – each May morning to show that he was alive, and such a sod was accordingly found there for a long time afterwards.

This is a local variant of a story found in other parts of Ireland also, a story which combines two different migratory legends. One of these legends concerned an attempt by a mermaid to entice a fisherman into her world; and the other described how an otherworld being was injured by a man, who was later brought into the otherworld to recover the offending instrument. Both of these LEGEND plots are found abroad also, but in Ireland are usually told in combination as above. At some stage in recent centuries, a mariner of some repute, known as the Ceannaí Fionn, was made the main character in the story as told in Munster and Connacht. The south-west-Kerry variant is a further elaboration of this, and duplicates the character by introducing Cluasach. His surname, Ó Failbhe (anglicised Falvey), was a common one in that area, and he may in reality have been a noted local teller of the story who was converted by tradition into an actor within the narrative. Some influence from learned tradition is evident, for there are echoes of the type of sea literature that concerned characters such as BRAN MAC FEABHAIL, MANANNÁN and MAOL DÚIN.

For sea-beings, *see also* CATTLE, HORSES and BRÉANAINN, and for an underwater monastery, *see* MARVELS.

SOURCES FOR WORDS: RIA Dictionary, s.v. '*muir*', '*murdúchu*'; C. Bowen in *Ériu*, *29*, 142–8.

LÍ BAN: O'Grady, *1* (1892), 234–7 & *2*, 484–5; Best & Bergin (1929), 96–100.

LAOGHAIRE MAC CRIOMHTHAINN: O'Grady, *1* (1892), 256–7.

MERMAID WIFE: Ó Duileanga (1948), 314–16, 438–9; D. Thomson (1965); Ua Ruaidhrí (1906); Ó Catháin (1985), 28–30, 80–1; Almqvist in *Béaloideas*, *58*, 1–9.

MOORE: Jackson, *SB* (1938), 77–9, 92–3; O'Sullivan (1966), 21–37; A.H. Krappe in *Modern Language Review*, *24*, 200–4; B. Hillers in *Béaloideas*, *59*, 91–105, 225–36; S. Ó Súilleabháin & Christiansen (1967), 345.

Ó FÁILBHE: Ua Murchadha (1939), 7–10; Ó Duileanga (1948), 259–63, 429–30; B. Almqvist in *Béaloideas*, *59*, 269; IFC Index.

OTHER LEGEND PLOTS: S. Thompson (1955–58), motif B81; Taylor (1927).

Midhe The fifth province of early and medieval Ireland. The term meant 'middle', and it was particularly the kingdom controlled by the royal UÍ NÉILL sept. It comprised modern Counties Meath and Westmeath, as well as parts of Counties Louth, Dublin, Longford and Offaly. The eastern half of that vast territory was usually referred to as Breagha.

Disregarding the true origin of the place name, an eleventh-century writer invented a story as a pseudo-explanation of it. According to this, a young man called Midhe mac Bratha lit a fire at Uisneach (Ushnagh, County Westmeath) to announce the lordship of that area over all Ireland. The fire remained lighting for six years and Midhe insisted that every other fire in the land should be kindled from it. Resenting this, the DRUIDS from different parts of the country began to utter complaints, but Midhe brought them all together into one house, cut out their tongues, and buried the tongues in a mound at Uisneach. He then sat upon

the mound and declared himself chief-POET of Ireland.

This imaginative story is attributed to one Aodh Ua Cárthaigh, a partisan of the Uí Néill dynasty, and its political import is clear. The notion of the master-fire seems to have been suggested by the way in which saint PATRICK reputedly lit a fire in defiance of king LAOGHAIRE; while the location at Uisneach is derived from the tradition that this place was the geographical centre of Ireland. The cutting out of tongues of mischievous poets was an old MOTIF.

Gwynn (1906), 42–5, 100; W. Stokes in *RC*, *15*, 297; T.F. O'Rahilly (1946), 166–71; F.J. Byrne (1973), 58, 87; Ó hÓgáin (1982), 40–1.

Midhir Mythical chieftain of the TUATHA DÉ DANANN. The name apparently had an original meaning such as 'measurer' or 'arbitrator', such as in the Celtic designation of a deity, *Medros*. In modern form, it would be Mír.

Midhir is represented as lord of the otherworld dwelling of Brí Leith (now called Slieve Golry, near Ardagh, County Longford). He was the foster-father of AONGHUS, whom he counselled on how to gain possession of Brugh na Bóinne (the Newgrange tumulus), and was lover and husband of ÉADAOIN. Some sources make him a brother of the DAGHDHA and others claim that he was the father of MACHA. One source makes him the father of Bláthnaid who was stolen, along with magical cows and a cauldron, by the celebrated warrior CÚ ROÍ. It was further claimed that three herons belonging to him were stolen from Brí Leith by the satirist AITHIRNE.

As a figure, Midhir would appear to have been an emanation from the Daghdha as male patron of KINGSHIP. The place name Brí Léith originally signified simply the hillock that had *liath* (grey or withered grass) growing on it, but this place name had a similarity with Liathdruim (the *Liath*-ridge), a poetic name for the sacred centre of kingship, TARA. The same word *Liath* could mean a grey-haired man, a suitable image for the father-deity, and one source does in fact explain Liathdruim as deriving from a personage called Liath mac Laighne, who constructed the ridge (*druim*) there. Liath may thus have been another name, or a descriptive, of Midhir; and his removal westwards to Brí Léith may have resulted from antiquarian speculation in the pre-literary period.

O'Brien in *Celtica*, *3*, 173–4; E. Hogan (1910), 488; MacCulloch (1911), 83–4; T.F. O'Rahilly (1946), 74, 290, 293; Macalister (1956), 52, 82; de Vries (1961), 109–10; Ó hÓgáin (1999), 131–5 & in B. Raftery (1996), 359–66.

Míl Fictional ancestor of the Irish people. His full name is given as Míl Easpaine, and is an invention of the historians, patterned on the Latin term *miles Hispaniae* (soldier of Spain). The idea of such a Spanish ancestor developed from the fanciful derivation of the Latin word for Ireland, Hibernia, from Iberia or Hiberia.

The account of Míl and his imagined relatives is given in the *Lebor Gabála* (Book of Invasions), a text composed and developed in early medieval Ireland and which purported to tell the ancient history of the country. This text was based on biblical chronology, and used many details from the early-seventh-century writings of Isidorus of Seville. Some elements from classical literature and from native Irish myth were also utilised. In it, the ultimate origin of the Irish people is put down to Scythia. The people of that area, we are told, were descendants of Noah's son Japheth; and the first important person among them was Fenius the Ancient, who was one of those leaders of different nationalities who went to build the Tower of Babel. Fenius was a great linguist, and when the languages were separated at Babel, he alone retained knowledge of them all. His grandson was Gaedheal Glas who, we are told, fashioned the Irish language (*Gaedhilg*) out of the whole 72 tongues then in existence. Gaedheal and his people lived in Egypt, where they were friendly with the captive Israelites. One recension of the text, in fact, states that Moses saved the life of the infant Gaedheal who had been stung by a serpent. From the green (*glas*) mark left by the bite, we are told, Gaedheal got his epithet. Moses cured him by touching the affected part with his rod, and then pronounced that the descendants of Gaedheal would forever be safe from serpents and would dwell in a land where no such creatures existed.

We read that in the time of Sru, grandson of Gaedheal, these people were persecuted in Egypt, and they left in four ships and returned to Scythia. They clashed with their old relatives, the inhabitants of that place, and, after several generations of turbulence there, were driven out and became seafarers. They suffered much hardship in the Caspian Sea for seven years, but eventually their DRUID Caicher found a remedy for the music of the MERMAIDS (*murdhúchu*) that was bringing lethargy on them. The remedy was to melt wax in their ears and, by virtue of this, they sailed far west into the Mediterranean and took Spain by force. Their king at that time, Breoghan, built a great tower at Brigantia (i.e. Braganza) to protect their territory; and on one clear winter evening, Íth, son of Breoghan, saw Ireland from that tower.

Míl is now introduced into the narrative. He is said to have been a son of Breoghan's son Bile, and his proper name was Golamh. When he grew up, he became curious concerning his relatives in Scythia, and went there. He was welcomed by the Scythian king, who gave him his daughter Seang as wife and made him an army commander. Míl was so successful that the king grew jealous and plotted to kill him; but Míl acted first, slaying the king and sailing away from that country with his followers in 60 ships. He arrived in Egypt, where he got land from the Pharaoh and was again made an army commander. His first wife having died in Scythia, he remarried – this time the bride was Scota, daughter of the Pharaoh. Remembering that the druid Caicher had prophesied that his people would settle in Ireland, he left Egypt after some time and set sail westwards. He was, however, interrupted on his journey by tidings that enemies were threatening Spain, and so returned to that country, where he gained victory in several battles. He had by this time no less than 32 sons. Twenty-four of these were born of his affairs in Spain before he left for Scythia, two more – DONN and Aireach – were children of Seang, and the other six – Éibhear, Amhairghin Glúngheal, Ír, Colptha, Érannan and Éireamhóin – were the offspring of Scota. These eight named sons were given importance as leaders of their people into Ireland.

All of this marvellous jumble is the result of liberal, and at times contradictory, speculation on the nomenclature applied to Ireland and the Irish people. Along with the Spanish connection of Míl (Hiberia versus Hibernia), we have pseudo-learned attempts to explain several other words. 'Féni', upon which was invented the character Fenius, was a designation used for themselves by the dominant CONNACHTA and EOGHANACHT septs in the early medieval period (see FÉINE). *Gaedheal* simply signified an Irish person, the word (earlier, *Goídel*) being in origin a borrowing from the Welsh term for an Irishman (see GAEL). Scota was the Latin word for an Irishwoman; it was, in fact, on the basis of a fabricated connection between Scoti (Irish people) and Scythia that the latter region was associated with the ancestors of the Irish. Éibhear was forged out of Eberus, a Hiberno-Latin form of Hibernus (an Irishman); while Ír is a variant of Éire (Ireland), as also is the first element in 'Éireamhóin' and 'Érannan'.

Míl himself never reached Ireland, according to the account. He died in Spain of an unspecified cause, and it was left to his sons to come and take the country. But in the meantime, his uncle Íth, who had seen Ireland across the sea, decided to go and investigate with thrice-50 warriors. They disembarked and went to Aileach (near Derry), where the triumvirate of TUATHA DÉ DANANN kings had convened to divide the treasures of Ireland between them. Íth counselled them on how the division should be made, but they were suspicious of his intentions and had him slain as he returned to his ship. His followers brought the body back to Spain, and his nine brothers joined with the eight sons of Míl on an expedition to take

Ireland from the Tuatha Dé. As they approached the country from the southwest, one of Míl's sons, Érannan, went up on the mast of his ship to reconnoitre and fell and was drowned. Another son, Ír, rowed ahead of his fellows and his oar broke. He fell backwards into the sea and was drowned also. Finally, they landed at Inbhear Scéine (Kenmare Bay, County Kerry) and Amhairghin was the first of them to set his foot on the soil of Ireland.

They defeated a Tuatha Dé force at Sliabh Mis (a mountain south of Tralee), and there met the lady BANBA, who asked that her name be henceforth on the country. This was granted, and they made similar promises to the lady FÓDLA at Eibhlinne (Slieve Felim, County Limerick) and to the lady ÉIRE at Uisneach (Ushnagh, County Westmeath). Thus these three GODDESSES were made by the pseudo-historians to sanction the takeover by the sons of Míl. At TARA, the invaders met with the three Tuatha Dé kings. These were Mac Cuill, Mac Céacht and Mac Gréine, and one recension of the text states that they were the husbands of the three goddesses. In order to trick the sons of Míl, these three kings sought a truce, asking that they be allowed to hold the country for a mere three days more and that the sons of Míl retire nine waves from the shore for that period. Amhairghin, who played the role of negotiator for his brothers, agreed to this. When the conditions were fulfilled, however, the druids of the Tuatha Dé sang spells against them, causing a storm that swept them far out to sea. Amhairghin then spoke a verse that calmed the waters. In a fit of anger, Donn threatened to put all who were in Ireland to the sword, but the wind rose against his ship and drowned him and his brother Aireach off the south-west coast. This meant that only four sons of Míl were left alive. Éireamhóin, who assumed the leadership, decided to sail with 30 ships righthand-wise around Ireland, and they landed at the Boyne estuary. Colptha was the first to step ashore – hence, it was claimed, the estuary was known as Inbhear Colptha. They routed the Tuatha Dé at the Battle of Tailtiu (Teltown, County Meath), after which all Ireland was in their possession. They divided it into two parts, with Éireamhóin ruling in the north and Éibhear in the south. Colptha is not mentioned again, but contention soon broke out between the other three sons of Míl (for which *see* ÉIREAMHÓIN, ÉIBHEAR *and* AMHAIRGHIN GLÚNGHEAL).

The *Lebor Gabála* account of how the sons of Míl took Ireland was a literary fabrication, but was accepted as conventional history by poets and scholars down until the nineteenth century.

Macalister (1939), 1–165 & (1956): 1–175; Dinneen, *2* (1908), 2–109; Arbois de Jubainville (1903), 123–48; C.-J. Guyonvarc'h in *Ogam*, *19*, 265–6; T.F. O'Rahilly (1946), 195–9; A.G. Van Hamel in *ZCP*, *10*, 167–81; Ó Muraíle, *1* (2003), 258–79.

Mis A young woman who is featured in a literary romance of the post-medieval period. Her name is fancifully derived from the mountain called Sliabh Mis, south-west of Tralee, County Kerry.

According to the medieval PLACE-LORE, she was a sister of EOCHAIDH MAC MAIREADHA and her husband, called Coemgen, gave her possession of that mountain as bride-price. Some later writer – probably of the fifteenth or sixteenth century – considered her good material for a different story, and so composed a romance about her. The text of this is lost, but is referred to in several poems. A late literary retelling from the eighteenth century does survive, and it is apparent that this contains the basic structure of the romance. We read that Mis was the daughter of Dáire Donn, leader of the invasion that was defeated by the FIANNA at Fionntráigh (Ventry, County Kerry). Finding her father's dead body on the battlefield, she began to drink the blood from his wounds and, as a result, became demented. She fled to Sliabh Mis and lived alone there for a very long time, and killed every animal or human being that came that way. The Munster king, FEIDHLIMIDH MAC CRIOMHTHAINN, offered a great reward to anybody who could capture her alive. At length, the king's harpist, Dubh Rois, went to Sliabh Mis and began to play

his music there. She came and recalled that her father had had such an instrument, and on seeing gold and silver with Dubh Rois, recalled also that her father had had such objects. On seeing the harpist's private parts, she remarked that she did not recall her father having these. Dubh Rois then invited her to sexual intercourse, which helped greatly to calm her wildness. He stayed with her for two months, cleaning her and teaching her how to cook, and in this way she regained her reason and grew beautiful again. He then took her with him to his home and married her. Later, when Dubh Rois was attacked and killed by hostile warriors, she lamented him in verse.

This story is a curious one, not least for the anachronism that brings the pseudo-historical Battle of Ventry into the same period as the ninth-century Feidhlimidh. It is best explained by postulating that the author of the romance was not a very learned man, but was acquainted with certain aspects of ancient tradition. These aspects would have included the lady Mis of medieval place-lore, and also the imagery of the GODDESS of sovereignty, an ugly HAG who becomes a beautiful young lady through intercourse with a particular hero.

Gwynn (1913), 240–1; T.F. O'Rahilly in *Celtica*, *1*, 382–4; B. Ó Cuiv in *Celtica*, *2*, 325–33.

Mochaoi *(earlier, Mochoe)* Reputed founder of the monastery of Naondroim (Nendrum, on the island of Inish Mahee, County Down). He probably lived in the latter fifth century AD. His original name is unknown, *Mochaoi* (my gentle one) being a term of endearment of a type commonly applied to Irish SAINTS.

Since the seventh century, it was claimed (probably inaccurately) that the place of bondage of St PATRICK in his youth was at Sliabh Mis (Slemish, County Down), and that his master was one Miliuc. In ninth-century sources, this is developed into a claim that on his mission, Patrick met in that vicinity a youthful swine-herd who was a grandson of Miliuc, and that this swine-herd accepted Christianity from the saint. We read that

348

Patrick presented him with a special crozier, which had fallen from heaven. The swine-herd was Mochaoi, and the crozier came to be known as his *eiteach* (winged thing) because it could miraculously fly through the air (*see* SAINTS). It is probable that Mochaoi was indeed an early convert to Christianity in that area, and that his hermitage grew into the monastery of Nendrum. One account claims that St Colmán of Drom Mór (Dromore, County Down) was his pupil, and that he taught the miraculous power of prayer to Colmán. The general tradition was that Mochaoi died in AD 497 and was succeeded as abbot of his foundation by a certain Caolán, who is sometimes confused with Mochaoi himself.

Although there is no surviving biography of Mochaoi, one striking little story is told of him in medieval texts. We read that he once went into the forest to collect timber to build a church, and while there a beautiful BIRD sang three strains for him. He thought that he was listening for a brief while only, but each strain in fact lasted for 50 years. When he returned to the monastery, he found that nobody there knew him, and an oratory had been erected in memory of him. This is a version of a narrative plot (*see* WONDER TALES, type 471A) which was very common in medieval European lore concerning saints. His feast day is 23 June.

Mulchrone (1939), 25–6; Stokes (1905), 158–9; O'Donovan (1864), 176–7; O'Hanlon (1875), *6*, 769–79; Lawlor (1925), 39–65.

Mochuda SAINT who died *c*.AD 637, abbot of Raithean (Rahan, County Offaly), and founder of the monastery of Lios Mór (Lismore, County Waterford). His real name was Cárthach, and he belonged to the Ciarraighe Luachra sept (in County Kerry).

A biography of him was compiled at Lismore in or about the eleventh century, and from this are derived the various texts concerning him in Latin and Irish. We read that a ball of fire descended from heaven onto his mother's head before his birth, and that he was reared by a bishop who gave him the nickname Mochuda out of fondness for him (i.e. *mo chuidigh*, meaning 'my loved one'). He built his first church near the place where he was born, by the River Maine. It is claimed that while abbot of Rahan, he performed many miracles, healing the sick, raising the dead, and banishing demons. On one occasion, an angel appeared to him and told him that the king of the Ciarraighe Luachra was at the point of death. The angel provided a fiery chariot in which he travelled south in an instant and administered the sacraments to the dying man. We further read that Mochuda was the most handsome man of his time, and that 30 maidens fell madly in love with him. He prayed that their love might be turned into a spiritual one, and accordingly they became nuns.

So great was the monastery of Rahan under his direction that the other abbots of Ireland grew jealous and persuaded the future high-king Bláthmhac to expel him from that place. When Bláthmhac came with his brother DIARMAID MAC AODHA SLÁINE and a strong army, Mochuda sent one of his monks to confront them. This monk was Constantinus, a foreign pilgrim who had settled at Rahan and who was a prodigious worker. Constantinus, by his rugged and threatening mien, twice got respite for Mochuda, but on the third occasion of Bláthmhac's approach, he was absent, and the aggressors gained entrance. Diarmaid relented when he came face to face with Mochuda himself, but Bláthmhac – supported by the rival abbots – drove the saint and his monks out of their dwellings. One of the monks had gout, and his foot touched that of Bláthmhac, transferring the disease to the king. The departing Mochuda, for his part, cursed Bláthmhac and the abbots who had so ill-treated him and his community. As they passed by the cemetery, a dead monk rose from his grave and seized Mochuda's foot, begging to be allowed to go with them, but the saint told him to stay and await the final Resurrection there. Going south, the monks were welcomed by the EOGHANACHT king of Munster, Fáilbhe Flann. When they reached the territory of the DÉISE (in County Waterford), a flooded river dried up for long enough to allow them to pass through, and they settled at Lismore and founded the great monastery there.

This account reflects the actual resentment of the Midland monasteries to the influence of monks from Munster in the seventh and eighth centuries, but the kernel of historical fact is, of course, much elaborated by imagery borrowed from the Bible and by literary creativity. Mochuda's feast day is 14 May.

Kenney (1929), 451–3; Plummer, *1* (1910), 170–99 & *1* (1922), 291–311; Power (1914), xxvi–xxxi, 74–147, 178–95; O'Hanlon, *5* (1875), 240–76; IFC 176:48–9, 245:363–5.

modern legends Fanciful stories, sometimes believed, of events that are claimed to have taken place in recent times in one's own community or a similar one. Because such narratives are usually situated in the environments of cities or big towns, they are often referred to – perhaps inadequately – as 'urban legends'. These stories can be understood to cast a dark light over contemporary life, as the imagery in them tends to be violent, and the attitude pervading them quite cynical, even when comical. They probably derive much of their appeal from the taste fostered by modern horror films and the sordid sense in some expressions of modern art.

Several of these narratives postulate a threatening world, and are therefore cautionary in character. Although found internationally, they may draw attention to supposed dangers of moving outside one's accustomed environment or habits. For instance, one very popular narrative tells of a girl who went on holiday abroad and ate a salad that had been contaminated by a lizard's egg. She grew very sick, and had to be operated on in hospital, where a large lizard was found in her stomach. The emphasis on dietary matters in contemporary culture is evident from this and from some other popular lore, such as the fear that a new restaurant in one's locality serves the disguised meat of DOG or CAT for food. A popular if extremely dubious story concerning going abroad on holiday is often told in modern Ireland. This concerns a

family who brought their grandmother with them on such a holiday. She died unexpectedly, and – to avoid the distressing legal formalities in such a situation – they hid the body in the roof-pack. On their journey home, however, they stopped to eat a meal in a restaurant, and when they returned, the roof-pack had been stolen!

Imagery of violence can sometimes be quite extreme. A motorist stopped at traffic lights, for example, is attacked by a man with a chain. The motorist slams and locks the door of his car and drives off hurriedly. He puts his car into his garage, and next morning notices that part of the chain is attached to the door, with a severed finger caught in one of the links! Another story of motoring concerns a driver who picks up a female hitch-hiker. He notices that her hands are quite hairy and suspects that his passenger is a man. He therefore stops the car and pretends that there is some difficulty – the back window needs to be cleaned from the outside or the engine is faltering and the car needs a shove. He then drives off, leaving the passenger behind, but later finds the passenger's bag that has been left in the car. It is full of hatchets!

Protection of cars and homes is a favourite theme, and fear of robbers and thieves is evident from many modern legends. For instance, a man's car is stolen and then surprisingly returned to him with an envelope inside. He opens the envelope and finds a letter with two tickets for the theatre. The letter explains that the thief had urgent need of the car, but is now returning it with the tickets as a token of his appreciation. The car owner is very pleased, and brings his wife to the theatre, but when they return home find their house burgled. Another legend tells of a man who goes on holidays abroad and requests his neighbour to feed his rather savage hound from over the wall. After some time, the neighbour is surprised that the dog does not come to be fed. Many days pass before the holidaymaker returns, to find a burglar sitting on a chair in his parlour. The unfortunate burglar is terrified to move, because the savage dog is guarding him and ready to pounce on him.

Although the plots of these 'urban legends' are international, travelling by boat and aeroplane as well as being told over tea and coffee breaks or being passed around by photocopy or e-mail, they are not all of recent origin. For instance, a burial legend tells of how scraping noises are heard for a while by visitors to a relative's grave. Eventually, they decide to have the grave opened, and discover the dead corpse with blood on its fingernails from scratching the coffin lid in an attempt to escape. A version of this plot was in the medieval Annals concerning the hero-prince MONGÁN. Another modern legend tells of a woman in a flat who notices that somebody is trying to force the door lock. She gets a knife, quickly opens the door, and stabs with the knife. She hears a scream, and then footsteps racing away. In a state of shock, she knocks on the door of a friendly man who lives in the next flat. He comes to her assistance, but she notices that his arm is bandaged from a recent wound. This gives a modern setting to a centuries-old story concerning a woman who goes in the form of a hare to steal milk from a neighbour's cows (see WILD ANIMALS).

VERSIONS FROM IRELAND: IFC, tape archive.

INTERNATIONAL TYPES: Brunvand (1981), S. Hobbs in Bennet, Smith & Widdowson (1987), 133–48.

Mogh Ruith

Mogh Ruith Mythical DRUID who in the secular literature performs magical services for the Munstermen when they are beleaguered by the high-king CORMAC MAC AIRT.

The genealogies consider him an ancestor of the Rothraighe, an ÉRAINN sept in Munster, and in line with this he is associated with Érainn areas. For instance, a ninth-century text describing his services to the Munstermen states that he resided firstly at Dairbhre (Valentia Island off the Kerry coast), but was awarded land in Magh Féine (near Fermoy, County Cork). Since *roth* was the word for a sphere or circle, the septal name Rothraighe would have meant simply the 'sphere-people' – i.e. the devotees of the sun in the heavens (see DAGHDHA *and* EOCHAIDH). The word *mogh* (from Celtic, *magus*) meant 'servant',

and his full name would therefore have indicated something like 'the sun who serves' – conceivably a respected appellation for the ancestor-deity of the tribe.

When his name came to be taken literally to mean 'servant of wheel', Mogh Ruith was said to have possessed a *roth rámhach* (literally, 'oared wheel'). Such imagery was suggested and vindicated by the survival of prehistoric solar symbols inscribed on stone, and one such stone – at Cnámhchoill (Cleghile, near Tipperary town) – was even said to have been a remnant of the great wheel of Mogh Ruith. It was known as the Roth Fáil (sacred wheel), and we read that 'everyone who saw it was blinded, everyone who heard it was deafened, and everyone who struck it was dead'. It is not, therefore, surprising that other debris from ancient solar beliefs became attached to him. It was claimed, for instance, that he was one-eyed, and a medieval pen portrait has him travelling in a lustrous chariot that made the night seem as bright as day.

The transformation of Mogh Ruith from an ancestor figure into a druid is an intriguing question, but it probably resulted from speculation by scholars schooled in Latin. From the eighth or ninth century, his name was being misinterpreted as the Latin *magus rotarum* (literally, 'magician of the wheels'), with the claim that 'it is by wheels that he used to make his druidic divinations'. This typification of him as a pagan druid allowed for the disparagement of the genealogy of septs by whom he was considered an ancestor. For instance, his devotees, the ÉRAINN sept of Magh Féine, inhabited an area in central Munster, with a predominant EOGHANACHT sept on either side of them. One genealogical entry states that the ancestors of the two Eoghanacht septs, Maine Muinchaoin and Dáire Cearba, were brothers, but that their mother had a vision before their birth to the effect that in her womb there was 'a beetle between them, Mugh Ruith the druid, so that neither of them could help the other'.

The false identification of the Irish *mogh* with the Latin *magus* (magician) had a further result in the extraordinary fiction that Mogh Ruith had learned his magic from the charlatan of Christian tradition, Simon Magus. Mogh Ruith was then further denigrated by the claim that he had entered the service of King Herod and had been the executioner of John the Baptist. This belief led to panic in AD 1096, which was the year of a great pestilence and, moreover, a leap year and a year in which the feast of John fell on a Friday. It was therefore feared that the wrath of God would fall on the country because of Mogh Ruith's action long before, and it was necessary for the bishops to proscribe special prayers and fasting in order to allay popular alarm.

GENEALOGY AND EARLY LORE: O'Brien (1962), 205, 279–80, 285–6, 385; Meyer (1912); 49; Gwynn (1924), 188; T.F. O'Rahilly (1946), 519–22; M-L. Sjoestedt-Jonval in *RC*, *43*, 62; W. Stokes in *Irische Texte*, *3*, 408.

JOHN THE BAPTIST: A.M. Scarre in *Ériu*, *4*, 173–81; K. Müller-Lisowski in *ZCP*, *14*, 145–63; Kenney (1929), 749–53; McNamara (1975), 64–7.

Moling SAINT who died *c*.AD 697, founder of the monastery called Teach Moling (St Mullins, County Carlow).

Anecdotes concerning him were in circulation soon after his death, and some of these are recorded in an early-ninth-century text. His name at first, we are told, was Dairchill. 'Moling' signified 'the holy leaper', and these anecdotes claim that an old woman gave him the name when she saw him jump over a river in Luachair (an area in south-east Kerry). An account is given of how the devil once came to him disguised as Christ, and sought his assistance. Moling advised him to genuflect, but the evil one protested that he could not do so because his knees were backwards.

The biographies of the saint, in Latin and Irish, are of late medieval date, and in them we read that a farmer of Luachair made the sister of his wife pregnant, and that she – called Eamhnait – fled for fear of her sister's vengeance. Helpless and caught in a snowdrift, she gave birth to her baby. She intended to kill the baby, but a dove came down from heaven and protected it. Some monks of the community of St Bréanainn noticed angels at

the place, and came and took mother and child to their monastery. When the child came of age, he began to go about seeking alms for all the monks. Once, he was confronted on his travels by evil spectres, who spoke in verse to him, but he replied in rhyme to all that they said. He then sprang away from them, and in three leaps had gone completely from their presence.

Soon after, he went to visit St MAODHÓG and spent some time with him. He decided to found his own monastery at Ros Broic, and was assisted in his work by the celebrated tradesman, GOBÁN SAOR. The great yew tree of Ros Broic had fallen, and Moling sought and obtained this as material for the building, which became known as his 'house' (Teach Moling). He performed several miracles and gained a great reputation among the Leinster people, in whose territory he had settled. So high was his standing that the LAIGHIN (Leinstermen) sought his assistance in their disputes with the joint Uí NÉILL high-kings DIARMAID MAC AODHA SLÁINE and his brother Bláthmhac. These HIGH-KINGS plotted treachery against him, but he avoided their ambushes by going in disguise, and eventually succeeded in having the Rye Water (between Counties Meath and Kildare) established as the northern boundary of Leinster. Where he sat down to arrange the treaty with the joint high-kings became known as his 'seat', Suidhe Moling.

Later, however, FIONNACHTA became high-king and sought to extract the traditional tribute called *BÓRAIMHE* from the Leinstermen. Moling then decided to go to TARA and seek remission of the tribute, and in the discussions played a trick on Fionnachta. He sought respite in the payment 'until Luan', and the high-king assented, believing that LUAN referred to the following Monday. Moling, however, explained that it actually referred to the Last Day, and through this use of verbal ambiguity achieved his purpose. We read that on the same occasion, he raised from the dead a son of Fionnachta who had just expired. St ADHAMHNÁN, however – who was of the royal Uí NÉILL sept – was much incensed at Moling's ruse concerning the tribute, and he prevailed on Fionnachta to send a group of men after the departing Moling. A mist fell on the pursuers and, through the miraculous power of Moling, they repeatedly mistook each other for him, and in this way a large number of them were slain by their fellows.

Several other anecdotes concerning Moling are found in the medieval literature. According to one of these, he had a friend called Maol Dobharchon, who was an exceedingly generous man. This Maol once claimed that he would have done all in his power to save JESUS CHRIST from the Crucifixion and, to test him, Moling set his cowl in a brake of thorns and told him to suppose that that was Christ. Maol cut his fingers trying to retrieve it, and thus proved his sincerity. We read that Moling was once captured by nine robbers, who challenged him to make a stanza for each of them. He did so and, as a result, was allowed to go unmolested. Yet another anecdote states that he had a pet fly which used to buzz musically for him, but a wren killed the fly. Moling then cursed the wren and, as a result, a fox killed and ate it.

Moling was generally portrayed in the manner of a seer-POET. Many verse compositions were ascribed to him, and he was said to have been one of the four chief prophets of Ireland. Several place names in Leinster indicate churches founded by him, but the actual founders may have been his disciples rather than himself. One tradition had it that he succeeded Maodhóg as abbot of the monastery of Fearna (Ferns, County Wexford). His feast day is 17 June.

Kenney (1929). 461–3; Stokes (1905), 150–7 & (1907) & in *RC, 13*, 44–7, 98–117 & in *AIM, 2*, 20–41; Plummer, *2* (1910), 190–205 & *1* (1922), 187–9, 244, 275–9; Heist (1965), 353–6; K. Meyer in *RC, 14*, 188–94; V. Hull in *ZCP, 18*, 90–9; O'Hanlon (1875), *6*, 691–724; M. de Paor (2001).

Molua SAINT who died *c.*AD 605. His original name was Lughaidh, of which Molua was a hypocoristic form. The tradition was that he was of the Uí Fidhgheinte sept (in the east of County Limerick).

Three medieval biographies in Latin survive, and they seem to derive from a text written in or about the ninth century. According to these accounts, he was son of one Cárthach of the Uí Fidhgheinte, and his mother was called Sochla. One imaginative source claims that he was a foundling, having been discovered in a brake of rushes by COMHGHALL as that saint was travelling in the territory of that sept; but this contradicts the general tradition, which had Molua being reared diligently by his parents, along with two elder brothers. He spent much of his youth herding cattle and sheep, and showed his miraculous power on several occasions. Once, his father found him asleep in a field, with an angel in white garments watching over him. When Comhghall visited Munster, he at once noticed Molua's holiness, and accordingly the youngster went north to be educated at the monastery of that saint at Bangor. He joined the community there, and soon showed his miraculous power by handling fire, being untouched by water though lying in the sea as penance, and lighting a candle with his breath. Molua prayed to God for intellectual prowess and, when reproached by Comhghall for this, replied that he desired it so as to promote the divine will.

Having learned much from Comhghall, he left Bangor and, accompanied by a few companions, founded the monastery of Droim Sneachta (Drumsna, County Monaghan), which became celebrated for its learning. We read that he banished a great monster from a nearby lake, and restored to life a boy who had died from the terror of it (*see* SAINTS). After some time, Molua left that place and went about founding several other houses along the boundary of the provinces of Leinster and Munster. This is undoubtedly an effort by the hagiographers to account for different dedications to a saint or saints called Lughaidh. We read that he eventually settled at Bealach Mór (Kyle, near Borris-in-Ossory, County Laois) and founded there the monastery that became known as Cluain Fhearta Molua. He is described as exercising discipline over his monks by a combination of kindness, patience and humour, and his method of teaching was inspired by his gentle motto: 'A little here, and a little there!' His rule divided the monastic day into three parts – one part for prayer, the second for study, and the third for labour.

Many of the miracles attributed to Molua involve healing the sick and inspiring vocations to the religious life, and his human sympathy is repeatedly stressed. There is, however, no absence of drama. We read that on one occasion, he resorted to a trick to secure the release of a captive from a certain king. Miraculously transforming some corn seed into gold, he used this to ransom the captive, but when the man was free, the gold returned to its former state. He died while returning to Cluain Fhearta Molua after a visit to St Crónán at Ros Cré (Roscrea, County Tipperary). The Leinster and Munster people argued over which of them should have his body for burial, but an angel appeared and directed that it be placed on a wagon drawn by two unbroken oxen. This was done, and the body was brought by the oxen to his own monastery to be buried. This account of the oxen is in fact a direct borrowing from an early biography of St PATRICK.

A medieval text in Irish has an angel announce that no saint ever got a greater welcome in heaven than he did; and we further read of how a BIRD was heard to lament him, because 'that Molua never killed a bird or any other living thing'. The memory of Molua survives in his native area, where a holy well is dedicated to him at Emlygrennan, near Kilfinane, County Limerick. At the site of his monastery in Kyle, County Laois, a large stone is pointed out as having been yielded to him by a DRUID after the saint had used it as an altar for the Eucharist. The stone has five circular cavities, which are claimed to have been made by the saint's head, knees and elbows as he prayed. The feast day of Molua is 4 August.

Kenney (1929), 398–9; Heist (1965), 131–45, 382–8; Plummer, 2 (1910), 206–25; Stokes (1905), 180–3; O'Hanlon, 8 (1875), 39–70; IFC 296:434–5, 1376:60.

Mongán Prince of the sept called Dál nAraidhe (in south Antrim and north Down). He was son of FIACHNA MAC BAODÁIN, the powerful king of Dál nAraidhe (+AD 626). Mongán himself, according to the Annals, was slain in the year 624 by a Briton called Artur ap Bicoir.

The kings of the Dál nAraidhe and other north-eastern septs were great patrons of the POETS and learned storytellers, and it is from this context that the extraordinary lore concerning Mongán grew. The name Mongán means 'hairy fellow', and its application to a person would suggest that he was born with a significant amount of hair already grown. A corpus of narratives was associated with a mythic seer who was portrayed as having been born with full-grown hair. It is evident that this symbolic child-seer was FIONN. Given this significance of his name, grateful poets would have been glad to compare Mongán to Fionn, and through such a conceit some ancient imagery of Fionn got attached to the Dál nAraidhe prince.

A reflection of the transformations anciently associated with the seer Fionn is found in an eighth-century account of Mongán. This describes him as visiting otherworld dwellings and gaining knowledge of secret lore there, and it also attributes to him the ability to travel in the forms of a wolf, deer, salmon, seal and swan. Such elaborate and unrealistic praise must have had an element of humour in it, and further play on the name Mongán made a connection between him and the sea-deity MANANNÁN. This connection was attractive to the eulogists because the root of Mongán's name, *moing* (mane), was a poetic metaphor for the sea. Thus the conceit that Manannán was a symbolic father of Mongán was added to that of his identity with Fionn. Both conceits must have been employed in a poem or rhetoric composed for the prince during his own lifetime. The surviving literary texts, however, belong to the eighth century, and by this time the material had been developed into pseudo-biographical narratives. One such narrative describes how

Fiachna went to Scotland to the assistance of his ally Aodán mac Gabhráin, who was at war with the Saxons. During his absence, a handsome stranger came to visit his queen at his palace in Magh Line (Moylinny, County Antrim). The stranger told her that Fiachna was in great danger, but that he himself would protect the king if she consented to lie with him. In order to save her husband, she lay with the stranger, who was Manannán. The latter left for Scotland and appeared between the two armies. He went to Fiachna and explained what had happened, and then slew a huge warrior of the Saxon army. This encouraged Fiachna and Aodán, and they routed the enemy host. Fiachna's queen (whose name is given in one version as Caintigern – i.e. Caointighearn) gave birth to a son, and this baby was Mongán. The narrative has been influenced by the MOTIF of a childless queen fertilised by a sea-spirit, which was the origin LEGEND of the Merovingian dynasty of the Franks. The eighth-century writer of the Mongán text, or his source, had very likely read in the Frankish chronicles an account of how the semi-mythical king Merovech had been conceived in this way, and considered it suitable for the development of the Mongán lore.

Another narrative in the eighth-century literature has sprung from the conceit concerning Fionn. According to this, in his palace at Magh Line, Mongán was once listening to a story being told by the importunate poet Forgoll (see DALLÁN FORGAILL). This was a story about the hero Fothadh Airgtheach, whom Forgoll claimed had been slain at Dubhthair Laighean (the Duffrey, County Wexford). Mongán contradicted him and, angered by this, Forgoll threatened to satirise him and refused all compensation except an offer of Mongán's wife Breothighearn, who was to be given to him within three days if Mongán could not prove the poet's statement to be incorrect. The evening of the third day arrived and Mongán still had not acquired the necessary proof. The queen was disconsolate, but Mongán said that he could hear the feet of a helper passing through a series of

rivers as he came to them all the way from the southwest of the country. Night arrived, and just when the poet was demanding his prize, a man vaulted over the ramparts and arrived in the centre of the palace. The newcomer was the FIANNA warrior CAOILTE, and he stated that he had been present when Fothadh Airgtheach was slain on the Ollarbha (the Larne river in County Antrim). He told where the grave was, and all was found to be as he had said. During the conversation, Caoilte called Mongán by the name Find (i.e. Fionn), and the text states that 'Mongán was Find, though he would not let it be told'. The author of this text must have been somewhat confused regarding the nature of his sources, for he takes Mongán's identity with Fionn not as a poetic conceit, but as a concrete fact. Undoubtedly, he does this purely in order to present an interesting narrative, but that he should do so at all indicates the strength of the tradition that the mythic seer Fionn could take on different forms, even perhaps in different generations.

Visits to the otherworld are to the fore in this literature. One account tells of how Mongán sent a poor scholar on an errand to three otherworld dwellings in Ulster, instructing him to collect from them a bag of silver, another of gold, and a precious jewel. The scholar did as he was told, and was received into each dwelling with great hospitality. In the third, he asked for the key to a marvellous chamber there and found the jewel. On his return to Mongán, he was allowed to keep the silver for his efforts. Another account has Mongán's wife – here called Findthighearn – asking for a description of her husband's adventures. He sought and obtained a respite of seven years before he would answer her request, and at the end of that time the couple were caught in a great hailstorm and found shelter in a strange and beautiful house. It had a roof of bronze, a pleasant bower over the windows, and it contained marvellous tapestries and jewels. Seven handsome men were there, and seven vats of ale. Mongán became intoxicated with the ale, and he recited a frenzied vision (*buile*) to his wife. Although they spent but one night in the house, they considered it a full year. It was obviously a dream-visit, for the text states that they found themselves at home in Mongán's palace 'when they awoke'. The text, unfortunately, does not give the words of Mongán's recitation, although it claims that in it he told of his adventures.

In or around the eleventh century, a fanciful story was written concerning Mongán's youth. It tells of how his father, Fiachna mac Baodáin, engaged EOCHAIDH ÉIGEAS as his professional poet, but Eochaidh made it a condition that the young Mongán should not be allowed to contend with him. Egged on by his companions, however, Mongán disguised himself and, with three other youths, contrived to meet Eochaidh on three occasions and asked questions concerning ancient edifices. Each time, Eochaidh's ignorance was displayed and Mongán showed his superior knowledge. The enraged poet cursed his tormentor and, as a result, Mongán had no royal issue. This story is an early example of a motif common in Irish folklore concerning poets – a visiting master is outwitted by a smart youngster or neophyte in the art. Another medieval tradition has Mongán encountering the famous saint COLM CILLE and being converted to Christianity by him. This lays much stress on Mongán's magical powers – he walks on water, frequents otherworld dwellings in barrows and on sea islands, and goes in the form of whatever animal he chooses. By showing him visions of hell and heaven, the saint persuades him to renounce magic and accept Christianity.

In actual history, Mongán's father, Fiachna mac Baodáin, was slain in battle against his own cousin, Fiachna mac Deamháin, in the year AD 626. This is, however, much distorted in a long narrative of Mongán compiled in the fourteenth century. It gives a somewhat altered account of his birth and – in contradiction of the Annals – has him surviving his father. According to the narrative, Fiachna mac Baodáin was on a visit to Scandinavia when the king of that country, called Eolgarg, fell sick. The leeches stated that

the meat of a white-eared cow was the only cure, and a hag who owned such a cow gave it on Fiachna's surety. A year later, when Fiachna had been installed as king of Ulster, the hag came to his palace and demanded the payment that Eolgarg, when healed, had refused to her. Fiachna accordingly invaded Scandinavia, but Eolgarg released a flock of venomous sheep against his army and he could make no headway. Then Manannán approached and offered to overcome the sheep if he be allowed to spend one night with Fiachna's queen. This was agreed, and Manannán took a fierce dog from his cloak, which killed the sheep. Fiachna conquered Scandinavia and compensated the hag, but on his return to Ireland found his queen pregnant, and thus Mongán was born a son of Manannán. On the same night that he was born, the wife of Fiachna mac Deamháin gave birth to a girl, who was called Dubh Lacha and was betrothed as a child to Mongán. Manannán took Mongán with him to his otherworld dwelling in Tír Tairngire and reared him there.

Mongán's earthly father Fiachna 'the Fair' was slain in battle by Fiachna mac Deamháin, called 'the Black'; and when Mongán was sixteen years old, he was brought to Ireland by Manannán. Peace was made with Fiachna 'the Black', who gave half of the Ulster kingdom to Mongán, as well as Dubh Lacha in marriage. Manannán, however, came again and, disguised as a cleric, encouraged Mongán to avenge his father. He therefore slew Fiachna 'the Black' and became sole king of Ulster. On a visit to Leinster, Mongán was given a herd of red-eared white cows by the king of that province, BRANDUBH. In return, however, Brandubh demanded his wife, Dubh Lacha, and Mongán had in honour to agree. Dubh Lacha obtained a promise from Brandubh not to lie with her for a year. Mongán had a servant, called Mac an Daimh, who was coeval with himself, and the wife of this servant had gone with Dubh Lacha. Thus Mac an Daimh also was pining for his wife and he prevailed on his master to take action.

Mongán got two sods, one from

Scotland and one from Ireland, and stood on these inside a basket, which the servant carried on his back to Leinster. Brandubh's DRUIDS were confused by the sods and did not realise that the king of Ulster was approaching. Coming to Leinster, Mongán and his servant met the monk Tiobraide with another cleric, and Mongán magically created a river and caused the monks to be carried downstream. Then he took onto himself and Mac an Daimh the shapes of the monks, and thus arrived at the court of Brandubh. Pretending to be the confessors of Dubh Lacha and her maid, they made themselves known to the two ladies and secretly took them to bed. When the real Tiobraide returned with a group of monks, Mongán told the door-keepers that the man outside was Mongán himself in disguise. Tiobraide was attacked, his men slain, and he himself forced to flee. By the time that Brandubh understood the trick that had been played on him, Mongán and his servant had made their getaway.

Once more, Mongán visited his wife, but on the third occasion Brandubh had soldiers waiting for his approach and he had to turn back. When the year had passed, preparations were made for the wedding between Brandubh and Dubh Lacha. Mongán, however, came in disguise and, with a magic wand, gave to a hag called Cuimne the appearance of a beautiful princess of Munster. He also put a love charm onto her cheek; thus when Brandubh saw her, he was completely captivated and agreed to exchange her for Dubh Lacha. During the night, Mongán and Mac an Daimh departed secretly on two swift horses, bringing their wives with them, and when morning came, Brandubh found to his dismay that his sleeping partner was a shrivelled hag.

This fanciful story has little regard for real history – it brings Mongán and Brandubh into association with each other and even claims that Mongán became king of Ulster. It also combines Mongán's magical abilities with some traditional narrative devices. Some notable instances of such motifs are the otherworld CATTLE, the sod-trick (see HUMOROUS TALES, type

1590), the love-spot put on a woman's cheek (see DIARMAID UA DUIBHNE), and a variety of magical ruses associated with figures like Manannán. The general structure of the narrative would suggest that its author was acquainted with the story of ÉADAOIN and Midhir.

A striking description of Mongán's death is given in one annalistic source. We read that once, when he and his mother were walking on the strand, she picked up a beautiful coloured stone and showed it to him. He shocked her by saying that his death would come by that stone. To prevent this, she took it in a boat and cast it into the sea far from the shore, but unknown to her it was carried back to the strand by the tide. Later, when a great fleet of Britons attacked his territory, Mongán defeated them and, through his magnanimity, allowed them to depart in safety. One of them, however, picked up the destined stone from the sand and shot it at Mongán. It struck him on the head, and as he fell dying, he told his mother that he would come alive again in exactly a year's time and that she should open his grave for him then. It was, however, a leap year, and so she came a day too late to the appointed task. She found the body warm and sweating, with blood coming from his nose, for he had been trying to come from the grave. This curious story was obviously a development from the earlier mystical imagery associated with the hero.

EARLY STORIES: Meyer & Nutt, 1 (1895–7), 16–17, 24–8; Mac Mathúna (1985), 54–6, 101–7; V. Hull in ZCP, 18, 414–19; O'Brien (1962), 282–4.

MEDIEVAL STORIES: E. Knott in Ériu, 8, 155–60; P. Grosjean in Analecta Bollandiana, 45, 75–83; O'Kelleher & Schoepperle (1918), 78–83, 168–9; K. Meyer in ZCP, 2, 313–20; S. Ó Duilearga in ZCP, 17, 347–70; O'Grady, 1 (1892), 391–2 & 2, 497.

GENERAL: Carney (1955), 280–95; P. Mac Cana in Ériu, 23, 102–42.

Mongfhionn *(earlier, Mongfhind)* Name of a shadowy mythic or otherworld lady in Irish literature. Its meaning is 'bright-maned', and it seems to have originally been another name for the mother-goddess.

The mother-GODDESS was often associated with water (see DANU), and her brightness in that context is evidenced by the ancient tradition of the river BÓINN (from Celtic *Bou-vinda*). Traces of the designation of a goddess as Vinda can be found in other ways in Irish literature. The word *mong* was a metaphor for crested waves and, significantly, the mother-goddess as MÓR-RÍOGHAIN (great queen) is described in an early text as inhabiting the water and as having the waves as her white hair (*mong fhind*). In the role of protectress, Mongfhionn appears as the tutelary nurse of young warriors (*see* MAC LUGHACH). Elsewhere, in a story derived from ancient KINGSHIP rituals, her name is borne by the fictional stepmother of the great king NIALL Naoi-Ghiallach, who wished that one of her sons rather than Niall should get their father's kingdom.

An eleventh-century text takes up this story, stating that in order to keep Niall from the throne, she used magic to get the men of Ireland to support her brother, Criomhthann mac Fiodhaigh, king of Munster. This Criomthann was thought of as having a kingdom in Scotland as well as in Ireland, and when he was on a royal circuit of Scotland, her sons grabbed the kingship. On Criomhthann's hasty return, Mongfhionn offered him a feast. She had poisoned his drink, but he insisted that she drink with him, and so both died – he as he returned to Munster. This, we read, was on the eve of Samhain (November), and after her death, she became 'an otherworld lady' whose festival is Samhain. 'Women and underlings pray to her' at that time. This medieval text may be taken to reflect an early tradition that the white-haired goddess was a patroness of the winter festival (*see* TIME).

A rhyme recited by children at Halloween in County Waterford to this day begins: *'Anocht Oíche Shamhna Mongfhinne banda'* (Tonight is the night of Samhain of Mongfhionn the goddess).

VINDA: C. O'Rahilly (1970), 105.

MÓR-RÍOGHAIN IN WATER: W. Stokes in *RC*, *17*, 175; O'Donovan (1842), 198.

NURSE: Stokes (1900), 16.

CRIOMHTHANN: O'Grady, *1* (1892), 326–30; Dillon (1946), 30–3; T.J. Westropp in *Folk-Lore*, *24*, 201–2.

MONGFHIONN AND THE SAMHAIN FEAST: O'Grady, *1* (1892), 330–2.

Moninne *(earlier, Monennai)* SAINT of the late fifth and early sixth century AD. She belonged to the Conaille sept of Muirtheimhne (north Louth).

Her biographies are in Latin and date from the eleventh to twelfth century, but contain some elements that seem to be quite early, perhaps deriving from some material committed to writing in the eighth century. We read that her real name was Darerca, and that her father was called Mochta and her mother Coman. The biographies further state that she was converted by St PATRICK himself, and that she received the veil at his hands. Nine other nuns followed her, one of them a widow whose son was adopted by Moninne. They were guided by bishop Iobhar of Beag-Éire (Beggery Island, Wexford Harbour), who was an associate of St BRIGHID, and then went to Brighid herself at Kildare. There Moninne impressed everybody by her selfless charity to the poor. Settling afterwards at a place called Ard Conais in her native area, her community increased to 150 nuns. On a visit to Kildare once, Moninne was presented by Brighid with a silver vessel, but due to her unselfishness did not take the gift with her but hid it in Brighid's convent. When it was later discovered there, Brighid ordered that it be cast into the River Liffey, from which it flowed into the sea and then northwards to the stagnant water at Ceann Tráchta (near Newry, County Down), where it was found by a brother of Moninne and returned to her.

Wishing to retire to quieter surroundings, the saint later moved her community of nuns to Cill Shléibhe (Killeavy, at the foot of Slieve Gullion, County Armagh). Apart from her charity, she practised great austerities, especially fasting, and we read that angels visited her and consulted with her each night. One tradition gives her original name as Sárbhile, and tells an interesting little story concerning how it was changed. We read that a dumb POET fasted against her in order to persuade her to get his speech for him. She consented, and as he began to talk, the first babbling words he uttered were 'nin-nin!' As a result, the poet himself became known as Nin*í*ne, and the saint as Moninne. The year 517 is given as the date of her death, and her feast day is 6 July.

Some saints with similar names were traditionally remembered in Scotland and England, and medieval writers attached to the convent of Burton-upon-Trent (in Staffordshire) claimed that Moninne was identical with their own foundress, Modwenna. This inspired a fanciful literature that described Moninne as leaving Killeavy and founding churches at seven different locations in Scotland, before settling at Burton.

O'Hanlon (1875), 7, 79–93; Stokes (1905), 166–7; Kenney (1929), 366–71; Heist (1965), 83–95; A. O'Sullivan (1983), 1688–9; L. de Paor (1993), 281–94.

Mór Mumhan Mythical woman whose name means 'Mór of Munster'. She was an emanation from ancient tradition, 'Mór' being originally a designation of the land-GODDESS (*see* MÓR-RÍOGHAIN).

The province of Munster took its name, Mumu (later, Mumhain) from a designation of the land-goddess that meant 'nurturess'. This designation seems to have originated with the ÉRAINN people in that region. The title was often confused with a different word, Mugha or Mughain (meaning 'female servant'), and this may have been a result of the overlordship that the EOGHANACHT people gradually gained over the Érainn. The adjective *mór* (large) was often combined with the name of the province, and this seems to have been the reason why Mór became associated with Munster in particular.

The territorial goddesses were symbolically portrayed as the mates of reigning KINGS, and in one late medieval text, this 'Mór of Munster' figures clearly in such a role. The text attempts to historicise her, connecting her to Eoghanacht kings of the early seventh century AD, the rationale doubtlessly being that the Eoghanacht had gained possession of the province. We read that Mór Mumhan was the daughter of Aodh Beannáin, a leader of the western Eoghanacht in whose territory the Érainn were still strong, and that she was being sought by various kings. She went mad and wandered through Ireland for two years in a distracted state. Coming to the royal Munster stronghold of Cashel, she lay with the king of the province, Fínghein mac Aodha, and he put aside his wife in favour of her. When Fínghein died, she went to the new king CATHAL MAC FIONGHUINE. Mór's sister was later taken captive, and the sons of Aodh Beannáin declared war on the sons of Cathal for failing to give her proper protection. The celebrated king Cathal mac Fionghuine has been mistakenly substituted here by the writer for Cathal mac Aodha, who succeeded Fínghein as king of the province in the year AD 619. The story is therefore a late fantasy based on earlier references to kingship.

The element Mughain has survived in petrified form in some place names – such as townlands called Fiodh Mughaine (Fithmoone) and Cluain Mughna (Clonmona) in north Tipperary, Bealach Mughna (Ballaghmoon, County Carlow) and Cill Mughaine (Kilmoone, County Cork). Memory of an actual personage called Mór is, however, preserved in the case of one toponymic only – Tigh Mhóire (the House of Mór), situated in the parish of Dunquin in west Kerry. A series of stories concerning her are current in that area, and it is clear from their sentiment that they are not more than a few centuries old. They do, however, preserve within them some snatches of ancient tradition; for instance, the phrase in local speech that describes the breadth of Ireland as being from Tigh Mhóire to Domhnach Diagh (Donaghadee, County Down) is in accord with similar statements in the early literature (*see* CAOILTE). The oral lore of Kerry transformed the latter place name rather awkwardly into a character called Donncha Daoi, who is made out to have been the husband of Mór. We are told that this couple lived somewhere in the centre of Ireland, but that Mór henpecked Donncha and he left her and went as far away from her as possible, thus leaving all Ireland between them.

Their three sons and one daughter went with the mother, but in time, these all met with misery, referred to proverbially as *íde chlainne Móire* (the misfortune of Mór's children). The two elder boys went overseas and became champions of a foreign king, for whom they slew giants and conquered foes. The youngest boy set out to find them, and all three got permission from the king to return home on holiday. They overstayed their time at home, however, and a strange ship soon arrived to collect them. There was nobody on board save a great black CAT, and they went onto the ship to examine it. No sooner had they done so than the cat (who was the foreign king in magical disguise) had the sails raised, and the ship carried them away forever. The daughter married a stranger who continually beat her, and Mór herself grew lonely and desolate living on her own. Finally, she decided to go to see her husband Donncha. She set out, and from a local hill top called Mám Clasach saw a wide expanse of countryside. 'Ireland is indeed long and wide!' she said. She felt the need to urinate there and thus created the streams which are on the Mám. She then returned to her house and went no further. Such humorous aetiological lore has not lost the aura of myth, and several exemplary phrases echo it; for instance, *leaghadh mhúin Mhóire* (the evaporation of Mór's urine) refers to the non-permanent nature of worldly things.

P. Mac Cana in *Études Celtiques, 7*, 76–114 & *8*, 64–5; T.P. O'Nolan in *Proceedings of the Royal Irish Academy, 30*, pt. C, 261–82; G. Mac Eoin in *ZCP, 36*, 63–82; F.J. Byrne (1973), 204–7; Olmsted (1994), 369–70, 481.
FOLKLORE: P. Ó Siochthradha in *An Claidheamh Soluis*, 30/7/1910, 2–4 & (1938), 75–6; Croker (1829), 74–80; Kennedy (1866), 287–8; Curtin (1894), xli–xliii, 35–7; Laoide (1915), 19; IFC Index.

Morann Mythical judge who was celebrated for his wisdom. His name is derived from *Mór-Fhind*, meaning 'great Find', and accordingly he would be an emanation from the archetypal wise seer of ancient tradition (*see* FIONN).

He figures in the medieval pseudo-historical writings, being portrayed as son of a usurper king Cairbre Catcheann who had banished the nobles from Ireland, but the MOTIFS concerning him obviously belong to earlier tradition. We read that two sons were born to Cairbre with cauls on their heads, and that Cairbre regarded them as monstrous births and had them drowned. The third child was Morann, and he also had a caul. When Cairbre's soldiers threw him into the sea, a great wave arose and broke the caul. The soldiers saw the child's face on the top of the wave, and he spoke to them, saying 'rough is the billow!' Then he spoke again, asking them to lift him up. They pitied him, and left him near the dwelling of a smith called Maon, who found him and took him home to his wife. The smith called for a candle to examine the child, and the infant remarked 'bright is the candle!' Later, it happened that Cairbre was at the house of the smith drinking ale, and the child jumped into his lap. The soldiers asked him how much he would pay for that child, and Cairbre said that he would give the child's weight in gold and silver. At that, they told him that it was his own son.

His father therefore took Morann with him and reared him. Morann became chief judge of Ireland, and when Cairbre died, decided that the only male survivor of the nobility, Fearadhach Fionn, should be recalled from Scotland to take the throne. He therefore sent his son to summon Fearadhach, quoting a long list of advices concerning how a king should rule properly. These advices predate the medieval literature, probably originating in the seventh century AD from maxims used by the actual legal schools of early Ireland. It is thus easy to understand why they should be fancifully attributed to a character with the name of the archetypal seer Fionn. One early legal tract, in deriving the name of the great judge from *mór* and *find*, appropriately explains the latter word as indicating how his decisions were full of wisdom (*fios*).

The ordinary designation of the judge was 'Morann mac Maoin', indicating that his father was Maon (earlier, *Moen*) which meant 'dumb'. This latter, curiously, was also a name given to the mythical founder of the Leinster kingship, LABHRAIDH, and so it is apparent that Morann – like FIONN FILE – originated in the strongly Leinster lore of Fionn. The reason why the medieval writers associated him with Cairbre seems to be that the story of his threatened youth resembles that of the threatened youth of Fearadhach (*see* CAIRBRE CATCHEANN).

Both early and late sources tell of the *sin* or *iodh* of Morann. This was the remnant of his caul, which remained around his neck, and if ever he was beginning to give a wrong judgement it would tighten on him and thus lead him to revise his decision. A development of this states that he used to place it on the neck of an accused person, and that it would choke the guilty but spare the innocent. The pseudo-historians also said that Morann was the first person in Ireland to believe in the Christian God 'through examination of the elements and through his own clear understanding'. This appears to be an echo from Christian didactic that put the image of the ancient seer Fionn to its own use (*see* FIONN MAC CUMHAILL). The medieval literature also relates a story of how Morann discovered his wife dallying with his servant. He turned the servant into a speckled calf, and the wife said that she was sick and desired the meat of that calf. Approaching the calf with a sword, Morann enquired of it what the sword feared. The calf replied 'stone', and a question-and-answer session commenced, viz. the stone feared fire, the fire water, the water wind, the wind hills, the hills boars, the boars hounds, and the hounds feared bad unrepentant women. When asked what a woman fears, the calf answered that it did not know. Morann then said that he would not slay his wife, because other men did not slay their unfaithful wives. This plot is in fact borrowed from folklore (*see* HUMOROUS TALES, types 2010–44). Despite his status in the old literature, however, no lore of Morann survives in oral tradition.

F. Kelly (1976); E.J. Gwynn in *Ériu 13*, 41–4, 47–52; O'Donovan, *1* (1865), 24–5; Binchy (1978), 1654–5; M. Dillon in *Ériu, 11*, 43–4; W. Stokes in *Irische Texte, 3*, 188–90; R. Thurneysen in *ZCP, 11*, 56–106 & *12*, 271–8 & *20*, 192–8; Dinneen, *2* (1908), 236–7 & *3*, 34–5.

Mór-Ríoghain A frequent designation of the mother-GODDESS in early Irish literature. It was taken to mean 'great queen', but in its original form, *Morrígu*, it may have meant 'phantom-queen'. In modern form, the appellation 'great queen' would be Mór-Ríon. Reference to a goddess as a queen was a long established tradition among the Celts – on the Continent, *Rigana* was used in that sense, and the Welsh parallel Rhiannon derives from a Celtic *Riganona* (revered queen).

The Mór-Ríoghain in Irish tradition had come to be imagined most frequently in the role of war-goddess, and she was identified with similar personages such as BADHBH and Neamhain. Her function as land-goddess had not entirely disappeared, however. The literature expressly states that MACHA was an alternative name for her, and her warlike imagery reflects contests for land. Several sources give her proper name as Anu, an alternative of the basic goddess-name DANU. Just as there were hills called the Paps of Anu at Killarney, County Kerry, so the Mór-Ríoghain was also identified with the landscape by having two hillocks as her Paps (*dá chích na Morrígna*) near Newgrange, County Meath. Her name occurs in several other toponymics, and further association of her with the landscape is evidenced by the term *fulacht na Mór-Ríoghna* (i.e. her 'hearth') for some ancient cooking-sites. As often with Irish divinities, she is represented as one of a triad of sisters. This triad are the active spirits of war, as in the account of the first Battle of Moytirra, fought between the FIR BOLG and the TUATHA DÉ DANANN – where they, of course, take the side of the latter, 'the people of the goddess Danu'. Named as 'Badhbh and Macha and Morrígu', they stand on the Hill of Tara and fling magical showers and masses of fire and blood onto the Fir Bolg. The triad thus have the function not specifically of encouraging war, but of encouraging their own people to victory.

This is clear in the tradition that the Mór-Ríoghain was in fact the wife of the father-god called the DAGHDHA. One account in the MYTHOLOGICAL CYCLE has her sharing his exalted status, and that in a very significant context. We read that, before the second Battle of Moytirra, the Daghdha had a tryst with her at the River Unshin (in County Sligo). She was washing there, with a foot on either side of the river, and he copulated with her in that position. She informed him where the enemy host of the FOMHÓIRE would land, and promised that she would terrify the Fomhóire king Inneach by draining away his valour and 'the blood from his heart'. She also told the Daghdha to summon the POETS of Ireland to her, and she directed these to sing spells against the foe. In the later text describing this battle, we are told that the Mór-Ríoghain, along with Badhbh and Macha, undertook to bring 'hailstones and fierce showers' down upon the Fomhóire, and to fling javelins and flails against them. These are clear illustrations of her combined functions as goddess of fertility and of war, protectress of her people's general interests.

When specifically cast in the role of war-goddess, she was encountered often by a riverside, portending slaughter. One eighth-century text has the mythical warrior FOTHADH CANAINNE say of the Mór-Ríoghain that 'it is she who has egged us on' and that 'horrible is her hateful laughing' that strikes terror into the hearts of men. The true warrior was one who was not overcome by fear and who was therefore on good terms with her. It was for this reason that she became attached to the developing lore of the hero CÚ CHULAINN in early medieval Ireland. We read that as a boy, he went to rescue king CONCHOBHAR MAC NEASA from a battlefield, and that he heard there 'the war-goddess crying from among the corpses' and encouraging him to great deeds. Here she is called the Badhbh, but Cú Chulainn encountered her under her own name and in a more direct manner when he was single-handedly contending with the forces of Meadhbh. She approached him in the form of a beautiful young woman and stated that she had fallen in love with him on hearing his fame. She offered him

her help, but he answered that he was not seeking a woman's torso, and she then threatened to encumber him when he was fighting. Accordingly, when he was locked in combat with a great warrior called Lóch, she came in the form of an eel and coiled herself around his feet. He fell, but arose again and struck the eel, breaking its ribs. Then she took the form of a grey wolf, and drove a herd of cattle against him, but he knocked an eye out of her head with a slingshot. Finally, she became a red hornless heifer and led the cattle in a stampede towards him, but he cast a stone at her and broke her leg. He succeeded in slaying his opponent Lóch, but when he was exhausted from the fighting, she came to him again – this time in the guise of an old crone milking a cow with three teats. He asked her for a drink, and she gave him a drink from each teat, with the result that the three wounds he had inflicted on her were healed.

Other female war-spirits in the ULSTER CYCLE are called Neamhain and Bé Néit, as well as Badhbh. These three shrieked over the enemy army, leading to great confusion and causing many of the soldiers to die of fright, and thus their portrayal is as protectresses of Ulster. Indeed, the Badhbh appeared to the great brown bull (see DONN CUAILNGE) and told him that he must move with his heifers to new pastures in order to avoid capture by the foe. She was in the form of a BIRD perching on a pillar-stone when she thus addressed the bull. The war-goddess in the Ulster Cycle is several times brought into association with cattle, no doubt because of the high profile of cattle-raiding in the practice of war. She is said, for instance, to have stolen a cow from Connacht and driven it to Cooley to be mated to the great brown bull there. As she brought it back, Cú Chulainn intercepted her. She was coloured red and was riding in a one-horse chariot, with a huge man walking alongside and driving the cow. Thinking that she was stealing a cow from Ulster, Cú Chulainn challenged her, but she and her retinue disappeared. All that remained was a dark bird on a branch near him. In this shape the Mór-Ríoghain spoke to him and explained that the calf born of that cow would be coeval with himself and would give rise to the war of *Táin Bó Cuailnge*.

Although the theme of this calf and its connection with Cú Chulainn is inconsistent with the ordinary sequence of the Ulster Cycle, it is clear that the narrative has as its theme the stirring up of war by the Mór-Ríoghain. When Cú Chulainn boasted to her of the feats he would perform, she threatened to discommode him in the manner described above. There is some ambiguity in her image here, for she and the hero are quite hostile to each other, even though she does promise him that she will be 'a shelter at your death'. No doubt due to the influence of such accounts, she occurs in the context of cattle in a rather confused and simplistic medieval story that tells of how she stole away a fierce bull from the herd of a cattle-drover of Tara called Buchat. The latter's wife Odhras followed her to the barrow of Cruachain (in County Roscommon), but fell asleep there – whereupon the Mór-Ríoghain came and chanted powerful spells over the woman, turning her into a river, which thus was called by the name Odhras.

Some sources identify Neamhain with Bé Néit, literally 'the wife of the warrior' (*see* NÉT), and it is clear that both of these were, like Macha and Fea, mere pseudonyms for the Mór-Ríoghain. Most frequent of all alternatives was the Badhbh, the scaldcrow form taken by the war-goddess as she hovered over the clash of contending armies. In her human form, she can be equally horrific – one late medieval text describes the 'grey-haired Mórrígu' as shrieking triumphantly over fighting soldiers, and appearing as 'a lean HAG, speedily leaping over the points of their weapons and shields'. The more comfortable image of protectress of the tribe had not entirely disappeared, however, as is evident from the death-tale of Cú Chulainn. Here, as the hero sets forth on his doomed journey, he finds that the Mór-Ríoghain has disconnected his chariot on the night before in order to discourage him from his venture. *See also* MONGFHIONN.

DESIGNATION: RIA Dictionary, s.v. 'morrigu'; Olmsted (1994), 201–13, 369–70, 477, 482.
ASSOCIATIONS WITH LAND: Gwynn (1906), 18–19, 62–3; W.M. Hennessy, 54–5; Van Hamel (1933), 37.
MYTHIC SYNCHRONISMS: Gray (1982), 118, 128–30; Macalister (1941), 122, 160, 188.
'FIRST' MOYTIRRA BATTLE: J. Frazer in *Ériu*, 8, 29–48.
'SECOND' MOYTIRRA BATTLE: Gray (1982), 44–5, 64–5, 70–3; Ó Cuív (1945), 20, 26–7.
FOTHADH CANAINNE: Meyer (1910), 16–17.
CÚ CHULAINN: C. O'Rahilly (1976), 31, 57–64, 105, 107; E. Windisch in *Irische Texte*, 2 (2), 239–54; Best & O'Brien (1956), 443.
ODHRAS: Gwynn (1924), 196, 201.
HISTORICAL BATTLES: John O'Donovan (1842), 198–9.

motif A term used by folklorists to denote the smallest single element on which a narrative can be built. In this sense, all stories contain one or more motifs. The tradition of storytelling is seldom satisfied with just one motif, as the resultant story would be so short as not to attract much attention. For a story to maintain a popular yet complex plot, its motifs must be selected to complement each other and must be arranged so as to bring the narrative forward logically. The number of motifs available in human culture is enormous, but they tend to be used contextually, and most oral storytellers would feel it unnatural to introduce motifs in a way that had no precedent in his or her narrative experience.

Certain motifs may be quite similar or even identical to things that happen in reality – the term 'self-realising motif' can be used for such a phenomenon. Examples would be the righting of injustice by a reversal of fortune; ruses or tricks that can be effective in reality; misunderstandings in language or speech; and non-recognition or mistaken identity of a particular person, with dramatic results. The occurrences in real life of such self-realising motifs, or of incidents similar to them, can, of course, feed into tradition and bolster the social role of storytelling. On the other hand, the appeal of unrealistic motifs is due to the expectation that storytelling involves the telling of events that are extraordinary and by implication not to be expected in real life.

In this book, attention is directed especially to the plot structures of traditional stories, which entail combinations of motifs (see, for example, FOLKTALE and LEGEND). Accordingly, concentration is more on these combinations than on an analysis of the actual motifs themselves. The compilation of a catalogue of individual motifs in Irish literature and folklore would be a massive enterprise.

PARTIAL CATALOGUE OF INTERNATIONAL FOLKLORE MOTIFS: S. Thompson (1955–58).

PARTIAL CATALOGUE OF MOTIFS IN IRISH TRADITIONAL LITERATURE: Cross (1952).

Muircheartach mac Earca

HIGH-KING of the Uí NÉILL, whose reign belonged to the period AD 513–36. Muircheartach was a very common name in early Ireland, meaning 'sea-craftsman' – i.e. a skilled mariner. This king won several battles against the Leinstermen (LAIGHIN), and his fame in the Annals caused several accounts of him to be written in medieval times.

An eleventh-century poem tells of how the Scottish king Eochu carried off the young Muireadhach, grandson of the celebrated NIALL, to serve him, and how Muireadhach slew Eochu and brought back to Ireland with him a maiden called Earc, daughter of Loarn. It was said that Muireadhach was slain by his father's swineherd through jealousy of Earc, but that Earc revived him by placing a herb in his mouth as she had seen a weasel do for its dead mate. Another account also mentions how Earc eloped with Muireadhach and states that Muircheartach was the eldest son of their union. Muircheartach was expelled from Ireland for killing some jesters, and he was later expelled from Scotland after he slew his grandfather Loarn. He went to the land of the Britons and became king over it, and eventually came to Ireland accompanied by his cousin, the cleric Cairneach.

There was some basis for this in the Annals, for one Loarn was there said to have crossed from Ireland to Scotland in the fifth century, and from cineál Loairn (his descendants) is apparently derived the name of the district, Lorne, in Argyll.

Muircheartach succeeded his father Muireadhach as king of Aileach (the area of west Ulster) at the end of the fifth century, but the designation of him by his mother's name (mac Earca) is puzzling. Earc (earlier, Erc) might have been the name of some goddess and mac Earca would thus have been a title rather than a name, but it is also quite possible that Muircheartach's mother was in fact called Earc. Cairneach (known in British records as Carantoc) was definitely historical. The medieval Irish literature describes him as son of a British king called Saran, and makes his mother Babona a sister of Earc, but this connection between him and Muircheartach may have arisen from a verse attributed to him and which prophesied the latter's death.

The death of Muircheartach is the subject of a saga composed in or about the eleventh century. It describes how, when he was HIGH-KING, he had his palace at Cleiteach (near Newgrange, County Meath), and his wife was Duaibhseach, daughter of the king of Connacht. When hunting alone one day, he met a beautiful lady. She told him that her name was Sín, and she agreed to become his paramour on condition that he expel his wife and children from the palace. This was done, and Duaibhseach went to complain to Cairneach. The cleric cursed the dwelling of Muircheartach, and dug a grave for him there in anticipation of his death. Soon after, Cairneach met a Munster troop coming to negotiate with the king, and he supervised a treaty between the two sides. Because he had cursed him, however, Muircheartach ordered Cairneach to stay far away from his dwelling forthwith. To demonstrate her magical power, Sín entertained Muircheartach and his Munster guests by creating illusions of men fighting, by making wine from water, and by turning the fern into swine. Next morning, the king felt that his strength was leaving him. Sín made of the stones blue men and goat-headed men on the lawn before Brugh na Bóinne (the Newgrange tumulus), and Muircheartach himself went to fight these. All day long, he slaughtered them, and then returned to his residence, where he was given more of Sín's food and drink. On the following morning, he was further weakened, and again Sín created illusions of battalions of soldiers to oppose him.

Cairneach, knowing of the king's dilemma, sent three clerics to assist him. They found him hacking at stones and sods and stalks, and on their advice he made the Sign of the Cross and the dementia left him. They told him that his death was near and instructed him to build a church there. He did this, and then was shriven and prepared for death by the clerics. Returning to Sín, however, he was again beguiled by her. She brought a storm and a great snowfall, and when he fell asleep, he dreamed that a host of demons was coming for him. He also dreamed that he was in a foundering ship and that a griffin came and carried him to her nest, where he was burned to death. He sent a message to the three clerics, and they explained that the ship was his kingship and that the griffin was the lady Sín. Finally, he imagined that the demons were attacking his palace and slaughtering his people. He went to oppose them and found the place in conflagration. To escape the fire, he went into a great cask of wine, and died there from the dual effects of drowning and burning. Next day, the clerics brought his body to the River Boyne nearby and washed it. Cairneach came there and lamented him, as also did the queen Duaibhseach. She died from grief for him, and she and Muircheartach were buried together. Sín came to the clerics and explained that this was her revenge on the high-king for the death of her family in the Battle of Cearb (Assey, County Meath), in which Muircheartach had decimated the old septs of TARA. She was shriven by the clerics, and died from grief at what she had done.

Although this story makes use of memories of the struggle between the Uí Néill and the remnants of the older ÉRAINN septs of the Boyne Valley, this is not the main focus. That focus is the struggle between the Christian and pagan world-views in the sixth century, as seen through the eyes of the medieval writer. It is significant that the cleric Cairneach curses the high-king when the latter departs from the Christian ethic, and that this curse becomes a reality, thereby underlying the superior power of the Church. A similar situation applied in the saga of another high-king, DIARMAID MAC CEARRBHEOIL, whose dramatic death was described as having three enigmatic aspects. This triple-death MOTIF was borrowed from the Diarmaid context into that of Muircheartach, apparently by ninth-century writers or storytellers, and thus was embedded in the sources the later medieval writer was using.

Nic Dhonnchadha (1964); Van Hamel (1932), 40–1; Mac Cionnaith (1938), 217–20; Ó Caithnia (1984), 103–4, 116; E. Mac Néill in *Archivium Hibernicum, 2,* 70; Macalister (1956), 360–3, 532–5; F.J. Byrne (1973), 100–3.

Murchadh mac Briain *(c.970–1014)* Eldest son of the high-king of Ireland BRIAN BÓRAMHA, his name Murchadh was a very popular and prestigious one in early Ireland, meaning 'sea-battler'. Murchadh was the leader of Brian's army at the Battle of Clontarf, in which he and his father were both slain. His fifteen-year-old son Toirdhealbhach also died in the fighting.

The earliest account of that battle stresses the great heroism of Murchadh fighting with a sword in each hand, for he was 'the last man in Ireland to have equal dexterity in each hand' and also 'the last man to be the equal of a hundred'. We read that he led a charge that broke the enemy ranks and then, swinging his two swords, he beheaded the NORSE leader Sigurd. He and a Norse warrior called the son of Elbric then came to grips with each other, and so fierce was the combat between them that Murchadh's sword became red hot and its handle melted. It burned his hand and he had to throw the sword aside. Knocking his opponent to the ground, he grabbed the Norseman's sword and stabbed him, but was himself stabbed with a knife in the stomach. He beheaded his opponent, but he himself was mortally wounded and died at sunrise on the following morning. When Brian got news that the standard of

Murchadh had fallen, he was heartbroken and remarked that 'Ireland has now fallen with it!'

The only one of Brian's sons to survive the pyrrhic victory was Donnchadh. This, according to the text, was in accordance with the prophecy given to Brian by the otherworld lady AOIBHEALL to the effect that his successor would be the first of his sons whom he saw on the day of the battle. The apparent meaning of this was that Brian first noticed Donnchadh in the battle, but a later medieval text tells a fanciful story to explain it. According to this, when Brian received the prediction from Aoibheall, he sent for Murchadh, who began to dress to go into his father's presence. Donnchadh, however, went straight to his father, and so, much to the latter's disappointment, was the one destined to succeed. This story, echoing the biblical account of Abraham's sons, must have derived from some dispute as to primacy among Brian's descendants.

The Aoibheall theme also prompted the inclusion of another account into the narrative of the Battle of Clontarf. According to this, a friend of Murchadh called Dúnlaing Ó hArtagáin arrived late just as the battle lines were drawn. He explained that he had been detained in an otherworld dwelling but that he had foregone the beautiful life there out of loyalty to Murchadh. While in the otherworld, he had discovered that he himself, as well as Brian, Murchadh and other members of the royal family, would be slain on that day. Dúnlaing then went into the battle and, fighting magnificently, was slain. A much later redaction has Dúnlaing bringing Murchadh from the thick of the battle to meet Aoibheall, and she confirms the prophecy for them. The theme of this Dúnlaing seems to have been invented by the sub-sept of Brian's people who bore the surname Ó hArtagáin (anglicised Hartigan), with the distinct purpose of increasing their prestige among the DÁL GCAIS families.

Murchadh's reputation for heroism continued in the literature. A thirteenth-century poem credits him with overcoming and slaying an horrific 'red woman' who came with a large fleet and strong magical powers to destroy Ireland. Writers of fiction in general found his personality suitable to their purpose. One romance, written in the seventeenth century, tells how, after following a magical stag and hound, Murchadh meets a hermit who is cutting wood. The hermit invites him to his castle, where Murchadh shows some untoward interest in his host's wife. The hermit explains the great difficulties he has had in procuring his stag, hound and woman, and describes how he had won back the woman when she had been abducted from him. Night comes and Murchadh goes to sleep, but when he awakes in the morning, the castle and all its occupants have disappeared. Another romance, written in or about the same time, tells of a great adventure Murchadh has in an underwater land where he recovers a magic cauldron stolen by a servant and rescues a maiden from a GIANT. Several versions of these romances circulated in folklore, and some oral storytellers introduced the heroic name Murchadh mac Briain at will into narratives of great deeds.

Todd (1867), clxxv–clxxviii, 168–97, 336–7; Goedheer (1938), 47–8, 58–9, 67–71; Bruford (1969), 136–43, 257, 261 & in *Éigse, 12*, 301–26; M. Ní Úrdail in *Éigse, 32*, 59–69; Hyde, *GF* (1899), vii–x, 4–49.

Mythological Cycle A collective term applied to the stories in Irish literature that describe the doings of otherworld characters. The basis for the cycle is ancient Celtic myth, and many of the characters are Irish manifestations of a Celtic pantheon of divine beings.

The central story of the cycle was concerned with a battle between two supernatural groups. This theme is found in other Indo-European sources – such as the conflict between the Devas and Asuras in Vedic literature, between the Aesir and Vanir in Norse, and between Zeus' family and the Titans in Greek. It is probable that the theme was adopted into Celtic sources due to the loss of the true meaning of druidic teaching regarding the encounter of night and day, and thus of the dead and the living, on a western island (*see* DONN *and* DRUIDS). At some early stage also, the theme became confused with a different tradition of a great contest – how the deity Lugh overcame Balar in a great atmospheric combat. This seems to have derived from a Celtic tradition of how Lugus (known alternately as Esus) overcame the thunder-god Taranos. Such a combat between Celtic deities must have been the ancient pattern from which developed the cult of St Michael overcoming Lucifer at rocks on the coasts of Normandy, Brittany, Cornwall and Ireland (Skellig Michael off the Kerry coast); from this, we can gather that the Lugh-versus-Balar scenario was once set on a sea-girt pinnacle.

Medieval Irish literature, in fact, contains echoes of a tradition in early Ireland that a great primordial battle was fought at such a site in the sea, but at a location in accord with the idea of a mystical island in the west. These echoes have a great tower on a small island being attacked by a race who inhabit Ireland and are being oppressed by the Fomhóire who live in that tower. The tower is called Tor Chonaing, and in one version the attackers are the people of NEIMHEADH, while in another version it is the TUATHA DÉ DANANN. One variant has a great tower of glass being attacked by the sons of MÍL when they reached Ireland. The idea of the taking of a Fomhóire tower (*tor*) by the Tuatha Dé is significant. The genitive of this word was *tuir*, and as such was easily confused with *tuir* or *tuire*, meaning 'pillar'. From this, one may assume that an eighth-century author or his source postulated that the great battle was fought at the inland location known as Magh Tuireadh (the Plain of the Pillars). That location (Moytirra, near Lough Arrow, County Sligo) was a dramatic one for the antiquarian and storyteller, for it comprises a flat landscape with a massive number of individual rocks and, in addition to this striking geological feature, also contains some ancient cairns and gravestones.

Thus the Irish myth of conflict between the divine Tuatha Dé Danann and the underworld FOMHÓIRE was written down in a particular form in the eighth century

AD. That original text does not survive, but a redaction derived from it is found in the medieval literature. This is known as the 'Second Battle of Moytirra', and in most details can be taken to accurately reflect the story as told in the eighth-century text. There is another relevant story in the medieval literature, the so-called 'First Battle of Moytirra', which was for the most part a literary fabrication. Both stories, however, must be taken into account in order to understand the full tradition.

The 'first' battle was known by the title *Cath Muige Tuired Cunga* (the Battle of Moytirra of Cong). Cong lies between Lough Mask and Lough Corrib in County Mayo. It abounds in cairns and other stone monuments, and thus appeared to the medieval literati as a suitable place to be called 'the Plain of the Pillar', even though that name properly belonged to the place in County Sligo. This story developed from the medieval pseudo-historical tract, *Lebor Gabála*, which claimed that the Tuatha Dé Danann were an ancient people who settled in Ireland and conquered a group of earlier inhabitants called the FIR BOLG. The idea of a clash between the Tuatha Dé and Fir Bolg necessitated a duplication of the Battle of Moytirra – hence the notion of an earlier or 'first' battle. The text that purports to give a full description of this was composed in or about the eleventh century, and goes as follows:

The Fir Bolg were in possession of Ireland, and Eochaidh mac Eirc was their king. Eochaidh had a dream in which he saw a great flock of black BIRDS coming from the ocean, and his POET explained that this was a fleet of ships carrying 1,000 magical heroes. Thus the Tuatha Dé Danann, led by their king NUADHU, arrived in Ireland. They broke and burned their boats, and encamped on a mountain in the northeast of the province of Connacht. The Fir Bolg sent one of their warriors, the huge Sreang, to parley with them, and he was confronted by BREAS of the Tuatha Dé. Since both peoples were descended from NEIMHEADH, the two warriors spoke the same language. Breas demanded half of Ireland for his people, and Sreang was inclined to agree, but the assembly of the Fir Bolg at TARA refused this. The three sorceresses of the Tuatha Dé – BADHBH, MACHA and the MÓR-RÍOGHAIN – then sent magical showers of fiery rain against the Fir Bolg, causing great damage until the Fir Bolg sorcerers managed to counteract them. Nuadhu sent envoys to Eochaidh, offering the same terms as before, but again the Fir Bolg refused. A group of the Fir Bolg went and challenged the Tuatha Dé to a hurling match, in which the Tuatha Dé players were slain. Then Eochaidh mac Eirc sent his poet to the Tuatha Dé nobles to arrange the conditions of the forthcoming battle. Each side built an entrenched fortress and prepared a well of healing for their wounded. Battle was fought at Cong, and on the first day the fighting went against the Tuatha Dé, but the Fir Bolg did not pursue their advantage. They returned to their own camp, and when king Eochaidh went to wash in their well next morning he was attacked by three warriors of the Tuatha Dé who had come to spy. A young man suddenly appeared and protected the king. This unnamed stranger slew the three and was himself slain.

When the armies joined battle on that day, the position was reversed, with the Fir Bolg being driven across the field. On the third day, the Tuatha Dé were led by the DAGHDHA, and in a furious combat, the Fir Bolg were driven right back to their own camp. The fourth day of the battle was the most terrible of all, and the Tuatha Dé fixed pillars on the plain so that the foe could not escape their onslaught. For the Fir Bolg, however, Sreang was rampant, and with a tremendous sword stroke severed the right arm of Nuadhu from the shoulder. The Daghdha had the disabled king carried from the fray to be looked after by physicians. In the ongoing fighting, king Eochaidh was overcome by thirst and had to leave the field for a while to drink. The wizards of the Tuatha Dé caused all the streams and rivers to dry up before him until he came to Tráigh Eothaile (Beltra Strand, County Sligo). He was followed there by a trio of Tuatha

Dé warriors, who slew him in fierce combat. On the final day of the battle, the great Sreang again came face to face with Nuadhu, but instead of contending they made peace, according to which Ireland was given to the Tuatha Dé and the Fir Bolg were allowed to keep the western province. Since Nuadhu was blemished, he was disqualified from the KINGSHIP of the Tuatha Dé, and Breas was installed in his place. The text states that Breas died from a drink he took while hunting seven years later. The missing arm of Nuadhu was then replaced, and he became king once more.

In this text, the original story of the Moytirra battle is quite distorted by pseudo-historical speculation. The account of the strange young warrior who saved Eochaidh from his three foes at the well, for instance, was invented on the basis of local landmarks called *Carn an Aonfhir* (the cairn of the single champion) and *Tulach an Trír* (the mound of the three). The most distorting element, of course, is the general structure of the narrative, which was drawn from the *Lebor Gabála*, but some basic traits unconnected with this come through clearly. The two contending races are described as not alien to each other but quite closely related, the Tuatha Dé are obviously masters in magic, and the loss of Nuadhu's arm is of great import. All of these traits occur also in the text on the 'second Battle of Moytirra'. This, from the eleventh century, is directly based on the lost eighth-century text, and preserves much more accurately the original lore. Having briefly recounted the pseudo-historical material concerning the victory over the Fir Bolg and how Sreang had cut off the arm of Nuadhu in that battle, the text reverts to its eighth-century source. It relates the cause of the great Battle of Moytirra in County Sligo, and describes – not without some embellishment of its own – the course of that conflict:

The Tuatha Dé decided that, since Nuadhu had lost his arm and was thus blemished, the kingship should be taken from him. They conferred it on Breas, who was the son of a Tuatha Dé woman and whose father Ealatha was the king of the Fomhóire. In this way, the Tuatha Dé hoped to cement friendship with the Fomhóire, and Breas for his part promised to give up the kingship if he misbehaved. Soon, however, and with his connivance, the Fomhóire began to oppress the Tuatha Dé. They imposed a tribute on every house from which smoke issued, and they forced OGHMA to carry loads and forced the Daghdha to construct a great rampart around Breas' fortress. Both of these enslaved champions were kept in hunger and misery. When their poet CAIRBRE MAC ÉADAOINE satirised Breas, the Tuatha Dé demanded that the oppressive king should resign. Breas agreed to this, but sought seven years respite, slyly planning to organise a great Fomhóire invasion. He soon quit the country, accompanied by his mother, and went to the northern regions of the world to enlist the support of his father. Ealatha was reluctant to assist him because he had not ruled Ireland justly, but he directed him to two other Fomhóire magnates, BALAR and Inneach. These two gathered a great invasion force, and made a bridge of ships all the way from the Hebrides to Ireland.

Meanwhile, the physician DIAN CÉACHT had replaced Nuadhu's severed limb with a silver arm that was 'as mobile as any hand', and the Tuatha Dé therefore reinstalled Nuadhu as their king. The restored monarch held a great banquet at Tara, during which a stranger arrived and demanded entry. This was LUGH, maternal grandson of the Fomhóire leader Balar, but whose father Cian was of the Tuatha Dé. Lugh gained entry to the feast because he was the master of all arts. Impressed by his stupendous skills, Nuadhu decided to bestow the leadership on him for thirteen days. Lugh accordingly made preparations for the impending clash with the Fomhóire, delegating functions to all the various craftsmen and magicians. For his part, the Daghdha held a tryst with the MÓR-RÍOGHAIN and enlisted her help, and then went to the Fomhóire camp in order to gain time for the Tuatha Dé in their preparations. He was mocked and humiliated there,

and after he left the camp encountered another strange woman, with whom he also had intercourse and who also promised magical assistance against the Fomhóire.

The battle was joined at Samhain (the November feast – *see* TIME), and each of the Tuatha Dé scions played a special part in the effort. The slaughter was atrocious on both sides, and among those who fell was Nuadhu. Lugh rushed to the forefront of the Tuatha Dé, and began to chant a magical spell. He met and slew his tyrant grandfather Balar before the latter could use his destructive eye that had the power to lay low multitudes. The fighting went against the Fomhóire, who took to flight towards the sea. Their poet, Lóch Leathghlas, was spared by Lugh and promised in return that the Fomhóire would never again threaten Ireland and that Lugh's judgements would always be correct. Breas was also captured, and he promised that in Ireland the cows would always have milk and that a harvest of grain would be produced every season. These promises were rejected, however, and Lugh gave him quarter in return for advice on ploughing, sowing and reaping. Then Lugh and the Daghdha and Oghma followed the Fomhóire to the banqueting-hall of Breas and his father Ealatha, and they recovered the harp of the Daghdha's musician, which had been taken. The Daghdha played the three kinds of magical music, lulling the Fomhóire with the sleep-music so that the three could escape. The Daghdha also took away all the CATTLE the Fomhóire had seized as tribute in Ireland. The Mór-Ríoghain then announced the great battle victory to all parts of the country.

The elements of most antiquity in this text have to do with the otherworld clash of a divine race with a destructive one. The principal characters of the Tuatha Dé who are mentioned were all Celtic deities, as appropriate to the exalted atmosphere of such a survival from archaic narrative; and the gaining of agricultural benefits from the Fomhóire parallels a similar theme in the Vedic and Norse versions of the myth, where the defeated races represent the fertility of the soil. Since Nuadhu is central to the Irish story, it may be that it was as part of his cult that the theme of a battle between two divine races was introduced into Ireland. If so, the other deities were soon added to the narrative so as to form a Tuatha Dé leadership. We have suggested that the dramatic parallel in situation caused the Lugh–Balar contest to be connected to the theme. Significantly, the battle is claimed to have taken place at the November feast, and not at Lughnasadh (August), which one would expect if Lugh had had an original part in the narrative.

The tradition of the great battle at Moytirra – with its descriptions of several Celtic deities in the guises of Tuatha Dé characters – is the principal connection between archaic myth and medieval lore concerning the otherworld community in Ireland. Other accounts of the 'second' battle, in medieval pseudo-history and in a post-medieval text, do not differ substantially from the plot given above. There are a number of other texts which preserve, albeit in a confused form, traditions of the Celtic pantheon. For such material, *see* the full list of entries on mythical lore in the List of Genres, page 509.

TOWER MOTIF: Macalister (1939), 249 & (1940), 122–5, 128–31, 138–43; Van Hamel (1932), 21–2.

'FIRST' BATTLE: J. Fraser in *Ériu*, 8, 1–63.

'SECOND' BATTLE: Gray (1982).

REFERENCES IN *LEABHAR GABHÁLA*: Macalister (1941), 106–21, 168–73.

LATER VERSION OF 'SECOND' BATTLE: Ó Cuív (1945).

GENERAL: B. Ó Cuív in Dillon (1968), 27–39; G. Murphy in *Éigse*, 7, 191–8; de Vries (1961), 148–56.

Naithí Historical king who died *c.*AD 445. The medieval historians held that he had been king of Ireland, but in reality his realm was confined to either the north Midlands or Connacht. The earlier form of his name was Nath Í, meaning 'nephew of Eo' (*eo* being a tree, figuratively a champion). By the Middle Ages, however, 'Naithí' was considered as an eclipsed form of *daithe* (meaning 'swiftness', hence 'the swift one'); accordingly, in later sources he is often called by a new form of his name, Dáithí. The fanciful interpretation thus given was that Naithí was swift to take up arms.

There was a tradition that his real name was the relatively common one, Fearadhach, but Nath Í was also current as a name in early Ireland. His father is said to have been Fiachra, brother of the celebrated NIALL, and accordingly was distinguished from other characters with the same name by the designation Naithí mac Fiachrach. He had the reputation of being from the beginning a fierce warrior. We read that after Niall was installed as high-king at Tara, the province of Connacht was assigned to Fiachra and his brother Brión. The two contended with each other, however, and war broke out between them. Brión defeated Fiachra's army at Damhchluain (near Tuam, County Galway), and Fiachra was taken prisoner and sent as a captive to Niall at Tara. Naithí managed to escape, and reassembled his father's army and, with a surprise attack, defeated Brión in a second battle at Damhchluain. Brión fled, but was pursued and slain, after which Niall released the captive Fiachra and installed him as king of the province of Connacht. Fiachra was later slain as he campaigned against Munster, and in savage revenge, 50 Munster hostages were buried alive with his corpse at Forrach (Farrow, near Mullingar, County Westmeath). Naithí became king in his place.

Naithí is also said to have engaged in predatory activities outside of Ireland, but if there is any historical basis to the claim, such activities would hardly have consisted of more than brief raids on the west coast of Britain. One long list given of his battles included some fought abroad. Referred to are engagements in Scotland – such as at Sraith Chluaidhe (Strathclyde) and Magh Circinn (Kincardine) – and also mentioned is an expedition across Muir nIocht (the English Channel) to Alpa (the Alps). The latter location probably resulted from a misinterpretation of Alba (which meant Scotland, or in the earlier literature all of Britain).

A medieval text describes how the king of Thrace, called Formenus – who was on a Christian pilgrimage – had a great tower built in the Alps. Naithí and his men knocked down this tower, and as a result

Formenus prayed to God against him. When Naithí was inspecting the area, a thunderbolt from heaven struck and killed him. On their way back to Ireland with the corpse, his followers fought and won nine further battles. He was buried at Carn Fraoich, near the royal Connacht centre, Cruachain (Rathcroghan, County Roscommon). An upright red pillar-stone (the *Lia Dhearg*) is still pointed out there as his monument, and it became the site of the inauguration of the kings of Connacht. The encounter of Naithí in the Alps with Formenus seems to have been invented by some medieval writer who had come across a reference to the fifth-century Frankish king Faramund.

A text written as late as the seventeenth century gives an extended account of Naithí's great campaign overseas. According to this, his DRUID Doghra prophesied for him at the feast of Samhain (November – *see* TIME) that he would conquer Scotland, and he accordingly set sail for that country at the head of a great army. In a bloody battle at Magh an Chairche (an obvious derivation from the Magh Circinn of earlier tradition), he defeated the Scottish king, called Fearadhach Fionn, and then proceeded through Britain and France, receiving submission from all and sundry, until his sudden demise in the Alps.

Medieval tradition regarded Naithí as residing at the hill called Mullach Rua (Mullaroe, in the parish of Skreen, County Sligo). It was claimed that the cairn on top of that hill was erected over his wife Ruadh, who died in giving birth to one of his sons, Fiachra Ealgach. An earlier wife, Eithne, was the mother of Naithí's more famous son, AILILL MOLT.

T.F. O'Rahilly (1946), 211–15; RIA Dictionary, s.v. 'Daithi'; O'Grady, 1 (1892), 333–4; V. Banatenau in ZCP, 18, 160–88; W. Stokes in Irische Texte, 3, 352–3, 418; Gwynn (1906), 40–1; J. Vendryes in Melanges à Ferdinand Lot (1925), 743–67; O'Donovan (1844), 17–27; O'Donovan & O'Conor Don (1891), 85; Dinneen, 2 (1908), 412–13; O'Curry (1873), 284–8. See also CONALL GULBAN.

Napoleon I *(1769–1821)* The Irish folk showed great interest in the personality and deeds of the celebrated French general and emperor, Napoleon Bonaparte.

Although he never set foot in Ireland, Napoleon had some interesting Irish connections – two of his brothers were married to Irish women, and his niece married an Irishman. It was said, indeed, that in his youth, Napoleon had been saved from drowning by a clerical student from Wexford, Edmund Redmond. Irish revolutionary leaders – including Theobald Wolfe Tone and Robert Emmet – met him personally and tried to convince him to send an army to Ireland to help break English imperial power in the country. In this they were disappointed, though Irish songs continued to show affection for the man they called 'Bona' and 'the Green Linnet'.

Napoleon was mentioned in Irish folklore as a great general who showed concern for his soldiers. One simple little LEGEND, for instance, told of how after the Battle of Austerlitz, a sentry fell asleep at night and woke to find the emperor substituting for him at his post. Napoleon spoke kindly to him, advising him to be more careful, for 'the enemy might come upon us unexpectedly and destroy us all!' Another legend told of how, on the disastrous retreat from Moscow, some soldiers were vainly trying to release an army cart from a snowdrift. One of them remarked bitterly: 'Where is our great Napoleon now?' and quickly received a reply from his companion: 'He is right here beside you!'

An interesting development is the representation of Napoleon as an insightful observer on the realities of life. Stories of this nature seem to have been spread by clergy engaged in education. The school atmosphere is stressed in accounts of how an old teacher remarked of the young Napoleon that he would one day do great things; and how the youngster himself once quietened bullies, who were mocking his name, by saying that 'the world will one day know my name well!' On a more philosophical note, Napoleon is said to have remarked that the day of his First Communion – long before he enjoyed worldly success – was the happiest in his life. When he was being crowned emperor, the Pope is said to have remarked that the cheering of the crowd for him was very impressive, but Napoleon replied that 'they would cheer twice as loudly if I were going to the guillotine!' When he and the Pope began to argue, folklore claims that Napoleon threatened that he would destroy the Church, but the Pope answered: 'You will not, for the clergy themselves have been trying to do so for a long time and have never succeeded!'

Napoleon was notoriously supersti- tious, a fact remembered in Irish folk tra- dition. The belief that he continually tried to foretell the future is probably an echo of his great foresight in military strategy, but a more direct allusion is made in one folk legend which has him seeking prophe- cies from a wise old HAG. She told him that he would be defeated by means of fire and rock, the fire being interpreted to mean his final battle at Waterloo and rock the island of St Helena where he died in forced exile.

It was believed in Ireland that Napoleon was betrayed by one of his offi- cers who had been given a large block of gold by the English as a bribe. Realising this at Waterloo, he remarked to the offi- cer: 'You have sold me, as you would sell a bullock at the market!' The tradition that grew up in France that Napoleon had been replaced by a lookalike at St Helena and that he had not really died was widespread for a while. A French traveller in Ireland around 1840 was told by a turf-cutter that Napoleon was not dead at all; and that it was not really his corpse, but that of one of his generals that had received a funeral in Paris. Napoleon was still alive, hidden in an impenetrable place, from which he would return at the proper time. This is a version of a widespread folklore MOTIF concerning lost leaders (see DESMOND, EARL OF).

The tradition that Napoleon's famous charger, Marengo, was bought in Ireland is mistaken, for that stallion was an Arabian horse acquired in Egypt.

R. Hayes in Studies, 3 (1946), 63–74; Kavanagh (1913), 303; P. Sébillot in Revue des Traditions Populaires, 6, 391–2; Gregory (1926), 91–3; Zimmermann (1967), 184–92; D. Ó hÓgáin in Anois, 1–2/5/1993, 10–11; IFC 11:243–4, 182:492, 686:251, 1018:14–16, 1264:558, S797:234.

Neara Character in the ULSTER CYCLE, who entered the otherworld at Cruachain (Rathcroghan, County Roscommon). His name (earlier, Nera), seems to have meant 'valiant'. It may have been a survival of some early Celtic mythical lore, as it is cognate with that of the Gaulish deity Nerios. In what may also be an echo of early mythology, the name of Neara's father is given as NUADHU.

The text concerning Neara belongs to the tenth century. According to it, queen MEADHBH and her husband Ailill mac Máta were feasting in their court at Cruachain at Samhain (November) when Ailill promised to give his gold-hilted sword to the man who would go and place a withe on the leg of a captive who had been hanged on the preceding day. Neara under- took to do that, but the dead man spoke to him and asked to be carried on his back to where he could drink. Neara consented to this, but the captive refused to enter any house where a fire had not been raked or wetted or cleaned, and eventually a drink was found for him in a suitable house. When returning home, Neara saw Meadhbh's fortress being attacked and set on fire. He followed the attackers into the otherworld dwelling of Cruachain, where he was given a wife. She explained that the fire he had seen was an illusion, but that it was planned for the next November, and she told him to warn Meadhbh and Ailill. He did this, and the Connacht warriors then attacked and plundered the other- world dwelling.

A year later, Neara returned to his wife. The otherworld inhabitants did not realise that it was Neara who had brought the attack on them, so he was welcomed, and his wife gave him a herd of cattle. However, his wife, unknown to him, had one heifer brought to be bulled by the great DONN CUAILNGE. When the heifer was returned, it dropped a bull-calf, which Neara took with him from the otherworld dwelling a year later. When Fearghus mac Róich heard the young bull bellowing, he prophesied that it would bring disaster. It fought Ailill's white bull, the Finnbheannach, and was slain – whereupon Neara's otherworld wife

372

and Meadhbh's herdsman both remarked that if the young bull's sire were present the result would have been different. Meadhbh then swore that she would not rest until she saw these two great bulls fighting. Thus the story is presented as a presage of the great cattle-raid of Cooley, the central story of the Ulster Cycle. Neara returned with his wife to the otherworld dwelling and remained there.

The corpse that speaks and gives information when carried on a man's back seems to have been a popular MOTIF in ancient times. It was also used by a medieval Irish cleric and made the basis for a quite different narrative, which became very popular in folklore (*see* RELIGIOUS TALES, type 764). The writer would have us believe that Neara's otherworld wife was the MÓR-RÍOGHAIN; and the episode of the bull-calf sired by the Donn Cuailnge is obviously based on a story concerning that goddess (q.v.).

K. Meyer in *RC*, 10, 212–28; S. Ó Duilearga in Ryan (1940), 522–34; Rees & Rees (1961), 298–303; Olmsted (1994), 210–11, 400.

Néidhe mac Adhna (earlier, *Néde mac Adnai*)

A POET much fictionalised in the early literature. His name was a rare one, probably a variant of NÉT, and *mac Adhna* meant 'son of the old man'.

He is described as engaging in a duel in rhetoric with the elder FEIRCHEIRDNE for the office of chief-poet of Ireland. His father Adhna had held that post, but in the contest Néidhe was defeated and accepted Feircheirdne as his superior. Another text describes a clash between him and his uncle Caier, KING of Connacht. We read that Caier had no son and that he therefore adopted Néidhe as his own. The young man, however, plotted with Caier's wife against the king. She informed him that there was a magical prohibition (*GEIS*) on Caier not to give away a special knife he had. Néidhe accordingly asked him for the knife, and when this was refused satirised the king so that three blisters of shame arose on his face. This blemish disqualified Caier from holding the KINGSHIP, and so he went south to Dún Chearmna (near Kinsale, County Cork)

to hide his shame. Néidhe became king of Connacht in his stead, but after a year the poet repented of his action and went to visit his uncle. On seeing him, Caier died from shame. The slab underneath him began to heat and burst into flame, and a piece of it flew up and struck Néidhe in the eye, killing him.

Stokes, *CTS* (1905); Meyer (1912), 58–60.

Neimheadh

Mythical or fictional leader of an imagined ancient settlement in Ireland. The word *neimheadh* (earlier, *nemed*, from Celtic *nemeton*) was used in the sense of a sacred place or sacred person, and thus would have been a designation of a DRUID.

Neimheadh, it was claimed, arrived 30 years after the people of PARTHALÁN had been wiped out by plague. He had a fleet of numerous ships, but on their journey they came across a tower of gold on the sea. Greedy for the gold, they went to take that tower, but the sea rose in a torrent and swept them all away but for one ship. This was Neimheadh's own, and on board with him were his wife Macha and his four sons and their wives, together with twenty others. After a year and a half wandering, they landed in Ireland. Neimheadh defeated the sea pirates, the FOMHÓIRE, in three battles, and he had four scions of that race build the fortress of Rath Chinneich (somewhere in south Armagh). This they did in one day, and Neimheadh then slew them lest they build a better fortress for somebody else. We read that he himself died from PLAGUE on the island of Ard Neimhidh (Great Island, Cork Harbour).

After his death, the Fomhóire oppressed his people, imposing a heavy tribute on them, and eventually Neimheadh's people rebelled and attacked the Fomhóire stronghold of Tor-Inis (Tory Island, off the Donegal coast). They captured the tower (*tor*) there, but Fomhóire reinforcements arrived and the sea went into flood. So frightful was the slaughter that only one ship of Neimheadh's people managed to get away. On board were 30 warriors, and they decided to leave Ireland completely. This account parallels their earlier effort to seize a tower at sea, and both episodes are an echo of the primordial clash between the Tuatha Dé Danann and the Fomhóire (*see* MYTHOLOGICAL CYCLE).

In handling elements of ancient myth, the medieval scholars were more concerned with devising a chronological pseudo-history than with avoiding duplication in narrative. These scholars therefore claimed that later groups of settlers in Ireland were descended from Neimheadh's people. We read that one grandson of Neimheadh, called Semeon, went to Greece, where his progeny became the FIR BOLG. Another grandson, Beothach, died of plague in Ireland, but his progeny went into the northern parts of the world and became the TUATHA DÉ DANANN. A son of Neimheadh, Fearghus Leathdhearg, went to Britain and – the pseudo-historians claimed – from him and his son Briotan Maol were descended the Britonic people. Neimheadh himself is probably drawn from genuine tradition, the word *nemed* having been personalised, and a different story has a personage of the same name being defeated in battle by three sons of CONAIRE MAC MOGHA LÁMHA and being buried also on the island of Ard Neimhidh. The fact that the name MACHA is given to Neimheadh's wife, however, suggests that his personality as we have it does not pre-date the medieval literature.

RIA Dictionary, s.v. '*neimed*'; Macalister (1939), 249 & (1940), 115–206; T.F. O'Rahilly (1946), 75–6; A.G. Van Hamel in *ZCP, 10*, 155–60, 182–6.

Nét Fictional figure in the genealogy of the FOMHÓIRE. His shadowy character grew out of speculation on the word *nia* or *niadh* (from Celtic *netos*, meaning 'leader'), which was well known as a rhetorical term for a champion in early Irish literature. A genitive form of that word was written *néit*, thus giving rise to the idea of an ancient personage called Nét.

A sobriquet of the Ulster hero CORMAC CONN LOINGEAS was Nia an Chairn, meaning 'the champion of the cairn', the cairn in question being in the Fews Mountains (County Armagh). This reflects the custom of erecting a cairn upon the burial of a hero. Similarly, the extreme south-west point of Ireland (Mizen Head, County Cork) was called Carn uí Néit (the Cairn of the Grandson of the Champion), in memory of some forgotten worthy of yore. The pseudo-historians, however, attributed that place name to the fanciful burial there of the Fomhóire leader BREAS, who was described as a grandson of Nét. This was obviously an invention, and other different genealogies were given for Breas. Similarly, BALAR was sometimes described as a grandson of Nét, and his death was also claimed to have taken place at Carn uí Néit (modern, Carn Uí Néid).

A ninth-century glossary describes Nét as 'a GOD of battle', and he was said to have had as wives Neamhain and Fea, both alter-egos of the battle-goddess BADHB. He was also said to have resided at the fortress of Aileach (in north Donegal), and to have died in a conflagration there – by which we may assume that there was a story of him being besieged at that place by the foes of the Fomhóire, the TUATHA DÉ DANANN. Such lore probably developed from the fact that the fortress was called Aileach Néid (the Stone Structure of the Warrior).

Walde & Pokorny, *2*(1930), 321; RIA Dictionary, s.v. '*nia*'; Olmsted (1994), 327–8; Gray (1982), 133–6; K. Meyer (1912), 82; Gwynn (1913), 198 & (1924), 102, 114; Macalister (1941), 130, 154, 210 & (1956), 14–15; W. Stokes in *Irische Texte, 3*, 298; E. Hogan (1910), 17, 164.

Ní Mháille, Gráinne Mhaol (*c.1530–1603*) Noblewoman of the Umhall district (Owles, west Mayo) who was famous for her involvement in piracy and intrigue. Her name in English was Grace O'Malley, and her nickname is given in English as 'Granuaile'. This is sometimes claimed to be a corruption of 'Gráinne Umhaill', referring to her native district; but folklore claims that she got the nickname – which indicates that she was *maol* (bald) – by cutting her hair as a youngster so that she would be mistaken for a boy and allowed to sail with a boat-crew. Her father was the chieftain of the O'Malley sept of County Mayo, and she was first married to Dónall Ó Flaithearta of Connemara and later to Sir Richard Burke of Burrishoole on Clew Bay.

During her long and eventful career, Gráinne with her small fleet of ships raided along the west coast of Ireland and even as far away as Scotland. She survived shifting alliances between Irish and English during the Elizabethan wars, was imprisoned for a while in Limerick and Dublin, and even went on a celebrated visit to Queen ELIZABETH in London. Much folklore concerning her, her battles and her raids is still current in Connacht. In this she is represented as a formidable and resourceful woman, as indeed she was. One story describes how she gave birth to a son by her second marriage while on board her ship. A Turkish corsair attacked the ship on the very same day, and word of this was passed on to Gráinne by her men. Cursing their ineffectiveness, she jumped from the bed and went out on deck, carrying a brace of blunderbusses. She began to caper about to attract the attention of the Turks, and then emptied the blunderbusses at them, saying 'Take this from unchurched hands!' Being thus given the advantage, her men triumphed over the foe.

The son born to her on that occasion was Theobald Burke, known as *Tiobóid na Long* (Theobald of the Ships). She was determined that he should grow up as brave a fighter as herself, and it is said that when he once showed a lack of courage, she remarked to him rather crudely: 'Are you trying to hide in my backside, where you came from?' Her efforts were successful, and Theobald grew up to be a very able soldier. He was remembered in tradition as an adept at single combat, and as a powerful leader who could be unscrupulous at times.

When married to Richard Burke, Gráinne operated from two strongholds on Clew Bay, one of them the castle of Carraig an Chabhlaigh (Fleetwood) on the mainland and the other being Clare Island. Various attempts to capture these strongholds by both English and rival Irish failed, and in July 1593 she sailed around the south coast of Ireland and of England and docked at London in order to submit to

Elizabeth. Little detail survives of the actual interview between the two strong-willed women, but Gráinne impressed Elizabeth, who confirmed her in her lands and issued restraining orders on her major English enemy in Connacht, Sir Richard Bingham. Tradition fills in the gaps in detail by claiming that Gráinne entered the presence of Elizabeth barefoot and dressed as a Gaelic chieftain. Elizabeth held her hand high, but Gráinne was taller and held her hand higher still, and the two conversed in Latin. A lady-in-waiting noticed that Gráinne required a handkerchief, and one of cambric and lace was given to her. Having used it, Gráinne threw the fine handkerchief into the fire, and when Elizabeth remarked that she should have put it in her pocket, Gráinne expressed dismay at such a lack of cleanliness.

It is said that on her return journey from England, Gráinne put in to port at Howth, County Dublin. However, she found the gates of Howth Castle closed before her, as the lord, Christopher St Lawrence, was at dinner and would not be disturbed. In a fit of pique, Gráinne seized the son of St Lawrence and took him captive with her to Connacht. She did not release him until Lord Howth went to her dwelling in Connacht and promised that his castle would henceforth be open to anyone who desired hospitality, an extra plate always being laid on his table for this purpose. There is a reference to such an event in the Annals for the fifteenth century, when the head of the Burkes of Connacht kidnapped the son of Lord Howth and released him for a nominal ransom, 'to keep the door of his court open at dinner time'. The story obviously was switched to Gráinne because she was the wife of a successor of that Burke and because of her swashbuckling reputation.

Gráinne was also said to have had a great taste for gambling, her dwelling being a favourite resort for card-players and those addicted to dice. Because of her dramatic stature, she came to be regarded in literary tradition as a symbol of the Irish spirit, and in the 1740s the Munster POET Seán Clarách Mac Domhnaill used her name for the metaphorical lady Ireland. In subsequent patriotic poetry in both Irish and English, 'Gráinne Mhaol' or 'Granuaile' is a frequent synonym for the country.

Chambers (1979); OSL: Mayo, *1* (1838), 2–12 & *2*, 249–63; Ó Foghludha (1933), 85–7; IFC Index.

Ní Mhathúna, Máire Rua *(c.1615–86)* Noblewoman of County Clare (earlier written Máire Ruadh Ní Mhathghamhna), daughter of the chieftain of the O'Mahony sept in that area. She was married three times and was an astute protector of her lands in the district of Leamaneh, which she inherited from her second and best-known husband, Conchúr Ó Briain. In the period 1661–63 she was put on trial for the murder twenty years earlier of a servant of an English settler, whose livestock she had been raiding, but she was not convicted.

She married her first husband Dónall Ó Nialláin, who had extensive lands at Dysert O'Dea, but he died within five years, leaving her with four children. She married again eight months later – this time Conchúr, for whom she gave birth to at least five more children. He was killed fighting against the Cromwellians in 1651. Two years later, she married a Cromwellian officer called John Cooper. In folklore, she and her second husband have a sinister reputation which does not seem to accord with their actual characters. It is said that they waylaid and robbed travellers who passed by their castle at Leamaneh, and that they did not hesitate to hang from the castle walls anybody who fell foul of them. Máire herself, with her flaming red hair, must have been quite a memorable person, but folklore is unfair to her when it claims that she had a dozen husbands. So lustful was she, we are told, that her maid servants were in reality male lovers in disguise. It can hardly be doubted that such lore has been attached to her from similar notions concerning Queen ELIZABETH I.

One very popular LEGEND of her, however, is a special development in her own context. We are told that she had in the castle a ferocious stallion that nobody could ride, and that she was wont to challenge wayfarers to mount the animal and in this way bring about their death. Once, a young man from the Burren, called Traolach Ó Lochlainn, took up the challenge. When he mounted the HORSE, it tore savagely from its stable and raced from the castle towards the precipitous Cliffs of Moher nearby. Reaching these cliffs, Traolach strained at the reins and for a moment horse and rider stood poised over the sea far below. The stallion's front feet made a strong impression on the cliff face, but the rider pulled him away and they raced back towards the castle. Seeing them coming, Máire Rua ordered her servants to close a huge iron gate in their path. Traolach was pulling so hard on the reins that he broke the stallion's jaw as it jumped the gate, and it crashed and was killed, but the rider survived, much to the chagrin of the malicious Máire Rua. The place name Leamaneh is in Irish *Léim an Eich*, meaning 'the stallion's leap', and there can be little doubt but that an old local tradition connected with the place name became confused with the memory of Máire Rua, thus giving rise to the story.

M. MacNeill (1990); T.J. Westropp in *Folk-Lore, 24*, 494–6; IFC Index.

Niadh Seaghamhain A mythical character in early Irish literature. His name was variously written 'Niad Segamain' and 'Nia Segamain'. It was a very ancient one – the first element derives from the Celtic *Netos*, meaning 'leader'; and the second element from Celtic *Segomonos*, meaning 'strong person'. Both elements are attested from Continental Celtic sources, Segomonos being the Celtic equivalent of the Roman war-god Mars in the Alpine region.

The character's name occurs – in the form 'Neta Segamonas' – in OGHAM inscriptions from County Waterford dating to the fifth or sixth century AD. These inscriptions would appear to belong to the EOGHANACHT sept, who claimed Nia Seaghamhain as one of their ancestors, thus showing the distant Celtic origin of some of their tradition. Later genealogists fancifully held that Niadh Seaghamhain had reigned as an early KING of Ireland.

They claimed that he slew in battle the incumbent king Conall Collomrach of the Érainn, and that after seven years, he himself was slain by an Érainn worthy, Éanna Airgtheach. This may contain a faint echo of the struggle for supremacy in Munster between the Érainn and the Eoghanacht, but the sources are confused – Niadh Seaghamhain himself being alternately listed among the Érainn.

Failing to understand the ancient name Segomonos, the etymologists guessed that it was connected with words such as *seg* (milk) and *ségnat* (little deer). Thus we read that during his reign, 'cows and does were milked together every day'. In another attempt to explain his name, a fictional father was invented for him, called Amadair Flidais. This appears to have been developed from an inversion of Seg-amain (understood as 'milk-agent') into Amanair Flidais (agent of flowing [milk]). The conceit was brought further, with an ungrammatical understanding of the father's name to mean Amadair of Flidais, and the consequent claim that a lady called Flidais was the wife of Amadair. Thus was invented the lady FLIODHAIS, imagined mother of Niadh Seaghamhain, a lady who like himself milked CATTLE and deer. *See also* NÉT.

Green (1992), 188; Olmsted (1994), 327–8; Macalister, *1* (1945), 257–60, 290–1 nos. 263, 300 & (1956), 288; McManus (1997), 108–10, 116; O'Brien (1962), 120, 188, 198, 200, 250, 362; Ó Donnchadha (1940), 45–6; F.J. Byrne (1973), 182.

Niall *(usually known as Niall Naoi-Ghiallach)* Historical king of TARA. The exact dates of his reign are unclear. Some sources date it from AD 379–405, but there are reasons to believe that it was somewhat later. The true date of his death seems to have been around AD 454.

His original name must have been Nél, with a meaning such as 'the lustrous', a name appropriate to one destined to be a great leader. The phonemic change to Niall would have occurred some generations after his death. His epithet (earlier, *Noígiallach*) meant literally 'nine-hostaged', indicating that he had hostages from nine septs – these being the nine septs of the AIRGHIALLA, on the northern

flank of his kingdom. In medieval times, however, the epithet was fancifully interpreted to mean that he had a hostage from each of the five provinces of Ireland, as well as one hostage each from the Scots, the Saxons, the Britons and the Franks.

Niall was leader of the predominant CONNACHTA sept and was the first of a long dynasty – known from him as Uí NÉILL – who claimed to be high-kings of Ireland. Niall himself was famous, or infamous, for his raiding abroad, and it may have been on one of his raids that the boy PATRICK was seized in Britain and brought as a captive to Ireland. Niall was stated to be son of Eochu Muighmheadhon, whose sobriquet seems to have meant 'lord of slaves'. That he preceded his son in such activity is strongly suggested by the description of Niall's own mother as a captive girl whom Eochu took in Britain and made his concubine. Her name confirms the authenticity of this tradition, for she is called Caireann (earlier, Cairenn), which is a hibernicisation of the Latin name Carina. Eochu was king of Tara, but that citadel may not have been long in the possession of his sept before him.

The role of Niall in the political history of early Ireland was crucial, and knowledge of his actual biography would therefore be of great value, but the accounts given by the literature of his birth and youth are fanciful. We read that he was the youngest of five sons of Eochu, the other four being born of the king's legal wife, MONGFHIONN. She wished to keep their full inheritance for her own sons, and so she reduced Caireann (also called Caireall) to slavery, compelling her to draw water from a well daily. Caireann's child was born in the open air as she lay beside her pail, and nobody dared care for her for fear of Mongfhionn. Ravens were already gathering above the child when a POET called Torna came by and picked him up. Torna foresaw the future, and he took the infant Niall with him and reared him. When Niall was of age, Torna brought him to Tara. They met Caireann, and she was carrying water as usual. Niall told her to leave that task, and he brought her with him and clothed her in a purple robe.

Mongfhionn called on Eochu to judge between all his five sons. He referred the matter to a druidic smith Síthcheann, who contrived to set fire to a forge in which the young men were working. Each of them emerged carrying some implements, but Niall had the anvil, and Síthcheann therefore proclaimed him the greatest. Then one day, the five were together hunting in the forest, when they came upon a frightfully ugly HAG at a well. She refused water to all but the one who would kiss her cheek. Niall embraced her and lay down with her on the grass. She immediately became a beautiful girl, and explained that she was sovereignty (see KINGSHIP). Under her instructions, he gave water to his brothers on condition that they allow him to place his weapons higher than theirs in Tara. Niall related this at his father's court, and when the brothers publicly accepted his primacy, Síthcheann announced that Niall and his descendants would have dominion over Ireland.

A variant account has Mongfhionn dreaming that her four sons were fighting – Brión in the form of a lion, Fiachra a greyhound, Ailill a beagle, and Fearghus a cur. Brión prevailed, and Síthcheann explained this to her as meaning that he would be the greatest of the four. When Eochu died, there was a struggle between these four and Niall for the succession. Seeing that Brión was not prevailing, Mongfhionn persuaded the men of Ireland – by entreaty and by sorcery – to give the kingship to her own brother Criomhthann. When Criomhthann was away on his royal circuit, however, Mongfhionn's four sons divided the kingdom amongst them, and on his return Mongfhionn proffered a poisoned drink to him. He compelled her to quaff first, which she did, and both of them died. Notwithstanding all her scheming, however, Niall was chosen as king. Brión became his champion in battle, seizing hostages and levying tribute for him. These accounts of Niall's youth show clearly the influence of popular narrative. As is usual in folklore, the socially weakest man triumphs over his fellows, and the oral MOTIF

of disenchantment by a kiss is deftly used in conjunction with the Irish literary theme of the GODDESS of sovereignty.

The folklore and romantic elements predominate in the literature concerning Niall, and there is little by way of description of his actual reign or of his conquests. He is said to have gone to Letha (i.e. Brittany) and to Italy 'to seek a kingdom', but his real achievements abroad amounted to little more than raids on the west coast of Britain. His achievements at home were more significant, though these have been subsumed in accounts of three fictional personages who are each called COLLA. These Collas, it was claimed, were cousins of Niall's grandfather Muireadhach Tíreach, and the tradition was that it was they who destroyed the northern citadel of Eamhain Mhacha (see ULSTER CYCLE) and seized the adjacent south Ulster territory of AIRGHIALLA. All the indications are that these actions were in fact carried out by Niall and his sons in the fifth century. Although he was reputed to be the highking of Ireland, it is unlikely that Niall's power extended far into the south of the country, but this did not prevent the medieval writers from claiming that he gained the overlordship of Munster also, by a speedy invasion of that province.

The death of Niall was the subject of a saga that stressed his adventures overseas. We read that one Eochu, son of the LAIGHIN (Leinster) king Éanna Cinsealach, was refused food at the house of Niall's poet Laidcheann. In anger, Eochu burned the poet's house and slew his son. Laidcheann satirised Leinster for this, so that that province was deprived of all growth and foliage for a year. Niall in retaliation invaded Leinster, and would not desist until Eochu was promised to him as a hostage. The Leinstermen tied Eochu to a stone pillar at Ath Fhadat (Ahade, County Carlow), and Niall sent a troop of nine men to take him. When these men attempted to slay him, however, Eochu broke loose and wielded his chain against them. Some Leinstermen slew the nine and, as a result, Niall came again into the province. Eochu was surrendered to him, but when Laidcheann began again to satirise Leinster, the hostage slew the poet with a stone-throw. Eochu was then banished from Ireland for as long as Niall lived. Soon after this, Niall was on a campaign in Scotland and was invited to the dwelling of the king of that country who wished to submit to him. While sojourning there in the company of Pictish bards, he fell victim to an arrow shot at him by the exiled Eochu. A variant account locates the episode in the Alps, claiming that Niall had advanced that far in his conquests and that Eochu shot the arrow at him from long range across a valley. The Alps have clearly been substituted here for Alba, which meant Scotland or, in the early literature, the whole island of Britain.

Yet another tradition was that Niall was slain by Eochu in the English Channel (Muir nIocht) on the last of seven great expeditions abroad. Niall's men brought his body back to Ireland, triumphing in seven battles 'before his face after his death'. One account has them raising the body of the king aloft before the enemy in battle so as to ensure victory. He was buried at Ochann (Faughan hill, near Navan, County Meath) and, on hearing news of the great king's demise, his faithful poet Torna fell dead from grief. Although these accounts date from several centuries after Niall's time, there is no special reason to reject their testimony that Niall was slain by a Leinster exile while raiding in Britain.

FLORUIT: Carney (1973), 7–13.

NAME: Pokorny (1959), 760; T.F. O'Rahilly (1946), 232–3; McCone (1996), 134.

BIRTH AND YOUTH: K. Meyer in *Otia Merseiana*, 2, 75–6; W. Stokes in *RC*, 24, 190–207; O'Grady, 1 (1892), 326–36; M. Joynt in *Ériu*, 4, 91–111; Ó Muraíle, 2 (2003), 262–4.

DISENCHANTMENT BY KISS: S. Thompson (1955–58), motif D735. *See also* same motif in Cross (1952).

REIGN: T.F. O'Rahilly (1946), 222–5; P. Breathnach in *Irisleabhar Muighe Nuadhat* (1932), 43–52 & (1933), 34–41; McKenna, 1 (1918), 4–11.

DEATH: Meyer in *Otia Merseiana*, 2, 84–92 & *ACL*, 3, 323–4; Gwynn (1906), 36–41; Stokes in *RC*, 15, 295–7; O'Brien (1962), 122.

GENERAL: Macalister (1956), 342–9, 528–9; F.J. Byrne (1973), 70–86; T.F. O'Rahilly (1946), 209–34; Ó Caithnia (1984), 118–19.

Niall Frasach *(AD 717–78)* Of the northern branch of the Uí NÉILL, son of FEARGHAL MAC MAOLDÚIN. He was HIGH-KING from the year 763 to 770.

His mother was Fearghal's queen, the daughter of a Midland king, and we read that she was the gentlest woman in Ireland. She was barren for a long time, but conceived after a holy nun had prayed for her. Niall's epithet refers to a shower (*fras*) that fell when he was born at his father's residence at Fathain (Fahan, north Donegal). This was developed in the literature, which claims that, at his birth, a shower of honey fell in Leinster and showers of silver and wheat fell at Fathain. We read that as he grew up, he was remarkably polite and respectful to his father, and in this was a striking contrast to his elder brother AODH ALLÁN. As high-king, he was extremely generous, his subjects were happy, and there was plenty of 'fruit and produce and corn and milk'. One annalistic source has it that a great FAMINE was in progress when he began his reign, and that he along with seven bishops fell on their knees and prayed earnestly to God for their people. Three showers then fell from heaven – one of silver, one of honey, and one of wheat that covered all the fields. This is clearly a development from the earlier MOTIFS.

A story of an unusual kind is told of him in a text of the eleventh to twelfth century. According to this, a young woman carrying a baby came to him at the great assembly of Tailtiu (Teltown, County Meath) as he was watching the horse racing there. She said that the baby was hers, but she did not know who the father was, for she had not been involved with a man. Niall thought for a while, and then enquired if she had dallied with another woman. She said that she had, and the king explained that the other woman must have had intercourse with a man beforehand. In this way, the baby's father was discovered. Just then, a phantom descended from the air amidst the assembly, causing everybody to flee. Niall stood his ground, and the phantom explained to him that he was a priest who had made a contract with a strange craftsman who had offered to do the woodwork on a house for him. The stranger had been a demon, and when he sought as payment that the priest bow to him, the former did so. He had thus unwittingly put himself into the power of demons, who carried him away and kept him for seven years. They had been passing through the air at that very moment, and when the demons felt the effect of the true judgement given by Niall, they had fled in fear, leaving their captive free.

This story shows how the native ideal of true KINGSHIP was combined in the person of Niall with the ideal of Christian holiness. His reputation for piety was high, and another common designation for him was Niall Connail – the epithet here meaning 'prudent' or 'pure-minded'. It seems to have been well deserved, for he resigned the throne in 770 and spent the remainder of his life as a monk at the monastery founded by COLM CILLE in Iona.

O'Donovan (1860), 20–33; W. Stokes in *Irische Texte*, 3, 340–1, 416; Macalister (1956), 384–7, 392–3; D. Murphy (1896), 121; Best & O'Brien, 5 (1967), 1202–3; D. Greene in *Saga och Sed* (1976), 30–7; K. Meyer in *ZCP*, 8, 102–3; Dinneen, 3 (1908), 144–5, 150–3; F.J. Byrne (1973), 156–7.

Niall Glúndubh (*c.AD 870–919*) Of the northern branch of the UÍ NÉILL, and son of the very able HIGH-KING Aodh Fionnliath (+879). His mother was Maolmhuire, daughter of the celebrated Scottish king Cionnaodh mac Ailpín. From 905, Niall shared the kingship of the northern Uí Néill with his brother Domhnall, and he became sole king after Domhnall's death in 915. On the death of the southern Uí Néill high-king Flann Sionna in the following year, Niall became high-king of Ireland. His sobriquet Glúndubh meant 'black-knee', probably a reference to his piety in kneeling at prayer.

Niall was a great warrior, winning many victories against Irish rivals and against the NORSEMEN, whose raiding had increased at the time. He appears to have had a flamboyant personality, and was held in high regard. Soon after he attained to the HIGH-KINGSHIP, he held the colourful royal assembly at Tailtiu (Teltown, County Westmeath), a custom that had fallen into

abeyance for some time. His predecessor in the high-kingship, Flann Sionna, was a far-out relative and leader of the southern Uí Néill, who in fact had married Niall's widowed mother. By a previous marriage, Flann had a daughter called Gormlaith, a celebrated beauty. Tradition held that Gormlaith had once been betrothed to the celibate bishop-king of Munster CORMAC MAC CUILEANNÁIN. She later married the Leinster king Cearbhall mac Muireagáin, and Cormac was slain in the Battle of Bealach Mughna (Ballaghmoon, County Kildare) by the combined forces of Flann Sionna and Cearbhall in 908. Cearbhall was wounded in the battle, and it was said that as Gormlaith nursed her husband back to health, she asked him how Cormac had been killed. Cearbhall gloated over the matter and, when she objected to this, he kicked her, knocking her to the floor. Outraged, she left him and returned to her father, the high-king Flann Sionna. From his kingdom in the north, Niall Glúndubh offered to force Cearbhall to give her restitution, but she insisted on settling the matter peacefully, and Cearbhall agreed to restore her property to her. After Cearbhall's death in 909, she became the wife of Niall. A lost narrative text told of their romance.

Niall was killed in battle against the Norsemen at Cill Moshamhóg (Islandbridge, now in Dublin city). According to the Annals, he engaged in that fatal battle following advice given him by his confessor, Céile Dabhaill, abbot of Bangor, County Down. When Niall was unseated in the battle, the abbot gave him viaticum but refused him a horse on which to escape. Fighting on hopelessly, he was reputedly slain by one Olaf – probably Olaf the White, Norse king of Dublin, who was in fact married to Niall's sister. Following on this tragedy, Gormlaith's brother Donnchadh Donn became highking, and in all likelihood she lived on in the role of a noble lady until her death in 943. Some medieval writers, however, portrayed her as a sad figure, who after Niall's death was reduced to such poverty that she had to beg her meals from her former servants. The story was told how, as an old lady, she dreamed that she saw Niall leaving her chamber. She tried to seize his mantle, but fell upon the sharp bedstead, which pierced her in the breast, and she died soon afterwards from the injury.

One of Niall's sons, Muircheartach, succeeded to the kingship of the northern Uí Néill in 938 and was in turn slain in battle by the Norsemen in 943. He was a brilliant military leader, and was given the nickname *Muircheartach na gCochall Craicinn* (of the leather cloaks) because of the manner in which he clothed his men on a winter expedition through much of Ireland in 941. One fanciful tradition explains the nickname differently, however. According to this, the Leinstermen aided the Norsemen in the Battle of Islandbridge, in which Niall had been killed, and later dishonoured Niall's head by making of it a vessel for chess pieces. Determined on revenge, Muircheartach came with selected men to the palace of the Leinster king at Nás (Naas, County Kildare) and, covered with cow hides, they lay overnight in the field beside the palace. When the Leinster king looked out through his window next morning, he saw the strange 'cows' there and went to hunt them away, but was slain, and Muircheartach had his bones taken away to Ulster to be used in the making of chess pieces. This story is totally unhistorical, as the Leinster king mentioned in it, Cearbhall Mac Muireagán, had predeceased Niall. In the late Middle Ages, several poems were composed and attributed to Gormlaith, lamenting the wonderful kingship of Niall Glúndubh.

The son of Muircheartach, Domhnall, became high-king in 956 and reigned until 980. Being grandson of Niall Glúndubh, he was known as Domhnall ua Néill, and this became accepted as a surname – Ua Néill, later Ó Néill. It is anglicised as O'Neill, and accordingly that surname indicates descent specifically from Niall Glúndubh. The nominative form Ó Néill becomes Uí Néill in the genitive and vocative of the surname. The correct usage in the plural of the surname is Niallaigh (badly rendered in English as 'O'Neills'), with its various inflected forms. This surname is distinct from the ancient septal designation Uí Néill, which designates the much broader lines of descent from the fifth-century NIALL.

GENERAL: W.M. Hennessy & McCarthy, *4* (1887–1901), 286; O'Donovan (1848–51), 560, 572–6, 580–97 & (1860), 150–1, 172–3; Best, Bergin & O'Brien, *1* (1954), 257–9; E. Hogan (1910), 204–5; D. Murphy (1896), 145, 152–5; Dinneen, *3* (1908), 214–16; F.J. Byrne (1973), 163–4; Mac Cana (1980), 103–4.

GORMLAITH'S POEMS: O. Bergin in Bergin & Marstrander (1912), 343–69. *See also* W.A. Trindade in *Études Celtiques*, *23*, 146–50.

MUIRCHEARTACH, SON OF NIALL: O'Donovan (1841).

Noíne A wonder-child described in early Irish texts. His name and lore show signs of being confused with memories of a more comprehensive tradition.

One account, found in the Munster genealogies, describes how a DRUID told a king called DÁIRE mac Deadha that if his daughter gave birth to a son, the king himself would die. Dáire accordingly watched her closely, but despite his efforts she conceived by Mac ind Óc (i.e. AONGHUS). She was pregnant for nine years, and then the son was born. He had long locks and a curly beard, and uttered nine sayings immediately after his birth, following which Dáire died. That Aonghus has been a spontaneous introduction into the account is evidenced by another version that does not mention him but gives a few other details. According to this, Noíne's mother was Finghile, daughter of Dáire mac Deadha, to whom a druid had made the prophecy. One day, the girl was playing on the seashore with the daughter of Noidhean mac Noímhaill, when a phantom came in from the sea and made her pregnant. When her child, called Noindiu, was born, Dáire died. The child gave nine audacious commands to its mother, and then itself died 'for it is not lawful for a son to argue with his mother'. The moralistic twist to the end of the story, and the child's own sudden death, we can take to be an addition, but in general this version seems to be nearer to the original story than the other.

The MOTIF of the sea-spirit as father is found also in the birth-story of MONGÁN, and the location on the beach suggests a connection with seer-lore. It echoes a similar location in the story of MORANN, who also speaks immediately after birth when he is thrown into the water and survives. The motif of the hairy child is found also in the Mongán story, where it seems to be borrowed from lore of FIONN MAC CUMHAILL. The original form of the name must have been Noidhiu (genitive, Noidhean), meaning 'child', and indeed this occurs in the above text as a designation of another character. Because of a misinterpretation of the name, the number of statements uttered by the child was claimed to have been nine (in Old Irish, *noí*). This number, of course, would be imagined as especially relevant to the idea of childbirth, and is stressed by the claim that Noíne was nine years in his mother's womb. In the case of Fionn (q.v.), we read that he was conceived nine hours before his father's death. In fact, there is good reason to suspect that the child Noíne was originally identical with Fionn. In one text, his father's name is given as Umhall, the name also given to Fionn's father in some early sources; and his tyrant grandfather Dáire also occurs as an alternative name of Fionn's grandfather.

Noíne seems to have been an emanation from Fionn – probably a Munster borrowing from Leinster in or about the seventh century AD – and the plot may have been in origin an account of Fionn's birth. All of this would indicate that the Noíne story reflects the lore of Fionn at an early stage of influence from the myth of LUGH, the hero prophesied to kill his tyrant grandfather.

J. Pokorny in ZCP, 12, 331–3; M.E. Dobbs in ZCP, 19, 48–52; R. Thurneysen in ZCP, 20, 192–200; O'Brien (1962), 189, 288; G. Murphy (1953), lxxix.

Normans Descendants of a group of NORSEMEN who had settled in the northern part of France, which area from their name became known as Normandy. The designation is a shortening of the English 'North-man', and when borrowed into Irish was rendered *Normannach*. The Normans took over England in 1066 and, just over 100 years later, their king Henry II sent an expeditionary force to Ireland. In 1169 their full invasion began, and within a year they had conquered most of the land. Despite continuous warfare, however, they never controlled the whole country, and it was left to their English successors to achieve that much later. The invaders of Ireland were in fact a mixture of several nationalities – including Welsh, English and Flemish as well as actual Normans.

Several of the initial leaders of the invasion had Welsh blood in their veins. Particularly evident was the role of Nesta, daughter of the defeated king of Dyfed in Wales, Rhys ap Tewdwr. Through her affair with King Henry I of England, she was the mother of Henry FitzHenry. By her marriage to Gerald of Windsor, she was the mother of William of Carew, of Maurice FitzGerald, of Bishop David of St David's, and of Angharet who married William de Bari. Finally, by another liaison, with Stephen of Cardigan, she was the mother of Robert FitzStephen. Thus some of the most powerful families engaged in the Norman conquest of Ireland – the Carews, FitzGeralds and Barrys – were of the direct line of a Welsh king of Dyfed. It should be added that the Marshalls and Vescis are descended from Raymond le Gros, son of William of Carew, and that the Condons are descended from Raymond's sister; while the Cogans are descended from Robert FitzStephen. The traditional Irish historians were not kind to Nesta, considering her a loose woman and referring to the Norman invaders as her 'brood'.

The event that gave the Normans a pretext to invade Ireland was the displacing of the troublesome Leinster king Diarmaid Mac Murchú by the Irish high-king Ruairí Ó Conchúir. Among Diarmaid's offences was his abduction of the wife of Tiarnán Ó Ruairc, chief of Breffney. This was interpreted by Diarmaid's supporters as a romantic and dashing episode, but by his enemies – and all of subsequent Irish tradition – as a deed carried out through treachery and lust. The Normans came ostensibly to support Diarmaid, who gave his daughter Aoife in marriage to their leader Richard de Clare (nicknamed 'Strongbow').

Diarmaid intended to use the Normans for his own purposes, but he was already being sidelined by them when he died in 1171. Leinster Annals claimed that he died happily and in the grace of God, whereas the other Irish Annals had him dying impenitent and with a terrible rotting disease. With Diarmaid departed, the Norman robber-barons used as their real excuse a document King Henry II claimed to have received from Pope Adrian IV in 1155, and which was affirmed by Pope Alexander III in 1172. This gave Henry and his Normans the right to rule Ireland and to 'reform' the Irish Church. The document, or 'bull', was known by the first word used in it, 'Laudabiliter', and it became a bone of contention for succeeding centuries, several attempts being made to persuade popes to revoke it. It contributed to a frequent theme in Irish poetry of the seventeenth and eighteenth centuries, whereby the oppression of Ireland by English authorities was explained as a punishment inflicted by God due to the sins of the Irish themselves. One curious little account in the medieval literature claims that the reason the Pope issued his bull was that a cardinal sent from Rome to reform the Church in Ireland in 1167 had his HORSES, mules, and DONKEYS stolen by some Irishmen.

The descendants of the Norman invaders, in fact, were not themselves to prove oppressors of Ireland in perpetuity. Gradually the feudal system they introduced became mixed with the native septal system of Ireland, they took to speaking Irish, engaging in Irish pastimes, and employing professional Irish POETS. Thus they were assimilated in varying degrees and at various rates – some so much so that a seventeenth-century native Irish historian could summarise their history as one of becoming 'more Irish than the Irish themselves' (*Hiberniores ipsis Hibernicis*). The most Gaelicised of all the Norman families were the FITZGERALDS, or 'Geraldines', who came to be held in special affection by the native Irish and were very numerous. Also of importance in Irish history were the great Norman lordships held by families with surnames such as Lacy (de Lacy),

Burke (de Burgh), Courcy (de Courcy) and Butler (le Bouteillier). There were several different Norman families known by the old generic name Walsh (le Waleis, meaning a Welshman), and some of these also were very powerful.

Of the many Norman surnames in Ireland, the most numerous include the following (with the Irish versions that developed from them bracketed): FitzGerald (Mac Gearailt); Lacy (de Léis); Burke (de Búrca); Courcy (de Cúrsa); Butler (de Buitléir); Walsh (Breathnach); Wallace (de Bhailís); Barry (de Barra); Roche (de Róiste); Power (de Paor); Carew (Carún); Clare or Cleere (de Cléir); Marshall (de Marascal); de Vesci or Fox (de Bhosca); Barrett (de Baróid in Munster, Bairéad in Connacht); Cantwell (de Cantual); Cantillon (de Cantalúin); Cogan (de Cógan); Condon (Condún); Tyrrell (Tirial); Grace (de Grás); Tobin (Tóibín); Eustace (Iústás); Hoare (de hÓra); Costello (Mac Oistealbha); Plunkett (Pluincéad); Purcell (Puirséal); Dillon (Diolún); Nugent (Nuinseann); Talbot (Talbóid); Stapleton (Galldubh: 'dark foreigner'); Bermingham (Mac Fheorais: 'son of Peter [Bermingham]'); White (de Faoite); Browne (de Brún); Blake (de Bláca); Fleming (Pléimeann); Gaskin (Gascón); Mansfield (de Móinbhíol); Mandeville (Mac Uighilín, Maighdiúl); Forristal (de Fuireastal); Ferriter (Feiritéar); Keating (Céitinn); Norris (de Noraidh); Synnott (Sionóid); Devereux (Dearbhrús); Redmond (Réamonn). Many Norman surnames begin with the element Fitz (son) – for example, FitzGibbon (Mac Giobúin); FitzMaurice (Mac Muiris); and FitzHenry (Mac Éinrí). So prestigious did that become that two native Irish families borrowed it into the anglicised versions of their surnames – Mac Giolla Phádraig (Fitzpatrick) of the OSRAIGHE and Mac Giolla Cholmóg (Fitzdermot) of the LAIGHIN.

DIARMAID: Scott & Martin (1978), 24–75; Orpen (1892); W. Stokes in *RC*, *18*, 51–9, 151–76; Best, Bergin & O'Brien (1954), 184; O'Donovan, *2* (1848–51), 1182–3.

DIVINE RETRIBUTION: Ó Buachalla (1996), 120–5.

STEALING FROM CARDINAL: O. Bergin in *Ériu*, *7*, 244.

NORMAN FAMILIES: Ó Muraíle, *3* (2003), 66–189, 722–71.

Norsemen *(or Vikings)* Scandinavian warriors who raided much of Europe in the early Middle Ages. Groups of them settled in Ireland from the eighth to the eleventh century, and in some scattered instances later still. The usual term for them in Irish is *Lochlannaigh*, as Scandinavia is known as Lochlainn (probably an Irish corruption of Rogaland, the area of Norway from which many of them came). In Irish literature they were also referred to as *Danair* (Danes) because some of them came from Denmark, and in later Hiberno-English speech were invariably remembered as 'the Danes'. The term *Gaill* was also applied to them, and this was a curious mistake. It derived from the Latin word for the Gauls, who – like the Irish – were a Celtic people, whereas the Norsemen were of Germanic rather than Celtic origin.

The greatest Irish victory over the Norsemen was gained by BRIAN BÓRAMHA at the Battle of Clontarf in the year 1014. A few generations later, a text entitled *Cogadh Gaedheal re Gallaibh* was written for his successors, and the description of the Norsemen given in that text became the standard one known to Irish literary and oral tradition. With much justification, the Norse were portrayed in the text as extremely oppressive. A precedent for the image of such raiders was already in Irish tradition, viz. the oppression of the mythical race TUATHA DÉ DANANN by the sea predators known as FOMHÓIRE, and so the Norsemen were cast in the mould of the latter. The Fomhóire imposed heavy taxes on each household of the Tuatha Dé, and the Norsemen were claimed to have done likewise to the Irish. In addition, they were described as ravaging the countryside, devastating churches, and seizing young men and women as slaves. They placed their stewards over every territory, quartered one of their soldiers in each house, and demanded the choice of the country's food produce.

This description in the *Cogadh* text gave rise to folk rationalisations of the oppressive power of the Norsemen and of its consequences. For instance, the text stated that they levied on the Irish each year 'an ounce of silver for every nose', and in folklore this is developed into a claim that they cut off the noses of those Irish people who would not pay taxes to them. A common MOTIF concerning oppressors *(ius primae noctis)* was introduced on a similar basis – we are told that their leaders demanded the right to sleep on the first night with any young bride of an Irishman. The harshness of the oppression became proverbial in expressions like 'as stubborn as a Dane' and 'as cruel as a Dane', and these Norsemen were said to have been rugged and savage in their habits. Adjectives derived from their appellations had similar nuances, such as *danardha* (used in the sense 'fierce') and *gallda* ('strong' or 'rough').

Special emphasis was placed on the colour of their hair, a distinction being made in the literature between fair-haired Norsemen *(fionn-Ghaill)* from Iceland and northern Scandinavia, and dark-haired ones *(dubh-Ghaill)* from Denmark. Both colours were considered extraordinary in medieval Ireland, when the conceit was that brown hair was the true mark of native descent. Similar ideas survive in folklore. Thus whereas red hair was common enough in Ireland since early times, it is popularly supposed to be of Norse origin. Several Irish surnames are of Norse derivation – in some cases such names were borne by actual Norse ancestors, whereas other cases represent an Irish ancestor who bore a borrowed Norse name. According to folk speculation, families with these surnames have certain notable traits, such as strong and rough hair, quick tempers, sharp intelligence, tall stature and proud bearing.

The ENVIRONMENT is fancifully held to contain much evidence from the Norse epoch. Though usually associated with the FAIRIES, many of the *raths* that dot the countryside are claimed to have been constructed by these 'Danes', and prehistoric flints and arrow-heads found near *raths* are in such cases claimed to have been artefacts left by them. The tendency to assimilate the Norsemen to the fairies is instanced also in late medieval literary sources, which have the FIANNA warriors engaged in battle with invading Viking armies as well as in conflict with the otherworld community. Several of the animals, too, were fancifully associated with the Norsemen. The stoats were said to have been their CATS, the foxes their DOGS, and they were reputed to have first brought hens to Ireland. A curious belief, prevalent throughout the country, was that the inhabitants of Scandinavia never abandoned their claims to the land won by the sword in Ireland. According to this, they have preserved from generation to generation charters and legal documents made out to their ancestors, in the hope of one day returning to Ireland and reclaiming their many estates.

In fact, the Norse settlements in Ireland – such as at Dublin, Wexford, Waterford and Limerick – continued to flourish through the Middle Ages until fully assimilated into the native population. Their settlements at Dublin and Cork, indeed, resisted more stoutly than any of the native Irish the invasion by their relatives, the NORMANS, in the later twelfth century. Disregarding all this, one very popular and dramatic LEGEND describes how, after the Battle of Clontarf, only two Norsemen survived – an old man and his son. They were the only two people who knew the secret method the Vikings had of making beer from wild heather. The old man refused to divulge the secret, but when threatened with torture relented. He asked, however, that his son should first be killed, for he could not bear the shame of letting his son see him submit. The son was accordingly put to death, but then the old man refused to give the information and was himself slain. He had tricked the Irish and thus brought the secret to the grave with him. This story parallels a medieval Norse account of the Rhinegold and how the hero Högni preserved the secret of where it is buried. Presumably the plot passed into Irish tradition of the Norsemen through that story being overheard, and partly understood, by some Irish person present at a Viking drinking feast where the beer flowed freely. Perhaps the same ultimate source gave rise to the common idea that TREASURE was hidden somewhere in Ireland by the Norsemen, but that it has never been found.

Dubhghall (dark-haired foreigner) became common as a personal name and is the basis of the surname Ó Dubhghaill (modern Ó Dúill, anglicised as 'Doyle'), which in fact is borne by many unrelated families, some of native Irish and some of Norse ancestry. There are several examples of the spread of Norse names through fashion or intermarriage. A senior branch of the northern UÍ NÉILL took on the surname Mac Lochlainn, while a sept of their southern Uí Néill relatives took the term Viking itself as a surname, viz. Ó hUiginn (Higgins). Some of the EOGHANACHT, too, took on Norse names – such as the surnames Mac Amhlaoibh (son of Olaf: MacAuliffe), and Ó Siochrú (grandson of Sigfrith: Sugrue), an offshoot of the O'Sullivans. Other Gaelic families who took Norse or Norse-sounding surnames include Ó Lochlainn (O'Loughlin); Mac Raghnaill (from Ragnall: Reynolds), Mac Mánais (from Magnus: McManus); Ó Bruadair (from Brodir: Brouder or Broderick), Ó hÍomhair (from Ivar: Howard), and Mac Íomhair (also from Ivar: MacKeever). More definitely Norse in origin are Mac Shitric (from Sigtrygg: McKittrick); Mac Coitir (from Ottir: Cotter); Ó Gofraidh (from Gothfrith: Gohery); Ó hArailt (Harald). Also of Norse derivation (with gaelicised versions bracketed) are Sweetman (Suaiteamán); Gould (Gúld); Coppinger (Coipinséar); Skiddy (Scideach); Trant (Trantach); Hammond (Mac Ámainn); Archbold or Aspel (Mac Aspail).

A. Sommerfelt in JCS, 1, 232; Todd (1867), 40–53; Christiansen (1931) & in Lochlann, 2, 137–64; P. Mac Cana in PICCS, 1, 78–112; Almqvist (1975) & (1991), 65–81; L-M. Smith in Ulster Folklife, 25, 103–12; L. Mac Mathúna in A. Ó Corráin (ed.) (2001), 65–82; Ó Muraíle, 3 (2003), 714–23.

Nuadhu Mythical KING of the TUATHA DÉ DANANN. The meaning of the name (earlier, Nuadu) is unclear, but the most likely interpretation would be 'catcher'. A cognate in British Celtic was the name of the deity Nodons, to whom a temple was dedicated at Lydney in Gloucestershire. Several representations of DOGS were found at the temple, which factor suggests that he was envisaged as a hunter, but in particular there was the figure of a man in the act of hooking a FISH.

In early Irish tradition, Nuadhu was associated with the Boyne, being married to the eponymous GODDESS of the river, BÓINN. He was displaced through a trick from his residence at Brugh na Bóinne (the Newgrange tumulus) by the Mac Óg (i.e. AONGHUS), and went to live at the nearby place called Sídh Chleitigh. Since the Mac Óg is probably cognate with the British Celtic deity Maponos, it may well be that lore of the two deities reached Ireland at the same time. In the first Battle of Moytirra (see MYTHOLOGICAL CYCLE), Nuadhu is described as the king of the Tuatha Dé who led them into Ireland, and the myth represented by that battle may have been part of his cult. The tradition concerning this battle has Nuadhu losing an arm and having to resign the kingship because of his blemish. The physician DIAN CÉACHT magically made a silver arm for him, as good and manageable as any other arm and, as a result, he was restored to the kingship. The import of this arm-MOTIF is difficult to decipher, but it must reflect ancient lore.

Similarly ancient must be the idea that the well at the source of the Boyne belonged to him. This well was said to have been in the Sídh (otherworld dwelling) of Nechtan. The origin of the name Nechtan is unclear, but it most probably contains an ancient word for water (necht). At any rate, it was from early times regarded as a pseudonym for Nuadhu, who was also known as Nuadhu Necht. Another well-known pseudonym for him was Elcmar (later, Ealcmhar) which meant 'the envious one'. This designation probably sprang from the triumph of the Mac Óg over him. His association with water parallels the engraving connected with Nodons at Lydney, and there is a striking similarity between the hooked fish at Lydney and a medieval story that connects Nuadhu with a mystical salmon in the River Boyne. This salmon was claimed to have become a source of wisdom from eating nuts that fell from hazel trees at the well of Nechtan. From the salmon, the young FIONN MAC CUMHAILL gained knowledge in a striking account that has him tasting it by chance, whereas it was intended for an elderly seer called Finnéigeas. The full name of this seer is elsewhere given as Nuadhu Finnéigeas, and the story was obviously suggested by the myth of how the youngster called Mac Óg got the dwelling of Newgrange from Nuadhu. The whole development can best be explained by supposing that the image of Nuadhu and his fish was superimposed onto the earlier lore of Fionn's wisdom. Considering that FIONN was a cult figure at the River Boyne from a quite archaic period in the Celtic culture of Ireland, it is likely that the whole lore of Nuadhu was introduced into the region at sometime in the final centuries BC.

A further development from this fusion was to make Nuadhu a maternal ancestor of Fionn. According to the medieval literature, when he came of age, Fionn gained possession by force of Nuadhu's fortress on the hill of Almhu (Allen, County Kildare). Some influence from the LUGH myth is involved here, but the basis must again be the contest between Nuadhu and the Mac Óg. Another result of the Fionn connection was the frequent designation of Nuadhu as Nuadhu Fionn (*Nuadhu Find*), the epithet being interpreted to mean 'white'. We are accordingly told that Nuadhu whitened the walls of his fortress at Almhu with lime. He was regarded by the LAIGHIN (Leinstermen) as their ancestor, and his removal from Sídh Chleitigh to Almhu was clearly part of the process by which the Leinstermen preserved the cult of Fionn when they were expelled from the Boyne Valley by the CONNACHTA. Further development of the Nuadhu lore is evidenced by the designation Nuadhu Fionn Feimhin (referring to the plain of Feimhean, County Tipperary), according to which he was claimed to reside in the cairn on Slievenamon. This resulted from the borrowing of Leinster ideology and lore by the ruling EOGHANACHT sept in Munster during the seventh century, a factor that caused them also to claim descent from Nuadhu. The Eoghanacht were finding common cause with the Leinstermen in their opposition to the growing power of the leading Connachta group, the Uí NÉILL. This accounts for the pseudonym Mugh Nuadhat (servant of Nuadhu) given by the Eoghanacht to their ancestor EOGHAN MÓR, whom they represented as contending with the ancestor of the Connachta, CONN CÉADCHATHACH.

The medieval genealogists made much of the name Nuadhu, duplicating it into various obscure and fictional figures in the pedigrees. One colourful designation used in this way is Nuadhu Fionn Fáil, which may derive from the early Boyne Valley context, for the stone of Fál was the symbol of kingship at TARA. This stone was, according to tradition, brought to Ireland by the Tuatha Dé with Nuadhu as their king. They also brought a great 'sword of Nuadhu', from which no opponent could escape and no wound inflicted by which could be healed. It seems that originally Nuadhu's blemishing involved a sacrifice or an accident with his own weapon. No such account survives, but it may be that some type of curative water symbolism was involved and that his arm was a metonym for a river. Medieval Irish literature had its own rationale for the blemish. According to it, Nuadhu's right arm was severed in combat between Nuadhu and the FIR BOLG warrior Sreang at the first Battle of Moytirra. Other Tuatha Dé warriors intervened to save Nuadhu and he was carried from the field. He and Sreang resumed their combat in the battle next day. He asked Sreang to tie up his own right hand so as to ensure fair terms, but Sreang refused, and in order to prevent fatal injury to Nuadhu, the Tuatha Dé offered the province of Connacht to Sreang and his Fir Bolg. BREAS then became king of the Tuatha Dé, but after seven years, Dian Céacht made the silver arm for Nuadhu and he was restored. Nuadhu gave authority over his army to the newcomer Lugh in the second Battle

of Moytirra, a battle in which he himself was slain by BALAR.

A post-medieval writer (probably fifteenth century) composed an anachronistic romance, the title of which claimed it to be the history of Nuadhu Fionn Feimhin. Here Nuadhu is represented as son of a Gaelic king of Ireland called Giallchadh, who resides at Tara. Giallchadh is a widower, and he marries a young lady of his son's age. Egged on by her malicious maidservant, she makes sexual advances to Nuadhu, but he forcefully rejects her. Then she pretends to Giallchadh that his son has molested her, and Nuadhu has to flee before his father's army. He fights stupendously whenever confronted, and takes refuge on the island of Gola (off the Donegal coast). There he encounters and overcomes a force of NORSEMEN who are coming to invade Ireland, and he sails away from the country. Meanwhile, his father's DRUID discovers the truth about the allegations against him, but on finding the remains of a Norse prince who resembles Nuadhu, it is presumed that the young hero is dead. Nuadhu gains several great victories abroad, and returns to Ireland at the head of a huge force. When he identifies himself, he is welcomed and inherits the kingship. The writer of this text had obviously read an account of the adventures of Eoghan Mór (q.v.), and he combined that with the 'Potiphar's Wife' plot which was quite popular in medieval Irish literature (*see* ROMANTIC TALES, type 870C). This comparatively late literary treatment of Nuadhu is somewhat strained, and Nuadhu was unknown in the post-medieval folklore.

NUADHU: T.F. O'Rahilly (1946), 278–81, 321–3, 467–8, 558; A. Ross (1974), 230–3, 465; J. Carey in *ZCP*, *40*, 1–22; J. Frazer in *Ériu*, *8*, 46–7, 52–9; Gray (1982), 24–7, 32–3, 40–3, 60–1, 130–1; Macalister (1941), 110–25; O'Brien (1962), 21–2, 117, 120, 714–15; K. Meyer in *AIM*, *1*, 30.

NECHTAN: J. Pinault in *Ogam*, *16*, 221–3; P.K. Ford in Larson (1974), 67–74.

LATE ROMANCE: K. Muller-Lisowski in *ZCP*, *13*, 195–250.

Ó Caoimh, Dónall Na Cásca

OUTLAW who flourished in north-west County Cork in the mid-seventeenth century and whose memory survives strongly in the lore of that area. The surname is anglicised as O'Keeffe, and Dónall was of noble stock. His nickname 'na Cásca' (literally, 'of Easter') may refer to his being born at that time of the year. He seems to have been a combatant on the Irish side during the Cromwellian wars, and was among a group of Irish outlaws who continued to harass the English settlers thereafter. He is reported as raiding for cattle in 1653, and continued the struggle on his own until early in the following year, when he surrendered. He was cleared of a murder charge, but was decreed to be transported to the West Indies with a group of other outlaws.

In folklore, he is portrayed as the typical heroic outlaw, being forced into hiding by the English authorities, against whom he carries out repeated cattle-raids from his mountainous retreat near the town of Cullen. He reputedly had another hideout further south, a cave in the side of a huge cliff at Gortmore near Mallow, access to which could only be gained by swimming the River Blackwater and climbing along the rock face. We are told that a lover informed on him to a handsome English army officer. It was arranged that she would induce Dónall to a place where he could be captured, but Dónall, while embracing her, found to his consternation that she had a letter in her bosom from the English officer. In a mad fit of anger, he ran her through immediately with his sword.

Several other accounts were current regarding his escapes and his marvellous horsemanship. For instance, when captured once, he secreted a sword inside his clothes and later used this to cut the ropes that bound him. Several usual MOTIFS concerning OUTLAWS got attached to him. It was claimed, for instance, that he escaped a pursuing band of cavalrymen by having his horse leap over a large precipice overlooking the Blackwater. Alternately, it was said that he made the jump on foot, and remarked to a woman who showed wonder at the feat that a long run had built up his momentum. Another tradition was that a man in his close confidence once invited

him to a meal in his house, at the same time apprising the soldiers of the situation. The man's wife, however, gave Dónall a hint during the meal through making an ambiguous remark. Some accounts claim that the warning came too late, and that as Dónall raced from the house, he was shot down by the soldiers.

Lomas (1905), 526–7, 533–5; E. Walsh in *Dublin Penny Journal, 1* (1833), 372–3 & 4 (1835), 71; Strachan (1904), 101–5; anon in *The Shamrock, 11*, 83; S. Ua Cadhlaigh in *An Claidheamh Soluis,* 6/5/1905, 6; Ó hÓgáin (1985), 179–81, 338; IFC Index.

Ó Conchúir, Cathal Crobhdhearg

(c.*1150–1224*) KING of the province of Connacht from 1201 until his death. He was of the leading family of O'Connor (earlier, Ua Conchubhair) of CONNACHTA descent in the west; and he succeeded his elder half-brother Ruairí, who was the last native high-king of Ireland but was deposed by the NORMAN invaders and reduced to the kingship of the western province of Connacht only. Cathal Crobhdhearg was an astute politician and managed to hold his lands in fealty to, but largely independent of, the kings who ruled from London.

His epithet Crobhdhearg means 'red-handed', and he did indeed have a red birthmark on his left hand, which he ordinarily kept covered with a glove. We know this from an inauguration ode composed for him by his professional POET, Giolla Bríde Beag Mac Con Mí. The poet makes it clear also that this red hand was taken as a messianic sign, and it is obvious that Cathal had borrowed some of the imagery of the prophesied AODH EANGACH and was having it applied to himself. His sept were of the same basic stock as the UÍ NÉILL high-kings, but for a century and a half after the death of BRIAN BÓRAMHA in 1014, the different leading families in Ireland had vied for the HIGH-KINGSHIP. Thus an Uí Néill prophecy in 1167 claimed that Aodh Eangach would destroy Cruachain (Rathcroghan, County Roscommon), the ancient seat of Connacht kingship and Cathal's headquarters. In 1201 Cathal's poet turned this prophecy about, claiming that 'the red-handed one has come to Cruachain, I see the sign on his hand', and went on to describe how Ireland was becoming fruitful again because of this new kingship of Cathal.

A direct echo of Cathal's propaganda is found in an oral tale of his birth and youth that survived until recently in the folklore of the western province. It tells of how the king of Connacht had no son by his wife, but got a girl called Gearróg Ní Mhóráin with child. The queen was very angry at this and employed a HAG skilled in magic to set a charm to prevent the girl from giving birth. The hag tied three intricate knots in a string and gave it to the queen, saying that the baby would not be born until these knots were removed. Gearróg was just beginning to give birth when the third knot was tied, and only the hand of the baby had emerged from its mother. Time passed, and mother and child remained in this critical situation. Then a wise man, who realised what had happened, went to the queen and told her that the girl had given birth. Believing him, the queen cursed the old hag and flung the string into the fire. It was burned, and immediately the child was born. This was Cathal, and his hand was red from the circumstances of his birth.

As he grew up, he and his mother were repeatedly persecuted by the queen, but the clergy took him from one monastery to another to protect him from the hostile agents. Eventually, the circumstances were so bad that he and his mother had to flee the province altogether. They went to Leinster, where the young Cathal supported them both by doing servile work. To conceal his identity, he always wore a glove on his red hand. Yet he could not totally hide his nature, and his fellow labourers often chided him, for as they applied themselves to their tasks, he was wont to be constantly talking of kings and wars and raiding. Then, when he was working at the harvest one day, a crier came by, announcing that the Connacht king was dead, and that the council of the province had proclaimed that the fugitive Cathal, if he was still living, should be enthroned. Hearing this, Cathal threw

away his glove and, revealing his red hand, said: 'Goodbye to the sickle, now for the sword!' He and his mother then returned home and he was installed king. He never forgot how Churchmen had protected him in his youth, and therefore, as king, became a great patron of the monasteries.

This story may be compared to the historical evidence. In actual fact, Cathal's father Toirdhealbhach was married three times and had children by each marriage. Official genealogy has Cathal the son of the second wife Dearbhfhorgaill, who married Toirdhealbhach in 1131 and who died in 1151. This must have been very close to Cathal's birth, and perhaps she died giving birth to him. It might be, however, that Cathal was born of another woman outside wedlock. The high-king Ruairí was a son of Toirdhealbhach's first marriage, and Cathal had to contend with the family of this older stepbrother in order to gain and retain power, a factor that could lie behind the idea of the stepmother's hostility in the folk story. His special patronising of the monasteries is an historical fact, and the Annals tell us that he actually died in the habit of a friar. Such elements, combined with Cathal's own messianic portrayal of his red hand, were at some stage set within a definite plot structure. That structure was derived from the Hercules myth, which was well known to the literati of medieval Ireland. For several generations after his death, the descendants of Cathal contended with their relatives for the Connacht kingship, and it would seem that the composer was one of these descendants, or a supporter of their faction. Eventually, in the second half of the fourteenth century, the line of Cathal Crobhdhearg became undisputed leaders of the sept.

E.C. Quiggin in Bergin & Marstrander (1912), 167–77; O'Donovan & O'Conor Don (1891), 44, 79–147; O'Donovan (1848–51), 210–14; B. Ó Cuiv in Celtica, 19, 31–54 & in Ériu, 34, 157–74; Ó hÓgáin (1985), 127–32, 333–4 & in Léachtaí Cholm Cille, 14, 192–3.

Ó Dálaigh, Cearbhall
A famous romantic POET in Irish folk tradition. From the late medieval period, the family surnamed Ó Dálaigh (anglicised O'Daly) had

as their main profession the composition of poetry, and accordingly branches of them were under the patronage of different nobles throughout the country. Cearbhall was a favourite Christian name among them, and the great poet of that name in folklore is in reality a combination of several different historical characters.

It is apparent that all members of the poetic O'Daly family are descended from a thirteenth-century poet from the Westmeath area called Aonghus Ó Dálaigh, who had seven sons. One of these was Cearbhall Fionn (the epithet meaning 'fair haired'), and he was the ancestor of the branch that settled in County Cork and became professional poets to the powerful MacCarthy sept. All indications are that this branch developed a family LEGEND that served as a kind of trademark for their craft, basing it on the figure of Cearbhall Fionn. Their MacCarthy patrons were sprung from the royal EOGHANACHT dynasty of Munster, and the O'Dalys would have been well acquainted with the myth of that dynasty concerning how CONALL CORC by an unintentional act gained the KINGSHIP of Cashel. They also would have known well the medieval story of how the hero FIONN MAC CUMHAILL got the gift of wisdom and poetry by an unintentional act. On the basis of such stories, and of old metaphors that likened poetry to milk from a mystical cow (see BÓINN), these O'Dalys of Munster invented an account of their own ancestor Cearbhall Fionn. The account became widespread in the folklore of Munster and Connacht and is still told today.

According to the Munster versions, Cearbhall Ó Dálaigh was a little boy who was the servant of a farmer and whose work was to herd the cattle. Each evening when he returned to the farmhouse, he was asked by his master had he seen anything strange during the day. He always replied truthfully that he had not, until one day he saw a cloud descend onto a clump of rushes and a brindle cow went and ate the rushes. When he told this in the evening, he was instructed to bring the first milk of that cow to his master.

Cearbhall did diligently as he was told, but a drop of the milk spilled onto his finger, and thus he got the first taste of it. Immediately a great change came over him. His face became lustrous and every word he spoke was in verse. Realising that the boy had got the drink intended for himself, the farmer ordered him to leave that place, and henceforth Cearbhall was a roving poet. Because of his first tasting the milk, he had not only genius at poetry, but also many kinds of magical powers. Connacht versions of the story claim that a black bull was in the cloud, and that he fertilised the cow, thereby giving the power to her beastings, but this was a later embellishment of the narrative.

It is probable that this family trade-legend was generated in the late fourteenth century, and one can surmise that it was promoted especially by the various poets of the sept who were actually christened Cearbhall. Towards the end of the fifteenth century, a romance text was composed in Connacht that featured a character of the name as its hero. Although no reference is made to the cow story, this character is portrayed as a poet and harpist with extraordinary powers. We read that Fearbhlaidh, daughter of the king of Scotland, saw the handsome young Cearbhall in a dream and fell in love with him. Her maidservant had her magically transported to Ireland to spend some time with him, and he later travelled to Scotland in a bardic company so that they could again meet. He put all the royal court to sleep with his magical music, except himself and Fearbhlaidh, so that he could dally with her. The Scottish king suspected that they were in love, and had Cearbhall thrown into prison, but Fearbhlaidh visited the poet, changed clothes with him, and thus allowed him to escape. Tricked by sorcerers later, Cearbhall forgot his loved one and married another lady, but Fearbhlaidh came magically to the wedding feast and wrote her name in her own blood on his harp. This brought back his memory, and the bride left him, complaining that he did not consummate the marriage. Finally, the Scottish king bribed some Irish visitors to tell Fearbhlaidh that Cearbhall had died in Ireland, and she died from a broken heart. These messengers then went to Ireland and told Cearbhall of her death, whereupon he laid his head on his harp and died. The author of this text identifies his Cearbhall with a poet of that name from north Clare who died in the year 1404, but it is obvious that he has confused several different people and one gets the impression that he had little historical information on any of them.

Another celebrated bearer of the magical name was a poet who lived at Pallis, in north County Wexford, in the early seventeenth century. Some verses survive in which he and a fellow poet humorously discuss the question of whether he is or is not the Cearbhall Ó Dálaigh who excelled at poetry, music, athletics, tricks and *eol amhra in ilgheasaibh* (wondrous knowledge in all studies). This Cearbhall from Wexford seems to have fallen in love with Eleanor Chaomhánach, daughter of Murchadh Caomhánach (Sir Morgan Kavanagh) of Clonmullen Castle in County Carlow. Two love poems concerning her are attributed to him in manuscript, and perhaps he also composed lines of rhythmical prose for her on the pattern of the Fearbhlaidh story. From some such context has sprung a folk narrative that has been well known throughout most of Ireland from at least the eighteenth century.

This narrative – which usually follows on the story of how the archetypal Cearbhall got the gift of poetry from the cow's milk – tells of how he married a young woman. During the wedding festivities, however, he heard mention of a more beautiful lady, and therefore pretended to be a sexual imbecile and did not consummate the marriage. The other lady was Eleanor, and she was at that time preparing for her own betrothal party. He cleverly took up employment with a shoemaker in her locality, and when she wished to have a special pair of shoes made for the occasion, he went to the castle to take her measure. By this means he and she fell in love, but there was no hope that her father would consent to this when a match was being arranged with a wealthy suitor. On the night of the betrothal party, Cearbhall came to the castle disguised as a beggar man, but he soon showed that he was an accomplished gleeman and entertainer. When he was asked to play music for the company, he played a magical air that put all to sleep, and then persuaded Eleanor to elope with him. He turned his horse's shoes backwards so that they could not be tracked, and in this way they made their getaway. Differing endings are given to the story. Some versions claim that they were captured, and that Cearbhall was put on trial, but that by his learning and skill he convinced the court that he was a proper husband for Eleanor. Other versions, however, have both lovers dying tragically in a foreign country; for instance, Cearbhall slips on a spear while performing a trick and Eleanor dies from heartbreak as a result. This theme of an unhappy ending is one of several features that parallel the romance of Cearbhall and Fearbhlaidh, and there can be no doubt that the literary story is in the background of the folk legend.

A love song with a very touching air that was popular since the sixteenth century had the title 'Eibhlín *a Rún*' (Darling Evelyn), it being addressed by its unknown composer to a young woman of that name. Because the first three syllables of the title sound very much like 'Eleanor', and because it suited the context, this song was incorporated into the folklore of Cearbhall and Eleanor Chaomhánach. Other material was added. In Munster, the MOTIF of a love-spot (*ball searc*) was borrowed from another great story of elopement, that concerning DIARMAID UA DUIBHNE and Gráinne, and applied to Cearbhall. This development may have been assisted by speculation as to the poet's name. Cearbhall was an old Irish name (in origin meaning 'war-valour'), but by folk etymology it could be taken to be *car-bhall* (literally, 'love-spot'). Thus we are told that Cearbhall Ó Dálaigh had a love-spot on his breast and that when he came to take Eleanor's measure for the shoes, he allowed his shirt to open so that she would see it and thereby fall in love with him.

The Cearbhall Ó Dálaigh of folklore is a very colourful character. A mixture of verse and prose called the *Seachrán* (wandering) of Cearbhall was current since the eighteenth century, and this seems to have been based on some text composed by the Wexfordman but now lost. Another tradition was that Cearbhall was a great composer of vision poetry and that he communed often with the otherworld. One by-product of this was a series of verses current in west Munster that described an attempt by the otherworld lady CLÍONA to entice him to become her lover, and how he overcame her in verse and thus rebutted her. Because of this tradition of his contact with supernatural powers, Cearbhall was reputed to be quite reckless and fearless, and a story from Limerick describes how he met one night with the otherworld lord DONN and tried to follow the latter into his residence at Knockfierna. Coming to the summit of the mountain, Cearbhall saw the entrance to a cavern there and threw a stone in to discover how deep it was, but the stone was flung back at him, giving him a black eye and knocking him down the slope.

Several humorous anecdotes concerning Cearbhall are common, some of them based on lore of the mythical craftsman, the GOBÁN SAOR. Like the Gobán, he is said to have shown his skill as a sculptor by chiselling the figure of a CAT with two tails while the other workers ate their dinner to which the unfortunate poet had not been invited. Again like the Gobán, he was a master shipbuilder, and could drive nails home by a throw of a hammer. Also a great trickster, a story popular in Connacht claimed that he had once cured a rich man after twelve doctors had failed to do so. In the sick-room, he made 'pills' by putting icing on excrement and then called in the doctors to test these pills. The patient, who had seen what Cearbhall had done, was convulsed with laughter when he saw the learned doctors eating the pills, and the merriment caused an internal boil to burst in his breast and thus he was healed. This anecdote has been borrowed from a nineteenth-century English translation of the adventures of the German trickster, Till Eulenspiegel.

T.F. O'Rahilly in *Proceedings of the Royal Irish Academy, 36*, 100–2; Ó hÓgáin (1982), 215–31, 242–64 & (1985), 234–6, 258–71, 345; Ní Laoire (1986); J.E. Doan in *Éigse, 18*, 1–24 & in *Béaloideas, 50*, 54–89 & *51*, 11–30; Ó Duilearga (1948), 324–9. 440–1; Ryan (1833), 333, 383.

Ó Dónaill, Aodh Balldearg

A messianic name among the O'Donnell (earlier, Ua Domhnaill) sept of Donegal. Prophecies concerning a leader of the sept who would bear this name were current since the twelfth or thirteenth century, and they seem to be an adaptation of the O'Neill lore concerning AODH EANGACH. It was said that this leader would defeat the English oppressors and thereby give the O'Donnells great prestige in the country. The epithet Balldearg means 'red-spotted', the belief being that the prophesied O'Donnell champion would have such a mark on his body.

The O'Donnells were descended from the celebrated CONALL GULBAN and were therefore of the same royal UÍ NÉILL stock as the O'Neills. Another claim to fame was that the celebrated saint COLM CILLE had been of their family, and they carried the reputed psalter of that saint – called the *Cathach* (battler) – in front of their armies when going to war. All of this strengthened their reputation and self-confidence, and facilitated their belief in a great champion of theirs to come. Several of the O'Donnell chieftains were called Aodh, and their POETS could, as occasion permitted, identify any of these with the prophesied Balldearg. The Annals make it clear that a chieftain of the sept who died in 1537 had been identified with Aodh Eangach himself, and a spy reported to the English in 1593 that a prophecy was current that 'when two Hughs succeed each other as O'Donnell the last shall be a monarch of Ireland and banish all foreign conquerors'. The man of the moment in this case was the colourful young chieftain Aodh Rua (Red Hugh), who had been kidnapped on board a ship by the English in Lough Swilly but, after a dramatic escape from Dublin Castle, had succeeded his father (also named Aodh) as chieftain. With the Earl of Dungannon, Aodh Ó Néill, he led a rebellion against the Elizabethans that was very successful for nine years. His friend and biographer, Lughaidh Ó Cléirigh, called him 'a chosen one whom the prophets had foretold long before his birth', and makes it clear that Aodh Rua's supporters made copious use of such prophecies.

The Irish chieftains of the sixteenth century looked to Spain for help, and this was rationalised by the literati through use of the old fiction that Míl of Spain was the ancestor of the Gaelic people. Therefore it was said that that country would not allow the Irish to be destroyed in their hour of need. When a Spanish expeditionary force did come in the winter of 1601, it landed in the extreme south of Ireland, and Aodh Ó Néill and Aodh Rua Ó Dónaill had to travel south in an attempt to relieve it from the English army, which was besieging it at Kinsale, County Cork. The result was a drastic defeat for the Irish forces, after which Aodh Rua went to Spain to seek meaningful help. He died there in the following year, his followers suspecting that he had been poisoned by an English agent.

Several other leading members of the family resorted to Spain, and to the O'Donnells at home in Ireland, the prophecy of the coming Balldearg was now joined specifically to the idea that assistance would come to them from that country. Thus it was claimed that the long-awaited Balldearg would arrive in Ireland at the head of a strong army. In July 1690, four days after the Battle of the Boyne, an accomplished soldier of the family did land at Kinsale. He was also called Aodh Ó Dónaill, and because he had the prophesied red spot on his body had the nickname Balldearg. He immediately attracted a large number of supporters, and fought skilfully. The machinations of King JAMES II and his officers, however, prevented him from being given the command of his Donegal people and, finding himself in an impossible situation, he had

little choice but to surrender to the forces of WILLIAM OF ORANGE. He returned to Spain, and died there in 1704 with the rank of major general.

The belief that a great Balldearg would come from Spain continued, however, and many versions of a story concerning this fanciful figure have been collected from the folklore of Donegal. The story probably had its genesis among oral storytellers in the eighteenth century. We are told that the baby Balldearg was seized by a group of English soldiers who arrived in Donegal by ship. Noticing the red spot on his skin, the commanding officer of these soldiers determined to kill the baby, but when the baby saw the naked sword, it laughed, and the officer could not find it in his heart to do the foul deed. Therefore he took the little Balldearg with him to Dublin and reared him with his own two sons. The three boys grew up together and, when they were in their early teens, stayed out late one starry night and each made a wish. The eldest wished that he had a cow for every star in the sky, the second preferred a HORSE for every star, but Balldearg wished for an army with himself at its head. Hearing this, the officer grew afraid and sent Balldearg north to Derry with a message for a fellow officer. Growing suspicious, Balldearg opened the letter and saw that it bore instructions to kill him, so he boarded a ship at Lough Foyle and sailed to Spain as a stowaway.

When the ship reached its destination he was imprisoned. Horse racing was in progress near the prison, and a fine black horse belonging to the king was bested by another animal. Balldearg said that if he were allowed to ride the horse, the result would be different. He was therefore released and won a great race, after which he was accepted into the king's service. Having been sent to Ireland on a mission to buy horses, he returned to his native place, Portacran, where he learned that his father was dead. Sojourning a while with his mother, he tamed a fierce stallion the family owned and which no man could ride, and then departed again for Spain with this horse. There he fought a fencing duel in place of the son of the Spanish king, and the royal family were so grateful to him that he was made a divisional commander in the army. He was said to be waiting with this army for the opportune time to return to Ireland.

GENERAL: W.M. Hennessy & Kelly (1875), 150–1, 228–31, 352–3; Freeman (1944), 702–3; Burke (1884), 747–8; Meehan (1868), 98–9; Breathnach & Ó Lochlainn, *1–2* (1948); Maxwell (1923), 91–4; Croker (1841), 85–96, 133–7; Haverty (1860), 665–6, 765–6; Gilbert (1892), 151; Maguidhir (1973), 47–53; Ó hÓgáin (1985), 133–41, 334–5 & in *Léachtaí Cholm Cille, 14*, 193.

MOTIFS: CHILD SMILING AT SWORD, TREACHEROUS LETTER: Knott (1936), 3; S. Thompson (1955–58), motif K978.

Ó Dónaill, Mánas (c. *1490–1563*)

Donegal chieftain, scholar and POET (name earlier written Maghnus Ua Domhnaill). He succeeded his father as leader of the O'Donnell sept (*see preceding entry*) in 1537, and five years later compiled his celebrated biography of St COLM CILLE at his castle near Lifford. He was twice married, his second wife being the sister of Gearóid Óg FitzGerald, Earl of KILDARE. He joined with the O'Neills and the Geraldines in a combined effort against the English, but was defeated in battle and had no choice but to surrender to King Henry VIII in 1540. He was displaced as chieftain in 1555 by his son Calbhach, and seven years later died and was buried at the Franciscan monastery of Donegal.

His fame as a scholar survived in the folklore of Donegal, where several stave-anecdotes are related of him. The fact that he was a patron of the Franciscan monastery is reflected in a very popular account of a quarrel he had with these friars. It is said that it was his wont to send a bullock to them regularly, but that on one occasion, he declined to do this. The friars, for their part, used to present him with apples from their orchard, but they also ceased this practice. Mánas then composed a satiric quatrain, claiming that 'these Donegal friars plant their trees so plentifully, but no fruit grows on their tops until meat is applied to their roots'.

Some slightly crude anecdotes have Mánas tilting with the prior of the monastery, Eoghan Ó Dufaigh. It is said

that Mánas made a satiric verse on Ó Dufaigh's huge nose, and that this led to a poetic flyting between them. When the friar cast doubts on the circumstances of Mánas' birth, the chieftain banished him from the area. They later met in Dublin, where Mánas had made a bet concerning his sexual prowess with an English nobleman. When Ó Dufaigh heard of this, he offered to take the chieftain's place in the dark, and he performed so well that the lady – thinking he was Mánas – allowed the Donegal chieftain to be the clear victor. This is in fact a version of an international humorous plot.

Most of the other folk accounts of Mánas involve verbal duels between him and his professional poet, Niall Mac an Bhaird. This Niall was a member of one of the leading poetic families in Ulster. The surname means literally 'son of the bard' and is anglicised as Ward. We are told that Niall was a very clever little boy and that Mánas noticed this and had him educated. When he grew up, Mánas gave a letter to him with directions to deliver it to the chieftain's rent collector. Niall was lazy and, having travelled a short distance, decided to wait until the rent collector came his way. When this happened, the collector read the letter and remarked to the poet that he ought to have come further to meet him, for Mánas had ordered in the letter that all the land travelled that day by Niall should be conferred on him. So the poet got no more than a townland in the Rosses, which thus became known as his letter – *Leitir Mhic an Bhaird*. This is the result of a folk etymology, for the word *leitir* in this place name actually means a hillside.

It appears that Mánas did really confer that land on the poet, and the folk memory is that Niall built a house there from wattles, sods and straw. The poet was quick-witted and sharp-tongued. We are told that Mánas, exasperated by his smart answers, once threatened to hang him 'with the moonlight', to which Niall replied that he preferred that to being hanged with a withy. When Mánas asked what his last request would be, the poet answered 'that you put your head into the noose with me!' On another occasion, Mánas came hurriedly to Niall's house, and so impatient was he that he did not dismount from his horse but rode directly into the doorway. He angrily demanded to know who was within, but received the clever answer from the poet: 'A man and a half and a half-horse!'

HISTORICAL Ó DÓNAILL, Ó DUFAIGH: Mac Giolla Chomhaill (1981), 16–24; P.A. Breatnach in Celtica, 16, 63–72; Ní Mhurchú & Breathnach (2001), 128–31, 136.

FOLKLORE: T.F. O'Rahilly (1921), 29, 77–9; S. Ó Catháin in Béaloideas, 53, 75–86; Ó Dónaill (1952), 100–2; Ó Muirgheasa (1924), 1–25 & in Béaloideas, 3, 58–9; Ó hÓgáin (1982), 6, 418; National Library of Scotland 4309 (new 14876), 45b; IFC Index.

INTERNATIONAL PLOT: S. Thompson (1955–58), motif K1311.

Ó Donnchú, Dónall Na nGeimhleach (c. 1140–78) Legendary

chieftain of the O'Donoghue sept of County Kerry, who is said to haunt, as a benign GHOST, the Killarney lakes. The agnomen *na nGeimhleach* is sometimes taken to mean 'of the fetters', and a fanciful alternative form is *na gcaoil-each*, meaning 'of the slender steeds'. The true meaning would appear to have been 'of the Geimheal people' – i.e. an ancient Ciarraighe sept called Uí Gheimhil who inhabited an area east of Killarney and among whom Dónall may have spent his youth in fosterage.

The largest of the Killarney lakes is called Loch Léin, which name seems to derive from the Clann Leáin, another section of the Ciarraighe who once inhabited the area. In medieval times, however, Loch Léin was fancifully taken to mean the lake of *léan* (disaster). It was claimed that a thriving human settlement was once on the site of the lake, but that a great inundation spread over the entire domain. This was a frequent MOTIF in early Irish lore (*see* EOCHAIDH MAC MAIREADHA). According to popular tradition, a strong well was in the area, and a special cover was kept on it. When this cover was accidentally removed, the water gushed forth and formed the lake. A text of the tenth century develops this further, claiming that a marvellous smith called Lén once lived

there, and on his anvil fashioned many types of wonderful metalwork, from chariots and helmets to vessels and jewellery. The idea of such a presiding figure at the place may originally have sprung from the cult of the GOD of the dead, DONN.

By the end of the Middle Ages, all of this lore had been expropriated by a branch of the EOGHANACHT who had moved into the area. They adopted the surname Ua Donnchadha (later, Ó Donnchú, anglicised as O'Donoghue). Their leader in the mid-twelfth century was one Amhlaoibh, who had several sons, from one of whom the O'Donoghues of Ross descend and from another the O'Donoghues of the Glen. Yet another son was Dónall, an able and ambitious man, who, having lost his land in 1170, returned from banishment to gain the leadership of the whole family. If his agnomen was not due to fosterage by the Uí Gheimhil sept, he may have gained it by living among them when in banishment. He won a memorable victory over the powerful O'Briens of DÁL gCAIS in 1177, but in the following year was slain in battle by a kindred sept, the Moriartys. Dónall had ruled as *rí* (KING) of the whole family from its headquarters at Loch Léin. The Ross branch of the O'Donoghues later regained the area from the Moriartys, and accordingly Dónall in folklore is claimed to have belonged to that branch.

Since the O'Donoghues were buried at Muckross Abbey by the shores of the lake, it was easy to identify the hero-ancestor of that family with the corpus of lore associated with a presiding spirit of the place. Folklore represents him as an ideal chieftain of the past (*see* KINGSHIP), renowned for his hospitality to strangers and his valour in war. A strong and handsome man, he was skilled in combat and a great protector of his people. According to one account, 'his subjects were happy, and fruitful seasons crowned the year with plenty'. The motif of inundation could thus explain how an end came to such a wonderful reign. Sometimes, the disaster is actually attributed to Dónall himself who – it is claimed – was once inebriated after a great feast and for a dare ordered the cover to be removed from the well. The result was that the water keep welling up, and next morning the valley was flooded. His palace had disappeared under the waves, and he and his retainers were all drowned.

Confused traditions developed from this idea of Dónall being drowned in the lake. Some say that he rode his horse into the lake when being pursued by enemy soldiers, others that he was drowned while boating there. An early tradition was that he once made prophecies for his friends at a feast, and then solemnly walked onto the water, bidding them goodbye. This is quite a reverential portrayal, and Dónall's function was extended to approach that of a patron SAINT to his people. As a returning GHOST, he defends them against oppression. For instance, on one occasion, he gave money to tenants to enable them to pay their exorbitant rents and, having given receipts, the landlord found to his dismay that the money turned to leaves. The trickery engaged in by Dónall could be of less serious import. A common story told of how he once accosted a stingy or pompous man who was travelling by night near Killarney. Inviting the man to his watery dwelling, he forced him to undress, and then put the clothes onto a skeleton from the graveyard and tied it onto the back of the man's horse. When the horse returned home, the family and all the neighbours thought the owner was dead and that his ghost had returned. Later, when the owner himself returned, he had trouble convincing them that he was still alive!

The appearances of Dónall in the vicinity of the lakes usually occurred at May time, this being considered the anniversary of his disappearance from this life. One nineteenth-century account states: 'As he approaches his ancient residence, everything returns to its former magnificence – his castle, library, and pigeon-house are reproduced as in olden times. Those who have courage to follow him over the lake may cross even the deepest parts dryfooted, and ride with him into the opposite mountains where his TREASURES lie concealed, and the daring visitor

will receive a liberal gift in return for his company. But, before the sun has risen, the O'Donoghue recrosses the water and vanishes amidst the ruins of his castle.' The fine horse on which he rides is called Craobhach, which name refers to its 'branching', or flowing, mane.

The portrayal of an Ó Donnchú ancestor on the pattern of DONN may have been strengthened by wordplay on the surname. Thus Dónall was described as, like Donn, riding abroad at night on a fine horse, and leading a FAIRY army. Like the fairies in general, Dónall was particularly adept at the game of hurling, and he and his retainers were often seen playing that game wonderfully on the surface of the lake on May mornings. There are several versions of a story that shows Dónall as a splendid hurler, and coming to the aid of an O'Donoghue kinsman in an embarrassing situation. We are told that this O'Donoghue laid a bet with an English lord on a hurling match. All looked lost for O'Donoghue, but Dónall appeared on the field of play with a team of hurlers, took part in the game, and secured the victory.

The image of Dónall also came under the influence of LEGENDS concerning the Earl of DESMOND (known as *Gearóid Iarla*). The reason for this may have been the fact that the then chieftain of the O'Donoghues took part in the great Desmond Rebellion of the sixteenth century and was attainted as a result. Such a unity of purpose would have caused the O'Donoghues to borrow some of the great ancestor lore of the Desmonds. Thus on the pattern of the lore of Gearóid Iarla at Lough Gur, County Limerick, it was sometimes claimed that Dónall slept underneath Muckross Lake at the head of a phantom army. Similarly, when he is seen riding on the waters of the lake, his horse is shod with silver shoes, and when these are worn out, he will return.

Like Gearóid also, he was said to have been enchanted through misuse of his magic. It happened at a feast in Ross Castle when he did some tricks to amuse his wife, first warning her not to scream, for to do so would entrap him in sorcery. She was unimpressed by his initial tricks, but he then stretched out on the floor in the form of an eel and leaped into his wife's bosom. She screamed, whereupon Dónall left the castle, took his horse out of its stable, and rode into the lake. Dónall occurs in yet another folk legend borrowed from the lore of Gearóid Iarla (q.v.), in which he is among a group of students who learned magic from the devil. The devil demanded one of the students, and he was told to take the hindmost. Dónall was last in the line, and so the devil took his shadow, as a result of which none of his relatives are said to have a shadow and are called *muintir dhubh Dhonnchú* (the black tribe of the O'Donoghues).

Many landmarks around the Killarney lakes are explained by reference to Dónall na nGeimhleach, such as rock formations reputed to have been his library, table, pigeon house, wine cellar and even his prison for offenders.

CIARRAIGHE SEPTS: O'Brien (1962), 295, 299.

LÉN STORY: Gwynn (1913), 260–5.

FLOODING MOTIF: (1952), 28–9.

HISTORICAL FIGURE: Mac Airt (1944), 302, 310–12, 498.

FOLKLORE: J. Leslie (1772), 18–23; W. Watson (1776), 39–41, 45–6; O'Conor (1793), 109, 153; Croker, *1* (1826), 317–18, 321 & *2* (1828), 236–43 & *1* (1829), 35–41, 48–9, 234; Chatterton, *1* (1839), 107–8, 114–15; Windele (1839), 311, 332; Strahan (1904), 85–7; Curtin (1895), 6–17; F. Mac Coluim in *An Claidheamh Soluis*, 4/1/1908, 8; D. Ó Cróinín in *Béaloideas*, *35–6*, 112–24, 358–9; Ó Siochfhradha (1932), 44–52; O'Cahill (ninth edn.), 25–7, 43–4; Ó Duilearga (1948), 270, 432 & in *Béaloideas*, *29*, 52, 139; D. Ó hÓgáin in *Béaloideas*, *42–4*, 302–7 & Ó hÓgáin (1982), 353–8 & (1985), 157–9, 337; Ó Caithnia (1980), 686–8; IFC 654:297–307; IFC Index.

Ó hAnluain, Réamonn *(1640–81)*

Celebrated OUTLAW who had a successful career on the roads of Ulster and north Leinster for seven years before he was betrayed and murdered. He was the leader of a band of about 50 men, and their principal source of income was a 'black rent' they levied on English planters and other well-to-do people. His name is anglicised as Redmond O'Hanlon. A chapbook describing him and some other celebrated outlaws was written in the mid-eighteenth century by a certain John Cosgrave, and this shows that most of the folklore concerning him was already current at that time.

We read that Réamonn's mother had special dreams before his birth, and that he had a mark in the shape of *T* on his breast when he was born. When he grew up, he was a master at disguise, 'sometimes appearing like an officer, sometimes like a country gentleman, sometimes like a footman, and could alter the tone of his voice at pleasure, so that the soldiers seldom knew him though he often gave them money to drink'. The chapbook describes how, disguised as an army officer, he once directed a party of soldiers in a search for himself, and on another occasion, when dressed like a rich man, he was given a bodyguard to protect him from himself! He led the bodyguard into a trap, so that they were disarmed and robbed by his men. We also read that having been arrested once, he contrived to get the soldiers drunk in a tavern and completed his triumph by tying them all up by the neck and heels, and taking their weapons. Another writer stressed his ubiquity: 'He was everywhere, in fact, for those whom he looked for, and nowhere for those who looked for him. That was the most curious thing about Redmond O'Hanlon – there was plenty of him where he could be spared, and the greatest possible scarcity where he was wanted.'

Cosgrave further describes how the leading highwayman in Munster, Richard Power, once set out to meet Réamonn, and put up at an inn near where he expected to find his great counterpart. Power noticed a rich gentleman there and contrived to meet him on the road the next day to rob him. The strange gentleman, however, exchanged pistol shots with him and then took to sword fencing. When both were exhausted, Power enquired as to the stranger's name and found that it was Réamonn himself. Later on, when Power was arrested in Munster, Réamonn travelled south in an attempt to rescue him from Clonmel jail. Dressed in fine clothes, he fell in with four soldiers who were escorting Power to his execution, plied them with liquor, and then had his men seize them and tie them up. The hue and cry was raised for the escaped prisoner and his accomplices, and Réamonn himself 'assisted' the soldiers in the hunt, slipping away from them in the Bog of Allen when all was safe.

Whatever the basis for these LEGENDS, the historical Réamonn had a fine sense of showmanship. He proclaimed himself 'chief ranger of the mountains, surveyor-general of the high roads, lord-examiner of all travellers and high protector of his benefactors and contributors', and his reputation for both dignity and elusiveness was so great that he was referred to in French newspapers of the time as a count. Since he accorded so well with the romantic image of highwaymen in seventeenth-to-eighteenth century culture, it is natural that several standard folk accounts of outlaws should have become attached to him. For instance, it is said of him that he could trick and frighten his opponents by pretending he was accompanied by a large force of men, though in fact quite alone. He did this, we are told, by putting hats on heads of cabbage and setting them in the hedges at dusk when the soldiers could not see clearly.

One story told by Cosgrave was well known in international robber-legends and is still widely popular concerning Réamonn. According to it, a merchant in Dundalk wished to have a large sum of money collected for him from Belfast, but nobody would undertake the task for fear of being accosted by Réamonn on the country roads. Eventually, an apparently dull-witted boy undertook the task, mounted on a broken-down nag. On the way to Belfast, he met a gentleman on a beautiful horse, and they conversed for a while, the boy revealing the nature of his business and his timetable. He then went on, collected the money in Belfast, and on his return journey met the same gentleman on the road. The gentleman said that he was Réamonn and demanded the money. The boy caught his saddlebags and threw them into a tangle of briars, and the outlaw jumped off his horse to recover the bags. The boy jumped from his own nag and, mounting Réamonn's fine steed, set off for Dundalk at high speed. Réamonn found nothing of value in the saddlebags,

for the boy had hidden the money within his shirt, and the highwayman had nothing for his trouble but the loss of his quality horse. This legend reflects the folk tendency to have great men sometimes outwitted by very ordinary people, and is closely related to the popular psychology of hero worship (*see also* O'CONNELL, SWIFT *and* POLITICAL LORE).

It was said that Réamonn had a shirt made from flax plucked and scutched and spun and woven between sunrise and sunset and that, as a result, it could not be penetrated by any bullet except one fired from his own gun. However, he was betrayed by his foster-brother Art, whom he had set as a lookout while he slept in a hut near Eight-Mile-Bridge, County Down. Eager to collect the large reward on the head of the famous outlaw, Art stole into the hut and shot Réamonn through the breast with his own blunderbuss.

T.W. Moody in *PBS*, 1, 17–33; Cosgrave (1776), 4–32; Danaher (1964), 14–19; M.J. Murphy (1975), 55–7; Ó hÓgáin (1985), 181–5, 338–9; Dunford (2000), 34–5, 61–4, 275–80, 304–5; IFC Index.

Ó Maoilriain, Éamonn an Chnoic

Outlaw of the late seventeenth and early eighteenth century, known in English as 'Ned of the Hill'. The surname, often shortened to Ó Riain, is anglicised as Ryan. The tradition is that Éamonn was born at Knockmeoll Castle in Atshanboe, about 8 miles west of Thurles, County Tipperary.

It is said that he was of noble stock and was forced into outlawry at the time of the Williamite Wars. A proclamation, dated 1702, offered as reward for his capture £200, then a very large sum. He was slain soon afterwards by a confidant, who sought to gain the money. According to tradition, Éamonn was one of the most famous of the heroic OUTLAWS known as 'raparees', and a great deal of folklore concerning him was current until recently, This was enhanced by a very popular love song entitled 'Éamonn an Chnoic'. The song consists of a conversation between the young man Éamonn and his loved one, in which he seeks admission to her house on a cold and windy night. It is likely that the song predated the outlaw, and that his nickname was in reality borrowed from it. We are told that Éamonn's girlfriend was one Mary Leahy.

In the folk stories, the raparee Éamonn is portrayed as a high-minded man who dressed well and was a master marksman with his fine brace of pistols. We are told that he studied for the priesthood abroad but, on his return home for holidays, intervened to prevent a cow being taken by a rent collector from a poor widow and in the resulting fracas the rent man was killed. This meant that Éamonn had to take to the hills and woods as a fugitive, but he soon gathered a strong band of men and fought for the Jacobites in the war against WILLIAM OF ORANGE. Together with a noted raparee leader, Dónall Ó hÓgáin ('Galloping Hogan') he attacked and destroyed an English convoy near Dundrum, County Tipperary.

Most accounts, however, portray him as on his own, mounted on a fine grey horse, evading search parties of soldiers and, when need be, attacking them and putting them to flight. He was always gallant, robbing only from the rich and rendering assistance to the poor. One especially popular story tells of how he once met an English lady who had been robbed by some men claiming to be his followers, and how he indignantly chased and captured these men and then returned her money to the lady. Her husband was a senior army officer, and it was said that, out of gratitude, he did all he could to secure a pardon for the chivalrous outlaw. It was said that Éamonn often fell in with rich travellers on the road, and as often as not treated them well and did not deprive them of their wealth. Once, he thus chatted with an English officer for a long while before revealing his identity. The officer feigned friendship and, taking Éamonn to a tavern for a drink, had him surrounded and captured by a company of soldiers. Éamonn, however, contrived to get the soldiers drunk, and in the confusion made his getaway, later slaying the treacherous officer with a well-directed shot.

Several conventional types of outlaw-LEGENDS were attached to him. For instance, a man tries to betray him by luring him to his house for a meal, but the man's wife hints to him to eat cold and flee. In this case, the migratory MOTIF has apparently been substituted for a real episode in which a certain Reuben Lee of Gurnaskehy tried to lure Éamonn into a trap, but the outlaw was warned by a relative who was also in the house. Another common migratory motif that has become attached to Éamonn tells of him giving money to poor tenants to settle debts with their rapacious landlord, and then retaking the money from the TYRANT in a hold-up. Yet another such story has Éamonn allowing himself to be taken so that a poor man can collect the reward for his capture, and then escaping again.

The typical heroic outlaw can only be overcome by foul and unfair means, and so it was with Éamonn in real life as in legend. We are told that he was sleeping at the house of a man called Dwyer whom he believed to be his friend but who actually intended to collect the price on the outlaw's head. Éamonn dreamed that Dwyer was approaching him with a hatchet, but on starting up from his sleep rejected such a suspicion. He fell asleep again, and the 'friend' really did behead him and brought the head to Clonmel to claim the reward. Tradition has it, however, that a pardon had just been procured by the English officer who was indebted to the outlaw for the courteous treatment of his wife, and that, as a result, the traitor got nothing for his efforts. Éamonn's head is said to have been buried by his sister Sadhbh under a whitethorn bush at Curraheen, in the parish of Toem in mid Tipperary; and it is claimed that the rest of his body lies in the earth at Doon, a few miles further west in County Limerick.

D. O'Sullivan in *Journal of the Irish Folk Song Society*, 24, 36–60; Ní Mhurchú & Breathnach (2001), 166–7; Cosgrave (ninth edn., 1776), 14, 34–6; Ó hÓgáin (1985), 186–7, 290, 339, 346; Dunford (2000), 94–113, 284–6; IFC Index.

Ó Néill, Eoghan Rua *(1582–1649)*

Brilliant Irish military leader. Of the noble O'Neill family of Tyrone, he was taken to the Netherlands in his youth and became a distinguished officer in the Spanish army. He returned to Ireland in 1642 to take command of the Ulster army after the rebellion, and in 1646 scored a great victory over the Covenanter forces at Benburb. Despite his continuing success in very difficult circumstances, wrangling and petty jealousies prevented him from being appointed overall commander of the Irish forces. In 1649 CROMWELL arrived in Dublin with a huge army, and Eoghan Rua prepared his own under-equipped men to face the daunting challenge. He was struck down by illness, however, and died at Cloughouter, County Cavan before he and Cromwell crossed swords. After his death, his army was poorly led and was utterly defeated in 1651.

The military skills of Eoghan Rua caused amazement to friend and foe alike, and he was loved by his followers on account of his concern for them and for the clever stratagems by which he kept casualties on his own side to a minimum. His son said of him that he would 'protract time and make a thousand wheels and turns to save the life of a single soldier'. A contemporary story had it that, noticing that one of his gunners was not performing well in a battle at Trim, he himself seized the weapon and showed him how to use it by shooting the enemy commander. Cavan town was his headquarters for a while, and a typical story from local folklore there describes a trick by which he got provisions for his army. He had only one bullock left, whereas the enemy had a large herd. He therefore took his bullock to a wood near the foe's encampment and, by lighting some straw on its back, caused it to bawl. Attracted by this, the herd came across to where Eoghan's men were waiting, and were quickly driven to his camp. This anecdote seems to have sprung from readings of how the DAGHDHA got the CATTLE of the Fomhóire and how the famous general Hannibal tricked the Romans with a herd of cattle.

He was known to the ordinary people as 'the General' or as Eoghan an Chogaidh (Eoghan of the War), and many places of Ulster and Leinster were popularly pointed out as the scenes of his ambushes and triumphs. His death was one of the most momentous losses in Irish history, and the people refused to believe it had come from natural causes. He apparently suffered from cancer, and the most acute pain was in his knee. The illness first struck him at a banquet in Derry, when he was negotiating with the Parliamentarian commander Charles Coote. It was therefore suspected that he had been given poison on that occasion, but an alternate explanation arose from the boast of one of his Irish rivals called Plunkett. This man claimed that he himself had been responsible for Eoghan's death by sending him a pair of poisoned boots as a present. An account from late folklore brings both theories together in narrative form by stating that a dance was organised in Eoghan's honour, and that a certain woman put poison in his shoes beforehand. He danced several times, and with the heat the poison worked itself up into his blood.

A POET lamenting Eoghan referred to him as 'the very David who would not allow Goliath to escape him', and a contemporary report shows that a messianic MOTIF (see DESMOND) became associated with him. We read of his followers' belief that God had 'lulled him to sleep and snatched him away to some secret corner of the world to keep him there for future better purposes'.

GENERAL: O'Neill (1937); D. Murphy (1897), 130–3; O'Cahan (1968), 375–7; C. O'Rahilly (1952), 23–7, 111–15; Mag Uidhir (1977), 5, 62–4; Hyde & Ó Conaire (1985), 28–33; Ó hÓgáin (1985), 169–70 & in *Anois*, 5–6/11/1994, 13; IFC 924:420–5.

CATTLE TRICK: S965:369–70; Gray (1982), 70; Livy 22.16–17.

Ó Raghallaigh, Giolla Íosa

(c. 1250–1331) Chieftain of the Ó Raghallaigh (anglice, O'Reilly) sept of Eastern Breffney (modern County Cavan and adjacent areas to the south). His Christian name Giolla Íosa was a popular one, meaning 'servant of JESUS', and because he was red haired he was usually known as Giolla Íosa Rua. The O'Reillys and their relatives, the Ó Ruairc family of Leitrim (anglice, O'Rourke), were an offshoot of the Uí Bhriúin (see CONNACHTA) who had migrated eastwards across the Shannon in the late eighth century, and took their name from their leader in the early eleventh century, Raghallach son of Cathalán.

Giolla Íosa was one of six sons of the O'Reilly chieftain Dónall Mór, He was preceded in the leadership by two elder brothers, Matha and Fearghal. Matha died a natural death, and Fearghal was slain by a kinsman in 1291, which event had been foretold by a celebrated wise retainer of the family, the Bodhar Mac Giolla Seanáin (anglice, deaf Gilsenan), who was blind and half-deaf. The most significant of the wise statements of the Bodhar concerned Giolla Íosa. We read that the latter was in youth the most miserable of the sons of Dónall Mór, being illegitimate. His mother was one of the Giolla Seanáin family, and as a boy, he was a scullion in his father's house. Once, when the cook asked for a piece of fuel without delay, Giolla Íosa put his own dirty tunic under the pot. This caused the onlookers to laugh, but the Bodhar – aware that a true leader should be willing to suffer for the common good – remarked that that was 'a laugh at a future ruler'.

On another occasion, the Bodhar announced that the son of Dónall Mór who first ate an apple from a certain tree would be ruler of the O'Reillys. Matha's mother brought the apples to him to eat and shut the door to ensure that he could eat them undisturbed. Giolla Íosa was playing outside the window, however, casting shots. Matha asked him for a shot, and Giolla Íosa offered to exchange it for an apple. Matha gave him the most miserable apple and, despite the efforts of Matha's mother to catch the fleeing urchin, the latter ate it up. So, after the deaths of Matha and of Fearghal, Giolla Íosa – by then in middle age – became chieftain of the sept. He proved a pious and generous ruler, and a great warrior to boot, raiding through much of Connacht and as far south as County Clare, and taking large preys. His residence was at Mullagh, and around 1300 he founded the Franciscan friary at Cavan, from which the modern town grew.

Carney (1959), 71–6.

Ó Rathaille, Aogán (c. 1670–1729)

Leading eighteenth-century POET. He was born in the area of Sliabh Luachra, in south-east Kerry, and spent most of his life in the service of the noble MacCarthy family of west Munster (see EOGHANACHT). Aogán was the leading proponent of the type of vision-poem called *aisling*, in which the composer claims that an otherworld lady, representing Ireland, comes to him with a message that the Irish will yet triumph over their oppressors.

Aogán was very much an aristocratic poet in his sentiments, and depended on the noble families for support and sustenance, but the defeat of that interest left him in dejection and poverty. In folklore, therefore, he is portrayed as a man of inspired intellect and quick wit who is buffeted by life and by the indifference and cruelty of upstarts. Several anecdotes tell of how he composed witty verses to satirise and deflate such people, and his wit can be both humorous and biting. An example of the latter describes how, one day, he saw the son of an English settler desecrating a churchyard by cutting down a venerable old tree that grew there. The youth slipped and was hanged between the branches, and the poet spoke a stanza wishing that trees bore such fruit every day. The anecdotes are usually of a more benevolent and light-hearted nature, however. We are told that he once got lodgings in the house of a very stingy man and was given nothing but watery porridge to eat. He asked for a spoon, and was told that all he could have was a piece of shell to scrape the pot. His host then enquired who he was, whereupon he replied in verse that he was Aogán Ó Rathaille from Sliabh Luachra who broke his shell in the bottom of the pot, and not due to the weight of the food!

As a typical poet, Aogán was said to have been able to show his immediate knowledge of any kind of situation. Thus we are told that he once saw a group of men trying to build a bridge, but the arch continually collapsed despite their efforts. He spoke a quatrain stating that he had never yet seen a bridge without a prop, thereby instructing them that they should use wattles as a cross-beam. On another occasion, he had two pigs at the market and was tricked by a slick buyer who asked what was the price of 'that white pig there with the black pig'. Aogán named his price, to be told that he had thereby sold both pigs. At the next market, the poet was selling more pigs, and when asked his price by the same buyer stated that all he was asking was one grain of corn with permission to double it for half an hour. The buyer agreed, and Aogán started on a long rhetoric that had the single grain increasing to sheafs and stacks and cornfields and parishes and counties until he was demanding all of Ireland as payment. The slick buyer was thus forced to settle for a reasonable price as a compromise.

The actual poetry of Aogán was of a very serious and heart-rending nature, but in folklore he is portrayed as a great trickster. One story has the daunting scholar Dean SWIFT going on a visit to Kerry to discover if the people of that area was intelligent. As he travelled in his carriage, he noticed a bedraggled fellow driving some cattle along the road. The dean stopped to ask for directions and was answered by the yokel in Latin, Greek, Hebrew and archaic Irish. Swift was so amazed by this that he turned on his heel and headed back for Dublin, remarking that if the tramps in Kerry were so knowledgeable, the scholars of the place must be unrivalled in their learning. The man whom he had encountered was, of course, Aogán. This type of folk LEGEND was conventional in the lore concerning Irish poets, with the visitor to an area always routed by a witty child or by the local sage in disguise. The plot was current in Ireland since medieval times (see MONGÁN). One story has Aogán exploiting folk ideas concerning the magical knowledge of poets. According to it, he was overtaken on his travels one night by a frightful downpour. When he was wringing wet he noticed a fine house, surrounded by tall trees, on the roadside, and went to ask for shelter there. His knock was answered by a surly man, who said that he would not admit a stranger to his house. Aogán looked up at the trees where the crows were cawing, and remarked: 'It is very strange that you do not know me, when even the crows recognise who I am.' He then instructed the man to listen carefully. The man did so, and it seemed to him as if the crows were cawing: 'Aogán, Aogán, Aogán Ó Rathaille!' Needless to say, the poet was then admitted and treated hospitably.

BIOGRAPHICAL: Dinneen & O'Donoghue (1911); Ní Mhurchú & Breathnach (2001), 164–6.

FOLKLORE: Ó Siochfhradha (1932), 261–5; Ó Duilearga (1948), 328–33, 441; Ó hÓgáin (1982), 473 & (1985), 98–9, 230–3, 248–51, 344 & in Ó Catháin (2001), 293–4, 302.

Ó Súilleabháin, Eoghan Rua

(1748–84) POET who was celebrated in Munster lore for his wit and his bohemian lifestyle. He was born at Meentogues, east of Killarney, County Kerry and spent much of his life as a part-time teacher and migrant labourer in different parts of Munster. Tradition claims that he was a great womaniser and, that to avoid one such involvement, he entered the British navy in or about the year 1776. Another, and perhaps more accurate, tradition has it that he was press-ganged, and this is what he himself states in one of his poems. In 1782 he was present at a fierce sea battle between the British and the French in the Caribbean, and he composed a poem in English praising the victor, Admiral Rodney. It is said that he thought to gain his freedom by this poem, but Rodney refused this. Eoghan persisted in his efforts to be released, blistering his shins with spearwort, and so terrible did his sores become that he was discharged. He returned to Ireland, but soon after was killed in an ale-house brawl caused by a satire he had composed.

The poetry of Eoghan Rua, although quite conventional in its themes, was extremely rich in its language and metre. As a result, this red-haired and rakish young man was popularly regarded as a wizard with words. Like all the Gaelic poets of his time, he was well versed in traditional Irish literature, and seems to have got as good an education as possible in the unofficial 'hedge-schools' of the time. He had good English and some knowledge also of Latin, Greek and perhaps a little Hebrew. By the folk, this proficiency in learning was expressed by the belief that Eoghan had perfect knowledge of 'seven languages', and that 'he had poetry and history and everything else at his disposal'. The many stories told of him have him use his fluency and quick wit to express folk sentiments, with which – considering his material circumstances – Eoghan must have been very much in accord. Thus we have him using his poetic skills to castigate stinginess, pomposity and oppressive authority – the three main objects of popular odium. It is said that he was once engaged in sowing seed for a dogged and ruthless farmer, who refused to give him his dinner but told him to continue at the work. Eoghan did so, but began to recite some verses in unison with his sowing. 'The first unit,' he said in Irish, 'may you, drill of the field, have neither fortune nor luck; the second unit, may you not grow copiously; the third unit, desolation and scattering on your progeny; the fourth unit, may a thunderbolt strike your house!' Hearing this, the farmer began to fear the poet's curse, and he begged Eoghan to come to dinner and to cease his versifying.

How poetry could so easily be composed by some, and yet was so difficult to others, was a puzzle to the folk, and so a story was told of how a simple man one day asked Eoghan how it was done. Eoghan said that it was just speech, and as they walked along the road together he picked up four observations made by the man and strung them together in a well-rhymed verse, thus proving that poetry was a natural and easy process. When occasion demanded, however, he would deliberately mystify his skill. He was very hungry once, and gained admittance to a wedding reception, but was put sitting with the tramps and was given nothing but sprats to eat. Picking up one of the sprats, he pretended to engage in a whispering conversation with it. This was soon noticed, and the host came to him and enquired as to what he was doing. Eoghan said that he

was seeking information from the sprat regarding his brother's affairs overseas. The host asked him to make enquiries concerning his own brother, who also was abroad, and, having whispered for a while, Eoghan said that the sprat did not know but had revealed that the hake yonder might have some information. He was therefore brought to the hake and, after further whispering, said that the hake had directed him on to the cattle as the man in question was known to have been herding abroad. Eoghan was therefore put sitting at the beef table, where he ate ravenously and announced that the host's brother was enjoying great fare in foreign climes. This is in fact an adaptation into the context of Eoghan of a common FOLKTALE concerning a trickster.

It is not clear whether or not there was a basis in truth for Eoghan's reputed amours, but folklore makes much of the theme, portraying him as a roguish and likeable gallant. It is said that he began early. When a mere seven years of age, he was late for school one day and faced a beating from the schoolmaster if he could not explain his delay. Little Eoghan then recited some polished octuplets describing how he had been detained watching two beautiful young women whom he had encountered on the road, and the master was so captivated by the description that he pardoned him. Having pursued the same line of interest in his adult life, Eoghan was once accosted in his travels by a little boy who answered everything in verse, and he thus recognised the child as a son of his own. This is in fact an example of a narrative plot found in many different countries (see ROMANTIC TALES, type 873). Another account has a lover thrusting her crying child at Eoghan and demanding that he take care of it, whereupon he composes a lullaby for the baby promising it all the beautiful things the mind of the poet could imagine.

A favourite type of anecdote has Eoghan contending with overbearing clergymen. According to one of these, a priest determined to criticise him publicly from the altar for his loose living. When all the congregation was assembled, the priest called out ominously: 'Is Eoghan Ó Súilleabháin here?' Receiving no reply, he called out again, to no avail, and then he shouted: 'Is Eoghan Rua here?' The poet answered from the body of the church: 'Yes, and may you not see the painter!' This was a clever reference to the meaning of his epithet *rua* (i.e. red). On another occasion, Eoghan was mending his torn shoe on the side of the road when a portly priest passed by and remarked in a semi-quatrain that the poet was not much of a shoemaker. Filling in the metre, Eoghan referred to 'a priest with his head full of Latin and his belly dancing with punch!' We are told also that he was refused admittance to Mass once because he had no offering to make at the door, and was told to listen from the outside of the church. Eoghan sat on a heap of turf, and was later challenged by the priest for not properly attending Mass. He replied in a rolling metre that poverty was not what most hurt him nor to be underfoot always, but to have his dignity insulted, and that if God was like the Church, he was just as well off sitting on the turf. Stung by Eoghan's theological sophistication, the priest relented. A humorous story of a type found in medieval European literature was also attached to Eoghan. According to this, he once offered to carry a priest on his back across a flooded river on the condition that the priest hear his confession simultaneously. Halfway through the water, Eoghan confessed some very serious sin, and the enraged priest shouted *'tá an diabhal thiar ort!'* which can be translated as 'the devil is riding you'. 'Well, if so,' said Eoghan, 'he will not be for much longer!' and he flung the priest into the flood.

The anti-clericalism attributed to Eoghan and to some other poets is very much a demand by the folk for charity and a rejection of authoritarianism. For instance, another story has him reprimanding a lazy priest who refused to rise from bed on a stormy night to attend to a sick woman. Eoghan's remark that 'she will have plenty of priests to accompany her on her journey to heaven without you'

set the priest thinking and he lost no time in fulfilling his duty. Other quatrains attributed to him have him castigating various clergymen for their greed and their indifference to the poor, a theme of social protest that has a long history in European literature and popular sentiment. In fact, the portrayal of Eoghan Rua has all the psychological power of the 'sinner-saint' image, and this is very much in accord with the actual poetry composed by him. His life, compositions and portrayal in folklore all share the paradox of a personality split in equal measure between its degrading physical surroundings and the soaring flights of its imagination. Such a paradox, of course, is of frequent occurrence in various milieux.

Two curious traditions are attached to the death of Eoghan Rua. According to one, after he had been struck on the head with a pair of tongs in the fatal brawl, he lay incapacitated for some time. It is said that a certain young woman, wishing to discover if he really was dying, came to his bed and took her clothes off, but Eoghan spoke a candid verse saying that his sexual powers were gone and she realised then that his death was near. Another tradition states that, when the bishop of Kerry heard of his death, he remarked sadly: 'More distressful is his death than that of a hundred priests. A priest can be made if money is available for his education, but a poet like Eoghan Rua can never again be made!' Both traditions are apocryphal, and the saying attributed to the bishop has parallels in accounts of some famous Renaissance artists in Europe.

GENERAL: Ua Duinnín (1901) & (1902); Corkery (1967). 184–221; Ó hÓgáin (1982), 473 & (1985), 218–24, 243–56, 341–4 & in *Feasta*, 1–2/1980, 8–12, 21–5 & in Ó Catháin (2001), 296–7, 303.

FOLKTALE PLOT OF TRICKSTER: Aarne & Thompson (1961), type 1567C.

PRIEST ON BACK: *See* Pauli (1972), *1*, 330, 385.

SAYING OF BISHOP: *See* Kris & Kurz (1979), 50–1.

Ó Súilleabháin Béarra, Dónall Cam *(1560–1618)* Chieftain from 1593 of the branch of the O'Sullivan sept (*see* EOGHANACHT) which resided at Beara in west Cork. He and his people took part in the war against Elizabethan forces and

held out until the final day of the year 1602 when he led over 1,000 of his sept – men, women and children – on a long march northwards from Glengariff. Braving continual attacks and ferocious weather, he and 34 survivors reached safety with the O'Rourkes of Leitrim within seventeen days.

A strong folk memory of Dónall, in the form of epic LEGENDS, survives in west Munster. His nickname *Cam* meant 'crooked', and folklore explains that, though a tall athletic man, he had bandy legs. We are told that he was very lazy as a youth, and that his parents could not prevail on him to do any work. His mother's brother was the chieftain of the neighbouring O'Donovan sept of Carbery, and we are told that this uncle raided the O'Sullivan territory. As the raiders left the Beara Peninsula, driving a huge herd and laden with booty, Dónall's mother chided him for lying at the fireside and not assisting his people to oppose the aggression. At that, the youth jumped up in anger and seized one of his father's swords. He wielded it so strongly that it broke, as did a second sword, but the third one was very strong and it held. Then he went to confront his uncle at the head of the raiders. O'Donovan had sworn not to rest until he laid his hand on the westernmost promontory of Beara, and Dónall now cut that hand off and slew his uncle. In order to fulfil the uncle's vow, he brought the hand and laid it on the point furthest west of the peninsula. The folk accounts are to an extent corroborated by annalistic entries, which state that, not the chieftain Diarmaid Ó Donnabháin, but his namesake son raided Beara in 1581 at the instigation of the English. Dónall, then twenty years of age, gathered 50 men and attacked the raiders, slaying hundreds of them and also their leader, who was his cousin.

After the accession of King James I, he visited England in the company of some other Irish leaders in an attempt to have his territories restored to him. The attempt failed, and in 1604 he travelled in secret to Cork, from where he and his family sailed to Spain. On account of his extraordinary ability to elude enemies, folk tradition claimed that he had the power to make himself invisible. It was said that he had got this gift while sleeping one night in a hut by the seashore. A voice spoke to him in a dream and told him that he had been betrayed and that the hut was surrounded by English soldiers. However, the voice also said that there was a herb on the table, and that if he put that in his mouth, he could not be seen. In this manner, he went outside, slew the bewildered soldiers, and escaped.

When he arrived in Spain, Dónall was received with great honour by King Philip III, and folklore had its own way of dramatising this. It is said that he burst his way through the royal guard and entered the king's presence. Philip demanded an explanation for this behaviour, and Dónall said that his sword was his pass. There was a great slab of brass in the court, which no champion had ever been able to cut with a sword stroke, and the king ordered Dónall to attempt this feat. Dónall gave a terrible look at all those present, and then rose himself into the air and brought his sword down onto the block with terrible force, splitting it in half. His servant began to throw water on him, and when the king queried the reason for this, Dónall explained that he had worked himself into a frenzy in order to procure the necessary strength and that, unless cooled down, nobody present would be safe from him. This is a version of a story concerning John DE COURCY, and seems to have been borrowed in the seventeenth or eighteenth century by the O'Sullivans of Beara from their near neighbours in that area, the lords of Kinsale, County Cork, who were of the de Courcy family.

The historical Dónall Cam worked hard to get Spanish assistance for a new campaign in Ireland and, along with other Irish émigré leaders, his affairs in Spain were closely watched by English intelligence sources. This is reflected by folk accounts of various attempts to assassinate him, but it is claimed that his death resulted from the greed of his valet, who knew him to have money. When Dónall bent down to tie his shoe, his cloak rose, revealing a chink in his armour, and the valet stabbed him through it. Thus he was referred to as 'Dónall Cam who was killed by treachery in Spain'. The reality was hardly less dramatic, for Dónall was actually stabbed to death outside a church in Madrid. He had lent money to an English friend called John Bath, and this matter led to a violent quarrel between Bath and Dónall's nephew, Philip O'Sullivan Beare. Two of Dónall's retainers separated them, but Bath unexpectedly lunged at the unsuspecting chieftain and stabbed him fatally through the neck.

D. Ó Súilleabháin (1940), 95–121; O'Donovan (1848–1851), 1762–3; M. Kelly (1850), 118, 337–8; M.J. Byrne (1903), 208; R.B. Breatnach in *Éigse*, 7, 162–81; Ó Duilearga (1948), 272–4, 433; Ó hÓgáin (1985), 163–8, 338 & in *Studia Hibernica*, 31, 175–89; IFC S274:199–201.

O'Connell, Daniel *(1775–1847)*

Irish political leader and brilliant lawyer, who won Catholic Emancipation from the British Parliament in 1829. He organised huge public meetings in an attempt to have the Act of Union between Ireland and England repealed, one of which at TARA in 1843 was attended by close on half a million people. Born into a prosperous old Gaelic family who resided at Derrynane, County Kerry, his name in Irish was Dónall Ó Conaill. Dubbed by the newspapers 'the Liberator', he was better known to the ordinary people as *An Consailéir* (the Counsellor).

A large number of anecdotes were told in folklore concerning Daniel in every part of Ireland. These centre chiefly on his skill as defence counsel in legal cases, but several also deal with his career as a Member of Parliament at Westminster. Sometimes his portrayal reaches epic dimensions, as in a tradition that the mountains of his native area pealed out a thunderous echo at his birth. This birth, it was claimed, was God's reward to his parents for a good deed. It was said that they had once taken shelter from rain at a tumbledown church and, seeing how badly the place was in need of repair, made a present of money to the local priest. The priest told the couple that they would have a baby son who would be the champion of Ireland. The ecclesiastical authorities were reticent about supporting

Daniel at first, but as he became successful, the Catholic clergy came to play a leading part in his organisation throughout the country and assisted him in fundraising. This close connection between him and the ecclesiastical world is reflected in folk LEGENDS of him. One tradition, for instance, claims that his cloak held a cure and that many people were healed of ailments by touching it – a direct borrowing from the Gospel account of how a woman was cured by touching the mantle of JESUS CHRIST.

Much ordinary narrative lore was also borrowed into his portrayal. For example, we are told that when he was a youngster, a very difficult law case was in progress locally. The case involved a man who was suing another for the loss of an eye, whereas the eye had in fact been lost accidentally through being caught by a fishhook. This had happened when the plaintiff was being saved from drowning by the other man, who had thrown the fishing line to him. The judge was unable to decide on the case, but he chanced to overhear some children acting out the courtroom drama as they played. One little boy, Daniel, was acting the part of the judge, and he ruled that the plaintiff should be put back into the water, and if he could save himself without the help of the fishing line, then he should be allowed damages against the other man. Realising that this was the correct verdict, the judge ruled accordingly, and the plaintiff dropped his case. This is in fact a version of an ordinary FOLKTALE, which has become attached to O'Connell.

Another such instance of a borrowed folktale concerns how a poor man emigrates to America, and before boarding the ship is given a meal of fried eggs by a certain woman. Years later, that man returns home, having become very rich, and the woman sues him for a large sum. She claims that if she had kept the eggs herself, they would have multiplied and she would now have a big chicken farm. Daniel is engaged to argue the man's case for him, and does so by producing peas in the courtroom and attempting to sow them in the wooden floor. When the judge demands an explanation of his behaviour, Daniel says that the peas would have the same chance of sprouting from the floor as the boiled eggs would have had of hatching out chickens. He thus wins the case. Yet another such story has Daniel defending a will against dishonest relatives of the deceased, who claimed that a later will had been prepared. Suspecting a trick, he asked one of these relatives was the will made while the dead man was still alive, and received the answer that it was 'while there was life in him'. The truth flashed across Daniel's mind, and he enquired 'was it the life that God put in him?' The imposter had to admit that it was not, but that a fly had been inserted into the dead man's mouth while his hand was guided to sign the will.

By his brilliant legal skills, the historical O'Connell often upset the odds in court cases. Particularly striking were his successes in bringing large numbers of people from the gallows, such as those charged in the Doneraile Conspiracy trial and the trials following the Carrickshock affray in Kilkenny. Many folk traditions tell of ruses by which he successfully defended hopeless cases. One such has him going in disguise to the chief prosecution witness before a trial and getting that witness to lay a bet on the outcome. Then, at the trial, he has the witness disqualified by making him admit that he stands to gain personally from a conviction. Another story tells of Daniel discovering that a certain hanging judge once took bribes, namely a white horse and a barrel of red wine. When defending a man on a capital charge before this judge, Daniel creates ructions in the court by pretending to fall asleep and then crying out loudly. Asked by the judge to explain his behaviour, he says that he has had a nightmare in which a white horse was being drowned in red wine. Fearing that Daniel will expose him, the judge hastily finds an excuse to dismiss the case. Other stories tell of him exposing perjurers and felonsetters, and there is evidence that some of such accounts derive from humorous anecdotes told by Daniel himself.

He had a fine taste for dramatic humour, as is clear from an actual occurrence when he laid a bet with some of his legal colleagues that he would defeat in vitriol a notorious scold. She was the proprietress of a huckster's stall opposite the Four Courts in Dublin and, having listened politely to a barrage of abuse from her, Daniel triumphed by himself using voluminous mathematical terms as nicknames for her, ending by calling her 'a porter swiping similitude of the bisection of a vortex!' This was probably the episode that caused another common folktale to be attached to him. We are told that a foolish woman once sold the same cow to three different buyers at a market and, when arraigned for this, engaged Daniel as her defence counsel. He advised her to feign madness, and to answer 'Moo!' to every question put to her. She did so, and was acquitted by the judge as not being responsible for her actions. When Daniel sought his fee from her, however, she again answered 'Moo!' Another borrowing of a common folktale plot has Daniel being outwitted by his servant, who claims that geese have only one leg after he has eaten part of his master's dinner.

In 1815 O'Connell was challenged to a duel by a member of Dublin Corporation, Norcot d'Esterre, who foolishly wished to impress those in power. He had no choice but to go ahead with the duel, and in it he shot d'Esterre, who died two days later. Daniel was quite upset at the episode and pitied d'Esterre, but to the folk mind it was a great victory that readily fitted into a heroic pattern, and d'Esterre was popularly believed to have been an expert gunman hired by the authorities to kill O'Connell. Another great victory was his election to Parliament in 1828, and his re-election after being disqualified on account of being a Catholic. He was received at Westminster with no small degree of hostility, and a large number of people had gathered to observe him with derisive curiosity. This situation is put in a humorous form in a popular Irish folk legend that tells of how, faced with a jeering crowd, Daniel was somewhat abashed and slipped on a banana skin, falling heavily on his backside. The onlookers went wild with delight, but he slowly picked himself up, looked around with a gracious air, and then curtsied to the ground. 'Pavements of London,' he said, 'you are so polite, and you give good example, for you kiss the Irishman where the English ought to!'

The Parliament provided him with a great theatre in which to display his wit and cunning, his major achievement being Catholic Emancipation. Several anecdotes tell of how he upset protocol and had unnecessary rules changed by clever ruses, and in these he is always represented as taking advantage of pompous and quite dullwitted opponents. This is well in tune with what O'Connell actually remarked before he won the right to sit in Parliament: 'How cruel the Penal Laws are which exclude me from a fair trial with men whom I look on as so much my inferiors.' A folk account of how he gained Emancipation is a masterpiece in hilarity. We are told that, having failed for a long time to win support for his bill, he finally decided on a ruse. He wrote the terms of it on a parchment and, procuring a fine cane with a spin-off top, hid it inside the top of that cane. When he was in his seat in Parliament, he nudged the member next to him and handed him the cane. That member admired its fine silverwork, and Daniel whispered to him to pass it on to the next man to seek his opinion also. In this way, the cane was passed right around the House, all admiring it for its style and craftsmanship. When it came back to Daniel, he stood up and asked did all present approve of this piece of handiwork, and the 'ayes' were unanimous. Then he screwed off the handle of the cane with a broad smile. 'Gentlemen,' he said, 'I congratulate you – we have Emancipation!'

In 1832 the London *Times* published an article in which a woman, who had in her youth been looked after by O'Connell and his family, claimed that Daniel was the father of her thirteen-year-old son. The newspaper further described alleged encounters between Daniel and this boy in the street. It was a crude attempt to damage O'Connell politically and had no basis in truth, but the idea was quickly seized on and promoted by his enemies. It imprinted itself on the Irish folk memory also, but there much of the damage was taken out of it by setting the allegation in a humorous setting. For instance, a version of a popular type of folk story (*see* ROMANTIC TALES, type 873) was adopted to the context, and accordingly it was said that Daniel once met a very clever little boy and gave him some money. He told him that he would give more to him the next time they met. As soon as he turned his back, the boy jumped inside the fence, and raced up to where he would again meet Daniel. The latter had no choice but to fulfil his promise and, having parted with more money, asked the boy who his people were. 'They say that I am a son of Daniel O'Connell!' said the boy. Daniel enquired as to his age and, on reflection, remarked that that might well be true.

O'Connell once said that he could 'drive a coach and six' through any law passed by Parliament, and the folk view would concur with him in this. He always protested that he would use only peaceful means to achieve his objectives for Ireland, but he was not adverse to delivering strongly worded speeches which could sound quite alarming to the authorities. A curious story came to be told of him in different parts of the country, which had him using a threat to back his demands. It was said that, when failing to get support from Parliament for a reasonable measure, he said that he could, if he wished, have all Ireland in rebellion within 24 hours. This was scoffed at, so to prove his point, he returned to Ireland, gave a wisp of straw to each of four persons, and told them to do likewise. Within 24 hours, every adult in Ireland had received a wisp, and thus Daniel showed that he could if he wished fulfil his boast. This story has no historical basis in the context of Daniel, but it is a reconstruction of an event that actually took place in June 1832, when he was at the height of his power. This, called 'the week of the blessed turf', was an extraordinary surge of religious devotion when an outbreak of cholera was feared. A man in Charleville, County Cork was said to have been instructed by the Virgin Mary to give packages of ashes to his neighbours and to tell them to do likewise, as this was the only way of preventing the disease. Soon the ashes were replaced by pieces of turf, which were given by each person to four others, and during the following six days, this continued and spread to most parts of the country, before quietly subsiding. Daniel was active in having measures taken against outbreaks of cholera at the time and, perhaps because of this, the event became linked to his name and to his career in Parliament.

The most popular and dramatic of all the legends concerning Daniel describes an attempt reputedly made by English politicians to poison him. We are told that he was invited to dinner by them, and that they had poison put in his drink. Before he drank, however, the servant-girl, who was from Ireland, spoke to him in Irish verse, warning him of the plot by remarking that 'there is pepper on your drink which would kill hundreds'. Daniel answered her in Irish, and also in verse, saying that his hosts themselves would drink it. Then, in feigned surprise, he stood up and said that he had seen a royal carriage pass by the window. Thinking that some very distinguished personage was coming to visit them, the others rose from the table to look through the window, and Daniel quietly switched the glasses around. When they returned, remarking that it had been but an ordinary carriage and chiding him for his mistake, Daniel proposed a toast, with devastating consequences for one of his would-be assassins. It is difficult to trace the origin of this story, but it resembles an account in the apocryphal 'Acts of the Holy Apostle Thomas'. Daniel may have known this early Christian text from his education in seminaries on the Continent, and it may be that a version of it was one of the many anecdotes he delighted in telling. In this way, it could easily have become attached to his own image.

As well as his large and lasting profile as a social leader, in his great brain and his gifted speech, Daniel echoed the age-old archetypal image of the Irish POETS. Yet his wit was not enough. He planned a huge public meeting at Clontarf – scene of the ancient triumph of BRIAN BÓRAMHA – in October 1843, but this had to be abandoned when massive military forces were deployed against it. Following this, Daniel was imprisoned for a while on a charge of conspiracy, and he died a broken man at Genoa in May 1847 as FAMINE raged at home.

STORIES CONCERNING O'CONNELL: O'Neill Daunt (1848); Uí Ógáin (1984); C. Ó Danachair in *Studia Hibernica, 14*, 40–63; Ó hÓgáin (1985), 99–119, 331–3.

ALLEGED WOMANISING: Gwynn (1930).

CHOLERA PANIC 1832: S.J. Connolly in *Irish Historical Studies*, May 1983, 214–32.

FOLKTALE PLOTS: Aarne & Thompson (1961), types 155, 785A, 821B, 873, 1585. *See also* Uí Ógáin (1984), 332–5.

ogham The earliest form of writing in Irish. It is found in inscriptions on standing-stones in many different parts of the country, especially in the south, and also in areas of Irish settlement in Wales, Devon, Cornwall and the Isle of Man. Its use dates from the fourth or fifth century AD down to the eighth century.

Ogham is in reality a borrowing of the Latin alphabet, but instead of the standard symbols, the letters are represented by a system of notches and grooves. The early literature refers to rhetorics and charms being written in ogham on timber, but the surviving evidence consists solely of standing stones with memorial inscriptions to the dead. The form of Irish in these is quite antique, with the longer Celtic word endings. Thus for instance, a name (in genitive form) in one inscription, *Dalagni maqi Dali*, would have been written *Dalláin maic Daill* by the time that Irish literature began in the sixth to seventh century. It is obvious that ogham was in reality an adaptation of the Latin alphabet by Irish POETS or learned men before Christianity brought widespread knowledge of Latin letters to Ireland. The Celtic forms of the words may have been deliberate preservation of archaic language – it is likely that they were already obsolete when ogham was first used, surviving only in the rhetorical speech of poets.

It is difficult to determine the exact development of the word ogham, but the most likely theory is that the learned caste derived it from the name of the divinity associated with rhetoric, OGHMA. As a system of writing, it was well known to the scholars who adopted the standard Latin lettering system, and explanations of it are found in manuscripts down to recent times. This meant that the knowledge of ogham was never really lost. The general attitude to it in the literature and folklore is that it was a form of writing with quasi-magical significance, and this indeed may have been the popular attitude when some member of the learned caste devised this system to first commit words to visual form in Ireland.

Macalister (1945–49); Calder (1917), 187–91, 272–99, 349–50, 373; McManus (1991) & in *Ériu*, *37*, 1–31; A. Harvey in *Ériu*, *38*, 45–71.

Oghma Mythical champion of the TUATHA DÉ DANANN. The Latin writer Lucian described a Gaulish deity called Ogmios who personified eloquence and whose tongue was joined by mystical chains to the ears of his listeners. This is paralleled by an early reference to the Irish Oghma as 'a man most knowledgeable in speech and in poetry'. In line with this, he is claimed to have been the son of a certain Ealadha, whose name meant 'art' or 'poetic composition'. To him was attributed the invention of the OGHAM script. The precise relation between the words Ogmios, Oghma and ogham are unclear, but the most likely explanation is that the appellative Ogmios was borrowed from the Gauls by the Irish Celts, who reconstructed it as Oghma and applied the deity's name to their magical script.

Oghma is said to have been brother of the DAGHDHA, and he was given sobriquets such as Grian-aineach (sun-faced) and Grian-eces (sun-poet). He is represented as one of the chieftains of the Tuatha Dé. In the time of oppression during the reign of BREAS, he – with the Daghdha – was forced to do heavy manual labour, his task being to carry loads of firewood. Despite this humiliation, he continued to show his skill at arms, and was the principal champion of the Tuatha Dé as they prepared for the second Battle of Moytirra (*see* MYTHOLOGICAL CYCLE). On the arrival of LUGH at the Tuatha Dé court, Oghma engaged in a contest with him throwing a flagstone over the side of the royal hall. One account states that he was slain in combat with one of the enemy leaders at the height of the battle, but alternately, he is said to have survived the battle and to have shared the triumph with Lugh and the Daghdha.

T.F. O'Rahilly (1935), 41–2; Arbois de Jubainville (1903), 172–3; Comyn (1902), 222; Calder (1917), 187–8, 272–3; Gray (1982), 28–9, 32–3, 38–45, 52–3, 64–5, 68–71, 131; McManus (1991), 151–2; Olmsted (1994), 404–5.

Oisín A leading mythical character in the FIANNA CYCLE, son of the celebrated FIONN MAC CUMHAILL. His name (earlier, Oiséne) means 'little fawn', and was a common one in early Ireland. Its application to him, however, reflects the hunting imagery of the Fianna.

The character Oisín was already established within the Fianna lore by the early ninth century, for a text of that time has him quarrelling with Fionn and leaving his father for a long time. The text describes how they met in the wilderness while Oisín was cooking a PIG, and they almost came to blows before they recognised each other. This is a version of a popular folklore plot (*see* ROMANTIC TALES, type 873).

In line with the lore of hunting and of deer, a story was already current in the early Middle Ages concerning the birth of Oisín. According to this, his mother was called Blái Dheirg and she used to come to visit Fionn's band in the form of a doe. Later tradition claims that she was a beautiful girl who married Fionn, but when the hero was absent one day, a malicious wizard came and turned her into the shape of a deer. When Fionn returned, she was gone, and he searched long and hard for her, but to no avail. She gave birth to his child in the wilderness while still in that shape. After several years, Fionn's hunting hounds found a handsome little boy in the forest, and when the boy said that he had been reared by a deer, Fionn realised that it was his son and called him Oisín. This is probably derived from late medieval legendary stories in Latin and French of a hunter discovering his child in the forest, plots which themselves owe something to the story of Herakles' son Telephos who was suckled by a doe. The older Fianna tradition would appear to have had Oisín's mother as an otherworld lady who deliberately took the form of a deer during a hunt in order to lure Fionn deep into the forest and seduce him there. Her name links her to DEARG, a divine figure often hostile to Fionn, and the likelihood is that she was in fact the daughter of Dearg, a lady who had a special grudge against the hero.

The otherworld could be either friendly or hostile in Irish storytelling, but it is always mysterious. Thus the medieval lore found little difficulty in accepting the idea that Oisín's mother was an otherworld lady, and did not trouble too much about whatever hostility she had towards Fionn. We read in a twelfth-century text that Oisín, after the final defeat of the Fianna troop, sojourned for a while with his mother Blái Dheirg in the otherworld dwelling of Ocht Cleitigh (a barrow near Newgrange, County Meath). This text, called *Agallamh na Seánorach* (The Colloquy of the Old Men), fancifully describes how Oisín and CAOILTE survived the demise of the rest of the Fianna warriors and lived on to meet the great missionary saint PATRICK. Although most of the conversation in the text takes place between the SAINT and Caoilte, the subsequent literature puts Oisín clearly into the leading role. This was probably due to the fact that, since the early Middle Ages, Oisín was being patterned after the imagery of his father Fionn as a wise and knowledgeable POET. The colloquy was the greatest medieval compilation of Fianna lore, using the format of Patrick's conversations with the survivors, and the learned Oisín therefore came to be regarded as the more suitable spokesman for the ancient memories.

The idea of Patrick thus meeting ancient Irish heroes and converting them posthumously to Christianity had been current for some time, and an earlier story had CÚ CHULAINN return from the dead and accept the new teachings. When it became attached to Oisín and to his memories of the Fianna, however, the idea gradually developed into dialogues of unprecedented drama and humour. From the thirteenth to the eighteenth century, new verses were continually being composed and put into the mouths of Patrick and Oisín as they argued the pros and cons of the warrior life of old and the monastic life of the saints. The earlier versions were obviously written by ecclesiastics, and these have Oisín being completely overcome by the rationale of Patrick's arguments. When the lay writers put their hands to composing such dialogues, however, they had Oisín pointing out several sanctimonious attitudes of the clergy and stressing that the generosity of the Fianna outdid the type of narrow moralism comically attributed to Patrick.

This tradition of a dialogue between Oisín and Patrick became the vehicle for many new adventures of the Fianna that were invented in the post-medieval period and told in the form of versified lays. Some older MOTIFS, too, were adapted and set to the context of the great debate. For instance, an old story told of how Patrick had baptised the Munster king Aonghus and had inadvertently put his crozier through the neophyte's foot. In the fifteenth or sixteenth century, this story was switched from Aonghus to Oisín, who similarly suffered the pain and loss of blood patiently, believing it to be part of the ceremony.

In order to rationalise the encounter of Patrick and Oisín, a whole complex of storytelling developed around the same time. According to this, Oisín had not been at the great Battle of Gabhra in which the Fianna had been destroyed, but had departed from Ireland sometime before. It happened that the Fianna were hunting one day when they were visited by a beautiful lady who loved him and asked him to accompany her to Tír na hÓige (the Land of Youth). He did so, but after some time there expressed the desire to pay a visit to his homeland. Although it seemed a short while to him, 300 long years had passed, and the lady warned him not to set foot on the soil of Ireland. He arrived in Ireland on horseback but found that the Fianna were all dead and gone. He met some men trying in vain to lift a load that seemed trifling to him. Without thinking, therefore, he leaped from the saddle to help them, but immediately on touching the ground was changed into a very old man. While in that state, he was approached by Patrick and the celebrated dialogue began.

This story was widespread throughout the Gaelic world in recent centuries, although there is only one literary version of it, and that as late as the mid-eighteenth century. The literary version calls the beautiful lady Niamh, has her and Oisín riding a fine white HORSE, and has Oisín accidentally falling from the horse when his saddle girths break in an attempt to lift a large boulder. These seem to be colourful extras inserted into the story by the author of the literary text, Micheál Coimín from County Clare. Coimín must have got the story from the folklore of his time, for it is in fact a variant of an international narrative plot that was long known in Ireland (see WONDER TALES, type 470).

The post-medieval folklore went on to tell of how Oisín was displeased with the type of food given to him by Patrick's housekeeper. He boasted that in the time of the Fianna, he had seen a blackbird's egg larger than the joint of meat she was cooking, a rowan berry larger than her chunk of butter, and an ivy leaf larger than her cake. She refused to believe this, but Oisín was determined to prove his point. We are told that Patrick had a bitch that gave birth to a litter of pups, and Oisín selected the best one of them. He did this by fastening a sheepskin to a wall and throwing each of the pups at it, the best being the one that alone clung to the skin. When the pup grew up somewhat, Oisín took it with him to the forest. He found an old trumpet there and told his servant to blow it.

Soon a huge blackbird approached, and the young hound was loosed against it and killed it. The hound became demented by its triumph, and so fierce was it that Oisín decided that it must be slain. Though failing of sight, he took a metal ball and accurately flung it into the hound's gullet, choking it. Oisín then procured a huge rowan berry and ivy leaf – relics from the lost epoch – and returned to Patrick's housekeeper to win the argument.

This story was widespread throughout the Gaelic world, as was the idea that Oisín finally managed to persuade Patrick to ask God for the release of the dead Fianna from hell, where they were confined on account of their paganism. Munster storytellers added a clever touch to this, claiming that Oisín had asked only for the release of Fionn, and when this request was granted, declared that they were all *fionn* (i.e. beloved) to him.

BIOGRAPHICAL AND DEER-MOTHER: Stokes (1900), 2; Meyer (1910), xviii, xxviii–xxx, 24–7 & in *RC, 6*, 186; G. Murphy (1953), xxi; Best & O'Brien (1957), 729; Gwynn (1913), 242–53; L-C. Stern in *ZCP, 5*, 180; D. de hÍde in *Béaloideas, 2*, 253–60; Ó hÓgáin (1988), 77–80, 330.
COLLOQUY: Stokes (1900), 2–9, 64–74, 220–4, 359–60; D. de hÍde in *Lia Fáil, 1*, 79–107; Ní Shéaghdha (1945), 224–5.
DEBATE WITH PATRICK: Mac Néill (1908), 74–5; G. Murphy (1933), 168–73, 178–83, 204–15; Ó Siochfhradha (1941), 227–40.
FOLKLORE: G. Murphy (1953), xx; Ó Siochfhradha (1941), 213–26; S. Ó Súilleabháin & Christiansen (1967), 96–7; Ó Cadhlaigh (1947), 447–50.
GENERAL: Ó hÓgáin (1988), 49–50, 117–18, 155–6, 241–55, 340–1, 361 & in Almqvist, Ó Catháin & Ó Héalaí (1987), 233–4.

oldest creature The various skills and characteristics of the fauna have long provided inspiration to POETS and storytellers. In ancient times (see FIONN) seers were believed to be able to go about in the form of animals and thereby gain knowledge from other than human perspectives. This gave a narrative base to archaic ideas concerning how the deities could exist in non-human form, and by implication that certain individual animals, BIRDS and FISH could have lived from time immemorial.

In medieval Ireland, all of this combined with the far-flung international method of reckoning time by the lifespan of different animals. The amalgam gave rise to a story that, with a degree of humour, compares various long-living creatures. There are both literary and oral versions of the story. In literary tradition, it was used in accounts of such characters as FIONNTAN and TUÁN MAC CAIRILL, who were claimed to have lived for long periods in the forms of different creatures and to have had great repositories of ancient history. The story may be summarised as follows:

A certain man, amazed at the coldness of a particular night, wonders if there was ever so cold a night before. He sets out to discover the answer to this, and first meets an otter lying in a deep hole on top of a rock. The otter tells him that it has been there for so long that the hole has been worn in the stone by its body, but it has never seen so cold a night as recently. Next the man meets Seabhac Acla (the Hawk of Achill Island, County Mayo), which is perched on an anvil and has been there for so long that the anvil is almost worn away from rubbing of its beak after eating. Neither has it seen so cold a night. Finally, the man encounters the one-eyed Bradán Easa Rua ('salmon of Assaroe', near Ballyshannon, County Donegal). This salmon tells him that it does indeed remember a colder night an extremely long time before. It had frozen so fast that night that when the salmon jumped out of the water to catch a fly, the river was ice when it returned. The salmon had thus lain on the ice, and a bird came and plucked out one of its eyes. The blood from the eye melted the ice, and so the salmon had got back into the water.

Apart from its curious background, this story exemplifies how a tradition can remould its imagery. In the early literature, for example, the one-eyed salmon was the form taken by the deity called AODH RUADH RÓ-FHEASA in the River Boyne, and by a confusion of this name it had become associated with the Donegal location. See also CAILLEACH BHÉARRA and WONDER TALES (type 726).

K. Meyer in *AIM*, *1*, 24–39; Ó Gallchobhair, Ua Cuain & Mac Giolla Fhionnáin (1915), 115–28; Hyde (1915), 40–62; E. Hull in *Folk-Lore*, *43* (1932), 376–409; Cross (1952), 59, 81; S. Ó Súilleabháin & Christiansen (1967), type 1927.

Ollamh Fódla Fictional king of Ireland situated in prehistory. His name meant 'high-poet of Fódla' (i.e. Ireland).

The medieval writers claimed that he reigned for 40 years, and that he instituted the Festival of TARA and constructed 'the Rampart of the High Poets' (*Múr na n-Ollamhan*) at that royal centre. He died, we are told, a natural death within the rampart. A seventeenth-century writer, apparently quoting some lost source, gives a more detailed account of this king. According to it, Ollamh Fódla was so called because he was the leading man in the country for wisdom and knowledge and drafting laws. We further read that the Festival of Tara he instituted was held every third year at Samhain (November), and at that session the laws were reviewed and the Annals were put in order.

Some earlier writers give clues to the origin of this fictional king. One source states that his real name was Eochaidh, that he was 'a marvellous poet', and that he had as brother a wonderful wizard called Araidhe. It is further claimed that the Dál nAraidhe people of east Ulster were named from this Araidhe. Other texts, equally inventive, state that the Ulstermen got their name from him, giving for ULAIDH the false etymology *oll-leith* (i.e. the side of Ollamh). These references indicate that the personality whose image suggested this fictional king was the sixth-century Ulsterman EOCHAIDH ÉIGEAS, known as 'the chief-poet of Ireland'. The medieval writers did not scruple about using what were to them obscure names and titles to invent characters, and so fill in the imagined ancient history.

Macalister (1956), 232–5; Dinneen, *2* (1908), 130–5; W. Stokes in *Irische Texte*, *3*, 392–3; Best & O'Brien (1957), 477; J. Carney in *Celtica*, *1*, 101.

Oscar Leading mythical warrior in the FIANNA CYCLE. His name has the element *os* (deer or fawn), and his origins obviously lay in the hunting lore of the Fianna. He is always described as the son of OISÍN, and therefore grandson of the celebrated FIONN MAC CUMHAILL.

It might be that his name was originally

an alternative one for Oisín, but distinctive lore of him has been in existence for a long time. Already in the eleventh century, he is described as slaying with a spear-cast the high-king CAIRBRE LIFEACHAIR in the Battle of Gabhra, where the Fianna were overthrown. The succeeding literature is unstinting in the prestige it accords to him. He is repeatedly portrayed as the hero who plays the foremost role in battle and who triumphs for the Fianna against strange warriors who come to seek single combat. His name in fact came to be used as a common noun *oscar* to denote a champion, and a thirteenth-century text says of him that 'there never will be after Oscar a warrior of so many hardy triumphs, nor in his own time was there a man his match in battles'.

Later tradition has Oisín poetically tell St PATRICK of his son: 'If I saw Oscar and God fighting hand to hand on yonder hill, if I saw Oscar laid low, then I would admit that God was a strong man!' Folklore has Oscar defeating the great GOLL MAC MORNA in a wrestling contest and thus gaining general recognition as the strongest man of all the Fianna. Finally, when the dead Fianna warriors perform their most dramatic feat by breaking out of hell, it is Oscar who acts as their rearguard. He wields a great flail, which has an unbreakable thong, and thus keeps the demons at bay while each one of the Fianna go free through the gates of hell. This account of him is based on a general folklore plot (*see* WONDER TALES, type 650A), which has an enormously strong man make a great flail and overcome the devils in hell with it. For the great fighting feats of Oscar, *see* FIANNA CYCLE.

E. Windisch in *Irische Texte*, 1, 158; Mac Néill (1908), 74; Ó Siochfhradha (1941), 85; G. Murphy (1953), 50–1, 56, 116; Christiansen (1931), 17–19; Ó hÓgáin (1988), 149– 50, 156, 240, 248–51, 284–5, 361.

Osraighe Tribal name for the inhabitants of the Nore Valley (in south County Laois and in County Kilkenny). The original meaning of the designation was probably 'deer-people', referring to the Celtic father-deity in the form of a stag. It is anglicised as Ossory.

The Osraighe were ÉRAINN, although their genealogists were at pains to make an ancient connection between them and their powerful neighbours, the LAIGHIN. Their tribal name caused no small amount of speculation. One tradition – misinterpreting it as *os-fhríthe* (deer-find) – claimed that their ancestor Aonghus was borne by his mother while sojourning amongst the wild deer, and thus acquired the nickname. There was a curious old tradition that the men of the Osraighe periodically took the shape of wolves, leaving their human body at home while they went in that shape. If the human body were touched during that time, they could not return to their proper form, and if one of them were killed when in wolf form, the human body would be found dead at home. Late medieval tellings have the men of Ossory suffering this affliction of shapechanging as a result of a curse put on them by a SAINT. All of this resulted from a mere word-play upon the name of another of their ancestors, Laighneach Faeladh (literally, 'the Leinsterman wolf-like'). Werewolf lore is not indigenous to Ireland, and must have been borrowed from abroad into this context.

The Osraighe maintained their independence from other population groups until the NORMAN invasion in the twelfth century. Their descendants bear surnames such as Mac Giolla Phádraig (Fitzpatrick); Ó Braonáin (Brennan); Ó Donnchaidh (Dunphy); Ó Caollaí (Queally); Ó Cionnfhaolaidh (Keneally); Mac Braoin (Breen).

NAME, ORIGIN, GENEALOGY: T.F. O'Rahilly (1946), 10, 18–19, 455–6; O'Brien (1962), 101–16.

AONGHUS: W. Stokes in *Irische Texte*, 3, 374–5.

AS WOLVES: Todd (1848), 204; Stokes in *Irische Texte*, 3, 215, 376–7; Cross (1952), 105–6, motif D113; O'Brien (1962), 15–17; Mac Suibhne (1961), 21–3, 33; O'Meara (1982), 69–72, 132–3; J. Carey in *CMCS*, 44, 48–64.

outlaws People who had been pushed outside the law by injustice and oppression are generally heroised in Irish folk tradition.

The continued confiscation of land by the English authorities through the seventeenth and eighteenth centuries gave rise to guerrilla bands of the dispossessed Irish, who resorted to remote areas and raided the English settlers. These bands were originally called 'Tories' (from the Irish word *tóirí*, which signifies 'harasser'), and later became known as 'raparees' (from the word *rápaire*, a half-pike – the weapon with which many of them were armed). They enjoyed the great advantage of expert knowledge of the terrain – which they used with great resourcefulness – and the co-operation of the native population. Methods used by the authorities to counter these outlaws were merciless. Captured raparees were invariably hanged, and periodic manhunts were organised to track down and kill these 'human wolves'. Proclamations even went so far as to penalise whole communities through which raparees passed. These regulations served to increase the sympathy of the native population for the raparees, and indeed many of the raparee bands were commanded by a dispossessed Irish chieftain of the locality.

Particular MOTIFS occur in the lore of different outlaws and become conventional. All over Ireland, for instance, the story was told of how the local outlaw hero was once being given food in a house by a man who intended to betray him. The man's wife noticed that treachery was afoot and that the soldiers were approaching the house. Thus while serving the outlaw at table, she remarked: '*Más maith leat bheith buan, caith fuar agus te!*' This literally means 'If you want a long life, eat cold and warm!' thus giving advice on health; but the word *te is* pronounced similarly to *teith* (flee), and the sentence could be taken to mean 'If you want a long life, eat it cold and flee!' Taking the hint, the outlaw jumped up and raced out of the house in time.

The hero-outlaws were not mere lawbreakers – their aggression was specifically directed towards the mighty and powerful. A perennial motif is the international one of 'robbing the rich and helping the poor'. It is noticeable how in this lore of Irish outlaws, the image of the raparee gradually slides into that of the highwayman. The tendency to romanticise highwaymen is found in the lore of many countries, but the Irish bandits derive special sympathy from Irish circumstances, and themes concerning the heroic outlaw are brought out with special clarity in Ireland. For instance, the hero-outlaw's social origins are of some consequence, he becomes an outlaw through no fault of his own, he is held in respect by a minority of his enemies who have a sense of fair play, and he is betrayed by a friend. Typcial examples of such figures were Réamonn Ó hANLUAIN of Armagh and Éamonn Ó MAOILRIAIN of Tipperary.

The soaring but defeated hopes of the folk are projected onto the outlaw so that he is considered a brilliant tactician, and fortune smiles brightly on him during his ascendancy. The heroic outlaw is a resourceful strategist, using the methods likely to be most successful – cleverness, mobility and studied unpredictability. He is surrounded by drama; disguise is a frequent theme – he may even be magically protected – and great emphasis is placed on his daring escapes. A contemporary account of the eighteenth-century highwayman William Peters from Laois states that 'people thought it was by witchcraft he preserved his life, and his mother used to say that no hemp was able to hang her son'. Local folk tradition holds that a travelling wise woman gave a stone to the outlaw's mother that, if held in his mouth, would ensure he could not be hanged. This is a clear instance of floating tradition being attached to Peters, based on the actual fact that he had on one occasion survived the gallows by keeping a medical mixture in his mouth while being hanged. He woke up next day in the coffin, was re-arrested, but managed to escape.

More usually, however, it is by his own wiles and abilities that the outlaw achieves his spectacular successes. A favourite trick, according to folk accounts, is that of holding up rich victims by using a cabbage stump in place of a pistol. Another is the frightening off of pursuing soldiers by placing hats on haystacks and thus pretending to have a large group of supporters ready in ambush. Regarding escapes, many outlaws are said to have confused their pursuers by reversing the shoes on their HORSE and thus leaving misleading trails. Again, other traditions attribute marvellous athletic feats, such as running and jumping, to particular outlaws. One widespread LEGEND tells of a woman washing clothes in a river when she sees an outlaw approach, running very fast and being pursued by a group of soldiers on horseback. He jumps over the river without slackening his pace. 'Great is your jump, man!' she remarks. 'You would not say so if you knew how long my run up to it was!' he says, thus showing that he has stayed clear of his pursuers for several miles.

The outlaw is often portrayed as possessing a great horse, the agility and intelligence of which are indispensable aids to him in his adventures. Cliffs and rivers are often pointed out locally where an escaping outlaw jumped over on horseback and thus affected his escape. Particularly rich was the folklore concerning the great black mare Venus owned by the outlaw Seoirse Mac Conmara (1690–1760) of Cong, County Mayo. An early-eighteenth-century Cork outlaw, Seán Ó Murchú – known as Seán Rua an Ghaorthaidh – had a very clever DOG. When in want of food at his hideout near Tomes, south of Bandon, Seán used to send the dog into the town of Macroom with a basket tied about its neck. The basket would be filled by sympathetic shopkeepers, and the dog would then trot back to its master with the provisions. When followed by soldiers eager to capture the outlaw, the dog would lead its trackers into swamps and quagmires, eventually giving them the slip.

These raparee and highwayman heroes are invariably portrayed as friends and benefactors of the poor tenants labouring under the landlord system. In order to illustrate this point, a migratory LEGEND told in several countries of kindly robbers was borrowed by the Irish folk and applied to various native outlaws. For instance, a chapbook tells it of the Cork highwayman, Risteard de Paor (c.1660–85) known as 'Captaen' Power. In his travels in Leinster once, Power came to the house of a poor farmer and his wife, and observed that the couple were in deep sorrow. They explained to him that they had run into arrears in their rent, and that the landlord was preparing to evict them. Power took compassion on them, and offered them a loan of £60 to pay the rapacious TYRANT when he came to demand it, but to get a receipt for it from him. This was done, and on the road home, the landlord was waylaid by Power and relieved of the cash, together with whatever other items of value he had on his person.

The lore of the hero-outlaw is usually dramatised by a tragic ending. The hero is so great that he cannot be overcome by ordinary means, but his demise is brought about by vile cunning on the part of his enemies or by treachery on the part of his friends. Often the traitor is described as a close confidant or a lover, and there is some social truth to this, for those in close contact with the outlaw would have sufficient knowledge of his movements. Most of the famous Irish outlaws did meet a violent end. The best known of them in folk tradition – in addition to those mentioned above – were Dónall Ó hÓgáin (+1692) from County Tipperary and known as 'Galloping Hogan'; Aonghus Ó hEachaidhin (c.1691–1720) from County Antrim; Seán Crosach Ó Maoláin (+1725) from County Derry; Cathaoir Ó Díomasaigh (+1735) from County Laois and an adept at stealing horses from the settlers; Liam Ó Crotaigh (1712–42) from County Waterford; Proinsias Dubh Ó Corragáin (+1782) from County Donegal; Liam Ó Braonáin (+1812) from County Cork and known as 'Brennan on the Moor'; and 'Captain' Jeremiah Grant (c.1785–1816) from County Tipperary. The above-mentioned Seán Rua Ó Murchú obtained a pardon, and another eighteenth-century highwayman, 'Captain' James Freney from County Kilkenny, survived to write his autobiography.

Cosgrave (ninth edn., 1776); Marshall (1927); anon in JCHAS, 11, (second ser.), 71–9; C. Ó Muimhneacháin (1956), 25–31; Ó hÓgáin (1985), 178–92, 293–4, 298–300, 338–9, 347; McCallen (1993); Dunford (2000); IFC Index.

Parthalán *(also, Partholón)* Leader of a fictional ancient settlement in Ireland. He and his people were an invention of the early medieval historians.

'Parthalán' is an Irish adaptation of Bartholomaeus, a name that had been explained by St Jerome as 'son of him who stays the waters'. This explanation was repeated in the influential work of Isidorus of Seville in the seventh century AD. Since the historians based their chronology on the biblical Deluge, they thus claimed that the first leader of a settlement in Ireland after that event was called Parthalán. This idea developed early, for Parthalán is mentioned in an account of Irish prehistory in the *Historia Brittonum* of Nennius, which was compiled in the early ninth century. That work had as one of its sources a primitive text of the Irish pseudo-historical work called the *Lebor Gabála*. According to this work, Parthalán fled from Greece after slaying his father and mother in an attempt to take the KINGSHIP from his brother. He also lost his left eye in the episode, and bad fortune was destined to follow him on account of his kin-slaying. After seven years wandering, he reached Ireland accompanied by his wife, his three sons and their wives. Various accounts are given of retainers whom he also brought with him. For instance, Beoil, who made the first guest house in Ireland, Bréa, who instituted cooking and duelling, and Malaliach, who was the first brewer, manufacturing ale from the fern. Furthermore, he brought with him four oxen, the first CATTLE in the country. The settlers found but one unforested area in Ireland, Sean-Mhagh nEalta (the plain on which the city of Dublin now stands), and so they set about levelling four other plains. Curiously, the accounts accept that the sinister FOMHÓIRE race were already in Ireland, and these were encountered and defeated by Parthalán in the Battle of Magh nÍotha (the plain of south Donegal). This conflict lasted for a week, but no combatant was slain 'for it was a magic battle'. It was fought 'on single legs and with single arms and single eyes', and the account of it is obviously an echo of the great mythic contest between the otherworld powers (*see* MYTHOLOGICAL CYCLE).

Some personal drama was also infused into the narrative concerning Parthalán. Once, when he went hunting, he left his wife Dealgnat with his manservant Topa at Magh-Inis (the estuary of the River Erne). Dealgnat seduced the servant, and they used Parthalán's own suction tube to drink ale from his vat. When he returned and found the taste of their mouths on the tube, he realised what had happened and flew into a rage. One recension states that he killed the unfortunate Topa, whereas others have his wife's lapdog as the victim of his rage. This was the first adultery and the first jealousy ever in Ireland. Dealgnat, however, justified her actions with a quatrain to the following effect: 'Honey with a woman, milk with a cat, food with a generous person, meat with a boy, a wright where an edged tool is – one with one, great the risk!'

We read that, having been 30 years in Ireland, Parthalán died on the primeval plain of Sean-Mhagh nEalta. His people continued to inhabit the country for 520 years. When they numbered over 9,000, they were overtaken by a PLAGUE on that same plain and all perished there between two Mondays in May. A variant telling, however, had one survivor, the long-living TUÁN MAC CAIRILL.

Macalister (1939), 249, 253–73 & (1940), 2–114; K. Meyer in *ZCP*, *13*, 141–2; Arbois de Jubainville (1903), 16–25; T.F. O'Rahilly (1946), 475–6; A.G. Van Hamel in *ZCP*, *10*, 152–5, 181–2.

Patrick *(in Irish Pátraic, later Pádraig, from the Latin Patricius)* The national SAINT, who flourished in the fifth century AD. The date of his mission was traditionally given as the years 432–61, but an alternative dating is from 456–93. He was not the first Christian missionary in Ireland, but he was the most influential, and his efforts were very significant in the general change to Christianity.

Patrick was born somewhere in the west of Britain into a family of Romanised Celts, his father's name being Calpurnius. At the age of sixteen, he was seized by an Irish raiding party and brought to Ireland as a slave. He was set to herding pigs and sheep in a lonely place, but after six years he escaped, travelling over 200 kilometres before he got a ship to bring him to the Continent. He studied there, was ordained to the priesthood, and after a long interval returned to Ireland to begin his mission. This much is clear from his own Latin work, the *Confessio*, and in it he tells that, while on the Continent, he had a vision in which a man brought him letters containing 'the voice of the Irish' and beseeching him to 'come back and walk once more among us'. In the vision, he recognised the voices of people who lived beside the wood of Voclut (apparently Foclath in the parish of Meelick, County Mayo), and it seems from this that he had spent at least part of his bondage in that area. The *Confessio* is very much a private document, and it is difficult to decipher much from it regarding the physical environment and actual events of his career. One other document survives from his hand – a letter written in condemnation of a north British prince called Coroticus who had seized some of Patrick's converts and taken them as captives.

The earliest surviving biographies of Patrick date from the second half of the seventh century. One of these was by Muirchú, who seems to have been a cleric from Armagh, and the other was by a bishop named Tíreachán, apparently a native of Tirawley, County Sligo. In some respects, both of these biographers drew from a common source: a work – now lost – written by Ultán (+657), who is reported to have been for a while the abbot of the monastery of Lughbhadh (the village of Louth in mid County Louth). That monastery had been founded in the early sixth century by a disciple of Patrick called Mochtae, and in it the writings of Patrick were carefully preserved. What Ultán had written, therefore, would appear to have been a compendium of early Patrick lore current in Louth, including LEGENDS that had developed out of discussions on his writings by monks and laity associated with that monastery. These legends drew on material relating to native mythical figures such

as LUGH and the DAGHDHA, and on native rituals such as the lighting of fires. For their part, Muirchú and Tíreachán added further drama to the material.

Muirchú describes Patrick's youth, captivity and escape according to the *Confessio*, and then goes on to tell in very dramatic terms of the saint's mission to Christianise the country. We read that the DRUIDS of the high-king LAOGHAIRE, son of the great NIALL, had foretold in verse the coming of such a one, an 'adze-head' who would triumph over the old ways. Accordingly, Patrick arrived at Inbhear Dé (Arklow), but then sailed north to Sliabh Mis (Slemish, County Down) to redeem himself from the man who is described as having been his master when in slavery, Miliuc. The latter, hearing that the escaped slave was approaching, feared that Patrick might become his master and burned himself to death. On seeing the burnt-out pier, Patrick turned away in disappointment and sailed to Inbhear Colptha (the Boyne estuary). It was Easter-tide, and the custom was for the high-KING to light a fire at TARA at that time. Anybody who lit a fire before Laoghaire did so would forfeit his life. Patrick, however, lit his own Easter fire at the burial place of Fir Féig (now Slane, County Meath), and when Laoghaire saw this, he rushed in anger, accompanied by his druids and soldiers, to confront the newcomer.

Patrick was ordered to explain his behaviour, and he immediately got into contention with the druids – one of whom, named Lochru, he caused to be raised into the air and to fall and dash his brains against a stone. Seeing this, Laoghaire and his men tried to seize the saint, but darkness fell and the ground shook, causing them to mistake each other for him. Following this, Laoghaire pretended to do reverence to Patrick and invited him to come to Tara. Patrick suspected treachery, and he blessed his eight companions, causing them to disappear into the wilderness in the form of deer. On the following day, the saint, with five of his companions, entered Tara through closed doors as the royal household was feasting. He was invited to join in the feast, and a druid called Lucet Moel put a drop of poison into his drink. Patrick blessed the drink, which froze, and the drop fell out. A contest in wondrous feats between the saint and Lucet ensued. To show his power, the druid covered the plain with snow, but he could not remove it and Patrick had to do that for him. Similarly, with a fog brought by the druid.

Finally, they agreed to a test of fire. A house was built, half of green wood and half of dry wood. Lucet went into the green part, wearing the saint's chasuble, and Patrick's servant-boy Benignus went into the other part, wearing the druid's garb. The house was set on fire, with the result that Lucet was burned to death while Benignus emerged unscathed. However, the druid's garment on Benignus was consumed, whereas Patrick's chasuble on Lucet was untouched. We read that Laoghaire was then converted, but Patrick told him that – on account of his previous opposition – none of his descendants would be kings.

Muirchú goes on to describe various events of Patrick's mission – including a claim that Coroticus, having made captives of some of the saint's converts, was turned into a fox. We read that a fierce tyrant in Ulster, called Mac Cuill (Mac Goill) tried to entrap the saint by having one of his men feign death and demanding that Patrick heal him. When the cover was removed from the face of the imposter, however, he was found to be really dead and had to be revived by the saint, whereupon Mac Cuill submitted to Patrick and sought baptism. As penance, Patrick ordered him to set himself adrift in a boat, and he did so and reached the Isle of Man, where he became a hermit. In an adventure at Droim Bó (near Downpatrick), Patrick rebuked pagans for building a dwelling on a Sunday and, as a result, a storm came and destroyed their work.

We also read that a powerful man named DÁIRE refused Patrick the hill of Droim Saileach (now Armagh), but instead gave him an inferior site for a monastery. One of Dáire's horses later died after grazing on this site, following which the magnate told

his men to go and kill the saint. Immediately, however, Dáire himself was struck down with illness, and the men begged Patrick to come and heal him. The saint gave them blessed water, with which both Dáire and the horse were revived. The magnate then sent a bronze cauldron as a present to Patrick, who reacted only by saying 'grazacham'. The displeased Dáire ordered that the cauldron be taken back, and again Patrick spoke the same word. Finally, the magnate himself went with the cauldron and gave it to him, giving also the piece of land at Droim Saileach, which became Patrick's great centre of Ard Mhacha.

Other details in Muirchú's text include a conversation of Patrick's with a pagan over whose grave a cross had inadvertently been placed. The dead man told him that the cross should rather have been placed next to him, on the grave of a man who had died a Christian. We also read that the saint was untouched by rain, and that he could light up the dark with his fingers, which glowed. Before he died, he obtained special requests from his companion angel, Victor. These were that Armagh should be pre-eminent in the Irish church, and that all the Irish people should be judged by Patrick himself at the end of time. For twelve days after his death at Sabhall (Saulpatrick, County Down), there was no darkness in that area. The angel had advised him regarding the manner of his burial, and his body was accordingly placed in a cart drawn by untamed oxen. They stopped at Dún Leathghlaise (Downpatrick) in the territory of the Ulstermen (see ULAIDH), and he was buried there. The Ulstermen and the royal Uí Néill sept quarrelled over which of them should have the body, but an illusion of another pair of oxen drawing a cart was seen by the Uí Néill, and they therefore thought that they had the body for burial.

This biography by Muirchú had various sources. It is clear that he dramatised his account of the saint's coming to the court of the high-king with various imagery from Christian tradition – he himself compares Laoghaire to the Old Testament tyrant Nebuchadnezzar, the angel speaks to Patrick from a burning bush as God did to Moses, and the contest with the druids is modelled jointly on that of Moses with the pharaoh's magicians and on the apocryphal account of St Peter's contest with Simon Magus. Other sources, too, can be identified. The account of Mac Cuill, called a 'Cyclops' in the text, contains a residue of ancient Irish myth concerning a one-eyed foe (see GOLL), while the Dáire story contains echoes of the DAGHDHA and his cauldron of plenty. On the other hand, the puzzling word 'grazacham' preserves an actual memory of a favourite phrase (grates agam – 'let me give thanks') used by Patrick in his Confessio. The contest with Lucet Mael and the story of the burning hut is given also in shorter form by Tíreachán, and must have been included in the common source used by both biographers. It is likely that Lucet was originally a Christian parody of Lugh.

Tíreachán gives a shorter and less ornamented account of the saint's coming to Tara, and states more realistically that Laoghaire refused conversion. This biography concentrates more on Patrick's activities in Tíreachán's native area of north Connacht, giving much detail of the saint's supposed itinerary. It also gives the first version of Patrick's famous retreat on the top of Cruachan Aigle (Croaghpatrick, County Mayo). We read that the saint spent 40 days and 40 nights there, and that the birds were so numerous there that they were troublesome to him. Tíreachán represents the saint as climbing many mountains, another echo of the early stratum of lore which envisaged him on a par with Moses, who communicated with God on Mount Sinai.

The Croaghpatrick story is given in a developed form in the third major work on the saint's life, entitled Bethu Phátraic, which was compiled mostly in Irish between the years 896 and 901. Here we are told that Patrick stayed at the top of the mountain for the duration of Lent. At the end of that time, the peak was filled with black demonic birds, and Patrick banished them by ringing his bell. Angelic white birds then came and sang melodiously for him. He refused to leave the mountain or abandon his fast until God agreed to give him the right to judge all the Irish on the Last Day. This request is the genesis of the long tradition that makes Patrick a symbol of Irish integrity. A text from the same early period adds two further boons – that no foreign people should rule over Ireland forever, and that the country would be submerged by the sea seven years before the end of the world and thus be spared the final desolation.

The text Bethu Phátraic is in three parts, making use of the works of both Muirchú and Tíreachán, but adding much material concerning Munster, the province in the interest of which it was compiled. A whole new (and quite unhistorical) missionary tour of Munster by Patrick is described, particularly influential being an account of the baptism of the EOGHANACHT king Aonghus mac Nad Fraoich at Cashel. We read that Patrick inadvertently put the spike of his crozier through Aonghus' foot. When he noticed what he had done, he asked why Aonghus had not complained, and Aonghus said that he thought that this was part of the rite. Patrick was so pleased at this piety that he ordained that none of Aonghus' descendants as kings should ever die of a wound. The text connects Patrick with various parts of Munster, and it thus represents a culmination of the process that turned the early missionary to the north Midlands and south Ulster into a national saint who travelled the length and breadth of Ireland, single-handedly converting the pagan people to Christianity.

The text of Bethu Phátraic also contains lore of the saint's youth that had developed since his time. We read that his mother was called Concess, and that she was a kinswoman of St MARTIN. He was baptised by a blind priest, but there was no water available and the priest made the Sign of the Cross with the infant's hand. Immediately a well sprang up from the ground, and when the priest washed his eyes in it, his sight was restored. We further read that Patrick, during his childhood, miraculously healed his sister who was on the point of death after an accident, restored his dead foster father to life, caused a wolf to return a stolen sheep, and made firewood from icicles, honey from water, and butter from snow.

Tíreachán gives a description of how Patrick resuscitated a dead giant in order to baptise him, a MOTIF borrowed from a seventh-century Latin biography of Pope GREGORY, who is claimed to have revived the Emperor Trajan for that purpose. This idea of how Patrick could revive and posthumously convert great men of old was put to use by writers from the eleventh century onwards, who represent him as gaining heaven for the dead CÚ CHULAINN, and as meeting with the Fianna heroes CAOILTE and OISÍN, who are claimed to have outlived their time. Beginning in the twelfth century, several accounts were written of his dialogues with this latter duo, and the folklore concerning Oisín preserves many snatches of such. The medieval account of the death of the mythical Ulster king CONCHOBHAR MAC NEASA was also developed in folklore by having Patrick baptise his soul. The soul spoke to the saint from a bush, and this story was further applied to the celebrated mythical high-king CORMAC MAC AIRT.

Several versions of Patrick's biography were written by Anglo-Norman scholars in the Middle Ages. The most striking innovation in these is the notion that the saint banished snakes from Ireland. This motif first became attached to him in the twelfth century, and various explanations of it have been suggested. Ireland was well-known for its lack of snakes from ancient times, and the Greek writer Solinus referred to the fact over a century before Patrick was born. Early medieval writers, such as Isidorus and Bede, also mention it as a scientific fact and with no reference to any tradition involving Patrick. The connection with the saint seems to have been due to the fancy of the hagiographical writers, who had read in earlier biographies that Patrick had studied for some time on the island of Aralanensis (understood to be the island of Lérins off the south coast of France). The monastery on Lérins had been founded by St Honoratus, whose biography claimed that he had banished the snakes from that island, and so the Anglo-Norman writers considered the motif a suitable one to borrow into the Irish context of Patrick. The notion is far more popular in late written and pictorial sources than in folk tradition, which has not quite digested a scenario so unrealistic in environmental as well as practical terms.

A rich harvest of custom and lore concerning the saint does, however, survive in genuine folk tradition. He is said, for instance, to have banished monsters into lakes at several different locations throughout the country. This is in line with the general popularity of that motif in stories of Irish SAINTS, but the tradition that Patrick banished a monster into Loch Dearg (Lough Derg, County Donegal) seems to date back as far as the seventh century, and to have been the main factor that gave rise to the great annual pilgrimage to that place. The pilgrimage was a very celebrated one in medieval times, with people coming to participate from all over the country and many different parts of Europe. A cavern on the island in Lough Derg was said to have been the entrance to purgatory, and penitents would have to endure the ordeal of spending one night in that cavern. The pilgrimage is still current, taking place on all the weekends between 1 June and 15 August, during which the pilgrims spend three days praying and fasting in the environs of the modern church built on the island, as well as one whole night without sleep. Another great annual penitential exercise which survives from the Middle Ages is the climbing of Croaghpatrick (in County Mayo). This is done barefoot on the first Sunday in August (see TIME), and also attracts pilgrims from all over Ireland.

Patrick looms large in folk legend. Versions of the test of the burning hut have been collected from living lore all over the country, as have versions of the story of the cauldron given to him as a gift by the great pagan. The name of the druid, Lucet Mael, does not, however, survive in these oral versions, and Dáire's name has been changed to CROM. The strong likelihood, then, is that these two legends passed into folklore from a post-medieval reading of some of the biographical texts. The folk also invented some original legends of the great saint. For instance, we are told that, exhausted from preaching once, he decided to take a nap and warned his servant-boy to listen carefully to what he would say. Three times the exasperated Patrick cursed Ireland through his sleep, but each time the clever boy deflected the curse with a prayer – firstly onto the tops of the rushes, secondly onto the bullocks' horns, and thirdly onto the bottom of the furze. That is why these three things are ever since black. When he awoke, Patrick praised the boy for his alert responses, because, he said, 'you have saved Ireland'.

In the early biographies, Patrick is represented as placing blessings on some septs and curses on others, thus reflecting bias in the backgrounds of the writers. This tendency passed over into folklore, although in a somewhat more humorous vein. Thus residents of various localities tease their western neighbours by claiming that Patrick never visited the latter, being put off by the bleakness of their territory and the crudity of the inhabitants. Another common jibe was that the residents of a particular area were guilty of the heinous offence of stealing the saint's goat while he was busy with his spiritual duties. The same type of banter lies behind a legend that was quite popular by way of chiding innkeepers. It was said that Patrick once visited a tavern but was given short measure by the landlady. Offended by this, he pointed out to her that the devil, in the shape of an ugly beast, was hiding in her cellar and being fattened by her dishonesty. The terrified woman begged Patrick to banish the evil spirit, but he told her that she must do so herself by mending her ways. Sometime later, when he visited that same tavern, he noted that she was filling the glasses of all her customers so that the whiskey poured out over the brim. He praised this change in behaviour, and brought her to the cellar, where they found the devil in a miserable

state. The evil spirit fled in a flash of fire at their approach, and Patrick ordained that, in memory of this, people should always take a drink of whiskey on his feast day. This drink was called the *Pota Phádraig* (Patrick's Pot), and is known in English as 'drowning the shamrock', for it was customary to place shamrock in drink as a flavourer. The custom of wearing a sprig of shamrock on one's coat on St Patrick's Day, 17 March, does not seem to be very ancient, the first known mention of it dating from the year 1681. It was popularly explained that Patrick had used this little trefoil plant as a means of explaining the Trinity, there being three persons in one God just as they are three leafs on the one stem. It would scarcely have been necessary for the saint to explain the mystery of the Trinity in this way, as the ancient Irish were well acquainted with the triplication of deities in their own mythology (*see* GODS *and* GODDESSES). Nevertheless, in recent centuries the shamrock has become in a very special way the symbol of Patrick and of his mission.

It was customary in the eighteenth and nineteenth centuries for people to wear little crosses on their coats on the saint's feast day. These crosses were made from paper coloured green and red, and were pinned onto a white paper background and decorated with ribbons. In recent generations, they have been replaced by manufactured green and gold badges in the shape of a shamrock or a harp. Another recent addition to the celebration of St Patrick's Day is the holding of great parades through towns, led by brass and pipe bands. This is an imported tradition, deriving from the practice in eighteenth-century North America of holding military parades on that day so as to impress the populace and to encourage the recruitment of Irishmen to the British and US armies. The custom, with its military function discarded, was adopted in Ireland in the nineteenth century, and colourful parades are now held on St Patrick's Day in most large towns in Ireland and abroad in places where substantial numbers of Irish people have settled.

PATRICK'S WRITINGS: Bieler, *1–2* (1951); Hanson (1983).

PERSONAL HISTORY: Carney (1973); Hanson (1968); E.A. Thompson (1985).

EARLY DEVELOPMENT OF LORE: D. Ó hÓgáin in Mac Conmara & Ní Thiarnaigh (1997), 168–184.

MUIRCHÚ: Bieler (1979), 1–35, 61–122, 193–213.

TÍREACHÁN: Bieler (1979), 35–46, 122–63, 213–33.

OTHER EARLY TEXTS: J.P. Migne in *Patrologiae Latinae*, *53*, 823–6; Bieler (1979), 46–56, 164–92, 233–41; Stokes & Strachan (1903), *2*, 354–8.

BETHU PHÁTRAIC: Stokes (1887); Mulchrone (1939).

OTHER BIOGRAPHIES: Bieler (1971): Stokes (1890), 1–19; R.I. Best in *AIM*, *3*, 29–42.

SNAKES: D. Ó hÓgáin in *Béaloideas*, *51*, 95–6.

LOUGH DERG: S. Leslie (1932); Haren & de Pontfarcy (1988); Hopkin (1989), 84–105; Ó hÓgáin in *Béaloideas*, *51*, 90–9.

CROAGHPATRICK: M. MacNeill (1962), 71–84, 686.

ST PATRICK'S DAY: Danaher (1972), 58–66; Hopkin (1989), 106–43.

FOLK LEGENDS: Ó hÓgáin (1985), 5–16, 323; M. MacNeill (1962), 434–648; IFC Index.

GENERAL: D.A. Binchy in *Studia Hibernica*, *2*, 7–173: Bieler (1949); Kenney (1929), 165–70, 319–56, 812; O'Hanlon (1875), *3*, 399–831.

Picts The designation *Picti* was given by the Romans to the people of north-east Scotland, whose indigenous culture had been overlaid with Celtic elements in ancient times. In Irish, these Picts were inaccurately referred to as CRUITHNIGH, of whom the medieval Irish historians developed fanciful traditions. The actual Picts of Scotland have been the subject of much research, but a clear picture of them has yet to emerge.

In Scottish folklore, the Picts were said to have been a dwarf people who lived long ago and were great builders. Some of this Scottish lore influenced folk belief in the province of Ulster in recent centuries, so that the Picts are sometimes given a role comparable to that of the FAIRIES. Flints discovered near forts in parts of Ulster are claimed to have been arrow heads belonging to them, and pieces of crockery their pipes. These 'Pechts' or 'Pixies' are described as having been a small, sturdy people with long hair and large feet. So large were their feet, indeed, that they could shelter themselves from rain by standing on their heads. This imagery seems to be based on the *sciapods* described in Greek literature. According to another humorous tradition,

they were very numerous. When building a fort, they would stand in a line and could bring the materials from a far distant source by handing them on from one to another without moving a step.

PICTS IN ULSTER FOLKLORE: Andrews (1913), 15–16, 27–31, 57–8; Briggs (1977), 322–3.

pigs One of the valued staples of the traditional Irish diet was pork or bacon, and this is underlined in the literature by the importance attributed to pigs. Accounts of swine-herding and boar-hunts were very popular in the medieval stories, and pigs were often given otherworld associations (*see, for example*, FIONN MAC CUMHAILL). Pigs were kept by a large number of farmers in olden times, their sty sometimes being an actual extension of the dwelling-house. In some places, it was customary to drive a pig into the house on May morning, so as to ensure luck for the summer season, and among the speculative capabilities of the animal was the ability to see the wind and thus forecast the weather.

Pigs were often regarded as crude and dirty animals, and the likening of a person to one was the ultimate insult. Accordingly, in the literature, when otherworld beings appeared in the form of a pig, their hostile aspect was being stressed. A folk LEGEND told of how a rich woman had once been unkind to a poor woman who came to seek alms, likening her and her children to a sow with a litter of bonhams. When the rich woman herself gave birth soon after, her child had a pig's head. Ominous GHOSTS were often said to appear in the form of a black pig, and a late legend in north Leinster and adjoining areas tells of how an ill-tempered schoolmaster was turned into such a creature by one of his pupils who got possession of a book with magical spells. The raging teacher carved out a large trench through the countryside, and this was popularly given as the origin of the 'Black Pig's Dyke', a series of earthworks that stretch approximately along the southern border of Ulster, and which were probably constructed in early centuries to prevent cattle-raiding.

GENERAL: F. Kelly (1997), 79–88; Cross (1952), 51–82, *passim*; Wood-Martin, *2* (1902), 131–7; S. Ó Súilleabháin (1942), 38–9; Ó Danachair (1978), 25; P.V. O'Sullivan (1991), 15–19, 102–7.
PIG'S HEAD ON CHILD: S. Ó Súilleabháin in *Béaloideas, 39–41,* 251–65.
BLACK PIG'S DYKE: M.E. Dobbs in *ZCP, 8,* 339–46; F. Williams in *Emania, 3,* 12–19.

place-lore Great interest has always been shown by the Irish people in antiquities and in historical probing into the past of various localities and landmarks. In early Ireland, the discovery and preservation of such knowledge was the specific duty of the POETS, who were the official men of learning, and this function continued to be associated with them until recent times.

The surviving texts of medieval date suggest that the learned men attained a far higher degree of accuracy in their preservation of genealogical lore than in place-lore proper. By the early Middle Ages, at any rate, the poets were finding it necessary to create new place-lore from the various stories known to them, and to invent new stories where there was no suitable material to hand. So, from the ninth century onwards, we have a series of onomastic poems written in this manner, and by the early twelfth century these poems were brought together into one great unit known as the *Dindshenchas* (Place-lore). There is no full surviving manuscript of this work, but in all there were nearly 300 poems, many accompanied by a prose synopsis. Each poem has the heading of a particular place name, and then relates a story that purports to explain the origin of that toponymic. The writers of these poems drew on many sources for their material, including the MYTHOLOGICAL, ULSTER and FIANNA CYCLES, stories of the ancient kings, and some local traditions, but many of the narratives are strained. Many more are fabricated, favourite devices being pseudo-etymologising and the invention of characters on the basis of existing place names. To cite an example, the toponymic of Dublin (*Dubhlinn*) is explained by claiming that a POETESS called Dubh was angry because her husband was consorting with another lady. As the latter was boating in the bay, Dubh sang a charm against her, causing her to be drowned. A retainer of the dead woman, however, made a slingshot at Dubh, killing her so that she fell into the water – hence Dubhlinn (the pool of Dubh). The place name, in fact, meant simply 'black pool' – it has been generally superseded in Irish by the city's other designation, Baile Átha Cliath, which means 'the town of the wattle-ford'. Originally, Dubhlinn and Baile Átha Cliath were two separate villages, a few hundred yards apart on opposite sides of the River Liffey, the former on the south bank and the latter on the north.

A second recension of the *Dindshenchas* was compiled about a century later. This repeats many of the verse texts, but its prose adds length to the stories and variety to the interpretations. Notwithstanding the mental efforts that went into the compilation of these works, a great deal of the material is still structured in the form of mere speculation, and most of the genuine narratives involved are adoptions of stories known from earlier texts. In the present volume, stories from the *Dindshenchas* are treated, as is the material found in other compilations, according to their subject-matter. In later medieval times, it was claimed that the sixth-century poet of king DIARMAID MAC CEARRBHEOIL, called Amhairghin mac Amhalghaidh, had been the author of the *Dindshenchas*. This highly anachronistic claim sprang from the account of how the antediluvian FIONNTAN recited ancient lore at the court of Diarmaid.

Neither the texts of the *Dindshenchas* nor the many other miscellaneous items of place-lore in the literature had much influence on the oral tradition. Yet folklore shows an enduring interest of its own in local lore, centring on matters such as historical happenings, supposed connections with SAINTS and other celebrated personages, social and economic history, and accounts of GHOSTS and FAIRIES. The folklore also displays some aspects that are entirely absent from the literature, such as humorous LEGENDS concerning places and humorous interpretations of their names. It is said, for instance, that in the city of Limerick, the inhabitants were once so angered by the heavy taxes imposed by a succession of mayors that they decided to elect as a new mayor the first man who crossed the principal bridge there. The man who did so was a poor chimney-sweep called Seán na Scuab (John of the Brushes), and he proved a very suitable and worthy mayor. A favourite nickname for the inhabitants of Kilkenny is the 'cats', and a story is told to explain why this is so. It is said that the soldiers of CROMWELL once set two cats fighting by hanging them by their tails on a pole, and when the soldiers returned to see the fight the cats had eaten each other down to the tails. This story possibly originated in jibes directed by the victorious Cromwellians at the mid-seventeenth-century Kilkenny Parliament, which was notorious for its squabbling.

Satiric verses on towns are common. For example, an anecdote told of various places in Munster called Baile an Fhaoitigh (anglicised Ballyneety or Whitestown) has a beggar man passing through and being attacked by a fierce dog. The unfortunate man bent down to pick up a stone, but found that it was stuck to the ground. After he was badly bitten, he made a wry verse on the place name, saying that the stones were tied there and the dogs were loose (*clocha ceangailte agus madraí scaoilte*). Some late anecdotes claim to explain the meanings of place names, giving hilarious etymologies – such as a beggar man complaining that the people of a County Derry town were 'done giving' (hence Dungiven); or St Patrick, having been struck by a stone, complaining of the 'wicked low' people who inhabited a town (Wicklow) on the east coast. Humorous stories and verses, which have people of one place making satiric comments on those of another place, are very common.

DINDSHENCHAS: Gwynn (1903), (1906), (1913), (1924), (1935); W. Stokes in *RC*, *15 & 16 passim*.

DUBHLINN: Gwynn (1913), 94–5; Stokes in *RC*, 15, 326–7.

SEÁN NA SCUAB: S. Ó Súilleabháin & Christiansen (1967), type 1383.

KILKENNY CATS: Egan (1884), 26–9.

OTHER FOLKLORE: IFC Index.

plague Such misfortunes were of frequent occurrence in Ireland, despite the country's island situation. A plague was often symbolised in Christian terms as a great beast or dragon that gobbled up people and animals. The shape of such a monster, it was said, was seen in the sky before the outbreaks of some plagues. This image was taken from the Apocalypse of John, which describes a dragon causing devastation for a while until overcome by an agent of God. In line with this imagery, Irish tradition referred to events of the sixth and seventh centuries AD, when outbreaks of yellow plague were banished by SAINTS. These outbreaks were called the *Crom Chonaill* and the *Buidhe Chonaill*, with the implication that they spread southwards from Tír Chonaill (the greater part of modern County Donegal). The idea that destructive forces came from the north is very old, the colder northern regions of the world being regarded as forbidding places. Happily, a pestilence expected to sweep the country in 1096 never materialised. It was named the *Roth Rámhach* (Wheel of Rowing – *see* MOGH RUITH), and was also referred to as the *Scuab a Fánait* (Brush from Fanad), presumably because its origin was expected to be in the area of Fanad in north Donegal.

Epidemics were often explained as the work of demons, such as in 1084 when a great pestilence was said to have killed a quarter of the country's population. This, the Annals claim, was caused by 'demons who came out of the northern isles of the world'. The reality that pestilence came from the east was often understood, however – the Annals report for the year AD 986, for instance, that 'magical sickness was caused by demons in the east of Ireland'. In general, wind and unseen forces were thought to be the culprits rather than human or animal contact, but the idea also existed that disease could not travel further than nine waves of the sea. A similar notion persists in folklore, to the effect that an evil spirit cannot cross running water (*see* GHOSTS). More rarely, public misfortunes were personalised by saying that a strange dark figure was seen to pass through a particular area as a prelude to disaster in that place. This accords with a general tendency in Irish folklore to present the brief and unexplained appearance of a stranger or of a ghost as a sinister omen.

The terror of plague continued, and in nineteenth-century Ireland the great fear was due to frequent cholera outbreaks. One such alarm in the year 1832 gave rise to extraordinary scenes for a brief period, when people thought that the passing around of 'blessed' turf would prevent a catastrophe (*see* Daniel O'CONNELL).

Joyce (1903), *1*, 607–11; Kenney (1929), 749–51; Cross (1952), 273; S. Ó Súilleabháin (1942), 488–9; S.J. Connolly in *Irish Historical Studies*, 5/1983, 214–32; Ó hÓgáin (1985), 116–17, 332–3.

poets/poetesses The word used for a poet, in Irish literature at all stages and in the spoken language, is *file*. This word contains a Celtic root *velit-*, meaning to see, and all the evidence suggests that the Irish *file* was originally a seer who expressed his mystical insights in the form of rhetoric. Early literary sources indicate that learned rhetorical speech was known as *bélra na bhfiled* (the language of the poets).

The mythical FIONN was the archetypal seer, and there can be little doubt but that his cult was developed by the poets or *filid* (modern Irish, *fili*). A single term, *fios*, is applied to the knowledge of Fionn and to that of the poets, and this knowledge is expressed in the same dimensions of antiquarianism, clairvoyance and prophecy. Poets in both Irish literature and folklore often appear as repositories of knowledge concerning the past, as possessors of immediate insight into issues of the present, and as deliverers of prophecies regarding the future. It is impossible to make a clear distinction in the early sources between *file* and *druí*, as both poets and DRUIDS tended to fulfil the same functions. The likely explanation for this is that the *file* was really a variety of druid, and that following the triumph of Christianity, much of the druidic cult was preserved under the comparatively innocuous guise of poetry. The Christian literature itself exemplifies this process. We read, for instance, that St PATRICK abolished pagan rituals, but that

a *file* called Dubhthach mac ua Lughair supported the saint. As a result, Patrick blessed the mouth of Dubhthach, who immediately began to compose inspired religious verse. Such a rapprochement between the two systems of learning was indeed reached in real history, and to it we owe the preservation of many of the rich secular stories that the monks and their students committed to writing. The native tradition of learning was originally an oral one, and memorisation of stories and traditions was an essential part of the poet's trade. He needed to be able to recite poetry and tales when called upon to do so by his royal and noble patrons, and the introduction of writing through the monasteries was therefore a much-valued asset to him.

Apart from the more strictly didactic texts, there is a similar or identical method of describing druids and poets in the early literature. The text that describes the verbal contest between the poets FEIRCHEIRDNE and NÉIDHE MAC ADHNA is especially enlightening in this regard. Both make many obscure references to ancient lore, Feircheirdne causes his younger opponent to sink somewhat into the ground through magic, and a colourful account is given of the paraphernalia associated with Feircheirdne as *ollamh* (chief-poet). We read that his robe was of purple colour, adorned with gold and silver, and that it was decorated with bird feathers and spangled with bronze. A golden branch was carried above him, and a special seat was allotted to him.

Whether or not these details are accurate, there can be little doubt but that the poets cultivated much lore concerning themselves in order to add to their prestige. Thus since earliest times, one encounters the conceit that the poet is a special and unique type of person. A compound of the word *fios*, written *soas*, is explained in the ancient laws as the property of the *ollamh*, and he displays it by 'making a verse without thinking'. Poetry being a verbal manifestation of mystical knowledge, it was considered to be a kind of genius within the poet himself, the most

426

important element in his unique nature. This idea persisted into recent folklore. A true poet, we are told, can pour forth perfect verses without planning them, and he always fills in the rhyme when challenged with a half-quatrain. His is popularly regarded as one of the three gifts that must be born with a person, and cannot be acquired by learning – the other two being a melodious voice and a generous heart.

Poetry always has an element of paradox, however, and it is not surprising to find that a contrary view concerning it existed side by side with the above. As well as being an inspired art, it was often referred to by poets themselves as being a trade or skill that had to be perfected by the practitioner. Metaphors for poetry abound in the literature, and many of these refer to it as the process of 'weaving' words, or 'spinning', 'cutting', 'shaping', 'rinsing', 'tying' or 'forging' them. A similar tendency is noticeable in folklore, which has developed anecdotes as glosses on the metaphors. So we are told that Eoghan Rua Ó SÚILLEABHÁIN took special care when composing a song because 'it will need to be good, as many the bad hand will have a go at it!' Similarly, it is said of the nineteenth-century Mayo poet Antoine Raifteirí that he once broke a shoemaker's scissors in anger, and when asked why he had done so, replied that it was in retaliation for the shoemaker having ruined his own trade by wrongly reciting one of his poems. Presumably, anecdotes of this sort have been spontaneously springing up in oral narrative since earliest times. Poetry is regarded in both literary and oral traditions as 'the king of trades', and there has long been a tendency to regard poets as experts, not just in their specific profession, but in many other trades as well.

There is a remarkable continuity in the whole of this tradition. Although the physical circumstances changed, as did the matter and form of the verse, there are recognisable threads of imagery stretching from antique times down to recent centuries and in the surviving folk LEGENDS of *filí*. We read, even in sources concerning the Continental Celts, of the great emphasis placed on druidic schools, where students spent many years studying under some celebrated master. Such a system of druidic schools is referred to in Irish literature also, and it is paralleled by the medieval poetic schools, where the full training period reputedly was 21 years. The material to be studied by the apprentice *file* consisted of ancient stories and legal issues, as well as problems of syntax and metre. There are also, however, echoes of more mysterious matters. Much of the contest between Feircheirdne and Néidhe, for instance, takes the form of riddles, and such enigmatic questions were associated with occult knowledge in many ancient cultures. We find in a ninth-century text that a professional poet called Cruitíne taught his pupils how to solve linguistic riddles, and several other accounts have poets showing their skill and contending with each other in such forms of speech. To be able to see into the hidden meaning of enigmatic statements is in these cases posited to be of equal importance as fluent and deft use of speech.

A late instance from folklore concerns the eighteenth-century Tipperary poet Liam Ó hIfearnáin 'the Blind'. We are told that once, on his way to a poetic assembly, he approached a tree from the northern side, caught a squirrel in it, and took the little creature with him in his pocket. When asked by the assembled poets what direction he had come from, he replied: '*Do ghabhas anoir aniar inné, agus níor thug mé aon choiscéim ach aduaidh* (I came from the east from the west yesterday, and the only step I took was from the north). All were puzzled by this answer, but the learned Seán Clárach Mac Dónaill enquired 'Where is it?' He realised that Liam was referring to the squirrel, for the words of his first phrase, written another way, could have meant 'I caught the squirrel in an oak yesterday'. A quite popular folk legend, told of various versifiers, concerns how a neophyte comes to the poetic school or to the poetic assembly and, when a question is posed to test his skill, utters such a polished quatrain that he is admitted to be their superior by all present. This legend is of a type found in other cultures also concerning brilliant youngsters, and it is difficult to determine its antiquity in Ireland.

Though education and training could bring extra refinement of their skill, if tradition is to be credited, Irish poets were born and not made. This idea was known to the learned men of long ago as it is to present-day storytellers. A text from the tenth century or thereabouts describes a child called Aí mac Ollamhan, the son of a druid. As the druid sits to a meal with his brother, the high-king Fiachna mac Dealbhaith, a great blast of wind is heard outside, and the druid states that this is a portent that his wife will give birth that night and the child will be of equal status with the king. Fiachna determines to prevent this, but immediately after its birth, the baby speaks a rhetoric naming the gift which it desires from the king. The astounded Fiachna complies. The name of this child means in fact 'Art son of Chief-Poet', and it is obvious that he is a personification of poetry. The anecdote must have been invented by some professional poet, probably as a teaching device for his students. The same MOTIF occurs also in the birth-story of the judge MORANN and in that of the seer-child NOÍNE, thus underlying the functional role of poetry relative to these other skills. Late folklore has various celebrated poets speaking immediately after their birth, or composing verse in the very early years of childhood, and thus astounding the watching adults.

Contradictory ideas can, however, abound in tradition. Thus it is said that many poets got their gifts of wisdom and fluency from otherworld sources as adults. A common folk legend – variants of which are told throughout the country – concerns how a man, not hitherto noted for his intellectual accomplishments, falls asleep one night by a mound. He dreams that a beautiful woman comes to him and gives him inspiration, sometimes even offering him a book of wisdom, and when he wakes up, he has the ability to compose verse without effort. This legend has a long pedigree, involving ideas of GODDESSES as bestowers of material and mental well-being, and of the FAIRIES as keepers of secret lore, but it owes much also to idioms employed by poets themselves. The image of the inspiring otherworld lady can be traced through different epochs in the history of Irish poetry. One early text, for instance, posits the queston 'What is poetry?' and gives the answer that it is a maiden who appears to the poet as he composes. She is 'multiformed multifaceted multimagical, a noble well-clasped maiden'. This is clearly a metaphysical argument. In post-medieval literature, the poets often used an encounter with an otherworld lady as a stock situation to introduce their material, which makes the image into a convention; while folklore has the poet actually gaining his art from such a lady, thereby turning it into a narrative LEGEND. All expressions of the image can, in fact, be taken as survivals of lore of poet-seers, such as Fionn gaining inspiration from otherworld beings, as in the shamanic rituals of archaic cultures generally.

Another system of metaphors prevalent in both literature and folklore concentrates on the anatomy of the poet. Most emphasis is on the tongue, which is claimed to be extraordinarily agile and sharp. One medieval source refers to a 'soft tuft' on the tongue of a poet, signifying praise; and another source of the same time refers to 'a bag of poison' on such a tongue, signifying satire. This concretises the division of poetry into *moladh agus aoir* (praise and satire), a division that reaches back into archaic Indo-European culture. It has remained the standard definition in Irish tradition, and a folk anecdote from Waterford expresses it succinctly: according to this, the poetess Máire Ní Dhonnagáin was asked rather flippantly by a priest to make a verse for him. She replied ominously but metrically to the effect that 'there are two sides to my tongue, the gentle side and the rough side'.

Equally important with the tongue is a mystical vein of poetry, which both literature and folklore claim is an essential part of the poet's physique. This is a clear instance of the way in which narrative tends to put abstract ideas into concrete form. It was fancied that the blood flowing through the vein (*féith*) was the special pulse (*cuisle*) of poetry. Folklore situated the vein in the back of the poet's head, and this probably encapsulates the mystical theory on which the belief is based, for that is the 'dark part' of one's body which the eyes cannot see, and extra insight is the unique quality of the poet. It was customary for *filí* of old to lie in dark huts when they were composing, which seems to be a survival from the ritual of DRUIDS who sought knowledge from the world of the dead. Probably by extension of the symbol, the poets themselves used the image of darkness for the much-lauded quality of obscurity in their verse. This idea of special 'seeing' was also the rationale used for the social fact that many poets were blind.

Literary and oral sources alike often presume that the composition of verse was due to a special activation within the poet's body. A general belief was that he was in a peculiar state of mental ferment as he composed – ecstatic, frenzied, mystically inspired, sometimes even intoxicated. Some folk traditions tell of particular poets who had abandoned composing, but resumed when moved to great sorrow or anger upon a special occasion. The poet's body was a general reservoir for genius, with the heart as the centre of both emotion and intellect. From it, the blood pulsated through the special vein, causing words to spring from the lungs, be refined in the head, and be fashioned by the tongue as they entered the world.

Connected with the idea that poetry is an inborn capacity is that which regards it as a talent running in specific families. This latter idea was much magnified by the fact that, from the Middle Ages at least, some families predominated as professional poets – the most famous being the O'Dalys, the Wards, the Higgins and the Keoghs. Since the surname is retained through the male line, the belief developed also that poetry would leave the family for seven generations if it passed to a daughter rather than a son. There were,

in fact, many women poets in both ancient and recent times, but few if any were considered to be of the first grade. This apparently has to do with social conventions that regarded certain occupations as being proper to one sex only, but it reflects also the worldwide notion that women have secret powers and can bring bad luck to men. In Irish folklore, a common type of legend tells of an old poet who on his deathbed speaks a semi-quatrain in the hope that his son will answer, but to his dismay it is the daughter who speaks with full and accurate metre.

Nowhere is the power of the poet more obvious than in the context of satire. The ancient Irish laws specified different kinds of satire and attributed magical effects to some. The poet maintained a high social position in Ireland down to the seventeenth century, being more or less on a par with the chieftain and the bishop, and his disapproval expressed in verse was much feared. It was believed that if he were justified in his satire, he could raise three blisters of shame on a person's face, deprive that person of honour and reputation, and even cause his death. The Annals record that in the year 1414 the English Viceroy, Sir John Stanley, died from the 'poison' of a satire made on him by an Irish poet whom he had wronged, and several similar instances could be cited from literature and lore. The early literature even refers to particular magical postures adopted by poets when satirising, such as going onto high ground overlooking the foe, or moving about on one leg with one eye closed, while reciting the verse in one breath. Sometimes the poets were said to contend fiercely with each other, and the effect could be devastating to both parties. Folk legends tell of how, with a verse, poets could cause storms, knock down trees and, in a less serious vein, shave a person's head or cut off his eyebrows.

The powers of Irish poets were commented upon by several English writers of the sixteenth and seventeenth centuries, including Ben Jonson, Philip Sidney and Shakespeare himself. Perhaps the most celebrated power was that of banishing rats.

All over Ireland it was believed that poets had such power, and many folk accounts tell of a benighted person who encountered a huge drove of rats on the road moving from one place to another in accordance with the versified directions given by a poet. It was sometimes reported that a poet would send rats to eat the corn of those who had offended him, but the major emphasis is on the *file* as a culture hero banishing pests and thus protecting his community. Other less widespread traditions claimed that poets could banish GHOSTS and even cure illnesses with their verse.

There is some divergence between the literature and the folklore with regard to the effect of poetic praise. Down to recent centuries, skilled literary eulogies were much valued and sometimes commissioned from poets at a high cost by chieftains and other prominent individuals, yet in popular lore there is a strong fear of one's name being mentioned at all in a poem. This seems to have been a side-effect from the time-honoured practice that poets had of composing mock-praises for those whom they wished to satirise but were constrained by law from so doing openly. Another folk belief that contradicts literary tradition holds that poetry is itself unlucky, and parents would accordingly discourage their children from making verses. This seems to have also been coloured by the strong tradition of satire, but its origin may be in the age-old idea that those with mystical power stand at a juncture between the physical and spiritual worlds, and are thus themselves in some danger. Yet again in this instance, paradox holds sway, for folklore equally represents people as envying poets for their art and wishing to emulate them.

Because of their quick wit and their dramatic role in society, folklore represents these men of art as being great entertainers and tricksters, and it is usual to meet with an element of humour even in the most serious legends concerning them.

For individual poets, *see* the entries on AITHIRNE, AMHAIRGHIN GLÚNGHEAL, AMHAIRGHIN MAC ÉIGIT SALAIGH, BRICRIU, COMHDHÁN, DALLÁN FORGAILL,

EOCHAIDH ÉIGEAS, FEIDHLIMIDH MAC CRIOMHTHAINN, FEIRCHEIRDNE, FLANN MAC LÓNÁIN, NÉIDHE MAC ADHNA, RUMHANN MAC COLMÁIN, SEANCHÁN and URARD MAC COISE; and the later poets Piaras FEIRITÉAR, Cathal Buí MAC GIOLLA GHUNNA, Cearbhall Ó DÁLAIGH, Mánas Ó DÓNAILL, Aogán Ó RATHAILLE and Eoghan Rua Ó SÚILLEABHÁIN.

L Mac Mathúna in *Veröffentlichungen der keltischen Kommission*, 2, 225–38; Calder (1917); Carney (1967); Robinson (1969); Bergin (1970); J.E.C. Williams (1971); H. Meroney in *JCS, 1*, 199–226; P.A. Breatnach in *Proceedings of the Royal Irish Academy, 83C*, 37–79; Ó Fiannachta (1978); Ó hÓgáin (1982) & (1985), 216–56 & in the following: *Irish University Review, 1* (1979), 44–61; *Léachtaí Cholm Cille*, 18, 89–107; *Comhar*, 2–3/1980, 7–8/1980; Stewart (1998), 1, 12–48; Ó Catháin (2001), 292–304.

political lore Many old themes are repeated in lore of modern political and social history, and there are some new ones, usually of a humorous nature.

As with Daniel O'CONNELL, the late-nineteenth-century political leader Charles Stewart Parnell was lauded for his brilliant use of parliamentary procedure to highlight Ireland's cause. English leaders at Westminster are represented as being exasperated and confused by his obstructive tactics in debate, and the folk believed that he could eventually frustrate the passing of laws so much that the British government would be willing to divest itself of Ireland and allow the country its freedom. The Irish public took great pleasure from his calmness and dignity in Parliament, which contrasted with the fury of his English opponents. This inverted the stereotyped imagery on which anti-Irish feeling was based. After his fall and his early death, admiration for Parnell, 'the Chief', did not evaporate, and poems and ballads portrayed him as an ever-present force castigating those of his Irish parliamentary colleagues who had betrayed him. There were even some fanciful notions that he had not really died. Thus, for instance, it was claimed after his death that he had been seen alive in Paris, where he was supposedly lying low and waiting to return.

Circumstances in Ireland changed, of course, and by the twentieth century the old lore of the heroic outlaw was again in vogue. Fighters for Irish freedom are the subjects of such lore, which focuses on their daring escapes, their disguises and their quick wit. Even though he was being sought by the British authorities everywhere in 1920 and 1921, Michael Collins had the reputation of walking around in very little disguise and by this very audacity bluffing the authorities into not recognising him. This is illustrated by one LEGEND that has him being stopped at a roadblock and being asked for his name by soldiers. He answers 'Michael Collins', and the soldiers – thinking him a good-for-nothing and a mocker – are angered by his insolence. They warn him not to tease them in this way again, and he apologises and departs. A developed form of this legend has Collins – accompanied by other top republican leaders, Cathal Brugha and Tom Barry – driving in a motor car through Dublin and being detained by soldiers. They give their names truthfully, but again are disbelieved. The soldiers give them some thumps and kicks, and tell them to be more careful in future and not to allow their drunkenness to waste the time of the army. Similar stories are told of the more recent war in Ireland and of leading personalities in it.

The competition between various political parties has given rise to much banter and wit, and some of this has become part of enduring lore. Most prominent of all in such lore was Éamon de Valera, whose career as a political leader spanned most of the twentieth century. Anecdotes concerning him take many forms – his supporters lauding his great intelligence and resourcefulness, while his opponents accused him of egoism. Because the taste for a good story usually out-valued the arguments, oral legends of de Valera are a curious mixture of pro and anti feeling. For instance, in common with other folk heroes such as O'Connell and Swift, there is a legend telling of how de Valera was once outdone by an ordinary person. While electioneering in County Clare, it is said, he called to a tumbledown house where an old woman was drinking tea.

When he spoke politely to her, she offered him tea from her own mug. Not wishing to refuse, de Valera deftly took the mug in his left hand so as to avoid drinking from the same side of it as she had been doing. He drank a little, and she remarked: 'I will vote for you, because you are left-handed like myself!'

One humorous story has a boy saving President de Valera from being drowned in the Grand Canal in Dublin. The grateful president offers the boy his choice of reward, but is surprised when the boy asks for a state funeral, and queries why such a young person should be contemplating death. The boy replies that when he hears what he has done, his father will kill him! Several humorous narrative types are shared by de Valera with other political leaders. For instance, he seeks to buy a funeral plot for himself in Glasnevin cemetery, and chooses a corner of the cemetery overgrown with nettles. The cemetery-keeper is surprised at this, but the president explains that it will suffice 'because I will only be there for three days anyway'. This messianism associated with de Valera is open to either positive or negative interpretation. On the positive side, it was sometimes claimed that his Spanish surname betokened that the old prophecies concerning Ireland's liberator coming from Spain were being fulfilled (see Aodh Balldearg Ó Dónaill).

However, it is humour, whether affectionate or caustic, that dominates in most of this lore concerning politicians. Several stories tell of political leaders situated fancifully at the gates of heaven. For instance, de Valera's rival William Cosgrave, who was noted for careful bookkeeping, dies. Fearing that times are hard in heaven as in Ireland, he brings a sack of potatoes with him on his back, but is told by St Peter – who guards the gates of heaven – that he cannot bring the sack inside, nor can he leave it at the gate to clutter the place. Peter tells him, therefore, that he must eat the potatoes before he gains admission. He is surprised to see Cosgrave smile at this, and enquires the reason for his merriment. 'Well,' says Cosgrave, 'I see de

Valera coming in the distance, and he has a sack of turnips!' The best known of these gates-of-heaven anecdotes concerning de Valera has two world leaders dying and being denied access by St Peter. When de Valera dies, Peter races into the interior of heaven, shouting out: 'Arise, God of Glories, and give your seat to de Valera!'

PARNELL: T.D. Sullivan (1905), 313–17; Callanan (1996), 260–99.

DE VALERA: D. Ó hÓgáin in *Léachtaí Cholm Cille*, *14*, 180–4; in *Inniu*, 10–11/1982.

Raghallach KING of Connacht, AD 622–49. An able leader, his name was an abbreviation of *ró-ghiallach*, meaning 'possessor of several hostages'. From his father Uadhu, he was usually known as Raghallach mac Uadhach. He belonged to the Uí Bhriúin sept (a branch of the CONNACHTA), and gained the kingship of the province by slaying Colmán mac Cobhthaigh, who was head of the Uí Fhiachrach and father of GUAIRE. This was at the Battle of Ceann Bugha (Cambo, near Roscommon town).

The genuine annalistic references to Raghallach are meagre, but a dramatic and pseudo-historical narrative concerning him was invented in medieval times. According to this, he had a nephew, the son of his elder brother, and he was extremely jealous of this nephew and fearful that he would take his crown. He therefore feigned sickness, and hearing that he was on the point of death, the nephew came to visit him. Not trusting Raghallach, the young man was accompanied by a strong troop. Raghallach bewailed the fact that the kinsman to whom he wished to bequeath the kingship did not trust him, so the nephew relented and went to him alone, whereupon Raghallach had his own men slay the unfortunate prince. After this, Raghallach's wife Muireann questioned her DRUID as to the king's future, and was told that since he had slaughtered all his relations, he would fall by one of his own children. Hearing this, Raghallach ordered the queen to have slain any baby which might be born to her. Muireann gave birth to a daughter, whom she accordingly gave to her swine-herd to kill, but the swine-herd pitied the infant

and left it at a cross outside the church of a holy woman. The baby was reared by this woman and, hearing of her beauty, Raghallach sent his men to seize and bring her to him. Neither he nor the queen knew who the girl was, but Muireann grew jealous of her husband's love for the young woman. In her jealousy, she swam across the River Shannon and fled to her former fosterling, the high-king DIARMAID MAC AODHA SLÁINE. Meanwhile, Raghallach was so captivated by the girl that he insisted on continually gazing upon her face, even when they were in separate chariots.

When St FÉICHÍN heard of these events, he and several other saints went to rebuke the Connacht king for so rejecting his wife, but Raghallach ignored them and they fasted against him, praying that he would perish dishonourably before the following May-feast (*see* TIME). When that feast was near, Raghallach was hunting a wounded stag on an island. The stag escaped him and swam away, whereupon the king followed it alone in a boat. He came upon some churls who had killed the stag and had divided it among themselves. He quarrelled with them over this, and they slew him with their spades. One account states that Muireann died from jealousy of her daughter.

This dramatic lore of Raghallach's career is quite contrived, and it is noticeable that neither his nephew nor his daughter are named. The episode concerning his nephew is clearly borrowed from the Leinster story of COBHTHACH, while that concerning the daughter is based on the well-known plot of a child who is prophesied to kill its tyrant grandfather (*see* BALAR *and* ROMANTIC TALES, type 934). The Annals make no reference to such events concerning Raghallach, merely recording his death as having taken place on a Sunday and at the hands of one Maolbhrighde mac Mothlacháin, of a subtribe who had been reduced by Raghallach to the role of peasants. They describe Raghallach as sitting on a white horse when slain, and say that Muireann lamented him, and that he was avenged by his son Cathal, who was in fact one of three sons of Raghallach. The narratives concerning the reputed nephew and daughter would seem to have been invented to discredit the Uí Chonchubhair (O'Connors of Connacht), who were direct descendants of Raghallach.

ANNALS: O'Donovan (1848–51), 258–61; W. Stokes in *RC*, *17*, 188–9; P. Walsh in *JGAHS*, *17*, 132; W.M. Hennessy & McCarthy, *1* (1887–91), 108.

NARRATIVES: O'Grady, *1* (1892), 394–6; Dinneen, *3* (1908), 130–5.

GENERAL: F.J. Byrne (1973), 246–8.

religious tales Most of these FOLK-TALES originated in medieval Europe, and have spread through much of the Continent. Versions of over half of the types listed in the Aarne/Thompson catalogue have been collected from Irish oral narrative. Some of them are exempla – tales told by the clergy of the Middle Ages to stress points of morality – and all are based in one way or another on ideas concerning the spiritual otherworld. The ordinary people preserved them for their dramatic traits rather than for their didactic ones, and accordingly the adventurous side of them was developed. Moral points have slipped quietly into the background in these folktales, but they are still operational, and the result is a strange atmosphere, a weird kind of world in which typified beings act out the parts which are their very purpose and lifeline.

They are not without humour, as illustrated by the very first such story listed, type 750A, which tells of God guaranteeing to a certain man the fulfilment of three wishes, which are stupidly wasted. In Ireland, it is usually the man's wife who causes this – for instance, she gets hungry and asks for sausages. This angers her husband very much, but to please her, he wishes for the sausages and they appear. Realising that the wish has been wasted he remarks bitterly: 'May they stick to your nose!' This, of course, the sausages do, and two wishes are thus spent. In order to remove them from her nose, he has to use the third wish. The foolish requests by the woman may vary from version to version. Type 750B is an international tale which tells of how a holy man restores to life a cow which a peasant had generously killed in order to provide a meal for him. It does not survive in Irish folk tradition, but a story in the medieval literature concerning the high-king FIONNACHTA was probably based on it, and an ecotype (*see* FOLKTALE) of it is found in legends of SAINTS (*see* DÉAGLÁN).

The miraculous is also featured in a very popular story that originated in western Europe and spread far and wide, gaining great popularity in Ireland (type 753). It tells of a blacksmith who is visited one day by a stranger wishing to have his horse shod. The stranger says he will do the shoeing himself, but his method of work is very odd. He cuts off the horse's legs, puts on the shoes, and then puts the legs back on the horse. Soon after, an old woman comes to the forge, and the stranger tells her that he can rejuvenate her. He does this by throwing her into the furnace, from which she emerges as a beautiful young girl. Observing all of this, the blacksmith thinks it easy and determines to try it himself. He cuts the legs off a horse, but cannot replace them, and the unfortunate animal dies. Thinking that he had merely got some minor detail wrong, the smith determines to try the second trick. He calls his wife and throws her into the furnace, but she burns. The smith is desperate, but the stranger steps forward and miraculously restores both woman and horse to life. The stranger, who is JESUS CHRIST, rebukes the smith for his pride and irresponsibility.

A group of stories dealing with penances are listed together under type 756, and these, on account of their dramatic range, were in great demand. We are told of a certain hermit (type 756A) who was so holy that in order not to interrupt his prayers, meals were sent to him from heaven. In a fit of anger at continuous bad weather, however, the hermit criticises God, and the food no longer arrives. The hermit is desolate, but an angel appears and tells him that he must do penance by standing in a river until his staff blossoms. He is standing in the water for a long time, and a robber who is passing by enquires as to why he is doing this. The hermit tells his story and, on hearing it, the robber compares the hermit's one sin with the many he has himself committed. He is stricken with remorse and joins the hermit to do penance in the river. The robber's staff blossoms before that of the hermit, however, which serves as a lesson in humility to the latter.

Equally popular in Ireland was a macabre story that tells of how a youth offered his soul as surety to the devil's sister in a card game and lost (type 756B). In desperation, he went to seek advice from a certain Seán Bráthair (Friar John), who told him that he must go to hell and recover the bill of contract. Arriving in hell, he tells the devil that Friar John has directed him thither, and the devil makes it clear that the friar has great influence in that place. The youth is given back his contract, and before he leaves the devil brings him to see the fiery bed that is being prepared in hell for the friar. On his return home, the youth tells Friar John of this bed. The friar is alarmed, but thinks of a plan. He brings the youth to a mountain top and, kneeling before him, directs him to slay him with an axe. As the blow is struck, a flash of lightning strikes the mountain top, and when the youth looks again there is no sign of the friar. However, he sees a white dove flying to heaven, by which he understands that Friar John's soul has been saved.

A more pleasant type of story is type 759B, which has been most copiously collected in Ireland, but which was also current in other parts of western Europe. This describes how a young man lives on the mountains herding cattle and sheep, and has no contact with the rest of the people. When he meets a villager, he is told that he must come to Mass in the village every Sunday. Arriving in the church, he puts his coat hanging on a sunbeam which is coming through the window. The priest notices the wild man and the coat which hangs miraculously, but says nothing. On the second Sunday the same happens, but on the third Sunday the coat falls down. The priest approaches the stranger and

asks why this is so. The nonplussed youth explains that he has done nothing new, except to listen to some uncharitable gossip that some of the congregation engaged in after the second Mass. Hearing this, the priest tells him to go back to the mountain and continue with his innocent life there alone, for human company is an occasion of sin for him.

Elements that appear in the secular literary story of NEARA gave rise to a religious tale (type 764) of Irish invention. This became quite popular in folklore throughout Ireland and spread also to Iceland. It tells of how a poor scholar on his travels meets with the corpse of a hanged man who asks to be carried on the scholar's back. They journey on in this manner until night falls. The dead man, however, refuses to enter a house where happiness reigns, and also a house where prayers are being said. Reaching a third house, where a husband and wife are fighting, he tells the poor scholar that this is appropriate lodgings for them. The householder and his wife sleep apart, and during the night the scholar notices that his companion goes and sleeps with the woman. The travellers leave the house next morning and, as they part, the dead man tells the scholar that a baby boy will be born to that woman in due course, that the boy will become a priest, and that all of the people blessed by that priest will belong to the dead man himself. The scholar then realises that his companion is none other than the devil. Years later, when the scholar is passing through the same place, he learns that the boy is to be ordained a priest in the local church. He rushes to the church, and succeeds in preventing the new priest from blessing the congregation. Then he privately tells the priest the horrible story of his conception. The distraught priest sets out for Rome to try to find a solution for his difficult situation, and has a very difficult ordeal imposed on him there. The ordeal may involve kissing horrid serpents that he meets on the road, crawling on his hands and knees to the North Pole and back, going naked through a great clump of thorns, or some other such excruciating experience. He succeeds, but so great is the effort that he dies. Beetles are seen to consume his body, since it belongs to the devil, but his soul goes to heaven in the form of a dove.

Type 774K tells of how St Peter once complained to JESUS CHRIST when a ship-full of sailors was drowned because only one sinner was on board. Soon after, Peter gets stung by a bee and in anger destroys the whole hive, and Christ then points out to him that he has done the very thing for which he had criticised God. This story was already known in Ireland in the sixteenth century, for a variant of it occurs in a biography of COLM CILLE from that time.

Established in Ireland from the tenth century was type 782, which tells of how a certain king had donkey's ears. It seems to have been borrowed from Welsh or Breton tradition concerning King March (meaning 'horse'), and versions concerning him always substitute horse's ears. The earliest Irish occurrence concerns a Midland king with horse's ears named Eochaidh (which name contains the element *each*, also meaning a horse). Soon, however, it got attached to the celebrated mythical Leinster king LABHRAIDH, and it is still told of him in folklore.

St Peter is featured again in type 785, which tells of how, when mutton is being divided, a companion of that saint eats the heart and then claims that the lamb had no heart. When Peter divides money between the company, the rogue confesses in order to get his share. Similar in plot though without a religious focus is type 785A, which has a servant eating the leg of a goose and telling his master that geese have only one leg. Later they see geese standing on one leg in water, and the rascal cites this to prove his point, but the master says 'whoosh' and the geese put down both legs and fly away. This HUMOROUS TALE is often told in Ireland as a LEGEND concerning Jonathan SWIFT or Daniel O'CONNELL.

As if to underline the religious purpose of this genre of storytelling, an Irish variant of type 844 contrasts the physical and spiritual realms. It tells of a king who seeks the shirt of the happiest man in his kingdom,

believing that this shirt will bring happiness and good fortune to himself. He finds, however, that the happiest man has no shirt.

Aarne & Thompson (1961), 254–84; S. Ó Súilleabháin & Christiansen (1967), 145–65; S. Ó Súilleabháin (1942), 573–5, 629–40 & (1952) & (1973), 18–19; P. Ó Héalaí in *Béaloideas*, 42–4, 176–212.

Rising of 1798 With the continuing oppression in eighteenth-century Ireland, the new political ideals sweeping France offered hope to Theobald Wolfe Tone and his fellow republicans, who hoped to organise the disparate bodies of resistance among the population. Feelings were running high, and the English and colonial Irish governments grew increasingly alarmed and decided on a pre-emptive strike in order to force the people into either submission or rebellion before a French army would land. As repression increased, popular feelings and fears broke out in blind fury in the summer of 1798. Without planning, it was disjointed and inconsistent – first and fiercest in Leinster, where the rebellion lasted all through summer, then in Ulster for a briefer period, and finally in Connacht when it was too late.

The events of 1798 – in all their horror and wild glory – have lived on in the consciousness of the Irish people, and the experience of great suffering meant that the soul of Ireland was alienated forever from the authorities. This feeling is strongly reflected in the folk memory, for 1798 in folk narrative is the age of atrocities, of savage government cruelties, and of brave men and women who would not lie down. Of these there were many. In Dublin, there were the colourful intellectuals such as Lord Edward Fitzgerald; in the North, Presbyterian rebel leaders such as Henry Joy MacCracken; in Connacht, the French General Humbert – a second Napoleon in the eyes of his Irish partisans. All of these and others have their part in national history and local traditions, but the greatest folk heroes belong to the area of the most shattering events of all – Wexford and the southeast. As one might expect, pride of place goes to the leader of the insurrectionary forces in that area, Father John Murphy. Initially opposed to a rebellion, Father Murphy agreed to lead the campaign of resistance in desperation at the brutality of the government conscript soldiers, known as the Yeomen. Folk tradition claims that he decided to rebel after his parish church at Boolavogue was burned by the Yeomen, but in fact he was already in arms when that event occurred. The folk description is nonetheless colourful, claiming that when he was in bed at night, he dreamed the chapel was on fire. He jumped up and discovered to his consternation that it really was on fire, past being saved. Saddling his horse, he gathered up three farming men on horseback, and they set about raising the whole countryside.

During the rebellion, Father Murphy displayed unusual tactical ability and leadership skills, leading his men to victory in several pitched battles. His followers loved him and thought he could not be beaten. Some said that he had immunity from harm by shot and shell. Although the revolutionary path he took was sternly opposed by the hierarchy and senior clergy of his Church, to the ordinary people of Wexford he was a saint, and indeed in time he became a martyr. After the insurgent forces were defeated at New Ross with frightful slaughter, the final disastrous defeat came at Vinegar Hill, after which Father Murphy continued to resist as best he could. Eventually, he and one faithful companion were left to their own devices. Lying low in the hope of rejoining his men, he was sheltered for a while by a Protestant farmer, who hid the refugees in a stable and looked after all their needs. This stable was afterwards called 'Father John's stable' – it is said that the patriot priest left his blessing on it, and ailing animals were often afterwards brought there to be healed. He was, however, betrayed and captured by a local man, after which he was tortured to death by the soldiers. It was said that the informer was reprimanded by a tinker woman for what he had done, and that he spat at her. She cursed him, and ever after his descendants had a nasty habit of salivating.

A number of folk LEGENDS tell of the ingratitude of authority figures who, when captured by the rebels, were protected by particular rebel leaders; for instance, the commander of the notorious North Cork Militia had been thus protected from popular vengeance by Father Philip Roche, a friend of Father Murphy. When Father Roche was captured, that worthy made no intervention on his behalf. One folk legend says that he was present at the priest's trial, and turned away when he was asked to speak for the defence, with the result that his neck remained twisted ever afterwards. Another case in point is that of John Kelly from Killanne, one of the rebel army's lieutenants. Kelly, aged 22 and over 7 feet in height, was a man of striking physical appearance. A popular hero, he led an attack on one of the gates of New Ross during the horrific battle there. Leading his 500 men uphill in a fierce charge, right into the teeth of the enemy muskets and cannon, he crashed through the gate and drove the foe before him towards the centre of the town. He had reached the military barracks when he was shot in the thigh, and was later found being sheltered in a local house and dragged before a court martial. Here one of the principal witnesses against him was a man whose life he had previously spared. After his execution, his head was kicked around the streets by the soldiers and mounted on a spike. Eventually, one of the soldiers took pity on his sister and gave her the head to take home and bury.

The heroism of the Wexfordmen is exemplified in a narrative that has a solitary young man become a living symbol of folk ideology. After the Battle of New Ross, the English soldiers were being mustered in a field when, to everyone's surprise, a bare-footed country boy with a long rebel's pike on his shoulder came out of one of the burning houses and walked across the far end of the field. One conceited trooper bawled out: 'Stop, and I'll show you a little sport!' He rode quickly across the field to a gap the youth was making for, and a fierce tussle ensued between the two. Eventually, the pikeman prodded the trooper's horse, causing it to rear and unseat its rider. Both combatants now being on the ground, the youth drove his pike into the trooper's side and slew him. The youth then calmly took the dead man's cartridge box, threw it over his shoulder and passed out through the gap. The soldiers were livid and aimed their guns at him, but their commander ordered them to let him go out of respect for his courage and dignity.

Traditions of single combat between individual rebels and soldiers are part of the 1798 lore in other parts of the country also, as are detailed folk accounts of how rebels evaded capture, and of those who aided or betrayed them. One of the most atrocious forms of torture engaged in by the authorities was flogging, and many accounts of such survived. For example, in Kilfinane, County Limerick, an elderly man called Patrick 'Staker' Wallis was almost dead from such treatment by a local magistrate and was offered relief by his tormentor if he would reveal but one name of a rebel. Unable to speak from his ordeals, Wallis directed that a pen and paper be brought to him, and then wrote down his own name. The magistrate, breaking his promise, had the unfortunate man hanged. The episode is commemorated in a beautiful slow air entitled 'Lament for Staker Wallace'. *See also* DWYER, Michael *and* TARA.

Kennedy (1855), 134–5; Kavanagh (1913), 237–9, 296; Gregory (1926), 60; P. Ó Tuathail in *Béaloideas*, 5, 155; Ó hÓgáin (1985), 192–202, 209, 339–40; IFC 54:374–5, S900:132–49; Brandt (1909), 40–1; Seoighe (1994).

romantic tales Over 150 international FOLKTALES are listed in the Aarne/Thompson catalogue under the heading 'Novelle (Romantic Tales)'. These have a mostly European provenance, and versions of over half of them have been collected from Irish folklore. The characters in romantic tales are usually of the ordinary human kind, but the things that happen to them are quite extraordinary, though generally credible. Tricks, accidents and coincidences are the guiding principles of these stories.

Type 851 concerns a princess who loves riddles and who offers to marry any man who will put a riddle to her which she cannot solve. On his way to the contest, a smart fellow sees twelve crows feeding on the carcass of a dead horse. He discovers that the horse has died as a result of eating poison, and decides that this will be a good subject for a riddle. He therefore asks the princess: 'What killed none and yet killed twelve?' The princess is puzzled, and asks for a day's respite to solve it. She hears that the questioner talks in his sleep, and so she goes in disguise to his bed at night. Realising who she is, he pretends to be asleep and says the answer. Next day, she boasts before the assembled court that she can solve the riddle, but as she begins to give the answer, she notices that he has a personal item of clothing belonging to her in his hand. Realising that he is ready to expose her nocturnal conduct, she defers and agrees to marry him instead.

Type 852 is somewhat similar, telling of a certain king who boasts that nobody can make him disbelieve a good story. He offers the hand of his daughter in marriage to any man who can disprove this, but the price of failure will be the man's head. Several ambitious young men make the attempt, but all pay with their lives, until a smart fellow comes to the court and relates the most incredible things. The king listens carefully, agreeing all the time, until eventually the fellow attributes vulgar personal habits to the king himself and even questions the legality of his birth. At this, the king shouts out in anger that he is lying, and so the smart fellow gets the princess in marriage.

Type 870C, as listed in the Aarne/Thompson catalogue, is entitled 'Stepmother Makes Love to Stepson', and a quite confined variant is given. It seems proper to suggest that the plot and range of this type number should be extended to cover the well-known international tale told in the Bible of Joseph and the wife of the pharaoh Potiphar. In that tale, a woman – often a stepmother – whose sexual advances to a young man have been rejected, gains revenge by falsely accusing him before her husband. Several versions of it occur in Irish literature from the eighth century onwards

– these include stories concerning DEARG, CONALL CORC, MAOL FHOTHARTAIGH, COMHDHÁN and NUADHU.

A celebrated and very ancient folktale tells of a hero who does not recognise a young man for his son (type 873). It may have either of two endings – both recognising each other after a contest, or else the father killing the son and recognising him too late. This story, in its happier form, was already being told of the hero FIONN MAC CUMHAILL and his son OISÍN in the ninth century, and in its tragic form concerning CÚ CHULAINN and his son CONLAÍ at around the same time. The opening of the literary tale concerning MAOL DÚIN also seems to be indebted to it, and the medieval account of the birth of BREAS definitely is. Due to redactions of the literary tale, the Conlaí version survives in the folklore of Ulster and Connacht, while in Munster the folktale is told in the Fionn context. In these latter versions, however, some other son of Fionn besides Oisín is named as the young man, and sometimes the characters are Oisín and his son OSCAR. The ending, as in the ancient text concerning Fionn, is always a happy one in these Munster variants, but it is clear that they derive from a re-adoption of the folktale in recent centuries. Humorous versions of this international folktale are also current in the south, being told as oral LEGENDS concerning contests in wit between smart characters such as Eoghan Rua Ó SÚILLEABHÁIN or Daniel O'CONNELL, and their even more clever offspring.

Type 875 tells of an unmarried king who meets with a peasant girl and is amazed by her cleverness and smart answers. He decides to set some impossible tasks for her, and when she succeeds at them decides to marry her. The tasks may include such things as coming to his palace neither walking nor riding, neither on the road nor off the road, neither naked nor clad, neither by day nor by night. She achieves them by being half mounted on a billy goat, half on the verge of the road, dressed only in a net, and arriving at sunrise or sunset. After their marriage, they are happy together for a while, but one day the king gives an unfair judgement in a dispute between two men. A mare belonging to one of the men has dropped a foal into a cart belonging to the other, and the king awards the foal to the cartman. The queen, however, objects to this, and she is proved correct when the foal is set free and follows the mare. Embarrassed and angry at being contradicted, the king orders his wife to leave the palace. She prepares to go, but as a last request asks that she be allowed to take with her the thing dearest to her in all the world. When the king assents, she takes him on her back, and they are reconciled. That this folktale was known in Ireland at an early date is suggested by the fact that variants of the first part of it are found in a tenth-century text on the encounter of FIONN MAC CUMHAILL with his sweetheart Ailbhe, and in a slightly later text on the encounter between king FEIDHLIMIDH MAC CRIOMHTHAINN and a clever girl.

The story entitled 'The Taming of the Shrew', immortalised by Shakespeare in English literature, can in fact be traced to Continental folklore of the Middle Ages (type 901). In Ireland, also, it has been quite popular. We are told of a certain rich man who has three daughters, two of them girls of gentle disposition, while the third is shrewish in the extreme. A young man comes to ask for the hand of the shrew, and the pleasantly surprised father offers a large dowry with her. After the wedding, the young man sets off for home on horseback with his bride. He forces the horse towards a large gate, and when the horse refuses, he remarks: 'That is once!' At the second effort, the horse again refuses, and he says: 'That is twice!' and when the horse acts similarly a third time he stabs it through the heart with a knife. When they reach his home, he similarly orders the dog to do an impossible task, and having enumerated each refusal he kills the dog also. Then he asks his bride to prepare tea, and when she angrily refuses, he remarks in a chilling voice: 'That is once!' She immediately obeys him, and it is later proved that neither of her two sisters are so obedient to their husbands.

Type 910B is somewhat less discriminatory against women. It tells of a married man who works for twenty years as a farm hand far from home. When that period is ended, he asks for payment, but the farmer refuses to give him anything except three advices: these are not to take a shortcut on his travels, not to spend the night in a house where a young woman is married to an old man, and not to do anything at night that he might regret in the morning. He sets out for home, ignores the first advice by taking a shortcut on his way, and barely escapes with his life when he falls among robbers. Then he ignores the second advice, and hears a young woman plotting with her lover to kill her husband and blame the traveller. He rushes from that place, and eventually reaches home. Arriving at night, he opens the door of his house and finds his wife sleeping in the same bed as a young man. He takes a hatchet to kill the young man, but then decides that he had better follow at least the third advice. Controlling his anger, he waits until morn, and when his wife awakes she welcomes him and proudly presents their son, who has in the time that he was absent grown into a young man. From that day forward, he follows the advices, and through his prudence becomes in time a very rich man. A twelfth-century Irish adaptation of the classical story of Ulysses contains a version of the three advices given to the hero on his travels, which shows that some version of the folktale was already known in Ireland at that time. Some references in a text of the eighth or ninth century suggest that a related story of advices was known in Ireland even earlier (type 911). This must have been more widespread in medieval Europe than the recorded instances suggest. It tells of how a man is advised not to confide secrets to his wife, not to accept a foster son of higher social standing, not to trust an underling, and so on. It is told in Irish literature concerning the judge FíOTHAL and, apart from echoes of this, has not otherwise been noticed in Irish oral narrative.

Type 920 also concerns a wise man, namely the biblical king SOLOMON, who through his quick wit exposes adultery, and Irish versions of this medieval folk-tale also usually name the wise character as that king. Some of the wise quips there attributed to Solomon belong properly to type 921, which tells of clever answers given by a peasant boy to the questions put to him by a king or other exalted personage. For instance, he says that his mother is fowling, that his father is hunting but throws away what he catches, and that his sister is lamenting her former laugh. These three answers are discovered to mean that the mother is picking fleas, the father is delousing, and the sister is giving birth to a baby.

Clever answers are again featured in type 922, which tells of how a tyrannical king tries to entrap his bishop. He orders the bishop to come to his palace and answer three questions correctly, else he will lose his head. The bishop is perplexed, but his identical twin, who is a fool, offers to go in his place. The fool, dressed in episcopal garb, is mistaken by the king for his brother, and the questioning begins. The first two questions may vary, but are always successfully countered with trick answers – for instance, the king asking how many loads of sand are on the seashore, and the fool replying 'One, if you had a cart large enough', and then the king asking how much he himself was worth and being told less than 30 pieces of silver, 'for Christ was sold for that amount and you are not half as good a man as he!' The third question and answer are standard: 'What am I thinking?' with the fool replying 'You are thinking that I am the bishop, but I am not!' There are witnesses present, ensuring that the king cannot renege on his word, and thus the fool saves his brother's life. Irish folklore often associates the story with a king of England and a bishop of Canterbury, having assimilated it to the historical conflict between Henry II and Thomas Becket. Another story of necessary trickery is type 925. Irish versions of this tell of a tyrant king whose mother is very ill. The king vows that if she dies, he will execute the person who brings him the sad news. The lot falls on a fool, who is quick-witted in his own way, and when the death does occur,

439

this fool goes to the king and makes an announcement such as 'The first house in which you lived has been knocked over'. 'So,' says the king, 'my mother is dead!' The fool then protests successfully that the king himself was the first person to say it.

Type 933 concerns the son of an incestuous union who is abandoned as a baby and who, after many trials, becomes Pope of Rome. The parents, not knowing that their son has survived, come to the Pope to be confessed; he recognises them, and all are reconciled. Versions of this were told in medieval Irish literature concerning St CUMAINE FADA, and, in adaptations to a secular context, of FIACHU FEAR MARA and MAC LUGHACH. The story survives in Irish folklore in its international setting, having the boy become Pope, although the later European tendency to identify the boy with GREGORY THE GREAT is rarely evidenced here.

The idea that a person is destined to be killed in a certain way is the basis of the various kinds of stories listed under type 934. In Irish folklore, the most common version concerns a boy for whom the prophecy is made that he will be killed by lightning on his seventh birthday. His father has an iron hut constructed underground, in which the unsuspecting boy is placed on his birthday. He escapes from the hut just in time before the lightning strikes it. A variant of this tale, also found internationally and common in Irish folklore, has a less happy ending, describing the death of a boy who is fated to drown at a certain age. That stories of this kind were current in medieval Ireland is evidenced by similar MOTIFS in texts concerning FIACHU MUILLEATHAN and MONGÁN.

A very dramatic ecotype of the story has for some reason declined in popularity since medieval times in Ireland as elsewhere. It concerns a man for whom a three-fold death – by wounding, drowning and burning – is prophesied, and was known in Ireland as early as the seventh century. Its appeal continued through the Middle Ages (see DIARMAID MAC CEARRBHEOIL and MUIRCHEARTACH MAC EARCA), but later oral versions are not found in this country.

On the other hand, Irish folklore has preserved and evidences a particular development of the international plot type 934B – telling of a prophecy that a prince will be killed by a black, eight-legged hound, but describing how he is saved by dogs that he meets. They kill the fierce hound and then insist that the prince cut their heads off with an axe. By so doing, he disenchants them, and finds that they are in reality a fellow prince and his two sisters.

An international story of great antiquity is listed as type 950. It concerns how the treasury of a king is robbed by the sons of the architect who built it and left one stone loose for this purpose. The story does not seem to have been in Ireland for very long, probably having sprung from a version of it told in an eighteenth-century chapbook. It has, nevertheless, become quite widespread and popular, though in a much altered form. The international plot derives from ancient Greek literature, in which Herodotus tells the story as he heard it in Egypt. In that plot, the thieves are two sons of the architect, but in the Irish versions they are usually described as three nephews of ARISTOTLE who rob the treasury of the mayor of Dublin. The great philosopher makes a prophecy that seems to mean that one of these three will be hanged in Dublin, but the prophecy is unexpectedly fulfilled when that young man marries the mayor's daughter Croch. Her name means 'gallows', and therefore he really does get the gallows in Dublin, though in a fortunate way. A similar reversal of fortune is found in a less ancient European folktale, type 952, Irish versions of which have an army deserter assisting an old man to rescue the latter's daughter from robbers. The old man later informs on the deserter, who is condemned to be shot. The girl intervenes to save his life, however, and then her father reveals that he is in fact the king, who has thus been testing their love.

A special story about a master thief (type 953) was very popular in northern and western Europe, and in Ireland the picaresque character was known as an Gadaí Dubh Ó Dubháin (the Black Thief

O'Dwan). A certain king is so impressed by the escapades of this thief that he sends out a challenge to him to steal a fine stallion from the royal stables. The Black Thief comes and, despite the close guard on the horse, almost succeeds, but is foiled and captured when bells on the horse's rug ring out. He is brought before the king, who triumphantly announces that the executioner is at hand, and jeeringly tells the thief that he is doomed unless he can describe a moment when he was nearer to death than now. The thief tells of some breathtaking escapes he has effected, but to no avail, and finally states that he was once captured by a man-eating giant who ordered him to slaughter and prepare for dinner a captive baby. The thief had saved the baby by boiling a piglet in its place, and to convince the giant that it really was baby-meat, he had cut off one of the infant's fingers and cooked it along with the piglet. When the king hears this, he looks down at his own hand, which lacks a finger, and realises that the thief had been his rescuer long ago. The Black Thief is forgiven and given the stallion as a present.

Dishonesty is featured also in type 978, which tells of how a young man finds himself among cheaters but is saved by the quick wit of a person who comes to his assistance. No examples of this folktale have been collected from Irish folklore, but a version of it was known to the fourteenth-century author of a story concerning a young man called Socht at the court of CORMAC MAC AIRT.

Another popular story (type 970) deserves the title of romantic tale in more senses than one. Still popular in Irish folklore, it describes how a youth and a girl love each other, but their parents oppose the match and both die of heartbreak. The vindictive parents have them buried at the furthest distance from each other in the graveyard, but a tree grows from each grave and the branches of both trees intertwine overhead. This folktale, found throughout Europe and Asia, was already known in Ireland in the tenth century, for its plot appears in texts from that period (see BAILE MAC BUAIN and LIADHAIN).

Aarne & Thompson (1961), 284–346; S. Ó Súilleabháin & Christiansen (1967), 165–96, with type 934B listed under type 333 on pp. 85–6; S. Ó Súilleabháin (1942), 575–9, 622–8 & (1973), 19–21.

Ruadhán SAINT who died c.AD 584, founder of the monastery of Lothra (Lorrha, in north County Tipperary). His name means 'red-haired man', and in modern form is rendered Ruán.

The several accounts given of him in Latin and Irish all derive from a lost biography compiled in the tenth or eleventh century. We read that he was son of one Fearghus Bearn of the royal EOGHANACHT sept of Munster, and that he was educated by St Finnian of Cluain Ioraird (Clonard, County Meath). When he went to Lorrha to found his monastery there, a fierce wild boar that had its lair in the hollow of a tree quitted the place so that he could have possession of it. He performed many miracles in different parts of Ireland, including finding their TREASURE for the people of Ros Éinne (in the Oriors area of south Armagh), who had forgotten where they had hidden it during a pestilence; healing the queen of Cualu (north Wicklow), who was afflicted by a dangerous blood clot; and rescuing a ship caught in a whirlpool near Limerick. He had a wondrous tree at Lorrha, the sap of which provided full sustenance for all who tasted of it. The other saints of Ireland grew jealous of Ruadhán on account of this tree and of his holiness generally, but he reconciled them to him by entertaining them with a fine feast in Lorrha.

The most celebrated story of him concerned his conflict with the high-king DIARMAID MAC CEARRBHEOIL who seized a hostage from out of Ruadhán's sanctuary and was elaborately cursed by the saint as a result. The two were eventually reconciled, and Diarmaid returned the hostage to Ruadhán in return for 30 beautiful dark-grey HORSES. These had come to the saint from a river, and they defeated the king's own horses at racing. Soon after the king had acquired them, however, they raced away into the sea. Another LEGEND has Ruadhán giving his own two chariot-horses as alms to lepers, and two stags coming from a wood to draw his chariot in their place.

441

Several of the other miracles attributed to him involve healing the sick and raising from the dead people who were recently deceased. For a miracle concerning the restoration of sight to the blinded Eochaidh mac Maolughra, king of Munster, see the general entry under EOCHAIDH. The feast day of Ruadhán is 15 April.

Kenney (1929), 391–2; Heist (1965), 160–7; Plummer, 2 (1910), 240–52 & 1 (1922), 317–29; P. Grosjean in Analecta Bollandiana, 49, 100–1; O'Hanlon, 4 (1875), 148–60.

Rumhann mac Colmáin POET

who, according to the Annals, died in AD 747. One medieval source accords him high distinction by referring to 'the three poets of the world – Homer of the Greeks and Virgil of the Latins and Rumhann of the Irish'. His name was a rare one, probably a variant of *ruamhann* and with a meaning such as 'flushed' or 'healthy colour'. His father Colmán was a descendant of the high-king LAOGHAIRE, and Rumhann himself resided at Áth Troim (Trim, County Meath), where his brother Baothghalach was abbot of the monastery. Rumhann himself had seven sons, two of whom became bishops.

A text from the twelfth century or thereabouts tells a few anecdotes of Rumhann. We read that he was the chief-poet of Ireland and that he once went on a pilgrimage to the monastery of Raithean (Rahen, County Offaly) while a famine raged. The people of that place did not wish to allow him to enter, and challenged him to state the number of timber planks being used in the building of an oratory there. Through his poetic genius, Rumhann spoke a quatrain saying that there were ten hundred planks, which was the exact number. He was admitted to Raithean, and soon after headed for Dublin, where the NORSEMEN asked him to make a poem. He demanded as payment 'one penny from every bad Viking and two pennies from every good Viking', whereupon they all paid the two pence each. They desired him to praise the sea and, in a frenzy, he recited a long, descriptive poem in a new metre that he called *laídh luascach* (literally, 'seesaw lay'). Rumhann then returned to the Midlands and divided his fee among some monasteries and schools. We read that he died at Raithean and was buried there.

The episode with the Norsemen is anachronistic, as these had not yet settled in Dublin at the time of Rumhann. It is therefore apparent that a later poem has been wrongly attributed to him, and it is clear that the whole account has been influenced by oral tradition. Folklore made much of the magical knowledge of poets, and the trick by which he got double payment from the Norsemen is an adaptation from a humorous international folktale.

GENERAL: K. Meyer in Otia Mersieiana, 2, 76–83; A. O'Sullivan (1983), 1588; O'Donovan, 1 (1848–51), 352–3.

FOLKTALE PLOT: See Aarne & Thompson (1961), types 1567–9, 1661.

saints

The ordinary word for a saint in Irish is *naomh* (earlier, *noíb*, from a Celtic root meaning 'bright' or 'good'). In referring to individual saints, this is applied as a title with the name of a native Irish saint – for instance, Naomh Abán for St Abán. With the exception of PATRICK, none of the holy men and women of pre-medieval Ireland have been officially canonised, but they are regarded as saints *vox populi*. Because of his pervasive Irish importance, the British-born Patrick is always called Naomh Pádraig. Saints from outside Ireland, whereas they are also referred to impersonally as *naomh*, usually have the Latin title *San* preceding their name, such as San Séamas (St James). Some foreign saints were, however, considered so homely as to be given the native title – these include Naomh Peadar (St Peter), Naomh Eoin Baiste (St John the Baptist) and Naomh Mártan (St MARTIN). The mother of JESUS is always referred to as '*an* Mhaighdean Mhuire' (the Virgin Mary) or simply Muire. It is remarkable that, out of respect for her, this form Muire tends to be used for her alone – it is customary for other Marys in Ireland to be called Máire.

From the fifth century onwards, considerable numbers of Irish people were turning to Christianity, and by the eighth century the new religion was general throughout the country. The intervening period is sometimes referred to as 'the age of the saints', and it is to that period that all the saints who are celebrated in Irish hagiography belong. The actual writing of the biographies began in the seventh century and continued well after the end of the Middle Ages. Latin and Irish are the languages of these texts, the Latin works being somewhat in the majority, and in the case of a number of saints, several different biographical texts survive.

The writers of Irish hagiography, like their counterparts abroad, drew on material from several different sources for their themes, plots and imagery. Such sources included not only the Old and New Testaments, the Apocrypha and biographies of Continental saints, but also Irish and classical works of secular literature, as well as oral tradition from within the monasteries and from the populace in general. It is sometimes quite difficult to unravel the various strands of lore in the texts and to determine how much of the accounts have direct historical value, but it must always be borne in mind that many of the biographies were written with the definite purpose of advancing the prestige of particular paruchiae or monasteries. Thus the profile of an individual saint depended to a large extent on the interests of those who inherited his or her foundation, and the hagiographers did not hesitate to borrow, or even to fabricate, material for their purpose. This is not to say that the hagiographers were men without taste or discrimination. The vast majority of them were monks, with varying degrees of learning, but usually with some theological sense and never devoid of piety. They could also, on occasion, give good insight into the human predicament, and portray individual characters and personalities with depth of feeling.

The biography of the saint, in Ireland as elsewhere, is basically a sacred version of the life pattern of all heroic or celebrated people. Thus the saint's birth is accompanied by wonders and MARVELS; he or she shows special holiness and miraculous powers while still a youth; on coming of age, the saint gains great triumphs against hostile forces and as a result of this is

recognised and given authority; and extraordinary circumstances again attend his or her death. For reasons of history and authentication, however, the hagiographer had to garner and include in the text as much detail concerning the real life of the saint as possible; and, for reasons of interest and variety, he had to select good adventures from whatever sources were available. The success of the narrative, of course, depended on the quality of such adventures and of their presentation, and the hagiographers thus built up a rich store of MOTIFS with which to punctuate their texts.

Particularly popular were accounts of healings, and in some cases the hagiographers did not scruple to have their saints going so far as to restore to life people who had recently died. The miraculous power of the saints could also strike down those who were persistently hostile to them or to those under their care, and their prophecies in both positive and negative senses were much in demand. As a spiritual champion, the saint always acts with extraordinary dedication and intensity, and so the hagiographers felt free to exaggerate greatly in descriptions of pious practices. Extraordinary self-mortification was a standard convention, at least in the literature (*see* CAOIMHGHIN, ÍDE *and* FIONNCHÚ), while one writer teeters precariously between opposite feelings when trying to impress readers with the piety and chastity of St Scoithín. He describes that holy man as having 'two maidens with pointed breasts' in his bed with him each night 'so that the battle with the devil might be the greater for him'.

Fire and light were particularly popular as dramatic devices, no doubt because of standard Christian symbolism of the faith, but probably also because such imagery had been associated with the sacred men of pre-Christian belief, the DRUIDS. We read of fiery manifestations and lights seen in the sky at the time of the births of saints. Sometimes, the saint is described as surrounded by the mystical light of holiness, and he is generally impervious to fire. A particularly impressive image has the saint lighting candles by breathing on them, or even having his fingers emit light in the darkness like a torch. The person of the saint is generally untouched by rain or snow, no matter how exposed he is to the elements or how severe the weather. His book, containing the sacred writings, was also impervious to wetting, and several LEGENDS tell of how such books were dropped into water but remained perfectly dry.

Objects closely associated with the saint were often claimed to have miraculous power attached to them – for instance, the *bachall* or crozier. This pastoral staff, if the hagiographers are to be credited, could raise the dead, drive back a flooding river, or divide the sea as Moses did in Exodus. It could also split rocks or cleave the ground, subdue wild animals, banish demons, or protect travellers. In some cases, the crozier was claimed to be able to attract and catch FISH, discover TREASURE, produce fountains on dry land, and fly through the air and return to the saint when misplaced. It is clear that this staff was regarded in early Christian Ireland as the most characteristic implement of the missionary. The old literature tells us that croziers were enshrined in precious metals, and some such coverings are preserved in modem museums.

Almost as impressive was the saint's bell, many examples of which have also been preserved. The bell, being used to summon people to prayer and devotions, was seen as having a central function in the Christian life and, accordingly, the hagiographers were keen to dramatise it. We read therefore of saints' bells that could raise the dead, protect the community from diseases and disasters, banish demons, repel enemies and cause them to be swallowed up by the ground. A common motif is for a bell to remain dumb until the place destined for the saint's settlement is reached, whereupon it rings out joyously of its own accord. Like the crozier, the bell could miraculously return to its owner if mislaid or stolen. Many bells had names of their own, which were usually based on their colour, and the application of actual personalities to them was sometimes carried to

the point of attributing human-like voices to them. In all of this, the hagiographers were merely developing in narrative terms the popular attitude to the special paraphernalia of churchmen in early Christian Ireland. Both croziers and bells were in fact ritually used in collecting ecclesiastical revenue, in cursing and excommunicating foes, and in the administration of solemn oaths.

A sense of genuine, if naive, spirituality was seldom far from the minds of the hagiographers. Thus they claim that various saints were in constant communication with angels, and concerning ÍDE we even read that an angel brought food to her every day. Although they could be quite partisan, the hagiographers in their piety intended the fantastic powers of the saints to show how goodness can pervade all reality. Nowhere is this more obvious than in the idea that the saints had a very special relationship with the animal world. We read again and again of how these holy men and women were sympathetic to all of God's creatures, and how these creatures were much attracted to the saints and assisted them in many ways. For instance, not only HORSES and oxen, but wild stags also, come of their own accord to work for them. The stags even allow their antlers to be used as book-rests when sacred study is in progress or prayers or hymns are being read. A charming account of St Colmán mac Duach (for whom, *see* GUAIRE) states that he had three pets – a cock, a mouse and a fly. The cock used to crow for him at midnight to call him to prayer and, as Colmán then sang his psalms, the fly would walk along under each line of the psalter, pausing at a word every time that the saint did so. If the saint nodded off to sleep, the mouse would begin to nibble at his ear in order to awaken him so that he would continue with his office.

All creation was attracted to the saints – for example, the birds lamented St MOLUA after his death because he had never killed any living thing. The same Molua had a tame partridge, St Crónán had a tame stag, and MOLING had a tame fox. Other saints had miscellaneous pets –

such as cranes, wrens, robins, doves, crows, cats and flies. The swans on the lakes of Killarney were wont to come at the call of CAINNEACH, and the swans on Lough Foyle came at the call of COMHGHALL. Swans were also helpful to St Columba of Terryglass, carrying him from place to place as he wished; and the same birds used to sing for St Colmán Eala and his monks as they worked. One of the animals portrayed as being closest to these Irish saints was, curiously, the wolf. For instance, CAOIMHGHIN and MAODHÓG fed starving wolves from their herds, and MOLUA was even claimed to have instituted a feast for the benefit of the wolves. It is apparent that some beliefs from pre-Christian Ireland are involved in this case, wolves imagined to be connected in some way with human beings. The ritualistic king CONAIRE, for example, was said to have had seven wolves as hostages for an agreement that more than one calf a year would not be taken from each CATTLE byre in Ireland.

According to his biography, St Colman mac Luacháin had a standing covenant with wolves. We read that the wolves of the forest came to him and licked his shoes like domestic dogs, and that he said to them: 'Be here continually, and the day that my name is mentioned to you in intercession, you must not draw blood on anyone!' Of this same Colmán it was said that when he was a child, he spent a whole day and night under the River Brosna (in County Kerry), and while there, the water creatures came and ran races before him as a welcome. The image of the holy hermit surrounded by wild animals who behave with great docility towards him was borrowed into Irish tradition from the lore concerning the Desert Fathers of eastern Christendom, the cult of whom was predominant in the Church at the time that Ireland was converted to the new faith. The point of such stories is that holiness puts a person in a properly balanced relationship to the world. The eighth-century English cleric and scholar, Bede, summed up the philosophy when he wrote that 'the more faithfully man obeys the Creator, the more he will regain his lost empire over the creatures'. This type of portrayal of the saint at peace with the ENVIRONMENT continued for some centuries in western Christendom, and it survived indefinitely in Ireland.

The fame of particular saints was spread and perpetuated through the Middle Ages by numerous dedications of local parishes to them. This is the major reason why the cults of individual saints are found over so widespread an area, but in tradition it was explained by greatly exaggerating their journeying and travels. The lore of some saints was spread into places far beyond their actual fields of activity, such as BRÉANAINN and the female saints BRIGHID and MONINNE, whose cults took root in parts of Britain and occasionally even further afield. The actual travels, from the seventh century onwards, of Irish missionaries in Britain and throughout Europe added much to this traditional imagery of our peripatetic saints.

Much of the literary imagery passed into the Irish folklore concerning saints through the media of clerical preachers and of local scholars. This is evidenced on a widespread level in the case of the great national triad of PATRICK, BRIGHID and COLM CILLE, and in more localised traditions concerning the other saints. Thus in folklore, the saints are generally portrayed as thaumaturges, as ascetics, and as miraculous protectors of their communities, and some of the most dramatic stories from the literature are related of them. It is apparent, however, that the folklore preserves some legends in a more accurate form than the literature does. In a number of such cases, the medieval literature may in fact have done no more than reflect lore that had long been current in the oral stream. An example is the widespread folk LEGEND, told of several saints, of how a great reptilic monster is banished into a lake (see COLM CILLE and PATRICK). We read of several such banishings in the hagiographical texts, but the folklore alone stresses that the monster is tricked by the saint into remaining in the water until 'Lá an Luain' (which actually means the Last

Day, although the monster takes it to mean the following Monday). This verbal trick, which is reflected in a different type of story concerning MOLING, derives from an idea that the final judgement will take place on a Monday. Thus the oral emphasis on the Last Day in the contest between saint and monster underlines the basic source of the legend – the New Testament Apocalypse – which has a great dragon being released on the Last Day and then confined to a fiery lake.

Another legend, also widespread in folklore, describes how two saints argue over where the boundary between their jurisdictions should lie. They agree to start from their own dwellings and to begin walking towards each other at an arranged time, and that the boundary line will be drawn where they meet. One of them, however, cheats by setting out too soon, and when this is discovered he is punished by having the boundary drawn to the advantage of the other. The full plot of this legend is nowhere found in the literature, but that it was already in popular tradition in the ninth or tenth century is strongly suggested by the occurrence of such a contest between saints in the *Bethu Phátraic*, a tripartite text on Patrick. A further oral legend, again told of several different holy men, describes how the saint as a boy was in service with a farmer, who ordered him to protect a newly planted cornfield from the birds. When Sunday came, the youngster wished to go to Mass, and so he miraculously collected all the birds and confined them in a roofless barn while he was absent. This legend appears only once in the literature, in a late medieval biography of AILBHE.

One folk legend, quite absent from the literature, represents the saint as the focal point of the whole human community. This was told in the oral tradition of BARRA, MOCHUDA, BRÉANAINN, ÉINNE and others, and whatever its origin it is well in keeping with the early Christian worldview. According to it, the holy man forgets his book when he leaves his monastery to conduct a religious service a good distance away. On reaching the arranged place, he remembers the book and remarks on it to the man who is standing nearest to him. Word is passed along the line, and so great is the multitude that they form an unbroken chain all the way back to the monastery. They therefore pass the book along from hand to hand until the saint receives it without moving from where he is standing.

There are individual entries in the present work on those saints who have especially developed lore attached to them. These – together with the names highlighted above – are ABÁN, ADHAMHNÁN, BEARACH, BEARCHÁN, CAILLÍN, CEALLACH, CIARÁN OF CLUAIN, CIARÁN OF SAIGHIR, DALUA, DÉAGLÁN, FÉICHÍN, FIONÁN CAM, FLANNÁN, FURSA, GOBNAIT, MAODHÓG, RUADHÁN and SEANÁN.

WORD 'NAOMH': Walde & Pokorny, *2* (1930), 321.

SOURCES: Kenney (1929); Best (1942), 152–63; Baumgarten (1986), 576–98; Cross (1952), 510–16.

BACKGROUND: Ryan (1931); Chadwick (1961).

COMPILATIONS OF HAGIOGRAPHY: Stokes (1890) & (1905); Plummer, *1–2* (1910) & *1–2* (1922) & (1925); Heist (1965); A. O'Sullivan (1983), xiii–xiv, 1527–1708. *See further* Kenney (1929).

HAGIOGRAPHY AND FOLKLORE: Delehaye (1907); O'Hanlon, 1–9 (1875); Plummer, *1*, (1910) lxxxix–clxxxviii; F. Ó Briain in Ryan (1940), 454–64; Ó hÓgáin (1985), 4–61, 322–7 & in *Béaloideas, 51*, 87–125.

Sarsfield, Patrick *Earl of Lucan (1650–93)* Officer in the army of JAMES II and leading figure on the Irish side in the war of 1689–91. He was born of a prosperous family at Lucan, County Dublin, and was known in Irish as Pádraig Sáirséal. In his youth, he was sent to France to pursue a military career, in which he rapidly won promotion.

He later proved his worth again while in the service of King James in England. While in that service, Sarsfield had a reputation for courage and fighting skill. In 1681 he overheard a senior English army officer make an insulting remark about the Irish, and he immediately challenged him to a duel. He spent some time in prison for this, but continued his independent behaviour and sometime afterwards was badly injured in a two-a-side duel on horseback. Folklore portrays him as an excellent swordsman, and tells of how once, in a horseback duel, he was being sore pressed until his servant called out to him to strike his opponent's horse on the head, and in the confusion to strike the opponent between neck and body. He followed the advice, with success. This is a migratory LEGEND, and versions of its plot – which has a servant's instructions proving decisive – were told also of other Irishmen fighting duels in England.

Despite his high reputation, Sarsfield was not allowed a position of real importance in the Jacobite army in the war between Kings James and WILLIAM OF ORANGE following the latter's arrival in Ireland. He was kept in the background at the Battle of the Boyne in July 1690 and, after the flight of James, had to assent to the authority of the inept commanders left behind. At the siege of Limerick a month later, he performed the feat for which his name survives in folk memory. Learning that a large consignment of provisions and heavy armaments was being brought to enable King William to batter down the walls of that city, he travelled by night with a troop of cavalry to intercept it. Evading the enemy patrols, he encountered the siege-train at Ballyneety, about 15 miles southeast of the city. He had his men pile all the wagons together, and then the whole consignment was blown up in a tremendous explosion. The result of this action was that William did not have the means to take Limerick, and had to abandon the siege.

Popular speculation held that Sarsfield fortuitously gained the information he needed to get his men inside the enemy encampment at Ballyneety. As he and his troop rode through the night, one of their horses cast a shoe and its rider was told to stay behind to walk the horse. This rider met a woman who told him that she was married to one of the Williamite soldiers, and in the conversation let it be known that the password at the Ballyneety encampment was the name of Sarsfield himself. The rider then proceeded at top speed and caught up again with Sarsfield. When Sarsfield was informed of this, he instructed some of his men to gain access

to the camp by use of the password. When himself challenged by a sentry, he shouted out triumphantly, 'Sarsfield is the word and Sarsfield is the man,' thus giving the signal for attack. The MOTIF of an enemy soldier's wife telling the password seems to have been borrowed from the lore of how BRIAN BÓRAMHA gained a great victory at Limerick.

Sarsfield is regularly portrayed in folk tradition as outsmarting the English. It was claimed that, on different occasions, he confused the Williamite search parties by having the shoes turned backwards on the horses of his cavalcade. This horseshoe-motif was common in Ireland and abroad in folklore concerning OUTLAWS and fugitives. We are further told that when besieged in Limerick for the second time, Sarsfield wished to give the impression to the enemy that his forces were well provisioned, even though supplies were running out. He therefore allowed a Williamite spy to enter the city, and ordered his own men to turn barrels upside down and cover their tops with meal. The spy duly reported to the Williamite general, Godet de Ginkel, that Limerick was well stocked, causing Ginkel to anticipate a long and costly siege, and to choose instead to offer a generous treaty to the Irish.

Following the surrender and the signing of the Treaty of Limerick, Sarsfield and his soldiers were allowed to depart for the Continent. This departure became known as 'the flight of the WILD GEESE'. Sarsfield himself was slain at the Battle of Landen in the Netherlands in July 1693. It was claimed that as he was being carried mortally wounded from the battlefield, he uttered: 'Oh, that this were for Ireland!' His courage was recognised not only by his Irish soldiers, but also by his opponents. In plays performed in London after the Williamite victory, King James was depicted as a petulant coward while Sarsfield was regarded as a hero of the Irish. In one scene, James is represented as saying in an aside: 'This fellow will make me brave in spite of myself!' The contrast between these two characters became a popular theme. It was widely reported that after his surrender at Limerick, Sarsfield had remarked to some Williamite officers: 'As low as we now are, change but kings with us, and we will fight it over again with you'. One fanciful anecdote has James criticising the Irish to the French king, Louis XIV, in the presence of Sarsfield. The latter drew his sword to run James through, but was prevented from doing so by the intervention of their French host.

It was said in his home town of Lucan, County Dublin that once in every three years, the ghost of Sarsfield can be seen coming at night on a white horse to his old estate and firing a musket shot in the direction of Limerick.

Curtayne (1934); Ellis (1976), 144–51; Mac Erlean, *3* (1917), 142–57; Bagwell, *3* (1916), 299; Ó Concheanainn (1981), 2–3, 69–70 & in *Éigse*, *14*, 215–36; Gregory (1926), 46–51; Kennedy (1855), 71; IFC 195:262.

Scots The word Scot (Latin, *Scotus*) originally meant an Irishman. It is thought to have been a Celtic word denoting a 'raider', and as such probably came into use for the Irish raiders on the coasts of Roman Britain in the third to fifth centuries AD. When the ÉRAINN group called Dál Riada extended its rule eastwards from Antrim across the sea to Argyll in the fifth century AD, the word Scot was used for these Irish settlers to distinguish them from the PICTS and the Celtic Britons, who lived to the east and south of them respectively. With the establishment of this Irish or Gaelic power throughout the whole region in the ninth century, the country became known as Scotland.

In the Gaelic language, however, Scotland was known exclusively as Alba, and the usual term for a Scottish person was Albanach. These terms derived from the old Celtic name (Albiu) for all of Britain, but in the Middle Ages the Irish confined its use to the part of that island with which they were in closest contact. Scotland in its turn began to influence events in Ireland. A standardised literary Gaelic held in common by the two countries meant that POETS and learned men could commute and communicate without difficulty, and accordingly there was a considerable exchange of songs, stories and other lore.

The most significant Irish–Scottish connection in the Middle Ages was through the Mac Dhomhnaill or Mac Dhónaill family (anglicised in Scotland as MacDonald and in Ireland as MacDonnell and McConnell). This family was descended from a twelfth-century chieftain of Argyll called Somerled who, despite his NORSE name, was largely of Irish descent. The genealogists traced his origins to Fearghus Mac Earca, the Dál Riada king who led the Irish settlements on the Scottish coast. The Scottish MacDonalds became the proud Lords of the Isles, and members of the extended family began to settle in the Glens of Antrim in the thirteenth century as mercenaries in the employ of local chiefs. They acquired more and more territory until, in the fifteenth century, they had established a lordship encompassing all of north Antrim. A large group of these MacDonnells was brought in the late fourteenth century to County Mayo by the NORMAN lords of that area, the Burkes. Scottish mercenaries were in great demand for the local wars between Irish and Norman-Irish lords in the later Middle Ages, and the MacDonnells were not the only family to benefit from this. Their relatives, the MacDowells, were also introduced into parts of Ulster and into Roscommon in this way. Such soldiers of fortune were known as *gallóglaigh* ('foreign warriors', anglicised as 'gallowglasses'). The MacSweeneys of Donegal and the MacCabes of Cavan were gallowglasses in origin, as were further afield the Sheehys in Munster.

After the overthrow of the native chieftains at the beginning of the seventeenth century, their lands were largely confiscated and the Plantation of Ulster began. The planted farmers and tradesmen consisted of three broad groups – speakers of Gaelic from the Scottish Highlands, speakers of Lallans (a dialect derived from Middle English) from the Scottish Lowlands, and speakers of English from northern England; these three languages have influenced Ulster to the present day. The new amalgam of peoples proved to be an important and industrious part of Irish life, with ideologies extending from radical republicanism that sought a free and independent Ireland to strong loyalism that identified with the British power-structures. Scotland has always been respected in Ireland as a source of popular songs, and this continued through from the common Gaelic language to Ulster-Scots (the variant of Lallans in Ireland). The composition of poetry in both languages continued to evince close cultural connections between Scotland and Ireland, and many ballads in English were also borrowed into Ireland through Scotland.

The sturdy Ulster-Scots farmers, like their older Ulster neighbours, had a strong lore of FAIRIES as fellow inhabitants of the landscape. One particular theme, common in folklore from Donegal all the way to Antrim and Down – and of obvious Scottish derivation – concerns a solitary otherworld helper. In its most usual form, it tells of how a strange little man comes to a farmer and does all the farm work for him, but accepts no payment. The farmer is so pleased that, after sometime, he decides to buy a fine suit of clothes for him, but when the stranger is offered the new clothes he takes it as an insult and leaves in high dudgeon. This is a version of the Scottish brownie LEGENDS. In County Donegal, a variant has the helpful stranger as a gallowglass who comes to serve an O'Donnell chieftain. With bow and arrow, he drives back a raiding party of O'Neills but, when offered a reward, disappears.

Apart from MacDonnell, gallowglass surnames include Mac Síthigh (Sheehy); Mac Suibhne (MacSweeney); Mac Dubhghaill (MacDowell); Mac Cába (MacCabe); Caimbéal (Campbell); and the obvious Mac Gallóglaigh (Gallogly). There are many surnames of Ulster-Scots origin, most of them shared with either Gaelic and English families, and they are given here with the sometime Gaelic equivalents. They include Smith (Mac Gabhann); Murray (Muireach); Morrison (Mac Giolla Mhuire); Wilson (Mac Liam); Clarke (Mac Cléirigh); Holmes or MacComish (Mac

Thomáis); Thompson (Mac Thámhais); Stuart (Stiubhart); Robinson (Mac Dhonnchaidh); Graham (Gréamach); Hamilton (Hamaltún); Patterson (Mac Phádraig); Wallace (de Bhailís); Kennedy (Ceannaideach); Ferguson (Mac Fhearghuis); Gordon (Górdan); Beatty (Mac Bheatha); Johnson (Mac Iain); Reid (de Réid); Boyd (Búid); Armstrong (Tréanlámhach).

'ALBA' AND 'SCOTLAND': Ó hÓgáin (2002), 14–15, 39–41, 205–10, 218, 227–33.
SCOTTISH GAELIC CULTURE: D.S. Thomson (1983).
GALLOWGLASSES: Hayes-McCoy (1937), 15–76.
IRISH AND ULSTER SCOTS: Ó Snodaigh (1973).
BROWNIE LEGEND: Westwood (1986), 334–40, 440; IFC Index.
O'DONNELL'S STRANGER: IFC 185:261–2, 493:153, 1223:283–4.

Seanán SAINT who died c.AD 544, founder of a monastery on Inis Cathaigh (Scattery Island in the mouth of the River Shannon). Seanán (earlier, Senan) must have been a nickname, for it meant 'old man'.

There are a few versions of his biography in Latin and one in Irish, and, though differing somewhat in content, all probably derive from a ninth-to-tenth-century work. A sense of chronology is quite lacking in these accounts – Seanán being brought into contact with the fourth-century MARTIN of Tours, as well as the seventh-century MAODHÓG. We read that the birth of a great saint was foretold by PATRICK to the Corca Bhaiscinn (an ÉRAINN sept of west Clare), and that a wizard of that sept identified the prophesied one as being in the womb of the wife of a peasant called Geirgreann. When Seanán was born, his mother was clutching a stake of rowan, and that stake burst into foliage and grew into a celebrated tree. The saint showed his miraculous powers at an early age, and was sent to study under the monk Nothail of Cill na Manach (Kilnamanagh, County Kilkenny). He later visited Maodhóg, and from there went to Martin of Tours, who presented him with a gospel and promised to be with him at his death.

We read that on his return to Ireland, Seanán was numbered among the five leading monks of the country, and that he founded several island monasteries off the south-west coast. Coming to Scattery

Island, he encountered and banished a great monster and settled there. The king of the Uí Fidhgheinte (an EOGHANACHT sept of County Limerick) claimed the island and sent his wizard to contend with Seanán, but both wizard and king perished in their attempts to expel him. The new king of that sept, Neachtan, submitted to the saint and was blessed by him, and thus Seanán's cult was advanced by the Uí Fidhgheinte as well as by the Corca Bhaiscinn. Several conventional miracles are attributed to Seanán, such as the restoration to life of people who had died accidentally. One striking account has a maiden called Canair walking over the waves to Scattery Island, and insisting that women as well as men be allowed by Seanán to follow the monastic life there. After a long argument, the saint consented to this.

When the time of his death came, he ordained that his body be conferred on the nun's community at Cill Eochaille (the convent on Scattery). Angels transported St Martin all the way to that place from the Continent in order to give the last rites to the dying Seanán, as the two saints had earlier arranged between them. An obscure praise-poem on him, entitled *Amra Senáin*, was fancifully attributed to DALLÁN FORGAILL, a sixth-century POET. Seanán's feast day is 8 March, and this was a day of great devotion when Scattery Island was well inhabited. It was customary, out of reverence for the holy site, to sail new boats around the island on the starboard side, and pebbles from the island were believed to protect sailors from drowning.

Kenney (1929), 364–6; Heist (1965), 301–24; Stokes (1890), 54–74 & in ZCP, 3, 220–5; C. Plummer in ZCP, 10, 1–35; O'Hanlon, 3 (1875), 210–57; IFC 354:279–91, 1133:417–20; T.J. Westropp in Folk-Lore, 24, 205–7.

Seanchán *(earlier, Senchán)* POET who flourished in the late sixth and early seventh centuries AD. The designation Seanchán was probably a nickname, since it means 'man of old lore', and would describe his profession. It is usually accompanied by the enigmatic sobriquet Toirpéist (for explanation, *see* below).

He wrote a genealogical text known as the *Cocangab Már* (Great Compilation), mere fragments of which survive, but a later tract may be a paraphrase of it. The tract mentions, in a context that would be contemporaneous with the poet, one 'Senchán mac Uarchridhe' of the Araidh sept, and this is quite likely the poet himself. The Araidh dwelt in the area on the northern Tipperary–Limerick border, and it can be inferred from some references to Seanchán Toirpéist in the medieval literature that he was a native of that general area. His sphere of activity was, however, more wide ranging. The literature claims that he was one of the poets present at the Convention of Drom Ceat (in County Derry) in the year 575, and that he succeeded DALLÁN FORGAILL as chief-poet of Ireland. It also represents him as a close associate of king GUAIRE who reigned in Connacht from 655–66. One or both of these attributions must be wrong. The real situation would appear to be that Seanchán was a younger colleague of Dallán Forgaill, who was still alive though probably quite old in the year 597. This would almost certainly rule out participation by Seanchán in a convention as early as 575, though it would suggest that he spent a period in Ulster, where Dallán flourished. On the other hand, Seanchán himself would be a very old man if he was among the entourage of Guaire as Connacht king, though he might well have frequented the Connacht court when Guaire was a youth and Guaire's father Colmán (+622) ruled.

The surviving fragments of *Cocangab Már* are verses on the genealogies of the Leinstermen (LAIGHIN), but no doubt the work had a much wider scope than that. The earliest occurrence of Seanchán in narrative dates from the late ninth century, and in which we read that a poetess of the Uí Fidhgheinte (an EOGHANACHT sept of County Limerick) was missing for some time, having gone on a circuit of Ireland, Scotland and Man. It happened that Seanchán – attired in his professional garb (*see* POETS) – sets out in a boat to visit the Isle of Man with an entourage of 50 colleagues. As they left, an extremely ugly man called to them from the shore to bring him with them. The brain of this man bulged through his forehead, emitting filthy fluid through his ears, and the rags on him were alive with lice. When he told Seanchán that he would be a more worthwhile companion than the haughty retinue of poets, Seanchán decided to risk letting him come along. On reaching the Isle of Man, they saw a tall old woman scavenging on the beach, and they told her who they were. She challenged them to poetically answer a half quatrain, and neither Seanchán nor his colleagues could do so. The monstrous stranger who had come with them did, however, answer, and gave poetical replies twice more in similar fashion. From the verses, Seanchán realised that the woman was none other than the missing Inghean Uí Dhulsaine. They took her back to Ireland with them, and on their return noticed that a great transformation came over their monstrous companion. He became a handsome and beautifully attired young man, and then disappeared. He was the Spirit of Poetry.

A passage in this story purports to explain Seanchán's sobriquet, Toirpéist. When the monstrous stranger came aboard the boat, the other poets shrank from him, remarking to Seanchán 'a monster approaches you' (viz. *tot-rorpai peist*). This is contrived, but the idea of a synthesis between ugliness and comeliness was well established in early Irish thought. It was strongly evidenced, for instance, in the concept of sovereignty (*see* KINGSHIP), and its extension to the context of poetry was easy, given the dialectic between praise and satire in the productions of poets (q.v.). It is possible that Seanchán taught some such allegory on the nature of poetry, and that echoes of it are preserved in this story. Several early Irish sources suggest that special poetic skill was learned in Alba, which earlier meant Britain but which came to mean, in particular, Scotland. An eleventh-century source may preserve some original detail when it explains Seanchán's sobriquet by stating that, when he was in Alba, the Spirit of Poetry met him on his road and conversed

with him in very obscure rhetoric. His interlocutor was in hideous guise, but this 'monster profited him' (viz. *dorarba peist*). If Seanchán allegorically referred to poetry as sometimes having a horrid guise, this in itself could explain the sobriquet, for a monster was denoted by words such as *torathar* and *péist*. Thus his designation might properly have been Seanchán Torphéiste (i.e. Seanchán of the Monster).

An even more striking and dramatic tradition was associated with this poet. According to it, he was the one who discovered the great epic called *Táin Bo Cuailnge* (*see* ULSTER CYCLE) after it had been lost to living memory. Earlier versions of the tradition had it that the text of the *Táin* had been taken to the Continent by a scholar from Armagh, and had been left there by him in exchange for the *Culmen* (i.e. the *Etymologiae* of Isidorus). Seanchán assembled the poets of Ireland to see if any of them knew the epic, but they could recall only a few fragments. He accordingly set out in search of the text. Coming to the grave of the hero FEARGHUS MAC RÓICH at Eanloch (Lough Finn, County Roscommon), Seanchán's son Muirghein recited a poem over the grave and, as a result, the dead hero appeared to him and told the story of the *Táin* from start to finish. In or about the eleventh century this account was developed and transformed, the discovery of the epic being set within the ambit of Seanchán's supposed patron, the Connacht king Guaire. The fullest recension of this dates from the thirteenth century, and is entitled *Tromdhámh Guaire*. It goes as follows:

The chief-poet of Ireland, Dallán Forgaill, died as the result of unjustly satirising a king, and Seanchán Toirpéist became chief-poet in his place. Because of the fame of Guaire's generosity, Seanchán brought his retinue of poets and servants to visit that king. This retinue was infamous for its demands and its readiness to satirise if the demands were not met. Guaire – through the advice of his brother, the hermit Marbhán – satisfied all their eccentricities, no matter how difficult. To suit one demand, Marbhán had to have his pet white boar killed, and he swore vengeance for this. Seanchán himself became impossibly presumptuous and testy, demanding that the nobility of Connacht be excluded from a feast, and then found fault with Guaire's servants. The grandfather of the cook, he claimed, had horny nails, and the grandmother of the waitress had once touched a leper.

Finally, when told that mice had eaten his egg, he satirised them, killing ten of the little creatures immediately with his words. On second thoughts, Seanchán decided that he should rather satirise the cats, since this would cause more mischief to his hosts. When the king of the cats, called Hirusán, felt the power of the satire, he left his cave at Cnoghbha (Knowth, County Meath) and seized Seanchán at Guaire's court. Slinging him over his back, the huge cat was taking him to the cave when intercepted by CIARÁN, the saint of Clonmacnoise. Ciarán was working in his forge, and he flung a lump of molten metal at the cat and slew it. Seanchán's life was spared, but he was angry, for if he had died his poets would have had an excuse to satirise Guaire. The aggrieved Marbhán began to test the poets with riddles. They answered each riddle correctly, and then he demanded to hear the poetic croon. Declaring himself unsatisfied with their efforts, he went on demanding the 'choking croon' (*crónán snagach*). To be unable to perform any of the poetic skills would expose them as failures in their profession, and so Seanchán himself had to attempt to save their honour. He raised his beard on high and started to croon, but the staccato effect that Marbhán sought was atrociously difficult to achieve, and so Seanchán overstrained himself and one of his eyes jumped from his head with the effort and onto his cheek. Marbhán miraculously replaced it, and then demanded to hear a story. What he asked for was *Táin Bó Cuailnge*.

Neither Seanchán nor any of his retinue knew this story, and so they had to go and seek it out or else retire from their profession in shame. They set out for Scotland, but nowhere there could it be found. Returning to Dublin, they met the saint CAILLÍN. Seanchán and Caillín are here described as sons of the same mother, and so Caillín assembled the saints of Ireland to give their assistance. Marbhán relented slightly and told the poets that there was but one way to learn the story and, following his advice, they went to the grave of Fearghus mac Róich and fasted against him. As a result, the huge warrior Fearghus appeared and sat down to recite the *Táin* to them. St Ciarán wrote down the epic from the dictation, and Marbhán ordered the poets to return to their own territories and never again to assemble as a *tromdhámh* (burdensome company).

This recension has made several additions to the tradition of Seanchán's rediscovery of the *Táin*. It is in fact a humorous belittling of the poets and was clearly intended as a jibe at that profession by a pro-clerical writer. This writer made use of the lore of the Convention of Drom Ceat held in AD 575 and where – it was claimed – the extortions of the poets had been strictly curtailed. Descriptions in the literature of that convention stressed the rapaciousness of the poets, and had Dallán Forgaill and Seanchán as leading participants.

The plot involving Marbhán predates the actual text *Tromdámh Guaire*, having been borrowed from the medieval lore of Guaire (q.v.). This lore, centring on the idea of a very generous king, drew on a source also used in the biography of the British St Kentigern. In that text, a jester demands mulberries in winter from the generous king Rhydderch. This is paralleled by a demand of blackberries in winter by Seanchán's daughter in *Tromdámh Guaire*, and a white boar belonging to Kentigern corresponds to Marbhán's pet animal. The source for both texts is now lost, but it was presumably in Latin and seems to have been a primitive account of the hermit-SAINT Kentigern. Marbhán would therefore have been modelled on Kentigern, though in origin he seems to have been derived from lore concerning the saint CUMAINE FADA, who was claimed to have been a half-brother of Guaire. One source from the tenth to eleventh centuries has Seanchán contending with this Cumaine

– the latter recites twelve lessons from the Gospel, and Seanchán fails to repeat them until he has heard them three times, whereas Cumaine can repeat the poetical compositions of Seanchán immediately. An early poem on the death of Cumaine repeatedly refers to his corpse (*marbhán*), and this could well be what suggested a character called Marbhán as an opponent of Seanchán at Guaire's court.

It is possible, even probable, that Seanchán was the man who put the various elements of the *Táin* into a unified narrative (*see* ULSTER CYCLE), and in that case, the tradition that he discovered, or caused to be discovered, the text of the epic would reach back to his own time. One can speculate that just as a metaphoric reference by himself to the Spirit of Poetry gave rise to one narrative concerning him, so also he might have cultivated the conceit that he had got the *Táin* from the mouth of Fearghus himself. The seeking of inspiration from the dead was a fancy much associated with poets in early Irish tradition, and if Seanchán did indeed belong to the Araidh sept, he would have regarded Fearghus as an ancestor of his own. It is noticeable that there are some elements common to the accounts of the Spirit of Poetry and the finding of the *Táin*. These include the quest-journey to Britain and the spiritual revelation.

The later literature knew little detail of this poet, apart from his supposed adventures at Guaire's court. One example of this is the surviving text concerning CANO MAC GARTNÁIN, which incorporates an account of Seanchán as a rapacious poet apparently predating the text of *Tromdamh Guaire*. We read that a third of Guaire's dwelling was allotted to him, but he schemed to eject Cano and thus get half of it. Among other things, he attempted to discommode Cano by causing his hunting party to be scattered through magic. Seanchán is described as a miserable little man wearing a woollen cloak, and with a poor appetite. He ate a mere quarter of a loaf each day, but his wife Brighid used to eat the other three-quarters. The same text relates that he once composed a praise-poem for the high-king

DIARMAID MAC AODHA SLÁINE. As payment, Diarmaid gave his servant a horse's fetter to bring to him. He then made another poem for the high-king and got a forked branch as reward, but he persisted and, on a third occasion, got gold and silver, and on the fourth, a fine steed. We further read that once, while passing through part of Guaire's territory, a drop of rain struck him on the forehead. An abscess grew on his forehead, and he demanded a large compensation from every settlement in the area as a result.

His memory has faded from living Irish folklore, but he was well known from the literature until recent times. Echoes from the text *Tromdámh Guaire* survived in Scottish folklore, where *cliar Sheanchain* (Seanchán's scholars) were described as a large, wandering band of lazy, ill-mannered and demanding poets. In the Isle of Man, it is said that Bun Ramhar (Gansey Strand) was the scene of his encounter with the old poetess.

TEXTS: O'Brien (1962), 19, 22, 386; Meyer (1912), xiii–xvii, 90–4 & 2 (1914), 19–21 & in *Archiv für celtische Lexikographie*, 3, 2–4 & in *ZCP*, 12, 378–9; R. Thurneysen in *ZCP*, 19, 193–207; Connellan (1860), 262–5; Windisch (1905), liii; Binchy (1963), 8–11; Joynt (1941); Dinneen, 3 (1908), 80–1, 94–5.

DISCUSSIONS: Ó Cadhlaigh (1939), 193–215; Carney (1955), 165–88 & in *Ériu*, 22, 68, 73–5; S. Ó Coileáin in *Ériu*, 28, 32–70; A.D. Rees in *PICCS*, 2, 56–7.

FOLKLORE: S. Ó Duilearga in *Béaloideas*, 25, 144; Ó hÓgáin (1982), 291–2, 334 & in *Béaloideas*, 72, 91–7; C.A. Gordon in *Scottish Gaelic Studies*, 8, 22–5; W.J. Watson in *Celtic Review*, 4, 80–8; I. Mac Aonghuis in S. Watson (1986), 103–4.

Seven Bishops A common Irish folk LEGEND describes how seven baby brothers were saved from drowning and grew up to each become a bishop, and accordingly seven churches were founded by them.

Variants of the story were told throughout Ireland. It was said that all seven were born at one birth and that their parents were poor and despaired of being able to support them. The father therefore put them into a sack and was bringing them to a river with the intention of drowning them when he met a holy man who enquired as to what was in the sack. The father protested that they were pups, but the holy man saw through the lie and insisted that the children be given to him. He took them, and reared and educated them, so that each of the seven became a priest and eventually a bishop. This is based on an international FOLKTALE which tells of how a parent tried to kill his or her children, but was prevented by the other parent from doing so. Although scarcely more than a few centuries old, the Irish adaptation is often cited as biographical material for groups of local SAINTS whose names survive in toponymics but concerning whom little else is known.

A special variant was developed in the area of south Kilkenny and south-east Tipperary due to a carving of seven episcopal figures on the famous high cross at Ahenny. The original significance of these figures is not known, but the folk speculated that they were the seven boys of the legend, and we are told that an aged cleric saved them from being drowned by their father and brought them to Rome for education. They became bishops, and on his death he directed that they return to Ireland and continue his religious work there. They were entertained at Grannagh Castle by the great sixteenth-century Countess of Ormond, Margaret BUTLER, but she grew suspicious that they had gold in their luggage and sent some of her servants after them to kill them. They were accordingly beheaded at Áth na gCeann, on the Lismatigue river in Aghavillar, County Kilkenny. Thus folklore explains this place name Áth na gCeann, which means literally the 'ford of the heads'. We are anachronistically told that they were buried at Ahenny and the high cross erected over them. The cross actually dates from the eighth century. It is sometimes said that only one of the bishops was buried there, and that other high crosses in the vicinity mark the graves of the other six.

Aarne & Thompson (1961), type 765; Ó Suilleabháin & Christiansen (1967), type 765B; F. Henry in *Béaloideas, 15*, 257–60; Carrigan (1905), *4*, 7.

sheep Not only is the sheep the most numerous domesticated animal in Ireland, it is also one of the oldest, dating back to the fifth millennium BC. Sensing this antiquity, the medieval scholars claimed that a small herd was brought in a boat by the fantastic lady CEASAIR, reputedly the leader of the first group of people to settle in the country.

There are some apparent traces of sheep-cults in the old ancestor-lore (*see* UGHAINE, AILILL MOLT *and* AILILL ÓLOM), but in general, sheep are not given a high profile in either the literature or the folklore. They usually figure only in the context of their commercial value. Because of their mutton and wool, they were considered lucky animals, and it was claimed in some places that if one looked through the shoulder blade of a dead sheep, one might see into the future. In one widespread story of FIONN MAC CUMHAILL, a ram is given an important role, being represented as a symbol of the world's energy.

F. Kelly (1997), 67–77; Cross (1952), 44, 51, 54, 65–6, 79, 82; Macalister (1940), 26; S. Ó Súilleabháin (1942), 37–8; S. Ó hEochaidh in *Béaloideas, 37–8* (1969–70), 131–209; Wood-Martin, *2* (1902), 137–8; P.V. O'Sullivan (1991), 80–2.

Sionainn The River Shannon, described in one early text as a *bandéa* (goddess). It being the longest and most majestic river in Ireland, it was natural for ancient Celtic lore – which associated GODDESSES with rivers – to be applied to it at an early date; hence the name, the original Celtic form of which was Senuna, meaning 'the old honoured one'. The quality of antiquity had a special meaning for the Celts, who associated it with wisdom – therefore the goddess could be not only synonymous with the waters that irrigate and render fruitful the soil, but also with the trait of knowledge that renders fruitful the human mind. As an echo of this, an early Greek writer related of the Continental Celts that they told of a western island ruled by druidesses called Senae (old ones).

In the medieval PLACE-LORE, variants of a story are told concerning a beautiful lady called Sionainn. According to this, she wished to gain wisdom from the bubbles of *imbas* (full knowledge) that were to be found in an otherworld well. This well burst up out of the ground, and she fled from it, but it chased her and finally drowned her. The course it took became the River Shannon, and thus her name is on that river. It is obvious that this is a mere copy of the tradition of the origin of the Boyne river (*see* BÓINN), but behind both lies the ancient mythic idea that goddesses were patrons of rivers and in some way resided in them. The river, with its source in the otherworld, was a very old Indo-European concept, probably rationalising the mysterious ways in which rivers rise in the landscape. It was therefore natural to imagine the streams of fertility flowing into this world from the otherworld, and bringing the power of the mother-goddess within them (*see* DANU).

GODDESS: Stokes & Strachan (1903), 264–5.

NAME: T.F. O'Rahilly (1946), 4–5.

SENAE: Ó hÓgáin (2002), 25-6.

MEDIEVAL STORY: Gwynn (1913), 286–97, 456-7; M. Joynt in Bergin (1912), 193–7; W. Stokes in *RC, 15*, 456-7.

OTHERWORLD SOURCE OF RIVER: Dillon (1969), 6.

Solomon The wise king of the Old Testament is known in Irish as Solamh or simply Sola, and his name is often used as a symbol of wisdom.

As such, one story in medieval Irish literature has him as a young prince correcting a decision made by his father, King David. It happened that David refused alms to an undeserving beggar, who repeatedly returned to seek more. David ordered that he be hanged, but Solomon interrupted the proceedings and told his father to give a blessing to the beggar instead of punishment. David said that Solomon himself should give the blessing, whereupon both blessed him on the breast, but Solomon told him not to open his vest until he reached home. When his wife washed the vest in a stream near his house, it brought lots of salmon there, and when she hung it on a tree, it brought wonderful apples. The beggar brought three red-gold apples to David, and Solomon advised that they be shared out in the following wise (though somewhat anachronistic) manner – one apple to David as he was the representative of the Church, one to Solomon as he would represent the

kingship, and one to the beggar, representing the ordinary people.

Another medieval text takes a somewhat different perspective, describing the young Solomon as growing impatient at the delays of his father in giving judgements. King David allowed him to sit in the royal seat to hear cases, but as soon as he did so, Solomon saw the hand of God in the air with a two-edged sword, ready to strike him down if he erred in passing judgement. This caused Solomon to regret his hastiness. Yet another medieval Irish text describes Solomon as 'a king of the Greeks'. Some drunken guests of his carried on a debate concerning what is the most powerful force in the world. One debater considered that wine was the most powerful, another considered a king. His queen knocked the helmet off Solomon with a blow of her fist, however, and on recovering, Solomon announced that a woman was the most powerful because her beauty saved her from all punishment. This seems to be a garbled version of an apocryphal story told in a Latin text from the Continent.

The special associations of Solomon with women are as old as the Bible, and Church sermons stressed such associations. For instance, very popular in Ireland was the biblical story of how Solomon discovered the true mother of a child claimed by two women, by threatening to divide it in two halves. Also from the Bible was an account of the womanising of Solomon's father David. It is claimed that David enforced a rule by which each new bride in his kingdom would have to spend a night with him, and when Solomon met a poor widow bringing her daughter to the palace, the widow explained the situation to him. Solomon went to his father and told him that a rich landowner wished to take the only lamb owned by a poor shepherd. David decreed that the rich man should be buried alive underneath seven sods of earth, and when Solomon told him that David himself was the offender, he had no choice but to accept the penalty. On Solomon's advice, however, he composed seven long psalms of contrition, and each psalm miraculously laid a sod aside so that he was brought back to his throne. This is, of course, based on the story of Bathsheba, wife of the soldier Uriah, in the Bible – with Solomon put in place of the prophet Nathan, and David's psalms being given a novel interpretation.

The Bible states that David's paramour Bathsheba was in fact the mother of Solomon, and as a result of the shady dealings of his parents, a fanciful FOLKTALE grew up in the Middle Ages (ROMANTIC TALES, type 920). Irish versions of this tell of how, after his birth, his mother notices that the infant Solomon is very clever, and accordingly fears that he will reveal details of her scandalous life. She therefore orders that he be killed, but he is saved by a sympathetic commoner, who rears him. As he grows up, he shows his wisdom in several ways, and King David finally realises that the talented youth is his son. Meanwhile, the mother plots to elope with a foreign king, and Solomon goes to their rendezvous and hides in a tree, bringing a blackbird with him. The queen suspects that he might be in the trees listening to their conversation, so she throws stones into the trees. At the third throw, Solomon's bird flies out, and the queen, remarking that the blackbird is a solitary creature, is confident that nobody is there. Hearing their plans, Solomon then sets out after them. He introduces himself to the queen, who falls in love with him, but when he tells her who he is, she has him seized and sentenced to death. He manages to send a message to King David, however, telling of his predicament and requesting that soldiers be sent disguised as angels and demons quarrelling over the soul of the man to be executed. In this way, David's soldiers gain access to the place of execution, slay the foreign king, and seize the queen. She is sentenced to be burned, but Solomon pities her and advises her to ask a boon of David. On his instructions, she asks for her right hand to be placed in the fire first, and David – realising that this refers to him as her husband – relents and forgives her.

Some simple stories tell of Solomon's wisdom. For instance, when his lover, the Queen of Sheba, brings him two beautiful and identical flowers, she challenges him to identify the real one from the artificial. He gets a BEE, which quickly alights on the real flower. In addition to all this, Solomon is sometimes substituted for other dignitaries in Irish stories. He may, for instance, be made the main character in the story of how the wise ARISTOTLE was poisoned by his wife. He may also be substituted for the TYRANT king in the international story type 925 (see ROMANTIC TALES), which has a clever fool tricking that king into announcing bad news to himself. In the opposite direction, it is obvious that, at various stages, the image of Solomon exerted influence on that of the legendary wise king of Ireland, CORMAC MAC AIRT.

P. Grosjean in *Irish Texts, 4*, 118–20; K. Meyer in *ACL, 3*, 321–2 & in *Irisleabhar na Gaedhilge, 4*, 216–17; Atkinson (1887), 156; McNamara (1975), 28–30; Hyde (1915), 66–9; S. Ó Súilleabháin & Christiansen (1967), 177, 182; IFC Index.

special powers All societies have speculated on whether the ordinary physical and mental limits of human existence could be transcended, and preserve accounts of some people who are reputed to have done so. In Irish literature, the portrayal of a lauded individual usually entailed a selection of some quite extraordinary powers, and the same is often true in folk LEGENDS. The telling of narratives about such heroes or heroines never failed to gain an audience, and no doubt many of the listeners secretly longed for similar abilities.

Apart from accounts of epic heroes, SAINTS and POETS, folklore includes many types of people to whom special powers are credited. The leading profession in this regard for several centuries is the Church, many priests being believed to have miraculous powers of healing. This was, of course, an extension into the social realm of the theology of spiritual healing, and folklore adds its own quality of concreteness to the belief. The custom was common until recently for people to ask their local priest to write some lines from John's Gospel in Latin on a piece of paper, and this was frequently worn about the neck in a little satchel to guarantee protection against illness, temptation and misfortunes of every kind. Here we see the reputed power of a mysterious language, Latin, being added to the religious power of the priest. Several stories were told of how priests banished GHOSTS, and a particularly popular LEGEND told of a priest temporarily bringing a dead landlord from hell so as to prove his power to that man's son and persuade the son to mend his ways. This legend seems to have sprung from religious arguments in Reformation England, where it was believed even by those opposed to Roman Catholicism that 'none can lay a spirit but a Popish priest'.

The untheological nature of folk belief is well exemplified by the belief that some priests had more power than others, and young priests were in greater demand than older men because of the idea that they would not yet have used up their spiritual energy. It was also held that silenced priests – men who had been deprived of their office by church authorities – had more power as healers than the ordinary clergymen. It is clear that, in social terms, lore of how priests could if necessary use their power made life more bearable. Accounts abounded of how cruel magistrates and wicked landlords were laid low by the well-deserved curse of a priest. A dramatic little legend, of a type current in Europe since medieval times, was employed as a good example of this. It tells of how a priest was once invited to a party by a group of disreputable landlords, and while there, his hosts insisted that he join in the drunken merriment by singing a song. He consented on condition that they all sing together, and then he struck up a lively hunting song. During the singing, which became more and more boisterous, the priest slipped out, and the landlords were miraculously compelled to continue at the song until next day. By that time, they were near to death from their exertions, but a servant went for the priest to relieve them of their agony. The prototype of this story on the Continent tells of how dancers were thus compelled to dance to exhaustion by a priest whose instructions they had ignored.

A noticeable social type in Ireland of the eighteenth and nineteenth centuries was the 'poor scholar', a man of some learning who travelled about in search of employment as a part-time schoolmaster. In the absence of an organised educational system for Catholics, such a scholar could eke out an existence by setting up a 'hedge school' and charging a small fee to the parents who wished to send their children to him to be given a basic education. These scholars were often quite learned men for their time and circumstances. Several of them were poets, all had a good knowledge of English reading and writing and of mathematics, and a few had a good knowledge of Latin and Greek also. In folklore, they are represented as wise men who were consulted on matters relating to propitious movements of the stars and on the interpretation of prophecies. One popular legend tells of how a poor scholar was staying in a house one night, and the householder asked him to interpret some lettering which was on a slab in the fireplace. The lettering, we are told, was in OGHAM script, and the scholar said that it meant that a TREASURE was hidden under the slab. Upon investigation, this was found to be so.

Those credited in the folk mind with extraordinary powers usually come from very definite sectors of society. They may belong to specialist professions that were seen by the general populace as in some way secretive, such as clergymen, poets, scholars and blacksmiths. The high standing of the latter has to do with the special value of iron implements in both war and peace, and as such must be of great antiquity. The smith was regarded as one of the wisest men in the community, and his forge was a great centre for social communication and for conversation. It was believed that the water in the trough of the forge, being impregnated with iron, held a cure for many ailments, and the smith himself was credited with the ability to curse an individual who offended him by turning the anvil against that person. The stonemason was also regarded as a particularly skilled and knowledgeable person. As with the smith, this seems to derive from the material on which he worked, stone being a valuable commodity, and it is interesting to note that another method of cursing was to turn stones against a person. Adding to the aura of mystery surrounding stonemasons was the fact that they had a 'language' of their own, called *Béarlagar na Saor* (the Slang of the Masons), which was a cryptic sort of Irish based on a fanciful selection of words.

Professions, of course, tended to be hereditary, and some special powers were regarded as likewise running in families. The blood of the Cahills and Keoghs, for instance, was believed to cure the shingles if applied to the affected part of the body, and the blood of the Darcys could cure wildfire. Those with the surnames Cassidy, Gough and Walsh were also sometimes claimed to have cures. It was widely believed that people whose parents had, before their marriage, the same surname, had the gift of healing. Another idea was that a cure could only be handed on by a dying person to a member of the family who was of the opposite sex.

A general assumption was that those who had extraordinary powers should not overuse them, as to do so might reduce the practitioner's own protective energy and leave himself or herself at risk. Noted healers were often of types which live on the periphery of ordinary social life, such as poor scholars, travelling poets, beggars or travelling people generally who pass through a community and on to the next. Members of the Travelling community – usually called 'tinkers' because they worked with tin – were often considered to have special powers. The particular reason for this was their skill at their trade, but the sense of mystery attaching to them was increased by their use of another secret 'language' – called *Shelta* or *Gammit*, this was composed of metaphoric Irish words but with English syntax, and is still used to advantage by Travellers when dealing with the settled community. In line with the view that special powers tended to be possessed by outsiders, people who were in some way unusual within the community were often thought of as having such powers. These included individuals born posthumously or born out of wedlock, individuals born on a Sunday or with a caul,

twins, and in particular a seventh son of a seventh son. Red-haired people, constituting a small minority in the community, could also be considered to have extraordinary abilities.

Some people were reputed to have first obtained special powers when already in adult life. One of the most curious cases concerns the family of Lee, who were traditionally doctors and physicians. It is said that one of this family, Muircheartach Ó Laoi, was taken away by the FAIRIES to an otherworld island off Galway Bay (*see* ENVIRONMENT), and that he found a book there that was full of medical knowledge. He brought the book ashore with him, read it, and as a result became a great doctor. This character lived in the late seventeenth century, and a contemporary account makes it clear that he himself claimed to have had the experience. The actual book in question is preserved in the Royal Irish Academy in Dublin, but on examination proves to have been written in the fifteenth century, being a collection of many cures translated into Irish from Latin textbooks. The book is colourfully decorated, and it was no doubt a combination of its contents and of its aspect that allowed Muircheartach to convincingly put forward his claim concerning it. Learned and obscure writings, like learned and obscure speech, were popularly regarded as containing magical power. A striking if alarming instance of this is a report from the year 1627 of how the beautifully illuminated Book of Durrow was being used by a farmer as a means of curing sick CATTLE. This farmer used to dip the book in water, which was then given to the cattle to drink. Fortunately the priceless 1,000-year-old manuscript was rescued from such usage.

Also in the seventeenth century, a man who lived in the Erris area of west Mayo was reputed to have amazing powers of prophecy. This was Brian Rua Ó Cearbháin, and he was said to have got his gift when he used whatever money he had to pay the rent due by a poor widow and thus prevented her eviction. The widow prayed earnestly that he might be rewarded, and on his way home from the landlord's office, Brian began to feel tired and fell asleep in mountainous terrain. He dreamed that a voice told him to search the sleeve of his coat, and on awakening did so and found a little mirror there. This mirror used to reflect future happenings for him and thus enable him to prophesy. Folklore claims that he foretold many of the great social, political and technological developments of the succeeding centuries. Stories were told of how he could disclose where gold was hidden in the earth, and one tradition even claims that he caused a mysterious and unpiloted ship carrying gold sovereigns to dock off the Mayo coast so that a generous Ulsterman, who had sold cattle to him on credit, should not be kept waiting for his payment. The Mayo lore concerning Brian Rua is the most dramatic concerning a folk-prophet, but in greater or less degree other local prophets were highly regarded throughout the country.

Of the many women with no formal education who were reputed healers in different parts of Ireland in the nineteenth century, the two most celebrated were Moll Anthony, who lived on the Curragh of Kildare, and Biddy Early from Feakle, County Clare. These women were said to travel with the fairies by night, and by this means were able to answer any question regarding an ailment put to them by those who came to seek their aid or advice. According to folklore, they seldom failed to cure either man or beast when their services were called upon. Although she died as recently as 1873, Biddy's fame spread through most of Munster and Connacht. People came from far and near to her, and found her to be a clairvoyant who could tell them the most private of things, as well as being a specialist in herbs. She apparently first got her powers after a bout of illness, and it was popularly supposed that during that illness she had been presented by the fairies with a special black bottle into which she looked to find information. As with folk-healers generally, she never used her power except for good purposes, but a humorous anecdote claims that an over-officious priest once came to upbraid her for dabbling in magical practices. She politely received him, but was not convinced that her healing contravened God's law. The priest left in some anger, but found that his horse would not budge for him and so had to return rather shamefacedly to seek Biddy's help. She advised him to spit on the HORSE and bless it, whereupon it obeyed his commands as before.

Some people with magical powers were naturally treated with suspicion. A folk legend current in Ireland since medieval times tells of a showman with a cock who, to the amazement of his onlookers, has the bird effortlessly draw a large block of timber after it. One man, however, is carrying a bundle of hay, and in it is a four-leafed shamrock that enables him to realise that the cock is in fact pulling a straw and that its owner is a hypnotist. In order to avoid discovery, the showman pays a large sum of money for the hay. Somewhat more eerie than sight-shifting was the power employed by certain mowers, who could maintain a sharp edge on their scythes by inserting a black beetle into the handle. Equally alarming was a type of man who could make any woman fall hopelessly in love with him by drying his hands in her apron. For their part, women could magically allure men by giving them an apple to eat on which charms had been put or into which a magical pin had been inserted.

GENERAL: Cross (1952), 119–210; S. Ó Súilleabháin (1942), 304–15, 362–439 & (1967), 56–60, 76–80; Wood-Martin, 2 (1902), 160–205; Ó Danachair (1978), 29–31.

PRIESTS: P. Ó Héalaí in *Léachtaí Cholm Cille, 8*, 109–31; Ó hÓgáin (1985), 204–15, 273–6.

COMPELLED TO DANCE: S. Thompson (1955–58), motif C94.1.1; M. Chesnutt in Newall (1980), 158–66; Ó hÓgáin (1982), 405–8 & (1985), 209–10, 340.

BLACKSMITHS: Danaher (1966), 81–7.

SECRET LANGUAGES: Macalister (1937).

HEALERS: Logan (1972); Danaher (1984), 98–123.

Ó LAOI: Ó hÓgáin (1982), 191–3, 435.

BOOK OF DURROW: D. Murphy (1896), 95–6.

Ó CEARBHÁIN: Ó Tiománaidhe (1906); Ó hÓgáin (1985), 286–9.

EARLY: Lenihan (1987); Ó hÓgáin (1985), 276–9.

COCK AND LOG: Szövérffy (1957), 151–5; B. Almqvist in *Béaloideas, 59*, 269.

LOVE-MAGIC: Ó Catháin (1980), 87–91; Ó hÓgáin (1985), 270–2.

sports and pastimes Some of the forms of recreation in Ireland had much tradition attached to them, storytelling putting particular emphasis on those who excelled in the different skills.

The literary stories repeatedly refer to the playing of a board game called *fidh-cheall*, which was a form of what we call chess. It consisted of two sets of men pegged into position on a board, but the rules followed are not known. Another board game frequently mentioned is *bran dubh* (literally, 'black raven'), and from at least the twelfth century the game of backgammon (called *táiplis* from French 'tables') was popular with the nobility. Apart from martial skills and athletics, the favourite pastime with young men is represented as playing hurley, involving a large number of players on each of two teams, each player having a hurley stick (*camán*). The game took the form of each team alternately defending a hole in the ground or a stick with both ends in the ground, into which the opposing team tried to drive a brass ball. The hunting of birds, deer and pigs was a frequent activity in the literature, as was the racing of horses.

Feasting and storytelling were evening recreations for the nobility – ale and mead being the favourite drinks. Medieval lists typify the stories told as narratives of courtships, feastings, otherworld adventures, hostings, destructions and CATTLE raids. These stories were the business of the professional POETS and their reciters, but other forms of entertainment were also in demand at banquets. Gleemen (usually called *crosáin*) seem to have had quite a rewarding profession, despite frequent clerical censure of some lewd performances that they proffered. They were skilled jugglers and acrobats, and specialised in a humorous medley of verse and prose. This genre of composition, called after them *crosánacht*, was in recent centuries practised by the poets, and there can be little doubt but that the trickster image of poets in later folklore owes much to these medieval entertainers (*see* MAC CONGLINNE *and* CEITHEARNACH CAOILRIABHACH). No doubt the ordinary people had humbler

versions of conviviality, although no clear accounts of these survive. With regard to storytelling, it can safely be taken that the narrative genres current among the ordinary folk in medieval times were of the same general nature as those found in more recent folklore. The literature, often the preserve of the higher orders of society, shows clearly the influences of oral LEGEND and oral FOLKTALE, as referred to in many instances in this book.

There seems to have been no major change in the patterns of entertainment until the fifteenth and sixteenth centuries, when new sports were introduced due to the spread of English rule and influence. Two of these, card-playing and dice, quickly became an addiction for many Irishmen. Elizabethan writers describe with shock and amazement how professional gamblers lay in wait for travellers on the road sides of Ireland, and how some of these gamblers staked all their possessions – even their clothes and parts of their body – on games. The term used for such a gambler, *cearrbhach*, is cognate with the word for 'cut', and this may indicate that they specialised in the quick and hazardous game of cutting the deck.

Clergymen of all denominations were strictly opposed to gambling, and through their censuring an oral legend was adopted from England, becoming very popular in Leinster and from there spreading to the other provinces. This told of how a dark stranger once appeared at a card-playing house and joined in a game. In the course of play, a card slipped from the table, and when one of the players stooped to pick it up, he saw that in place of a foot the stranger had a cloven hoof. The devil – for it was he – disappeared in a flash of fire, having been foiled by a mere chance in his attempt to win the souls of the players. This cautionary tale had as its purpose to discourage people from card-playing, and it was said that the evil one was not far away when this and other crazed forms of gambling were in progress. On a lighter note, the playing of cards for small stakes – such as a goose or duck – became very popular in rural Ireland, variants of the five-card game being the most popular. It is interesting to note that oral narrative reflected social reality by substituting cards for chess in stories that involved wagers.

The seventeenth century brought some new and unsavoury forms of entertainment to the towns, such as bull-baiting, dogfighting and cockfighting. In the countryside, hunting the fox with a pack of hounds became a favourite pastime with landlords. The latter also began to take an interest in hurling as played on specially chosen fields, and helped to reorganise it into teams of their tenants. Alongside this, other more spontaneous forms of hurling survived, such as hurling on strands or rough terrain with makeshift sticks (*camánacht*). The more structured form of the game, field-hurling, was played with finely made ash sticks – this was called *iomáint* (driving), and from it emerged the great national game of hurling instituted by the Gaelic Athletic Association in 1884. That association also took under its care the Irish forms of football and handball, both of which had been played in primitive form for some centuries.

Folklore told of many great hurlers of old, some of whom were so skilled that they could keep a ball in the air by repeatedly striking it while they disrobed and then dressed again, and others who could race around large buildings and strike the ball from all sides without allowing it to touch the ground. A common folk legend told of how some famous hurler was taken away by night by the FAIRIES, and how he goaled for an otherworld team before being returned to his bed. The great popularity of organised hurling in the twentieth century has given rise to a wealth of folklore concerning famous players such as Lory Meagher, Mick Mackey and Christy Ring. A frequent MOTIF is how the hurler trains by hitting the ball through a loop at a distance or by ringing a doorbell in the same manner, how during a game he tricks opponents by apparently making the ball invisible, or how he deliberately plays poorly for a while so as to lull opponents into a false sense of security. Some legend types, illustrating the self-effacing nature of great hurlers, are very popular. For instance, a boy meets a stranger who teaches him the skills of hurling, and soon after, the boy attends a major game and discovers that the stranger is a famous player. Also, a famous player meets a team of media interviewers and pretends to be somebody else in order to avoid publicity.

Wrestling and boxing became popular from the seventeenth century onwards, and lore developed concerning great champions at these sports. Several of such legends centre on Irish champions defeating English ones, most notably the exploits of the boxer Dan DONNELLY in the early nineteenth century. A more obscure tradition, in Connacht lore, tells of how the seventeenth-century worthy Tomás Láidir Ó Coisdealbha (Strong Thomas Costello) of Carrowduff, County Roscommon, defeated a giant English wrestler who had come to Sligo to challenge all and sundry. The unfortunate visitor had his neck broken in the contest and died. The victor was also a great athlete, and was reputed to have out-raced a horse on one occasion – a fanciful motif also associated with great local athletes in other parts of the country. Tomás was the epitome of the sort of man upon whom folk legend thrived – he was lithe and handsome, and was long remembered for his sad love affair around the year 1660 with Úna MacDermott, to whom he composed a well-known love song. Her rich parents would not allow the marriage, and so both pined away and died from heartbreak. They were buried on an island in Lough Key, County Roscommon, and a tree grew from each of their graves and entwined over the graveyard (*see* ROMANTIC TALES, type 970).

A common formula in Irish folktales is for the heroic company to make three-thirds of the night 'a third with drink, a third with music, and a third with slumber and deep sleep'. Music, song and dance have all been extremely popular in the Ireland of recent centuries, but no great antiquity can be attributed to the surviving genres. Singing can be traced with some precision. It is apparent that early Irish songs were in fact chanted poems, of both popular and learned type, with the rhythm dependent on the words. Working songs – such as those sung by ploughmen and spinning-women – were popular until the nineteenth century, as were also chanted rhetorics in the keening of the dead. All of these may be descendants of ancient Irish styles of singing. It is clear that such styles did not become calcified in form, for despite changes in prosody through the centuries, the composition of poetry in Irish was usually intended for the singing voice. Precedence for the actual melody gradually developed under the influence of Latin, French and English sources during the Middle Ages, and it can be shown that the very emotional love songs in the Irish language derive their themes and imagery from the *amour courtois* conventions that became popular in western Europe from the thirteenth to the fifteenth century. These songs describe love as a malady which can only be cured by its fulfilment, and they treat much of idyllic surroundings and of secrets and pacts between lovers. They became the favourite genre of song in Ireland, and so much attention was focused on them that the post-medieval spread of international ballad types had little influence on Ireland. With the spread and consolidation of the English language in the eighteenth and nineteenth centuries, however, versions of these ballads from England and Scotland began to take root, and in time became very popular.

The harp (*cruit* or *cláirseach*) is the musical instrument mentioned most frequently in early and medieval literature, but there are also references to instruments the nature of which is less certain – such as a stringed *tiompán* and a type of pipe called *feadán*. Music was considered a highly artistic skill, and many stories referred to experts who could play three magical strains. These were *goltraighe*, which made listeners weep, *geantraighe*, which made them merry, and *suantraighe*, which brought on slumber. The harp had virtually disappeared by the late eighteenth century, being replaced by combined pipes of a type that had long been popular among the ordinary people. The violin, known as a 'fiddle', was introduced to Ireland in the seventeenth century, and was the favourite instrument for dance music until largely displaced by the accordion in the nineteenth century. Melodious or inspiring music was fancifully said to have otherworld strains within it, and the folk were so awed by the playing of some practitioners that it was reputed to have been learned from the *sí* people (*see* FAIRIES *and* POETS).

It may be that the function of dance in early Ireland lay in ritual rather than entertainment, such postures being associated with magical acts (*see* LUGH, POETS *and* ULSTER CYCLE). Regarding the pastime of dancing in post-medieval times, two words are used synonymously – *damhsa* and *rince*. Both are borrowings from English ('dance' and 'rink'), which suggests that existing Irish traditional dance is not of native origin. Post-medieval accounts of *rince an ghadraigh* (withy dance), *rince fada* (long dance) and *rince an chlaímh* (sword dance) make it clear that forms of group and processional dancing became popular, but in the seventeenth and eighteenth centuries were displaced by jigs, reels and hornpipes from Scotland and England. In the late eighteenth and early nineteenth centuries, professional dance masters toured the country teaching deportment to children, and they spread modified forms of quadrilles, from which are sprung the set-dances that have been popular now for several generations.

There was no formal drama in Gaelic Ireland, but plays were being staged in English in the towns since the fourteenth century. A form of folk drama called 'mumming' was adopted from England, and became very popular in recent centuries in large parts of Ulster and Leinster. Performed in the Christmas season by local people travelling from house to house and suitably accoutred, these plays consisted of long speeches and supporting action by a mixture of saints, devils and historical characters.

More general and spontaneous pastimes included weight-throwing, skittles and bowls, while divination games of many types were in great demand, particularly by girls speculating as to whom they would marry. Speech games such as riddles and tongue-twisters were family entertainment, and adults were much given to tracing genealogy and to discussions of linguistic usages and proverbs. Above all else, however, traditional Irish culture specialised in storytelling, and the variety and sophistication achieved in that skill is the basic subject of this book.

EARLY AND MEDIEVAL IRELAND: A. Ross (1970), 93–109; Mac Cana (1980); Cross (1952), 287–93; E. MacWhite in *Éigse, 5,* 25–35; RIA Dictionary, s.v. '*crosán*', '*crosánacht*'; MacLysaght (1950), 128–65.

RECENT CENTURIES: S. Ó Súilleabháin (1942), 652–99; Ó Danachair (1978), 41–3; K. Danaher & P. Lysaght in *Béaloideas, 48–49,* 214–16; Ó hÓgáin (1985), 289–305, 346–7.

CARD-PLAYING: Ó hÓgáin (1985), 274–5, 345; É. Ní Anluain in *Béaloideas, 59,* 45–54, 219–20.

HURLING AND FOOTBALL: Ó Maolfabhail (1973); L.P. Ó Caithnia (1980) & BCÉ (1984).

TOMÁS LÁIDIR: de híde (1909); M. MacEnery in *Éigse, 4,* 133–46.

MUSIC, SONG AND DANCE: D. O'Sullivan (1974); Ó Tuama (1960); Breathnach (1971); B. Ó Madagáin in *Béaloideas, 53,* 130–216; Ralls-MacLeod (2000).

MUMMING: Alan Gailey (1969).

SPEECH GAMES: N.J. Williams (1988).

Suibhne Fictional character in a story written in the ninth century and a full version of which is in the twelfth-century text *Buile Shuibhne*. The name Suibhne was a common one in early Ireland (*see* SUIBHNE MEANN).

The story describes him as a seventh-century king of the sept called Dál nAraidhe (who lived in south Antrim and north Down). One day, on hearing the bell of St Rónán – who was building a church in his territory – Suibhne rushed in anger to expel the SAINT. His queen, Eorann, tried to restrain him and caught his cloak, whereupon he ran naked from his house and attacked the saint, flinging Rónán's psalter into a lake. He was dragging the unfortunate saint along when a messenger came to summon him to the assistance of the Ulster king Conghal Claon in a battle against the high-king DOMHNALL MAC AODHA. Suibhne went

with the messenger, and Rónán cursed him for what he had done – praying that he would wander through the world naked, as he was when he abused a servant of God.

An otter came and restored Rónán's psalter as if it had never been in water, and then the saint went to try to make peace between the contending parties. As he blessed the armies, Suibhne was angered by the sprinkling of holy water on him, and he speared one of Rónán's clerics to death. He made a second cast at the saint himself, but the spear broke against the saint's bell and its shaft flew into the air. Rónán cursed him again, praying that Suibhne might thus fly through the air and die of a spear-cast. When the battle was joined at Magh Rátha (Moira, County Down), Suibhne looked up amid the horrid clamour and saw everything whirling about. He became deranged and fled from the battlefield, racing far away and leaping onto a yew tree, which he made his dwelling. A kinsman tried to restore him to his senses, but he fled again and perched on a tree in Tír Chonaill (County Donegal). When the victorious army of the high-king encamped near there, Domhnall mac Aodha himself encountered the mad Suibhne, pitied him, and tried unsuccessfully to dissuade him from such a life. Suibhne fled once more and travelled through all Ireland until he came to Gleann Bolcáin (apparently at Rosharkin, County Antrim), a place where the lunatics used to congregate and find solace. There a faithful friend and relative, Loingseachán, found his footprints near a river where he used to eat watercress, but failed to locate Suibhne himself. As Loingseachán slept in a hut one night, the madman came near, but he avoided him when awake.

Loingseachán succeeded in meeting him by disguising himself as a mill-hag who used to give food to Suibhne. The madman told him that he would go to see his wife Eorann. She had gone to live with another man, and Suibhne reproached her for doing this, but when she said that she would prefer to live with himself even in misery, he took pity on her and advised her to remain with the new lover. A crowd gathered as they spoke, and Suibhne once more fled to the wilderness and took up his abode in trees again. Loingseachán came to him a second time and pleaded with him to return to his stately comfortable life as king. When Suibhne asked for tidings of his kingdom, Loingseachán told him that his father, mother, brother and daughter had died. As Suibhne lamented this loss of his family, Loingseachán told him that his son also was dead. The madman said that this news 'would bring a man to the earth, that a little son who used to say "papa" is cold and lifeless'. Overcome by grief, Suibhne fell from the tree, and Loingseachán tied him up and told him that his family were in fact alive. He took him back to the people of Dál nAraidhe and reinstalled him as king.

One day, when alone in his palace, the old mill-hag mentioned to him his period of madness and persuaded him to jump as he had then done. She competed with him, and both went away jumping into the wilderness, where Suibhne resumed his life of lunacy as before. Coming to Dún Sobhairce (Dunseverick, County Antrim), he cleared the fortress there with a leap, and in attempting to emulate his feat, the hag fell from the cliff and was killed. Having travelled Ireland, Suibhne then went to Britain and met there a lunatic like himself, Alladhán, who had the nickname Fear Caille (Man of the Wood). Alladhán had been cursed into madness by his people after he insisted that they go into battle dressed in satin. The two lunatics stayed together for a year, until Alladhán decided to go and drown himself in a waterfall. Suibhne now returned to his own people. Coming to his house, he would not enter for fear of being captured there. Eorann protested that she was ashamed of his madness, and said that if he would not stay with her, she would prefer that he depart forever. Suibhne left, sadly bemoaning the fickleness of women.

Again he went flighting around Ireland, until he was caught out in a fearfully wet and cold night, and the misery of this caused his reason to return to him. Once more, therefore, he set out for his own territory of the Dál nAraidhe. His adventures were miraculously revealed to Rónán, and that saint prayed that he not be allowed to return to persecute the Church again. As Suibhne passed by Sliabh Fuaid (the Fews, County Armagh) he was beset by horrendous phantoms who roared at him that he was a lunatic and sent him deliriously astray. Finally, when he was in Fiodh Gaibhle (Feegile, County Laois), he became repentant for the bad deeds of his life. He met with St MOLING at Teach Moling (St Mullins, County Carlow), and that holy man took pity on him and told him to return from his wanderings to the monastery each evening. He got supper there, and Moling wrote down his adventures. The saint's cook used to feed his supper to him by making a hole in cow dung with her foot and filling it with milk. The cook's husband grew jealous of her attention to the madman, and he ran him through with a spear. Swooning from the wound, Suibhne confessed his sins to Moling and was given the last rites. Moling led him by the hand to the door of the church, where he expired.

That this Suibhne was not an historical personage is strongly suggested by the fact that he does not appear in the genealogies of Dál nAraidhe, and neither is he mentioned in the earlier accounts of the Battle of Magh Rátha, which was fought in AD 637. Scholars accept that the story of his madness was borrowed from the British tradition of St Kentigern and the wild man called Lailoken. This Lailoken went mad as the result of a horrible vision he saw in the sky during the Battle of Arfderydd in AD 574. The episode is doubled by an account that the wise man Merlin went mad due to grief for the slain at the same battle. Both are described as going to live in the woods, eating wild fruit and roots, and due to their madness they could make prophecies. Furthermore, Lailoken is described as being befriended by St Kentigern before he died. Merlin was known in Welsh as Myrddin Wyllt, the second word being a mutated form of *gwyllt* (meaning 'wild'). This parallels the Irish designation Suibhne *geilt* – the sobriquet here denotes him as a lunatic and may be a borrowing of the British word. The roles played by the saints Rónán and Moling are largely an innovation in the Irish story – the former saint providing a rationalisation of Suibhne's madness, and the latter parallelling and developing the role of Kentigern. The celebrated St Moling was attracted to the context by his reputed ability at jumping and his encounter with phantoms. The text of Buile Shuibhne puts much nature poetry into the mouth of the madman, and this seems to be a reflection of similar verse attributed to Moling. The MOTIF of a contest with a hostile hag was very popular in ordinary Irish folklore, and the curious episode of the mill-hag and her maleficent influence on Suibhne was obviously derived from the oral tradition.

A fourteenth-century text in the FIANNA CYCLE, *Cath Finntrágha*, situates Gleann Bolcáin in west Kerry, apparently identifying it with the wild valley in Kilgobban parish on the Dingle Peninsula. This place is known as *Gleann na nGealt* (the Glen of the Lunatics). It is difficult to say whether the valley already bore that name in the fifteenth century or whether the name became associated with it as a result of the *Cath Finntrágha* text. The latter proposition seems the more likely, for that text was very popular in manuscripts. Texts of the Suibhne story were less numerous, but were known to POETS and scholars, and in this way would have had their influence on the folk consciousness. At any rate, the imagery associated with Suibhne became part of the folklore concerning the west Kerry glen. In the popular lore of the past few centuries, it was said that lunatics from all over Ireland used to retire to that place, drink water from a well there, eat watercress, and race wildly about.

SUIBHNE STORY: O'Keeffe (1913); Carney (1955), 129–53.
CONTESTS WITH HAGS: R. Power in *Scottish Studies, 28*, 69–89.
LAILOKIN AND MERLIN: Clarke (1973).
GLEANN NA nGEALT: G. Mac Eoin in *Béaloideas, 30*, 105–20; Ó Siochradha (1938), 284–5; K. Jackson in *Béaloideas, 8*, 48–9; Ó hÓgáin (1981), 29.

Suibhne Meann High-king of the Uí NÉILL from AD 615 to his death in 628. The name Suibhne was a very popular one in early Ireland – its meaning seems to have been 'pleasantly humoured man'. The sobriquet of this king (earlier, Mend) meant 'dumb' and is likely to have referred to a speech defect.

Suibhne's father was called Fiachna and, though a descendant of the famous fifth-century king NIALL, was not prominent in political life. To explain how a son of this Fiachna could become high-king, a fanciful story is told in one annalistic source. According to it, Fiachna was ploughing one day when the thought struck him that he should rise in the world and contest the kingship. He lay with his wife while his mind was occupied by this thought, and the fire of ambition passed on to the child who was thereby conceived. This was Suibhne, and when he grew up he would not be satisfied until he was high-king. Another set of annals claims that his ambition was fed by his wife, who in conversation one day chided him for not seeking the leadership of the northern Uí NÉILL and leading them in battle. Next morning he armed himself, set out from home, and collected a strong force of warriors by overcoming them one by one in single combat.

Suibhne gained the throne by defeating the incumbent high-king Maol Cobha in the Battle of Sliabh Bealgadáin (near Cong, County Mayo), but was himself slain by the Ulster king Conghal Caoch at the Battle of Tráigh Bréine (on the east shore of Lough Swilly, County Donegal). Narrative tradition, however, claimed that he was murdered by Conghal – while engaged in a game of chess – at the instigation of DOMHNALL MAC AODHA, brother of Maol Cobha.

O'Donovan (1848–51), 1, 246–7 & (1860), 16–19; O'Grady, *1* (1892), 390; Macalister (1956), 374–7; W. Stokes in *Irische Texte, 3*, 410–11, 423; Dinneen, *3* (1908), 116–19; Lehmann (1964), 10–11.

Swift, Jonathan *(1667–1745)* Dean of St Patrick's Cathedral in Dublin from 1713, and one of the greatest writers in the English language. Because of his satires against the English establishment, he became very popular with the ordinary Irish people, although he was of a different religion and also of a different outlook to most of them, and many anecdotes concerning him are told both in the English and Irish languages.

He had several traits of personality that helped to endear him to Irish popular lore, especially his honesty and quick wit, and his hot temper and often crude use of language added drama to his image. The anecdotes are all of a humorous nature, and centre on the relationship between himself and a supposed servant called Jack. The perennial theme is of a clever master being upstaged by his even cleverer servant, and this seems to derive from the actual social circle of the dean himself. Contemporary accounts describe his tendency towards tomfoolery with those in his employment, and he even wrote a humorous tract entitled 'Instructions to Servants'. He became quite a celebrity, particularly among the young intelligentsia of Dublin, and it is clear that the humorous theme owes much of its origin to that context also. The anecdotes told in folklore, although echoing the social surroundings of the dean, are, however, mostly adaptations of common humorous lore and of stories from joke books that circulated widely in the eighteenth and nineteenth centuries. Once the dean became established in tradition as the archetypal clever and somewhat jolly master, any kind of narrative regarding clever servants could get attached to his name, and in order to make matters more definite and memorable, the apocryphal Jack was invented.

One common story describes how the dean first took Jack into his employ. Three applicants answered his advertisement for a servant, and the learned clergyman decided to test their memories. He therefore told them to repeat after him the words 'Lamb of God, who takest away the sins of the world, have mercy on us', and to return to him a year later and repeat the sentence. The year passed, and at the appointed time the first two applicants came to the dean and repeated the sentence. The third fellow,

however, had altered the words to 'sheep of God' and, when the dean queried this, stated that what was a lamb a year ago would be fully grown by now. The dean was amazed at his wit, and gave the position to him. This was the redoubtable Jack. The story itself is an example of a widespread HUMOROUS TALE. A variant tradition has the dean question the applicants regarding their ability to drive a coach. One of them said that he could gallop a coach with six horses through a wood, and another said that he could drive the horses within an inch of a cliff edge. Jack, however, said that he would prefer to drive carefully, and so got the job.

Other accounts also make use of material from popular international folklore plots. For instance, we are told that when Jack applied for the position, Swift put some rudimentary questions to him concerning ordinary work and was amazed at his stupidity. 'Can you do anything at all?' the dean finally asked in desperation, and Jack said that he could not. The dean then asked about Jack's family, and got saucy replies, and finally in exasperation ordered him out, saying that he would only employ him if he could come to work neither dressed nor undressed, neither walking nor riding, neither on the road nor off the road. Jack came next day clad only in a fishing net, seated on a billy goat so that he was half-walking and half-riding, and with one leg on the grass and the other on the road. Swift remarked that he was the smartest fellow he had ever seen, and took him on.

When employed, Jack continues to show his cleverness. In order to teach him a lesson, Swift locks him into the kitchen with no meat and orders him to cook meat for a meal. Jack takes the leather from the Dean's walking boots, cooks this and serves it up as tripe. Swift is very pleased with the meal, but when he looks for his boots later, he realises what has happened. He flies into a rage, and tells Jack that as punishment he will be allowed nothing to eat until he sees 'water running against a hill'. Then the dean goes riding, with Jack running along behind the horse. When they stop to let the horse drink, Jack remarks that this is water running uphill. Another anecdote has Jack being reprimanded for not cleaning his master's boots. He replies that 'It's no use cleaning them, for they will be dirty again tomorrow,' but Swift then denies him breakfast, saying that 'It's no use eating, for you will be hungry again tomorrow!' This has the dean triumphing, and it can be compared to an account printed in the year 1789 according to which Swift made two servants go without breakfast because they had disputed over which of them should clean his boots. We know from contemporary sources that the dean did really have a large pair of boots that attracted some attention when he went riding.

The most popular of all the stories concerning him tells of how one day he instructs Jack to cook a fine goose for him. Jack is hungry and eats a leg of the goose before he serves it at table. When Swift queries this, Jack says that geese have only one leg. Later, when they go riding, they see a flock of wild geese with one leg under their wings, and Jack points this out as proof of his earlier assertion. Swift claps his hands and says 'Whoosh!' with the result that the geese put down both legs and fly away. Jack, however, counters this by asking why he had not said 'whoosh' to the cooked goose. This is a version of an international oral story, but was also found in jest books, and it may have become attached to Swift from either such source. FOWL also figure in an hilarious FOLKTALE that became attached to him. According to this, Swift brought home a tramp to lunch one day, and Jack was displeased because he knew that he himself would get neither of the two chickens that had been cooked. He therefore suggested darkly to the visitor that the dean was accustomed to castrate his guests. The dean liked to carve the chicken himself, and when he suddenly appeared in the doorway with a large knife, the startled tramp took flight. Referring to the chickens, Swift called out that he was going to take only one, to which the fleeing guest retorted: 'No, I want the two of them myself!'

A direct connection can be made between the historical Swift and one story commonly told about him. This deals with the unfaithfulness of women, a story of the 'Ephesian Matron' type, and we know that Swift's young protegée, William Dunkin, wrote a version of such a story in verse for him and that the dean read it 'with some glee'. It was no doubt due to its popularity within his circle that the dean himself was made an actor in the narrative in folk tradition. We are told that one day, as they travelled in a fine coach, Jack and the dean argued about the nature of women. Swift had a very chivalric attitude, claiming that women were angelic creatures and that but for them men would go about like wild beasts. Jack's attitude was somewhat more cynical, claiming that women were flippant and unreliable. As the debate heated up, they noticed a woman in a graveyard, weeping copiously over the grave of her dead husband. Jack, who was well dressed, approached the woman and made a proposal of marriage to her, remarking that his chaplain was with him in the coach. She immediately accepted the proposal, much to the chagrin of the dean who was thus proved wrong in his estimate of the fair sex.

Despite the fact that Swift never married, another adaptation of a folklore plot concerns him and a supposed wife. According to this, when away from home, he asks Jack to find a sleeping partner for him. Jack finds an ugly old woman, and is immediately dismissed from his service by the enraged dean. When they return home, Swift's wife asks Jack how he had displeased his master, and Jack explains it by saying that 'the dean sent me out to find a pullet and I brought an old hen'. The wife then asks Swift how did he expect poor Jack to be an expert on fowl, and he begins to explain, but thinks better of it and takes Jack back into his service. Another adaptation has the dean reprimanding Jack for his rude manners and reversing roles so as to show him how to behave. 'You are a good boy,' says Jack in the dean's role, 'and here is money for you!' Yet another has Jack lazily indicating direction by pointing his foot, and when the dean offers him a sovereign if he can do anything more lazy than that, Jack mutters: 'Put it in my pocket for me!'

Although Dean Swift was a senior clergyman of the Established Church, many Roman Catholics believed that secretly he was more inclined to their views. Thus a humorous story grew up concerning his death and his supposed vacillation between the two religions. It was said that he told the Protestant minister who was attending him on his deathbed that he had a debt to pay to one particular man before he died. The minister kindly offered to bring this man to him so that the matter could be settled, and then Swift named a certain Catholic priest. Rather reluctantly, the minister did as requested of him, but he was outraged to see Swift confessing to the priest and preparing for death in the Catholic manner. 'If you recover you will pay for this!' shouted the minister, to which Swift cunningly replied: 'Well, then, you will be dismissed from your ministry, for it was you who brought the priest to me!'

Sheridan (1784); Kennedy (n.d.), 32–6; M.L. Jarrell in *Journal of American Folklore*, 77, 99–117; Ó hÓgáin (1985), 86–99, 330–1.

BORROWED FOLKTALE PLOTS: Aarne & Thompson (1961), types 785A, 875, 921, 1510, 1623, 1741, 1832E, 1832N, 1950. *See also* these type numbers in S. Ó Súilleabháin & Christiansen (1967).

Tadhg mac Céin Fictional Munster nobleman, whose father Cian (meaning 'the enduring') was mythical ancestor of the Ciannachta sept of the ÉRAINN. This Cian was fancifully claimed to have been son of AILILL ÓLOM, the mythical Munster king.

The medieval literature represents Tadhg as the lord of Éile (in north Tipperary), and as an ally of CORMAC MAC AIRT in the Battle of Crionna (near Mellifont on the River Boyne), Cormac had promised him as much land of that area as his chariot would encircle after the battle until sunset, but then tried to trick him out of his due. The wounded Tadhg was for a while helpless in the care of Cormac's leeches, who plotted to bring about his death. He managed to get word to his own doctors in Munster, and they

came and cured him. When he returned home, Tadhg threatened war on Cormac, who thereupon consented to pay the agreed fee for his support at Crionna. The land comprised a substantial part of eastern Breagha (in County Meath), and the story was invented in order to rationalise the presence of the Ciannachta sept there. As well as in that area, the Ciannachta had branches in north Tipperary and in County Derry in the far north.

A sept to the south of the Ciannachta was known as Gaileanga, and early tradition claimed them also to be descendants of Tadhg. Already in the eighth century, a story was in existence that rationalised this. We read that a son of Tadhg, called Cormac, was making a feast for his father, and had the meat of many kinds of animals prepared for it. He had no badger meat, however, and so went to a set and called the badgers out to him. When he guaranteed their safety under the protection of his father Tadhg, they came to him and he killed a large number of them for the feast. When Tadhg saw this meat, his heart shuddered and he angrily rebuked his son, calling him Gaileang (derived here from *gae lang* – i.e. 'fouling of honour') and banishing him from his household. This strange story is apparently based on the survival of an ancient Celtic word *tazgos* (meaning 'badger') in the form 'tadg', thus giving rise to the personal name. This would mean that badgers were namesakes of Tadhg mac Céin and that it was taboo for him to eat them on that account.

The inference from the story of Tadhg and a badger-taboo is that a special corpus of heroic lore had developed concerning him. The only surviving long story, however, dates from the fourteenth century or thereabouts. It is typical of the fanciful romances of that period, but makes special use of earlier traditions of journeys to the otherworld. According to it, Tadhg was visiting the west of Munster when he and his company were set upon by raiders from a foreign country called Fresen (probably Friesland). The raiders took away several of Tadhg's people, including his wife Lí Ban and his two brothers, and Tadhg himself barely managed to escape from them. In Fresen, Lí Ban was kept by Camthann to be his wife, while Tadhg's brothers, Eoghan and Airnealach, were put to menial tasks and given the worst of food. Only 40 of Tadhg's men remained free, but they slew an equal number of the foe and captured one of them alive. This prisoner told them about the land of Fresen, and they constructed a large boat in order to travel there. On their journey, they visited an island where there were huge sheep, and a pair of other islands with beautiful birds. When they ate the eggs of these birds, feathers sprouted on them, but the feathers fell off as soon as they bathed. Setting sail again, they came to a frightfully stormy sea, but Tadhg urged his men to stand firm, and they survived this ordeal, coming eventually to a wondrous land where they met a beautiful and wise lady. She told them that she was CEASAIR, the first woman ever to reach Ireland, and she related that in this land lived all the people who had formerly dwelt in Ireland. It was in fact the otherworld paradise, with luscious foliage, delightful climate, and dwellings of gold and marble (for which otherworld, see MANANNÁN). Among those whom they encountered there were CONN CÉADCHATHACH and his son Connla. They also met the lady CLÍONA, who gave them three musical birds and a goblet that had been found in the heart of a whale.

They spent a whole year in that land, thinking it but a day, and then set sail again. Reaching Fresen, Tadhg met his brother Eoghan, who was working as a ferryman. Eoghan told him that he and Airnealach had been conspiring with two nephews of Camthann to overthrow that TYRANT. He also related that Lí Ban had gained respite from Camthann until then, but that she now had perforce to marry the tyrant and the wedding was being prepared. Tadhg combined his forces with those of Camthann's nephews and decided to attack the feast, but the Fresener prisoner escaped and went to inform Camthann of their plans. Reaching the castle, he first met Airnealach there and, not recognising him, told his news.

Airnealach beheaded him and went to welcome the attackers. In a frightful melée, Tadhg's men slaughtered the king's soldiers, and Tadhg himself engaged Camthann in his bed-chamber and beheaded him. He was then reunited with his wife. Installing the elder of Camthann's nephews, Eochaidh Armdhearg, as king, Tadhg set sail triumphantly for Ireland.

O'Grady, 1 (1892), 319–26 & 2, 491–3; O'Brien (1962), 403–5; K. Meyer in ZCP, 10, 42; A. Mac an Bhaird in Ériu, 31, 150–5; W. Stokes in Irische Texte, 3, 384–5 & (1862), xlii–xlv.
ROMANCE TEXT: O'Grady, 1 (1892), 342–59.

Tara (in Irish, Teamhair) The centre of the HIGH-KINGSHIP in Irish tradition, it is situated a few miles northwest of Dunshaughlin, County Meath. The anglicised form 'Tara' is based on the genitive Teamhrach. The word itself (earlier written Temuir, from a Celtic Temoria) meant 'spectacle'. A fine view of the centre of Ireland is available from this vantage point, and it was of importance long before it was given such an appropriate Celtic designation.

Archaeology has shown that Tara was an important burial site from the second millennium BC, and it continued so after the Celtic culture became general throughout the area. In the usual manner of such sites, it became the centre of a cult of sacred kingship. This is evidenced by the ancient tradition concerning a mythical king of the ÉRAINN people at Tara. That king was called CONAIRE, and the early medieval lore represents his reign as propitious and hedged about by many magical conditions. Such memories of ritual can hardly be taken to contain historical information, but the account of Conaire's death seems to reflect something of the seizing of control of Tara by the LAIGHIN (Leinstermen) in or around the third century AD.

It was in all likelihood the Leinster kings who developed the idea of a special goddess of sovereignty called MEADHBH presiding over the site. A special 'feast of Tara' was celebrated by each king at the high point of his reign. This was anciently known as Feis Temro, the word feis having the basic meaning of sleeping with the GODDESS, and the celebration was thus closely connected with the cult of kingship. All of this was highly prestigious to the Leinstermen, and the importance in which they held Tara as the most strategic point of the luscious Boyne Valley is reflected in their lore concerning FIONN MAC CUMHAILL. It would appear that the Festival of Tara tended to be celebrated at Samhain (November), a TIME devoted to the revered dead; and a medieval recension of a very ancient mythic complex has the citadel at Tara being delivered by Fionn mac Cumhaill from a phantom who came every Samhain to burn it.

The CONNACHTA sept took Tara from the Leinstermen in the fourth century AD, and their great leader NIALL soon made it the focus of their control over the whole Boyne Valley. The descendants of Niall (the Uí NÉILL) claimed to be high-kings of all Ireland, and they put the cult of the sacral kingship of Tara to their own advantage. The principal tenet of their propaganda was based on one great figure who came to be regarded as the archetype of Irish kingship. This was CORMAC MAC AIRT, the basic elements of whose myth seem to have been taken over by the Uí Néill from the lore of their Leinster predecessors at the site. By the early Middle Ages, they had developed the myth of Cormac to such a degree that the cultural landscape of Tara was explained by reference to it. Thus a striking neolithic tumulus on the site was reinterpreted as a mound on which Cormac kept his hostages, and the huge surrounding enclosure known as Ráth na Ríogh (the rampart of the kings) was said to have been constructed by him. At the centre of the *ráth* were two earthwork structures that were fancifully claimed to have been Cormac's house and his royal assembly seat. To the north is a long, sunken rectangular area, which was interpreted as having been the site of Cormac's great banquet hall called the Teach Miodhchuarta, and near this was an enclosure which was said to have belonged to his daughter Gráinne (for whom, *see* DIARMAID UA DUIBHNE). Among the other remains at Tara associated with the reign of the Uí Néill kings

are a mound where Niall's son LAOGHAIRE was buried, and a circle of banks and fosses reputed to have been the site of synods held by ADHAMHNÁN and other SAINTS.

The accumulated heritage of Tara made it the scene par excellence of adventure. Central to this were the rites of inauguration of kings. Such ancient rituals, and rhetorics associated with them, welcomed the new king to the place as a protector and guardian. This imagery survived in narratives of a great champion coming to Tara as a stranger – such as in the LEGENDS concerning CONAIRE, LUGH, CORMAC and later of St PATRICK. Added to this was a wide variety of lore and fiction concerning the actual courts of kings at the site, making it central to much of the high drama of early Irish literature, and presenting it as a symbol of Irish identity and pride to generations of poets and scholars.

By these writers, however, the hill of Tara was regarded as a site of ancient rather than of contemporary glory. The Uí Néill dynasty continued to refer to themselves as 'kings of Tara', and the 'feast of Tara' was apparently still celebrated by their kings down to the ninth century, but the prestige of the place in medieval culture was rather abstract. The actual site was overgrown and reclaimed by nature, and was the subject of speculation by antiquarians. Thus the fiction grew up that Tara had been abandoned due to a curse placed on it by the sixth-century saint RUADHÁN, and the ultimate alienation from the ancient cult was reached when an eleventh-century scholar invented a new interpretation of its name. According to this, a lady called Tea was the wife of the pseudo-historical Gaelic leader ÉIREAMHÓIN, and had come from Spain with him. She had seen in Spain a rampart around the grave of a lady of that country called Teiphe. On reaching Tara, Tea begged her husband to bestow the hill on her and, when he complied, built a wall (*mur*) around it in imitation of Teiphe's rampart. When she died, she was buried within that enclosure; hence – the writer fancifully argues – the place name Teamhair.

Another object of great curiosity at Tara is the upright granite stone called the Lia

Fáil, which now stands on the mound known as Cormac's House but which formerly stood near the Mound of the Hostages. This was the stone that symbolised kingship, and it screamed out under the foot or chariot wheel of the true king. Its cultic role was quite ancient, and in their appreciation of this, the medieval pseudo-historians claimed that it had been one of the marvellous objects brought to Ireland by the TUATHA DÉ DANANN. It has remained the object of lively speculation down through the centuries. The seventeenth-century historian Seathrún CÉITINN believed that it had been sent to Scotland by MUIRCHEARTACH MAC EARCA and had been used for the inauguration of Scottish kings at Scone until taken by the English king Edward I to serve as the coronation stone at Westminster. It is practically certain, however, that the stone at Scone was a different one, and that the ancient Lia Fáil is the landmark still pointed out at Tara.

No other place in Ireland is so venerable and occupies so basic a role in the culture of the country. At the height of the Nine Years War, in 1598, Aodh Ó Néill, Earl of Dungannon and chieftain of his sept, made a push against the Elizabethan forces and caused such alarm that an English agent reported to Dublin that he had come to the hill of Tara 'where the old doating prophecy was that if O'Neill could come and shoe his horse, he should be king of all Ireland'. This was a reference to the age-old Uí Néill prophecy that one of their leaders, called AODH EANGACH, would re-establish the old Gaelic order throughout the land.

Something of a messianic sense is found also in Tara tradition about the RISING OF 1798 and the battle fought on 26 May of that year on the hill, in which hundreds of rebels were slain. Among them was a young girl from County Dublin called Molly Weston, who played a daring part in the battle. According to a folklore account: 'She was a handsome young girl, arrayed in green who, mounted on a white horse, rode hither and thither upon the field with drawn sword in hand, rallying the pikemen and leading them in successive charges with the utmost fearlessness. Unexpectedly and providentially this young girl – from out the void as it were – appeared in the role of leader. Who she was, and whence she came, the Meath insurgents knew not. On several occasions, when the heavy fire of the enemy's artillery pitifully gapped the insurgent's ranks, she rallied and re-formed the stricken pikemen and, placing herself at their head, led repeated charges against the blazing guns.' Despite her best efforts, the day was lost, and her dead body was later discovered on the battlefield.

All of this tradition lay behind the significant step taken by Daniel O'CONNELL when he held a huge meeting on the hill of Tara in 1843 for repeal of the Act of Union and the restoration of an Irish parliament. The location was intended to have maximum symbolical effect, underlining Ireland's integrity and nationality, and it was estimated that over a half-million people attended that meeting.

GENERAL: Ó Ríordáin (1960); E. Hogan (1910), 629–30; J. Baudis in *Ériu*, 7, 101–7; D.A. Binchy in *Ériu*, 18, 113–38; F.J. Byrne (1973); 48–69; Macalister (1931); Comyn (1902), 100–1, 206–9; M. O'Daly in *Celtica*, 5, 186–91.

Ó NÉILL, WESTON, O'CONNELL: Ó hÓgáin (1985), 136, 199–201; Uí Ógáin (1995), 40, 258.

Tighearnmhas Fictional KING of Ireland situated in prehistory. His name meant 'lordly', and in modern form would be Tiarnmhas. He is described as a descendant of ÉIREAMHÓIN, and is said to have slain Conmhaol, son of ÉIBHEAR, and to have won thrice-nine battles in one year.

It is further stated that during his reign, the first gold mine in Ireland was discovered in the territory of the Fotharta of the eastern Liffey (i.e. near Naas, County Kildare). Tighearnmhas employed a wright called Iuchadán to make a brooch for him from the gold. Also attributed to Tighearnmhas were the making of the first goblets and silver vessels, and the first use of the colours purple, blue and green on garments. He ordained that colours of garments be worn according to social status – one colour for bondsmen, two for peasants, three for paid warriors, four for lords, five for chieftains, six for learned men, and seven for royalty.

Tighearnmhas was said to have originated the worship of the idol Crom Cruach (see CROM) at Mágh Sléacht (the plain at Tullyhaw, County Cavan). He went to that place at Samhain (November) accompanied by the men of Ireland, but was overtaken by some unspecified disaster and died there along with three-fourths of his followers. He is clearly the invention of the medieval writers, and though his reign is ascribed to the pagan era, his sudden death was meant to signify the wrath of God against the sin of idolatry.
Macalister (1956), 199–209, 432–7; Gwynn (1913), 266–9 & (1924), 19–23; Dinneen, 2 (1908), 120–3.

time The basic Celtic division of the year was into two parts, for which parts the term *samonio*s (meaning 'half') was used. The winter half was considered the beginning of the year, and the summer half the second part. Thus the division in Ireland was held to be 'from Samhain to Bealtaine, and from Bealtaine to Samhain' – Samhain here meaning the beginning of November and Bealtaine meaning the beginning of May. There were two further sub-divisions, beginning at Oímelg (1 February) and Lughnasa (1 August), so that the year was in effect divided into the standard four seasons.

At each of these four junctures, a festival was celebrated that involved an impressive amount of custom and lore. The festivals properly began at sunset on the day before the actual date, evincing the Celtic tendency to regard the night as preceding the day. This was in accord with the dark half of the year preceding the bright half, and the whole complex of thought seems to have been a very ancient one, by which the living community showed the primacy of the dead ancestors (as represented by darkness) over the living community (represented by light).

Computation of time in this way meant that, for instance, Oíche Shamhna (literally, 'the night of November') actually began on the evening of the last day of October, and similarly with Oíche

Bhealtaine. The festival of Oímelg is better known to history as the feast of St BRIGHID, and the eve of the festival is known as St Brighid's Night. There is no particular stress on the eve of Lughnasa, for the celebration of that is not tied to the actual first day of August. Having been strongly Christianised (see LUGH *and* PATRICK), this festival of the harvest has since medieval times been celebrated on the Sunday nearest to that date.

Samhain was the festival that attracted most interest in Irish literature. Being the beginning of the dark season, it was especially associated with the dead and the otherworld. Many of the supernatural adventures of heroes in the early literature are said to have taken place at this time (see DONN *and* FIONN). The dead ancestors were of great importance in Irish custom and belief, and the literature claims that this was the date on which the Festival of Tara was celebrated. Folklore places great emphasis on Oíche Shamhna (Halloween) as a time when GHOSTS are abroad and FAIRIES are moving from their summer to their winter quarters. Due to the Church festivals of All Saints and All Souls on the first two days of November, much of the solemnity has gone from the attitude towards Halloween itself. There is, however, a clear remnant of native belief in the tradition – which survived until recently – of leaving the fire lighting and going to bed early on All Souls' Night, so that the family kitchen or parlour would be left to the dead ancestors who would congregate there on that night.

The term Oímelg occurs only in the early literature, and its original meaning was 'lactation'. It later was understood to be *imbolg*, meaning 'large bellied' or 'parturition'. Tradition shows clearly that this feast of Brighid was concerned with the birth of young animals, and that it was originally under the tutelage of the goddess BRIGHID. Until recently, it was customary to invoke the protection of her namesake St BRIGHID on farm animals at this time. The St Brighid's crosses were hung in the cow byre, and the hope for general agricultural prosperity was expressed by leaving a piece of cloth outdoors overnight to gather dew. The cloth was called 'Brighid's mantle', and the saint was believed to touch it as she passed by. A general manner of communal celebration was associated with this as with several other festivals – the young people going from house to house in disguise, singing and playing music. On this particular feast, they were usually led by a young girl representing the saint, and the boys were humorously accoutred as women.

The word for May, Bealtaine (earlier, Beltine), originally meant 'bright fire', but it was also known in medieval Ireland as Céad Shamhain (first half). This secondary term must be very old, for it is common also in Welsh and Scottish Gaelic. We must suppose that its 'initial' position referred to it being the culmination of the dark, or 'first', half of the year. Socially, the May festival was very important as it announced the coming of good weather and of the sowing season, and also was the time when the prospective milk yield became clear. The medieval literature claims that it was on this festival that the Gaelic people had first come to Ireland (see Míl). The celebration of the May festival was, of course, common throughout Europe, but it had certain distinctive traits in Ireland. In former centuries, for instance, a great fire was lit by the various communities at this time, recalling the Irish name of the festival itself and no doubt deriving anciently from a desire to encourage the sun. Symbolising the desired prosperity, some greenery was brought into the house, and there are accounts from the eighteenth century that describe how young people dressed up in greenery and celebrated the coming of summer by open-air dancing. The May bush – usually a whitethorn – was cut and brought home, decorated with garlands and eggshells, and set up near the dwelling house.

This being the beginning of summer, it was considered to foreshadow all of that season. Agriculture can be in many ways an unreliable affair, and so people were extremely careful to protect their prosperity. It was believed that some malicious neighbours might attempt to magically steal away one's good fortune, and this gave rise to several traditions and stories. For instance, a loan of salt should never be given to a neighbour who asked for it on May Eve, nor should a piece of the household fire be allowed to be brought outside of the house. Especially important was the dew in one's fields and the water in one's well, for it was believed that certain greedy individuals were keen to take a portion of these overnight, with the same magical effect. Two well-known international LEGENDS, appropriate to the context, were particularly associated with May Eve in Irish folklore. One of these tells of how a woman, regardless of how hard she worked at the churning, could not make butter, but eventually was advised to put a piece of red-hot iron into the churn-dash. A neighbouring woman, who had put the harmful charm on the buttermilk, came screaming to the house, contorted with pain as if pierced by hot iron, and could only get relief by herself taking a hand at the churning and thereby undoing the charm. The other legend tells of how an old lady took the form of a hare and drank the milk from the neighbour's cows until discovered (see WILD ANIMALS).

Lughnasa (earlier, Lughnasadh) was the feast of LUGH, and its celebration marked the ripening of corn and the weaning of calves and lambs. In early Ireland, several great fairs coincided with this festival, but since the Middle Ages its celebration on a Sunday meant that it was religious and recreational in character. Its original designation does not survive in popular tradition, that being now the common word in Irish (Lúnasa) for the month of August. The festival is rather known as the Sunday of CROM DUBH, or in varying areas as Lammas Sunday, Garland Sunday, Bilberry Sunday, or Fraughan Sunday. Hill-top climbing for both prayers and for gathering bilberries was general throughout the country, as were assemblies at lakes and holy wells, and other favourite pastimes were horse racing, horse swimming and hurling. The earlier commercial aspect of the festival was not completely lost, however, as fairs or markets were held on a day near to the Sunday at many places – most notably Ballycastle in County Antrim, Muff in County Cavan, Ennistymon in County Clare and Killorglin in County Kerry.

The Christian festivals were very popular, though they never developed the same wealth of lore as the four great seasonal feasts. Christmas and Easter were, of course, the most important, and popular traditions associated with them were of the type general in Europe. Christmas, being dedicated to the birth of JESUS CHRIST, was a time of special mystery and deep human and religious feeling. Everybody became more devout, more charitable and more good-humoured, and presents were exchanged according to people's means. Special emphasis was on the children – for instance, the youngest child in the household would light the Christmas candle. This was placed in the window to light the way for any poor travellers who, like Mary and Joseph long ago, might be seeking their way through the world in the darkness. The children were told that at the hour of midnight the CATTLE and DONKEYS received the power of speech for a while in remembrance of how the cow and donkey kept the infant Jesus warm, but it was unlucky to be near these animals at that time and so their speech was never heard. During the twelve days of Christmas, it was said, the doors of heaven were open, and anybody who died in that period passed over directly to eternal happiness.

Regarding Easter Sunday, it was said that, as it rose in the morning, the sun danced in joy at the Resurrection of Jesus. Many people therefore woke early and climbed onto a hill top to watch the sun, or went to a well to see its reflection quiver in the water. This belief was common in most parts of Europe since the Middle Ages, as was the custom of painting, rolling and eating eggs. This latter probably arose, not from any ritual, but from the simple reality that the eating of eggs was forbidden during Lent and a great number of them would therefore have been stored up by Easter. Folk beliefs

relative to the other important days in the Christian calendar were generally derived from biblical imagery; for instance, the Slaughter of the Innocents being commemorated on 28 December led to that day being regarded as a sinister one. It was known as *lá crosta na bliana* (the forbidden day of the year), and no new enterprise was undertaken on it. Similarly, no carpentry or other work involving the driving of nails was carried out on Good Friday, because of Christ's Crucifixion on that day. On the other hand, the Epiphany – known as Little Christmas or Women's Christmas – was regarded as second only to Christmas Day itself in happiness and beauty. This stress on the Epiphany – in European terms generally – was in fact a relic of the celebration of the birth of Christ on this date in the early centuries of Christianity in the Middle East. An old saying in Irish claimed that 'on the Night of the Three Kings wine is made of the water, silk of the rushes, and gold of the gravel'. This was not, however, observed by humans, and any toper who slyly went to drink water at midnight from the well was in danger of being turned into stone.

A European tradition that survived with particular vigour in Ireland was the lighting of bonfires at Midsummer, the festival of St John. On 11 November – the Feast of St MARTIN – the oncome of winter was greeted with a special family meal, calling on that saint to protect the household against want in the lean season. Also very popular was the collecting of money and presents on St Stephen's Day by groups of disguised singers and dancers, a custom that has apparently been moving gradually northwards in Europe since medieval times, but which has not yet reached Scotland or most of Ulster. In Ireland, the custom is associated with hunting the wren (*see* BIRDS).

For some reason, Whit Sunday is generally regarded as an unlucky day on which to be born, a belief that was especially strong in Leinster. If a child were born on this day, it was said that he was destined to be a killer, and in order to prevent this, a worm was placed in the baby's hand, which was then closed tightly so that the destined killing was over and done. The question of destiny, of good luck and bad, has for the past two centuries been associated above all with New Year's Day, known in Irish as Lá Coille (Kalend-Day). The Church has observed 1 January as the beginning of its year since the sixteenth century, and it has been the legal beginning since the reform of the calendar in 1751. Since then, popular lore has taken that day as a kind of premonition of the coming year in terms of business, weather and general welfare, and its eve is celebrated with a great family feast. This was called Oíche na Coda Móire (the Night of the Large Portion), for to eat well on this night was regarded as a way of preventing scarcity and hunger during all of the ensuing year.

The seven-day week unit was introduced into Ireland by Christianity, and the names of all the weekdays in Irish derive from Latin or Church culture. Luan, Máirt and Satharn come from Luna, Mars and Saturn; whereas Domhnach (Sunday) comes from Dominus, Céadaoin (Wednesday) means 'first fast', Déardaoin (Thursday) means 'day between two fasts', and Aoine (Friday) means simply 'fast'. Because of its association with the Crucifixion, Friday was generally observed as a day of special prayer by the devout, and it was regarded as an unlucky day to embark on an undertaking, especially marriage. A direct echo from the Gospels is the expectation that if a storm began on a Friday, it would subside on the following Sunday. Because of its initial position in the week, Monday was also considered a risky day to begin a new enterprise. Thus if a deal had to be made, payment was held over until the following day, or if a grave had to be dug, the first sod was turned on the Sunday beforehand. People did, however, feel that Monday was a good day on which to give alms to the poor. Tuesday and Thursday were regarded as the most propitious days for business affairs.

Danaher (1972); S. Ó Súilleabháin (1942), 316–64 & (1967), 61–75; M. MacNeill (1962); Ó Catháin (1980), 17–26, 118–24; Ó hÓgáin (1995), 78–86 & (1999), 54–7, 126–7.

Tomás Mór (Big Thomas)

Fanciful ancestor of the churls of Ireland in a satiric prose text written in the early seventeenth century. The text is entitled *Pairlement Chloinne Tomáis* (the Parliament of Clan Thomas), and its author was from south Kerry or west Cork.

Tomás is described as the son of one Liobar 'the Rotten', of demonic descent. He was, we read, a contemporary of St PATRICK, and was ugly and surly. When that SAINT banished the demons from the summit of Croaghpatrick, he allowed Tomás to remain, since his mother was of the human race. Patrick, however, ordained that his descendants should be ignorant and crude, of lowly status and with a taste for the roughest food and manners. Tomás had no fewer than 24 sons, who spread throughout Ireland and had numerous progeny, to whom silly and rugged names are applied. Eventually, one of the sept, called Murchadh Ó Multuaiscirt, became very rich, and he convened an assembly of all the important men of the Clan Thomas in his dwelling at Clonmacnoise, County Offaly. He told the assembly that he required their support in his courtship of the daughter of a Connacht chieftain, Maghnus Ó Madagáin, and they all set out for Connacht. Maghnus' counsellors advised him not to allow his blood to be sullied with that of Clan Thomas, but his avaricious wife insisted on such a wealthy alliance, and so the maiden was married off to Murchadh. The wedding feast was held on Crom Dubh Sunday (*see* TIME), and at it a disgraceful brawl broke out, with various members of the Clan Thomas abusing each other and hacking at each other. Eventually, Murchadh succeeded in quieting them, and he then made a great speech, advising the whole clan to get education for their children, to dress like the aristocracy, and to gain power in the country.

They accordingly rose in the world, and by the time of Queen ELIZABETH I had amassed vast wealth. It so happened that a great warrior of the clan, Cairbre Crom Ó Céirín, lived on the plain of Cashel, County Tipperary, and he had a daughter called Seiligeán. There was a huge crop of wheat on that plain, and in order to have it harvested, he sent out a proclamation that the best reaper of Clan Thomas could have the hand of Seiligeán. Hundreds of aspirants assembled from all over Ireland and set to work. However, contention arose and the proceedings deteriorated into a brutal riot, leaving many dead and wounded by sickles, billhooks and flails, and the beautiful plain of Cashel turned into a quagmire. Eventually, Cairbre awarded his daughter to one Yellow Cathal Ó Breisleáin, who lived at Dún Eochair Máighe (Bruree, County Limerick).

With the thinning out of the Irish nobles due to the Elizabethan wars, the Clan Thomas began to take possession of much territory and even to marry into the upper class. In the time of King James I, they had become so precocious that they decided to convene a great parliament of their own at Cros Uí Fhloinn (Crusline, a few miles northeast of Tralee, County Kerry) under the chairmanship of a crude fellow named Seán Séideánach Ó Smutacháin (literally, 'Snorting John O'Flatnosed'). There they discussed their social position and their grievances, and rejoiced at the new county juries, which blamed the crimes of Clan Thomas on the nobles. Soon two horsemen approached, one of whom was the noble poet Muiris, son of Dáibhí Dubh Mac Gearailt, who had written a detailed account of the clan. Two of the boors asked Muiris to settle a dispute between them. A sow belonging to one of them, Bearnard Ó Broic, had been attacked by a dog belonging to the other, called Tomás 'of the Trumpet'. The wife of the latter had seized the dog, and Bearnard aimed a blow of an axe at it but missed his target, killing his own pig and breaking his wife's shin bone. They were thus suing each other for damages. Muiris could not decide between them, and he departed, whereupon the two litigants laid hands on each other, and this led to a general melée.

Clan Thomas reconvened at the same place thirteen years later. This time they had arranged rules of procedure, but their conversation and general behaviour was as vile as ever. Crude personal remarks soon led once more to a vicious brawl, and many of the clan were maimed and worse, so that the parliamentary deliberations had to be interrupted to bury the dead. The statutes they enacted related principally to agricultural and dietary matters, but they also decided to take noble surnames for themselves. An Englishman approached, selling tobacco, and the leaders of Clan Thomas bargained with him for its purchase. They spoke execrable English, but were held in high estimation by their followers for their efforts. Then they all began to smoke the tobacco, but Tomás accused Bearnard of farting and recited a hideous quatrain on this. Bearnard left in high dudgeon, cursing the parliament and all its proceedings.

The author of this satire has not been identified. He was clearly a learned man with some knowledge of foreign literature, and the savagery of his attack on the churls is derived from some such source. The theme of parliaments held by rustics and rogues was fashionable in the anti-peasant satires of late medieval Europe, but the immediate texts that suggested such material to this author were a sixteenth-century translation into English of Sebastian Brant's German work *Narrenschiff*, and an early seventeenth-century English work by Samuel Rowlands entitled *Martin Mark-All*. In writing *Pairlement Chloinne Tomáis*, the author seems to have intended not so much to ridicule the peasantry as to lampoon some trends that were developing in the socio-political life of his time. This is the drift of a poem by Muiris, son of Dáibhí Dubh Mac Gearailt (Black David Fitzgerald), to which he refers laudingly and which was probably his immediate inspiration. The boorish characters described in the *Pairlement* could well have been caricatures of individuals of his own time known to the author. There are several indications that the leading target of the satire was the anglicising Black Thomas Butler (1532–1614), Earl of Ormond.

An addendum to the text was written around the year 1660. This describes how one of the Clan Thomas, Dónall Ó Plubarnáin, was knighted and became a magistrate, owing this to his great protector,

Oliver CROMWELL. Dónall decided to convene a parliament near Mullingar, County Westmeath, and scions of the clan assembled there from all over Ireland. They discussed a curse that had been put on them long ago by the Pope because one of their number had slain a friar with his coulter. Through all their bickering and rowing, they managed to agree to send a delegate to Rome in order to have this curse set aside, but he succeeded in having it removed from three millers only. On hearing this, the parliament of Sir Dónall enacted that all millers should be boycotted by the Clan Thomas. They then dispersed, bickering still and admitting that their misfortune arose from their treachery towards the nobility who would willingly help them in dire straits.

The boisterous humour of *Pairlement Chloinne Tomáis*, based largely on verbal profusion, overrides its illogical social assumptions, and the literati of succeeding centuries looked to it as a rich source of humorous and abusive phraseology in more general contexts. For instance, several works of social and personal satire composed within the following half-century made use of the setting and nomenclature from it. Accusations of rural boorishness, derived from the text, became a favourite stylistic device. Most notable of such works were two late-seventeenth-century satires on the pretensions and intricacies of ecclesiastical life, entitled *Comhairle Mhic Clamha* and *Comhairle Comissarius na Cléire*.

FIRST AND SECOND TEXTS: N.J. Williams (1981).

FITZGERALD POEM: N.J. Williams (1979), 48–57.

DERIVED WORKS: N.J. Williams in *Éigse, 15,* 126–30; A. Harrison in *Éigse, 15,* 189–202; M. Ní Ghráda in *Lia Fáil, 1,* 49–78; Dinneen & O'Donoghue (1911), 287–98.

SATIRES ON ECCLESIASTICS: Ó Dufaigh & Rainey (1981); Ó Dufaigh in *Studia Hibernica, 10,* 70–83.

treasure There is a general belief that several treasure troves lie hidden beneath the soil of Ireland, and rumours persist that some rich people came by their wealth in this way. There is a feeling that such treasure is in some way eerie, however, and it is often said that to find a trove brings comfort for a while but that misfortune eventually overtakes the finder.

The idea that hidden treasure was guarded by spirits is probably quite old in Ireland (*see* MAOL DÚIN), but it is expressed in folklore through imagery associated with later beliefs. For instance, men who go at night to dig up treasure may be put to flight by the sudden appearance of spirits such as a fierce cat, a savage bull, a massive dog, or a huge bird. There was also a belief – though not a very common one – that a human spirit could be a guardian of a hoard, such a spirit being that of a man killed and buried there long ago specifically for that purpose. Though this coincides with some archaeological discoveries, the actual folk belief may be of more recent origin (*see, for example,* GOIBHNIU).

Perhaps due to the occasional discovery of ancient troves concealed in the earth, popular belief tended to associate hidden treasure with supposed or real ancient dwellers in the country – such as the TUATHA DÉ DANANN (*see* CONN CÉADCHATHACH *and* CRIOMHTHANN NIA NÁIR) and the NORSEMEN. One interesting story describes how an Irishman in a foreign country (often Scandinavia) is given mouse soup to drink, after which he gets insight into a treasure trove hidden in a mound or a lake in Ireland. Thinking that if he eats the mouse's meat he will know where all the troves of Ireland lie concealed, he greedily does so, but as a result loses the vision. Alternately, it is said that it was once revealed to a man that a treasure trove was hidden at the bottom of a lake and that it could only be dragged from there by a team of all-black horses. The man got such horses and a strong rope, but failed to remove the trove because one horse had a single strand of hair of different colour.

A common LEGEND tells of an OUTLAW being executed offering to tell where his trove is hidden to anybody from his own locality, but no such person is present; while another legend has a poor scholar using his SPECIAL POWERS of learning to discover hidden treasure for a generous householder. There is mention of hidden treasure troves also in the entries on CANO MAC GARTNÁIN, DAMER, HUMOROUS TALES, type 1645, LEPRECHAUN, Ó DONNCHÚ, RUADHÁN, SAINTS and WONDER TALES, type 326.

S. Ó Súilleabháin (1942), 507–11.

Tuán mac Cairill

Tuán mac Cairill A holy man of east Ulster in or about the sixth century. His name meant 'the silent one', and his father seems to have been Caireall Mac Muireadhaigh, king of the ULAIDH at that time. Tuán resided at a place called Tamhlacht Bhairche in the Mourne Mountains.

Tamhlacht meant 'burial-ground', but the word was also used for a PLAGUE. Recalling the notion that the fictional PARTHALÁN and his followers had died from a plague, a writer in the ninth century fancied that Tuán might have been a survivor of that plague, having silently observed the ages since the time of Parthalán. On this basis a whole new fiction was created. We read that Tuán was a rich warrior who resided in the vicinity of St Finnian of Magh Bhile (Moville, near Newtownards, County Down). He refused hospitality to the SAINT at their first encounter, but Finnian fasted against him and was then admitted to his house. When Finnian enquired who he was, Tuán disclosed that he had lived for a long time and that he had undergone many transformations. He was born son of Caireall, after Caireall's wife had eaten him when he was in the form of a salmon. Before that he had been in turn a stag, a boar and an eagle for long periods. Originally he had been son of Starn, brother of Parthalán. Growing old in his various shapes, and being renewed in others, Tuán had witnessed all the great events that had occurred between the coming of Parthalán and the coming of Christianity, and was also an expert on genealogy. Tuán relayed all this knowledge to Finnian, thereby preserving it for posterity. It is clear that this narrative was written under the influence of the story of the antediluvian FIONNTAN.

J. Carey in *Ériu*, 35, 93–111; Macalister (1933), 272–3; Arbois de Jubainville (1903), 25–35.

Tuatha Dé Danann

Tuatha Dé Danann The principal otherworld race in Irish literary myth. Their designation was taken by medieval scholars to mean 'the People of the Goddess Danu'. DANU was considered the mother-GODDESS per se, the special patroness of human welfare, and it was natural to consider her performing this function for the gods also.

The divinities were often referred to in shorter form as Tuatha Dé. This designation is very old. Although its import in Irish is 'divine communities', its original meaning seems to have been more specific. The Continental Celts referred to the deities by the same word, Toutates, and a god in the singular could accordingly be referred to as Toutatis, meaning 'he of the community'. Thus the Toutates were the patrons of specific human communities who were their devotees. Being the 'representatives of communities', there was a natural shift in the meaning of their designation to the 'divine communities'.

The Celtic culture, in its westward expansion, was apparently reaching Ireland as early as the fifth century BC. There must have been small but powerful settlements of Celtic speakers in the country, and such influxes continued until the early centuries AD. The new groups brought with them their own mythical and religious ideas, but upon reaching Ireland encountered many archaeological remains of much earlier settlements. Particularly noticeable were the passage-graves and tumuli of north Leinster and east Ulster, constructed by a specially advanced people in the fourth and third millennia BC; but there were also cairns, dolmens, megaliths and, indeed, pliable artefacts surviving throughout the country, having been left behind also by ancient inhabitants. The newcomers would have been quite impressed by such remains and, engaging with the indigenous peoples in the inevitable social relationships, learned something of their import.

Impressed by the notable non-natural aspects of the landscape, and getting information from locals and using their own imagination, the newcomers associated the structures with mystical otherworld beings.

The pantheon of such beings known to them were their own deities, and in this way archaeological remains came to be associated with the characters and activities of Celtic mythology. Specific deities or Toutates were connected with noteworthy archaeological sites, and were imagined to inhabit them still as spiritual beings, while the myth patterns of Celtic lore were adapted to a geographical plane based on the occurrence of such sites in the landscape. Thus arose the Irish complex of imagery and story associated with the Tuatha Dé Danann. Although Danu herself and the father-god DAGHDHA were of ancient Indo-European vintage, it is clear that the general pantheon known to early Irish tradition was assorted from various sources, delineating various ideas.

The myth that gave a unified basis to the lore of the Tuatha Dé was that of a great battle (*see* MYTHOLOGICAL CYCLE). This myth, of Indo-European derivation, told of a primordial conflict between a divine race and a destructive one – which in Irish came to be identified respectively with the Tuatha Dé and the FOMHÓIRE. It is likely that the myth was first introduced from Celtic Britain in the third or second century BC (*see* NUADHU), and, once situated on Irish soil, its plot allowed for various elements of the Celtic otherworld to be synchronised and for a logical Irish theogony to be constructed. The great battle became confused with a separate myth concerning LUGH, and the battle itself eventually became located at Moytirra, County Sligo. Some other surviving elements of ancient Celtic lore were not fitted into the context of this primordial conflict, but were relayed as separate fragments of narrative under the general umbrella of the Tuatha Dé theme (*see* MYTHOLOGICAL CYCLE in the List of Genres, page 509).

When the early medieval writers set themselves the task of constructing a pseudo-history of Ireland, they enthusiastically put the mythological material to use. These writers being Christians – and probably monks – this part of their work had particular appeal for them, for the 'historicising' of the Tuatha Dé removed the remnants of pre-Christian religious belief from their general ambit. The culmination of the process was the long description of the Tuatha Dé given in the *Lebor Gabála* (Book of Invasions), which was assembled and expanded from the eighth century to the twelfth. This book purported to tell the ancient history of Ireland, and its account became the standard source for later references to the Tuatha Dé. The gods and goddesses having been mythic patrons of arts and skills, the *Lebor Gabála* was following good precedence when it portrayed the Tuatha Dé as having among them many magical craftsmen. The division of the race into nobles and peasants, however, was probably not so much a mythic theme as a reflection of medieval Gaelic society. The *Lebor Gabála* suggests that only the nobles had these magical abilities, and elaborates by stating that 'gods were their men of art, non-gods their husbandmen'.

In speculative fashion typical of medieval writers, the Tuatha Dé are described as having been descendants of NEIMHEADH and as having sojourned in the northern parts of the world learning wizardry. The character who led them into Ireland, and their first KING in the country, is stated to have been Nuadhu, and he gained control of the whole country when the Tuatha Dé defeated the FIR BOLG at the so-called 'first' Battle of Moytirra. Due to the loss of his arm in that battle, however, he was replaced for seven years by BREAS, whose father was of the Fomhóire. When an arm made of silver was put on him, Nuadhu was restored to the kingship, but he was slain at the 'second' Battle of Moytirra. He had given the command of his army to the newcomer Lugh in that battle, and now Lugh became king and reigned for 40 years. After his death, the Daghdha became king and reigned for 80 years. Then a certain Dealbhaeth (or Dealbh-aodh) reigned for ten years, and he was in turn succeeded by his son Fiacha. Finally, three grandsons of the Daghdha – called Mac Cuill, Mac Céacht and Mac Gréine – divided Ireland between them and married the three eponymous goddesses of the country called BANBA, FÓDLA and ÉIRE. They ruled for 29 years until the coming of the sons of MÍL, who took the kingship for the Gaelic people.

The trio of Mac Cuill, Mac Céacht, and Mac Gréine reflect the tendency in early Irish myth to triplicate deities. This finds most striking expression in 'the three gods of Danu', called Trí Dé Danann, which designation parallels the name of the supernatural race itself. Indeed, the Tuatha Dé are called *fir Trí nDéa* (men of the Three Gods) in the earliest surviving text of the Moytirra battle, where we are told that Lugh went to the three gods of Danu to provide him with weapons. It is apparent, however, that the original form of the phrase was the otherwise attested Trí Dé Dána (Three Gods of Art). The *Lebor Gabála* states that the three were Brian, Iuchair and Iucharba – sons of the goddess Danu – but three of the Tuatha Dé champions who played a leading part in the Moytirra battle were GOIBHNIU the blacksmith, Luchta the wright, and Créidhne the silversmith. These made weapons for Lugh and, though not expressly identified as such, it may be that they were the original 'three gods of art' who were alternately known as the three sons of Danu. Other leading characters of the Tuatha Dé mentioned in the *Lebor Gabála* were the physician DIAN CÉACHT, the warrior OGHMA, the poetess BRIGHID, and the satirist CRIDHINBHÉAL.

An atmosphere of magic and mystery surrounds the Tuatha Dé in the *Lebor Gabála*. We read that they first came to Ireland in obscure clouds, landing on a mountain in the west of the country, and that they caused an eclipse of the sun that lasted for three days. They brought with them the Lia Fáil (Stone of Destiny), which cried out at Tara when touched by the rightful king, the great spear of Lugh, which guaranteed victory to its wielder, the sword of Nuadhu, from which no opponent escaped, and the cauldron of the Daghdha, from which no company departed unsatisfied.

After their defeat by the Gaelic people led by the sons of Míl, the *Lebor Gabála* gives no further details, but a twelfth-century writer tells that an agreement was reached whereby the Tuatha Dé left the upper half of the ground to the Gaelic people and they themselves went underground to live in the ancient barrows and cairns that dot the landscape. Thus medieval Irish Christianity explained the age-old belief that associated the deities with the prehistoric monuments, while at the same time demoting these deities to the level of the Fomhóire by claiming that their habitat was in the nether regions. Regarding the barrows and cairns, it was claimed that the Daghdha assigned to each of their chiefs one such dwelling – thus illustrating the old idea, found throughout Irish literature, that the mystical Tuatha Dé live on side by side with the human inhabitants of Ireland. Another twelfth-century writer – notwithstanding a strong antipathy to the subject that caused him to call the Tuatha Dé 'devils' – puts the tradition in a nutshell when he states that they 'used to fight with men in bodily form, and used to show delights and mysteries to them, and people believed that they were immortal'. One early source states that, as part of the war between them, the Tuatha Dé destroyed the corn and milk of the sons of Míl, but the Daghdha made restitution once the peace agreement was arranged.

The late medieval literature makes the Daghdha's son, BODHBH DEARG, king of the Tuatha Dé, and gives to the sea-deity MANANNÁN the function of dividing the ten principal otherworld dwellings among their chiefs. It is Manannán, too, who institutes the *féth fiadha* (cloak of concealment), an obscure magical device that enabled the Tuatha Dé, when they so wished, to become invisible to the human world. He also arranged that they would have magical swine, which returned to life after being killed so that the warriors could again hunt them. The variety of locations for the otherworld which is usual in human thought is evidenced by the tradition that, notwithstanding their dwelling in cairns and barrows, the Tuatha Dé are portrayed also as living in idyllic overseas realms such as Magh Meall (the Delightful Plain) or Eamhain Abhlach (the Region of Apples), which is cognate with Avalon, the version of the Celtic otherworld which surfaced later in Arthurian romance.

The later writers often confused the Tuatha Dé with the Fomhóire, and in post-medieval literature the Tuatha Dé are represented as having both salutary and demonic groups among them. They were thus suitable as powerful beings to be introduced into a variety of literary narratives. As well as being a vestige of the idea of a divine race, however, the Tuatha Dé were also a versionz of the ancient and far-flung notion of quasi-human communities living beside the human one. As such they are of the same stock as the FAIRIES of ordinary folklore, and it is clear that Irish fairy lore owes much to them in its general themes.

ARCHAEOLOGY: Herity & Eogan (1978).

MOYTIRRA: see references following MYTHOLOGICAL CYCLE.

LEBOR GABÁLA: Macalister (1941), 106–37 & (1956), 14–39; A.G. Van Hamel in ZCP, 10, 164–7, 190–3; Ó Muraíle, 1 (2003), 248–57.

THREE GODS: Meyer (1912), 83; Gray (1982), 44–5, 50–3; T.F. O'Rahilly (1946), 308–17.

UNDERGROUND: W.J. Watson (1941), 1; L. Duncan in Ériu, 11, 188.

'DEVILS': Dillon (1953), 29; Ó Raithbheartaigh (1932), 197–201.

PEACE AGREEMENT: V. Hull in ZCP, 19, 55–7.

OTHERWORLD: Dillon & Chadwick (1973), 182–92. See also MANANNÁN.

Tuathal Teachtmhar

A KING reputed to have reigned in the early centuries AD. The name Tuathal is not a mythic one, being the Irish version of the Celtic Teuto-valos, meaning 'tribe-ruler'. The sobriquet (earlier, Techtmar) has been variously explained, but the most likely meaning was 'wealth-appropriator'. Judging by the names, therefore, it seems quite possible that Tuathal Teachtmhar was an historical person who established the power of the CONNACHTA in the north Midlands in the second or third century, but the lore concerning him is definitely the result of propaganda invented later by these Connachta. He is represented in the genealogies as grandfather of CONN CÉADCHATHACH.

The earliest surviving account of him is of this fictional nature. It occurs in a poem from the ninth century, according to which the descendants of UGHAINE were oppressed by the subject-peoples (aitheach-thuatha) of Ireland. A leader of these subject-peoples, Éilim mac Conrach, slew the king of Ughaine's line, who was called Fiachu, and usurped the kingship. A FAMINE was visited on the country, for there was no harvest or fruit or fish. Then Fiachu's son, Tuathal, came to claim his heritage. He was joined by the brothers Fiachra Casán and Findmhall with 600 men. Together they marched on TARA, and slew Éilim in the Battle of Achall (at Skreen, County Meath). Tuathal went on to win a large number of battles against the subject-peoples of all the provinces, and he then held an assembly of all the chieftains of the country at Tara and made them swear loyalty to his descendants.

These events are again referred to in a text that belongs to the tenth or eleventh century. Here the assembly of chieftains he held is called the Festival of Tara – i.e. the ritual gathering that began a king's reign. He is also described as originator of a controversial and long-lasting tax on the LAIGHIN, on account of a dishonourable act done on his daughters by their king, Eochaidh mac Eachach (see BÓRAIMHE). Another medieval account of Tuathal tells that after the death of his father Fiachu, the subject-peoples put to death all the descendants of Ughaine, except for the young Tuathal himself. His mother brought the youngster to Fiachra Casán, who commanded 150 mercenaries in the service of the usurper Éilim. Fiachra took Tuathal into his corps, and one day the youngster went to the fort of Tara and sought admission. The usurper ordered that this be refused, but Tuathal announced that his father and grandfather had ruled at Tara. Éilim allowed him to enter then but, fearing the usurper's intentions, Fiachra spirited him out of the country. Later, when Tuathal returned to Ireland with a fleet, Fiachra took his corps to meet him at Rinn Ruamann (probably Wexford Harbour), and together they fought and defeated Éilim at the Battle of Achall.

Further detail still is given in other texts. These state that Tuathal's mother was called Eithne Imgheal, and that she was daughter of the king of Scotland. After her husband Fiachu was killed in his own house at Tara, we are told, she fled to her native country, where she gave birth to Tuathal. When he was twenty years old, he returned to Ireland with his mother and landed at Inbhear Domhnann (Malahide, County Dublin). There they were joined by the *díbheargaigh* (marauding outlaws) of the country, under their leader Fiachra Casán, who made him king. A seventeenth-century source retells the story, with some variation. After Fiachu's death, misfortune filled the country, and eventually the subject-peoples themselves sent messengers to Tuathal in Scotland. He was then 25 years of age, and when he returned with his mother and landed at Iorras Domhnann (Erris, County Mayo), he was joined by the remnants of the nobility (*saorchlanna*) who had been resisting and plundering the subject-peoples who ruled. These plunderers were led by Fiachra Casán and his brother (here called Fionnbhall), and they assisted Tuathal in defeating Éilim at Achall.

The idea that Tuathal ruled over all the provinces of Ireland is, of course, a fiction, for there was no HIGH-KING of the country in his time. The purpose of the fiction was to give a moral claim from immemorial tradition to the Connachta overlordship, and the ancient division of Ireland into five parts was made to fit into the scheme. The fifth province was Midhe (meaning 'the middle'), and it was claimed that Tuathal had formed this province by taking pieces from each of the other four. This was explained by a false etymology for Midhe – namely *mede* (neck) – and Tuathal was said to have 'cut off the neck of each province'. He was further said to have built four great fortresses, one in the territory expropriated from each province. These were Tlachtga (near Athboy, County Meath), taken – in contradiction of all history and geography – from Munster; Uisneach (Ushnagh, County Westmeath), taken from the western province, here anachronistically called Connacht; Tailtiu (Teltown, County Meath), taken from

Ulster; and Tara, taken from Leinster. Having ruled for 30 years, Tuathal was slain at Móin an Chatha (near Larne, County Antrim), through an unspecified act of treachery by the Ulster king Mál mac Rochraidhe.

Tuathal Teachtmhar belongs solely to the literature of genealogy and pseudo-history, and no traditions of him are found in folklore.

O'Brien (1962), 130, 747; T.F. O'Rahilly (1946), 154–70; S. de Búrca in *Studia Celtica*, 1, 135; C.-J. Guyonvarc'h in *Ogam*, 19, 231–3; Macalister (1956), 308–31, 484–5; W. Stokes in *RC*, 13, 36–43 & in *Irische Texte*, 3, 332–3; Binchy (1978), 877; Best, Bergin & O'Brien (1954), 250–1; Gwynn (1906), 46–9 & (1913), 473 & (1935), 179; Dinneen, 2 (1908), 238–59.

Turgesius *(properly Thorgestr or Thorgils; in Irish, Tuirgéis)* Leader of the NORSEMEN who raided Ireland in the mid-ninth century. He was defeated and slain in AD 845 by Maoilsheachlainn (earlier, Mael Sechnaill), the KING of Meath who in the following year became HIGH-KING of Ireland.

A detailed, and quite imaginative, account of him is given in the Annals and historical tracts. We read that he came from Norway, and that he assumed the leadership of all the Norsemen of Ireland. He captured Armagh, the principal ecclesiastical centre, usurped the authority of the abbot there, and made himself the most powerful man in the north of the country. Gathering a great fleet on Lough Ree (on the River Shannon), he attacked and plundered the major monasteries of the Midlands – including Clonmacnoise, where his wife Ota used to sit on the high-altar as if it were her throne, and give pagan oracles.

Seeing one day the daughter of Maoilsheachlainn, Turgesius lusted after her and demanded her of her father. Maoilsheachlainn agreed to send the girl to him, at an island on Loch Uair (Lough Owel, County Westmeath), accompanied by fifteen other maidens. At the appointed time, however, he sent with her fifteen beardless young men disguised in women's clothing and secretly carrying daggers. The ageing Turgesius promised a woman to each of his fifteen Viking commanders, and he himself waited in his chamber for the daughter of Maoilsheachlainn. The fifteen young men wasted no time in slaughtering their hosts, and then they went and captured Turgesius. Maoilsheachlainn took him and drowned him in the lake. The drowning itself was an historical fact, but the story of the young men disguised as women is derived from Herodotus or some other classical source. An elaboration of the story has Maoilsheachlainn, sometime before, seeking advice from Turgesius concerning what should be done with some troublesome cormorants that had recently come to Ireland. Turgesius had recommended that their nests should be destroyed. Accordingly, after the drowning of the tyrant, Maoilsheachlainn put the advice to good purpose by telling the Irish to attack every Viking fortress in Ireland, and in this way the power of the raiders was broken.

The earliest version of this story concerning Turgesius dates from the eleventh century, but it proved very attractive to later historians whether Norman, English or Irish. In the seventeenth century Seathrún CÉITINN gives a much dramatised version, having the girl and fifteen disguised youths being sent to Turgesius' headquarters in Dublin. They seize Turgesius there, and at the same time Maoilsheachlainn attacks with a strong force. All the Vikings are slain, except for Turgesius, who is brought as a prisoner to Maoilsheachlainn's palace and from there to Loch Ainninn (Lough Ennell), rather than Lough Owel, where he is drowned. On hearing the news, the Norsemen are seized with dread throughout Ireland, race to their ships, and depart the country. The situating of the action in Dublin is the result of references in the Annals to how Maoilsheachlainn defeated the Dublin Vikings and plundered their settlement in 849 – four years after the death of Turgesius.

The folklore of Westmeath claims that the tyrant had a fortress at Ballania, near Castlepollard, as well as a house on an island in Lough Lene nearby. To this house, by his command, was brought every new bride in Ireland so that Turgesius might have the opportunity of spending the first night with her. Folk accounts do not specify how he was seized by Maoilsheachlainn, but they are clear that he was shown no mercy. They describe him being bound in chains and then thrown into Lough Owel, while some storytellers elaborate further by stating that he was put into a barrel and rolled down a hillside into the water.

GENERAL: Todd (1867), xlii–lv, 12–15, 224–7; O'Meara (1982), 120–1; O'Donovan, 1 (1848–51), 466–70; Dinneen, 3 (1908), 172–83; Holinshed (1586), 55–6; Hanmer (1633), 83–5; Campion (1633), 49–51; O'Halloran, 2 (1778), 158–75; O'Kelly (1844), 207–11; OSL: Westmeath (1837), 69–76, 87–97.

MOTIF OF DISGUISED YOUNG MEN: see O'Meara (1982), 136.

tyrants There are several archetypal tyrants portrayed in medieval Irish literature, most notably the mythical BALAR and the historical TURGESIUS. Some native Irish chieftains are also portrayed as tyrants, especially in contexts in which they clash with saints (see COLM CILLE, GREGORY THE GREAT, PATRICK and RAGHALLACH). Some well-known later historical figures are given special emphasis as tyrants in folklore – most notably CROMWELL, but also figures who played ambiguous roles in history, such as Maolmhuire MAC SUIBHNE and Baothlach MAC FHLANNCHAIDH, as well as a number of powerful ladies, such as Countess Margaret BUTLER, ELIZABETH I and Máire Rua Ní MHATHÚNA. Various tyrant figures appear, of course, as opponents of popular heroes (see OUTLAWS, RISING OF 1798 and Ó MAOILRIAIN).

In later Irish tradition, the twin aspects of English oppression – often embodied in the same person – were the landlord and the magistrate. These had a huge raft of legislation on their side, which could be used to peremptorily snuff out any dissent. There were some people in authority who were of sympathetic disposition, but these found their good intentions swept aside by the power of those whose method of rule was tyranny. Discontent among the vast majority of the population was continually simmering and breaking out periodically in outlawry, agrarian violence and insurgency; accordingly, folk LEGENDS from the eighteenth and early nineteenth century abound in accounts of tyrannical landlords and magistrates. In these legends, the images of cruel tyrants as described in ecclesiastical sources are often applied to such figures. For instance, a landlord-magistrate condemns the innocent to death without any qualms and, in turn, he himself dies a horrible death from a rotting disease, like the Herods of biblical history. The tyrant rack-rents and evicts his starving tenants, but ends his own days in a fit of madness, which has him – as said of the persecuting Emperor Diocletian – eating grass in the fields like a wild animal. A common MOTIF is an attempt by a tyrant to impose the *ius primae noctis* on tenants – i.e. the right to sleep with every young woman on the estate on her bridal night. There are several accounts of a curse being put on a tyrant by a widow whose family has suffered from his actions – such a curse may bring disaster or disfigurement not just to the tyrant himself but also to his descendants. Some tyrants are even reputed to have grown a tail on account of their evil deeds.

During the Penal Laws of the seventeenth and eighteenth centuries, Catholic priests had a price put on their heads by the authorities and were often man-hunted by bigoted magistrates or by paid priest-hunters. Stories tell of how certain priests escaped such dire straits by using SPECIAL POWERS, such as miraculously disappearing out of sight of their pursuers (*see, for example*, CÉITINN). It was also claimed that, if arrested, a priest might place a curse on his tormentors that would later be fulfilled. The priest-hunters were the objects of particular opprobrium, and it was said that grass would never grow on the grave of such a person. Just as in the early literary accounts of saints overcoming tyrants, a popular theme is that of a priest using his miraculous power to confound such individuals. The priest may even call up the lost GHOST of a tyrant in order to warn living oppressors of the consequences of their actions.

A satiric tale – told commonly in Europe against social tyrants – concerns a bailiff in Ireland (*see* HUMOROUS TALES, type 1186). For tyrant kings as characters in entertainment stories, *see* ROMANTIC TALES, types 851–2, 922, 953.

TYRANT LORE: S. Ó Súilleabháin (1948), 529–32; Ó hÓgáin (1985), 211–14; S. Mac Philib in *Béaloideas*, 56, 97–140.

Ughaine *(earlier, Augaine, Ugoine)* Mythic ancestor of many Irish septs. His cult seems to have originally belonged to the CONNACHTA. The name is from Celtic Ovogenios (literally, 'sheep-conceived'), a type of ram-god appropriate to a people whose chief economic concern was animal husbandry. His name is usually accompanied by the epithet Mór (great).

Much of the detail concerning Ughaine in the genealogies and medieval literature is at variance with received tradition. The writers claimed that he had been a foster-child of a certain queen called Macha. This Macha was killed by Reachtaidh Ríghdhearg, who usurped the kingship of Ireland, but Ughaine slew him in turn and ruled at TARA for either 30 or 40 years. During that time, he is reputed to have extended his dominion to cover Scotland and the Isle of Wight, and it was even claimed that he took the kingship of all Europe. A story that was known in the tenth century, but which has since been lost, was entitled 'The Hosting of Ughaine Mór to Italy', and it is clear that he was given a very fanciful reputation as a conqueror. This was apparently a projection onto him of lore associated with the historical king NAITHÍ. We are told, quite anachronistically, that Ughaine married the daughter of the king of the Franks. She, called Ceasair, bore 25 children to him, and Ughaine divided Ireland between these in equal parts. Only two of his sons, however, had progeny. These two were Laoghaire Lorc (grandfather of LABHRAIDH and thus ancestor of the LAIGHIN) and COBHTHACH CAOL (claimed by the genealogists to be ancestor of both the ÉRAINN and the CONNACHTA). Contrived connections were in this way being made here by the genealogists, who were trying to give a single ancestry to all the groups in early Ireland. It is, however, of interest to note the echo of Ughaine's ancient connection with SHEEP, for the pseudo-historians claimed that CEASAIR was the name of the lady who first brought these animals to Ireland.

Even more fanciful is the account of why Ughaine divided the country. We read that his 25 children, when grown up, used to go on repeated circuits of Ireland, expecting to be lavishly fed and entertained everywhere. The nobles complained of this to Ughaine, with the result that each was given a separate area, without permission to seek provisions outside of it. During the following 300 years, it was claimed, these 25 units continued to be used for taxation and other administrative purposes.

It was said that Ughaine fell at the hands of his own brother Bodhbhcha at Teallach an Choscair (near Gormanstown, County Meath). The fratricide, however, reigned for only a day and a half before being himself slain by whom the writers call Ughaine's son, Laoghaire Lorc.

O. Bergin in *Ériu*, 12, 224–5; J. Pokorny in *Celtica*, 3, 306–8; O'Brien (1962), 1, 3, 10, 16–17, 129, 137, 159, 358; T.F. O'Rahilly (1946), 154–63; Macalister (1956), 267–75, 467; Dinneen, 2 (1908), 156–9; Mac Cana (1980), 48, 59.

Uí Mhaine A strong sept in the west of Ireland, deriving its name from a legendary ancestor Maine 'the Great'. This sept seems to have been in origin a mixture of ÉRAINN and LAIGHIN.

Their original territory lay on both sides of the River Shannon, stretching east and west from Lough Ree; and the personage Maine was probably derived from the culture of the Laighin, as his name seems to be that of MANANNÁN in abbreviated form. In the sixth century AD, the CONNACHTA seized the area east of Lough Ree, and made wide gains of territory to the west of the Shannon, bordering on the Uí Mhaine to the north. Realising the danger, and still holding the broad region between the Shannon and the Suck and as far as Galway Bay, the Uí Mhaine determined to bolster their position politically by inventing an impressive genealogical history for themselves.

They noted that a broadly similar situation prevailed in south Ulster, where a conglomeration of Érainn peoples called AIRGHIALLA had stabilised their position by claiming to be lateral relatives of the celebrated fifth-century Connachta king NIALL. Accordingly, they claimed that their eponymous ancestor Maine 'the Great' had belonged to the Airghialla. Due to a great increase in population there, they said, Maine had decided to migrate with his warriors and their dependents to a new region. With their flocks and herds, they moved southwestwards, crossed the Shannon, and demanded territory between Lough Ree and the River Suck from the aboriginal inhabitants. The latter were led by a king called Cian, who assembled a great host to oppose them.

As a preliminary to negotiations, Maine gave hostages – including his own son Amhalgaidh – to Cian. Amhalgaidh was a handsome fellow, and the wife of Cian's administrator fell in love with him, whereupon the aggrieved husband prevailed on Cian to secretly kill the hostages. Cian then invited Maine and his chiefs to a conference, intending to kill them by treachery. Maine, however, learned of the plan, and he gathered his forces and defeated Cian in battle. A further rationalisation of this fiction was that an old SAINT of the area, Greallán, perceived the treachery of Cian, and by his miraculous power brought about the victory of Maine. By thus giving his support to the sept, St Greallán became the patron of the Uí Mhaine.

From medieval times, the leading branches of the Uí Mhaine took on the surnames Ó Ceallaigh (Kelly of Galway); Ó Neachtain (Naughton); Ó Maolalaigh (Mullally, Lally); Ó Madáin (Madden). Other surnames which became prevalent among the sept included Ó Laighin (Lyne, Lyons); Mac Aogáin (Egan, Keegan); Ó Lachtnáin (Loughnane); Ó Lorcáin (Larkin of Connacht); Ó Fuaráin (Foran); Ó Dónalláin (Donnellan); Ó Conbhuí (Conway); Ó Duibhginn (Deegan); Mac Uallacháin (Coolahan); Ó Conraí (Conroy); Ó Bréanainn (Brennan of Connacht); Ó Fathaigh (Fahy of Connacht); Ó Cinaeith (Kenny of Connacht); Mac Eochaidh (Keogh of Connacht).

SOURCES: O'Donovan (1843); O'Brien (1962), 172–3; F.J. Byrne (1973), 92–3, 341.

Uí Néill The designation – literally 'Grandsons of Niall' – adopted by the descendants of NIALL, the famous king of TARA, and CONNACHTA leader in the fifth century AD.

Niall had several sons, most of whom inherited his ability and ambition. Three of them – Cairbre, Maine and Fiacha – extended the rule of Tara into areas from the Shannon to Offaly and Kildare, while Conall Créamhthainne worked closer to his father, just north of Tara. Three more sons – Eoghan, CONALL GULBAN and Éanna – carved out kingdoms for themselves in central and western Ulster. LAOGHAIRE, apparently the eldest son, succeeded to the Tara kingship and was thus nominally head of the whole sept. These Uí Néill came to be naturally divided into their northern section, descended from Eoghan, Conall Gulban and Éanna; and their southern section, descended from the other sons of Niall. The northern and southern Uí Néill claimed the HIGH-KINGSHIP of Ireland, which they alternated between themselves for several centuries. In effect, they were overlords of much of the country.

In the early tenth century the high-king was NIALL GLÚNDUBH of the northern section. His grandsons picked up on the old tribal designation Uí Néill as referring in particular to themselves, and thus adopted it as a surname – in the singular form Ua Néill or Ó Néill. Surnames taken since medieval times by descendants of the northern Uí Néill include the following: From Eoghan – Ó Néill (O'Neill, descendants of Niall Glúndubh); Mac Lochlainn (McLoughlin of Ulster); Ó hÁgáin (O'Hagan); Ó Goirmfhleadhaigh, modern Ó Goirmlí (Gormley of Ulster); Ó Catháin (Kane); Ó Donghaile (Donnelly); Ó Ceallaigh (Kelly of Derry); Mac Cathmhaoil (Campbell of Tyrone); Ó Sléibhín (Slevin).

From Conall Gulban – Ó Dónaill (O'Donnell); Ó Dochartaigh (Doherty); Ó Gallchobhair, modern Ó Gallchóir (Gallagher); Mac Eiteagáin (McGettigan). Surnames taken in medieval times by descendants of the southern Uí Néill include the following:

From Laoghaire – Ó Caoindealbháin (Kindellan, Connellan, Quinlevan, Quinlan).
From Conall Créamhthainne – Ó Maoilsheachlainn (Melaghlin, McLoughlin of Westmeath); Ó Ceallaigh (Kelly of Meath); Mac Fhógartaigh (Gogarty) (*see also* AODH SLÁINE *and* DIARMAID MAC AODHA SLÁINE).
From Maine – Mac Amhalghadha, modern Mac Amhlaigh (McAuley); Mac Aogáin (Egan, Keegan); Ó Rónáin (Ronan); Mac Con Midhe (Conway, McNamee); Ó Duibhgheannáin (Duignan); Ó Maolchonaire (Conroy of Laois); Ó Siail (Shields); Ó Muirí (Murray); Ó Coinn (Quinn of Longford).
From Fiacha – Ó Maolmhuaidh (Molloy); Mac Eochagáin (Geoghegan).

GENERAL: O'Brien (1962), 159–67, 173–80, 425, 435, 438; F.J. Byrne (1973), 70–105; Ó Muraíle, *1* (2003), 286–429 & *3*, 422–60.

Ulaidh The Ulaidh (literally, 'bearded men') were an ÉRAINN people inhabiting the centre of the province of Ulster, which province took its name from them. They were also known as Dáirine (worshippers of the father-deity under the name DÁIRE). In time they came to call themselves Rudhraighe (which probably meant 'rightful occupiers'), and hence the literary sources often refer to them as Clann Rudhraighe. Dundrum Bay, County Down got its ancient name, Loch Rudhraighe, from them.

The Ulaidh had a great ritual site, which was of importance from antiquity. It had been inhabited since the neolithic era, and in the seventh century BC, a palisaded enclosure was erected on the top of the hill, with wooden huts inside it. At the beginning of the first century BC a whole new and larger enclosure was raised, within which were four concentric rings of oak posts and a circle of timber uprights towards the centre. In this circle again was a large timber post sunk into a hole. It is thought that the whole inner structure may have been roofed. The function of this complex was undoubtedly ceremonial, and the largest timber post might have been intended as a sort of 'world-tree' at the sacred centre of the territory with a ceremonial function of linking the earth with the skies. As such it would have been a symbol of the prosperity of the tribe or sept that inhabited the area, and important ceremonies would have centred on it. Soon after, the inner structure was filled with limestone blocks and its walling burned, and finally it was sealed by covering it over with sods. Although it has been suggested that this destruction was a ceremonial act carried out by the devotees themselves, the destruction may rather have been a hostile act, and if so may have marked the overthrow of a people at the site by a powerful new group. This latter group may have been the Ulaidh.

The first reference to the site in writing – predating Irish literature by a long time – was by the Graeco-Egyptian geographer Ptolemy in the second century AD, who spelt it as 'Isamnion'. This might be taken to represent a meaning 'swift tides' or the like, a compound that gave rise to the place name Eamhain in other parts of Ireland. Much more likely from the location of the site, however, is that Ptolemy's form should have been *Isomnion*, with a meaning such as 'beneath the posts'. The development of this Celtic compound within archaic Irish would have been: *isomnis > ihomniah > eumania*. The latter form is in fact attested in early Irish literature as the designation of the place, written in Old Irish *emain* and in Modern Irish *Eamhain*. In the literature, it is called Eamhain Mhacha (the hill fort of Navan, a few miles west of Armagh city).

The importance of this ancient site is reflected by the high prestige that continued to attach to it. In view of its strategic location overlooking the central plain of the northern province, the Ulaidh held it as their royal seat. They inaugurated their kings there, adapting to the site the appropriate rhetorics that represented the reigning monarch as a substitute for the sun-deity (*see* CONCHOBHAR MAC NEASA *and* FEARGHUS MAC RÓICH). Equine imagery was strong in such rituals, and this was stressed in the cult of their land-GODDESS (*see* MACHA). Towards the middle of the

fifth century AD, this kingdom of the Ulaidh was overthrown by the ambitious and powerful CONNACHTA who were pushing northwards from the Boyne Valley. Henceforth the Ulaidh were confined to the east of the province (the area of modern County Down), where their descendants became known as Dál bhFiatach. These Dál bhFiatach preserved memories of their glorious past, which memories were in time imaginatively developed into a corpus of heroic tales in medieval literature known as the ULSTER CYCLE.

The medieval Irish writers, who made a fine art of fanciful derivation, claimed that the tribal designation Rudhraighe originated in a character of that name, who they said had been an early king of Ireland. Aware that the Ulaidh were a different people from the Connachta septs, who had become predominant, these writers made the fictional king Rudhraighe a descendant of Ír (long-lasting), who was a third and rather inconsequential son of MÍL. In order to give support through detail to the existence of Rudhraighe, some writers described him as dying from a PLAGUE, while others had him slain by a phantom. Though some accounts tried to represent many generations of his descendants ruling Ireland (*see, for example*, BREASAL BÓ-DHÍOBHADH *and* OLLAMH FÓDLA), the medieval historians generally had to concede that the ambit of the Ulaidh was confined to the northern part of the country. This general area came to be known according to the designation of this people as Ulaidh, and that province as their 'fifth' – namely, *Cúige Uladh*. In English this is rendered Ulster, which province contains nine modern counties (Down, Monaghan, Cavan, Armagh, Antrim, Derry, Tyrone, Fermanagh and Donegal). A duplicated ending is used in Modern Irish to indicate an Ulster person, *Ultach* (plural *Ultaigh*).

Surnames adopted in medieval times by the leading Dál bhFiatach families are: Mac Doinnshléibhe (Donlevy, Leavy, Livingstone); Mac Eochadha (McCaughey, Haughey, Hoey); Ó Mathúna (Mahon); Ó hEachaidhin (Haughian).

ARCHAEOLOGY OF EAMHAIN: B. Raftery (1994), 74–80; J.P. Mallory in Waddell & Shee Twohig (1995), 73–86.
NAME EAMHAIN: T.F. O'Rahilly (1946), 12–13; A. Mac an Bhaird in *Ainm*, 5, 11; Pokorny, 1 (1959), 177; RIA Dictionary, s.v. 'omna'; W.M. Hennessy, 1 (1887), 66–7.
ULAIDH: T.F. O'Rahilly (1946), 175–81, 341–52; F.J. Byrne (1973), 106–110; O'Brien (1962), 269–86, 325, 407–13; K. Meyer in *ZCP, 8*, 324–37; Ó Muraíle, 2 (2003), 308–50, 356–418, 506–541 & 3, 504–21, 578–633, 636–45.
FICTIONAL KING RUDHRAIGHE: Macalister (1956), 290–7, 490–1; O'Brien (1962), 269–86, 406–13.

Ulster Cycle A large corpus of heroic tales in medieval Irish literature, based on the ULAIDH, the ancient people from whom the province of Ulster got its name and who once controlled the centre of that province (modern County Armagh and adjacent parts). A favourite name used by the Ulaidh for themselves was Rudhraighe, and from it the Ulster Cycle is called in Irish *Rudhraigheacht* (modern, *Rúraíocht*). In the fifth century AD the Ulaidh, called Dál bhFiatach, were pushed eastwards into modern County Down by the ascendant CONNACHTA. The Dál bhFiatach had valued memories – probably in cryptic and rhetorical form – of their rituals centring on Eamhain Mhacha (Navan Fort in County Armagh), and of their courageous but futile stand against the Connachta. These various elements of their tradition were recast into a saga that reflected their great pride in their past. In its development through the succeeding centuries, this saga imaginatively developed ritual names into dramatic characters, invented some new characters, and made use of much extraneous material.

The saga described FEARGHUS as a former KING of the Ulaidh who went over to the Connachta, led by the GODDESS-type figure MEADHBH. A great war ensued between the Ulaidh under CONCHOBHAR and the Connachta forces under Meadhbh, and this war involved not only fierce fighting but also great CATTLE-raiding. The latter aspect of the conflict was stressed so much that the saga came to be known as *Táin Bó Cuailnge* (The Cattle Raid of Cooley). This may have recalled a practice by the Ulstermen of, in times of danger,

hiding their cattle away from foes in the peninsula of Cuailnge (Cooley in north County Louth), a mountainous area difficult of access. The Dál bhFiatach and other septs of eastern Ulster were noted for their generosity towards visiting poets and storytellers (see MONGÁN), and one can speculate that it was such learned reciters who strung together the various elements of lore into the basic saga, as a tribute to their hosts.

It may well be, indeed, that – as literary tradition has it – the Munster poet SEANCHÁN Toirpéist played a significant role in developing the saga in the early seventh century AD. His contemporary and fellow Munsterman, Luccreth moccu Chiara, has left an obscure poem that gives some insights into what the early form was. Luccreth calls his material *sen-eolas* (old lore), probably intending by this the legendary material which in his own time had been assembled into the narrative unit. One can discern from the poem that Fearghus mac Róich and his associates were proclaimed by Conchobhar, and that they went to TARA, where Fearghus became the ally of queen Meadhbh and the rival of her husband Ailill. When Meadhbh launched a raid for cattle against Ulster, Fearghus was in the forefront of her forces, but his son Fiacc fought bravely on the side of Ulster. Probably during this campaign, Fearghus slew CEITHEARN MAC FIONNTAIN, and in revenge Ceithearn's son slew Fiacc – a deed that incensed the Ulstermen, for whom Fiacc was a hero. A ninth-century gloss on the poem states that Fearghus deserted Ulster out of lust for Meadhbh, and also claims that another son of Fearghus, Fer Deodae (i.e. FEAR DIADH), defected along with his father and was in fact the man who slew Ceithearn.

Much of this was, through the succeeding centuries, developed into a complex epic story, of which several long recensions have survived in the literature, all presenting the same narrative pattern. The earliest surviving recension dates from the eleventh century, it being a conflation of two ninth-century texts with some extra material added by the compiler himself.

The military-political situation had already come to be explained by a series of 'pre-tales' that preserved fragments of myth and were put together in support of the saga. The *Táin* itself, and its pre-tales, thus contain several echoes of very early tradition, which can be compared with what Greek and Latin writers on the Continent attributed to the Celts known to them. The MOTIFS include fighting from two-horse chariots, head-hunting for prestige, single combat between warriors while opposing armies stand by, the awarding of the best portion of meat to the greatest champion at a feast, and the general custom of cattle-raiding as a test of martial prowess. Also, some superstitions and types of phraseology in the *Táin* can be matched with reports concerning the Continental Celts. Many of the external details, however – such as weaponry and dress – were imaginative descriptions by medieval writers, based on the ethnology of their own time.

The surviving versions of the *Táin* all feature the superhero CÚ CHULAINN, who was early introduced into the narrative. The eleventh-century recension is somewhat disjointed. The second one, dating from the twelfth century, gives a better synthesis of the incidents. We read of MEADHBH presiding at Cruachain (Rathcroghan, County Roscommon) over the western province that had come to be known as Connachta. She and her husband Ailill mac Máta argued over which of them had brought more wealth into their marriage. Meadhbh matched all of Ailill's boasts, except that he had a magnificent bull, called the Finnbheannach (white and horned), which had no equal in her herd. She was told, however, that there was as fine a bull in the possession of a farmer in Cooley (in County Louth), which was the southern cantred of Ulster. Messengers were sent by her to seek a loan of that great brown bull – called the Donn Cuailnge – but they failed to secure it. Thereupon, she gathered her army and decided to take it by force. As her great army set out, she sought a prophecy from a strange woman, a seeress, whom they met. The woman answered ominously: 'I see crimson, I see red!' In the forefront of Meadhbh's army was the exiled former king of Ulster, Fearghus mac Róich, who, although thirsting for revenge against his usurper, Conchobhar mac Neasa, delayed the progress of the host and sent warnings to the men of his native province. But the Ulstermen were stricken, in this the hour of their greatest need, by the magical debility that resulted from the curse which the lady MACHA had put on them.

Only the young Cú Chulainn, who was not a real Ulsterman – being from Muirtheimhne, on the southern border of the province – was exempt from this debility. Therefore he alone could go to face Meadhbh's Connachtmen and her assembled allies from other parts of Ireland. At Ard Cuillinn (now Crossakeel, County Westmeath), he cut a sapling of oak with a single stroke and, using but one arm, one leg and one eye, made a hoop of it and wrote a message in OGHAM script. He fixed this on a stone pillar, and when the enemy approached, Fearghus interpreted it to mean that the invading army should go no further until one of them could make a hoop in the same way. They circumvented that place, and next day Cú Chulainn found them near Cnoghbha (Knowth, County Meath). He killed two warriors and their charioteers, and stuck the four heads on a tree fork. When the army came upon this grisly sight, Fearghus stated that there was a magical prohibition (*GEIS*) against crossing that ford until one of them could remove the fork with one hand without dismounting from his chariot, because Cú Chulainn had placed it there in that manner.

Ailill asked Fearghus about Cú Chulainn and had described for him the youth-biography of this new hero. Next day the army went eastwards, devastating the countryside but harassed all the way by Cú Chulainn. Meadhbh grew worried as he continued his sorties, leaving hundreds dead, and she sought a parley with him. The only condition he would accept was that they should send a warrior to fight him each day and that the army should advance only while the combat lasted. Many such combats ensued, with Cú Chulainn always the victor, and since the progress of her army was thereby impossibly impeded, Meadhbh reneged on the agreement. She marched north, and Cú Chulainn was sore pressed as her forces ravaged Ulster, with one contingent searching through the Cooley Mountains until they found the great brown bull with his herd in a lonely retreat there. They took the bull away, but not without severe casualties, for the animal was enraged. Then the supernatural champion LUGH came from the otherworld to the assistance of Cú Chulainn and held the front for him while he slept for three days and nights.

When he awoke, Cú Chulainn learned that 150 boys from Ulster had joined the fray and had killed three times their number of Meadhbh's men before being themselves overwhelmed and slain. He thus arose in a frenzy of anger and, as was his wont in such situations, his body became marvellously distorted. Mounting his chariot, which bristled with knives, hooks and spears, he wrought havoc on the foe. In this, 'the great slaughter on the plain of Muirtheimhne', multitudes were killed and not a third of the foe escaped unscathed. The rampant Cú Chulainn sustained not a scratch, and next morning appeared in all his splendour before the women and POETS of Meadhbh's host. Struck by the beauty of his countenance and figure, the women climbed onto the soldiers' backs to behold him.

Meadhbh then prevailed upon Fearghus to oppose Cú Chulainn. Since he was the young hero's former tutor, however, Fearghus brought no sword and the two reached a face-saving agreement according to which Cú Chulainn fled before Fearghus and Fearghus promised to yield to him in the final battle. Growing confident now, Meadhbh sent out parties of men to find and slay Cú Chulainn, but to no avail, as they all met with death at his hands. Finally, she tried to persuade a renowned warrior to oppose him. This was FEAR DIADH, a foster-brother to Cú Chulainn. They had been trained in arms together and had faced many dangers together in former times, but Fear Diadh was one of the band of exiles who had defected from Ulster with Fearghus. He was reluctant to fight his friend, but Meadhbh insinuated that Cú Chulainn had claimed superiority over him, and she thus tricked him into the undertaking. In a harrowing scene, the two friends faced each other at a ford on the River Dee (Ardee, County Louth). They fought heroically, but in the end Cú Chulainn shot his barbed javelin – the *ga bolga* – from his toes at his opponent and killed him. He lamented the death of his friend, and himself lay fainting from wounds on the ground.

Meanwhile, nine days of the crisis having passed, king Conchobhar and his Ulstermen recovered from their debility, and an advance party of their forces rescued Cú Chulainn and bore him away to a safe place. The Ulstermen fell furiously upon Meadhbh's army, and in the heat of battle Conchobhar came face to face with his old rival Fearghus. Loath to wreak havoc on his own province, Fearghus turned his rage against the hills and sheared three of these of their heads with his sword. Hearing the din of battle, Cú Chulainn himself rose from his sickbed and rushed forth wielding his chariot as a weapon. Seeing him approach, Fearghus fulfilled his part of their agreement and led his company out of the battle. The men of Leinster and Munster followed them, and so Meadhbh's Connachtmen stood alone to face defeat by Conchobhar's Ulster forces. She appealed to Cú Chulainn to spare her army, and he consented. Crestfallen, they went westwards past Athlone into Connacht, and Fearghus remarked to Meadhbh that a drove of horses led by a mare could have no luck.

Not to be foiled, however, Meadhbh had the stolen brown bull dispatched to her herd at her headquarters in Cruachain (Rathcroghan, County Roscommon), and now the two bulls met. A ferocious contest ensued, and when night fell the noise of the Finnbheannach and the Donn Cuailnge was heard as they travelled all over Ireland goring and rending each other. In the morning the brown was seen passing by Cruachain with the mangled carcass of its rival on its horns. The Donn Cuailnge then headed back to Ulster, scattering pieces of the dead bull at different places. On reaching its homeland, the heart burst within the great bull of Cooley and it expired.

It is indeed difficult to decipher how the several strands running through the developed *Táin* narrative became intertwined. The four basic themes can be enumerated as the rivalry between Fearghus and Conchobhar, the struggle between the Ulaidh and Connachta peoples, the contest between the bulls, and the heroic exploits of Cú Chulainn. The rivalry between Fearghus and Conchobhar has all the marks of a survival from ancient ritual concerning the Ulster kingship, Fearghus being in origin a divine patron of that kingship and Conchobhar representing the reigning king. When the royal Ulster stronghold of Eamhain Mhacha fell to the Connachta, the focus of authority shifted to Tara, which was the headquarters of the Connachta. Dramatised in personal terms, this meant that Fearghus went over to the side of Meadhbh, who was the female personification of Tara sovereignty and thus symbol of Connachta power. The *Táin* narrative, however, represents the attack on Ulster as emanating from the capital of the western province, Cruachain, and situates the power base of Meadhbh there. This shows that the saga as we have it dates from later than the sixth century AD, for 'Connachta' had at that time come to mean the western province rather than the strong sept that ruled the Boyne Valley in County Meath.

Cattle-raiding, as reflected in the story's title, was a typical practice of great warrior-kings of the period, and the actual practice in that region may be reflected by the place name Bearnas Bó Cuailnge (the Gap of the Cattle of Cooley) in the *Táin* text. We read that the cattle had gone through that gap for safety from Meadhbh's army. To hide their cattle away in such a location would be a sensible precaution for the Ulstermen when confronted with a raid by their southern neighbours, for the Cooley Peninsula itself is a natural redoubt, and the gap leads to a concealed retreat deep in the mountains. The cattle-raid itself, and the efforts to foil it, would therefore echo real historical practices, but the actual bulls mentioned in the saga have a definite mythic background. The names of these two protagonists were designations of divine personages (*see* FIONN *and* DONN), and their contest exemplifies a tendency to view such deities as opposites to each other. One of the 'pre-tales' confirms this by describing how the two bulls had previously existed as rivals in other shapes (*see* DONN CUAILNGE), and such transformations are typical of characters with divine traits in ancient Irish lore (*see* FIONNTAN, ÉADAOIN, MONGÁN *and* CÚ ROÍ). The stallion imagery of Fearghus could well have given rise to an emphasis on great male animals within ancient Ulster lore, and it would have been natural to attribute divine traits to a pair of highly dramatised bulls. It has been suggested that the *Táin* contains evidence of a special bull-cult, but no other traces of such are found in Irish literature, and that interpretation is hardly necessary to explain the contest of the Finnbheannach and the Donn Cuailnge.

Once its political and geographical outlines were fancifully fixed, the story underwent rapid development. It became popular, not just in the north, but also in the south of Ireland, no doubt due to a feeling of solidarity with the Ulaidh against the expansionist Connachta. How and when Cú Chulainn was introduced into these events is unclear, but it must have been at a stage when the narrative had assumed a stable form. It seems likely that he displaced the above-mentioned Fiacc, for in the *Táin* he is represented as a beloved foster-son of Fearghus, who is nevertheless on the opposite side. It is significant that the native territory assigned to Cú Chulainn – Muirtheimhne – lies outside Ulster proper, but is in the same general area as Cooley, to which the bull belonged. Being a sacred personification of war, and demonstrably a cult figure of some group in that area, the dramatic potential of Cú Chulainn was so great that he forced himself onto a story the title of which referred to Cooley. Moreover, a gradual development in the role of Cú Chulainn can be deduced. The motif of the debility of the Ulstermen must have grown up from the original fertility imagery that lies behind the LEGEND of Macha, and once this motif became part of the *Táin* narrative, Cú Chulainn fitted well into the context as a dramatic substitute in the war. Further amplification can be traced. His boyhood deeds, for example, are described as an in-tale in the narrative, thus betraying that the passage is an insertion. Similarly, the sorrowful combat with Fear Diadh is a late inclusion, and the surviving recensions themselves clearly illustrate its development.

Regarding the general picture given in the cycle, it should be noted that the tribal designation Rudhraighe was early misinterpreted as having the element *ruadh* (red), and hence the palace of the legendary king of the Ulaidh, Conchobhar, was called by medieval writers *an Chraobhruadh*, meaning the red-branched or red-poled edifice. This (earlier, *craebruad*) might well have been a misunderstanding for an original term such as *craeb ruda*, which would have designated the Ulaidh as 'the rightfully occupying sept'. The medieval writers, at any rate, made sense of it by imagining the royal palace as a magnificent and richly ornamented house supported by 'posts of red yew', the focal point of the Ulster capital Eamhain Mhacha. From a loose rendering by translators of the texts into English, the Ulster Cycle itself is now often referred to as stories of the 'Red Branch Knights'.

The final recension of the *Táin* was written in Modern Irish in the fifteenth century, and manuscript copies of this were being made until recent centuries. Yet the story of the great cattle-raid is hardly known at all in oral lore, and this seems to have been the case since the end of the Middle Ages. It is a quite complex and involved story, with various levels of action, and is assembled very much as a literary rather than an oral unit. The same is

generally true of the whole Ulster Cycle, stories from which, together with derived accounts, span the literature from the eighth to the eighteenth centuries. This long span shows how much chieftains and audiences in different parts of the country continued to take the supposed ancient warriors of Ulster to their hearts and loved to romance about them. The material could only be handled by professional storytellers in formal settings, however, and consequently only a small selection from the narratives is found in the late folklore. Episodes from the cycle that have been collected from folklore, as well as some onomastic data in popular tradition referring to it, all derive from written sources in the not-too-remote background.

For the voluminous material belonging to this tradition, apart from *Táin Bó Cuailnge, see* the full list of entries for the Ulster Cycle in the GENRE LIST in this book.

LUCCRETH'S POEM: J. Carney in *Ériu, 22,* 73–80; P.L. Henry in Mac Mathúna & Ó Corráin (1997), 53–70.

CÚ CHULAINN INTRODUCED: K. Meyer in *AIM, 5,* 28–30; Van Hamel (1933), 57–60; Carney in *PICCS, 6,* 113–30.

SURVIVING TEXTS OF *TÁIN BÓ CUAILNGE:* Recension 1: C. O'Rahilly (1976); Recension 2: C. O'Rahilly (1970); Recension 3: R. Thurneysen in *ZCP, 8,* 524–54 & M. Nettlau in *RC, 14,* 254–66 & *15,* 62–78, 198–208. Fifteenth-century version: O'Rahilly (1961).

CRAOBHRUADH: Van Hamel (1933), 20; W. Stokes in *Ériu, 4,* 26–7 & *Irische Texte, 2* (2), 135; C. O'Rahilly (1970), 131; Gwynn (1924), 128, 130.

DISCUSSION: Jackson (1964); D. Greene in Dillon (1968), 93–104; P. Henry (1978), 9–27; Ó hÓgáin (1999), 171–8, 243–4.

FOLKLORE: S. Ó Súilleabháin (1942), 597–9; Bruford (1969), 93–105.

Urard mac Coise *(+AD 990)* POET

who is represented in the medieval literature as an exemplar of his profession in its dealings with KINGS and nobility. The name Urard (also Iorard) is an old one meaning 'of high status', and his father's name Coise seems to reflect Coised, meaning 'foremost [in battle]'.

Urard was the leading man of learning in Ireland in his time, and he died at the renowned monastery of Clonmacnoise. One text states that he was on pilgrimage when he died, and describes him as being extraordinarily charitable. Another poet, Airbheartach mac Coise, is referred to in the Annals as having been taken captive by the NORSEMEN and ransomed by BRIAN BÓRAMHA at Scattery Island on the River Shannon in the year 990. The correspondence in dates caused the two to be confused. The Annals state that Airbheartach (whose name meant 'skilled') died in either 1015 or 1023. Due to the confusion, the late medieval writers felt it feasible to claim that Urard mac Coise, 'chief-poet of Ireland', composed several verses on the HIGH-KINGSHIP of Brian.

A rhetorical prose text, known as *Airecc Menman* or 'Stratagem' of Urard mac Coise, seems to have been composed by the poet himself and is the basis for his portrayal in later tradition. This text tells of how Urard was despoiled by members of the northern UÍ NÉILL sept, who carried off his wealth and destroyed his house at Clártha (Clare, County Westmeath). The poet went to TARA and, when asked to recite a story by the high-king Domhnall mac Muircheartaigh, told of 'the destruction of the fort of Maol Milscothach'. It was in reality an allegory of his own misfortunes, and when Domhnall realised this, he called for a judgement on the matter. The leading scholar of Clonmacnoise, called Flann, decreed full compensation to the poet, and it was decided that the chief-poet should henceforth have equal honour-price with the king of Tara.

It is clear that Urard flourished at the court of the high-king, for he is associated with Domhnall's son and successor, Maoilsheachlainn (earlier, Mael Sechnaill), in a story that is a kind of parody of the foregoing. We read that Maoilsheachlainn, due to his love of learning, bestowed the revenues of the kingship on him for one year. When the year had passed, Urard insisted on keeping the privilege permanently, whereupon the king challenged him to a combat on horseback. Maoilsheachlainn was the best horseman 'in those parts of Europe', and so he put on no armour and wielded only a headless staff for fear he might injure the poet. Urard, despite wearing full armour, was vanquished by the king.

In later stories, he is usually referred to simply as 'Mac Coise'. One fanciful story

from the late medieval period tells of him seeing one day on the shore of Loch Léibhinn (Loch Lene, County Westmeath) a huge but beautiful woman weeping. He spoke to her, and she said that her sweetheart had been killed and had been buried at Clonmacnoise that very day. Going to that monastery, Mac Coise was told that nobody had been buried there for a quarter of a year. Soon after, however, a grave was being dug for a deceased monk and the diggers found the newly interred corpse of a huge man with a fearsome wound. They covered in the grave, and discussed what to do, but when they dug again next day, nothing could be found. This story is obviously a combination of belief in an otherworld community and of antiquarian speculation, but the special connection of poets with the otherworld is an old convention. Yet the atmosphere is that of pseudo-lore, and it is obvious that the writer was not serious in his description. We read in another story of Mac Coise shooting a swan on the Boyne. When he took it up, the swan became a woman who explained to him that she had been put into that shape by demons. Mac Coise then brought her back to her people. Such accounts can be taken as narrative developments from the status of the poet Urard mac Coise as a reciter of ancient lore.

In the Annals, a curious little story is told of his later years. We read that he made his residence in Clonmacnoise so that he could be near enough to the church to attend Mass every day. One night, however, an angel appeared to him and told him that his paces to and from the church would be measured by God in deciding the reward due to him. As a result of this information, Mac Coise went to live in a bog at a good distance from Clonmacnoise, and walked from there to the monastery each day.

M.E. Byrne in *AIM, 2*, 42–76; O. Bergin in *Ériu, 9*, 175–80; D. Murphy (1896), 161–2; T.F. O'Rahilly in *Celtica, 1*, 316–17; Mac Cana (1980), 33–8; C. Ó Lochlainn in *Éigse, 3*, 208–18 & *4*, 33–4; K. Meyer in *ZCP, 8*, 218–22, 559–60; Todd (1848), 208–11; E. Poppe in *CMCS, 37*, 33–54; A.M. O'Leary in *CMCS, 38*, 53–71.

weather This has always been a matter of immediate concern to people, farmers and others alike. Much depended on it in the economy of traditional society, and yet it could be very unreliable. So great efforts were made to foresee what the weather had in store, or at least to see what was most likely to happen. In deciding on the type of weather to be expected, people used all the methods that had been worked out over many generations in order to grapple with the ENVIRONMENT. These vary from the scientific approach and from experience to premonitions and some fantastic guesses.

The sky is the great vista whose mystery is ever present, and so people observed it closely in the hope that it would reveal at least some of its secrets. Its change of colour is one obvious and interesting phenomenon. 'A reddening at night is the shepherd's delight,' we are told, 'and a reddening at morn is the shepherd's scorn!' But the distinctions could be more sophisticated, especially in winter. The old people took a red sky in the east to presage frost or even snow, while a red sky to the west meant that sunshine was imminent. If the redness was in the north, rain was coming, and if in the south there would be rain and strong wind. In spring time, a red southern sky was taken as an indication of pleasant moist weather that would help the crops to grow. The size of the rainbow was calculated with great care. If only a small piece of it could be seen on the horizon, this was taken to mean plenty more rain, and a rainbow in the east was considered even more ominous than a sky that was already clouded. Fishermen, however, were generally pleased with a fine rainbow high over the waves, for they took that to betoken a change for the better and a good fine period in the future.

The sun could itself be a great indicator. Bright rays emanating from it in the morning were referred to as *cosa na gréine* (the sun's feet), and it was said that they were a sure sign that the evening would be fine. This was especially assured if intermittent winds blew during the morning. A close eye was also kept to the moon. If a white haze could be seen around it, and if this haze cleared from the north, very good weather was expected, but if it cleared from the south it meant the opposite. A red moon was an ominous thing, not just in the works of POETS but also in the eyes of the unlettered. This red moon meant storms and the elements running wild. As for the stars, if these were perceived to be shining too brightly something was wrong also, and people – natural pessimists in the Irish climate – feared a sudden change for the worse. These folk readings of the weather were a mixture of observation, experience and imagination. The same was true of the wind. If it blew from the north, it would drive away the rain but leave in its place some very harsh and cold weather; and if from the south, the weather would be moist and good for farming. The east wind was dry and the west wind good for fishing, as it stirred the waters. Regarding possible change in the weather, much notice was taken of fog. If it occurred as the moon was waning, this was taken to mean rain in the near future. If seen over a river, fog was considered a sign of good weather, but a cap of fog on a hill top was not so good. This, of course, was a quite realistic interpretation, as was the idea that rain is imminent when 'distant hills are looking nigh'. But again complication could set in. For example, when fog rested on a high hill but did not touch a lower hill adjacent to it, it meant that the rain would pass and fall somewhere else.

Things varied according to the time of day also. The Connemara people claimed that if a morning were so clear that they could see Mount Brandon far away in Kerry, that was a sign that the day would be very wet. If, however, they had that clear view in the evening, then fine weather would follow, or at least the rain would fall overnight, for the rather tongue-in-cheek wish in Irish is *'Báisteach ó Dhia chugainn is gan í a bheith fliuch, is cuid an lae amáirigh go dtite sí anocht!'* (May we get rain from God without it being wet, and may tomorrow's portion fall tonight!). Frost is much feared by the countryman and the town dweller alike. It is also quite unpredictable, especially on a night in late autumn. It is said that the great FIONN MAC

CUMHAILL himself was fooled by it, for he once sold his shoes when he saw frost at nightfall. He thought that the morning would be fine, but he was wrong, and had to buy his shoes back again, no doubt at a higher price! Tradition holds that frost is inevitably followed by rain, and its onset would be suspected if scattered raindrops were blown on the wind. Such a wind was likened to a fierce dog, ready to bite at anything that came in its way.

Apart from the elements, people very wisely observed what the other creatures around them were doing. Loud quacking of ducks was a proverbial sign of rain, and equally ominous was the sight of hens going to roost too early in the evening. Seagulls coming too far inland were taken to mean the same thing, as did the sudden appearance of an agitated flock of swallows. A heron could also be a good indicator – if this large bird moved upriver the weather would be dry, but the opposite was expected if it moved downwards. The curlew was well known to 'whistle for rain', and the early arrival of wild geese meant that a prolonged and severe winter was in store. People also looked to domestic animals for some indications. Thus if the dog suddenly took to eating grass and did not otherwise appear to be sick, this was taken as a sign of rain; and if the cat remained stubbornly near the fireplace, then cold and harsh weather could be expected. The GOAT was considered the most perceptive of all animals, being able even to see the wind. So when the climate was about to take a turn for the worse, the goats wasted no time in going under a bush or fence, and would make every possible effort to reach the shelter of the farmyard. Something could also be learned from the bushes and trees. A quick withering of leaves in autumn was a very bad sign, being both physically and visually bleak. The old people used to say that a plentiful crop of haws indicated that a snowy winter was at hand, as providence would compensate the birds for whatever hardship was in store.

In agriculture, the seasons are all important, and folklore has an intricate pattern of determining how these relate to each other – the general idea being that there is a balance in nature and that the effects of one season are cancelled out by the next. The farmers of old regarded the following as the most natural weather: a foggy winter, a frosty spring, a variable summer, and a sunny autumn. Notwithstanding all of this, the weather seldom behaves exactly as expected; but the traditional fancy is that there is a very special way of knowing what variations are in store. According to this, each of the twelve days of Christmas represents a month of the following year. Whatever type of weather comes on the first day, so will January be, the second day gives a foretaste of February, the third a foretaste of March, and so on with the rest of the twelve days and the twelve months.

S. Ó Súilleabháin (1942), 254–69; Ó Máille, *1* (1952), 15–38; Ó Muirgheasa & Ó hUrmholtaigh (1976), 123–33; Ó Síochfhradha & Ua Maoileoin (1984), 153–61.

wild animals Tradition shows that the Irish people regarded the fauna with a good deal of intelligent curiosity, but also with a degree of fanciful imagination. In the literature there are mentions of some fantastic animals, especially great dragon-like creatures that inhabit watery realms and have their origin in the biographies of SAINTS. Some other fanciful creatures – such as massive cats, fire-breathing hounds and griffins – are mere devices to heighten the drama in texts, and their rare occurrences in FOLKTALES are for the same purpose. There is a richer and more varied lore, however, concerning the ordinary creatures that are or were met with in the ENVIRONMENT.

Wolves have been extinct in Ireland since the eighteenth century – due largely to rewards offered for their heads. The wolf still figures as an actor in Irish versions of international ANIMAL TALES, however, and several traditions linger as to how the last wolf in a particular locality was killed. These creatures had a high profile in the medieval literature of heroes and saints (*see* AILBHE, CORMAC MAC AIRT *and* SAINTS), their usual portrayal in these sources being helpful to man once their nature was understood. Such traditions may echo an ancient belief in the wolf as a sacred animal. We read that St MOLUA founded an annual feast for the benefit of wolves, and that the celebrated king CONAIRE had seven wolves as hostages for the agreement that their fellows should take no more than one calf annually from each byre in Ireland, while a sixteenth-century English writer claims that the Irish prayed for wolves as if they were human (see also OSRAIGHE).

The fox is the most famed of all creatures in the international animal tales, but from ordinary observation many further accounts of this dramatic creature grew up in various localities. A fanciful tradition purported to explain the origin of foxes in Ireland by claiming that they were the 'dogs' brought into the country by the NORSEMEN. This animal was, however, noted for its intelligence and wile long before the Middle Ages, and in the LEGENDS of the saints, he appears as a helpful but somewhat unreliable creature. His tricks in order to evade the hunting-hounds were particularly the subject of interest – for example, how he would urinate in a circle and then jump outside the circle in order to put the hounds off his scent. He was also believed to be able to foresee events, including the weather, and his barking was taken as a sign that rain was approaching. In a few cases, most notably that of the Preston family of Gormanstown, County Meath, a group of foxes was believed to assemble near the house and set up a continuous chorus of barking as a sign that a member of the household would soon die.

Foxes were the subject of many songs – some humorous ones concerning their stealing of FOWL and others in praise of great hunts they gave to the 'hard-riding country gentlemen'. The fox's colour suggests the red of blood-spilling and also makes it one of the most conspicuous of land animals. It was therefore considered unlucky to see one when undertaking a new task, and particularly when going fishing. Fishermen conversing at sea would never refer to a fox by its name, but would instead use a circumlocution such as 'bushy tail'.

The badger was also regarded as a clever animal and had several reputed abilities. It could, for instance, save hay for farmers overnight, if it so chose. It was also said to have a quite unusual way of making its getaway or otherwise travelling in a hurry – this was to put its snout into a special pocket under its tail, curl itself into a ball, and roll down hills or slopes. Hedgehogs were understood to be animals of great perseverance in their difficult lives. One of them was said to have helped JESUS CHRIST after his 40-day fast by rolling on the ground and collecting apples on its spikes for him. On the other hand, hedgehogs were believed to suck the milk from cows as they lay down on the field at night.

Particularly notorious for this kind of milk-stealing was the hare, in which form it was said that malicious women could go abroad at night to take the dairy profit of their neighbours. This idea – once common in western Europe – has been in Ireland for several centuries, and a common LEGEND tells of how a farmer grew suspicious when the milk yield of his cows diminished greatly. He stayed up at night to watch the cows, and saw a hare come to drink from them. His dog followed the hare, but could only manage to draw blood from its quarters as it fled. The farmer followed on and, coming to a house, asked an old woman who lived there had she seen a hare pass by. As she answered, he noticed that the woman was bleeding, and from this realised that the hare had in fact been her.

Hares were thought to be in special contact with otherworld dwellings (see FAIRIES). One medieval story, for instance, had a man killing and cooking three hares, only to be told by an otherworld voice that these were sons of the legendary king CONCHOBHAR MAC NEASA who had come from a tumulus in that form after their deaths. It was also thought that the souls of dead people returned in the form of rabbits – this belief being particularly applied to a white rabbit, no doubt because such an animal was unusual and eye-catching. Apart from such human transformations, hares in their natural state could betoken

496

bad fortune – for instance, if one crossed the path of a pregnant woman, the child could be born with a fissure in the upper lip. To avoid this 'hare-lip' in the child, it was advised that such a woman should tear the hem of her dress, thus transferring the destined fissure to another object.

Deer play a large part in much of the literature, especially in stories of the FIANNA, where they are often portrayed as otherworld beings in disguise. They do not, however, figure much in folklore, which instead has a tendency to regard wild CATS as being otherworldly. It is apparent that there have been no real wild cats in Ireland in historical times, and such cats in Irish folklore seem to be a combination in the popular mind of various things. These would include ordinary domestic cats either gone wild or engaged in nocturnal escapades, and reports from abroad of larger cats, such as the wild cats of Scotland and the Alps or even the lions of Africa. The latter would seem to account for the tradition that a wild cat has a claw at the tip of its tail. In some accounts, however, there are strong indications that what are meant by these 'wild cats' of Irish folklore are in fact pine martens. When the wild cats congregate at night, they are said to discuss their private affairs and various stratagems that they will employ against humans. Irish versions of a very popular story (see WONDER TALES, type 613) tell of how valuable secrets are discussed at these assemblies.

Another agile creature that attracted attention was the otter – the 'water-dog'. In the biographies of the saints, otters are sometimes portrayed as assisting the holy men by providing fish for them. Folk belief held that otters slept with their eyes open, and a special and rare kind, called the 'king-otter', never slept at all. The king-otter, it was claimed, was an extraordinarily large male specimen, white in colour but with the tips of his ears black and a black cross on his back. He was vulnerable only to a bullet made from silver, and the person who killed him would not live for more than 24 hours afterwards. The person who came into possession of a piece of his skin was, however, very fortunate indeed. That skin would guarantee safety at sea to any boat on which it was kept, safety from fire to any house in which it was, and safety from all accidents to any man who had a piece of it in his pocket.

Much speculation surrounded the seals. They were sometimes said to have been the people who had been left outside the biblical Ark by Noah, and as a result had been changed into that form. They could regain their human shape for short intervals, and stories were told of how benighted individuals saw the seals congregate on the seashore, cast aside their skins and dance as humans. This notion probably sprang from contemplation of the human-like cry given by seals, and it was in time strengthened by the adaptation to the seal context of the legend of a man who married a MERMAID. Accordingly, it is sometimes said that the strange bride in that legend was a seal-woman. A folk legend, common since medieval times, told of how a seal was captured by a fisherman and brought home, but the voice of another seal was heard from outside the house calling its name, and it answered him. The fisherman, pitying the captive seal, allowed it to escape back to the sea.

The fanciful belief that humans had been enchanted into animal form is found also in the case of the creature known as a weasel in Ireland but designated a stoat by the zoologists. It is said that these 'weasels' hold funerals for their dead, much as humans do, and that they show intelligence very like that of people. Its spit was believed to be poisonous, and a story was widely told of how it was prepared to use this as protection. A group of men were mowing a field in which a weasel had its nest, and the weasel was worried that its young would be killed. It therefore went and spat into the men's tea-can, so that they would be poisoned before they reached the nest. One of the men, however, came upon the nest, and kindly put it to the side of the field where it would not be damaged. When the men went to drink their tea, the mother weasel was seen to approach and knock the can over so that they would not be poisoned. Not-withstanding this, weasels were reputed to be vengeful against humans, and to see one early in the morning or when setting out on a journey was taken to be a bad portent. The folk fancy was that weasels had been the cats of the NORSEMEN, and that they had come to Ireland in this way.

Rats were the principal pest-creatures in Irish life, since they stole and dirtied the grain, and they were therefore believed to be vile and vengeful creatures. A long-standing tradition, very strong through-out the whole Gaelic world, was that POETS had the power to banish or control them with verse. On the other hand, rats were thought to be a sign of good luck on board ship, probably because if they deserted the vessel it would indicate that it was foundering. For its part, the mouse had a more variable image. It was said that mice first came into existence due to a mir-acle of St MARTIN, who once placed food under a tub and warned his companions to leave it there until the morrow. An inquisitive person lifted the tub during the night, and a plague of mice rushed forth. In order to control them, Martin threw his glove after them and it turned into a CAT. This derives from an international legend that has mice and rats created by the devil and sent into Noah's Ark. Noticing them, Noah threw his glove at them and they turned into a cat. The legend, in its international form, is told in a fourteenth-century Irish text.

Also feared were bats, whose appear-ance in or near a house was believed to betoken death. It was thought that they would stick in a person's hair, and if the hair were not cut immediately, that person would die.

MEDIEVAL TEXTS: Cross (1952), 48–83; O'Meara (1982), 47–50, 69–72, 77, 81.

GENERAL: S. Ó Súilleabháin (1942), 294–7 & in *Béaloideas, 10*, 130–5; Wood-Martin, *1* (1902), 116–51 & *2*, 118–22; Ó Danachair (1978), 25–6; M. Ó Cadhain in *Béaloideas, 4*, 71–4; P.V. O'Sullivan (1991), 56–78; Ó hÓgáin (1995), 69–78.

SAINTS AND ANIMALS: Plummer, *1* (1910), cxli–cxlvii.

HARE STORIES: Danaher (1972), 109–10; Evans & Thomson (1974), 41–9, 156–77; O. Bergin in *Ériu, 7*, 242–3; B. Almqvist in *Béaloideas, 59*, 269. In the twelfth century, Giraldus Cambrensis (*Topographia*

Hibernica xix.18) cites the witch-as-hare story from Ireland, but he probably heard it rather in Wales.

SEALS: D. Thomson (1965); K. Meyer in *Irisleabhar na Gaedhilge, 4*, 88–9; Ó Duilearga (1948), 313–14, 438; Danaher (1966), 122–7; B. Almqvist in *Béaloideas, 59*, 270.

WEASEL AND WORKMEN: S. Ó Súilleabháin & Christiansen (1967), 50–1 (type 168).

RATS BANISHED BY POETRY: Ó hÓgáin (1980), 380–404.

GLOVE BECOMES CAT: Ó Duilearga (1948), 1, 415; K. Meyer in *Irisleabhar na Gaedhilge, 5*, 155.

Wild Geese *(in Irish, Géanna Fiáine)*

A metaphoric term used for exiled Irishmen fighting in Continental armies. It originated as a code word used for recruiting young men to go abroad into the French army in the early eighteenth century. Wild geese being migratory birds, the promise of a return to Ireland was held out, thus giving the code word an aura of secrecy and subversion of English power similar to metaphoric names used in song for Ireland – such as Róisín Dubh (Little Black Rose) or Droimeann Donn Dílis (Faithful White-backed Brown Cow) – or ordinary women's names used in the same context – for example, Síle Ní Ghadhra, Cáit Ní Dhuibhir or Sadhbh Ultach.

The three wars that in particular resulted in the departure of defeated sol-diers from Ireland were the Nine Years War which ended in 1603, the Cromwellian War which ended in 1653, and the Jacobite War which ended in 1691. The latter war was concluded by the Treaty of Limerick, in which relatively generous terms were offered to the Irish – terms that were rescinded as soon as the Irish soldiers departed the country. By the early eigh-teenth century huge numbers of Irishmen were serving in Continental armies – spread all the way from France and Spain to Austria, Poland, Russia and other places. They were often referred to by Irish POETS of those times in terms such as *na leoin thar toinn* (the lions overseas), and their return to resume Ireland's struggle and to defeat the English was hoped for.

Several of these émigrés reached high rank. Most celebrated of them was Patrick SARSFIELD – leader of the Irish Brigade in the army of Louis XIV of France until his death in 1693 – but others were almost as well known both at home and abroad. Among these was Séarlas Ó Briain, Viscount Clare, whose three Irish regiments in the French army – known as 'Clare's Dragoons' – were famous for their ferocious charges in battle. He was slain in the Battle of Ramillies in 1706. Further east, Piaras de Léis (Peter Lacy, 1678–1751) from County Limerick commanded the Russian army that won the famous Battle of Pultava in 1709. A story is told of him that shows his quick wits. There was uncertainty in the Petersbourg palace in 1741, when the new empress, Anna Leopoldovna, was being challenged by the daughter of Peter the Great, Elizabeth. An overnight *coup d'état* placed Elizabeth on the throne, and Lacy was approached at three o'clock in the morning and asked which side he was on. Not knowing exactly which way the wind was blowing, he replied that he was 'of the party of the reigning empress', and thus survived. His close kinsman, Count George Browne (1698–1784), another commander in the Russian army, endured slavery at the hands of the Turks and terrible war wounds to become governor of Estonia.

These were hard-headed military men and were sometimes fighting on opposing sides in the tangle of Continental politics. To Irish folk memory, however, they were romantic exiles longing to avenge the injustices that had been inflicted on their native land. This was not without some basis, as many of the Wild Geese felt deep grievances at the plight of their people at home. Such feeling was exemplified in the Battle of Fontenoy in 1745, which ended in a stunning French victory over the English forces. The battle was in fact nearly lost by the French, until the Irish Brigades were called into the field. They tore through the enemy, shouting: '*Cuimhnígí ar Luimneach is ar fheall na Sacsan!*' (Remember Limerick, and the treachery of the English!).

The leader of the French in that signal victory was Marechal Maurice de Saxe, who was preparing an army to come to Ireland. A brilliant military man, he was a giant in physical stature and so strong that he was reputedly able to bend a horseshoe with his bare hands. One folk LEGEND brings him into close association with one of his Irish soldiers, referred to only by his surname Ó hÓgáin (Hogan). We are told that Saxe brought his horse to Hogan to be shod, and when the first shoe was made, he took it and pulled it straight with one jerk of his powerful hands. Hogan made a second and a third shoe, to see each of them pulled out of shape by Saxe. At last Saxe said that although the shoes were bad, they must suffice for his horse as he could wait no longer. When the work was done, Saxe handed him a *louis d'or*, and Hogan bent the gold coin double between finger and thumb. He remarked that 'the gold they are making nowadays is just as bad as the iron', and tossed the coin away. Startled at this, Saxe gave him another coin, but the same fate met this second one, as also the third. The fourth was grumblingly accepted as better than nothing at all!

This story – typical of lore of the Wild Geese – was a product of Irish tradition. The blacksmith in question probably owes his name and occupation to one of the most celebrated Irish soldiers of the Jacobite War who never went to the Continent. This was the blacksmith and expert horseman Dónall Ó hÓgáin (Galloping Hogan) – for whom, *see* OUT-LAWS. The plot seems to be a variant of a common legend, told of particular strong men all over Ireland, that describes a horseman stopping at a forge to light his pipe. The blacksmith shows his prodigious strength by holding out the anvil in his hand, having placed a live coal on top of it, but the horseman equals this by taking the anvil in one hand and his pipe in the other, and calmly lighting up.

The swashbuckling careers of the Wild Geese, spread out across the Continent, appealed to the imagination of the Irish community at home and abroad. Their lifestyles could indeed be reckless. One story concerns Balthasar de Bhál (1701–54), of a significant Irish family, who was an officer in an Irish regiment in France and had fought in different parts of Europe. He was an inveterate gambler, and having once lost everything at the tables, produced an orange, saying that was all he had left in the world. He sold it to a lady for one *louis d'or*, with which he returned to the tables, and stage by stage won everything back. As a result of this, he was given the nickname 'de Wall l'Orange'.

One folk account has King George II of England, on hearing of the victory of the Wild Geese at Fontenoy, cursing the legal system that compelled such men to leave their own country. In reality, however, the human 'wild geese' of émigré Ireland were reduced to the role of mercenaries whose return was but a forlorn hope, and in the Irish language itself a wild goose (*gé fhiáin*) came to mean simply a vagrant or wanderer. Another metaphoric saying was: *Imeacht ghé an oileáin, imeacht gan filleadh go brách* (the departure of the goose from the island, a departure without return ever).

GENERAL: O'Callaghan (1870); M. Hennessy (1973); J. O'Daly (n.d.), 200–4; IFC 195:258–60, IFC Index.

LACY AND BROWNE: de Lacy-Bellingari (1928), 213–21.

SAXE AND HOGAN: K. Danaher in *Biatas*, 6/1961, 209–10; DE BHÁL: Gallwey (1970), 87–8.

William of Orange *(1650–1702)*

Chief of state of the Netherlands who became King William III of England in 1689 after his father-in-law James II was deposed. In Ireland, William is remembered for his resounding victory over James at the Battle of the Boyne, fought near Oldbridge, County Meath on 1 July (11 July according to the revised calendar) of the year 1690. Although William was a Protestant and James a Catholic, opposition to James' patron, Louis XIV of France, caused the Pope and most of the Catholic powers of Europe to rejoice at the victory of William. In Ireland, the victory brought about the supremacy of the Established Church, with Roman Catholics persecuted and Presbyterian rights also curtailed.

William landed at Carrickfergus two-and-a-half weeks before the Battle of the Boyne, at the head of a fleet of some 700 ships and a huge and well-equipped army of Danes, Dutch, French and Prussians. Folk tradition claims that he left the imprint of his foot on the quay there, and that he signed his first warrant in his blood, using a sprig of hyssop for pen and saying that 'the first Orange warrant should not be written by anything made by the hand of man'. As he led his army southwards towards the Boyne, it is said that he plucked a spray of lily and wore it as his emblem, hence the Orange Lily.

All of this is remembered by Irish loyalists on 12 July each year, when the victory at the Battle of the Boyne is celebrated with marches, music and pageantry. William is represented on banners dressed in colourful military regalia, brandishing his sword, and riding a fine white horse. He did indeed wear his full decorations in the battle – a factor that caused some worry to his supporters as it made him a conspicuous target – but the iconographic portrayal of him stems from a painting done by Benjamin West in 1771. As such, the popular image of William belongs rather to the end of the eighteenth century than to the end of the seventeenth. In answer to the new radical movement of United Irishmen, which sought to unite members of all religions under a common banner of equality and Irish independence, the Orange Order was founded by the ruling classes in 1795. This Order made William into a figure representing all Protestant sections and an implacable opponent of 'popery'.

William showed great personal courage in the Battle of the Boyne, this being in stark contrast to the behaviour of James. He was wounded once in the shoulder, another shot struck the cap of his pistol, and yet another carried away the heel of his boot. Though suffering from an asthmatic attack, he rode tirelessly through the thick of the battle, personally looking to every section of his army, and refusing to retire to a safe vantage point. He was admired for this even by his Jacobite opponents, and Patrick SARSFIELD is reputed to have remarked later to some English officers: 'Change but kings with us, and we will fight it over again with you.'

Ellis (1976), 56–121; Bagwell, *3*(1916), 294–9; McBride (1997); Bell (1956), 12–19, 118–9: Gregory (1926), 47–9.

wonder tales This is the folklore genre that has most attracted the attention of scholars, creative writers and psychoanalysts. Several hundreds of such international FOLKTALES are listed in the Aarne/Thompson catalogue, where they are entitled 'Tales of Magic'. In the Ireland of recent centuries, they have been the most popular genre in oral narrative, and it is clear from the literature that a number of them have been current in the country for a very long time. There are good reasons for their popularity in Ireland, for wonder tales are long, very stylised and open to ornamentation, and are quite bombastic in their content and form. All of these traits are particularly marked in the culture of the Irish language, which has taken to the wonder tales with special relish. They are sometimes referred to as 'fairy tales', which is a rather inaccurate term since FAIRIES very rarely have a role in them. The world of the wonder tale is a fantastic one, full of strange beings and happenings, and is generally prefaced with the remark 'long ago' – i.e. the events are said to have taken place in a context totally different from the ordinary experienced world – in reality, a quite incredible world.

One of the oldest and most widespread international oral tales seems to have been composed in the early Middle Ages, based on elements known in the ancient Middle East and reflected in early Greek literature. It is listed as type 300. Irish versions tell of a beautiful princess who is being offered in sacrifice to a dragon (called in Irish *ollphiast*, or 'great worm'). This dragon threatens to ravage her father's kingdom if the princess is not handed over to it. So on the appointed day, the king sadly exposes his daughter on the beach, tied down in waiting for the dragon to come in from the sea. A widow's son unexpectedly arrives and fights the dragon, and in a prolonged and fierce contest slays it. The king and his people can only observe the combat at a distance, due to their fear of the terrible creature, and so are not sure of the identity of the young hero. A false warrior pretends that he is the victor and, as the widow's son is a retiring fellow, this

warrior threatens the princess into going along with the deception. The unsuspecting king promises the girl in marriage to the false warrior, but on the day of the wedding, the widow's son comes forward to tell the truth. The false warrior dismisses his claim, displaying the dragon's head as his trophy, but the true hero proves that he was the real dragon-slayer by producing the tongue of the fierce creature, which he had cut from its terrible maw. We may assume that this story has been known in Ireland since the late Middle Ages, as it occurs in versions of the Tristan and Isolde romance from that period in western Europe.

Type 301 seems definitely to be of medieval European derivation. Irish versions tell of three brothers who go to recover a princess who has been abducted by a GIANT to an underground world. The youngest of the three brothers alone has the courage to descend to the underworld, and the other two lower him in a basket through a hole in the ground. He rescues the princess and sends her up in the basket, but his treacherous brothers refuse to lower the basket again to bring him up. He finally manages to ascend on an eagle's back, and arrives home in time to prevent one of his brothers from forcibly marrying the princess. A late literary version of this plot (*see* IOLLANN AIRMDHEARG) has influenced several of the later oral tellings of the tale in Ireland.

Another international wonder tale has a young hero pitted against a giant who has kidnapped a princess and forced her to become his mistress (type 302). Here again the hero is an insignificant youth, who has been kind to several creatures while on the quest for the girl. Discovering the giant's residence, he goes to visit the princess when the giant is away hunting, and she tells him that the giant has an external heart and can only be killed when that heart is destroyed. She does not know where it is located, but promises to try to discover it. When the giant returns to the house, she tries in vain to inveigle the secret from him; similarly on the second day; but on the third evening, she has the threshold strewn with beautiful flowers and explains to the giant that she has done this to honour his heart, which she believes is situated there. The giant is touched by her tenderness and confides his secret to her – the heart is in an egg in a duck's belly in a well on an island in a lake. She informs the young man of this, and the creatures to whom he has been kind now come to his aid. A wolf carries him to the lakeside, a raven brings him to the island, and a salmon dives down into the well and picks up the egg as soon as the duck lays it. The youth then smashes the egg to pieces, and immediately the giant falls down dead in his residence. The youth is given the hand of the princess in marriage, and they live happily ever after. This story must have been known in Ireland for several centuries, for elements of it are used in an early medieval account of how the massive warrior Cú Roí was slain.

A story that was very popular in western Europe concerns the adventures of two young men who are twins (type 303). In Ireland, they are called 'É the Salmon's Son' and 'Ó the Salmon's Son'. We are told of how an old fisherman catches a salmon that speaks to him and asks that it be allowed back into the water. The fisherman does as asked, and the same happens on the second day. On the third day, the salmon tells him to bring it home and give it to his childless wife to eat. The fisherman does so, and as a result his wife becomes pregnant and gives birth to twin boys, who are given the names É and Ó. When they grow up, É tells his brother that he intends to go abroad to seek adventures, and so sets out, bringing with him his horse, hound and hawk. He meets and marries a beautiful princess in a foreign land, and then sets out to subdue an evil hag who is ravaging that land. The hag, however, tricks him by feigning helplessness and fear of his animals. She pulls a long strand of hair from her head and begs him to tie the animals with it before they engage in conversation. When he does so, she strikes him with a magic wand and turns him into stone. His brother Ó at home notices blood on a flower, and from this realises that he is in trouble. So Ó sets out, with his own horse, hound and

hawk. Since they are identical twins, the princess mistakes Ó for her husband, and Ó learns from her what has happened. Going to the hag, he also ties his animals at her request, but uses a running knot so that when she tries to enchant him the animals come to his assistance. He then slays her, and uses the magic wand to resuscitate his brother. É enquires as to how Ó learned of his fate, and is struck by jealousy when he learns of Ó's dealings with his wife. He therefore slays Ó, and returns to the princess. She remarks to him that he is much more affectionate than on the previous night, and from this he realises that his brother has not been unfaithful to him. So he uses the magic wand to resuscitate Ó, and providentially the princess has an equally beautiful sister, who becomes Ó's wife, so all ends happily.

Many versions have been collected from Irish folklore of a worldwide story concerning a youth who is kind to animals, and who rescues a girl from enchantment (type 313). The youth, in trying to effect the girl's release, gambles with the captor, but loses and is given several difficult tasks to perform as forfeit – such as cleaning out a stable which continually fills with manure, cutting down a dense forest, and catching a wild horse. The girl helps him to successfully carry out the tasks, and when they flee together, she performs great feats of magic to keep the pursuers from catching up with them. She first throws back a comb, which turns into a forest to block the pursuers' path, then throws back a stone, which turns into a mountain, and a piece of flint, which becomes a great fire. They finally escape over a magic bridge, which folds up behind them and stops the pursuers once and for all. The girl, however, has warned the youth not to kiss anybody when he gets home, for if he does he will forget her. When his dog rushes out to greet him, he kisses the animal, thinking it no harm, but as a result immediately forgets his lover. Time passes, and a marriage is arranged for him with another girl. As the wedding festivities begin, his true love appears on the scene with a magical ruse to jog his memory. She has two speaking birds, one a cock and the other a hen, which she sets talking. The whole conversation that passes between them follows word for word what the youth and herself had said to each other when they were together. In this way, she succeeds in getting him to remember her, and they marry. This folktale has been current in Ireland for a long time, for several elements from it have been borrowed into the tenth-century literary story of ÉADAOIN, and again into the somewhat later literary account of the high-king ART. Because many versions of the international folktale begin with a wounded eagle being cared for by the youth, several Irish versions start with an account of how the eagle was wounded in a war between birds and animals (*see* ANIMAL TALES, type 222).

The story of a magician and his pupil (type 325) has been current in Europe from antiquity. It involves several transformations of the characters, and to this extent its plot seems to have affected the above-mentioned literary tale of Éadaoin as well as the account of the DONN CUAILNGE. The folktale describes how a boy becomes apprenticed to a magician, and gains access to his master's secret book. He learns from the book how to transform himself into different shapes, and in order to help his impoverished father, turns himself into a horse that the father can sell at the market. When the magician discovers how his book has been used, he is livid with anger and attacks the pupil. In the course of their fight, they change themselves into several different shapes, and finally the pupil attempts to escape by becoming a grain of corn. At that the magician changes himself into a cock and dives at the corn to swallow it, but the pupil becomes a fox and kills the cock, thus triumphing over his master.

An equally popular folktale (type 326) concerns another irrepressible youth. This fellow does not know what fear is and wishes to discover it. He spends three successive nights in a house haunted by a most boisterous GHOST, and eventually the ghost speaks to him and thanks him, for the former was destined to remain there until a mortal should undergo that ordeal. Furthermore, the ghost tells him where a fine TREASURE is hidden, and the newly rich youth decides to marry. He still has not discovered what fear is, but when his bride slips a live fish down his back he wakes up shivering. This is his first experience of fear! The context and the provenance of that story suggest that it originated in medieval Europe.

Such an origin is even more definite in the case of another narrative that was popular in Ireland (type 330). This tells of a blacksmith who sells his soul to the devil, and who then gets the opportunity to set the deal aside when guaranteed by an angel the fulfilment of any three wishes. He wishes for three foolish things: that anybody who plucks an apple from his tree, who sits on his chair, or who enters his bag, will stick thereto. When the devil comes at the appointed time to take his soul, he sticks the terrible visitor to the tree and so gains respite, and on the next occasion he gains further respite by using the chair wish. When the devil comes for the third time, he plays on the pride of the evil one by saying that there is one feat impossible even to him, namely to escape from the blacksmith's bag. The devil angrily denies this, and to prove the point enters the bag. He gets stuck inside, however, and is subjected to a tremendous beating by the smith – so much so that he flees in terror, vowing never again to trouble the smith. When the smith dies, he is refused access to both heaven and hell because of his behaviour. Some storytellers say that he is thus fated to wander the earth continually, and that he is the strange light *ignus fatuus* often seen at night and popularly called 'Jack of the Lantern' and 'Will of the Wisp'. Other storytellers, however, describe him throwing a deck of cards through the gates of heaven, and when told by St Peter to collect them, he enters and claims successfully that nobody, once in, can be put out of heaven. In Munster, this roguish character is usually said to have been a shoemaker rather than a smith.

Type 332 originated from some literary source in medieval Europe, and has marked allegorical traits. It tells of a cautious man whose wife gives birth to a son, and who, wishing to avoid all conflict, rejects the offers of both God and the devil to be the child's godfather. However, he accepts the offer made by Death, believing the latter to be the most neutral possible patron. At the baptism, Death gives the man a special present, the gift of healing, and so he becomes a famous doctor. Death says that if ever he himself is seen by the doctor at the head of a patient, then that patient must be allowed to die. After several years of successful healing, Death appears at the head of a sick man, but the doctor slyly reverses the patient's position and thus tricks his benefactor. Death is angry, and soon afterwards demands the life of the doctor himself as compensation. However, the doctor again tricks him by gaining respite to say the Pater Noster, and then delaying recital of the prayer indefinitely. Death, however, is not fooled thrice. The doctor sees a little boy crying, and on enquiring the reason for this is told by the boy that he will be cruelly beaten by his father if he fails to learn the words of the Pater Noster. Overcome by sympathy for the child, the doctor teaches him the prayer, only to realise that in doing so he has recited it and that the little boy is Death in disguise. Thus the doctor is taken away by Death, an unhappy ending that is unusual in wonder tales and which reflects the unusual literary origin of this folk story.

Type 400 concerns a boy who is abandoned by his father and who, on an island, meets a girl who has been enchanted so that she becomes a swan while in water. By stealing her swan-cloak, he disenchants her and they marry. On a visit home, an enemy puts him to sleep with a magic slumber pin, and when he does not return to her, his wife thinks she is deserted. She recovers her swan-cloak and forgets him. Furnished with magic boots and assisted by a variety of animals, however, he arrives just in time before she is remarried, and they are reconciled and live happily ever after.

Type 425 is in Ireland known by the title *Cú Bán an tSléibhe* (The White Hound of the Mountain). It tells of a man who is put under a spell by a witch so that he becomes a hound by day and regains his own form by night only. His wife learns that she can disenchant him by burning his hide, but she does so too soon and, as a result, he is compelled to leave her. She follows him, and finding him in the power of the witch decides on a plan to redeem him. She barters with the witch for one night alone with him in exchange for a beautiful comb, gets a second night in exchange for a fine scissors, and a third night for her magical needle. On that third night, she manages to disenchant him and win him back by a kiss.

Some quite dramatic material is found in type 461, which has a prophecy being made to a king that a certain poor boy will marry his daughter. In order to be rid of him, the king gives the boy the extremely dangerous task of getting three hairs from the devil's beard. The boy sets out for hell, and on his way meets various people who wish to have difficult questions solved. These include a farmer who cannot understand why his well is bloody, a gardener who cannot understand why his apple tree does not flourish, and a ferryman who does not know when he will be relieved of his magically imposed work. Reaching hell, the boy secures the help of the devil's wife, and thereby succeeds in all his tasks. On his return home, the king is seized with envy and decides to emulate the boy's exploits. He sets out, and on reaching the river has an oar handed to him by the ferryman, who by this means is released from his obligations. The king in his place must remain continually rowing.

A trip to the otherworld is featured also in a folktale which has a man fulfilling a promise to a dead friend or to a speaking skull (type 470). On the way, he sees some strange sights, such as a fat and a thin cow, a broad and a narrow road, a house of plenty and another of great dearth, and he has these sights explained to him by his friend. On his return home, he finds that he has been many centuries absent. A variant of this international type has a man visiting the land of the immortals and marrying its queen. She allows him to visit his home, but warns him not to get off his horse. He breaks the prohibition, becomes old and dies. In Irish folklore, this variant is always told of OISÍN, but the fact that general versions of type 470 have been known in Ireland for a very long time is evidenced by the use of the plot in the story of BRAN MAC FEABHAIL in eighth-century literature (*see also* LAOGHAIRE MAC CRIOMHTHAINN). Another narrative of the same kind is instanced by type 471, which tells of two brothers who attempt to go thither, but neglect to cross the correct bridge and are turned into stone. Their younger brother crosses correctly, sees strange sights illustrative of religious truths, and returns home. A variant of this type was very popular in medieval Europe, telling of a monk who listens to a bird singing and does not realise that centuries are passing as he does so. When the singing is over, the monk finds that all has changed around him, and is told that a monk had disappeared from that monastery without trace many years before. Versions of this story were told in the folklore of different parts of Ireland, and it occurs in a late medieval text concerning St MOCHAOI.

One of the best-known folktales in Ireland is type 503, which tells of a man with a hump who hears the fairies singing and dancing one night. Their tune was to the words '*Dé Luain, Dé Máirt*' (Monday, Tuesday), and the man joined in, adding an extra day '*Dé Céadaoin*' (Wednesday). The fairies were so pleased with this new rhythm that they took away the man's hump from him. He went home very pleased with himself and told his brother, who also was a hunchback. The brother went on the following night to the fairy dwelling, and he added all the rest of the weekdays to the words. He thereby ruined the melody, and in high dudgeon the fairies put the other hump on him also, leaving him with two.

There are many Irish versions of the worldwide Cinderella story (type 510), in which the heroine is called Cóitín Luachra or 'Rushy Coat', and in which the supernatural helper is usually her dead mother returning in the form of a CAT.

Also popular in Ireland was type 513, which tells of marvellous helpers who assist a young man in his attempt to recover a princess who has been stolen away by an enchantress. On his quest, the young man is joined one by one by the helpers. These include a fellow who is so strong that he can pull up trees, another so accurate that he can shoot the eye from a fly's head at a great distance, another who runs so fast that he has one leg tied up under his belt to prevent him from running away, another who can hear the grass growing, one who can blow strongly enough to drive a windmill, a great climber, and so on. By employing all their special skills, the young man manages to carry out a seemingly impossible task set by the enchantress, which is to bring water from the well at the world's end. The princess, however, states that she will marry the young man only if he or one of his retainers can defeat her in a race. She is a great runner, but proves no match for the fleet-footed helper, and so she marries her rescuer. In addition to the standard versions, this story has, since the Middle Ages, exerted a strong influence on the narratives concerning the celebrated FIONN MAC CUMHAILL. A story with certain similarities to it also exerted an influence on the FIANNA CYCLE in medieval times. The international form of this (type 570) tells of a king who promises his daughter in marriage to any man who can herd all the rabbits in his kingdom, and of a youth who gets possession of a magic pipe with which he assembles the herd. This was adopted and adapted into the lore of Fionn's fleet-footed companion CAOILTE, and it is not evidenced from Ireland outside of that context.

The lore of Fionn's grandson OSCAR was influenced, in or about the fifteenth century, by type 650, which related the adventures of a stupendously strong man. As well as this, the folktale survived independently in Irish oral tradition, telling of how the man was so strong that he used a tree as a walking stick and performed several difficult tasks for his master, who feared him and wanted to be rid of him. Among the tasks were hauling a huge load of timber, threshing with a roof beam as flail, and visiting hell and driving the devils out of that place. Somewhat earlier was the influence on the lore concerning FIONN MAC CUMHAILL of type 653, which describes four brothers with extraordinary skills. One of them can count the number of eggs in a bird's nest on a tree, another can steal the eggs, another can shoot them as they fall, and the fourth can sew the shells together again. A princess is kidnapped and taken to a high rock in a distant sea, and they set out to rescue her. The climber scales the rock and brings the others up with him, the thief steals her from the kidnapper, the marksman shoots the kidnapper with an arrow, and the handyman repairs their boat when it is in danger of sinking. Each then claims the princess as wife, but the question is undecided as to which of them best earned her. When told in the context of Fionn, the four assist him to recover a kidnapped baby, and the plot has obviously been attracted to that context by the earlier use there of the related folktale (type 513, *see above*).

Type 655, which tells of how a man makes extraordinarily wise deductions, influenced Continental hagiography in medieval times, and it is in the context of SAINTS only that it occurs in Ireland (*see* DÉAGLÁN). Wise men are fooled in type 660, which relates how three doctors test their skills on themselves, one removing his eyes, another his hand, and the third his heart. The organs are stolen overnight, and so they must find substitutes. The first doctor inserts a cat's eye in his own head, the second attaches a thief's hand to himself, and the third inserts a pig's heart. The result is that – much to their embarrassment – the substitute organs retain their natural propensities. That this story has been known in Ireland for some centuries is proved by the occurrence of the cat's eye MOTIF in a literary text concerning the mythical physician DIAN CÉACHT.

Sight and cats figure prominently also in Irish versions of a story that compares the relative values of truth and falsehood (type 613). According to this, a liar is judged to be more wise than a truthful man, and the liar demands that the other man pay the penalty of defeat by having his eyes knocked out. Later the blind man overhears a nocturnal assembly of wild cats say where a bottle that could restore the sight of an afflicted princess is hidden. He gets the bottle, heals himself, and also heals the princess, for which he is given a large reward. On hearing how he learned the cure, the liar goes to the assembly of the cats to learn valuable information for himself, but is noticed by them and they tear his eyes out.

Type 673 is a far-flung story concerning how a man learns the language of birds by eating the flesh of a white serpent that another person was cooking. This story does not occur in Ireland in its standard form, but a much altered ecotype (*see* FOLKTALE) is told concerning Fionn. This ecotype has been current since before the twelfth century, but its relationship to the international pattern is an extremely complex problem (*see* FIONN MAC CUMAILL *and* Ó DÁLAIGH).

The earliest instance of an occurrence in Irish literature of a catalogued wonder tale involves type 736A, which describes how a ring is thrown into the sea but is recovered from the belly of a fish. This story was very popular in Christian literature, and that no doubt was the context from which it entered the seventh-century biography of St BRIGHID. Probably borrowed from that biography, it occurs again in the eighth-century account of the hero FRAOCH, and it has survived in some Irish folk accounts of JESUS CHRIST and the saints.

Aarne & Thompson (1961), 88–254; S. Ó Súilleabháin & Christiansen (1967), 58–145; S. Ó Súilleabháin (1942), 559–73, 611–22; Christiansen (1959).

List of Genres

Oral Narrative and its Typology

Peoples and Traditions

Religious Lore

Pronunciation of Irish-language Entries

A synopsis of the historical development of Irish is in the entry IRISH LANGUAGE, and the following notes should be read in that context.

In issues of pronunciation, it should in particular be remembered that all Irish consonants are either palatal ('slender') or non-palatal ('broad'). In the phonetic script, the palatal quality of a consonant is shown by the sign ' following it – for example, d' as distinct from the non-palatal d. Lengthening of vowels is represented by : after the letter (for example, ɑ: for written 'á'). The syllables with greatest stress in pronunciation are here indicated by a preceding '.

Aspiration of a consonant is written in Irish by an 'h' following it. Thus the aspirated versions of c and g are written 'ch' and 'gh', and are pronounced respectively as the fricatives x and ɣ. Aspirated p is written 'ph' and pronounced f, while aspirated 'b' is written 'bh' and pronounced v or w – in each case with bi-labial more than labio-dental quality. Aspirated m, written 'mh', is also pronounced bi-labial w or v; aspirated s, written 'sh', is pronounced h; while aspirated f is written 'fh' and is mute. Since medieval times, 'dh' (originally a ð sound) is pronounced the same as 'gh'; and 'th' (originally a θ sound) is pronounced as h. In non-initial position, aspirated consonants may be muted or otherwise vary from dialect to dialect. The written combinations 'mb', 'gc', 'nd', 'bhf', 'bp', 'ts' and 'dt' are pronounced respectively as m, g, n, v, b, t, d. The combination 'ng' is the nasal velar, represented here as ŋ. It should be noted that all the foregoing consonants and their mutations, as well as combinations of them, are always of either palatal or non-palatal quality, and are thus indicated in the lists below.

Short broad vowels in unstressed position tend to lose their quality in Modern Irish and are thus pronounced ə. Short slender vowels in such position occasionally keep something of their quality.

The dialects of Modern Irish have been diverging from each other since the medieval period at least, and this has left a good deal of dialectal variety in pronunciation. For instance, northern dialects best preserve the old vowel qualities, whereas vowels followed by liquids and nasals are often lengthened or diphthongised in the rest of the country. The written combination 'ao' shows particular variety – in the north it is usually pronounced as a back unrounded and lengthened 'u' sound, represented here by ʊ:; while in the west and centre it is pronounced i: and in the south e: is the usual form. The combination 'aoi' is pronounced i: throughout the country. The most notable consonantal variation is instanced by the combination 'cn', which is pronounced kn now only in the south, but as kr in the rest of the country. Perhaps the greatest difference in Irish dialects relates to stressed and unstressed syllables, which seems also to have developed for the most part since medieval times (see IRISH LANGUAGE).

Minute aspects of pronunciation are not represented in detail here. For instance, in Old Irish the double consonants 'll' and 'nn' had extra-strong pronunciation (ʟ and ɴ), whether palatal or non-palatal, but modern dialects vary in their selection of these; palatal ɴ survives most strongly in the north, whereas non-palatal ʟ is often substituted for simple l in the south. In the extreme south palatal 'nn' is pronounced as a nasal velar ŋ'. Variety is found also in palatal 't' and 'd' – these are pronounced simply in the south, but there is some influence on them in the north from s' and in the west from s (approaching respectively t's'/ d's' and t's/ d's, while in the southeast they are sometimes affected by a slight glide (approaching t'ɣ'/ d'ɣ').

The pronunciations here given are generally intended to reflect the post-medieval dialects in the areas to which the characters and subjects belonged, and only in especially relevant cases are the Old Irish pronunciations cited.

The following subjects would be known to a greater or less extent to living tradition today, whether in folklore, in local tradition or in popular books.

Abán ['aba:n / a'ba:n]; Adhamhnán ['euna:n]; Ailbhe ['al'v'e]; Áine ['a:n'e]; Amhairghin Glúngheal ['awərɣ'in' 'glu:nɣ'al]; Aoibheall ['i:v'əl]; Aonghus [earlier, 'aenɣus / later, 'e:ni:s / e:'ni:s].

Badhbh [baiv / bou]; Balar ['balər]; Banshee [i.e. *bean sí* – b'an 's'i:]; Barra ['barə]; Bréanainn ['b'r'e:nən']; Brian Bóramha [b'r'iən bo:'ru:]; Brighid (saint) [earlier, 'b'r'iɣ'id' / later, b'r'i:d'].

Cailleach Bhéarra [kaL'əx 'w'eərə (north and centre) / kə'l'ax 'v'iarə (south)]; Caillín ['kaL'in']; Cainneach ['kaN'əx]; Caoilte ['ki:l't'e]; Caoimhghin [earlier, 'ki:v'ɣ'in' / later, 'ki:v'i:n' / ki:'v'i:n']; Céadach ['k'eədəx]; Ceallach ['k'aləx]; Seathrún Céitinn [s'ahəru:n 'k'e:t'iɲ']; Ciarán the Older [sean-Chiarán / Ciarán Saighire – 's'anx'iəra:n / k'iəra:n 'sair'e]; Ciarán Chluana [k'iəra:n 'xluənə]; Clíona ['k'l'iənə]; Cod [kod]; Colm Cille [koləm 'k'iL'e] Conall Cearnach [konəl 'k'a:rnəx]; Conall Gulban [konəl 'goləbən]; Conán Maol [kona:n 'mu:l (north) / kona:n 'mi:l (centre) / kona:n 'me:l (south)]; Conchobhar mac Neasa ['konxowər mak 'n'esə / later, krəhu:r mak 'n'asə]; Cormac mac Airt ['kormək mak 'ar't']; Cormac mac Cuileannáin ['kormək mak kil'ə'na:n']; Crom [krom / kroum]; Cú Chulainn [ku: 'huləN' (north) / ku: 'xolən' (centre and south)]; Cú Roí [ku: 'ri:].

Dallán Forgaill [dala:n 'forgiL']; Dalua [də'luə]; Déaglán [d'iag'la:n]; Deirdre ['d'e:r'd'r'e]; Gerald Earl of Desmond [in Irish, Gearóid Iarla Deasmhumhan – g'a'ro:d' 'iərlə d'a'su:n]; Diarmaid ua Duibhne ['d'iərmid' o: 'div'n'e /

'd'iərmid' o: 'di:n'e (in south)]; Donn [doN / later, don or doun]; Donn Cuailnge [doN 'kuəl'N'e / later, don 'kuəL'e].

Éinne ['e:N'e]; Elizabeth [in Irish, Éilís – 'e:l'i:s' / ei'l'i:s' (in south)].

Fear Diadh [f'ar 'd'iə]; Feardhomhain [f'a'roun']; Fearghus mac Róich [earlier, 'f'erɣus mak 'ro:ex' / later, f'ari:s mak 'ro:i]; Féichín ['f'e:x'i:n'] Piaras Feiritéar [p'iərəs f'er'i't'eər]; Fianna Cycle ['f'iənə]; Finnbheara [f'in''varə]; Fíonán Cam [fi:na:n 'kaum]; Fionn mac Cumhaill [f'iN (north) / f'on (centre) / f'u:n and f'eun (south) – ma 'ku:l']; Fionnchú ['f'unxu:]; Fionntan ['f'ontən]; FitzGerald [in Irish, Mac Gearailt – ma 'g'arəl't']; Flannán [fla'na:n]; Fliodhais [f'l'ihis' / f'l'i:s']; Fomhóire ['fowo:r'e / fo'vo:r'e (earlier, 'fowor'e; *see* the entry)].

Garlach Coileánach [ga:rləx ki'l'a:nəx]; Glas Ghoibhneann [glas 'ɣiv'n'ən (north and centre) / glas 'ɣoin'ən (south)]; Gobán Saor [goban 'su:r (north) / goba:n 'si:r (centre) / go'ba:n 'se:r (south)]; Gobnait ['gobnit']; Goll mac Morna [goL mak 'mo:rnə]; Guaire ['guər'e].

Íde ['i:d'e].

James [in Irish, Séamas – 's'eəməs]; Jesus Christ [in Irish, Íosa Críost – i:sə 'k'r'i:st].

Gerald Earl of Kildare [in Irish, Gearóid Iarla Chill Dara – 'g'aro:d' 'iərlə x'il' 'darə].

Labhraidh ['louri]; Laoghaire ['le:r'e / 'li:r'e]; Leprechaun [i.e. leipreachán – 'l'ep'r'əxa:n]; Lir [l'ir']; Lugh [earlier, luɣ / later, lu:]; Lughaidh mac Con [lu:i ma 'kon].

Alasdair Mac Dhomhnaill ['aləstər' ma 'ko:nəL]; Baothlach Mac Fhlannchaidh ['behələx ma 'klanəxi]; Cathal Buí

Mac Giolla Ghunna [kɑhəl 'bi: mɑ g'ilə 'ɣonə]; Maolmhuire Mac Suibhne [mi:l'r'e mak 'siv'n'e]; Macha [maxə]; Manannán ['manəna:n / manə'na:n]; Maodhóg ['me:og / me:'og and 'mo:g (in south)]; Meadhbh [m'e:v]; Mis [m'is']; Mochaoi [mə'xi:]; Mochuda [mə 'xodə]; Moling [mə'l'iŋ' / mə'l'in' / mə 'l'aiŋ']; Molua [mə'luə]; Moninne [mə'n'iN'e]; Mór Mumhan [mo:r 'mu:n]; Murchadh mac Briain ['morəxə mak 'b'r'iən'].

Naithí ['nah'i]; Gráinne Mhaol Ní Mháille [gra:N'e 'wi:l n'i:'wa:L'e]; Máire Rua Ní Mhathúna [ma:r'e 'ruə n'i: wa'hu:nə]; Niall ('Niall Naoi-Ghiallach') – [n'iəl ni:'ɣ'iələx].

Dónall na Cásca Ó Caoimh [do:nəl nə 'ka:skə o: 'ki:v']; Cathal Crobhdhearg Ó Conchúir [kahəl 'krovɣ'arəg o: 'krohu:r']; Cearbhall Ó Dálaigh [k'a'ru:l o: 'da:lə]; Aodh Balldearg Ó Dónaill [i: 'bald'arəg o: 'do:nəl]; Mánas Ó Dónaill ['ma:nəs o: 'do:nəl]; Dónall na nGeimhleach Ó Donnchú ['do:nəl nə 'ŋ'i:l'əx o: donə'xu:]; Réamonn Ó hAnluain ['re:mən o: 'hanluən']; Éamonn an Chnoic Ó Maoilriain [iamən ə 'xnik' o: mə'r'iən']; Eoghan Rua Ó Néill [o:n 'ruə o: 'n'e:l']; Giolla Íosa Ó Raghallaigh [g'il 'i:sə o:'raili]; Aogán Ó Rathaille [e:'ga:n o: 'rahəl'ə]; Eoghan Rua Ó Súilleabháin [o:n 'ruə o: 'su:l'əva:n']; Dónall Cam Ó Súilleabháin Béarra [do:nəl 'kaum o: 'su:l'əva:n' 'b'iarə]; Daniel O'Connell [in Irish, Dónall Ó Conaill – 'do:nəl o: 'konəl']; ogham [earlier, oɣəm / later, o:m]; Oisín ['os'i:n (north and centre) / i's'i:n (south)]; Oscar ['oskər].

Parthalán ['parhəla:n].

Ruadhán [earlier, 'ruəða:n / later, ruən and ru'a:n].

Patrick Sarsfield [in Irish, Pádraig Sáirséal – pa:drig' 'sa:r's'e:l]; Seanán [s'ana:n]; Seanchán ['s'anəxa:n/ s'anə'xa:n]; Suibhne [siv'n'e].

Tuatha Dé Danann ['tuəhə d'e: 'danən]; Turgesius [in Irish, Tuirgéis – tir"g'e:s'].

William of Orange [in Irish, Liam Buí – l'iəm 'bi:]

Entries such as old population names and place names which are recognisable today – though the traditions associated with them are not well known – are given here.

Airghialla [earliier, 'ar'ɣ'iəLə / later, 'er'iələ]; Banba ['banəbə]; Bóinn [bo:N']; Connachta ['koNəxtə]; Cruithnigh ['krih'in'i]; Dál gCais [da:l 'gas']; Déise ['d'e:s'e]; Éire ['e:r'e]; Eoghanacht [earlier, 'eoɣənəxt'/ later, 'o:nəxt]; Érainn ['e:rəN]; Fir Bolg [f'ir' 'boləg]; Fódla ['fo:dlə > 'fo:lə]; Gael [geəl (earlier, 'gaiɣ'əl; see the entry)]; Laighin [earlier, laɣ'in' / later, lain']; Osraighe [earlier, 'osriɣ'e]; / later, os'ri:]; Sionainn ['s'onəN']; Uí Mhaine [i: 'wan'e]; Uí Néill [i: 'n'e:L']; Ulaidh ['oli].

The following subjects would be known only to students of traditional Irish history and literature. The reader may reconstruct the Old and Middle Irish pronunciation of these from the orthographic system, giving the consonants something of their ancient qualities – for example, the genitive form 'ildathaigh' would until medieval times have had the clear vowels and the clearly aspirated consonants viz. 'ildaθaɣ'. So also the name Eochaidh would have been pronounced long ago 'eoxað', but now is 'oxi (in the south 'oxə). Similarly, the name Aodh (earlier, Aedh) was anciently pronounced aeð, whereas in modern pronunciation it is usually ʊ: in the north; i: in the centre; and e: in the south. Here we give acceptable modern pronunciations, with some further detail.

Ábhartach mac Ildathaigh ['a:wərtəx mak il"dahi]; Ailill ['al'iL']; Ailill Molt ['al'iL' 'molt]; Ailill Ólom ['al'iL' 'o:lom]; Aithirne ['ah'ir'n'e]; Amhairghin mac Éigit Salaigh

515

['awəry'in' mak 'eːg'it' 'sali]; Aodh Allán [eː 'aʟaːn]; Aodh Eangach [eː 'aŋəx]; Aodh Ruadh Ró-Fheasa [eː 'ruə roː 'asə]; Aodh Sláine [eː slaːn'e]; Art [art].

Baile mac Buain ['bal'e mak 'buən']; Beag mac Dé [b'eg mak 'd'eː]; Bearach ['b'arəx], Bearchán ['b'arəxaːn]; Bodhbh Dearg [bouv / bou 'd'arəg]; *bóraimhe* ['boːrəv'e]; Bran mac Feabhail [bran mak 'f'awil']; Brandubh ['branduv]; Breas [b'r'as]; Breasal Bó-Dhíobhadh ['b'r'asəl 'boːɣ'iːvə]; Bricriu ['b'r'ik'r'u]; Brighid (goddess) ['b'r'iɣ'id'].

Cairbre Catcheann ['kar'b'ir'e 'katx'eun]; Cairbre Lifeachair ['kar'b'ir'e 'l'if'əxər']; Cairbre mac Éadaoine ['kar'b'ir'e mak 'eːdiːn'e]; Cano mac Gartnáin ['kanə ma 'gartnaːn']; Cathal mac Fionghuine ['kahəl mak f'i'niːn'e]; Cathaoir Mór [kahiːr' 'moːr]; Cathbhadh [kafə]; Cealtchar ['k'altxər]; Ceasair ['k'asər]; Ceat mac Mághach [k'at mak 'maːx]; Ceithearn mac Fionntain ['k'eh'ərn mak 'f'ontən']; Ceithearnach Caoilriabhach ['k'eh'ərnəx 'kiːl'riəwəx]; Cian mac Maolmhuaidhe [k'iən mak meːl'wui]; Cnú Dearóil [kru: 'd'aroːl' (north and centre) / knu: d'ə'roːl' (south)]; Cobhthach Caol [kofəx 'keːl]; Colla ['kolə]; Comhdhán [earlier, 'kovðaːn / later, kuən]; Comhghall [earlier, 'kovɣaʟ/ later, kuəl]; Conaire ['konər'e]; Conaire mac Mogha Lámha ['konər'e mak mou 'laːwə]; Conall Clogach ['konəl 'klogəx]; Conall Corc [konəl 'kork]; Conghal Cláiringneach ['koniːl 'klaːr'iŋ'in'əx]; Conlae ['konlə]; Conn Céadchathach [koN / koun k'eːd'xahəx]; Corc Duibhne [kork 'div'n'e / later, kork 'diːn'e]; Cormac Conn Loingeas ['kormək koN 'liŋ'əs]; Cormac mac Cuileannáin ['kormək mak kil'ə'naːn']; Craiftine [kraf't'ine]; Cridhinbhéal ['k'r'i:n'v'eːl]; Criomhthann Nia Náir ['k'r'ifən n'iə 'naːr']; Cumaine Fada ['kumən'e 'fadə / later, 'Cuimín Fada' – 'kim'iːn' 'fadə];

Cúscraidh Meann Macha ['kuːscri: m'aN 'maxə].

Daghdha [earlier, 'dayðа / later, 'daiə or dai]; Dearg ['d'arəg]; Danu [earlier, 'danu / later, 'danən' (*see* the entry)]; Dian Céacht [d'iən 'k'eːxt]; Diarmaid mac Aodha Sláine ['d'iərmid' ma keː 'slaːn'e]; Diarmaid mac Cearrbheoil ['d'iərmid' ma 'k'aːrv'oːl']; Domhnall mac Aodha ['doːnəl ma 'keː]; Dubhthach Daol Uladh ['dufəx diːl 'olə].

Éadaoin ['eːdiːn']; Éibhear ['eːv'ər]; Éireamhóin ['eːr'əvoːn']; Eithne ['eh'in'e]; Eochaidh [earlier, 'eoxəð / later, 'oxi]; Eochaidh Aireamh [oxi 'ar'əw]; Eochaidh Éigeas [oxi 'eːg'əs]; Eochaidh Feidhleach [oxi 'f'eil'əx]; Eochaidh mac Maireadha ['oxi mak 'mar'iː]; Eoghan Béal [oːn 'b'eəl]; Eoghan Mór [earlier, eoɣən 'moːr / later, oːn 'moːr].

Fearghal mac Maoldúin ['f'ariːl mak meːl'duːn']; Fearghus mac Léide ['f'ariːs mak 'l'eːd'e]; Feidhlimidh mac Criomhthainn ['f'eil'im'e ma 'k'r'ifən']; Féine ['f'eːn'e]; Feircheirdne [f'er''x'eːr'd'n'e]; Fiachna mac Baodáin ['f'iəxnə mak 'buːdaːn']; Fiachu Fear Mara ['f'iəxə f'ar 'marə]; Fiachu Muilleathan ['f'iəxə mi'l'ahən]; Finn Eamhna [f'iN' 'eunə]; Fionn [f'ind > f'iN]; Fionn File [f'in 'f'il'e]; Fionnachta ['f'onəxtə]; Fíothal ['f'iːhəl]; Flann mac Lónáin [flaN / flaun mak 'loːnaːn']; Fothadh Canainne [fohə 'kanən'e]; Fraoch [fruːx (north) / friːx (centre) / freːx (south)].

geis [g'es']; Goibhniu ['giv'n'u].

Laoghaire Buach [leːr'e 'buəx]; Liadhain [l'iən']; Lughaidh Lágha [lui 'laː]; Lughaidh Lámhdhearg [lui 'laːw ɣ'arəg]; Lughaidh mac Con [lui ma 'kon]; Lughaidh Riabhdhearg [lui 'riəv ɣ'arəg].

Mac Conglinne [mak 'kon 'g'l'iN'e]; Mac Lughach [mak 'luːx]; Mac na

Míchomhairle ['mɑk nə m'i:'xo:r'l'e];
Mac Rustaing [mɑk 'rustəŋ']; Maine
[man'e]; Maol Dúin [me:l 'du:n']; Maol
Fhothartaigh [me:l 'ohərti];
Maolodhrán [me: lou'rɑ:n]; Midhir
[early, 'm'iɣ'ir' / later, 'm'i:r'] Míl
[m'i:l']; Mogh Ruith [mou 'rih'];
Mongán ['moŋɑ:n]; Mongfhionn
['moŋin]; Morann ['morən]; Mór-
Ríoghain [earlier, 'mo:riɣən' / later,
mo:'ri:n]; Muircheartach mac Earca
['mir'x'ərtəx mɑk 'arkə].

Neara ['n'ɑrə]; Néidhe mac Adhna
[earlier, 'n'e:ð'e mɑ 'kɑðnə / later, 'n'e:
mɑ 'kainə]; Neimheadh [earlier,
'n'ew'əð / later, 'n'ew'e or 'n'ev'e]; Nét
[n'e:d]; Niadh Seaghamhain [n'iə
's'eiwən' / niə 's'ɑ:wən']; Niall Frasach
[n'iəL 'frasəx]; Niall Glúndubh [n'iəL
'glu:nduv]; Noíne [ni:n'e]; Nuadhu
[earlier, nuəðə / later, nuə].

Oghma [o:mə]; Ollamh Fódla [olə w
'fo:lə].

Raghallach [earlier, 'raɣəLəx / later,
'railəx]; Rumhann mac Colmáin
['ruwən mɑ 'koləmɑ:n'].

Suibhne Meann [siv'n'e 'm'ɑN].

Tadhg mac Céin [taig mɑ 'k'e:n'];
Tighearnmhas ['t'iərnwəs]; Tomás Mór
[tə'mɑ:s 'muər]; Tuán mac Cairill
['tuɑ:n mɑ 'kar'il']; Tuathal Teachtmhar
['tuəhəl 't'axtwər].

Ughaine ['uɣən'e / later, u:n'e]; Urard
mac Coise ['urɑrd mɑ 'kos'e].

517

Bibliography

Abbreviations

ACL   *Archiv für celtische Lexikographie*, 1–3 (Halle, 1898–1907)

AIM   *Anecdota from Irish Manuscripts*, 1–5 (Halle, 1907–13)

CLAJ   *County Louth Archaeological Journal* (Dundalk, 1904–)

CMCS   *Cambridge/Cambrian Medieval Celtic Studies* (Cambridge, 1981–)

CR   Manuscript Collection at Coláiste na Rinne (Ring College), County Waterford

JCHAS   *Journal of the Cork Historical and Archaeological Society* (Cork, 1892–)

JCS   *Journal of Celtic Studies*, 1–2 (Santa Barbara, 1950–53)

JGAHS   *Journal of the Galway Archaeological and Historical Society* (Dublin, 1900–)

JKAS   *Journal of the Kildare Archaeological Society* (Dublin, 1895–1938)

JRSAI   *Journal of the Royal Society of Antiquaries of Ireland* (originally *Journal of the Kilkenny Archaeological Society*) (Dublin, 1849-)

JWAS   *Journal of the Waterford and South-East of Ireland Archaeological Society*, 1–19 (Waterford, 1894–1920)

IFC   Irish Folklore Collection, Delargy Centre, University College, Dublin

OSL   Ordnance Survey Letters, Coimisiún na Logainmneacha (Placenames Commission), Dublin

PBS   *Proceedings of the Belfast Natural History and Philosophical Society* (second series: Belfast, 1935–77)

PHCC   *Proceedings of the Harvard Celtic Colloquium* (Harvard, 1981–)

PICCS   *Proceedings of the International Congress of Celtic Studies*, 1, 2, 6 (Dublin, 1959; Cardiff, 1966; Dublin, 1983)

PMLA   *Publications of the Modern Language Association of America* (Wisconsin, 1884–)

PRIA   *Proceedings of the Royal Irish Academy* (Dublin, 1826–)

RC   *Revue Celtique*, 1–55 (Paris, 1870–1934)

RIA   Gaelic Manuscript Collection, Royal Irish Academy, Dublin

ZCP   *Zeitschrift für celtische Philologie* (Halle, 1896–)

Periodicals

ACL: Archiv für celtische Lexikographie, vols. 1–3 (Halle, 1898–1907)

AIM: Anecdota from Irish Manuscripts, vols. 1–5 (Halle, 1907–13)

An Claidheamh Soluis (Dublin, 1899–1932)

An Gaodhal, vols. 1–23 (New York, 1884–1904)

An Lóchrann (Dublin, 1907–31)

An Síoladóir, vols. 1–9 (Dublin, 1920–22)

An Stoc (Dublin, 1923–30)

Analecta Bollandiana (Brussels/Paris, 1882–)

Anecdota Oxoniensia, vols. 1–15 (Mediaeval & Modern Series: Oxford, 1882–1929)

Ar Aghaidh (Galway, 1931–70)

Archivium Hibernicum (Maynooth, 1912–)

Arv (Stockholm, 1945–)

Atlantis, vols. 1–5 (Dublin, 1858–70)

Béaloideas (Dublin, 1927–)

Bentley's Miscellany, vols. 1–64 (London, 1837–68)

Biatas, vols. 1–47 (Dublin, 1946–93)

Celtic Review, vols. 1–10 (Edinburgh, 1904–10)

Celtica (Dublin, 1946–)

CLAJ: County Louth Archaeological Journal (Dundalk, 1904–)

CMCS: Cambridge/Cambrian Medieval Celtic Studies (Cambridge, 1981–)

Comhar (Dublin, 1938–)

Dinnseanchas (Dublin, 1964–)

Dublin Historical Record (Dublin, 1938–)

Dublin Penny Journal, vols. 1–4 (Dublin, 1832–36)

Dublin University Magazine, vols. 1–75 (Dublin, 1833–70)

Edda (Oslo, 1913–)

Éigse (Dublin, 1939–)

Emania (Belfast, 1987–)

Ériu (Dublin, 1904–)
Études Celtiques (Paris, 1936–)
Feasta (Dublin, 1948–)
Folk-Lore (London, 1890–)
Galvia (Galway, 1954–)
Hermathena (Dublin, 1873–)
Inniu (Dublin, weekly newspaper, now discontinued)
Irische Texte, vols. 1–4 (Leipzig, 1880–1909)
Irish Historical Studies (Oxford, Antrim, Dublin, 1938–)
Irish Independent (Dublin, daily newspaper, 1891–)
Irish Monthly, vols. 1–83 (Dublin, 1873–1954)
Irish Press (Dublin, daily newspaper, 1931–95)
Irish Rosary (Dublin, 1897–)
Irish Texts, vols. 1–5 (London, 1931–34)
Irish University Review (Dublin, 1970–)
Irisleabhar Muighe Nuadhat / Irisleabhar Mhá Nuad (Maynooth, 1907–)
Irisleabhar na Gaedhilge: The Gaelic Journal, vols. 1–19 (Dublin, 1882–1909)
JCHAS: Journal of the Cork Historical and Archaeological Society (Cork, 1892–)
JGAHS: Journal of the Galway Archaeological and Historical Society (Dublin, 1900–)
JKAS: Journal of the Kildare Archaeological Society (Dublin, 1895–1938)
Journal of American Folklore (New York, 1888)
JCS: Journal of Celtic Studies, vols. 1–2 (Santa Barbara, 1950–53)
JRSAI: Journal of the Royal Society of Antiquaries of Ireland [originally *Journal of the Kilkenny Archaeological Society*] (Dublin, 1849–)
JWAS: Journal of the Waterford and South-East of Ireland Archaeological Society, vols. 1–19 (Waterford, 1894–1920)
Léachtaí Cholm Cille (Maynooth, 1970–)
Lia Fáil, vols. 1–3 (Dublin, 1928–30)
Lochlann (Oslo, 1958–)
Modern Language Review (Cambridge, 1906–)
Modern Philology (Chicago, 1903–)
New Ireland Review, vols. 1–32 (Dublin, 1894–1910)
Ogam (Rennes, 1948–)
Old Kilkenny Review, vols. 1–25 (first series: Kilkenny, 1946–73)
Otia Merseiana, vols. 1–4 (Liverpool, 1899–1904)
Patrologiae Latinae, vols. 1–221 (Paris, 1844–64)
PBS: Proceedings of the Belfast Natural History and Philosophical Society (second Series: Belfast, 1935–77)

Peritia: Journal of the Medieval Academy of Ireland (Paris, 1982)
PHCC: Proceedings of the Harvard Celtic Colloquium (Harvard, 1981–)
PICCS: Proceedings of the International Congress of Celtic Studies, vols. 1, 2, 6 (Dublin, 1959; Cardiff, 1966; Dublin, 1983)
PRIA: Proceedings of the Royal Irish Academy (Dublin, 1826–)
Proceedngs of the British Academy (London, 1903–)
PMLA: Publications of the Modern Language Association of America (Wisconsin, 1884–)
RC: Revue Celtique, vols. 1–55 (Paris, 1870–1934)
Revue des Traditions Populaires (Paris, 1885–)
Saga och Sed (Uppsala, 1932–)
Scottish Gaelic Studies (Edinburgh, 1926–)
Scottish Studies (Edinburgh, 1957–)
Sinsear (Dublin, 1979–)
Speculum (Cambridge, Massachusetts, 1926–)
Studia Celtica (Cardiff, 1966–)
Studia Hibernica (Dublin, 1961–)
Studies (Dublin, 1912–)
Shamrock, The, vols. 1–34 (Dublin, 1867–96)
Ulster Journal of Archaeology (third ser., Belfast, 1938–)
Ulster Folklife (Belfast, 1955–)
Veröffentlichungen der keltischen Kommission (Vienna, 1981–)
Vexilla Regis (Dublin, 1951–66)
ZCP: Zeitschrift für celtische Philologie (Halle, 1896–)

Manuscript Collections

IFC: Irish Folklore Collection MSS, Department of Irish Folklore, University College, Dublin

OSL: Ordnance Survey Letters, Coimisiún na Logainmneacha (Placenames Commission), Dublin

RIA: Gaelic MSS Collection, Royal Irish Academy, Dublin

CR: MSS Collection at Coláiste na Rinne (Ring College), Co. Waterford

Books

Note: Where an author has two publications for the same year, an abbreviation for the title is contained within square parentheses; the abbreviated form is used for references following the entries in the main body of the text; for example:

Ó Caithnia, Liam P., *Scéal na hIománá* (Dublin, 1980)
— *Apalóga na bhFilí* (Dublin, 1984)
— *Báirí Cos in Éirinn* [BCÉ] (Dublin, 1984)

Aarne, Antti, Thompson, Stith, *The Types of the Folktale* (Helsinki, 1961)

Almqvist, Bo, *Crossing the Border: a Sampler of Irish Migratory Legends about the Supernatural* (Dublin, 1988)
— *Viking Ale* (Aberystwyth, 1991)

Almqvist, Bo, Ó Catháin, Séamas and Ó Héalaí, Pádraig (eds.), *The Heroic Process* (Dublin, 1987)

Anderson, Alan O and Anderson, Marjorie O., *Adomnan's Life of Columba* (Edinburgh, 1961)

Andrews, Elizabeth, *Ulster Folklore* (London, 1913)

Anonymous, *History of the Seven Wise Masters and Mistresses of Rome* (chapbook, n.d.)

Arbois de Jubainville, H. d', *The Irish Mythological Cycle*, trans. Richard I. Best (Dublin, 1903)

Ashdown, Margaret, *English and Norse Documents* (Cambridge, 1930)

Atkinson, Robert, *The Passions and Homilies from Leabhar Breac* (Dublin, 1887)

Bagwell, Richard, *Ireland Under the Stuarts* (London, 1909–16), vols. 1–3

Baring-Gould, S., *Curious Myths of the Middle Ages* (London, 1872)

Barrington, Jonah, *Personal Sketches of His Own Times* (London, 1830), vol. 2

Barry, Michael, *An Affair of Honour* (Fermoy, 1981)

Baumgarten, Rolf, *Bibliography of Irish Linguistics and Literature: 1942–1971* (Dublin, 1986)

Bédier, Joseph, *Les Légendes Épiques* (Paris, 1926–29), vols. 1–4

Bekker-Nielsen, Hans (ed.), *Oral Tradition: A Symposium* (Odense, 1977)

Bell, Sam Hanna, *Erin's Orange Lily* (London, 1956)

Bennett, Gillian, Smith, Paul and Widdowson, J.D.A. (eds.), *Perspectives in Contemporary Legend*, vol. 2 (Sheffield, 1987)

Bergin, Osborn, *Irish Bardic Poetry* (eds. D. Greene and F. Kelly) (Dublin, 1970)

Bergin, Osborn and Marstrander, Carl (eds.), *Miscellaney presented to Kuno Meyer* (Halle, 1912)

Bernard, J.H. and Atkinson, Robert, *The Irish Liber Hymnorum* (London, 1898), vols. 1–2

Best, Richard I., *Bibliography of Irish Philology and of Printed Irish Literature* (Dublin, 1913)
— *Bibliography of Irish Philology and Manuscript Literature Publications: 1913–1941* (Dublin, 1942)

Best, Richard I. and Lawlor, H.J., *The Martyrology of Tallaght* (London, 1931)

Best, Richard I. and Bergin, Osborn, *Lebor na hUidre* (Dublin, 1929)

Best, Richard I., Bergin, Osborn and O'Brien, Michael A., *The Book of Leinster* (Dublin, 1954), vol. 1

Best, Richard I. and Lawlor, H.J. *The Martyrology of Tallaght* (London, 1931)

Best, Richard I. and O'Brien, Michael A., *The Book of Leinster* (Dublin, 1956–57), vols. 2–3

Bieler, Ludwig, *The Life and Legend of St. Patrick* (Dublin, 1949)
— *Four Latin Lives of St. Patrick* (Dublin, 1971)
— *The Patrician Texts in the Book of Armagh* (Dublin, 1979)

Binchy, Daniel A., *Scéla Cano Meic Gartnáin* (Dublin, 1963)
— *Celtic and Anglo-Saxon Kingship* (Oxford, 1970)
— *Corpus Iuris Hibernici* (Dublin, 1978), vols. 1–6

Bleeker, C. Juoco and Widengren, Geo, *Historia Religionum, I* (Leiden, 1969)

Bliss, Alan, *The English Language in Ireland* (Dublin, 1976)
— *English Spoken in Ireland* (Dublin, 1979)

Bollandus, Johannes and Henschenius, Godefridus, *Acta Sanctorum* (Paris, 1863)

Bonanno, Giuseppe (ed.), *Casa Italia* (Rome, 2000)

Boswell, Charles S., *An Irish Precursor of Dante* (London, 1908)

Brandt, Eunice Graham, *Memoirs of the Staker Wallace* (Chicago, 1909)

Breathnach, Breandán, *Folkmusic and Dances of Ireland* (Dublin, 1971)

Breathnach, Caoimhín, *Patronage, Politics and Prose* (Maynooth, 1996)

Breathnach, Deasún, *Chugat an Púca* (Dublin, 1993)

Brewer, E. Cobham, *A Dictionary of Miracles* (London, 1901)

Brewer, J.S. and Bullen, William, *Calendar of the Carew Manuscripts* (London, 1871), vol. 5

Briggs, Katharine A., *A Dictionary of Fairies* (Middlesex, 1977)

— *The Vanishing People* (London, 1978)

Bromwich, Rachel, *Trioedd Ynys Prydain* (Cardiff, 1961)

Brown, Arthur C.L., *The Origin of the Grail Legend* (Cambridge, 1943)

Brown, Arthur and Foote, Peter (eds.), *Early English and Norse Studies* (London, 1963)

Bruen, Máire Comer and Ó hÓgáin, Dáithí, *An Mangaire Súgach* (Dublin, 1996)

Bruford, Alan, *Gaelic Folk-Tales and Medieval Romances* (Dublin, 1969)

Brunner, Karl, *The Seven Sages of Rome* (London, 1933)

Brunvand, Jan H., *The Vanishing Hitchhiker* (London, 1981)

Bryan, Donough, *The Great Earl of Kildare* (Dublin, 1933)

Burke, Bernard, *The General Armor* (London, 1884)

Byrne, Francis J., *Irish Kings and High Kings* (London, 1973)

Byrne, Matthew J., *Ireland under Elizabeth* (Dublin, 1903)

Byrne, Patrick, *Irish Ghost Stories* (Dublin, n.d.)

Calder, George, *Auraceipt na n-Éces* (Edinburgh, 1917)

Callanan, Frank, *T.M. Healy* (Cork, 1996)

Campbell, John F., *Leabhar na Féinne* (London, 1872)

Campbell, Killis, *The Seven Sages of Rome* (London, 1907)

Campion, Edmund, *History of Ireland* (London, 1633)

Carlen, Louis and Steinegger, Fritz, *Festschrift Nikolaus Grass* (Innsbruck, 1974), vols. 1–2

Carney, James, *Poems on the Butlers* (Dublin 1945)

— *Studies in Irish Literature and History* (Dublin, 1955)

— *A Genealogical History of the O'Reillys* (Cavan, 1959)

— *The Poems of Bláthmhac son of Cú Brettan* (Dublin, 1964)

— *The Irish Bardic Poet* (Dublin, 1967)

— *The Problem of Saint Patrick* (Dublin, 1973); see Ó Ceithearnaigh, Séamus

Carrigan, William, *The History and Antiquities of the Diocese of Ossory* (Dublin, 1905), vols. 1–4

Chambers, Anne, *Granuaile* (Dublin, 1979)

Chatterton, Lady, *Rambles in the South of Ireland* (London, 1839), vols. 1–2

Christiansen, Reidar Th, *The Vikings and the Viking Wars in Irish and Gaelic Tradition* (Oslo, 1931)

— *The Migratory Legends* (Helsinki, 1958)

— *Studies in Irish and Scandinavian Folktales* (Copenhagen, 1959)

Ciarán, Sr, *Leabhar Ghobnatan* (Dublin, n.d.)

Clarke, Basil, *Life of Merlin* (Cardiff, 1972)

Clanricarde, Marquis of, *Memoirs* (London, 1722), preface by Thomas O'Sullevane

Comyn, David, *Forus Feasa ar Éirinn* (London, 1902), vol. 1

Connelan, Owen, *Imtheacht na Tromdháimhe* (Dublin, 1860)

Corkery, Daniel, *The Hidden Ireland* (Dublin, 1967)

Cosgrave, John, *Lives and Actions of the most notorious Irish Highwaymen, Tories and Raparees* (Belfast, 1776; ninth edn.)

Couchoud, P.-L., *Congrés d'histoire du Christianisme* (Paris, 1928)

Cox, Michael F., *Notes on the History of the Irish Horse* (Dublin, 1897)

Cramer, Thomas, *Lohengrin* (Munich, 1971)

Croker, Thomas C., *Fairy Legends and Traditions of the South of Ireland* (London, 1826–28), vols. 1–2

— *Legends of the Lakes* (London, 1829), vols. 1–2

— *The Historical Songs of Ireland* (London, 1841)

Cross, Tom Peete, *Motif-Index of Early Irish Literature* (Bloomington, 1952)

Cullen, Luke, *'98 in Wicklow* (ed. Myles V. Ronan) (Wexford, 1938)

Cunningham, Bernadette, *The World of Geoffrey Keating* (Dublin, 2000)

Curtayne, Alice, *Patrick Sarsfield* (Dublin, 1934)

Curtin, Jeremiah, *Hero-Tales of Ireland* (London, 1894)

— *Tales of the Fairies and of the Ghost World* (London, 1895)

Curtis, Edmund, *A History of Medieval Ireland* (London, 1923)

— *A History of Ireland* (London 1936)

Danaher, Kevin, *Gentle Places and Simple Things* (Cork, 1964)

— *Irish Country People* (Cork, 1966)

— *The Year in Ireland* (Dublin, 1972)

— *That's How it Was* (Dublin, 1984); *see* Ó Danachair, Caoimhín

Daunt, W.J. O'Neill, *Personal Recollections of the late Daniel O'Connell* (London, 1848), vols. 1–2

de hÍde, Dubhglas, *Abhráin Ghrádha Chúige Connacht* (Dublin, 1909)

— *An Sgéaluidhe Gaedhealach* (Dublin, 1933)

— *Abhráin agus Dánta an Reachtabhraigh* [AR] (Dublin, 1933); *see* Hyde, Douglas

de Bhaldraithe, Tomás, *English–Irish Dictionary* (Dublin, 1959)

de Lacy-Bellingarri, *The Roll of the House of Lacy* (Baltimore, 1928)

de Paor, Liam, *St Patrick's World* (Dublin, 1993)

de Paor, Máire, *Saint Moling Luachra* (Dublin, 2001)

Dégh, Linda, Glassie, Henry and Oinas, F.J. (eds.), *Folklore Today* (Bloomington, 1976)

Delargy, J.H., *The Gaelic Storyteller* (Chicago, 1969) (*see Proceedings of the British Academy*, 31, 1945); *see* Ó Duilearga, Séamus

Delehaye, Hippolyte, *The Legends of the Saints*, trans. V.M. Crawford (London, 1907)

Dickson, Charles, *The Life of Michael Dwyer* (Dublin, 1944)

Dillon, Myles, *The Cycle of the Kings* (London, 1946)

— *Early Irish Literature* (Chicago, 1948)

— *Serglige Con Culainn* (Dublin, 1953)

— *Lebor na Cert* (Dublin, 1962)

— (ed.), *Irish Sagas* (Cork, 1968)

— *The Archaism of Irish Tradition* (Chicago, 1969; reprint from *Proceedings of the British Academy*, 33, 1947)

Dillon, Myles and Chadwick, Nora K., *The Celtic Realms* (London, 1973)

Dinneen, Patrick S., *Foras Feasa ar Éirinn* (London, 1908–14), vols. 2–4

— *An Irish–English Dictionary* (Dublin, 1927); *see* Ua Duinnín, Pádraig

Dinneen, Patrick S. and O'Donoghue, Tadhg, *Dánta Aodhagáin Uí Rathaille* (London, 1911)

Dolan, T.P. and Ó Muirithe, Diarmaid, *Poole's Glossary* (Wexford, 1979)

Dudley Edwards, R. and Williams, T. Desmond, *The Great Famine* (Dublin, 1956)

Dumézil, Georges, *The Destiny of a King* (Chicago, 1973)

Dunford, Stephen, *The Irish Highwaymen* (Dublin, 2000)

Dunne, John J. *Haunted Ireland* (Belfast, 1977)

Duval, Paul-Marie, *La Gaule jusqu'au Milieu du Ve Siècle* (Paris, 1974)

Edsman, Carl-Martin, *Ignis Divinus* (Lund, 1949)

Egan, Patrick M., *The Illustrated Guide to the City and County of Kilkenny* (Kilkenny, 1884)

Ellis Hercules, *The Rhyme Book* (London, 1851)

Ellis, Peter Berresford, *The Boyne Water* (London, 1976)

Enright, Michael J., *Lady with a Mead Cup* (Dublin, 1996)

Evans, E. Estyn, *Irish Heritage* (Dundalk, 1942)

— *Irish Folk Ways* (London, 1957)

Evans, George Ewart, Thomson, David, *The Leaping Hare* (London, 1974)

Evans, J. Gwenogvryn, *The White Book Mabinogion* (Pwllheli, 1907)

FitzGerald, Brian, *The Geraldines* (London, 1951)

Fletcher, Alan, *Drama, Performance, and Polity in Pre-Cromwellian Ireland* (Cork, 2000)

Flood, John and Flood, Phil, *Kilcash* (Dublin, 1999)

Flower, Robin, *Catalogue of Irish Manuscripts in the British Museum* (London, 1926), vol. 2

Freeman, A Martin, *Annála Connacht* (Dublin, 1944)

French, W.H. and Hale, C.B., *English Metrical Romances* (New York, 1964)

Frost, James, *The County of Clare* (Dublin, 1893)

Gailey, Alan, *Irish Folk Drama* (Cork, 1969)

Gailey, Alan and Ó hÓgáin, Dáithí, *Gold Under the Furze* (Dublin, 1985)

Gallwey, Hubert, *The Wall Family in Ireland* (Naas, 1970)

Gardner, Phyllis, *The Irish Wolfhound* (Dundalk, 1931)

Garmonsway, G.N., *The Anglo-Saxon Chronicle* (London, 1972)

Gaughan, J. Anthony, *The Knights of Glin* (Dublin, 1978)

Gautier, Léon, *Bibliographie des Chansons de Geste* (Paris, 1897)

Gilbert, Thomas A., *A Jacobite Narrative of the War in Ireland* (Dublin, 1892)

Goedheer, Albertus J., *Irish and Norse Traditions about the Battle of Clontarf* (Haarlem, 1938)

Graham, George A., *The Irish Wolfhound* (Dursley, 1885)

Gramadach na Gaeilge agus Litriú na Gaeilge: an Caighdeán Oifigiúil (Government Publications: Dublin, 1968)

Gray, Elizabeth A., *Cath Muige Tuired* (Dublin, 1982)

Green, Miranda J., *Dictionary of Celtic Myth and Legend* (London, 1992)

— *Celtic Goddesses* (London, 1995)

Greene, David, *Fingal Rónáin and Other Stories* (Dublin, 1955)

Gregory, Lady A., *The Kiltartan History Book* (London, 1926)

Gruffydd, W.J., *Math Vab Mathonwy* (Cardiff, 1928)

Guyonvarc'h, Christian-J., *Les Druides* (Ouest-France, 1986)

Gwynn, Edward J., *The Metrical Dindshenchas* (Dublin, 1903, 1906, 1913, 1924, 1935), vols. 1–5

Hanmer, Meredith, *Chronicle of Ireland* (London, 1633)

Hansen, R.P.C., *The Life and Writings of the Historical St Patrick* (New York, 1983)

Hardiman, James, *Irish Minstrelsy* (London, 1831), vols. 1–2

Haren, Michael and de Pontfarcy, Yolande (eds.), *The Medieval Pilgrimage to St Patrick's Purgatory* (Enniskillen, 1988)

Harrison, Alan, *An Chrosántacht* (Dublin, 1979)

Harward, Vernon J., *The Dwarfs of Arthurian Romance and Celtic Tradition* (Leiden, 1958)

Haverty, Martin, *The History of Ireland* (Dublin, 1860)

Hayes-McCoy, Gerard A, *Scots Mercenary Forces in Ireland* (Dublin, 1937)

Heist, W.W., *Vitae Sanctorum Hiberniae* (Brussels, 1965)

Henderson, George, *Fled Bricrenn* (London, 1899)

Hennessy, Maurice, *The Wild Geese* (London, 1973)

Hennessy, William M., *The Annals of Loch Cé* (London, 1871), vols. 1–2

— *Mesca Ulad* (Dublin, 1889)

Hennessy, William M. and Kelly, D.H., *The Book of Fenagh* (Dublin, 1875)

Hennessy, William M. and McCarthy, Bartholomew, *Annals of Ulster* (London, 1887–1901), vols. 1–4

Henry, Françoise, *Irish Art in the Early Christian Period* (London, 1940)

Henry, Patrick, *Saoithiúlacht na Sean-Ghaeilge* (Dublin, 1978)

Herity, Michael and Eogan, George, *Ireland in Prehistory* (London, 1978)

Hill, George, *The MacDonnells of Antrim* (Belfast, 1873)

Hogan, Edmund, *Cath Ruis na Rígh for Bóinn* (Dublin, 1892)

— *The Irish Nennius and Homilies and Legends* (Dublin, 1895)

— *The Irish Wolfdog* (Dublin, 1897)

— *Onomasticon Goedelicum* (Dublin, 1910)

Hogan, James J., *The English Language in Ireland* (Dublin, 1927)

Holder, Alfred, *Alt-Celtischer Sprachschatz* (Leipzig, 1896), vols. 1–3

Holinshed, Raphael, *Chronicles* (London, 1586)

Holmer, Nils M., *The Dialects of Co. Clare* (Dublin, 1965), vol. 2

Hopkin, Alannah, *The Living Legend of St Patrick* (London, 1989)

Hughes, Kathleen, *The Church in Early Irish Society* (London, 1966)

Hull, Vernam, *Longes Mac n-Uislenn* (New York, 1949)

Hunt, B., *Folk Tales of Breffny* (London, 1912)

Hyde, Douglas, *A Literary History of Ireland* (London, 1899)

— *Giolla an Fhiugha* [GF] (London, 1899)

— *Saints and Sinners* (London, 1915)

— *Amhráin Chúige Chonnacht* (ed. Ó Conaire, Breandán) (Dublin, 1985); *see* de hÍde, Dubhglas

Jackson, Kenneth H., *Cath Maighe Léna* (Dublin, 1938)

— *Scéalta ón mBlascaod* [SB] (Dublin, 1938)

— *Language and History in Early Britain* (Edinburgh, 1953)

— *The Oldest Irish Tradition* (Cambridge, 1964)

— *Aislinge Meic Con Glinne* (Dublin, 1990)

Jestice, Phyllis G., *Encyclopedia of Irish Spirituality* (Santa Barbara, 2000)

Jónsson, Guðni, *Kununga sögur* (Reykjavík, 1957), vol. 2

Joyce, Patrick W., *A Social History of Ancient Ireland* (London, 1903), vols. 1–3

Joynt, Maud, *Feis Tighe Chonáin* (Dublin, 1936)

— *Tromdámh Guaire* (Dublin, 1941)

Kavanagh, Patrick, *A Popular History of the Insurrection of 1798* (Dublin, 1913)

Kelly, Fergus, *Audacht Morainn* (Dublin, 1976)

— *A Guide to Early Irish Law* (Dublin, 1988)

— *Early Irish Farming* (Dublin, 1997)

Kelly, James, *'That Damn'd Thing Called Honour': Duelling in Ireland* (Cork, 1995)

524

Kelly, Matthew, *Historicae Catholicae Iberniae Compendium* (Dublin, 1850)

Kennedy, Patrick, *Legends of Mount Leinster* (Dublin, 1855)

— *The Fireside Stories of Ireland* (Dublin, 1870)

Kenney, James F., *The Sources for the Early History of Ireland: Ecclesiastical* (New York, 1929)

Kierse, Seán, *Historic Killaloe* (Killaloe, 1983)

Kildare, Marquis of, *The Earls of Kildare and their Ancestors* (Dublin, 1858; second edn., Dublin, 1872)

Kilfeather, T.P., *Ireland, Graveyard of the Spanish Armada* (Dublin,1967)

Knott, Eleanor, *Togail Bruidne Da Derga* (Dublin, 1936)

— *Irish Classical Poetry* (Dublin, 1957)

Koch, John T. and Carey, John, *The Celtic Heroic Age* (Massachusetts, 1997)

Krappe, Alexander H., *Balor with the Evil Eye* (Columbia, 1927)

Kris, Enst and Kurz, Otto, *Legend, Myth and Magic in the Image of the Artist* (New Haven, 1979)

Kurth, Godefroid, *Histoire Poétique des Mérovingiens* (Paris, 1893)

Laoide, Seosamh, *Sgéaluidhe Oirghiall* (Dublin, 1905)

— *Cruach Chonaill* (Dublin, 1913)

— *Alasdair Mac Colla* (Dublin, 1914)

— *Réalta de'n Spéir* (Dublin, 1915)

Larminie, William, *West Irish Folk-tales and Romances* (London, 1893)

Larson, Gerald J. (ed.), *Myth in Indo-European Antiquity* (Berkeley, 1974)

Le Roux, Françoise and Guyonvarc'h, Christian-J., *Les Druides* (Ouest-France, 1986)

Lecouteux, Claude, *Mélusine et le Chevalier au Cygne* (Paris, 1982)

Lehmann, Ruth, *Fled Dúin na nGéd* (Dublin, 1964)

Lenihan, Edmund, *In Search of Biddy Early* (Cork, 1987)

Leslie, John, *Killarney, a Poem* (Dublin, 1772)

Leslie, Shane, *St Patrick's Purgatory* (London, 1932)

Little, A.G., *Liber Exemplorum* (Aberdeen, 1908)

Little, George A., *Malachi Horan Remembers* (Dublin, 1943)

Logan, Pat, *Making the Cure* (Dublin, 1972)

Lomas, S.C., *Report on the Manuscripts of the Earl of Egmont* (Historical Mss. Commission: London, 1905), vol. 1

Loomis Studies; see Medieval Studies in Memory of Gertrude Schoepperle Loomis (Paris, 1927)

Lorne, Marquis of, *Adventures in Legend* (Westminster, 1898)

Lot, Ferdinand; see *Mélanges d'histoire du Moyen Age offerts a Ferdinand Lot* (Paris, 1925)

Lover, Samuel, *Legends and Stories of Ireland* (Dublin, 1834)

Lysaght, Patricia, *The Banshee* (Dublin, 1986)

Lysaght, Patricia, Ó Catháin, Séamas and Ó hÓgáin, Dáithí (eds.), *Islanders and Water-Dwellers* (Dublin, 1999)

Mac Airt, Seán, *The Annals of Innisfallen* (Dublin, 1944)

— *Leabhar Branach* (Dublin, 1951)

Mac Cana, Proinsias, *Celtic Mythology* (London, 1970)

— *The Learned Tales of Medieval Ireland* (Dublin, 1980)

Mac Cionnaith, Láimhbheartach, *Díoghluim Dána* (Dublin, 1938); *see* McKenna, Lambert

Mac Conmara, Máirtín and Ní Thiarnaigh, Éilís (eds.), *Cothú an Dúchais* (Dublin, 1997); *see* MacNamara, Martin

Mac Gill-Fhinnein, Gordon, *Gàidhlig Uidhist a Deas* (Dublin, 1966)

Mac Giolla Chomhaill, Anraí, *Beatha Cholm Cille* (Dublin, 1981)

Mac Giolla Eáin, Eoin, *Dánta, Amhrán is Caointe Sheathrúin Céitinn* (Dublin, 1900); *see* MacErlean, John C.

Mac Giolla Léith, Caoimhín, *Oidheadh Chloinne hUisneach* (London, 1993)

Mac Giollarnáth, Seán, *Loinnir Mac Leabhair agus Scéalta Gaiscidh Eile* (Dublin, 1936)

— *Annála Beaga ó Iorras Aithneach* (Dublin, 1941)

Mac Mathúna, Séamus, *Immram Brain* (Tübingen, 1985)

Mac Mathúna, Séamus and Ó Corráin, Ailbhe, *Miscellanea Celtica in Memoriam Heinrich Wagner* (Uppsala, 1997)

Mac Néill, Eoin, *Eachtra Lomnochtáin* (Dublin, 1904)

— *Duanaire Finn* (Dublin, 1908), vol. 1; *see* MacNeill, Eoin

Mac Néill, Eoin and Macalister, R.A.S., *Leabhar Gabhála* (Dublin, 1916)

Mac Piarais, Pádraig, *Bodach an Chóta Lachtna* (Dublin, 1906)

— *Bruidhean Chaorthainn* (Dublin, 1908)

Mac Suibhne, Seán, *Tótamas in Éirinn* (Dublin, 1961).

Macalister, R.A. Stewart, *Latin and Irish Lives of Ciarán* (Dublin, 1921)

— *The Secret Languages of Ireland* (Cambridge, 1937)

— *Lebor Gabála Érenn* (Dublin, 1938, 1939, 1940, 1941, 1956), vols. 1–5

— *Corpus Inscriptionum Insularum* (Dublin, 1945–49), vols. 1–2

MacCarthy, B., *The Codex Palatino-Vaticanus* (Dublin, 1892)

MacCulloch, John A., *The Childhood of Fiction* (London, 1905)

— *The Religion of the Ancient Celts* (Edinburgh, 1911)

MacErlean, John C., *Duanaire Dháibhidh Uí Bhruadair* (London, 1917), vol. 3; *see* Mac Giolla Eáin, Eoin

MacKillop, James, *Fionn Mac Cumhaill: Celtic Myth in English Literature* (New York, 1986)

MacLysaght, Edward, *Irish Life in the Seventeenth Century* (Dublin, 1969)

— *The Surnames of Ireland* (Dublin, 1973)

MacManus, Dermot, *The Middle Kingdom* (London, 1959)

MacManus, Seamus, *Heavy Hangs the Golden Grain* (Dublin, 1951)

MacNamara, Martin, *The Apocrypha in the Irish Church* (Dublin, 1975); *see* Mac Conmara, Máirtín

MacNeill, Eoin, *Phases of Irish History* (Dublin, 1919); *see* Mac Néill, Eoin

MacNeill, Máire, *The Festival of Lughnasa* (Oxford, 1962)

— *Máire Rua: Lady of Leamaneh* (Whitegate, 1990)

MacSweeney, Patrick M., *Caithréim Conghail Cláiringhnigh* (London, 1904)

Magnusson, Magnus and Pálsson, Hermann, *Njal's Saga* (Middlesex, 1960)

Maguidhir, Seosamh, *Maith Thú, a Mhicí* (Monaghan, 1973)

— *Pádraig Mac a Liondain* (Dublin, 1977)

Maher, James, *Romantic Slievenamon* (Mullinahone, 1954)

Mallory, J.P and Adams, D.Q. (eds.), *Encyclopedia of Indo-European Culture* (London,1997)

Malone, S., *Life of St Flannan* (Dublin, 1902)

Marshall. John J., *Irish Tories, Rapparees, and Robbers* (Dungannon, 1927)

Maxwell, Constantia, *Irish History from Contemporary Sources* (London, 1923)

McCallen, Jim, *Stand and Deliver* (Cork, 1993)

McCone, Kim, *Pagan Past and Christian Present* (Maynooth, 1990)

— *Ancient and Medieval Celtic Sound Change* (Maynooth, 1996)

McKenna, Lambert, *The Book of Magauran* (Dublin, 1947); *see* Mac Cionnaith, Láimhbheartach

Medieval Studies in Memory of Gertrude Schoepperle Loomis (Paris, 1927)

Meehan, Charles P., *Fate and Fortunes of Tyrone and Tyrconnel* (Dublin, 1868)

— *The Geraldines, Earls of Desmond* (Dublin, 1878)

Meid, Wolfgang, *Táin Bó Fraích* (Dublin, 1974)

Mélanges d'histoire du Moyen Age offerts a Ferdinand Lot (Paris, 1925)

Mercier, Vivian, *The Irish Comic Tradition* (Oxford, 1962)

Meyer, Kuno, *Cath Finntrágha* (Oxford, 1885)

— *Aislinge Meic Conglinne* (London, 1892)

— *Hibernica Minora* (Oxford, 1894)

— *Liadain and Curithir* (London, 1902)

— *Four Old-Irish Songs of Summer and Winter* (London, 1903)

— *The Death-Tales of the Ulster Heroes* (London, 1906)

— *The Instructions of King Cormac Mac Airt* (Dublin, 1909)

— *Fianaigecht* (Dublin, 1910)

— *Beatha Colmáin maic Lúacháin* (Dublin, 1911)

— *Sanas Cormaic* (Halle, 1912)

— *Hail Brigit* [HB] (Dublin, 1912)

— *Über die älteste Irische Dichtung* (Berlin, 1914), vols. 1–2

Meyer, Kuno and Nutt, Alfred, *The Voyage of Bran* (London, 1895–97), vols. 1–2

Mulchrone, Kathleen, *Caithréim Cellaig* (Dublin, 1933)

— *Bethu Phátraic* (Dublin, 1939)

Murphy, Denis, *The Annals of Clonmacnoise* (Dublin, 1896)

— *Cromwell in Ireland* (Dublin, 1897)

Murphy, Gerard, *Duanaire Finn* (London, 1933–53), vols. 2–3

— *Saga and Myth in Ancient Ireland* (Dublin, 1961)

— *Early Irish Lyrics* (Oxford, 1962)\

— *The Ossianic Lore and Romantic Tales of Medieval ireland* (Dublin, 1971)

Murphy, Michael J., *Now You're Talking* (Belfast, 1975)

Myler, Patrick, *Regency Rogue: Dan Donnelly* (Dublin, 1976)

Nagy, Joseph Falaky, *The Wisdom of the Outlaw* (Berkeley, 1985)

Neilson, William, *An Introduction to the Irish Language* (Achill, 1845), vols. 1–2

Newall, Venetia J. (ed.), *Folklore Studies in the Twentieth Century* (London, 1980)

Ní Chléirigh, Meadhbh, *Eachtra na gCuradh* (Dublin, 1941)

— *Coimheasgar na gCuradh* (Dublin, 1942)

Ní Chróinín, Áine, *Beatha Chríost* (Dublin, 1952); *see* O'Sullivan, Anne

Ní Laoire, Siobhán, *Bás Cearbhaill agus Farbhlaidhe* (Dublin, 1986)

Ní Mhuirgheasa, Máire, *Imtheacht an Dá Nónbhar agus Tóraidheacht Taise Taoibhghile* (Dublin, 1954)

Ní Mhuirgheasa, Máire and Ó Ceithearnaigh, Séamus, *Sgéalta Rómánsaíochta* (Dublin, 1952)

Ní Mhurchú, Máire and Breathnach, Diarmaid, *Beathaisnéis 1560–1781* (Dublin, 2001)

Ní Shéaghdha, Nessa, *Agallamh na Seanórach* (Dublin, 1942, 1942, 1945), vols. 1–3

— *Tóruigheacht Dhiarmada agus Ghráinne* (Dublin, 1967)

Ní Shéaghdha, Nessa and Ní Mhuirgheasa, Máire, *Trí Bruidhne* (Dublin, 1941)

Nic Dhonnchadha, Lil, *Aided Muirchertaig meic Erca* (Dublin, 1964)

Nolan, William and McGrath, T.G. (eds.), *Tipperary: History and Society* (Dublin, 1985)

Ó Buachalla, Breandán, *Cathal Buí* (Dublin, 1975)

— *Aisling Ghéar* (Dublin, 1996)

Ó Cadhlaigh, Cormac, *Cormac Mac Airt* (Dublin, 1927)

— *Guaire an Oinigh* (Dublin, 1939)

— *An Fhiannuidheacht* (Dublin, 1947)

— *Diarmaid Mac Chearbhaill* (Dublin, 1950)

— *An Rúraíocht* (Dublin, 1956)

Ó Caithnia, Liam P., *Scéal na hIománna* (Dublin, 1980)

— *Apalóga na bhFilí* (Dublin, 1984)

— *Báirí Cos in Éirinn* [BCÉ] (Dublin, 1984)

Ó Catháin, Séamas, *The Bedside Book of Irish Folklore* (Dublin, 1980)

— *Irish Life and Lore* (Dublin, 1982)

— *Uair an Chloig Cois Teallaigh* (Dublin, 1985)

— *The Festival of Brigit* (Dublin, 1995)

— (ed.), *Northern Lights: Essays in Honour of Bo Almqvist* (Dublin, 2002)

Ó Cathasaigh, Tomás, *The Heroic Biography of Cormac mac Airt* (Dublin, 1977)

Ó Ceithearnaigh, Séamus, *Siabhradh Mhic na Míochomhairle* (Dublin, 1955); *see* Carney, James

Ó Concheanainn, Tomás, *Nua-Dhuanaire* (Dublin, 1981), vol. 3

Ó Corráin, Ailbhe (ed.), *Proceedings of the Fifth Symposium of Societas Celtologica Nordica* (Uppsala, 2001)

Ó Corráin, Donncha and Maguire, Fidelma, *Gaelic Personal Names* (Dublin, 1981)

Ó Crualaoich, Gearóid, *The Book of the Cailleach* (Cork, 2003)

Ó Cuív, Brian, *Cath Muighe Tuireadh* (Dublin, 1945)

— *A View of the Irish Language* (Dublin, 1969)

Ó Danachair, Caoimhín, *A Bibliography of Irish Ethnology and Folk Tradition* (Dublin, 1978); *see* Danaher, Kevin

Ó Domhnaill, Maoghnus, *Beatha Mhuire* (Dublin, 1940)

Ó Dónaill, Niall, *Na Glúnta Rosannacha* (Dublin, 1952)

— *Foclóir Gaeilge-Béarla* (Dublin, 1977)

Ó Donnchadha, Tadhg, *An Leabhar Muimhneach* (Dublin, 1940)

Ó Duilearga, Séamus, *Leabhar Sheáin Í Chonaill* (Dublin, 1948); *see* Delargy, J.H.

Ó Duilearga, Séamus and Ó hÓgáin, Dáithí, *Leabhar Stiofáin Uí Ealaoire* (Dublin, 1981)

Ó Dufaigh, Seosamh and Rainey, Brian E., *Comhairle Mhic Clamha* (Lille, 1981)

Ó Duinn, Seán, *Gnás na Féile Bríde* (Dublin, 2002)

Ó Fiannachta, Pádraig, *An Barántas* (Maynooth, 1978)

Ó Foghludha, Risteard, *Seán Clárach* (Dublin, 1933)

— *Cois na Cora* (Dublin, 1937)

— *Cois na Ruachtaighe* (Dublin, 1938)

— *Cois Caoin-Reathaighe* (Dublin, 1946)

Ó Fotharta, Domhnall, *Siamsa an Gheimhridh* (Dublin, 1892)

Ó Gallchobhair, Tomás, Ua Cuain, Pádraig and Mac Giolla Fhionnáin, Tadhg, *Gadaidhe Géar na Geamh-oidhche* (Dublin, 1915)

Ó hAodha, Donncha, *Bethu Brigte* (Dublin, 1978)

Ó hEochaidh, Seán, Ní Néill, Máire and Ó Catháin, Séamas, *Síscéalta ó Thír Chonaill* (Dublin, 1977)

Ó hÓgáin, Dáithí, *Duanaire Osraíoch* (Dublin, 1980)

— *Duanaire Thiobraid Árann* (Dublin, 1981)

— *An File* (Dublin, 1982)

— *The Hero in Irish Folk History* (Dublin, 1985)

— *Fionn Mac Cumhaill* (Dublin, 1988)

— *The Sacred Isle* (Cork, 1999)

— *The Celts: a History* (Cork, 2002)

Ó Laoghaire, Diarmaid, *Ár bPaidreacha Dúchais* (Dublin, 1975)

Ó Luaighnigh, Liam, *Dánta Aindréis Mhic Cruitín* (Ennis, 1935)

Ó Madagáin, Breandán, *Gnéithe den Chaointeoireacht* (Dublin, 1978)

Ó Máille, Tomás S., *Sean-Fhocla Chonnacht* (Dublin, 1952), vols. 1–2

Ó Maolfabhail, Art, *Camán: Two Thousand Years of Hurling in Ireland* (Dundalk, 1973)

Ó Maonaigh, Cainneach, *Smaointe Beatha Chríost* (Dublin, 1944)

Ó Muimhneacháin, Conchubhar, *Béaloideas Bhéal Átha an Ghaorthaidh* (Dublin, 1956)

Ó Muirgheasa, Énrí, *Oidhche Áirneáil* (Dublin, 1924)

— *Dhá Chéad de Cheoltaibh Uladh* (Dublin, 1934)

— *Seanfhocail Uladh* (ed. Nollaig Ó hUrmoltaigh) (Dublin, 1976)

Ó Muirithe, Diarmaid, *The Wexford Carols* (Portlaoise, 1982)

Ó Muraíle, Nollaig, *The Great Book of Irish Genealogies* (Dublin, 2003)

Ó Murchú, Liam P., *Cúirt an Mheon Oíche* (Dublin, 1982)

Ó Nuanáin, P., *Glendalough* (Wicklow, 1936)

Ó Raithbheartaigh, Toirdhealbhach, *Genealogicasl Tracts* (Dublin, 1932)

Ó Rathile, Tomás, *Laoithe Cumainn* (Cork, 1925)

— *Dánta Grádha* (Cork, 1926); *see* O'Rahilly, Thomas F.

Ó Riain, Pádraig, *Cath Almaine* (Dublin, 1978)

— *Beatha Bharra* (London, 1994)

Ó Ríordáin, Seán P., *Tara: the Monuments on the Hill* (Dundalk, 1982)

Ó Searcaigh, Séamas, *Beatha Cholm Cille* (Dublin, 1967)

Ó Siochfhradha, Pádraig, *An Seanchaidhe Muimhneach* (Dublin, 1932)

— *Triocha Céad Chorca Dhuibhne* (Dublin, 1938)

— *Tóraidheacht an Ghiolla Dheacair* (Dublin, 1939)

— *Laoithe na Féinne* (Dublin, 1941)

Ó Snodaigh, Pádraig, *Hidden Ulster* (1973)

Ó Súilleabháin, Domhnall, *Seanchas na Deasmhumhan* (Dublin, 1940)

Ó Súilleabháin, Seán, *A Handbook of Irish Folklore* (Dublin, 1942)

— *Scéalta Cráibhtheacha* (Dublin, 1952: *Béaloideas,* vol. 21)

— *Caitheamh Aimsire ar Thórraimh* (Dublin, 1961; translated as *Irish Wake Amusements,* Cork, 1967)

— *Irish Folk Custom and Belief* (Dublin, 1967)

— *Storytelling in Irish Tradition* (Cork, 1973); *see* O'Sullivan, Seán

Ó Súilleabháin, Seán and Christiansen, Reidar Th, *The Types of the Irish Folktale* (Helsinki, 1967)

Ó Súilleabháin, Seán C., *Lá Fhéile Bríde* (Dublin, 1977)

Ó Tiománaidhe, Mícheál, *Targaireacht Bhriain Ruaidh Uí Chearbháin* (Dublin, 1906)

Ó Tuama, Seán, *An Grá in Amhráin na nDaoine* (Dublin, 1960)

Ó Tuathail, Éamonn, *Sgéalta Mhuintir Luinigh* (Dublin, 1933)

— *Seanchas Ghleann Ghaibhle* (Dublin, 1934, appendix to *Béaloideas,* vol. 4)

O'Brien, Michael A., *Corpus Genealogiarum Hiberniae* (Dublin, 1962)

O'Cahill, Donal, *Legends of Killarney* (Tralee, ninth edn., n.d.)

O'Callaghan, John C., *History of the Irish Brigades* (London, 1870)

O'Conor, Daniel R., *Works* (Cork, 1793)

O'Curry, Eugene, *Lectures on the Manuscript Materials of Ancient Irish History* (Dublin, 1855)

— *Manners and Customs of the Ancient Irish* (London, 1873), vols. 1–3

O'Daly, John, *The Poets and Poetry of Munster* (Dublin, 1850)

O'Daly [O Daly], Máirín, *Cath Maige Mucrama* (Dublin, 1975)

O'Donnell, Patrick, *The Irish Faction Fighters* (Tralee, 1975)

O'Donnell, Ruán, *Wicklow: 1799–1803* (Dublin, 2000)

O'Donovan, John, *The Circuit of Ireland* (Dublin, 1841)

— *The Banquet of Dún na nGédh and the Battle of Magh Rath* (Dublin, 1842)

— *Tribes and Customs of Hy Many* (Dublin, 1843)

— *The Genealogies, Tribes and Customs of Hy-Fiachrach* (Dublin, 1844)

— *Leabhar na gCeart, or the Book of Rights* (Dublin, 1847)

— *Annála Ríoghachta Éireann, the Annals of Ireland* (Dublin, 1848–51), vols. 1–7

— *Miscellany of the Celtic Society* (Dublin, 1849)

— *Three Fragments by Dubhaltach Mac Firbhisigh* (Dublin, 1860)

— *The Martyrology of Donegal* (Dublin, 1864)

O'Donovan, John and O'Conor Don, Charles, *The O'Conors of Connaught* (Dublin, 1891)

O'Duffy, Richard J., *Oidhe Chloinne Tuireann* (Dublin, 1888)

O'Dwyer, Peter, *Mary: a History of Devotion in Ireland* (Dublin, 1988)

O'Fihelly, Patrick, *Mil na mBeach* (Dublin, 1911)

O'Grady, Standish Hayes, *Silva Gadelica* (London, 1892), vols. 1–2

— *Caithréim Thoirdhealbhaigh* (London, 1929), vols. 1–2

O'Halloran, Sylvester, *The History and Antiquities of Ireland* (Dublin, 1778), vols. 1–3

O'Hanlon, John, *Lives of the Irish Saints* (Dublin, 1875–), vols. 1–9

O'Kearney, Nicholas, *The Prophecies of St Columbkille* (Dublin, 1856)

O'Keeffe, James G., *Buile Suibhne* (London, 1913)

O'Kelleher, Andrew and Schoepperle, Gertrude, *Betha Colaim Chille* (Illinois, 1918)

O'Kelly, Patrick, *The History of Ireland by the Abbé Mac-Geoghagan* (Dublin, 1844)

O'Meara, John J., *The History and Topography of Ireland: Gerald of Wales* (Middlesex, 1982)

— *The Voyage of Saint Brendan* (Dublin, 1978)

O'Neill, Elizabeth, *Owen Roe O'Neill* (Dublin, 1937)

O'Rahilly, Cecile, *Tóruigheacht Gruaidhe Griansholus* (London, 1924)

— *Five Seventeenth-century Political Poems* (Dublin, 1952)

— *The Stowe Version of Táin Bó Cuailnge* (Dublin, 1961)

— *Cath Finntrágha* (Dublin, 1962)

— *Táin Bó Cuailnge from the Book of Leinster* (Dublin, 1970)

— *Táin Bó Cúailnge: Recension 1* (Dublin, 1976)

O'Rahilly, Thomas F., *Dánfhocail* (Dublin, 1921)

— *Irish Dialects, Past and Present* (Dublin, 1932)

— *The Goidels and their Predecessors* (Dublin, 1935)

— *Early Irish History and Mythology* (Dublin, 1946); *see* Ó Rathile, Tomás

O'Sullivan, Anne, *The Book of Leinster* (Dublin, 1983), vol. 6; *see* Ní Chróinín, Áine

O'Sullivan, Donal, *Carolan* (London, 1958), vols. 1–2

— *Irish Folk Music, Song and Dance* (Cork, 1974)

O'Sullivan, Patrick V., *Irish Superstitions and Legends of Animals and Birds* (Cork, 1991)

O'Sullivan Sean, *Folktales of Ireland* (London, 1966)

— *The Folklore of Ireland* (London, 1974)

— *Legends from Ireland* (London, 1977); *see* Ó Súilleabháin, Seán

Olmsted, Garrett S., *The Gods of the Celts and the Indo-Europeans* (Budapest, 1994)

Orpen, Goddard H., *The Song of Dermot and the Earl* (Oxford, 1892)

Oskamp, H.P.A., *The Voyage of Máel Dúin* (Groningen, 1970)

Owens, Cóilín (ed.), *Family Chronicles: Maria Edgeworth's Castle Rackrent* (Dublin, 1987)

Partridge, Angela, *Caoineadh na dTrí Muire* (Dublin, 1983)

Pauli, Johannis, *Schimpf und Ernst* (New York, 1972), vol. 1

Petrie, George, *The Ecclesiastical Architecture of Ireland* (Dublin, 1845)

Pender, Séamus (ed.), *Féilscríbhinn Torna* (Cork, 1947)

Pettersson, Gerd, *Finn and the Fían* (Göteborg, 1999)

Piggott, Stuart, *The Druids* (London, 1968)

Plummer, Carolus, *Vitae Sanctorum Hiberniae* (Oxford, 1910), vols. 1–2

— *Bethada Náem nÉrenn* (Oxford, 1922), vols. 1–2

— *Miscellanea Hagiographica Hibernica* (Brussels, 1935)

Pokorny, Julius, *Indogermanisches Etymologisches Wörterbuch* (Bern, 1959)

Powell, T.G.E., *The Celts* (London, 1958)

Power, Patrick, *Lives of Saints Declan and Mochuda* (London, 1914)

Póirtéir, Cathal, *Famine Echoes* (Dublin,1995)

Prevost, J.J., *Un Tour en Irlande* (Paris, 1846)

Puhvel, Jaan (ed.), *Myth and Law among the Indo-Europeans* (Berkeley, 1970)

Quiggin, Edmund C., *A Dialect of Donegal* (Cambridge, 1906)

Raftery, Barry, *Pagan Celtic Ireland* (London, 1994)

— (ed.), *Trackway Excavations in the Mountdillon Bogs* (Dublin, 1997)

Raftery, Joseph (ed.), *The Celts* (Dublin, 1964)

Ralls-MacLeod, Karen, *Music and the Celtic Otherworld* (Edinburgh, 2000)

Rank, Otto, *The Myth of the Birth of the Hero* (New York, 1914)

Ransome, Hilda M., *The Sacred Bee* (Bridgewater, 1986)

Reinhard, John R., *The Survival of Geis in Medieval Romance* (Halle, 1933)

RIA Dictionary: *Contributions to a Dictionary of the Irish Language* (Royal Irish Academy: Dublin, 1913–75)

Richmond, W. Edson (ed.), *Studies in Folklore* (Bloomington, 1957)

Richter, Michael, *Ireland and her Neighbours in the Seventh Century* (New York, 1999)

Rivet, A.L.F. and Smith, Colin, *The Place-Names of Roman Britain* (London, 1979)

Robinson, Fred Norris, *Satirists and Enchanters in Early Irish Literature* (New York, 1969), originally in D.G. Lyon and G.F. Moore (eds.), *Studies in the History of Religions* (New York, 1912)

Roider, Ulrike, *De Chophur in Da Muccida* (Innsbruck, 1979)

Ross, Anne, *Everyday Life of the Pagan Celts* (London, 1970)

— *Pagan Celtic Britain* (London, 1974)

Ross, Neil, *Heroic Poetry from the Book of the Dean of Lismore* (Edinburgh, 1939)

Ryan, John, *Irish Monasticism* (Dublin, 1931)

— (ed.), *Féil-sgríbhinn Eoin Mhic Néill* (Dublin, 1940)

Ryan, John, *History and Antiquities of the County of Carlow* (Dublin, 1833)

Scott, AB. and Martin, F.X., *Expugnatio Hibernica: Giraldus Cambrensis* (Dublin, 1978)

Seabhac, An; *see* Ó Siochfhradha, Pádraig

Selmer, Carl, *Navigatio Sancti Brendani Abbatis* (Notre Dame, 1959)

Seoighe, Mainchín, *Staker Wallis* (Kilfinane, 1996)

Shaw, Francis, *The Dream of Oengus* (Dublin, 1934)

Sheridan, Thomas, *The Life of the Reverend Dr Jonathan Swift* (London, 1784)

Sherley-Price, Leo and Latham R.E., *Bede* (Middlesex, 1968)

Sjoestedt, Marie-Louise, *Gods and Heroes of the Celts*, trans. Myles Dillon (Berkeley, 1982)

Smyth, Alfred P., *Celtic Leinster* (Dublin, 1982)

Spargo, John W., *Virgil the Necromancer* (Cambridge, 1934)

Stevenson, David, *Alasdair MacColla* (Edinburgh, 1980)

Stewart, Bruce (ed.), *That Other World* (London, 1998), vol. 1

Stokes, Whitley, *Three Irish Glossaries* (London, 1862)

— *The Calendar of Óengus* (Dublin, 1880)

— *The Tripartite Life of Patrick* (London, 1887), vols. 1–2

— *Lives of the Saints from the Book of Lismore* (Oxford, 1890)

— *The Bodleian Dinnshenchas* (London, 1892)

— *Acallamh na Seanórach* (Leipzig, 1900: *Irische Texte*, 4)

— *Félire Óengusso Céli Dé* (London, 1905)

— *The Colloquy of the Two Sages* [CTS] (Paris, 1905)

— *The Birth and Life of St Moling* (London, 1907)

Stokes, Whitley and Strachan, John, *Thesaurus Palaeohibernicus*, vols. 1–2 (Cambridge, 1901–03)

Strachan, Geoffrey, *Irish Fairy Tales* (London, 1904)

Sullivan, T.D., *Recollections of Troubled Times in Irish Politics* (Dublin, 1905)

Swinfen, Averil, *The Irish Donkey* (London, 1975)

Szövérffy, Joseph, *Irisches Erzählgut im Abendland* (Berlin, 1957)

— *Some Stages of the St Columba Traditions in the Middle Ages* (Boston, 1988)

Taylor, Archer, *The Black Ox* (Helsinki, 1927)

Thevenot, Émile, *Divinités et Sanctuaires de la Gaule* (Paris, 1968)

Thompson, E.A., *Who Was St Patrick?* (Suffolk, 1985)

Thompson, Stith, *Motif-Index of Folk-Literature* (Bloomington, 1955–58), vols. 1–6

Thoms, William J., *Lays and Legends of Ireland* (London, 1834)

Thomson, David, *The People of the Sea* (London, 1965)

Thomson, Derick S., *The Companion to Gaelic Scotland* (Oxford, 1983)

Thomson, Derick S. (ed.), *Gaelic Scotland* (Oxford, 1983)

Thurneysen, Rudolf, *Die irische Helden- und Königsage bis zum siebzehnten Jahrhundert* (Halle, 1921)

— *Scéla Mucce Meic Dathó* (Dublin, 1935)

— *A Grammar of Old Irish* (Dublin, 1961)

Todd, James Henthorpe, *The Irish Version of the Historia Britonum of Nennius* (Dublin, 1848)

— *The War of the Gaedhil with the Gaill* (Dublin, 1867)

Tovar, Antonio, *The Ancient Languages of Spain and Portugal* (New York, 1961)

Ua Ceallaigh, Seán, *Brian Bóirmhe* (Dublin, 1908)

— *Trí Truagha na Scéaluigheachta* (Dublin, 1927)

— *Rudhraigheacht* (Dublin, 1935)

Ua Duinnín, Pádraig, *Amhráin Eoghain Ruaidh Uí Shúilleabháin* (Dublin, 1901)

— *Beatha Eoghain Ruaidh Uí Shúilleabháin* (Dublin, 1902)

— *Dánta Phiarais Feiritéir* (Dublin, 1903); *see* Dinneen, Patrick S.

Ua Muirgheasa, Énrí, *Ceithearnach Uí Dhomhnaill* (Dublin, 1912)

Ua Murchadha, Domhnall, *Sean-Aimsireacht* (Dublin, 1939)

Ua Ruaidhrí, Seaghán, *Súil Uí Dhubhdha le hÁrd na Ríogh* (Dublin, 1906)

Uí Ógáin, Ríonach, *An Rí gan Choróin* (Dublin, 1984)

— *Immortal Dan* (Dublin, 1995)

Van Hamel, A.G., *Lebor Bretnach* (Dublin, 1932)

— *Compert Con Culainn* (Dublin, 1933)

Vendryes, Joseph, *Airne Fíngein* (Dublin, 1953)

Vendryes, Joseph, Bachellery E. and Lambert, P.-Y., *Lexique Étymologique de l'Irlandais Ancien* (Paris, 1959–)

Vries, Jan de, *Keltische Religion* (Stuttgart, 1961)

— *Heroic Song and Heroic Legend*, trans. B.J. Timmer (London, 1963)

Waddell, John and Shee Twohig, Elizabeth, *Ireland in the Bronze Age* (Dublin, 1995)

Wainright, F.T., *The Problem of the Picts* (Edinburgh, 1955)

Walde, Alois and Pokorny, Julius, *Vergleichendes Wörterbuch der Indogermanischen Sprachen* (Berlin, 1927–30), vols. 1–2

Walker, Joseph Cooper, *Historical Memoirs of the Irish Bards* (Dublin, 1786)

Walsh, John Edward, *Rakes and Ruffians* (Dublin, 1979 edn.)

Walsh, Paul, *Irish Chiefs and Leaders* (Dublin, 1960)

Watson, J. Carmichael, *Mesca Uladh* (Dublin, 1941)

Watson, Seosamh, *Mac na Míchomhairle* (Dublin, 1979)

— (ed.), *Féilscríbhinn Thomáis de Bhaldraithe* (Dublin, 1986)

Watson, W. (publisher), *A Description of Killarney* (Dublin, 1776)

Wentz, W.Y. Evans, *The Fairy Faith in Celtic Countries* (London, 1911)

Westwood, Jennifer, *Albion: a Guide to Legendary Britain* (London, 1986)

Westropp, T.G., *King Brian: The Hero of Clontarf* (Dublin, 1914)

Wilde, Lady J.F., *Ancient Legends of Ireland* (London, 1888)

Wilgus, D.K. and Sommer, Carol (eds.), *Folklore International: Essays in Honour of W.D. Hand* (Pennsylvania, 1967)

Williams, Ifor, *Pedeir Keinc y Mabinogi* (Cardiff, 1930)

Williams, J.E. Caerwyn, *The Court Poet in Medieval Ireland* (London, 1971)

Williams, Nicholas J., *Dánta Mhuiris Mhic Dháibhí Dhuibh Mhic Gearailt* (Dublin, 1979)

— *The Poems of Giolla Brighde Mac Con Midhe* (Dublin, 1980)

— *Pairlement Chloinne Tomáis* (Dublin, 1981)

— *Cniogaide Cnagaide* (Dublin, 1988)

Windele, J., *Notices of the City of Cork and Killarney* (Cork, 1839)

Windisch, Ernst, *Die altirische Heldensage Táin Bó Cúailnge* (Leipzig, 1905)

Wood, Herbert, *The Chronicle of Ireland: 1584–1608* (Dublin, 1933)

Wood-Martin, W.G., *Traces of the Elder Faiths of Ireland* (London, 1902), vols. 1–2

Zimmermann, George-Denis, *Songs of Irish Rebellion* (Dublin, 1967)

Printed in the United States
by Baker & Taylor Publisher Services